# Black Water

The Book of Fantastic Literature

# Black Water
## Alberto Manguel

*Clarkson N. Potter, Inc./Publishers*
NEW YORK
DISTRIBUTED BY
CROWN PUBLISHERS, INC.

Published by Clarkson N. Potter, Inc., 225 Park Avenue South,
New York, New York 10003, and simultaneously in Great
Britain by Pan Books Ltd as *Black Water: The Anthology of
Fantastic Literature* First published in Canada in 1983 by Lester
and Orpen Dennys Ltd as *Black Water: The Anthology of
Fantastic Literature*

Manufactured in the United States of America

Library of Congress Cataloging in Publication Data
Main entry under title:
Black water.
   1. Fantastic fiction.    I. Manguel, Alberto.
PN6071.F25B54    1984    808.83'876    83–19091
ISBN 0–517–55269–8
10  9  8  7  6  5  4
First American Edition

# Dedication

A knowledge that another has felt as we have felt, and seen things, even as they are little things, not much otherwise than we have seen them, will continue to the end to be one of life's choicest pleasures.

Robert Louis Stevenson

*To Johnny and Mikey and Lili, for all I wish we could have shared, far away and long ago.*

# Epigraphs

Whatever a man prays for, he prays for a miracle. Every prayer reduces itself to this: Great God, grant that two and two be not four.

Ivan Turgenev, from *Prayer*

It was agreed that my endeavours should be directed to persons and characters supernatural . . . ; yet so as to transfer from our inward nature a human interest and a semblance of the truth sufficient to procure for these shadows of imagination that willing suspension of disbelief for the moment, which constitutes poetic faith.

Samuel Taylor Coleridge, from *Biographia Literaria*

'One *can't* believe impossible things.'

'I daresay you haven't had much practice,' said the Queen. 'When I was your age, I always did it for half-an-hour a day. Why, sometimes I've believed as many as six impossible things before breakfast.'

Lewis Carroll, from *Through the Looking-Glass*

So long as we regard a tree as an obvious thing, naturally and reasonably created for a giraffe to eat, we cannot properly wonder at it. It is when we consider it as a prodigious wave of the living soil sprawling up to the skies for no reason in particular that we take off our hats, to the astonishment of the park-keeper.

G. K. Chesterton, from 'A Defense of Nonsense'

I don't want realism. I want magic . . . I don't tell truth, I tell what *ought* to be truth.

Tennessee Williams, from *A Streetcar Named Desire*

I wonder if that's why we sleep at night, because the darkness still . . . frightens us? They say we sleep to let the demons out – to let our mind go raving mad, our dreams and nightmares all our logic gone awry, the dark side of our reason.

Edward Albee, from *A Delicate Balance*

– What is a ghost? Stephen said with tingling energy. One who has faded into impalpability, through death, through absence, through change of manners.

James Joyce, from *Ulysses*

From one who maintains, there is nothing beyond
The Human Imagination; or another

Soul who contends, by night, that beyond
The human imagination, there is Nothing?

Richard Outram, from *Turns and Other Poems*

# Acknowledgements

Every effort has been made to contact copyright holders; in the event of an inadvertent omission or error, the editor should be notified at Lester & Orpen Dennys Ltd, 78 Sullivan Street, Toronto M5T 1C1 Ontario, Canada.

For permission to reprint the stories and excerpts in this anthology, acknowledgement is made as follows:

*Akutagawa, Ryunosuke*, 'Autumn Mountain', translated by Ivan Morris, to Charles E. Tuttle Co. Inc. and the author.

*Aymé, Marcel*, 'The State of Grace', from *Across Paris and other stories* by Marcel Aymé, translated from the French by Norman Denny, copyright Librairie Gallimard 1947. By permission of Harper & Row, Publishers, Inc. and The Bodley Head Ltd.

*Beerbohm, Max*, 'Enoch Soames', from *Seven Men*, to William Heinemann Ltd.

*Belloc, Hilaire*, 'Home', from *On Something*. Reprinted by permission of A. D. Peters & Co. Ltd.

*Benét, Stephen Vincent*, 'The Curfew Tolls', to Brandt & Brandt Literary Agents, Inc., from *The Selected Works of Stephen Vincent Benét*, Holt Rhinehart & Winston Inc., copyright Stephen Vincent Benét 1935, copyright renewed © Thomas C. Benét, Stephanie B. Mahin and Rachael Benét Lewis 1963.

*Bioy Casares, Adolfo*, 'Venetian Masks', translated by Alberto Manguel, to the author, © Adolfo Bioy Casares 1983. This translation © Alberto Manguel 1983.

*Bloy, Léon*, 'The Captives of Longjumeau', translated by Alberto Manguel, to Mercure de France. © Mercure de France 1967. This translation © Alberto Manguel 1983.

*Borges, Jorge Luis*, 'August 25, 1983', translated by Alberto Manguel, to the author, © Jorge Luis Borges 1982. This translation © Alberto Manguel 1983.

*Bradbury, Ray*, 'The Playground', to the author. © Ray Bradbury 1953, © renewed Ray Bradbury 1980. Reprinted by permission of the Harold Matson Company, Inc.

*Calvino, Italo*, 'The Argentine Ant', translated by Archibald Colquhoun. First published in Botteghe Oscure X, 1952. © Giulio Einaudi editore S.p.A., Torino. For the translation, from *Adam, One Afternoon*, © Wm Collins Sons & Co. Ltd 1957 and © Harcourt Brace Jovanovich, Inc. 1971.

*Cocteau, Jean*, excerpt from *Le Grand écart*, to Editions Stock, copyright Editions Stock 1923. This translation © Alberto Manguel 1983.

*Collier, John*, 'The Lady on the Grey', to A. D. Peters Ltd, and the Harold Matson Co. Inc. Copyright John Collier 1951, copyright renewed 1979.

*Comfort, Alex*, 'The Lemmings', to Books and Broadcasts, Inc. and the author.

*Cortázar, Julio*, 'House taken over', from *End of Game*, translated by Paul Blackburn, to Random House, Inc., ALIA and the author. © Random House, Inc. 1967, 1963.

*De la Mare, Walter*, 'Seaton's Aunt', to the Literary Trustees of Walter de la Mare and the Society of Authors as their representatives.

*Denevi, Marco*, 'A Dog in Dürer's Engraving', translated by Alberto Manguel, to the author, © Marco Denevi 1968. This translation © Alberto Manguel 1983.

*Dinesen*, Isak, an excerpt from 'Peter and Rosa', from *Winter's Tales* by Isak Dinesen, copyright Random House, Inc. 1942, and by permission of the Rungstedlund Foundation.

*Du Maurier, Daphne*, 'Split Second', from *Kiss Me Again, Stranger*, to Mollie Waters and the author, © Daphne du Maurier 1952. Reprinted by permission of Doubleday & Co. Inc.

*Fast, Howard*, 'The Large Ant', from *A Touch of Infinity*. Reprinted by permission of The Sterling Lord Agency. © William Morrow & Co 1972.

*Forster, E. M.*, 'The Story of a Panic', from *The Collected Short Stories* by E. M. Forster, to Sidgwick and Jackson.

*Garnett, David*, 'Lady into Fox', to the author and Chatto and Windus Ltd; also to A. P. Watt Ltd.

*Greenburg, Joanne*, 'Certain Distant Suns', from *High Crimes and Misdemeanors* by Joanne Greenburg. © Joanne Greenburg 1977, 1979. Reprinted by permission of Holt, Rinehart & Winston, Publishers; also the Wallace & Shiel Agency, Inc. and Victor Gollancz Ltd.

*Greene, Graham*, 'A Little Place off the Edgware Road', from *The*

*Collected Stories of Graham Greene*, copyright 1941, 1942, 1946, 1947, 1949, © 1955, 1956, 1957, 1962, 1963, 1964, 1965, 1969, 1970, 1972 by Graham Greene; reprinted by permission of Viking Penguin Ltd. And from *Collected Stories* published by The Bodley Head and William Heinemann, © Graham Greene 1954, 1972. Reprinted by permission of the author. © Graham Greene 1954, 1972.

*Guimarães Rosa, João*, 'The Third Bank of the River', from *Modern Brazilian Short Stories*, © João Guimarães Rosa 1962. Translated by William L. Grossman (1967), © University of California Press 1967. Reprinted by permission of the Regents of the University of California.

*Hartley, L. P.*, 'A Visitor from Down Under', from *The Travelling Grave*, to Hamish Hamilton Ltd. © the Executors of the Estate of the late L. P. Hartley 1973.

*Hesse, Hermann*, 'A Man by the Name of Ziegler', from *Stories of Five Decades* by Herman Hesse, translated by Ralph Manheim. © Farrar, Straus and Giroux, Inc. 1954, 1972. Reprinted by permission of Farrar, Straus and Giroux, Inc.

*Hichens, Robert S.*, 'How Love Came to Professor Guildea', to A. P. Watt Ltd. and the Executors of the Estate of Robert S. Hichens.

*Hitchcock, George*, 'An Invitation to the Hunt' (first published in *The San Francisco Review*) to the author.

*James, M. R.*, an excerpt from 'A School Story', from *The Ghost Stories of M. R. James* (2nd edition) to Edward Arnold (Publishers) Ltd.

*Kafka, Franz*, 'In the Penal Colony' from *Franz Kafka: Stories 1904–1924*, translated by J. A. Underwood, first published by Macdonald & Co., 1981, to the translator. © J. A. Underwood 1981.

*King, Francis*, 'A Scent of Mimosa', from *The Times Book of Ghost Stories*. © Francis King 1975. Reprinted by permission of A. M. Heath & Co. Ltd and the author.

*Kipling, Rudyard*, 'The Wish House', from *Debits and Credits*, to The National Trust of Great Britain and Macmillan London Ltd. Copyright Rudyard Kipling 1924, reprinted by permission of Doubleday & Co. Inc.

*LeGuin, Ursula K.*, 'The Ones Who Walk Away from Omelas', from *The Wind's Twelve Quarters* by U. K. LeGuin. © Ursula K. LeGuin 1973, 1975. Reprinted by permission of the author and the author's agent, Virginia Kidd.

*Mandiargues, André Pieyre de*, 'Clorinda' translated by Alberto

Manguel, from *Soleil des Loups*, to Editions Gallimard. © Editions Gallimard 1979. This translation copyright © Alberto Manguel 1983.
*Manuel, Juan*, 'The Wizard Postponed', from *A Universal History of Infamy* by Jorge Luis Borges, translated by Norman Thomas di Giovanni. © Emece Editores S. A. and Norman Thomas di Giovanni, 1970, 1971. Published by Allen Lane, 1973. Reprinted by permission of the publishers, E. P. Dutton, Inc.
*Maugham, W. Somerset*, 'Lord Mountdrago', from *The Complete Short Stories of W. Somerset Maugham*, to the Estate of the late W. Somerset Maugham and William Heinemann Ltd; also Doubleday & Co. Inc. Copyright W. Somerset Maugham, 1939.
*Moore, Brian*, 'The Sight', from *Irish Ghost Stories*, edited by Joseph Hone, to Hamish Hamilton and Curtis Brown, Ltd. © Brian Moore 1977.
*Mujica Lainez, Manuel*, 'Importance', translated by Alberto Manguel, to the author. © Manuel Mujica Lainez, 1978. This translation © Alberto Manguel 1983.
*Nabokov, Vladimir*, 'The Visit to the Museum', from *Nabokov's Dozen*, to Mrs Vladimir Nabokov. © Vladimir Nabokov 1958.
*O'Brien, Flann*, 'John Duffy's Brother', from *Stories and Plays* by Flann O'Brien. Copyright Brian O'Nolan 1941. © Evelyn O'Nolan 1973. Reprinted by permission of Viking Penguin Inc. and the Brandt & Brandt Literary Agency.
*Ocampo, Silvina*, 'The Friends', translated by Alberto Manguel, to the author. © Silvina Ocampo 1982. This translation © Alberto Manguel 1983.
*Ozick, Cynthia*, 'The Pagan Rabbi', to the author and her agents Raines & Raines; also to Alfred A. Knopf, Inc. 'The Pagan Rabbi' was first published in *The Hudson Review*. © Cynthia Ozick 1966.
*Priestley, J. B.*, 'The Grey Ones', to A. D. Peters Ltd.
*Pushkin, Alexander*, 'The Queen of Spades', from *The Queen of Spades and other stories*, translated by Rosemary Edmonds (Penguin Classics 1962) pp.153–83. © Rosemary Edmonds, 1958, 1962. Reprinted by permission of Penguin Books Ltd.
*Quiroga, Horacio*, 'The Feather Pillow', translated by Margaret Sayers Peden, to the University of Texas Press. © University of Texas Press 1976.
*Saki (H. H. Munro)*, 'Laura', from *The Complete Works of Saki*, published by The Bodley Head, and *The Complete Short Stories of Saki*, copyright by the Viking Press, Inc. 1930. Copyright renewed

Viking Press, Inc. 1958. Reprinted by permission of Viking Penguin, Inc.

*Schulz, Bruno,* 'Father's Last Escape', from *Sanatorium Under the Sign of the Hourglass* by Bruno Schulz. © Jakob Schulz 1978. Used with permission of the publishers Walker & Co. and Hamish Hamilton Ltd.

*Tanizaki, Junichiro,* 'Tattoo', translated by Ivan Morris, to the author and the Orion Literary Agency. Copyright Matsuko Tanizaki 1910, originally published in Japan. All rights reserved. Also, for this translation, to Georges Borchardt, Inc.

*Wells, H. G.,* 'The Door in the Wall', to the Estate of the late H. G. Wells.

*Wharton, Edith,* 'Pomegranate Seed', from *The Ghost Stories of Edith Wharton,* © William R. Tyler 1973. For the story, copyright Curtis Publishing Company 1931; copyright renewed A. Watkins, Inc. and Constable Publishers 1959.

*Williams, Charles,* 'Et in Sempiternum Pereant', reprinted by permission of David Higham Associates Ltd.

*Williams, Tennessee,* 'The Mysteries of the Joy Rio' from *Hard Candy.* © Tennessee Williams 1954. Reprinted by permission of New Directions Publishing Corporation.

*Yourcenar, Marguerite,* 'How Wang-Fo was saved', translated by Alberto Manguel, from *Nouvelles Orientales,* to the author and Editions Gallimard. © Marguerite Yourcenar, 1963. This translation © Alberto Manguel 1983.

# Contents

# Foreword

Nothing is more difficult to give up than a pleasure once experienced.

When I was thirteen years old I was fortunate enough to have a small room of my own set apart from the rest of the house. Here I kept my books – a great many I thought, about a hundred, most of which, of course, I had not read. One evening I picked up an illustrated edition of the *Arabian Nights*, a small selection with ugly colour plates. The first story I tried, the one about Alladin, I had heard or read before and found uninteresting. But with the second I was luckier. I fell upon a story whose title intrigued me: 'The King of the Black Isles'. That night another world was revealed. The tale of the coloured fish and the evil princess and the monstrous slave suddenly made me realize that I had the key to places where access could not be denied me. Now, for the first time, I knew that there was literature. An image still haunts me: the young king, half marble, half flesh, captive inside a high room of black columns, whipped, till his blood ran, by his beautiful and unfaithful cousin.

Awakening to my physical senses, longing to leave and see the world, I found that something else – reading – had much the same majesty and terror and delight as those yearned-for pleasures, loving and travelling. Huxley says somewhere that in the essential moments of life we are alone: in the climax of love and in the instant of mystical revelation. I found that the discovery of literature is also a solitary act, that literature is a lonely place. There nothing can touch us because, like Alice through the looking-glass, we ourselves create the country through which we walk, giving it a geography in our mind. Once we are in possession we can call to others: read them a story, give them a book, offer them an anthology. But, like the youth who wanted to learn about fear, we have to spend the first night on our own.

When literature is discovered, a revelation occurs: the joyful, exultant knowledge that anything can happen. Of the many forms of literature, fantastic literature in particular explores that blissful knowledge. It makes use of our everyday world as a façade through which the undefinable appears, hinting at the half-forgotten dreams of our imagination. Unlike tales of fantasy (those chronicles of mundane life in mythical surroundings such as Narnia or Middle Earth), fantastic literature deals with what can be best defined as the impossible seeping into the possible, what Wallace Stevens calls 'black water breaking into reality'. Fantastic literature never really explains everything. Like the ghost train at the fair, it takes us through the darkness of a real world, from terror to laughable terror, diving into walls that swing away at the very last minute, racing under eerie nothings that touch us with cobweb fingers, suddenly slowing down and lengthening that last encounter (with what? with what?), using our expectancy of horror more effectively than horror itself.

Fantastic literature thrives on surprise, on the unexpected logic that is born from its own rules. It behaves exactly as Mr Lucian Gregory, Chesterton's anarchic poet, wishes reality would behave. 'Why do all clerks and navvies in the railway trains look so sad and tired,' asks the gentleman, 'so very sad and tired? I will tell you. It is because they know the train is going right. It is because they know that whatever place they have taken a ticket for, that place they will reach. It is because after they have passed Sloane Square they know that the next station must be Victoria, and nothing but Victoria. Oh, their wild rapture! Oh, their eyes like stars and their souls again in Eden, if the next station were unaccountably Baker Street!' Fantastic literature has nothing but contempt for timetables.

The stories that make up this anthology are essentially stories I enjoy, stories which, for me, represent the best of fantastic literature. Though each is unique, like coloured threads, certain general themes appear again and again. This repetition is in no way a hindrance to pleasure – indeed, it heightens our enjoyment by contrast, by stirring secret memories, making the reader an accomplice to the story by reminding him that he has been here before. Part of the delight of reading is being startled not by the sheer novelty of a subject but by the dexterity with which it is treated. Novelty after all is simply a question of 'first come, first served', and who knows what pushes one book rather than another first into our hands.

As far as I can make out, these are the main themes:

*Time warps:* where Time leads two separate existences – one for us, one for the rest of the world, in the tradition of Rip Van Winkle.

*Hauntings:* by the dead (usually) – for revenge (like Banquo's ghost); to make a belated announcement (like Hamlet's father); to love beyond the grave (like Dante's Beatrice).

*Dreams:* which become part of reality (like Caedmon's dream in the beginning of English literature); which issue a warning (like that of Caesar's wife); which tell us we are such stuff as dreams are made on (like the Red King's dream in *Through the Looking-Glass*).

*Unreal creatures, transformations:* like the creature in Kafka's 'Metamorphosis'; like Circe's swine; the Frog Prince; and the many foxes of Chinese ghost stories.

*Mimesis:* seemingly unrelated acts which secretly dramatize each other (the strange events that take place during King Duncan's murder, the cracked mirror of the Lady of Shalott). Also, a totally alien happening can provoke a tragedy somewhere else, as if all the threads in the universe were connected.

*Dealings with God and the Devil:* not of course theological writings, but stories which make use of that misty borderland of belief to frame a fantastic tale (as in the tragic history of Doctor Faustus). Usually this theme overlaps others, such as time warps or transformations.

I have deliberately avoided dividing the anthology into these sections because, like all systems of classification, this one would be unfair to the stories themselves. Yet the list of themes, apart from satisfying a spring-cleaning spirit, can give us an inkling as to why certain stories bring to mind others seemingly so different, what makes them so rich and in many ways, so moving.

I don't know exactly what it is that moves us when we read a fantastic story. Perhaps it is the gnawing suspicion that what has been imagined, however preposterous, has a place in the world and in our lives. Andrew Lang says in his *Blue Fairy Book:* 'When the Princess awakens, after her betrothal to the Yellow Dwarf, and hopes it was a dream, and finds on her finger the fatal ring of one red hair, we have a brave touch of horror and of truth. All of us have wakened and struggled with a dim evil memory, and trusted it was a dream, and found, in one form or another, a proof, a shape of that ring of red hair.'

Behind a story read, a tale told, something else is said as well, like a nagging voice half heard amid a conversation. We have the certainty that this voice is important, a necessity, and yet we cannot exactly make it out.

Conrad, in a text unworthy of Conrad, said that he did not write fantastic tales because writing them would be denying that life itself is fantastic. But that is not so. On the contrary, a truly good fantastic story will echo that which escapes explanation in life; it will *prove*, in fact, that life is fantastic. It will point to that which lies beyond our dreams and fears and delights; it will deal with the invisible, with the unspoken; it will not shirk from the uncanny, the absurd, the impossible; in short, it has the courage of total freedom.

Alberto Manguel
Paea and Toronto, 1982–3

# House Taken Over

## Julio Cortázar

*'Anyone who doesn't read Cortázar is doomed,'* Pablo Neruda *wrote shortly before his death. 'Not to read him is a serious invisible disease which in time can have terrible consequences. Something similar to a man who has never tasted peaches. He would quietly become sadder, noticeably paler, and probably, little by little, he would lose his hair.'*

*'House Taken Over' is one of Cortázar's first stories, published – while he was still living in Argentina – in Victoria Ocampo's famous* Sur *magazine. (Sur was Victoria Ocampo's way of bringing Europe to the pampas, and also of showing Europe that life had been discovered in a faraway corner of the world: the first number published a map showing Argentina's location.) Soon afterwards Cortázar left for Paris where he became the most famous of Argentina's literary exiles. His best books are the collections of short stories* End of Game, All Fires the Fire *and* Cronopios and Famas, *and his novel* The Winners.

*I met him in Paris in 1968, towards the end of May, and he suggested I take his picture next to one of May 68's most exhilarating graffiti:* L'imagination au pouvoir! *('Let imagination rise to power!').*

We liked the house because, apart from its being old and spacious (in a day when old houses go down for a profitable auction of their construction materials), it kept the memories of great-grandparents, our paternal grandfather, our parents and the whole of childhood.

Irene and I got used to staying in the house by ourselves, which was crazy, eight people could have lived in that place and not have gotten in each other's way. We rose at seven in the morning and got the cleaning done, and about eleven I left Irene to finish off whatever rooms and went to the kitchen. We lunched at noon precisely; then there was nothing left to do but a few dirty plates. It was pleasant to take lunch and commune with the great hollow, silent house, and it was enough for us just to keep it clean. We ended up thinking, at times, that that was what had kept us from marrying. Irene turned down two suitors for no particular reason, and María Esther went and died on me before we could manage to get engaged. We were easing into our forties with the unvoiced concept that the quiet, simple marriage of sister and brother was the indispensable end to a line established in this house by our grandparents. We would die here someday, obscure and distant cousins would inherit the place, have it torn down, sell the bricks and get rich on the building plot; or more justly and better yet, we would topple it ourselves before it was too late.

Irene never bothered anyone. Once the morning housework was finished, she spent the rest of the day on the sofa in her bedroom, knitting. I couldn't tell you why she knitted so much; I think women knit when they discover that it's a fat excuse to do nothing at all. But Irene was not like that, she always knitted necessities, sweaters for winter, socks for me, handy morning robes and bedjackets for herself. Sometimes she would do a jacket, then unravel it the next moment because there was something that didn't please her; it was pleasant to see a pile of tangled wool in her knitting basket fighting a losing battle for a few hours to retain its shape. Saturdays I went downtown to buy wool; Irene had faith in my good taste, was pleased with the colours and never a skein had to be returned. I took advantage of these trips to make the rounds of the bookstores, uselessly asking if they had anything new in French literature. Nothing worthwhile had arrived in Argentina since 1939.

But it's the house I want to talk about, the house and Irene, I'm not very important. I wonder what Irene would have done without her knitting. One can reread a book, but once a pullover is finished you can't do it over again, it's some kind of disgrace. One day I found that the drawer at the bottom of the chiffonier, replete with moth-balls, was filled with shawls, white, green, lilac. Stacked amid a great smell of camphor – it was like a shop; I didn't have the nerve to ask her what she planned to do with them. We didn't have to earn our living, there was plenty coming in from the farms each month, even piling up. But Irene was only interested in the knitting and showed a wonderful dexterity, and for me the hours slipped away watching her, her hands like silver sea-urchins, needles flashing, and one or two knitting baskets on the floor, the balls of yarn jumping about. It was lovely.

How not to remember the layout of that house. The dining room, a living room with tapestries, the library and three large bedrooms in the section most recessed, the one that faced toward Rodríguez Peña. Only a corridor with its massive oak door separated that part from the front wing, where there was a bath, the kitchen, our bedrooms and the hall. One entered the house through a vestibule with enamelled tiles, and a wrought-iron grated door opened on to the living room. You had to come in through the vestibule and open the gate to go into the living room; the doors to our bedrooms were on either side of this, and opposite it was the corridor leading to the back section; going down the passage, one swung open the oak door beyond which was the other part of the house; or just before the door, one could turn to the left and go down a narrower passageway which led to the kitchen and the bath. When the door was open, you became aware of the size of the house; when it was closed, you had the impression of an apartment, like the ones they build today, with barely enough room to move around in. Irene and I always lived in this part of the house and hardly ever went beyond the oak door except to do the cleaning. Incredible how much dust collected on the furniture. It may be Buenos Aires is a clean city, but she owes it to her population and nothing else. There's too much dust in the air, the slightest breeze and it's back on the marble console tops and in the diamond patterns of the tooled-leather desk set. It's a lot of work to get it off with a feather duster; the motes rise and hang in the air, and settle again a minute later on the pianos and the furniture.

I'll always have a clear memory of it because it happened so simply and without fuss. Irene was knitting in her bedroom, it was eight at night, and I suddenly decided to put the water up for *mate*. I went down the corridor as far as the oak door, which was ajar, then turned into the hall toward the kitchen, when I heard something in the library or the dining room. The sound came through muted and indistinct, a chair being knocked over on to the carpet or the muffled buzzing of a conversation. At the same time, or a second later, I heard it at the end of the passage which led from those two rooms toward the door. I hurled myself against the door before it was too late and shut it, leaned on it with the weight of my body; luckily, the key was on our side; moreover, I ran the great bolt into place, just to be safe.

I went down to the kitchen, heated the kettle, and when I got back with the tray of *mate*, I told Irene:

'I had to shut the door to the passage. They've taken over the back part.'

She let her knitting fall and looked at me with her tired, serious eyes.

'You're sure?'

I nodded.

'In that case,' she said, picking up her needles again, 'we'll have to live on this side.'

I sipped at the *mate* very carefully, but she took her time starting her work again. I remember it was a grey vest she was knitting. I liked that vest.

The first few days were painful, since we'd both left so many things in the part that had been taken over. My collection of French literature, for example, was still in the library. Irene had left several folios of stationery and a pair of slippers that she used a lot in the winter. I missed my briar pipe, and Irene, I think, regretted the loss of an ancient bottle of Hesperidin. It happened repeatedly (but only in the first few days) that we would close some drawer or cabinet and look at one another sadly.

'It's not here.'

One thing more among the many lost on the other side of the house.

But there were advantages, too. The cleaning was so much simplified that, even when we got up late, nine-thirty for instance, by eleven we were sitting around with our arms folded. Irene got into the habit of coming to the kitchen with me to help get lunch. We thought about it and decided on this: while I prepared the lunch, Irene would cook up dishes that could be eaten cold in the evening. We were happy with the arrangement because it was always such a bother to have to leave our bedrooms in the evening and start to cook. Now we made do with the table in Irene's room and platters of cold supper.

Since it left her more time for knitting, Irene was content. I was a little lost without my books, but so as not to inflict myself on my sister, I set about reordering papa's stamp collection; that killed some time. We amused ourselves sufficiently, each with his own thing, almost always getting together in Irene's bedroom, which was the more comfortable. Every once in a while, Irene might say:

'Look at this pattern I just figured out, doesn't it look like clover?'

After a bit it was I, pushing a small square of paper in front of her so that she could see the excellence of some stamp or another from Eupen-et-Malmédy. We were fine, and little by little we stopped thinking. You can live without thinking.

(Whenever Irene talked in her sleep, I woke up immediately and stayed awake. I never could get used to this voice from a statue or a parrot, a voice that came out of the dreams, not from a throat. Irene said that in my sleep I flailed about enormously and shook the blankets off. We had the living room between us, but at night you could hear everything in the house. We heard each other breathing, coughing, could even feel each other reaching for the light switch when, as happened frequently, neither of us could fall asleep.

Aside from our nocturnal rumblings, everything was quiet in the house. During the day there were the household sounds, the metallic click of knitting needles, the rustle of stamp-album pages turning. The oak door was massive, I think I said that. In the kitchen or the bath, which adjoined the part that was taken over, we managed to talk loudly, or Irene sang lullabies. In a kitchen there's always too much noise, the plates and glasses, for there to be interruptions from other sounds. We seldom allowed ourselves silence there, but when we went back to our rooms or to the living room, then the house grew quiet, half-lit, we ended by stepping around more slowly so as not to disturb one another. I think it was because of this that I woke up irremedially and at once when Irene began to talk in her sleep.)

Except for the consequences, it's nearly a matter of repeating the same scene over again. I was thirsty that night, and before we went to sleep, I told Irene that I was going to the kitchen for a glass of water. From the door of the bedroom (she was knitting) I heard the noise in the kitchen; if not the kitchen, then the bath, the passage off at that angle dulled the sound. Irene noticed how brusquely I had paused, and came up beside me without a word. We stood listening to the noises, growing more and more sure that they were on our side of the oak door, if not the kitchen then the bath, or in the hall itself at the turn, almost next to us.

We didn't wait to look at one another. I took Irene's arm and forced her to run with me to the wrought-iron door, not waiting to look back. You could hear the noises, still muffled but louder, just behind us. I slammed the grating and we stopped in the vestibule. Now there was nothing to be heard.

'They've taken over our section,' Irene said. The knitting had reeled off from her hands and the yarn ran back toward the door and disappeared under it. When she saw that the balls of yarn were on the other side, she dropped the knitting without looking at it.

'Did you have time to bring anything?' I asked hopelessly.

'No, nothing.'

We had what we had on. I remembered fifteen thousand pesos in the wardrobe in my bedroom. Too late now.

I still had my wrist watch on and saw that it was 11 p.m. I took Irene around the waist (I think she was crying) and that was how we went into the street. Before we left, I felt terrible; I locked the front door up tight and tossed the key down the sewer. It wouldn't do to have some poor devil decide to go in and rob the house, at that hour and with the house taken over.

*Translated from the Spanish by Paul Blackburn.*

# How Love Came to Professor Guildea

## Robert S. Hichens

*Robert Smythe Hichens, who died in 1950, wrote three best-selling novels now scarcely remembered:* The Garden of Allah *(filmed three times; the latest version in 1936, with Charles Boyer and Marlene Dietrich),* The Paradine Case *(filmed by Alfred Hitchcock); and* Bella Donna. *He was Oscar Wilde's confidant and caricatured him in his novel* The Green Carnation *(1894). He was also a friend of the young Somerset Maugham. His fame, however, is secured by the following short story, selected by Dorothy L. Sayers for her own anthology of detection, mystery, and horror. Dorothy L. Sayers spoke of the 'delicious nausea' it provoked in her; I found Guildea's ghost (invisible and nameless as those of Cortázar) a startling and wonderful invention, the story's originality heightened by the classical use of a pair of opposed characters like Holmes and Watson, Don Quixote and Sancho Panza, Father Brown and Flambeau.*

## I

Dull people often wondered how it came about that Father Murchison and Professor Guildea were intimate friends. The one was all faith, the other all scepticism. The nature of the Father was based on love. He viewed the world with an almost childlike tenderness above his long, black cassock; and his mild, yet perfectly fearless, blue eyes seemed always to be watching the goodness that exists in humanity, and rejoicing at what they saw. The Professor, on the other hand, had a hard face like a hatchet, tipped with an aggressive black goatee beard. His eyes were quick, piercing and irreverent. The lines about his small, thin-lipped mouth were almost cruel. His voice was harsh and dry, sometimes, when he grew energetic, almost soprano. It fired off words with a sharp and clipping utterance. His habitual manner was one of distrust and investigation. It was impossible to suppose that, in his busy life, he found any time for love, either of humanity in general or of an individual.

Yet his days were spent in scientific investigations which conferred immense benefits upon the world.

Both men were celibates. Father Murchison was a member of an Anglican order which forbade him to marry. Professor Guildea had a poor opinion of most things, but especially of women. He had formerly held a post as lecturer at Birmingham. But when his fame as a discoverer grew, he removed to London. There, at a lecture he gave in the East End, he first met Father Murchison. They spoke a few words. Perhaps the bright intelligence of the priest appealed to the man of science, who was inclined, as a rule, to regard the clergy with some contempt. Perhaps the transparent sincerity of this devotee, full of common sense, attracted him. As he was leaving the hall he abruptly asked the Father to call on him at his house in Hyde Park Place. And the Father, who seldom went into the West End, except to preach, accepted the invitation.

'When will you come?' said Guildea.

He was folding up the blue paper on which his notes were written in a tiny, clear hand. The leaves rustled dryly in accompaniment to his sharp, dry voice.

'On Sunday week I am preaching in the evening at St Saviour's, not far off,' said the Father.

'I don't go to church.'

'No,' said the Father, without any accent of surprise or condemnation.

'Come to supper afterward?'

'Thank you, I will.'

'What time will you come?'

The Father smiled.

'As soon as I have finished my sermon. The service is at six-thirty.'

'About eight then, I suppose. Don't make the sermon too long. My number in Hyde Park Place is 100. Good night to you.'

He snapped an elastic band round his papers and strode off without shaking hands.

On the appointed Sunday, Father Murchison preached to a

densely crowded congregation at St Saviour's. The subject of his sermon was sympathy, and the comparative uselessness of a man in the world unless he can learn to love his neighbour as himself. The sermon was rather long, and when the preacher, in his flowing, black cloak, and his hard, round hat, with a straight brim over which hung the ends of a black cord, made his way toward the Professor's house, the hands of the illuminated clock disc at the Marble Arch pointed to twenty minutes past eight.

The Father hurried on, pushing his way through the crowd of standing soldiers, chattering women and giggling street boys in their Sunday best. It was a warm April night, and when he reached number 100 Hyde Park Place, he found the Professor bareheaded on his doorstep, gazing out toward the Park railings, and enjoying the soft, moist air, in front of his lighted passage.

'Ha, a long sermon!' he exclaimed. 'Come in.'

'I fear it was,' said the Father, obeying the invitation. 'I am that dangerous thing – an extempore preacher.'

'More attractive to speak without notes, if you can do it. Hang your hat and coat – oh, cloak – here. We'll have supper at once. This is the dining room.'

He opened a door on the right and they entered a long, narrow room, with gold paper and a black ceiling, from which hung an electric lamp with a gold-coloured shade. In the room stood a small oval table with covers laid for two. The Professor rang the bell. Then he said, 'People seem to talk better at an oval table than at a square one.'

'Really. Is that so?'

'Well, I've had precisely the same party twice, once at a square table, once at an oval table. The first dinner was a dull failure, the second a brilliant success. Sit down, won't you?'

'How d'you account for the difference?' said the Father, sitting down, and pulling the tail of his cassock well under him.

'H'm. I know how you'd account for it.'

'Indeed. How then?'

'At an oval table, since there are no corners, the chain of human sympathy – the electric current, is much more complete. Eh! Let me give you some soup.'

'Thank you.'

The Father took it, and, as he did so, turned his beaming blue eyes on his host. Then he smiled.

'What!' he said, in his pleasant, light tenor voice. 'You do go to church sometimes, then?'

'Tonight is the first time for ages. And, mind you, I was tremendously bored.'

The Father still smiled, and his blue eyes gently twinkled.

'Dear, dear!' he said, 'what a pity!'

'But not by the sermon,' Guildea added. 'I don't pay a compliment. I state a fact. The sermon didn't bore me. If it had, I should have said so, or said nothing.'

'And which would you have done?'

The Professor smiled almost genially.

'Don't know,' he said. 'What wine d'you drink?'

'None, thank you. I'm a teetotaler. In my profession and *milieu* it is necessary to be one. Yes, I will have some soda water. I think you would have done the first.'

'Very likely, and very wrongly. You wouldn't have minded much.'

'I don't think I should.'

They were intimate already. The Father felt most pleasantly at home under the black ceiling. He drank some soda water and seemed to enjoy it more than the Professor enjoyed his claret.

'You smile at the theory of the chain of human sympathy, I see,' said the Father. 'Then what is your explanation of the failure of your square party with corners, the success of your oval party without them?'

'Probably on the first occasion the wit of the assembly had a chill on his liver, while on the second he was in perfect health. Yet, you see, I stick to the oval table.'

'And that means –'

'Very little. By the way, your omission of any allusion to the notorious part liver plays in love was a serious one tonight.'

'Your omission of any desire for close human sympathy in your life is a more serious one.'

'How can you be sure I have no such desire?'

'I divine it. Your look, your manner, tell me it is so. You were disagreeing with my sermon all the time I was preaching. Weren't you?'

'Part of the time.'

The servant changed the plates. He was a middle-aged, blond, thin man, with a stony white face, pale, prominent eyes, and an accomplished manner of service. When he had left the room the Professor continued.

'Your remarks interested me, but I thought them exaggerated.'

'For instance?'

'Let me play the egoist for a moment. I spend most of my time in hard work, very hard work. The results of this work, you will allow, benefit humanity.'

'Enormously,' assented the Father, thinking of more than one of Guildea's discoveries.

'And the benefit conferred by this work, undertaken merely for its own sake, is just as great as if it were undertaken because I loved my fellow man, and sentimentally desired to see him more comfortable than he is at present. I'm as useful precisely in my present condition of – in my present nonaffectional condition – as I should be if I were as full of gush as the sentimentalists who want to get murderers out of prison, or to put a premium on tyranny – like Tolstoi – by preventing the punishment of tyrants.'

'One may do great harm with affection; great good without it. Yes, that is true. Even *le bon motif* is not everything, I know. Still I contend that, given your powers, you would be far more useful in the world with sympathy, affection for your kind, added to them than as you are. I believe even that you would do still more splendid work.'

The Professor poured himself out another glass of claret.

'You noticed my butler?' he said.

'I did.'

'He's a perfect servant. He makes me perfectly comfortable. Yet he has no feeling of liking for me. I treat him civilly. I pay him well. But I never think about him, or concern myself with him as a human being. I know nothing of his character except what I read of it in his last master's letter. There are, you may say, no truly human relations between us. You would affirm that his work would be better done if I had made him personally like me as man – of any class – can like man – of any other class?'

'I should, decidedly.'

'I contend that he couldn't do his work better than he does it at present.'

'But if any crisis occurred?'

'What?'

'Any crisis, change in your condition. If you needed his help, not only as a man and a butler, but as a man and a brother? He'd fail you then, probably. You would never get from your servant that finest service which can only be prompted by an honest affection.'

'You have finished?'

'Quite.'

'Let us go upstairs then. Yes, those are good prints. I picked them up in Birmingham when I was living there. This is my workroom.'

They came to a double room lined entirely with books, and brilliantly, rather hardly, lit by electricity. The windows at one end looked on to the Park, at the other on to the garden of a neighbouring house. The door by which they entered was concealed from the inner and smaller room by the jutting wall of the outer room, in which stood a huge writing table loaded with letters, pamphlets and manuscripts. Between the two windows of the inner room was a cage in which a large, grey parrot was clambering, using both beak and claws to assist him in his slow and meditative peregrinations.

'You have a pet,' said the Father, surprised.

'I possess a parrot,' the Professor answered dryly. 'I got him for a purpose when I was making a study of the imitative powers of birds, and I have never got rid of him. A cigar?'

'Thank you.'

They sat down. Father Murchison glanced at the parrot. It had paused in its journey, and, clinging to the bars of its cage, was regarding them with attentive round eyes that looked deliberately intelligent, but by no means sympathetic. He looked away from it to Guildea, who was smoking, with his head thrown back, his sharp, pointed chin, on which the small black beard bristled, upturned. He was moving his under lip up and down rapidly. This action caused the beard to stir and look peculiarly aggressive. The Father suddenly chuckled softly.

'Why's that?' cried Guildea, letting his chin drop down on his breast and looking at his guest sharply.

'I was thinking it would have to be a crisis indeed that could make you cling to your butler's affection for assistance.'

Guildea smiled too.

'You're right. It would. Here he comes.'

The man entered with coffee. He offered it gently, and retired like a shadow retreating on a wall.

'Splendid, inhuman fellow,' remarked Guildea.

'I prefer the East End lad who does my errands in Bird Street,' said the Father. 'I know all his worries. He knows some of mine. We are friends. He's more noisy than your man. He even breathes hard when he is especially solicitous, but he would do more for me than put the coals on my fire, or black my square-toed boots.'

'Men are differently made. To me the watchful eye of affection would be abominable.'

'What about that bird?'

The Father pointed to the parrot. It had got up on its perch and, with one foot uplifted in an impressive, almost benedictory, manner, was gazing steadily at the Professor.

'That's a watchful eye of imitation, with a mind at the back of it, desirous of reproducing the peculiarities of others. No, I thought your sermon tonight very fresh, very clever. But I have no wish for affection. Reasonable liking, of course, one desires – ' he tugged sharply at his beard, as if to warn himself against sentimentality – 'but anything more would be most irksome, and would push me, I feel sure, towards cruelty. It would also hamper one's work.'

'I don't think so.'

'The sort of work I do. I shall continue to benefit the world without loving it, and it will continue to accept the benefits without loving me. That's all as it should be.'

He drank his coffee. Then he added rather aggressively, 'I have neither time nor inclination for sentimentality.'

When Guildea let Father Murchison out, he followed the Father on to the doorstep and stood there for a moment. The Father glanced across the damp road into the Park.

'I see you've got a gate just opposite you,' he said idly.

'Yes, I often slip across for a stroll to clear my brain. Good night to you. Come again some day.'

'With pleasure. Good night.'

The priest strode away, leaving Guildea standing on the step.

Father Murchison came many times again to number 100 Hyde Park Place. He had a feeling of liking for most men and women whom he knew, and of tenderness for all, whether he knew them or not, but he grew to have a special sentiment toward Guildea. Strangely enough, it was a sentiment of pity. He pitied this hard-working, eminently successful man of big brain and bold heart, who never seemed depressed, who never wanted assistance, who never complained of the twisted skein of life or faltered in his progress along its way. The Father pitied Guildea, in fact, because Guildea wanted so little. He had told him so, for the intercourse of the two men, from the beginning, had been singularly frank.

One evening, when they were talking together, the Father happened to speak of one of the oddities of life, the fact that those who do not want things often get them, while those who seek them vehemently are disappointed in their search.

'Then I ought to have affection poured upon me,' said Guildea smiling rather grimly. 'For I hate it.'

'Perhaps some day you will.'

'I hope not, most sincerely.'

Father Murchison said nothing for a moment. He was drawing together the ends of the broad band round his cassock. When he spoke he seemed to be answering someone.

'Yes,' he said slowly, 'yes, that *is* my feeling – pity.'

'For whom?' said the Professor.

Then, suddenly, he understood. He did not say that he understood, but Father Murchison felt, and saw, that it was quite unnecessary to answer his friend's question. So Guildea, strangely enough, found himself closely acquainted with a man – his opposite in all ways – who pitied him.

The fact that he did not mind this, and scarcely ever thought about it, shows perhaps as clearly as anything could, the peculiar indifference of his nature.

# II

One autumn evening, a year and a half after Father Murchison and the Professor had first met, the Father called in Hyde Park Place and inquired of the blond and stony butler – his name was Pitting – whether his master was at home.

'Yes, sir,' replied Pitting. 'Will you please come this way?'

He moved noiselessly up the rather narrow stairs, followed by the Father, tenderly opened the library door, and in his soft, cold voice, announced, 'Father Murchison.'

Guildea was sitting in an armchair, before a small fire. His thin, long-fingered hands lay outstretched upon his knees, his head was sunk down on his chest. He appeared to be pondering deeply. Pitting very slightly raised his voice.

'Father Murchison to see you, sir,' he repeated.

The Professor jumped up rather suddenly and turned sharply round as the Father came in.

'Oh,' he said. 'It's you, is it? Glad to see you. Come to the fire.'

The Father glanced at him and thought him looking unusually fatigued.

'You don't look well tonight,' the Father said.

'No?'

'You must be working too hard. That lecture you are going to give in Paris is bothering you?'

'Not a bit. It's all arranged. I could deliver it to you at this moment verbatim. Well, sit down.'

The Father did so, and Guildea sank once more into his chair and stared hard into the fire without another word. He seemed to be thinking profoundly. His friend did not interrupt him, but quietly lit a pipe and began to smoke reflectively. The eyes of Guildea were fixed upon the fire. The Father glanced about the room, at the walls of soberly bound books, at the crowded writing table, at the windows, before which hung heavy, dark blue curtains of old brocade, at the cage, which stood between them. A green baize covering was thrown over it. The Father wondered why. He had never seen Napoleon – so the parrot was named – covered up at night before. While he was looking at the baize Guildea suddenly jerked up his head and, taking his hands from his knees and clasping them, said abruptly, 'D'you think I'm an attractive man?'

Father Murchison jumped. Such a question coming from such a man astounded him.

'Bless me!' he ejaculated. 'What makes you ask? Do you mean attractive to the opposite sex?'

'That's what I don't know,' said the Professor gloomily, and staring again into the fire. 'That's what I don't know.'

The Father grew more astonished.

'Don't know!' he exclaimed.

And he laid down his pipe.

'Let's say – d'you think I'm attractive, that there's anything about me which might draw a – a human being, or an animal irresistibly to me?'

'Whether you desired it or not?'

'Exactly – or – no, let us say definitely – if I did not desire it.'

Father Murchison pursed up his rather full, cherubic lips, and little wrinkles appeared about the corners of his blue eyes.

'There might be, of course,' he said, after a pause. 'Human nature is weak, engagingly weak, Guildea. And you're inclined to flout it. I could understand a certain class of lady – the lion-hunting, the intellectual lady, seeking you. Your reputation, your great name – '

'Yes, yes,' Guildea interrupted, rather irritably, 'I know all that, I know.'

He twisted his long hands together, bending the palms outward till his thin, pointed fingers cracked. His forehead was wrinkled in a frown.

'I imagine,' he said – he stopped and coughed dryly, almost shrilly – 'I imagine it would be very disagreeable to be liked, to be run after – that is the usual expression, isn't it – by anything one objected to.'

And now he half turned in his chair, crossed his legs one over the other, and looked at his guest with an unusual, almost piercing interrogation.

'Anything?' said the Father.

'Well – well, anyone. I imagine nothing could be more unpleasant.'

'To you – no,' answered the Father. 'But – forgive me, Guildea, I cannot conceive your permitting such intrusion. You don't encourage adoration.'

Guildea nodded his head gloomily.

'I don't,' he said, 'I don't. That's just it. That's the curious part of it, that I – '

He broke off deliberately, got up and stretched.

'I'll have a pipe, too,' he said.

He went over to the mantelpiece, got his pipe, filled it and lighted it. As he held the match to the tobacco, bending forward with an inquiring expression, his eyes fell upon the green baize that covered Napoleon's cage. He threw the match into the grate, and puffed at the pipe as he walked forward to the cage. When he reached it he put out his hand, took hold of the baize and began to pull it away. Then suddenly he pushed it back over the cage.

'No,' he said, as if to himself, 'no.'

He returned rather hastily to the fire and threw himself once more into his armchair.

'You're wondering,' he said to Father Murchison. 'So am I. I don't know at all what to make of it. I'll just tell you the facts and you must tell me what you think of them. The night before last, after a day of hard work – but no harder than usual – I went to the front door to get a breath of air. You know I often do that.'

'Yes, I found you on the doorstep when I first came here.'

'Just so. I didn't put on hat or coat. I just stood on the step as I was. My mind, I remember, was still full of my work. It was rather a dark night, not very dark. The hour was about eleven, or a quarter past. I was staring at the Park, and presently I found that my eyes were directed towards somebody who was sitting, back to me, on one of the benches. I saw the person – if it was a person – through the railings.'

'If it was a person!' said the Father. 'What do you mean by that?'

'Wait a minute. I say that because it was too dark for me to know. I merely saw some blackish object on the bench, rising into view above the level of the back of the seat. I couldn't say it was man, woman or child. But something there was, and I found that I was looking at it.'

'I understand.'

'Gradually, I also found that my thoughts were becoming fixed upon this thing or person. I began to wonder, first, what it was doing there; next, what it was thinking; lastly, what it was like.'

'Some poor creature without a home, I suppose,' said the Father.

'I said that to myself. Still, I was taken with an extraordinary interest about this object, so great an interest that I got my hat and crossed the road to go into the Park. As you know, there's an entrance almost opposite to my house. Well, Murchison, I crossed the road, passed through the gate in the railings, went up to the seat, and found that there was – nothing on it.'

'Were you looking at it as you walked?'

'Part of the time. But I removed my eyes from it just as I passed through the gate, because there was a row going on a little way off, and I turned for an instant in that direction. When I saw that the seat was vacant I was seized by a most absurd sensation of disappointment, almost of anger. I stopped and looked about me to see if anything was moving away, but I could see nothing. It was a cold night and misty, and there were few people about. Feeling, as I say, foolishly and unnaturally disappointed, I retraced my steps to this house. When I got here I discovered that during my short absence I had left the hall door open – half open.'

'Rather imprudent in London.'

'Yes. I had no idea, of course, that I had done so, till I got back. However, I was only away three minutes or so.'

'Yes.'

'It was not likely that anybody had gone in.'

'I suppose not.'

'Was it?'

'Why do you ask me that, Guildea?'

'Well, well!'

'Besides, if anybody had gone in, on your return you'd have caught him, surely.'

Guildea coughed again. The Father, surprised, could not fail to recognize that he was nervous and that his nervousness was affecting him physically.

'I must have caught cold that night,' he said, as if he had read his friend's thought and hastened to contradict it. Then he went on, 'I entered the hall, or passage, rather.'

He paused again. His uneasiness was becoming very apparent.

'And you did catch somebody?' said the Father.

Guildea cleared his throat.

'That's just it,' he said, 'now we come to it. I'm not imaginative, as you know.'

'You certainly are not.'

'No, but hardly had I stepped into the passage before I felt certain that somebody had got into the house during my absence. I felt convinced of it, and not only that, I also felt convinced that the intruder was the very person I had dimly seen sitting upon the seat in the Park. What d'you say to that?'

'I begin to think you are imaginative.'

'H'm! It seemed to me that the person – the occupant of the seat – and I, had simultaneously formed the project of interviewing each other, had simultaneously set out to put that project into execution. I became so certain of this that I walked hastily upstairs into this room, expecting to find the visitor awaiting me. But there was no one. I then came down again and went into the dining room. No one. I was actually astonished. Isn't that odd?'

'Very,' said the Father, quite gravely.

The Professor's chill and gloomy manner, and uncomfortable, constrained appearance kept away the humour that might well have lurked round the steps of such a discourse.

'I went upstairs again,' he continued, 'sat down and thought the matter over. I resolved to forget it, and took up a book. I might perhaps have been able to read, but suddenly I thought I noticed – '

He stopped abruptly. Father Murchison observed that he was staring toward the green baize that covered the parrot's cage.

'But that's nothing,' he said. 'Enough that I couldn't read. I resolved to explore the house. You know how small it is, how easily one can go all over it. I went all over it. I went into every room without exception. To the servants, who were having supper, I made some excuse. They were surprised at my advent, no doubt.'

'And Pitting?'

'Oh, he got up politely when I came in, stood while I was there, but never said a word. I muttered "Don't disturb yourselves – " or something of the sort, and came out. Murchison, I found nobody new in the house – yet I returned to this room entirely convinced that somebody had entered while I was in the Park.'

'And gone out again before you came back?'

'No, had stayed, and was still in the house.'

'But, my dear Guildea,' began the Father, now in great astonishment. 'Surely—'

'I know what you want to say – what I should want to say in your place. Now, do wait. I am also convinced that this visitor has not left the house and is at this moment in it.'

He spoke with evident sincerity, with extreme gravity. Father Murchison looked him full in the face, and met his quick, keen eyes.

'No,' he said, as if in reply to an uttered question, 'I'm perfectly sane, I assure you. The whole matter seems almost as incredible to me as it must to you. But, as you know, I never quarrel with facts, however strange. I merely try to examine into them thoroughly. I have already consulted a doctor and been pronounced in perfect bodily health.'

He paused, as if expecting the Father to say something.

'Go on, Guildea,' he said, 'you haven't finished.'

'No. I felt that night positive that somebody had entered the house, and remained in it, and my conviction grew. I went to bed as usual, and, contrary to my expectation, slept as well as I generally do. Yet directly I woke up yesterday morning I knew that my household had been increased by one.'

'May I interrupt you for one moment? How did you know it?'

'By my mental sensation. I can only say that I was perfectly conscious of a new presence within my house, close to me.'

'How very strange,' said the Father. 'And you feel absolutely certain that you are not overworked? Your brain does not feel tired? Your head is quite clear?'

'Quite. I was never better. When I came down to breakfast that morning I looked sharply into Pitting's face. He was as coldly placid and inexpressive as usual. It was evident to me that his mind was in no way distressed. After breakfast I sat down to work, all the time ceaselessly conscious of the fact of this intruder upon my privacy. Nevertheless, I laboured for several hours, waiting for any development that might occur to clear away the mysterious obscurity of this event. I lunched. About half-past two I was obliged to go out to attend a lecture. I therefore took my coat and hat, opened my door, and stepped on to the pavement. I was instantly aware that I was no longer intruded upon, and this although I was now in the street, surrounded by people. Consequently, I felt certain that the thing in my house must be thinking of me, perhaps even spying upon me.'

'Wait a moment,' interrupted the Father. 'What was your sensation? Was it one of fear?'

'Oh, dear no. I was entirely puzzled – as I am now – and keenly interested, but not in any way alarmed. I delivered my lecture with my usual ease and returned home in the evening. On entering the house again I was perfectly conscious that the intruder was still there. Last night I dined alone and spent the hours after dinner in reading a scientific work in which I was deeply interested. While I read, however, I never for one moment lost the knowledge that some mind – very attentive to me – was within hail of mine. I will say more than this – the sensation constantly increased, and, by the time I got up to go to bed, I had come to a very strange conclusion.'

'What? What was it?'

'That whoever – or whatever – had entered my house during my short absence in the Park was more than interested in me.'

'More than interested in you?'

'Was fond, or was becoming fond, of me.'

'Oh!' exclaimed the Father. 'Now I understand why you asked me just now whether I thought there was anything about you that might draw a human being or an animal irresistibly to you.'

'Precisely. Since I came to this conclusion, Murchison, I will confess that my feeling of strong curiosity has become tinged with another feeling.'

'Of fear?'

'No, of dislike, or irritation. No – not fear, not fear.'

As Guildea repeated unnecessarily this asseveration he looked again towards the parrot's cage.

'What is there to be afraid of in such a matter?' he added. 'I am not a child to tremble before bogies.'

In saying the last words he raised his voice sharply; then he walked quickly to the cage, and, with an abrupt movement, pulled the baize covering from it. Napoleon was disclosed, apparently dozing upon his perch with his head held slightly on one side. As the light reached him, he moved, ruffled the feathers about his neck, blinked his eyes, and began slowly to sidle to and fro, thrusting his head forward and drawing it back with an air of complacent, though rather unmeaning, energy. Guildea stood by the cage, looking at him closely, and indeed with an attention that was so intense as to be remarkable, almost unnatural.

'How absurd these birds are!' he said at length, coming back to the fire.

'You have no more to tell me?' asked the Father.

'No. I am still aware of the presence of something in my house. I am still conscious of its close attention to me. I am still irritated, seriously annoyed – I confess it – by that attention.'

'You say you are aware of the presence of something at this moment?'

'At this moment – yes.'

'Do you mean in this room, with us, now?'

'I should say so – at any rate, quite near us.'

Again he glanced quickly, almost suspiciously, toward the cage of the parrot. The bird was sitting still on its perch now. Its head was bent down and cocked sideways, and it appeared to be listening attentively to something.

'That bird will have the intonations of my voice more correctly than ever by tomorrow morning,' said the Father, watching Guildea closely with his mild blue eyes. 'And it has always imitated me very cleverly.'

The Professor started slightly.

'Yes,' he said. 'Yes, no doubt. Well, what do you make of this affair?'

'Nothing at all. It is absolutely inexplicable. I can speak quite frankly to you, I feel sure.'

'Of course. That's why I have told you the whole thing.'

'I think you must be overworked, overstrained, without knowing it.'

'And that the doctor was mistaken when he said I was all right?'

'Yes.'

Guildea knocked his pipe out against the chimney piece.

'It may be so,' he said, 'I will not be so unreasonable as to deny the possibility, although I feel as well as I ever did in my life. What do you advise then?'

'A week of complete rest away from London, in good air.'

'The usual prescription. I'll take it. I'll go tomorrow to Westgate and leave Napoleon to keep house in my absence.'

For some reason, which he could not explain to himself, the pleasure which Father Murchison felt in hearing the first part of his friend's final remark was lessened, was almost destroyed, by the last sentence.

He walked toward the City that night, deep in thought, remembering and carefully considering the first interview he had with Guildea in the latter's house a year and a half before.

On the following morning Guildea left London.

# III

Father Murchison was so busy a man that he had little time for brooding over the affairs of others. During Guildea's week at the sea, however, the Father thought about him a great deal, with much wonder and some dismay. The dismay was soon banished, for the mild-eyed priest was quick to discern weakness in himself, quicker still to drive it forth as a most undesirable inmate of the soul. But the wonder remained. It was destined to a crescendo. Guildea had left London on a Thursday. On a Thursday he returned, having previously sent a note to Father Murchison to mention that he was leaving Westgate at a certain time. When his train ran into Victoria Station, at five o'clock in the evening, he was surprised to see the cloaked figure of his friend standing upon the grey platform behind a line of porters.

'What, Murchison!' he said. 'You here! Have you seceded from your order that you are taking this holiday?'

They shook hands.

'No,' said the Father. 'It happened that I had to be in this neighbourhood today, visiting a sick person. So I thought I would meet you.'

'And see if I were still a sick person, eh?'

The Professor glanced at him kindly, but with a dry little laugh.

'Are you?' replied the Father gently, looking at him with interest. 'No, I think not. You appear very well.'

The sea air had, in fact, put some brownish red into Guildea's always thin cheeks. His keen eyes were shining with life and energy, and he walked forward in his loose grey suit and fluttering overcoat with a vigour that was noticeable, carrying easily in his left hand his well-filled Gladstone bag.

The Father felt completely reassured.

'I never saw you look better,' he said.

'I never was better. Have you an hour to spare?'

'Two'.

'Good. I'll send my bag up by cab, and we'll walk across the Park to my house and have a cup of tea there. What d'you say?'

'I shall enjoy it.'

They walked out of the station yard, past the flower girls and newspaper sellers towards Grosvenor Place.

'And you have had a pleasant time?' the Father said.

'Pleasant enough, and lonely. I left my companion behind me in the passage at number 100, you know.'

'And you'll not find him there now, I feel sure.'

'H'm!' ejaculated Guildea. 'What a precious weakling you think me, Murchison.'

As he spoke he strode forward more quickly, as if moved to emphasize his sensation of bodily vigour.

'A weakling – no. But anyone who uses his brain as persistently as you do yours must require an occasional holiday.'

'And I required one very badly, eh?'

'You required one, I believe.'

'Well, I've had it. And now we'll see.'

The evening was closing in rapidly. They crossed the road at Hyde Park Corner, and entered the Park, in which were a number of people going home from work; men in corduroy trousers, caked with dried mud, and carrying tin cans slung over their shoulders, and flat panniers, in which lay their tools. Some of the younger ones talked loudly or whistled shrilly as they walked.

'Until the evening,' murmured Father Murchison to himself.

'What?' asked Guildea.

'I was only quoting the last words of the text, which seems written upon life, especially upon the life of pleasure: "Man goeth forth to his work, and to his labour."'

'Ah, those fellows are not half bad fellows to have in an audience. There were a lot of them at the lecture I gave when I first met you, I remember. One of them tried to heckle me. He had a red beard. Chaps with red beards are always hecklers. I laid him low on that occasion. Well, Murchison, and now we're going to see.'

'What?'

'Whether my companion has departed.'

'Tell me – do you feel any expectation of – well – of again thinking something is there?'

'How carefully you choose language. No, I merely wonder.'

'You have no apprehension?'

'Not a scrap. But I confess to feeling curious.'

'Then the sea air hasn't taught you to recognize that the whole thing came from overstrain.'

'No,' said Guildea, very dryly.

He walked on in silence for a minute. Then he added, 'You thought it would?'

'I certainly thought it might.'

'Make me realize that I had a sickly, morbid, rotten imagination – eh? Come now, Murchison, why not say frankly that you packed me off to Westgate to get rid of what you considered an acute form of hysteria?'

The Father was quite unmoved by this attack.

'Come now, Guildea,' he retorted, 'what did you expect me to think? I saw no indication of hysteria in you. I never have. One would suppose you the last man likely to have such a malady. But which is more natural – for me to believe in your hysteria or in the truth of such a story as you told me?'

'You have me there. No, I mustn't complain. Well, there's no hysteria about me now, at any rate.'

'And no stranger in your house, I hope.'

Father Murchison spoke the last words with earnest gravity, dropping the half-bantering tone – which they had both assumed.

'You take the matter very seriously, I believe,' said Guildea, also speaking more gravely.

'How else can I take it? You wouldn't have me laugh at it when you tell it me seriously?'

'No. If we find my visitor still in the house, I may even call upon you to exorcise it. But first I must do one thing."

'And that is?'

'Prove to you, as well as to myself, that it is still there.'

'That might be difficult,' said the Father, considerably surprised by Guildea's matter-of-fact tone.

'I don't know. If it has remained in my house I think I can find a means. And I shall not be at all surprised if it is still there – despite the Westgate air.'

In saying the last words the Professor relapsed into his former tone of dry chaff. The Father could not quite make up his mind whether Guildea was feeling unusually grave or unusually gay. As the two men drew near to Hyde Park Place their conversation died away and they walked forward silently in the gathering darkness.

'Here we are!' said Guildea at last.

He thrust the key into the door, opened it and let Father Murchison into the passage, following him closely, and banging the door.

'Here we are!' he repeated in a louder voice.

The electric light was turned on in anticipation of his arrival. He stood still and looked round.

'We'll have some tea at once,' he said. 'Ah, Pitting!'

The pale butler, who had heard the door bang, moved gently forward from the top of the stairs that led to the kitchen, greeted his master respectfully, took his coat and Father Murchison's cloak, and hung them on two pegs against the wall.

'All's right, Pitting? All's as usual?' said Guildea.

'Quite so, sir.'

'Bring us up some tea to the library.'

'Yes, sir.'

Pitting retreated. Guildea waited till he had disappeared, then opened the dining-room door, put his head into the room and kept it there for a moment, standing perfectly still. Presently he drew back into the passage, shut the door, and said, 'Let's go upstairs.'

Father Murchison looked at him inquiringly, but made no remark. They ascended the stairs and came into the library. Guildea glanced rather sharply round. A fire was burning on the hearth. The blue curtains were drawn. The bright gleam of the strong electric light fell on the long rows of books, on the writing table –

very orderly in consequence of Guildea's holiday – and on the uncovered cage of the parrot. Guildea went up to the cage. Napoleon was sitting humped up on his perch with his feathers ruffled. His long toes, which looked as if they were covered with crocodile skin, clung to the bar. His round and blinking eyes were filmy, like old eyes. Guildea stared at the bird very hard, and then clucked with his tongue against his teeth. Napoleon shook himself, lifted one foot, extended his toes, sidled along the perch to the bars nearest to the Professor and thrust his head against them. Guildea scratched it with his forefinger two or three times, still gazing attentively at the parrot; then he returned to the fire just as Pitting entered with the tea tray.

Father Murchison was already sitting in an armchair on one side of the fire. Guildea took another chair and began to pour out tea, as Pitting left the room, closing the door gently behind him. The Father sipped his tea, found it hot and set the cup down on a little table at his side.

'You're fond of that parrot, aren't you?' he asked his friend.

'Not particularly. It's interesting to study sometimes. The parrot mind and nature are peculiar.'

'How long have you had him?'

'About four years. I nearly got rid of him just before I made your acquaintance. I'm very glad now I kept him.'

'Are you? Why is that?'

'I shall probably tell you in a day or two.'

The Father took his cup again. He did not press Guildea for an immediate explanation, but when they had both finished their tea he said, 'Well, has the sea air had the desired effect?'

'No,' said Guildea.

The Father brushed some crumbs from the front of his cassock and sat up higher in his chair.

'Your visitor is still here?' he asked, and his blue eyes became almost ungentle and piercing as he gazed at his friend.

'Yes,' answered Guildea calmly.

'How do you know it, when did you know it – when you looked into the dining room just now?'

'No. Not until I came into this room. It welcomed me here.'

'Welcomed you! In what way?'

'Simply by being here, by making me feel that it is here, as I might feel that a man was if I came into the room when it was dark.'

He spoke quietly, with perfect composure in his usual dry manner.

'Very well,' the Father said, 'I shall not try to contend against your sensation, or to explain it away. Naturally, I am in amazement.'

'So am I. Never has anything in my life surprised me so much. Murchison, of course I cannot expect you to believe more than that I honestly suppose – imagine, if you like – that there is some intruder here, of what kind I am totally unaware. I cannot expect you to believe that there really is anything. If you were in my place, I in yours, I should certainly consider you the victim of some nervous delusion. I could not do otherwise. But – wait. Don't condemn me as a hysteria patient, or as a madman, for two or three days. I feel convinced that – unless I am indeed unwell, a mental invalid, which I don't think is possible – I shall be able very shortly to give you some proof that there is a newcomer in my house.'

'You don't tell me what kind of proof?'

'Not yet. Things must go a little farther first. But, perhaps even tomorrow I may be able to explain myself more fully. In the meanwhile, I'll say this, that if, eventually, I can't bring any kind of proof that I'm not dreaming, I'll let you take me to any doctor you like, and I'll resolutely try to adopt your present view – that I'm suffering from an absurd delusion. That is your view, of course?'

Father Murchison was silent for a moment. Then he said, rather doubtfully, 'It ought to be.'

'But isn't it?' asked Guildea, surprised.

'Well, you know, your manner is enormously convincing. Still, of course, I doubt. How can I do otherwise? The whole thing must be fancy.'

The Father spoke as if he were trying to recoil from a mental position he was being forced to take up.

'It must be fancy,' he repeated.

'I'll convince you by more than my manner, or I'll not try to convince you at all,' said Guildea.

When they parted that evening, he said, 'I'll write to you in a day or two probably. I think the proof I am going to give you has been accumulating during my absence. But I shall soon know.'

Father Murchison was extremely puzzled as he sat on the top of the omnibus going homeward.

# IV

In two days' time he received a note from Guildea asking him to call, if possible, the same evening. This he was unable to do as he had an engagement to fulfil at some East End gathering. The following day was Sunday. He wrote saying he would come on the Monday, and got a wire shortly afterward: 'YES, MONDAY COME TO DINNER SEVEN-THIRTY GUILDEA.' At half-past seven he stood on the doorstep of number 100.

Pitting let him in.

'Is the Professor quite well, Pitting?' the Father inquired as he took off his cloak.

'I believe so, sir. He has not made any complaint,' the butler formally replied. 'Will you come upstairs, sir?'

Guildea met them at the door of the library. He was very pale and sombre, and shook hands carelessly with his friend.

'Give us dinner,' he said to Pitting.

As the butler retired, Guildea shut the door rather cautiously. Father Murchison had never before seen him look so disturbed.

'You're worried, Guildea,' the Father said. 'Seriously worried.'

'Yes, I am. This business is beginning to tell on me a good deal.'

'Your belief in the presence of something here continues then?'

'Oh, dear, yes. There's no sort of doubt about the matter. The night I went across the road into the Park something got into the house, though what the devil it is I can't yet find out. But now, before we go down to dinner, I'll just tell you something about that proof I promised you. You remember?'

'Naturally.'

'Can't you imagine what it might be?'

Father Murchison moved his head to express a negative reply.

'Look about the room,' said Guildea. 'What do you see?'

The Father glanced round the room, slowly and carefully.

'Nothing unusual. You do not mean to tell me there is any appearance of—'

'Oh, no, no, there's no conventional, white-robed, cloudlike figure. Bless my soul, no! I haven't fallen so low as that.'

He spoke with considerable irritation.

'Look again.'

Father Murchison looked at him, turned in the direction of his fixed eyes and saw the grey parrot clambering in its cage, slowly and persistently.

'What?' he said, quickly. 'Will the proof come from there?'

The Professor nodded.

'I believe so,' he said. 'Now let's go down to dinner. I want some food badly.'

They descended to the dining room. While they ate and Pitting waited upon them, the Professor talked about birds, their habits, their curiosities, their fears and their powers of imitation. He had evidently studied this subject with the thoroughness that was characteristic of him in all that he did.

'Parrots,' he said presently, 'are extraordinarily observant. It is a pity that their means of reproducing what they see are so limited. If it were not so, I have little doubt that their echo of gesture would be as remarkable as their echo of voice often is.'

'But hands are missing.'

'Yes. They do many things with their heads, however. I once knew an old woman near Goring on the Thames. She was afflicted with the palsy. She held her head perpetually sideways and it trembled, moving from right to left. Her sailor son brought her home a parrot from one of his voyages. It used to reproduce the old woman's palsied movement of the head exactly. Those grey parrots are always on the watch.'

Guildea said the last sentence slowly and deliberately, glancing sharply over his wine at Father Murchison, and, when he had spoken it, a sudden light of comprehension dawned in the priest's mind. He opened his lips to make a swift remark. Guildea turned his bright eyes toward Pitting, who at the moment was tenderly bearing a cheese meringue from the lift that connected the dining room with the lower regions. The Father closed his lips again. But presently, when the butler had placed some apples on the table, had meticulously arranged the decanters, brushed away the crumbs and evaporated, he said, quickly, 'I begin to understand. You think Napoleon is aware of the intruder?'

'I know it. He has been watching my visitant ever since the night of that visitant's arrival.'

Another flash of light came to the priest.

'That was why you covered him with green baize one evening?'

'Exactly. An act of cowardice. His behaviour was beginning to grate upon my nerves.'

Guildea pursed up his thin lips and drew his brows down, giving to his face a look of sudden pain.

'But now I intend to follow his investigations,' he added, straightening his features. 'The week I wasted at Westgate was not wasted by him in London, I can assure you. Have an apple.'

'No, thank you; no, thank you.'

The Father repeated the words without knowing that he did so. Guildea pushed away his glass.

'Let us come upstairs, then.'

'No, thank you,' reiterated the Father.

'Eh?'

'What am I saying?' exclaimed the Father, getting up. 'I was thinking over this extraordinary affair.'

'Ah, you're beginning to forget the hysteria theory?'

They walked out into the passage.

'Well, you are so very practical about the whole matter.'

'Why not? Here's something very strange and abnormal come into my life. What should I do but investigate it closely and calmly?'

'What indeed?'

The Father began to feel rather bewildered, under a sort of compulsion which seemed laid upon him to give earnest attention to a matter that ought to strike him – so he felt – as entirely absurd. When they came into the library his eyes immediately turned, with profound curiosity, towards the parrot's cage. A slight smile curled the Professor's lips. He recognized the effect he was producing upon his friend. The Father saw the smile.

'Oh, I'm not won over yet,' he said in answer to it.

'I know. Perhaps you may be before the evening is over. Here comes the coffee. After we have drunk it we'll proceed to our experiment. Leave the coffee, Pitting, and don't disturb us again.'

'No, sir.'

'I won't have it black tonight,' said the Father, 'plenty of milk, please. I don't want my nerves played upon.'

'Suppose we don't take coffee at all?' said Guildea. 'If we do, you may trot out the theory that we are not in a perfectly normal condition. I know you, Murchison, devout priest and devout sceptic.'

The Father laughed and pushed away his cup.

'Very well, then. No coffee.'

'One cigarette, and then to business.'

The grey-blue smoke curled up.

'What are we going to do?' said the Father.

He was sitting bolt upright as if ready for action. Indeed there was no suggestion of repose in the attitudes of either of the men.

'Hide ourselves, and watch Napoleon. By the way – that reminds me.'

He got up, went to a corner of the room, picked up a piece of green baize and threw it over the cage.

'I'll pull that off when we are hidden.'

'And tell me first if you have had any manifestation of this supposed presence during the last few days?'

'Merely an increasingly intense sensation of something here, perpetually watching me, perpetually attending to all my doings.'

'Do you feel that it follows you about?'

'Not always. It was in this room when you arrived. It is here now – I feel. But, in going down to dinner, we seemed to get away from it. The conclusion is that it remained here. Don't let us talk about it just now.'

They spoke of other things till their cigarettes were finished. Then, as they threw away the smouldering ends, Guildea said. 'Now, Murchison, for the sake of this experiment, I suggest that we should conceal ourselves behind the curtains on either side of the cage, so that the bird's attention may not be drawn towards us and so distracted from that which we want to know more about. I will pull away the green baize when we are hidden. Keep perfectly still, watch the bird's proceedings, and tell me afterward how you feel about them, how you explain them. Tread softly.'

The Father obeyed, and they stole towards the curtains that fell before the two windows. The Father concealed himself behind those on the left of the cage, the Professor behind those on the right. The latter, as soon as they were hidden stretched out his arm, drew the baize down from the cage, and let it fall on the floor.

The parrot, which had evidently fallen asleep in the warm darkness, moved on its perch as the light shone upon it, ruffled the feathers round its throat, and lifted first one foot and then the other. It turned its head round on its supple, and apparently elastic, neck, and, diving its beak into the down upon its back, made some searching investigations with, as it seemed, a satisfactory result, for it soon lifted its head again, glanced around its cage, and began to address itself to a nut which had been fixed between the bars for its refreshment. With its curved beak it felt and tapped the nut, at first gently, then with severity. Finally it plucked the nut from the bars, seized it with its rough, grey toes, and, holding it down firmly on the perch, cracked it and pecked out its contents, scattering some on the floor of the cage and letting the fractured shell fall into the china bath that was fixed against the bars. This accomplished, the bird paused meditatively, extended one leg backward, and went through an elaborate process of wing-stretching that made it look as if it were lopsided and deformed. With its head reversed, it again applied itself to a subtle and exhaustive search among the feathers of its wing. This time its investigation seemed interminable, and Father Murchison had time to realize the absurdity of the whole position, and to wonder why he had lent himself to it. Yet he did not find his sense of humour laughing at it. On the contrary, he was smitten by a sudden gust of horror. When he was talking to his friend and watching him, the Professor's manner, generally so calm, even so prosaic, vouched for the truth of his story and the well-adjusted balance of his mind. But when he was hidden this was not so. And Father Murchison, standing behind his curtain, with his eyes upon the unconcerned Napoleon, began to whisper to himself the word – madness, with a quickening sensation of pity and of dread.

The parrot sharply contracted one wing, ruffled the feathers around its throat again, then extended its other leg backward, and proceeded to the cleaning of its other wing. In the still room the dry sound of the feathers being spread was distinctly audible. Father Murchison saw the blue curtains behind which Guildea stood tremble slightly, as if a breath of wind had come through the window they shrouded. The clock in the far room chimed, and a coal dropped into the grate, making a noise like dead leaves stirring abruptly on hard ground. And again a gust of pity and of dread swept over the Father. It seemed to him that he had behaved very foolishly, if not wrongly, in encouraging what must surely be the strange dementia of his friend. He ought to have declined to lend himself to a proceeding that, ludicrous, even childish in itself, might well be dangerous in the encouragement it gave to a diseased expectation. Napoleon's protruding leg, extended wing and twisted neck, his busy and unconscious devotion to the arrangement of his person, his evident sensation of complete loneliness, most comfortable solitude, brought home with vehemence to the Father the undignified buffoonery of his conduct; the more piteous buffoonery of his friend. He seized the curtains with his hand and was about to thrust them aside and issue forth, when an abrupt movement of the parrot stopped him. The bird, as if sharply attracted by something, paused in its pecking, and, with its head still bent backward and twisted sideways on its neck, seemed to listen intently. Its round eye looked glistening and strained, like the eye of a disturbed pigeon. Contracting its wing, it lifted its head and sat for a moment erect on its perch, shifting its feet mechanically up and down, as if a dawning excitement produced in it an uncontrollable desire of movement. Then it thrust its head forward in the direction of the further room and remained perfectly still. Its attitude so strongly suggested the concentration of its attention on something immediately before it, that Father Murchison instinctively stared about the room, half expecting to see Pitting advance softly, having entered through the hidden door. He did not come, and there was no sound in the chamber. Nevertheless, the parrot was obviously getting excited and increasingly attentive. It bent its head lower and lower, stretching out its neck until, almost falling from the perch, it half extended its wings, raising them slightly from its back, as if about to take flight, and fluttering them rapidly up and down. It continued this fluttering movement for what seemed to the Father an immense time. At length, raising its wings as far as possible, it dropped them slowly and deliberately down to its back, caught hold of the edge of its bath with its beak, hoisted itself onto the floor of the cage, waddled to the bars, thrust its head against them, and stood quite still in the exact attitude it always assumed when its head was being scratched by the Professor. So complete was the suggestion of this delight conveyed by the bird, that Father Murchison felt as if he saw a white finger gently pushed among the soft feathers of its head, and he was seized by a most strong conviction that something, unseen by him but seen and welcomed by Napoleon, stood immediately before the cage.

The parrot presently withdrew its head, as if the coaxing finger had been lifted from it, and its pronounced air of acute physical enjoyment faded into one of marked attention and alert curiosity. Pulling itself up by the bars it climbed again upon its perch, sidled to the left side of the cage, and began apparently to watch something with profound interest. It bowed its head oddly, paused for a moment, then bowed its head again. Father Murchison found himself conceiving – from this elaborate movement of the head – a distinct idea of a personality. The bird's proceedings suggested extreme sentimentality combined with that sort of weak determination which is often the most persistent. Such weak determination is a very common attribute of persons who are partially idiotic. Father Murchison was moved to think of these poor creatures who will often, so strangely and unreasonably, attach themselves with persistence to those who love them least. Like many priests, he had had some experience of them, for the amorous idiot is peculiarly sensitive to the attraction of preachers. This bowing movement of the parrot recalled to his memory a terrible, pale woman who for a time haunted all churches in which he ministered, who was perpetually endeavouring to catch his eye, and who always bent her head with an obsequious and cunningly conscious smile when she did so. The parrot went on bowing, making a short pause between each genuflection, as if it waited for a signal to be given that called into play its imitative faculty.

'Yes, yes, it's imitating an idiot,' Father Murchison caught himself saying as he watched.

And he looked again about the room, but saw nothing; except the furniture, the dancing fire, and the serried ranks of the books. Presently the parrot ceased from bowing, and assumed the concentrated and stretched attitude of one listening very keenly. He opened his beak, showing his black tongue, shut it, then opened it again. The Father thought he was going to speak, but he remained silent, although it was obvious that he was trying to bring out something. He bowed again two or three times, paused, and then, again opening his beak, made some remark. The Father could not distinguish any words, but the voice was sickly and disagreeable, a cooing and, at the same time, querulous voice, like a woman's, he thought. And he put his ear nearer to the curtain, listening with almost feverish attention. The bowing was resumed, but this time Napoleon added to it a sidling movement, affectionate and affected, like the movement of a silly and eager thing, nestling up to someone, or giving someone a gentle and furtive nudge. Again the Father thought of that terrible, pale woman who had haunted churches. Several times he had come upon her waiting for him after evening services. Once she had hung her head smiling, and lolled out her tongue and pushed against him sideways in the dark. He remembered how his flesh had shrunk from the poor thing, the sick loathing of her that he could not banish by remembering that her mind was all astray. The parrot paused, listened, opened his beak, and again said something in the same dovelike, amorous voice, full of sickly suggestion and yet hard, even dangerous, in its intonation. A loathsome voice, the Father thought it. But this time, although he heard the voice more distinctly than before, he could not make up his mind whether it was like a woman's voice or a man's – or perhaps a child's. It seemed to be a human voice, and yet oddly sexless. In order to resolve his doubt he withdrew into the darkness of the curtains, ceased to watch Napoleon and simply listened with keen attention, striving to forget that he was listening to a bird, and to imagine that he was overhearing a human being in conversation. After two or three minutes' silence the voice spoke again, and at some length, apparently repeating several times an affectionate series of ejaculations with a cooing emphasis that was unutterably mawkish and offensive. The sickliness of the voice, its falling intonations and its strange indelicacy, combined with a die-away softness and meretricious refinement, made the Father's flesh creep. Yet he could not distinguish any words, nor could he decide on the voice's sex or age. One thing alone he was certain of as he stood still in the darkness – that such a sound could only proceed from something peculiarly loathsome, could only express a personality unendurably abominable to him, if not to everybody. The voice presently failed, in a sort of husky gasp, and there was a prolonged silence. It was broken by the Professor, who suddenly pulled away the curtains that hid the Father and said to him, 'Come out now, and look.'

The Father came into the light, blinking, glanced toward the cage, and saw Napoleon poised motionless on one foot with his head under his wing. He appeared to be asleep. The Professor was pale, and his mobile lips were drawn into an expression of supreme disgust.

'Faugh!' he said.

He walked to the windows of the further room, pulled aside the curtains and pushed the glass up, letting in the air. The bare trees were visible in the grey gloom outside. Guildea leaned out for a minute drawing the night air into his lungs. Presently he turned round to the Father, and exclaimed abruptly, 'Pestilent! Isn't it?'

'Yes – most pestilent.'

'Ever hear anything like it?'

'Not exactly.'

'Nor I. It gives me nausea, Murchison, absolute physical nausea.'

He closed the window and walked uneasily about the room.

'What d'you make of it?' he asked, over his shoulder.

'How d'you mean exactly?'

'Is it man's, woman's, or child's voice?'

'I can't tell, I can't make up my mind.'

'Nor I.'

'Have you heard it often?'

'Yes. Since I returned from Westgate. There are never any words that I can distinguish. What a voice!'

He spat into the fire.

'Forgive me,' he said, throwing himself down in a chair. 'It turns my stomach – literally.'

'And mine,' said the Father truly.

'The worst of it is,' continued Guildea, with a high, nervous accent, 'that there's no brain with it, none at all – only the cunning of idiocy.'

The Father started at this exact expression of his own conviction by another.

'Why d'you start like that?' said Guildea, with a quick suspicion which showed the unnatural condition of his nerves.

'Well, the very same idea had occurred to me.'

'What?'

'That I was listening to the voice of something idiotic.'

'Ah! That's the devil of it, you know, to a man like me. I could fight against brain – but this!'

He sprang up again, poked the fire violently, then stood on the hearth rug with his back to it, and his hands thrust into the high pockets of his trousers.

'That's the voice of the thing that's got into my house,' he said. 'Pleasant, isn't it?'

And now there was really horror in his eyes, and his voice.

'I must get it out,' he exclaimed. 'I must get it out. But how?'

He tugged at his short black beard with a quivering hand.

'How?' he continued. 'For what is it? Where is it?'

'You feel it's here – now?'

'Undoubtedly. But I couldn't tell you in what part of the room.'

He stared about, glancing rapidly at everything.

'Then you consider yourself haunted?' said Father Murchison.

He, too, was much moved and disturbed, although he was not conscious of the presence of anything near them in the room.

'I have never believed in any nonsense of that kind, as you know,' Guildea answered. 'I simply state a fact, which I cannot understand, and which is beginning to be very painful to me. There is something here. But whereas most so-called hauntings have been described to me as inimical, what I am conscious of is that I am admired, loved, desired. This is distinctly horrible to me, Murchison, distinctly horrible.'

Father Murchison suddenly remembered the first evening he had spent with Guildea, and the latter's expression almost of disgust, at the idea of receiving warm affection from anyone. In the light of that long-ago conversation, the present event seemed supremely strange, and almost like a punishment for an offence committed by the Professor against humanity. But, looking up at his friend's twitching face, the Father resolved not to be caught in the net of his hideous belief.

'There can be nothing here,' he said. 'It's impossible.'

'What does that bird imitate, then?'

'The voice of someone who has been here.'

'Within the last week then. For it never spoke like that before, and mind, I noticed that it was watching and striving to imitate something before I went away, since the night that I went into the Park, only since then.'

'Somebody with a voice like that must have been here while you were away,' Father Murchison repeated, with a gentle obstinacy.

'I'll soon find out.'

Guildea pressed the bell. Pitting stole in almost immediately.

'Pitting,' said the Professor, speaking in a high, sharp voice, 'did anyone come into this room during my absence at the sea?'

'Certainly not, sir, except the maids – and me, sir.'

'Not a soul? You are certain?'

'Perfectly certain, sir.'

The cold voice of the butler sounded surprised, almost resentful. The Professor flung out his hand toward the cage.

'Has the bird been here the whole time?'

'Yes, sir.'

'He was not moved, taken elsewhere, even for a moment?'

Pitting's pale face began to look almost expressive, and his lips were pursed.

'Certainly not, sir.'

'Thank you. That will do.'

The butler retired, moving with a sort of ostentatious rectitude. When he had reached the door, and was just going out, his master called, 'Wait a minute, Pitting.'

The butler paused. Guildea bit his lips, tugged at his beard uneasily two or three times, and then said, 'Have you noticed – er – the parrot talking lately in a – a very peculiar, very disagreeable voice?'

'Yes, sir – a soft voice like, sir.'

'Ha! Since when?'

'Since you went away, sir. He's always at it.'

'Exactly. Well, and what did you think of it?'

'Beg pardon, sir?'

'What do you think about his talking in this voice?'

'Oh, that it's only his play, sir.'

'I see. That's all, Pitting.'

The butler disappeared and closed the door noiselessly behind him.

Guildea turned his eyes on his friend.

'There, you see!' he ejaculated.

'It's certainly very odd.' said the Father. 'Very odd indeed. You are certain you have no maid who talks at all like that?'

'My dear Murchison! Would you keep a servant with such a voice about you for two days?'

'No.'

'My housemaid has been with me for five years, my cook for seven. You've heard Pitting speak. The three of them make up my entire household. A parrot never speaks in a voice it has not heard. Where has it heard that voice?'

'But we hear nothing?'

'No. Nor do we see anything. But it does. It feels something too. Didn't you observe it presenting its head to be scratched?'

'Certainly it seemed to be doing so.'

'It was doing so.'

Father Murchison said nothing. He was full of increasing discomfort that almost amounted to apprehension.

'Are you convinced?' said Guildea, rather irritably.

'No. The whole matter is very strange. But till I hear, see or feel – as you do – the presence of something, I cannot believe.'

'You mean that you will not?'

'Perhaps. Well, it is time I went.'

Guildea did not try to detain him, but said, as he let him out, 'Do me a favour, come again tomorrow night.'

The Father had an engagement. He hesitated, looked into the Professor's face and said, 'I will. At nine I'll be with you. Good night.'

When he was on the pavement he felt relieved. He turned round, saw Guildea stepping into his passage, and shivered.

# V

Father Murchison walked all the way home to Bird Street that night. He required exercise after the strange and disagreeable evening he had spent, an evening upon which he looked back already as a man looks back upon a nightmare. In his ears, as he walked, sounded the gentle and intolerable voice. Even the memory of it caused him physical discomfort. He tried to put it from him, and to consider the whole matter calmly. The Professor had offered his proof that there was some strange presence in his house. Could any reasonable man accept such proof? Father Murchison told himself that no reasonable man could accept it. The parrot's proceedings were, no doubt, extraordinary. The bird had succeeded in producing an extraordinary illusion of an invisible presence, in the room. But that there really was such a presence the Father insisted on denying to himself. The devoutly religious, those who believe implicitly in the miracles recorded in the Bible, and who regulate their lives by the messages they suppose themselves to receive directly from the Great Ruler of a hidden World, are seldom inclined to accept any notion of supernatural intrusion into the affairs of daily life. They put it from them with anxious determination. They regard it fixedly as hocus-pocus, childish if not wicked.

Father Murchison inclined to the normal view of the devoted churchman. He was determined to incline to it. He could not – so he now told himself – accept the idea that his friend was being supernaturally punished for his lack of humanity, his deficiency in affection, by being obliged to endure the love of some horrible thing, which could not be seen, heard, or handled. Nevertheless, retribution did certainly seem to wait upon Guildea's condition. That which he had unnaturally dreaded and shrunk from in his thought he seemed to be now forced unnaturally to suffer. The Father prayed for his friend that night before the little, humble altar in the barely furnished, cell-like chamber where he slept.

On the following evening, when he called in Hyde Park Place, the door was opened by the housemaid, and Father Murchison mounted the stairs, wondering what had become of Pitting. He was met at the library door by Guildea and was painfully struck by the alteration in his appearance. His face was ashen in hue, and there were lines beneath his eyes. The eyes themselves looked excited and horribly forlorn. His hair and dress were disordered and his lips twitched continually, as if he were shaken by some acute nervous apprehension.

'What has become of Pitting?' asked the Father, grasping Guildea's hot and feverish hand.

'He has left my service.'

'Left your service!' exclaimed the Father in utter amazement.

'Yes, this afternoon.'

'May I ask why?'

'I'm going to tell you. It's all part and parcel of this – this most odious business. You remember once discussing the relations men ought to have with their servants?'

'Ah!' cried the Father, with a flash of inspiration. 'The crisis has occurred?'

'Exactly,' said the Professor, with a bitter smile. 'The crisis has occurred. I called upon Pitting to be a man and a brother. He responded by declining the invitation. I upbraided him. He gave me warning. I paid him his wages and told him he could go at once. And he has gone. What are you looking at me like that for?'

'I didn't know,' said Father Murchison, hastily dropping his eyes, and looking away. 'Why,' he added, 'Napoleon is gone too.'

'I sold him today to one of those shops in Shaftesbury Avenue.'

'Why?'

'He sickened me with his abominable imitation of – his intercourse with – well, you know what he was at last night. Besides, I have no further need of his proof to tell me I am not dreaming. And, being convinced as I now am, that all I have thought to have happened has actually happened, I care very little about convincing others. Forgive me for saying so, Murchison, but I am now certain that my anxiety to make you believe in the presence of something here really arose from some faint doubt on that subject – within myself. All doubt has now vanished.'

'Tell me why.'

'I will.'

Both men were standing by the fire. They continued to stand while Guildea went on.

'Last night I felt it.'

'What?' cried the Father.

'I say that last night, as I was going upstairs to bed, I felt something accompanying me and nestling up against me.'

'How horrible!' exclaimed the Father, involuntarily.

Guildea smiled drearily.

'I will not deny the horror of it. I cannot, since I was compelled to call on Pitting for assistance.'

'But – tell me – what was it, at least what did it seem to be?'

'It seemed to be a human being. It seemed, I say; and what I mean exactly is that the effect upon me was rather that of human contact than of anything else. But I could see nothing, hear nothing. Only, three times, I felt this gentle, but determined, push against me, as if to coax me and to attract my attention. The first time it happened I was on the landing outside this room, with my foot on the first stair. I will confess to you, Murchison, that I bounded upstairs like one pursued. That is the shameful truth. Just as I was about to enter my bedroom, however, I felt the thing entering with me, and, as I have said, squeezing, with loathsome, sickening tenderness, against my side. Then—'

He paused, turned towards the fire and leaned his head on his arm. The Father was greatly moved by the strange helplessness and despair of the attitude. He laid his hand affectionately on Guildea's shoulder.

'Then?'

Guildea lifted his head. He looked painfully abashed.

'Then, Murchison, I am ashamed to say, I broke down, suddenly, unaccountably, in a way I should have thought wholly impossible to me. I struck out with my hands to thrust the thing away. It pressed more closely to me. The pressure, the contact became unbearable to me. I shouted out for Pitting. I – I believe I must have cried – "Help." '

'He came, of course?'

'Yes, with his usual soft, unemotional quiet. His calm – its opposition to my excitement of disgust and horror – must, I suppose, have irritated me. I was not myself, no, no!'

He stopped abruptly. Then—

'But I need hardly tell you that,' he added, with most piteous irony.

'And what did you say to Pitting?'

'I said that he should have been quicker. He begged my pardon. His cold voice really maddened me, and I burst out into some foolish, contemptible diatribe, called him a machine, taunted him, then – as I felt that loathsome thing nestling once more to me – begged him to assist me, to stay with me, not to leave me alone – I meant in the company of my tormentor. Whether he was frightened, or whether he was angry at my unjust and violent manner and speech a moment before, I don't know. In any case he answered that he was engaged as a butler, and not to sit up all night with people. I suspect he thought I had taken too much to drink. No doubt that was it. I believe I swore at him as a coward – I! This morning he said he wished to leave my service. I gave him a month's wages, a good character as a butler, and sent him off at once.'

'But the night? How did you pass it?'

'I sat up all night.'

'Where? In your bedroom?'

'Yes – with the door open – to let it go.'

'You felt that it stayed?'

'It never left me for a moment, but it did not touch me again. When it was light I took a bath, lay down for a little while, but did not close my eyes. After breakfast I had the explanation with Pitting and paid him. Then I came up here. My nerves were in a very shattered condition. Well, I sat down, tried to write, to think. But the silence was broken in the most abominable manner.'

'How?'

'By the murmur of that appalling voice, that voice of a lovesick idiot, sickly but determined. Ugh!'

He shuddered in every limb. Then he pulled himself together, assumed, with a self-conscious effort, his most determined, most aggressive, manner, and added, 'I couldn't stand that. I had come to the end of my tether; so I sprang up, ordered a cab to be called, seized the cage and drove with it to a bird shop in Shaftesbury

Avenue. There I sold the parrot for a trifle. I think, Murchison, that I must have been nearly mad then, for, as I came out of the wretched shop, and stood for an instant on the pavement among the cages of rabbits, guinea pigs, and puppy dogs, I laughed aloud. I felt as if a load was lifted from my shoulders, as if in selling that voice I had sold the cursed thing that torments me. But when I got back to the house it was here. It's here now. I suppose it will always be here.'

He shuffled his feet on the rug in front of the fire.

'What on earth am I to do?' he said. 'I'm ashamed of myself, Murchison, but – but I suppose there are things in the world that certain men simply can't endure. Well, I can't endure this, and there's an end of the matter.'

He ceased. The Father was silent. In the presence of this extraordinary distress he did not know what to say. He recognized the uselessness of attempting to comfort Guildea, and he sat with his eyes turned, almost moodily, to the ground. And while he sat there he tried to give himself to the influences within the room, to feel all that was within it. He even, half unconsciously, tried to force his imagination to play tricks with him. But he remained totally unaware of any third person with them. At length he said, 'Guildea, I cannot pretend to doubt the reality of your misery here. You must go away, and at once. When is your Paris lecture?'

'Next week. In nine days from now.'

'Go to Paris tomorrow then; you say you have never had any consciousness that this – this thing pursued you beyond your own front door?'

'Never – hitherto.'

'Go tomorrow morning. Stay away till after your lecture. And then let us see if the affair is at an end. Hope, my dear friend, hope.'

He had stood up. Now he clasped the Professor's hand.

'See all your friends in Paris. Seek distractions. I would ask you also to seek – other help.'

He said the last words with a gentle, earnest gravity and simplicity that touched Guildea, who returned his handclasp almost warmly.

'I'll go,' he said. 'I'll catch the ten o'clock train, and tonight I'll sleep at a hotel, at the Grosvenor – that's close to the station. It will be more convenient for the train.'

As Father Murchison went home that night he kept thinking of that sentence: 'It will be more convenient for the train.' The weakness in Guildea that had prompted its utterance appalled him.

# VI

No letter came to Father Murchison from the Professor during the next few days, and this silence reassured him, for it seemed to betoken that all was well. The day of the lecture dawned, and passed. On the following morning, the Father eagerly opened the *Times*, and scanned its pages to see if there were any report of the great meeting of scientific men which Guildea had addressed. He glanced up and down the columns with anxious eyes, then suddenly his hands stiffened as they held the sheets. He had come upon the following paragraph:

> We regret to announce that Professor Frederic Guildea was suddenly seized with severe illness yesterday evening while addressing a scientific meeting in Paris. It was observed that he looked very pale and nervous when he rose to his feet. Nevertheless, he spoke in French fluently for about a quarter of an hour. Then he appeared to become uneasy. He faltered and glanced about like a man apprehensive, or in severe distress. He even stopped once or twice, and seemed unable to go on, to remember what he wished to say. But, pulling himself together with an obvious effort, he continued to address the audience. Suddenly, however, he paused again, edged furtively along the platform, as if pursued by something which he feared, struck out with his hands, uttered a loud, harsh cry and fainted. The sensation in the hall was indescribable. People rose from their seats. Women screamed, and, for a moment, there was a veritable panic. It is feared that the Professor's mind must have temporarily given way owing to overwork. We understand that he will return to England as soon as possible, and we sincerely hope that necessary rest and quiet will soon have the desired effect, and that he will be completely restored to health and enabled to prosecute further the investigations which have already so benefited the world.

The Father dropped the paper, hurried out into Bird Street, sent a wire of inquiry to Paris, and received the same day the following reply: 'RETURNING TOMORROW. PLEASE CALL EVENING. GUILDEA.' On that evening the Father called in Hyde Park Place, was at once admitted, and found Guildea sitting by the fire in the library, ghastly pale, with a heavy rug over his knees. He looked like a man emaciated by a long and severe illness, and in his wide-open eyes there was an expression of fixed horror. The Father started at the sight of him, and could scarcely refrain from crying out. He was beginning to express his sympathy when Guildea stopped him with a trembling gesture.

'I know all that,' Guildea said, 'I know. This Paris affair—' He faltered and stopped.

'You ought never to have gone,' said the Father. 'I was wrong. I ought not to have advised your going. You were not fit.'

'I was perfectly fit,' he answered, with the irritability of sickness. 'But I was – I was accompanied by that abominable thing.'

He glanced hastily round him, shifted his chair and pulled the rug higher over his knees. The Father wondered why he was thus wrapped up. For the fire was bright and red and the night was not very cold.

'I was accompanied to Paris,' he continued, pressing his upper teeth upon his lower lip.

He paused again, obviously striving to control himself. But the effort was vain. There was no resistance in the man. He writhed in his chair and suddenly burst forth in a tone of hopeless lamentation.

'Murchison, this being, thing – whatever it is – no longer leaves me even for a moment. It will not stay here unless I am here for it loves me, persistently, idiotically. It accompanied me to Paris, stayed with me there, pursued me to the lecture hall, pressed against me, caressed me while I was speaking. It has returned with me here. It is here now – ' he uttered a sharp cry – 'now, as I sit here with you. It is nestling up to me, fawning upon me, touching my hands. Man, man, can't you feel that it is here?'

'No,' the Father answered truly.

'I try to protect myself from its loathsome contact,' Guildea continued, with fierce excitement, clutching the thick rug with both hands. 'But nothing is of any avail against it. Nothing. What is it? What can it be? Why should it have come to me that night?'

'Perhaps as a punishment,' said the Father, with a quick softness.
'For what?'

'You hated affection. You put human feeling aside with contempt.
You had, you desired to have, no love for anyone. Nor did you desire
to receive any love from anything. Perhaps this is a punishment.'

Guildea stared into his face.

'D'you believe that?' he cried.

'I don't know,' said the Father. 'But it may be so. Try to endure
it, even to welcome it. Possibly then the persecution will cease.'

'I know it means me no harm,' Guildea exclaimed, 'it seeks me
out of affection. It was led to me by some amazing attraction which
I exercise over it ignorantly. I know that. But to a man of my nature
that is the ghastly part of the matter. If it would hate me, I could
bear it. If it would attack me, if it would try to do me some dreadful
harm, I should become a man again. I should be braced to fight
against it. But this gentleness, this abominable solicitude, this brain-
less worship of an idiot, persistent, sickly, horribly physical, I
cannot endure. What does it want of me? What would it demand
of me? It nestles to me. It leans against me. I feel its touch, like
the touch of a feather, trembling about my heart, as if it sought to
number my pulsations, to find out the inmost secrets of my impulses
and desires. No privacy is left to me.' He sprang up excitedly. 'I
cannot withdraw,' he cried, 'I cannot be alone, untouched, unwor-
shipped, unwatched for even one-half second. Murchison, I am
dying of this, I am dying.'

He sank down again in his chair, staring apprehensively on all
sides, with the passion of some blind man, deluded in the belief
that by his furious and continued effort he will attain sight. The
Father knew well that he sought to pierce the veil of the invisible,
and have knowledge of the thing that loved him.

'Guildea,' the Father said, with insistent earnestness, 'try to
endure this – do more – try to give this thing what it seeks.'

'But it seeks my love.'

'Learn to give it your love and it may go, having received what
it came for.'

'T'sh! You talk like a priest. Suffer your persecutors. Do good
to them that despitefully use you. You talk as a priest.'

'As a friend I spoke naturally, indeed, right out of my heart. The
idea suddenly came to me that all this – truth or seeming, it doesn't
matter which – may be some strange form of lesson. I have had

lessons – painful ones. I shall have many more. If you could welcome—'

'I can't! I can't!' Guildea cried fiercely. 'Hatred! I can give it that – always that, nothing but that – hatred, hatred.'

He raised his voice, glared into the emptiness of the room, and repeated, 'Hatred!'

As he spoke the waxen pallor of his cheeks increased, until he looked like a corpse with living eyes. The Father feared that he was going to collapse and faint, but suddenly he raised himself upon his chair and said, in a high and keen voice, full of suppressed excitement 'Murchison, Murchison!'

'Yes. What is it?'

An amazing ecstasy shone in Guildea's eyes.

'It wants to leave me,' he cried. 'It wants to go! Don't lose a moment! Let it out! The window – the window!'

The Father, wondering, went to the near window, drew aside the curtains and pushed it open. The branches of the trees in the garden creaked dryly in the light wind. Guildea leaned forward on the arms of his chair. There was silence for a moment. Then Guildea, speaking in a rapid whisper, said, 'No, no. Open this door – open the hall door. I feel – I feel that it will return the way it came. Make haste – ah, go!'

The Father obeyed – to soothe him, hurried to the door and opened it wide. Then he glanced back to Guildea. He was standing up, bent forward. His eyes were glaring with eager expectation, and, as the Father turned, he made a furious gesture towards the passage with his thin hands.

The Father hastened out and down the stairs. As he descended in the twilight he fancied he heard a slight cry from the room behind him, but he did not pause. He flung the hall door open, standing back against the wall. After waiting a moment – to satisfy Guildea, he was about to close the door again, and had his hand on it, when he was attracted irresistibly to look forth towards the park. The night was lit by a young moon, and, gazing through the railings, his eyes fell upon a bench beyond them.

Upon the bench something was sitting, huddled together very strangely.

The Father remembered instantly Guildea's description of that former night, that night of Advent, and a sensation of horror-stricken curiosity stole through him.

Was there then really something that had indeed come to the Professor? And had it finished its work, fulfilled its desire and gone back to its former existence?

The Father hesitated a moment in the doorway. Then he stepped out resolutely and crossed the road, keeping his eyes fixed upon this black or dark object that leaned so strangely upon the bench. He could not tell yet what it was like, but he fancied it was unlike anything with which his eyes were acquainted. He reached the opposite path, and was about to pass through the gate in the railings, when his arm was brusquely grasped. He started, turned round, and saw a policeman eyeing him suspiciously.

'What are you up to?' said the policeman.

The Father was suddenly aware that he had no hat upon his head, and that his appearance, as he stole forward in his cassock, with his eyes intently fixed upon the bench in the Park, was probably unusual enough to excite suspicion.

'It's all right, policeman,' he answered quickly, thrusting some money into the constable's hand.

Then, breaking from him, the Father hurried towards the bench, bitterly vexed at the interruption. When he reached it, nothing was there. Guildea's experience had been almost exactly repeated and, filled with unreasonable disappointment, the Father returned to the house, entered it, shut the door and hastened up the narrow stairway into the library.

On the hearth rug, close to the fire, he found Guildea lying with his head lolled against the armchair from which he had recently risen. There was a shocking expression of terror on his convulsed face. On examining him the Father found that he was dead.

The doctor, who was called in, said that the cause of death was failure of the heart.

When Father Murchison was told this, he murmured, 'Failure of the heart! It was that then!'

He turned to the doctor and said, 'Could it have been prevented?'

The doctor drew on his gloves and answered, 'Possibly, if it had been taken in time. Weakness of the heart requires a great deal of care. The Professor was too much absorbed in his work. He should have lived very differently.'

The Father nodded.

'Yes, yes,' he said, sadly.

# Climax for a Ghost Story

## I. A. Ireland

*This brief and frightening climax appears in* Visitations, *which Ireland published in 1919. He declared himself a descendant of the famous eighteenth-century impostor William Henry Ireland who was a forger of Shakespearian documents – including two 'Shakespeare' plays,* Vortigern and Rowena *and* Henry II *– which deceived several literary experts of the time. (In 1796 Sheridan produced* Vortigern and Rowena, *which proved a total flop.) I. A. Ireland is also the author of* A Brief History of Nightmares *(1899).*

'How EERIE!' said the girl, advancing cautiously. ' – And what a heavy door!' She touched it as she spoke and it suddenly swung to with a click.

'Good Lord!' said the man, 'I don't believe there's a handle inside. Why, you've locked us both in!'

'Not both of us. Only one of us,' said the girl, and before his eyes she passed straight through the door, and vanished.

# The Mysteries of the Joy Rio

## Tennessee Williams

*The author of such superb plays as* A Streetcar Named Desire, Cat on a Hot Tin Roof, Sweet Bird of Youth *and* The Night of the Iguana *was also a brilliant short-story writer. In a letter to Donald Windham, written in Rome in 1955, Tennessee Williams tried to define his craft: 'I think my work is good in exact ratio to the degree of emotional tension which is released in it. In a sense, writing of this kind (lyric?) is a losing game, for steadily life takes away from you, bit by bit, step by step, the quality of fresh involvement, new, startling reactions to experience, [and] the emotional reservoir is only rarely replenished.'*

*From the perfect opening sentence to the ghostly and powerful end, 'The Mysteries of the Joy Rio' shows Tennessee Williams at his lyric best. Unlike Hichens' ghost, whose love is an end in itself, the ghost of the Joy Rio makes use of its love to save another soul – a theme which also appears in Williams' play* Orpheus Descending.

*Tennessee Williams wrote a second version of this story, called 'Hard Candy'. Of the two, I think 'The Mysteries of the Joy Rio' is the richer and more effective.*

## I

Perhaps because he was a watch repairman, Mr Gonzales had grown to be rather indifferent to time. A single watch or clock can be a powerful influence on a man, but when a man lives among as many watches and clocks as crowded the tiny, dim shop of Mr Gonzales, some lagging behind, some skipping ahead, but all ticking monotonously on in their witless fashion, the multitude of them may be likely to deprive them of importance, as a gem loses its value when there are too many just like it which are too easily or cheaply obtainable. At any rate, Mr Gonzales kept very irregular hours, if he could be said to keep any hours at all, and if he had not been where he was for such a long time, his trade would have suffered badly. But Mr Gonzales had occupied his tiny shop for more than twenty years, since he had come to the city as a boy of nineteen to work as an apprentice to the original owner of the shop, a very strange and fat man of German descent named Kroger, Emiel Kroger, who had now been dead a long time. Emiel Kroger, being a romantically practical Teuton, had taken time, the commodity he worked with, with intense seriousness. In practically all his behaviour he had imitated a perfectly adjusted fat silver watch. Mr Gonzales, who was then young enough to be known as Pablo, had been his only sustained flirtation with the confusing, quicksilver world that exists outside of regularities. He had met Pablo during a watchmakers' convention in Dallas, Texas, where Pablo, who had illegally come into the country from Mexico a few days before, was drifting hungrily about the streets, and at that time Mr Gonzales, Pablo, had not grown plump but had a lustrous dark grace which had completely bewitched Mr Kroger. For as I have noted already, Mr Kroger was a fat and strange man, subject to the kind of bewitchment that the graceful young Pablo could cast. The spell was so strong that it interrupted the fleeting and furtive practices of a lifetime in Mr Kroger and induced him to take the boy home with him, to his shop-residence, where Pablo, now grown to the mature and fleshy proportions of Mr Gonzales, had lived ever since, for three years before the death of his protector and for more than seventeen years after that, as the inheritor of shop-residence, clocks, watches, and everything else that Mr Kroger had owned except a few pieces of dining-room silver which Emiel Kroger had left as a token bequest to a married sister in Toledo.

Some of these facts are of dubious pertinence to the little history which is to be unfolded. The important one is the fact that Mr Gonzales had managed to drift enviably apart from the regularities that rule most other lives. Some days he would not open his shop at all and some days he would open it only for an hour or two in the morning, or in the late evening when other shops had closed, and in spite of these caprices he managed to continue to get along fairly well, due to the excellence of his work, when he did it, the fact that he was so well established in his own quiet way, the advantage of his location in a neighbourhood where nearly everybody had an old alarm-clock which had to be kept in condition to order their lives (this community being one inhabited mostly by people with small-paying jobs), but it was also due in measurable part to the fact that the thrifty Mr Kroger, when he finally succumbed to a chronic disease of the bowels, had left a tidy sum in government bonds, and this capital, bringing in about a hundred and seventy dollars a month, would have kept Mr Gonzales going along in a commonplace but comfortable fashion even if he had declined to do anything whatsoever. It was a pity that the late, or rather long-ago, Mr Kroger, had not understood what a fundamentally peaceable sort of young man he had taken under his wing. Too bad he couldn't have guessed how perfectly everything suited Pablo Gonzales. But youth does not betray its true nature as palpably as the later years do, and Mr Kroger had taken the animated allure of his young protégé, the flickering lights in his eyes and his quick, nervous movements, his very grace and slimness, as meaning something difficult to keep hold of. And as the old gentleman declined in health, as he did quite steadily during the three years that Pablo lived with him, he was never certain that the incalculably precious bird flown into his nest was not one of sudden passage but rather the kind that prefers to keep a faithful commitment to a single place, the nest-building kind, and not only that, but the very-rare-indeed-kind that gives love back as generously as he takes it. The long-ago Mr Kroger had paid little attention to his illness, even when it entered the stage of acute pain, so intense was his absorption in what he thought was the tricky business of holding Pablo close to him. If only he had known that for all this time after his decease the boy would still be in the watchshop, how it might have relieved him! But on the other hand, maybe this anxiety, mixed as it was with so much tenderness and sad delight, was actually a blessing, standing as it did between the dying old man and a concern with death.

Pablo had never flown. But the sweet bird of youth had flown from Pablo Gonzales, leaving him rather sad, with a soft yellow face that was just as round as the moon. Clocks and watches he fixed with marvellous delicacy and precision, but he paid no attention to them; he had grown as obliviously accustomed to their many small noises as someone grows to the sound of waves who has always lived by the sea. Although he wasn't aware of it, it was actually light by which he told time, and always in the afternoons when the light had begun to fail (through the narrow window and narrower, dusty skylight at the back of the shop), Mr Gonzales automatically rose from his stooped position over littered table and gooseneck lamp, took off his close-seeing glasses with magnifying lenses, and took to the street. He did not go far and he always went in the same direction, across town towards the river where there was an old opera house, now converted into a third-rate cinema, which specialized in the showing of cowboy pictures and other films of the sort that have a special appeal to children and male adolescents. The name of this movie-house was the Joy Rio, a name peculiar enough but nowhere nearly so peculiar as the place itself.

The old opera house was a miniature of all the great opera houses of the old world, which is to say its interior was faded gilt and incredibly old and abused red damask which extended upwards through at least three tiers and possibly five. The upper stairs, that is, the stairs beyond the first gallery, were roped off and unlighted and the top of the theatre was so peculiarly dusky, even with the silver screen flickering far below it, that Mr Gonzales, used as he was to close work, could not have made it out from below. Once he had been there when the lights came on in the Joy Rio, but the coming on of the lights had so enormously confused and embarrassed him, that looking up was the last thing in the world he felt like doing. He had buried his nose in the collar of his coat and had scuttled out as quickly as a cockroach makes for the nearest shadow when a kitchen light comes on.

I have already suggested that there was something a bit special and obscure about Mr Gonzales' habitual attendance at the Joy Rio, and that was my intention. For Mr Gonzales had inherited more than the material possessions of his dead benefactor: he had also come into custody of his old protector's fleeting and furtive practices in dark places, the practices which Emiel Kroger had given up only when Pablo had come into his fading existence. The old man had left Mr Gonzales the full gift of his shame, and now Mr Gonzales did the sad, lonely things that Mr Kroger had done for such a long time before his one lasting love came to him. Mr Kroger had even practised those things in the same place in which they were practised now by Mr Gonzales, in the many mysterious recesses of the Joy Rio, and Mr Gonzales knew about this. He knew about it because Mr Kroger had told him. Emiel Kroger had confessed his whole life and soul to Pablo Gonzales. It was his theory, the theory of most immoralists, that the soul becomes intolerably burdened with lies that have to be told to the world in order to be permitted to live in the world, and that unless this burden is relieved by entire honesty with *some one* person, who is trusted and adored, the soul will finally collapse beneath its weight of falsity. Much of the final months of the life of Emiel Kroger, increasingly dimmed by morphia, were devoted to these whispered confessions to his adored apprentice, and it was as if he had breathed the guilty soul of his past into the ears and brain and blood of the youth who listened, and not long after the death of Mr Kroger, Pablo, who had stayed slim until then, had begun to accumulate fat. He never became anywhere nearly so gross as Emiel Kroger had been, but his delicate frame disappeared sadly from view among the irrelevant curves of a sallow plumpness. One by one the perfections which he had owned were folded away as Pablo put on fat as a widow puts on black garments. For a year beauty lingered about him, ghostly, continually fading, and then it went out altogether, and at twenty-five he was already the nondescriptly plump and moonfaced little man that he now was at forty, and if in his waking hours somebody to whom he would have to give a true answer had enquired of him, Pablo Gonzales, how much do you think about the dead Mr Kroger, he probably would have shrugged and said, *Not much now. It's such a long time ago.* But if the question were asked him while he slept, the guileless heart of the sleeper would have responded, *Always, always!*

# II

Now across the great marble stairs, that rose above the first gallery of the Joy Rio to the uncertain number of galleries above it, there had been fastened a greasy and rotting length of old velvet rope at the centre of which was hung a sign that said to *Keep Out*. But that rope had not always been there. It had been there about twenty years, but the late Mr Kroger had known the Joy Rio in the days before the flight of stairs was roped off. In those days the mysterious upper galleries of the Joy Rio had been a sort of fiddler's green where practically every device and fashion of carnality had run riot in a gloom so thick that a chance partner could only be discovered by touch. There were not rows of benches (as there were now on the orchestra level and the one gallery still kept in use), but strings of tiny boxes, extending in semicircles from one side of the great proscenium to the other. In some of these boxes broken-legged chairs might be found lying on their sides and shreds of old hangings still clung to the sliding brass loops at the entrances. According to Emiel Kroger, who is our only authority on these mysteries which share his remoteness in time, one lived up there, in the upper reaches of the Joy Rio, an almost sightless existence where the other senses, the senses of smell and touch and hearing, had to develop a preternatural keenness in order to spare one from making awkward mistakes, such as taking hold of the knee of a boy when it was a girl's knee one looked for, and where sometimes little scenes of panic occurred when a mistake of gender or of compatibility had been carried to a point where radical correction was called for. There had been many fights, there had even been rape and murder in those ancient boxes, till finally the obscure management of the Joy Rio had been compelled by the pressure of notoriety to shut down that part of the immense old building which had offered its principal enticement, and the Joy Rio, which had flourished until then, had then gone into sharp decline. It had been closed down and then reopened and closed down and reopened again. For several years it had opened and shut like a nervous lady's fan. Those were the years in which Mr Kroger was dying. After his death the fitful era subsided, and now for about ten years the Joy Rio had been continually active as a third-rate cinema, closed only for one week during a threatened epidemic of poliomyelitis some years past and once for a few days when a small fire had damaged the projection booth. But nothing happened there now of a nature to provoke a disturbance. There were no complaints to the management or the police, and the dark glory of the upper galleries was a legend in such memories as that of the late Emiel Kroger and the present Pablo Gonzales, and one by one, of course, those memories died out and the legend died out with them. Places like the Joy Rio and the legends about them make one more than usually aware of the short bloom and the long fading out of things. The angel of such a place is a fat silver angel of sixty-three years in a shiny dark-blue alpaca jacket, with short, fat fingers that leave a damp mark where they touch, that sweat and tremble as they caress between whispers, an angel of such a kind as would be kicked out of heaven and laughed out of hell and admitted to earth only by grace of its habitual slyness, its gift for making itself a counterfeit being, and the connivance of those that a quarter tip and an old yellow smile can corrupt.

But the reformation of the Joy Rio was somewhat less than absolute. It had reformed only to the point of ostensible virtue, and in the back rows of the first gallery at certain hours in the afternoon and very late at night were things going on of the sort Mr Gonzales sometimes looked for. At those hours the Joy Rio contained few patrons, and since the seats in the orchestra were in far better condition, those who had come to sit comfortably watching the picture would naturally remain downstairs; the few that elected to sit in the nearly deserted rows of the first gallery did so either because smoking was permitted in that section – or *because* . . .

There was a danger, of course, there always is a danger with places and things like that, but Mr Gonzales was a tentative person not given to leaping before he looked. If a patron had entered the first gallery only in order to smoke, you could usually count on his occupying a seat along the aisle. If the patron had bothered to edge his way towards the centre of a row of seats irregular as the jawbone of poor Yorick, one could assume as infallibly as one can assume anything in a universe where chance is the one invariable, that he had chosen his seat with something more than a cigarette in mind. Mr Gonzales did not take many chances. This was a respect in which he paid due homage to the wise old spirit of the late Emiel Kroger, that romantically practical Teuton who used to murmur to Pablo, between sleeping and waking, a sort of incantation that went like this: Sometimes you will find it and other times you won't find it and the times you don't find it are the times when you have got to be careful. Those are the times when you have got to remember that other times you *will* find it, not *this* time but the *next* time, or the time *after* that, and then you've got to be able to go home without it, yes, those times are the times when you have got to be able to go home without it, go home *alone* without it . . .

Pablo didn't know, then, that he would ever have need of this practical wisdom that his benefactor had drawn from his almost lifelong pursuit of a pleasure which was almost as unreal and basically unsatisfactory as an embrace in a dream. Pablo didn't know then that he would inherit so much from the old man who took care of him, and at that time, when Emiel Kroger, in the dimness of morphia and weakness following haemorrhage, had poured into the delicate ear of his apprentice, drop by slow, liquid drop, this distillation of all he had learned in the years before he found Pablo, the boy had felt for this whisper the same horror and pity that he felt for the mortal disease in the flesh of his benefactor, and only gradually, in the long years since the man and his whisper had ceased, had the singsong rigmarole begun to have sense for him, a practical wisdom that such a man as Pablo had turned into, a man such as Mr Gonzales, could live by safely and quietly and still find pleasure . . .

# III

Mr Gonzales was careful, and for careful people life has a tendency to take on the character of an almost arid plain with only here and there, at wide intervals, the solitary palm tree and its shadow and the spring alongside it. Mr Kroger's life had been much the same until he had come across Pablo at the watchmakers' convention in Dallas. But so far in Mr Gonzales' life there had been no Pablo. In his life there had been only Mr Kroger and the sort of things that Mr Kroger had looked for and sometimes found but most times continued patiently to look for in the great expanse of arid country which his lifetime had been before the discovery of Pablo. And since it is not my intention to spin this story out any longer than its content seems to call for, I am not going to attempt to sustain your interest in it with a description of the few palm trees on the uneventful desert through which the successor to Emiel Kroger wandered after the death of the man who had been his life. But I am going to remove you rather precipitately to a summer afternoon which we will call *Now* when Mr Gonzales learned that he was dying, and not only dying but dying of the same trouble that had put the period under the question mark of Emiel Kroger. The scene, if I can call it that, takes place in a doctor's office. After some hedging on the part of the doctor, the word malignant is uttered. The hand is placed on the shoulder, almost contemptuously comforting, and Mr Gonzales is assured that surgery is unnecessary because the condition is not susceptible to any help but that of drugs to relax the afflicted organs. And after that the scene is abruptly blacked out . . .

Now it is a year later. Mr Gonzales has recovered more or less from the shocking information that he received from his doctor. He has been repairing watches and clocks almost as well as ever, and there has been remarkably little alteration in his way of life. Only a little more frequently is the shop closed. It is apparent, now, that the disease from which he suffers does not intend to destroy him any more suddenly that it destroyed the man before him. It grows slowly, the growth, and in fact it has recently shown signs of what is called a remission. There is no pain, hardly any and hardly ever. The most palpable symptom is loss of appetite and, as a result of that, a steady decrease of weight. Now rather startlingly, after all this time, the graceful approximation of Pablo's delicate structure has come back out of the irrelevant contours which had engulfed it after the long-ago death of Emiel Kroger. The mirrors are not very good in the dim little residence-shop, where he lives in his long wait for death, and when he looks in them, Mr Gonzales sees the boy that was loved by the man whom he loved. It is almost Pablo. Pablo has almost returned from Mr Gonzales.

And then one afternoon . . .

# IV

The new usher at the Joy Rio was a boy of seventeen and the little Jewish manager had told him that he must pay particular attention to the roped-off staircase to see to it that nobody slipped upstairs to the forbidden region of the upper galleries, but this boy was in love with a girl named Gladys who came to the Joy Rio every afternoon, now that school was let out for the summer, and loitered around the entrance where George, the usher, was stationed. She wore a thin, almost transparent, white blouse with nothing much underneath it. Her skirt was usually of sheer silken material that followed her heart-shaped loins as raptly as George's hand followed them when he embraced her in the dark ladies' room on the balcony level of the Joy Rio. Sensual delirium possessed him those afternoons when Gladys loitered near him. But the recently changed management of the Joy Rio was not a strict one, and in the summer vigilance was more than commonly relaxed. George stayed near the downstairs entrance, twitching restively in his tight, faded uniform till Gladys drifted in from the afternoon streets on a slow tide of lilac perfume. She would seem not to see him as she sauntered up the aisle he indicated with his flashlight and took a seat in the back of the orchestra section where he could find her easily when the 'coast was clear', or if he kept her waiting too long and she was more than usually bored with the film, she would stroll back out to the lobby and inquire in her childish drawl, Where is the Ladies'

Room, Please? Sometimes he would curse her fiercely under his breath because she hadn't waited. But he would have to direct her to the staircase, and she would go up there and wait for him, and the knowledge that she was up there waiting would finally overpower his prudence to the point where he would even abandon his station if the little manager, Mr Katz, had his office door wide open. The ladies' room was otherwise not in use. Its light-switch was broken, or if it was repaired, the bulbs would be mysteriously missing. When ladies other than Gladys enquired about it, George would say gruffly, The ladies' room's out of order. It made an almost perfect retreat for the young lovers. The door left ajar gave warning of footsteps on the grand marble staircase in time for George to come out with his hands in his pockets before whoever was coming could catch him at it. But these interruptions would sometimes infuriate him, especially when a patron would insist on borrowing his flashlight to use the cabinet in the room where Gladys waited with her crumpled silk skirt gathered high about her flanks (leaning against the invisible dried-up washbasin) which were the blazing black heart of the insatiably concave summer.

In the old days Mr Gonzales used to go to the Joy Rio in the late afternoons but since his illness he had been going earlier because the days tired him earlier, especially the steaming days of August which were now in progress. Mr Gonzales knew about George and Gladys; he made it his business, of course, to know everything there was to be known about the Joy Rio, which was his earthly heaven, and, of course, George also knew about Mr Gonzales; he knew why Mr Gonzales gave him a fifty cent tip every time he inquired his way to the men's room upstairs, each time as if he had never gone upstairs before. Sometimes George muttered something under his breath, but the tributes collected from patrons like Mr Gonzales had so far ensured him complicity in their venal practices. But then one day in August, on one of the very hottest and blindingly bright afternoons, George was so absorbed in the delights of Gladys that Mr Gonzales had arrived at the top of the stairs to the balcony before George heard his footsteps. Then he heard them and he clamped a sweating palm over the mouth of Gladys which was full of stammerings of his name and the name of God. He waited, but Mr Gonzales also waited. Mr Gonzales was actually waiting at the top of the stairs to recover his breath from the climb, but George, who could see him, now, through the door kept slightly ajar, suspected that he was waiting to catch him coming out of his secret place. A fury burst in the boy. He thrust Gladys violently back against the washbasin and charged out of the room without even bothering to button his fly. He rushed up to the slight figure waiting near the stairs and began to shout a dreadful word at Mr Gonzales, the word 'morphodite'. His voice was shrill as a jungle bird's, shouting this word 'morphodite'. Mr Gonzales kept backing away from him, with the lightness and grace of his youth, he kept stepping backwards from the livid face and threatening fists of the usher, all the time murmuring, No, no, no, no, no. The youth stood between him and the stairs below so it was towards the upper staircase that Mr Gonzales took flight. All at once, as quickly and lightly as ever Pablo had moved, he darted under the length of velvet rope with the sign 'Keep Out'. George's pursuit was interrupted by the manager of the theatre, who seized his arm so fiercely that the shoulder-seam of the uniform burst apart. This started another disturbance under the cover of which Mr Gonzales fled farther and farther up the forbidden staircase into regions of deepening shadow. There were several points at which he might safely have stopped but his flight had now gathered an irresistible momentum and his legs moved like pistons bearing him up and up, and then—

At the very top of the staircase he was intercepted. He half turned back when he saw the dim figure waiting above, he almost turned and scrambled back down the grand marble staircase, when the name of his youth was called to him in a tone so commanding that he stopped and waited without daring to look up again.

Pablo, said Mr Kroger, come on up here, Pablo.

Mr Gonzales obeyed, but now the false power that his terror had given him was drained out of his body and he climbed with effort. At the top of the stairs where Emiel Kroger waited, he would have sunk exhausted to his knees if the old man hadn't sustained him with a firm hand at his elbow.

Mr Kroger said, This way, Pablo. He led him into the Stygian blackness of one of the little boxes in the once-golden horseshoe of the topmost tier. Now sit down, he commanded.

Pablo was too breathless to say anything except, Yes, and Mr Kroger leaned over him and unbuttoned his collar for him, unfastened the clasp of his belt, all the while murmuring, There now, there now, Pablo.

The panic disappeared under those soothing old fingers and the breathing slowed down and stopped hurting the chest as if a fox was caught in it, and then at last Mr Kroger began to lecture the boy as he used to. Pablo, he murmured, don't ever be so afraid of being lonely that you forget to be careful. Don't forget that you will find it sometimes but other times you won't be lucky, and those are the times when you have got to be patient, since patience is what you must have when you don't have luck.

The lecture continued softly, reassuringly familiar and repetitive as the tick of a bedroom clock in his ear, and if his ancient protector and instructor, Emiel Kroger, had not kept all the while soothing him with the moist, hot touch of his tremulous fingers, the gradual, the very gradual dimming out of things, his fading out of existence, would have terrified Pablo. But the ancient voice and fingers, as if they had never left him, kept on unbuttoning, touching, soothing, repeating the ancient lesson, saying it over and over like a penitent counting prayer beads, Sometimes you will have it and sometimes you won't have it, so don't be anxious about it. You must always be able to go home alone without it. Those are the times when you have got to remember that other times you will have it and it doesn't matter if sometimes you don't have it and have to go home without it, go home alone without it, go home alone without it. The gentle advice went on, and as it went on, Mr Gonzales drifted away from everything but the wise old voice in his ear, even at last from that, but not till he was entirely comforted by it.

# Pomegranate Seed

## Edith Wharton

*When 'Pomegranate Seed' first appeared in an American magazine in 1931, Edith Wharton said that she was 'bombarded by a host of inquirers anxious, in the first place, to know the meaning of the story's title'. This she clarifies with a little note on 'classical fairy lore'.*

*'Persephone, daughter of Demeter, goddess of fertility, was abducted and taken to Hades by Pluto, the god of the underworld. Her mother begged Jupiter to intercede, and he did so. But Persephone had broken her vow of abstinence in Hades by eating some pomegranate seeds. She was therefore required to spend a certain number of months each year – essentially the winter months – with Pluto.'*

*Edith Wharton was a close friend of Henry James, and her earlier work shows the influence of his style. She is probably the best known of America's 'classical' novelists, writing with what she herself called 'a great economy of means'. Of the fantastic tale she said, 'It must depend for its effect solely on what one might call its thermometrical quality; if it sends a cold shiver down one's spine, it has done its job and done it well.'*

# I

Charlotte Ashby paused on her doorstep. Dark had descended on the brilliancy of the March afternoon, and the grinding, rasping street life of the city was at its highest. She turned her back on it, standing for a moment in the old-fashioned, marble-flagged vestibule before she inserted her key in the lock. The sash curtains drawn across the panes of the inner door softened the light within to a warm blur through which no details showed. It was the hour when, in the first months of her marriage to Kenneth Ashby, she had most liked to return to that quiet house in a street long since deserted by business and fashion. The contrast between the soulless roar of New York, its devouring blaze of lights, the oppression of its congested traffic, congested houses, lives, minds and this veiled sanctuary she called home, always stirred her profoundly. In the very heart of the hurricane she had found her tiny islet – or thought she had. And now, in the last months, everything was changed, and she always wavered on the doorstep and had to force herself to enter.

While she stood there she called up the scene within: the hall hung with old prints, the ladder-like stairs, and on the left her husband's long shabby library, full of books and pipes and worn armchairs inviting to meditation. How she had loved that room! Then, upstairs, her own drawing room, in which, since the death of Kenneth's first wife, neither furniture nor hangings had been changed, because there had never been money enough, but which Charlotte had made her own by moving furniture about and adding more books, another lamp, a table for the new reviews. Even on the occasion of her only visit to the first Mrs Ashby – a distant, self-centred woman, whom she had known very slightly – she had looked about her with an innocent envy, feeling it to be exactly the drawing room she would have liked for herself and now for more than a year it had been hers to deal with as she chose – the room to which she hastened back at dusk on winter days where she sat reading by the fire, or answering notes at the pleasant roomy desk, or going over her stepchildren's copybooks, till she heard her husband's step.

Sometimes friends dropped in; sometimes – oftener – she was alone; and she liked that best, since it was another way of being with Kenneth, thinking over what he had said when they parted in the morning, imagining what he would say when he sprang up the stairs, found her by herself and caught her to him.

Now, instead of this, she thought of one thing only – the letter she might or might not find on the hall table. Until she had made sure whether or not it was there, her mind had no room for anything else. The letter was always the same – a square greyish envelope with 'Kenneth Ashby, Esquire', written on it in bold but faint characters. From the first it had struck Charlotte as peculiar that anyone who wrote such a firm hand should trace the letters so lightly; the address was always written as though there were not enough ink in the pen, or the writer's wrist were too weak to bear upon it. Another curious thing was that, in spite of its masculine curves, the writing was so visibly feminine. Some hands are sexless, some masculine, at first glance; the writing on the grey envelope, for all its strength and assurance, was without doubt a woman's. The envelope never bore anything but the recipient's name; no stamp, no address. The letter was presumably delivered by hand – but by whose? No doubt it was slipped into the letter box, whence the parlourmaid, when she closed the shutters and lit the lights, probably extracted it. At any rate, it was always in the evening, after dark, that Charlotte saw it lying there. She thought of the letter in the singular, as 'it', because, though there had been several since her marriage – seven, to be exact – they were so alike in appearance that they had become merged in one another in her mind, become one letter, become 'it'.

The first had come the day after their return from their honeymoon – a journey prolonged to the West Indies, from which they had returned to New York after an absence of more than two months. Re-entering the house with her husband, late on that first evening – they had dined at his mother's – she had seen, alone on the hall table, the grey envelope. Her eye fell on it before Kenneth's, and her first thought was 'Why I've seen that writing before', but where she could not recall. The memory was just definite enough for her to identify the script whenever it looked up at her faintly from the same pale envelope; but on that first day she would have thought no more of the letter if, when her husband's glance lit on it, she had not chanced to be looking at him. It all happened in a flash – his seeing the letter, putting out his hand for it, raising it to his shortsighted eyes to decipher the faint writing, and then abruptly withdrawing the arm he had slipped through Charlotte's, and moving away to the hanging light, his back turned to her. She had waited – waited for a sound, an exclamation; waited for him to open the letter; but he had slipped it into his pocket without a word and followed her into the library. And there they had sat down by the fire and lit their cigarettes, and he had remained silent, his head thrown back broodingly against the armchair, his eyes fixed on the hearth, and presently had passed his hand over his forehead and said: 'Wasn't it unusually hot at my mother's tonight? I've got a splitting head. Mind if I take myself off to bed?'

That was the first time. Since then Charlotte had never been present when he had received the letter. It usually came before he got home from his office, and she had to go upstairs and leave it lying there. But even if she had not seen it, she would have known it had come by the change in his face when he joined her – which, on those evenings, he seldom did before they met for dinner. Evidently, whatever the letter contained, he wanted to be by himself to deal with it; and when he reappeared he looked years older, looked emptied of life and courage, and hardly conscious of her presence. Sometimes he was silent for the rest of the evening; and if he spoke, it was usually to hint some criticism of her household arrangements, suggest some change in the domestic administration, to ask, a little nervously, if she didn't think Joyce's nursery governess was rather young and flighty, or if she herself always saw to it that Peter – whose throat was delicate – was properly wrapped up when he went to school. At such times Charlotte would remember the friendly warnings she had received when she became engaged to Kenneth Ashby: 'Marrying a heartbroken widower! Isn't that rather risky? You know Elsie Ashby absolutely dominated him'; and how she had jokingly replied: 'He may be glad of a little liberty for a change.' And in this respect she had been right. She had needed no one to tell her, during the first months, that her husband was perfectly happy with her. When they came back from their protracted honeymoon the same friends said: 'What have you done to Kenneth? He looks twenty years younger'; and this time she answered with careless joy: 'I suppose I've got him out of his groove.'

But what she noticed after the grey letters began to come was not so much his nervous tentative faultfinding – which always seemed to be uttered against his will – as the look in his eyes when he joined her after receiving one of the letters. The look was not unloving, not even indifferent; it was the look of a man who had been so far away from ordinary events that when he returns to familiar things they seem strange. She minded that more than the faultfinding.

Though she had been sure from the first that the handwriting on the grey envelope was a woman's, it was long before she associated the mysterious letters with any sentimental secret. She was too sure of her husband's love, too confident of filling his life, for such an idea to occur to her. It seemed far more likely that the letters – which certainly did not appear to cause him any sentimental pleasure – were addressed to the busy lawyer than to the private person. Probably they were from some tiresome client – women, he had often told her, were nearly always tiresome as clients – who did not want her letters opened by his secretary and therefore had them carried to his house. Yes; but in that case the unknown female must be unusually troublesome, judging from the effect her letters produced. Then again, though his professional discretion was exemplary, it was odd that he had never uttered an impatient comment, never remarked to Charlotte, in a moment of expansion, that there was a nuisance of a woman who kept badgering him about a case that had gone against her. He had made more than one semiconfidence of the kind – of course without giving names or details; but concerning this mysterious correspondent his lips were sealed.

There was another possibility: what is euphemistically called an 'old entanglement'. Charlotte Ashby was a sophisticated woman. She had few illusions about the intricacies of the human heart: she knew that there were often old entanglements. But when she had married Kenneth Ashby, her friends, instead of hinting at such a possibility, had said: 'You've got your work cut out for you. Marrying a Don Juan is a sinecure to it. Kenneth's never looked at another woman since he first saw Elsie Corder. During all the years of their marriage he was more like an unhappy lover than a comfortably contented husband. He'll never let you move an armchair or change the place of a lamp; and whatever you venture to do, he'll mentally compare with what Elsie would have done in your place.'

Except for an occasional nervous mistrust as to her ability to manage the children – a mistrust gradually dispelled by her good humour and the children's obvious fondness for her – none of these forebodings had come true. The desolate widower, of whom his nearest friends said that only his absorbing professional interests had kept him from suicide after his first wife's death, had fallen in love, two years later, with Charlotte Gorse, and after an impetuous wooing had married her and carried her off on a tropical honeymoon. And ever since he had been as tender and lover-like as during those first radiant weeks. Before asking her to marry him he had spoken to her frankly of his great love for his first wife and his despair after her sudden death; but even then he had assumed no stricken attitude, or implied that life offered no possibility of renewal. He had been perfectly simple and natural, and had confessed to Charlotte that from the beginning he had hoped the future held new gifts for him. And when, after their marriage, they returned to the house where his twelve years with his first wife had been spent, he had told Charlotte at once that he was sorry he couldn't afford to do the place over for her, but that he knew every woman had her own views about furniture and all sorts of household arrangements a man would never notice, and had begged her to make any changes she saw fit without bothering to consult him. As a result, she made as few as possible; but his way of beginning their new life in the old setting was so frank and unembarrassed that it put her immediately at her ease, and she was almost sorry to find that the portrait of Elsie Ashby, which used to hang over the desk in his library, had been transferred in their absence to the children's nursery. Knowing herself to be the indirect cause of this banishment, she spoke of it to her husband; but he answered: 'Oh, I thought they ought to grow up with her looking down on them.' The answer moved Charlotte, and satisfied her; and as time went by she had to confess that she felt more at home in her house, more at ease and in confidence with her husband, since that long coldly beautiful face on the library wall no longer followed her with guarded eyes. It was as if Kenneth's love had penetrated to the secret she hardly acknowledged to her own heart – her passionate need to feel herself the sovereign even of his past.

With all this stored-up happiness to sustain her, it was curious that she had lately found herself yielding to a nervous apprehension. But there the apprehension was; and on this particular afternoon – perhaps because she was more tired than usual, or because of the trouble of finding a new cook or, for some other ridiculously trivial reason, moral or physical – she found herself unable to react against the feeling. Latchkey in hand, she looked back down the silent street to the whirl and illumination of the great thoroughfare beyond, and up at the sky already aflare with the city's nocturnal life. 'Outside there,' she thought, 'skyscrapers, advertisements, telephones, wireless, airplanes, movies, motors, and all the rest of the twentieth century; and on the other side of the door something I can't explain, can't relate to them. Something as old as the world, as mysterious as life . . . Nonsense! What am I worrying about? There hasn't been a letter for three months now – not since the day we came back from the country after Christmas . . . Queer that they always seem to come after our holidays! . . . Why should I imagine there's going to be one tonight!'

No reason why, but that was the worst of it – one of the worst! – that there were days when she would stand there cold and shivering with the premonition of something inexplicable, intolerable, to be faced on the other side of the curtained panes; and when she opened the door and went in, there would be nothing; and on other days when she felt the same premonitory chill, it was justified by the sight of the grey envelope. So that ever since the last had come she had taken to feeling cold and premonitory every evening, because she never opened the door without thinking the letter might be there.

Well, she'd had enough of it: that was certain. She couldn't go on like that. If her husband turned white and had a headache on the days when the letter came, he seemed to recover afterwards, but she couldn't. With her the strain had become chronic, and the reason was not far to seek. Her husband knew from whom the letter came and what was in it; he was prepared beforehand for whatever he had to deal with, and master of the situation, however bad; whereas she was shut out in the dark with her conjectures.

'I can't stand it! I can't stand it another day!' she exclaimed aloud, as she put her key in the lock. She turned the key and went in; and there, on the table, lay the letter.

# II

She was almost glad of the sight. It seemed to justify everything, to put a seal of definiteness on the whole blurred business. A letter for her husband; a letter from a woman – no doubt another vulgar case of 'old entanglement'. What a fool she had been ever to doubt it, to rack her brains for less obvious explanations! She took up the envelope with a steady contemptuous hand, looked closely at the faint letters, held it against the light and just discerned the outline of the folded sheet within. She knew that now she would have no peace till she found out what was written on that sheet.

Her husband had not come in; he seldom got back from his office before half-past six or seven, and it was not yet six. She would have time to take the letter up to the drawing room; hold it over the tea kettle which at that hour always simmered by the fire in expectation of her return, solve the mystery and replace the letter where she had found it. No one would be the wiser, and her gnawing uncertainty would be over. The alternative, of course, was to question her husband; but to do that seemed even more difficult. She weighed the letter between thumb and finger, looked at it again under the light, started up the stairs with the envelope – and came down again and laid it on the table.

'No, I evidently can't,' she said, disappointed.

What should she do, then? She couldn't go up alone to that warm welcoming room, pour out her tea, look over her correspondence, glance at a book or review – not with that letter lying below and the knowledge that in a little while her husband would come in, open it and turn into the library alone, as he always did on the days when the grey envelope came.

Suddenly she decided. She would wait in the library and see for herself, see what happened between him and the letter when they thought themselves unobserved. She wondered the idea had never occurred to her before. By leaving the door ajar, and sitting in the corner behind it, she could watch him unseen . . . Well, then, she would watch him! She drew a chair into the corner, sat down, her eyes on the crack, and waited.

As far as she could remember, it was the first time she had ever tried to surprise another person's secret, but she was conscious of no compunction. She simply felt as if she were fighting her way through a stifling fog that she must at all costs get out of.

At length she heard Kenneth's latchkey and jumped up. The impulse to rush out and meet him had nearly made her forget why she was there; but she remembered in time and sat down again. From her post she covered the whole range of his movements – saw him enter the hall, draw the key from the door and take off his hat and overcoat. Then he turned to throw his gloves on the hall table, and at that moment he saw the envelope. The light was full on his face, and what Charlotte first noted there was a look of surprise. Evidently he had not expected the letter – had not thought of the possibility of its being there that day. But though he had not expected it, now that he saw it he knew well enough what it contained. He did not open it immediately, but stood motionless, the colour slowly ebbing from his face. Apparently he could not make up his mind to touch it; but at length he put out his hand, opened the envelope, and moved with it to the light. In doing so he turned his back on Charlotte, and she saw only his bent head and slightly stooping shoulders. Apparently all the writing was on one page, for he did not turn the sheet but continued to stare at it for so long that he must have reread it a dozen times – or so it seemed to the woman breathlessly watching him. At length she saw him move; he raised the letter still closer to his eyes, as though he had not fully deciphered it. Then he lowered his head, and she saw his lips touch the sheet.

'Kenneth!' she exclaimed, and went on out into the hall.

The letter clutched in his hand, her husband turned and looked at her. 'Where were you?' he said, in a low bewildered voice, like a man waked out of his sleep.

'In the library, waiting for you.' She tried to steady her voice: 'What's the matter! What's in that letter? You look ghastly.'

Her agitation seemed to calm him, and he instantly put the envelope into his pocket with a slight laugh. 'Ghastly? I'm sorry. I've had a hard day in the office – one or two complicated cases. I look dog-tired, I suppose.'

'You didn't look tired when you came in. It was only when you opened that letter—'

He had followed her into the library, and they stood gazing at each other. Charlotte noticed how quickly he had regained his self-control; his profession had trained him to rapid mastery of face and voice. She saw at once that she would be at a disadvantage in any attempt to surprise his secret, but at the same moment she lost all desire to manoeuvre, to trick him into betraying anything he wanted to conceal. Her wish was still to penetrate the mystery, but only that she might help him to bear the burden it implied. 'Even if it *is* another woman,' she thought.

'Kenneth,' she said, her heart beating excitedly, 'I waited here on purpose to see you come in. I wanted to watch you while you opened that letter.'

His face, which had paled, turned to dark red; then it paled again. 'That letter? Why especially that letter?'

'Because I've noticed that whenever one of those letters comes it seems to have such a strange effect on you.'

A line of anger she had never seen before came out between his eyes, and she said to herself: 'The upper part of his face is too narrow; this is the first time I ever noticed it.'

She heard him continue, in the cool and faintly ironic tone of the prosecuting lawyer making a point: 'Ah, so you're in the habit of watching people open their letters when they don't know you're there?'

'Not in the habit. I never did such a thing before. But I had to find out what she writes to you, at regular intervals, in those grey envelopes.'

He weighed this for a moment; then: 'The intervals have not been regular,' he said.

'Oh, I dare say you've kept a better account of the dates than I have,' she retorted, her magnanimity vanishing at his tone. 'All I know is that every time that woman writes to you—'

'Why do you assume it's a woman?'

'It's a woman's writing. Do you deny it?'

He smiled. 'No, I don't deny it. I asked only because the writing is generally supposed to look more like a man's.'

Charlotte passed this over impatiently. 'And this woman – what does she write to you about?'

Again he seemed to consider a moment. 'About business.'

'Legal business?'

'In a way, yes. Business in general.'

'You look after her affairs for her?'

'Yes.'

'You've looked after them for a long time?'

'Yes. A very long time.'

'Kenneth, dearest, won't you tell me who she is?'

'No. I can't.' He paused, and brought out, as if with a certain hesitation: 'Professional secrecy.'

The blood rushed from Charlotte's heart to her temples. 'Don't say that – don't!'

'Why not?'

'Because I saw you kiss the letter.'

The effect of the words was so disconcerting that she instantly repented having spoken them. Her husband, who had submitted to her cross-questioning with a sort of contemptuous composure, as though he were humouring an unreasonable child, turned on her a face of terror and distress. For a minute he seemed unable to speak; then, collecting himself, with an effort, he stammered out: 'The writing is very faint; you must have seen me holding the letter close to my eyes to try to decipher it.'

'No; I saw you kissing it.' He was silent. 'Didn't I see you kissing it?'

He sank back into indifference. 'Perhaps.'

'Kenneth! You stand there and say that – to me?'

'What possible difference can it make to you? The letter is on business, as I told you. Do you suppose I'd lie about it? The writer is a very old friend whom I haven't seen for a long time.'

'Men don't kiss business letters, even from women who are very old friends, unless they have been their lovers, and still regret them.'

He shrugged his shoulders slightly and turned away, as if he considered the discussion at an end and were faintly disgusted at the turn it had taken.

'Kenneth!' Charlotte moved towards him and caught hold of his arm.

He paused with a look of weariness and laid his hand over hers. 'Won't you believe me?' he asked gently.

'How can I? I've watched these letters come to you – for months now they've been coming. Ever since we came back from the West Indies – one of them greeted me the very day we arrived. And after each one of them I see their mysterious effect on you, I see you disturbed, unhappy, as if someone were trying to estrange you from me.'

'No, dear, not that. Never!'

She drew back and looked at him with passionate entreaty. 'Well, then, prove it to me, darling. It's so easy!'

He forced a smile. 'It's not easy to prove anything to a woman who's once taken an idea into her head.'

'You've only got to show me the letter.'

His hand slipped from hers and he drew back and shook his head.

'You won't?'

'I can't.'

'Then the woman who wrote it is your mistress.'

'No, dear. No.'

'Not now perhaps. I suppose she's trying to get you back, and you're struggling, out of pity for me. My poor Kenneth!'

'I swear to you she never was my mistress.'

Charlotte felt the tears rushing to her eyes. 'Ah, that's worse, then – that's hopeless! The prudent ones are the kind that keep their hold on a man. We all know that.' She lifted her hands and hid her face in them.

Her husband remained silent; he offered neither consolation nor denial, and at length, wiping away her tears, she raised her eyes almost timidly to his.

'Kenneth, think! We've been married such a short time. Imagine what you're making me suffer. You say you can't show me this letter. You refuse even to explain it.'

'I've told you the letter is on business. I will swear to that too.'

'A man will swear to anything to screen a woman. If you want me to believe you, at least tell me her name. If you'll do that, I promise you I won't ask to see the letter.'

There was a long interval of suspense, during which she felt her heart beating against her ribs in quick admonitory knocks, as if warning her of the danger she was incurring.

'I can't,' he said at length.

'Not even her name?'

'No.'

'You can't tell me anything more?'

'No.'

Again a pause; this time they seemed both to have reached the end of their arguments and to be helplessly facing each other across a baffling waste of incomprehension.

Charlotte stood breathing rapidly, her hands against her breast. She felt as if she had run a hard race and missed the goal. She had meant to move her husband and had succeeded only in irritating him; and this error of reckoning seemed to change him into a stranger, a mysterious incomprehensible being whom no argument or entreaty of hers could reach. The curious thing was that she was aware in him of no hostility or even impatience, but only of a remoteness, an inaccessibility, far more difficult to overcome. She felt herself excluded, ignored, blotted out of his life. But after a moment or two, looking at him more calmly, she saw that he was suffering as much as she was. His distant guarded face was drawn with pain; the coming of the grey envelope, though it always cast a shadow, had never marked him as deeply as this discussion with his wife.

Charlotte took heart; perhaps, after all, she had not spent her last shaft. She drew nearer and once more laid her hand on his arm. 'Poor Kenneth! If you knew how sorry I am for you—'

She thought he winced slightly at this expression of sympathy, but he took her hand and pressed it.

'I can think of nothing worse than to be incapable of loving long,' she continued, 'to feel the beauty of a great love and to be too unstable to bear its burden.'

He turned on her a look of wistful reproach. 'Oh, don't say that of me. Unstable!'

She felt herself at last on the right tack, and her voice trembled with excitement as she went on: 'Then what about me and this other woman? Haven't you already forgotten Elsie twice within a year?'

She seldom pronounced his first wife's name; it did not come naturally to her tongue. She flung it out now as if she were flinging some dangerous explosive into the open space between them, and drew back a step, waiting to hear the mine go off.

Her husband did not move; his expression grew sadder, but showed no resentment. 'I have never forgotten Elsie,' he said.

Charlotte could not repress a faint laugh. 'Then, you poor dear, between the three of us—'

'There are not—' he began; and then broke off and put his hand to his forehead.

'Not what?'

'I'm sorry; I don't believe I know what I'm saying. I've got a blinding headache.' He looked wan and furrowed enough for the statement to be true, but she was exasperated by his evasion.

'Ah, yes the grey envelope headache!'

She saw the surprise in his eyes. 'I'd forgotten how closely I've been watched,' he said coldly. 'If you'll excuse me, I think I'll go up and try an hour in the dark, to see if I can get rid of this neuralgia.'

She wavered; then she said, with desperate resolution: 'I'm sorry your head aches. But before you go I want to say that sooner or later this question must be settled between us. Someone is trying to separate us, and I don't care what it costs me to find out who it is.' She looked him steadily in the eyes. 'If it costs me your love, I don't care! If I can't have your confidence I don't want anything from you.'

He still looked at her wistfully. 'Give me time.'

'Time for what? It's only a word to say.'

'Time to show you that you haven't lost my love or my confidence.'

'Well, I'm waiting.'

He turned toward the door, and then glanced back hesitatingly. 'Oh, do wait, my love,' he said, and went out of the room.

She heard his tired step on the stairs and the closing of his bedroom door above. Then she dropped into a chair and buried her face in her folded arms. Her first movement was one of compunction; she seemed to herself to have been hard, unhuman, unimaginative. 'Think of telling him that I didn't care if my insistence cost me his love! The lying rubbish!' She started up to follow him and unsay the meaningless words. But she was checked by a reflection. He had had his way, after all; he had eluded all attacks on his secret, and now he was shut up alone in his room, reading that other woman's letter.

## III

She was still reflecting on this when the surprised parlourmaid came in and found her. No, Charlotte said, she wasn't going to dress for dinner; Mr Ashby didn't want to dine. He was very tired and had gone up to his room to rest; later she would have something brought on a tray to the drawing room. She mounted the stairs to her bedroom. Her dinner dress was lying on the bed, and at the sight the quiet routine of her daily life took hold of her and she began to feel as if the strange talk she had just had with her husband must have taken place in another world, between two beings who were not Charlotte Gorse and Kenneth Ashby, but phantoms projected by her fevered imagination. She recalled the year since her marriage – her husband's constant devotion; his persistent, almost too insistent tenderness; the feeling he had given her at times of being too eagerly dependent on her, too searchingly close to her, as if there were not air enough between her soul and his. It seemed preposterous, as she recalled all this, that a few moments ago she should have been accusing him of an intrigue with another woman! But, then, what—

Again she was moved by the impulse to go up to him, beg his pardon and try to laugh away the misunderstanding. But she was restrained by the fear of forcing herself upon his privacy. He was troubled and unhappy, oppressed by some grief or fear; and he had shown her that he wanted to fight out his battle alone. It would be wiser, as well as more generous, to respect his wish. Only, how strange, how unbearable, to be there, in the next room to his, and feel herself at the other end of the world! In her nervous agitation she almost regretted not having had the courage to open the letter and put it back on the hall table before he came in. At least she would have known what his secret was, and the bogy might have been laid. For she was beginning now to think of the mystery as something conscious, malevolent: a secret persecution before which he quailed, yet from which he could not free himself. Once or twice in his evasive eyes she thought she had detected a desire for help, an impulse of confession, instantly restrained and suppressed. It was as if he felt she could have helped him if she had known, and yet had been unable to tell her!

There flashed through her mind the idea of going to his mother. She was very fond of old Mrs Ashby, a firm-fleshed clear-eyed old lady, with an astringent bluntness of speech which responded to the forthright and simple in Charlotte's own nature. There had been a tacit bond between them ever since the day when Mrs Ashby Senior, coming to lunch for the first time with her new daughter-in-law, had been received by Charlotte downstairs in the library, and glancing up at the empty wall above her son's desk, had remarked laconically: 'Elsie gone, eh?' adding, at Charlotte's murmured explanation: 'Nonsense. Don't have her back. Two's company.' Charlotte, at this reading of her thoughts, could hardly refrain from exchanging a smile of complicity with her mother-in-law; and it seemed to her now that Mrs Ashby's almost uncanny directness might pierce to the core of this new mystery. But here again she hesitated, for the idea almost suggested a betrayal. What right had she to call in anyone, even so close a relation, to surprise a secret which her husband was trying to keep from her? 'Perhaps, by and by, he'll talk to his mother of his own accord,' she thought, and then ended: 'But what does it matter? He and I must settle it between us.'

She was still brooding over the problem when there was a knock on the door and her husband came in. He was dressed for dinner and seemed surprised to see her sitting there, with her evening dress lying unheeded on the bed.

'Aren't you coming down?'

'I thought you were not well and had gone to bed,' she faltered.

He forced a smile. 'I'm not particularly well, but we'd better go down.' His face, though still drawn, looked calmer than when he had fled upstairs an hour earlier.

'There it is; he knows what's in the letter and has fought his battle out again, whatever it is,' she reflected, 'while I'm still in darkness.' She rang and gave a hurried order that dinner should be served as soon as possible – just a short meal, whatever could be got ready quickly, as both she and Mr Ashby were rather tired and not very hungry.

Dinner was announced, and they sat down to it. At first neither seemed able to find a word to say; then Ashby began to make conversation with an assumption of ease that was more oppressive than his silence. 'How tired he is! How terribly overtired!' Charlotte said to herself, pursuing her own thoughts while he rambled on about municipal politics, aviation, an exhibition of modern French painting, the health of an old aunt and the installing of the automatic telephone. 'Good heavens, how tired he is!'

When they dined alone they usually went into the library after dinner, and Charlotte curled herself up on the divan with her knitting while he settled down in his armchair under the lamp and lit a pipe. But this evening, by tacit agreement, they avoided the room in which their strange talk had taken place, and went up to Charlotte's drawing room.

They sat down near the fire, and Charlotte said: 'Your pipe?' after he had put down his hardly-tasted coffee.

He shook his head. 'No, not tonight.'

'You must go to bed early; you look terribly tired. I'm sure they overwork you at the office.'

'I suppose we all overwork at times.'

She rose and stood before him with sudden resolution. 'Well, I'm not going to have you use up your strength slaving in that way. It's absurd. I can see you're ill.' She bent over him and laid her hand on his forehead. 'My poor old Kenneth. Prepare to be taken away soon on a long holiday.'

He looked up at her, startled. 'A holiday?'

'Certainly. Didn't you know I was going to carry you off at Easter? We're going to start in a fortnight on a month's voyage to somewhere or other. On any one of the big cruising steamers.' She paused and bent closer, touching his forehead with her lips. 'I'm tired, too, Kenneth.'

He seemed to pay no heed to her last words, but sat, his hands on his knees, his head drawn back a little from her caress, and looked up at her with a stare of apprehension. 'Again? My dear, we can't, I can't possibly go away.'

'I don't know why you say "again," Kenneth; we haven't taken a real holiday this year.'

'At Christmas we spent a week with the children in the country.'

'Yes, but this time I mean away from the children, from servants, from the house. From everything that's familiar and fatiguing. Your mother will love to have Joyce and Peter with her.'

He frowned and slowly shook his head. 'No, dear; I can't leave them with my mother.'

'Why, Kenneth, how absurd! She adores them. You didn't hesitate to leave them with her for over two months when we went to the West Indies.'

He drew a deep breath and stood up uneasily. 'That was different.'

'Different? Why?'

'I mean, at that time I didn't realize—' He broke off as if to choose his words and then went on: 'My mother adores the children, as you say. But she isn't always very judicious. Grandmothers always spoil children. And sometimes she talks before them without thinking.' He turned to his wife with an almost pitiful gesture of entreaty. 'Dont ask me to, dear.'

Charlotte mused. It was true that the elder Mrs Ashby had a fearless tongue, but she was the last woman in the world to say or hint anything before her grandchildren at which the most scrupulous parent could take offence. Charlotte looked at her husband in perplexity.

'I don't understand.'

He continued to turn on her the same troubled and entreating gaze. 'Don't try to,' he muttered.

'Not try to?'

'Not now – not yet.' He put up his hands and pressed them against his temples. 'Can't you see that there's no use in insisting? I can't go away, no matter how much I might want to.'

Charlotte still scrutinized him gravely. 'The question is, *do* you want to?'

He returned her gaze for a moment; then his lips began to tremble, and he said, hardly above his breath: 'I want – anything you want.'

'And yet—'

'Don't ask me. I can't leave – I can't.'

'You mean that you can't go away out of reach of those letters!'

Her husband had been standing before her in an uneasy half-hesitating attitude; now he turned abruptly away and walked once or twice up and down the length of the room, his head bent, his eyes fixed on the carpet.

Charlotte felt her resentfulness rising with her fears. 'It's that,' she persisted. 'Why not admit it? You can't live without them.'

He continued his troubled pacing of the room; then he stopped short, dropped into a chair and covered his face with his hands. From the shaking of his shoulders, Charlotte saw that he was weeping. She had never seen a man cry, except her father after her mother's death, when she was a little girl: and she remembered still how the sight had frightened her. She was frightened now; she felt that her husband was being dragged away from her into some mysterious bondage, and that she must use up her last atom of strength in the struggle for his freedom, and for hers.

'Kenneth – Kenneth!' she pleaded, kneeling down beside him. 'Won't you listen to me? Won't you try to see what I'm suffering? I'm not unreasonable, darling, really not. I don't suppose I should ever have noticed the letters if it hadn't been for their effect on you. It's not my way to pry into other people's affairs; and even if the effect had been different – yes, yes, listen to me – if I'd seen that the letters made you happy, that you were watching eagerly for them, counting the days between their coming, that you wanted them, that they gave you something I haven't known how to give – why, Kenneth, I don't say I shouldn't have suffered from that, too; but it would have been in a different way, and I should have had the courage to hide what I felt, and the hope that someday you'd come to feel about me as you did about the writer of the letters. But what I can't bear is to see how you dread them, how they make you suffer, and yet how you can't live without them and won't go away lest you should miss one during your absence. Or perhaps,' she added, her voice breaking into a cry of accusation – 'perhaps it's because she's actually forbidden you to leave. Kenneth, you must answer me! Is that the reason? Is it because she's forbidden you that you won't go away with me?'

She continued to kneel at his side, and raising her hands, she drew his gently down. She was ashamed of her persistence, ashamed of uncovering that baffled disordered face, yet resolved that no such scruples should arrest her. His eyes were lowered, the muscles of his face quivered; she was making him suffer even more than she suffered herself. Yet this no longer restrained her.

'Kenneth, is it that? She won't let us go away together?'

Still he did not speak or turn his eyes to her; and a sense of defeat swept over her. After all, she thought, the struggle was a losing one. 'You needn't answer. I see I'm right,' she said.

Suddenly, as she rose, he turned and drew her down again. His hands caught hers and pressed them so tightly that she felt her rings cutting into her flesh. There was something frightened, convulsive in his hold; it was the clutch of a man who felt himself slipping over a precipice. He was staring up at her now as if salvation lay in the face she bent above him. 'Of course we'll go away together. We'll go wherever you want,' he said in a low confused voice; and putting his arm about her, he drew her close and pressed his lips on hers.

# IV

Charlotte had said to herself: 'I shall sleep tonight,' but instead she sat before her fire into the small hours, listening for any sound that came from her husband's room. But he, at any rate, seemed to be resting after the tumult of the evening. Once or twice she stole to the door and in the faint light that came in from the street through his open window she saw him stretched out in heavy sleep – the sleep of weakness and exhaustion. 'He's ill,' she thought – 'he's undoubtedly ill. And it's not overwork; it's this mysterious persecution.'

She drew a breath of relief. She had fought through the weary fight and the victory was hers – at least for the moment. If only they could have started at once – started for anywhere! She knew it would be useless to ask him to leave before the holidays; and meanwhile the secret influence – as to which she was still so completely in the dark – would continue to work against her, and she would have to renew the struggle day after day till they started on their journey. But after that everything would be different. If once she could get her husband away under other skies, and all to herself, she never doubted her power to release him from the evil spell he was under. Lulled to quiet by the thought, she too slept at last.

When she woke, it was long past her usual hour, and she sat up in bed surprised and vexed at having overslept herself. She always liked to be down to share her husband's breakfast by the library fire, but a glance at the clock made it clear the he must have started long since for his office. To make sure, she jumped out of bed and went into his room, but it was empty. No doubt he had looked in on her before leaving, seen that she still slept, and gone downstairs without disturbing her; and their relations were sufficiently lover-like for her to regret having missed their morning hour.

She rang and asked if Mr Ashby had already gone. Yes, nearly an hour ago, the maid said. He had given orders that Mrs Ashby should not be waked and that the children should not come to her till she sent for them . . . Yes, he had gone up to the nursery himself to give the order. All this sounded usual enough, and Charlotte hardly knew why she asked: 'And did Mr Ashby leave no other message?'

Yes, the maid said, he did; she was so sorry she'd forgotten. He'd told her, just as he was leaving, to say to Mrs Ashby that he was going to see about their passages, and would she please be ready to sail tomorrow?

Charlotte echoed the woman's 'Tomorrow', and sat staring at her incredulously. 'Tomorrow – you're sure he said to sail tomorrow?'

'Oh, ever so sure, ma'am. I don't know how I could have forgotten to mention it.'

'Well, it doesn't matter. Draw my bath, please.' Charlotte sprang up, dashed through her dressing, and caught herself singing at her image in the glass as she sat brushing her hair. It made her feel young again to have scored such a victory. The other woman vanished to a speck on the horizon, as this one, who ruled the foreground, smiled back at the reflection of her lips and eyes. He loved her, then – he loved her as passionately as ever. He had divined what she had suffered, had understood that their happiness depended on their getting away at once, and finding each other again after yesterday's desperate groping in the fog. The nature of the influence that had come between them did not much matter to Charlotte now; she had faced the phantom and dispelled it. 'Courage – that's the secret! If only people who are in love weren't always so afraid of risking their happiness by looking it in the eyes.' As she brushed back her light abundant hair it waved electrically above her head, like the palms of victory. Ah, well, some women knew how to manage men, and some didn't – and only the fair – she gaily paraphrased – deserve the brave! Certainly she was looking very pretty.

The morning danced along like a cockleshell on a bright sea – such a sea as they would soon be speeding over. She ordered a particularly good dinner, saw the children off to their classes, had her trunks brought down, consulted with the maid about getting out summer clothes – for of course they would be heading for heat and sunshine – and wondered if she oughtn't to take Kenneth's flannel suits out of camphor. 'But how absurd,' she reflected, 'that I don't yet know where we're going!' She looked at the clock, saw that it was close on noon, and decided to call him up at his office. There was a slight delay; then she heard his secretary's voice saying that Mr Ashby had looked in for a moment early, and left again almost immediately . . . Oh, very well, Charlotte would ring up later. How soon was he likely to be back? The secretary answered that she couldn't tell; all they knew in the office was that when he left he had said he was in a hurry because he had to go out of town.

Out of town! Charlotte hung up the receiver and sat blankly gazing into new darkness. Why had he gone out of town? And where had he gone? And of all days, why should he have chosen the eve of their suddenly planned departure? She felt a faint shiver of apprehension. Of course he had gone to see that woman – no doubt to get her permission to leave. He was as completely in bondage as that; and Charlotte had been fatuous enough to see the palms of victory on her forehead. She burst into a laugh and, walking across the room, sat down again before her mirror. What a different face she saw! The smile on her pale lips seemed to mock the rosy vision of the other Charlotte. But gradually her colour crept back. After all, she had a right to claim the victory, since her husband was doing what she wanted, not what the other woman exacted of him. It was natural enough, in view of his abrupt decision to leave the next day, that he should have arrangements to make, business matters to wind up; it was not even necessary to suppose that this mysterious trip was a visit to the writer of the letters. He might simply have gone to see a client who lived out of town. Of course they would not tell Charlotte at the office; the secretary had hesitated before imparting even such meagre information as the fact of Mr Ashby's absence. Meanwhile she would go on with her joyful preparations, content to learn later in the day to what particular island of the blest she was to be carried.

The hours wore on, or rather were swept forward on a rush of eager preparations. At last the entrance of the maid who came to draw the curtains roused Charlotte from her labours, and she saw to her surprise that the clock marked five. And she did not yet know where they were going the next day! She rang up her husband's office and was told that Mr Ashby had not been there since the early morning. She asked for his partner, but the partner could add nothing to her information, for he himself, his suburban train having been behind time, had reached the office after Ashby had come and gone. Charlotte stood perplexed; then she decided to telephone to her mother-in-law. Of course Kenneth, on the eve of a month's absence, must have gone to see his mother. The mere fact that the children – in spite of his vague objections – would certainly have to be left with old Mrs Ashby, made it obvious that he would have all sorts of matters to decide with her. At another time Charlotte might have felt a little hurt at being excluded from their conference, but nothing mattered now but that she had won the day, that her husband was still hers and not another woman's. Gaily she called up Mrs Ashby, heard her friendly voice, and began: 'Well, did Kenneth's news surprise you? What do you think of our elopement?'

Almost instantly, before Mrs Ashby could answer, Charlotte knew what her reply would be. Mrs Ashby had not seen her son, she had had no word from him and did not know what her daughter-in-law meant. Charlotte stood silent in the intensity of her surprise. 'But then, where *has* he been?' she thought. Then, recovering herself, she explained their sudden decision to Mrs Ashby, and in doing so, gradually regained her own self-confidence, her conviction that nothing could ever again come between Kenneth and herself. Mrs Ashby took the news calmly and approvingly. She, too, had thought that Kenneth looked worried and overtired, and she agreed with her daughter-in-law that in such cases change was the surest remedy. 'I'm always so glad when he gets away. Elsie hated travelling; she was always finding pretexts to prevent his going anywhere. With you, thank goodness, it's different.' Nor was Mrs Ashby surprised at his not having had time to let her know of his departure. He must have been in a rush from the moment the decision was taken; but no doubt he'd drop in before dinner. Five minutes' talk was really all they needed. 'I hope you'll gradually cure Kenneth of his mania for going over and over a question that could be settled in a dozen words. He never used to be like that, and if he carried the habit into his professional work he'd soon lose all his clients . . . Yes, do come in for a minute, dear, if you have time; no doubt he'll turn up while you're here.' The tonic ring of Mrs Ashby's voice echoed on reassuringly in the silent room while Charlotte continued her preparations.

Toward seven the telephone rang, and she darted to it. Now she would know! But it was only from the conscientious secretary, to say that Mr Ashby hadn't been back, or sent any word, and before the office closed she thought she ought to let Mrs Ashby know. 'Oh, that's all right. Thanks a lot!' Charlotte called out cheerfully, and hung up the receiver with a trembling hand. But perhaps by this time, she reflected, he was at his mother's. She shut her drawers and cupboards, put on her hat and coat and called up to the nursery that she was going out for a minute to see the children's grandmother.

Mrs Ashby lived nearby, and during her brief walk through the cold spring dusk Charlotte imagined that every advancing figure was her husband's. But she did not meet him on the way, and when she entered the house she found her mother-in-law alone. Kenneth had neither telephoned nor come. Old Mrs Ashby sat by her bright fire, her knitting needles flashing steadily through her active old hands, and her mere bodily presence gave reassurance to Charlotte. Yes, it was certainly odd that Kenneth had gone off for the whole day without letting any of them know; but, after all, it was to be expected. A busy lawyer held so many threads in his hands that any sudden change of plan would oblige him to make all sorts of unforeseen arrangements and adjustments. He might have gone to see some client in the suburbs and been detained there; his mother remembered his telling her that he had charge of the legal business of a queer old recluse somewhere in New Jersey, who was immensely rich but too mean to have a telephone. Very likely Kenneth had been stranded there.

But Charlotte felt her nervousness gaining on her. When Mrs Ashby asked her at what hour they were sailing the next day and she had to say she didn't know – that Kenneth had simply sent her word he was going to take their passages – the uttering of the words again brought home to her the strangeness of the situation. Even Mrs Ashby conceded that it was odd; but she immediately added that it only showed what a rush he was in.

'But, mother, it's nearly eight o'clock! He must realize that I've got to know when we're starting tomorrow.'

'Oh, the boat probably doesn't sail till evening. Sometimes they have to wait till midnight for the tide. Kenneth's probably counting on that. After all, he has a level head.'

Charlotte stood up. 'It's not that. Something has happened to him.'

Mrs Ashby took off her spectacles and rolled up her knitting. 'If you begin to let yourself imagine things—'

'Aren't you in the least anxious?'

'I never am till I have to be. I wish you'd ring for dinner, my dear. You'll stay and dine? He's sure to drop in here on his way home.'

Charlotte called up her own house. No, the maid said, Mr Ashby hadn't come in and hadn't telephoned. She would tell him as soon as he came that Mrs Ashby was dining at his mother's. Charlotte followed her mother-in-law into the dining room and sat with parched throat before her empty plate, while Mrs Ashby dealt calmly and efficiently with a short but carefully prepared repast. 'You'd better eat something, child, or·you'll be as bad as Kenneth . . . Yes, a little more asparagus, please, Jane.'

She insisted on Charlotte's drinking a glass of sherry and nibbling a bit of toast; then they returned to the drawing room, where the fire had been made up, and the cushions in Mrs Ashby's armchair shaken out and smoothed. How safe and familiar it all looked; and out there, somewhere in the uncertainty and mystery of the night, lurked the answer to the two women's conjectures, like an indistinguishable figure prowling on the threshold.

At last Charlotte got up and said: 'I'd better go back. At this hour Kenneth will certainly go straight home.'

Mrs Ashby smiled indulgently. 'It's not very late, my dear. It doesn't take two sparrows long to dine.'

'It's after nine.' Charlotte bent down to kiss her. 'The fact is, I can't keep still.'

Mrs Ashby pushed aside her work and rested her two hands on the arms of her chair. 'I'm going with you,' she said, helping herself up.

Charlotte protested that it was too late, that it was not necessary, that she would call up as soon as Kenneth came in, but Mrs Ashby had already rung for her maid. She was slightly lame, and stood resting on her stick while her wraps were brought. 'If Mr Kenneth turns up, tell him he'll find me at his own house,' she instructed the maid as the two women got into the taxi which had been summoned. During the short drive Charlotte gave thanks that she was not returning home alone. There was something warm and substantial in the mere fact of Mrs Ashby's nearness, something that corresponded with the clearness of her eyes and the texture of her fresh firm complexion. As the taxi drew up she laid her hand encouragingly on Charlotte's. 'You'll see; there'll be a message.'

The door opened at Charlotte's ring and the two entered. Charlotte's heart beat excitedly; the stimulus of her mother-in-law's confidence was beginning to flow through her veins.

'You'll see – you'll see,' Mrs Ashby repeated.

The maid who opened the door said no, Mr Ashby had not come in, and there had been no message from him.

'You're sure the telephone's not out of order?' his mother suggested: and the maid said, well, it certainly wasn't half an hour ago; but she'd just go and ring up to make sure. She disappeared, and Charlotte turned to take off her hat and cloak. As she did so her eyes lit on the hall table, and there lay a grey envelope, her husband's name faintly traced on it. 'Oh!' she cried out, suddenly aware that for the first time in month's she had entered her house without wondering if one of the grey letters would be there.

'What is it, my dear?' Mrs Ashby asked with a glance of surprise.

Charlotte did not answer. She took up the envelope and stood staring at it as if she could force her gaze to penetrate to what was within. Then an idea occurred to her. She turned and held out the envelope to her mother-in-law.

'Do you know that writing?' she asked.

Mrs Ashby took the letter. She had to feel with her other hand for her eyeglasses, and when she had adjusted them she lifted the envelope to the light. 'Why!' she exclaimed; and then stopped. Charlotte noticed that the letter shook in her usually firm hand. 'But this is addressed to Kenneth,' Mrs Ashby said at length, in a low voice. Her tone seemed to imply that she felt her daughter-in-law's question to be slightly indiscreet.

'Yes, but no matter,' Charlotte spoke with sudden decision. 'I want to know – do you know the writing?'

Mrs Ashby handed back the letter. 'No,' she said distinctly.

The two women had turned into the library. Charlotte switched on the electric light and shut the door. She still held the envelope in her hand.

'I'm going to open it,' she announced.

She caught her mother-in-law's startled glance. 'But, dearest – a letter not addressed to you? My dear, you can't!'

'As if I cared about that – now!' She continued to look intently at Mrs Ashby. 'This letter may tell me where Kenneth is.'

Mrs Ashby's glossy bloom was effaced by a quick pallor; her firm cheeks seemed to shrink and wither. 'Why should it? What makes you believe— It can't possibly—'

Charlotte held her eyes steadily on that altered face. 'Ah, then you *do* know the writing?' she flashed back.

'Know the writing? How should I? With all my son's correspondents . . . What I do know is—' Mrs Ashby broke off and looked at her daughter-in-law entreatingly, almost timidly.

Charlotte caught her by the wrist. 'Mother! What do you know? Tell me! You must!'

'That I don't believe any good ever came of a woman's opening her husband's letters behind his back.'

The words sounded to Charlotte's irritated ears as flat as a phrase culled from a book of moral axioms. She laughed impatiently and dropped her mother-in-law's wrist. 'Is that all? No good can come of this letter, opened or unopened. I know that well enough. But whatever ill comes, I mean to find out what's in it.' Her hands had been trembling as they held the envelope, but now they grew firm, and her voice also. She still gazed intently at Mrs Ashby. 'This is the ninth letter addressed in the same hand that has come for Kenneth since we've been married. Always these same grey envelopes. I've kept count of them because after each one he has been like a man who has had some dreadful shock. It takes him hours to shake off their effect. I've told him so. I've told him I must know from whom they come, because I can see they're killing him. He won't answer my questions; he says he can't tell me anything about the letters; but last night he promised to go away with me – to get away from them.'

Mrs Ashby, with shaking steps, had gone to one of the armchairs and sat down in it, her head drooping forward on her breast. 'Ah,' she murmured.

'So now you understand – '

'Did he tell you it was to get away from them?'

'He said, to get away – to get away. He was sobbing so that he could hardly speak. But I told him I knew that was why.'

'And what did he say?'

'He took me in his arms and said he'd go wherever I wanted.'

'Ah, thank God!' said Mrs Ashby. There was a silence, during which she continued to sit with bowed head, and eyes averted from her daughter-in-law. At last she looked up and spoke. 'Are you sure there have been as many as nine?'

'Perfectly. This is the ninth. I've kept count.'

'And he has absolutely refused to explain?'

'Absolutely.'

Mrs Ashby spoke through pale contracted lips. 'When did they begin to come? Do you remember?'

Charlotte laughed again. 'Remember? The first one came the night we got back from our honeymoon.'

'All that time?' Mrs Ashby lifted her head and spoke with sudden energy. 'Then – yes, open it.'

The words were so unexpected that Charlotte felt the blood in her temples, and her hands began to tremble again. She tried to slip her finger under the flap of the envelope, but it was so tightly stuck that she had to hunt on her husband's writing table for his ivory letter opener. As she pushed about the familiar objects his own hands had so lately touched, they sent through her the icy chill emanating from the little personal effects of someone newly dead. In the deep silence of the room the tearing of the paper as she slit the envelope sounded like a human cry. She drew out the sheet and carried it to the lamp.

'Well?' Mrs Ashby asked below her breath.

Charlotte did not move or answer. She was bending over the page with wrinkled brows, holding it nearer and nearer to the light. Her sight must be blurred, or else dazzled by the reflection of the lamplight on the smooth surface of the paper, for, strain her eyes as she would, she could discern only a few faint strokes, so faint and faltering as to be nearly undecipherable.

'I can't make it out,' she said.

'What do you mean, dear?'

'The writing's too indistinct . . . Wait.'

She went back to the table, and, sitting down close to Kenneth's reading lamp, slipped the letter under a magnifying glass. All this time she was aware that her mother-in-law was watching her intently.

'Well?' Mrs Ashby breathed.

'Well, it's no clearer. I can't read it.'

'You mean the paper is an absolute blank?'

'No, not quite. There is writing on it. I can make out something like, "mine" – oh, and "come". It might be "come".'

Mrs Ashby stood up abruptly. Her face was even paler than before. She advanced to the table and, resting her two hands on it, drew a deep breath 'Let me see,' she said, as if forcing herself to a hateful effort.

Charlotte felt the contagion of her whiteness. 'She knows,' she thought. She pushed the letter across the table. Her mother-in-law lowered her head over it in silence, but without touching it with her pale wrinkled hands.

Charlotte stood watching her as she herself, when she had tried to read the letter, had been watched by Mrs Ashby. The latter fumbled for her glasses, held them to her eyes, and bent still closer to the outspread page, in order, as it seemed, to avoid touching it. The light of the lamp fell directly on her old face, and Charlotte reflected what depths of the unknown may lurk under the clearest and most candid lineaments. She had never seen her mother-in-law's features express any but simple and sound emotions – cordiality, amusement, a kindly sympathy; now and again a flash of wholesome anger. Now they seemed to wear a look of fear and hatred, of incredulous dismay and almost cringing defiance. It was as if the spirits warring within her had distorted her face to their own likeness. At length she raised her head. 'I can't – I can't,' she said in a voice of childish distress.

'You can't make it out either?'

She shook her head, and Charlotte saw two tears roll down her cheeks.

'Familiar as the writing is to you?' Charlotte insisted with twitching lips.

Mrs Ashby did not take up the challenge. 'I can make out nothing – nothing.'

'But you do know the writing?'

Mrs Ashby lifted her head timidly; her anxious eyes stole with a glance of apprehension around the quiet familiar room. 'How can I tell? I was startled at first . . .'

'Startled by the resemblance?'

'Well, I thought—'

'You'd better say it out, mother! You knew at once it was *her* writing?'

'Oh, wait, my dear – wait.'

'Wait for what?'

Mrs Ashby looked up; her eyes, travelling slowly past Charlotte, were lifted to the blank wall behind her son's writing table.

Charlotte, following the glance, burst into a shrill laugh of accusation. 'I needn't wait any longer! You've answered me now! You're looking straight at the wall where her picture used to hang!'

Mrs Ashby lifted her hand with a murmur of warning. 'Sh-h.'

'Oh, you needn't imagine that anything can ever frighten me again!' Charlotte cried.

Her mother-in-law still leaned against the table. Her lips moved plaintively. 'But we're going mad – we're both going mad. We both know such things are impossible.'

Her daughter-in-law looked at her with a pitying stare. 'I've known for a long time now that everything was possible.'

'Even this?'

'Yes, exactly this.'

'But this letter – after all, there's nothing in this letter—'

'Perhaps there would be to him. How can I tell? I remember his saying to me once that if you were used to a handwriting the faintest stroke of it became legible. Now I see what he meant. He *was* used to it.'

'But the few strokes that I can make out are so pale. No one could possibly read that letter.'

Charlotte laughed again. 'I suppose everything's pale about a ghost.' she said stridently.

'Oh, my child – my child – don't say it!'

'Why shouldn't I say it, when even the bare walls cry it out? What difference does it make if her letters are illegible to you and me? If even you can see her face on that blank wall, why shouldn't he read her writing on this blank paper? Don't you see that she's everywhere in this house, and the closer to him because to everyone else she's become invisible?' Charlotte dropped into a chair and covered her face with her hands. A turmoil of sobbing shook her from head to foot. At length a touch on her shoulder made her look up, and she saw her mother-in-law bending over her. Mrs Ashby's face seemed to have grown still smaller and more wasted, but it had resumed its usual quiet look. Through all her tossing anguish, Charlotte felt the impact of that resolute spirit.

'Tomorrow – tomorrow. You'll see. There'll be some explanation tomorrow.'

Charlotte cut her short. 'An explanation? Who's going to give it, I wonder?'

Mrs Ashby drew back and straightened herself heroically. 'Kenneth himself will,' she cried out in a strong voice. Charlotte said nothing, and the old woman went on: 'But meanwhile we must act; we must notify the police. Now, without a moment's delay. We must do everything – everything.'

Charlotte stood up slowly and stiffly; her joints felt as cramped as an old woman's. 'Exactly as if we thought it could do any good to do anything?'

Resolutely Mrs Ashby cried: 'Yes!' and Charlotte went up to the telephone and unhooked the receiver.

# Venetian Masks

## Adolfo Bioy Casares

*In 1931 Adolfo Bioy Casares, aged seventeen, met Borges, aged thirty-two. Bioy wanted to become a writer. 'If you want to write,' said Borges, 'don't mess around with publishing companies or literary magazines. Just read and write.' The advice bore fruit and nine years later Bioy published* The Invention of Morel, *a novel which Borges described as 'perfect'. Their friendship led to stories written in collaboration under the pen-name Bustos Domecq – stories full of humour and brilliant word-play. Silvina Ocampo (a talented writer and Bioy's wife) says that she can tell when they are working together by the howls of laughter that echo through the apartment.*

*One afternoon in 1939 Bioy, Borges and Silvina planned a story – never to be written – set in France. The hero was a young literary gentleman who, intrigued by the secret reputation of a writer who had recently died, decided to look up the man's works. With difficulty the hero found all the master's publications: a speech consisting of a series of well-written clichés; a brochure in praise of the academicians' sword; a brief essay, dedicated to the memory of Nisard, on the fragments of Varro's* Treatise on the Latin Tongue; *a* Wreath of Sonnets *severe both in its form and its content. Unable to reconcile these writings, so cold and barren, with the author's reputation, the hero decided to look farther. He arrived at the castle in which the master had spent his last years, and gained access to his papers. He discovered a pile of brilliant first drafts, hopelessly mutilated. Finally he came upon a list of 'things that a writer must avoid'. (Bioy says that he copied out the list they then invented on the end-papers of Dunne's* An Experiment with Time.) *Among the 'prohibitions' are included:*

*– Psychological curiosities and paradoxes: murderers through kindness, suicides for happiness' sake.*

*– Surprising interpretations of literary works and characters: Don Juan's loathing of women, etc.*

*– Couples of evidently dissimilar characters: Sherlock Holmes and Watson, Don Quixote and Sancho Panza.*

– *Characters made different from one another through their little peculiarities (as in Dickens).*

– *Novelty and surprise; trick-stories. The search for what has not yet been said seems an unworthy task for a poet in a cultured society. Civilized readers will not be pleased with the incivility of having a surprise sprung upon them.*

– *Pretentious distortions of space and time: Faulkner, Borges, Bioy Casares.*

– *The discovery that in a certain book the true hero is the jungle, the sea, the weather, the surplus-value theory. Writing books of which someone may say this.*

– *Poems, situations, characters with which the reader may identify himself.*

– *Phrases currently used or which may become catch-phrases or quotations (because they are inconsistent with a coherent text).*

– *Characters that may become myths.*

– *Characters, scenes, words typical of a certain place or of a certain historical moment. Local colour.*

– *Chaotic enumeration.*

– *Richness of vocabulary. Any word chosen as a synonym. Inversely, the* mot juste. *Any effort to be precise.*

– *Vivid descriptions. Physically rich worlds (as in Faulkner).*

– *Background, atmosphere, surroundings. Tropical heat, drunkenness, voices on the radio, words repeated as a refrain.*

– *Meteorological beginnings and endings. Meteorological and spiritual coincidences:* Le vent se lève . . . Il faut tenter de vivre. *('The wind is rising . . . We must try and live.')*

– *Metaphors in general. In particular visual metaphors, and especially agricultural, naval, banking metaphors. (See Proust.)*

– *Any anthropomorphism.*

– *Novels in which the plot runs parallel with that of another book. (James Joyce's* Ulysses.*)*

– *Books that pretend to be menus, albums, itineraries, concerts.*

– *Anything that may suggest illustrations; anything that may inspire a film.*

– *Disapproval or praise in critical writings. Nothing is more naïve than these 'dealers in the obvious' who proclaim the ineptitude of Homer, Cervantes, Milton, Molière.*

– *In critical writings, all historical or biographical references. The author's personality. Psychoanalysis.*

*– Family scenes or erotic scenes in detective novels. Dramatic scenes in philosophical dialogues.*
*– Satisfying the reader's expectations: sob-stories and eroticism in romantic novels; puzzles and death in detective stories; ghosts in fantastic stories.*
*– Vanity, modesty, homosexuality, lack of homosexuality, suicide.*

*And so the list continues until it encompasses the whole of literature.*

When I hear people talk about psychosomatics as if it were a real and unavoidable phenomenom, I say to myself with bitterness that life is more intricate than they suppose. I do not try to convince them, but I cannot unlearn my own experience. For years I drifted aimlessly from one love affair to another – not many affairs for so long a period, and those few proved both incongruous and unhappy. Then I met Daniela and I knew my search had ended, that everything I could hope for had been granted. It was at that time too that I began to suffer from feverish spells.

I remember the doctor's first visit.

'I suspect your ganglions are to blame for this temperature,' he announced. 'I'll prescribe something to bring it down.'

I took his words as an encouragement, but as he wrote out the prescription I asked myself whether the fact that he was giving me something for the symptoms meant that he was not giving me anything for the disease because it was incurable. I realized that if I did not dispel my doubts I would have to prepare myself for a future full of anxiety, but that if I did ask I was risking an answer that would make the rest of my life impossible to bear. The thought of such drawn-out uncertainty seemed too tiresome, and I plucked up courage to ask the question.

'Incurable?' he answered. 'No, not necessarily. There are cases, I can say there have been cases, of recovery.'

'Of total recovery?'

'You've said it. Look, I'll put my cards on the table. In cases like yours, a doctor is apt to do everything he can to raise his patient's hopes. But – and pay attention, this is important – of the recovery in previous cases I have absolutely no doubts; what remains unclear are the reasons: why and how the cure came about.'

'So there's no treatment?'

'Of course there is. Palliative treatment.'

'That sometimes results in a cure?'

He did not say no, and in that imperfect hope I placed my will to be cured.

It seemed certain that the examination had been far from encouraging, and yet when I left the surgery I did not know what to think; I felt in no fit state to draw conclusions, as if I had received news which, for lack of time, I had not read closely. I felt less sad than overwhelmed.

In two or three days the treatment rid me of the fever. It left me a little weak or tired, and perhaps because of that I accepted the doctor's diagnosis literally. Then I felt well, even better than before the illness, and I told myself that doctors are not always right in their diagnosis, that maybe I would not suffer another attack. I said to myself: 'If it were to happen again, I would be noticing some preliminary symptoms, but the truth is that I feel better than ever before.'

I will not deny that I nursed a clear inclination to disbelieve in my illness. It was probably my way of defending myself against forebodings or worrying about its influence on my future with Daniela. I had become accustomed to happiness, and life without her seemed unimaginable. I used to say to Daniela that a hundred years were not enough to look at her, not enough for being together. My exaggerations reflected my feelings.

I enjoyed her telling me about her experiments. Spontaneously I pictured biology – her subject – as an enormous river flowing between prodigious revelations. Thanks to a grant, Daniela had studied in France with Jean Rostand and with Leclerc, his no less famous colleague. Describing the project on which Leclerc was then working, Daniela used the word 'carbon-copy'. Rostand, on the other hand, was investigating the possibilities of anabolic acceleration. I remember saying, 'I don't even know what anabolic means.'

'All living creatures go through three stages,' Daniela explained. 'The anabolic, or period of growth; then a more or less long plateau, adulthood; and finally the catabolic stage, or period of decline. Rostand imagined that if we spent fewer years growing, we would gain many more useful years of life.'

'How old is he?'

'He's almost eighty. But don't think he's an old man. All his female students fall in love with him.'

Daniela smiled. Without looking at her, I answered, 'I, if I were Rostand, would dedicate my efforts to delay, even suppress, the catabolic stage. And I don't say this because I think he's old.'

'Rostand shares your opinion, but he maintains that in order to understand the mechanisms of decline it is imperative to understand the mechanisms of growth.'

A few weeks after my first attack, Daniela received a letter from her professor. When she read it to me, I felt truly gratified. I was tremendously pleased that a man so famous for his intelligence should show such affection and esteem for Daniela.

He had written to ask her to attend the forthcoming Biology Congress in Montevideo, where she would meet one of the researchers in his team, a certain doctor Proux or Prioux, who would bring her up to date on their work.

'How shall I tell him that I don't want to go?' Daniela asked me. She always thought these international seminars and congresses were useless. I know of no one less keen on appearing in public.

'Don't you think it would be ungrateful to say no to Rostand?'

'I owe him all I know.'

'Then don't refuse. I'll come with you.'

I remember the scene as if I saw it now. Daniela threw herself into my arms, whispered a nickname (which I will not mention; all nicknames which are not one's own sound ridiculous) and cried gleefully, 'A week in Uruguay, with you! What fun!' She paused and added, 'Especially if there were no congress.'

She let herself be convinced. The day of departure I woke with a temperature and by mid-morning I felt dreadful. If I did not want to be a millstone round Daniela's neck I would have to give up the journey. I admit I hoped for a miracle and it was not until the very last minute that I told her I was not going. She accepted my decision, but unhappily.

'A whole week without you, just so as not to miss that boring old congress. Why in the world didn't I say no to Rostand?'

Suddenly it was late. We kissed goodbye in a hurry which left me with a feeling of bewilderment tinged with sadness. Bewilderment and forlornness. To make myself feel better I tried to remember how lucky I had been, not having had enough time to explain to her the extent of my illness. Perhaps I imagined that if I didn't talk about it, I would be giving it less importance. The illusion did not last long. I felt so sick that I became totally disheartened; I realized I was seriously ill and that my illness had no cure. The fever gave way to the treatment with more difficulty than the first time, and left me nervous and exhausted. When Daniela returned I was delighted, but I probably looked a sight because she asked me more than once how I was feeling. I had intended not to talk about my illness, but noticing, or imagining, in her words a veiled remonstrance for not having accompanied her to Montevideo, I reminded her of the doctor's diagnosis. I only gave her the bare essentials, leaving aside the cases of recovery which in all probability had simply been mentioned by the doctor to mitigate the terrible truth.

'What are you suggesting?' Daniela asked. 'That we stop seeing each other?'

'I haven't got the courage to say it, but there's something I can't forget: the day you met me I was a whole, healthy man; today I'm someone else.'

'I don't understand,' she answered.

I tried to explain to her that I had no right to burden her with an invalid, and she took my speculations or scruples to mean that I had reached a firm decision. She said in a low voice, 'All right.'

We did not argue because Daniela believed in respecting other people's decisions, but mainly because she was angry. That was our last day together.

I reflected sadly: 'It's for the best. Even if Daniela's absence will seem terrible to me, it would be worse to close my eyes to the facts, tire her out, begin to notice her weariness and her desire to leave.' The illness might force me to give up my job at the paper; then Daniela would not only have to put up with me but keep me as well.

I recalled a comment she had made, which at the time I had thought funny. Daniela had said, 'How tiresome those people who are forever fond of fighting and making up.' I did not, therefore, dare try and make up. I did not go to see her or phone her. Nevertheless, I tried to set up a chance meeting. I had never before walked so much through Buenos Aires. When I left the paper at night, I could not resign myself to going home and postponing until the next day the possibility of meeting her. I would sleep badly and wake up as if I had not slept at all, certain that on that day I would come across her, simply because I did not have the strength to go on living without her. In the midst of these anxious expectations I heard that Daniela had left for France.

I told Hector Massey (a life-long friend) what had happened. He reflected, out loud: 'You know, people disappear. You break off with someone and then you never see the person again. It happens all the time.'

'Buenos Aires without Daniela is another city.'

'If you really think so, maybe you'll find the following piece of information helpful; I read it in some magazine. In other cities there are sometimes doubles of the people we know here.'

Maybe he said it just to divert my attention. He must have guessed my irritation because he apologized.

'I understand what it must be like to give up Daniela. You'll never meet another woman like her.'

I do not like talking about my private life. But I have discovered that, sooner or later, I end up discussing all my problems with Massey. Probably I look for his approval because I consider him to be both honest and equitable, and because he will not let personal feelings stand in the way of his opinions. When I told him about my last words with Daniela, he looked up the illness to see whether the symptoms actually were as I had described them, and then he said he agreed with me. He added, 'You'll never find Daniela again.'

'I know that all too well,' I said.

I have thought many times that my friend's naïve insensitivity was an advantage, because it allowed him to express his opinions with utter sincerity. The people who consult him professionally – Massey is a lawyer – praise him for saying what he thinks and for having a clear, straightforward view of the facts.

I spent years secluded in my nightmare. I hid my illness as something shameful and I believed, perhaps rightly, that if I could not see Daniela it was not worth seeing anyone. I avoided Massey himself; one day I heard that he was somewhere in the States or in Europe. During working hours, at the paper, I tried to keep away from my colleagues. In spite of everything I hoped for something I could not put into words, and the expectation helped me overcome my affliction and adjust my life to the unflinching goal of rebuilding the crumbled sandcastle of my health: I hoped against hope for a cure – never mind when – and to be again with Daniela. Not content with hoping, I used my imagination. I dreamt of our meeting. Like a demanding film director, I rehearsed the scene again and again, to make it more triumphant, more moving. Many think that intelligence is a stumbling-block on the road to happiness. The real stumbling-block is our own imagination.

From Paris came the news that Daniela had given herself over completely to her work, her biological experiments. I approved. I never felt jealous of either Rostand or Leclerc.

I think I began to recover (an invalid lives in a continuous sway, from high hopes to disappointments). During the day I no longer thought much about my next attack, and my nights were less full of anxiety. One morning, very early, the doorbell woke me. I opened the door: there was Massey. As far as I could make out, he had just arrived from France and had come straight away to see me, without first stopping at his place. I asked him if he had seen her. He said yes. The silence that followed was so long that I wondered whether Massey's presence was not somehow related to Daniela. Then he told me that he had come back with the single purpose of letting me know that they had just got married.

The surprise, the confusion, left me speechless. At last I excused myself, saying that I had an appointment with the doctor. I looked so sick he must have believed me.

I never doubted that Massey had acted in good faith. He must have thought that he was not actually depriving me of anything, because it had been I who had left Daniela. When he said that their marriage should not be an obstacle to our meeting as before, I had to explain to him that it might be better if we let some time go by before we met again.

I did not tell him that his marriage would not last. I reached that conviction not because I bore them a grudge but because I knew all too well the people involved. Of course I was burning with indignation.

A few months later I heard that they had separated.

Neither of them returned to Buenos Aires. As to my hopeful recovery (one of many) it turned out to be an illusion, and I kept on plodding through my dreary daily life in which the feverish spells alternated with periods of promising improvement.

The years passed quickly. Perhaps I should say numbly. Ten years! – ten years swept along by the dizzy repetition of almost identical weeks. Two facts proved, however, that time still existed: my health improved yet again – once more I imagined that this was finally *the* recovery – and I heard that Massey and Daniela were going to give their marriage a second chance. So many months passed without fever that I began to wonder whether I was not cured; while Massey and Daniela had been separated for so many years, that the news of their getting together again surprised me.

To bolster my recovery I thought I should change my routine, break away from the past. Perhaps a trip to Europe would be the best solution.

I went to see the doctor. I carefully thought out the words I would use to tell him of my plans. I did not want to leave myself open to a possible objection. The truth is that I was afraid he might dissuade me for the best or the worst of reasons.

Without taking his eyes off my clinical history, he muttered, 'It seems like an excellent idea.'

He stared at me as if he wished to say something, but the ringing phone caught his attention; he had a long conversation. In the meantime I remembered, somewhat to my surprise, that on my first visit I had seen that surgery as part of an evil dream, and the doctor (now it seemed incredible) as an enemy. Remembering all this I felt sure of myself, but suddenly I thought of an alarming possibility. What was he trying to say? Could I swear that his words were 'an excellent idea'? And if they were, had he perhaps said them ironically? My anxiety was dispelled when the doctor hung up. 'Not only the physical part is important,' he explained. 'Just now a trip to Europe would do you more good than all the medicines I could prescribe you.'

Several circumstances, among them a temporary strengthening of the Argentine *peso*, allowed me to undertake the trip. Fate seemed to be on my side.

I thought that the pleasure of staying indefinitely in almost any place in the world would prevent me from falling for the classical tourist routine favoured by agencies – two days in Paris, a night in Nice, lunch in Genoa, *et cetera* – but a certain impatience, as that of someone in search of something, or someone escaping something (the illness close to my heels?), forced me to continue my journey hardly a day after having arrived in the most delightful places. I continued in my absurd haste until one afternoon towards the end of December, drifting down a canal, in a gondola (now I ask myself if it was not a boatful of tourists and luggage – what matter!), I entered Venice and found myself in a state of mind which combined, in perfect harmony, exultation and peace. I cried out, 'Here I'll stay! This is what I was looking for.'

I got off at the Mocenigo Hotel, where a room had been reserved for me. I remember I slept well, anxious, however, for morning to come so that I could get up and see Venice. All at once it seemed to me that a faint light rimmed the window. I ran and looked out. Dawn was glittering on the Grand Canal and was drawing the Rialto from the shadows. A damp cold made me close the window and seek refuge under the blankets.

As soon as I felt warmer I leapt from bed. After a light breakfast I took a hot bath and with no further delay set out to walk through the city. For an instant I thought I was in a dream. No, it was even stranger. I knew I was not dreaming, but I could find no explanation for what I was seeing. 'In good time all will be made clear,' I said to myself without conviction because I still felt puzzled. While two or three gondoliers were shouting and waving their hands to attract my attention a Harlequin rode past me in a motor-boat.

Determined, I do not really know why, not to seem surprised, with feigned indifference I asked one of the men how much he charged for a ride to the Rialto, and with a hesitant step I entered the gondola. We set off in the opposite direction from the masked Harlequin. Seeing the palaces on both sides of the canal I thought to myself, 'It seems as if Venice had been built like an endless series of stage sets . . . And yet, why is it that the first thing I see on leaving my hotel is a Harlequin? Perhaps to convince me that I am in a theatre and to charm me even more. Of course, if I were suddenly to meet Massey here, I would hear him say that everything in this world is grey and mediocre, and that Venice dazzles me because I came here expecting to be dazzled.'

Only after passing more masks and a second Harlequin did I remember that it was Carnival. I mentioned to the gondolier that it surprised me to see that many people dressed-up so early in the day.

If I understood him correctly (the man's accent was rather strong), he said that they were all heading for the Piazza San Marco, where there would be a costume competition at noon, and that I should not miss it, because the prettiest Venetian ladies would be there, and that they were famous all over the world for their beauty. Maybe he imagined I was terribly ignorant, because he called out the name of the costumes we passed, spelling out the syllables to make himself clear: 'Pan-ta-loon. Co-lum-bine. Har-le-quin.'

Of course there were some I would not have recognized: *Il dottore*, with glasses and a long nose; *Meneghino*, wearing a tie with white stripes; another, frankly disagreeable, Plague or *la malattia;* and one I cannot remember well, called *Brighella* or something of the sort.

I got out near the Rialto bridge. At the post office I sent a card to my doctor ('Dear *dottore*, Wonderful trip. I'm feeling splendid. All the best.') and then I walked down the Merceria towards the Piazza San Marco, glancing at the passing masks as if I were looking for one in particular. Not without reason it is said that if we suddenly remember someone, after a while we will meet him. On a bridge, near a church – San Giuliano o Salvatore – I almost knocked Massey over. I cried out, 'You, here!'

'We have been living in Venice for some time now. When did you arrive?'

I did not answer immediately because the plural upset me. The simple allusion to Daniela was enough to cast a shadow over me. And I had thought the old wounds had healed. In the end I muttered, 'Last night.'

'Why not come and stay at our place? We've got plenty of room.'

'I'd have loved to, but tomorrow I'm leaving for Paris.' I lied because I was not certain of how the meeting would affect me.

'If my wife knows you were in Venice and that you left without seeing her, she'd never forgive me. Tonight they're showing Catalini's *Lorelei* at La Fenice.'

'I don't like opera.'

'Who cares about opera? The important thing is spending some time together. Come to our box. You'll enjoy it. It's a gala performance, because of the Carnival, and people will go all dressed up.'

'I don't like getting dressed up.'

'Very few men do. The ones who dress up are the women.'

I must have thought I had done enough and that if Massey kept on insisting I would not be able to refuse much longer. I believe it was then that I discovered that the secret stimulus of my journey had been the hope of meeting Daniela. Now, knowing she was in Venice, the idea of leaving without seeing her seemed to me a sacrifice beyond my will.

'We'll pick you up at your hotel.'

'No, I'll get there on my own. Just leave my ticket at the box-office.'

He insisted I be on time, because if I arrived after the first note had been struck, I would not be able to get in until the end of the first act. I felt tempted to ask about Daniela but found myself filled with fear and loathing that Massey should pronounce her name. We said goodbye.

Of course, I forgot all about the costume competition. Daniela and the thrill of seeing her again were my only concerns. On and off, in sharp stabs, I had flashes of what would be at risk during the meeting. After all my suffering, I would rekindle a pain which even though it had not vanished had at least become dull. Did I hope to find a way – in a moment, in a theatre-box, at the opera – to win Daniela back? Would I do that to Massey? Why think about impossibilities . . . The very expectation of seeing Daniela was enough to seal my fate.

When I arrived, the performance had begun. An usher led me to the box, one of the kind called 'balconies'. Upon opening the door the first thing I saw was Daniela, dressed as Columbine, eating chocolate. Beside her was Massey. Daniela was smiling at me and, behind her mask – which she did not take off, as I longed for her to do – her eyes sparkled. She whispered, 'Pull up a chair.'

'I'm all right here,' I answered. Not to make noise, I sat on the first chair I could find.

'You won't see a thing,' said Massey.

I passed from bliss to dull annoyance at Massey's presence in the box. A soprano began to sing:

*Vieni, deh, vieni*

and Daniela, fascinated, turned towards the stage with her back to me. No doubt unjustly I thought that the woman of my life, after an interminable separation, had granted me (lent is maybe a better word) her attention for less than a minute. More remarkable still, sadder perhaps, was the fact that I reacted with indifference. I felt so far from her that I even managed to concentrate on the star-crossed loves of Anna, Walter, and Lorelei who out of spite and to obtain magical powers marries a river (the Rhine, if I remember correctly). At first, the only similarity I found between the story on the stage and my own, was that it concerned three people; I needed no more to follow it with extraordinary interest. At times, however, I felt bewildered . . . I found myself in an unforseen situation which I thought somewhat scandalous: Daniela and I looked at each other as if we were strangers. Even worse, I wanted to leave. During the intermission Daniela asked, 'Who'll be an angel and bring me more of these chocolates? They sell them across the road, in the café on the piazza.'

'I'll go,' I hastened to answer.

To my annoyance, I heard Massey announce, 'I'll come with you.'

Surrounded by masks and gentlemen in black ties, we walked slowly down the marble staircase. We ran across the piazza because it was cold. In the café, Massey chose a table by the door. A girl in a hoop-skirt, a dressed-up nobleman and a turbaned Turk came in and stood close to us, joking.

'I don't like the draught,' I said. 'Let's change tables.'

We chose one at the back. The waiter immediately took our order: a *strega* for me, coffee and the chocolates for Massey. We hardly talked, as if there were only one subject and it were forbidden. When the time came to pay for the bill, there were no free tables left; in spite of our calls the waiters just sailed by. The cold had brought the people indoors. Suddenly, among the buzz of the many voices, we heard one unmistakable voice: we both looked towards the door. I do not know why, but I think we both had the slightest hesitation, as if each of us had felt that he had been surprised by the other. At our first table (others had been pulled up to it) I saw several Harlequins, Pantaloons and two or three young girls dressed as Columbine. I immediately knew which one was Daniela. The lustre of her eyes watching me from behind the mask left no room for doubt.

Visibly nervous, Massey looked at his watch. 'It's about to start.'

In my mind I prayed that he would not go on with his story about not being able to get in if we were late. What he said made me even angrier:

'Why don't you go and wait for me in the box?'

'Who does he think he is, shoving me aside, just because Daniela is here,' I thought indignantly. After a moment I reconsidered: every man sees things his own way, and maybe Massey felt he was within his rights because he had married her after I had let her go.

I said, 'I'll take her the chocolates.'

He handed them over, a little doubtfully, as if my request had baffled him. When I came up to her table, Daniela looked me in the eyes and whispered, 'Tomorrow, here, at this time.'

She also said another word, a nickname she alone knew. In a halo of happiness I left the bar. As if a curtain had been drawn open, I asked myself why it had taken me so long to understand that in the box Daniela had shown herself distant to better disguise her feelings. Suddenly I realized that I had not given her the chocolates and I was about to turn when I thought that if I reappeared with them I would perhaps add a touch of the ridiculous to an otherwise wonderful moment. Of one thing I am certain: I did not stand too long in the piazza because it was too cold, and once in the theatre I went straight back to our box. So I was surprised to see Daniela there, sitting as we had left her, her elbows on the red velvet of the railing. One would have said that in all that time she had not changed her position. I managed to hand over the chocolates, but I felt very confused. A suspicion, a stupid hunch – I remembered that in the morning Massey had not said 'Daniela' but 'my wife' – suddenly urged me to ask her to take off her mask. To steady myself I fixed my attention on the movements of her hands which first pulled back the sleeves of her costume and then tied up her slightly ruffled hair. How I longed for days gone by. It was not necessary, I thought, for her to take off her mask; only Daniela had such grace. I was about to dissuade her but Daniela had already unmasked her face. Even though I always remembered her as incomparable, as unique, the perfection of her beauty dazzled me. I whispered her name.

I regretted it almost immediately. Something strange had taken place: that word so loved, here, at this very moment, made me sad. The world became incomprehensible. In the midst of my confusion I had a second hunch which I found highly disagreeable: 'Twins?' As if I had opened the door for a suspicion that had to be confirmed at once, I stood up carefully, not to be heard, and crept out into the corridor; even as I crossed the threshold I asked myself if I was not making a mistake, if I was not being unfair to Daniela. I turned back and whispered:

'I'll be back.'

I ran down the horseshoe corridor that surrounded the boxes. As I was about to set foot on the stairs, I saw Massey climbing slowly, and I hid behind a group of masks. If they had asked me what I was doing, I would not have had an acceptable answer; perhaps they did not notice my presence. Before Massey had reached the door of the box, I pushed my way past the masks and ran down the stairs. Like someone plunging into freezing water, I entered the piazza. When I reached the café I noticed there were fewer people and that Daniela's chair was empty. I asked another girl dressed up as Columbine.

'She just left, with Massey,' she said; she must have noticed my bewilderment because she added, kindly, 'She's probably not far away . . . Maybe you can catch up with her through the passage Delle Veste.'

I set off determined to overcome all difficulties and find her at all costs. I felt healthy; I could put all my energy into achieving that one goal. Probably my strength came from my urgent desire to regain Daniela, the true Daniela, and to prove to her that I loved her and that, if I had once abandoned her, it had not been for want of love. I wanted to prove it to Daniela and to the world. On the second street I turned right; everyone else seemed to turn there. I felt a sharp pain, a blow that cut my breath: it was the cold. I had discovered that if I thought about the illness I became ill, so to think about something else I said to myself that we Argentines are not as brave as the Venetians, that on a night like this we do not roam the streets. I was trying to walk as fast as I could while scrutinizing, as far as possible, the women dressed in black as well as, of course, the women dressed as Columbine. Opposite a church I felt sure I recognized her, but when I drew near I found it was someone else. The disappointment made me physically ill. 'I mustn't let myself fall into despair,' I said to myself. Not to lose heart, I thought how funny it was that unintentionally I was literally expressing my true feelings: with difficulty I managed not to fall.

I did not want to draw anyone's attention to me or lean on somebody's arm, fearful of meeting some good Samaritan who would insist on delaying me. As soon as I felt I could manage, I carried on. I was trying to overtake the ceaseless flow drifting in my direction and to avoid the crowds coming the opposite way. I tried hard to catch the eye of every woman dressed as Columbine, and to make out her face beneath the mask. There were so many that in spite of my efforts I missed a few. I made my way among the crowd. A Harlequin stepped aside, laughed and yelled something at me, probably imitating the gondoliers. I saw myself as a ship cutting its way with its prow; in that dream-like image the ship's figurehead and my own head became one. I put a hand to my brow: it was burning. I began to say to myself that even though it sounded strange, it was the beating of the waves that created the heat; then I fainted.

The days that followed were hazy, days of dreaming both asleep and awake. From time to time I believed myself to be awake at last, hoping that the dreams, troublesome because of their persistence, would vanish once and for all. But I was always disappointed, perhaps because real happenings, worrying and difficult to admit, would provoke, with the fever, new deliriums.

To top my anxious uncertainty, I did not recognize the room I lay in. A woman who looked after me with motherly efficiency and whom I had never seen before, told me we were at the Hotel La Fenice. The woman's name was Eufemia and I called her Saint Eufemia.

I think that on a couple of occasions a certain doctor Kurtz came to see me. On the first, he explained that he lived 'just around the corner, in the very heart of Venice', at I do not know what number of Fiubera, and that if I needed him I was to call him at any hour of the night. On the second occasion he said I was cured. When he left I realized I had not asked him for his bill, which worried me because I was afraid I would not remember his address, I would forget to pay, or I would not find him if I looked for him, like a character in a dream. He seemed like the typical old-fashioned family doctor, a little unreal perhaps in our times, but then everything in Venice has that quality.

One afternoon I asked Eufemia how I had arrived at La Fenice. She answered by avoiding the question and emphatically insisting that during my illness, even twice a day, both Mr and Mrs Massey had come to see me. Immediately I remembered the visits or, rather, saw in a limpid dream Massey and Daniela. The worst thing about the fever – its effects had not changed – was that my mental images had a life of their own. The fact that will-power had no effect on them made me anxious, like a hint of madness. That afternoon I remembered some of the Masseys' visits, I saw them as if they were sitting by my sick-bed; I also saw Daniela in the theatre-box, eating chocolates, and then a mask, leaning over me and talking, a mask which I easily identified. Reliving or dreaming the scene disturbed me so much that at first I did not make out the words of the mask. At the very moment I was asking her to repeat them, she

disappeared. Massey had come into the room. The disappearance
distressed me, because I preferred to have Daniela in my dreams
rather than meet her face to face; but Massey's presence woke me
up completely – a blessing perhaps, because I began to feel less lost.
My friend spoke to me as frankly as usual, as if I were healthy and
able to face the truth. I tried to match his trust. He told me
something that of course I already knew: that after our separation,
Daniela was never the same woman.

'I've never been unfaithful to her,' I pointed out.

'That's true. And she confesses she never really believed in your
illness till she found you lying there, on the street.'

Suddenly angry, I said, 'Now she tries to make amends by calling
in a good nurse and a good doctor.'

'Don't ask for what she can't give you.'

'You know what's wrong? She doesn't understand that I love
her.'

He told me not to be presumptuous – and that she had loved me
when I left her. I argued.

'I was ill.'

He said love demanded the impossible, adding, 'As you yourself
are now proving, with your demands for her to come back to you.
She won't, you know.'

I asked him why he was so sure, and he said because of his own
relationship with her. I said, with barely disguised irritation, 'That's
not the same.'

'Of course,' he said. '*I* didn't leave her.'

I stared at him, amazed, because for a moment I thought he
would break down. He assured me Daniela had suffered very much,
and that after her experience with me she could not fall in love
again, not as before.

'Not ever, you see?'

I did not hold back. I said, 'Maybe she still loves me.'

'Of course she loves you. As a friend, as her best friend – so you
could ask her to do for you what she did for me.'

Massey had pulled himself together. In a calm, relaxed tone of
voice he began a series of horrible explanations which I did not
want to hear and which, weak as I felt after my illness, I barely
understood. He mentioned the so-called carbon-copy offsprings, or
doubles, or clones. He said that Daniela, together with Leclerc, had
developed from one of her own cells – I think he used the word

'cell' but I cannot be sure – daughters identical to herself. Now I think it may have been just one – one was enough for the nightmare Massey was describing for me – and that she managed to accelerate its growth to such an extent that in less than ten years she turned it into a splendid woman of seventeen or eighteen.

'Your Daniela?' I asked with unexpected relief.

'It seems incredible, but she really is a woman made to measure. Identical to her mother, but, how shall I put it? so much more adequate for a man like me. I'll tell you something that may seem sacrilegious: I wouldn't change her for the original even if I could. She's identical, but next to her I live in a different kind of peaceful bliss, in genuine serenity. If you knew how things really are, you'd envy me.'

To stop him from pressing me to accept a similar favour from Daniela, I said, 'I'm not interested in an identical woman. I want her.'

He replied sadly but firmly, 'Then you'll get nothing. Daniela told me that when she saw your face in the café she realized you still loved her. She thinks that to renew an old love is senseless. To avoid an unnecessary discussion, as soon as they told her you were out of danger, she left on the first available plane.'

*Translated from the Spanish by Alberto Manguel.*

# The Wish House

## Rudyard Kipling

*Borges asked me to read him the following story in Buenos Aires in 1972. I had met him years before at Pygmalion, the Anglo-German bookshop where I worked during the last term of high school and where Borges used to come with his mother to buy Anglo-Saxon textbooks. (I remember Borges' mother complaining that, 'Georgie' now spent his time 'studying this Anglo-Saxon rubbish instead of something useful, like Latin or Greek.') When I returned to Buenos Aires I went to see him, and he timidly suggested that perhaps, if I had nothing better to do, I could read Kipling to him. The first evening led to a second and third and on through several months of intellectual delight during which I felt I was reading the only copy of a dazzling annotated edition. Borges would constantly interrupt to remember an event long past or to point out another meaning behind Kipling's words, a meaning he had probably carefully considered beforehand and which he seemed to confide in order to commit it to memory. I submitted meekly to the task of becoming his notebook, and when we parted he gave me a copy of* Stalky and Co. *from his schooldays.*

*In* Something of Myself *(Kipling's autobiography, which Borges thinks should be called* Very Little of Myself*) Kipling comments on a reviewer's reaction to 'The Wish House': 'After many years [in 1924], I wrote a tale ('The Wish House') about a woman of what was called "temperament" who loved a man and who also suffered from a cancer on her leg – the exact situation carefully specified. The review [in the* Manchester Guardian*] came to me with a gibe on the margin from a faithful friend: "You threw up a catch that time!" The review said that I had revived Chaucer's Wife of Bath even to the "mormal on her shinne". And it looked just like that too! There was no possible answer, so, breaking my rule not to have commerce with any paper, I wrote to the* Manchester Guardian *and gave myself "out – caught to leg". The reply came from an evident human being (I had thought red-hot linotypes composed their staff) who was pleased with the tribute to his knowledge of Chaucer.'*

The new Church Visitor had just left after a twenty minutes' call. During that time, Mrs Ashcroft had used such English as an elderly, experienced, and pensioned cook should, who had seen life in London. She was the readier, therefore, to slip back into easy, ancient Sussex ('t's softening to 'd's as one warmed) when the 'bus brought Mrs Fettley from thirty miles away for a visit, that pleasant March Saturday. The two had been friends since childhood; but, of late, destiny had separated their meetings by long intervals.

Much was to be said, and many ends, loose since last time, to be ravelled up on both sides, before Mrs Fettley, with her bag of quilt-patches, took the couch beneath the window commanding the garden, and the football-ground in the valley below.

'Most folk got out at Bush Tye for the match there,' she explained, 'so there weren't no one for me to cushion agin, the last five mile. An' she *do* just-about bounce ye.'

'You've took no hurt,' said her hostess. 'You don't brittle be agein', Liz.'

Mrs Fettley chuckled and made to match a couple of patches to her liking. 'No, or I'd ha' broke twenty year back. You can't ever mind when I was so's to be called round, can ye?'

Mrs Ashcroft shook her head slowly – she never hurried – and went on stitching a sack-cloth lining into a list-bound rush tool-basket. Mrs Fettley laid out more patches in the spring light through the geraniums on the window-sill, and they were silent awhile.

'What like's this new Visitor o' yourn?' Mrs Fettley inquired, with a nod towards the door. Being very shortsighted, she had, on her entrance, almost bumped into the lady.

Mrs Ashcroft suspended the big packing-needle judicially on high, ere she stabbed home. 'Settin' aside she don't bring much news with her yet, I dunno as I've anythin' special agin her.'

'Ourn, at Keyneslade,' said Mrs Fettley, 'she's full o' words an' pity, but she don't stay for answers. Ye can get on with your thoughts while she clacks.'

'This 'un don't clack. She's aimin' to be one o' those High Church nuns, like.'

'Ourn's married, but, by what they say, she've made no great gains of it . . ..' Mrs Fettley threw up her sharp chin. 'Lord! How they dam' cherubim do shake the very bones o' the place!'

The tile-sided cottage trembled at the passage of two specially chartered forty-seat charabancs on their way to the Bush Tye match;

a regular Saturday 'shopping' 'bus, for the county's capital, fumed behind them; while, from one of the crowded inns, a fourth car backed out to join the procession, and held up the stream of through pleasure-traffic.

'You're as free-tongued as ever, Liz,' Mrs Ashcroft observed.

'Only when I'm with you. Otherwhiles, I'm Granny – three times over. I lay that basket's for one o' your gran'chiller – ain't it?'

''Tis for Arthur – my Jane's eldest.'

'But he ain't workin' nowheres, is he?'

'No. 'Tis a picnic-basket.'

'You're let off light. My Willie, he's allus at me for money for them aireated wash-poles folk puts up in their gardens to draw the music from Lunnon, like. An' I give it 'im – pore fool me!'

'An' he forgets to give you the promise-kiss after, don't he?' Mrs Ashcroft's heavy smile seemed to strike inwards.

'He do. No odds 'twixt boys now an' forty year back. Take all an' give naught – an' we to put up with it! Pore fool we! Three shillin' at a time Willie'll ask me for!'

'They don't make nothin' o' money these days,' Mrs Ashcroft said.

'An' on'y last week,' the other went on, 'me daughter, she ordered a quarter pound suet at the butcher's; an' she sent it back to 'im to be chopped. She said she couldn't bother with choppin' it.'

'I lay he charged her, then.'

'I lay he did. She told me there was a whisk-drive that afternoon at the Institute, an' she couldn't bother to do the choppin'.'

'Tck!'

Mrs Ashcroft put the last firm touches to the basket-lining. She had scarcely finished when her sixteen-year-old grandson, a maiden of the moment in attendance, hurried up the garden-path shouting to know if the thing were ready, snatched it, and made off without acknowledgement. Mrs Fettley peered at him closely.

'They're goin' picnickin' somewheres,' Mrs Ashcroft explained.

'Ah,' said the other, with narrowed eyes. 'I lay *he* won't show much mercy to any he comes across, either. Now 'oo the dooce do he remind me of, all of a sudden?'

'They must look arter theirselves – 'same as we did.' Mrs Ashcroft began to set out the tea.

'No denyin' *you* could, Gracie,' said Mrs Fettley.

'What's in your head now?'

'Dunno . . . But it come over me, sudden-like – about dat woman from Rye – I've slipped the name – Barnsley, wadn't it?'

'Batten – Polly Batten, you're thinkin' of.'

'That's it – Polly Batten. That day she had it in for you with a hay-fork – 'time we was all hayin' at Smalldene – for stealin' her man.'

'But you heered me tell her she had my leave to keep him?' Mrs Ashcroft's voice and smile were smoother than ever.

'I did – an' we was all looking that she'd prod the fork spang through your breastes when you said it.'

'No-oo. She'd never go beyond bounds – Polly. She shruck too much for reel doin's.'

'Allus seems to *me,*' Mrs Fettley said after a pause, 'that a man 'twixt two fightin' women is the foolishest thing on earth. Like a dog bein' called two ways.'

'Mebbe. But what set ye off on those times, Liz?'

'That boy's fashion o' carryin' his head an' arms. I haven't rightly looked at him since he's growed. Your Jane never showed it, but – *him!* Why, 'tis Jim Batten and his tricks come to life again! . . . Eh?'

'Mebbe. There's some that would ha' made it out so – bein' barren-like, themselves.'

'Oho! Ah well! Dearie, dearie me, now! . . . An' Jim Batten's been dead this – '

'Seven and twenty years,' Mrs Ashcroft answered briefly. 'Won't ye draw up, Liz?'

Mrs Fettley drew up to buttered toast, currant bread, stewed tea, bitter as leather, some home-preserved pears, and a cold boiled pig's tail to help down the muffins. She paid all the proper compliments.

'Yes. I dunno as I've ever owed me belly much,' said Mrs Ashcroft thoughtfully. 'We only go through this world once.'

'But don't it lay heavy on ye, sometimes?' her guest suggested.

'Nurse says I'm a sight liker to die o' me indigestion than me leg.' For Mrs Ashcroft had a long-standing ulcer on her shin, which needed regular care from the Village Nurse, who boasted (or others did, for her) that she had dressed it one hundred and three times already during her term of office.

'An' you that *was* so able, too! It's all come on ye before your full time, like. *I've* watched ye goin'.' Mrs Fettley spoke with real affection.

'Somethin's bound to find ye sometime. I've me 'eart left me still,' Mrs Ashcroft returned.

'You was always big-hearted enough for three. That's somethin' to look back on at the day's eend.'

'I reckon you've *your* back-lookin's, too,' was Mrs Ashcroft's answer.

'You know it. But I don't think much regardin' such matters excep' when I'm along with you, Gra'. Takes two sticks to make a fire.'

Mrs Fettley stared, with jaw half-dropped, at the grocer's bright calendar on the wall. The cottage shook again to the roar of the motor-traffic, and the crowded football-ground below the garden roared almost as loudly; for the village was well set to its Saturday leisure.

Mrs Fettley had spoken very precisely for some time without interruption, before she wiped her eyes. 'And,' she concluded, 'they read 'is death-notice to me, out o' the paper last month. O' course it wadn't any o' *my* becomin' concerns – let be I 'adn't set eyes on him for so long. O' course *I* couldn't say nor show nothin'. Nor I've no rightful call to go to Eastbourne to see 'is grave, either. I've been schemin' to slip over there by the 'bus some day; but they'd ask questions at 'ome past endurance. So I 'aven't even *that* to stay me.'

'But you've 'ad your satisfactions?'

'Godd! Yess! Those four years 'e was workin' on the rail near us. An' the other drivers they gave him a brave funeral, too.'

'Then you've naught to cast-up about. 'Nother cup o' tea?'

The light and air had changed a little with the sun's descent, and the two elderly ladies closed the kitchen-door against chill. A couple of jays squealed and skirmished through the undraped apple-trees in the garden. This time, the word was with Mrs Ashcroft, her elbows on the tea-table, and her sick leg propped on a stool . . .

'Well I never! But what did your 'usband say to that?' Mrs Fettley asked, when the deep-toned recital halted.

''E said I might go where I pleased for all of 'im. But seein' 'e was bedrid, I said I'd 'tend 'im out. 'E knowed I wouldn't take no advantage of 'im in that state. 'E lasted eight or nine week. Then he was took with a seizure-like; an' laid stone-still for days. Then 'e propped 'imself up abed an' says: "You pray no man'll ever deal with you like you've dealed with some." "An' you?" I says, for *you* know, Liz, what a rover 'e was. "It cuts both ways," says 'e, "but *I'm* death-wise, an' I can see what's comin' to you." He died a-Sunday an' was buried a-Thursday . . . An' yet I'd set a heap by him – one time or – did I ever?'

'You never told me that before,' Mrs Fettley ventured.

'I'm payin' ye for what ye told me just now. Him bein' dead, I wrote up, sayin' I was free for good, to that Mrs Marshall in Lunnon – which gave me my first place as kitchen-maid – Lord, how long ago! She was well pleased, for they two was both gettin' on, an' I knowed their ways. You remember, Liz, I used to go to 'em in service between whiles, for years – when we wanted money, or – or my 'usband was away – on occasion.'

"E *did* get that six months at Chichester, didn't 'e?' Mrs Fettley whispered. 'We never rightly won to the bottom of it.'

"E'd ha' got more, but the man didn't die.'

'None o' your doin', was it, Gra'?'

'No! 'Twas the woman's husband this time. An' so, my man bein' dead, I went back to them Marshall's, as cook, to get me legs under a gentleman's table again, and be called with a handle to me name. That was the year you shifted to Portsmouth.'

'Cosham,' Mrs Fettley corrected. 'There was a middlin' lot o' new buildin' bein' done there. My man went first, an' got the room, an' I follered.'

'Well, then, I was a year-abouts in Lunnon, all at a breath, like, four meals a day an' livin' easy. Then, 'long towards autumn, they two went travellin', like, to France; keepin' me on, for they couldn't do without me. I put the house to rights for the caretaker, an' then I slipped down 'ere to me sister Bessie – me wages in me pockets, an' all 'ands glad to be 'old of me.'

'That would be when I was at Cosham,' said Mrs Fettley.

'*You* know, Liz, there wasn't no cheap-dog pride to folk, those days, no more than there was cinemas nor whisk-drives. Man or woman 'ud lay hold o' any job that promised a shillin' to the backside of it, didn't they? I was all peaked up after Lunnon, an' I thought the fresh airs 'ud serve me. So I took on at Smalldene, obligin' with a hand at the early potato-liftin', stubbin' hens, an' such-like. They'd ha' mocked me sore in my kitchen in Lunnon, to see me in men's boots, an' me petticoats all shorted.'

'Did it bring ye any good?' Mrs Fettley asked.

''Twadn't for that I went. You know, 's'well's me, that na'un happens to ye till it *'as* 'appened. Your mind don't warn ye before'and of the road ye've took, till you're at the far eend of it. We've only a backwent view of our proceedin's.'

''Oo was it?'

''Arry Mockler.' Mrs Ashcroft's face puckered to the pain of her sick leg.

Mrs Fettley gasped. ''Arry? Bert Mockler's son! An' *I* never guessed!'

Mrs Ashcroft nodded. 'An' I told myself – *an*' I beleft it – that I wanted field-work.'

'What did ye get out of it?'

'The usuals. Everythin' at first – worse than naught after. I had signs an' warning a-plenty, but I took no heed of 'em. For we was burnin' rubbish one day, just when we'd come to know how 'twas with – with both of us. 'Twas early in the year for burnin', an' I said so. "No!" says he. "The sooner dat old stuff's off an' done with," 'e says, "the better." 'Is face was harder'n rocks when he spoke. Then it come over me that I'd found me master, which I 'adn't ever before. I'd allus owned 'em, like.'

'Yes! Yes! They're yourn or you're theirn,' the other sighed. 'I like the right way best.'

'I didn't. But 'Arry did . . . 'Long then, it come time for me to go back to Lunnon. I couldn't. I clean couldn't! So, I took an' tipped a dollop o' scaldin' water out o' the copper one Monday mornin' over me left 'and and arm. Dat stayed me where I was for another fortnight.'

'Was it worth it?' said Mrs Fettley, looking at the silvery scar on the wrinkled fore-arm.

Mrs Ashcroft nodded. 'An' after that, we two made it up 'twixt us so's 'e could come to Lunnon for a job in a liv'ry-stable not far from me. 'E got it. *I* 'tended to that. There wadn't no talk nowhere. His own mother never suspicioned how 'twas. He just slipped up to Lunnon, an' there we abode that winter, not 'alf a mile 'tother from each.'

'Ye paid 'is fare an' all, though'; Mrs Fettley spoke convincedly.

Again Mrs Ashcroft nodded. 'Dere wadn't much I didn't do for him. 'E was me master, an' – O God, help us! – we'd laugh over it walkin' together after dark in them paved streets, an' me corns fair wrenchin' in me boots! I'd never been like that before. Ner he! Ner he!'

Mrs Fettley clucked sympathetically.

'An' when did ye come to the eend?' she asked.

'When 'e paid it all back again, every penny. Then I knowed, but I wouldn't *suffer* meself to know. "You've been mortal kind to me," he says. "Kind!" I said. '"Twixt *us*?" But 'e kep' all on tellin' me 'ow kind I'd been an' 'e'd never forget it all his days. I held it from off o' me for three evenin's, because I would *not* believe. Then 'e talked about not bein' satisfied with 'is job in the stables, an' the men there puttin' tricks on 'im, an' all they lies which a man tells when 'e's leavin' ye. I heard 'im out, neither 'elpin' nor 'inderin'. At the last, I took off a liddle brooch which he'd give me an' I says: "Dat'll do. *I* ain't askin' na'un'." An' I turned me round an' walked off to me own sufferin's. 'E didn't make 'em worse. 'E didn't come nor write after that. 'E slipped off 'ere back 'ome to 'is mother again.'

'An' 'ow often did ye look for 'en to come back?' Mrs Fettley demanded mercilessly.

'More'n once – more'n once! Goin' over the streets we'd used, I thought de very pave-stones 'ud shruck out under me feet.'

'Yes,' said Mrs Fettley. 'I dunno but dat don't 'urt as much as aught else. An' dat was all ye got?'

'No. 'Twadn't. That's the curious part, if you'll believe it, Liz.'

'I do. I lay you're further off lyin' now than in all your life, Gra'.'

'I am . . . An' I suffered, like I'd not wish my most arrantest enemies to. God's Own Name! I went through the hoop that spring! One part of it was 'eddicks which I'd never known all me days before. Think o' *me* with an 'eddick! But I come to be grateful for 'em. They kep' me from thinkin' . . .'

''Tis like a tooth,' Mrs Fettley commented. 'It must rage an' rugg till it tortures itself quiet on ye; an' then – then there's na'un left.'

'*I* got enough lef' to last me all *my* days on earth. It come about through our charwoman's liddle girl – Sophy Ellis was 'er name – all eyes an' elbers an' hunger. I used to give 'er vittles. Otherwhiles, I took no special notice of 'er, an' a sight less, o' course, when me trouble about 'Arry was on me. But – you know how liddle maids first feel it sometimes – she come to be crazy-fond o' me, pawin' an' cuddlin' all whiles: an' I 'adn't the 'eart to beat 'er off . . . One afternoon, early in spring 'twas, 'er mother 'ad sent 'er round to scutchel up what vittles she could off of us. I was settin' by the fire, me apern over me head, half-mad with the 'eddick, when she slips in. I reckon I was middlin' short with 'er. "Lor'!" she says. "Is *that* all? I'll take it off you in two-twos!" I told her not to lay a finger on me, for I thought she'd want to stroke my forehead; an' – I ain't that make. "*I* won't tech ye," she says, an' slips out again. She 'adn't been gone ten minutes 'fore me old 'eddick took off quick as bein' kicked. So I went about my work. Prasin'ly, Sophy comes back, an' creeps into my chair quiet as a mouse. 'Er eyes was deep in 'er 'ead an' 'er face all drawed. I asked 'er what 'ad 'appened. "Nothin'," she says. "Only *I've* got it now." "Got what?" I says. "Your 'eddick," she says, all hoarse an' sticky-lipped. "I've took it on me." "Nonsense," I says, "it went of itself when you was out. Lay still an' I'll make ye a cup o' tea." "'Twon't do no good," she says, "till your time's up. 'Ow long do *your* 'eddicks last?" "Don't talk silly," I says, "or I'll send for the Doctor." It looked to me like she might be hatchin' de measles. "Oh, Mrs Ashcroft," she says, stretchin' out 'er liddle thin arms. "I *do* love ye." There wasn't any holdin' agin that. I took 'er into me lap an' made much of 'er. "Is it truly gone?" she says. "Yes," I says, "an' if 'twas you took it away, I'm truly grateful." "'*Twas* me," she says, layin' 'er cheek to mine. "No one but me knows how." An' then she said she'd changed me 'eddick for me at a Wish 'Ouse.'

'Whatt?' Mrs Fettley spoke sharply.

'A Wish House. No! *I* 'adn't 'eard o' such things, either. I couldn't get it straight at first, but, puttin' all together, I made out that a Wish 'Ouse 'ad to be a house which 'ad stood unlet an' empty long enough for Some One, like, to come an' in'abit there. She said a liddle girl that she'd played with in the livery-stables where 'Arry worked 'ad told 'er so. She said the girl 'ad belonged in a caravan that laid up, o' winters, in Lunnon. Gipsy, I judge.'

'Ooh! There's no sayin' what Gippos know, but *I've* never 'eard of a Wish 'Ouse, an' I know – some things,' said Mrs Fettley.

'Sophy said there was a Wish 'Ouse in Wadloes Road – just a few streets off, on the way to our green-grocer's. All you 'ad to do, she said, was to ring the bell an' wish your wish through the slit o' the letter-box. I asked 'er if the fairies give it 'er? "Don't ye know," she says, "there's no fairies in a Wish 'Ouse? There's on'y a Token."'

'Goo' Lord A'mighty! Where did she come by *that* word?' cried

Mrs Fettley; for a Token is a wraith of the dead or, worse still, of the living.

'The caravan-girl 'ad told 'er, she said. Well, Liz, it troubled me to 'ear 'er, an' lyin' in me arms she must ha' felt it. "That's very kind o' you," I says, holdin' 'er tight, "to wish me 'eddick away. But why didn't ye ask somethin' nice for yourself?" "You can't do that," she says. "All you'll get at a Wish 'Ouse is leave to take some one else's trouble. I've took Ma's 'eddicks, when she's been kind to me; but this is the first time I've been able to do aught for you. Oh, Mrs Ashcroft, I *do* just-about love you." An' she goes on all like that. Liz, I tell you my 'air e'en a'most stood on end to 'ear 'er. I asked 'er what like a Token was. "I dunno," she says, "but after you've ringed the bell, you'll 'ear it run up from the basement, to the front door. Then say your wish," she says, "an' go away." "The Token don't open de door to ye, then?" I says. "Oh no," she says. "You on'y 'ear gigglin', like, be'ind the front door. Then you say you'll take the trouble off of 'oo ever 'tis you've chose for your love; an' ye'll get it," she says. I didn't ask no more – she was too 'ot an' fevered. I made much of 'er till it come time to light de gas, an' a liddle after that, 'er 'eddick – mine, I suppose – took off, an' she got down an' played with the cat.'

'Well, I never!' said Mrs Fettley. 'Did – did ye foller it up, anyways?'

'She askt me to, but I wouldn't 'ave no such dealin's with a child.'

'What *did* ye do, then?'

'Sat in me own room 'stid o' the kitchen when me 'eddicks come on. But it lay at de back o' me mind.'

''Twould. Did she tell ye more, ever?'

'No. Besides what the Gippo girl 'ad told 'er, she knew naught, 'cept that the charm worked. An', next after that – in May 'twas – I suffered the summer out in Lunnon. 'Twas hot an' windy for weeks, an' the streets stinkin' o' dried 'orse-dung blowin' from side to side an' lyin' level with the kerb. We don't get that nowadays. I 'ad my 'ol'day just before hoppin'; an' come down 'ere to stay with Bessie again. She noticed I'd lost flesh, an' was all poochy under the eyes.'

'Did ye see 'Arry?'

Mrs Ashcroft nodded. 'The fourth – no, the fifth day. Wednesday 'twas. I knowed 'e was workin' at Smalldene again. I asked 'is mother in the street, bold as brass. She 'adn't room to say much, for Bessie – you know 'er tongue – was talkin' full-clack. But that Wednesday, I was walkin' with one o' Bessie's chillern hangin' on me skirts, at de back o' Chanter's Tot. Prasin'ly, I felt 'e was be'ind me on the footpath, an' I knowed by 'is tread 'e'd changed 'is nature. I slowed, an' I heard 'im slow. Then I fussed a piece with the child, to force him past me, like. So 'e *'ad* to come past. 'E just says "Good-evenin'," and goes on, tryin' to pull 'isself together.'

'Drunk, was he?' Mrs Fettley asked.

'Never! S'runk an' wizen; 'is clothes 'angin' on 'im like bags, an' the back of 'is neck whiter'n chalk. 'Twas all I could do not to oppen my arms an' cry after him. But I swallered me spittle till I was back 'ome again an' the chillern abed. Then I says to Bessie, after supper, "What in de world's come to 'Arry Mockler?" Bessie told me 'e'd been a-Hospital for two months, 'long o' cuttin' 'is foot wid a spade, muckin' out the old pond at Smalldene. There was poison in de dirt, an' it rooshed up 'is leg, like, an' come out all over him. 'E 'adn't been back to 'is job – carterin' at Smalldene – more'n a fortnight. She told me the Doctor said he'd go off, likely, with the November frostes; an' 'is mother 'ad told 'er that 'e didn't rightly eat nor sleep, an' sweated 'imself into pools, no odds 'ow chill 'e lay. An' spit terrible o' mornin's. "Dearie me," I says. "But, mebbe, hoppin' 'll set 'im right again," an' I licked me thread-point an' I fetched me needle's eye up to it an' I threads me needle under de lamp, steady as rocks. An' dat night (me bed was in de wash-house) I cried an' I cried. An' *you* know, Liz – for you've been with me in my throes – it takes summat to make me cry.'

'Yes; but chile-bearin' is on'y just pain,' said Mrs Fettley.

'I come round by cock-crow, an' dabbed cold tea on me eyes to take away the signs. Long towards nex' evenin' – I was settin' out to lay some flowers on me 'usband's grave, for the look 'o the thing – I met 'Arry over against where the War Memorial is now. 'E was comin' back from 'is 'orses, so 'e couldn't *not* see me. I looked 'im all over, an' "'Arry," I says twix' me teeth, "come back an' rest-up in Lunnon." "I won't take it," he says, "for I can give ye naught." "I don't ask it," I says. "By God's Own Name, I don't ask na'un! On'y come up an' see a Lunnon doctor." 'E lifts 'is two 'eavy eyes at me: "'Tis past that, Gra'," 'e says. "I've but a few months left." "'Arry!" I says. "*My* man!" I says. I couldn't say no more. 'Twas all up in me throat. "Thank ye kindly Gra'," 'e says (but 'e never says "my woman"), an' 'e went on up-street an' 'is mother – Oh, damn 'er! – she was watchin' for 'im, an' she shut de door be'ind 'im.'

Mrs Fettley stretched an arm across the table, and made to finger Mrs Ashcroft's sleeve at the wrist, but the other moved it out of reach.

'So I went on to the churchyard with my flowers, an' I remembered my 'usband's warnin' that night he spoke. 'E *was* death-wise, an' it *'ad* 'appened as 'e said. But as I was settin' down de jam-pot on the grave-mound, it come over me there was one thing I *could* do for 'Arry. Doctor or no Doctor, I thought I'd make a trial of it. So I did. Nex' mornin', a bill came down from our Lunnon greengrocer. Mrs Marshall, she'd lef' me petty cash for suchlike – o' course – but I tole Bess 'twas for me to come an' open the 'ouse. So I went up, afternoon train.'

'An' – but I know you 'adn't – 'adn't you no fear?'

'What for? There was nothin' front o' me but my own shame an' God's croolty. I couldn't ever get 'Arry – 'ow *could* I? I knowed it must go on burnin' till it burned me out.'

'Aie!' said Mrs Fettley, reaching for the wrist again, and this time Mrs Ashcroft permitted it.

'Yit 'twas a comfort to know I could try *this* for 'im. So I went an' I paid the green-grocer's bill, an' put 'is receipt in me handbag, an' then I stepped round to Mrs Ellis – our char – an' got the 'ouse-keys an' opened the 'ouse. First, I made me bed to come back to (God's Own Name! Me bed to lie upon!). Nex' I made me a cup o' tea an' sat down in the kitchen thinkin', till long towards dusk. Terrible close, 'twas. Then I dressed me an' went out with the receipt in me 'and-bag, feignin' to study it for an address, like. Fourteen, Wadloes Road, was the place – a liddle basement-kitchen 'ouse, in a row of twenty-thirty such, an' tiddy strips o' walled garden in front – the paint off the front door, an' na'un done to na'un since ever so long. There wasn't 'ardly no one in the streets 'cept the cats. *'Twas* 'ot, too! I turned into the gate bold as brass; up de steps I went an' I ringed the front-door bell. She pealed loud, like it do in an empty house. When she'd all ceased, I 'eard a cheer, like, pushed back on de floor o' the kitchen. Then I 'eard feet on de kitchen-stairs, like it might ha' been a heavy woman in slippers. They come up to de stair-head, acrost the hall – I 'eard the bare boards creak under 'em – an' at de front door dey stopped. I stooped me to the letter-box slit, an' I says: "Let me take everythin' bad that's in store for my man, 'Arry Mockler, for love's sake." Then, whatever it was 'tother side de door let its breath out, like, as if it 'ad been holdin' it for to 'ear better.'

'Nothin' was *said* to ye?' Mrs Fettley demanded.

'Na'un. She just breathed out – a sort of *A-ah*, like. Then the steps went back an' downstairs to the kitchen – all draggy – an' I heard the cheer drawed up again.'

'An' you abode on de doorstep, throughout all, Gra'?'

Mrs Ashcroft nodded.

'Then I went away, an' a man passin' says to me: "Didn't you know that house was empty?" "No," I says. "I must ha' been give the wrong number." An' I went back to our 'ouse, an' I went to bed: for I was fair flogged out. 'Twas too 'ot to sleep more'n snatches, so I walked me about, lyin' down betweens, till crack o' dawn. Then I went to the kitchen to make me cup o' tea, an' I hitted meself just above the ankle on an old roastin'-jack o' mine that Mrs Ellis had moved out from the corner, her last cleanin'. An' so – nex' after that – I waited till the Marshalls come back o' their holiday.'

'Alone there? I'd ha' thought you'd 'ad enough of empty houses,' said Mrs Fettley, horrified.

'Oh, Mrs Ellis an' Sophy was runnin' in an' out soon's I was back, an' 'twixt us we cleaned de house again top-to-bottom. There's allus a hand's turn more to do in every house. An' that's 'ow 'twas with me that autumn an' winter, in Lunnon.'

'Then na'un hap – overtook ye for your doin's?'

Mrs Ashcroft smiled. 'No. Not then. 'Long in November I sent Bessie ten shillin's.'

'You was allus free-'anded,' Mrs Fettley interrupted.

'An' I got what I paid for, with the rest o' the news. She said the hoppin' 'ad set 'im up wonderful. 'E'd 'ad six weeks of it, and now 'e was back again carterin' at Smalldene. No odds to me *'ow* it 'ad 'appened – 'slong's it *'ad*. But I dunno as my ten shillin's eased me much. 'Arry bein' *dead*, like, 'e'd ha' been mine, till Judgement. 'Arry bein' alive, 'e'd like as not pick up with some woman middlin' quick. I raged over that. Come spring, I 'ad somethin' else to rage for. I'd growed a nasty little weepin' boil, like, on me shin, just above the boot-top, that wouldn't heal no shape. It made me sick to look at it, for I'm clean-fleshed by nature. Chop me all over with a spade, an' I'd heal like turf. Then Mrs Marshall she set 'er own doctor at me. 'E said I ought to ha' come to him at first go-off, 'stead o' drawin' all manner o' dyed stockin's over it for months. 'E said I'd stood up too much to me work, for it was settin' very close atop of a big swelled vein, like, behither the small o' me ankle. "Slow come, slow go," 'e says. "Lay your leg up on high an' rest it," he says, "an' 'twill ease off. Don't let it close up too soon. You've got a very fine leg, Mrs Ashcroft," 'e says. An' he put wet dressin's on it.'

"E done right.' Mrs Fettley spoke firmly. 'Wet dressin's to wet wounds. They draw de humours, same's a lamp-wick draws de oil.'

'That's true. An' Mrs Marshall was allus at me to make me set down more, an' dat nigh healed it up. An' then after a while they packed me off down to Bessie's to finish the cure; for I ain't the sort to sit down when I ought to stand up. You was back in the village then, Liz.'

'I was. I was, but – never did I guess!'

'I didn't desire ye to.' Mrs Ashcroft smiled. 'I saw 'Arry once or twice in de street, wonnerful fleshed up an' restored back. Then, one day I didn't see 'im, an' 'is mother told me one of 'is 'orses 'ad lashed out an' caught 'im on the 'ip. So 'e was abed an' middlin' painful. An' Bessie, she says to his mother, 'twas a pity 'Arry 'adn't a woman of 'is own to take the nursin' off 'er. And the old lady *was* mad! She told us that 'Arry 'ad never looked after any woman in 'is born days, an' as long as she was atop the mowlds, she'd contrive for 'im till 'er two 'ands dropped off. So I knowed she'd do watch-dog for me, 'thout askin' for bones.'

Mrs Fettley rocked with small laughter.

'That day,' Mrs Ashcroft went on, 'I'd stood on me feet nigh all the time, watchin' the doctor go in an' out; for they thought it might be 'is ribs, too. That made my boil break again, issuin' an' weepin'. But it turned out 'twadn't ribs at all, an' 'Arry 'ad a good night. When I heard that, nex' mornin', I says to meself, "I won't lay two an' two together *yit*. I'll keep me leg down a week, an' see what comes of it." It didn't hurt me that day, to speak of – 'seemed more to draw the strength out o' me like – an' 'Arry 'ad another good night. That made me persevere; but I didn't dare lay two an' two together till the week-end, an' then, 'Arry come forth e'en

a'most 'imself again – na'un hurt outside ner in of him. I nigh fell
on me knees in de wash-house when Bessie was up-street. "I've got
ye now, my man," I says. "You'll take your good from me 'thout
knowin' it till my life's end. O God, send me long to live for 'Arry's
sake!" I says. An' I dunno that didn't still me ragin's.'

'For good?' Mrs Fettley asked.

'They come back, plenty times, but, let be how 'twould, I knowed
I was doin' for 'im. I *knowed* it. I took an' worked me pains on an'
off, like regulatin' my own range, till I learned to 'ave 'em at my
commandments. An' that was funny, too. There was times, Liz,
when my trouble 'ud all s'rink an' dry up, like. First, I used to try
an' fetch it on again; bein' fearful to leave 'Arry alone too long for
anythin' to lay 'old of. Prasin'ly I come to see that was a sign he'd
do all right awhile, an' so I saved myself.'

"Ow long for?' Mrs Fettley asked, with deepest interest.

'I've gone de better part of a year onct or twice with na'un more
to show than the liddle weepin' core of it, like. *All* s'rinked up an'
dried off. Then he'd inflame up – for a warnin' – an' I'd suffer it.
When I couldn't no more – an' I *'ad* to keep on goin' with my
Lunnon work – I'd lay me leg high on a cheer till it eased. Not too
quick. I knowed by the feel of it, those times, dat 'Arry was in
need. Then I'd send another five shillin's to Bess, or somethin' for
the chillern, to find out if, mebbe, 'e'd took any hurt through my
neglects. 'Twas *so*! Year in, year out, I worked it dat way, Liz, an'
'e got 'is good from me 'thout knowin' – for years and years.'

'But what did *you* get out of it, Gra'?' Mrs Fettley almost wailed.
'Did ye see 'im reg'lar?'

'Times – when I was 'ere on me 'ol'days. An' more, now that
I'm 'ere for good. But 'e's never looked at me, ner any other woman
'cept 'is mother. 'Ow I used to watch an' listen! So did she.'

'Years an' years!' Mrs Fettley repeated. 'An' where's 'e workin'
at now?'

'Oh, 'e's give up carterin' quite a while. He's workin' for one o'
them big tractorizin' firms – plowin' sometimes, an' sometimes off
with lorries – fur as Wales, I've 'eard. He comes 'ome to 'is mother
'tween whiles; but I don't set eyes on him now, fer weeks on end.
No odds! 'Is job keeps 'im from continuin' in one stay anywheres.'

'But – just for de sake o' sayin' somethin' – s'pose 'Arry *did* get
married?' said Mrs Fettley.

Mrs Ashcroft drew her breath sharply between her still even and natural teeth. '*Dat* ain't been required of me,' she answered. 'I reckon my pains 'ull be counted agin that. Don't *you*, Liz?'

'It ought to be, dearie. It ought to be.'

'It *do* 'urt sometimes. You shall see it when Nurse comes. She thinks I don't know it's turned.'

Mrs Fettley understood. Human nature seldom walks up to the word 'cancer'.

'Be ye certain sure, Gra'?' she asked.

'I was sure of it when old Mr Marshall 'ad me up to 'is study an' spoke a long piece about my faithful service. I've obliged 'em on an' off for a goodish time, but not enough for a pension. But they give me a weekly 'lowance for life. I knew what *that* sinnified – as long as three years ago.'

'Dat don't *prove* it, Gra'.'

'To give fifteen bob a week to a woman 'oo'd live twenty year in the course o' nature? It *do*!'

'You're mistook! You're mistook!' Mrs Fettley insisted.

'Liz, there's *no* mistakin' when the edges are all heaped up, like – same as a collar. You'll see it. An' I laid out Dora Wickwood, too. *She* 'ad it under the arm-pit, like.'

Mrs Fettley considered awhile, and bowed her head in finality.

''Ow long d'you reckon 'twill allow ye, countin' from now, dearie?'

'Slow come, slow go. But if I don't set eyes on ye 'fore next hoppin', this'll be good-bye, Liz.'

'Dunno as I'll be able to manage by then – not 'thout I have a liddle dog to lead me. For de chillern, dey won't be troubled, an' – O Gra'! – I'm blindin' up – I'm blindin' up!'

'Oh, *dat* was why you didn't more'n finger with your quilt-patches all this while! I was wonderin' . . . But the pain *do* count, don't ye think, Liz? The pain *do* count to keep 'Arry – where I want 'im. Say it can't be wasted, like.'

'I'm sure of it – sure of it, dearie. You'll 'ave your reward.'

'I don't want no more'n this – *if* de pain is taken into de reckonin'.'

''Twill be – 'twill be, Gra'.'

There was a knock on the door.

'That's Nurse. She's before 'er time,' said Mrs Ashcroft. 'Open to 'er.'

The young lady entered briskly, all the bottles in her bag clicking.

'Evenin', Mrs Ashcroft,' she began. 'I've come raound a little earlier than usual because of the Institute dance to-na-ite. You won't ma-ind, will you?'

'Oh, no. Me dancin' days are over.' Mrs Ashcroft was the self-contained domestic at once. 'My old friend, Mrs Fettley 'ere, has been settin' talkin' with me a while.'

'I hope she 'asn't been fatiguing you?' said the Nurse a little frostily.

'Quite the contrary. It 'as been a pleasure. Only – only – just at the end I felt a bit – a bit flogged out like.'

'Yes, yes.' The Nurse was on her knees already, with the washes to hand. 'When old ladies get together they talk a deal too much, I've noticed.'

'Mebbe we do,' said Mrs Fettley, rising. 'So now I'll make myself scarce.'

'Look at it first, though,' said Mrs Ashcroft feebly. 'I'd like ye to look at it.'

Mrs Fettley looked, and shivered. Then she leaned over, and kissed Mrs Ashcroft once on the waxy yellow forehead, and again on the faded grey eyes.

'It *do* count, don't it – de pain?' The lips that still kept trace of their original moulding hardly more than breathed the words.

Mrs Fettley kissed them and moved towards the door.

# The Playground

## Ray Bradbury

*We had a teacher in school called Pellegrini: he was supposed to teach us Spanish Literature but he was a science-fiction fan. In those days in Argentina (in the brief respite between the first and second coming of Perón), schooling was strict, science-fiction was very young, and boys of thirteen were not allowed to read what was considered rubbish. One morning Mr Pellegrini stood in front of the class – the teacher's desk was set up on a dais behind which loomed a gigantic blackboard – and started to read, with no previous announcement, a story by Ray Bradbury called 'There will come soft rains'. We sat at our desks, at first wary, then intrigued, finally completely in his power, listening to the description of a world that had stood still. That afternoon every bookshop in the neighbourhood sold out its copies of the Spanish translation of* The Martian Chronicles; *some thirty pimply boys had decided that maybe the thing called literature was not, after all, as terrible as they had come to believe.*

He had often walked by the playground on the way from his train and paid it no particular attention. He neither liked nor disliked it, he had no opinion of it. But his wife had looked at him across the breakfast table this morning and said, 'I'm going to start Jim at the playground this week. You know, the one down the street. Jim's old enough now.'

At his office, Mr Charles Underhill had made a memorandum: *Look at playground.* And on the way home down the street from the train at four in the afternoon, he purposely folded his newspaper so he would not read himself past the playground.

Now, at four-ten in the late day, he moved slowly along the sidewalk and stopped at the playground gate.

At first there was nothing. And then, as his ears adjusted outward from his usual interior monologues, it was like turning the volume dial of a radio louder. And the scene before him, like a grey, blurred television image, came to a slow focus. Primarily, there were faint voices, faint cries, streaks and shadows, vague impressions. And then, as if someone had jolted the machine, there were screams, sharp visions, children dashing, children fighting, pummelling, bleeding, screaming! He saw the tiniest scabs on their faces and knees in amazing clarity.

Mr Underhill stood there in the full volume of blasting sound, blinking. And then his nostrils took up where his eyes and ears left off.

He smelled the cutting odours of iodine, raw adhesive, and pink mercurochrome, so strong it was bitter to his tongue. The wind of iodine moving through the steely wire fence which glinted dully in the grey light of the overcast day. And the rushing children there, it was like hell cut loose in a great pintable machine, a colliding and banging and totalling of hits and pushes and rushes to a grand and as yet unforseen total of brutalities. And was he mistaken or was the light of a strange intensity within the playground; everything seeming to possess four shadows, one dark one, and three subsidiaries, which made it impossible, strategically, to tell which way the small bodies were screaming until they bashed their targets. Yes, the oblique, pressing light made the entire playground seem deep, far away, and somehow remote from his touching it. Or perhaps it was the hard steel wire fence, not unlike certain park zoo barriers, beyond which anything might happen.

'A pen of misery, that's what it is,' said Mr Underhill. 'Why do children insist on making life miserable for each other? It's nothing but torture to be a child.' He heard himself give a great relieved sigh. Thank God, childhood was over and done for him. No more pinchings, bruisings, shattered dreams and senseless excitements.

A gust of wind tore the paper from his hand and blew it through the gate. He went after it, down into the playground, three steps. Clutching it, he immediately retreated, heart pounding, for in the moment he had remained stranded in the playground's atmosphere he had felt his hat too large, his coat too cumbersome, his belt too loose, his shoes too big, he had felt like a small boy playing business man in his father's clothes, and the gate behind him had loomed impossibly large, while the sky itself pressed greyer at his eyes, and the scent of the iodine, like that of a feral tiger's mouth exhaled upon him, touched and blew his hair. He almost stumbled and fell, getting out of there!

He stood outside, like someone who has just emerged, shocked, from a terrible, cold sea.

'Hello, Charlie!'

He heard the voice and turned to see who had called him. There was the caller, on top a slide, a boy about nine years old, waving. 'Hello, Charlie!'

Mr Charles Underhill raised a hand. 'But I don't *know* that boy,' he murmured. 'And why should he call me by my first name?'

The boy was smiling up in the murky air, and now, jostled by other yelling children, rushed shrieking down the slide.

Mr Underhill stood bemused by what he saw. Now the playground was an immense iron industry whose sole product was pain, sorrow and sadism. If you stood here half an hour there wasn't a face in the entire enclosure that didn't wince, cry, redden with anger, or pale with fear, one minute or another. Really! Who said childhood was the best time of life, when in reality it was the most horrifying, the most merciless era, the barbaric time when there were no police to protect you, only parents preoccupied with themselves and the taller world. No, if he had his way, he gripped the fence with one fist, they'd nail a new sign here: TORQUEMADA'S GREEN.

And as for that boy, the one who had shouted at him, who was he? There was something familiar there, perhaps in the hidden bones, an echo of some old friend, probably the son of a successfully ulcered father.

And this is the playground where my son will play, thought Mr Underhill, and shuddered.

Hanging his hat in the hall, checking his lean image in the watery mirror, Mr Underhill felt wintry and tired. When his wife appeared, and his son came tapping on mousefeet, he greeted them with something less than full attention. The boy clambered thinly over him, playing 'King of the hill'. And the father, fixing his gaze to the end of the cigar he was slowly lighting, finally cleared his throat and said, 'I've been thinking about that playground, Susan.'

'I'm taking Jim over tomorrow,' said his wife.

'Not really? *That* playground?'

His mind rebelled. The smell and look of the place were still vivid to him. That writhing world with its atmosphere of cuts and beaten noses, the air as full of pain as a dentist's office, and those horrid tic-tac-toes and hopscotches under his feet as he picked up his newspaper, horrid for no reason he could see!

'What's wrong with that playground?' asked his wife.

'Have you seen it?' He paused in confusion. 'Damn it, I mean, the children there. It's a Black Hole, that's what it is.'

'The children are clean and from well-to-do families.'

'Why, they shove and push like vulgar little Gestapos,' cried Mr Underhill. 'It'd be like shoving the child in a granary to be ground down into meal by a couple of two-ton grinders! Every time I think of Jim settling into that barbaric pit, I turn cold!'

'You know it's the only convenient centre.'

'They'll kill Jim. I saw some with all kinds of bats and clubs and guns. Good God, Jim'll be in splinters by the end of the first day. They'll have him on a spit with an orange in his mouth.'

'How you exaggerate!' She was laughing at him.

'I'm serious!'

'You can't live Jim's life for him, you know that. He has to learn the hard way. He's got to be beat up and beat others up; children are like that.'

'I don't *like* children like that.'

'It's the happiest time of life.'

'Nonsense! I used to look back on childhood with nostalgia. Now I realize I was a sentimental fool. It was nothing but scratching and beating and kicking and coming home a bleeding scab from head to foot. If I could possibly save Jim from that, I would.'

'That's impractical and anyway, thank God, impossible.'

'I won't have him near that place, I tell you. I'll have him grow up a neurotic recluse first.'

'Charlie!'

'I will! Those little beasts, you should've *seen* them! He's my only son, Jim is.' He felt the boy's skinny legs about his shoulders, the boy's delicate hands rumpling his hair. 'I won't have him butchered.'

'He'll get it in school, later. Better to let him get a little shoving about now, when he's three, so he's prepared for it.'

'I've thought of that, too.' Mr Underhill fiercely held to his son's ankles that dangled like warm, thin sausages on either lapel. 'I might even get a private tutor for him!'

'Oh, Charles!'

They did not speak during dinner.

After dinner, he took Jim for a walk while his wife was washing the dishes. They strolled down past the playground under the dim street lamps. It was a cooling September night, with the first sniff of autumn in it. Next week, and the children would be raked in off the fields like so many leaves and set to burning in the schools, using their fire and energy for more constructive purposes. But they would be here after school, ramming about, making projectiles of themselves, exploding and crashing, leaving a wake of misery behind their miniature wars.

'Wanna go in,' said Jim, leaning against the cold wire fence, watching the horrible children beat each other and run.

'No, Jim, you don't want that.'

'Play,' said Jim, his eyes glassy with fascination, as he saw a large boy kick a small boy and the small boy kick a smaller boy to even things up.

'Play, Daddy.'

'Come along, Jim, you'll never get in that mess if *I* can help it.' Mr Underhill tugged the small arm firmly.

'Play.' Jim was beginning to blubber now. His eyes were melting out of his cheeks. His face became a wrinkled orange of colour and feeling.

Some of the children heard the crying and glanced over. Underhill had the terrible sense of watching a den of foxes suddenly startled and looked up from the white hairy ruin of a dead rabbit. The mean yellow eyes, the conical chins, the white teeth, the dreadful wiry hair, the brambly sweaters, the iron-coloured hands covered with a day's battle dust.

They saw Jim and he was new. They didn't say anything, but as Jim cried louder and Mr Underhill, by main force, dragged him like a cement bag along the walk, they watched the little boy. Mr Underhill felt like pushing his fist at them and crying, 'You little beasts, you won't get *my* son!'

And then, with beautiful irrelevance, the boy at the top of the slide, the boy with the familiar face, called to him, waving.

'Hello, Charlie.'

Mr Underhill paused and Jim stopped crying.

'See you later, Charlie.'

And the face of the boy way up there on that high slide, was

suddenly like the face of Thomas Marshall, an old business friend
who lived just around the block but whom he hadn't seen in years.

'See you later, Charlie.'

Later, later? What did the fool boy mean?

'I know *you*, Charlie!' called the boy. 'Hi!'

'What?' gasped Mr Underhill.

'Tomorrow night, Charlie, hey!' And the boy fell off the slide
and lay choking for breath, face like a cheese from the fall, while
children jumped on him and tumbled over.

Mr Underhill stood undecided for five seconds or more, until Jim
thought to cry again and then, with the fox eyes upon them, in the
first chill of autumn, he dragged Jim all the way home.

The next afternoon Mr Underhill finished at the office early and
took the three o'clock train, arriving out in Green Town at three-
twenty-five, in plenty of time to drink in the brisk rays of the
autumnal sun. Strange how one day it is suddenly autumn, he
thought. One day it is summer and the next, how could you measure
or tell it? Something about the temperature or smell? Or the sedi-
ment of age knocked loose from your bones during the night and
circulating in your blood and heart, giving you a slight tremble and
a chill? A year older, a year dying, was *that* it?

He walked up toward the playground, planning the future. It
seemed you did more planning in autumn than any other season.
This had to do with dying, perhaps. You thought of death and you
automatically planned. Well, then, there was to be a tutor for Jim
*that* was positive; none of those horrible schools for him. It would
pinch the bank account a bit, but Jim would at least grow up a
happy boy. They would pick and choose his friends. Any slambang
bullies would be thrown out as soon as they so much as touched
Jim. And as for this playground. Completely out of the question!

'Oh, hello, Charles.'

He looked up suddenly. Before him, at the entrance to the wire
enclosure, stood his wife. He noted instantly that she called him
Charles, instead of Dear. Last night's unpleasantness had not quite
evaporated. 'Susan, what're you doing down here?'

She flushed guiltily and glanced in through the fence.

'You didn't!' he cried.

His eyes sought among the scrabbling, running, screaming children. 'Do you mean to say . . . ?'

His wife nodded, half amused. 'I thought I'd bring him early—'

'Before I got home, so I wouldn't know is *that* it?'

That was it.

'Good God, Susan, where *is* he?'

'I just came to see.'

'You mean you left him there all afternoon?'

'Just half an hour while I shopped.'

'And you *left* him, good God!' Mr Underhill flung his hand to his drained cheek. 'Well, come on, find him, get him out of there!'

They peered in together past the wire to where some boys charged about, to girls slapping each other, to a squabbling heap of children who seemed to take turns at getting off, taking a good run, and jumping one against another.

'That's where he is, I *know* it!' said Mr Underhill.

Just then, across the field at full speed, sobbing and wailing, came Jim, with six boys after him. He fell, got up, ran, fell again, stumbled up, shrieking, and the boys behind him shot beans through metal shooters.

'I'll stuff those blowers up their noses!' cried Mr Underhill. 'Come on, Jim! Run!'

Jim made it to the gate. Mr Underhill caught him and it was like catching a rumpled, bloody wad of material. Jim's nose was bleeding and his pants were ripped and he was covered with grime.

'*There's* your playground,' said Mr Underhill, bent to his knees, staring up from his son, patting him, to his wife, viciously. 'There's your sweet happy little innocents, your well-to-do piddling Fascists! Let me catch this boy in there again and there'll be hell. Come on, Jim. All right, you little bastards, get back there!' he shouted.

'We didn't do nothing,' said the children.

'What's the world coming to?' Mr Underhill questioned the universe.

'Hi, Charlie,' said the strange boy, standing to one side. He waved casually and smiled.

'Who's that?' asked Susan.

'How in hell do *I* know?' snapped Mr Underhill.

'Be seeing you, Charlie, so long,' called the boy.

Mr Underhill marched his wife and child home.

'Take your hand off my elbow!' she said.

He was trembling, absolutely, continually trembling with rage when he got to bed. He had tried some coffee, but nothing stopped it. He wanted to beat their pulpy little brains out, those gross Cruikshank children; yes, that phrase fitted them, those fox-fiend, melancholy Cruikshank children, with all the guile and poison and slyness in their cold faces. In the name of all that was decent, what manner of child was this new generation? A bunch of cutters and hangers and kickers, a drove of bleeding, moronic thumb-screwers, with the sewage of neglect running in their veins? He lay violently jerking his head from one side of his hot pillow to the other, and at last got up and lit a cigarette, but it wasn't enough. He and Susan had had a huge battle when they got home. He had yelled at her and she had yelled back, peacock and peahen shrieking in a wilderness where law and order were insanities laughed at and forgotten.

He was ashamed. You didn't fight violence with violence, not if you were a gentleman. You talked calmly. But she didn't give him a chance, damn it! She wanted the boy put in a vice and squashed. She wanted him reamed and punctured and given the laying-on-of-hands. To be beaten from playground to kindergarten, to grammar school, to junior high, to high school. If he was lucky, in high school, the beatings and sadisms would refine themselves, the sea of blood and spittle would drain back down the shore of years and Jim would be left upon the edge of maturity, with God knows what outlook to the future, with a desire, perhaps, to be a wolf among wolves, a dog among dogs, a fiend among fiends. But there was enough of that in the world, already. And the very thought of the next ten or fifteen years of torture was enough to make Mr Underhill cringe, he felt his own flesh impaled with a BB shot, stung, burned, fisted, scrounged, twisted, violated, and bruised. He quivered, like a jelly-fish hurled violently into a concrete-mixer. Jim would never survive it. Jim was too delicate for this horror.

'I've made up my mind,' said Susan, in bed. 'You needn't walk the room all night. Jim's not having a private tutor. He's going to school. And he's going back to that playground tomorrow and keep going back until he's learned to stand on his own two feet.'

'Let me alone.' Mr Underhill dressed. Downstairs, he opened the front door. It was about five minutes to midnight as he walked swiftly down the street, trying to outdistance his rage and outrage. He knew Susan was right, of course. This was the world, you lived in it, you accepted it, but *that* was the very trouble! He had been through the mill already, he knew what it was to be a boy among lions, his own childhood had come rushing back to him the last few hours, a time of terror and violence, and now he could not bear to think of Jim going through it all, those long years, especially if you were a delicate child, through no fault of your own, your bones thin, your face pale, what could you expect but to be harried and chased?

He stopped by the playground which was still lit by one great overhead lamp. It was locked for the night, but that one light remained on until twelve. He wanted to tear the contemptible place down, rip up the steel fences, obliterate the slides, and say to the children, 'Go home! Play in your back yards!'

How ingenious, the cold, deep playground. You never knew where anyone lived. The boy who knocked your teeth out, who was *he*? Nobody knew. Where did he live? Nobody knew. How to find him? Nobody knew. Why, you could come here one day, beat the living tar out of some smaller child, and run on the next day to some *other* playground. They would never find you. From playground to playground, you could take your criminal tricks, with everyone forgetting you, since they never knew you. You could return to this playground a month later, and if the little child whose teeth you knocked out was there and recognized you, you could deny it. No, I'm not the one. Must be some other kid. This is my first time here! No, not me! And when his back is turned, knock him down. And run off down the nameless streets, a nameless person.

'What am I going to do?' asked Mr Underhill. 'I can't buck Susan forever on this. Should we move to the country? I can't do that. But I can't have Jim here, either.'

'Hello, Charlie,' said a voice.

Mr Underhill turned. Inside the fence, seated in the dirt, making diagrams with one finger in the cold dust, was the nine-year-old boy. He didn't look up. He said hello, Charlie, just sitting there, easily, in that world beyond the hard steel fence.

Mr Underhill said, 'How do you know my name?'

'You're having a lot of trouble.' The boy crossed his legs comfortably, smiling.

'How'd you get in there so late? Who are you?'

'My name's Marshall—'

'Of course, Tom Marshall's son. Tommy. I *thought* you looked familiar.'

'More familiar than you think.' The boy laughed.

'How's your father, Tommy?'

'Have you seen him lately?' the boy asked.

'Briefly, on the street, a month ago.'

'How did he look?'

'What?'

'How did Mr Marshall look?' asked the boy. It was strange he wouldn't say 'my Father'.

'He looked all right. Why?'

'I guess he's happy,' said the boy. Mr Underhill saw the boy's arms and legs and they were covered with scabs and scratches.

'Aren't you going home, Tommy?'

'I sneaked out to see you. I just knew you'd come. You're afraid.'

Mr Underhill didn't know what to say.

'Those little monsters,' he said at last.

'Maybe I can help you.' The boy made a dust triangle.

It was ridiculous. 'How?'

'You'd give anything, wouldn't you, if you could spare Jim all this? You'd trade places with him if you could?'

Mr Underhill nodded, frozen.

'Well, you come down here tomorrow afternoon at four. Then I can help you.'

'How do you mean, help?'

'I can't tell you outright,' said the boy. 'It has to do with the playground. Any place where there's lots of evil, that makes power. You can feel it, can't you?'

A kind of warm wind stirred off the bare field under the one high light. Underhill shivered. Yes, even now, at midnight, the playground was evil, for it was used for evil things. 'Are all playgrounds like this?'

'Some. Maybe this is the only one like this. What I wanted to say is that Tom Marshall was like you. He worried about Tommy Marshall and the playground and the kids, too. He wanted to save Tommy the trouble and the hurt, also.'

This business of talking about people as if they were remote, made Mr Underhill feel like laughing.

'So we made a bargain,' said the boy.

'Who with?'

'With the playground, I guess, or whoever runs it.'

'Who runs it?'

'I've never seen him. There's an office over there under the grandstand. A light burns in it all night. It's a bright, blue light, kind of funny. There's a desk there with no papers on it and an empty chair. The sign says Manager, but nobody ever sees the man.'

'He must be around.'

'That's right,' said the boy. 'Or I wouldn't be where I am, and someone else wouldn't be where they are.'

'You certainly talk grown-up.'

The boy was pleased. 'Want to know who I really am? I'm not Tommy Marshall. I'm Tom Marshall, the father. I know you won't believe it. But I was afraid for Tommy. I was the way you are now about Jim. So I made this deal with the playground. Oh, there are others, too. You'll see them among the kids.'

'You'd better run home to bed.'

'You want it to be true. I saw your eyes then! If you could trade places with Jim, you would. Save him all that torture, let him be in your place, grown-up, the real work over and done.'

'Any decent parent sympathizes with his children.'

'You more than most. You feel every kick. You come here tomorrow. You can make a deal, too.'

'Trade places?' It was an amusing, but an oddly satisfactory thought. 'What would I have to do?'

'Just make up your mind.' He tried to make it sound casual, a joke. But his mind was in a rage, again, frantic. 'What would I pay?'

'Nothing. You'd just have to play in the playground.'

'All day?'

'And go to school, of course.'

'And grow up again?'

'Yes. Be here at four.'

'I have work in the city tomorrow.'

'Tomorrow,' said the boy.

'You'd better get home to bed, Tommy.'

'My name is *Tom* Marshall,' said the boy, sitting there.

The playground lights went out.

Mr Underhill and his wife did not speak at breakfast. He usually phoned her at noon to chat about this or that, but he did not phone. But at one-thirty, after a bad lunch, he dialled the house number. When Susan answered he hung up. Five minutes later he phoned again.

'Charlie, was that you called five minutes ago?'

'Yes,' he said.

'I thought I heard you breathing before you hung up. What'd you call about, dear?' She was being sensible again.

'Oh, just called.'

'It's been a bad two days, hasn't it? You do see what I mean, don't you, Charlie? Jim must go to the playground and get a few scabs.'

'A few scabs, yes.'

He saw the blood and the hungry foxes and the torn rabbits.

'And learn to give and take,' she was saying, 'and fight if he has to.'

'Fight if he has to,' he murmured.

'I knew you'd come around.'

'Around,' he said. 'You're right. No way out. He must be sacrificed.'

'Oh, Charlie, you're so odd.'

He cleared his throat. 'Well, that's settled. Love me?'

'Yes.'

I wonder what it would be like, he thought.

'Miss me?' he asked the phone.

He thought of the diagrams in the dust, the boy seated there with the hidden bones in his face.

'Yes,' she said.

'I've been thinking,' he said. 'The playground.'

'Speak up.'

'I'll be home at three,' he said, slowly, piercing out the words, like a man hit in the stomach, gasping for breath. 'We'll take a walk, you and Jim and I,' he said, eyes shut.

'Wonderful!'

'To the playground,' he said and hung up.

It was really autumn now, the real chill, the real snap, the trees overnight burnt red and snapped free of their leaves, which spiralled about Mr Underhill's face as he walked up the front steps, and there were Susan and Jim bundled up because of the sharp wind, waiting for him.

'Hello!' they cried to one another, with much embracing and kissing. 'There's Jim down there!' 'There's Daddy up there!' They laughed and he felt paralysed and in terror of the late day. It was almost four. He looked at the leaden sky, which might pour down molten silver any moment, a sky of lava and soot and a wet wind blowing out of it. He held his wife's arm very tightly as they walked. 'Aren't you friendly, though?' She smiled.

'It's ridiculous, of course,' he said, thinking of something else.

'What?'

They were at the playground gate.

'Hello, Charlie. Hi!' Far away, atop the monstrous slide stood the Marshall boy, waving, not smiling now.

'You wait here,' said Mr Underhill to his wife. 'I'll only be a moment. I'll just take Jim in.'

'All right.'

He grasped the small boy's hand. 'Here we go, Jim. Stick close to Daddy.'

They stepped down the hard concrete steps and stood in the flat dust. Before them, in a magical sequence, stood diagrams, gigantic-tic-tac-toes, monstrous hopscotches, the amazing numerals and triangles and oblongs of children's scrabbling in the incredible dust.

The sky blew a huge wind upon him and he was shivering. He grasped the little boy's hand still tighter and turned to his wife. 'Goodbye!' he said. For he was believing it. He was in the playground and believing it, and it was for the best. Nothing was too good for Jim! Nothing at all in the crazy world! And now his wife was laughing back at him, 'Charlie, you idiot!'

They were running, running across the dirt playground floor, at the bottom of a stony sea that pressed and blew upon them. Now Jim was crying, 'Daddy, Daddy!' and the children racing to meet them, the boy on the slide yelling, the tic-tac-toe and hopscotches whirling, a sense of bodiless terror gripping him, but he knew what he must do and what must be done and what would happen. Far across the field footballs sailed, baseballs whizzed, bats flew, fists jabbed up, and the door of the Manager's office stood open, the desk empty, the seat empty, a lone light burning in it.

Mr Underhill stumbled, shut his eyes and fell, crying out, his body clenched by a hot pain, mouthing strange words, everything in turmoil.

'There you are, Jim,' said a voice.

And he was climbing, climbing, eyes closed, climbing metal, ringing ladder rungs, screaming, wailing, his throat raw.

Mr Underhill opened his eyes.

He was on top of the slide. The gigantic slide which was ten thousand feet high, it seemed. Children after him, children beating him to go on, slide! slide!

And he looked, and there, going off across the field, was a man in a black overcoat. And there, at the gate, was a woman waving and the man standing there with the woman, both of them looking in at him, waving, and their voices calling, 'Have a good time! Have a good time, Jim!'

He screamed. He looked at his hands, in a panic of realization. The small hands, the thin hands. He looked at the earth far below. He felt his nose bleeding and there was the Marshall boy next to him. 'Hi!' cried the other, and bashed him in the mouth. 'Only twelve years here!' cried the other in the uproar.

Twelve years! thought Mr Underhill, trapped. And time is different to children. A year is like ten years. No, not twelve years of childhood ahead of him, but a century, a century of *this!*

'Slide!'

He was pinched, pummelled and shoved. He felt fists rising, he saw the fox faces, and beyond them, at the fence, the man and woman walking off. He screamed, he shrieked, he covered his face, he felt himself pushed, bleeding, to the rim of nothingness. Face first, he careened down the slide, screeching, with ten thousand monsters behind. A thought jumped through his brain a moment before he hit bottom in a nauseous mound of claws.

*This is Hell, this is Hell!*

And no one in the hot, milling heap contradicted him.

# Importance

## Manuel Mujica Lainez

*One evening, walking through one of Buenos Aires' tree-lined streets,
Mujica Lainez pointed out to me a small unobtrusive square off Cabildo
Avenue and told me that after his death the square would be named after
him. He had just had 'second sight'. Manuel Mujica Lainez reads the
future in cards, palms and dreams, and believes in ghosts. He lives in
a large Spanish mansion in the hills of Córdoba in Argentina, surrounded
by paintings, books and objects, each somehow related to his long life of
wandering: a large stone statue brought over from China in the thirties
(the story of the finding of the statue involves a blindfolded beggar who
could read any book with his toes); a letter from the Spanish poet García
Lorca, murdered in Spain (Mujica Lainez's ancestors were Spanish and
included a notorious Grand Inquisitor and a medieval Rabbi); a yellow
ring with the effigy of Shakespeare (whose sonnets Mujica Lainez
translated into Spanish, as well as plays by Racine and Molière).*

*The literary fate of Mujica Lainez is a curious one. Although he is a
best-selling author in Spanish-speaking countries, his books have taken
a long time to reach the English-speaking public, and France has yet to
discover them. Only* Bomarzo *(a vast fresco of the Renaissance seen
through the eyes of an immortal duke) and* The Wandering Unicorn
*(the story of the fairy Melusine told against the background of the
Crusades and medieval Europe) have been translated into English.*

Mrs Hermosilla del Fresno is both a widow and a lady of great
importance. In this vast city inhabited by so many important
widows, there is none so important as Mrs Hermosilla del Fresno.
As befits her importance, she lives in a large mansion full of servants
and important furniture and presides over important charities that
require important parties. Through a curious twist of fate the only
thing that lacks importance within this splendid setting is her family:
the lady is of doubtful pedigree – a fact of which no one has the

slightest doubt, least of all the other important ladies. Witness to these origins (which not even the splendour of her wedding has been able to improve) are certain obscure relatives of unshakeable modesty, whom Mrs Hermosilla del Fresno hardly ever sees. If she is forced to introduce them – something she cleverly avoids – she manages to wrap up their names and kinship in a half smile and an aloof glance, while her vanity spits and snarls inside her like a crouching tiger.

Mrs Hermosilla del Fresno believes in God and in Hell. She believes (as her administrators and charity helpers have often assured her) that she has amply earned a place in Paradise. She would have preferred, quite naturally, to remain in the world which after all suited her perfectly – with the single absurd exception of the relatives in question – but one morning, suddenly, after waking (or not waking) in her important bed, Mrs Hermosilla del Fresno realizes, because of the wails and cries of her important servants, that she is dead. She is a little frightened and very astonished, for deep down inside her, though she has never admitted as much, she believed herself to be immortal. The hours go by and Mrs Hermosilla del Fresno waits in vain for the arrival of the celestial hosts who are supposed to set her up somewhere in a chosen room of the Divine Mansions. Instead, her cousins and nephews appear (and that abominable half-sister) and their existence is finally made clear to the many important ladies who now surround her with their rosaries.

Mrs Hermosilla del Fresno wants to speak but cannot utter a single word. She wants to explain that these relatives are of no importance, that they are not really relatives, that they exaggerate, that there is no need to shake hands with them, or embrace them or give them heartfelt condolences or make such a fuss about them or ask so many stupid questions which, because they concern these relatives, are of no importance whatsoever . . . And in the meantime no one comes to fetch her. Mrs Hermosilla del Fresno, accustomed as she is to the fast and haughty rhythm of giving orders, begins to feel impatient.

Six disagreeable days go by and in the end Mrs Hermosilla del Fresno realizes, with helpless horror and fury, that the solicitor to whom she has entrusted her precious will (in which she left her whole fortune to colossal charities that would have spread and perpetuated her important name) has said that there is no such will, that

Mrs Hermosilla del Fresno refused up to the very last moment – God knows why! shyness perhaps or superstition, or her strength of character – to dictate and sign one. 'Who would have thought it!' is the only comment of the charities' administrators. And in the absence of a legal document it must be assumed that her fortune goes to her melancholy relatives. Mrs Hermosilla del Fresno wants to speak out, raise her voice against this outrage, but now she is the prisoner of a new ghostly space in which her voice deserts her. She wants to lift her arms towards Heaven, towards that Heaven so curiously postponed, and let everyone know that her generous intentions have been betrayed by the solicitor, probably in league with her miserable, despised relatives. And she cannot. She cannot do anything at all.

Week after week she lies there, witness to the moving of her nephews and cousins (and that abominable half-sister) into her magnificent home. She sees them opening her drawers, reading her letters, trying on her jewellery, her furs, giving orders to her servants, emptying her wine cellar, playing host to the city's important widows who try desperately to persuade them to join the boards of her most important charities. She hears the widows begging, she hears her relatives finally accepting; she sees them signing cheques. She notices now how they have learned to smile the way she used to smile, and how, when her name is mentioned, they assume an aloof, almost indifferent look.

And still no one comes to fetch her. She remains motionless, invisible in her bed slept in by other people, people who perform on that very bed, upon her illustrious ghostly body, detailed acts of sensuality, people who sully her memory with coarse, rude jokes, who speak freely of her vanity, as if she, of all people, had ever been guilty of that sin. Only those who are unhappy are vain; surely she was never unhappy – she was simply important, very important.

Until, gradually, Mrs Hermosilla del Fresno (who cannot even escape into the haven of madness) understands, with surprise and despair, that she will never be taken away, not even to be guided to an unexpected Hell. Because this, however strange, absurd, unconventional and antitheological it might seem, this is Hell.

*Translated from the Spanish by Alberto Manguel.*

# Enoch Soames

## Max Beerbohm

*'All fantasy should have a solid basis in reality,' wrote Max Beerbohm in 1946. The reality of 'Enoch Soames' is the literary London of the 1880s which Max Beerbohm knew so well. He was the author of novels, stories and essays, a caricaturist, a wit, an elegant dandy who at the age of twenty-four published his first book of essays under the title of* The Works of Max Beerbohm.

*'Enoch Soames' was written in Rapallo, Italy, where Beerbohm lived from 1911 until his death in 1956. It comes from* Seven Men, *a collection in which there are only six main characters: Beerbohm considered the seventh to be himself, the author – his own creation.*

When a book about the literature of the eighteen-nineties was given by Mr Holbrook Jackson to the world, I looked eagerly in the index for SOAMES, ENOCH. I had feared he would not be there. He was not there. But everybody else was. Many writers whom I had quite forgotten, or remembered but faintly, lived again for me, they and their work, in Mr Holbrook Jackson's pages. The book was as thorough as it was brilliantly written. And thus the omission found by me was an all the deadlier record of poor Soames' failure to impress himself on his decade.

I daresay I am the only person who noticed the omission. Soames had failed so piteously as all that! Nor is there a counterpoise in the thought that if he had had some measure of success he might have passed, like those others, out of my mind, to return only at the historian's beck. It is true that had his gifts, such as they were, been acknowledged in his lifetime, he would never have made the bargain I saw him make – that strange bargain whose results have kept him always in the foreground of my memory. But it is from those very results that the full piteousness of him glares out.

Not my compassion, however, impels me to write of him. For

his sake, poor fellow, I should be inclined to keep my pen out of the ink. It is ill to deride the dead. And how can I write about Enoch Soames without making him ridiculous? Or rather, how am I to hush up the horrid fact that he *was* ridiculous? I shall not be able to do that. Yet, sooner or later, write about him I must. You will see, in due course, that I have no option. And I may as well get the thing done now.

In the Summer Term of '93 a bolt from the blue flashed down on Oxford. It drove deep, it hurtlingly embedded itself in the soil. Dons and undergraduates stood around, rather pale, discussing nothing but it. Whence came it, this meteorite? From Paris. Its name? Will Rothenstein. Its aim? To do a series of twenty-four portraits in lithograph. These were to be published from the Bodley Head, London. The matter was urgent. Already the Warden of A, and the Master of B, and the Regius Professor of C, had meekly 'sat'. Dignified and doddering old men, who had never consented to sit to any one, could not withstand this dynamic little stranger. He did not sue: he invited; he did not invite: he commanded. He was twenty-one years old. He wore spectacles that flashed more than any other pair ever seen. He was a wit. He was brimful of ideas. He knew Whistler. He knew Edmond de Goncourt. He knew every one in Paris. He knew them all by heart. He was Paris in Oxford. It was whispered that, so soon as he had polished off his selection of dons, he was going to include a few undergraduates. It was a proud day for me when I – I – was included. I liked Rothenstein not less than I feared him; and there arose between us a friendship that has grown ever warmer, and been more and more valued by me, with every passing year.

At the end of Term he settled in – or rather, meteoritically into – London. It was to him I owed my first knowledge of that forever enchanting little world-in-itself, Chelsea, and my first acquaintance with Walter Sickert and other august elders who dwelt there. It was Rothenstein that took me to see, in Cambridge Street, Pimlico, a young man whose drawings were already famous among the few – Aubrey Beardsley, by name. With Rothenstein I paid my first visit to the Bodley Head. By him I was inducted into another haunt of intellect and daring, the domino room of the Café Royal.

There, on that October evening – there, in that exuberant vista of gilding and crimson velvet set amidst all those opposing mirrors and upholding caryatids, with fumes of tobacco ever rising to the painted and pagan ceiling, and with the hum of presumably cynical conversation broken into so sharply now and again by the clatter of dominoes shuffled on marble tables, I drew a deep breath, and 'This indeed', said I to myself, 'is life!'

It was the hour before dinner. We drank vermouth. Those who knew Rothenstein were pointing him out to those who knew him only by name. Men were constantly coming in through the swing-doors and wandering slowly up and down in search of vacant tables, or of tables occupied by friends. One of these rovers interested me because I was sure he wanted to catch Rothenstein's eye. He had twice passed our table, with a hesitating look; but Rothenstein, in the thick of a disquisition on Puvis de Chavannes, had not seen him. He was a stooping, shambling person, rather tall, very pale, with longish and brownish hair. He had a thin vague beard – or rather, he had a chin on which a large number of hairs weakly curled and clustered to cover its retreat. He was an odd-looking person; but in the 'nineties odd apparitions were more frequent, I think, than they are now. The young writers of that era – and I was sure this man was a writer – strove earnestly to be distinct in aspect. This man had striven unsuccessfully. He wore a soft black hat of clerical kind but of Bohemian intention, and a grey waterproof cape which, perhaps because it was waterproof, failed to be romantic. I decided that 'dim' was the *mot juste* for him. I had already essayed to write, and was immensely keen on the *mot juste*, that Holy Grail of the period.

The dim man was now again approaching our table, and this time he made up his mind to pause in front of it. 'You don't remember me,' he said in a toneless voice.

Rothenstein brightly focussed him. 'Yes, I do,' he replied after a moment, with pride rather than effusion – pride in a retentive memory. 'Edwin Soames,'

'Enoch Soames,' said Enoch.

'Enoch Soames,' repeated Rothenstein in a tone implying that it was enough to have hit on the surname. 'We met in Paris two or three times when you were living there. We met at the Café Groche.'

'And I came to your studio once.'

'Oh yes; I was sorry I was out.'

'But you were in. You showed me some of your paintings, you know . . . I hear you're in Chelsea now.'

'Yes.'

I almost wondered that Mr Soames did not, after this monosyllable, pass along. He stood patiently there, rather like a dumb animal, rather like a donkey looking over a gate. A sad figure, his. It occurred to me that 'hungry' was perhaps the *mot juste* for him; but – hungry for what? He looked as if he had little appetite for anything. I was sorry for him; and Rothenstein, though he had not invited him to Chelsea, did ask him to sit down and have something to drink.

Seated, he was more self-assertive. He flung back the wings of his cape with a gesture which – had not those wings been waterproof – might have seemed to hurl defiance at things in general. And he ordered an absinthe. '*Je me tiens toujours fidèle*,' he told Rothenstein, '*à la sorcière glauque*.'

'It is bad for you,' said Rothenstein drily.

'Nothing is bad for one,' answered Soames. '*Dans ce monde il n'y a ni de bien ni de mal*.'

'Nothing good and nothing bad? How do you mean?'

'I explained it all in the preface to *Negations*.'

'*Negations?*'

'Yes; I gave you a copy of it.'

'Oh yes, of course. But did you explain – for instance – that there was no such thing as bad or good grammar?'

'N-no,' said Soames. 'Of course in Art there is the good and the evil. But in Life – no.' He was rolling a cigarette. He had weak white hands, not well washed, and with finger-tips much stained by nicotine. 'In Life there are illusions of good and evil, but' – his voice trailed away to a murmur in which the words 'vieux jeu' and 'rococo' were faintly audible. I think he felt he was not doing himself justice, and feared that Rothenstein was going to point out fallacies. Anyway, he cleared his throat and said '*Parlons d'autre chose*.'

It occurs to you that he was a fool? It didn't to me. I was young, and had not the clarity of judgement that Rothenstein already had. Soames was quite five or six years older than either of us. Also, he had written a book.

It was wonderful to have written a book.

If Rothenstein had not been there, I should have revered Soames. Even as it was, I respected him. And I was very near indeed to reverence when he said he had another book coming out soon. I asked if I might ask what kind of book it was to be.

'My poems,' he answered. Rothenstein asked if this was to be the title of the book. The poet meditated on this suggestion, but said he rather thought of giving the book no title at all. 'If a book is good in itself – ' he murmured, waving his cigarette.

Rothenstein objected that absence of title might be bad for the sale of a book. 'If,' he urged, 'I went into a bookseller's and said simply "Have you got?" or "Have you a copy of?" how would they know what I wanted?'

'Oh, of course I should have my name on the cover,' Soames answered earnestly. 'And I rather want,' he added, looking hard at Rothenstein, 'to have a drawing of myself as frontispiece.' Rothenstein admitted that this was a capital idea, and mentioned that he was going into the country and would be there for some time. He then looked at his watch, exclaimed at the hour, paid the waiter, and went away with me to dinner. Soames remained at his post of fidelity to the glaucous witch.

'Why were you so determined not to draw him?' I asked.

'Draw him? Him? How can one draw a man who doesn't exist?'

'He is dim,' I admitted. But my *mot juste* fell flat. Rothenstein repeated that Soames was non-existent.

Still, Soames had written a book. I asked if Rothenstein had read *Negations*. He said he had looked into it. 'But,' he added crisply, 'I don't profess to know anything about writing.' A reservation very characteristic of the period! Painters would not then allow that any one outside their own order had a right to any opinion about painting. This law (graven on the tablets brought down by Whistler from the summit of Fujiyama) imposed certain limitations. If other arts than painting were not utterly unintelligible to all but the men who practised them, the law tottered – the Monroe Doctrine, as it were, did not hold good. Therefore no painter would offer an opinion of a book without warning you at any rate that his opinion was worthless. No one is a better judge of literature than Rothenstein; but it wouldn't have done to tell him so in those days; and I knew that I must form an unaided judgement on *Negations*.

Not to buy a book of which I had met the author face to face would have been for me in those days an impossible act of self-denial. When I returned to Oxford for the Christmas Term I had duly secured *Negations*. I used to keep it lying carelessly on the table in my room, and whenever a friend took it up and asked what it was about I would say 'Oh, it's rather a remarkable book. It's by a man whom I know.' Just 'what it was about' I never was able to say. Head or tail was just what I hadn't made of that slim green volume. I found in the preface no clue to the exiguous labyrinth of contents, and in that labyrinth nothing to explain the preface.

*Lean near to life. Lean very near – nearer.*

*Life is web, and therein nor warp nor woof is, but web only.*

*It is for this I am Catholick in church and in thought, yet do let swift Mood weave there what the shuttle of Mood wills.*

These were the opening phrases of the preface, but those which followed were less easy to understand. Then came 'Stark: A *Conte*', about a midinette who, so far as I could gather, murdered, or was about to murder, a mannequin. It seemed to me like a story by Catulle Mendès in which the translator had either skipped or cut out every alternate sentence. Next, a dialogue between Pan and St Ursula – lacking, I rather felt, in 'snap'. Next, some aphorisms (entitled α'φορίσματα). Throughout, in fact, there was a great variety of form; and the forms had evidently been wrought with much care. It was rather the substance that eluded me. Was there, I wondered, any substance at all? It did now occur to me: suppose Enoch Soames was a fool! Up cropped a rival hypothesis: suppose *I* was! I inclined to give Soames the benefit of the doubt. I had read *L'Après-midi d'un Faune* without extracting a glimmer of meaning. Yet Mallarmé – of course – was a Master. How was I to know that Soames wasn't another? There was a sort of music in his prose, not indeed arresting, but perhaps, I thought, haunting, and laden perhaps with meanings as deep as Mallarmé's own. I awaited his poems with an open mind.

And I looked forward to them with positive impatience after I had had a second meeting with him. This was on an evening in January. Going into the aforesaid domino room, I passed a table at which sat a pale man with an open book before him. He looked from his book to me, and I looked back over my shoulder with a vague sense that I ought to have recognized him. I returned to pay my respects. After exchanging a few words, I said with a glance to the open book, 'I see I am interrupting you,' and was about to pass on, but 'I prefer,' Soames replied in his toneless voice, 'to be interrupted,' and I obeyed his gesture that I should sit down.

I asked him if he often read here. 'Yes; things of this kind I read here,' he answered, indicating the title of his book – *The Poems of Shelley*.

'Anything that you really' – and I was going to say 'admire?' But I cautiously left my sentence unfinished, and was glad that I had done so, for he said, with unwonted emphasis, 'Anything second-rate.'

I had read little of Shelley, but 'Of course,' I murmured, 'he's very uneven.'

'I should have thought evenness was just what was wrong with him. A deadly evenness. That's why I read him here. The noise of this place breaks the rhythm. He's tolerable here.' Soames took up the book and glanced through the pages. He laughed. Soames' laugh was a short, single and mirthless sound from the throat, unaccompanied by any movement of the face or brightening of the eyes. 'What a period!' he uttered, laying the book down. And 'What a country!' he added.

I asked rather nervously if he didn't think Keats had more or less held his own against the drawbacks of time and place. He admitted that there were 'passages in Keats', but did not specify them. Of 'the older men', as he called them, he seemed to like only Milton. 'Milton,' he said, 'wasn't sentimental.' Also, 'Milton had a dark insight.' And again, 'I can always read Milton in the reading-room.'

'The reading-room?'

'Of the British Museum. I go there every day.'

'You do? I've only been there once. I'm afraid I found it rather a depressing place. It – it seemed to sap one's vitality.'

'It does. That's why I go there. The lower one's vitality, the more sensitive one is to great art. I live near the Museum. I have rooms in Dyott Street.'

'And you go round to the reading-room to read Milton?'

'Usually Milton.' He looked at me. 'It was Milton,' he certificatively added, 'who converted me to Diabolism.'

'Diabolism? Oh yes? Really?' said I, with that vague discomfort and that intense desire to be polite which one feels when a man speaks of his own religion. 'You – worship the Devil?'

Soames shook his head. 'It's not exactly worship,' he qualified, sipping his absinthe. 'It's more a matter of trusting and encouraging.'

'Ah, yes . . . But I had rather gathered from the preface to *Negations* that you were a – a Catholic.'

'*Je l'étais à cette époque.* Perhaps I still am. Yes, I'm a Catholic Diabolist.'

This profession he made in an almost cursory tone. I could see that what was upmost in his mind was the fact that I had read *Negations*. His pale eyes had for the first time gleamed. I felt as one who is about to be examined, *viva voce*, on the very subject in which he is shakiest. I hastily asked him how soon his poems were to be published. 'Next week,' he told me.

'And are they to be published without a title?'

'No. I found a title, at last. But I shan't tell you what it is,' as though I had been so impertinent as to inquire. 'I am not sure that it wholly satisfies me. But it is the best I can find. It does suggest something of the quality of the poems . . . Strange growths, natural and wild; yet exquisite,' he added, 'and many-hued, and full of poisons.'

I asked him what he thought of Baudelaire. He uttered the snort that was his laugh, and 'Baudelaire,' he said, 'was a *bourgeois malgré lui*.' France had had only one poet: Villon; 'and two-thirds of Villon were sheer journalism.' Verlaine was 'an *épicier malgré lui*'. Altogether, rather to my surprise, he rated French literature lower than English. There were 'passages' in Villiers de l'Isle-Adam. But 'I', he summed up, 'owe nothing to France.' He nodded at me. 'You'll see,' he predicted.

I did not, when the time came, quite see that. I thought the author of *Fungoids* did – unconsciously, no doubt – owe something to the young Parisian decadents, or to the young English ones who owed something to *them*. I still think so. The little book – bought by me in Oxford – lies before me as I write. Its pale grey buckram cover and silver lettering have not worn well. Nor have its contents. Through these, with a melancholy interest, I have again been looking. They are not much. But at the time of their publication I had a vague suspicion that they *might* be. I suppose it is my capacity for faith, not poor Soames' work, that is weaker than it once was . . .

TO A YOUNG WOMAN

*Thou art, who hast not been!*
   Pale tunes irresolute
   And traceries of old sounds
   Blown from a rotted flute
Mingle with noise of cymbals rouged with rust,
Nor not strange forms and epicene

> Lie bleeding in the dust,
>     Being wounded with wounds.
>     For this it is
> That is thy counterpart
>     Of age-long mockeries
> *Thou hast not been nor art!*

There seemed to me a certain inconsistency as between the first and last lines of this. I tried, with bent brows, to resolve the discord. But I did not take my failure as wholly incompatible with a meaning in Soames' mind. Might it not rather indicate the depth of his meaning? As for the craftsmanship, 'rouged with rust' seemed to me a fine stroke, and 'nor not' instead of 'and' had a curious felicity. I wondered who the Young Woman was, and what she had made of it all. I sadly suspect that Soames could not have made more of it than she. Yet, even now, if one doesn't try to make any sense at all of the poem, and reads it just for the sound, there is a certain grace of cadence. Soames was an artist – in so far as he was anything, poor fellow!

It seemed to me, when first I read *Fungoids*, that, oddly enough, the Diabolistic side of him was the best. Diabolism seemed to be a cheerful, even a wholesome, influence in his life.

## NOCTURNE

> Round and round the shutter'd Square
> I stroll'd with the Devil's arm in mine.
> No sound but the scrape of his hoofs was there
> And the ring of his laughter and mine.
>     We had drunk black wine.

> *I scream'd 'I will race you, Master!'*
> *'What matter,' he shriek'd, 'to-night*
> *Which of us runs the faster?*
> *There is nothing to fear to-night*
>     *In the foul moon's light!'*

> Then I look'd him in the eyes,
> And I laugh'd full shrill at the lie he told
> And the gnawing fear he would fain disguise.

It was true, what I'd time and again been told:
He was old – old.

There was, I felt, quite a swing about that first stanza – a joyous and rollicking note of comradeship. The second was slightly hysterical perhaps. But I liked the third: it was so bracingly unorthodox, even according to the tenets of Soames' peculiar sect in the faith. Not much 'trusting and encouraging' here! Soames triumphantly exposing the Devil as a liar, and laughing 'full shrill,' cut a quite heartening figure, I thought – then! Now, in the light of what befell, none of his poems depresses me so much as 'Nocturne'.

I looked out for what the metropolitan reviewers would have to say. They seemed to fall into two classes: those who had little to say and those who had nothing. The second class was the larger, and the words of the first were cold; insomuch that

Strikes a note of modernity throughout ... These tripping numbers. – *Preston Telegraph*.

was the sole lure offered in advertisements by Soames' publisher. I had hoped that when next I met the poet I could congratulate him on having made a stir; for I fancied he was not so sure of his intrinsic greatness as he seemed. I was but able to say, rather coarsely, when next I did see him, that I hoped *Fungoids* was 'selling splendidly'. He looked at me across his glass of absinthe and asked if I had bought a copy. His publisher had told him that three had been sold. I laughed, as at a jest.

'You don't suppose I *care*, do you?' he said, with something like a snarl. I disclaimed the notion. He added that he was not a tradesman. I said mildly that I wasn't, either, and murmured that an artist who gave truly new and great things to the world had always to wait long for recognition. He said he cared not a sou for recognition. I agreed that the act of creation was its own reward.

His moroseness might have alienated me if I had regarded myself as a nobody. But ah! hadn't both John Lane and Aubrey Beardsley suggested that I should write an essay for the great new venture that was afoot – *The Yellow Book*? And hadn't Henry Harland, as editor, accepted my essay? And wasn't it to be in the very first number? At Oxford I was still *in statu pupillari*. In London I regarded myself as very much indeed a graduate now – one whom no Soames could ruffle. Partly to show off, partly in sheer goodwill, I told Soames he ought to contribute to *The Yellow Book*. He uttered from the throat a sound of scorn for that publication.

Nevertheless, I did, a day or two later, tentatively ask Harland if he knew anything of the work of a man called Enoch Soames. Harland paused in the midst of his characteristic stride around the room, threw up his hands towards the ceiling, and groaned aloud: he had often met 'that absurd creature' in Paris, and this very morning had received some poems in manuscript from him.

'Has he *no* talent?' he asked.

'He has an income. He's all right.' Harland was the most joyous of men and most generous of critics, and he hated to talk of anything about which he couldn't be enthusiastic. So I dropped the subject of Soames. The news that Soames had an income did take the edge off solicitude. I learned afterwards that he was the son of an unsuccessful and deceased bookseller in Preston, but had inherited an annuity of £300 from a married aunt, and had no surviving relatives of any kind. Materially, then, he was 'all right'. But there was still a spiritual pathos about him, sharpened for me now by the possibility that even the praises of the *Preston Telegraph* might not have been forthcoming had he not been the son of a Preston man. He had a sort of weak doggedness which I could not but admire. Neither he nor his work received the slightest encouragement; but he persisted in behaving as a personage: always he kept his dingy little flag flying. Wherever congregated the *jeunes féroces* of the arts, in whatever Soho restaurant they had just discovered, in whatever music-hall they were most frequenting, there was Soames in the midst of them, or rather on the fringe of them, a dim but inevitable figure. He never sought to propitiate his fellow-writers, never bated a jot of his arrogance about his own work or of his contempt for theirs. To the painters he was respectful, even humble; but for the poets and prosaists of *The Yellow Book*, and later of *The Savoy*, he had never a word but of scorn. He wasn't resented. It didn't occur to anybody that he or his Catholic Diabolism mattered. When, in the autumn of '96, he brought out (at his own expense, this time) a third book, his last book, nobody said a word for or against it. I meant, but forgot, to buy it. I never saw it, and am ashamed to say I don't even remember what it was called. But I did, at the time of its publication, say to Rothenstein that I thought poor old Soames was really a rather tragic figure, and that I believed he would literally die for want of recognition. Rothenstein scoffed. He said I was trying to get credit for a kind heart which I didn't possess; and perhaps this was so. But at the private view of the New English Art Club, a few weeks later, I beheld a pastel portrait of 'Enoch Soames, Esq.' It was very like him, and very like Rothenstein to have done it. Soames was standing near it, in his soft hat and his waterproof cape, all through the afternoon. Anybody who knew him would have recognized the portrait at a glance, but nobody who didn't know him would have recognized the portrait from its bystander: it 'existed' so much more than he; it was bound to. Also, it had not that expression of faint happiness which on this day was discernible, yes, in Soames' countenance. Fame had breathed on him. Twice again in the course of the month I went to the New English, and on both occasions Soames himself was on view there. Looking back, I regard the close of that exhibition as having been virtually the close of his career. He had felt the breath of Fame against his cheek – so late, for such a little while; and at its withdrawal he gave in, gave up, gave out. He, who had never looked strong or well, looked ghastly now – a shadow of the shade he had once been. He still frequented the domino room, but, having lost all wish to excite curiosity, he no longer read books there. 'You read only at the Museum now?' asked I, with attempted cheerfulness. He said he never went there now. 'No absinthe there,' he muttered. It was the sort of thing that in the old days he would have said for effect; but it carried conviction now. Absinthe, erst but a point in the 'personality' he had striven so hard to build up, was solace and necessity now. He no longer called it 'la sorcière glauque'. He had shed away all his French phrases. He had become a plain, unvarnished, Preston man.

Failure, if it be a plain, unvarnished, complete failure, and even though it be a squalid failure, has always a certain dignity. I avoided Soames because he made me feel rather vulgar. John Lane had published, by this time, two little books of mine, and they had had a pleasant little success of esteem. I was a – slight but definite – 'personality'. Frank Harris had engaged me to kick up my heels in the *Saturday Review*, Alfred Harmsworth was letting me do likewise in the *Daily Mail*. I was just what Soames wasn't. And he shamed my gloss. Had I known that he really and firmly believed in the greatness of what he as an artist had achieved, I might not have shunned him. No man who hasn't lost his vanity can be held to have altogether failed. Soames' dignity was an illusion of mine. One

day in the first week of June, 1897, that illusion went. But on the
evening of that day Soames went too.

I had been out most of the morning, and, as it was too late to
reach home in time for luncheon, I sought 'the Vingtième'. This
little place – Restaurant du Vingtième Siècle, to give it its full title
– had been discovered in '96 by the poets and prosaists, but had
now been more or less abandoned in favour of some later find. I
don't think it lived long enough to justify its name; but at that time
there it still was, in Greek Street, a few doors from Soho Square,
and almost opposite to that house where, in the first years of the
century, a little girl, and with her a boy named De Quincey, made
nightly encampment in darkness and hunger among dust and rats
and old legal parchments. The Vingtième was but a small whitewashed room, leading out into the street at one end and into a
kitchen at the other. The proprietor and cook was a Frenchman,
known to us as Monsieur Vingtième; the waiters were his two
daughters, Rose and Berthe; and the food, according to faith, was
good. The tables were so narrow, and were set so close together,
that there was space for twelve of them, six jutting from either wall.

Only the two nearest to the door, as I went in, were occupied.
On one side sat a tall, flashy, rather Mephistophelian man whom I
had seen from time to time in the domino room and elsewhere. On
the other side sat Soames. They made a queer contrast in that sunlit
room – Soames sitting haggard in that hat and cape which nowhere
at any season had I seen him doff, and this other, this keenly vital
man, at sight of whom I more than ever wondered whether he was
a diamond merchant, a conjurer, or the head of a private detective
agency. I was sure Soames didn't want my company; but I asked,
as it would have seemed brutal not to, whether I might join him,
and took the chair opposite to his. He was smoking a cigarette, with
an untasted salmi of something on his plate and a half-empty bottle
of Sauterne before him; and he was quite silent. I said that the
preparations for the Jubilee made London impossible. (I rather
liked them, really.) I professed a wish to go right away till the whole
thing was over. In vain did I attune myself to his gloom. He seemed
not to hear me nor even to see me. I felt that his behaviour made
me ridiculous in the eyes of the other man. The gangway between
the two rows of tables at the Vingtième was hardly more than two
feet wide (Rose and Berthe, in their ministrations, had always to
edge past each other, quarrelling in whispers as they did so), and

any one at the table abreast of yours was practically at yours. I thought our neighbour was amused at my failure to interest Soames, and so, as I could not explain to him that my insistence was merely charitable, I became silent. Without turning my head, I had him well within my range of vision. I hoped I looked less vulgar than he in contrast with Soames. I was sure he was not an Englishman, but what *was* his nationality? Though his jet-black hair was *en brosse*, I did not think he was French. To Berthe, who waited on him, he spoke French fluently, but with a hardly native idiom and accent. I gathered that this was his first visit to the Vingtième; but Berthe was off-hand in her manner to him: he had not made a good impression. His eyes were handsome, but – like the Vingtième's tables – too narrow and set too close together. His nose was predatory, and the points of his moustache, waxed up beyond his nostrils, gave a fixity to his smile. Decidedly, he was sinister. And my sense of discomfort in his presence was intensified by the scarlet waistcoat which tightly, and so unseasonably in June, sheathed his ample chest. This waistcoat wasn't wrong merely because of the heat, either. It was somehow all wrong in itself. It wouldn't have done on Christmas morning. It would have struck a jarring note at the first night of 'Hernani'. I was trying to account for its wrongness when Soames suddenly and strangely broke silence. 'A hundred years hence!' he murmured, as in a trance.

'We shall not be here!' I briskly but fatuously added.

'We shall not be here. No,' he droned, 'but the Museum will still be just where it is. And the reading-room, just where it is. And people will be able to go and read there.' He inhaled sharply, and a spasm as of actual pain contorted his features.

I wondered what train of thought poor Soames had been following. He did not enlighten me when he said, after a long pause, 'You think I haven't minded.'

'Minded what, Soames?'

'Neglect. Failure.'

'*Failure?*' I said heartily. 'Failure?' I repeated vaguely. 'Neglect – yes, perhaps; but that's quite another matter. Of course you haven't been – appreciated. But what then? Any artist who – who gives – ' What I wanted to say was, 'Any artist who gives truly new and great things to the world has always to wait long for recognition'; but the flattery would not out: in the face of his misery, a misery so genuine and so unmasked, my lips would not say the words.

And then – he said them for me. I flushed. 'That's what you were going to say, isn't it?' he asked.

'How did you know?'

'It's what you said to me three years ago, when *Fungoids* was published.' I flushed the more. I need not have done so at all, for 'It's the only important thing I ever heard you say,' he continued. 'And I've never forgotten it. It's a true thing. It's a horrible truth. But – d'you remember what I answered? I said "I don't care a sou for recognition." And you believed me. You've gone on believing I'm above that sort of thing. You're shallow. What should *you* know of the feelings of a man like me? You imagine that a great artist's faith in himself and in the verdict of posterity is enough to keep him happy . . . You've never guessed at the bitterness and loneliness, the' – his voice broke; but presently he resumed, speaking with a force that I had never known in him. 'Posterity! What use is it to *me*? A dead man doesn't know that people are visiting his grave – visiting his birthplace – putting up tablets to him – unveiling statues of him. A dead man can't read the books that are written about him. A hundred years hence! Think of it! If I could come back to life *then* – just for a few hours – and go to the reading-room, and *read*! Or better still: if I could be projected, now, at this moment, into that future, into that reading-room, just for this one afternoon! I'd sell myself body and soul to the devil, for that! Think of the pages and pages in the catalogue: "SOAMES, ENOCH" endlessly – endless editions, commentaries, prolegomena, biographies' – but here he was interrupted by a sudden loud creak of the chair at the next table. Our neighbour had half risen from his place. He was leaning towards us, apologetically intrusive.

'Excuse – permit me,' he said softly. 'I have been unable not to hear. Might I take a liberty? In this little restaurant-sans-façon' – he spread wide his hands – 'might I, as the phrase is, "cut in"?'

I could but signify our acquiescence. Berthe had appeared at the kitchen door, thinking the stranger wanted his bill. He waved her away with his cigar, and in another moment had seated himself beside me, commanding a full view of Soames.

'Though not an Englishman,' he explained, 'I know my London well, Mr Soames. Your name and fame – Mr Beerbohm's too – very known to me. Your point is: who am *I*?' He glanced quickly over his shoulder, and in a lowered voice said 'I am the Devil.'

I couldn't help it: I laughed. I tried not to, I knew there was nothing to laugh at, my rudeness shamed me, but – I laughed with increasing volume. The Devil's quiet dignity, the surprise and disgust of his raised eyebrows, did but the more dissolve me. I rocked to and fro, I lay back aching. I behaved deplorably.

'I am a gentleman, and,' he said with intense emphasis, 'I thought I was in the company of *gentlemen*.'

'Don't!' I gasped faintly. 'Oh, don't!'

'Curious, *nicht wahr?*' I heard him say to Soames. 'There is a type of person to whom the very mention of my name is – oh-so-awfully-funny! In your theatres the dullest *comédien* needs only to say "The Devil!" and right away they give him "the loud laugh that speaks the vacant mind". Is it not so?'

I had now just breath enough to offer my apologies. He accepted them, but coldly, and readdressed himself to Soames.

'I am a man of business,' he said, 'and always I would put things through "right now", as they say in the States. You are a poet. *Les affaires* – you detest them. So be it. But with me you will deal, eh? What you have said just now gives me furiously to hope.'

Soames had not moved, except to light a fresh cigarette. He sat crouched forward, with his elbows squared on the table, and his head just above the level of his hands, staring up at the Devil. 'Go on,' he nodded. I had no remnant of laughter in me now.

'It will be the more pleasant, our little deal,' the Devil went on, 'because you are – I mistake not? – a Diabolist.'

'A Catholic Diabolist,' said Soames.

The Devil accepted the reservation genially. 'You wish,' he resumed, 'to visit now – this afternoon as-ever-is – the reading-room of the British Museum, yes? but of a hundred years hence, yes? *Parfaitement*. Time – an illusion. Past and future – they are as ever-present as the present, or at any rate only what you call "just-round-the-corner". I switch you on to any date. I project you – pouf! You wish to be in the reading-room just as it will be on the afternoon of June 3rd, 1997? You wish to find yourself standing in that room, just past the swing-doors, this very minute, yes? and to stay there till closing time? Am I right?'

Soames nodded.

The Devil looked at his watch. 'Ten past two,' he said. 'Closing time in summer same then as now: seven o'clock. That will give you almost five hours. At seven o'clock – pouf! – you find yourself again here, sitting at this table. I am dining tonight *dans le monde*

– *dans le higlif*. That concludes my present visit to your great city. I come and fetch you here, Mr Soames, on my way home.'

'Home?' I echoed.

'Be it never so humble!' said the Devil lightly.

'All right,' said Soames.

'Soames!' I entreated. But my friend moved not a muscle.

The Devil had made as though to stretch forth his hand across the table and touch Soames' forearm; but he paused in his gesture.

'A hundred years hence, as now,' he smiled, 'no smoking allowed in the reading-room. You would better therefore—'

Soames removed the cigarette from his mouth and dropped it into his glass of Sauterne.

'Soames!' again I cried. 'Can't you' – but the Devil had now stretched forth his hand across the table. He brought it slowly down on – the table-cloth. Soames' chair was empty. His cigarette floated sodden in his wine-glass. There was no other trace of him.

For a few moments the Devil let his hand rest where it lay, gazing at me out of the corners of his eyes, vulgarly triumphant.

A shudder shook me. With an effort I controlled myself and rose from the chair. 'Very clever,' I said condescendingly. 'But – *The Time Machine* is a delightful book, don't you think? So entirely original!'

'You are pleased to sneer,' said the Devil, who had also risen, 'but it is one thing to write about a not possible machine; it is a quite other thing to be a Supernatural Power.' All the same, I had scored.

Berthe had come forth at the sound of our rising. I explained to her that Mr Soames had been called away, and that both he and I would be dining here. It was not until I was out in the open air that I began to feel giddy. I have but the haziest recollection of what I did, where I wandered, in the glaring sunshine of that endless afternoon. I remember the sound of carpenters' hammers all along Piccadilly, and the bare chaotic look of the half-erected 'stands'. Was it in the Green Park, or in Kensington Gardens, or *where* was it that I sat on a chair beneath a tree, trying to read an evening paper? There was a phrase in the leading article that went on repeating itself in my fagged mind – 'Little is hidden from this august Lady full of the garnered wisdom of sixty years of Sovereignty.' I remember wildly conceiving a letter (to reach Windsor by express messenger told to await answer):

MADAM – Well knowing that your Majesty is full of the garnered wisdom of sixty years of Sovereignty, I venture to ask your advice in the following delicate matter. Mr Enoch Soames, whose poems you may or may not know . . .

Was there *no* way of helping him – saving him? A bargain was a bargain, and I was the last man to aid or abet any one in wriggling out of a reasonable obligation. I wouldn't have lifted a little finger to save Faust. But poor Soames! – doomed to pay without respite an eternal price for nothing but a fruitless search and a bitter disillusioning . . .

Odd and uncanny it seemed to me that he, Soames, in the flesh, in the waterproof cape, was at this moment living in the last decade of the next century, poring over books not yet written, and seeing and seen by men not yet born. Uncannier and odder still, that tonight and evermore he would be in Hell. Assuredly, truth was stranger than fiction.

Endless that afternoon was. Almost I wished I had gone with Soames – not indeed to stay in the reading-room, but to sally forth for a brisk sight-seeing walk around a new London. I wandered restlessly out of the Park I had sat in. Vainly I tried to imagine myself an ardent tourist from the eighteenth century. Intolerable was the strain of the slow-passing and empty minutes. Long before seven o'clock I was back at the Vingtième.

I sat there just where I had sat for luncheon. Air came in listlessly through the open door behind me. Now and again Rose or Berthe appeared for a moment. I had told them I would not order any dinner till Mr Soames came. A hurdy-gurdy began to play, abruptly drowning the noise of a quarrel between some Frenchmen further up the street. Whenever the tune was changed I heard the quarrel still raging. I had bought another evening paper on my way. I unfolded it. My eyes gazed ever away from it to the clock over the kitchen door . . .

Five minutes, now, to the hour! I remembered that clocks in restaurants are kept five minutes fast. I concentrated my eyes on the paper. I vowed I would not look away from it again. I held it upright, at its full width, close to my face, so that I had no view of anything but it . . . Rather a tremulous sheet? Only because of the draught, I told myself.

My arms gradually became stiff; they ached; but I could not drop

them – now. I had a suspicion, I had a certainty. Well, what then?
. . . What else had I come for? Yet I held tight that barrier of
newspaper. Only the sound of Berthe's brisk footstep from the
kitchen enabled me, forced me, to drop it, and to utter:

'What shall we have to eat, Soames?'

'Il est souffrant, ce pauvre Monsieur Soames?' asked Berthe.

'He's only – tired.' I asked her to get some wine – Burgundy –
and whatever food might be ready. Soames sat crouched forward
against the table, exactly as when last I had seen him. It was as
though he had never moved – he who had moved so unimaginably
far. Once or twice in the afternoon it had for an instant occurred
to me that perhaps his journey was not to be fruitless – that perhaps
we had all been wrong in our estimate of the works of Enoch
Soames. That we had been horribly right was horribly clear from
the look of him. But 'Don't be discouraged,' I falteringly said.
'Perhaps it's only that you – didn't leave enough time. Two, three
centuries hence, perhaps—'

'Yes,' his voice came. 'I've thought of that.'

'And now – now for the more immediate future! Where are you
going to hide? How would it be if you caught the Paris express
from Charing Cross? Almost an hour to spare. Don't go on to Paris.
Stop at Calais. Live in Calais. He'd never think of looking for you
in Calais.'

'It's like my luck,' he said, 'to spend my last hours on earth with
an ass.' But I was not offended. 'And a treacherous ass,' he strangely
added, tossing across to me a crumpled bit of paper which he had
been holding in his hand. I glanced at the writing on it – some sort
of gibberish, apparently. I laid it impatiently aside.

'Come, Soames! pull yourself together! This isn't a mere matter
of life and death. It's a question of eternal torment, mind you! You
don't mean to say you're going to wait limply here till the Devil
comes to fetch you?'

'I can't do anything else. I've no choice.'

'Come! This is "trusting and encouraging" with a vengeance!
This is Diabolism run mad!' I filled his glass with wine. 'Surely,
now that you've *seen* the brute—'

'It's no good abusing him.'

'You must admit there's nothing Miltonic about him, Soames.'

'I don't say he's not rather different from what I expected.'

'He's a vulgarian, he's a swell-mobsman, he's the sort of man who hangs about the corridors of trains going to the Riviera and steals ladies' jewel-cases. Imagine eternal torment presided over by *him*!'

'You don't suppose I look forward to it, do you?'

'Then why not slip quietly out of the way?'

Again and again I filled his glass, and always, mechanically, he emptied it; but the wine kindled no spark of enterprise in him. He did not eat, and I myself ate hardly at all. I did not in my heart believe that any dash for freedom could save him. The chase would be swift, the capture certain. But better anything than this passive, meek, miserable waiting. I told Soames that for the honour of the human race he ought to make some show of resistance. He asked what the human race had ever done for him. 'Besides,' he said, 'can't you understand that I'm in his power? You saw him touch me, didn't you? There's an end of it. I've no will, I'm sealed.'

I made a gesture of despair. He went on repeating the word 'sealed'. I began to realize that the wine had clouded his brain. No wonder! Foodless he had gone into futurity, foodless he still was. I urged him to eat at any rate some bread. It was maddening to think that he, who had so much to tell, might tell nothing. 'How was it all,' I asked, 'yonder? Come! Tell me your adventures.'

'They'd make first-rate "copy", wouldn't they?'

'I'm awfully sorry for you, Soames, and I make all possible allowances; but what earthly right have you to insinuate that I should make "copy", as you call it, out of you?'

The poor fellow pressed his hands to his forehead. 'I don't know,' he said. 'I had some reason, I'm sure . . . I'll try to remember.'

'That's right. Try to remember everything. Eat a little more bread. What did the reading-room look like?'

'Much as usual,' he at length muttered.

'Many people there?'

'Usual sort of number.'

'What did they look like?'

Soames tried to visualise them. 'They all,' he presently remembered, 'looked very like one another.'

My mind took a fearsome leap. 'All dressed in Jaeger?'

'Yes. I think so. Greyish-yellowish stuff.'

'A sort of uniform?' He nodded. 'With a number on it, perhaps? – a number on a large disc of metal sewn on to the left sleeve? DKF 78,910 – that sort of thing?' It was even so. 'And all of them – men and women alike – looking very well-cared-for? very Utopian? and smelling rather strongly of carbolic? and all of them quite hairless?' I was right every time. Soames was only not sure whether the men and women were hairless or shorn. 'I hadn't time to look at them very closely,' he explained.

'No, of course not. But – '

'They stared at *me,* I can tell you. I attracted a great deal of attention.' At last he had done that! 'I think I rather scared them. They moved away whenever I came near. They followed me about at a distance, wherever I went. The men at the round desk in the middle seemed to have a sort of panic whenever I went to make inquiries.'

'What did you do when you arrived?'

Well, he had gone straight to the catalogue, of course – to the S volumes, and had stood long before SN–SOF, unable to take this volume out of the shelf, because his heart was beating so . . . At first, he said, he wasn't disappointed – he only thought there was some new arrangement. He went to the middle desk and asked where the catalogue of *twentieth*-century books was kept. He gathered that there was still only one catalogue. Again he looked up his name, stared at the three little pasted slips he had known so well. Then he went and sat down for a long time . . .

'And then,' he droned, 'I looked up the *Dictionary of National Biography* and some encyclopædias . . . I went back to the middle desk and asked what was the best modern book on late nineteenth-century literature. They told me Mr T. K. Nupton's book was considered the best. I looked it up in the catalogue and filled in a form for it. It was brought to me. My name wasn't in the index, but – Yes!' he said with a sudden change of tone. 'That's what I'd forgotten. Where's that bit of paper? Give it me back.'

I, too, had forgotten that cryptic screed. I found it fallen on the floor, and handed it to him.

He smoothed it out, nodding and smiling at me disagreeably. 'I found myself glancing through Nupton's book,' he resumed. 'Not very easy reading. Some sort of phonetic spelling . . . All the modern books I saw were phonetic.'

'Then I don't want to hear any more, Soames, please.'

'The proper names seemed all to be spelt in the old way. But for that, I mightn't have noticed my own name.'

'Your own name? Really? Soames, I'm *very* glad.'

'And yours.'

'No!'

'I thought I should find you waiting here tonight. So I took the trouble to copy out the passage. Read it.'

I snatched the paper. Soames' handwriting was characteristically dim. It, and the noisome spelling, and my excitement, made me all the slower to grasp what T. K. Nupton was driving at.

The document lies before me at this moment. Strange that the words I here copy out for you were copied out for me by poor Soames just seventy-eight years hence . . .

From p. 234 of *Inglish Littracher 1890–1900,* bi T. K. Nupton, published by th Stait, 1992:

Fr. egzarmpl, a riter ov th time, naimd Max Beerbohm, hoo woz stil alive in th twentieth senchri, rote a stauri in wich e pautraid an immajnari karrakter kauld 'Enoch Soames' – a thurd-rait poit hoo beleevz imself a grate jeneus an maix a bargin with th Devvl in auder ter no wot posterriti thinx ov im! It iz a sumwot labud sattire but not without vallu az showing hou seriusli the yung men ov th aiteen-ninetiz took themselvz. Nou that the littreri profeshn haz bin auganized az a department of publik servis, our riters hav found their levvl an hav lernt ter doo their duti without thort ov th morro. 'Th laibrer iz werthi ov hiz hire,' an that iz aul. Thank hevvn we hav no Enoch Soameses amung us to-dai!

I found that by murmuring the words aloud (a device which I commend to my reader) I was able to master them, little by little. The clearer they became, the greater was my bewilderment, my distress and horror. The whole thing was a nightmare. Afar, the great grisly background of what was in store for the poor dear art of letters; here, at the table, fixing on me a gaze that made me hot all over, the poor fellow whom – whom evidently . . . but no: whatever down-grade my character might take in coming years, I should never be such a brute as to—

Again I examined the screed. 'Immajnari' – but here Soames was, no more imaginary, alas! than I. And 'labud' – what on earth was that? (To this day, I have never made out that word.) 'It's all very – baffling,' I at length stammered.

Soames said nothing, but cruelly did not cease to look at me.

'Are you sure,' I temporized, 'quite sure you copied the thing out correctly?'

'Quite'.

'Well, then it's this wretched Nupton who must have made – must be going to make – some idiotic mistake . . . Look here, Soames! you know me better than to suppose that I . . . After all, the name "Max Beerbohm" is not at all an uncommon one, and there must be several Enoch Soameses running around – or rather, "Enoch Soames" is a name that might occur to any one writing a story. And I don't write stories: I'm an essayist, an observer, a recorder . . . I admit that it's an extraordinary coincidence. But you must see—'

'I see the whole thing,' said Soames quietly. And he added, with a touch of his old manner, but with more dignity than I had ever known in him, '*Parlons d'autre chose.*'

I accepted that suggestion very promptly. I returned straight to the more immediate future. I spent most of the long evening in renewed appeals to Soames to slip away and seek refuge somewhere. I remember saying at last that if indeed I was destined to write about him, the supposed 'stauri' had better have at least a happy ending. Soames repeated those last three words in a tone of intense scorn. 'In Life and in Art,' he said, 'all that matters is an *inevitable* ending.'

'But,' I urged, more hopefully than I felt, 'an ending that can be avoided *isn't* inevitable.'

'You aren't an artist,' he rasped. 'And you're so hopelessly not an artist that, so far from being able to imagine a thing and make it seem true, you're going to make even a true thing seem as if you'd made it up. You're a miserable bungler. And it's like my luck.'

I protested that the miserable bungler was not I – was not going to be I – but T. K. Nupton; and we had a rather heated argument, in the thick of which it suddenly seemed to me that Soames saw he was in the wrong: he had quite physically cowered. But I wondered why – and now I guessed with a cold throb just why – he stared so, past me. The bringer of that 'inevitable ending' filled the doorway.

I managed to turn in my chair and to say, not without a semblance of lightness, 'Aha, come in!' Dread was indeed rather blunted in me by his looking so absurdly like a villain in a melodrama. The sheen of his tilted hat and of his shirtfront, the repeated twists he was giving to his moustache, and most of all the magnificence of his sneer, gave token that he was there only to be foiled.

He was at our table in a stride. 'I am sorry,' he sneered witheringly, 'to break up your pleasant party, but—'

'You don't: you complete it,' I assured him. 'Mr Soames and I want to have a little talk with you. Won't you sit? Mr Soames got nothing – frankly nothing – by his journey this afternoon. We don't wish to say that the whole thing was a swindle – a common swindle. On the contrary, we believe you meant well. But of course the bargain, such as it was, is off.'

The Devil gave no verbal answer. He merely looked at Soames and pointed with rigid forefinger to the door. Soames was wretchedly rising from his chair when, with a desperate quick gesture, I swept together two dinner-knives that were on the table, and laid their blades across each other. The Devil stepped sharp back against the table behind him, averting his face and shuddering.

'You are not superstitious!' he hissed.

'Not at all,' I smiled.

'Soames!' he said as to an underling, but without turning his face, 'put those knives straight!'

With an inhibitive gesture to my friend, 'Mr Soames,' I said emphatically to the Devil, 'is a *Catholic* Diabolist'; but my poor friend did the Devil's bidding, not mine; and now, with his master's eyes again fixed on him, he arose, he shuffled past me. I tried to speak. It was he that spoke. 'Try,' was the prayer he threw back at me as the Devil pushed him roughly out through the door, '*try* to make them know that I did exist!'

In another instant I too was through that door. I stood staring all ways – up the street, across it, down it. There was moonlight and lamplight, but there was not Soames nor that other.

Dazed, I stood there. Dazed, I turned back, at length, into the little room; and I suppose I paid Berthe or Rose for my dinner and luncheon, and for Soames': I hope so, for I never went to the Vingtième again. Ever since that night I have avoided Greek Street altogether. And for years I did not set foot even in Soho Square, because on that same night it was there that I paced and loitered, long and long, with some such dull sense of hope as a man has in not straying far from the place where he has lost something . . .
'Round and round the shutter'd Square' – that line came back to me on my lonely beat, and with it the whole stanza, ringing in my

brain and bearing in on me how tragically different from the happy scene imagined by him was the poet's actual experience of that prince in whom of all princes we should put not our trust.

But – strange how the mind of an essayist, be it never so stricken, roves and ranges! – I remember pausing before a wide doorstep and wondering if perchance it was on this very one that the young De Quincey lay ill and faint while poor Ann flew as fast as her feet would carry her to Oxford Street, the 'stony-hearted stepmother' of them both, and came back bearing that 'glass of port wine and spices' but for which he might, so he thought, actually have died. Was this the very doorstep that the old De Quincey used to revisit in homage? I pondered Ann's fate, the cause of her sudden vanishing from the ken of her boyfriend; and presently I blamed myself for letting the past override the present. Poor vanished Soames!

And for myself, too, I began to be troubled. What had I better do? Would there be a hue and cry – Mysterious Disappearance of an Author, and all that? He had last been seen lunching and dining in my company. Hadn't I better get a hansom and drive straight to Scotland Yard? . . . They would think I was a lunatic. After all, I reassured myself, London was a very large place, and one very dim figure might easily drop out of it unobserved – now especially, in the blinding glare of the near Jubilee. Better say nothing at all, I thought.

And I was right. Soames' disappearance made no stir at all. He was utterly forgotten before any one, so far as I am aware, noticed that he was no longer hanging around. Now and again some poet or prosaist may have said to another, 'What has become of that man Soames?' but I never heard any such question asked. The solicitor through whom he was paid his annuity may be presumed to have made inquiries, but no echo of these resounded. There was something rather ghastly to me in the general unconsciousness that Soames had existed, and more than once I caught myself wondering whether Nupton, that babe unborn, were going to be right in thinking him a figment of my brain.

In that extract from Nupton's repulsive book there is one point which perhaps puzzles you. How is it that the author, though I have here mentioned him by name and have quoted the exact words he is going to write, is not going to grasp the obvious corollary that I have invented nothing? The answer can but be this: Nupton will not have read the later passages of this memoir. Such lack of thoroughness is a serious fault in any one who undertakes to do scholar's work. And I hope these words will meet the eye of some contemporary rival to Nupton and be the undoing of Nupton.

I like to think that some time between 1992 and 1997 somebody will have looked up this memoir, and will have forced on the world his inevitable and startling conclusions. And I have reasons for believing that this will be so. You realize that the reading-room into which Soames was projected by the Devil was in all respects precisely as it will be on the afternoon of June 3rd, 1997. You realize, therefore, that on that afternoon, when it comes round, there the self-same crowd will be, and there Soames too will be, punctually, he and they doing precisely what they did before. Recall now Soames' account of the sensation he made. You may say that the mere difference of his costume was enough to make him sensational in that uniformed crowd. You wouldn't say so if you had ever seen him. I assure you that in no period could Soames be anything but dim. The fact that people are going to stare at him, and follow him around, and seem afraid of him, can be explained only on the hypothesis that they will somehow have been prepared for his ghostly visitation. They will have been awfully waiting to see whether he really would come. And when he does come the effect will of course be – awful.

An authentic, guaranteed, proven ghost, but – only a ghost, alas! Only that. In his first visit, Soames was a creature of flesh and blood, whereas the creatures into whose midst he was projected were but ghosts, I take it – solid, palpable, vocal, but unconscious and automatic ghosts, in a building that was itself an illusion. Next time, that building and those creatures will be real. It is of Soames that there will be but the semblance. I wish I could think him destined to revisit the world actually, physically, consciously. I wish he had this one brief escape, this one small treat, to look forward to. I never forget him for long. He is where he is, and for ever. The more rigid moralists among you may say he has only himself to blame. For my part, I think he has been very hardly used. It is well that vanity should be chastened; and Enoch Soames' vanity was, I admit, above the average, and called for special treatment. But there was no need for vindictiveness. You say he contracted to pay the price he is paying; yes; but I maintain that he was induced to do so by fraud. Well-informed in all things, the Devil must have known that my friend would gain nothing by his visit to futurity.

The whole thing was a very shabby trick. The more I think of it, the more detestable the Devil seems to me.

Of him I have caught sight several times, here and there, since that day at the Vingtième. Only once, however, have I seen him at close quarters. This was in Paris. I was walking, one afternoon, along the Rue d'Antin, when I saw him advancing from the opposite direction – over-dressed as ever, and swinging an ebony cane, and altogether behaving as though the whole pavement belonged to him. At thought of Enoch Soames and the myriads of other sufferers eternally in this brute's dominion, a great cold wrath filled me, and I drew myself up to my full height. But – well, one is so used to nodding and smiling in the street to anybody whom one knows, that the action becomes almost independent of oneself: to prevent it requires a very sharp effort and great presence of mind. I was miserably aware, as I passed the Devil, that I nodded and smiled to him. And my shame was the deeper and hotter because he, if you please, stared straight at me with the utmost haughtiness.

To be cut – deliberately cut – by *him*! I was, I still am, furious at having had that happen to me.

# A Visitor from Down Under

## L. P. Hartley

The Shrimp and the Anemone, The Sixth Heaven, Eustace and Hilda, *and* The Go-Between *are the novels which established Hartley's reputation in England. His main theme is the past. 'The past is a foreign country,' he wrote in* The Go-Between. *'They do things differently there.' The past is also the land of ghosts; as in 'A Visitor from Down Under', they come from the past to haunt us.*

*'There is no difficulty,' says Lord David Cecil in his introduction to Hartley's tales, 'in believing in his ghosts. They and their stories assault the imagination with the compelling horror of nightmare.'*

'And who will you send to fetch him away?'

After a promising start, the March day had ended in a wet evening. It was hard to tell whether rain or fog predominated. The loquacious bus conductor said, 'A foggy evening,' to those who rode inside, and 'A wet evening,' to such as were obliged to ride outside. But in or on the buses, cheerfulness held the field, for their patrons, inured to discomfort, made light of climatic inclemency. All the same, the weather was worth remarking on: the most scrupulous conversationalist could refer to it without feeling self convicted of banality. How much more the conductor who, in common with most of his kind, had a considerable conversational gift.

The bus was making its last journey through the heart of London before turning in for the night. Inside it was only half full. Outside, as the conductor was aware by virtue of his sixth sense, there still remained a passenger too hardy or too lazy to seek shelter. And now, as the bus rattled rapidly down the Strand, the footsteps of this person could be heard shuffling and creaking upon the metal-shod steps.

'Anyone on top?' asked the conductor, addressing an errant umbrella-point and the hem of a mackintosh.

'I didn't notice anyone,' the man replied.

'It's not that I don't trust you,' remarked the conductor pleasantly, giving a hand to his alighting fare, 'but I think I'll go up and make sure.'

Moments like these, moments of mistrust in the infallibility of his observation, occasionally visited the conductor. They came at the end of a tiring day, and if he could he withstood them. They were signs of weakness, he thought; and to give way to them a matter for self-reproach. 'Going barmy, that's what you are,' he told himself, and he casually took a fare inside to prevent his mind dwelling on the unvisited outside. But his unreasoning disquietude survived this distraction, and murmuring against himself he started to climb the steps.

To his surprise, almost stupefaction, he found that his misgivings were justified. Breasting the ascent, he saw a passenger sitting on the right-hand front seat; and the passenger, in spite of his hat turned down, his collar turned up, and the creased white muffler that showed between the two, must have heard him coming; for though the man was looking straight ahead, in his outstretched left hand, wedged between the first and second fingers, he held a coin.

'Jolly evening, don't you think?' asked the conductor, who wanted to say something. The passenger made no reply, but the penny, for such it was, slipped the fraction of an inch lower in the groove between the pale freckled fingers.

'I said it was a damn wet night,' the conductor persisted irritably, annoyed by the man's reserve.

Still no reply.

'Where you for?' asked the conductor, in a tone suggesting that wherever it was, it must be a discreditable destination.

'Carrick Street.'

'Where?' the conductor demanded. He had heard all right, but a slight peculiarity in the passenger's pronunciation made it appear reasonable to him, and possibly humiliating to the passenger, that he should not have heard.

'Carrick Street.'

'Then why don't you say Carrick Street?' the conductor grumbled as he punched the ticket.

There was a moment's pause, then:

'Carrick Street,' the passenger repeated.

'Yes, I know, I know, you needn't go on telling me,' fumed the conductor, fumbling with the passenger's penny. He couldn't get hold of it from above; it had slipped too far, so he passed his hand underneath the other's and drew the coin from between his fingers.

It was cold, even where it had been held. 'Know?' said the stranger suddenly. 'What do you know?'

The conductor was trying to draw his fare's attention to the ticket, but could not make him look round.

'I suppose I know you are a clever chap,' he remarked. 'Look here, now. Where do you want this ticket? In your button-hole?'

'Put it here,' said the passenger.

'Where?' asked the conductor. 'You aren't a blooming letter-rack.'

'Where the penny was,' replied the passenger. 'Between my fingers.'

The conductor felt reluctant, he did not know why, to oblige the passenger in this. The rigidity of the hand disconcerted him: it was stiff, he supposed, or perhaps paralysed. And since he had been standing on the top his own hands were none too warm. The ticket doubled up and grew limp under his repeated efforts to push it in. He bent lower, for he was a good-hearted fellow, and using both hands, one above and one below, he slid the ticket into its bony slot.

'Right you are, Kaiser Bill.'

Perhaps the passenger resented this jocular allusion to his physical infirmity; perhaps he merely wanted to be quiet. All he said was:

'Don't speak to me again.'

'Speak to you!' shouted the conductor, losing all self-control. 'Catch me speaking to a stuffed dummy!'

Muttering to himself he withdrew into the bowels of the bus.

At the corner of Carrick Street quite a number of people got on board. All wanted to be first, but pride of place was shared by three women who all tried to enter simultaneously. The conductor's voice made itself audible over the din: 'Now then, now then, look where you're shoving! This isn't a bargain sale. Gently, *please,* lady; he's only a pore old man.' In a moment or two the confusion abated, and the conductor, his hand on the cord of the bell, bethought himself of the passenger on top whose destination Carrick Street was. He had forgotten to get down. Yielding to his good nature, for the conductor was averse from further conversation with his uncommunicative fare, he mounted the steps, put his head over the top and shouted 'Carrick Street! Carrick Street!' That was the utmost he could bring himself to do. But his admonition was without effect; his summons remained unanswered; nobody came. 'Well, if he wants to stay up there he can,' muttered the conductor, still aggrieved. 'I won't fetch him down, cripple or no cripple.' The bus moved on. He slipped by me, thought the conductor, while all that Cup-tie crowd was getting in.

The same evening, some five hours earlier, a taxi turned into Carrick Street and pulled up at the door of a small hotel. The street was empty. It looked like a cul-de-sac, but in reality it was pierced at the far end by an alley, like a thin sleeve, which wound its way into Soho.

'That the last, sir?' inquired the driver, after several transits between the cab and the hotel.

'How many does that make?'

'Nine packages in all, sir.'

'Could you get all your worldly goods into nine packages, driver?'

'That I could; into two.'

'Well, have a look inside and see if I have left anything.' The cabman felt about among the cushions. 'Can't find nothing, sir.'

'What do you do with anything you find?' asked the stranger.

'Take it to New Scotland Yard, sir,' the driver promptly answered.

'Scotland Yard?' said the stranger. 'Strike a match, will you, and let me have a look.'

But he, too, found nothing, and reassured, followed his luggage into the hotel.

A chorus of welcome and congratulation greeted him. The manager, the manager's wife, the Ministers without portfolio of whom all hotels are full, the porters, the lift-man, all clustered around him.

'Well, Mr Rumbold, after all these years! We thought you'd forgotten us! And wasn't it odd, the very night your telegram came from Australia we'd been talking about you! And my husband said, "Don't you worry about Mr Rumbold. He'll fall on his feet all right. Some fine day he'll walk in here a rich man." Not that you weren't always well off, but my husband meant a millionaire.'

'He was quite right,' said Mr Rumbold slowly, savouring his words. 'I am.'

'There, what did I tell you?' the manager exclaimed, as though one recital of his prophecy was not enough. 'But I wonder you're not too grand to come to Rossall's Hotel.'

'I've nowhere else to go,' said the millionaire shortly. 'And if I had, I wouldn't. This place is like home to me.'

His eyes softened as they scanned the familiar surroundings. They were light grey eyes, very pale, and seeming paler from their setting in his tanned face. His cheeks were slightly sunken and very deeply lined; his blunt-ended nose was straight. He had a thin, straggling moustache, straw-coloured, which made his age difficult to guess. Perhaps he was nearly fifty, so wasted was the skin on his neck, but his movements, unexpectedly agile and decided, were those of a younger man.

'I won't go up to my room now,' he said, in response to the manageress's question. 'Ask Clutsam – he's still with you? – good – to unpack my things. He'll find all I want for the night in the green suitcase. I'll take my despatch-box with me. And tell them to bring me a sherry and bitters in the lounge.'

As the crow flies it was not far to the lounge. But by the way of the tortuous, ill-lit passages, doubling on themselves, yawning with dark entries, plunging into kitchen stairs – the catacombs so dear to *habitués* of Rossall's Hotel – it was a considerable distance. Anyone posted in the shadow of these alcoves, or arriving at the head of the basement staircase, could not have failed to notice the air of utter content which marked Mr Rumbold's leisurely progress: the droop of his shoulders, acquiescing in weariness; the hands turned inwards and swaying slightly, but quite forgotten by their owner; the chin, always prominent, now pushed forward so far that it looked relaxed and helpless, not at all defiant. The unseen witness would have envied Mr Rumbold, perhaps even grudged him his holiday air, his untroubled acceptance of the present and the future.

A waiter whose face he did not remember brought him the aperitif, which he drank slowly, his feet propped unconventionally upon a ledge of the chimneypiece; a pardonable relaxation, for the room was empty. Judge therefore of his surprise when, out of a fire-engendered drowsiness, he heard a voice which seemed to come from the wall above his head. A cultivated voice, perhaps too cultivated, slightly husky, yet careful and precise in its enunciation.

Even while his eyes searched the room to make sure that no one
had come in, he could not help hearing everything the voice said.
It seemed to be talking to him, and yet the rather oracular utterance
implied a less restricted audience. It was the utterance of a man
who was aware that, though it was a duty for him to speak, for Mr
Rumbold to listen would be both a pleasure and a profit.

' . . . A Children's Party,' the voice announced in an even, neutral
tone, nicely balanced between approval and distaste, between
enthusiasm and boredom; 'six little girls and six little' (a faint lift
in the voice, expressive of tolerant surprise) 'boys. The Broadcasting
Company has invited them to tea, and they are anxious that you
should share some of their fun.' (At the last word the voice became
completely colourless.) 'I must tell you that they have had tea, and
enjoyed it, didn't you, children?' (A cry of 'Yes', muffled and timid,
greeted this leading question.) 'We should have liked you to hear
our table-talk, but there wasn't much of it, we were so busy eating.'
For a moment the voice identified itself with the children. 'But we
can tell you what we ate. Now, Percy, tell us what you had.'

A piping little voice recited a long list of comestibles; like the
children in the treacle-well, thought Rumbold, Percy must have
been, or soon would be, very ill. A few others volunteered the items
of their repast. 'So you see,' said the voice, 'we have not done so
badly. And now we are going to have crackers, and afterwards'
(the voice hesitated and seemed to dissociate itself from the words)
'Children's Games.' There was an impressive pause, broken by the
muttered exhortation of a little girl. 'Don't cry, Philip, it won't hurt
you.' Fugitive sparks and snaps of sound followed; more like a fire
being kindled, thought Rumbold, than crackers. A murmur of
voices pierced the fusillade. 'What have you got, Alec, what have
you *got*?' 'I've got a cannon.' 'Give it to me.' 'No.' 'Well, lend it to
me.' 'What do you want it for?' 'I want to shoot Jimmy.'

Mr Rumbold started. Something had disturbed him. Was it
imagination, or did he hear, above the confused medley of sound,
a tiny click? The voice was speaking again. 'And now we're going
to begin the Games.' As though to make amends for past lukewarm-
ness a faint flush of anticipation gave colour to the decorous voice.
'We will commence with that old favourite, Ring-a-Ring of Roses.'

The children were clearly shy, and left each other to do the
singing. Their courage lasted for a line or two and then gave out.
But fortified by the speaker's baritone, powerful though subdued,

they took heart, and soon were singing without assistance or direction. Their light wavering voices had a charming effect. Tears stood in Mr Rumbold's eyes. 'Oranges and Lemons' came next. A more difficult game, it yielded several unrehearsed effects before it finally got under way. One could almost see the children being marshalled into their places, as though for a figure in the Lancers. Some of them no doubt had wanted to play another game; children are contrary; and the dramatic side of 'Oranges and Lemons', though it appeals to many, always affrights a few. The disinclination of these last would account for the pauses and hesitations which irritated Mr Rumbold, who, as a child, had always had a strong fancy for this particular game. When, to the tramping and stamping of many small feet, the droning chant began, he leaned back and closed his eyes in ecstasy. He listened intently for the final accelerando which leads up to the catastrophe. Still the prologue maundered on, as though the children were anxious to extend the period of security, the joyous carefree promenade which the great Bell of Bow, by his inconsiderate profession of ignorance, was so rudely to curtail. The Bells of Old Bailey pressed their usurer's question; the Bells of Shoreditch answered with becoming flippancy; the Bells of Stepney posed their ironical query, when suddenly, before the great Bell of Bow had time to get his word in, Mr Rumbold's feelings underwent a strange revolution. Why couldn't the game continue, all sweetness and sunshine? Why drag in the fatal issue? Let payment be deferred; let the bells go on chiming and never strike the hour. But heedless of Mr Rumbold's squeamishness, the game went its way.

After the eating comes the reckoning.

> Here is a candle to light you to bed,
> And here comes a chopper to chop off your head!
> > Chop – chop – chop.

A child screamed, and there was silence.

Mr Rumbold felt quite upset, and great was his relief when, after a few more half-hearted rounds of 'Oranges and Lemons,' the Voice announced, 'Here We Come Gathering Nuts and May'. At least there was nothing sinister in that. Delicious sylvan scene, comprising in one splendid botanical inexactitude all the charms of winter, spring, and autumn. What superiority to circumstances was implied in the conjunction of nuts and May! What defiance of cause and effect! What a testimony to coincidence! For cause and effect is against us, as witness the fate of Old Bailey's debtor; but coincidence is always on our side, teaching us how to eat our cake and have it! The long arm of coincidence! Mr Rumbold would have liked to clasp it by the hand.

Meanwhile his own hand conducted the music of the revels and his foot kept time. Their pulses quickened by enjoyment, the children put more heart into their singing; the game went with a swing; the ardour and rhythm of it invaded the little room where Mr Rumbold sat. Like heavy fumes the waves of sound poured in, so penetrating, they ravished the sense; so sweet, they intoxicated it; so light, they fanned it into a flame. Mr Rumbold was transported. His hearing, sharpened by the subjugation and quiescence of his other faculties, began to take in new sounds; the names, for instance, of the players who were 'wanted' to make up each side, and of the champions who were to pull them over. For the listeners-in, the issues of the struggles remained in doubt. Did Nancy Price succeed in detaching Percy Kingham from his allegiance? Probably. Did Alec Wharton prevail against Maisie Drew? It was certainly an easy win for someone: the contest lasted only a second, and a ripple of laughter greeted it. Did Violet Kingham make good against Horace Gold? This was a dire encounter, punctuated by deep irregular panting. Mr Rumbold could see, in his mind's eye, the two champions straining backwards and forwards across the white, motionless handkerchief, their faces red and puckered with exertion. Violet or Horace, one of them had to go: Violet might be bigger than Horace, but then Horace was a boy: they were evenly matched: they had their pride to maintain. The moment when the will was broken and the body went limp in surrender would be like a moment of dissolution. Yes, even this game had its stark, uncomfortable side. Violet or Horace, one of them was smarting now: crying perhaps under the humiliation of being fetched away.

The game began afresh. This time there was an eager ring in the children's voices: two tried antagonists were going to meet: it would be a battle of giants. The chant throbbed into a war-cry.

> Who will you have for your Nuts and May,
>   Nuts and May, Nuts and May;
> Who will you have for your Nuts and May
>   On a cold and frosty morning?

They would have Victor Rumbold for Nuts and May, Victor

Rumbold, Victor Rumbold: and from the vindictiveness in their voices they might have meant to have had his blood, too.

> And who will you send to fetch him away,
>     Fetch him away, fetch him away;
> Who will you send to fetch him away
>     On a cold and frosty morning?

Like a clarion call, a shout of defiance, came the reply:

> We'll send Jimmy Hagberd to fetch him away,
>     Fetch him away, fetch him away;
> We'll send Jimmy Hagberd to fetch him away
>     On a wet and foggy evening.

This variation, it might be supposed, was intended to promote the contest from the realms of pretence into the world of reality. But Mr Rumbold probably did not hear that his abduction had been ante-dated. He had turned quite green, and his head was lolling against the back of the chair.

'Any wine, sir?'

'Yes, Clutsam, a bottle of champagne.'

'Very good, sir.'

Mr Rumbold drained the first glass at one go.

'Anyone coming in to dinner besides me, Clutsam?' he presently inquired. 'Not now, sir, it's nine o'clock,' replied the waiter, his voice edged with reproach.

'Sorry, Clutsam, I didn't feel up to the mark before dinner, so I went and lay down.'

The waiter was mollified.

'Thought you weren't looking quite yourself, sir. No bad news, I hope.'

'No, nothing. Just a bit tired after the journey.'

'And how did you leave Australia, sir?' inquired the waiter, to accommodate Mr Rumbold, who seemed anxious to talk.

'In better weather than you have here,' Mr Rumbold replied, finishing his second glass, and measuring with his eye the depleted contents of the bottle.

The rain kept up a steady patter on the glass roof of the coffee-room.

'Still, a good climate isn't everything. It isn't like home, for instance,' the waiter remarked.

'No, indeed.'

'There's many parts of the world as would be glad of a good day's rain,' affirmed the waiter.

'There certainly are,' said Mr Rumbold, who found the conversation sedative.

'Did you do much fishing when you were abroad, sir?' the waiter pursued.

'A little.'

'Well, you want rain for that,' declared the waiter, as one who scores a point. 'The fishing isn't preserved in Australia, like what it is here?'

'No.'

'Then there ain't no poaching,' concluded the waiter philosophically. 'It's every man for himself.'

'Yes, that's the rule in Australia.'

'Not much of a rule, is it?' the waiter took him up. 'Not much like law, I mean.'

'It depends what you mean by law.'

'Oh, Mr Rumbold, sir, you know very well what I mean. I mean the police. Now if you was to have done a man in out in Australia – murdered him, I mean – they'd hang you for it if they caught you, wouldn't they?'

Mr Rumbold teased the champagne with the butt-end of his fork and drank again.

'Probably they would, unless there were special circumstances.'

'In which case you might get off?'

'I might'

'That's what I mean by law,' pronounced the waiter. 'You know what the law is: you go against it, and you're punished. Of course I don't mean you, sir; I only say "you" as – as an illustration to make my meaning clear.'

'Quite, quite.'

'Whereas if there was only what you call a rule,' the waiter pursued, deftly removing the remains of Mr Rumbold's chicken, 'it might fall to the lot of any man to round you up. Might be anybody; might be me.'

'Why should you or they,' asked Mr Rumbold, 'want to round me up? I haven't done you any harm, or them.'

'Oh, but we should have to, sir.'

'Why?'

'We couldn't rest in our beds, sir, knowing you was at large. You might do it again. Somebody'd have to see to it.'

'But supposing there was nobody?'

'Sir?'

'Supposing the murdered man hadn't any relatives or friends: supposing he just disappeared, and no one ever knew that he was dead?'

'Well, sir,' said the waiter, winking portentously, 'in that case he'd have to get on your track himself. He wouldn't rest in his grave, sir, no, not he, and knowing what he did.'

'Clutsam,' said Mr Rumbold suddenly, 'bring me another bottle of wine, and don't trouble to ice it.'

The waiter took the bottle from the table and held it to the light.

'Yes, it's dead, sir.'

'Dead?'

'Yes, sir; finished; empty; dead.'

'You're right,' Mr Rumbold agreed. 'It's quite dead.'

It was nearly eleven o'clock. Mr Rumbold again had the lounge to himself. Clutsam would be bringing his coffee presently. Too bad of Fate to have him haunted by these casual reminders; too bad, his first day at home. 'Too bad, too bad,' he muttered, while the fire warmed the soles of his slippers. But it was excellent champagne; he would take no harm from it: the brandy Clutsam was bringing him would do the rest. Clutsam was a good sort, nice old-fashioned servant . . . nice old-fashioned house . . . Warmed by the wine, his thoughts began to pass out of his control.

'Your coffee, sir,' said a voice at his elbow.

'Thank you, Clutsam, I'm very much obliged to you,' said Mr Rumbold, with the exaggerated civility of slight intoxication. 'You're an excellent fellow. I wish there were more like you.'

'I hope so, too, I'm sure,' said Clutsam, trying in his muddle-headed way to deal with both observations at once.

'Don't seem many people about,' Mr Rumbold remarked. 'Hotel pretty full?'

'Oh, yes, sir, all the suites are let, and the other rooms, too. We're turning people away every day. Why, only tonight a gentleman rang up. Said he would come round late, on the off-chance. But, bless me, he'll find the birds have flown.'

'Birds?' echoed Mr Rumbold.

'I mean there ain't any more rooms, not for love nor money.'

'Well, I'm sorry for him,' said Mr Rumbold, with ponderous sincerity. 'I'm sorry for any man, friend or foe, who has to go tramping about London on a night like this. If I had an extra bed in my room, I'd put it at his disposal.'

'You have, sir,' the waiter said.

'Why, of course I have. How stupid. Well, well. I'm sorry for the poor chap. I'm sorry for all homeless ones, Clutsam, wandering on the face of the earth.'

'Amen to that,' said the waiter devoutly.

'And doctors and such, pulled out of their beds at midnight. It's a hard life. Ever thought about a doctor's life, Clutsam?'

'Can't say I have, sir.'

'Well, well, but it's hard; you can take that from me.'

'What time shall I call you in the morning, sir?' the waiter asked, seeing no reason why the conversation should ever stop.

'You needn't call me Clutsam,' replied Mr Rumbold, in a sing-song voice, and rushing the words together as though he were excusing the waiter from addressing him by the waiter's own name. 'I'll get up when I'm ready. And that may be pretty late, pretty late.' He smacked his lips over the words.

'Nothing like a good lie, eh, Clutsam?'

'That's right, sir, you have your sleep out,' the waiter encouraged him. 'You won't be disturbed.'

'Goodnight, Clutsam. You're an excellent fellow, and I don't care who hears me say so.'

'Goodnight, sir.'

Mr Rumbold returned to his chair. It lapped him round, it ministered to his comfort: he felt at one with it. At one with the fire, the clock, the tables, all the furniture. Their usefulness, their goodness, went out to meet his usefulness, his goodness, met, and were friends. Who could bind their sweet influences or restrain them in the exercise of their kind offices? No one: certainly not a shadow from the past. The room was perfectly quiet. Street sounds reached it only as a low continuous hum, infinitely reassuring. Mr Rumbold fell asleep.

He dreamed that he was a boy again, living in his old home in the country. He was possessed, in the dream, by a master-passion; he must collect firewood, whenever and wherever he saw it. He found himself one autumn afternoon in the wood-house; that was how the dream began. The door was partly open, admitting a little light, but he could not recall how he got in. The floor of the shed was littered with bits of bark and thin twigs; but, with the exception of the chopping-block which he knew could not be used, there was nowhere a log of sufficient size to make a fire. Though he did not like being in the wood-house alone he stayed long enough to make a thorough search. But he could find nothing. The compulsion he knew so well descended on him, and he left the wood-house and went into the garden. His steps took him to the foot of a high tree, standing by itself in a tangle of long grass at some distance from the house. The tree had been lopped; for half its height it had no branches, only leafy tufts, sticking out at irregular intervals. He knew what he would see when he looked up into the dark foliage. And there, sure enough, it was: a long dead bough, bare in patches where the bark had peeled off, and crooked in the middle like an elbow.

He began to climb the tree. The ascent proved easier than he expected, his body seemed no weight at all. But he was visited by a terrible oppression, which increased as he mounted. The bough did not want him; it was projecting its hostility down the trunk of the tree. And every second brought him nearer to an object which he had always dreaded; a growth, people called it. It stuck out from the trunk of the tree, a huge circular swelling thickly matted with twigs. Victor would have rather died than hit his head against it.

By the time he reached the bough twilight had deepened into night. He knew what he had to do: sit astride the bough, since there was none near by from which he could reach it, and press with his hands until it broke. Using his legs to get what purchase he could, he set his back against the tree and pushed with all his might downwards. To do this he was obliged to look beneath him, and he saw, far below him on the ground, a white sheet spread out as though to catch him; and he knew at once that it was a shroud.

Frantically he pulled and pushed at the stiff, brittle bough; a lust to break it took hold of him; leaning forward his whole length he seized the bough at the elbow joint and strained it away from him. As it cracked he toppled over and the shroud came rushing upwards . . .

Mr Rumbold waked in a cold sweat to find himself clutching the curved arm of the chair on which the waiter had set his brandy. The glass had fallen over and the spirit lay in a little pool on the leather seat. 'I can't let it go like that,' he thought. 'I must get some more.' A man he did not know answered the bell. 'Waiter,' he said, 'bring me a brandy and soda in my room in a quarter of an hour's time. Rumbold, the name is.' He followed the waiter out of the room. The passage was completely dark except for a small blue gas-jet, beneath which was huddled a cluster of candlesticks. The hotel, he remembered, maintained an old-time habit of deference towards darkness. As he held the wick to the gas-jet, he heard himself mutter, 'Here is a candle to light you to bed.' But he recollected the ominous conclusion of the distich, and fuddled though he was he left it unspoken.

Shortly after Mr Rumbold's retirement the door-bell of the hotel rang. Three sharp peals, and no pause between them. 'Someone in a hurry to get in,' the night porter grumbled to himself. 'Expect he's forgotten his key.' He made no haste to answer the summons; it would do the forgetful fellow good to wait: teach him a lesson. So dilatory was he that by the time he reached the hall door the bell was tinkling again. Irritated by such importunity, he deliberately went back to set straight a pile of newspapers before letting this impatient devil in. To mark his indifference he even kept behind the door while he opened it, so that his first sight of the visitor only took in his back; but this limited inspection sufficed to show that the man was a stranger and not a visitor at the hotel.

In the long black cape which fell almost sheer on one side, and on the other stuck out as though he had a basket under his arm, he looked like a crow with a broken wing. A bald-headed crow, thought the porter, for there's a patch of bare skin between that white linen thing and his hat.

'Good evening, sir,' he said. 'What can I do for you?'

The stranger made no answer, but glided to a side-table and began turning over some letters with his right hand.

'Are you expecting a message?' asked the porter.

'No,' the stranger replied. 'I want a room for the night.'

'Was you the gentleman who telephoned for a room this evening?'

'Yes.'

'In that case, I was to tell you we're afraid you can't have one; the hotel's booked right up.'

'Are you quite sure?' asked the stranger. 'Think again.'

'Them's my orders, sir. It don't do me no good to think.'

At this moment the porter had a curious sensation as though some important part of him, his life maybe, had gone adrift inside him and was spinning round and round. The sensation ceased when he began to speak.

'I'll call the waiter, sir,' he said.

But before he called the waiter appeared, intent on an errand of his own.

'I say, Bill,' he began, 'what's the number of Mr Rumbold's room? He wants a drink taken up, and I forgot to ask him.'

'It's thirty-three,' said the porter unsteadily. 'The double room.'

'Why, Bill, what's up?' the waiter exclaimed. 'You look as if you'd seen a ghost.'

Both men stared round the hall, and then back at each other. The room was empty.

'God!' said the porter. 'I must have had the horrors. But he was here a moment ago. Look at this.'

On the stone flags lay an icicle, an inch or two long, around which a little pool was fast collecting.

'Why, Bill,' cried the waiter, 'how did that get here? It's not freezing.'

'*He* must have brought it,' the porter said.

They looked at each other in consternation, which changed into terror as the sound of a bell made itself heard, coming from the depths of the hotel.

'Clutsam's there,' whispered the porter. 'He'll have to answer it, whoever it is.'

Clutsam had taken off his tie and was getting ready for bed. He slept in the basement. What on earth could anyone want in the smoking-room at this hour? He pulled on his coat and went upstairs.

Standing by the fire he saw the same figure whose appearance and disappearance had so disturbed the porter.

'Yes, sir?' he said.

'I want you to go to Mr Rumbold,' said the stranger, 'and ask him if he is prepared to put the other bed in his room at the disposal of a friend.'

In a few moments Clutsam returned.

'Mr Rumbold's compliments, sir, and he wants to know who it is.'

The stranger went to the table in the centre of the room. An Australian newspaper was lying there which Clutsam had not noticed before. The aspirant to Mr Rumbold's hospitality turned over the pages. Then with his finger, which appeared even to Clutsam standing by the door unusually pointed, he cut out a rectangular slip, about the size of a visiting card, and, moving away, motioned the waiter to take it.

By the light of the gas-jet in the passage Clutsam read the clipping. It seemed to be a kind of obituary notice; but of what possible interest could it be to Mr Rumbold to know that the body of Mr James Hagberd had been discovered in circumstances which suggested that he had met his death by violence?

After a longer interval Clutsam returned, looking puzzled and a little frightened.

'Mr Rumbold's compliments, sir, but he knows no one of that name.'

'Then take this message to Mr Rumbold,' said the stranger. 'Say, "Would he rather that I went up to him, or that he came down to me?"' For the third time Clutsam went to do the stranger's bidding. He did not, however, upon his return open the door of the smoking-room, but shouted through it:

'Mr Rumbold wishes you to Hell, sir, where you belong, and says, "Come up if you dare!"'

Then he bolted.

A minute later, from his retreat in an underground coal-cellar, he heard a shot fired. Some old instinct, danger-loving or danger-disregarding, stirred in him, and he ran up the stairs quicker than he had ever run up them in his life. In the passage he stumbled over Mr Rumbold's boots. The bedroom door was ajar. Putting his head down he rushed in. The brightly lit room was empty. But almost all the movables in it were overturned and the bed was in a frightful mess. The pillow with its five-fold perforation was the first object on which Clutsam noticed bloodstains. Thenceforward he seemed to see them everywhere. But what sickened him and kept him so long from going down to rouse the others was the sight of an icicle on the window-sill, a thin claw of ice curved like a China-man's nail, with a bit of flesh sticking to it.

That was the last he saw of Mr Rumbold. But a policeman patrolling Carrick Street noticed a man in a long black cape, who seemed, by the position of his arm, to be carrying something heavy. He called out to the man and ran after him; but though he did not seem to be moving very fast, the policeman could not overtake him.

# Laura

## Saki

*No one knows why Hector Hugh Munro called himself Saki – the name
of the cup-bearer in Fitzgerald's Rubaiyat. Saki was born in Burma,
went to school in England, travelled through Europe and was killed, a
sergeant in the Royal Fusiliers, at Beaumont Hamel in 1916, at the age
of forty-six. William Drake, in* Memories of the War, *says that the
soldiers of the First World War read Saki in the trenches, 'attracted
perhaps by his upper-class schoolboy tone carried to the extreme of talent.'
Saki was one of the funniest, most caustic of British short-story writers.
He was also the author of many famous one-liners, such as 'The cook
was a good cook, as cooks go; and as cooks go, she went.' 'Waldo is
one of those people who would be enormously improved by death!' 'Never
be a pioneer. It's the Early Christian that gets the fattest lion.'*

'You are not really dying, are you?' asked Amanda.

'I have the doctor's permission to live till Tuesday,' said Laura.

'But today is Saturday; this is serious!' gasped Amanda.

'I don't know about it being serious; it is certainly Saturday,' said
Laura.

'Death is always serious,' said Amanda.

'I never said I was going to die. I am presumably going to leave
off being Laura, but I shall go on being something. An animal of
some kind, I suppose. You see, when one hasn't been very good in
the life one has just lived, one reincarnates in some lower organism.
And I haven't been very good, when one comes to think of it. I've
been petty and mean and vindictive and all that sort of thing when
circumstances have seemed to warrant it.'

'Circumstances never warrant that sort of thing,' said Amanda
hastily.

'If you don't mind my saying so,' observed Laura, 'Egbert is a
circumstance that would warrant any amount of that sort of thing.

You're married to him – that's different; you've sworn to love, honour and endure him: I haven't.'

'I don't see what's wrong with Egbert,' protested Amanda.

'Oh, I dare say the wrongness has been on my part,' admitted Laura dispassionately; 'he has merely been the extenuating circumstance. He made a thin, peevish kind of fuss, for instance, when I took the collie puppies from the farm out for a run the other day.'

'They chased his young broods of speckled Sussex and drove two sitting hens off their nests, besides running all over the flower beds. You know how devoted he is to his poultry and garden.'

'Anyhow, he needn't have gone on about it for the entire evening, and then have said, "Let's say no more about it" just when I was beginning to enjoy the discussion. That's where one of my petty vindictive revenges came in,' added Laura with an unrepentant chuckle. 'I turned the entire family of speckled Sussex into his seedling shed the day after the puppy episode.'

'How could you?' exclaimed Amanda.

'It came quite easy,' said Laura; 'two of the hens pretended to be laying at the time, but I was firm.'

'And we thought it was an accident!'

'You see,' resumed Laura, 'I really *have* some grounds for supposing that my next incarnation will be in a lower organism. I shall be an animal of some kind. On the other hand, I haven't been a bad sort in my way, so I think I may count on being a nice animal, something elegant and lively, with a love of fun. An otter, perhaps.'

'I can't imagine you as an otter,' said Amanda.

'Well, I don't suppose you can imagine me as an angel, if it comes to that,' said Laura.

Amanda was silent. She couldn't.

'Personally I think an otter life would be rather enjoyable,' continued Laura; 'salmon to eat all the year round, and the satisfaction of being able to fetch the trout in their own homes without having to wait for hours till they condescend to rise to the fly you've been dangling before them; and an elegant svelte figure—'

'Think of the otter hounds,' interposed Amanda; 'how dreadful to be hunted and harried and finally worried to death!'

'Rather fun with half the neighbourhood looking on, and anyhow not worse than this Saturday-to-Tuesday business of dying by inches; and then I should go on into something else. If I had been a moderately good otter I suppose I should get back into human shape of some sort; probably something rather primitive – a little brown, unclothed Nubian boy, I should think.'

'I wish you would be serious,' sighed Amanda; 'you really ought to be if you're only going to live till Tuesday.'

As a matter of fact Laura died on Monday.

'So dreadfully upsetting,' Amanda complained to her uncle-in-law, Sir Lulworth Quayne. 'I've asked quite a lot of people down for golf and fishing, and the rhododendrons are just looking their best.'

'Laura always was inconsiderate,' said Sir Lulworth; 'she was born during Goodwood week, with an Ambassador staying in the house who hated babies.'

'She had the maddest kind of ideas,' said Amanda; 'do you know if there was any insanity in her family?'

'Insanity? No, I never heard of any. Her father lives in West Kensington, but I believe he's sane on all other subjects.'

'She had an idea that she was going to be reincarnated as an otter,' said Amanda.

'One meets with those ideas of reincarnation so frequently even in the West,' said Sir Lulworth, 'that one can hardly set them down as being mad. And Laura was such an unaccountable person in this life that I should not like to lay down definite rules as to what she might be doing in an after state.'

'You think she really might have passed into some animal form?' asked Amanda. She was one of those who shape their opinions rather readily from the standpoint of those around them.

Just then Egbert entered the breakfast-room, wearing an air of bereavement that Laura's demise would have been insufficient, in itself, to account for.

'Four of my speckled Sussex have been killed,' he exclaimed; 'the very four that were to go to the show on Friday. One of them was dragged away and eaten right in the middle of that new carnation bed that I've been to such trouble and expense over. My best flower bed and my best fowls singled out for destruction; it almost seems as if the brute that did the deed had special knowledge how to be as devastating as possible in a short space of time.'

'Was it a fox, do you think?' asked Amanda.

'Sounds more like a polecat,' said Sir Lulworth.

'No,' said Egbert, 'there were marks of webbed feet all over the place, and we followed the tracks down to the stream at the bottom of the garden; evidently an otter.'

Amanda looked quickly and furtively across at Sir Lulworth.

Egbert was too agitated to eat any breakfast, and went out to superintend the strengthening of the poultry yard defences.

'I think she might at least have waited till the funeral was over,' said Amanda in a scandalized voice.

'It's her own funeral, you know,' said Sir Lulworth; 'it's a nice point in etiquette how far one ought to show respect to one's own mortal remains.'

Disregard for mortuary convention was carried to further lengths next day; during the absence of the family at the funeral ceremony the remaining survivors of the speckled Sussex were massacred. The marauder's line of retreat seemed to have embraced most of the flower beds on the lawn, but the strawberry beds in the lower garden had also suffered.

'I shall get the otter hounds to come here at the earliest possible moment,' said Egbert savagely.

'On no account! You can't dream of such a thing!' exclaimed Amanda. 'I mean, it wouldn't do, so soon after a funeral in the house.'

'It's a case of necessity,' said Egbert; 'once an otter takes to that sort of thing it won't stop.'

'Perhaps it will go elsewhere now that there are no more fowls left,' suggested Amanda.

'One would think you wanted to shield the beast,' said Egbert.

'There's been so little water in the stream lately,' objected Amanda; 'it seems hardly sporting to hunt an animal when it has so little chance of taking refuge anywhere.'

'Good gracious!' fumed Egbert, 'I'm not thinking about sport. I want to have the animal killed as soon as possible.'

Even Amanda's opposition weakened when, during church time on the following Sunday, the otter made its way into the house, raided half a salmon from the larder and worried it into scaly fragments on the Persian rug in Egbert's studio.

'We shall have it hiding under our beds and biting pieces out of our feet before long,' said Egbert, and from what Amanda knew of this particular otter she felt that the possibility was not a remote one.

On the evening preceding the day fixed for the hunt Amanda spent a solitary hour walking by the banks of the stream, making what she imagined to be hound noises. It was charitably supposed by those who overheard her performance, that she was practising for farmyard imitations at the forthcoming village entertainment.

It was her friend and neighbour, Aurora Burret, who brought her news of the day's sport.

'Pity you weren't out; we had quite a good day. We found it at once, in the pool just below your garden.'

'Did you – kill?' asked Amanda.

'Rather. A fine she-otter. Your husband got rather badly bitten in trying to "tail it". Poor beast, I felt quite sorry for it, it had such a human look in its eyes when it was killed. You'll call me silly, but do you know who the look reminded me of? My dear woman, what is the matter?'

When Amanda had recovered to a certain extent from her attack of nervous prostration Egbert took her to the Nile Valley to recuperate. Change of scene speedily brought about the desired recovery of health and mental balance. The escapades of an adventurous otter in search of a variation of diet were viewed in their proper light. Amanda's normally placid temperament reasserted itself. Even a hurricane of shouted curses, coming from her husband's dressing-room, in her husband's voice, but hardly in his usual vocabulary, failed to disturb her serenity as she made a leisurely toilet one evening in a Cairo hotel.

'What is the matter? What has happened?' she asked in amused curiosity.

'The little beast has thrown all my clean shirts into the bath! Wait till I catch you, you little—'

'What little beast?' asked Amanda, suppressing a desire to laugh; Egbert's language was so hopelessly inadequate to express his outraged feelings.

'A little beast of a naked brown Nubian boy,' spluttered Egbert.

And now Amanda is seriously ill.

# An Injustice Revealed

## Anonymous

*I found this story in a French children's book which gave no indication as to when or where it might have been written. Chinese ghost stories go back to the dawn of civilization and reached near-perfection during the golden age of the Tang dynasty (AD 618–907). To the modern reader they seem different from Western ghost stories in that the element of surprise never lies in the sudden appearance of the ghost itself but usually in what it has come to say or do. The Chinese ghost is as much a part of reality as the narrator or his surroundings, and the other characters accept his existence as a matter of course. In the following story the ghost appears as a lovable, chatty, very everyday kind of ghost, himself haunted by the terrors of bureaucracy.*

Two civil servants, Ye Ning-fei and Wang Li, were very good friends who enjoyed each other's company. Both were outstanding examples of honest, incorruptible inspectors, and for that reason much feared by the corrupt officials whom it was their task to keep under observation.

But lately their meetings had been few and far between because both had been busy in different parts of their provinces. Then one day Ye Ning-fei heard that Wang Li, during his last tour of inspection, had suddenly fallen ill and died. His family had had his body transported to his birthplace and had buried him there according to his wishes. Ye Ning-fei grieved deeply at the loss of his friend and promised himself that he would go, as soon as his work permitted, to pay his respects to Wang Li's memory.

Almost three months after Wang Li's death, Ye Ning-fei was sent on an inspection tour to the faraway town of Houa-si where the governor had become the object of many serious complaints. Although Ye Ning-fei did not know it, Houa-si was the town in which Wang Li had died.

After a tiresome journey, Ye Ning-fei arrived in Houa-si, took a room at the inn, and without delay began to study the governor's files and documents, all of which he found in great disorder. There was little doubt as to the extent of the governor's corruption: though the entire province lived in abject poverty, the governor's house was of a luxury beyond a sane person's dreams. Ye Ning-fei locked himself up in his room, gave instructions not to be disturbed, and settled down to investigate the matter.

One evening as he was sitting at his table, deep in the study of official documents, the door of his room opened silently and a cold gust of air blew on the flame in his lamp and made it flutter. Ye Ning-fei lifted his eyes in surprise, but the door closed itself again slowly. Thinking that it was nothing but the wind he returned to his papers, but before he could find the paragraph at which he had left off he saw, sitting across the table from him, his old friend Wang Li, smiling sweetly. Ye Ning-fei greeted him affectionately but expressed surprise at seeing him.

'I had not realized that it was here,' he said, 'in this small town, that you died. But why are you not in your grave? I heard that your family had collected your body and had held your funeral. What are you doing wandering so far from home? Even your spirit should by now have returned to your sacred birthplace.'

'You're quite right,' agreed Wang Li. 'But something so terrible has happened that I can hardly find words to describe it. You see, I was kept here while my body was being carried away home, and now I cannot rejoin it. I have not even got enough money to pay the infernal guards the toll into my province. And you know what a long journey that is. I was delighted to find out that you were coming to Houa-si: you, my dear friend, are my only hope. I must apologize for troubling you but I cannot think of any other way out of this terrible situation. I am forced to ask you for a friendly loan.'

Ye Ning-fei said that of course he would help – what else were friends for? He asked Wang Li how much money he required and promised to get it the very next day. Then he put his papers away into a box and said, 'I have no wish to pry, but I would very much like to know exactly what happened.'

Wang Li shrugged his shoulders. 'It is a long and muddled tale, so complicated that at first I could make no sense at all out of it. And I mustn't take up too much of your valuable time – I see you have a great deal of work to do.'

Ye Ning-fei insisted that his friend tell him as much as possible: the chance of conversing together might not arise again in the near future, and besides he had almost finished his work for the day. So Wang Li agreed.

'At first,' he said, 'everything was very confusing. As you know, I had been sent here to Houa-si on an inspection tour. But even before I was able to start work I became terribly ill. I was struck down by a violent fever and died practically without realizing it. As I lay dead here in my room, the door was violently wrenched open and two horrible bailiffs burst in. I remember thinking that the innkeeper left much to be desired if he allowed two such men to enter a civil servant's room as if they owned the place. They looked truly frightening. They were dressed entirely in black, with thick belts around their waists, and out of their livid faces their bloodshot eyes shone red and menacing. On their heads they wore strange ornaments wrought in black iron and in their hands they carried heavy chains with round brass weights. They dragged me off my bed, tied my hands behind my back and, with great roughness, pushed me into the street.

'Throughout the journey they never said a word, and whenever I tried to ask them a civil question their only answer would be a hard tug on my chains. Suddenly – I cannot say how – I found myself in a vast hall, surrounded by even more bailiffs, all looking very much alike. Near the door an enormous judge was sitting behind a desk. His face was green, with large piercing eyes burning beneath bushy black eyebrows. Long, thick, red whiskers drooped down to his feet. The judge drew his hands out of the folds of his robe and laid them on his desk, looking at me with such severity that I felt an icy chill creep down to the small of my back.

'The bailiffs pushed me down on my knees and stood on either side of me. The judge asked my name, and then instructed one of his assistants – the registrar, no doubt – to find my case in the Book of Complaints and Punishments. I realized at last that I was in the Court of Hell.

'Turning the pages of a large, musty volume, the registrar began to read out in a monotonous voice:

' "The person who calls himself Wang stands here accused, according to the laws of this Court, not only of numerous breaches of honour due to a dissolute and corrupt life but also of causing the death of a certain Tchou Heng. The above-mentioned Tchou Heng after his death filed this complaint at the present Court and his claim has been recognized as valid."

'I cannot hope to make you understand what I felt at that moment. There I stood, accused of an immoral and corrupt life! I had no idea who this Tchou Heng was, so how in the world could I have been the cause of his death? I was bathed in perspiration from the shock and the indignation I felt. Fear made me tremble.

'During the entire reading the terrible judge kept staring at me, and when the registrar stopped he asked in a stentorian voice:

' "Do you, the accused, confess to this crime?"

'I made an attempt to rise, but the bailiffs threw me back on my knees. From this humiliating position I wailed, "Your Honour, members of the Court, there must be some mistake, I know of no one called Tchou Heng."

'The Judge frowned hideously and asked the registrar to read out Tchou Heng's complaint in order to refresh my memory. I learnt that a certain Tchou Heng had addressed the Court, humbly begging that Wang, governor of the province, be punished, for he had sullied Tchou Heng's good reputation. Tchou Heng, it seems, had been Wang's subordinate, and under his orders had become involved in the illegal commerce of antiques. An inspector arrived and Wang put all the blame on Tchou who apparently was not aware of the true nature of these transactions. Tchou suffered the humiliation of being fired, and the shame he felt and his wounded honour caused him such sadness that he died of a broken heart. He therefore wished to lodge a complaint against Wang who had ruined his good name and caused his premature death.

'As the reading proceeded under the judge's menacing eyes, I realized that my trial was in fact a mistake. I had never been the governor of a province, I had never been anything more than an inspector! When I was asked once again to answer the accusations, I pointed out to the judge that a great many civil servants bore the name Wang. I swore that I had never been a governor and that I had never met Tchou Heng. But you know what bureaucracy is like. The Judge ordered that I be taken to a cell until the affair could be clarified, and two whole months went by before it was discovered that they had got the wrong Wang: the Wang in question is to die tomorrow, that is, ninety days after myself. I was set free and came back here, finding myself, as I have already told you, in an infernally awkward situation.'

Ye Ning-fei listened with great interest to Wang's story and asked him a number of questions concerning the organization of justice in Hell. They discussed the story from every possible angle, and before they knew it the night was gone and the first morning light was creeping into the room. Wang Li rose to say goodbye and thanked his friend for helping him. Before leaving he added, 'It might interest you to know that this infamous Wang is in fact Wang Lu, governor of the province you are now in charge of inspecting.'

And with this he smiled and disappeared as suddenly as he had come. Ye Ning-fei slept for a short while. When he woke, his servants informed him that Wang, governor of the province, had died in his sleep during the night. Ye Ning-fei had several more documents brought to him and after consulting them discovered that a certain Tchou Heng had in fact been employed by the provincial authorities and had been fired as a result of some illegal transactions in the commerce of antiques. Some time later he had died of shame and humiliation.

That evening Ye Ning-fei went out to a little monastery near the town walls and there burnt some ritual paper money for his friend Wang Li.

Once finished his tour of inspection, he returned home, stopping on the way at Wang Li's village to pay his respects at his friend's tomb. That night Wang Li visited him again and thanked him once more for his kindness. They talked for a while and just before parting, Wang Li told him that the other Wang had been judged by the Court of Hell and found guilty. As a punishment, he had been condemned to be reborn in the form of a pig.

*Translated from an anonymous French version by Alberto Manguel.*

# A Little Place off the Edgware Road

## Graham Greene

*This story appeared in Graham Greene's first collection,* Nineteen
Stories, *published when he was very young. In the introduction he called
them 'scraps' and later confessed that at the time the short story as a
form bothered him and even bored him. Looking back on them, however,
in the preface to his* Collected Stories *published in 1972, he admits that
some had the qualities his first novels lacked: 'simplicity of language, the
sense of life as it is lived'. 'I realize', he says, 'that since the beginning
I have really been all the time a writer of short stories.'*

*'A Little Place off the Edgware Road' is a terrifying tale, and it is
that 'sense of life as it is lived' that gives the supernatural element in it
such a frightening reality. Everything in it is possible, and yet we know
that what has happened cannot be. Built into the story's pattern I found
echoes of Browning's* The Ring and the Book *and Ulysses' visit to
Hades (Odyssey, book XI) where he speaks with the ghost of Achilles;
but these findings remind me too of Cesare Pavese's comment: 'Critics
sometimes find hidden clues and new arguments in my stories. I cannot
say they are wrong and that the clues and arguments are non-existent. I
can only say I haven't put them there.'*

Craven came up past the Achilles statue in the thin summer rain.
It was only just after lighting-up time, but already the cars were
lined up all the way to the Marble Arch, and the sharp acquisitive
faces peered out ready for a good time with anything possible which
came along. Craven went bitterly by with the collar of his mackintosh tight round his throat: it was one of his bad days.

All the way up the Park he was reminded of passion, but you
needed money for love. All that a poor man could get was lust.
Love needed a good suit, a car, a flat somewhere, or a good hotel.
It needed to be wrapped in cellophane. He was aware all the time
of the stringy tie beneath the mackintosh, and the frayed sleeves:

he carried his body about with him like something he hated. (There were moments of happiness in the British Museum reading-room, but the body called him back.) He bore, as his only sentiment, the memory of ugly deeds committed on park chairs. People talked as if the body died too soon – that wasn't the trouble, to Craven, at all. The body kept alive – and through the glittering tinselly rain, on his way to a rostrum, passed a little man in a black suit carrying a banner, 'The Body shall rise again.' He remembered a dream he had three times woken trembling from: he had been alone in the huge dark cavernous burying ground of all the world. Every grave was connected to another under the ground: the globe was honey-combed for the sake of the dead, and on each occasion of dreaming he had discovered anew the horrifying fact that the body doesn't decay. There are no worms and dissolution. Under the ground the world was littered with masses of dead flesh ready to rise again with their warts and boils and eruptions. He had lain in bed and remembered – as 'tidings of great joy' – that the body after all was corrupt.

He came up into the Edgware Road walking fast – the Guardsmen were out in couples, great languid elongated beasts – the bodies like worms in their tight trousers. He hated them, and hated his hatred because he knew what it was, envy. He was aware that every one of them had a better body than himself: indigestion creased his stomach: he felt sure that his breath was foul – but who could he ask? Sometimes he secretly touched himself here and there with scent: it was one of his ugliest secrets. Why should he be asked to believe in the resurrection of this body he wanted to forget? Some-times he prayed at night (a hint of religious belief was lodged in his breast like a worm in a nut) that *his* body at any rate should never rise again.

He knew all the side streets round the Edgware Road only too well: when a mood was on, he simply walked until he tired, squin-ting at his own image in the windows of Salmon & Gluckstein and the ABCs. So he noticed at once the posters outside the disused theatre in Culpar Road. They were not unusual, for sometimes Barclays Bank Dramatic Society would hire the place for an evening – or an obscure film would be trade-shown there. The theatre had been built in 1920 by an optimist who thought the cheapness of the site would more than counter-balance its disadvantage of lying a mile outside the conventional theatre zone. But no play had ever succeeded, and it was soon left to gather rat-holes and spider-webs. The covering of the seats was never renewed, and all that ever happened to the place was the temporary false life of an amateur play or a trade show.

Craven stopped and read – there were still optimists it appeared, even in 1939, for nobody but the blindest optimist could hope to make money out of the place as 'The Home of the Silent Film'. The first season of 'primitives' was announced (a high-brow phrase): there would never be a second. Well, the seats were cheap, and it was perhaps worth a shilling to him, now that he was tired, to get in somewhere out of the rain. Craven bought a ticket and went in to the darkness of the stalls.

In the dead darkness a piano tinkled something monotonously recalling Mendelssohn: he sat down in a gangway seat, and could immediately feel the emptiness all round him. No, there would never be another season. On the screen a large woman in a kind of toga wrung her hands, then wobbled with curious jerky movements towards a couch. There she sat and stared out like a sheep-dog distractedly through her loose and black and stringy hair. Sometimes she seemed to dissolve altogether into dots and flashes and wiggly lines. A sub-title said, 'Pompilia betrayed by her beloved Augustus seeks an end to her troubles.'

Craven began at last to see – a dim waste of stalls. There were not twenty people in the place – a few couples whispering with their heads touching, and a number of lonely men like himself wearing the same uniform of the cheap mackintosh. They lay about at intervals like corpses – and again Craven's obsession returned: the tooth-ache of horror. He thought miserably – I am going mad: other people don't feel like this. Even a disused theatre reminded him of those interminable caverns where the bodies were waiting for resurrection.

'A slave to his passion Augustus calls for yet more wine.'

A gross middle-aged Teutonic actor lay on an elbow with his arm round a large woman in a shift. The Spring Song tinkled ineptly on, and the screen flickered like indigestion. Somebody felt his way through the darkness, scrabbling past Craven's knees – a small man: Craven experienced the unpleasant feeling of a large beard brushing his mouth. Then there was a long sigh as the newcomer found the next chair, and on the screen events had moved with such rapidity that Pompilia had already stabbed herself – or so Craven supposed – and lay still and buxom among her weeping slaves.

A low breathless voice sighed out close to Craven's ear: 'What's happened? Is she asleep?'

'No. Dead.'

'Murdered?' the voice asked with a keen interest.

'I don't think so. Stabbed herself.'

Nobody said 'Hush': nobody was enough interested to object to a voice: they drooped among the empty chairs in attitudes of weary inattention.

The film wasn't nearly over yet: there were children somehow to be considered: was it all going on to a second generation? But the small bearded man in the next seat seemed to be interested only in Pompilia's death. The fact that he had come in at that moment apparently fascinated him. Craven heard the word 'coincidence' twice, and he went on talking to himself about it in low out-of-breath tones. 'Absurd when you come to think of it,' and then 'no blood at all'. Craven didn't listen: he sat with his hands clasped between his knees, facing the fact as he had faced it so often before, that he was in danger of going mad. He had to pull himself up, take a holiday, see a doctor (God knew what infection moved in his veins). He became aware that his bearded neighbour had addressed him directly. 'What?' he asked impatiently, 'what did you say?'

'There would be more blood than you can imagine.'

'What are you talking about?'

When the man spoke to him, he sprayed him with damp breath. There was a little bubble in his speech like an impediment. He said, 'When you murder a man . . .'

'This was a woman,' Craven said impatiently.

'That wouldn't make any difference.'

'And it's got nothing to do with murder anyway.'

'That doesn't signify.' They seemed to have got into an absurd and meaningless wrangle in the dark.

'I know, you see,' the little bearded man said in a tone of enormous conceit.

'Know what?'

'About such things,' he said with guarded ambiguity.

Craven turned and tried to see him clearly. Was he mad? Was this a warning of what he might become – babbling incomprehensibly to strangers in cinemas? He thought, By God, no, trying to see: I'll be sane yet. I *will* be sane. He could make out nothing but a small black hump of body. The man was talking to himself again. He said, 'Talk. Such talk. They'll say it was all for fifty pounds. But that's a lie. Reasons and reasons. They always take the first reason. Never look behind. Thirty years of reasons. Such simpletons,' he added again in that tone of breathless and unbounded conceit. So this was madness. So long as he could realize that, he must be sane himself – relatively speaking. Not so sane perhaps as the seekers in the park or the Guardsmen in the Edgware Road, but saner than this. It was like a message of encouragement as the piano tinkled on.

Then again the little man turned and sprayed him. 'Killed herself, you say? But who's to know that? It's not a mere question of what hand holds the knife.' He laid a hand suddenly and confidingly on Craven's: it was damp and sticky. Craven said with horror as a possible meaning came to him: 'What are you talking about?'

'I know,' the little man said. 'A man in my position gets to know almost everything.'

'What is your position?' Craven said, feeling the sticky hand on his, trying to make up his mind whether he was being hysterical or not – after all, there were a dozen explanations – it might be treacle.

'A pretty desperate one *you'd* say.' Sometimes the voice almost died in the throat altogether. Something incomprehensible had happened on the screen – take your eyes from these early pictures for a moment and the plot had proceeded on at such a pace . . . Only the actors moved slowly and jerkily. A young woman in a nightdress seemed to be weeping in the arms of a Roman centurion: Craven hadn't seen either of them before. '*I am not afraid of death, Lucius – in your arms.*'

The little man began to titter – knowingly. He was talking to himself again. It would have been easy to ignore him altogether if it had not been for those sticky hands which he now removed: he seemed to be fumbling at the seat in front of him. His head had a habit of lolling suddenly sideways – like an idiot child's. He said distinctly and irrelevantly: 'Bayswater Tragedy.'

'What was that?' Craven said sharply. He had seen those words on a poster before he entered the park.

'What?'

'About the tragedy.'

'To think they call Cullen Mews Bayswater.' Suddenly the little man began to cough – turning his face towards Craven and coughing right at him: it was like vindictiveness. The voice said brokenly, 'Let me see. My umbrella.' He was getting up.

'You didn't have an umbrella.'

'My umbrella,' he repeated. 'My—' and seemed to lose the word altogether. He went scrabbling out past Craven's knees.

Craven let him go, but before he had reached the billowy dusty curtains of the Exit the screen went blank and bright – the film had broken, and somebody immediately turned up one dirt-choked chandelier above the circle. It shone down just enough for Craven to see the smear on his hands. This wasn't hysteria: this was a fact. He wasn't mad: he had sat next a madman who in some mews – what was the name Colon, Collin . . . Craven jumped up and made his own way out: the black curtain flapped in his mouth. But he was too late: the man had gone and there were three turnings to choose from. He chose instead a telephone-box and dialled with an odd sense for him of sanity and decision 999.

It didn't take two minutes to get the right department. They were interested and very kind. Yes, there had been a murder in a mews – Cullen Mews. A man's neck had been cut from ear to ear with a bread knife – a horrid crime. He began to tell them how he had sat next the murderer in a cinema: it couldn't be anyone else: there was blood now on his hands – and he remembered with repulsion as he spoke the damp beard. There must have been a terrible lot of blood. But the voice from the Yard interrupted him. 'Oh no,' it was saying, 'we have the murderer – no doubt of it at all. It's the body that's disappeared.'

Craven put down the receiver. He said to himself aloud, 'Why should this happen to *me*? Why to *me*?' He was back in the horror of his dream – the squalid darkening street outside was only one of the innumerable tunnels connecting grave to grave where the imperishable bodies lay. He said, 'It was a dream, a dream,' and leaning forward he saw in the mirror above the telephone his own face sprinkled by tiny drops of blood like dew from a scent-spray. He began to scream, 'I won't go mad. I won't go mad. I'm sane. I won't go mad.' Presently a little crowd began to collect, and soon a policeman came.

# From 'A School Story'

## M. R. James

*According to the Oxford English Dictionary, the word 'ghost' carries in its root the sense of 'anger' and 'evil'. The meaning has survived and even today a ghost is almost certainly something that will harm us. The reasons for this irascible temperament are not always known and do not always matter, but ghosts have been with us, taunting, frightening and tormenting us, since the first stories in the world were told.*

*The ghost story is a genre in itself and, though very ancient, English literature did not recognize it as such until the Romantic age. The best ghost stories I know of were written later, towards the turn of the century, by Sheridan Le Fanu and Montague Rhodes James, dean of King's College, Cambridge. I have no particular fondness for the straightforward ghost story: for me the simple apparition of a ghost is not enough. However, the following extract from M. R. James' Ghost Stories from an Antiquary has all the best qualities of the genre and is pleasantly terrifying.*

'Let's see. I wonder if I can remember the staple ones that I was told. First, there was the house with a room in which a series of people insisted on passing a night; and each of them in the morning was found kneeling in a corner, and had just time to say, "I've seen it," and died.'

'Wasn't that the house in Berkeley Square?'

'I dare say it was. Then there was the man who heard a noise in the passage at night, opened his door, and saw someone crawling towards him on all fours with his eye hanging out on his cheek. There was besides, let me think – Yes! the room where a man was found dead in bed with a horseshoe mark on his forehead, and the floor under the bed was covered with marks of horseshoes also; I don't know why. Also there was the lady who, on locking her bedroom door in a strange house, heard a thin voice among the bed-curtains say, "Now we're shut in for the night.

# The Signalman

## Charles Dickens

*Dickens wrote 'The Signalman' in the 1840s, after his success with* A Christmas Carol, The Chimes, *and* The Cricket on the Hearth – *the famous* Christmas Stories. *He was then the English-speaking world's most popular writer and he knew exactly how to capture the public's attention. His stories were written before his great novels –* Bleak House *was published in 1852,* Hard Times *in 1854,* Great Expectations *in 1860 – but they already show Dickens' superb control of his craft.*

*Dickens often makes use of the fantastic in his work, giving ghosts and dreams a credible coat of reality, making them similar to objects in the tangible world. 'Two things can be very much alike and yet abysmally different,' wrote George Orwell in his essay on Dickens. '[In Dickens' writings] Heaven and Hell are in the same place.'*

'Halloa! Below there!'

When he heard a voice thus calling to him, he was standing at the door of his box, with a flag in his hand, furled round its short pole. One would have thought, considering the nature of the ground, that he could not have doubted from what quarter the voice came; but instead of looking up to where I stood on the top of the steep cutting nearly over his head, he turned himself about, and looked down the Line. There was something remarkable in his manner of doing so, though I could not have said for my life what. But I know it was remarkable enough to attract my notice, even though his figure was foreshortened and shadowed, down in the deep trench, and mine was high above him, so steeped in the glow of an angry sunset that I had shaded my eyes with my hand before I saw him at all.

'Halloa! Below!'

From looking down the Line, he turned himself about again, and, raising his eyes, saw my figure high above him.

'Is there any path by which I can come down and speak to you?' He looked up at me without replying, and I looked down at him without pressing him too soon with a repetition of my idle question. Just then there came a vague vibration in the earth and air, quickly changing into a violent pulsation, and an oncoming rush that caused me to start back, as though it had force to draw me down. When such vapour as rose to my height from this rapid train had passed me, and was skimming away over the landscape, I looked down again, and saw him refurling the flag he had shown while the train went by.

I repeated my inquiry. After a pause, during which he seemed to regard me with fixed attention, he motioned with his rolled-up flag towards a point on my level, some two or three hundred yards distant. I called down to him, 'All right!' and made for that point. There, by dint of looking closely about me, I found a rough zigzag descending path notched out, which I followed.

The cutting was extremely deep, and unusually precipitate. It was made through a clammy stone, that became oozier and wetter as I went down. For these reasons, I found the way long enough to give me time to recall a singular air of reluctance or compulsion with which he had pointed out the path.

When I came down low enough upon the zigzag descent to see him again, I saw that he was standing between the rails on the way by which the train had lately passed, in an attitude as if he were waiting for me to appear. He had his left hand at his chin, and that left elbow rested on his right hand, crossed over his breast. His attitude was one of such expectation and watchfulness that I stopped a moment, wondering at it.

I resumed my downward way, and stepping out upon the level of the railroad, and drawing nearer to him, saw that he was a dark sallow man, with a dark beard and rather heavy eyebrows. His post was in as solitary and dismal a place as ever I saw. On either side, a dripping-wet wall of jagged stone, excluding all view but a strip of sky; the perspective one way only a crooked prolongation of this great dungeon; the shorter perspective in the other direction terminating in a gloomy red light, and the gloomier entrance to a black tunnel, in whose massive architecture there was a barbarous, depressing, and forbidding air. So little sunlight ever found its way to this spot, that it had an earthy, deadly smell; and so much cold wind rushed through it, that it struck chill to me, as if I had left the natural world.

Before he stirred, I was near enough to him to have touched him. Not even then removing his eyes from mine, he stepped back one step, and lifted his hand.

This was a lonesome post to occupy, I said, and it had riveted my attention when I looked down from up yonder. A visitor was a rarity, I should suppose; not an unwelcome rarity, I hoped? In me, he merely saw a man who had been shut up within narrow limits all his life, and who, being at last set free, had a newly-awakened interest in these great works. To such purpose I spoke to him; but I am far from sure of the terms I used; for, besides that I am not happy in opening any conversation, there was something in the man that daunted me.

He directed a most curious look towards the red light near the tunnel's mouth, and looked all about it, as if something were missing from it, and then looked at me.

That light was part of his charge? Was it not?

He answered in a low voice, 'Don't you know it is?'

The monstrous thought came into my mind, as I perused the fixed eyes and the saturnine face, that this was a spirit, not a man. I have speculated since, whether there may have been infection in his mind.

In my turn I stepped back. But in making the action, I detected in his eyes some latent fear of me. This put the monstrous thought to flight.

'You look at me,' I said, forcing a smile, 'as if you had a dread of me.'

'I was doubtful,' he returned, 'whether I had seen you before.'

'Where?'

He pointed to the red light he had looked at.

'There?' I said.

Intently watchful of me, he replied (but without sound), 'Yes.'

'My good fellow, what should I do there? However, be that as it may, I never was there, you may swear.'

'I think I may,' he rejoined. 'Yes; I am sure I may.'

His manner cleared, like my own. He replied to my remarks with readiness, and in well-chosen words. Had he much to do there? Yes; that was to say, he had enough responsibility to bear; but exactness and watchfulness were what was required of him, and of actual work – manual labour – he had next to none. To change that signal, to trim those lights, and to turn this iron handle now and then, was all he had to do under that head. Regarding those many long and lonely hours of which I seemed to make so much, he could only say that the routine of his life had shaped itself into that form, and he had grown used to it. He had taught himself a language down here – if only to know it by sight, and to have formed his own crude ideas of its pronunciation, could be called learning it. He had also worked at fractions and decimals, and tried a little algebra; but he was, and had been as a boy, a poor hand at figures. Was it necessary for him when on duty always to remain in that channel of damp air, and could he never rise into the sunshine from between those high stone walls? Why, that depended upon times and circumstances. Under some conditions there would be less upon the Line than under others, and the same held good as to certain hours of the day and night. In bright weather, he did choose occasions for getting a little above those lower shadows; but, being at all times liable to be called by his electric bell, and at such times listening for it with redoubled anxiety, the relief was less than I would suppose.

He took me into his box, where there was a fire, a desk for an official book in which he had to make certain entries, a telegraphic instrument with its dial, face, and needles, and the little bell of which he had spoken. On my trusting that he would excuse the remark that he had been well educated, and (I hoped I might say without offence) perhaps educated above that station, he observed that instances of slight incongruity in such wise would rarely be found wanting among large bodies of men; that he had heard it was so in workhouses, in the police force, even in that last desperate resource, the army; and that he knew it was so, more or less, in any great railway staff. He had been, when young (if I could believe it, sitting in that hut – he scarcely could), a student of natural philosophy, and had attended lectures; but he had run wild, misused his opportunities, gone down, and never risen again. He had no complaint to offer about that. He had made his bed, and he lay upon it. It was far too late to make another.

All that I have here condensed he said in a quiet manner, with his grave dark regards divided between me and the fire. He threw in the word 'Sir' from time to time, and especially when he referred to his youth – as though to request me to understand that he claimed to be nothing but what I found him. He was several times interrupted by the little bell, and had to read off messages and send replies. Once he had to stand without the door, and display a flag as a train passed, and make some verbal communication to the driver. In the discharge of his duties, I observed him to be remarkably exact and vigilant, breaking off his discourse at a syllable, and remaining silent until what he had to do was done.

In a word, I should have set this man down as one of the safest of men to be employed in that capacity, but for the circumstance that while he was speaking to me he twice broke off with a fallen colour, turned his face towards the little bell when it did *not* ring, opened the door of the hut (which was kept shut to exclude the unhealthy damp), and looked out towards the red light near the mouth of the tunnel. On both of those occasions he came back to the fire with the inexplicable air upon him which I had remarked, without being able to define, when we were so far asunder.

Said I, when I rose to leave him, 'You almost make me think that I have met with a contented man.'

(I am afraid I must acknowledge that I said it to lead him on.)

'I believe I used to be so,' he rejoined, in the low voice in which he had first spoken; 'but I am troubled, sir, I am troubled.'

He would have recalled the words if he could. He had said them, however, and I took them up quickly.

'With what? What is your trouble?'

'It is very difficult to impart, sir. It is very, very difficult to speak of. If ever you make me another visit, I will try to tell you.'

'But I expressly intend to make you another visit. Say, when shall it be?'

'I go off early in the morning, and I shall be on again at ten tomorrow night, sir.'

'I will come at eleven.'

He thanked me, and went out at the door with me. 'I'll show my white light, sir,' he said, in his peculiar low voice, 'till you have found the way up. When you have found it, don't call out! And when you are at the top, don't call out!'

His manner seemed to make the place strike colder to me, but I said no more than 'Very well.'

'And when you come down tomorrow night, don't call out! Let me ask you a parting question. What made you cry, "Halloa! Below there!" tonight?'

'Heaven knows,' said I, 'I cried something to that effect—'

'Not to that effect, sir. Those were the very words. I know them well.'

'Admit those were the very words. I said them, no doubt, because I saw you below.'

'For no other reason?'

'What other reason could I possibly have?'

'You have no feeling that they were conveyed to you in any supernatural way?'

'No.'

He wished me goodnight, and held up his light. I walked by the side of the down Line of rails (with a very disagreeable sensation of a train coming behind me) until I found the path. It was easier to mount than to descend, and I got back to my inn without any adventure.

Punctual to my appointment, I placed my foot on the first notch of the zigzag next night as the distant clocks were striking eleven. He was waiting for me at the bottom, with his white light on. 'I have not called out,' I said, when we came close together; 'may I speak now?' 'By all means, sir.' 'Goodnight, then, and here's my hand.' 'Goodnight, sir, and here's mine.' With that we walked side by side to his box, entered it, closed the door, and sat down by the fire.

'I have made up my mind, sir,' he began, bending forward as soon as we were seated, and speaking in a tone but a little above a whisper, 'that you shall not have to ask me twice what troubles me. I took you for someone else yesterday evening. That troubles me.'

'That mistake?'

'No. That someone else.'

'Who is it?'

'I don't know.'

'Like me?'

'I don't know. I never saw the face. The left arm is across the face, and the right arm is waved – violently waved. This way.'

I followed his action with my eyes, and it was the action of an arm gesticulating, with the utmost passion and vehemence, 'For God's sake, clear the way!'

'One moonlight night,' said the man, 'I was sitting here, when I heard a voice cry, "Halloa! Below there!" I started up, looked from that door, and saw this some one else standing by the red light near the tunnel, waving as I just now showed you. The voice seemed hoarse with shouting, and it cried, "Look out! Look out!" And then again, "Halloa! Below there! Look out!" I caught up my lamp, turned it on red, and ran towards the figure, calling, "What's wrong? What has happened? Where?" It stood just outside the blackness of the tunnel. I advanced so close upon it that I wondered at its keeping the sleeve across its eyes. I ran right up at it, and had my hand stretched out to pull the sleeve away when it was gone.'

'Into the tunnel?' said I.

'No. I ran on into the tunnel, five hundred yards. I stopped, and held my lamp above my head, and saw the figures of the measured distance, and saw the wet stains stealing down the walls and trickling through the arch. I ran out again faster than I had run in (for I had a mortal abhorrence of the place upon me), and I looked all round the red light with my own red light, and I went up the iron ladder to the gallery atop of it, and I came down again, and ran back here. I telegraphed both ways. "An alarm has been given. Is anything wrong?" The answer came back, both ways, "All well." '

Resisting the slow touch of a frozen finger tracing out my spine, I showed him how that this figure must be a deception of his sense of sight; and how that figures, originating in disease of the delicate nerves that minister to the functions of the eye, were known to have often troubled patients, some of whom had become conscious of the nature of their affliction, and had even proved it by experiments upon themselves. 'As to an imaginary cry,' said I, 'do but listen for a moment to the wind in this unnatural valley while we speak so low, and to the wild harp it makes of the telegraph wires.'

That was all very well, he returned, after we had sat listening for a while, and he ought to know something of the wind and the wires – he who so often passed long winter nights there, alone and watching. But he would beg to remark that he had not finished.

I asked his pardon, and he slowly added these words, touching my arm:

'Within six hours after the Appearance, the memorable accident on this line happened, and within ten hours the dead and wounded were brought along through the tunnel over the spot where the figure had stood.'

A disagreeable shudder crept over me, but I did my best against it. It was not to be denied, I rejoined, that this was a remarkable coincidence, calculated deeply to impress his mind. But it was unquestionable that remarkable coincidences did continually occur, and they must be taken into account in dealing with such a subject. Though to be sure I must admit, I added (for I thought I saw that he was going to bring the objection to bear upon me), men of common sense did not allow much for coincidences in making the ordinary calculations of life.

He again begged to remark that he had not finished.

I again begged his pardon for being betrayed into interruptions.

'This,' he said, again laying his hand upon my arm, and glancing over his shoulder with hollow eyes, 'was just a year ago. Six or seven months passed, and I had recovered from the surprise and shock, when one morning, as the day was breaking, I, standing at the door, looked towards the red light, and saw the spectre again.' He stopped, with a fixed look at me.

'Did it cry out?'

'No. It was silent.'

'Did it wave its arm?'

'No. It leaned against the shaft of the light with both hands before the face. Like this.'

Once more I followed his actions with my eyes. It was an action of mourning. I have seen such an attitude on stone figures on tombs.

'Did you go up to it?'

'I came in and sat down, partly to collect my thoughts, partly because it had turned me faint. When I went to the door again, daylight was above me, and the ghost was gone.'

'But nothing followed? Nothing came of this?'

He touched me on the arm with his forefinger twice or thrice, giving a ghastly nod each time:

'That very day, as a train came out of the tunnel, I noticed, at a carriage window on my side, what looked like a confusion of hands and heads, and something waved. I saw it just in time to signal the drive, Stop! He shut off, and put his brake on, but the train drifted past here a hundred and fifty yards or more. I ran after it, and, as I went along, heard terrible screams and cries. A beautiful young lady had died instantaneously in one of the compartments, and was brought in here, and laid down on this floor between us.'

Involuntarily I pushed my chair back, as I looked from the boards at which he pointed to himself.

'True, sir. True. Precisely as it happened, so I tell it you.'

I could think of nothing to say, to any purpose, and my mouth was very dry. The wind and the wires took up the story with a long lamenting wail.

He resumed, 'Now, sir, mark this, and judge how my mind is troubled. The spectre came back a week ago. Ever since, it has been there, now and again, by fits and starts.'

'At the light?'

'At the Danger-light.'

'What does it seem to do?'

He repeated, if possible with increased passion and vehemence, that former gesticulation of 'For God's sake, clear the way!'

Then he went on, 'I have no peace or rest for it. It calls to me, for many minutes together, in an agonized manner, "Below there! Look out! Look out!" It stands waving to me. It rings my little bell—'

I caught at that. 'Did it ring your bell yesterday evening when I was here, and you went to the door?'

'Twice.'

'Why, see,' said I, 'how your imagination misleads you. My eyes were on the bell, and my ears were open to the bell, and if I am a living man, it did *not* ring at those times. No, nor at any other time, except when it was rung in the natural course of physical things by the station communicating with you.'

He shook his head. 'I have never made a mistake as to that yet, sir. I have never confused the spectre's ring with the man's. The ghost's ring is a strange vibration in the bell that it derives from nothing else, and I have not asserted that the bell stirs to the eye. I don't wonder that you failed to hear it. But *I* heard it.'

'And did the spectre seem to be there when you looked out?'

'It *was* there.'

'Both times?'

He repeated firmly: 'Both times.'

'Will you come to the door with me, and look for it now?'

He bit his under lip as though he were somewhat unwilling, but arose. I opened the door, and stood on the step, while he stood in the doorway. There was the Danger-light. There was the dismal mouth of the tunnel. There were the high, wet stone walls of the cutting. There were the stars above them.

'Do you see it?' I asked him, taking particular note of his face. His eyes were prominent and strained, but not very much more so, perhaps, than my own had been when I had directed them earnestly towards the same spot.

'No,' he answered. 'It is not there.'

'Agreed,' said I.

We went in again, shut the door, and resumed our seats. I was thinking how best to improve this advantage, if it might be called one, when he took up the conversation in such a matter-of-course way, so assuming that there could be no serious question of fact between us, that I felt myself placed in the weakest of positions.

'By this time you will fully understand, sir,' he said, 'that what troubles me so dreadfully is the question: What does the spectre mean?'

I was not sure, I told him, that I did fully understand.

'What is its warning against?' he said, ruminating, with his eyes on the fire, and only by times turning them on me. 'What is the danger? Where is the danger? There is danger overhanging somewhere on the Line. Some dreadful calamity will happen. It is not to be doubted this third time, after what has gone before. But surely this is a cruel haunting of *me*. What can I do?'

He pulled out his handkerchief, and wiped the drops from his heated forehead.

'If I telegraph Danger on either side of me, or on both, I can give no reason for it,' he went on, wiping the palms of his hands. 'I should get into trouble and do no good. They would think I was mad. This is the way it would work – Message: "Danger! Take care!" Answer: "What Danger? Where?" Message: "Don't know. But for God's sake, take care!" They would displace me. What else could they do?'

His pain of mind was most pitiable to see. It was the mental torture of a conscientious man, oppressed beyond endurance by an unintelligible responsibility involving life.

'When it first stood under the Danger-light,' he went on, putting his dark hair back from his head, and drawing his hands outward across and across his temples in an extremity of feverish distress, 'why not tell me where that accident was to happen – if it must happen? Why not tell me how it could be averted – if it could have been averted? When on its second coming it hid its face, why not tell me, instead, "She is going to die. Let them keep her at home"? If it came, on those two occasions, only to show me that its warnings were true, and so to prepare me for the third, why not warn me plainly now? And I, Lord help me! A mere poor signalman on this solitary station! Why not go to somebody with credit to be believed, and power to act?'

When I saw him in this state, I saw that for the poor man's sake, as well as for the public safety, what I had to do for the time was to compose his mind. Therefore, setting aside all question of reality or unreality between us, I represented to him that whoever thoroughly discharged his duty must do well, and that at least it was his comfort that he understood his duty, though he did not understand these confounding Appearances. In this effort I succeeded far better than in the attempt to reason him out of his conviction. He became calm; the occupations incidental to his post as the night advanced began to make larger demands on his attention: and I left him at two in the morning. I had offered to stay through the night, but he would not hear of it.

That I more than once looked back at the red light as I ascended the pathway, that I did not like the red light, and that I should have slept but poorly if my bed had been under it, I see no reason to conceal. Nor did I like the two sequences of the accident and the dead girl. I see no reason to conceal that either.

But what ran most in my thoughts was the consideration how ought I to act, having become the recipient of this disclosure? I had proved the man to be intelligent, vigilant, painstaking, and exact; but how long might he remain so, in his state of mind? Though in a subordinate position, still he held a most important trust, and would I (for instance) like to stake my own life on the chances of his continuing to execute it with precision?

Unable to overcome a feeling that there would be something treacherous in my communicating what he had told me to his superiors in the Company, without first being plain with himself and proposing a middle course to him, I ultimately resolved to offer to accompany him (otherwise keeping his secret for the present) to the wisest medical practitioner we could hear of in those parts, and to take his opinion. A change in his time of duty would come round next night, he had apprised me, and he would be off an hour or two after sunrise, and on again soon after sunset. I had appointed to return accordingly.

Next evening was a lovely evening, and I walked out early to enjoy it. The sun was not yet quite down when I traversed the fieldpath near the top of the deep cutting. I would extend my walk for an hour, I said to myself, half an hour on and half an hour back, and it would then be time to go to my signalman's box.

Before pursuing my stroll, I stepped to the brink, and mechanically looked down, from the point from which I had first seen him. I cannot describe the thrill that seized upon me, when, close at the mouth of the tunnel, I saw the appearance of a man, with his left sleeve across his eyes, passionately waving his right arm.

The nameless horror that oppressed me passed in a moment, for in a moment I saw that this appearance of a man was a man indeed, and that there was a little group of other men standing at a short distance, to whom he seemed to be rehearsing the gesture he made. The Danger-light was not yet lighted. Against its shaft a little low hut entirely new to me, had been made of some wooden supports and tarpaulin. It looked no bigger than a bed.

With an irresistible sense that something was wrong – with a flashing self-reproachful fear that fatal mischief had come of my leaving the man there, and causing no one to be sent to overlook or correct what he did – I descended the notched path with all the speed I could make.

'What is the matter?' I asked the men.

'Signalman killed this morning, sir.'

'Not the man belonging to that box?'

'Yes, sir.'

'Not the man I know?'

'You will recognize him, sir, if you knew him,' said the man who spoke for the others, solemnly uncovering his own head, and raising an end of the tarpaulin, 'for his face is quite composed.'

'Oh, how did this happen, how did this happen?' I asked, turning from one to another as the hut closed in again.

'He was cut down by an engine, sir. No man in England knew his work better. But somehow he was not clear of the outer rail. It was just at broad day. He had struck the light, and had the lamp in his hand. As the engine came out of the tunnel, his back was towards her, and she cut him down. That man drove her, and was showing how it happened. Show the gentleman, Tom.'

The man who wore a rough dark dress, stepped back to his former place at the mouth of the tunnel.

'Coming round the curve in the tunnel, sir,' he said, 'I saw him at the end, like as if I saw him down a perspective-glass. There was no time to check speed, and I knew him to be very careful. As he didn't seem to take heed of the whistle, I shut it off when we were running down upon him, and called to him as loud as I could call.'

'What did you say?'

'I said, "Below there! Look out! Look out! For God's sake, clear the way!"'

I started.

'Ah! It was a dreadful time, sir. I never left off calling to him. I put this arm before my eyes not to see, and I waved this arm to the last; but it was no use.'

Without prolonging the narrative to dwell on any one of its curious circumstances more than on any other, I may, in closing it, point out the coincidence that the warning of the engine-driver included, not only the words which the unfortunate signalman had repeated to me as haunting him, but also the words which I myself – not he – had attached, and that only in my own mind, to the gesticulation he had imitated.

# The Tall Woman

## Pedro Antonio de Alarcón

*A contemporary of Tolstoy, Nietzsche and Dante Gabriel Rossetti, Pedro Antonio de Alárcón had none of their literary qualities, and if Manuel de Falla had not transformed his novella* The Three-Cornered Hat *into a piece of matinée music the world could easily have done without the knowledge of Alarcón's existence. But even a bad writer can sometimes be a good craftsman and produce, almost as if by magic, a work of genius. In Alarcón's case the muse visited him twice: in 1852, when he wrote 'The Friend of Death', a haunting and powerful short story; and in 1881, when he wrote 'The Tall Woman', ten years before his death.*

# I

'What do we know, my friends? What do we know?' exclaimed Gabriel, the distinguished mining engineer, sitting down under a pine tree near a fountain, on the slope of Guadarrama, about six miles from the Escorial Palace and just on the boundary line between the provinces of Madrid and Segovia. I know the place, the fountain, and the pine tree very well. I can see them still, but I cannot remember the name.

'Let's all sit down and rest here,' said Gabriel. 'We've agreed to enjoy the lovely weather as best we can in this charming place, famous for the tonic qualities of this sparkling fountain and for the picnics which have taken place here, where great scientists have come to observe Nature and to find an appetite from time to time. Sit down and I'll tell you a true story to bear out my theory. You call me a materialist, but I still maintain that in this world in which we live strange things happen – things so strange that no reason can account for them, nor can science or philosophy give any explanation of such things. Surely there are more mysteries in heaven and on earth than all our philosophy can account for – to alter slightly the words of Hamlet.'

Gabriel was addressing five friends of various ages, none of them very young and only one elderly. Three of them, like him, were mining engineers, the fourth was an artist, and the fifth something of a writer. All of us had come up with Gabriel, who was the youngest, on hired mules from the village of San Lorenzo, to spend the day in hunting for specimens in the lovely woods of Peguerinos, gathering interesting forest plants under the pine trees, catching butterflies in gauze nets, finding rare beetles under the bark of the decayed trees, and in all these occupations giving a fair amount of attention to the well-filled hamper of cold provisions and the skin of wine, to the cost of which all had contributed in equal shares.

This was in the middle of the hot summer of 1875. I am not sure if it was the festival of Santiago or that of San Luis, but it was a holiday of some sort – I think San Luis. In any case, the day was very hot, and the shade of the pine wood and murmur of the fountain were delicious after climbing the mountainside. Up there, mind, heart, body, and especially appetite were refreshed by the pure air and the stillness, so sweet after the busy life of the plains which we had left far below us.

The six friends sat in the shade of the pine trees, and Gabriel continued:

'You may call me a visionary if you like, but it has been my fortune or misfortune in life that I have always been regarded as a materialist, a man of modern thought, not believing in things unseen. In fact, a positivist. Well, I may be so, but my positivism includes an acknowledgment of the mysterious influences of Nature – all the strange and inexplicable facts which *are* facts because they happen; all the emotions of the mind which are inseparable from the life of every reasoning creature. I believe in all these things because they are material and natural. They cannot be explained, but still they happen. Now, as to other things which are supernatural, or extra-natural – just listen, and then judge for yourselves. I was not the hero of the strange occurrence which I'm going to relate to you – but listen, and then tell me what explanation you can give me – natural, physical, scientific, whatever you think will best explain the case, if explanation is at all possible.'

# II

'Perhaps you may have heard of an engineer of Public Works named Telesforo de Ruiz. He died in 1860.'

'No, I never heard of him.'

'I have.'

'So have I. He was an Andalusian, very dark and handsome. He was engaged to be married to the daughter of the Marquis of Moreda, and he died of gastric fever.'

'Yes, that he was,' replied Gabriel. 'Well, until about six months before he died, my friend Telesforo was a brilliant young man – as every one said. Tall, strong, handsome, talented and with a first-class diploma from the School of Mines, and excellent prospects, he was very much sought after in the way of his profession by both public and private enterprises, and he was just as much sought after in private life by the fair sex, marriageable or unhappily married, and even by some charming widows anxious to tempt Providence again. One of these was a well-known conquest of his, who would gladly have accompanied my friend to the altar. However, she does not enter into this story, and indeed Telesforo merely amused himself in her case by flirting with her. If she did make herself a bit cheap to him . . . Well, he was all the time deeply and seriously in love with the girl to whom he was engaged, poor Joaquina de Moreda, and so the poor widow merely filled a temporary gap—'

'Now, now, Don Gabriel! No scandal allowed.'

'I am not going to talk scandal. Those of you who knew the young couple will remember that poor Joaquina died suddenly when taking the waters at Santa Agueda at the end of the summer of 1859. I was in Pau when the sad news came, and I was very much affected because of my friendship for Telesforo. I had only met the girl once, at the house of her aunt, General Lopez's widow, and her extreme pallor, almost a bluish tint, struck me as an indication of weak health, such as one sees in sufferers from aneurism. But she was very graceful, refined, and gentle looking, and in addition to her personal charms she was to inherit her father's title, as she was the only child, and she would also have a good deal of money. When I heard of her death I knew that her sweetheart would be inconsolable, and when I got back to Madrid, about three weeks later, I went to see him early one morning. He had a charming flat in the Calle del Lobo, near the Plaza San Jerónimo. He lived there and had his office under the same roof.

'He looked very sad, but he was calm and evidently master of his grief, as he sat working with his assistants at some plan of a railway. He was dressed in deep mourning, and when I entered he embraced me in silence then turned to give some instructions to one of his staff respecting the work in hand. I waited until, taking my arm, he led me to his private sitting-room at the other end of the house, saying as we went:

' "I'm so glad you have come. I cannot tell you how much I have missed you in my present state of mind. Something very strange and unaccountable has happened to me, and I want to tell you about it, for only a friend who knows me as you do will be able to judge if I am mad or a fool. I urgently need a sane, calm opinion, as I know yours will be.

' "Sit down here," he went on when we had reached the sitting-room, "and don't be afraid that I'm going to weary you by describing my grief, which can only end with my life. You have not had much personal experience of sorrow or human suffering, but you can imagine what I suffer and must always suffer. I do not seek or wish for consolation now or later on, or ever in all time. That subject is ended now. What I want to tell you is something so strange, so terrible, that I must speak of it to some one of calm judgement, some one who will listen and advise me. The whole adventure is like an awful seal set on my present misery, on the agony of my life, and it tortures me to the point of despair. It is all a most frightful mystery, and I think it will alarm you too."

' "Tell me," I replied, feeling vaguely anxious and more than half wishing that I had not come to see my unhappy friend. His expression of terror struck a chill to my heart and made me fear for his reason.

' "Listen then," said he, wiping the perspiration from his forehead.

# III

' "I do not know if it is a mental twist which I have always had, or if it is the effect of some of those silly tales which old nurses use to frighten children into quiet and obedience, but ever since I was very young nothing has caused me so much fright and horror as the sight, or even the thought, of a woman alone out of doors at a late hour of the night.

' "You can testify that I have never been a coward. Like every other man of the world, I have always been ready to fight a duel if it became necessary to do so, and not very long after I had left the School of Mines I was obliged to quell a dangerous revolt among my workmen on my first important piece of work with blows and even shots, so that singlehanded I reduced them to obedience. All my life, in Jaén, in Madrid, and elsewhere, I was accustomed to go about the streets at any hour of the night, alone and unarmed, and if by chance I did meet any late wanderers of suspicious appearance, I knew that they were merely thieves or human prowlers in search of prey, and I simply avoided them or let them pass without notice. But if the solitary form was that of a woman, walking or standing, then, if I was alone or there was no one else in sight, I was in the most abject state of terror possible to imagine. You may laugh if you like, but my agony of mind was dreadful; I shivered from head to foot, thought of ghosts or lost souls, apparitions from the other world, wraiths of persons still alive; in fact, of all the terrible superstitious ideas which have ever been invented to torture the credulous, and which at any other time or in any other circumstances would have only provoked my ridicule. Then I would hasten my steps or turn back; I would make all kinds of detours to avoid meeting the lonely figure, and overcome by repulsion and horror, I would rush back to my home, never stopping until I was safe within its doors.

' "Once in the shelter of my own house, I could laugh at my silly fears, and console myself by reflecting that at any rate no one of my acquaintance knew of such folly on my part. I would feel sure then that as I did not believe in fairies or witches or apparitions of any sort there was no need to have been frightened by the sight of the poor solitary creature, whom want, or vice, or some other cruel spur had driven from shelter on such a night and at such an hour. I felt that I should have offered her assistance if she was in need of it, or alms if I had waited for her to ask me for them. But all this solid reasoning did not prevent my acting in just the same way when the next solitary female form was sighted. When I was twenty-five years of age, I met many such lonely nocturnal wanderers, and though I had always fled from them in the same way, I never had the slightest reason to think that they intended me any harm or were able to injure me in any way, or had I ever any notable or disagreeable adventure with any one I met in the street late at night. But my fear was indomitable, only vanishing when I was safe at home and could laugh at or scold myself for my lack of common sense. If I were not alone or if there were other people in the street, the case was different, for I did not care then. The incident attracted no one's notice, and was soon forgotten, as children forget their terrors of the dark when they have companions by their side.

' "Now, this brings me to one night about three years ago. I have only too good a reason to remember the exact date. It was the 16th of November, at three o'clock in the morning. At that time I was living in a little flat in the Calle de los Jardines, near the Calle de la Montera. The night was terribly cold and wet, and I was alone. You will ask me what I was doing out of doors at that hour on a November morning. Well, you will be surprised to hear that I had just left a sort of gambling saloon, unknown as such to the police, but where many people had already been ruined. I had been induced to go there the night before for the first and last time. Gambling was never a vice of mine, and the inducement held out to me by the friend who took me there, and who was a bit of a scamp, was that I would see something of the smart night life of the capital, and make the acquaintance of some interesting members of Bohemian society and ultra-fashionable actresses and other stars of the *demi-monde*, who dropped in to win or lose a few crowns at roulette.

' "Well, about midnight the fun waxed furious. People of all classes dropped in, apparently after the theatre or late receptions; play grew high, and I, like all novices, threw prudence to the winds, and staked my all, winning at first and then losing steadily, until at last, after being severely handled by cruel Fortune, I came away without a single coin in my pockets, and with debts to my friend and others, the amounts of which I had jotted down without having any very clear idea of what they amounted to but feeling certain that it was utterly out of my power ever to discharge them.

' "I was going home, half dead with weariness, annoyance and disgust at my own folly, freezing with cold, and also very hungry. I did not know what to do, except to write to my poor father, who was very ill, asking him to send me money, and that would not only grieve but surprise him, for he believed that I was doing well in my profession and already in comfortable circumstances. Overcome by these sad thoughts, I was just crossing the corner of the Calle de los Peligros to reach my own street, and was about to pass a newly-erected house at the corner, when on looking up, I became aware that in the doorway, erect and still as a pine tree, stood a very tall, large woman, about sixty years of age, whose bold, malignant, and lashless eyes were fixed on me like two daggers, while her huge toothless mouth grinned at me horribly.

' "The terror, or rather, the mad panic, which seized on me then surpassed all I have ever experienced previously. I stood staring at this horrible figure, and each line of her form, each smallest detail of her dress, were indelibly branded in my recollection. The lamp at the street corner shone steadily on the scene, and the apparition, or whatever it might be, and I were the only occupants of the entire street. I forgot my ruined position, I forgot my folly of that night, there was only room in my brain for one thought, if thought it could be called – a crazy terror of the woman who seemed to fill the whole doorway beside me.

' "Oh, don't be alarmed, my friend. I was not really mad; I am not mad now. But what will I be if some consolation is not found for me, some solution to my distress? It is for that reason that I have asked you to listen to me and to bear with me.

' "The first surprising thing about this woman, as I must call her, was her great height and the breadth of her bony shoulders; next the size and roundness of her enormous owl-like eyes, the size of her nose, and the hideous gap which served her as a mouth, made still more hideous by the malignant grin which would have disfigured the fairest mouth in existence, and finally, the strange coquetry of her dress; the bright-coloured handkerchief which was draped over her ugly forehead and fastened beneath the chin, and a very small fan which she held open in her hand, and which she flirted in an affectation of modesty before her face and figure.

' "Nothing could be more grotesque or ridiculous than the sight of that tiny fan in those enormous hands, like a sceptre of weakness for a giantess so old, so bony, so hideous. The same effect was produced by the gay cotton handkerchief in contrast to the huge deformed nose, and the coarse face which made me ask myself for a moment if this were not a man in woman's dress. But no. The expression was that of a wicked woman, of a witch, of a sorceress, of one of the Fates, of a Fury.

' "I cannot express my exact thought, but in that instant I felt that this was the cause and the justification of all the unreasonable fears which had overcome me when I had seen a woman, however innocent looking, alone in the street at night. It would seem that, from my very birth, I had foreseen the horror of this encounter, and that I feared it by instinct, as all living creatures are given the instinct to recognize their natural enemies, even by their approach, before ever they have received any injury from them.

' "When I saw now, for the first time, this sphinx of my whole life, I did not run away – less through shame or manly pride than because I dreaded unreasoningly that my very fear would reveal to the creature that it was I, her victim, who fled, and would give her wings to pursue me, to seize me, to . . . I could not tell what I feared. Panic is a thing of itself, and has no form of thought even to shape the thing it fears or to put into words its own madness.

' "The house where I lived was at the extreme end of the street, which, as you know, is very long and narrow. Not another soul was to be seen. I was alone, utterly alone, with that awful statue-like figure, which might annihilate me with a word. How was I to get away, to get home? I looked along to where I saw the broad well-lighted Calle de la Montera, where policemen and watchmen are on the beat at all times.

' "Finally, I don't remember how, I resolved to do something to escape from the horrible obsession which dominated me – not to take flight, but to creep by degrees down the street, even at the cost of years of life and health, and thus, little by little, to get nearer and nearer to my home, exerting myself to the utmost not to fall fainting on the ground before I reached it.

' "I had moved slowly about twenty steps along the street towards my house when all at once a new spasm of terror seized me. I did not dare stop, I could not look round, but what if my enemy were following me! Dare I look round? I stopped and tried to reason calmly.

' " 'One thing or another must happen,' I thought quickly. 'Either I have good cause for this fear, or else it is sheer madness. In the first case, this terrible witch is following me, she will overtake me, and nothing in the whole world can save me. But if this is only a craze, a mania, an access of folly, a groundless panic, then let me face it out, convince myself of its unreality, and thus be cured once for all, and never have to suffer in this way again. I shall feel certain of my silly conduct if I find that this poor old woman is still standing in the doorway sheltering from cold, or waiting for the door to be opened. Then I shall go home, and never again will I permit such groundless fears to torment me.'

' "Having almost calmed myself, I stood still and turned my head.

' "Oh, Gabriel, Gabriel, how shall I convey my feelings to you at what I saw? The tall woman had followed me with soundless footsteps, she was towering over me, almost touching me with her fan, her head bent so that it nearly touched my shoulder.

' "Why? Ah, why, indeed? Was she a pickpocket? Was it a man in disguise? Or was it only a spiteful old woman who saw that I was frightened and wanted to terrify me more? Was it the spectral reflection of my own cowardice? Was it the sum total of all the deceptions and shortcomings of our human nature?

' "To tell you all the ideas which ran through my mind at that moment would be impossible, I managed to scream, which roused me from my stupor as from a nightmare, and I ran like a terrified child of four years old and did not stop until I was in the Calle de la Montera.

' "Once there, all my fear fell away from me. And yet the Calle de la Montera was deserted too. I looked all along the Calle de los Jardines, the whole of which I could see, and which was sufficiently well lighted by its three lamp-posts and by the reflection from the Calle de los Peligros. It would not be possible for the tall woman to hide if she had gone in that direction, but I give you my word there was not a cat or the shadow of a mouse to be seen in the whole street, not to speak of a giantess like my tormentor.

' " 'She has gone into some other doorway,' I thought. 'But she will not be able to get away without my seeing her if she moves while the lamps are lit.'

' "Just then I saw a night-watchman coming along the Calle del Caballero de Gracia, and I shouted to him without moving from where I stood. To explain my call and put him on the alert, I told him that there was a man disguised as a woman in the Calle de los Jardines, that he had gone into that street by the Calle de los Peligros, and must have gone off towards the Calle de la Aduana; that I would remain where I was if he would go to the other end of the street, and that in that way he would not be able to escape. It would be well for us both to capture him, I said, for he must be a robber or worse to go about disguised at that hour.

' "The night-watchman did as I advised. He went down to the Calle de la Aduana, and when I saw his lantern gleam at the other end of the Calle de los Jardines I went along the other side and down the next street to meet him.

' "Neither of us had seen anything in the shape of a human being, although both of us had looked into the doorway of every house.

' " 'He must have gone into some house,' said the watchman.

' " 'I expect so,' I replied, opening my own door, with the firm determination to change to another street next day.

' "I ascended the stairs to my flat on the third floor, and opened the outer door with my latch-key. I never made my good servant José sit up for me.

' "However, this time, he was waiting for me. My troubles were not over yet.

' " 'Is there anything wrong?' I asked him in surprise.

' "He seemed rather agitated.

' " 'Sir,' he said, 'Captain Falcón was here from eleven o'clock until half-past two. He said he would come back after daylight, and that if you came back you were to wait up for him, because he must see you.'

' "Those words filled me with new terrors. I felt as if my own death were at hand. Certainly something very serious was on foot. My dear old father had been very ill for a long time, and as he had seemed to be much worse lately, I had written to my brothers in Jaén, where all my family lived, that if matters became very serious they were to telegraph to my friend, Captain Falcón, who would let me know at once what had happened. I had no doubt now that my father was dead.

' "I sat in an armchair, waiting for the dawn and my friend who was to be the bearer of sad news. How can I tell now what I suffered in those long hours of waiting? Three things, all of terribly painful association, kept repeating themselves in my mind, as being inextricably connected with one another, standing apart from the rest of the world in a monstrous and terrifying group: my ruin at play, the meeting with the tall woman, and the death of my revered father.

' "As six o'clock struck, Captain Falcón entered my sitting-room, and looked at me in silence. I flung myself into his arms in a hysterical outburst, and he said, essaying to calm my grief:

' " "Weep, my friend. You have indeed cause to weep, for such a loss as this can only come once in a lifetime.' " ' "

# IV

'My friend Telesforo,' continued Gabriel, after he had drained another glass of wine, 'paused when he reached this point of his story. After a silence of some minutes he went on:

' "If this were all I had to tell you, you might not find anything strange or supernatural in it, and you might tell me what others have told me – men of much common sense have said that everyone with a lively and ardent imagination has his or her pet subject of unreasoning terror; that mine was the idea of solitary female night-walkers, and that the old woman in the Calle de los Jardines was only some poor old creature who tried to ask me for alms when she was without home or food, and whom I had alarmed by my own strange demeanour; that at the worst, she could only be an associate of thieves or other bad characters, waiting in a quiet street for her companions, and fearful of their being discovered by the night-watchman.

' "I, too, wished to believe this, and after hearing it constantly repeated I did almost come to believe it at the end of some months. Still I would have given years of my life for the certainty of never again seeing the tall woman! And now I would give everything I have just to be able to see her once more!"

' "But why?"

' "Just to be able to strangle her!"

' "I don't understand."

' "You will understand when I tell you that I met her again three weeks ago, a few hours before I received the fatal news of the death of my poor Joaquina."

' "Well, tell me about it."

' "There is not much more to tell. It was about five o'clock in the morning, and I had been to an entertainment where I had not been much entertained. I had the unpleasant task of breaking the news of my approaching marriage to a lady with whom I had had a very pronounced flirtation, and who took the news very ill. I had to stand many reproaches and even tears when I explained that the position was inevitable; my resolution was taken, and my wedding-day fixed. And at that moment, though I did not know it, they were burying my promised wife in Santa Agueda.

' "It was not yet daylight, but there was that faint light in the sky which shows that night is weakening. The street lamps had been extinguished and the watchmen had retired when, as I was passing by the Plaza de las Cortes to get to my flat in the Calle del Lobo, at the corner of the Calle de Santa Ana who should cross my path but the terrible woman whom I had seen in the Calle de los Jardines.

' "She did not look at me, and I thought she had not seen me. She wore the same dress, even carried the same little fan as when I had seen her three years ago. And all my previous terror was as nothing in comparison with what took possession of me now. I walked quickly down the Calle del Prado after she had passed, but I did not take my eyes off her to make sure that she did not turn her head; and when I reached the other part of the Calle del Lobo I breathed hard as if I had just breasted an impetuous stream, and my fear giving way to satisfaction I pressed on, thinking that I had narrowly but completely escaped the notice of the hateful witch, and that now I was free from her baleful proximity.

' "But just as I was about to enter my house a new terror stirred in me. Surely she was too cunning to allow me to escape like this, and she was only feigning not to notice me in order to be able to track me with more certainty down the dark and silent street and thus find where I lived.

' "I stopped and looked round. There she was just behind me, her dress almost touching me, her wicked eyes fixed on me, her hideous mouth distended in a spiteful grin of triumph, as she fanned herself with an air of languor, as though ridiculing my childish terror.

' "That fear gave place at once to the most senseless fury, to the rage of desperation, and I flung myself on the vile creature, seized her by the arms and dashed her against the wall. I held her back by the throat, and felt her face, her breast, the straggling locks of her grey hair until I was convinced that she was a human being, and a woman.

' "She had uttered a hoarse cry of mingled pain and rage, and pretended to weep, but I felt that it was only pretense; then fixing her hyena eyes on me, she said:

' " 'Why do you treat me like this?'

' "My anger died away and my fear returned.

' " 'Do you remember,' I said, 'that you have seen me elsewhere?'

' " 'Indeed I do,' she replied sardonically. 'The night of San Eugenio, about three o'clock, in the Calle de los Jardines.'

' "I shivered involuntarily, but I still kept hold of her.

' " 'Who are you?' I asked. 'Why do you run after me like this? What do you want with me?'

' " 'I am only a poor weak woman,' she said with a diabolical grin. 'You hate and fear me without cause or reason. If not, will you please tell me why you were so overcome with fear the first time you saw me?'

' " 'Because I have hated you ever since I was born,' I cried involuntarily. 'Because you are the evil spirit of my life!'

' " 'So you have known me for a long time past? Well, my son, I have known you too.'

' " 'You have known me? Since when?'

' " 'Since before you were born. And when I saw you pass close to me three years ago, I said to myself: "Here he is at last!" '

' " 'But what am I to you? What are you to me?'

' " 'I am Hell,' she said, spitting in my face. And with that she suddenly slipped from my grasp, caught up her skirts, and ran from my sight without making the least noise as she disappeared.

' "It would have been madness to try to overtake her. And it was now broad daylight and a good many people were passing in the streets, both in San Jerónimo Square and in the Calle del Prado. The tall woman continued to run, or as it seemed to fly, until she reachèd the Calle de las Huertas, now gleaming in the morning sun. She stopped there and looked back at me, waving her fan at me in a threatening manner, holding it closed like a dagger, and finally she disappeared round the corner of the last street.

' "No, just wait a moment, Gabriel. Do not give me your opinion yet, for I have not quite finished my strange tale, in which my heart and my life are equally involved. Listen to me for a few minutes longer!

' "When I reached home, whom do you think I found awaiting me but Colonel Falcón (as he is now). He had come to bring me the terrible news that my love, my darling Joaquina, all my hope of happiness and good fortune on this earth, had died the day before in Santa Agueda! Her unhappy father had telegraphed to Falcón, knowing what an old friend of ours he was, asking him to break the news to me . . . to me, who had guessed that a great misfortune was in store for me as soon as ever I set eyes on the curse of my life. Now you know why I want to kill the enemy of my happiness,

my born foe, that wicked old sorceress who embodies the cruelty
of my destiny.

'  "But why do I talk like this? Is she really a woman? Is she a
human being at all? Why did the presentiment of her existence
weigh on me ever since I was born? Why did she *recognize* me when
she saw me first? Why have I only seen her when some great
misfortune has happened to me? What or who is she?" '

## V

'Well, my friends, I leave you to imagine what remarks I made and
what arguments I used in the effort to calm Telesforo, for all I said
was what you are all thinking now and preparing to tell me, to
prove to me that there is nothing superhuman or supernatural in
my story. You will tell me more than that . . . you will say that my
poor friend was not in his right mind; that he must have been always
a little mad, for he evidently suffered from the moral infirmity which
specialists call groundless panic or, as the case may be, intermittent
delirium; that even admitting that all that he said about the strange
woman was quite true, still it was only a case of a singular series of
chance coincidences of dates and events; and that perhaps the poor
old woman was mad too, and was excited by his mania. She might
have been an old rat-catcher abroad at her nightly work, or a beggar,
or a procuress – as Telesforo said to himself in an interval of lucidity
and common sense.

'Well, you will see that I was wrong in thinking that, as you are
wrong now. The only person who was not wrong was Telesforo.
Ah! it is much easier to talk of madness than to find an explanation
for many things which happen on this earth.'

## VI

'A few days after this conversation with Telesforo I was obliged to
go to the province of Albacete in my capacity of mining engineer;
and not many weeks later I heard from a contractor of public works
that my poor friend had been attacked by a very severe gastric fever
and jaundice. He was green in hue, unable to move from his chair,
and he could not work, nor would he see any one. His grief and
melancholy were pitiable, and the doctors despaired of his recovery.
Then I knew why he had not answered my letters. I had to resort

to Colonel Falcón for news, and reports continued ever more and more depressing.

'After five months of absence, I returned to Madrid on the very day when the news of the battle of Tetuán arrived. I remember it as if it were yesterday. That evening I bought the *Correspondencia de España* to see the news, and the first thing my eye lighted on was the obituary notice of my poor friend Telesforo, and the invitation to all his friends to attend his funeral on the following day.

'You will readily understand that I would not willingly fail to give him this last tribute. I had a place in one of the carriages nearest to the hearse, and when we alighted in the cemetery of San Luis I noticed a woman of the poorer class, old and very tall, who laughed in a most unseemly manner when the hearse arrived, and who then advanced with an air of triumph towards the pall-bearers pointing out to them with a very small fan the way they were to take to reach the open grave, which was to be my friend's last resting-place.

'At the first glance I recognized, with grief and fear, that this woman corresponded to the description given by Telesforo of his implacable enemy. She was just what he had described, with her enormous nose, her infernal eyes, her hideous mouth, the bright printed cotton handkerchief over her head, and the tiny fan, which in her hands seemed to be the sceptre of profanity and inhuman mockery.

'She perceived at once that I was looking at her, and she fixed her eyes on me in a peculiar way, as if recognizing me while she ascertained that I recognized her, as if she knew that my dead friend had told me all about the scenes in the Calle de los Jardines and the Calle del Lobo, as if defying me, as if declaring that I had inherited the hatred she had borne my unfortunate friend.

'I confess that the fear which overcame me was greater than my surprise at this new coincidence or disaster. It seemed certain that some mysterious connection had existed in some supernatural way between the appalling old woman and Telesforo before this life; but at that moment I saw that my own life, my own good fortune, my own soul even, were in danger if I should inherit the strange and terrible curse.

'The tall woman began to laugh, pointing at me mockingly with her fan, as if she had read my thoughts and wished every one to notice my cowardice. I was obliged to lean on the arm of a friend to avoid falling, and then she made a gesture of contempt or pity,

turned on her heels, and walked into the church-yard, still looking
at me with her head turned over her shoulder. She fanned herself
and signed to me with the fan at one and the same time, walking
with mincing steps among the tombs with a sort of infernal coquetry, until at last I saw her disappear for ever in the crowded heart
of that great world of the dead.

'I say "for ever", because fifteen years have passed since then,
and I have never seen her since that moment: If she were really a
human being, she must be dead by now; and if she were not, if she
were a supernatural creature, I feel sure that she must have scorned
me too much to persecute me.

'Now, my friends! I've told you all I know. Let me have your
opinion.'

It is not necessary for me to repeat the remarks made by the
group of friends and comrades to Gabriel. For indeed the fact
remains that every reader will have his own ideas and beliefs in the
matter, and to use his own judgement as to the conclusion to which
he comes. So I will say no more. I leave it to the judgement of every
one of my readers.

*Translated from the Spanish by P. A. Schultz.*

# A Scent of Mimosa

## Francis King

*In the spring of 1975 The Times of London organized a ghost-story competition. The unlikely judges were Kingsley Amis, Patricia High-smith and Christopher Lee, and from several thousand entries they selected thirteen which were published together in one volume. Francis King – a fellow of the Royal Society of Literature, who has received both the Katherine Mansfield and the Somerset Maugham awards – won the second prize with 'A Scent of Mimosa'.*

It was long past midnight when the municipal Citroën dumped the four of them outside the Menton hotel. Tom, the youngest and most assertive of the Katherine Mansfield Prize judges, grabbed Lenore's arm and helped her up the steps. It was Lenore, thirtyish and thinnish, who had that year won the prize, given by the munici-pality. Though they had never met until the start of their journey out to the South of France together, he was always touching her, as though to communicate to her some assurance, at the nature of which she could still only guess. As they followed behind, Theo and Lucy, the other two judges, maintained a cautious distance from each other. There had been some acrimony, many years before, about an unsigned review in *The Times Literary Supplement*. Lenore could no longer even remember which of the two had written it and which had felt aggrieved.

In the hall they all stared at each other, like bewildered strangers wondering what they were doing in each other's company so late at night, in an unknown hotel, in a foreign town.

Tom broke the silence, swaying back and forth on his tiny feet: 'Well, what's the programme for tomorrow? Christ, I'm tired!'

Lucy hunted for one of three or four minuscule, lace-fringed handkerchiefs in the crocodile bag that dangled from her wrist. When travelling with her stockbroker husband, she was used to more luxurious hotels, more powerful cars and more amusing company. 'Apparently we're going to be taken up into the mountains for another banquet.' She held the handkerchief to the tip of her sharp nose and gave a little sniff.

Theo, who was almost as drunk as Tom, wailed, 'Oh, God! Altitude and hairpin bends always make me sick.'

'Well, there'll be plenty of both tomorrow,' Lucy replied, with some relish.

Lenore gazed down at the key that she was balancing on her palm. 'The Ambassador told me that he would be placing a wreath on some local war-memorial. Tomorrow's armistice-day, isn't it?'

Lucy, who had been affronted that the prizewinner and not she had been seated on the New Zealand Ambassador's right, exclaimed, 'What a dreadfully boring man! Nice, but oh so boring!'

'Oh, I thought him rather interesting.' Lenore was still secretly both frightened and envious of Lucy, who was older, much more successful and much richer than herself. 'Some young New Zealander's going to meet us up there, the Ambassador told me. In the village. He's coming specially for the Katherine Mansfield celebrations.'

'I suppose if your country's produced only one writer of any note, you're bound to make a fuss of her,' Tom commented.

'Well, we'd better get some sleep. If we can.' Lucy began to walk towards the lift. 'The beds here are horribly hard and lumpy.'

Tom again held Lenore by the arm, as he shepherded her towards the small, gilded cage. So close, she could smell the alcohol heavy on his breath.

Lucy got out first, since on their arrival she had managed to secure for herself the only room on the first floor with a balcony over the bay. Bowing to Lenore, she sang out, 'Bonne nuit, Madame la Lauréate!'

Lenore gave a small, embarrassed laugh. 'Goodnight, Lucy!'

Theo got out at the next floor, tripping and all but falling flat, with only Tom's arm to save him. He began to waddle off down the corridor; then turned as the lift-gates were closing. 'Bonne nuit, Madame la Lauréate!'

Lenore and Tom walked down their corridor, his hand again at her elbow, as though once more to assure her and perhaps also himself of something that he could not or dared not put into words. They came to her door.

'Well . . . ' He released her and clumsily she stopped and inserted the key. 'Tomorrow we'll drive up into the mountains and watch poor Theo being car-sick and meet the Ambassador's young New Zealander. And, of course, hear lots and lots of speeches.'

She opened the door; and at once, as though frightened that she would ask him in, he backed away.

'Well, bonne nuit, Madame la Lauréate!'

'Bonne nuit, Monsieur le Juge!'

She shut the door and leant against it, feeling the wood hard against her shoulder-blades. Her head was throbbing from too much food and drink, too much noise and too much French, and her mouth felt dry and sour. What would each of the others be doing now that they had separated? She began to speculate. Well, Lucy would no doubt be taking great care of each garment as she removed it; and then she would take equal care of her face, patting and smoothing, smoothing and patting. Theo, drunken and dishevelled, his tiny eyes bleary and his tie askew, would perch himself on a straight-backed chair – he always seemed masochistically determined to inflict the maximum of discomfort on himself – and would then start work on the pile of postcards that he had rushed out to buy as soon as they had been shown into their rooms. The postcards would, of course, arrive in England long after his return. Someone had told Lenore that he had a wife much older than himself and a horde of children and step-children – six? seven? eight? – to all of whom he was sentimentally devoted. And Tom? Tom, she decided after some deliberation, would walk along to his room, wait there for a few minutes and then take the lift downstairs again and go out into the night, wandering the autumnal streets in search of a – well, what? She did not know, not yet; any more than she knew the nature of the assurance that constant touching was designed to convey.

The bed was soft, not hard and lumpy at all as Lucy had complained, too soft, so that its swaying was almost nauseating. Perhaps poor Theo would be bed-sick and would have to take to the floor . . . She shut her eyes and yawned and yawned again . . . She was asleep.

When she awoke, it seemed as if many hours had passed, even though the dark of the room was still impenetrable. Her body was on fire, the sweat pouring off it, her head was throbbing and she had an excruciating pain, just under her right ribs, as though a knife had been inserted there and was now being twisted round and round. The central heating was always turned too high in these continental hotels; and after having eaten and drunk so much, she ought not to be surprised at an attack of acute indigestion. She threw back the sheet and duvet and then, after lying for a while uncovered with none of the expected coolness, she switched on the bedside lamp and dragged herself off the bed. For a long time she struggled with the regulator of the radiator that ran the whole length of the window; but the effort only made her sweat the more, it would not budge. She would have to open the window instead. Again she struggled; and at last the square of glass screeched along its groove and she felt the icy air enfolding her body.

From her suitcase she fetched a tube of Alka-Seltzer and padded into the bathroom. It was as she was dropping two of the tablets into a tumbler of water, the only light coming through the half-open door behind her, that suddenly she felt a strange tickling at the back of her throat, as though a feather had lodged there, coughed, coughed again, and then effortlessly began spitting, spitting, spitting.

Giddy and feeling sick, the sweat now chill on her forehead and bare arms, she stared down at the blood that had spattered the porcelain of the basin and was even dripping from one of the taps. She felt that she was about to faint and staggered back into the bedroom, to fall diagonally across the bed, her cheek pressed against the thrown-back duvet. Oh God, oh God . . . She must have had some kind of haemorrhage.

She lay there, shivering, for a while. She would have to see a doctor. But how could she call one at this hour? The best thing would be to go along to the room of one of the others. But she shrank from appealing to either Lucy or Tom. It would have to be Theo.

She got off the bed, still feeling giddy, sick and weak, and went back into the bathroom to wash away the blood. This time she turned on the light. The two tablets of Alka-Seltzer were now dissolved; but, with an extraordinary hyperaesthesia, she could hear the water fizzing even when she was still far away from it. She approached the basin slowly, fearful of what she would find in it: the trails and spatters of blood on the glistening porcelain and over the tap. But when she was above the basin and forced her eyes down, there was, amazingly, nothing there, nothing there at all.

Porcelain and tap were both as clean as she had left them after brushing her teeth.

It was cold and damp by the mountain war-memorial, a lichen-covered obelisk, one end sunk into the turf, with a stone shield attached, bearing names that for the most part were Italian, not French. The Mayor, cheeks scarlet from the many toasts at the banquet and medals dangling from his scuffed blue-serge suit, stood before it and bellowed out an oration to which Lenore did not listen, her gaze tracking back and forth among the faces, mostly middle-aged and brooding, of the handful of villagers huddled about her. Lucy had retreated into the back of the municipal Citroën, saying that she was certainly not going to risk a cold just before she and her husband were due to set off for the Caribbean on a holiday. Theo was holding a handkerchief to his chin, as though he had an attack of toothache, his tiny eyes rheumy and bloodshot. Tom, who had been chatting to their dapper young chauffeur in his excellent French, now stood beside the man, faintly smirking.

At last the oration ended and the Ambassador, grizzled, grey-faced and grave, walked forward with his wreath, stooped and placed it against the tilted obelisk. An improbable girl bugler, in white boots and a mini-skirt that revealed plump knees at the gap between them, stepped proudly forward and the valedictory notes volleyed back and forth among the mountains. Again Lenore felt that tickling at the back of her throat; but now it was tears. She always cried easily.

Suddenly she was aware of a smell, bitter and pungent, about her; and she wondered, in surprise, what could be its source. It was too late in the year for the smell to come from any flower at this altitude; and it seemed unlikely that any of the village women – with the possible exception of the girl bugler – would use a perfume so strange and strong. She peered around; and then, turning, saw the tall young man with the mousy, closecropped hair and the sunburned face, his cheekbones and his nose prominent, who was standing a little apart from the rest of the gathering. A khaki rucksack was propped against one leg. Their eyes met and he smiled and gave a little nod, as though they already knew each other.

The ceremony was over. In twos and threes the people began to drift away, for the most part silent, and silent not so much in grief as in the attempt to recapture its elusive memory. The young man, his rucksack now on his back, was beside her.

'Hello.' The voice was unmistakably antipodean.

'Hello.'

'You won the prize.' It was not a question.

'By some marvellous fluke. I've never had any luck in my life before. Everything I've achieved, I've had to struggle for.' She gave an involuntary shudder, feeling the cold and damp insinuate themselves through the thickness of her topcoat. 'You must be the New Zealander.'

'*The* New Zealander? Well, *a* New Zealander.'

'We heard that you were coming.'

'I always try to come.'

The Ambassador was approaching, still grey-faced and grave. 'Your New Zealander has arrived,' Lenore called out to him.

'*My* New Zealander?' He looked at the young man, who held out his hand. The Ambassador took it. 'So you're from back home?'

The young man nodded, at once friendly and remote. 'Wellington.'

'What brings you here?'

'I wanted to be present at the ceremonies. I was telling Miss Marlow, I always have been.'

'Then you're a fan of K.M.?'

'Oh, yes.'

Lenore was becoming increasingly bewildered. She turned to the Ambassador. 'But didn't you say . . . ? Didn't you tell me last night – at the banquet – that you were expecting a New Zealander?'

'I?'

'Yes, surely . . .'

'But I'd no idea that this young man would turn up, none at all.'

'But I'm sure . . . Didn't you . . . ?'

'We've never set eyes on each other. And we know nothing about each other. Do we?' He appealed to the other man.

'Nothing at all.'

'Anyway' – cold and tired, the Ambassador began to move away – 'it's been nice to meet you. What's your name?'

'Leslie.' It might have been either surname or Christian name.

'We'll be seeing you again?'

'Oh, yes. I'll be at the prizegiving ceremony tomorrow. As I said, I've been at every one.'

Lenore and the young man were now alone by the lop-sided war-memorial. Far down the road she could make out Theo, shapeless in his ancient overcoat, a cap pulled down over his bulging forehead, as he urinated against a tree that soared up into the gathering mist and darkness. Tom was climbing into the car beside Lucy; Lenore could hear his laugh, strangely loud.

'How are you going to get down to Menton? Would you like me to ask if we can give you a lift?'

'Oh, that's very kind of you. But I think I'd like to stay here a little longer.'

'Here?' She could not imagine why anyone should wish to stay on in this cramped, craggy village, with all the inhabitants drifting back into their homes and nothing to see in the coagulating mist and dark and nothing to do.

He nodded. 'She came up here. She was driven up here by Connie and Jennie.'

'Oh, yes, they were the ones who let her the Villa Isola Bella, weren't they? Connie was the aunt.'

'Well, cousin really.'

'I didn't know she'd ever been in this village. I know the journals and the letters pretty well but obviously not as well as you.' Suddenly she did not wish to let him go; this imminent parting from a total stranger had become like the resurgence of some deep-seated, long-forgotten sorrow. 'Can't we really give you a lift? We can squeeze you into our car.'

He shook his head. 'I want to stay here a little. But I'll be down. We'll meet again?'

'Perhaps this evening you might join us for dinner? We have the evening free and we thought that we might all go to a fish-restaurant in Monte Carlo. Lucy – she's one of the judges – says that Somerset Maugham once took her there and it was absolutely fabulous.' 'Fabulous' was not Lenore's kind of word, it was Lucy's. 'Do try to join us.'

'Perhaps.'

'Please! We'll be leaving the hotel at about eight-thirty. So just come there before that. It's the Hôtel du Parc. Do you know where it is?'

He nodded.

'How will you get down to Menton? There can't be a bus now.'

'Oh, I'll manage.'

'Lenore! Time we started back!' It was Tom's peremptory voice.
'I must go. They're getting impatient. Please come this evening.'
He raised his hand as she hurried away from him, in what was
half a wave and half a salute. Then he remained standing motionless
beside the war-memorial.

Lucy said fretfully, 'We want to get down the mountain before
this mist really thickens.'

'I'm sorry. But that was . . . He was from New Zealand.'

'Is that the one you told us about last night?' Theo asked, wiping
with a soiled handkerchief at eyes still streaming from the cold.

Lenore nodded. 'Yes, I did tell you about him, didn't I?' She all
but added, 'But the funny thing is that the Ambassador pretended
that he'd said nothing to me at all about his coming.' Then something made her check herself.

It was as though, walking over sunlit fields, she had all at once
unexpectedly found ahead of her a dark and dense wood; had
hesitated whether to enter it or not; and had then turned and in
panic retraced her steps.


'Well, he's obviously not coming.' Lucy drew her chinchilla coat
up over her shoulders and got to her feet. The two men also rose.

Lenore sighed. 'No, I suppose not.'

'He probably decided there were more amusing things for a young
man to do on the Côte,' Theo said.

'I can think of less amusing things too,' Lucy retorted tartly.

'Perhaps he hadn't got the money for a slap-up meal.'

Of course, of course! Tom was right. Lenore saw it now. What
she should have said was, 'You must be my guest, because I want
to spend some of my prize-money in celebration,' or something of
that kind. She had spoken of the 'fabulous' restaurant to which
Lucy had been taken by Maugham – enough to put off anyone who
was travelling on a slender budget. Of course!

Once again Tom tried to take her arm as they emerged into the
soft November air; but this time she pulled free with a sharp,
impatient jerk.


The next morning they were driven out to Isola Bella, the villa on
the steep hill where Katherine Mansfield had lived for nine months
in a fever of illness and activity. The villa itself was occupied; but
the municipality had made over a room on the lowest of its three

levels into a shrine. A bearded French critic, who was regarded as an authority on the English writer, explained to Lenore that an outhouse had been converted into a lavatory and shower, in the hope that some other English writer might soon be installed in what was, in effect, a tiny apartment.

'But Katherine Mansfield herself never lived here?'

He hesitated between truth and his loyalty to his hosts. Then: 'Well, no,' he agreed in his excellent English. 'Katherine lived above.' (He invariably referred to the writer merely by her Christian name.)

'And probably she never even came down here?'

Again he hesitated. 'Possibly not.'

Lenore wandered away from the rest of the party, up the hill to the rusty gates that led to the main part of the house. Ahead of her, as she peered through the curlicues of wrought iron, stretched the terrace on which the invalid would lie out for most of the day on a chaise-longue spread with a kaross made of flying-squirrel skins brought home from Africa by her father. Oh, and there were the mimosa trees, like elongated ferns – Katherine Mansfield had described how she would lie awake at break of day and watch the shafts of the rising sun shimmer through them. All at once, Lenore could smell the tiny yellow flowers still hanging from the fragile racemes. Though infinitely fainter, a mere ghost, it was none the less that same odour, pungent and bitter, that had enveloped her up in the mountains. But surely, so high up in the mountains, no mimosa could grow or, if it did, could come to bloom in November? As she breathed in the scent, deeper and deeper until her lungs began to ache with it as they had done that first night in the hotel, she thought once again of the New Zealander and wondered what had happened to him. She had hoped to see him in the town early that morning as she had wandered alone about it, pretending that she was in quest of presents but in reality in quest of him; but he had been nowhere. And now he had not turned up at the villa, as she had also hoped that he would do. Perhaps he had already moved on, with his exiguous rucksack, farther up the coast; perhaps she would never see him again.

Suddenly she wanted a spray of the mimosa. She rattled the gate and the rusty padlock swung from side to side, with a dry sound of scraping against the bars. The occupiers of the house must be away. But she tugged at the bell, hearing it tinkle from somewhere out of sight. No one came. She thought, If he were here, he could climb over for me. He'd find some way. She hoisted herself up with both hands, feeling the flaking metal graze a palm. But it was useless.

'Can I help madame?'

It was the French critic, stroking his beard with a narrow, nicotine-stained hand.

Lenore explained what she wanted; and then he too tugged at the bell-pull and even shouted out in French. No one came. Oddly, she could no longer smell that pungent, bitter odour, not since he had come.

He shrugged. 'I'm afraid that I am too old and too fat to climb over for you. Perhaps if you come tomorrow, the owners will be here.'

'We're leaving tomorrow morning.'

'Then . . .' Again he shrugged. When he had first seen her, he had thought her a dowdy, insignificant little woman, and had hardly bothered to speak to her. But now he experienced a sudden pull, as though a boat in which he had long been becalmed had all at once felt the tug and sweep of the tide. Now he too grabbed her arm just above the elbow, as Tom had kept on doing until that rebuff of the previous night. 'Let me assist you down the hill.' How thin the arm was, how pathetically thin and fragile – the arm of a child or invalid. He felt excited at the contact.

'I have given most of my life to Katherine,' he told her, as they began to descend. It was not strictly true, since he had given much of his life to other things: to the editing of a magazine, to the collection of Chinese works of art, to women, to eating and drinking. But at that moment, when his fingers felt the delicate bone inside its envelope of flesh, he not only wished that it had been so but believed that it had been so. 'In a strange way you remind me of her, you know.'

In the town hall the audience for the prize-giving ceremony was composed almost entirely of elderly men in dark suits and elderly women in hats. Lenore had been told that she would have to make a small speech of thanks in French after Lucy had spoken, also in French, on behalf of the judges. Lenore had never made a speech in her life, let alone a speech in French, and she dreaded the ordeal. The hall was stuffy, its radiators too hot to touch even on this autumn day. She felt headachy, sweaty and vaguely sick, as she listened, in a kind of trance, first to the orotund platitudes of the Mayor, then to the clipped phrases of the Ambassador and finally to Lucy's few witty, lucid comments. In rising panic she thought, If he were here, if only he were here! In one hand she was clutching the typescript, the French of which Lucy had corrected for her.

She heard her name and then one of the French officials was giving her a little push from behind, his hand to her shoulder. She rose and, as she did so, she felt the room revolve first gently and then faster and faster around her. She clutched the back of her chair, staring up at the face of the Mayor on the dais above her. All at once she could smell, far stronger than ever before, that pungent, bitter odour of mimosa. It was all around her, an enveloping cloud. She moved forward and then up the steps, the French critic putting out one of those long, narrow hands of his to help her.

She was handed an envelope, cold and dry on her hot and damp palm and then she was handed a red-leather box, open, with a bronze medallion embedded in it. Whose head was that? But of course – it was Katherine Mansfield's, jagged prongs of fringe across a wide forehead. She looked down and read: 'Menton c'est le Paradis d'une aube à l'autre.'

The Mayor was prompting her in a sibilant whisper, perhaps she would wish to say a few words?

She turned to face the audience: and it was then, as she moistened her lips with her tongue and raised the sheet of typescript, that all at once she saw him, standing by himself at the far end of the hall, one shoulder against the jamb of a closed door and his eyes fixed on her.

She began to read, at first all but inaudibly but then in a stronger and stronger voice. Her French was all but perfect; she felt wholly calm.

In the premature dusk, they talked outside the Town Hall, pacing the terrace among the stunted oleanders.

'You saved my life,' she said. She felt the euphoria that precedes a bout of fever. 'I can't explain it but I was, oh, petrified, I felt sure I could not say a word, and then suddenly I saw you and all at once . . .'

'I like that story of yours. Very much.'

'Oh, have you read it?' She was amazed. The story had appeared in a little magazine that, after three issues, had folded and vanished.

'Yes. It was – *right*. For her, I mean. It's the only story that she herself might have written, of all the ones that have ever won the prize.'

'That's a terrific compliment.'

'I mean it.'

'I'd hoped that perhaps you'd have joined us last night.'

'Well, I wanted to,' he said, with no further excuse.

'And then I thought that I might see you at the villa.'

'I've been there many times.'

'But not this time?'

He did not answer; and then she began to tell him about the mimosa on the terrace – how she remembered reading about it in the journals and the letters and how she had wanted a spray, just one spray, but there had been no one at the house and the gate was padlocked. 'If you'd been there, perhaps you could have climbed over. But none of our party looked capable of doing so.'

'I'll get you a spray.'

'Will you? Can you?'

'Of course.' He smiled. His teeth were very white in the long, sunburned face.

'But we leave early tomorrow.'

'What time?'

'We must leave the hotel at ten for the airport.'

'Oh, that'll give me time. Don't worry.'

Boldly she said, 'Oh, I wish there were no banquet this evening! I wish we could just have dinner alone together.'

'There'll be other times,' he said quietly. 'Anyway, I won't forget the mimosa.'

'Promise?'

'Promise.'

After that Tom was again calling and the cars were starting up and people were shaking her hand and saying how glad they were for her and that soon she must come back to Menton again.

When she looked round for the New Zealander, she found that he had vanished.

Lenore was back in her dark, two-roomed Fulham flat. At the airport Lucy had been whisked off by her husband in a chauffeur-driven Daimler, barely bothering to say goodbye. Theo had explained that it would be impossible to fit any more passengers into his battered station-wagon, already packed with his wife, a number of children, a dog and a folding bicycle. Tom had said that it looked as if the friend who was supposed to meet him must have got held up and he'd wait around for a while. So Lenore had travelled alone on the bus. She had felt chilled and there was again that pain, dull now, under her right ribs.

She shivered as she stooped to light the gas. Then she remained kneeling before it, staring at the radiants as the blue light flickering up from them steadied to an orange glow. He had failed to keep his promise and she had no idea of where he might be or even of what he was called – other than that either his surname or his Christian name was Leslie. It was hopeless. She got up, with a small, dry cough, and went into the bedroom. There she hauled her suitcase up on to the bed and began to unpack it, hurriedly, throwing things into drawers or jerking them on to hangers, as though she did not have a whole empty evening ahead of her and a number of empty days after that. At the bottom of the suitcase she came on the typescript of her speech – she crumpled it into a ball and threw it into the waste-paper basket – and the red-leather box, containing her trophy. She pressed the stud of the lid and lifted it upwards with a thumb; and, as she did so, it was as if she were releasing from it the smell pungent and bitter, that soon was all around her. She gave a little gasp; the pain in her chest sharpened. Looking down, she saw the spray of mimosa that lay across the medallion.

She took the spray in her hand; but it was dry, dry and faded and old as though it had lain there not for a few hours but for many, many years. 'Leslie.' She said the name aloud to herself and then, with no shock and no alarm but with the relieved recognition of someone lost who all at once sights a familiar landmark, she remembered that yes, of course, Leslie had been the name of the beloved brother killed in the war, whom Katherine Mansfield had always called 'Chummie'.

She touched the arid, dead raceme and some of the small, yellow-ish-grey blossoms, hard as berries, fell to the carpet at her feet. They might have been beads, scattering hither and thither. Three or four rolled back and forth in her palm. She felt a tickle at the back of her throat; it must be pollen, she decided wrongly.

Then suddenly the concluding lines of Katherine Mansfield's sonnet on the death of her brother, read long ago and forgotten, forced themselves up within her, like the spurs of a plant, buried for years, all at once thrusting up into the light of day,

> By the remembered stream my brother stands
> Waiting for me with berries in his hands . . .
>> 'These are my body. Sister, take and eat.'

She gave another little dry cough, and tasted something thick and salt on her tongue. The scent of mimosa was already fading as those blooms had long since faded. But she knew that it would come back and that he would come back with it.

# Death and the Gardener

## Jean Cocteau

*In a small and wonderful book called* The Difficulty of Being *Cocteau writes about his notion of death (his 'mistress', as he called her): 'As I grow shorter, she grows longer. She takes up more room, she worries about little details, she busies herself with unimportant, trivial tasks. She makes less and less of an effort to deceive me. But her hour of triumph will be that in which I cease to be. Then she can consider her troubles over and done with, and leave, shutting the door behind her.'*

*Though this tale is a very ancient one, retold by several other writers (including Somerset Maugham in his play* Sheppey – *quoted by John O'Hara as the epigraph of his novel* Appointment in Samarra), *Cocteau lends a matter-of-fact quality to his version. Death was always a very real thing to Cocteau. A friend of mine, Michel-Claude Touchard, once interviewed Cocteau on the set of* The Testament of Orpheus *(1959). He asked Cocteau why he had chosen the actress María Casares – 'so beautiful, so full of life' – to play the role of death. 'Because she is a friend,' he answered, 'and we need Death to be a friend. It is best to have a friend as travelling companion when you have so far to go together.'*

A young gardener said to his prince, 'Save me! I met Death in the garden this morning and he made a menacing gesture. Tonight I wish by some miracle I could be far away, in Ispahan.'

The prince lent him his swiftest horse.

That afternoon, walking in the garden, the prince came face to face with Death. 'Why,' he asked, 'did you make a threatening gesture at my gardener this morning?'

'It wasn't a threatening gesture,' answered Death. 'It was a gesture of surprise. I saw him far from Ispahan this morning and I knew that I must take him in Ispahan tonight.'

*Translated from the French by Alberto Manguel.*

# Lord Mountdrago

## William Somerset Maugham

*I had an aunt who loved Somerset Maugham: she made me read 'The Three Fat Women of Antibes' and 'The Creative Impulse', and 'Miss King' with its brilliant last scene, and 'Rain' (I did not make much of 'Rain' at the age of ten). According to her, Maugham did the two essential things a good writer should do: write well and entertain her, not necessarily in that order. Maugham was not always a good writer. His vast output was very uneven: some stories, like 'The Necklace', are very badly written; others, like 'Honolulu' and 'Lord Mountdrago', are perfect in every sense. His nephew, Robin Maugham, says in his biographical essay that his uncle used to send his secretary out into bars and dark alleys to collect stories which he could later develop. I wonder who told him the one that became 'Lord Mountdrago'.*

Dr Audlin looked at the clock on his desk. It was twenty minutes to six. He was surprised that his patient was late, for Lord Mountdrago prided himself on his punctuality; he had a sententious way of expressing himself which gave the air of an epigram to a common-place remark, and he was in the habit of saying that punctuality is a compliment you pay to the intelligent and a rebuke you administer to the stupid. Lord Mountdrago's appointment was for five-thirty.

There was in Dr Audlin's appearance nothing to attract attention. He was tall and spare, with narrow shoulders and something of a stoop; his hair was grey and thin; his long, sallow face deeply lined. He was not more than fifty, but he looked older. His eyes, pale-blue and rather large, were weary. When you had been with him for a while you noticed that they moved very little; they remained fixed on your face, but so empty of expression were they that it was no discomfort. They seldom lit up. They gave no clue to his thoughts nor changed with the words he spoke. If you were of an observant turn it might have struck you that he blinked much less often than most of us. His hands were on the large side, with long, tapering fingers; they were soft, but firm, cool but not clammy. You could never have said what Dr Audlin wore unless you had made a point of looking. His clothes were dark. His tie was black. His dress made his sallow lined face paler, and his pale eyes more wan. He gave you the impression of a very sick man.

Dr Audlin was a psychoanalyst. He had adopted the profession by accident and practised it with misgiving. When the war broke out he had not been long qualified and was getting experience at various hospitals; he offered his services to the authorities, and after a time was sent out to France. It was then that he discovered his singular gift. He could allay certain pains by the touch of his cool, firm hands, and by talking to them often induce sleep in men who were suffering from sleeplessness. He spoke slowly. His voice had no particular colour, and its tone did not alter with the words he uttered, but it was musical, soft, and lulling. He told the men that they must rest, that they mustn't worry, that they must sleep; and rest stole into their jaded bones, tranquillity pushed their anxieties away, like a man finding a place for himself on a crowded bench, and slumber fell on their tired eyelids like the light rain of spring upon the fresh-turned earth. Dr Audlin found that by speaking to men with that low, monotonous voice of his, by looking at them with his pale, quiet eyes, by stroking their weary foreheads with his long firm hands, he could soothe their perturbations, resolve the conflicts that distracted them, and banish the phobias that made their lives a torment. Sometimes he effected cures that seemed miraculous. He restored speech to a man who, after being buried under the earth by a bursting shell, had been struck dumb, and he gave back the use of his limbs to another who had been paralysed after a crash in a plane. He could not understand his powers; he was of a sceptical turn, and though they say that in circumstances of this kind the first thing is to believe in yourself, he never quite succeeded in doing that; and it was only the outcome of his activities, patent to the most incredulous observer, that obliged him to admit that he had some faculty, coming from he knew not where, obscure and uncertain, that enabled him to do things for which he could offer no explanation. When the war was over he went to Vienna and studied there, and afterwards to Zürich; and then settled down in London to practise the art he had so strangely acquired. He had been practising now for fifteen years, and had attained, in the speciality he followed, a distinguished reputation. People told one another of the amazing things he had done, and though his fees were high, he had as many patients as he had time to see. Dr Audlin knew that he had achieved some very extraordinary results; he had saved men from suicide, others from the lunatic asylum, he had assuaged griefs that embittered useful lives, he had turned unhappy marriages into happy ones, he had eradicated abnormal instincts and thus delivered not a few from a hateful bondage, he had given health to the sick in spirit; he had done all this, and yet at the back of his mind remained the suspicion that he was little more than a quack.

It went against his grain to exercise a power that he could not understand, and it offended his honesty to trade on the faith of the people he treated when he had no faith in himself. He was rich enough now to live without working, and the work exhausted him; a dozen times he had been on the point of giving up practice. He knew all that Freud and Jung and the rest of them had written. He was not satisfied; he had an intimate conviction that all their theory was hocus-pocus, and yet there the results were, incomprehensible, but manifest. And what had he not seen of human nature during the fifteen years that patients had been coming to his dingy back room in Wimpole Street? The revelations that had been poured into his ears, sometimes only too willingly, sometimes with shame, with reservations, with anger, had long ceased to surprise him. Nothing could shock him any longer. He knew by now that men were liars, he knew how extravagant was their vanity; he knew far worse than that about them; but he knew that it was not for him to judge or to condemn. But year by year as these terrible confidences were imparted to him his face grew a little greyer, its lines a little more marked, and his pale eyes more weary. He seldom laughed, but now and again when for relaxation he read a novel he smiled. Did their authors really think the men and women they wrote of were like that? If they only knew how much more complicated they were, how much more unexpected, what irreconcilable elements coexisted within their souls and what dark and sinister contentions afflicted them!

It was a quarter to six. Of all the strange cases he had been called upon to deal with Dr Audlin could remember none stranger than that of Lord Mountdrago. For one thing the personality of his patient made it singular. Lord Mountdrago was an able and a distinguished man. Appointed Secretary of Foreign Affairs when still under forty, now after three years in office he had seen his policy prevail. It was generally acknowledged that he was the ablest politician in the Conservative Party and only the fact that his father was a peer, on whose death he would no longer be able to sit in the House of Commons, made it impossible for him to aim at the premiership. But if in these democratic times it is out of the question for a Prime Minister of England to be in the House of Lords, there was nothing to prevent Lord Mountdrago from continuing to be Secretary for Foreign Affairs in successive Conservative administrations and so for long directing the foreign policy of his country.

Lord Mountdrago had many good qualities. He had intelligence and industry. He was widely travelled, and spoke several languages fluently. From early youth he had specialized in foreign affairs, and had conscientiously made himself acquainted with the political and economic circumstances of other countries. He had courage, insight, and determination. He was a good speaker, both on the platform and in the House, clear, precise, and often witty. He was a brilliant debater and his gift of repartee was celebrated. He had a fine presence: he was a tall, handsome man, rather bald and somewhat too stout, but this gave him solidity and an air of maturity that were of service to him. As a young man he had been something of an athlete and had rowed in the Oxford boat, and he was known to be one of the best shots in England. At twenty-four he had married a girl of eighteen whose father was a duke and her mother a great American heiress, so that she had both position and wealth, and by her he had had two sons. For several years they had lived privately apart, but in public united, so that appearances were saved, and no other attachment on either side had given the gossips occasion to whisper. Lord Mountdrago indeed was too ambitious, too hard-working, and it must be added too patriotic, to be tempted by any pleasures that might interfere with his career. He had, in short, a great deal to make him a popular and successful figure. He had unfortunately great defects.

He was a fearful snob. You would not have been surprised at this if his father had been the first holder of the title. That the son of an ennobled lawyer, a manufacturer, or a distiller should attach an inordinate importance to his rank is understandable. The earldom held by Lord Mountdrago's father was created by Charles II, and the barony held by the first Earl dated from the Wars of the Roses.

For three hundred years the successive holders of the title had allied themselves with the noblest families of England. But Lord Mountdrago was as conscious of his birth as a *nouveau riche* is conscious of his money. He never missed an opportunity of impressing it upon others. He had beautiful manners when he chose to display them, but this he did only with people whom he regarded as his equals. He was coldly insolent to those whom he looked upon as his social inferiors. He was rude to his servants and insulting to his secretaries. The subordinate officials in the government offices to which he had been successively attached feared and hated him. His arrogance was horrible. He knew that he was a great deal cleverer than most of the persons he had to do with, and never hesitated to apprise them of the fact. He had no patience with the infirmities of human nature. He felt himself born to command and was irritated with people who expected him to listen to their arguments or wished to hear the reasons for his decisions. He was immeasurably selfish. He looked upon any service that was rendered him as a right due to his rank and intelligence and therefore deserving of no gratitude. It never entered his head that he was called upon to do anything for others. He had many enemies: he despised them. He knew no one who merited his assistance, his sympathy, or his compassion. He had no friends. He was distrusted by his chiefs, because they doubted his loyalty; he was unpopular with his party, because he was overbearing and discourteous; and yet his merit was so great, his patriotism so evident, his intelligence so solid, and his management of affairs so brilliant that they had to put up with him. And what made it possible to do this was that on occasion he could be enchanting; when he was with persons whom he considered his equals, or whom he wished to captivate, in the company of foreign dignitaries or women of distinction, he could be gay, witty, and debonair; his manners then reminded you that in his veins ran the same blood as had run in the veins of Lord Chesterfield; he could tell a story with point, he could be natural, sensible, and even profound. You were surprised at the extent of his knowledge and the sensitiveness of his taste. You thought him the best company in the world; you forgot that he had insulted you the day before and was quite capable of cutting you dead the next.

Lord Mountdrago almost failed to become Dr Audlin's patient. A secretary rang up the doctor and told him that his lordship, wishing to consult him, would be glad if he would come to his house at ten o'clock on the following morning. Dr Audlin answered that he was unable to go to Lord Mountdrago's house, but would be pleased to give him an appointment at his consulting-room at five o'clock on the next day but one. The secretary took the message and presently rang back to say that Lord Mountdrago insisted on seeing Dr Audlin in his own house and the doctor could fix his own fee. Dr Audlin replied that he only saw patients in his consulting-room and expressed his regret that unless Lord Mountdrago was prepared to come to him he could not give him his attention. In a quarter of an hour a brief message was delivered to him that his lordship would come not next day but one, but next day, at five.

When Lord Mountdrago was then shown in he did not come forward, but stood at the door and insolently looked the doctor up and down. Dr Audlin perceived that he was in a rage; he gazed at him, silently, with still eyes. He saw a big heavy man, with greying hair, receding on the forehead so that it gave nobility to his brow, a puffy face with bold regular features and an expression of haughtiness. He had somewhat the look of one of the Bourbon sovereigns of the eighteenth century.

'It seems that it is as difficult to see you as a Prime Minister, Dr Audlin. I'm an extremely busy man.'

'Won't you sit down?' said the doctor.

His face showed no sign that Lord Mountdrago's speech in any way affected him. Dr Audlin sat in his chair at the desk. Lord Mountdrago still stood and his frown darkened.

'I think I should tell you that I am His Majesty's Secretary for Foreign Affairs,' he said acidly.

'Won't you sit down?' the doctor repeated.

Lord Mountdrago made a gesture, which might have suggested that he was about to turn on his heel and stalk out of the room; but if that was his intention he apparently thought better of it. He seated himself. Dr Audlin opened a large book and took up his pen. He wrote without looking at his patient.

'How old are you?'

'Forty-two.'

'Are you married?'

'Yes.'

'How long have you been married?'

'Eighteen years.'

'Have you any children?'

'I have two sons.'

Dr Audlin noted down the facts as Lord Mountdrago abruptly answered his questions. Then he leaned back in his chair and looked at him. He did not speak; he just looked, gravely, with pale eyes that did not move.

'Why have you come to see me?' he asked at length.

'I've heard about you. Lady Canute is a patient of yours, I understand. She tells me you've done her a certain amount of good.'

Dr Audlin did not reply. His eyes remained fixed on the other's face, but they were so empty of expression that you might have thought he did not even see him.

'I can't do miracles,' he said at length. Not a smile, but the shadow of a smile flickered in his eyes. 'The Royal College of Physicians would not approve of it if I did.'

Lord Mountdrago gave a brief chuckle. It seemed to lessen his hostility. He spoke more amiably.

'You have a very remarkable reputation. People seem to believe in you.'

'Why have you come to me?' repeated Dr Audlin.

Now it was Lord Mountdrago's turn to be silent. It looked as though he found it hard to answer. Dr Audlin waited. At last Lord Mountdrago seemed to make an effort. He spoke.

'I'm in perfect health. Just as a matter of routine I had myself examined by my own doctor the other day, Sir Augustus Fitzherbert, I dare say you've heard of him, and he tells me I have the physique of a man of thirty. I work hard, but I'm never tired, and I enjoy my work. I smoke very little and I'm an extremely moderate drinker. I take a sufficiency of exercise and I lead a regular life. I am a perfectly sound, normal, healthy man. I quite expect you to think it very silly and childish of me to consult you.'

Dr Audlin saw that he must help him.

'I don't know if I can do anything to help you. I'll try. You're distressed?'

Lord Mountdrago frowned.

'The work that I'm engaged in is important. The decisions I am called upon to make can easily affect the welfare of the country and even the peace of the world. It is essential that my judgement should be balanced and my brain clear. I look upon it as my duty to eliminate any cause of worry that may interfere with my usefulness.'

Dr Audlin had never taken his eyes off him. He saw a great deal.

He saw behind his patient's pompous manner and arrogant pride an anxiety that he could not dispel.

'I asked you to be good enough to come here because I know by experience that it's easier for someone to speak openly in the dingy surroundings of a doctor's consulting-room than in his accustomed environment.'

'They're certainly dingy,' said Lord Mountdrago acidly. He paused. It was evident that this man who had so much self-assurance, so quick and decided a mind that he was never at a loss, at this moment was embarrassed. He smiled in order to show the doctor that he was at his ease, but his eyes betrayed his disquiet. When he spoke again it was with unnatural heartiness.

'The whole thing's so trivial that I can hardly bring myself to bother you with it. I'm afraid you'll just tell me not to be a fool and waste your valuable time.'

'Even things that seem very trivial may have their importance. They can be a symptom of a deep-seated derangement. And my time is entirely at your disposal.'

Dr Audlin's voice was low and grave. The monotone in which he spoke was strangely soothing. Lord Mountdrago at length made up his mind to be frank.

'The fact is I've been having some very tiresome dreams lately. I know it's silly to pay any attention to them, but – well, the honest truth is that I'm afraid they've got on my nerves.'

'Can you describe any of them to me?'

Lord Mountdrago smiled, but the smile that tried to be careless was only rueful.

'They're so idiotic, I can hardly bring myself to narrate them.'

'Never mind.'

'Well, the first I had was about a month ago. I dreamt that I was at a party at Connemara House. It was an official party. The King and Queen were to be there and of course decorations were worn. I was wearing my ribbon and my star. I went into a sort of cloakroom they have to take off my coat. There was a little man there called Owen Griffiths, who's a Welsh Member of Parliament, and to tell you the truth, I was surprised to see him. He's very common, and I said to myself: "Really, Lydia Connemara is going too far, whom will she ask next?" I thought he looked at me rather curiously, but I didn't take any notice of him; in fact I cut the little bounder and walked upstairs. I suppose you've never been there?'

'Never.'

'No, it's not the sort of house you'd ever be likely to go to. It's a rather vulgar house, but it's got a very fine marble staircase, and the Connemaras were at the top receiving their guests. Lady Connemara gave me a look of surprise when I shook hands with her, and began to giggle; I didn't pay much attention, she's a very silly, ill-bred woman and her manners are no better than those of her ancestor whom King Charles II made a duchess. I must say the reception rooms at Connemara House are stately. I walked through, nodding to a number of people and shaking hands; then I saw the German Ambassador talking with one of the Austrian Archdukes. I particularly wanted to have a word with him, so I went up and held out my hand. The moment the Archduke saw me he burst into a roar of laughter. I was deeply affronted. I looked him up and down sternly, but he only laughed the more. I was about to speak to him rather sharply, when there was a sudden hush and I realized that the King and Queen had come. Turning my back on the Archduke, I stepped forward, and then, quite suddenly, I noticed that I hadn't got any trousers on. I was in short silk drawers, and I wore scarlet sock-suspenders. No wonder Lady Connemara had giggled; no wonder the Archduke had laughed! I can't tell you what that moment was. An agony of shame. I awoke in a cold sweat. Oh, you don't know the relief I felt to find it was only a dream.'

'It's the kind of dream that's not so very uncommon,' said Dr Audlin.

'I dare say not. But an odd thing happened next day. I was in the lobby of the House of Commons, when that fellow Griffiths walked slowly past me. He deliberately looked down at my legs and then he looked me full in the face and I was almost certain he winked. A ridiculous thought came to me. He'd been there the night before and seen me make that ghastly exhibition of myself and was enjoying the joke. But of course I knew that was impossible because it was only a dream. I gave him an icy glare and he walked on. But he was grinning his head off.'

Lord Mountdrago took his handkerchief out of his pocket and wiped the palms of his hands. He was making no attempt now to conceal his perturbation. Dr Audlin never took his eyes off him. 'Tell me another dream.'

'It was the night after, and it was even more absurd than the first one. I dreamt that I was in the House. There was a debate on foreign affairs which not only the country, but the world, had been looking forward to with the gravest concern. The government had decided on a change in their policy which vitally affected the future of the Empire. The occasion was historic. Of course the House was crowded. All the ambassadors were there. The galleries were packed. It fell to me to make the important speech of the evening. I had prepared it carefully. A man like me has enemies, there are a lot of people who resent my having achieved the position I have at an age when even the cleverest men are content with situations of relative obscurity, and I was determined that my speech should not only be worthy of the occasion, but should silence my detractors. It excited me to think that the whole world was hanging on my lips. I rose to my feet. If you've ever been in the House you'll know how members chat to one another during a debate, rustle papers and turn over reports. The silence was the silence of the grave when I began to speak. Suddenly I caught sight of that odious little bounder on one of the benches opposite, Griffiths the Welsh member; he put out his tongue at me. I don't know if you've ever heard a vulgar music-hall song called "A Bicycle Made for Two". It was very popular a great many years ago. To show Griffiths how completely I despised him I began to sing it. I sang the first verse right through. There was a moment's surprise, and when I finished they cried "Hear, hear," on the opposite benches. I put up my hand to silence them and sang the second verse. The House listened to me in stony silence and I felt the song wasn't going down very well. I was vexed, for I have a good baritone voice, and I was determined that they should do me justice. When I started the third verse the members began to laugh; in an instant the laughter spread; the ambassadors, the strangers in the Distinguished Strangers' Gallery, the ladies in the Ladies' Gallery, the reporters, they shook, they bellowed, they held their sides, they rolled in their seats; everyone was overcome with laughter except the ministers on the Front Bench immediately behind me. In that incredible, in that unprecedented uproar, they sat petrified. I gave them a glance, and suddenly the enormity of what I had done fell upon me. I had made myself the laughing-stock of the whole world. With misery I realized that I should have to resign. I woke and knew it was only a dream.'

Lord Mountdrago's grand manner had deserted him as he narrated this, and now having finished he was pale and trembling.

But with an effort he pulled himself together. He forced a laugh to his shaking lips.

'The whole thing was so fantastic that I couldn't help being amused. I didn't give it another thought, and when I went into the House on the following afternoon I was feeling in very good form. The debate was dull, but I had to be there, and I read some documents that required my attention. For some reason I chanced to look up and I saw that Griffiths was speaking. He has an unpleasant Welsh accent and an unprepossessing appearance. I couldn't imagine that he had anything to say that it was worth my while to listen to, and I was about to return to my papers when he quoted two lines from "A Bicycle Made for Two". I couldn't help glancing at him and I saw that his eyes were fixed on me with a grin of bitter mockery. I faintly shrugged my shoulders. It was comic that a scrubby little Welsh member should look at me like that. It was an odd coincidence that he should quote two lines from that disastrous song that I'd sung all through in my dream.

I began to read my papers again, but I don't mind telling you that I found it difficult to concentrate on them. I was a little puzzled. Owen Griffiths had been in my first dream, the one at Connemara House, and I'd received a very definite impression afterwards that he knew the sorry figure I'd cut. Was it a mere coincidence that he had quoted those two lines? I asked myself if it was possible that he was dreaming the same dreams as I was. But of course the idea was preposterous and I determined not to give it a second thought.'

There was a silence. Dr Audlin looked at Lord Mountdrago and Lord Mountdrago looked at Dr Audlin.

'Other people's dreams are very boring. My wife used to dream occasionally and insist on telling me her dreams next day with circumstantial detail. I found it maddening.'

Dr Audlin faintly smiled.

'You're not boring me.'

'I'll tell you one more dream I had a few days later. I dreamt that I went into a public-house at Limehouse. I've never been to Limehouse in my life and I don't think I've ever been in a public-house since I was at Oxford, and yet I saw the street and the place I went into as exactly as if I were at home there. I went into a room, I don't know whether they call it the saloon bar or the private bar; there was a fireplace and a large leather armchair on one side of it, and on the other a small sofa; a bar ran the whole length of the room and over it you could see into the public bar. Near the door was a round marble-topped table and two armchairs beside it. It was a Saturday night and the place was packed. It was brightly lit, but the smoke was so thick that it made my eyes smart. I was dressed like a rough, with a cap on my head and a handkerchief round my neck. It seemed to me that most of the people there were drunk. I thought it rather amusing. There was a gramophone going, or the radio, I don't know which, and in front of the fireplace two women were doing a grotesque dance. There was a little crowd round them, laughing, cheering, and singing. I went up to have a look and some man said to me: " 'Ave a drink, Bill?" There were glasses on the table full of a dark liquid which I understand is called brown ale. He gave me a glass and not wishing to be conspicuous I drank it. One of the women who were dancing broke away from the other and took hold of the glass. " 'Ere, what's the idea?" she said. "That's my beer you're putting away." "Oh, I'm so sorry," I said, "this gentleman offered it me and I very naturally thought it was his to offer." "All right, mate," she said, "I don't mind. You come an' 'ave a dance with me." Before I could protest she'd caught hold of me and we were dancing together. And then I found myself sitting in the armchair with the woman on my lap and we were sharing a glass of beer. I should tell you that sex has never played any great part in my life. I married young because in my position it was desirable that I should marry, but also in order to settle once for all the question of sex. I had the two sons I had made up my mind to have, and then I put the whole matter on one side. I've always been too busy to give much thought to that kind of thing, and living so much in the public eye as I do it would have been madness to do anything that might give rise to scandal. The greatest asset a politician can have is a blameless record as far as women are concerned. I have no patience with the men who smash up their careers for women. I only despise them. The woman I had on my knees was drunk; she wasn't pretty and she wasn't young: in fact, she was just a blowsy old prostitute. She filled me with disgust, and yet when she put her mouth to mine and kissed me, though her breath stank of beer and her teeth were decayed, though I loathed myself, I wanted her – I wanted her with all my soul. Suddenly I heard a voice. "That's right, old boy, have a good time." I looked up and there was Owen Griffiths. I tried to spring out of the chair, but that horrible woman wouldn't let me. "Don't you pay no

attention to 'im," she said, " 'e's only one of them nosy-parkers."
"You go to it," he said. "I know Moll. She'll give you your money's
worth all right." You know, I wasn't so much annoyed at his seeing
me in that absurd situation as angry that he should address me as
"old boy". I pushed the woman aside and stood up and faced him.
"I don't know you and I don't want to know you," I said. "I know
you all right," he said. "And my advice to you, Molly, is, see that
you get your money, he'll bilk you if he can." There was a bottle
of beer on the table close by. Without a word I seized it by the
neck and hit him over the head with it as hard as I could. I made
such a violent gesture that it woke me up.'

'A dream of that sort is not incomprehensible,' said Dr Audlin. 'It
is the revenge nature takes on persons of unimpeachable character.'

'The story's idiotic. I haven't told it you for its own sake. I've told
it you for what happened next day. I wanted to look up something in
a hurry and I went into the library of the House. I got the book
and began reading. I hadn't noticed when I sat down that Griffiths
was sitting in a chair close by me. Another of the Labour Members
came in and went up to him. "Hullo, Owen," he said to him,
"you're looking pretty dicky today." "I've got an awful headache,"
he answered. "I feel as if I'd been cracked over the head with a
bottle." '

Now Lord Mountdrago's face was grey with anguish.

'I knew then that the idea I'd had and dismissed as preposterous
was true. I knew that Griffiths was dreaming my dreams and that
he remembered them as well as I did.'

'It may also have been a coincidence.'

'When he spoke he didn't speak to his friend, he deliberately
spoke to me. He looked at me with sullen resentment.'

'Can you offer any suggestion why this same man should come
into your dreams?'

'None.'

Dr Audlin's eyes had not left his patient's face and he saw that
he lied. He had a pencil in his hand and he drew a straggling line
or two on his blotting-paper. It often took a long time to get people
to tell the truth, and yet they knew that unless they told it he could
do nothing for them.

'The dream you've just described to me took place just over three
weeks ago. Have you had any since?'

'Every night.'

'And does this man Griffiths come into them all?'

'Yes.'

The doctor drew more lines on his blotting-paper. He wanted the silence, the drabness, the dull light of that little room to have its effect on Lord Mountdrago's sensibility. Lord Mountdrago threw himself back in his chair and turned his head away so that he should not see the other's grave eyes.

'Dr Audlin, you must do something for me. I'm at the end of my tether. I shall go mad if this goes on. I'm afraid to go to sleep. Two or three nights I haven't. I've sat up reading and when I felt drowsy put on my coat and walked till I was exhausted. But I must have sleep. With all the work I have to do I must be at concert pitch; I must be in complete control of all my faculties. I need rest; sleep brings me none. I no sooner fall asleep than my dreams begin, and he's always there, that vulgar little cad, grinning at me, mocking me, despising me. It's a monstrous persecution. I tell you, doctor, I'm not the man of my dreams; it's not fair to judge me by them. Ask anyone you like. I'm an honest, upright, decent man. No one can say anything against my moral character either private or public. My whole ambition is to serve my country and maintain its greatness. I have money, I have rank, I'm not exposed to many of the temptations of lesser men, so that it's no credit to me to be incorruptible; but this I can claim, that no honour, no personal advantage, no thought of self would induce me to swerve by a hair's breadth from my duty. I've sacrificed everything to become the man I am. Greatness is my aim. Greatness is within my reach and I'm losing my nerve. I'm not that mean, despicable cowardly, lewd creature that horrible little man sees. I've told you three of my dreams; they're nothing; that man has seen me do things that are so beastly, so horrible, so shameful, that even if my life depended on it I wouldn't tell them. And he remembers them. I can hardly meet the derision and disgust I see in his eyes and I even hesitate to speak because I know my words can seem to him nothing but utter humbug. He's seen me do things that no man with any self-respect would do, things for which men are driven out of the society of their fellows and sentenced to long terms of imprisonment; he's heard the foulness of my speech; he's seen me not only ridiculous, but revolting. He despises me and he no longer pretends to conceal it. I tell you that if you can't do something to help me I shall either kill myself or kill him.'

'I wouldn't kill him if I were you,' said Dr Audlin, coolly, in that soothing voice of his. 'In this country the consequences of killing a fellow-creature are awkward.'

'I shouldn't be hanged for it, if that's what you mean. Who would know that I'd killed him? That dream of mine has shown me how. I told you, the day after I'd hit him over the head with a beer-bottle he had such a headache that he couldn't see straight. He said so himself. That shows that he can feel with his waking body what happens to his body asleep. It's not with a bottle I shall hit him next time. One night, when I'm dreaming, I shall find myself with a knife in my hand or a revolver in my pocket, I must because I want to so intensely, and then I shall seize my opportunity. I'll stick him like a pig; I'll shoot him like a dog. In the heart. And then I shall be free of this fiendish persecution.'

Some people might have thought that Lord Mountdrago was mad; after all the years during which Dr Audlin had been treating the diseased souls of men he knew how thin a line divides those whom we call sane from those whom we call insane. He knew how often in men who to all appearance were healthy and normal, who were seemingly devoid of imagination, and who fulfilled the duties of common life with credit to themselves and with benefit to their fellows, when you gained their confidence, when you tore away the mask they wore to the world, you found not only hideous abnormality, but kinks so strange, mental extravagances so fantastic, that in that respect you could call them lunatic. If you put them in an asylum not all the asylums in the world would be large enough. Anyhow, a man was not certifiable because he had strange dreams and they had shattered his nerve. The case was singular, but it was only an exaggeration of others that had come under Dr Audlin's observation; he was doubtful, however, whether the methods of treatment that he had so often found efficacious would here avail.

'Have you consulted any other member of my profession?' he asked.

'Only Sir Augustus. I merely told him that I suffered from nightmares. He said I was overworked and recommended me to go for a cruise. That's absurd. I can't leave the Foreign Office just now when the international situation needs constant attention. I'm indispensable, and I know it. On my conduct at the present juncture my whole future depends. He gave me sedatives. They had no effect. He gave me tonics. They were worse than useless. He's an old fool.'

'Can you give any reason why it should be this particular man who persists in coming into your dreams?'

'You asked me that question before. I answered it.'

That was true. But Dr Audlin had not been satisfied with the answer.

'Just now you talked of persecution. Why should Owen Griffiths want to persecute you?'

'I don't know.'

Lord Mountdrago's eyes shifted a little. Dr Audlin was sure that he was not speaking the truth.

'Have you ever done him an injury?'

'Never.'

Lord Mountdrago made no movement, but Dr Audlin had a queer feeling that he shrank into his skin. He saw before him a large, proud man who gave the impression that the questions put to him were an insolence, and yet for all that, behind that façade, was something shifting and startled that made you think of a frightened animal in a trap. Dr Audlin leaned forward and by the power of his eyes forced Lord Mountdrago to meet them. 'Are you quite sure?'

'Quite sure. You don't seem to understand that our ways lead along different paths. I don't wish to harp on it, but I must remind you that I am a Minister of the Crown and Griffiths is an obscure member of the Labour Party. Naturally there's no social connection between us; he's a man of very humble origin, he's not the sort of person I should be likely to meet at any of the houses I go to; and politically our respective stations are so far separated that we could not possibly have anything in common.'

'I can do nothing for you unless you tell me the complete truth.'

Lord Mountdrago raised his eyebrows. His voice was rasping.

'I'm not accustomed to having my word doubted, Dr Audlin. If you're going to do that I think to take up any more of your time can only be a waste of mine. If you will kindly let my secretary know what your fee is he will see that a cheque is sent to you.'

For all the expression that was to be seen on Dr Audlin's face you might have thought that he simply had not heard what Lord Mountdrago said. He continued to look steadily into his eyes and his voice was grave and low.

'Have you done anything to this man that *he* might look upon as an injury?'

Lord Mountdrago hesitated. He looked away, and then, as though there were in Dr Audlin's eyes a compelling force that he could not resist, looked back. He answered sulkily:

'Only if he was a dirty, second-rate little cad.'

'But that is exactly what you've described him to be.'

Lord Mountdrago sighed. He was beaten. Dr Audlin knew that the sigh meant he was going at last to say what he had till then held back. Now he had no longer to insist. He dropped his eyes and began again drawing vague geometrical figures on his blotting-paper. The silence lasted two or three minutes.

'I'm anxious to tell you everything that can be of any use to you. If I didn't mention this before, it's only because it was so unimportant that I didn't see how it could possibly have anything to do with the case. Griffiths won a seat at the last election and he began to make a nuisance of himself almost at once. His father's a miner, and he worked in a mine himself when he was a boy; he's been a schoolmaster in the board schools and a journalist. He's that half-baked, conceited intellectual, with inadequate knowledge, ill-considered ideas, and impracticable plans, that compulsory education has brought forth from the working-classes. He's a scrawny, grey-faced man, who looks half-starved, and he's always very slovenly in appearance; heaven knows members nowadays don't bother much about their dress, but his clothes are an outrage to the dignity of the House. They're ostentatiously shabby, his collar's never clean and his tie's never tied properly; he looks as if he hadn't had a bath for a month and his hands are filthy. The Labour Party have two or three fellows on the Front Bench who've got a certain ability, but the rest of them don't amount to much. In the kingdom of the blind the one-eyed man is king: because Griffiths is glib and has a lot of superficial information on a number of subjects, the Whips on his side began to put him up to speak whenever there was a chance. It appeared that he fancied himself on foreign affairs, and he was continually asking me silly, tiresome questions. I don't mind telling you that I made a point of snubbing him as soundly as I thought he deserved. From the beginning I hated the way he talked, his whining voice and his vulgar accent; he had nervous mannerisms that intensely irritated me. He talked rather shyly, hesitatingly, as though it were torture to him to speak and yet he was forced on by some inner passion, and often he used to say some very disconcerting things. I'll admit that now and again he had a sort of tub-thumping eloquence. It had a certain influence over the ill-regulated minds of the members of his party. They were impressed by his earnestness and they weren't, as I was, nauseated by his sentimentality. A certain sentimentality is the common coin of political debate. Nations are governed by self-interest, but they prefer to believe that their aims are altruistic, and the politician is justified if with fair words and fine phrases he can persuade the electorate that the hard bargain he is driving for his country's advantage tends to the good of humanity. The mistake people like Griffiths make is to take these fair words and fine phrases at their face value. He's a crank, and a noxious crank. He calls himself an idealist. He has at his tongue's end all the tedious blather that the intelligentsia have been boring us with for years. Non-resistance. The brotherhood of man. You know the hopeless rubbish. The worse of it was that it impressed not only his own party, it even shook some of the sillier, more sloppy-minded members of ours. I heard rumours that Griffiths was likely to get office when a Labour Government came in; I even heard it suggested that he might get the Foreign Office. The notion was grotesque but not impossible. One day I had occasion to wind up a debate on foreign affairs which Griffiths had opened. He'd spoken for an hour. I thought it a very good opportunity to cook his goose, and by God, sir, I cooked it. I tore his speech to pieces. I pointed out the faultiness of his reasoning and emphasized the deficiency of his knowledge. In the House of Commons the most devastating weapon is ridicule: I mocked him; I bantered him; I was in good form that day and the House rocked with laughter. Their laughter excited me and I excelled myself. The Opposition sat glum and silent, but even some of them couldn't help laughing once or twice; it's not intolerable, you know, to see a colleague, perhaps a rival, made a fool of. And if ever a man was made a fool of I made a fool of Griffiths. He shrank down in a seat, I saw his face go white, and presently he buried it in his hands. When I sat down I'd killed him. I'd destroyed his prestige for ever; he had no more chance of getting office when a Labour Government came in than the policeman at the door. I heard afterwards that his father, the old miner, and his mother had come up from Wales, with various supporters of his in the constituency, to watch the triumph they expected him to have. They had seen only his utter humiliation. He'd won the constituency by the narrowest margin. An incident like that might very easily lose him his seat. But that was no business of mine.'

'Should I be putting it too strongly if I said you had ruined his career?' asked Dr Audlin.

'I don't suppose you would.'

'That is a very serious injury you've done him.'

'He brought it on himself.'

'Have you never felt any qualms about it?'

'I think perhaps if I'd known that his father and mother were there I might have let him down a little more gently.'

There was nothing further for Dr Audlin to say, and he set about treating his patient in such a manner as he thought might avail. He sought by suggestion to make him forget his dreams when he awoke; he sought to make him sleep so deeply that he would not dream. He found Lord Mountdrago's resistance impossible to break down. At the end of an hour he dismissed him. Since then he had seen Lord Mountdrago half a dozen times. He had done him no good. The frightful dreams continued every night to harass the unfortunate man, and it was clear that his general condition was growing rapidly worse. He was worn out. His irritability was uncontrollable. Lord Mountdrago was angry because he received no benefit from his treatment, and yet continued it, not only because it seemed his only hope, but because it was a relief to him to have someone with whom he could talk openly. Dr Audlin came to the conclusion at last that there was only one way in which Lord Mountdrago could achieve deliverance, but he knew him well enough to be assured that of his own free will he would never, never take it. If Lord Mountdrago was to be saved from the breakdown that was threatening he must be induced to take a step that must be abhorrent to his pride of birth and his self-complacency. Dr Audlin was convinced that to delay was impossible. He was treating his patient by suggestion, and after several visits found him more susceptible to it. At length he managed to get him into a condition of somnolence. With his low, soft, monotonous voice he soothed his tortured nerves. He repeated the same words over and over again. Lord Mountdrago lay quite still, his eyes closed; his breathing was regular, and his limbs were relaxed. Then Dr Audlin in the same quiet tone spoke the words he had prepared.

'You will go to Owen Griffiths and say that you are sorry that you caused him that great injury. You will say that you will do whatever lies in your power to undo the harm that you have done him.'

The words acted on Lord Mountdrago like the blow of a whip across his face. He shook himself out of his hypnotic state and sprang to his feet. His eyes blazed with passion and he poured forth upon Dr Audlin a stream of angry vituperation such as even he had never heard. He swore at him. He cursed him. He used language of such obscenity that Dr Audlin, who had heard every sort of foul word, sometimes from the lips of chaste and distinguished women, was surprised that he knew it.

'Apologize to that filthy little Welshman? I'd rather kill myself.'

'I believe it to be the only way in which you can regain your balance.'

Dr Audlin had not often seen a man presumably sane in such a condition of uncontrollable fury. He grew red in the face and his eyes bulged out of his head. He did really foam at the mouth. Dr Audlin watched him coolly, waiting for the storm to wear itself out, and presently he saw that Lord Mountdrago, weakened by the strain to which he had been subjected for so many weeks, was exhausted.

'Sit down,' he said then, sharply.

Lord Mountdrago crumpled up into a chair.

'Christ, I feel all in. I must rest a minute and then I'll go.'

For five minutes perhaps they sat in complete silence. Lord Mountdrago was a gross, blustering bully, but he was also a gentleman. When he broke the silence he had recovered his self-control.

'I'm afraid I've been very rude to you. I'm ashamed of the things I've said to you and I can only say you'd be justified if you refused to have anything more to do with me. I hope you won't do that. I feel that my visits to you do help me. I think you're my only chance.'

'You mustn't give another thought to what you said. It was of no consequence.'

'But there's one thing you mustn't ask me to do, and that is to make excuses to Griffiths.'

'I've thought a great deal about your case. I don't pretend to understand it, but I believe that your only chance of release is to do what I proposed. I have a notion that we're none of us one self, but many, and one of the selves in you has risen up against the injury you did Griffiths and has taken on the form of Griffiths in your mind and is punishing you for what you cruelly did. If I were a priest I should tell you that it is your conscience that has adopted the shape and lineaments of this man to scourge you to repentance and persuade you to reparation.'

'My conscience is clear. It's not my fault if I smashed the man's career. I crushed him like a slug in my garden. I regret nothing.'

It was on these words that Lord Mountdrago had left him. Reading through his notes, while he waited, Dr Audlin considered how best he could bring his patient to the state of 'mind that, now that his usual methods of treatment had failed, he thought alone could help him. He glanced at his clock. It was six. It was strange that Lord Mountdrago did not come. He knew he had intended to because a secretary had rung up that morning to say that he would be with him at the usual hour. He must have been detained by pressing work. This notion gave Dr Audlin something else to think of: Lord Mountdrago was quite unfit for work and in no condition to deal with important matters of state. Dr Audlin wondered whether it behoved him to get in touch with someone in authority, the Prime Minister or the Permanent Under-Secretary for Foreign Affairs, and impart to him his conviction that Lord Mountdrago's mind was so unbalanced that it was dangerous to leave affairs of moment in his hands. It was a ticklish thing to do. He might cause needless trouble and get roundly snubbed for his pains. He shrugged his shoulders.

'After all,' he reflected, 'the politicians have made such a mess of the world during the last five-and-twenty years, I don't suppose it makes much odds if they're mad or sane.'

He rang the bell.

'If Lord Mountdrago comes now will you tell him that I have another appointment at six-fifteen and so I'm afraid I can't see him.'

'Very good, sir.'

'Has the evening paper come yet?'

'I'll go and see.'

In a moment the servant brought it in. A huge headline ran across the front page: Tragic Death of Foreign Minister.

'My God!' cried Dr Audlin.

For once he was wrenched out of his wonted calm. He was shocked, horribly shocked, and yet he was not altogether surprised. The possibility that Lord Mountdrago might commit suicide had occurred to him several times, for that it was suicide he could not doubt. The paper said that Lord Mountdrago had been waiting in a Tube station, standing on the edge of the platform, and as the train came in was seen to fall on the rail. It was supposed that he had had a sudden attack of faintness. The paper went on to say that Lord Mountdrago had been suffering for some weeks from the effects of overwork, but had felt it impossible to absent himself while the foreign situation demanded his unremitting attention. Lord Mountdrago was another victim of the strain that modern politics placed upon those who played the more important parts in it. There was a neat little piece about the talents and industry, the patriotism and vision, of the deceased statesman, followed by various surmises upon the Prime Minister's choice of his successor. Dr Audlin read all this. He had not liked Lord Mountdrago. The chief emotion that his death caused in him was dissatisfaction with himself because he had been able to do nothing for him.

Perhaps he had done wrong in not getting into touch with Lord Mountdrago's doctor. He was discouraged, as always when failure frustrated his conscientious efforts, and repulsion seized him for the theory and practice of this empiric doctrine by which he earned his living. He was dealing with dark and mysterious forces that it was perhaps beyond the powers of the human mind to understand. He was like a man blindfold trying to feel his way to he knew not whither. Listlessly he turned the pages of the paper. Suddenly he gave a great start, and an exclamation once more was forced from his lips. His eyes had fallen on a small paragraph near the bottom of a column. Sudden Death of an MP, he read. Mr Owen Griffiths, member for so-and-so, had been taken ill in Fleet Street that afternoon and when he was brought to Charing Cross Hospital life was found to be extinct. It was supposed that death was due to natural causes, but an inquest would be held. Dr Audlin could hardly believe his eyes. Was it possible that the night before Lord Mountdrago had at last in his dream found himself possessed of the weapon, knife or gun, that he had wanted, and had killed his tormentor, and had that ghostly murder, in the same way as the blow with the bottle had given him a racking headache on the following day, taken effect a certain number of hours later on the waking man? Or was it, more mysterious and more frightful, that when Lord Mountdrago sought relief in death, the enemy he had so cruelly wronged, unappeased, escaping from his own mortality, had pursued him to some other sphere there to torment him still? It was strange. The sensible thing was to look upon it merely as an odd coincidence. Dr Audlin rang the bell.

'Tell Mrs Milton that I'm sorry I can't see her this evening. I'm not well.'

It was true; he shivered as though of an ague. With some kind of spiritual sense he seemed to envisage a bleak, a horrible void. The dark night of the soul engulfed him, and he felt a strange, primeval terror of he knew not what.

# The Sick Gentleman's Last Visit

## Giovanni Papini

*Papini is a neglected master of Italian literature. He wrote over eighty books on philosophy, theology and literary criticism, as well as novels and short stories. He was first an anti-nationalist, then a staunch national-ist; first an agnostic, then a practising Christian; he joined the Futurist movement but later turned against it, and though an enemy of academic erudition sought official recognition from the Italian universities. He wrote both a life of Christ and a history of the Devil. His short stories are masterpieces of invention, written in what today seems perhaps a florid style, and in many Papini himself is the main character. In one story Papini meets himself as the young man he was and whom he only vaguely remembers; in another he continues to live after his suicide in order to pay a minor debt. His best collection of fantastic tales is intrigu-ingly called* The Blind Pilot *– there is no story of that title in the book.*

No one ever knew the real name of the man we all called the Sick Gentleman. Since his sudden disappearance everything that was his has vanished as well, everything except the memory of his unforgettable smile, and a portrait by Sebastiano del Piombo which shows him half hidden in the soft shadow of a fur coat, one gloved hand drooping delicately like the hand of someone asleep. A few of those who loved him truly – and I count myself as one of the few – also remember his remarkable skin of a transparent and pale yellow hue, the almost feminine lightness of his step, and his constantly vacant look. He enjoyed talking for hours on end but no one ever grasped the full meaning of his words. I even know of some who did not wish to understand him because the things he said were too horrible. His presence lent a fantastic tint to the simplest things: when his hand touched an object, the object seemed to enter and become part of the world of dreams. His eyes reflected not things that were there but other unknown and faraway things not seen by those who were with him. No one ever asked him what his illness was, or why he did not seem to try to cure it. He spent his time walking, always, day and night, without stopping. No one knew where he lived; no one ever met his parents or his brothers or sisters. One day he just appeared in town and then another day, some years later, he vanished.

The day before his disappearance he came to my room to wake me, very early, when dawn was just beginning to break. I felt the soft touch of his glove on my forehead and saw him standing in front of me, wrapped in his furs, with the ghost of a smile on his lips and his eyes more absent than ever. I realized, seeing his red eyelids, that he had been awake all night, and that he must have waited for dawn with great anxiety because his hands were trembling and his entire body seemed to shake with fever.

'What is the matter?' I asked. 'Is your illness causing you more discomfort than usual?'

'My illness?' he answered. 'My illness? Do you too believe, like the others, that I *have* an illness? That there is such a thing as *my illness?* Why not say that I *myself* am an illness? There is nothing that is mine, don't you understand? There is nothing that actually belongs to me! It is I, I who belong to someone, and that someone is my master!'

Accustomed as I was to his strange talk, I didn't answer. I continued to look at him and my look must have been gentle because he came even nearer to my bed and again touched my forehead with his soft glove.

'You do not seem to have a temperature,' he said. 'You are perfectly healthy and calm. Your blood runs peacefully through your veins. I can therefore tell you something that perhaps will frighten you: I can tell you who I am. Listen carefully, please, because I may not be able to say the same things twice. But it is necessary that I say them at least once.'

With this, he let himself fall into a purple armchair beside my bed, and carried on in a stronger voice.

'I am not a real man. I am not a man like others, a man of flesh and blood, a man born of woman. I did not come into this world like your fellow men. No one rocked me in my cradle, or watched over my growing years. I have not known the restlessness of adolescence, or the comfort of family ties. I am – and I will say this out loud though perhaps you may not want to believe me – I am but *a figure in a dream*. In me, Shakespeare's image has become literally and tragically exact: I am *such stuff as dreams are made on!* I exist because someone is dreaming me, someone who is now asleep and dreaming and sees me act and live and move, and in this very moment is dreaming that I am saying these very words. When this *someone* began to dream me, I began my existence. When he wakes, I will cease to be. I am an imagination, a creation, a guest of his long nightly fantasies. This someone's dream is lasting and intense to such a degree that I have become visible even to those who are awake. But the world of watchfulness, the world of solid reality is not mine. I feel uncomfortable in the midst of your tangible and vulgar existence! My life flows slowly in the soul of my sleeping creator . . .

'Don't think I speak symbolically or in riddles. What I am saying is the truth – the whole, simple and tremendous truth.

'To be an actor in a dream is not what pains me most. There are poets who have said that man's life is but the shadow of a dream, and philosophers who have hinted that all reality is but hallucination. I, instead, am haunted by another thought: *who is this someone who dreams me?* Who is this nameless, unknown being to whom I belong, who suddenly brought me out of the darkness of his tired brain and whose awakening will just as suddenly extinguish me, like a flame in the wind? How many days have I spent thinking of this master of mine, asleep; thinking of my creator busy with the course of my ephemeral life! He must be someone great and powerful, a being for whom our years are minutes, someone who can live the entire life of a man in just one of his nights. His dreams must be so vivid and powerful and deep that they can cast forth images in such a way that they seem real. Perhaps the whole world is but the ever-changing result of the crossing of dreams dreamt by beings identical to him. But I won't generalize: let us leave metaphysical trifling to reckless philosophers! For me, it is enough to know with absolute certainty that I am the imaginary creature of a vast, enormous dreamer.

'But who is he? That is the question that's been troubling me for so long, ever since I discovered the nature of the stuff I was made on. Surely you understand how important this question is to me? On its answer hinges my entire fate. The actors in dreams enjoy ample freedom, and for that reason my life has not been entirely determined by my birth but to a large extent by my free will.

However, it has become necessary for me to know who it was that was dreaming me in order to choose my way of life. At first I was terrified by the idea that the slightest thing might wake him – that is, destroy me. A shout, a noise, a whisper might suddenly fling me into nothingness. In those days I used to care for life, so I would torture myself in vain trying to guess the tastes and passions of my unknown master, trying to give to my existence the attributes and shapes that might please him. All the time I trembled with the thought that I might commit an act that would offend him, frighten him – and therefore wake him. For a while I imagined him to be a sort of paternalistic, evangelic deity, and I tried to lead the most virtuous and saintly of lives. At another time I pictured him as a classic pagan hero, and I would crown myself with vine-leaves and sing songs in praise of wine and dance with young nymphs in forest clearings. Once I even believed that I was part of the dream of a pure and immortal sage who managed to live in a superior spiritual world, and I spent long sleepless nights counting the stars and measuring the Earth and trying to find out how living creatures were made.

'But in the end I grew tired, humiliated to think I was but the spectacle of this unknown and unknowable master. I realized that this fiction of a life was not worth such base and servile flattery. And I began to wish ardently for that which in the beginning had caused me such terror – his awakening. I deliberately filled my life with gruesome images so that the sheer horror might wake him. I tried everything to achieve the peace of annihilation, I did all within my power to interrupt the sad comedy of my apparent life, to destroy this ridiculous larva of a life that somehow likens me to men.

'I left no crime untouched, no infamy untasted. With refined tortures I murdered innocent old people, I poisoned the waters of entire cities, I set fire to the hair of hundreds of women. Grown wild through my death-wish, I tore apart with my teeth the children I met on my way. At night I sought the company of monstrous dark giants forgotten by mankind. I took part in the incredible villanies of trolls, demons and ghosts. I threw myself from the top of a mountain into a broken and naked valley surrounded by caverns full of white bones. Witches taught me the shrieks of wild beasts that at night put fear into the hearts of the bravest of men. But it seems that he who dreams me isn't frightened by those things which make ordinary men tremble. Perhaps he enjoys watching horrible sights, perhaps he doesn't care or perhaps it doesn't affect him. Until this day I have not been able to wake him, so I must drag on with this ignoble life, wretched and unreal.

'Who will free me from my dreamer? When will the dawn come that will put an end to his work? When will the bell toll, the cock crow, the voice call that will wake him? I have been waiting so long for my day of freedom! I have been waiting so eagerly for the end of this foolish dream in which I play so monotonous a part!

'What I am doing now is my last attempt. I am telling my dreamer that I am a dream. I want him to dream that he is dreaming. That is something that happens to men, doesn't it? And don't they wake, once they realize they are dreaming? That's why I have come to see you and that's why I have told you everything. I hope he who has created me understands that at this very minute I do not exist as a real man, for as soon as he does I shall cease to exist, even as an unreal image. Do you think I will succeed? Do you think that by repeating it and shouting it I will manage to startle and awaken my invisible master?'

And while he was saying these words, the Sick Gentleman tossed and turned in the armchair, pulling off and putting on the glove of his left hand, staring at me with eyes that seemed to grow more and more vacant. It was as if he expected something terrible and marvellous to happen at any minute. His face took on an agonized expression. From time to time he would stare at his own body as if expecting to see it dissolve into thin air, and he would nervously pass a hand across his damp forehead.

'Do you believe all this to be true?' he asked me. 'Or do you think I'm lying? But why can't I disappear, why can't I be free of it all? Is it that I'm part of an everlasting dream, the dream of an immortal sleeper, of an eternal dreamer? Help me get rid of this terrible notion! Console me, find me some plan, some way to escape from this horror! I beg you, help me! Will no one pity this poor, bored apparition?'

As I remained silent, he stared at me once again and then stood up. He seemed to me taller than before, and once again I noticed his almost diaphanous skin. One could see he was suffering terribly. His whole body seemed convulsed: he looked like an animal trying to escape from a net. The soft gloved hand shook mine, for the last time. Murmuring something very gently he left my room, and *only one person* has seen him since.

*Translated from the Italian by Alberto Manguel.*

# Insomnia

## Virgilio Piñera

*A Cuban writer, Piñera lived for many years in Argentina (where he published his Cold Tales in 1956); he returned to Cuba in the sixties. In Buenos Aires he met several writers interested in metaphysics – Jorge Luis Borges, Macedonio Fernández (who according to Borges reached the same conclusions as Plato and Schopenhauer without having read either), Santiago Dabove, Leopoldo Marechal – and they certainly influenced his work. The following very short story develops a theme Macedonio Fernández liked to talk about: if death and sleep are, in Oscar Wilde's phrase, brothers, there is no reason why one should have power over the other.*

The man goes to bed early but he cannot fall asleep. He turns and tosses. He twists the sheets. He lights a cigarette. He reads a bit. He puts out the light again. But he cannot sleep. At three in the morning he gets up. He calls on his friend next door and confides in him that he cannot sleep. He asks for advice. The friend suggests he take a walk and maybe he will tire himself out – then he should drink a cup of linden-tea and turn out the light. He does all these things but he does not manage to fall asleep. Again he gets up. This time he goes to see the doctor. As usual the doctor talks a good deal but in the end the man still cannot manage to sleep. At six in the morning he loads a revolver and blows out his brains. The man is dead but still he is unable to sleep. Insomnia is a very persistent thing.

*Translated from the Spanish by Alberto Manguel.*

# The Storm

## Jules Verne

*In 1863 the thirty-five-year-old Jules Verne walked into the offices of
publisher Pierre Hetzel and told him about his idea for his first book:*
Five Weeks in a Balloon. *Heztel listened, first politely, then interested,
finally spellbound. When Verne had finished, Hetzel asked him if he
had any more ideas for these 'scientific adventure stories', as Verne called
them. Timidly, but with increasing confidence, Jules Verne told Hetzel
of his imaginary travels. That afternoon Verne took Hetzel deep under
the sea, away to the moon, into the heart of darkest India, down to the
centre of the Earth. The interview ended with a twenty-year contract for
three books a year. Hetzel then decided to create a deluxe series on the
strength of his faith in his unknown writer's imagination, and one of the
world's best-beloved authors was launched on his career.*

*'The Storm' is unlike anything else I have read by Jules Verne.
Usually his novels and stories are straightforward tales of adventure in
which a scientific explanation is given to a seemingly fantastic occurrence.
In 'The Storm' nothing is explained; the reader is left with a sense of
vertigo not easily dispelled.*

The wind is blowing. The rain is pouring down. The roaring storm
bends the trees on the Volsinian shore and crashes against the
flanks of the Crimma Mountains. On the coast, the high rocks are
relentlessly gnawed away by the sharp teeth of the Megalocridian
Sea.

Deep within the shelter of the bay lies the little village of Luktrop
– barely a few hundred houses whose green belvederes try vainly to
defend themselves from the ocean winds. Four or five narrow streets
climb the mountainside, looking more like gullies than streets, paved
with pebbles and choked with rubble spat from the eruptive cone
that rises in the background. The Vanglor volcano is not far away.
During the day the inner cauldron releases sulphur fumes. At night,

at regular intervals, it spews forth long flames. Visible at a distance of a hundred and fifty *kertses*, like a lighthouse, the Vanglor pinpoints the port of Luktrop to coasting vessels, *felzane* ships, *verley* boats and even light *balanzes* whose bows cut through the icy Megalocridian waters.

At the far end of the village, next to a handful of Crimmerian ruins, are the Arab quarters: a casbah with whitewashed walls, round roofs and terraces gobbled up by the sun. The Casbah resembles a pile of stone cubes, of dice with the edges worn thin by time.

Among the notable buildings of Luktrop is the Six-Four, a bizarre construction with a square roof, six windows at the front and four at the back. A steeple dominates the village: the square tower of Saint Philifenus, whose bells are tolling in the storm. When this happens the villagers tremble with fear. 'An evil omen!' they say.

This is Luktrop. Farther away – but not too far – are a few miserable hovels scattered around the village in a landscape of bushes and ferns, somewhat like Britanny. But this is not Britanny.

Someone has knocked discreetly on the narrow door of Six-Four, at the left-hand corner of Messagliere Street. It is certainly one of the most comfortable houses in the village – if the word can be used when referring to Luktrop; one of the richest – if earning a few thousand *fretzers* can be considered a sign of wealth.

The knock has been answered by a savage snarl – something like the barking of a wolf. A window is raised above the Six-Four entrance.

'Go to hell, you nuisance, whoever you may be!' cries out an ill-humoured voice.

A young girl, shivering under the rain, wrapped in a tattered shawl, asks whether Doctor Trifulgas is in.

'Maybe yes, maybe no; it all depends.'

'It's about my father, he's dying!'

'Where is he dying?'

'Near Val Karniou, some four *kertses* from here.'

'And his name?'

'Vort Kartif.'

A hard man, this Doctor Trifulgas, not very compassionate. He only sees a patient after receiving payment in cash. Old Hurzof, the doctor's dog, half bulldog and half spaniel, has probably got a kinder heart. Six-Four only opens its doors to the rich. Every illness has a fixed price: one for curing typhoid fever, another for a cold, yet another for pericarditis or other such diseases which doctors invent by the dozen. Vort Kartif is a poor man, born of a poor family. Why should Doctor Trifulgas bother, especially on a night like this?

'Just getting me out of bed would have cost her ten *fretzers*!' he mutters, and lies down again.

Some twenty minutes later the iron knocker is heard once more. With a curse the doctor leaves his bed for the second time and leans out of the window.

'Who's there?' he cries.

'I'm Vort Kartif's wife.'

'Vort Kartif of Val Karniou?'

'Yes, and if you refuse to come he'll die!'

'Fine, then you'll be a widow.'

'Here are twenty *fretzers*—'

'Twenty *fretzers* to go all the way to Val Karniou, four *kertses* away?'

'For pity's sake!'

'Go to hell!'

And the window slams shut. Twenty *fretzers*! *What a fortune*! To risk catching a cold for twenty *fretzers*, especially when he is expected in Kiltreno tomorrow to look after rich Mr Edzingov's gout at fifty *fretzers* a visit!

With this happy thought, Doctor Trifulgas falls into a deeper sleep than before.

The beating of the storm is suddenly joined by three knocks on the door, this time from a firmer hand. The doctor is asleep. He wakes up, but in what a mood! Through the open window the storm enters like the blast of a machine-gun.

'It's about Vort Kartif—'

'Not again!'

'I'm his mother!'

'May his mother, his wife and his daughter perish with him!'

'He's had a seizure!'

'So let him fight back!'

'We've been given some money on the house; we're selling it to Dontrup on Messagliere Street. But if you don't come now my grand-daughter won't have a father, my daughter-in-law won't have a husband, and I won't have a son!'

It is pitiful and terrible to hear the old woman's voice, to imagine the wind freezing her blood and the rain soaking her thin flesh to the bones.

'A seizure is two hundred *fretzers*!' answers the heartless Trifulgas.

'We only have a hundred and twenty!'

'Good night!'

And the window closes once more.

However, after some careful thought, he concludes that a hundred and twenty *fretzers* for an hour and a half's walk, plus half an hour's visit, is about sixty *fretzers* an hour – a *fretzer* a minute. A small profit, yet not to be neglected.

Instead of going back to bed, the doctor puts on his outdoor clothes, his heavy marsh-boots, his fur cape, his woollen hood and his warm mittens. He leaves the lamp burning next to his *Codex* open at page 197. Then he pushes the door of Six-Four and steps outside.

The old woman is still there, leaning on her stick, wasted by her eighty years of misery.

'The hundred and twenty *fretzers*?'

'Here, here . . . and may God make them a thousand in your pocket!'

'God! God's money! Has anyone ever seen God's money?'

The doctor whistles for Hurzof, hangs a small lamp from the brute's mouth, and takes the road towards the sea.

The old woman follows.


What weather, my God, what weather! The bells of Saint Philifenus are tolling in the wind: a bad sign. But Doctor Trifulgas is not superstitious. In fact he believes in nothing, not even in science – except in the profit it makes.

What weather! And what a road! Pebbles and rubble, rubble and pebbles. Pebbles slippery with seaweed, rubble that crackles like slag. No light except the one carried by Hurzof, dim and faltering. Sometimes they see Vanglor's leaping flames in which quaint figures seem to struggle.

The doctor and the old woman follow the pattern of small inlets that form the coast. The sea looks white, livid, mourning-white. It dazzles the eye as it shatters against the phosphorescent rim of the surf, spilling bucketfuls of glistening worms on to the strand.

Both figures continue to climb until the road turns between soft dunes where the broom and the reeds are thrown against each other by the wind with the click of bayonets. Here the old woman stops, and with a trembling finger points to a reddish light in the shadows. Vort Kartif's house.

'There?' asks the doctor.

'Yes,' answers the woman.

The dog howls.

Suddenly the Vanglor shakes to its very roots. A sheaf of flames sprouts up into the sky, cleaving the clouds. Doctor Trifulgas falls backwards.

He swears like a damned soul. Then he scrambles to his feet and looks around him. The old woman is no longer there. Has she been swallowed by a gap in the ground or has she disappeared into the booming clouds? The dog is still there, sitting on its hind legs, the extinguished lamp still hanging from its mouth.

'Cowards,' grumbles Doctor Trifulgas.

The honest man has received his hundred and twenty *fretzers*: now he feels he must earn them.

The small dot of light is about half a *kertse* away. The dying man's lamp . . . the *dead* man's lamp, perhaps . . . There is his house, as the old woman pointed out. There is no mistaking it.

Beneath the whistling wind, the beating rain, the rolling storm, Doctor Trifulgas marches on with hasty steps. As he advances, the house becomes clearer, standing alone in the middle of the heath. It looks a little like the doctor's house, Six-Four, in Luktrop. Same windows at the front, same narrow door . . .

Doctor Trifulgas hurries on as fast as the wind will allow him. The door is ajar, he has only to push. He pushes, he steps inside, and the wind slams it shut behind his back.

Outside, Hurzof the dog starts to howl once again, pausing at regular intervals, like a cantor between the versicles of a psalm.

How very odd! It is almost as if Doctor Trifulgas had returned to his own house. However, he is certain he has not lost his way, he has not turned back. He is now in Val Karniou, not in Luktrop. And yet here is the same corridor, low and vaulted, the same wooden spiral staircase with its heavy handrail worn down by the palms of many hands . . .

He climbs it. He arrives on the landing. A faint beam shines softly under the chamber door.

Is it his imagination? In the weak light he recognizes his own room, the yellow sofa to the right, the pearwood cupboard to the left, the steel-banded chest where he would have put his hundred and twenty *fretzers*. Here is his leather-patched armchair, here his bandy-legged table, and here, next to the dying lamp, his *Codex* open at page 197.

'What is happening to me?' he says in a low voice.

Doctor Trifulgas is afraid. His eyes shine wide open, his body seems contracted, diminished. A cold sweat runs down him. He is trembling.

Nevertheless he must hurry! The lamp will go out for lack of oil – like the lamp, the sick man is dying.

Yes, the bed is there – his own bed, surrounded by columns, his canopied bed closed by heavy curtains. Can this be a poor man's bed? With a shaking hand Doctor Trifulgas pulls the curtains apart and peers inside.

The dying man, his head barely above the sheets, is lying motionless as if hardly able to breathe. The doctor leans over him.

Doctor Trifulgas' cry is echoed outside by a sinister howl.

The dying man is not Vort Kartif: it is Doctor Trifulgas himself. He has been struck down by a congestion of the lungs; an apoplectic seizure has paralysed half his body.

It is himself he has come to see, it is for himself that a hundred and twenty *fretzers* have been paid. Himself, who had refused to attend the dying man; himself, who is going to die.

Doctor Trifulgas thinks he is going mad. He feels utterly lost. His hands no longer obey him. With a supreme effort he manages to control himself.

What can he do? Diminish the blood pressure by bleeding the patient? Doctor Trifulgas is dead if he hesitates.

He opens his bag, takes out a lancet and pierces a vein in the dying man's arm. But the blood does not rise. He vigorously rubs the dying man's chest – he feels the beating of his own chest slowing down. He burns the dying man's feet with scorching stones – his own feet grow as cold as ice.

The man in the bed tries to sit up, struggles, and utters one final cry . . .

And Doctor Trifulgas, in spite of all the tricks which science has taught him, falls back dead in his own arms.

Next morning a body was found in Six-Four: that of Doctor Trifulgas. He was bathed in beer, placed in a wooden coffin and conducted with great pomp to Luktrop cemetery, where he now lies buried with so many others.

*Translated from the French by Alberto Manguel.*

# A Dream

(from *The Arabian Nights Entertainments*)

## Anonymous

*Jorge Luis Borges adapted this story and included it in several anthologies. But I have returned to E. W. Lane's version of* The Thousand and One Nights, or Arabian Nights Entertainments, *where it appears in a note at the end of Chapter XVI in the second volume. I like the elegance of the symmetrical story, I like the fact that a faithful dreamer is rewarded, I like the thought that a dream can be the source of true knowledge and lead to happiness.*

It is related also, that a man of Baghdad was possessed of ample riches and great wealth; but his wealth passed away, and his state changed, and he became utterly destitute, and could not obtain his sustenance save by laborious exertion. And he slept one night, overwhelmed and oppressed, and saw in his sleep a person who said to him, Verily thy fortune is in Cairo: therefore seek it and repair to it. So he journeyed to Cairo; and when he arrived there, the evening overtook him, and he slept in a mosque. Now there was, adjacent to the mosque, a house; and as God (whose name be exalted!) had decreed, a party of robbers entered the mosque, and thence passed to that house; and the people of the house, awaking at the disturbance occasioned by the robbers, raised cries; whereupon the Wálee came to their aid with his followers, and the robbers fled. The Wálee then entered the mosque, and found the man of Baghdad sleeping there: so he laid hold upon him, and inflicted upon him a painful beating with mikra'ahs, until he was at the point of death, and imprisoned him; and he remained three days in the prison; after which, the Wálee caused him to be brought, and said to him, From what country art thou? He answered, from Baghdad. – And what affair, said the Wálee, was the cause of thy coming to

Cairo? He answered, I saw in my sleep a person who said to me,
Verily thy fortune is in Cairo: therefore repair to it. And when I
came to Cairo, I found the fortune of which he told me to be those
blows of the mikra'ahs, that I have received from thee. – And upon
this the Wálee laughed so that his grinders appeared, and said to
him. O thou of little sense, *I* saw three times in my sleep a person
who said to me, Verily a house in Baghdad, in such a district, and
of such a description, hath in its court a garden, at the lower end
of which is a fountain, wherein is wealth of great amount: therefore
repair to it and take it. But I went not; and thou, through the
smallness of thy sense, hast journeyed from city to city on account
of a thing thou hast seen in sleep, when it was only an effect of
confused dreams. – Then he gave him some money, and said to
him, Help thyself with this to return to thy city. So he took it and
returned to Baghdad. Now the house which the Wálee had
described, in Baghdad, was the house of that man; therefore when
he arrived at his abode, he dug beneath the fountain, and beheld
abundant wealth. Thus God enriched and sustained him; and this
was a wonderful coincidence.

*Translated from the Arabic by E. W. Lane.*

# The Facts in the Case of M. Valdemar

## Edgar Allan Poe

*With 'The Purloined Letter', 'The Mystery of Marie Roget', 'Thou Art the Man' and 'The Murders of the Rue Morgue' Poe invented the detective story; with* The Narrative of Arthur Gordon Pym *he perfected the fantastic novel; with 'The Black Cat' and 'The Tell-Tale Heart' he set out the laws that govern a tale of horror. In 'The Facts in the Case of M. Valdemar' he combines the talents for all three genres. There is a mystery, and a search for a solution conducted with scientific rigour; there is the intrusion of what we know to be impossible in an otherwise normal setting; there is the gradual building-up that leads to the horrific ending. (The credibility of the story is so well achieved that shortly after its publication in America in 1854 it was printed in England as a pamphlet about a remarkable scientific experiment.)*

*On 22 September 1835, Poe married his thirteen-year-old cousin Virginia Clemm, who died ten years later of tuberculosis. Julian Symons, in his biography of Poe, suggests that this story stems from Virginia's illness. Both Valdemar and Virginia, Symons points out, suffered from the same illness, and both names begin with 'V'. Whether it stems from a desire to halt death, or from a need to know what lies beyond the grave, the point of the story is the stopping of time. (As Hotspur says in Henry IV, Part I: 'Time, that takes survey of all the world, must have a stop.')*

Of course I shall not pretend to consider it any matter for wonder, that the extraordinary case of M. Valdemar has excited discussion. It would have been a miracle had it not – especially under the circumstances. Through the desire of all parties concerned, to keep the affair from the public, at least for the present, or until we had further opportunities for investigation – through our endeavours to effect this – a garbled or exaggerated account made its way into society, and became the source of many unpleasant misrepresentations, and, very naturally, of a great deal of disbelief.

It is now rendered necessary that I give the *facts* – as far as I comprehend them myself. They are, succinctly, these:

My attention, for the last three years, had been repeatedly drawn to the subject of Mesmerism; and, about nine months ago, it occurred to me, quite suddenly, that in the series of experiments made hitherto, there had been a very remarkable and most unaccountable omission – no person had as yet been mesmerized *in articulo mortis*. It remained to be seen, first, whether, in such condition, there existed in the patient any susceptibility to the magnetic influence; secondly, whether, if any existed, it was impaired or increased by the condition; thirdly, to what extent, or for how long a period, the encroachments of Death might be arrested by the process. There were other points to be ascertained, but these most excited my curiosity – the last in especial, from the immensely important character of its consequences.

In looking around me for some subject by whose means I might test these particulars, I was brought to think of my friend, M. Ernest Valdemar, the well-known compiler of the *Bibliotheca Forensica*, and author (under the *nom de plume* of Issachar Marx) of the Polish versions of *Wallenstein* and *Gargantua*. M. Valdemar, who has resided principally at Harlem, N.Y., since the year 1839, is (or was) particularly noticeable for the extreme spareness of his person – his lower limbs much resembling those of John Randolph; and, also, for the whiteness of his whiskers, in violent contrast to the blackness of his hair – the latter, in consequence, being very generally mistaken for a wig. His temperament was markedly nervous, and rendered him a good subject for mesmeric experiment. On two or three occasions I had put him to sleep with little difficulty, but was disappointed in other results which his peculiar constitution had naturally led me to anticipate. His will was at no period positively, or thoroughly, under my control, and in regard to *clairvoyance*, I could accomplish with him nothing to be relied upon. I always attributed my failure at these points to the disordered state of his health. For some months previous to my becoming acquainted with him, his physicians had declared him in a confirmed phthisis. It was his custom, indeed, to speak calmly of his approaching dissolution, as of a matter neither to be avoided nor regretted.

When the ideas to which I have alluded first occurred to me, it was of course very natural that I should think of M. Valdemar. I knew the steady philosophy of the man too well to apprehend any scruples from *him;* and he had no relatives in America who would be likely to interfere. I spoke to him frankly upon the subject; and, to my surprise, his interest seemed vividly excited. I say to my surprise; for, although he had always yielded his person freely to my experiments, he had never before given me any tokens of sympathy with what I did. His disease was of that character which would admit of exact calculation in respect to the epoch of its termination in death; and it was finally arranged between us that he would send for me about twenty-four hours before the period announced by his physicians as that of his decease.

It is now rather more than seven months since I received, from M. Valdemar himself, the subjoined note:

My Dear P—,

You may as well come *now*. D— and F— are agreed that I cannot hold out beyond tomorrow midnight; and I think they have hit the time very nearly.

VALDEMAR

I received this note within half an hour after it was written, and in fifteen minutes more I was in the dying man's chamber. I had not seen him for ten days, and was appalled by the fearful alteration which the brief interval had wrought in him. His face wore a leaden hue; the eyes were utterly lustreless; and the emaciation was so extreme that the skin had been broken through by the cheek-bones. His expectoration was excessive. The pulse was barely perceptible. He retained, nevertheless, in a very remarkable manner, both his mental power and a certain degree of physical strength. He spoke with distinctness – took some palliative medicines without aid – and, when I entered the room, was occupied in pencilling memoranda in a pocket-book. He was propped up in the bed by pillows. Doctors D— and F— were in attendance.

After pressing Valdemar's hand, I took these gentlemen aside, and obtained from them a minute account of the patient's condition. The left lung had been for eighteen months in a semi-osseous or cartilaginous state, and was, of course, entirely useless for all purposes of vitality. The right, in its upper portion, was also partially, if not thoroughly, ossified, while the lower region was merely a mass of purulent tubercles, running one into another. Several extensive perforations existed; and, at one point, permanent adhesion to the ribs had taken place. These appearances in the right lobe were of comparatively recent date. The ossification had proceeded with very unusual rapidity; no sign of it had been discovered a month before, and the adhesion had only been observed during the three previous days. Independently of the phthisis, the patient was suspected of aneurism of the aorta; but on this point the osseous symptoms rendered an exact diagnosis impossible. It was the opinion of both physicians that M. Valdemar would die about midnight on the morrow (Sunday). It was then seven o'clock on Saturday evening.

On quitting the invalid's bed-side to hold conversation with myself, Doctors D— and F— had bidden him a final farewell. It had not been their intention to return; but, at my request, they agreed to look in upon the patient about ten the next night.

When they had gone, I spoke freely with M. Valdemar on the subject of his approaching dissolution, as well as, more particularly, of the experiment proposed. He still professed himself quite willing and even anxious to have it made, and urged me to commence it at once. A male and a female nurse were in attendance; but I did not feel myself altogether at liberty to engage in a task of this character with no more reliable witnesses than these people, in case of sudden accident, might prove. I therefore postponed operations until about eight the next night, when the arrival of a medical student with whom I had some acquaintance (Mr Theodore L—l), relieved me from further embarrassment. It had been my design, originally, to wait for the physicians; but I was induced to proceed, first, by the urgent entreaties of M. Valdemar, and secondly, by my conviction that I had not a moment to lose, as he was evidently sinking fast.

Mr L—l was so kind as to accede to my desire that he would take notes of all that occurred; and it is from his memoranda that what I now have to relate is, for the most part, either condensed or copied *verbatim*.

It wanted about five minutes of eight when, taking the patient's hand, I begged him to state, as distinctly as he could, to Mr L—l, whether he (M. Valdemar) was entirely willing that I should make the experiment of mesmerizing him in his then condition.

He replied feebly, yet quite audibly, 'Yes, I wish to be mesmerized' – adding immediately afterward, 'I fear you have deferred it too long.'

While he spoke thus, I commenced the passes which I had already found most effectual in subduing him. He was evidently influenced with the first lateral stroke of my hand across his forehead; but although I exerted all my powers, no farther perceptible effect was induced until some minutes after ten o'clock, when Doctors D— and F— called, according to appointment. I explained to them, in a few words, what I designed, and as they opposed no objection, saying that the patient was already in the death agony, I proceeded without hesitation – exchanging, however, the lateral passes for downward ones, and directing my gaze entirely into the right eye of the sufferer.

By this time his pulse was imperceptible and his breathing was stertorous, and at intervals of half a minute.

This condition was nearly unaltered for a quarter of an hour. At the expiration of this period, however, a natural although a very deep sigh escaped the bosom of the dying man, and the stertorous breathing ceased – that is to say, its stertorousness was no longer apparent; the intervals were undiminished. The patient's extremities were of an icy coldness.

At five minutes before eleven I perceived unequivocal signs of the mesmeric influence. The glassy roll of the eye was changed for that expression of uneasy *inward* examination which is never seen except in cases of sleep-walking, and which it is quite impossible to mistake. With a few rapid lateral passes I made the lids quiver, as in incipient sleep, and with a few more I closed them altogether. I was not satisfied, however, with this, but continued the manipulations vigorously, and with the fullest exertion of the will, until I had completely stiffened the limbs of the slumberer, after placing them in a seemingly easy position. The legs were at full length; the arms were nearly so, and reposed on the bed at a moderate distance from the loins. The head was very slightly elevated.

When I had accomplished this, it was fully midnight, and I requested the gentlemen present to examine M. Valdemar's condition. After a few experiments, they admitted him to be in an unusually perfect state of mesmeric trance. The curiosity of both the physicians was greatly excited. Dr D— resolved at once to remain with the patient all night, while Dr F— took leave with a promise to return at daybreak. Mr L—l and the nurses remained.

We left M. Valdemar entirely undisturbed until about three o'clock in the morning, when I approached him and found him in precisely the same condition as when Dr F— went away – that is to say, he lay in the same position; the pulse was imperceptible; the breathing was gentle (scarcely noticeable, unless through the application of a mirror to the lips); the eyes were closed naturally; and the limbs were as rigid and as cold as marble. Still, the general appearance was certainly not that of death.

As I approached M. Valdemar I made a kind of half effort to influence his right arm into pursuit of my own, as I passed the latter gently to and fro above his person. In such experiments with this patient I had never perfectly succeeded before, and assuredly I had little thought of succeeding now; but to my astonishment, his arm very readily, although feebly, followed every direction I assigned it with mine. I determined to hazard a few words of conversation.

'M. Valdemar,' I said, 'are you asleep?' He made no answer, but I perceived a tremor about the lips, and was thus induced to repeat the question, again and again. At its third repetition, his whole frame was agitated by a very slight shivering; the eyelids unclosed themselves so far as to display a white line of the ball; the lips moved sluggishly, and from between them, in a barely audible whisper, issued the words:

'Yes; – asleep now. Do not wake me! – let me die so!'

I here felt the limbs and found them as rigid as ever. The right arm, as before, obeyed the direction of my hand. I questioned the sleep-waker again:

'Do you still feel pain in the breast, M. Valdemar?'

The answer now was immediate, but even less audible than before:

'No pain – I am dying.'

I did not think it advisable to disturb him further just then, and nothing more was said or done until the arrival of Dr F—, who came a little before sunrise, and expressed unbounded astonishment at finding the patient still alive. After feeling the pulse and applying a mirror to the lips, he requested me to speak to the sleep-waker again. I did so, saying:

'M. Valdemar, do you still sleep?'

As before, some minutes elapsed ere a reply was made; and during the interval the dying man seemed to be collecting his energies to speak. At my fourth repetition of the question, he said very faintly, almost inaudibly:

'Yes; still asleep – dying.'

It was now the opinion, or rather the wish, of the physicians, that M. Valdemar should be suffered to remain undisturbed in his present apparently tranquil condition, until death should supervene – and this, it was generally agreed, must now take place within a few minutes. I concluded, however, to speak to him once more, and merely repeated my previous question.

While I spoke, there came a marked change over the countenance of the sleep-waker. The eyes rolled themselves slowly open, the pupils disappearing upwardly; the skin generally assumed a cadaverous hue, resembling not so much parchment as white paper; and the circular hectic spots which, hitherto, had been strongly defined in the centre of each cheek, *went out* at once. I use this expression, because the suddenness of their departure put me in mind of nothing so much as the extinguishment of a candle by a puff of the breath. The upper lip, at the same time, writhed itself away from the teeth, which it had previously covered completely; while the lower jaw fell with an audible jerk, leaving the mouth widely extended, and disclosing in full view the swollen and blackened tongue. I presume that no members of the party then present had been unaccustomed to death-bed horrors; but so hideous beyond conception was the appearance of M. Valdemar at this moment, that there was a general shrinking back from the region of the bed.

I now feel that I have reached a point of this narrative at which every reader will be startled into positive disbelief. It is my business, however, simply to proceed.

There was no longer the faintest sign of vitality in M. Valdemar; and, concluding him to be dead, we were consigning him to the charge of the nurses, when a strong vibratory motion was observable in the tongue. This continued for perhaps a minute. At the expiration of this period, there issued from the distended and motionless jaws a voice – such as it would be madness in me to attempt describing. There are, indeed, two or three epithets which might be considered as applicable to it in parts; I might say for example, that the sound was harsh, and broken, and hollow; but the hideous whole is indescribable, for the simple reason that no similar sounds have ever jarred upon the ear of humanity. There were two particulars, nevertheless, which I thought then, and still think, might fairly be stated as characteristic of the intonation – as well adapted to convey some idea of its unearthly peculiarity. In the first place, the voice seemed to reach our ears – at least mine – from a vast distance, or from some deep cavern within the earth. In the second place, it impressed me (I fear, indeed, that it will be impossible to make myself comprehended) as gelatinous or glutinous matters impress the sense of touch.

I have spoken both of 'sound' and of 'voice'. I mean to say that the sound was one of distinct – of even wonderfully, thrillingly distinct – syllabification. M. Valdemar *spoke* – obviously in reply to the question I had propounded to him a few minutes before. I had asked him, it will be remembered, if he still slept. He now said:

'Yes; – no; – I *have been* sleeping – and now – now – *I am dead.*'

No person present even affected to deny, or attempted to repress, the unutterable, shuddering horror which these few words, thus uttered, were so well calculated to convey. Mr L——l (the student) swooned. The nurses immediately left the chamber, and could not be induced to return. My own impressions I would not pretend to render intelligible to the reader. For nearly an hour, we busied ourselves, silently – without the utterance of a word – in endeavours to revive Mr L——l. When he came to himself, we addressed ourselves again to an investigation of M. Valdemar's condition.

It remained in all respects as I have last described it, with the exception that the mirror no longer afforded evidence of respiration. An attempt to draw blood from the arm failed. I should mention, too, that this limb was no farther subject to my will. I endeavoured in vain to make it follow the direction of my hand. The only real indication, indeed, of the mesmeric influence, was now found in the vibratory movement of the tongue, whenever I addressed M. Valdemar a question. He seemed to be making an effort to reply, but had no longer sufficient volition. To queries put to him by any other person than myself he seemed utterly insensible – although I endeavoured to place each member of the company in mesmeric *rapport* with him. I believe that I have now related all that is necessary to an understanding of the sleep-waker's state at this epoch. Other nurses were procured; and at ten o'clock I left the house in company with the two physicians and Mr L——l.

In the afternoon we all called again to see the patient. His condition remained precisely the same. We had now some discussion as to the propriety and feasibility of awakening him; but we had little difficulty in agreeing that no good purpose would be served by so doing. It was evident that, so far, death (or what is usually termed death) had been arrested by the mesmeric process. It seemed clear to us all that to awaken M. Valdemar would be merely to insure his instant, or at least his speedy, dissolution.

From this period until the close of last week – *an interval of nearly seven months* – we continued to make daily calls at M. Valdemar's house, accompanied, now and then, by medical and other friends. All this time the sleep-waker remained *exactly* as I have last described him. The nurses' attentions were continual.

It was on Friday last that we finally resolved to make the experiment of awakening, or attempting to awaken him; and it is the (perhaps) unfortunate result of this latter experiment which has given rise to so much discussion in private circles – to so much of what I cannot help thinking unwarranted popular feeling.

For the purpose of relieving M. Valdemar from the mesmeric trance, I made use of the customary passes. These, for a time, were unsuccessful. The first indication of revival was afforded by a partial descent of the iris. It was observed, as especially remarkable, that this lowering of the pupil was accompanied by the profuse outflowing of a yellowish ichor (from beneath the lids) of a pungent and highly offensive odour.

It was now suggested that I should attempt to influence the patient's arm, as heretofore. I made the attempt and failed. Dr F— then intimated a desire to have me put a question. I did so, as follows:

'M. Valdemar, can you explain to us what are your feelings or wishes now?'

There was an instant return of the hectic circles on the cheeks; the tongue quivered, or rather rolled violently in the mouth (although the jaws and lips remained rigid as before); and at length the same hideous voice which I have already described, broke forth:

'For God's sake! – quick! – quick! – put me to sleep – or, quick! – waken me! – quick! – *I say to you that I am dead!*'

I was thoroughly unnerved, and for an instant remained undecided what to do. At first I made an endeavour to recompose the patient; but, failing in this through total abeyance of the will, I retraced my steps and as earnestly struggled to awaken him. In this attempt I soon saw that I should be successful – or at least I soon fancied that my success would be complete – and I am sure that all in the room were prepared to see the patient awaken.

For what really occurred, however, it is quite impossible that any human being could have been prepared.

As I rapidly made the mesmeric passes, amid ejaculations of 'Dead! dead!' absolutely *bursting* from the tongue and not from the lips of the sufferer, his whole frame at once – within the space of a single minute, or even less, shrunk – crumbled – absolutely *rotted* beneath my hands. Upon the bed, before that whole company, there lay a nearly liquid mass of loathsome – of detestable – putridity.

# Split Second

## Daphne du Maurier

*The author of* Rebecca *is also a brilliant short-story writer: the proof lies in 'The Way of the Cross', in 'Don't Look Now', in 'The Birds' (the story is even better than the film). Alfred Hitchcock (who filmed* Rebecca *and 'The Birds', as well as several other du Maurier books) made a television adaptation of 'Split Second', with Bette Davis as Mrs Ellis; it was excellent, and I suggest the reader keep Bette Davis' image in mind while reading the following pages.*

*The literature of time travel is vast and honourable: one of the first time travellers, Aeneas, sees his future in the shield Vulcan makes for him and visits his dead father who speaks to him in tender tones. The most famous of all time travellers, H. G. Wells' hero, brings back a flower that will bloom many years later. In 'Split Second' the traveller is no longer a hero with glorious tasks to fulfil, but a modern-day heroine left to cope with mundane chores in a world that is no longer her own.*

Mrs Ellis was methodical and tidy. She disliked disorder. Unanswered letters, unpaid bills, the litter and rummage of a slovenly writing desk were things that she abhorred.

Today, more than usual, she was in what her late husband used to call her 'clearing' mood.

She had wakened to this mood; it remained with her throughout breakfast and lasted the whole morning.

Besides, it was the first of the month, and as she ripped off the page of her daily calendar and saw the bright clean 1 staring at her, it seemed to symbolize a new start to her day.

The hours ahead of her must somehow seem untarnished like the date; she must let nothing slide.

First she checked the linen. The smooth white sheets lying in rows upon their shelves, pillow slips beside, and one set still in its pristine newness from the shop, tied with blue ribbon, waiting for a guest that never came.

Next, the store cupboard. The stock of homemade jam pleased her, the labels, and the date in her own handwriting.

There were also bottled fruit, and tomatoes, and chutney to her own recipe. She was sparing of these, keeping them in reserve for the holidays when Susan should be home, and even then, when she brought them down and put them proudly on the table, the luxury of the treat was spoilt by a little stab of disappointment; it would mean a gap upon the store-cupboard shelf.

When she had closed the store cupboard and hidden the key (she could never be quite certain of Grace, her cook), Mrs Ellis went into the drawing-room and settled herself at her desk.

She was determined to be ruthless. The pigeonholes were searched, and those old envelopes that she had kept because they were not torn and could be used again (to tradesmen, not to friends) were thrown away. She would buy fresh buff envelopes of a cheap quality instead.

Here were some receipts of two years back. Unnecessary to keep them now. Those of a year ago were filed, and tied with tape.

A little drawer, stiff to open, she found crammed with old counterfoils from her chequebook. This was wasting space.

Instead, she wrote in her clear handwriting, 'Letters to Keep'. In the future, the drawer would be used for this purpose.

She permitted herself the luxury of filling her blotter with new sheets of paper. The pen tray was dusted. A new pencil sharpened. And steeling her heart, she threw the stub of the little old one, with worn rubber at the base, into the waste-paper basket.

She straightened the magazines on the side table, pulled the books to the front on the shelf beside the fire – Grace had an infuriating habit of pushing them all to the back – and filled the flower vases with clean water. Then with a bare ten minutes before Grace popped her head round the door and said, 'Lunch is in,' Mrs Ellis sat down, a little breathless, before the fire, and smiled in satisfaction. Her morning had been very full indeed. Happy, well-spent.

She looked about her drawing-room (Grace insisted on calling it the lounge and Mrs Ellis was forever correcting her) and thought how comfortable it was, and bright, and how wise they had been not to move when poor Wilfred suggested it a few months before he died. They had so nearly taken the house in the country, because of his health, and his fad that vegetables should be picked fresh every morning and brought to the table, and then luckily – well, hardly luckily, it was most terribly sad and a fearful shock to her – but before they had signed the lease, Wilfred had a heart attack and died. Mrs Ellis was able to stay on in the home she knew and loved, and where she had first gone as a bride ten years before.

People were inclined to say the locality was going downhill, that it had become worse than suburban. Nonsense. The blocks of flats that were going up at the top end of the road could not be seen from her windows, and the houses, solid like her own, standing in a little circle of front garden, were quite unspoilt.

Besides, she liked the life. Her mornings, shopping in the town, her basket over her arm. The tradesmen knew her, treated her well.

Morning coffee at eleven, at the Cosy Café opposite the bookshop, was a small pleasure she allowed herself on cold mornings – she could not get Grace to make good coffee – and in the summer, the Cosy Café sold ice cream.

Childishly, she would hurry back with this in a paper bag and eat it for lunch; it saved thinking of a sweet.

She believed in a brisk walk in the afternoons, and the heath was so close to hand, it was just as good as the country; and in the evenings she read, or sewed, or wrote to Susan.

Life, if she thought deeply about it, which she did not because to think deeply made her uncomfortable, was really built round Susan. Susan was nine years old, and her only child.

Because of Wilfred's ill-health and, it must be confessed, his irritability, Susan had been sent to boarding school at an early age. Mrs Ellis had passed many sleepless nights before making this decision, but in the end she knew it would be for Susan's good. The child was healthy and high-spirited, and it was impossible to keep her quiet and subdued in one room, with Wilfred fractious in another. It meant sending her down to the kitchen with Grace, and that, Mrs Ellis decided, did not do.

Reluctantly, the school was chosen, some thirty miles away. It was easily reached within an hour and a half by a Green Line bus; the children seemed happy and well cared for, the principal was grey-haired and sympathetic, and as the prospectus described it, the place was a 'home from home'.

Mrs Ellis left Susan, on the opening day of her first term, in agony of mind, but constant telephone calls between herself and the headmistress during the first week reassured her that Susan had settled placidly to her new existence.

When her husband died, Mrs Ellis thought Susan would want to return home and go to a day school, but to her surprise and disappointment the suggestion was received with dismay, and even tears.

'But I love my school,' said the child; 'we have such fun, and I have lots of friends.'

'You would make other friends at a day school,' said her mother, 'and think, we would be together in the evenings.'

'Yes,' answered Susan doubtfully, 'but what would we do?'

Mrs Ellis was hurt, but she did not permit Susan to see this.

'Perhaps you are right,' she said. 'You are contented and happy where you are. Anyway, we shall always have the holidays.'

The holidays were like brightly coloured beads on a frame and stood out with significance in Mrs Ellis' engagement diary throwing the weeks between into obscurity.

How leaden was February, in spite of twenty-eight days; how blue and interminable was March, for all that morning coffee at the Cosy Café, the choosing of library books, the visit with friends to the local cinema, or sometimes, more dashing, a matinee 'in town'.

Then April came, and danced its flowery way across the calendar. Easter, and daffodils, and Susan with glowing cheeks whipped by a spring wind, hugging her once again; honey for tea, scones baked by Grace ('You've been and grown again'), those afternoon walks across the heath, sunny and gay because of the figure running on ahead. May was quiet, and June pleasant because of wide-flung windows, and the snapdragons in the front garden; June was leisurely.

Besides, there was the school play on Parents' Day, and Susan, with bright eyes, surely much the best of the pixies, and although she did not speak, her actions were so good.

July dragged until the twenty-fourth, and then the weeks spun themselves into a sequence of glory until the last week in September. Susan at the sea . . . Susan on a farm . . . Susan on Dartmoor . . . Susan just at home, licking an ice cream, leaning out of a window.

'She swims quite well for her age', thus casually, to a neighbour on the beach; 'she insists on going in, even when it's cold.'

'I don't mind saying,' this to Grace, 'that I hated going through that field of bullocks, but Susan did not mind a scrap. She has a way with animals.'

Bare scratched legs in sandals, summer frocks outgrown, a sun hat, faded, lying on the floor. October did not bear thinking about . . . But, after all, there was always plenty to do about the house. Forget November, and the rain, and the fogs that turned white upon the heath. Draw the curtains, poke the fire, settle to something. The *Weekly Home Companion*. Fashions for Young Folk. Not that pink, but the green with the smocked top, and a wide sash would be just the thing for Susan at parties in the Christmas holidays. December . . . Christmas . . .

This was the best, this was the height of home enjoyment.

As soon as Mrs Ellis saw the first small trees standing outside the florist's and those orange boxes of dates in the grocer's window, her heart would give a little leap of excitement.

Susan would be home in three weeks now. Then the laughter and the chatter. The nods between herself and Grace. The smiles of mystery. The furtiveness of wrappings.

All over in one day like the bursting of a swollen balloon; paper ribbon, cracker novelties, even presents, chosen with care, thrown aside. But no matter. It was worth it.

Mrs Ellis, looking down upon a sleeping Susan tucked in with a doll in her arms, turned down the light and crept off to her own bed, sapped, exhausted.

The egg cosy, Susan's handiwork at school, hastily stitched, stood on her bedside table.

Mrs Ellis never ate boiled eggs, but, as she said to Grace, there is such a gleam in the hen's eye; it's very cleverly done.

The fever, the pace of the New Year. The Circus, the Pantomime. Mrs Ellis watched Susan, never the performers.

'You should have seen her laugh when the seal blew the trumpet; I have never known a child with such a gift for enjoyment.'

And how she stood out at parties, in the green frock, with her fair hair and blue eyes. Other children were so stumpy. Ill-made little bodies, or big shapeless mouths.

'She said, "Thank you for a lovely time," when we left, which was more than most of them did. And she won at Musical Chairs.'

There were bad moments, too, of course. The restless night, the high spot of colour, the sore throat, the temperature of 102.

Shaking hands on the telephone. The doctor's reassuring voice. And his very footsteps on the stairs, a steady, reliable man.

'We had better take a swab, in case.'

A swab? That meant diphtheria, scarlet fever?

A little figure being carried down in blankets, an ambulance, hospital . . . ?

Thank God, it proved to be a relaxed throat. Lots of them about. Too many parties, keep her quiet for a few days. Yes, Doctor, yes.

The relief from dread anxiety, and on and on without a stop, the reading to Susan from her *Playbook Annual*, story after story, terrible and trite, 'and so Nicky Nod *did* lose his treasure after all, which just served him right, didn't it, children?'

'All things pass,' thought Mrs Ellis, 'pleasure and pain, and happiness and suffering, and I suppose my friends would say my life is a dull one, rather uneventful, but I am grateful for it, and contented, and although sometimes I feel I did not do my utmost for poor Wilfred – his was a difficult nature, luckily Susan has not inherited it – at least I believe I have succeeded in making a happy home for Susan.' She looked about her, that first day of the month, and·noticed with affection and appreciation those bits and pieces of furniture, the pictures on the walls, the ornaments on the mantelpiece, all the things she had gathered about her during ten years of marriage, and which meant herself, her home.

The sofa and two chairs, part of an original suite, were worn but comfortable. The pouf by the fire, she had covered it herself. The fire irons, not quite so polished as they should be, she must speak to Grace. The rather melancholy portrait of Wilfred in that dark corner behind the bookshelf, he looked at least distinguished. And was, thought Mrs Ellis to herself, hastily. The flower picture showed more to advantage over the mantelpiece; the green foliage harmonized so well with the green coat of the Staffordshire figure who stood with his lady beside the clock.

'I could do with new covers,' thought Mrs Ellis, 'and curtains too, but they must wait. Susan has grown so enormously the last few months. Her clothes are more important. The child is tall for her age.'

Grace looked round the door. 'Lunch is in,' she said.

'If she would open the door outright,' thought Mrs Ellis, 'and come right into the room, I have mentioned it a hundred times. It's the sudden thrust of the head that is so disconcerting, and if I have anyone to lunch . . .'

She sat down to guinea fowl and apple charlotte, and she wondered if they were remembering to give Susan extra milk at school this term, and the Minidex tonic; the matron was inclined to be forgetful.

Suddenly, for no reason, she laid her spoon down on the plate, swept with a wave of such intense melancholy as to be almost unbearable. Her heart was heavy. Her throat tightened. She could not continue her lunch.

'Something is wrong with Susan,' she thought; 'this is a warning that she wants me.'

She rang for coffee and went into the drawing-room. She crossed to the window and stood looking at the back of the house opposite. From an open window sagged an ugly red curtain, and a lavatory brush hung from a nail.

'The district *is* losing class,' thought Mrs Ellis. 'I shall have lodginghouses for neighbours soon.'

She drank her coffee, but the feeling of uneasiness, of apprehension, did not leave her. At last she went to the telephone and rang up the school.

The secretary answered. Surprised, and a little impatient, surely. Susan was perfectly all right. She had just eaten a good lunch. No, she had no sign of a cold. No one was ill in the school. Did Mrs Ellis want to speak to Susan? The child was outside with the others, playing, but could be called in if necessary.

'No,' said Mrs Ellis, 'it was just a foolish notion on my part that Susan might not be well. I am so sorry to have bothered you.'

She hung up the receiver, and then went to her bedroom to put on her outdoor clothes. A good walk would do her good.

She gazed in satisfaction upon the photograph of Susan on the dressing table. The photographer had caught the expression in her eyes to perfection. Such a lovely light on the hair too.

Mrs Ellis hesitated. Was it really a walk she needed? Or was this vague feeling of distress a sign that she was over-tired, that she had better rest?

She looked with inclination at the downy quilt upon her bed. Her hot-water bottle, hanging by the washstand, would take only a moment to fill.

She could loosen her girdle, throw off her shoes, and lie down for an hour on the bed, warm with the bottle under the downy quilt. No. She decided to be firm with herself. She went to the wardrobe and got out her camel coat, wound a scarf round her head, pulled on a pair of gauntlet gloves, and walked downstairs.

She went into the drawing-room and made up the fire, and put the guard in front of it. Grace was apt to be forgetful of the fire. She opened the window at the top so that the room should not strike stuffy when she came back.

She folded the daily papers ready to read when she returned, and replaced the marker in her library book.

'I'm going out for a little while. I shan't be long,' she called down to the basement to Grace.

'All right ma'am,' came the answer.

Mrs Ellis caught the whiff of cigarette, and frowned. Grace could do as she liked in the basement, but there was something not quite right about a maidservant smoking.

She shut the front door behind her, and went down the steps, and into the road, and turned left towards the heath.

It was a dull, grey day. Mild for the time of year, almost to oppression. Later, there would be fog, perhaps, rolling up from London the way it did, in a great wall, stifling the clean air.

Mrs Ellis made her 'short round', as she always called it. Eastward, to the Viaduct ponds, and then back, circling, to the Vale of Health.

It was not an inviting afternoon, and she did not enjoy her walk. She kept wishing she was home again, in bed with a hot-water bottle, or sitting in the drawing-room beside the fire, soon to shut out the muggy, murky sky, and draw the curtains.

She walked swiftly past nurses pushing prams, two or three of them in groups chatting together, their charges running ahead. Dogs barked beside the ponds. Solitary men in mackintoshes stared into vacancy. An old woman on a seat threw crumbs to chirping sparrows. The sky took on a darker, olive tone. Mrs Ellis quickened her steps. The fairground by the Vale of Health looked sombre, the merry-go-round shrouded in its winter wrappings of canvas, and two lean cats stalked each other in and out of the palings.

A milkman, whistling, clanked his tray of bottles and, lifting them to his cart, urged the pony to a trot.

'I must,' thought Mrs Ellis inconsequently, 'get Susan a bicycle for her birthday. Nine is a good age for a first bicycle.'

She saw herself choosing one, asking advice, feeling the handle bars, the colour red perhaps. Or a good blue. A little basket on the front and a leather bag, for tools, strapped to the back of the seat. The brakes must be good, but not too gripping, otherwise Susan would topple headfirst over the handle bars and graze her face.

Hoops were out of fashion, which was a pity. When she had been a child there had been no fun like a good springy hoop, struck smartly with a little stick, bowling its way ahead of you. Quite an art to it too. Susan would have been good with a hoop.

Mrs Ellis came to the junction of two roads, and crossed to the opposite side; the second road was her own, and her house the last one on the corner.

As she did so she saw the laundry van swinging down towards her, much too fast. She saw it swerve, heard the screech of its brakes. She saw the look of surprise on the face of the laundry boy.

'I shall speak to the driver next time he calls,' she said to herself. 'One of these days there will be an accident.'

She thought of Susan on the bicycle, and shuddered.

Perhaps a note to the manager of the laundry would do more good.

'If you could possibly give a word of warning to your driver, I should be grateful. He takes his corners much too fast.'

And she would ask to remain anonymous. Otherwise the man might complain about carrying the heavy basket down the steps each time.

She had arrived at her own gate. She pushed it open, and noticed with annoyance that it was nearly off its hinges. The men calling for the laundry must have wrenched at it in some way and done the damage. The note to the manager would be stronger still. She would write immediately after tea. While it was on her mind.

She took out her key and put it in the Yale lock of the front door. It stuck. She could not turn it. How very irritating.

She rang the bell. That would mean bringing Grace up from the basement, which she did not like.

Better to call down, perhaps, and explain the situation.

She leant over the steps and called down to the kitchen.

'Grace, it's only me,' she said, 'my key has jammed in the door; could you come up and let me in?'

She paused. There was no sound from below. Grace must have gone out. This was sheer deceit. It was an agreed bargain between them that when Mrs Ellis was out Grace must stay in. The house must not be left. But sometimes Mrs Ellis suspected that Grace did not keep to the bargain. Here was proof.

She called once again, rather more sharply this time.

'Grace?'

There was a sound of a window opening below, and a man thrust his head out of the kitchen. He was in his shirt sleeves. And he had not shaved.

'What are you bawling your head off about?' he said.

Mrs Ellis was too stunned to answer. So this was what happened when her back was turned. Grace, respectable, well over thirty, had a man in the house. Mrs Ellis swallowed, but kept her temper.

'Perhaps you will have the goodness to ask Grace to come upstairs and let me in,' she said.

The sarcasm was wasted, of course. The man blinked at her, bewildered.

'Who's Grace?' he said.

This was too much. So Grace had the nerve to pass under another name. Something fanciful, no doubt, Shirley, or Marlene.

She was pretty sure now what must have happened. Grace had slipped out to the public house down the road to buy this man beer. The man was left to loll in the kitchen. He might even have been poking his fingers in the larder. Now she knew why there was so little left on the joint two days ago.

'If Grace is out,' said Mrs Ellis, and her voice was icy, 'kindly let me in yourself. I prefer not to use the back entrance.'

That would put him in his place. Mrs Ellis trembled with rage. She was angry seldom; she was a mild, even-tempered woman. But this reception, from a lout in shirt sleeves, at her own kitchen window, was rather more than she could bear.

It was going to be unpleasant, the interview with Grace. Grace would give notice in all probability. But some things could not be allowed to slide, and this was one of them.

She heard shuffling footsteps coming along the hall. The man had mounted from the basement. He opened the front door and stood there, staring at her.

'Who is it you want?' he said.

Mrs Ellis heard the furious yapping of a little dog from the drawing-room. Callers . . . This was the end. How perfectly frightful, how really overwhelmingly embarrassing. Someone had called, and Grace had let them in, or, worse still, this man in his shirt sleeves had done so. What would people think?

'Who is in the drawing-room, do you know?' she murmured swiftly.

'I think Mr and Mrs Bolton are in, but I'm not sure,' he said. 'I can hear the dog yapping. Was it them you wanted to see?'

Mrs Ellis did not know a Mr and Mrs Bolton. She turned impatiently towards the drawing-room, first whipping off her coat and putting her gloves in her pocket.

'You had better go down to the basement again,' she said to the man, who was still staring at her; 'tell Grace not to bring tea until I ring. These people may not stay.'

The man appeared bewildered.

'All right,' he said, 'I'm going down. But if you want Mr and Mrs Bolton again, ring twice.'

He shuffled off down the basement stairs. He was drunk, no doubt. He meant to be insulting. If he proved difficult, later in the evening, after dark, it would mean ringing for the police.

Mrs Ellis slipped into the lobby to hang up her coat. No time to go upstairs if callers were in the drawing-room. She fumbled for the switch and turned it, but the bulb had gone. Another pinprick. Now she could not see herself in the mirror.

She stumbled over something, and bent to see what it was. It was a man's boot. And here was another, and a pair of shoes, and beside them a suitcase and an old rug. If Grace had allowed that man to put his things in her lobby, then Grace would go tonight. Crisis had come. High crisis.

Mrs Ellis opened the drawing-room door, forcing a smile of welcome, not too warm, upon her lips. A little dog rushed towards her, barking furiously.

'Quiet Judy,' said a man, grey-haired, with horn spectacles, sitting before the fire. He was clicking a typewriter.

Something had happened to the room. It was covered with books and papers; odds and ends of junk littered the floor. A parrot, in a cage, hopped on its perch and screeched a welcome.

Mrs Ellis tried to speak, but her voice would not come. Grace had gone raving mad. She had let that man into the house, and this one too, and they had brought the most terrible disorder; they had turned the room upside down; they had deliberately, maliciously, set themselves to destroy her things.

No. Worse! It was part of a great thieving plot. She had heard of such things. Gangs went about breaking into houses. Grace, perhaps, was not at fault. She was lying in the basement, gagged and bound. Mrs Ellis felt her heart beating much too fast. She also felt a little faint.

'I must keep calm,' she said to herself, 'whatever happens, I must keep calm. If I can get to the telephone, to the police, it is the only hope. This man must not see that I am planning what to do.'

The little dog kept sniffing at her heels.

'Excuse me,' said the intruder, pushing his horn spectacles on to his forehead, 'but do you want anything? My wife is upstairs.'

The diabolic cunning of the plot. The cool bluff of his sitting there, the typewriter on his knees. They must have brought all this stuff in through the door to the back garden; the French window was ajar. Mrs Ellis glanced swiftly at the mantelpiece. It was as she feared. The Staffordshire figures had been removed, and the flower picture too. There must be a car, a van, waiting down the road . . . Her mind worked quickly. It might be that the man had not guessed her identity. Two could play at bluff. Memories of amateur theatricals flashed through her mind. Somehow she must detain these people until the police arrived. How fast they had worked. Her desk was gone, the bookshelves too, nor could she see her armchair.

But she kept her eyes steadily on the stranger. He must not notice her brief glance around the room.

'Your wife is upstairs?' said Mrs Ellis, her voice strained, yet calm.

'Yes,' said the man, 'if you've come for an appointment, she always makes them. You'll find her in the studio. Room in the front.'

Steadily, softly, Mrs Ellis left the drawing-room, but the wretched little dog had followed her, sniffing at her heels.

One thing was certain. The man had not realized who she was. They believed the householder out of the way for the afternoon, and that she, standing now in the hall, listening, her heart beating, was some caller to be fobbed off with a lie about appointments.

She stood silently by the drawing-room door. The man had resumed typing on his machine. She marvelled at the coolness of it, the drawn-out continuity of the bluff.

There had been nothing in the papers very recently about large-scale house robberies. This was something new, something outstandding. It was extraordinary that they should pick on her house. But they must know she was a widow, on her own, with one maid-servant. The telephone had already been removed from the stand in the hall. There was a loaf of bread on it instead, and something that looked like meat wrapped up in newspaper. So they had brought provisions . . . There was a chance that the telephone in her bedroom had not yet been taken away, nor the wires cut. The man had said his wife was upstairs. It may have been part of his bluff, or it might be true that he worked with a woman accomplice. This woman, even now, was probably turning out Mrs Ellis' wardrobe, seizing her fur coat, ramming the single string of cultured pearls into a pocket.

Mrs Ellis thought she could hear footsteps in her bedroom.

Her anger overcame her fear. She had not the strength to do battle with the man, but she could face the woman. And if the worst came to the worst, she would run to the window, put her head out, and scream. The people next door would hear. Or someone might be passing in the street.

Stealthily, Mrs Ellis crept upstairs. The little dog led the way with confidence. She paused outside her bedroom door. There was certainly movement from within. The little dog waited, his eyes fixed upon her with intelligence.

At that moment the door of Susan's small bedroom opened, and a fat elderly woman looked out, blowsy, and red in the face. She had a tabby cat under her arm. As soon as the dog saw the cat it started a furious yapping.

'Now that's torn it,' said the woman. 'What do you want to bring the dog upstairs for? They always fight when they meet. Do you know if the post's been yet? Oh, sorry. I thought you were Mrs Bolton.'

She brought an empty milk bottle from under her other arm and put it down on the landing.

'I'm blowed if I can manage the stairs today,' she said, 'somebody else will have to take it down for me. Is it foggy out?'

'No,' said Mrs Ellis, shocked into a natural answer, and then, feeling the woman's eyes upon her, hesitated between entering her bedroom door and withdrawing down the stairs. This evil-looking old woman was part of the gang and might call the man from below.

'Got an appointment?' said the other. 'She won't see you if you haven't booked an appointment.'

A tremor of a smile appeared on Mrs Ellis' lips.

'Thank you,' she said, 'yes, I have an appointment.'

She was amazed at her own steadiness, and that she could carry off the situation with such aplomb. An actress on the London stage could not have played her part better.

The elderly woman winked and, drawing nearer, plucked Mrs Ellis by the sleeve.

'Is she going to do you straight or fancy?' she whispered. 'It's the fancy ones that get the men. You know what I mean!'

She nudged Mrs Ellis and winked again.

'I see by your ring you're married,' she said. 'You'd be surprised even the quietest husbands like their pictures fancy. Take a tip from an old pro. Get her to do you fancy.'

She lurched back into Susan's room, the cat under her arm, and shut the door.

'It's possible,' thought Mrs Ellis, the faint feeling coming over her once again, 'that a group of lunatics have escaped from an asylum, and in their terrible, insane fashion, they have broken into my house not to thieve, not to destroy my belongings, but because in some crazed, deluded fashion they believe themselves to be at home.'

The publicity would be frightful once it became known. Headlines in the papers. Her photograph taken. So bad for Susan. Susan . . . That horrible, disgusting old woman in Susan's bedroom.

Emboldened, fortified, Mrs Ellis opened her own bedroom door. One glance revealed the worst. The room was bare, was stripped. There were several lights at various points of the room, flexes attached, and a camera on a tripod. A divan was pushed against the wall. A young woman, with a crop of thick fuzzy hair, was kneeling on the floor, sorting papers.

'Who is it?' she said. 'I don't see anyone without an appointment. You've no right to come in here.'

Mrs Ellis, calm, resolute, did not answer. She had made certain that the telephone, though it had been moved like the rest of her things, was still in the room.

She went to it and lifted the receiver.

'Leave my telephone alone,' cried the shock-haired girl, and she began to struggle to her knees.

'I want them to come at once to 17 Elmhurst Road. I am in great danger. Please report this message to the police at once.'

The girl was beside her now, taking the receiver from her. 'Who's sent you here?' said the girl, her face sallow, colourless, against the fuzzy hair. 'If you think you can come in snooping, you're mistaken. You won't find anything. Nor the police, neither. I have a trade licence for the work I do.'

Her voice had risen, and the dog, alarmed, joined her with high-pitched barks. The girl opened the door and called down the stairs.

'Harry?' she shouted. 'Come here and throw this woman out.'

Mrs Ellis remained quite calm. She stood with her back to the wall, her hands folded. The exchange had taken her message. It would not be long now before the police arrived.

She heard the drawing-room door open from below, and the man's voice called up, petulant, irritated.

'What's the matter?' he shouted. 'You know I'm busy. Can't you deal with the woman? She probably wants a special pose.'

The girl's eyes narrowed. She looked closely at Mrs Ellis.

'What did my husband say to you?' she said.

'Ah!' thought Mrs Ellis triumphantly. 'They are getting frightened. It's not such an easy game as they think.'

'I had no conversation with your husband,' said Mrs Ellis quietly; 'he merely told me I should find you upstairs. In this room. Don't try any bluff with me. It's too late. I can see what you have been doing.'

She gestured at the room. The girl stared at her.

'You can't put any phony business over on me,' she said; 'this studio is decent, respectable, everyone knows that I take camera studies of children. Plenty of clients can testify to that. You've got no proof of anything else. Show me a negative, and then I might believe you.'

Mrs Ellis wondered how long it would be before the police came. She must continue to play for time. Later, she might even feel sorry, perhaps, for this wretched, deluded girl who had wrought such havoc in the bedroom, believing herself to be a photographer; but this moment, now, she must be calm, calm.

'Well?' said the girl. 'What are you going to say when the police come? What's your story?'

It did not do to antagonize lunatics. Mrs Ellis knew that. They must be humoured. She must humour this girl until the police came.

'I shall tell them that I live here,' she said gently; 'that is all they will need to know. Nothing further.'

The girl looked at her, puzzled, and lit a cigarette.

'Then it is a pose you want?' she said. 'That call was just a bluff? Why don't you come clean and say why you're here?'

The sound of their voices had attracted the attention of the old woman in Susan's room. She tapped on the door, which was already open, and stood on the threshold.

'Anything wrong, dear?' she said slyly to the girl.

'Push on out of it,' said the girl impatiently, 'this is none of your business. I don't interfere with you, and you don't interfere with me.'

'I'm not interfering, dear,' said the woman, 'I only wanted to know if I could help. Difficult client, eh? Wants something outsize?'

'Oh, shut your mouth,' said the girl.

The girl's husband, Bolton or whatever his name was, the spectacled man from the drawing-room, came upstairs and into the bedroom.

'Just what's going on?' he said.

The girl shrugged her shoulders and glanced at Mrs Ellis.

'I don't know,' she said, 'but I think it's blackmail.'

'Has she got any negatives?' said the man swiftly.

'Not that I know of. Never seen her before.'

'She might have got them from another client,' said the elderly woman, watching.

The three of them stared at Mrs Ellis. She was not afraid. She had the situation well in hand.

'I think we've all become a little overwrought,' she said, 'and much the best thing to do would be to go downstairs, sit quietly by the fire, and have a little chat, and you can talk to me about your work. Tell me, are you all three photographers?'

As she spoke, half of her mind was wondering where they had managed to hide her things. They must have bundled her bed into Susan's room; the wardrobe was in two parts, of course, and could be taken to pieces very soon; but her clothes . . . her ornaments . . . these must have been concealed in a lorry. Somewhere, there was a lorry filled with all her things. It might be parked down another road, or might have been driven off already by yet another accomplice. The police were good at tracing stolen goods, she knew that, and everything was insured; but such a mess had been made of the house; insurance would never cover that, nor would her fire policy, unless there was some clause, some proviso against damage by lunatics; surely the insurance people would not call that an act of God . . . Her mind ran on and on, taking in the mess, the disorder, these people had created, and how many days and weeks would it take for her and Grace to get everything straight again?

Poor Grace. She had forgotten Grace. Grace must be shut up somewhere in the basement with that dreadful man in shirt sleeves, another of the gang, not a follower at all.

'Well,' said Mrs Ellis with the other half of her mind, the half that was acting so famously, 'shall we do as I suggest and go downstairs?'

She turned, and led the way, and to her surprise they followed her, the man and his wife, not the horrible old woman. She remained above, leaning over the banisters.

'Call me if you want me,' she said.

Mrs Ellis could not bear to think of her fingering Susan's things in the little bedroom.

'Won't you join us?' she said, steeling herself to courtesy. 'It's far more cheerful down below.'

The old woman smirked. 'That's for Mr and Mrs Bolton to say,' she said, 'I don't push myself.'

'If I can get all three of them pinned into the drawing-room,' thought Mrs Ellis, 'and somehow lock the door, and make a tremendous effort at conversation, I might possibly keep their attention until the police arrive. There is, of course, the door into the garden, but then they will have to climb the fence, fall over that potting shed next door. The old woman, at least, would never do it.'

'Now,' said Mrs Ellis, her heart turning over inside at the havoc of the drawing-room, 'shall we sit down and recover ourselves, and you shall tell me all about this photography.'

But she had scarcely finished speaking before there was a ring at the front door, and a knock, authoritative, loud.

The relief sent her dizzy. She steadied herself against the door. It was the police. The man looked at the girl, a question in his eye.

'Better have 'em in,' he said, 'she's got no proof.'

He crossed the hall and opened the front door.

'Come in, officer,' he said. 'There's two of you, I see.'

'We had a telephone call,' Mrs Ellis heard the constable say, 'some trouble going on, I understand.'

'I think there must be some mistake,' said Bolton. 'The fact is, we've had a caller and I think she got hysterical.'

Mrs Ellis walked out into the hall. She did not recognize the constable, nor the young policeman from the beat. It was unfortunate, but it did not really matter. Both were stout, well-built men.

'I am not hysterical,' she said firmly, 'I am perfectly all right. I put the telephone call through to the exchange.'

The constable took out a notebook and a pencil.

'What's the trouble?' he said. 'But give me first your name and address.'

Mrs Ellis smiled patiently. She hoped he was not going to be a stupid man.

'It's hardly necessary,' she said, 'but my name is Mrs Wilfred Ellis of this address.'

'Lodge here?' asked the constable.

Mrs Ellis frowned. 'No,' she said, 'this is my house, I live here.' And then because she saw the look flash from Bolton to his wife, she knew the time had come to be explicit. 'I must speak to you alone, Constable,' she said, 'the matter is terribly urgent; I don't think you quite understand.'

'If you have any charge to bring, Mrs Ellis,' said the officer, 'you can bring it at the police station at the proper time. We were informed that somebody lodging here at Number 17 was in danger. Are you, or are you not, the person who gave that information to the exchange?'

Mrs Ellis began to lose control.

'Of course I am that person,' she said. 'I returned home to find that my house had been broken into by thieves, these people here, dangerous thieves, lunatics, I don't know what they are, and my things carried away, the whole of my house turned upside down, the most terrible disorder everywhere.'

She talked so rapidly, her words fell over themselves.

The man from the basement had now joined them in the hall. He stared at the two policemen, his eyes goggling.

'I saw her come to the door,' he said; 'I thought she was barmy. Wouldn't have let her in if I had known.'

The constable, a little nettled, turned to the interruption.

'Who are you?' he said.

'Name of Upshaw,' said the man, 'William Upshaw. Me and my missus has the basement flat here.'

'That man is lying,' said Mrs Ellis, 'he does not live here, he belongs to this gang of thieves. Nobody lives in the basement except my maid – perhaps I should say cook-general – Grace Jackson, and if you will search the premises you will probably find her gagged and bound somewhere, and by that ruffian.'

She had now lost all restraint. She could hear her voice, usually low and quiet, rising to a hysterical pitch.

'Barmy,' said the man from the basement, 'you can see the straw in her hair.'

'Quiet, please,' said the constable, and turned an ear to the young policeman, who murmured something in his ear.

'Yes, yes,' he said, 'I've got the directory here. It's all in order.'

He consulted another book. Mrs Ellis watched him feverishly. Never had she seen such a stupid man. Why had they sent out such a slow-witted fool from the police station?

The constable now turned to the man in the horn spectacles.

'Are you Henry Bolton?' he asked.

'Yes, officer,' replied the man eagerly, 'and this is my wife. We have the ground floor here. This is my wife. She uses an upstairs room for a studio. Camera portraits, you know.'

There was a shuffle down the stairs, and the old evil woman came to the foot of the banister.

'My name's Baxter,' she said, 'Billie Baxter they used to call me in my old stage days. Used to be in the profession, you know. I have the first-floor back here at Number 17. I can witness this woman came as a sort of Paul Pry, and up to no good. I saw her looking through the keyhole of Mrs Bolton's studio.'

'Then she doesn't lodge here?' asked the constable. 'I didn't think she did: the name isn't in the directory.'

'We have never seen her before, officer,' said Bolton. 'Mr Upshaw let her into the house through some error; she walked into our living-room, and then forced her way into my wife's studio, threatened her, and in hysterical fashion rang for the police.'

The constable looked at Mrs Ellis.

'Anything to say?' he said.

Mrs Ellis swallowed. If only she could keep calm, if only her heart would not beat so dreadfully fast, and the terrible desire to cry would not rise in her throat.

'Constable,' she said, 'there has been some terrible mistake. You are new to the district, perhaps, and the young policeman too – I don't seem to recognize him – but if you would kindly get through to your headquarters, they must know all about me; I have lived here for years. My maid Grace has been with me a very long time; I am a widow; my husband, Wilfred Ellis, has been dead two years; I have a little girl of nine at school. I went out for a walk on the heath this afternoon, and during my absence these people have broken into my house, seized or destroyed my belongings – I don't know which – the whole place is upside down; if you would please get through immediately to your headquarters . . .'

'There, there,' said the constable, putting his notebook away, 'that's all right; we can go into all that quietly down at the station. Now, do any of you want to charge Mrs Ellis with trespassing?'

There was silence. Nobody said anything.

'We don't wish to be unkind,' said Bolton diffidently; 'I think my wife and myself are quite willing to let the matter pass.'

'I think it should be clearly understood,' interposed the shock-haired girl, 'that anything this woman says about us at the police station is completely untrue.'

'Quite,' said the officer. 'You will both be called, if needed, but I very much doubt the necessity. Now, Mrs Ellis' – he turned to her, not harshly in any way, but with authority – 'we have a car outside, and we can run you down to the station, and you can tell your story there. Have you a coat?'

Mrs Ellis turned blindly to the lobby. She knew the police station well; it was barely five minutes away. It was best to go there direct. See someone in authority, not this fool, this hopeless, useless fool. But in the meantime, these people were getting away with their criminal story. By the time she and an additional police force returned, they would have fled. She groped for her coat in the dark lobby, stumbling again over the boots, the suitcases.

'Constable,' she said softly, 'here, one minute.'

He moved towards her.

'Yes?' he said.

'They've taken away the electric bulb,' she said rapidly in a low whisper; 'it was perfectly all right this afternoon, and these boots, and this pile of suitcases, all these have been brought in, and thrown here; the suitcases are probably filled with my ornaments. I must ask you most urgently to leave the policeman in charge here until we return, to see that these people don't escape.'

'That's all right, Mrs Ellis,' said the officer. 'Now, are you ready to come along?'

She saw a look pass between the constable and the young policeman. The young policeman was trying to hide his smile.

Mrs Ellis felt certain that the constable was *not* going to remain in the house. And a new suspicion flashed into her mind. Could this officer and his subordinate be genuine members of the police force? Or were they, after all, members of the gang? This would explain their strange faces, their obvious mishandling of the situation. In which case they were now going to take her away to some lair, drug her, kill her possibly.

'I'm not going with you,' she said swiftly.

'Now, Mrs Ellis,' said the constable, 'don't give any trouble. You shall have a cup of tea down at the station, and no one is going to hurt you.'

He seized her arm. She tried to shake it off. The young policeman moved closer.

'Help,' she shouted, 'help . . . help . . .'

There must be someone. Those people from next door, she barely knew them, but no matter, if she raised her voice loud enough . . .

'Poor thing,' said the man in shirt sleeves, 'seems sad, don't it? I wonder how she got like it.'

Mrs Ellis saw his bulbous eyes fixed on her with pity, and she nearly choked.

'You rogue,' she said, 'how dare you, how dare you?' But she was being bundled down the steps, and through the front garden, and into the car, and there was another policeman at the wheel of the car; and she was thrust at the back, the constable keeping a steady hold upon her arm.

The car turned downhill, past the stretch of heath; she tried to see out of the windows the direction, but the bulk of the constable prevented her.

After twisting and turning, the car stopped, to her great surprise, in front of the police station.

Then these men were genuine, after all. They were not members of the gang. Stupefied for a moment, but relieved, thankful, Mrs Ellis stumbled from the car. The constable, still holding her arm, led her inside.

The hall was not unfamiliar; she remembered coming once before, years ago, when the ginger cat was lost; there was somebody in charge always, sitting at a sort of desk, everything very official, very brisk. She supposed she would stop here in the hall, but the constable led her on to an inner room, and here was another officer seated at a large desk, a more superior type altogether, thank heaven, and he looked intelligent.

She was determined to get her word in before the constable spoke. 'There has been great confusion,' she began. 'I am Mrs Ellis, of 17 Elmhurst Road, and my house has been broken into, robbery is going on at this moment on a huge scale; I believe the thieves to be very desperate and extraordinarily cunning; they have completely taken in the constable here, and the other policeman . . .'

To her indignation this superior officer did not look at her. He raised his eyebrows at the constable, and the constable, who had taken off his hat, coughed and approached the desk. A policewoman, appearing from nowhere, stood beside Mrs Ellis and held her arm.

The constable and the superior officer were talking together in low tones. Mrs Ellis could not hear what they were saying. Her legs trembled with emotion. She felt her head swim.

Thankfully, she accepted the chair dragged forward by the policewoman, and in a few moments, too, she was given a cup of tea. She did not want it though. Precious time was being lost.

'I must insist that you hear what I have to say,' she said, and the policewoman tightened her grip on Mrs Ellis' arm. The superior officer behind the desk motioned Mrs Ellis forward, and she was assisted to another chair, the policewoman remaining beside her all the while.

'Now,' he said, 'what is it you want to tell me?'

Mrs Ellis gripped her hands together. She had a premonition that this man, in spite of his superior face, was going to prove as great a fool as the constable.

'My name is Ellis,' she said, 'Mrs Wilfred Ellis, of 17 Elmhurst Road. I am in the telephone book. I am in the directory. I am very well known in the district, and have lived at Elmhurst Road for ten years. I am a widow, and I have one little girl of nine years at present at school. I employ one maidservant, Grace Jackson, who cooks for me and does general work. This afternoon I went for a short walk on the heath, round by the Viaduct and the Vale of Health ponds, and when I returned home I found my house had been broken into; my maid had disappeared; the rooms were already stripped of my belongings, and the thieves were in possession of my home, putting up a stupendous act of bluff that deceived even the constable here. I put the call through to the exchange, which frightened the thieves, and I endeavoured to keep them pinned in my drawing-room until help arrived.'

Mrs Ellis paused for breath. She saw that the officer was paying attention to her story, and kept his eyes fixed upon her.

'Thank you,' he said, 'that is very helpful, Mrs Ellis. Now, have you anything you can show me to prove your identity?'

She stared at him. Prove her identity? Well, of course. But not here, not actually on her person. She had come away without her handbag, and her calling cards were in the writing desk, and her passport – she and Wilfred had been to Dieppe once – was, if she remembered rightly, in the left-hand pigeonhole of the small writing desk in her bedroom.

But she suddenly remembered the havoc of the house. Nothing would be found . . .

'It's very unfortunate,' she said to the officer, 'but I did not take my handbag with me when I went out for my walk this afternoon. I left it in the chest of drawers in the bedroom. My calling cards are in the desk in the drawing-room, and there is a passport – rather out of date; my husband and I did not travel much – in a pigeonhole in a small desk in my bedroom. But everything has been upset, taken by these thieves. The house is in utter chaos.'

The officer made a note on a pad beside him.

'You can't produce your identity card or your ration book?' he asked.

'I have explained,' said Mrs Ellis, governing her temper, 'my calling cards are in my writing desk. I don't know what you mean by ration book.'

The officer went on writing on his pad. He glanced at the police-woman, who began feeling Mrs Ellis' pockets, touching her in a familiar way. Mrs Ellis tried to think which of her friends could be telephoned to, who could vouch for her, who could come at once by car and make these idiots, these stone-witted fools, see sense.

'I must keep calm,' she told herself again, 'I must keep calm.'

The Collinses were abroad; they would have been the best, but Netta Draycott should be; she was usually at home about this time because of the children.

'I have asked you,' said Mrs Ellis, 'to verify my name and address in the telephone book, or the district directory. If you refuse to do that, ask the postmaster, or the manager of my bank, a branch of which is in the High Street, and where I cashed a cheque on Saturday. Finally, would you care to ring up Mrs Draycott, a friend of mine, 21 Charlton Court, the block of flats in Charlton Avenue, who will vouch for me?'

She sat back in the chair, exhausted. No nightmare, she told herself, could ever have the horror, the frustrated hopelessness, of her present plight. Little incident piled on little incident. If she had only remembered to bring her handbag, there was a calling-card case in her handbag. And all the while those thieves, those devils, breaking up her home, getting away with her precious things, her belongings . . .

'Now, Mrs Ellis,' said the officer, 'we have checked up on your statements, you know, and they won't do. You are not in the telephone book, nor in the directory.'

'I assure you I am,' said Mrs Ellis with indignation; 'give me the books and I'll show you.'

The constable, still standing, placed the books before her. She ran her finger down the name of Ellis to the position on the left-hand page where she knew it would be. The name Ellis was repeated, but not hers. And none with her address or number. She looked in the directory and saw that beside 17 Elmhurst Road were the names of Bolton, of Upshaw, of Baxter . . . She pushed both books away from her. She stared at the officer.

'There is something wrong with these books,' she said, 'they are not up to date, they are false, they are not the books I have at home.'

The officer did not answer. He closed the books.

'Now, Mrs Ellis,' he said, 'I can see you are tired, and a rest would do you good. We will try to find your friends for you. If you will go along now, we will get in touch with them as soon as possible. I will send a doctor along to you, and he may chat with you a little and give you a sedative, and then, after some rest, you will feel better in the morning and we may have news for you.'

The policewoman helped Mrs Ellis to her feet.

'Come along now,' she said.

'But my house?' said Mrs Ellis. 'Those thieves, and my maid Grace, Grace may be lying in the basement; surely you are going to do something about the house; you won't permit them to get away with this monstrous crime; even now we have wasted a precious half hour—'

'That's all right, Mrs Ellis,' said the officer, 'you can leave everything in our hands.'

The policewoman led her away, still talking, still protesting, and now she was being taken down a corridor, and the policewoman kept saying:

'Now, don't fuss, take it calmly; no one's going to hurt you,' and she was in a little room with a bed; heavens . . . it was a cell, a cell where they put the prisoners, and the policewoman was helping her off with her coat, unpinning the scarf that was still tied round her hair, and because Mrs Ellis felt so faint the policewoman made her lie down on the bed, covered her with the coarse grey blanket, placed the little hard pillow under her head.

Mrs Ellis seized the woman's hands. Her face, after all, was not unkind.

'I beg of you,' she said, 'ring up Hampstead 4072, the number of my friend Mrs Draycott, at Charlton Court, and ask her to come here. The officer won't listen to me. He won't hear my story.'

'Yes, yes, that will be all right,' said the policewoman.

Now somebody else was coming into the room, the cell. Cleanshaven, alert, he carried a case in his hands. He said good evening to the policewoman, and opened his case. He took out a stethoscope and a thermometer. He smiled at Mrs Ellis.

'Feeling a little upset, I hear,' he said, 'Well, we'll soon put that to rights. Now, will you give me your wrist?'

Mrs Ellis sat up on the hard narrow bed, pulling the blanket close.

'Doctor,' she said, 'there is nothing whatever the matter with me. I admit I have been through a terrible experience, quite enough to unnerve anyone; my house has been broken into; no one here will listen to my story, but I am Mrs Ellis, Mrs Wilfred Ellis, of 17 Elmhurst Road; if you can possibly persuade the authorities here
. . .'

He was not listening to her. With the assistance of the policewoman he was taking her temperature, under her arm, not in the mouth, treating her like a child; and now he was feeling her pulse, dragging down the pupils of her eyes, listening to her chest . . . Mrs Ellis went on talking.

'I realize this is a matter of routine. You are obliged to do this. But I want to warn you that my whole treatment, since I have been brought here, since the police came to my house before that, has been infamous, scandalous. I don't personally know our MP; but I sincerely believe that when he hears my story he will take the matter up, and someone is going to answer for the consequences. Unfortunately I am a widow, no immediate relatives, my little daughter is away at school; my closest friends, a Mr and Mrs Collins, are abroad, but my bank manager . . .'

He was dabbing her arm with spirit; he was inserting a needle, and with a whimper of pain Mrs Ellis fell back on to the hard pillow. The doctor went on holding her arm, her wrist, and Mrs Ellis her head going round and round, felt a strange numb sensation as the injection worked into her bloodstream. Tears ran down her cheeks. She could not fight. She was too weak.

'How is that?' said the doctor. 'Better, eh?'

Her throat was parched, her mouth without saliva. It was one of those drugs that paralysed you, made you helpless.

But the emotion bubbling within her was eased, was still. The anger, the fear and frustration that had keyed her nerves to a point of contraction seemed to die away.

She had explained things badly. The folly of coming out without her handbag had caused half the trouble. And the terrible, wicked cunning of those thieves. 'Be still,' she said to her mind, 'be still. Rest now.'

'Now,' said the doctor, letting go her wrist, 'supposing you tell me your story again. You say your name is Mrs Ellis?'

Mrs Ellis sighed and closed her eyes. Must she go into it all again? Had not they got the whole thing written down in their notebooks? What was the use, when the inefficiency of the whole establishment was so palpable? Those telephone books, directories, with wrong names, wrong addresses. Small wonder there were burglaries, murders, every sort of crime, with a police force that was obviously rotten to the core. What was the name of the Member? It was on the tip of her tongue. A nice man, sandy-haired, always looked so trustworthy on a poster. Hampstead was a safe seat, of course. He would take up her case . . .

'Mrs Ellis,' said the doctor, 'do you think you can remember now your real address?'

Mrs Ellis opened her eyes. Wearily, patiently, she fixed them upon the doctor.

'I live at 17 Elmhurst Road,' she said mechanically. 'I am a widow, my husband has been dead two years. I have a little girl of nine at school. I went for a short walk on the heath this afternoon after lunch, and when I returned—'

He interrupted her.

'Yes,' he said, 'we know that. We know what happened after your walk. What we want you to tell us is what happened before.'

'I had lunch,' said Mrs Ellis; 'I remember perfectly well what I ate. Guinea fowl and apple charlotte, followed by coffee. Then I nearly decided to take a nap upstairs on my bed, because I was not feeling very well, but decided the air would do me good.'

As soon as she said this, she regretted it. The doctor looked at her keenly.

'Ah!' he said. 'You weren't feeling very well. Can you tell me what the trouble was?'

Mrs Ellis knew what he was after. He and the rest of the police force at the station wanted to certify her as insane. They would make out she had suffered from some brain storm, that her whole story was fabrication.

'There was nothing much the matter,' she said quickly. 'I was rather tired from sorting things during the morning. I tidied the linen, cleared out my desk in the drawing-room – all that took time.'

'Can you describe your house, Mrs Ellis?' he said. 'The furniture, for instance, of your bedroom, your drawing-room?'

'Very easily,' she answered, 'but you must remember that the thieves who broke into the house this afternoon have done what I begin to fear is irreparable damage. Everything had been seized, hidden away. The rooms were strewn with rubbish, and there was a young woman upstairs in my bedroom pretending to be a photographer.'

'Yes,' he said, 'don't worry about that. Just tell me about your furniture, how the various things were placed, and so on.'

He was more sympathetic than she had thought. Mrs Ellis launched into a description of every room in her house. She named the ornaments, the pictures, the position of the chairs and tables.

'And you say your cook is called Grace Jackson?'

'Yes, Doctor, she has been with me several years. She was in the kitchen when I left this afternoon; I remember most distinctly calling down to the basement and saying that I was going for a short walk and would not be long. I am extremely worried about her, Doctor. Those thieves will have got hold of her, perhaps kidnapped her.'

'We'll see to that,' said the doctor. 'Now, Mrs Ellis, you have been very helpful, and you have given such a clear account of your home that I think we shan't be long in tracing it, and your relations. You must stay here tonight, and I hope in the morning we shall have news for you. Now, you say your small daughter is at school? Can you remember the address?'

'Of course,' said Mrs Ellis, 'and the telephone number too. The school is High Close, Bishop's Lane, Hatchworth, and the telephone number is Hatchworth 202. But I don't understand what you mean about tracing my home. I have told you, I come from 17 Elmhurst Road.'

'There is nothing to worry about,' said the doctor; 'you are not ill, and you are not lying. I quite realize that. You are suffering from a temporary loss of memory that often happens to all sorts of people, and it quickly passes. We've had many cases before.'

He smiled. He stood up, his case in his hand.

'But it isn't true,' said Mrs Ellis, trying to raise herself from the pillow. 'My memory is perfectly all right. I have given you every detail I can think of; I have told you my name, where I live, a description of my home, the address of my daughter at school . . .'

'All right,' he said, 'now, don't worry. Just try to relax and have a little sleep. We shall find your friends for you.'

He murmured something to the policewoman and left the cell. The policewoman came over to the bed and tucked in the blanket.

'Now cheer up,' she said, 'do as the doctor said. Get a little rest. Everything will be all right, you'll see.'

Rest . . . But how? Relax . . . But to what purpose? Even now her house was being looted, sacked, every room stripped. The thieves getting clear away with their booty, leaving no trace behind them. They would take Grace with them; poor Grace could not come down to the police station to give witness to her identity. But the people next door, the Furbers, surely they would be good enough; it would not be too much trouble . . . Mrs Ellis supposed she should have called, been more friendly, had them to tea, but after all, people did not expect that unless they lived in the country, it was out of date; if the police officer had not got hold of Netta Draycott then the Furbers must be got in touch with at once . . .

Mrs Ellis plucked at the policewoman's sleeve.

'The Furbers,' she said, 'next door, at number 19, they know me well by sight. We have been neighbours for quite six years. The Furbers.'

'Yes,' said the policewoman, 'try to get some sleep.'

Oh, Susan, my Susan, if this had happened in the holidays, how much more fearful; what would we have done? Coming back from an afternoon walk to find those devils in the house, and then, who knows, that dreadful photographer woman and her husband taking a fancy to Susan, so pretty, so fair, and wanting to kidnap her. Then what fear, what terror . . . At least the child was safe, knew nothing of what was happening, and if only the story could be kept out of the newspapers, she need never know. So shameful, so degrading, a night spent in a prison cell through such crass stupidity, through such appalling blunders . . .

'You've had a good sleep then,' said the policewoman, handing her a cup of tea.

'I don't know what you mean,' said Mrs Ellis, 'I haven't slept at all.'

'Oh yes, you have.' The woman smiled. 'They all say that.'

Mrs Ellis blinked, sat up on the narrow bed. She had been speaking to the policewoman only a moment before. Her head ached abominably. She sipped at the tea, tasteless, unrefreshing. She yearned for her bed at home, for Grace coming in noiselessly, drawing the curtains.

'You're to have a wash,' said the policewoman, 'and I'll give you a comb through, and then you are to see the doctor again.'

Mrs Ellis suffered the indignity of washing under supervision, of having her hair combed; then her scarf and coat and gloves were given to her again, and she was taken out of the cell, along the corridor, back through the hall to the room where they had questioned her the night before. This time a different officer sat at the desk, but she recognized the police constable, and the doctor too.

The last came towards her with that same bland smile on his face.

'How are you feeling today?' he said. 'A little more like your true self?'

'On the contrary,' said Mrs Ellis, 'I am feeling very unwell indeed, and shall continue to do so until I know what has happened at home. Is anyone here prepared to tell me what has happened at 17 Elmhurst Road since last night? Has anything at all been done to safeguard my property?'

The doctor did not answer, but guided her towards the chair at the desk.

'Now,' he said, 'the officer here wants to show you a picture in a newspaper.'

Mrs Ellis sat down in the chair. The officer handed her a copy of *The News of the World* – a paper Grace took on Sundays; Mrs Ellis never looked at it – and there was a photograph of a woman with a scarf round her head, and chubby cheeks, wearing some sort of light-coloured coat. The photograph had a red circle round it, and underneath was written:

'Missing from Home, Ada Lewis, aged 36, widow, of 105 Albert Buildings, Kentish Town.'

Mrs Ellis handed the paper back across the desk.

'I'm afraid I can't help you,' she said. 'I don't know this woman.'

'The name Ada Lewis conveys nothing to you?' said the officer. 'Nor Albert Buildings?'

'No,' said Mrs Ellis, 'certainly not.'

Suddenly she knew the purpose of the interrogation. The police thought that she was the missing woman, this Ada Lewis from Albert Buildings. Simply because she wore a light-coloured coat and had a scarf round her hair. She rose from the chair.

'This is absolutely preposterous,' she said. 'I have told you my name is Ellis, Mrs Wilfred Ellis, of 17 Elmhurst Road, and you persist in disbelieving me. My detention here is an outrage; I demand to see a lawyer, my own lawyer . . .' But wait, she hadn't needed the services of a lawyer since Wilfred died, and the firm had moved or been taken over by somebody else; better not give the name; they would think she was lying once again; it was safer to give the name of the bank manager . . .

'One moment,' said the officer, and she was interrupted once again, because somebody else came into the room, a seedy, common-looking man in a checked shabby suit, holding his trilby hat in his hand.

'Can you identify this woman as your sister, Ada Lewis?' asked the officer.

A flush of fury swept Mrs Ellis as the man stepped forward and peered into her face.

'No, sir,' he said, 'this isn't Ada. Ada isn't so stout, and this woman's teeth seem to be her own. Ada wore dentures. Never seen this woman before.'

'Thank you,' said the officer, 'that's all. You can go. We will let you know if we find your sister.'

The seedy-looking man left the room. Mrs Ellis turned in triumph to the officer behind the desk.

'Now,' she said, 'perhaps you will believe me?'

The officer considered her a moment, and then, glancing at the doctor, looked down at some notes on his desk.

'Much as I would like to believe you,' he said, 'it would save us all a great deal of trouble if I could; unfortunately I can't. Your facts have been proved wrong in every particular. So far.'

'What do you mean?' said Mrs Ellis.

'First, your address. You do not live at 17 Elmhurst Road because the house is occupied by various tenants who have lived there for some time and who are known to us. Number 17 is an apartment house, and the floors are let separately. You are not one of the tenants.'

Mrs Ellis gripped the sides of her chair. The obstinate, proud, and completely unmoved face of the officer stared back at her.

'You are mistaken,' said Mrs Ellis quietly. 'Number 17 is not a lodginghouse. It is a private house. My own.'

The officer glanced down again at his notes.

'There are no people called Furber living at number 19,' he went on. 'Number 18 is also a lodginghouse. You are not in the directory under the name of Ellis, nor in the telephone book. There is no Ellis on the register of the branch of the bank you mentioned to us last night. Nor can we trace anyone of the name of Grace Jackson in the district.'

Mrs Ellis looked up at the doctor, at the police constable, at the policewoman, who was still standing by her side.

'Is there some conspiracy?' she said. 'Why are you all against me? I don't understand what I have done . . .'

Her voice faltered. She must not break down. She must be firm with them, be brave, for Susan's sake.

'You rang up my friend at Charlton Court?' she asked. 'Mrs Draycott, that big block of flats?'

'Mrs Draycott is not living at Charlton Court, Mrs Ellis,' said the police officer, 'for the simple reason that Charlton Court no longer exists. It was destroyed by a fire bomb.'

Mrs Ellis stared at him in horror. A fire bomb? But how perfectly terrible! When? How? In the night? Disaster upon disaster . . . Who could have done it, anarchists, strikers, unemployed, gangs of people, possibly those who had broken into her house? Poor Netta and her husband and children; Mrs Ellis felt her head reeling . . .

'Forgive me,' she said, summoning her strength, her dignity, 'I had no idea there had been such a fearful outrage. No doubt part of the same plot, those people in my house . . .'

Then she stopped, because she realized they were lying to her; everything was lies; they were not policemen; they had seized the building; they were spies; the government was to be overthrown; but then why bother with her, with a simple harmless individual like herself; why were they not getting on with the civil war, bringing machine guns into the street, marching to Buckingham Palace; why sit here, pretending to her?

A policeman came into the room and clicked his heels and stood before the desk.

'Checked up on all the nursing homes,' he said, 'and the mental homes, sir, in the district, and within a radius of five miles. Nobody missing.'

'Thank you,' said the officer. Ignoring Mrs Ellis, he looked across at the doctor.

'We can't keep her here,' he said; 'you'll have to persuade them to take her at Moreton Hill. The matron *must* find a room. Say it's a temporary measure. Case of amnesia.'

'I'll do what I can,' said the doctor.

Moreton Hill. Mrs Ellis knew at once what they meant by Moreton Hill. It was a well-known mental home somewhere near Highgate, very badly run, she always heard, a dreadful place.

'Moreton Hill?' she said. 'You can't possibly take me there. It has a shocking reputation. The nurses are always leaving. I refuse to go to Moreton Hill. I demand to see a lawyer – no, my doctor, Dr Godber; he lives in Parkwell Gardens.'

The officers stared at her thoughtfully.

'She must be a local woman,' he said; 'she gets the names right every time. But Godber went to Portsmouth, didn't he? I remember Godber.'

'If he's at Portsmouth,' said Mrs Ellis, 'he would only have gone for a few days. He's most conscientious. But his secretary knows me. I took Susan there last holidays.'

Nobody listened to her though, and the officer was consulting his notes again.

'By the way,' he said, 'you gave me the name of that school correctly. Wrong telephone number, but right school. Co-educational. We got through to them last night.'

'I'm afraid then,' said Mrs Ellis, 'that you got the wrong school. High Close is most certainly not co-educational, and I should never have sent Susan there if it had been.'

'High Close,' repeated the officer, reading from his notes, 'is a co-educational school, run by a Mr Foster and his wife.'

'It is run by a Miss Slater,' said Mrs Ellis, 'a Miss Hilda Slater.'

'You mean it *was* run by a Miss Slater,' said the officer; 'a Miss Slater had the school and then retired, and it was taken over by Mr and Mrs Foster. They have no pupil there of the name of Susan Ellis.'

Mrs Ellis sat very still in her chair. She looked at each face in turn. None was harsh. None was unfriendly. And the policewoman smiled encouragement. They all watched her steadily. At last she said:

'You are not deliberately trying to mislead me? You do realize that I am anxious, most desperately anxious, to know what has happened? If all that you are saying is some kind of a game, some kind of torture, would you tell me so that I know, so that I can understand?'

The doctor took her hand, and the officer leant forward in his chair.

'We are trying to help you,' he said; 'we are doing everything we can to find your friends.'

Mrs Ellis held tight to the doctor's hand. It had suddenly become a refuge.

'I don't understand,' she said, 'what has happened. If I am suffering from loss of memory, why do I remember everything so clearly? My address, my name, people, the school . . . Where is Susan; where is my little girl?'

She looked round her in blind panic. She tried to rise from the chair.

'If Susan is not at High Close, where is she?' said Mrs Ellis.

Someone was patting her on the shoulder. Someone was giving her a glass of water.

'If Miss Slater had retired to give place to a Mr and Mrs Foster, I should have heard, they would have told me,' she kept repeating; 'I only telephoned the school yesterday. Susan was quite well, and playing in the grounds.

'Are you suggesting that Miss Slater answered you yourself?' enquired the officer.

'No, the secretary answered. I telephoned because I had . . . what seemed to me a premonition that Susan might not be well. The secretary assured me that the child had eaten a good lunch and was playing. I am not making this up. It happened yesterday. I tell you, the secretary would have told me if Miss Slater was making changes in the school.'

Mrs Ellis searched the doubtful faces fixed upon her. And momentarily her attention was caught by the large 2 on the calendar standing on the desk.

'I *know* it was yesterday,' she said, 'because today is the second of the month, isn't it? And I distinctly remember tearing off the page in my calendar, and because it was the first of the month I decided to tidy my desk, sort out my papers, during the morning.'

The police officer relaxed and smiled.

'You are certainly very convincing,' he said, 'and we can all tell from your appearance, the fact that you have no money on you, that your shoes are polished, and other little signs, that you definitely belong somewhere in this district; you have not wandered from any great distance. But you do not come from 17 Elmhurst Road, Mrs Ellis, that is quite certain. For some reason, which we hope to discover, that address has become fixed in your mind, and other addresses too. I promise you everything will be done to clear your mind and to get you well again and you need have no fear about going to Moreton Hill; I know it well, and they will look after you there.'

Mrs Ellis saw herself shut up behind those grey forbidding walls, grimly situated, frowning down upon the further ponds the far side of the heath. She had skirted those walls many times, pitying the inmates within.

The man who came with the groceries had a wife who became insane. Mrs Ellis remembered Grace coming to her one morning full of the story, 'and he says they've taken her to Moreton Hill.'

Once inside, she would never get out. These men at the police station would not bother with her any more.

And now there was this new, hideous misunderstanding about Susan, and the talk of a Mr and Mrs Foster taking over the school.

Mrs Ellis leant forward, clasping her hands together.

'I do assure you,' she said, 'that I don't want to make trouble. I have always been a very quiet, peaceable sort of person, not easily excited, never quarrelsome, and if I have really lost my memory I will do what the doctor tells me, take any drugs or medicines that will help. But I am worried, desperately worried, about my little girl and what you have told me about the school and Miss Slater's having retired. Would you do just one thing for me? Telephone the school and ask where you can get in touch with Miss Slater. It is just possible that she has taken the house down the road and removed there with some of the children, Susan amongst them; and whoever answered the telephone was new to the work and gave you vague information.'

She spoke clearly, without any sort of hysteria or emotion; they must see that she was in deadly earnest, and this request of hers was not wild fancy.

The police officer glanced at the doctor, then he seemed to make up his mind.

'Very well,' he said, 'we will do that. We will try to contact this Miss Slater, but it may take time. Meanwhile, I think it is best if you wait in another room while we put through the enquiry.'

Mrs Ellis stood up, this time without the help of the policewoman. She was determined to show that she was well, mentally and bodily, and quite capable of managing her affairs without the assistance of anybody, if it could be permitted.

She wished she had a hat instead of the scarf, which she knew instinctively was unbecoming, and her hands were lost without her handbag. At least she had gloves. But gloves were not enough.

She nodded briskly to the police officer and the doctor – at all costs she must show civility – and followed the policewoman to a waiting room. This time she was spared the indignity of a cell. Another cup of tea was brought to her.

'It's all they think about,' she said to herself, 'cups of tea. Instead of getting on with their job.'

Suddenly she remembered poor Netta Draycott and the terrible tragedy of the fire bomb. Possibly she and her family had escaped and were now with friends, but there was no immediate means of finding out.

'Is it all in the morning papers about the disaster?' she asked the policewoman.

'What disaster?' said the woman.

'The fire at Charlton Court the officer spoke to me about.'

The policewoman stared at her with a puzzled expression.

'I don't remember him saying anything about a fire,' she said.

'Oh yes, he did,' said Mrs Ellis. 'He told me that Charlton Court had been destroyed by fire, by some bomb. I was aghast to hear it because I have friends living there. It must surely be in all the morning papers.'

The woman's face cleared.

'Oh, that,' she said. 'I think the officer was referring to some fire bomb during the war.'

'No, no,' said Mrs Ellis impatiently. 'Charlton Court was built a long time after the war. I remember the block being built when my husband and I first came to Hampstead. No, this accident apparently happened last night, the most dreadful thing.'

The policewoman shrugged her shoulders.

'I think you're mistaken,' she said; 'there's been no talk of any accident or disaster here.'

An ignorant, silly sort of girl, thought Mrs Ellis. It was a wonder she had passed her test into the force. She thought they only employed very intelligent women.

She sipped her tea in silence. No use carrying on any sort of conversation with her.

It seemed a long while before the door opened, but when it did it was to reveal the doctor, who stood on the threshold with a smile on his face.

'Well,' he said, 'I think we're a little nearer home. We were able to contact Miss Slater.'

Mrs Ellis rose to her feet, her eyes shining.

'Oh, Doctor, thank heaven . . . Have you news of my daughter?'

'Steady a moment now. You mustn't get excited or we shall have all last night's trouble over again, and that would never do. I take it, when you refer to your daughter, you mean someone who is called, or was called, Susan Ellis?'

'Yes, yes, of course,' said Mrs Ellis swiftly. 'Is she all right, is she with Miss Slater?'

'No, she is not with Miss Slater, but she is perfectly well, and I have spoken to her on the telephone myself, and I have her present address here in my notebook.'

The doctor patted his breast pocket and smiled again.

'Not with Miss Slater?' Mrs Ellis stared in bewilderment. 'Then the school *has* been handed over; you spoke to these people called Foster. Is it next door? Have they moved far? What has happened?'

The doctor took her hand and led her to the seat once more.

'Now,' he said, 'I want you to think quite calmly and quite clearly and not be agitated in any way, and your trouble will be cleared up, and your mind will be free again. You remember last night you gave us the name of your maid, Jackson?'

'Yes, Doctor.'

'Now, take your time. Tell us a little about Grace Jackson.'

'Have you found her? Is she at home? Is she all right?'

'Never mind for the moment. Describe Grace Jackson.'

Mrs Ellis was horribly afraid poor Grace had been found murdered, and they were going to ask her to identify the body.

'She is a big girl,' she said, 'at least not really a girl, about my own age, but you know how one is inclined to talk of a servant as a girl; she has a large bust, rather thick ankles, brownish hair, grey eyes, and she would be wearing, let me see, I think she may not have changed into her cap and apron when those thieves arrived; she was still probably in her overalls; she is inclined to change rather late in the afternoon; I have often spoken about it; it looks so bad to open the front door in overalls, slovenly, like a boardinghouse; Grace has good teeth and a pleasant expression, though of course if anything has happened to her she would hardly—'

Mrs Ellis broke off. Murdered, battered. Grace would not be smiling.

The doctor did not seem to notice this. He was looking closely at Mrs Ellis.

'You know,' he said, 'you have given a very accurate description of yourself.'

'Myself?' said Mrs Ellis.

'Yes. Figure, colouring, and so on. We think, you know, it is just possible that your amnesia has taken the form of mistaken identity and that you are really Grace Jackson, believing yourself to by a Mrs Ellis, and now we are doing our best to trace the relatives of Grace Jackson.'

This was too much. Mrs Ellis swallowed. Outraged pride rose in
her.

'Doctor,' she said rapidly, 'you have gone a little too far. I bear
no sort of resemblance to my maid, Grace Jackson, and if and when
you ever find trace of the unfortunate girl, she would be the first
to agree with me. Grace has been in my employment seven years;
she came originally from Scotland; her parents were Scottish, I
believe – in fact, I know it, because she used to go for her holiday
to Aberdeen. Grace is a good, hard-working, and I like to think
honest girl; we have had our little ups and downs, but nothing
serious; she is inclined to be obstinate; I am obstinate myself – who
is not? – but . . .'

If only the doctor would not look at her in that smiling, patron-
izing way.

'You see,' he said, 'you do know a very great deal about Grace
Jackson.'

Mrs Ellis could have hit him. He was so self-assured, so confident.

'I must keep my temper,' she told herself. 'I must, I must . . .'

Aloud she said: 'Doctor, I know about Grace Jackson because,
as I have told you, she has been in my employment for seven years.
If she is found ill or in any way hurt, I shall hold the police force
here responsible, because in spite of my entreaties, I do not believe
they kept a watch on my house last night. Now perhaps you will
be good enough to tell me where I can find my child. She, at least,
will recognize me.'

Mrs Ellis considered she had been very restrained, very calm. In
spite of terrible provocation she had not lost control of herself.

'You insist that your age is thirty-five?' said the doctor, switching
the subject. 'And that Grace Jackson was approximately the same?'

'I was thirty-five in August last,' said Mrs Ellis; 'I believe Grace
to be a year younger, I am not sure.'

'You certainly don't look more,' said the doctor, smiling.

Surely, at such a moment, he was not going to attempt to appease
her by gallantry?

'But,' he continued, 'following upon the telephone conversation
I have just had, Grace Jackson should be, today, at least fifty-five
or fifty-six.'

'There are probably,' said Mrs Ellis icily, 'several persons of the
name of Grace Jackson employed as domestic servants. If you
propose tracing every one of them it will take you and the police

force a considerable time. I am sorry to insist, but I must know the whereabouts of my daughter Susan before anything else.'

He was relenting; she could see it in his eye.

'As a matter of fact,' he said, 'it happens, very conveniently, that Miss Slater was able to put us in touch with the lady; we have spoken to her on the telephone, and she is only a short distance away, in St John's Wood. She is not sure, but she thinks she would remember Grace Jackson if she saw her.'

For a moment Mrs Ellis was speechless. What in the world was Susan doing in St John's Wood? And how monstrous to drag the child to the telephone and question her about Grace. Of course she would be bewildered and say she 'thought' she would remember Grace, though goodness only knows it was only two months since Grace was waving her goodbye from the doorstep when she left for school.

Then she suddenly remembered the Zoo. Perhaps, if these changes at school were all being decided upon in a great hurry, one of the junior mistresses had taken a party of children up to London to the Zoo, to be out of the way. The Zoo or Madame Tussaud's.

'Do you know where she spoke from?' asked Mrs Ellis sharply. 'I mean, somebody was in charge, somebody was looking after her?'

'She spoke from 2a Halifax Avenue,' said the doctor, 'and I don't think you will find she needs any looking after. She sounded very capable, and I heard her turn from the telephone and call to a little boy named Keith to keep quiet and not to make so much noise, because she couldn't hear herself speak.'

A tremor of a smile appeared on Mrs Ellis' lips. How clever of Susan to have shown herself so quick and lively. It was just like her, though. She was so advanced for her age. Such a little companion. But Keith . . . It sounded very much as though the school *had* suddenly become co-educational; this was a mixed party being taken to the Zoo or Madame Tussaud's. They were all having lunch, perhaps, at Halifax Avenue, relations of Miss Slater's, or these Fosters, but really the whole thing was most inexcusable, that changes should come about like this, and the children be taken backwards and forwards from High Close to London without any attempt to notify the parents. Mrs Ellis would write very strongly to Miss Slater about it, and if the school had changed hands and was to be co-educational, she would remove Susan at the end of the term.

'Doctor,' she said, 'I am ready to go to Halifax Avenue at once, if the authorities here will only permit me to do so.'

'Very well,' said the doctor. 'I am afraid I can't accompany you, but we have arranged for that, and Sister Henderson, who knows all about the matter, will go with you.'

He nodded to the policewoman, who opened the door of the waiting room and admitted a severe middle-aged woman in nurse's uniform. Mrs Ellis said nothing, but her mouth tightened. She was very sure that Sister Henderson had been summoned from Moreton Hill.

'Now, Sister,' said the doctor cheerfully, 'this is the lady, and you know where to take her and what to do; and I think you will only be a few minutes at Halifax Avenue, and then we hope things will be straightened out.'

'Yes, Doctor,' said the nurse.

She looked across at Mrs Ellis with a quick professional eye.

'If only I had a hat,' thought Mrs Ellis, 'if only I had not come out with nothing but this wretched scarf, and I can feel bits and pieces of hair straggling at the back of my neck. No powder compact on me, no comb, nothing. Of course I must look terrible to them, ungroomed, common . . .'

She straightened her shoulders, resisted an impulse to put her hands in her pockets. She walked stiffly towards the open door. The doctor, the Sister, and the policewoman conducted her down the steps of the police station to a waiting car.

A uniformed chauffeur was to drive, she was thankful to see, and she climbed into the car, followed by the Sister.

The awful thought flashed through her mind that there might be some charge for the night's lodging in the cell and for the cups of tea; also, should she have tipped the policewoman? But anyway, she had no money. It was impossible. She nodded brightly to the policewoman as a sort of sop, to show she had no ill feeling. She felt rather different towards the doctor. She bowed rather formally, coldly. The car drove away.

Mrs Ellis wondered if she was expected to make conversation with the Sister, who sat stalwart and forbidding at her side. Better not, perhaps. Anything she said might be taken as evidence of mental disturbance. She stared straight in front of her, her gloved hands primly folded on her lap.

The traffic jams were very bad, worse than she had ever known.

There must be a Motor Exhibition on. So many American cars on the road. A rally, perhaps . . .

She did not think much of Halifax Avenue when they came to it. Houses very shabby, and quite a number with windows broken.

The car drew up at a small house that had 2a written on the pillar outside. Curious place to take a party of children for lunch. A good Lyons Café would have been so much better.

The Sister got out of the car and waited to help Mrs Ellis.

'We shan't be long,' she said to the chauffeur.

'That's what you think,' said Mrs Ellis to herself, 'but I shall certainly stay with Susan as long as I please.'

They walked through the piece of front garden to the front door. The Sister rang the bell. Mrs Ellis saw a face looking at them from the front window and then quickly dart behind a curtain. Good heavens . . . It was Dorothy, Wilfred's younger sister, who was a schoolteacher in Birmingham; of course it was, it must be . . . Everything became clearer; the Fosters must know Dorothy; people to do with education always knew each other, but how awkward, what a bore. Mrs Ellis had never cared for Dorothy, had stopped writing to her in fact; Dorothy had been so unpleasant when poor Wilfred died, and had insisted that the writing bureau was hers, and rather a nice piece of jewellery that Mrs Ellis had always understood had been given by Wilfred's mother to her, Mrs Ellis; and in fact the whole afternoon after the funeral had been spent in most unpleasant argument and discussion, that Mrs Ellis had been only too glad to send Dorothy away with the jewellery, and the bureau, and a very nice rug to which she had no right at all.

Dorothy was the last person Mrs Ellis wanted to see, and especially in these very trying circumstances, with this Sister at her side, and herself looking so untidy, without a hat or a bag.

There was no time to compose herself because the door opened. No . . . no, it was not Dorothy after all, but . . . how strange, so very like her. That same thin nose and rather peeved expression. A little taller, perhaps, and the hair was lighter. The resemblance, though, was really quite extraordinary.

'Are you Mrs Drew?' asked the Sister.

'Yes,' answered the young woman, and then because a child was calling from an inner room she called back over her shoulder impatiently, 'Oh, be quiet, Keith, do, for heaven's sake.'

A little boy of about five appeared along the hall dragging a toy on wheels. 'Dear little fellow,' thought Mrs Ellis, 'what a tiresome nagging mother. But where are all the children; where is Susan?'

'This is the person I have brought along for you to identify,' said the Sister.

'You had better come inside,' said Mrs Drew rather grudgingly. 'I'm afraid everything's in a fearful mess. I've got no help, and you know how it is.'

Mrs Ellis, whose temper was beginning to rise again, stepped neatly over a broken toy on the door mat and, followed by the Sister, went into what she supposed was this Mrs Drew's living room. It was certainly a mess. Remains of breakfast not cleared away – or was it lunch? – and toys everywhere, and some material for cutting out spread on a table by the window.

Mrs Drew laughed apologetically.

'What with Keith's toys and my material – I'm a dressmaker in my spare time – and trying to get a decent meal for my husband when he comes home in the evening, life isn't a bed of roses,' she said.

Her voice was *so* like Dorothy's. Mrs Ellis could hardly take her eyes off her. The same note of complaint.

'We don't want to take up your time,' said the Sister civilly, 'if you will just say whether this person is Grace Jackson or not.'

The young woman, Mrs Drew, stared at Mrs Ellis thoughtfully.

'No,' she said at length, 'I'm sure she is not. I haven't seen Grace for years, not since I married; I used to look her up in Hampstead occasionally before then; but she had quite a different appearance from this person. She was stouter, darker, older too.'

'Thank you,' said the Sister, 'then you are sure you have never seen this lady before?'

'No, never,' said Mrs Drew.

'Very well then,' said the Sister, 'we needn't detain you any longer.'

She turned, as though to go, but Mrs Ellis was not to be fobbed off with the nonsense that had just passed.

'Excuse me,' she said to Mrs Drew, 'there has been a most unfortunate misunderstanding all round, but I understand you spoke to the doctor at the police station at Hampstead this morning, or someone did from this house, and that you have a party of school children here from High Close, my child amongst them. Can you tell me if she is still here; is anyone from the school in charge?'

The Sister was about to intervene, but Mrs Drew did not notice this, because the little boy had come into the room, dragging his toy.

'Keith, I *told* you to stay outside,' she nagged.

Mrs Ellis smiled at the boy. She loved all children.

'What a pretty boy,' she said, and she held out her hand to him. He took it, holding it tight.

'He doesn't usually take to strangers,' said Mrs Drew, 'he's very shy. It makes me wild at times when he won't speak and hangs his head.'

'I was shy myself as a child, I understand it,' said Mrs Ellis.

Keith looked up at her with confidence and trust. Her heart warmed to him. But she was forgetting Susan . . .

'We were talking about the party from High Close,' she said.

'Yes,' said Mrs Drew, 'but the police officer was rather an idiot, I'm afraid, and got everything wrong. My name was Susan Ellis before I married, and I used to go to school at High Close, and that's where the mistake came in. There are no children from the school here.'

'What a remarkable coincidence,' said Mrs Ellis, smiling, 'because my name is Ellis, and my daughter is called Susan, and an even stranger coincidence is that you are so like a sister of my late husband's.'

'Oh?' said Mrs Drew. 'Well, the name is common enough, isn't it? The butcher is Ellis, down the road.'

Mrs Ellis flushed. Not a very tactful remark. And she felt suddenly nervous, too, because the Sister was advancing and was leaning forward as though to take her by the arm and walk to the front door. Mrs Ellis was determined not to leave the house. Or at any rate, not to leave it with the Sister.

'I've always found High Close such a homey sort of school,' she said rapidly, 'but I am rather distressed about the changes they are making there, and I am afraid it is going to be on rather a different tone in the future.'

'I don't think they've changed it much,' said Mrs Drew; 'most small children are horrible little beasts, anyway, and it does them good not to see too much of their parents and to be thoroughly well mixed up with every sort of type.'

'I'm afraid I don't agree with you on that,' said Mrs Ellis. So peculiar. The tone, the expression might have been Dorothy's.

'Of course,' said Mrs Drew, 'I can't help being grateful to old Salty. She's a funny old stick, but a heart of gold, and she did her best for me, I'll say that, and kept me in the holidays, even after my mother was killed in a street accident.'

'How good of her,' said Mrs Ellis, 'and what a dreadful thing for you.'

Mrs Drew laughed.

'I was pretty tough, I think,' she said. 'I don't remember much about it. But I do remember my mother was a very kind person, and pretty too. I think Keith takes after her.'

The little boy had not relinquished Mrs Ellis' hand.

'It's time we were getting along,' said the Sister. 'Come now, Mrs Drew has told us all we need to know.'

'I don't want to go,' said Mrs Ellis calmly, 'and you have no right to make me go.'

The Sister exchanged a glance with Mrs Drew.

'I'm sorry,' she said in a low tone, 'I shall have to get the chauffeur. I wanted them to send another nurse with me, but they said it wouldn't be necessary.'

'That's all right,' said Mrs Drew. 'So many people are bats these days, one extra doesn't make much difference. But perhaps I had better remove Keith to the kitchen, or she may kidnap him.'

Keith, protesting, was carried from the room.

Once again the Sister looked at Mrs Ellis.

'Come along now,' she said, 'be reasonable.'

'No,' said Mrs Ellis, and with a quickness that surprised herself she reached out to the table where Mrs Drew had been cutting out material, and seized the pair of scissors.

'If you come near me, I shall stab you,' she said.

The Sister turned and went quickly out of the room and down the steps, calling for the chauffeur. The next few moments passed quickly, but for all this Mrs Ellis had time to realize that her tactics were brilliant, rivalling the heroes of detective fiction.

She crossed the room, opened the long French windows that gave on to a back yard. The window of the bedroom was open; she could hear the chauffeur calling.

'Tradesmen's entrance is ajar,' he shouted; 'she must have gone this way.'

'Let them go on with their confusion,' thought Mrs Ellis, leaning against the bed. 'Let them. Good luck to them in their running about. This will take down some of that Sister's weight. Not much running about for her at Moreton Hill. Cups of tea at all hours, and sweet biscuits, while the patients were given bread and water.'

The movement went on for some time. Somebody used the telephone. There was more talk. And then, when Mrs Ellis was nearly dozing off against the bed valance, she heard the car drive away.

Everything was silent. Mrs Ellis listened. The only sound was the little boy playing in the hall below. She crept to the door and listened once more. The wheeled toy was being dragged backwards and forwards, up and down the hall.

And there was a new sound coming from the living-room. The sound of a sewing machine going at great speed. Mrs Drew was at work.

The Sister and the chauffeur had gone.

An hour, two hours must have passed since they had left. Mrs Ellis glanced at the clock on the mantelpiece. It was two o'clock. What an untidy, scattered sort of room, everything all over the place. Shoes in the middle of the floor, a coat flung down on a chair, and Keith's cot had not been made up; the blankets were rumpled, anyhow.

'Badly brought up,' thought Mrs Ellis, 'and such rough, casual manners. But poor girl, if she had no mother . . .'

She took a last glance round the room, and she saw with a shrug of her shoulder that even Mrs Drew's calendar had a printing error. It said 1952 instead of 1932. How careless . . .

She tiptoed to the head of the stairs. The door of the living-room was shut. The sound of the sewing machine came at breathless speed.

'They must be hard up,' thought Mrs Ellis, 'if she has to do dressmaking. I wonder what her husband does for a living.'

Softly she crept downstairs. She made no sound. And if she had, the sound of the sewing machine would have covered it.

As she passed the living-room door it opened. The boy stood there, staring at her. He said nothing. He smiled. Mrs Ellis smiled back at him. She could not help herself. She had a feeling that he would not give her away.

'Shut the door, Keith, *do*,' nagged his mother from within. The door slammed. The sound of the sewing machine became more distant, muffled. Mrs Ellis let herself out of the house and slipped away . . . She turned northward, like an animal scenting direction, because northward was her home.

She was soon swallowed up in traffic, the buses swinging past her in the Finchley Road, and her feet began to ache, and she was tired, but she could not take a bus or summon a taxi because she had no money.

No one looked at her; no one bothered with her; they were all intent upon their business, either going from home or returning, and it seemed to Mrs Ellis, as she toiled up the hill towards Hampstead, that for the first time in her life she was friendless and alone. She wanted her house, her home, the consolation of her own surroundings; she wanted to take up her normal, everyday life that had been interrupted in so brutal a fashion.

There was so much to straighten out, so much to do, and Mrs Ellis did not know where to begin or whom to ask for help.

'I want everything to be as it was before that walk yesterday,' thought Mrs Ellis, her back aching, her feet throbbing. 'I want my home. I want my little girl.'

And here was the heath once more. This was where she had stood before crossing the road. She even remembered what she had been thinking about. She had been planning to buy a red bicycle for Susan. Something light, but strong, a good make.

The memory of the bicycle made her forget her troubles, her fatigue. As soon as all this muddle and confusion were over, she would buy a red bicycle for Susan.

Why, though, for the second time, that screech of brakes when she crossed the road, and the vacant face of the laundry boy looking down at her?

# August 25, 1983

## Jorge Luis Borges

*For Borges, life has a dream-like quality. 'The light comes in and clumsily I go, / From my dreams to the sharing of my dreams,' he says in one of his poems. His blindness, that 'constant night', heightens the impression of being always in a dream. His first 'fiction' (as he calls his stories that pretend to be essays), 'Pierre Menard, Author of* Don Quixote*', was born from a nightmare caused by high fever, and many of his stories – like 'The Circular Ruins' – explore the world of dreams in search of the secret laws that govern them. In the early seventies he compiled an anthology of dreams which included several of his own.*

*I spoke to Borges in Buenos Aires in May 1982, while the Falkland Islands War was going on. He had just returned from a happy trip to the United States (he had listened to jazz in New Orleans and flown in a balloon in San Francisco) and he found himself back in the midst of an absurd nightmare. Torn between his love for Argentina and his love for England he felt once more betrayed by 'the clumsy fools who rule us'. 'Let us imagine we are dreaming,' he suggested to me. 'Let us imagine we will wake and all this will belong to the past. I will then call you up and say "I had this curious dream, so absurd, a war with England, just imagine . . ." And you will wait a while and say "Borges, do you know, I had that very same dream myself." ' Then he paused and said, a little wistfully, 'I am so looking forward to that waking-up.'*

*August 24 is Borges' birthday. On August 25, 1983, he was eighty-four years old – and a day.*

I saw by the little station clock that it was a few minutes past eleven at night. I walked to the hotel. I felt, as on so many other occasions, the relief and resignation inspired by places we know well. The heavy gate was open; the house stood in darkness.

I entered the hall where dim mirrors duplicated the potted plants in the room. Strangely enough, the hotel-keeper didn't recognize me and handed me the register. I took the pen which was chained to the desk, dipped it in the bronze inkwell and, as I bent over the open book, there occurred the first of the many surprises which that night was to offer me. My name, Jorge Luis Borges, had already been written on the page and the ink was still fresh.

The hotel-keeper said, 'I thought you'd already gone upstairs.' Then he peered at me more closely and corrected himself. 'I'm sorry, sir, the other looks a lot like you. But you're younger of course.'

'What room is he in?'

'He asked for number nineteen,' was the answer. It was as I feared.

I dropped the pen and ran up the stairs. Room nineteen was on the second floor and looked on to a poor and badly tended courtyard with a veranda and, I seem to remember, a bench. It was the highest room in the hotel. I tried the handle and the door opened. The lamp had not been switched off. Under the harsh light I recognized myself. There I was, lying on my back on the small iron bed, older, wizened and very pale, the eyes lost on the high stucco moldings. The voice reached me. It wasn't exactly mine; it was like the voice I often hear in my recordings, unpleasant and monotonous.

'How strange,' it said. 'We are two and we are one. But then, there is nothing really strange in dreams.'

I asked bewildered, 'Is all this a dream?'

'It is certainly my last dream.'

He pointed at the empty bottle on the marble top of the night-table.

'But you have still got plenty to dream before reaching this night. What date is it for you?'

'I don't know exactly,' I answered uncertainly. 'But yesterday was my sixty-first birthday.'

'When you reach this night, your eighty-fourth birthday will have been yesterday. Today is August 25, 1983.'

'So many more years to wait,' I said in a low voice.

'I have nothing left,' he said suddenly. 'I can die any day now. I can fade into that which I don't know and yet keep on dreaming of the double. That hackneyed theme given to me by Stevenson and mirrors!'

I felt that to mention Stevenson was a last farewell, not a pedantic allusion. I was he, and I understood. Even the most dramatic moments are not enough to turn one into Shakespeare and coin memorable phrases.

To change the subject I said, 'I knew what would happen to you. In this very place, in one of the lower rooms, we began to draft the story of this suicide.'

'Yes,' he answered slowly, as if collecting vague memories, 'but I don't see the resemblance. In that draft I bought a one-way ticket to Adrogué, and in the Hotel Las Delicias I climbed to room nineteen, the farthest room of all. There I committed suicide.'

'That is why I am here,' I said to him.

'Here? But we are always here. Here I am dreaming of you, in the apartment of Calle Maipú. Here I am dying in the room that used to be mother's.'

'That used to be mother's,' I repeated, trying not to understand. 'And I am dreaming of you in room nineteen, on the top floor.'

'Who is dreaming whom? I know I am dreaming you but I don't know whether you are dreaming me. The hotel in Adrogué was pulled down many years ago – twenty, maybe thirty. Who knows!'

'I am the dreamer,' I answered with a certain defiance.

'But don't you see that the important thing is to discover whether there is only one dreamer or two?'

'I am Borges who has seen your name in the register and has climbed up to this room.'

'Borges am I, dying in Calle Maipú.'

There was a moment of silence. Then the other said, 'Let's put ourselves to the test. Which was the most terrible moment of our life?'

I leant over towards him and we both spoke at the same time. I know we both lied. A faint smile lit the old face. I felt that the smile somehow reflected my own.

'We have lied to each other,' he said, 'because we feel two and not one. The truth is that we are two and we are one.'

The conversation was beginning to irritate me. I told him so. And I added, 'And you, in 1983, won't you reveal something of the years that lie before me?'

'What can I tell you, my poor Borges? The misfortunes to which you have grown accustomed will keep on happening. You will live alone in this house. You will touch the letterless books and the Swedenborg medallion and the wooden box with the Federal Cross.

Blindness isn't darkness – it's a form of loneliness. You will return to Iceland.'

'Iceland! Iceland of the seas!'

'In Rome you will say a few lines by Keats whose name, like that of all other men, was written on water.'

'I have never been to Rome.'

'There are other things as well. You will write our best poem, and it will be an elegy.'

'To the death of . . .' I said. I did not dare utter the name.

'No. She will live longer than you.' We sat in silence. Then he continued.

'You will write that book we dreamt of for so long. Towards 1979 you will understand that your so-called works are nothing but a series of sketches, miscellaneous drafts, and you will yield to the vain and superstitious temptation of writing your one great book. The superstition that has inflicted upon us Goethe's *Faust, Salammbô, Ulysses*. To my amazement, I have filled too many pages.'

'And in the end you realized you had failed.'

'Something worse. I realized it was a masterpiece in the most oppressive sense of the word. My good intentions did not go farther than the first few pages. In the others lay the labyrinths, the knives, the man who believes he is a dream, the reflection that believes itself to be real, the tigers of night, the battles turned to blood, Juan Muraña fatal and blind, Macedonio's voice, the ship made of the fingernails of the dead, old English spoken through so many days.'

'I know that museum well,' I observed, not without irony.

'And then false memories too, the double play of symbols, the long enumerations, the craft of good prose, the imperfect symmetries that the critics discover with glee, the not always apocryphal quotations.'

'Have you published this book?'

'I toyed – without conviction – with the melodramatic idea of destroying it, perhaps with fire. I finally published it in Madrid under another name. It was described as the work of a vulgar imitator of Borges who had the disadvantage of not being Borges and of having repeated the superficial features of the model.'

'I'm not surprised,' I said. 'Every writer ends by being his own least intelligent disciple.'

'That book was one of the roads that led me to this night. As to the others, the humiliation of old age, the certainty of having already lived all those days to come . . .'

'I won't write that book,' I said.

'Yes you will. My words, which now are the present, will be barely the memory of a dream.'

His dogmatic tone, no doubt the same one I use in the classroom, annoyed me. I was bothered by the fact that we resembled each other so much, and that he should take advantage of the impunity given him by the nearness of death. In revenge I asked him: 'Are you really so certain you are about to die?'

'Yes,' he answered. 'I feel a sort of sweet peacefulness and relief which I have never felt before. I cannot explain it to you. All words require a shared experience. Why do you seem annoyed by what I'm telling you?'

'Because we are far too alike. I hate your face which is a caricature of mine. I hate your voice which apes my own. I hate your pathetic way of building sentences, which is mine.'

'So do I,' said the other. 'That is why I have decided to kill myself.'

A bird sang in the street.

'The last one,' said the other.

With a gesture he called me to his side. His hand took hold of mine. I drew back, fearing that both hands would fade into one. He said:

'The stoics have taught us not to regret leaving this life: the gates of prison are at last open. I have always thought of life in this way, but my sloth and cowardice made me hesitate. Some twelve days ago I gave a conference in La Plata on the sixth book of the *Aeneid*. Suddenly, repeating an hexameter, I knew which was the road to take, and I made up my mind. From that moment onwards I felt invulnerable. My fate will be yours, you will receive this sudden revelation in the midst of Virgil's Latin, and you will have forgotten this curious and prophetic dialogue which takes place in two places and two moments in time. When you dream it again you will be the one I am now and I will be your dream.'

'I won't forget it and tomorrow I'll write it down.'

'It will lie deep inside your memory, beneath the tide of dreams. When you write it, you will believe you are inventing a fantastic story. But it won't be tomorrow. You still have several years to wait.'

He stopped talking; I realized he was dead. In a certain sense I died with him. Anxiously I leant forward over the top of the pillow but there was no one there.

I fled from the room. Outside there was no courtyard, no marble staircase, no large silent hotel, no eucalyptus, no statues, no arches, no fountains, no gate of a country house in Adrogué.

Outside were other dreams, waiting for me.

*Translated from the Spanish by Alberto Manguel.*

# How Wang-Fo Was Saved

## Marguerite Yourcenar

In 1951, immediately after settling in the United States, Marguerite Yourcenar published the novel Memoirs of Hadrian on which she had been working for fifteen years. The book brought her immediate fame and revealed to the French public a versatile author who had already written other historical novels, plays, essays and exquisite translations of the Greek poet Cavafy, as well as a selection of Negro spirituals translated into French.

Oriental Tales (from which the following story is taken) was published in 1938. The tales are based on traditional stories from several countries. The Chinese legend that serves as a basis for 'How Wang-Fo Was Saved' was familiar to both Algernon Blackwood (who used it in 'The Man Who Was Milligan') and M. R. James (who used it in 'The Mezzotint'). Neither, however, has the quality of Yourcenar's story, which is also a study of the artist's role in the world.

Another version of the legend is told in the classic Sanskrit epic, the Ramayana. In the sixteenth century the Indian poet Tulsi Das, who had written the saga of Hanuman and his monkey army, was thrown into prison by an angry king. Tulsi Das called upon his creation to help him, and Hanuman and his army broke into the poet's cell and set him free.

The old painter Wang-Fo and his disciple Ling were wandering along the roads of the kingdom of Han.

They made slow progress, because Wang-Fo would stop at night to watch the stars and during the day to observe the dragonflies. They carried hardly any luggage, because Wang-Fo loved the image of things and not the things themselves, and no object in the world seemed to him worth buying, except brushes, pots of lacquer and China ink, and rolls of silk and rice-paper. They were poor, because Wang-Fo would exchange his paintings for a ration of boiled millet, and paid no attention to pieces of silver. Ling, his disciple, bent beneath the weight of a sack full of sketches, bowed his back with respect as if he were carrying the Heavens' vault, because for Ling the sack was full of snow-covered mountains, torrents in spring, and the face of the summer moon.

Ling had not been born to trot down the roads, following an old man who seized the dawn and captured the dusk. His father had been a banker who dealt in gold, his mother the only child of a jade merchant who had left her all his worldly possessions, cursing her for not being a son. Ling had grown up in a house where wealth had eliminated all trouble. This carefully cushioned existence had made him shy: he was afraid of insects, of thunder and the face of the dead. At the age of fifteen, his father chose a bride for him, a very beautiful one because the thought of the happiness he was giving his son consoled him for having reached the age in which the night is meant for sleep. Ling's wife was as frail as a reed, childish as milk, sweet as saliva, salty as tears. After the wedding, Ling's parents became discreet to the point of dying, and their son was left alone in a house painted vermilion, in the company of his young wife who never stopped smiling and a plum-tree that blossomed every spring with pale-pink flowers. Ling loved this woman of a crystal-clear heart like one loves a mirror that will never tarnish, or a talisman that will protect one for ever. He visited the tea-houses to follow the dictates of fashion, and only moderately favoured acrobats and dancers.

One night, in the tavern, Wang-Fo shared Ling's table. The old man had drunk in order to better paint a drunkard, and he cocked his head to one side as if trying to measure the distance between his hand and his bowl. The rice wine undid the tongue of the taciturn craftsman, and that night Wang spoke as if silence were a wall and words the colours with which to cover it. Thanks to him, Ling got to know the beauty of the drunkards' faces blurred by the vapours of hot drinks, the brown splendour of the roasts unevenly brushed by tongues of fire, and the exquisite blush of wine stains strewn on the tablecloths like withered petals. A gust of wind broke the window: the storm entered the room. Wang-Fo leaned out to make Ling admire the livid zebra stripes of the lightning, and Ling, spellbound, stopped being afraid of storms.

Ling paid the old painter's bill, and as Wang-Fo was both without money and without lodging, he humbly offered him a resting-place.

They walked away together; Ling held a lamp – its light projected unexpected fires in the puddles. That evening Ling discovered with surprise that the walls of his house were not red, as he had always thought, but the colour of an almost rotten orange. In the courtyard, Wang-Fo noticed the delicate shape of a bush to which no one had paid any attention until then, and compared it to a young woman letting down her hair to dry. In the passageway he followed with delight the hesitant trail of an ant along the cracks in the wall, and Ling's horror for these creatures vanished into thin air. Realizing that Wang-Fo had just presented him with the gift of a new soul and a new vision of the world, Ling respectfully offered the old man the room in which his father and mother had died.

For many years now Wang-Fo had dreamt of painting the portrait of a princess of olden days, playing the lute under a willow. No woman was sufficiently unreal to be his model, but Ling would do because he was not a woman. Then Wang-Fo spoke of painting a young prince shooting an arrow at the foot of a large cedar-tree. No young man of the present was sufficiently unreal to serve as his model, but Ling got his own wife to pose under the plum-tree in the garden. Later on Wang-Fo painted her in a fairy costume against the clouds of twilight, and the young woman wept because it was an omen of death. As Ling came to prefer the portraits painted by Wang-Fo to the young woman herself, her face began to fade, like a flower exposed to warm winds and summer rains. One morning they found her hanging from the branches of the pink plum-tree: the ends of the scarf that was strangling her floated in the wind, entangled with her hair. She looked even more delicate than usual, and as pure as the beauties celebrated by the poets of days gone by. Wang-Fo painted her one last time, because he loved the green hue that covers the face of the dead. His disciple Ling mixed the colours and the task needed such concentration that he forgot to shed tears.

One after the other Ling sold his slaves, his jades and the fish in his pond to buy his master pots of purple ink that came from the West. When the house was emptied, they left it, and Ling closed the door of his past behind him. Wang-Fo felt tired of a city where the faces could no longer teach him secrets of ugliness or beauty, and the master and his disciple walked away together down the roads of the kingdom of Han.

Their reputation preceded them into the villages, to the threshold of fortresses and into the atrium of temples where restless pilgrims halt at dusk. It was murmured that Wang-Fo had the power to bring his paintings to life by adding a last touch of colour to their eyes. Farmers would come and beg him to paint a watch-dog, and the lords would ask him for portraits of their soldiers. The priests honoured Wang-Fo as a sage; the people feared him as a sorcerer. Wang enjoyed these differences of opinion which gave him the chance to study expressions of gratitude, fear or veneration.

Ling begged for food, watched over his master's rest, and took advantage of his ecstasies to massage his feet. With the first rays of the sun, when the old man was still asleep, Ling went in pursuit of timid landscapes hidden behind bunches of reeds. In the evening, when the master, disheartened, threw away his brushes, he would carefully pick them up. When Wang became sad and spoke of his old age, Ling would smile and show him the solid trunk of an old oak; when Wang felt happy and made jokes, Ling would humbly pretend to listen.

One day, at sunset, they reached the outskirts of the imperial city and Ling went ahead in search of an inn in which Wang-Fo could spend the night. The old man wrapped himself up in rags, and Ling lay down next to him to keep him warm because spring had only just started and the floor of beaten earth was still frozen. At dawn, heavy steps echoed in the corridors of the inn; they heard the frightened whispers of the innkeeper and orders shouted in a foreign tongue. Ling trembled, remembering that the night before he had stolen a rice-cake for his master's supper. Certain that they would come to take him to prison, he asked himself who would help Wang-Fo ford the next river tomorrow.

The soldiers entered carrying lanterns. The flames gleaming through the many-coloured paper cast red and blue lights on their leather helmets. The string of a bow quivered over their shoulders, and the fiercest among them suddenly let out a roar for no reason at all. A heavy hand fell on Wang-Fo's neck, and the painter could not help noticing that the soldiers' sleeves did not match the colour of their coats.

Helped by his disciple, Wang-Fo followed the soldiers, stumbling along uneven roads. The passing crowds made fun of these two criminals who were certainly going to be beheaded. To Wang's questions the soldiers answered with savage scowls. His bound hands hurt him, and Ling in despair looked smiling at his master, which for him was a gentler way of crying.

They reached the threshold of the imperial palace whose purple walls rose in broad daylight like a sweep of sunset. The soldiers led Wang-Fo through countless square and circular rooms whose shapes symbolized the seasons, the cardinal points, the male and the female, longevity, and the prerogatives of power. The doors swung on their hinges with a musical note, and were placed in such a manner that one followed the entire scale when crossing the palace from East to West. Everything combined to give an impression of superhuman power and subtlety, and one could feel that here the simplest orders became as final and as terrible as the wisdom of the ancients. At last the air became scarce and the silence so deep that not even a man under torture would have dared to scream. A eunuch lifted a tapestry; the soldiers began to tremble like women, and the small troop entered the chamber in which the Son of Heaven sat on a high throne.

It was a room without walls, held up by thick columns of blue stone. A garden spread out on the far side of the marble shafts, and each and every flower blooming in the greenery belonged to a rare species brought here from across the oceans. But none of them had any perfume, so that the Celestial Dragon's meditations would not be troubled by fine smells. Out of respect for the silence in which his thoughts evolved no bird had been allowed within the enclosure and even the bees had been driven away. An enormous wall separated the garden from the rest of the world, so that the wind that passes over dead dogs and corpses on the battlefield would not dare brush the Emperor's sleeve.

The Celestial Master sat on a throne of jade, and his hands were wrinkled like those of an old man though he had scarcely reached the age of twenty. His robe was blue to symbolize winter, and green to remind one of spring. His face was beautiful but undisturbed, like a looking-glass placed too high, reflecting nothing except the stars and the immutable heaven. To his right stood his Minister of Perfect Pleasures, and to his left his Counsellor of Just Torments. Because his courtiers, lined along the base of the columns, always lent a keen ear to the slightest sound from his lips, he had adopted the habit of speaking in a low voice.

'Celestial Dragon,' said Wang-Fo bowing low, 'I am old, I am poor, I am weak. You are like summer; I am like winter. You have Ten Thousand Lives; I have but one, and it is near its close. What have I done to you? My hands have been tied, these hands that never harmed you.'

'You ask what you have done to me, old Wang-Fo?' said the Emperor.

His voice was so melodious that it made one want to cry. He raised his right hand to which the reflections from the jade pavement gave a pale sea-green hue like that of an underwater plant, and Wang-Fo marvelled at the length of those thin fingers, and hunted among his memories to discover whether he had not at some time painted a mediocre portrait of either the Emperor or one of his ancestors, that would now deserve the pain of death. But it seemed unlikely because Wang-Fo had not been an assiduous visitor at the imperial court. He preferred the farmers' huts or, in the cities, the courtesans' quarters and the taverns along the harbour where the dockers liked to quarrel.

'You ask me what it is you have done, old Wang-Fo?' continued the Emperor, inclining his slender neck towards the old man waiting attentively. 'I will tell you. But, as another man's poison cannot enter our veins except through our nine openings, in order to show you your offences I must take you with me down the corridors of my memory and tell you the story of my life. My father had assembled a collection of your work and hidden it in the most secret chamber in the palace, because he judged that the people in your paintings should be concealed from the world since they cannot lower their eyes in the imperial presence. It was in those same rooms that I was brought up, old Wang-Fo, surrounded by solitude. To prevent my innocence from being sullied by other human souls, the restless crowd of my future subjects had been driven away from me, and no one was allowed to pass my threshold for fear that his or her shadow would stretch out and touch me. The few aged servants that were placed in my service showed themselves as little as possible; the hours turned in circles; the colours of your paintings bloomed in the first hours of the morning and grew pale at dusk. At night, when I was unable to go to sleep, I watched them, and for nearly ten years I watched them every night. During the day, sitting on a carpet whose design I knew by heart, I dreamt of the joys the future had in store for me. I imagined the world, with the kingdom of Han at the centre, like the monotonous hollow of my hand crossed by the fatal lines of the Five Rivers. Around it lay the sea in which monsters are born, and farther away the mountains that hold up the heavens. And to help me visualize these things I used your paintings. You made me believe that the sea looked like the vast sheet of water spread across your scrolls, so blue that if a stone were to fall into it, it would become a sapphire; that women opened and closed like flowers, like the creatures that come forward, pushed by the wind, along the paths of your painted gardens; and that the young, slim-waisted warriors who mount guard in the fortresses along the frontier were themselves like arrows that could pierce your heart. At sixteen I saw the doors that separated me from the world open once again; I climbed on to the balcony of my palace to watch the clouds, but they were far less beautiful than those in your sunsets. I ordered my litter; shaken along roads on which I had not forseen either mud or stones, I travelled across the provinces of the Empire without ever finding your gardens full of women like fireflies, or a woman whose body is in itself a garden. The pebbles on the beach spoilt my taste for oceans; the blood of the tortured seemed less red than the pomegranates in your paintings; the village vermin forbade me to see the beauty of the rice fields; the flesh of mortal women disgusted me like the dead meat hanging from the butcher's hook, and the coarse laughter of my soldiers made me sick. You lied, Wang-Fo, you old imposter. The world is nothing but a mass of muddled colours thrown into the void by an insane painter, and smudged by our tears. The kingdom of Han is not the most beautiful of kingdoms, and I am not the Emperor. The only empire which is worth reigning over is that which you alone can enter, old Wang, by the road of One Thousand Curves and Ten Thousand Colours. You alone reign peacefully over mountains covered in snow that cannot melt, and over fields of daffodils that cannot die. And that is why, Wang-Fo, I have imagined a punishment for you, for you whose enchantment has given me the disgust of everything I own, and the desire for everything I shall never possess. And in order to lock you up in the only cell from which there is no escape I have decided to have your eyes burnt, because your eyes, Wang-Fo, are the two magic gates that open on to your kingdom. And as your hands are the two roads of ten forking paths that lead to the heart of your kingdom, I have decided to have your hands cut off. Have you understood, old Wang-Fo?'

Hearing the sentence, Ling, the disciple, tore from his belt a

broken knife and leapt towards the Emperor. Two guards immediately took hold of him. The Son of Heaven smiled and added with
a sigh:

'And I also hate you, old Wang-Fo, because you have known
how to make yourself be loved. Kill that dog.'

Ling jumped to one side so that his blood would not stain his
master's robe. One of the soldiers lifted his sword and Ling's head
fell from his neck like a cut flower. The servants carried away the
remains, and Wang-Fo, in despair, admired the beautiful scarlet
stain that his disciple's blood made on the green stone floor.

The Emperor made a sign and two eunuchs dried Wang's tears.

'Listen, old Wang-Fo,' said the Emperor, 'and dry your tears
because this is not the time to weep. Your eyes must be clear so
that the little light that is left to them is not clouded by your
weeping. Because it is not only the grudge I bear you that makes
me wish your death; it is not only the cruelty in my heart that
makes me want to see you suffer. I have other plans, old Wang-Fo.
I possess among your works a remarkable painting in which the
mountains, the river estuary and the sea reflect each other, on a
very small scale certainly but with a clarity that surpasses the real
landscapes themselves, like objects reflected on the walls of a metal
sphere. But that painting is unfinished, Wang-Fo; your masterpiece
is but a sketch. No doubt, when you began your work, sitting in a
solitary valley, you noticed a passing bird, or a child running after
the bird. And the bird's beak or the child's cheeks made you forget
the blue eyelids of the sea. You never finished the frills of the
water's cloak, nor the seaweed-hair of the rocks. Wang-Fo, I want
you to use the few hours of light that are left to you to finish this
painting which will thus contain the final secrets amassed during
your long life. I know that your hands, about to fall, will not tremble
on the silken cloth, and infinity will enter your work through those
unhappy cuts. I know that your eyes, about to be put out, will
discover bearings far beyond all human senses. This is my plan, old
Wang-Fo, and I can force you to fulfill it. If you refuse, before
blinding you, I will have all your paintings burnt, and you will be
like a father whose children are slaughtered and all hopes of posterity
extinguished. However, believe, if you wish, that this last order
stems from nothing but my kindness, because I know that the silken
scroll is the only mistress you ever deigned to touch. And to offer

you brushes, paints and inks to occupy your last hours is like offering the favours of a harlot to a man condemned to death.'

Upon a sign from the Emperor's little finger, two eunuchs respectfully brought forward the unfinished scroll on which Wang-Fo had outlined the image of the sea and the sky. Wang-Fo dried his tears and smiled, because that small sketch reminded him of his youth. Everything in it spoke of a fresh new spirit which Wang-Fo could no longer claim as his, and yet something was missing from it, because when Wang had painted it he had not yet looked long enough at the mountains nor at the rocks bathing their naked flanks in the sea, and he had not yet penetrated deep enough into the sadness of the evening twilight. Wang-Fo selected one of the brushes which a slave held ready for him and began spreading wide strokes of blue on to the unfinished sea. A eunuch crouched by his feet mixing the colours; he carried out his task with little skill, and more than ever Wang-Fo lamented his disciple Ling.

Wang began by adding a touch of pink to the tip of the wing of a cloud perched on a mountain. Then he painted on to the surface of the sea a few small lines that deepened the perfect feeling of calm. The jade floor became increasingly damp but Wang-Fo, absorbed as he was in his painting, did not seem to notice that he was working with his feet in water.

The fragile rowboat grew under the strokes of the painter's brush and now occupied the entire foreground of the silken scroll. The rhythmic sound of the oars rose suddenly in the distance, quick and eager like the beating of wings. The sound came nearer, gently filling the whole room, then ceased, and a few trembling drops appeared on the boatman's oars. The red iron intended for Wang's eyes lay extinguished on the executioner's coals. The courtiers, motionless as etiquette required, stood in water up to their shoulders, trying to lift themselves on to the tips of their toes. The water finally reached the level of the imperial heart. The silence was so deep one could have heard a tear drop.

It was Ling. He wore his everyday robe, and his right sleeve still had a hole that he had not had time to mend that morning before the soldiers' arrival. But around his neck was tied a strange red scarf.

Wang-Fo said to him softly, while he continued painting, 'I thought you were dead.'

'You being alive,' said Ling respectfully, 'how could I have died?'

And he helped his master into the boat. The jade ceiling reflected itself in the water so that Ling seemed to be inside a cave. The pigtails of the submerged courtiers rippled up towards the surface like snakes, and the pale head of the Emperor floated like a lotus.

'Look at them,' said Wang-Fo sadly. 'These wretches will die, if they are not dead already. I never thought there was enough water in the sea to drown an Emperor. What are we to do?'

'Master, have no fear,' murmured the disciple. 'They will soon be dry again and will not even remember that their sleeves were ever wet. Only the Emperor will keep in his heart a little of the bitterness of the sea. These people are not of the kind to lose themselves inside a painting.'

And he added, 'The sea is calm, the wind high, the seabirds fly to their nests. Let us leave, Master, and sail to the land beyond the waves.'

'Let us leave,' said the old painter.

Wang-Fo took hold of the helm, and Ling bent over the oars. The sound of rowing filled the room again, strong and steady like the beating of a heart. The level of the water diminished unnoticed around the large vertical rocks that became columns once more. Soon only a few puddles shone in the hollows of the jade floor. The courtiers' robes were dry, but a few wisps of foam still clung to the hem of the Emperor's cloak.

The painting finished by Wang-Fo was leaning against a tapestry. A rowboat occupied the entire foreground. It drifted away little by little, leaving behind it a thin wake that smoothed out into the quiet sea. One could no longer make out the faces of the two men sitting in the boat but one could still see Ling's red scarf and Wang-Fo's beard waving in the breeze.

The beating of the oars grew fainter then ceased, blotted out by the distance. The Emperor, leaning forward, a hand above his eyes, watched Wang's boat sail away till it was nothing but an imperceptible dot in the paleness of the twilight. A golden mist rose and spread over the water. Finally the boat veered around a rock that stood in the gateway to the ocean; the shadow of a cliff fell across it; its wake disappeared from the deserted surface, and the painter Wang-Fo and his disciple Ling vanished for ever on the jade-blue sea that Wang-Fo had just created.

*Translated from the French by Alberto Manguel.*

# From 'Peter and Rosa'

## Isak Dinesen

*Defining Isak Dinesen's style, the* New York Times *said, 'True, but not true to life . . . We know we have been here before, in fairy stories read in childhood, and also in our dreams and in our life-as-dreams. The action is strange, and yet not so strange either. It happened a long time ago, yesterday, and is happening now. The meanings appear to be many, and we feel if we could only be a little more perceptive we could see what they are.'*

*The Baroness Karen Blixen-Finecke, who chose the name of Isak Dinesen, wrote her* Winter's Tales *during World War Two, using the Denmark of her childhood for background and themes. She sent the manuscript to America, telling her publisher that she would not be able to communicate with him until the war ended. When it did, she received dozens of letters from American soldiers and sailors all over the world. To her surprise, the book had been so successful that it had been published in an Armed Forces edition. Isak Dinesen finally received two copies of her book and sent one to the King of Denmark. Later on the King remarked how delighted he was to see that, after all, 'a voice had spoken from his silent country during the dark years of the War.'*

*From* Winter's Tales *I have chosen a short passage rather than a full-length story because I find it concentrates better one of fantastic literature's most difficult themes: the correspondence between our actions and the actions of the universe, the idea that man and the many things in our world, are one.*

I have heard a story . . . of a skipper who named his ship after his wife. He had the figure-head of it beautifully carved, just like her, and the hair of it gilt. But his wife was jealous of the ship. 'You think more of the figure-head than of me,' she said to him. 'No,' he answered, 'I think so highly of her because she is like you, yes, because she is you yourself. Is she not gallant, full-bosomed; does she not dance in the waves, like you at our wedding? In a way she is really even kinder to me than you are. She gallops along where I tell her to go, and she lets her long hair hang down freely, while you put up yours under a cap. But she turns her back to me, so that when I want a kiss I come home to Elsinore.' Now once, when this skipper was trading at Trankebar, he chanced to help an old native King to flee from traitors in his own country. As they parted the King gave him two big blue, precious stones, and these he had set into the face of his figure-head, like a pair of eyes to it. When he came home he told his wife of his adventure, and said: 'Now she has your blue eyes too.' 'You had better give me the stones for a pair of earrings,' said she. 'No,' he said again, 'I cannot do that, and you would not ask me to if you understood.' Still the wife could not stop fretting about the blue stones, and one day, when her husband was with the skippers' corporation, she had a glazier of the town take them out, and put two bits of blue glass into the figure-head instead, and the skipper did not find out, but sailed off to Portugal. But after some time the skipper's wife found that her eyesight was growing bad, and that she could not see to thread a needle. She went to a wise woman, who gave her ointments and waters, but they did not help her, and in the end the old woman shook her head, and told her that this was a rare and incurable disease, and that she was going blind. 'Oh, God,' the wife then cried, 'that the ship was back in the harbour of Elsinore. Then I should have the glass taken out, and the jewels put back. For did he not say that they were my eyes?' But the ship did not come back. Instead the skipper's wife had a letter from the Consul of Portugal, who informed her that she had been wrecked, and gone to the bottom with all hands. And it was a very strange thing, the Consul wrote, that in broad daylight she had run straight into a tall rock, rising out of the sea.

# Tattoo

## Junichiro Tanizaki

*Edgar Allan Poe's influence spread far and wide. In Latin America he inspired the modernist movement at the turn of the century, and Julio Cortázar acknowledged his debt by translating Poe's stories in the sixties; in France he was translated by Baudelaire, who called him his master; in the early years of the twentieth century he was translated into Japanese by Tanizaki, and today his name is still used as a pseudonym by one of Japan's most popular detective-story writers.*

*Tanizaki wrote 'Tattoo' at the age of twenty-four. Poe's influence is noticeable in the story, as well as that of Oscar Wilde whose* Portrait of Dorian Gray *Tanizaki also translated. In Wilde's novel a painting of a man displays the increasing depravity and decay of the subject, while the man himself remains eternally young; in Tanizaki's story an artist's design is the cause of a young woman's transformation, following Wilde's revelation that 'Nature imitates art.'*

These things happened at a time when the noble virtue of frivolity still flourished, when today's relentless struggle for existence was yet unknown. The faces of the young aristocrats and squires were darkened by no cloud; at court the maids of honour and the great courtesans always wore smiles on their lips; the occupations of clown and professional teahouse wit were held in high esteem; life was peaceful and full of joy. In the theatre and in the writings of the time, beauty and power were portrayed as inseparable.

Physical beauty, indeed, was the chief aim of life, and in its pursuit people went so far as to have themselves tattooed. On their bodies, brilliant lines and colours were ravelled in a sort of dance. When visiting the gay quarters, they would choose as bearers for their palanquins men whose bodies were skilfully tattooed, and the courtesans of Yoshiwara and Tatsumi gave their love to men whose bodies boasted beautiful tattoos. Frequenters of the gambling dens, firemen, merchants, and even samurai all had recourse to the tattooer's art. Tattoo exhibitions were frequently arranged where the participants, fingering the tattoo marks on each other's bodies, would praise the original design of one and criticize the shortcomings of another.

There was a young tattooer of outstanding talent. He was much in fashion and his reputation rivalled even those of the great masters of old, Charibun of Asakusa, Yakkohei of Matsushimachō, and Konkonjirō. His works were greatly prized at the tattoo exhibitions and most admirers of the art aspired to become his clients. While the artist Darumakin was known for his fine drawings and Karakusa Gonta was the master of the vermilion tattoo, this man Seikichi was famous for the originality of his compositions and for their voluptuous quality.

Previously he had achieved a certain reputation as a painter, belonging to the school of Toyokuni and Kunisada and specializing in genre paintings. In descending to the rank of tattooer, he still preserved the true spirit of an artist and a great sensitivity. He declined to execute his work on people whose skin or general physique did not appeal to him, and such customers as he did accept had to agree implicitly to the design of his choosing and also to his price. Moreover, they had to endure for as long as one or two months the excruciating pain of his needles.

Within this young tattooer's heart lurked unsuspected passions and pleasures. When the pricking of his needles caused the flesh to swell and the crimson blood to flow, his patients, unable to endure the agony, would emit groans of pain. The more they groaned, the greater was the artist's strange pleasure. He took particular delight in vermilion designs, which are known to be the most painful of tattoos. When his patients had received five or six hundred pricks of the needle and then taken a scalding hot bath the more vividly to bring out the colours, they would often collapse half dead at Seikichi's feet. As they lay there unable to move, he would ask with a satisfied smile: 'So it really hurts?'

When he had to deal with a fainthearted customer whose teeth would grind or who gave out shrieks of pain, Seikichi would say: 'Really, I thought you were a native of Kyoto where people are supposed to be courageous. Please try to be patient. My needles are unusually painful.' And glancing from the corner of his eyes at the victim's face, now moist with tears, he would continue his work with utter unconcern. If, on the contrary, his patient bore the agony without flinching, he would say: 'Ah, you are much braver than you look. But wait a while. Soon you will be unable to endure it in silence, try as you may.' And he would laugh, showing his white teeth.

For many years now, Seikichi's great ambition had been to have under his needle the lustrous skin of some beautiful girl, on which he dreamed of tattooing, as it were, his very soul. This imaginary woman had to meet many conditions as to both physique and character; a lovely face and a fine skin would not in themselves satisfy Seikichi. In vain had he searched among the well-known courtesans for a woman who would measure up to his ideal. Her image was constantly in his mind, and although three years had now elapsed since he started this quest, his desire had only grown with time.

It was on a summer's evening while walking in the Fukagawa district that his attention was caught by a feminine foot of dazzling whiteness disappearing behind the curtain of a palanquin. A foot can convey as many variations of expression as a face, and this white foot seemed to Seikichi like the rarest of jewels. The perfectly shaped toes, the iridescent nails, the rounded heel, the skin, as lustrous as if it had been washed for ages by the limpid waters of some mountain brook – all combined to make a foot of absolute perfection designed to stir the heart of a man and to trample upon his soul. Seikichi knew at once that this was the foot of the woman for whom he had searched these many years. Joyously he hurried after the palanquin, hoping to catch a glimpse of its occupant, but after following it for several streets, he lost sight of it around a corner. From then on what had been a vague yearning was transformed into the most violent of passions.

One morning a year later Seikichi received a visit at his house in the Fukagawa district. It was a young girl sent on an errand by a friend of his, a certain geisha from the Tatsumi quarter.

'Excuse me, sir,' the girl said timidly. 'My mistress has asked me to deliver this coat to you personally and to request you to be so good as to make a design on the lining.'

She handed him a letter and a woman's coat, the latter wrapped in a paper bearing the portrait of the actor Iwai Tojaku. In her letter the geisha informed Seikichi that the young messenger was her newly adopted ward and was soon to make her debut as a geisha in the restaurants of the capital. She asked him to do what he could to launch the girl on her new career.

Seikichi looked closely at the visitor who, though no more than sixteen or seventeen, had in her face something strangely mature. In her eyes were reflected the dreams of all the handsome men and beautiful women who had lived in this city, where the virtues and vices of the whole country converged. Then Seikichi's glance went to her delicate feet, shod in street clogs covered with plaits of straw.

'Could it have been you who left the Hirasei restaurant last June in a palanquin?'

'Yes, sir, it was I,' she said, laughing at his strange question. 'My father was alive then and he used to take me occasionally to the Hirasei restaurant.'

'I have been waiting for you now for five years,' said Seikichi. 'This is the first time that I have seen your face but I know you by your feet . . . There is something that I should like you to see. Please come inside, and do not be afraid.'

So saying, he took the hand of the reluctant girl and led her upstairs into a room which looked out on the great river. He fetched two large picture scrolls and spread one of them before her.

It was a painting of Mo Hsi, the favourite princess of the ancient Chinese emperor, Chou the Cruel. Languidly she leaned against a balustrade, and the bottom of her richly brocaded gown rested on the steps of the staircase leading to a garden. Her tiny head seemed almost too delicate to support the weight of her crown, which was encrusted with lapis lazuli and coral. In her right hand she held a cup, slightly tilted, and with an indolent expression she watched a prisoner who was about to be beheaded in the garden below. Secured hand and foot to a stake, he stood there awaiting his last moment; his eyes were closed, his head bent down. Pictures of such scenes tend to vulgarity, but so skilfully had the painter portrayed the expressions of the princess and of the condemned man that this picture scroll was a work of consummate art.

For a while the young girl fixed her gaze on the strange painting. Unconsciously her eyes began to shine and her lips trembled; gradually her face took on a resemblance to that of the young Chinese princess.

'Your spirit is reflected in that painting,' said Seikichi, smiling with pleasure as he gazed at her.

'Why have you shown me such a terrible picture?' asked the girl, passing her hand over her pale forehead.

'The woman depicted here is yourself. Her blood flows through your veins.'

Seikichi then unrolled the other scroll, which was entitled 'The Victims', In the centre of the picture a young woman leaned against a cherry tree, gazing at a group of men's corpses which lay about her feet; pride and satisfaction were to be discerned in her pale face. Hopping about among the corpses, a swarm of little birds chirped happily. Impossible to tell whether the picture represented a battlefield or a spring garden!

'This painting symbolizes your future,' said Seikichi, indicating the face of the young woman, which again strangely resembled that of his visitor. 'The men fallen on the ground are those who will lose their lives because of you.'

'Oh, I beg you,' she cried. 'put that picture away.' And as if to escape its terrifying fascination, she turned her back to the scroll and threw herself on the straw matting. There she lay with lips trembling and her whole body shuddering. 'Master, I will confess to you . . . As you have guessed, I have in me the nature of that woman. Take pity on me and hide the picture.'

'Do not talk like a coward! On the contrary, you should study the painting more carefully and then you will soon stop being frightened of it.'

The girl could not bring herself to raise her head, which remained hidden in the sleeve of her kimono. She lay prostrate on the floor saying over and over: 'Master, let me go home. I am frightened to be with you.'

'You shall stay for a while,' said Seikichi imperiously. 'I alone have the power to make of you a beautiful woman.'

From among the bottles and needles on his shelf Seikichi selected a vial containing a powerful narcotic.

The sun shone brightly on the river. Its reflected rays threw a pattern like golden waves on the sliding doors and on the face of the young sleeping woman. Seikichi closed the doors and sat down beside her. Now for the first time he was able to relish her strange beauty fully, and he thought that he could have spent years sitting there gazing at that perfect, immobile face.

But the urge to accomplish his design overcame him before many moments. Having fetched his tattooing instruments from the shelf, Seikichi uncovered the girl's body and began to apply to her back the point of his pen, held between the thumb, ring finger, and little finger of his left hand. With the needle, held in his right hand, he pricked along the lines as they were drawn. As the people of Memphis once embellished the sphinxes and pyramids of the fine land of Egypt, so Seikichi now adorned the pure skin of this young girl. It was as if the tattooer's very spirit entered into the design, and each injected drop of vermilion was like a drop of his own blood penetrating the girl's body.

He was quite unconscious of the passage of time. Noon came and went, and the quiet spring day moved gradually toward its close. Indefatigably Seikichi's hand pursued its work without ever waking the girl from her slumber. Presently the moon hung in the sky, pouring its dreamy light over the rooftops on the other side of the river. The tattoo was not yet half done. Seikichi interrupted his work to turn up the lamp, then sat down again and reached for his needle.

Now each stroke demanded an effort, and the artist would let out a sigh, as if his own heart had felt the prick. Little by little there began to appear the outline of an enormous spider. As the pale glow of dawn entered the room, this animal of diabolic mien spread its eight legs over the girl's back.

The spring night was almost over. Already one could hear the dip of the oars as the rowboats passed up and down the river; above the sails of the fishing smacks, swollen with the morning breeze, one could see the mists lifting. And at last Seikichi brought himself to put down his needle. Standing aside, he studied the enormous female spider tattooed on the girl's back, and as he gazed at it, he realized that in this work he had expressed the essence of his whole life. Now that it was completed, the artist was aware of a great emptiness.

'To give you beauty I have poured my whole soul into this tattoo,' Seikichi murmured. 'From now on there in not a woman in Japan to rival you! Never again will you know fear. All men, all men will be your victims . . .'

Did she hear his words? A moan rose to her lips, her limbs moved. Gradually she began to regain consciousness, and as she lay breathing heavily in and out, the spider's legs moved on her back like those of a living animal.

'You must be suffering,' said Seikichi. 'That is because the spider is embracing your body so closely.'

She half opened her eyes. At first they had a vacant look, then the pupils began to shine with a brightness that matched the moonlight reflected on Seikichi's face.

'Master, let me see the tattoo on my back! If you have given me your soul, I must indeed have become beautiful.'

She spoke as in a dream, and yet in her voice there was a new note of confidence, of power.

'First you must take a bath to brighten the colours,' Seikichi answered her. And he added with unwanted solicitude: 'It will be painful, most painful. Have courage!' 'I will bear anything to become beautiful,' said the girl.

She followed Seikichi down some stairs into the bathroom, and as she stepped into the steaming water her eyes glistened with pain.

'Ah, ah, how it burns!' she groaned. 'Master, leave me and wait upstairs. I shall join you when I am ready. I do not want any man to see me suffer.'

But when she stepped out of the bath, she did not even have strength to dry herself. She pushed aside Seikichi's helping hand and collapsed on the floor. Groaning, she lay with her long hair flowing across the floor. The mirror behind her reflected the soles of two feet, iridescent as mother-of-pearl.

Seikichi went upstairs to wait for her, and when at last she joined him she was dressed with care. Her damp hair had been combed out and hung about her shoulders. Her delicate mouth and curving eyebrows no longer betrayed her ordeal, and as she gazed out at the river there was a cold glint in her eyes. Despite her youth she had the mien of a woman who had spent years in teahouses and acquired the art of mastering men's hearts. Amazed, Seikichi reflected on the change in the timid girl since the day before. Going to the other room, he fetched the two picture scrolls which he had shown her.

'I offer you these paintings,' he said. 'And also, of course, the tattoo. They are yours to take away.'

'Master,' she answered, 'my heart is now free from all fear. And you . . . you shall be my first victim!'

She threw him a look, piercing as a newly sharpened sword blade. It was the look of the young Chinese princess, and of that other woman who leaned against a cherry tree surrounded by singing birds and dead bodies. A feeling of triumph raced through Seikichi.

'Let me see your tattoo,' he said to her. 'Show me your tattoo.'

Without a word, she inclined her head and unfastened her dress. The rays of the morning sun fell on the young girl's back and its golden gleam seemed to set fire to the spider.

*Translated from the Japanese by Ivan Morris.*

# John Duffy's Brother

## Flann O'Brien

*'Humour' said Flann O'Brien, 'is the handmaid of sorrow and fear.' Humour, sorrow and fear combine in his two novels – The Third Policeman, a hilarious fantastic detective story, and At Swim-Two-Birds, which Anthony Burgess called 'one of the ten great comic books of the century' – and in the following short story. Because of the mundane setting and the humorous characters, the fantastic occurrence is almost obscured by the impression of a vaudeville farce. Here, as in other fantastic stories, the seemingly impossible might be explained away by madness or delusion. And yet, as in a dream that seems real, the reader knows that something more is being said: a sudden magic has taken place, the laws of everyday life have been broken. Estragon, in Beckett's Waiting for Godot, says to Vladimir, 'We always find something, eh, Didi, to give us the impression that we exist?' And Vladimir answers, impatiently, 'Yes, yes, we're magicians.'*

Strictly speaking, this story should not be written or told at all. To write it or to tell it is to spoil it. This is because the man who had the strange experience we are going to talk about never mentioned it to anybody, and the fact that he kept his secret and sealed it up completely in his memory is the whole point of the story. Thus we must admit that handicap at the beginning – that it is absurd for us to tell the story, absurd for anybody to listen to it and unthinkable that anybody should believe it.

We will, however, do this man one favour. We will refrain from mentioning him by his complete name. This will enable us to tell his secret and permit him to continue looking his friends in the eye. But we can say that his surname is Duffy. There are thousands of these Duffys in the world; even at this moment there is probably a new Duffy making his appearance in some corner of it. We can even go so far as to say that he is John Duffy's brother. We do not break faith in saying so, because if there are only one hundred John Duffy's in existence, and even if each one of them could be met and questioned, no embarrassing enlightenments would be forthcoming. That is because the John Duffy in question never left his house, never left his bed, never talked to anybody in his life and was never seen by more than one man. That man's name was Gumley. Gumley was a doctor. He was present when John Duffy was born and also when he died, one hour later.

John Duffy's brother lived alone in a small house on an eminence in Inchicore. When dressing in the morning he could gaze across the broad valley of the Liffey to the slopes of the Phoenix Park, peacefully. Usually the river was indiscernible but on a sunny morning it could be seen lying like a long glistening spear in the valley's palm. Like a respectable married man, it seemed to be hurrying into Dublin as if to work.

Sometimes, recollecting that his clock was fast, John Duffy's brother would spend an idle moment with his father's spy glass, ranging the valley with an eagle eye. The village of Chapelizod was to the left and invisible in the depth but each morning the inhabitants would erect, as if for Mr Duffy's benefit, a lazy plume of smoke to show exactly where they were.

Mr Duffy's glass usually came to rest on the figure of a man hurrying across the uplands of the Park and disappearing from view in the direction of the Magazine Fort. A small white terrier bounced along ahead of him but could be seen occasionally sprinting to overtake him after dallying behind for a time on private business.

The man carried in the crook of his arm an instrument which Mr Duffy at first took to be a shotgun or patent repeating rifle, but one morning the man held it by the butt and smote the barrels smartly on the ground as he walked, and it was then evident to Mr Duffy – he felt some disappointment – that the article was a walking stick.

It happened that this man's name was Martin Smullen. He was a retired stationary-engine-driver and lived quietly with a delicate sister at Number Four, Cannon Row, Parkgate. Mr Duffy did not know his name and was destined never to meet him or have the privilege of his acquaintance, but it may be worth mentioning that they once stood side by side at the counter of a public-house in Little Easter Street, mutually unrecognised, each to the other a black stranger. Mr Smullen's call was whiskey, Mr Duffy's stout.

Mr. Smullen's sister's name was not Smullen but Goggins, relict of the late Paul Goggins wholesale clothier. Mr Duffy had never even heard of her. She had a cousin by the name of Leo Corr who was not unknown to the police. He was sent up in 1924 for a stretch of hard labour in connection with the manufacture of spurious currency. Mrs Goggins had never met him, but heard he had emigrated to Labrador on his release.

About the spy glass. A curious history attaches to its owner, also a Duffy, late of the Mercantile Marine. Although unprovided with the benefits of a University education – indeed, he had gone to sea at the age of sixteen as a result of an incident arising out of an imperfect understanding of the sexual relation – he was of a scholarly turn of mind and would often spend the afternoons of his sea-leave alone in his dining-room thumbing a book of Homer with delight or annotating with erudite sneers the inferior Latin of the Angelic Doctor. On the fourth day of July, 1927, at four o'clock, he took leave of his senses in the dining-room. Four men arrived in a closed van at eight o'clock that evening to remove him from mortal ken to a place where he would be restrained for his own good.

It could be argued that much of the foregoing has little real bearing on the story of John Duffy's brother, but modern writing, it is hoped, has passed the stage when simple events are stated in the void without any clue as to the psychological and hereditary forces working in the background to produce them. Having said so much, however, it is now permissable to set down briefly the nature of the adventure of John Duffy's brother.

He arose one morning – on the ninth of March, 1932 – dressed and cooked his frugal breakfast. Immediately afterwards, he became possessed of the strange idea that he was a train. No explanation of this can be attempted. Small boys sometimes like to pretend that they are trains, and there are fat women in the world who are not, in the distance, without some resemblance to trains. But John Duffy's brother was certain that he *was* a train – long, thunderous and immense, with white steam escaping noisily from his feet and deep-throated bellows coming rhythmically from where his funnel was.

Moreover, he was certain that he was a particular train, the 9.20 into Dublin. His station was the bedroom. He stood absolutely still for twenty minutes, knowing that a good train is equally punctual in departure as in arrival. He glanced often at his watch to make sure that the hour should not go by unnoticed. His watch bore the words 'Shockproof' and 'Railway Timekeeper'.

Precisely at 9.20 he emitted a piercing whistle, shook the great mass of his metal ponderously into motion and steamed away heavily into town. The train arrived dead on time at its destination, which was the office of Messrs. Polter and Polter, Solicitors, Commissioners for Oaths. For obvious reasons, the name of this firm is fictitious. In the office were two men, old Mr Cranberry and young Mr Hodge. Both were clerks and both took their orders from John Duffy's brother. Of course, both names are imaginary.

'Good morning, Mr Duffy,' said Mr Cranberry. He was old and polite, grown yellow in the firm's service.

Mr Duffy looked at him in surprise. 'Can you not see I am a train?' he said. 'Why do you call me Mr Duffy?'

Mr Cranberry gave a laugh and winked at Mr Hodge who sat, young, neat and good-looking, behind his typewriter.

'All right, Mr Train,' he said. 'That's a cold morning, sir. Hard to get up steam these cold mornings, sir.'

'It is not easy,' said Mr Duffy. He shunted expertly to his chair and waited patiently before he sat down while the company's servants adroitly uncoupled him. Mr Hodge was sniggering behind his roller.

'Any cheap excursions, sir?' he asked.

'No,' Mr Duffy replied. 'There are season tickets, of course.'

'Third class and first class, I suppose, sir?'

'No,' said Mr Duffy. 'In deference to the views of Herr Marx, all class distinctions in the passenger rolling-stock have been abolished.'

'I see,' said Mr Cranberry.

'That's communism,' said Mr Hodge.

'He means,' said Mr Cranberry, 'that it is now first-class only.'

'How many wheels has your engine?' asked Mr Hodge. 'Three big ones?'

'I am not a goods train,' said Mr Duffy acidly. 'The wheel formation of a passenger engine is four-four-two – two large driving wheels on each side, coupled, of course, with a four-wheel bogey in front and two small wheels at the cab. Why do you ask?'

'The platform's in the way,' Mr Cranberry said. 'He can't see it.'

'Oh quite,' said Mr Duffy, 'I forgot.'

'I suppose you use a lot of coal?' Mr Hodge said.

'About half a ton per thirty miles,' said Mr Duffy slowly, mentally checking the consumption of that morning. 'I need scarcely say that frequent stopping and starting at suburban stations takes a lot out of me.'

'I'm sure it does,' said Mr Hodge, with sympathy.

They talked like that for half an hour until the elderly Mr Polter arrived and passed gravely into his back office. When that happened, conversation was at an end. Little was heard until lunch-time except the scratch of pens and the fitful clicking of the typewriter.

John Duffy's brother always left the office at one thirty and went home to his lunch. Consequently he started getting steam up at twelve forty-five so that there should be no delay at the hour of departure. When the 'Railway Timekeeper' said that it was one thirty, he let out another shrill whistle and steamed slowly out of the office without a word or a look at his colleagues. He arrived home dead on time.

We now approach the really important part of the plot, the incident which gives the whole story its significance. In the middle of his lunch John Duffy's brother felt something important, something queer, momentous and magical taking place inside his brain, an immense tension relaxing, clean light flooding a place which had been dark. He dropped his knife and fork and sat there for a time wild-eyed, a filling of potatoes unattended in his mouth. Then he swallowed, rose weakly from the table and walked to the window, wiping away the perspiration which had started out on his brow.

He gazed out into the day, no longer a train, but a badly frightened man. Inch by inch he went back over his morning. So far as he could recall he had killed no one, shouted no bad language, broke no windows. He had only talked to Cranberry and Hodge. Down in the roadway there was no dark van arriving with uniformed men infesting it. He sat down again desolately beside the unfinished meal.

John Duffy's brother was a man of some courage. When he got back to the office he had some whiskey in his stomach and it was later in the evening than it should be. Hodge and Cranberry seemed preoccupied with their letters. He hung up his hat casually and said:

'I'm afraid the train is a bit late getting back.'

From below his downcast brows he looked very sharply at Cranberry's face. He thought he saw the shadow of a smile flit absently on the old man's placid features as they continued poring down on a paper. The smile seemed to mean that a morning's joke was not good enough for the same evening. Hodge rose suddenly in his corner and passed silently into Mr Polter's office with his letters. John Duffy's brother sighed and sat down wearily at his desk.

When he left the office that night, his heart was lighter and he thought he had a good excuse for buying more liquor. Nobody knew his secret but himself and nobody else would ever know.

It was a complete cure. Never once did the strange malady return. But to this day John Duffy's brother starts at the rumble of a train in the Liffey tunnel and stands rooted to the road when he comes suddenly on a level-crossing – silent, so to speak, upon a peak in Darien.

# Lady Into Fox

## David Garnett

*A bookseller, a publisher, the editor of the letters of T. E. Lawrence, a member of the Bloomsbury Group, David Garnett will no doubt be remembered as the author of* Lady Into Fox.

*A year before Kafka's death in 1924, Gustav Janouch, Kafka's friend, visited Kafka in hospital and gave him Garnett's recently published book; Janouch thought it might amuse him, as it dealt with the same idea Kafka had used in 'Metamorphosis': the transformation of a human being into an animal. Kafka read it and was delighted. 'But no,' he said to Janouch, 'the theme is not mine. It belongs to our time – that is where I got it from. Animals are now closer to us than man. Because of the bars of the cage, you see.'*

Wonderful or supernatural events are not so uncommon, rather they are irregular in their incidence. Thus there may be not one marvel to speak of in a century, and then often enough comes a plentiful crop of them; monsters of all sorts swarm suddenly upon the earth, comets blaze in the sky, eclipses frighten nature, meteors fall in rain, while mermaids and sirens beguile, and sea-serpents engulf every passing ship, and terrible cataclysms beset humanity.

But the strange event which I shall here relate came alone, unsupported, without companions into a hostile world, and for that very reason claimed little of the general attention of mankind. For the sudden changing of Mrs Tebrick into a vixen is an established fact which we may attempt to account for as we will. Certainly it is in the explanation of the fact, and the reconciling of it with our general notions that we shall find most difficulty, and not in accepting for true a story which is so fully proved, and that not by one witness but by a dozen, all respectable, and with no possibility of collusion between them.

But here I will confine myself to an exact narrative of the event and all that followed on it. Yet I would not dissuade any of my readers from attempting an explanation of this seeming miracle because up till now none has been found which is entirely satisfactory. What adds to the difficulty to my mind is that the metamorphosis occurred when Mrs Tebrick was a full-grown woman, and that it happened suddenly in so short a space of time. The sprouting of a tail, the gradual extension of hair all over the body, the slow change of the whole anatomy by a process of growth, though it would have been monstrous, would not have been so difficult to reconcile to our ordinary conceptions, particularly had it happened in a young child.

But here we have something very different. A grown lady is changed straightway into a fox. There is no explaining that away by any natural philosophy. The materialism of our age will not help us here. It is indeed *a miracle*; something from outside our world altogether; an event which we would willingly accept if we were to meet it invested with the authority of Divine Revelation in the Scriptures, but which we are not prepared to encounter almost in our time, happening in Oxfordshire amongst our neighbours.

The only things which go any way towards an explanation of it are but guesswork, and I give them more because I would not conceal anything, than because I think they are of any worth.

Mrs Tebrick's maiden name was certainly Fox, and it is possible that such a miracle happening before, the family may have gained their name as a *soubriquet* on that account. They were an ancient family, and have had their seat at Tangley Hall time out of mind. It is also true that there was a half-tame fox once upon a time chained up at Tangley Hall in the inner yard, and I have heard many speculative wiseacres in the public houses turn that to great account – though they could not but admit that 'there was never one there in Miss Silvia's time'. At first I was inclined to think that Silvia Fox, having once hunted when she was a child of ten and having been blooded, might furnish more of an explanation. It seems she took great fright or disgust at it, and vomited after it was done. But now I do not see that it has much bearing on the miracle itself, even though we know that after that she always spoke of the 'poor foxes' when a hunt was stirring and never rode to hounds till after her marriage when her husband persuaded her to it.

She was married in the year 1879 to Mr Richard Tebrick, after a short courtship, and went to live after their honeymoon at Rylands, near Stokoe, Oxon. One point indeed I have not been able to ascertain and that is how they first became acquainted. Tangley Hall is over thirty miles from Stokoe, and is extremely remote. Indeed to this day there is no proper road to it, which is all the more remarkable as it is the principal, and indeed the only, manor house for several miles around.

Whether it was from a chance meeting on the roads, or less romantic but more probable, by Mr Tebrick becoming acquainted with her uncle, a minor canon at Oxford, and thence being invited by him to visit Tangley Hall, it is impossible to say. But however they became acquainted the marriage was a very happy one. The bride was in her twenty-third year. She was small, with remarkably small hands and feet. It is perhaps worth noting that there was nothing at all foxy or vixenish in her appearance. On the contrary, she was a more than ordinarily beautiful and agreeable woman. Her eyes were of a clear hazel but exceptionally brilliant, her hair dark, with a shade of red in it, her skin brownish, with a few dark freckles and little moles. In manner she was reserved almost to shyness, but perfectly self-possessed, and perfectly well-bred.

She had been strictly brought up by a woman of excellent principles and considerable attainments, who died a year or so before the marriage. And owing to the circumstance that her mother had been dead many years, and her father bedridden, and not altogether rational for a little while before his death, they had few visitors but her uncle. He often stopped with them a month or two at a stretch, particularly in winter, as he was fond of shooting snipe, which are plentiful in the valley there. That she did not grow up a country hoyden is to be explained by the strictness of her governess and the influence of her uncle. But perhaps living in so wild a place gave her some disposition to wildness, even in spite of her religious upbringing. Her old nurse said: 'Miss Silvia was always a little wild at heart,' though if this was true it was never seen by anyone else except her husband.

On one of the first days of the year 1880, in the early afternoon, husband and wife went for a walk in the copse on the little hill above Rylands. They were still at this time like lovers in their behaviour and were always together. While they were walking they heard the hounds and later the huntsman's horn in the distance. Mr Tebrick had persuaded her to hunt on Boxing Day, but with great difficulty, and she had not enjoyed it (though of hacking she was fond enough).

Hearing the hunt, Mr Tebrick quickened his pace so as to reach the edge of the copse, where they might get a good view of the hounds if they came that way. His wife hung back, and he, holding her hand, began almost to drag her. Before they gained the edge of the copse she suddenly snatched her hand away from his very violently and cried out, so that he instantly turned his head.

*Where his wife had been the moment before was a small fox, of a very bright red.* It looked at him very beseechingly, advanced towards him a pace or two, and he saw at once that his wife was looking at him from the animal's eyes. You may well think if he were aghast: and so maybe was his lady at finding herself in that shape, so they did nothing for nearly half-an-hour but stare at each other, he bewildered, she asking him with her eyes as if indeed she spoke to him: 'What am I now become? Have pity on me, husband, have pity on me for I am your wife.'

So that with his gazing on her and knowing her well, even in such a shape, yet asking himself at every moment: 'Can it be she? Am I not dreaming?' and her beseeching and lastly fawning on him and seeming to tell him that it was she indeed, they came at last together and he took her in his arms. She lay very close to him, nestling under his coat and fell to licking his face, but never taking her eyes from his.

The husband all this while kept turning the thing in his head and gazing on her, but he could make no sense of what had happened, but only comforted himself with the hope that this was but a momentary change, and that presently she would turn back again into the wife that was one flesh with him.

One fancy that came to him, because he was so much more like a lover than a husband, was that it was his fault, and this because if anything dreadful happened he could never blame her but himself for it.

So they passed a good while, till at last the tears welled up in the poor fox's eyes and she began weeping (but quite in silence), and she trembled too as if she were in a fever. At this he could not contain his own tears, but sat down on the ground and sobbed for a great while, but between his sobs kissing her quite as if she had been a woman, and not caring in his grief that he was kissing a fox on the muzzle.

They sat thus till it was getting near dusk, when he recollected himself, and the next thing was that he must somehow hide her, and then bring her home.

He waited till it was quite dark that he might the better bring her into her own house without being seen, and buttoned her inside his topcoat, nay, even in his passion tearing open his waistcoat and his shirt that she might lie the closer to his heart. For when we are overcome with the greatest sorrow we act not like men or women but like children whose comfort in all their troubles is to press themselves against their mother's breast, or if she be not there to hold each other tight in one another's arms.

When it was dark he brought her in with infinite precautions, yet not without the dogs scenting her after which nothing could moderate their clamour.

Having got her into the house, the next thing he thought of was to hide her from the servants. He carried her to the bedroom in his arms and then went downstairs again.

Mr Tebrick had three servants living in the house, the cook, the parlourmaid, and an old woman who had been his wife's nurse. Besides these women there was a groom or a gardener (whichever you choose to call him), who was a single man and so lived out, lodging with a labouring family about half a mile away.

Mr Tebrick going downstairs pitched upon the parlourmaid.

'Janet,' says he, 'Mrs Tebrick and I have had some bad news, and Mrs Tebrick was called away instantly to London and left this afternoon, and I am staying tonight to put our affairs in order. We are shutting up the house, and I must give you and Mrs Brant a month's wages and ask you to leave tomorrow morning at seven o'clock. We shall probably go away to the Continent, and I do not know when we shall come back. Please tell the others, and now get me my tea and bring it into my study on a tray.'

Janet said nothing for she was a shy girl, particularly before gentlemen, but when she entered the kitchen Mr Tebrick heard a sudden burst of conversation with many exclamations from the cook.

When she came back with his tea, Mr Tebrick said: 'I shall not require you upstairs. Pack your own things and tell James to have the waggonette ready for you by seven o'clock tomorrow morning to take you to the station. I am busy now, but I will see you again before you go.'

When she had gone Mr Tebrick took the tray upstairs. For the first moment he thought the room was empty, and his vixen got away, for he could see no sign of her anywhere. But after a moment he saw something stirring in a corner of the room, and then behold! she came forth dragging her dressing-gown, into which she had somehow struggled.

This must surely have been a comical sight, but poor Mr Tebrick was altogether too distressed then or at any time afterwards to divert himself at such ludicrous scenes. He only called to her softly:

'Silvia – Silvia. What do you do there?' And then in a moment saw for himself what she would be at, and began once more to blame himself heartily – because he had not guessed that his wife would not like to go naked, notwithstanding the shape she was in. Nothing would satisfy him then till he had clothed her suitably, bringing her dresses from the wardrobe for her to choose. But as might have been expected, they were too big for her now, but at last he picked out a little dressing-jacket that she was fond of wearing sometimes in the mornings. It was made of a flowered silk, trimmed with lace, and the sleeves short enough to sit very well on her now. While he tied the ribands his poor lady thanked him with gentle looks and not without some modesty and confusion. He propped her up in an armchair with some cushions, and they took tea together, she very delicately drinking from a saucer and taking bread and butter from his hands. All this showed him, or so he thought, that his wife was still herself; there was so little wildness in her demeanour and so much delicacy and decency, especially in her not wishing to run naked, that he was very much comforted, and began to fancy they could be happy enough if they could escape the world and live always alone.

From this too sanguine dream he was aroused by hearing the gardener speaking to the dogs, trying to quiet them, for ever since he had come in with his vixen they had been whining, barking and growling, and all as he knew because there was a fox within doors and they would kill it.

He started up now, calling to the gardener that he would come down to the dogs himself to quiet them, and bade the man go indoors again and leave it to him. All this he said in a dry, compelling kind of voice which made the fellow do as he was bid, though it was against his will, for he was curious. Mr Tebrick went downstairs and taking his gun from the rack loaded it and went out into the yard. Now there were two dogs, one a handsome Irish setter that was his wife's dog (she had brought it with her from Tangley Hall on her marriage); the other was an old fox terrier called Nelly that he had had ten years or more.

When he came out into the yard both dogs saluted him by barking and whining twice as much as they did before, the setter jumping up and down at the end of his chain in a frenzy, and Nelly shivering, wagging her tail, and looking first at her master and then at the house door, where she could smell the fox right enough.

There was a bright moon, so that Mr Tebrick could see the dogs as clearly as could be. First he shot his wife's setter dead, and then looked about him for Nelly to give her the other barrel, but he could see her nowhere. The bitch was clean gone, till, looking to see how she had broken her chain, he found her lying hid in the back of her kennel. But that trick did not save her, for Mr Tebrick, after trying to pull her out by her chain, and finding it useless – she would not come – thrust the muzzle of his gun into the kennel, pressed it into her body and so shot her. Afterwards, striking a match, he looked in at her to make certain she was dead. Then, leaving the dogs as they were, chained up, Mr Tebrick went indoors again and found the gardener, who had not yet gone home, gave him a month's wages in lieu of notice and told him he had a job for him yet – to bury the two dogs and that he should do it that same night.

But by all this going on with so much strangeness and authority on his part, as it seemed to them, the servants were much troubled. Hearing the shots while he was out in the yard his wife's old nurse, or Nanny, ran up to the bedroom though she had no business there, and so opening the door saw the poor fox dressed in my lady's little jacket lying back in the cushions, and in such a reverie of woe that she heard nothing.

Old Nanny, though she was not expecting to find her mistress there, having been told that she was gone that afternoon to London, knew her instantly and cried out:

'Oh, my poor precious! Oh, poor Miss Silvia! What dreadful change is this?' Then, seeing her mistess start and look at her, she cried out:

'But never fear, my darling, it will all come right, your old Nanny knows you, it will all come right in the end.'

But though she said this she did not care to look again, and kept her eyes turned away so as not to meet the foxy slit ones of her mistress, for that was too much for her. So she hurried out soon, fearing to be found there by Mr Tebrick, and who knows, perhaps shot, like the dogs, for knowing the secret.

Mr Tebrick had all this time gone about paying off his servants and shooting his dogs as if he were in a dream. Now he fortified himself with two or three glasses of strong whisky and went to bed, taking his vixen into his arms, where he slept soundly. Whether she did or not is more than I or anybody else can say.

In the morning when he woke up they had the place to themselves, for on his instructions the servants had all left first thing: Janet and the cook to Oxford, where they would try and find new places, and Nanny going back to the cottage near Tangley, where her son lived, who was the pigman there.

So with that morning there began what was now to be their ordinary life together. He would get up when it was broad day, and first thing light the fire downstairs and cook the breakfast, then brush his wife, sponge her with a damp sponge, then brush her again, in all this using scent very freely to hide somewhat her rank odour. When she was dressed he carried her downstairs and they had their breakfast together, she sitting up to table with him, drinking her saucer of tea, and taking her food from his fingers, or at any rate being fed by him. She was still fond of the same food that she had been used to before her transformation, a lightly boiled egg or slice of ham, a piece of buttered toast or two, with a little quince and apple jam. While I am on the subject of her food, I should say that reading in the encyclopedia he found that foxes on the Continent are inordinately fond of grapes, and that during the autumn season they abandon their ordinary diet for them, and then grow exceedingly fat and lose their offensive odour.

This appetite for grapes is so well confirmed by Aesop, and by passages in the Scriptures, that it is strange Mr Tebrick should not have known it. After reading this account he wrote to London for a basket of grapes to be posted to him twice a week and was rejoiced to find that the account in the encyclopedia was true in the most important of these particulars. His vixen relished them exceedingly and seemed never to tire of them, so that he increased his order first from one pound to three pounds and afterwards to five. Her odour abated so much by this means that he came not to notice it at all except sometimes in the mornings before her toilet.

What helped most to make living with her bearable for him was that she understood him perfectly – yes, every word he said, and though she was dumb she expressed herself very fluently by looks and signs though never by the voice.

Thus he frequently conversed with her, telling her all his thoughts and hiding nothing from her, and this the more readily because he was very quick to catch her meaning and her answers.

'Puss, Puss,' he would say to her, for calling her that had been a habit with him always. 'Sweet Puss, some men would pity me living alone here with you after what has happened, but I would not change places while you were living with any man for the whole world. Though you are a fox I would rather live with you than any woman. I swear I would, and that too if you were changed to anything.' But then, catching her grave look, he would say: 'Do you think I jest on these things, my dear? I do not. I swear to you, my darling, that all my life I will be true to you, will be faithful, will respect and reverence you who are my wife. And I will do that not because of any hope that God in His mercy will see fit to restore your shape, but solely because I love you. However you may be changed, my love is not.'

Then anyone seeing them would have sworn that they were lovers, so passionately did each look on the other.

Often he would swear to her that the devil might have power to work some miracles, but that he would find it beyond him to change his love for her.

These passionate speeches, however they might have struck his wife in an ordinary way, now seemed to be her chief comfort. She would come to him, put her paw in his hand and look at him with sparkling eyes shining with joy and gratitude, would pant with eagerness, jump at him and lick his face.

Now he had many little things which busied him in the house – getting his meals, setting the room straight, making the bed and so forth. When he was doing this housework it was comical to watch his vixen. Often she was as it were beside herself with vexation and distress to see him in his clumsy way doing what she could have done so much better had she been able. Then, forgetful of the decency and the decorum which she had at first imposed upon herself never to run upon all fours, she followed him everywhere, and if he did one thing wrong she stopped him and showed him the way of it. When he had forgot the hour for his meal she would come and tug his sleeve and tell him as if she spoke: 'Husband, are we to have luncheon today?'

This womanliness in her never failed to delight him, for it showed she was still his wife, buried as it were in the carcase of a beast but with a woman's soul. This encouraged him so much that he debated with himself whether he should not read aloud to her, as he often had done formerly. At last, since he could find no reason against it, he went to the shelf and fetched down a volume of the *History of Clarissa Harlowe*, which he had begun to read aloud to her a few weeks before. He opened the volume where he had left off, with Lovelace's letter after he had spent the night waiting fruitlessly in the copse.

*'Good God!*

*What is now become of me?*

*My feet benumbed by midnight wanderings through the heaviest dews that ever fell; my wig and my linen dripping with the hoarfrost dissolving on them!*

*Day but just breaking . . .'* etc.

While he read he was conscious of holding her attention, then after a few pages the story claimed all his, so that he read on for about half an hour without looking at her. When he did so he saw that she was not listening to him, but was watching something with strange eagerness. Such a fixed intent look was on her face that he was alarmed and sought the cause of it. Presently he found that her gaze was fixed on the movements of her pet dove which was in its cage hanging in the window. He spoke to her, but she seemed displeased, so he laid *Clarissa Harlowe* aside. Nor did he ever repeat the experiment of reading to her.

Yet that same evening, as he happened to be looking through his writing-table drawer with Puss beside him looking over his elbow, she spied a pack of cards, and then he was forced to pick them out to please her, then draw them from their case. At last, trying first one thing, then another, he found that what she was after was to play piquet with him. They had some difficulty at first in contriving for her to hold her cards and then to play them, but this was at last overcome by his stacking them for her on a sloping board, after which she could flip them out very neatly with her claws as she wanted to play them. When they had overcome this trouble they played three games, and most heartily she seemed to enjoy them.

Moreover she won all three of them. After this they often played a quiet game of piquet together, and cribbage too. I should say that in marking the points at cribbage on the board he always moved her pegs for her as well as his own, for she could not handle them or set them in the holes.

The weather, which had been damp and misty, with frequent downpours of rain, improved very much in the following week, and, as often happens in January, there were several days with the sun shining, no wind, and light frosts at night, these frosts becoming more intense as the days went on till bye and bye they began to think of snow.

With this spell of fine weather it was but natural that Mr Tebrick should think of taking his vixen out of doors. This was something he had not yet done, both because of the damp rainy weather up till then and because of the mere notion of taking her out filled him with alarm. Indeed he had so many apprehensions beforehand that at one time he resolved totally against it. For his mind was filled not only with the fear that she might escape from him and run away, which he knew was groundless, but with more rational visions, such as wandering curs, traps, gins, spring guns, besides a dread of being seen with her by the neighbourhood. At last however he resolved on it, and all the more as his vixen kept asking him in the gentlest way: 'Might not she go out into the garden?' Yet she always listened very submissively when he told her that he was afraid if they were seen together it would excite the curiosity of their neighbours; besides this, he often told her of his fears for her on account of dogs. But one day she answered this by leading him into the hall and pointing boldly to his gun. After this he resolved to take her, though with full precautions. That is he left the house door open so that in case of need she could beat a swift retreat, then he took his gun under his arm, and lastly he had her well wrapped up in a little fur jacket lest she should take cold.

He would have carried her too, but that she delicately disengaged herself from his arms and looked at him very expressively to say that she would go by herself. For already her first horror of being seen to go upon all fours was worn off; reasoning no doubt upon it, that either she must resign herself to go that way or else stay bed-ridden all the rest of her life.

Her joy at going into the garden was inexpressible. First she ran this way, then that, though keeping always close to him, looking very sharply with ears cocked forward first at one thing, then another and then up to catch his eye.

For some time indeed she was almost dancing with delight, running round him, then forward a yard or two, then back to him and gambolling beside him as they went round the garden. But in spite of her joy she was full of fear. At every noise, a cow lowing, a cock crowing, or a ploughman in the distance hulloaing to scare the rooks, she started, her ears pricked to catch the sound, her muzzle wrinkled up and her nose twitched, and she would then press herself against his legs. They walked round the garden and down to the pond where there were ornamental waterfowl, teal, widgeon and mandarin ducks, and seeing these again gave her great pleasure. They had always been her favourites, and now she was so overjoyed to see them that she behaved with very little of her usual self-restraint. First she stared at them, then bounding up to her husband's knee sought to kindle an equal excitement in his mind. Whilst she rested her paws on his knee she turned her head again and again towards the ducks as though she could not take her eyes off them, and then ran down before him to the water's edge.

But her appearance threw the ducks into the utmost degree of consternation. Those on shore or near the bank swam or flew to the centre of the pond, and there huddled in a bunch; and then, swimming round and round, they began such a quacking that Mr Tebrick was nearly deafened. As I have before said, nothing in the ludicrous way that arose out of the metamorphosis of his wife (and such incidents were plentiful) ever stood a chance of being smiled at by him. So in this case, too, for realizing that the silly ducks thought his wife a fox indeed and were alarmed on that account he found painful that spectacle which to others might have been amusing.

Not so his vixen, who appeared if anything more pleased than ever when she saw in what a commotion she had set them, and began cutting a thousand pretty capers. Though at first he called to her to come back and walk another way, Mr Tebrick was overborne by her pleasure and sat down, whilst she frisked around him happier far than he had seen her ever since the change. First she ran up to him in a laughing way, all smiles, and then ran down again to the water's edge, and began frisking and frolicking, chasing her own brush, dancing on her hind legs even, and rolling on the ground, then fell to running in circles, but all this without paying any heed to the ducks.

But they, with their necks craned out all pointing one way, swam to and fro in the middle of the pond, never stopping their quack, quack, quack, and keeping time too, for they all quacked in chorus. Presently she came farther away from the pond, and he, thinking they had had enough of this sort of entertainment, laid hold of her and said to her:

'Come, Silvia, my dear, it is growing cold, and it is time we went indoors. I am sure taking the air has done you a world of good, but we must not linger any more.'

She appeared then to agree with him, though she threw half a glance over her shoulder at the ducks, and they both walked soberly enough towards the house.

When they had gone about halfway she suddenly slipped round and was off. He turned quickly and saw the ducks had been following them.

So she drove them before her back into the pond, the ducks running in terror from her with their wings spread, and she not pressing them, for he saw that had she been so minded she could have caught two or three of the nearest. Then, with her brush waving above her, she came gambolling back to him so playfully that he stroked her indulgently, though he was first vexed, and then rather puzzled that his wife should amuse herself with such pranks.

But when they got within doors he picked her up in his arms, kissed her and spoke to her.

'Silvia, what a light-hearted childish creature you are. Your courage under misfortune shall be a lesson to me; but I cannot, I cannot bear to see it.'

Here the tears stood suddenly in his eyes, and he lay down upon the ottoman and wept, paying no heed to her until presently he was aroused by her licking his cheek and his ear.

After tea she led him to the drawing-room and scratched at the door till he opened it, for this was part of the house which he had shut up, thinking three or four rooms enough for them now, and to save the dusting of it. Then it seemed she would have him play to her on the pianoforte: she led him to it, nay, what is more, she would herself pick out the music he was to play. First it was a fugue of Handel's, then one of Mendelssohn's Songs Without Words, and then 'The Diver', and then music from Gilbert and Sullivan; but each piece of music she picked out was gayer than the last one. Thus they sat happily engrossed for perhaps an hour in the candle light until the extreme cold in that unwarmed room stopped his playing and drove them downstairs to the fire. Thus did she admirably comfort her husband when he was dispirited.

Yet next morning when he woke he was distressed when he found that she was not in the bed with him but was lying curled up at the foot of it. During breakfast she hardly listened when he spoke, and then impatiently, but sat staring at the dove.

Mr Tebrick sat silently looking out of window for some time, then he took out his pocket book; in it there was a photograph of his wife taken soon after their wedding. Now he gazed and gazed upon those familiar features, and now he lifted his head and looked at the animal before him. He laughed then bitterly, the first and last time for that matter that Mr Tebrick ever laughed at his wife's transformation, for he was not very humorous. But this laugh was sour and painful to him. Then he tore up the photograph into little pieces, and scattered them out of the window, saying to himself: 'Memories will not help me here,' and turning to the vixen he saw that she was still staring at the caged bird, and as he looked he saw her lick her chops.

He took the bird into the next room, then acting suddenly upon the impulse, he opened the cage door and set it free, saying as he did so:

'Go, poor bird! Fly from this wretched house while you still remember your mistress who fed you from her coral lips. You are not a fit plaything for her now. Farewell, poor bird! Farewell! Unless,' he added with a melancholy smile, 'you return with good tidings like Noah's dove.'

But, poor gentleman, his troubles were not over yet, and indeed one may say that he ran to meet them by his constant supposing that his lady should still be the same to a tittle in her behaviour now that she was changed into a fox.

Without making any unwarrantable suppositions as to her soul or what had now become of it (though we could find a good deal to the purpose on that point in the system of Paracelsus), let us consider only how much the change in her body must needs affect her ordinary conduct. So that before we judge too harshly of this unfortunate lady, we must reflect upon the physical necessities and infirmities and appetites of her new condition, and we must magnify the fortitude of her mind which enabled her to behave with decorum, cleanliness and decency in spite of her new situation.

Thus she might have been expected to befoul her room, yet never could anyone, whether man or beast, have shown more nicety in such matters. But at luncheon Mr Tebrick helped her to a wing of chicken, and leaving the room for a minute to fetch some water which he had forgot, found her at his return on the table crunching the very bones. He stood silent, dismayed and wounded to the heart at this sight. For we must observe that this unfortunate husband thought always of his vixen as that gentle and delicate woman she had lately been. So that whenever his vixen's conduct went beyond that which he expected in his wife he was, as it were, cut to the quick, and no kind of agony could be greater to him than to see her thus forget herself. On this account it may indeed be regretted that Mrs Tebrick had been so exactly well-bred, and in particular that her table manners had always been scrupulous. Had she been in the habit, like a continental princess I have dined with, of taking her leg of chicken by the drumstick and gnawing the flesh, it had been far better for him now. But as her manners had been perfect, so the lapse of them was proportionately painful to him. Thus in this instance he stood as it were in silent agony till she had finished her hideous crunching of the chicken bones and had devoured every scrap. Then he spoke to her gently, taking her on to his knee, stroking her fur and fed her with a few grapes, saying to her:

'Silvia, Silvia, is it so hard for you? Try and remember the past, my darling, and by living with me we will quite forget that you are no longer a woman. Surely this affliction will pass soon, as suddenly as it came, and it will all seem to us like an evil dream.'

Yet though she appeared perfectly sensible of his words and gave him sorrowful and penitent looks like her old self, that same afternoon, on taking her out, he had all the difficulty in the world to keep her from going near the ducks.

There came to him then a thought that was very disagreeable to him, namely, that he dare not trust his wife alone with any bird or she would kill it. And this was the more shocking to him to think of since it meant that he durst not trust her as much as a dog even. For we may trust dogs who are familiars, with all the household pets; nay more, we can put them upon trust with anything and know they will not touch it, not even if they be starving. But things were come to such a pass with his vixen that he dared not in his heart trust her at all. Yet she was still in many ways so much more woman than fox that he could talk to her on any subject and she would understand him, better far than the Oriental women who are kept in subjection can ever understand their masters unless they converse on the most trifling household topics.

Thus she understood excellently well the importance and duties of religion. She would listen with approval in the evening when he said the Lord's Prayer, and was rigid in her observance of the Sabbath. Indeed, the next day being Sunday he, thinking no harm, proposed their usual game of piquet, but no, she would not play. Mr Tebrick, not understanding at first what she meant, though he was usually very quick with her, he proposed it to her again, which she again refused, and this time, to show her meaning, made the sign of the cross with her paw. This exceedingly rejoiced and comforted him in his distress. He begged her pardon, and fervently thanked God for having so good a wife, who, in spite of all, knew more of her duty to God than he did. But here I must warn the reader from inferring that she was a papist because she then made the sign of the cross. She made that sign to my thinking only on compulsion because she could not express herself except in that way. For she had been brought up as a true Protestant, and that she still was one is confirmed by her objection to cards, which would have been less than nothing to her had she been a papist. Yet that evening, taking her into the drawing-room so that he might play her some sacred music, he found her after some time cowering away from him in the farthest corner of the room, her ears flattened back and an expression of the greatest anguish in her eyes. When he spoke to her she licked his hand, but remained shivering for a long time at his feet and showed the clearest symptoms of terror if he so much as moved towards the piano.

On seeing this and recollecting how ill the ears of a dog can bear with our music, and how this dislike might be expected to be even greater in a fox, all of whose senses are more acute from being a wild creature, recollecting this he closed the piano and taking her in his arms locked up the room and never went into it again. He could not help marvelling though, since it was but two days after she had herself led him there, and even picked out for him to play and sing those pieces which were her favourites.

That night she would not sleep with him, neither in the bed nor on it, so that he was forced to let her curl herself up on the floor.

But neither would she sleep there, for several times she woke him by trotting around the room, and once when he had got sound asleep by springing on the bed and then off it, so that he woke with a violent start and cried out, but got no answer either, except hearing her trotting round and round the room. Presently he imagines to himself that she must want something, and so he fetches her food and water, but she never so much as looks at it, but still goes on her rounds, every now and then scratching at the door.

Though he spoke to her, calling her by her name, she would pay no heed to him, or else only for a moment. At last he gave her up and said to her plainly: 'The fit is on you now Silvia to be a fox, but I shall keep you close and in the morning you will recollect yourself and thank me for having kept you now.'

So he lay down again, but not to sleep, only to listen to his wife running about the room and trying to get out of it. Thus he spent what was perhaps the most miserable night of his existence. In the morning she was still restless, and was reluctant to let him wash and brush her, and appeared to dislike being scented but as it were to bear with it for his sake. Ordinarily she had taken the greatest pleasure imaginable in her toilet, so that on this account, added to his sleepless night, Mr Tebrick was utterly dejected, and it was then that he resolved to put a project into execution that would show him, so he thought, whether he had a wife or only a wild vixen in his house. But yet he was comforted that she bore at all with him, though so restlessly that he did not spare her, calling her a 'bad wild fox'. And then speaking to her in this manner: 'Are you not ashamed, Silvia to be such a madcap, such a wicked hoyden? You who were particular in dress. I see it was all vanity – now you have not your former advantages you think nothing of decency.'

His words had some effect with her too, and with himself, so that by the time he had finished dressing her they were both in the lowest state of spirits imaginable and neither of them far from tears.

Breakfast she took soberly enough, and after that he went about getting his experiment ready, which was this. In the garden he gathered together a nosegay of snowdrops, those being all the flowers he could find, and then going into the village of Stokoe bought a Dutch rabbit (that is a black and white one) from a man there who kept them.

When he got back he took her flowers and at the same time set down the basket with the rabbit in it, with the lid open. Then he called to her: 'Silvia, I have brought some flowers for you. Look, the first snowdrops.'

At this she ran up very prettily, and never giving as much as one glance at the rabbit which had hopped out of its basket, she began to thank him for the flowers. Indeed she seemed indefatigable in shewing her gratitude, smelt them, and stood a little way off looking at them, then thanked him again. Mr Tebrick (and this was all part of his plan) then took a vase and went to find some water for them, but left the flowers beside her. He stopped away five minutes, timing it by his watch and listening very intently, but never heard the rabbit squeak. Yet when he went in what a horrid shambles was spread before his eyes. Blood on the carpet, blood on the armchairs and antimacassars, even a little blood spurtled on to the wall, and what was worse, Mrs Tebrick tearing and growling over a piece of skin and the legs, for she had eaten up all the rest of it. The poor gentleman was so heartbroken over this that he was like to have done himself an injury, and at one moment thought of getting his gun, to have shot himself and his vixen too. Indeed the extremity of his grief was such that it served him a very good turn, for he was so entirely unmanned by it that for some time he could do nothing but weep, and fell into a chair with his head in his hands, and so kept weeping and groaning.

After he had been some little while employed in this dismal way, his vixen, who had by this time bolted down the rabbit skin, head, ears and all, came to him and putting her paws on his knees, thrust her long muzzle into his face and began licking him. But he, looking at her now with different eyes, and seeing her jaws still sprinkled with fresh blood and her claws full of the rabbit's fleck, would have none of it.

But though he beat her off four or five times even to giving her blows and kicks, she still came back to him, crawling on her belly and imploring his forgiveness with wide-open sorrowful eyes. Before he had made this rash experiment of the rabbit and the flowers, he had promised himself that if she failed in it he would have no more feeling or compassion for her than if she were in truth a wild vixen out of the woods. This resolution, though the reasons for it had seemed to him so very plain before, he now found more difficult to carry out than to decide on. At length after cursing her and beating her off for upwards of half-an-hour, he admitted to himself that he still did care for her, and even loved her dearly in spite of all, whatever pretence he affected towards her. When he had acknowledged this he looked up at her and met her eyes fixed upon him, and held out his arms to her and said:

'Oh Silvia, Silvia, would you had never done this! Would I had never tempted you in a fatal hour! Does not this butchery and eating of raw meat and rabbit's fur disgust you? Are you a monster in your soul as well as in your body? Have you forgotten what it is to be a woman?'

Meanwhile, with every word of his, she crawled a step nearer on her belly and at last climbed sorrowfully into his arms. His words then seemed to take effect on her and her eyes filled with tears and she wept most penitently in his arms, and her body shook with her sobs as if her heart were breaking. This sorrow of hers gave him the strangest mixture of pain and joy that he had ever known, for his love for her returning with a rush, he could not bear to witness her pain and yet must take pleasure in it as it fed his hopes of her one day returning to be a woman. So the more anguish of shame his vixen underwent, the greater his hopes rose, till his love and pity for her increasing equally, he was almost wishing her to be nothing more than a mere fox than to suffer so much by being half-human.

At last he looked about him somewhat dazed with so much weeping, then set his vixen down on the ottoman, and began to clean up the room with a heavy heart. He fetched a pail of water and washed out all the stains of blood, gathered up the two antimacassars and fetched clean ones from the other rooms. While he went about this work his vixen sat and watched him very contritely with her nose between her two front paws, and when he had done he brought in some luncheon for himself, though it was already late, but none for her, she having lately so infamously feasted. But water he gave her and a bunch of grapes. Afterwards she led him to the small tortoiseshell cabinet and would have him open it. When he had done so she motioned to the portable stereoscope which lay inside. Mr Tebrick instantly fell in with her wish and after a few trials adjusted it to her vision. Thus they spent the rest of the afternoon together very happily looking through the collection of views which he had purchased, of Italy, Spain and Scotland. This diversion gave her great apparent pleasure and afforded him considerable comfort. But that night he could not prevail upon her to sleep in bed with him, and finally allowed her to sleep on a mat beside the bed where he could stretch down and touch her. So they passed the night, with his hand upon her head.

The next morning he had more of a struggle than ever to wash and dress her. Indeed at one time nothing but holding her by the scruff prevented her from getting away from him, but at last he achieved his object and she was washed, brushed, scented and dressed, although to be sure this left him better pleased than her, for she regarded her silk jacket with disfavour.

Still at breakfast she was well mannered though a trifle hasty with her food. Then his difficulties with her began for she would go out, but as he had his housework to do, he could not allow it. He brought her picture books to divert her, but she would have none of them but stayed at the door scratching it with her claws industriously till she had worn away the paint.

At first he tried coaxing her and wheedling, gave her cards to play patience and so on, but finding nothing would distract her from going out, his temper began to rise, and he told her plainly that she must wait his pleasure and that he had as much natural obstinacy as she had. But to all that he said she paid no heed whatever but only scratched the harder.

Thus he let her continue until luncheon, when she would not sit up, or eat off a plate, but first was for getting on to the table, and when that was prevented, snatched her meat and ate it under the table. To all his rebukes she turned a deaf or sullen ear, and so they each finished their meal eating little, either of them, for till she would sit at table he would give her no more, and his vexation had taken away his own appetite. In the afternoon he took her out for her airing in the garden.

She made no pretence now of enjoying the first snowdrops or the view from the terrace. No – there was only one thing for her now – the ducks, and she was off to them before he could stop her. Luckily they were all swimming when she got there (for a stream running into the pond on the far side it was not frozen there).

When he had got down to the pond, she ran out on to the ice, which would not bear his weight, and though he called her and begged her to come back she would not heed him but stayed frisking about, getting as near the ducks as she dared, but being circumspect in venturing on to the thin ice.

Presently she turned on herself and began tearing off her clothes, and at last by biting got off her little jacket and taking it in her mouth stuffed it into a hole in the ice where he could not get it. Then she ran hither and thither a stark naked vixen, and without giving a glance to her poor husband who stood silently now upon the bank, with despair and terror settled in his mind. She let him stay there most of the afternoon till he was chilled through and through and worn out with watching her. At last he reflected how she had just stripped herself and how in the morning she struggled against being dressed, and he thought perhaps he was too strict with her and if he let her have her own way they could manage to be happy somehow together even if she did eat off the floor. So he called out to her then:

'Silvia, come now, be good, you shan't wear any more clothes if you don't want to, and you needn't sit at table neither, I promise. You shall do as you like in that, but you must give up one thing, and that is you must stay with me and not go out alone, for that is dangerous. If any dog came on you he would kill you.'

Directly he had finished speaking she came to him joyously, began fawning on him and prancing round him so that in spite of his vexation with her, and being cold, he could not help stroking her.

'Oh, Silvia, are you not wilful and cunning? I see you glory in being so, but I shall not reproach you but shall stick to my side of the bargain, and you must stick to yours.'

He built a big fire when he came back to the house and took a glass or two of spirits also, to warm himself up, for he was chilled to the very bone. Then, after they had dined, to cheer himself he took another glass, and then another, and so on till he was very merry, he thought. Then he would play with his vixen, she encouraging him with her pretty sportiveness. He got up to catch her then and finding himself unsteady on his legs, he went down on to all fours. The long and the short of it is that by drinking he drowned all his sorrow; and then would be a beast too like his wife, though she was one through no fault of her own, and could not help it. To what lengths he went in that drunken humour I shall not offend my readers by relating, but shall only say that he was so drunk and sottish that he had a very imperfect recollection of what had passed when he woke the next morning. There is no exception to the rule that if a man drink heavily at night the next morning will show the other side to his nature. Thus with Mr Tebrick, for as he had been beastly, merry and a very daredevil the night before, so on his awakening was he ashamed, melancholic and a true penitent before his Creator. The first thing he did when he came to himself was to call out to God to forgive him for his sin, then he fell into earnest prayer and continued so for half-an-hour upon his knees. Then he got up and dressed but continued very melancholy for the whole of the morning. Being in this mood you may imagine it hurt him to see his wife running about naked, but he reflected it would be a bad reformation that began with breaking faith. He had made a bargain and he would stick to it, and so he let her be, though sorely against his will.

For the same reason, that is because he would stick to his side of the bargain, he did not require her to sit up at table, but gave her her breakfast on a dish in the corner, where to tell the truth she on her side ate it all up with great daintiness and propriety. Nor did she make any attempt to go out of doors that morning, but lay curled up in an armchair before the fire dozing. After lunch he took her out, and she never so much as offered to go near the ducks, but running before him led him on to take her a longer walk. This he consented to do very much to her joy and delight. He took her through the fields by the most unfrequented ways, being much alarmed lest they should be seen by anyone. But by good luck they walked above four miles across country and saw nobody. All the way his wife kept running on ahead of him, and then back to him to lick his hand and so on, and appeared delighted at taking exercise. And though they started two or three rabbits and a hare in the course of their walk she never attempted to go after them, only giving them a look and then looking back to him, laughing at him as it were for his warning cry of 'Puss! come in, no nonsense now!'

Just when they got home and were going into the porch they came face to face with an old woman. Mr Tebrick stopped short in consternation and looked about for his vixen, but she had run forward without any shyness to greet her. Then he recognized the intruder, it was his wife's old nurse.

'What are you doing here, Mrs Cork?' he asked her.

Mrs Cork answered him in these words:

'Poor thing. Poor Miss Silvia! It is a shame, to let her run about like a dog. It is a shame, and your own wife too. But whatever she looks like, you should trust her the same as ever. If you do she'll do her best to be a good wife to you, if you don't I shouldn't wonder if she did turn into a proper fox. I saw her, sir, before I left, and I've had no peace of mind. I couldn't sleep thinking of her. So I've come back to look after her, as I have done all her life, sir,' and she stooped down and took Mrs Tebrick by the paw.

Mr Tebrick unlocked the door and they went in. When Mrs Cork saw the house she exclaimed again and again: 'The place was a pigstye. They couldn't live like that, a gentleman must have somebody to look after him. She would do it. He could trust her with the secret.'

Had the old woman come the day before it is likely enough that Mr Tebrick would have sent her packing. But the voice of conscience being woken in him by his drunkenness of the night before he was heartily ashamed of his own management of the business, moreover the old woman's words that 'it was a shame to let her run about like a dog,' moved him exceedingly. Being in this mood the truth is he welcomed her.

But we may conclude that Mrs Tebrick was as sorry to see her old Nanny as her husband was glad. If we consider that she had been brought up strictly by her when she was a child, and was now again in her power, and that her old nurse could never be satisfied with her now whatever she did, but would always think her wicked to be a fox at all, there seems good reason for her dislike. And it is possible, too, that there may have been another cause as well, and that is jealousy. We know her husband was always trying to bring her back to be a woman, or at any rate to get her to act like one, may she not have been hoping to get him to be like a beast himself or to act like one? May she not have thought it easier to change him thus than ever change herself back into being a woman? If we think that she had had a success of this kind only the night before, when he got drunk, can we not conclude that this was indeed the case, and then we have another good reason why the poor lady should hate to see her old nurse?

It is certain that whatever hopes Mr Tebrick had of Mrs Cork affecting his wife for the better were disappointed. She grew steadily wilder and after a few days so intractable with her that Mr Tebrick again took her under his complete control.

The first morning Mrs Cork made her a new jacket, cutting down the sleeves of a blue silk one of Mrs Tebrick's and trimming it with swan's down, and directly she had altered it, put it on her mistress, and fetching a mirror would have her admire the fit of it. All the time she waited on Mrs Tebrick the old woman talked to her as though she were a baby, and treated her as such, never thinking perhaps that she was either the one thing or the other, that is either a lady to whom she owed respect and who had rational powers exceeding her own, or else a wild creature on whom words were wasted. But though at first she submitted passively, Mrs Tebrick only waited for her Nanny's back to be turned to tear up her pretty piece of handiwork into shreds, and then ran gaily about waving her brush with only a few ribands still hanging from her neck.

So it was time after time (for the old woman was used to having her own way) until Mrs Cork would, I think, have tried punishing her if she had not been afraid of Mrs Tebrick's rows of white teeth, which she often showed her, then laughing afterwards, as if to say it was only play.

Not content with tearing off the dresses that were fitted on her, one day Silvia slipped upstairs to her wardrobe and tore down all her old dresses and made havoc with them, not sparing her wedding dress either, but tearing and ripping them all up so that there was hardly a shred or rag left big enough to dress a doll in. On this, Mr Tebrick, who had let the old woman have most of her management to see what she could make of her, took her back under his own control.

He was sorry enough now that Mrs Cork had disappointed him in the hopes he had had of her, to have the old woman, as it were, on his hands. True she could be useful enough in many ways to him, by doing the housework, the cooking and mending, but still he was anxious since his secret was in her keeping, and the more now that she had tried her hand with his wife and failed. For he saw that vanity had kept her mouth shut if she had won over her mistress to better ways, and her love for her would have grown by getting her own way with her. But now that she had failed she bore her mistress a grudge for not being won over, or at the best was become indifferent to the business, so that she might very readily blab.

For the moment all Mr Tebrick could do was to keep her from going into Stokoe to the village, where she would meet all her old cronies and where there were certain to be any number of inquiries about what was going on at Rylands and so on. But as he saw that it was clearly beyond his power, however vigilant he might be, to watch over the old woman and his wife, and to prevent anyone from meeting with either of them, he began to consider what he could best do.

Since he had sent away his servants and the gardener, giving out a story of having received bad news and his wife going away to London where he would join her, their probably going out of England and so on, he knew well enough that there would be a great deal of talk in the neighbourhood.

And as he had now stayed on, contrary to what he had said, there would be further rumour. Indeed, had he known it, there was a story already going round the country that his wife had run away with Major Solmes, and that he was gone mad with grief, that he had shot his dogs and his horses and shut himself up alone in the house and would speak with no one. This story was made up by his neighbours not because they were fanciful or wanted to deceive, but like most tittle-tattle to fill a gap, as few like to confess ignorance, and if people are asked about such or such a man they must have something to say, or they suffer in everybody's opinion, are set down as dull or 'out of the swim'. In this way I met not long ago with someone who, after talking some little while and not knowing me or who I was, told me that David Garnett was dead, and died of being bitten by a cat after he had tormented it. He had long grown a nuisance to his friends as an exorbitant sponge upon them, and the world was well rid of him.

Hearing this story of myself diverted me at the time, but I fully believe it has served me in good stead since. For it set me on my guard as perhaps nothing else would have done, against accepting for true all floating rumour and village gossip, so that now I am by second nature a true sceptic and scarcely believe anything unless the evidence for it is conclusive. Indeed I could never have got to the bottom of this history if I had believed one tenth part of what I was told, there was so much of it that was either manifestly false and absurd, or else contradictory to the ascertained facts. It is therefore only the bare bones of the story which you will find written here, for I have rejected all the flowery embroideries which would be entertaining reading enough, I daresay, for some, but if there be any doubt of the truth of a thing it is poor sort of entertainment to read about in my opinion.

To get back to our story: Mr Tebrick having considered how much the appetite of his neighbours would be whetted to find out the mystery by his remaining in that part of the country, determined that the best thing he could do was to remove.

After some time turning the thing over in his mind, he decided that no place would be so good for his purpose as old Nanny's cottage. It was thirty miles away from Stokoe, which in the country means as far as Timbuctoo does to us in London. Then it was near Tangley, and his lady having known it from her childhood would feel at home there, and also it was utterly remote, there being no village near it or manor house other than Tangley Hall, which was now untenanted for the greater part of the year. Nor did it mean imparting his secret to others, for there was only Mrs Cork's son, a widower, who being out at work all day would be easily outwitted, the more so as he was stone deaf and of a slow and saturnine disposition. To be sure there was little Polly, Mrs Cork's granddaughter, but either Mr Tebrick forgot her altogether, or else reckoned her as a mere baby and not to be thought of as a danger.

He talked the thing over with Mrs Cork, and they decided upon it out of hand. The truth is the old woman was beginning to regret that her love and her curiosity had ever brought her back to Rylands, since so far she had got much work and little credit by it.

When it was settled, Mr Tebrick disposed of the remaining business he had at Rylands in the afternoon, and that was chiefly putting out his wife's riding horse into the keeping of a farmer nearby, for he thought he would drive over with his own horse, and the other spare horse tandem in the dog-cart.

The next morning they locked up the house and they departed, having first secured Mrs Tebrick in a large wicker hamper where she would be tolerably comfortable. This was for safety, for in the agitation of driving she might jump out, and on the other hand, if a dog scented her and she were loose, she might be in danger of her life. Mr Tebrick, drove with the hamper beside him on the front seat, and spoke to her gently very often.

She was overcome by the excitement of the journey and kept poking her nose first through one crevice, then through another, turning and twisting the whole time and peeping out to see what they were passing. It was a bitterly cold day, and when they had gone about fifteen miles they drew up by the roadside to rest the horses and have their own luncheon, for he dared not stop at an inn. He knew that any living creature in a hamper, even if it be only an old fowl, always draws attention; there would be several loafers most likely who would notice that he had a fox with him, and even if he left the hamper in the cart the dogs at the inn would be sure to sniff out her scent. So not to take any chances he drew up at the side of the road and rested there, though it was freezing hard and a north-east wind howling.

He took down his precious hamper, unharnessed his two horses, covered them with rugs and gave them their corn. Then he opened the basket and let his wife out. She was quite beside herself with joy, running hither and thither, bouncing up on him, looking about her and even rolling over on the ground. Mr Tebrick took this to mean that she was glad at making this journey and rejoiced equally with her. As for Mrs Cork, she sat motionless on the back seat of the dogcart well wrapped up, eating her sandwiches, but would not speak a word. When they had stayed there half-an-hour Mr Tebrick harnessed the horses again, though he was so cold he could scarcely buckle the straps, and put his vixen in her basket, but seeing that she wanted to look about her, he let her tear away the osiers with her teeth till she had made a hole big enough for her to put her head out of.

They drove on again and then the snow began to come down and that in earnest, so that he began to be afraid they would never cover the ground. But just after nightfall they got in, and he was content to leave unharnessing the horses and baiting them to Simon, Mrs Cork's son. His vixen was tired by then, as well as he, and they slept together, he in the bed and she under it, very contentedly.

The next morning he looked about him at the place and found the thing there that he most wanted, and that was a little walled-in garden where his wife could run in freedom and yet be in safety.

After they had had breakfast she was wild to go out into the snow. So they went out together, and he had never seen such a mad creature in all his life as his wife was then. For she ran to and fro as if she were crazy, biting at the snow and rolling in it, and round and round in circles and rushed back at him fiercely as if she meant to bite him. He joined her in the frolic, and began snowballing her till she was so wild that it was all he could do to quiet her again and bring her indoors for luncheon. Indeed with her gambollings she tracked the whole garden over with her feet; he could see where she had rolled in the snow and where she had danced in it, and looking at those prints of her feet as they went in, made his heart ache, he knew not why.

They passed the first day at old Nanny's cottage happily enough, without their usual bickerings, and this because of the novelty of the snow which had diverted them. In the afternoon he first showed his wife to little Polly, who eyed her very curiously but hung back shyly and seemed a good deal afraid of the fox. But Mr Tebrick took up a book and let them get acquainted by themselves, and presently looking up saw that they had come together and Polly was stroking his wife, patting her and running her fingers through her fur. Presently she began talking to the fox, and then brought her doll in to show her so that very soon they were very good playmates together. Watching the two gave Mr Tebrick great delight, and in particular when he noticed that there was something very motherly in his vixen. She was indeed far above the child in intelligence and restrained herself too from any hasty action. But while she seemed to wait on Polly's pleasure yet she managed to give a twist to the game, whatever it was, that never failed to delight the little girl. In short, in a very little while, Polly was so taken with her new play-mate that she cried when she was parted from her and wanted her always with her. This disposition of Mrs Tebrick's made Mrs Cork more agreeable than she had been lately either to the husband or the wife.

Three days after they had come to the cottage the weather changed, and they woke up one morning to find the snow gone, and the wind in the south, and the sun shining, so that it was like the first beginning of spring.

Mr Tebrick let his vixen out into the garden after breakfast, stayed with her awhile, and then went indoors to write some letters.

When he got out again he could see no sign of her anywhere, so that he ran about bewildered, calling to her. At last he spied a mound of fresh earth by the wall in one corner of the garden, and running thither found that there was a hole freshly dug seeming to go under the wall. On this he ran out of the garden quickly till he came to the other side of the wall, but there was no hole there, so he concluded that she was not yet got through. So it proved to be, for reaching down into the hole he felt her brush with his hand, and could hear her distinctly working away with her claws. He called to her then, saying: 'Silvia, Silvia, why do you do this? Are you trying to escape from me? I am your husband, and if I keep you confined it is to protect you, not to let you run into danger. Show me how I can make you happy and I will do it, but do not try to escape from me. I love you, Silvia: is it because of that that you want to fly from me to go into the world where you will be in danger of your life always? There are dogs everywhere and they all would kill you if it were not for me. Come out, Silvia, come out.'

But Silvia would not listen to him, so he waited there silent. Then he spoke to her in a different way, asking her had she forgot the bargain she made with him that she would not go out alone, but now when she had all the liberty of a garden to herself would she wantonly break her word? And he asked her, were they not married? And had she not always found him a good husband to her? But she heeded this neither until presently his temper getting somewhat out of hand he cursed her obstinacy and told her if she would be a damned fox she was welcome to it, for his part he could get his own way. She had not escaped yet. He would dig her out for he still had time, and if she struggled put her in a bag.

These words brought her forth instantly and she looked at him with as much astonishment as if she knew not what could have made him angry. Yes, she even fawned on him, but in a good-natured kind of way, as if she were a very good wife putting up wonderfully with her husband's temper.

These airs of hers made the poor gentleman (so simple was he) repent his outburst and feel most ashamed.

But for all that when she was out of the hole he filled it up with great stones and beat them in with a crowbar so she should find her work at that point harder than before if she was tempted to begin it again.

In the afternoon he let her go again into the garden but sent little Polly with her to keep her company. But presently on looking out he saw his vixen had climbed up into the limbs of an old pear tree and was looking over the wall, and was not so far from it but she might jump over if she could get a little farther.

Mr Tebrick ran out into the garden as quick as he could, and when his wife saw him it seemed she was startled and made a false spring at the wall, so that she missed reaching it and fell back heavily to the ground and lay there insensible. When Mr Tebrick got up to her he found her head was twisted under her by her fall and the neck seemed to be broken. The shock was so great to him that for some time he could not do anything, but knelt beside her turning her limp body, stupidly in his hands. At length he recognized that she was indeed dead, and beginning to consider what dreadful afflictions God had visited him with, he blasphemed horribly and called on God to strike him dead, or give his wife back to him.

'Is it not enough,' he cried, adding a foul blasphemous oath, 'that you should rob me of my dear wife, making her a fox, but now you must rob me of that fox too, that has been my only solace and comfort in this affliction?'

Then he burst into tears and began wringing his hands and continued there in such an extremity of grief for half-an-hour that he cared nothing, neither what he was doing, nor what would become of him in the future, but only knew that his life was ended now and he would not live any longer than he could help.

All this while the little girl Polly stood by, first staring, then asking him what had happened, and lastly crying with fear, but he never heeded her nor looked at her but only tore his hair, sometimes shouted at God, or shook his fist at Heaven. So in a fright Polly opened the door and ran out of the garden.

At length worn out, and as it were all numb with his loss, Mr Tebrick got up and went within doors, leaving his dear fox lying near where she had fallen.

He stayed indoors only two minutes and then came out again with a razor in his hand intending to cut his own throat, for he was out of his senses in this first paroxysm of grief.

But his vixen was gone, at which he looked about for a moment bewildered, and then enraged, thinking that somebody must have taken the body.

The door of the garden being open he ran straight through it. Now this door, which had been left ajar by Polly when she ran off, opened into a little courtyard where the fowls were shut in at night; the woodhouse and the privy also stood there. On the far side of it from the garden gate were two large wooden doors big enough when open to let a cart enter, and high enough to keep a man from looking over into the yard.

When Mr Tebrick got into the yard he found his vixen leaping up at these doors, and wild with terror, but as lively as ever he saw her in his life. He ran up to her but she shrank away from him, and would then have dodged him too, but he caught hold of her. She bared her teeth at him but he paid no heed to that, only picked her straight up into his arms and took her so indoors. Yet all the while he could scarce believe his eyes to see her living, and felt her all over very carefully to find if she had not some broken bones.

But no, he could find none. Indeed it was some hours before this poor silly gentleman began to suspect the truth, which was that his vixen had practised a deception upon him, and all the time he was bemoaning his loss in such heartrending terms, she was only shamming death to run away directly she was able. If it had not been that the yard gates were shut, which was a mere chance, she had got her liberty by that trick. And that this was only a trick of hers to sham dead was plain when he had thought it over. Indeed it is an old and time-honoured trick of the fox. It is in Aesop and a hundred other writers have confirmed it since. But so thoroughly had he been deceived by her, that at first he was as much overcome with joy at his wife still being alive, as he had been with grief a little while before, thinking her dead.

He took her in his arms, hugging her to him and thanking God a dozen times for her preservation. But his kissing and fondling her had very little effect now, for she did not answer him by licking or soft looks, but stayed huddled up and sullen, with her hair bristling on her neck and ears laid back every time he touched her. At first he thought this might be because he had touched some broken bone or tender place where she had been hurt, but at last the truth came to him.

Thus he was again to suffer, and though the pain of knowing her treachery to him was nothing to the grief of losing her, yet it was more insidious and lasting. At first, from a mere nothing, this pain grew gradually until it was a torture to him. If he had been one of your stock ordinary husbands, such a one who by experience has learnt never to enquire too closely into his wife's doing, her comings or goings, and never to ask her, 'How she has spent the day?' for fear he should be made the more of a fool, had Mr Tebrick been such a one he had been luckier, and his pain would have been almost nothing. But you must consider that he had never been deceived once by his wife in the course of their married life. No, she had never told him as much as one white lie, but had always been frank, open and ingenuous as if she and her husband were not husband and wife, or indeed of opposite sexes. Yet we must rate him as very foolish, that living thus with a fox, which beast has the same reputation for deceitfulness, craft and cunning, in all countries, all ages, and amongst all races of mankind, he should expect this fox to be as candid and honest with him in all things as the country girl he had married.

His wife's sullenness and bad temper continued that day, for she cowered away from him and hid under the sofa, nor could he persuade her to come out from there. Even when it was her dinner time she stayed, refusing resolutely to be tempted out with food, and lying so quiet that he heard nothing from her for hours. At night he carried her up to the bedroom, but she was still sullen and refused to eat a morsel, though she drank a little water during the night, when she fancied he was asleep.

The next morning was the same, and by now Mr Tebrick had been through all the agonies of wounded self-esteem, disillusion-ment and despair that a man can suffer. But though his emotions rose up in his heart and nearly stifled him he showed no sign of them to her, neither did he abate one jot his tenderness and consider-ation for his vixen. At breakfast he tempted her with a freshly killed young pullet. It hurt him to make this advance to her, for hitherto he had kept her strictly on cooked meats, but the pain of seeing her refuse it was harder still for him to bear. Added to this was now an anxiety lest she should starve herself to death rather than stay with him any longer.

All that morning he kept her close, but in the afternoon let her loose again in the garden after he had lopped the pear tree so that she could not repeat her performance of climbing.

But seeing how disgustedly she looked while he was by, never offering to run or to play as she was used, but only standing stock still with her tail between her legs, her ears flattened, and the hair bristling on her shoulders, seeing this he left her to herself out of mere humanity.

When he came out after half-an-hour he found that she was gone, but there was a fair-sized hole by the wall, and she just buried all but her brush, digging desperately to get under the wall and make her escape.

He ran up to the hole, and put his arm in after her and called to her to come out, but she would not. So at first he began pulling her out by the shoulder, then his hold slipping, by the hind legs. As soon as he had drawn her forth she whipped round and snapped at his hand and bit it through near the joint of the thumb, but let it go instantly.

They stayed there for a minute facing each other, he on his knees and she facing him, the picture of unrepentant wickedness and fury. Being thus on his knees, Mr Tebrick was down on her level very nearly, and her muzzle was thrust almost into his face. Her ears lay flat on her head, her gums were bared in a silent snarl, and all her beautiful teeth threatening him that she would bite him again. Her back too was half-arched, all her hair bristling and her brush held drooping. But it was her eyes that held his, with their slit pupils looking at him with savage desperation and rage.

The blood ran very freely from his hand but he never noticed that or the pain of it either, for all his thoughts were for his wife.

'What is this, Silvia?' he said very quietly, 'what is this? Why are you so savage now? If I stand between you and your freedom it is because I love you. Is it such torment to be with me?' But Silvia never stirred a muscle.

'You would not do this if you were not in anguish, poor beast, you want your freedom. I cannot keep you, I cannot hold you to vows made when you were a woman. Why, you have forgotten who I am.'

The tears then began running down his cheeks, he sobbed, and said to her:

'Go – I shall not keep you. Poor beast, poor beast, I love you, I love you. Go if you want to. But if you remember me come back. I shall never keep you against your will. Go – go. But kiss me now.'

He leant forward then and put his lips to her snarling fangs, but though she kept snarling she did not bite him. Then he got up quickly and went to the door of the garden that opened into a little paddock against a wood.

When he opened it she went through it like an arrow, crossed the paddock like a puff of smoke and in a moment was gone from his sight. Then, suddenly finding himself alone, Mr Tebrick came as it were to himself and ran after her, calling her by name and shouting to her, and so went plunging into the wood, and through it for about a mile, running almost blindly.

At last when he was worn out he sat down, seeing that she had gone beyond recovery and it was already night. Then, rising, he walked slowly homewards, wearied and spent in spirit. As he went he bound up his hand that was still running with blood. His coat was torn, his hat lost, and his face scratched right across with briars. Now in cold blood he began to reflect on what he had done and to repent bitterly having set his wife free. He had betrayed her so that now, from his act, she must lead the life of a wild fox for ever, and must undergo all the rigours and hardships of the climate, and all the hazards of a hunted creature. When Mr Tebrick got back to the cottage he found Mrs Cork was sitting up for him. It was already late.

'What have you done with Mrs Tebrick, sir? I missed her, and I missed you, and I have not known what to do, expecting something dreadful had happened. I have been sitting up for you half the night. And where is she now, sir?'

She accosted him so vigorously that Mr Tebrick stood silent. At length he said: 'I have let her go. She has run away.'

'Poor Miss Silvia!' cried the old woman. 'Poor creature! You ought to be ashamed, sir! Let her go, indeed! Poor lady, is that the way for her husband to talk! It is a disgrace. But I saw it coming from the first.'

The old woman was white with fury, she did not mind what she said, but Mr Tebrick was not listening to her. At last he looked at her and saw that she had just began to cry, so he went out of the room and up to bed, and lay down as he was, in his clothes, utterly exhausted, and fell into a dog's sleep, starting up every now and then with horror, and then falling back with fatigue. It was late when he woke up, but cold and raw, and he felt cramped in all his limbs. As he lay he heard again the noise which had woken him – the trotting of several horses, and the voices of men riding by the house. Mr Tebrick jumped up and ran to the window and then looked out, and the first thing that he saw was a gentleman in a pink coat riding at a walk down the lane. At this sight Mr Tebrick waited no longer, but pulling on his boots in mad haste, ran out instantly, meaning to say that they must not hunt, and how his wife was escaped and they might kill her.

But when he found himself outside the cottage words failed him and fury took possession of him, so that he could only cry out:

'How dare you, you damned blackguard?'

And so, with a stick in his hand, he threw himself on the gentleman in the pink coat and seized his horse's rein, and catching the gentleman by the leg was trying to throw him. But really it is impossible to say what Mr Tebrick intended by his behaviour or what he would have done, for the gentleman finding himself suddenly assaulted in so unexpected a fashion by so strange a tousled and dishevelled figure, clubbed his hunting crop and dealt him a blow on the temple so that he fell insensible.

Another gentleman rode up at this moment and they were civil enough to dismount and carry Mr Tebrick into the cottage, where they were met by old Nanny, who kept wringing her hands and told them Mr Tebrick's wife had run away and she was a vixen, and that was the cause that Mr Tebrick had run out and assaulted them.

The two gentlemen could not help laughing at this, and mounting their horses rode on without delay, after telling each other that Mr Tebrick, whoever he was, was certainly a madman, and the old woman seemed as mad as her master.

This story, however, went the rounds of the gentry in those parts and perfectly confirmed everyone in their previous opinion, namely that Mr Tebrick was mad and his wife had run away from him. The part about her being a vixen was laughed at by the few that heard it, but was soon left out as immaterial to the story, and incredible in itself, though afterwards it came to be remembered and its significance to be understood.

When Mr Tebrick came to himself it was past noon, and his head was aching so painfully that he could only call to mind in a confused way what had happened.

However, he sent off Mrs Cork's son directly on one of his horses to enquire about the hunt.

At the same time he gave orders to old Nanny that she was to put out food and water for her mistress, on the chance that she might yet be in the neighbourhood.

By nightfall Simon was back with the news that the hunt had had a very long run but had lost one fox, then, drawing a covert, had chopped an old dog-fox, and so ended the day's sport.

This put poor Mr Tebrick in some hopes again, and he rose at once from his bed, and went out to the wood and began calling his wife, but was overcome with faintness, and lay down and so passed the night in the open, from mere weakness.

In the morning he got back again to the cottage, but he had taken a chill, and so had to keep his bed for three or four days after.

All this time he had food put out for her every night, but though rats came to it and ate of it, there were never any prints of a fox.

At last his anxiety began working another way, that is he came to think it possible that his vixen would have gone back to Stokoe, so he had his horses harnessed in the dogcart and brought to the door and then drove over to Rylands, though he was still in a fever, and with a heavy cold upon him.

After that he lived always solitary, keeping away from his fellows and only seeing one man, called Askew, who had been brought up a jockey at Wantage, but was grown too big for his profession. He mounted this loafing fellow on one of his horses three days a week and had him follow the hunt and report to him whenever they killed, and if he could view the fox so much the better, and then he made him describe it minutely, so he should know if it were his Silvia. But he dared not trust himself to go himself, lest his passion should master him and he might commit a murder.

Every time there was a hunt in the neighbourhood he set the gates wide open at Rylands and the house doors also, and taking his gun stood sentinel in the hope that his wife would run in if she were pressed by the hounds, and so he could save her. But only once a hunt came near, when two fox-hounds that had lost the main pack strayed on to his land and he shot them instantly and buried them afterwards himself.

It was not long now to the end of the season, as it was the middle of March.

But living as he did at this time, Mr Tebrick grew more and more to be a true misanthrope. He denied admittance to any that came to visit him, and rarely showed himself to his fellows, but went out chiefly in the early mornings before people were about, in the hope of seeing his beloved fox. Indeed it was only this hope that he would see her again that kept him alive, for he had become so careless of his own comfort in every way that he very seldom ate a proper meal, taking no more than a crust of bread with a morsel of cheese in the whole day, though sometimes he would drink half a bottle of whisky to drown his sorrow and to get off to sleep, for sleep fled from him, and no sooner did he begin dozing but he awoke with a start thinking he had heard something. He let his beard grow too, and though he had always been very particular in his person before, he now was utterly careless of it, gave up washing himself for a week or two at a stretch, and if there was dirt under his fingernails let it stop there.

All this disorder fed a malignant pleasure in him. For by now he had come to hate his fellow men and was embittered against all human decencies and decorum. For strange to tell he never once in these months regretted his dear wife whom he had so much loved. No, all that he grieved for now was his departed vixen. He was haunted all this time not by the memory of a sweet and gentle woman, but by the recollection of an animal; a beast it is true that could sit at table and play piquet when it would, but for all that nothing really but a wild beast. His one hope now was the recovery of this beast, and of this he dreamed continually. Likewise both waking and sleeping he was visited by visions of her; her mask, her full white-tagged brush, white throat and the thick fur in her ears all haunted him.

Every one of her foxy ways was now so absolutely precious to him that I believe that if he had known for certain she was dead, and had thoughts of marrying a second time, he would never have been happy with a woman. No, indeed, he would have been more tempted to get himself a tame fox, and would have counted that as good a marriage as he could make.

Yet this all proceeded one may say from a passion, and a true conjugal fidelity, that it would be hard to find matched in this world. And though we may think him a fool, almost a madman, we must, when we look closer, find much to respect in his extraordinary devotion. How different indeed was he from those who, if their wives go mad, shut them in madhouses and give themselves up to concubinage, and nay, what is more, there are many who extenuate such conduct too. But Mr Tebrick was of a very different temper, and though his wife was now nothing but a hunted beast, cared for no one in the world but her.

But this devouring love ate into him like a consumption, so that by sleepless nights, and not caring for his person, in a few months he was worn to the shadow of himself. His cheeks were sunk in, his eyes hollow but excessively brilliant, and his whole body had lost flesh, so that looking at him the wonder was that he was still alive.

Now that the hunting season was over he had less anxiety for her, yet even so he was not positive that the hounds had not got her. For between the time of his setting her free, and the end of the hunting season (just after Easter), there were but three vixens killed near. Of those three one was a half-blind or wall-eyed, and one was a very grey dull-coloured beast. The third answered more to the description of his wife, but that it had not much black on the legs, whereas in her the blackness of the legs was very plain to be noticed. But yet his fear made him think that perhaps she had got mired in running and the legs being muddy were not remarked on as black.

One morning the first week in May, about four o'clock, when he was out waiting in the little copse, he sat down for a while on a tree stump, and when he looked up saw a fox coming towards him over the ploughed field. It was carrying a hare over its shoulder so that it was nearly all hidden from him. At last, when it was not twenty yards from him, it crossed over, going into the copse, when Mr Tebrick stood up and cried out, 'Silvia, Silvia, is it you?'

The fox dropped the hare out of his mouth and stood looking at him, and then our gentleman saw at the first glance that this was not his wife. For whereas Mrs Tebrick had been of a very bright red, this was a swarthier, duller beast altogether, moreover it was a good deal larger and higher at the shoulder and had a great white tag to his brush. But the fox after the first instant did not stand for his portrait you may be sure, but picked up his hare and made off like an arrow.

Then Mr Tebrick cried out to himself: 'Indeed I am crazy now! My affliction has made me lose what little reason I ever had. Here am I taking every fox I see to be my wife! My neighbours call me a madman and now I see that they are right. Look at me now, oh God! How foul a creature I am. I hate my fellows. I am thin and wasted by this consuming passion, my reason is gone and I feed myself on dreams. Recall me to my duty, bring me back to decency, let me not become a beast likewise, but restore me and forgive me, Oh my Lord.'

With that he burst into scalding tears and knelt down and prayed, a thing he had not done for many weeks.

When he rose up he walked back feeling giddy and exceedingly weak, but with a contrite heart, and then washed himself thoroughly and changed his clothes, but his weakness increasing he lay down for the rest of the day, but read in the Book of Job and was much comforted.

For several days after this he lived very soberly, for his weakness continued, but every day he read in his bible, and prayed earnestly, so that his resolution was so much strengthened that he determined to overcome his folly, or his passion, if he could, and at any rate to live the rest of his life very religiously. So strong was this desire in him to amend his ways that he considered if he should not go to spread the Gospel abroad, for the Bible Society, and so spend the rest of his days.

Indeed he began a letter to his wife's uncle, the canon, and he was writing this when he was startled by hearing a fox bark.

Yet so great was this new turn he had taken that he did not rush out at once, as he would have done before, but stayed where he was and finished his letter.

Afterwards he said to himself that it was only a wild fox and sent by the devil to mock him, and that madness lay that way if he should listen. But on the other hand he could not deny to himself that it might have been his wife, and that he ought to welcome the prodigal. Thus he was torn between these two thoughts, neither of which did he completely believe. He stayed thus tormented with doubts and fears all night.

The next morning he woke suddenly with a start and on the instant heard a fox bark once more. At that he pulled on his clothes and ran out as fast as he could to the garden gate. The sun was not yet high, the dew thick everywhere, and for a minute or two everything was very silent. He looked about him eagerly but could see no fox, yet there was already joy in his heart.

Then while he looked up and down the road, he saw his vixen step out of the copse about thirty yards away. He called to her at once.

'My dearest wife! Oh, Silvia! You are come back!' and at the sound of his voice he saw her wag her tail, which set his last doubts at rest.

But then though he called her again, she stepped into the copse once more though she looked back at him over her shoulder as she went. At this he ran after her, but softly and not too fast lest he should frighten her away, and then looked about for her again and called to her when he saw her among the trees still keeping her distance from him. He followed her then, and as he approached so she retreated from him, yet always looking back at him several times.

He followed after her through the underwood up the side of the hill, when suddenly she disappeared from his sight, behind some bracken.

When he got there he could see her nowhere, but looking about him found a fox's earth, but so well hidden that he might have passed it by a thousand times and would never have found it unless he had made particular search at that spot.

But now, though he went on his hands and knees, he could see nothing of his vixen, so that he waited a little while wondering.

Presently he heard a noise of something moving in the earth, and so waited silently, then saw something which pushed itself into sight. It was a small sooty black beast, like a puppy. There came another behind it, then another and so on till there were five of them. Lastly there came his vixen pushing her litter before her, and while he looked at her silently, a prey to his confused and unhappy emotions, he saw that her eyes were shining with pride and happiness.

She picked up one of her youngsters then, in her mouth, and brought it to him, and laid it in front of him, and then looked up at him very excited, or so it seemed.

Mr Tebrick took the cub in his hands, stroked it and put it against his cheek. It was a little fellow with a smutty face and paws, with staring vacant eyes of a brilliant electric blue and a little tail like a carrot. When he was put down he took a step towards his mother and then sat down very comically.

Mr Tebrick looked at his wife again and spoke to her, calling her a good creature. Already he was resigned and now, indeed, for the first time he thoroughly understood what had happened to her, and how far apart they were now. But looking first at one cub, then at another, and having them sprawling over his lap, he forgot himself, only watching the pretty scene, and taking pleasure in it. Now and then he would stroke his vixen and kiss her, liberties which she freely allowed him. He marvelled more than ever now at her beauty; for her gentleness with the cubs and the extreme delight she took in them seemed to him then to make her more lovely than before. Thus lying amongst them at the mouth of the earth he idled away the whole of the morning.

First he would play with one, then with another, rolling them over and tickling them, but they were too young yet to lend themselves to any other more active sport than this. Every now and then he would stroke his vixen, or look at her, and thus the time slipped away quite fast and he was surprised when she gathered her cubs together and pushed them before her into the earth, then coming back to him once or twice very humanly bid him 'Goodbye and that she hoped she would see him soon again, now he had found out the way.'

So admirably did she express her meaning that it would have

been superfluous for her to have spoken had she been able, and Mr Tebrick, who was used to her, got up at once and went home.

But now that he was alone, all the feelings which he had not troubled himself with when he was with her, but had, as it were, put aside till after his innocent pleasures were over, all these came swarming back to assail him in a hundred tormenting ways.

Firstly he asked himself: Was not his wife unfaithful to him, had she not prostituted herself to a beast? Could he still love her after that? But this did not trouble him so much as it might have done. For now he was convinced inwardly that she could no longer in fairness be judged as a woman, but as a fox only. And as a fox she had done no more than other foxes, indeed in having cubs and tending them with love, she had done well.

Whether in this conclusion Mr Tebrick was in the right or not, is not for us here to consider. But I would only say to those who would censure him for a too lenient view of the religious side of the matter, that we have not seen the thing as he did, and perhaps if it were displayed before our eyes we might be led to the same conclusions.

This was, however, not a tenth part of the trouble in which Mr Tebrick found himself. For he asked himself also: 'Was he not jealous?' And looking into his heart he found that he was indeed jealous, yes, and angry too, that now he must share his vixen with wild foxes. Then he questioned himself if it were not dishonourable to do so, and whether he should not utterly forget her and follow his original intention of retiring from the world, and see her no more.

Thus he tormented himself for the rest of that day, and by evening he had resolved never to see her again.

But in the middle of the night he woke up with his head very clear, and said to himself in wonder, 'Am I not a madman? I torment myself foolishly with fantastic notions. Can a man have his honour sullied by a beast? I am a man, I am immeasurably superior to the animals. Can my dignity allow of my being jealous of a beast? A thousand times no. Were I to lust after a vixen, I were a criminal indeed. I can be happy in seeing my vixen, for I love her, but she does right to be happy according to the laws of her being.'

Lastly, he said to himself what was, he felt, the truth of this whole matter:

'When I am with her I am happy. But now I distort what is simple and drive myself crazy with false reasoning upon it.'

Yet before he slept again he prayed, but though he had thought first to pray for guidance, in reality he prayed only that on the morrow he would see his vixen again and that God would preserve her, and her cubs too, from all dangers, and would allow him to see them often, so that he might come to love them for her sake as if he were their father, and that if this were a sin he might be forgiven, for he sinned in ignorance.

The next day or two he saw vixen and cubs again, though his visits were cut shorter, and these visits gave him such an innocent pleasure that very soon his notions of honour, duty and so on, were entirely forgotten, and his jealousy lulled asleep.

One day he tried taking with him the stereoscope and a pack of cards.

But though his Silvia was affectionate and amiable enough to let him put the stereoscope over her muzzle, yet she would not look through it, but kept turning her head to lick his hand, and it was plain to him that now she had quite forgotten the use of the instrument. It was the same too with the cards. For with them she was pleased enough, but only delighting to bite at them, and flip them about with her paws, and never considering for a moment whether they were diamonds or clubs, or hearts or spades, or whether the card was an ace or not. So it was evident that she had forgotten the nature of cards too.

Thereafter he only brought them things which she could better enjoy, that is sugar, grapes, raisins and butcher's meat.

By and by, as the summer wore on, the cubs came to know him, and he them, so that he was able to tell them easily apart, and then he christened them. For this purpose he brought a little bowl of water, sprinkled them as if in baptism and told them he was their godfather and gave each of them a name, calling them Sorel, Kasper, Selwyn, Esther, and Angelica.

Sorel was a clumsy little beast of a cheery and indeed puppyish disposition; Kasper was fierce, the largest of the five, even in his play he would always bite, and gave his godfather many a sharp nip as time went on. Esther was of a dark complexion, a true brunette and very sturdy; Angelica the brightest red and the most exactly like her mother; while Selwyn was the smallest cub, of a very prying, inquisitive and cunning temper, but delicate and undersized.

Thus Mr Tebrick had a whole family now to occupy him, and, indeed, came to love them with very much of a father's love and partiality.

His favourite was Angelica (who reminded him so much of her mother in her pretty ways) because of a gentleness which was lacking in the others, even in their play. After her in his affections came Selwyn, whom he soon saw was the most intelligent of the whole litter. Indeed he was so much more quick-witted than the rest that Mr Tebrick was led into speculating as to whether he had not inherited something of the human from his dam. Thus very early he learnt to know his name, and would come when he was called, and what was stranger still, he learnt the names of his brothers and sisters before they came to do so themselves.

Besides all this he was something of a young philosopher, for though his brother Kasper tyrannized over him he put up with it all with an unruffled temper. He was not, however, above playing tricks on the others, and one day when Mr Tebrick was by, he made believe that there was a mouse in a hole some little way off. Very soon he was joined by Sorel, and presently by Kasper and Esther. When he had got them all digging, it was easy for him to slip away, and then he came to his godfather with a sly look, sat down before him, and smiled and then jerked his head over towards the others and smiled again and wrinkled his brows so that Mr Tebrick knew as well as if he had spoken that the youngster was saying, 'Have I not made fools of them all?'

He was the only one that was curious about Mr Tebrick: he had made him take out his watch, put his ear to it, considered it and wrinkled up his brows in perplexity. On the next visit it was the same thing. He must see the watch again, and again think over it. But clever as he was, little Selwyn could never understand it, and if his mother remembered anything about watches it was a subject which she never attempted to explain to her children.

One day Mr Tebrick left the earth as usual and ran down the slope to the road, when he was surprised to find a carriage waiting before his house and a coachman walking about near his gate. Mr Tebrick went in and found that his visitor was waiting for him. It was his wife's uncle.

They shook hands, though the Rev. Canon Fox did not recognize him immediately, and Mr Tebrick led him into the house.

The clergyman looked about him a good deal, at the dirty and disorderly rooms, and when Mr Tebrick took him into the drawing-room it was evident that it had been unused for several months, the dust lay so thickly on all the furniture.

After some conversation on indifferent topics Canon Fox said to him:

'I have called really to ask about my niece.'

Mr Tebrick was silent for some time and then said:

'She is quite happy now.'

'Ah – indeed. I have heard she is not living with you any longer.'

'No. She is not living with me. She is not far away. I see her every day now.'

'Indeed. Where does she live?'

'In the woods with her children. I ought to tell you that she has changed her shape. She is a fox.'

The Rev. Cannon Fox got up; he was alarmed, and everything Mr Tebrick said confirmed what he had been led to expect he would find at Rylands. When he was outside, however, he asked Mr Tebrick:

'You don't have many visitors now, eh?'

'No – I never see anyone if I can avoid it. You are the first person I have spoken to for months.'

'Quite right too, my dear fellow. I quite understand – in the circumstances.' Then the cleric shook him by the hand, got into his carriage and drove away.

'At any rate,' he said to himself, 'there will be no scandal.' He was relieved also because Mr Tebrick had said nothing about going abroad to disseminate the Gospel. Canon Fox had been alarmed by the letter, had not answered it, and thought that it was always better to let things be, and never to refer to anything unpleasant. He did not at all want to recommend Mr Tebrick to the Bible Society if he were mad. His eccentricities would never be noticed at Stokoe. Besides that, Mr Tebrick had said he was happy.

He was sorry for Mr Tebrick too, and he said to himself that the queer girl, his niece, must have married him because he was the first man she had met. He reflected also that he was never likely to see her again and said aloud, when he had driven some little way:

'Not an affectionate disposition,' then to his coachman: 'No, that's all right. Drive on, Hopkins.'

When Mr Tebrick was alone he rejoiced exceedingly in his solitary life. He understood, or so he fancied, what it was to be happy, and that he had found complete happiness now, living from day to day, careless of the future, surrounded every morning by playful and affectionate little creatures whom he loved tenderly, and sitting beside their mother, whose simple happiness was the source of his own.

'True happiness,' he said to himself, 'is to be found in bestowing love; there is no such happiness as that of the mother for her babe, unless I have attained it in mine for my vixen and her children.'

With these feelings he waited impatiently for the hour on the morrow when he might hasten to them once more.

When, however, he had toiled up the hillside, to the earth, taking infinite precaution not to tread down the bracken, or make a beaten path which might lead others to that secret spot, he found to his surprise that Silvia was not there and that there were no cubs to be seen either. He called to them, but it was in vain, and at last he laid himself on the mossy bank beside the earth and waited.

For a long while, as it seemed to him, he lay very still, with closed eyes, straining his ears to hear every rustle among the leaves, or any sound that might be the cubs stirring in the earth.

At last he must have dropped asleep, for he woke suddenly with all his senses alert, and opening his eyes found a full-grown fox within six feet of him sitting on its haunches like a dog and watching his face with curiosity. Mr Tebrick saw instantly that it was not Silvia. When he moved the fox got up and shifted his eyes, but still stood his ground, and Mr Tebrick recognized him then for the dog-fox he had seen once before carrying a hare. It was the same dark beast with a large white tag to his brush. Now the secret was out and Mr Tebrick could see his rival before him. Here was the real father of his godchildren, who could be certain of their taking after him, and leading over again his wild and rakish life. Mr Tebrick stared for a long time at the handsome rogue, who glanced back at him with distrust and watchfulness patent in his face, but not without defiance too, and it seemed to Mr Tebrick as if there was also a touch of cynical humour in his look, as if he said:

'By Gad! we two have been strangely brought together!'

And to the man, at any rate, it seemed strange that they were thus linked, and he wondered if the love his rival there bare to his vixen and his cubs were the same thing in kind as his own.

'We would both of us give our lives for theirs,' he said to himself as he reasoned upon it, 'we both of us are happy chiefly in their company. What pride this fellow must feel to have such a wife, and such children taking after him. And has he not reason for his pride? He lives in a world where he is beset with a thousand dangers. For half the year he is hunted, everywhere dogs pursue him, men lay traps for him or menace him. He owes nothing to another.'

But he did not speak, knowing that his words would only alarm the fox; then in a few minutes he saw the dog-fox look over his shoulder, and then he trotted off as lightly as a gossamer veil blown in the wind, and, in a minute or two more, back he comes with his vixen and the cubs all round him. Seeing the dog-fox thus surrounded by vixen and cubs was too much for Mr Tebrick; in spite of all his philosophy a pang of jealousy shot through him. He could see that Silvia had been hunting with her cubs, and also that she had forgotten that he would come that morning, for she started when she saw him, and though she carelessly licked his hand, he could see that her thoughts were not with him.

Very soon she led her cubs into the earth, the dog-fox had vanished and Mr Tebrick was again alone. He did not wait longer but went home.

Now was his peace of mind all gone, the happiness which he had flattered himself the night before he knew so well how to enjoy, seemed now but a fool's paradise in which he had been living. A hundred times this poor gentleman bit his lip, drew down his torvous brows, and stamped his foot, and cursed himself bitterly, and called his lady bitch. He could not forgive himself either, that he had not thought of the damned dog-fox before, but all the while had let the cubs frisk round him, each one a proof that a dog-fox had been at work with his vixen. Yes, jealousy was now in the wind, and every circumstance which had been a reason for his felicity the night before was now turned into a monstrous feature of his nightmare. With all this Mr Tebrick so worked upon himself that for the time being he had lost his reason. Black was white and white black, and he was resolved that on the morrow he would dig the vile brood of foxes out and shoot them, and so free himself at last from this hellish plague.

All that night he was in this mood, and in agony, as if he had broken in the crown of a tooth and bitten on the nerve. But as all things will have an ending, so at last Mr Tebrick, worn out and wearied by this loathed passion of jealousy, fell into an uneasy and tormented sleep.

After an hour or two the procession of confused and jumbled images which first assailed him passed away and subsided into one clear and powerful dream. His wife was with him in her own proper shape, walking as they had been on that fatal day before her transformation. Yet she was changed too, for in her face there were visible tokens of unhappiness, her face swollen with crying, pale and downcast, her hair hanging in disorder, her damp hands wringing a small handkerchief into a ball, her whole body shaken with sobs, and an air of long neglect about her person. Between her sobs she was confessing to him some crime which she had committed, but he did not catch the broken words, nor did he wish to hear them, for he was dulled by his sorrow. So they continued walking together in sadness as it were for ever, he with his arm about her waist, she turning her head to him and often casting her eyes down in distress.

At last they sat down, and he spoke, saying: 'I know they are not my children, but I shall not use them barbarously because of that. You are still my wife. I swear to you they shall never be neglected. I will pay for their education.'

Then he began turning over the names of schools in his mind. Eton would not do, nor Harrow, nor Winchester, nor Rugby . . . But he could not tell why these schools would not do for these children of hers, he only knew that every school he thought of was impossible, but surely one could be found. So turning over the names of schools he sat for a long while holding his dear wife's hand, till at length, still weeping, she got up and went away and then slowly he awoke.

But even when he had opened his eyes and looked about him he was thinking of schools, saying to himself that he must send them to a private academy, or even at the worst engage a tutor. 'Why, yes,' he said to himself, putting one foot out of bed, 'that is what it must be, a tutor, though even then there will be a difficulty at first.'

At those words he wondered what difficulty there would be and recollected that they were not ordinary children. No, they were foxes – mere foxes. When poor Mr Tebrick had remembered this he was, as it were, dazed or stunned by the fact, and for a long time he could understand nothing, but at last burst into a flood of tears compassionating them and himself too. The awfulness of the fact itself, that his dear wife should have foxes instead of children, filled him with an agony of pity, and, at length, when he recollected the cause of their being foxes, that is that his wife was a fox also, his tears broke out anew, and he could bear it no longer but began calling out in his anguish, and beat his head once or twice against the wall, and then cast himself down on his bed again and wept and wept, sometimes tearing the sheets asunder with his teeth.

The whole of that day, for he was not to go to the earth till evening, he went about sorrowfully, torn by true pity for his poor vixen and her children.

At last when the time came he went again up to the earth, which he found deserted, but hearing his voice, out came Esther. But though he called the others by their names there was no answer, and something in the way the cub greeted him made him fancy she was indeed alone. She was truly rejoiced to see him, and scrambled up into his arms, and thence to his shoulder, kissing him, which was unusual in her (though natural enough in her sister, Angelica). He sat down a little way from the earth, fondling her, and fed her with some fish he had brought for her mother, which she ate so ravenously that he concluded she must have been short of food that day and probably alone for some time.

At last while he was sitting there Esther pricked up her ears, started up, and presently Mr Tebrick saw his vixen come towards them. She greeted him very affectionately but it was plain had not much time to spare, for she soon started back whence she had come with Esther at her side. When they had gone about a rod the cub hung back and kept stopping and looking back to the earth, and at last turned and ran back home. But her mother was not to be fobbed off so, for she quickly overtook her child and gripping her by the scruff began to drag her along with her.

Mr Tebrick, seeing then how matters stood, spoke to her, telling her he would carry Esther if she would lead, so after a little while Silvia gave her over, and then they set out on their strange journey.

Silvia went running on a little before while Mr Tebrick followed after with Esther in his arms whimpering and struggling now to be free, and indeed, once she gave him a nip with her teeth. This was not so strange a thing to him now, and he knew the remedy for it, which is much the same as with others whose tempers run too high, that is a taste of it themselves. Mr Tebrick shook her and gave her a smart little cuff, after which, though she sulked, she stopped her biting.

They went thus above a mile, circling his house and crossing the highway until they gained a small covert that lay with some waste fields adjacent to it. And by this time it was so dark that it was all Mr Tebrick could do to pick his way, for it was not always easy for him to follow where his vixen found a big enough road for herself.

But at length they came to another earth, and by the starlight Mr Tebrick could just make out the other cubs skylarking in the shadows.

Now he was tired, but he was happy and laughed softly for joy, and presently his vixen coming to him, put her feet upon his shoulders as he sat on the ground, and licked him, and he kissed her back on the muzzle and gathered her in his arms and rolled her in his jacket and then laughed and wept by turns in the excess of his joy.

All his jealousies of the night before were forgotten now. All his desperate sorrow of the morning and the horror of his dream were gone. What if they were foxes? Mr Tebrick found that he could be happy with them. As the weather was hot he lay out there all the night, first playing hide and seek with them in the dark till, missing his vixen and the cubs proving obstreperous, he lay down and was soon asleep.

He was woken up soon after dawn by one of the cubs tugging at his shoelaces in play. When he sat up he saw two of the cubs standing near him on their hind legs, wrestling with each other, the other two were playing hide and seek round a tree trunk, and now Angelica let go his laces and came romping into his arms to kiss him and say 'Good morning' to him, then worrying the points of his waistcoat a little shyly after the warmth of his embrace.

That moment of awakening was very sweet to him. The freshness of the morning, the scent of everything at the day's rebirth, the first beams of the sun upon a tree-top near, and a pigeon rising into the air suddenly, all delighted him. Even the rough scent of the body of the cub in his arms seemed to him delicious.

At that moment all human customs and institutions seemed to him nothing but folly; for said he, 'I would exchange all my life as a man for my happiness now, and even now I retain almost all of the ridiculous conceptions of a man. The beasts are happier and I will deserve that happiness as best I can.'

After he had looked at the cubs playing merrily, how, with soft stealth, one would creep behind another to bounce out and startle him, a thought came into Mr Tebrick's head, and that was that these cubs were innocent, they were as stainless snow, they could not sin, for God had created them to be thus and they could break none of His commandments. And he fancied also that men sin because they cannot be as the animals.

Presently he got up full of happiness, and began making his way home when suddenly he came to a full stop and asked himself: 'What is going to happen to them?'

This question rooted him stockishly in a cold and deadly fear as if he had seen a snake before him. At last he shook his head and hurried on his path. Aye, indeed, what would become of his vixen and her children?

This thought put him into such a fever of apprehension that he did his best not to think of it any more, but yet it stayed with him all that day and for weeks after, at the back of his mind, so that he was not careless in his happiness as before, but as it were trying continually to escape his own thoughts.

This made him also anxious to pass all the time he could with his dear Silvia, and, therefore, he began going out to them for more of the daytime, and then he would sleep the night in the woods also as he had done that night; and so he passed several weeks, only returning to his house occasionally to get himself a fresh provision of food. But after a week or ten days at the new earth both his vixen and the cubs, too, got a new habit of roaming. For a long while back, as he knew, his vixen had been lying out alone most of the day, and now the cubs were all for doing the same thing. The earth, in short, had served its purpose and was now distasteful to them, and they would not enter it unless pressed with fear.

This new manner of their lives was an added grief to Mr Tebrick, for sometimes he missed them for hours together, or for the whole day even, and not knowing where they might be was lonely and anxious. Yet his Silvia was thoughtful for him too and would often send Angelica or another of the cubs to fetch him to their new lair, or come herself if she could spare the time. For now they were all perfectly accustomed to his presence, and had come to look on him as their natural companion, and although he was in many ways irksome to them by scaring rabbits, yet they always rejoiced to see him when they had been parted from him. This friendliness of theirs was, you may be sure, the source of most of Mr Tebrick's happiness at this time. Indeed he lived now for nothing but his foxes, his love for his vixen had extended itself insensibly to include her cubs, and these were now his daily playmates so that he knew them as well as if they had been his own children. With Selwyn and Angelica indeed he was always happy; and they never so much as when they were with him. He was not stiff in his behaviour either, but had learnt by this time as much from his foxes as they had from him. Indeed never was there a more curious alliance than this or one with stranger effects upon both of the parties.

Mr Tebrick now could follow after them anywhere and keep up with them too, and could go through a wood as silently as a deer. He learnt to conceal himself if ever a labourer passed by so that he was rarely seen, and never but once in their company. But what was most strange of all, he had got a way of going doubled up, often almost on all fours with his hands touching the ground every now and then, particularly when he went uphill.

He hunted with them too sometimes, chiefly by coming up and scaring rabbits towards where the cubs lay ambushed, so that the bunnies ran straight into their jaws.

He was useful to them in other ways, climbing up and robbing pigeons' nests for the eggs which they relished exceedingly, or by occasionally dispatching a hedgehog for them so they did not get the prickles in their mouths. But while on his part he thus altered his conduct, they on their side were not behindhand, but learnt a dozen human tricks from him that are ordinarily wanting in Reynard's education.

One evening he went to a cottager who had a row of skeps, and bought one of them, just as it was after the man had smothered the bees. This he carried to the foxes that they might taste the honey, for he had seen them dig out wild bee's nests often enough. The skep full was indeed a wonderful feast for them, they bit greedily into the heavy scented comb, their jaws were drowned in the sticky flood of sweetness, and they gorged themselves on it without restraint. When they had crunched up the last morsel they tore the skep in pieces, and for hours afterwards they were happily employed in licking themselves clean.

That night he slept near their lair, but they left him and went hunting. In the morning when he woke he was quite numb with cold, and faint with hunger. A white mist hung over everything and the wood smelt of autumn.

He got up and stretched his cramped limbs, and then walked homewards. The summer was over and Mr Tebrick noticed this now for the first time and was astonished. He reflected that the cubs were fast growing up, they were foxes at all points, and yet when he thought of the time when they had been sooty and had blue eyes it seemed to him only yesterday. From that he passed to thinking of the future, asking himself as he had done once before what would become of his vixen and her children. Before the winter he must tempt them into the security of his garden, and fortify it against all the dangers that threatened them.

But though he tried to allay his fear with such resolutions he remained uneasy all that day. When he went out to them that afternoon he found only his wife Silvia there and it was plain to him that she too was alarmed, but alas, poor creature, she could tell him nothing, only lick his hands and face, and turn about pricking her ears at every sound.

'Where are your children, Silvia?' he asked her several times, but she was impatient of his questions, but at last sprang into his arms, flattened herself upon his breast and kissed him gently, so that when he departed his heart was lighter because he knew that she still loved him.

That night he slept indoors, but in the morning early he was awoken by the sound of trotting horses, and running to the window saw a farmer riding by very sprucely dressed. Could they be hunting so soon, he wondered, but presently assured himself that it could not be a hunt already.

He heard no other sound till eleven o'clock in the morning when suddenly there was the clamour of hounds giving tongue and not so far off neither. At this Mr Tebrick ran out of his house distracted and set open the gates of his garden, but with iron bars and wire at the top so the huntsmen could not follow. There was silence again; it seems the fox must have turned away, for there was no other sound of the hunt. Mr Tebrick was now like one helpless with fear, he dared not go out, yet could not stay still at home. There was nothing that he could do, yet he would not admit this, so he busied himself in making holes in the hedges, so that Silvia (or her cubs) could enter from whatever side she came.

At last he forced himself to go indoors and sit down and drink some tea. While he was there he fancied he heard the hounds again; it was but a faint ghostly echo of their music, yet when he ran out of the house it was already close at hand in the copse above.

Now it was that poor Mr Tebrick made his great mistake, for hearing the hounds almost outside the gate he ran to meet them, whereas rightly he should have run back to the house. As soon as he reached the gate he saw his wife Silvia coming towards him but very tired with running and just upon her the hounds. The horror of that sight pierced him, for ever afterwards he was haunted by those hounds – their eagerness, their desperate efforts to gain on her and their blind lust for her came at odd moments to frighten him all his life. Now he should have run back, though it was already late, but instead he cried out to her, and she ran straight through the open gate to him. What followed was all over in a flash, but it was seen by many witnesses.

The side of Mr Tebrick's garden there is bounded by a wall, about six feet high and curving round, so that the huntsmen could see over this wall inside. One of them indeed put his horse at it very boldly, which was risking his neck, and although he got over safe was too late to be of much assistance.

His vixen had at once sprung into Mr Tebrick's arms, and before he could turn back the hounds were upon them and had pulled them down. Then at that moment there was a scream of despair heard by all the field that had come up, which they declared afterwards was more like a woman's voice than a man's. But yet there was no clear proof whether it was Mr Tebrick, or his wife who had suddenly regained her voice. When the huntsman who had leapt the wall got to them and had whipped off the hounds Mr Tebrick had been terribly mauled and was bleeding from twenty wounds. As for his vixen, she was dead, though he was still clasping her dead body in his arms.

Mr Tebrick was carried into the house at once and assistance sent for, but there was no doubt now about his neighbours being in the right when they called him mad.

For a long while his life was despaired of, but at last he rallied, and in the end he recovered his reason and lived to be a great age; for that matter he is still alive.

# Father's Last Escape

## Bruno Schulz

*When the Germans occupied the Polish town of Orogobych in 1941, Bruno Schulz was earning his living as a painter; his writings didn't sell, in spite of the prize awarded to his book* The Street of Crocodiles *by the Polish Academy of Letters, and his salary as a Jewish teacher was meagre. A year later, in November, while bringing home a loaf of bread, he was shot to death in the street by a Nazi officer who bore a grudge against another Nazi, Schulz's temporary 'protector' who liked his paintings.*

*A translator of Kafka, Schulz shared with Kafka the fate of being, in his own words, 'a parasite of metaphors'. 'Father's Last Escape' is a metaphor of Schulz's vision of his father, but it is also the chronicle of his search for truth – 'to fill in the gaps that official history leaves,' says John Updike in his introduction to* Sanatorium Under The Sign of the Hourglass, *the collection from which this story is taken. Updike quotes Schulz: 'Where is truth to shelter, where is it to find asylum if not in a place where nobody is looking for it . . . ?'*

It happened in the late and forlorn period of complete disruption, at the time of the liquidation of our business. The signboard had been removed from over our shop, the shutters were halfway down, and inside the shop my mother was conducting an unauthorized trade in remnants. Adela had gone to America, and it was said that the boat on which she had sailed had sunk and that all the passengers had lost their lives. We were unable to verify this rumour, but all trace of the girl was lost and we never heard of her again.

A new age began – empty, sober, and joyless, like a sheet of white paper. A new servant girl, Genya, anaemic, pale, and boneless, mooned about the rooms. When one patted her on the back, she wriggled, stretched like a snake, or purred like a cat. She had a dull white complexion, and even the insides of her eyelids were white. She was so absent-minded that she sometimes made a white sauce from old letters and invoices: it was sickly and inedible.

At that time, my father was definitely dead. He had been dying a number of times, always with some reservations that forced us to revise our attitude towards the fact of his death. This had its advantages. By dividing his death into instalments, Father had familiarized us with his demise. We became gradually indifferent to his returns – each one shorter, each one more pitiful. His features were already dispersed throughout the room in which he had lived, and were sprouting in it, creating at some points strange knots of likeness that were most expressive. The wallpaper began in certain places to imitate his habitual nervous tic; the flower designs arranged themselves into the doleful elements of his smile, symmetrical as the fossilized imprint of a trilobite. For a time, we gave a wide berth to his fur coat lined with polecat skins. The fur coat breathed. The panic of small animals sewn together and biting into one another passed through it in helpless currents and lost itself in the folds of the fur. Putting one's ear against it, one could hear the melodious purring unison of the animals' sleep. In this well-tanned form, amid the faint smell of polecat, murder, and nighttime matings, my father might have lasted for many years. But he did not last.

One day, Mother returned home from town with a preoccupied face.

'Look, Joseph,' she said, 'what a lucky coincidence. I caught him on the stairs, jumping from step to step' – and she lifted a handkerchief that covered something on a plate. I recognized him at once. The resemblance was striking, although now he was a crab or a large scorpion. Mother and I exchanged looks: in spite of the metamorphosis, the resemblance was incredible.

'Is he alive?' I asked.

'Of course. I can hardly hold him,' Mother said. 'Shall I place him on the floor?'

She put the plate down, and leaning over him, we observed him closely. There was a hollow place between his numerous curved legs, which he was moving slightly. His uplifted pincers and feelers seemed to be listening. I tipped the plate, and Father moved cautiously and with a certain hesitation on to the floor. Upon touching the flat surface under him, he gave a sudden start with all of his legs, while his hard arthropod joints made a clacking sound. I barred his way. He hesitated, investigated the obstacle with his feelers,

then lifted his pincers and turned aside. We let him run in his
chosen direction, where there was no furniture to give him shelter.
Running in wavy jerks on his many legs, he reached the wall and,
before we could stop him, ran lightly up it, not pausing anywhere.
I shuddered with instinctive revulsion as I watched his progress up
the wallpaper. Meanwhile, Father reached a small built-in kitchen
cupboard, hung for a moment on its edge, testing the terrain with
his pincers, and then crawled into it.

He was discovering the apartment afresh from the new point of
view of a crab; evidently, he perceived all objects by his sense of
smell, for, in spite of careful checking, I could not find on him any
organ of sight. He seemed to consider carefully the objects he
encountered in his path, stopping and feeling them with his
antennae, then embracing them with his pincers, as if to test them
and make their acquaintance; after a time, he left them and continued on his run, pulling his abdomen behind him, lifted slightly
from the floor. He acted the same way with the pieces of bread and
meat that we threw on the floor for him, hoping he would eat them.
He gave them a perfunctory examination and ran on, not recognizing
that they were edible.

Watching these patient surveys of the room, one could assume
that he was obstinately and indefatigably looking for something.
From time to time, he ran to a corner of the kitchen, crept under
a barrel of water that was leaking, and, upon reaching the puddle,
seemed to drink.

Sometimes he disappeared for days on end. He seemed to manage
perfectly well without food, but this did not seem to affect his
vitality. With mixed feelings of shame and repugnance, we concealed by day our secret fear that he might visit us in bed during
the night. But this never occurred, although in the daytime he
would wander all over the furniture. He particularly liked to stay
in the spaces between the wardrobes and the wall.

We could not discount certain manifestations of reason and even
a sense of humour. For instance, Father never failed to appear in
the dining-room during mealtimes, although his participation in
them was purely symbolic. If the dining-room door was by chance
closed during dinner and he had been left in the next room, he
scratched at the bottom of the door, running up and down along
the crack, until we opened it for him. In time, he learned how to
insert his pincers and legs under the door, and after some elaborate

manoeuvres he finally succeeded in insinuating his body through it sideways into the dining-room. This seemed to give him pleasure. He would then stop under the table, lying quite still, his abdomen slightly pulsating. What the meaning of these rhythmic pulsations was, we would could not imagine. They seemed obscene and malicious, but at the same time expressed a rather gross and lustful satisfaction. Our dog, Nimrod, would approach him slowly and, without conviction, sniff at him cautiously, sneeze, and turn away indifferently, not having reached any conclusions.

Meanwhile, the demoralization in our household was increasing. Genya slept all day long, her slim body bonelessly undulating with her deep breaths. We often found in the soup reels of cotton, which she had thrown in unthinkingly with the vegetables. Our shop was open non-stop, day and night. A continuous sale took place amid complicated bargainings and discussions. To crown it all, Uncle Charles came to stay.

He was strangely depressed and silent. He declared with a sigh that after his recent unfortunate experiences he had decided to change his way of life and devote himself to the study of languages. He never went out but remained locked in the most remote room – from which Genya had removed all the carpets and curtains, as she did not approve of our visitor. There he spent his time, reading old price lists. Several times he tried viciously to step on Father. Screaming with horror, we told him to stop it. Afterwards he only smiled wryly to himself, while Father, not realizing the danger he had been in, hung around and studied some spots on the floor.

My father, quick and mobile as long as he was on his feet, shared with all crustaceans the characteristic that when turned on his back he became largely immobile. It was sad and pitiful to see him desperately moving all his limbs and rotating helplessly around his own axis. We could hardly force ourselves to look at the conspicuous, almost shameless mechanism of his anatomy, completely exposed under the bare articulated belly. At such moments, Uncle Charles could hardly restrain himself from stamping on Father. We ran to his rescue with some object at hand, which he caught tightly with his pincers, quickly regaining his normal position; then at once he started a lightning, zigzag run at double speed, as if wanting to obliterate the memory of his unsightly fall.

I must force myself to report truthfully the unbelievable deed, from which my memory recoils even now. To this day I cannot understand how we became the conscious perpetrators of it. A strange fatality must have been driving us to it; for fate does not evade consciousness or will but engulfs them in its mechanism, so that we are able to admit and accept, as in a hypnotic trance, things that under normal circumstances would fill us with horror.

Shaken badly, I asked my mother in despair, again and again, 'How could you have done it? If it were Genya who had done it – but you yourself?' Mother cried, wrung her hands, and could find no answer. Had she thought that Father would be better off? Had she seen in that act the only solution to a hopeless situation, or did she do it out of inconceivable thoughtlessness and frivolity? Fate has a thousand wiles when it chooses to impose on us its incomprehensible whims. A temporary blackout, a moment of inattention or blindness, is enough to insinuate an act between the Scylla and Charybdis of decision. Afterwards, with hindsight, we may endlessly ponder that act, explain our motives, try to discover our true intentions; but the act remains irrevocable.

When Father was brought in on a dish, we came to our senses and understood fully what had happened. He lay large and swollen from the boiling, pale grey and jellified. We sat in silence, dumbfounded. Only Uncle Charles lifted his fork towards the dish, but at once he put it down uncertainly, looking at us askance. Mother ordered it to be taken to the sitting-room. It stood there afterwards on a table covered with a velvet cloth, next to the album of family photographs and a musical cigarette box. Avoided by us all, it just stood there.

But my father's earthly wanderings were not yet at an end, and the next instalment – the extension of the story beyond permissible limits – is the most painful of all. Why didn't he give up, why didn't he admit that he was beaten when there was every reason to do so and when even Fate could go no farther in utterly confounding him? After several weeks of immobility in the sitting room, he somehow rallied and seemed to be slowly recovering. One morning, we found the plate empty. One leg lay on the edge of the dish, in some congealed tomato sauce and aspic that bore the traces of his escape. Although boiled and shedding his legs on the way, with his remaining strength he had dragged himself somewhere to begin a homeless wandering, and we never saw him again.

*Translated from the Polish by Celina Wieniewska.*

# A Man by the Name of Ziegler

Hermann Hesse

*Fantastic literature pulls down the barriers we set up to feel at ease in our place in the universe. It makes us insecure about the laws of time and space, it blots out the distinctions between man and the other creatures of this and other worlds, it denies death as an end, it demands that we reconsider who we really are.*

*The problem of identity appears in several of Hermann Hesse's books: in* Demian, *in* Siddhartha, *in the complex and vast* Magister Ludi, *which won him the Nobel Prize in 1946, in the magical* Steppenwolf, *and in the following short story.*

There was once a young man by the name of Ziegler, who lived on Brauergasse. He was one of those people we see every day on the street, whose faces we can never really remember, because they all have the same face: a collective face.

Ziegler was everything and did everything that such people always are and do. He was not stupid, but neither was he gifted; he loved money and pleasure, liked to dress well, and was as cowardly as most people: his life and activities were governed less by desires and strivings than by prohibitions, by the fear of punishment. Still, he had a number of good qualities and all in all he was a gratifyingly normal young man, whose own person was most interesting and important to him. Like every other man, he regarded himself as an individual, though in reality he was only a specimen, and like other men he regarded himself and his life as the centre of the world. He was far removed from all doubts, and when facts contradicted his opinions, he shut his eyes disapprovingly.

As a modern man, he had unlimited respect not only for money, but also for a second power: science. He could not have said exactly what science was, he had in mind something on the order of statistics and perhaps a bit of bacteriology, and he knew how much money and honour the state accorded to science. He especially admired cancer research, for his father had died of cancer, and Ziegler firmly believed that science, which had developed so remarkably since then, would not let the same thing happen to him.

Outwardly Ziegler distinguished himself by his tendency to dress somewhat beyond his means, always in the fashion of the year. For since he could not afford the fashions of the month or season, it goes without saying that he despised them as foolish affectation. He was a great believer in independence of character and often spoke harshly, among friends and in safe places, of his employers and of the government. I am probably dwelling too long on this portrait. But Ziegler was a charming young fellow, and he has been a great loss to us. For he met with a strange and premature end, which set all his plans and justified hopes at naught.

One Sunday soon after his arrival in our town, he decided on a day's recreation. He had not yet made any real friends and had not yet been able to make up his mind to join a club. Perhaps this was his undoing. It is not good for a man to be alone.

He could think of nothing else to do but go sightseeing. After conscientious inquiry and mature reflection he decided on the historical museum and the zoo. The museum was free of charge on Sunday mornings, and the zoo could be visited in the afternoon for a moderate fee.

Wearing his new suit with cloth buttons – he was very fond of it – he set out for the historical museum. He was carrying his thin, elegant, red-lacquered walking cane, which lent him dignity and distinction, but which to his profound displeasure he was obliged to part with at the entrance.

There were all sorts of things to be seen in the lofty rooms, and in his heart the pious visitor sang the praises of almighty science, which here again, as Ziegler observed in reading the meticulous inscriptions on the showcases, proved that it could be counted on. Thanks to these inscriptions, old bric-a-brac, such as rusty keys, broken and tarnished necklaces, and so on, became amazingly interesting. It was marvellous how science looked into everything, understood everything and found a name for it – oh, yes, it would definitely get rid of cancer very soon, maybe it would even abolish death.

In the second room he found a glass case in which he was reflected so clearly that he was able to stop for a moment and check up, carefully and to his entire satisfaction, on his coat, trousers, and the knot of his tie. Pleasantly reassured, he passed on and devoted his attention to the products of some early wood-carvers. Competent men, though shockingly naïve, he reflected benevolently. he also contemplated an old grandfather clock with ivory figures which danced the minuet when it struck the hour, and it too met with his patient approval. Then he began to feel rather bored; he yawned and looked more and more frequently at his watch, which he was not ashamed of showing, for it was solid gold, inherited from his father.

As he saw to his regret, he still had a long way to go until lunchtime, and so he entered another room. Here his curiosity revived. It contained objects of medieval superstition, books of magic, amulets, trappings of witchcraft, and in one corner a whole alchemist's workshop, complete with forge, mortars, pot-bellied flasks, dried-out pig's bladders, bellows, and so on. This corner was roped off, and there was a sign forbidding the public to touch the objects. But one never reads such signs very attentively, and Ziegler was alone in the room.

Unthinkingly he stretched out his arm over the rope and touched a few of the weird things. He had heard and read about the Middle Ages and their comical superstitions; it was beyond him how the people of those days could have bothered with such childish nonsense, and he failed to see why such absurdities as witchcraft had not simply been prohibited. Alchemy, on the other hand, was pardonable, since the useful science of chemistry had developed from it. Good Lord, to think that these gold-makers' crucibles and all this magic hocus-pocus may have been necessary, because without them there would be no aspirin or gas bombs today!

Absentmindedly he picked up a small dark-coloured pellet, rather like a pill, rolled the dry, weightless little thing between his fingers, and was about to put it down again when he heard steps behind him. He turned round. A visitor had entered the room. Ziegler was embarrassed at having the pellet in his hand, for actually he had read the sign. So he closed his hand, put it in his pocket, and left.

He did not think of the pellet again until he was on the street. He took it out and decided to throw it away. But first he raised it to his nose and sniffed it. It had a faint resinous smell that he found rather pleasing, so he put it back in his pocket.

Then he went to a restaurant, ordered, leafed through a few

newspapers, toyed with his tie, and cast respectful or haughty glances at the guests around him, depending on how they were dressed. But when his meal was rather long in coming, he took out the alchemist's pill that he had involuntarily stolen, and smelled it. Then he scratched it with his fingernail, and finally, naïvely giving in to a childlike impulse, he put it in his mouth. It did not taste bad and dissolved quickly; he washed it down with a sip of beer. And then his meal arrived.

At two o'clock the young man jumped off the street car, went to the zoo, and bought a Sunday ticket.

Smiling amiably, he went to the primate house and planted himself in front of the big cage where the chimpanzees were kept. A large chimpanzee blinked at him, gave him a good-natured nod, and said in a deep voice: 'How goes it, brother?'

Repelled and strangely frightened, Ziegler turned away. As he was hurrying off, he heard the ape scolding: 'What's he got to be so proud about! The stupid bastard!'

He went to see the long-tailed monkeys. They were dancing merrily. 'Give us some sugar, old buddy!' they cried. And when he had no sugar, they grew angry, mimicked him, called him a cheapskate, and bared their teeth. That was more than he could stand; he fled in consternation and made for the deer, whom he expected to behave better.

A large stately elk stood close to the bars, looking him over. And suddenly Ziegler was stricken with horror. For since swallowing the magic pill, he understood the language of the animals. And the elk spoke with his eyes, two big brown eyes. His silent gaze expressed dignity, resignation, sadness, and with regard to the visitor a lofty and solemn contempt, a terrible contempt. In the language of these silent, majestic eyes, Ziegler read, he, with his hat and cane, his gold watch and his Sunday suit, was no better than vermin, an absurd and repulsive bug.

From the elk he fled to the ibex, from the ibex to the chamois, the llama, and the gnu, to the wild boars and bears. They did not all insult him, but without exception they despised him. He listened to them and learned from their conversations what they thought of people in general. And what they thought was most distressing. Most of all, they were surprised that these ugly, stinking, undignified bipeds with their foppish disguises should be allowed to run around loose.

He heard a puma talking to her cub, a conversation full of dignity and practical wisdom, such as one seldom hears among humans. He heard a beautiful panther expressing his opinions of this riffraff, the Sunday visitors, in succinct, well-turned, aristocratic phrases. He looked the blond lion in the eye and learned of the wonderful immensity of the wilderness, where there are no cages and no human beings. He saw a kestrel perched proud and forlorn, congealed in melancholy, on a dead branch and saw the jays bearing their imprisonment with dignity, resignation, and humour.

Dejected and wrenched out of all his habits of thought, Ziegler turned back to his fellow men in his despair. He looked for eyes that would understand his terror and misery; he listened to conversations in the hope of hearing something comforting, something understandable and soothing; he observed the gestures of the visitors in the hope of finding nobility and quiet, natural dignity.

But he was disappointed. He heard voices and words, he saw movements, gestures, and glances, but since he now saw everything as through the eyes of an animal, he found nothing but a degenerate, dissembling mob of bestial fops, who seemed to be an unbeautiful mixture of all the animal species.

In despair Ziegler wandered about. He felt hopelessly ashamed of himself. He had long since thrown his red-lacquered cane into the bushes and his gloves after it. But when he threw away his hat, took off his shoes and his tie, and shaken with sobs pressed against the bars of the elk's cage, a crowd collected, the guards seized him, and he was taken away to an insane asylum.

*Translated from the German by Ralph Manheim.*

# The Argentine Ant

## Italo Calvino

*Italo Calvino began writing in the style of the Italian neo-realists: stark, detached stories set against the background of the war. He quickly changed his tone; with the publication of* The Cloven Viscount *in 1952 he began a series of wonderfully comic and fantastic novels which established him as Italy's most original writer of our time.* The Baron in the Trees (1957) *and* The Non-Existent Knight (1959) *continued to explore the legendary world of what Calvino calls 'our ancestors'.*

*'I've always preferred to choose a different route each time I start something new,' Calvino wrote in* The Castle of Crossed Destinies. *'The Argentine Ant' is quite unlike his other stories. The style has changed, but the same magical universe, Calvino's world of encroaching menace and free spirits, is still present.*

When we came to settle here we did not know about the ants. We'd be all right here, it seemed that day; the sky and green looked bright, too bright, perhaps, for the worries we had, my wife and I – how could we have guessed about the ants? Thinking it over, though, Uncle Augusto may have hinted at this once: 'You should see the ants over there . . . they're not like the ones here, those ants . . .' but that was just said while talking of something else, a remark of no importance, thrown in perhaps because as we talked we happened to notice some ants. Ants, did I say? No, just one single lost ant, one of those fat ants we have at home (they seem fat to me, now, the ants from my part of the country). Anyway, Uncle Augusto's hint did not seem to detract from the description he gave us of a region where, for some reason which he was unable to explain, life was easier and jobs were not too difficult to find, judging by all those who had set themselves up there – though not, apparently, Uncle Augusto himself.

On our first evening here, noticing the twilight still in the air after supper, realizing how pleasant it was to stroll along those lanes towards the country and sit on the low walls of a bridge, we began to understand why Uncle Augusto liked it. We understood it even more when we found a little inn which he used to frequent, with a garden behind, and squat, elderly characters like himself, though rather more blustering and noisy, who said they had been his friends; they too were men without a trade, I think, workers by the hour, though one said he was a clockmaker, but that may have been bragging; and we found they remembered Uncle Augusto by a nickname, which they all repeated among general guffaws; we noticed, too, rather stifled laughter from a woman in a knitted white sweater who was fat and no longer young, standing behind the bar.

And my wife and I understood what all this must have meant to Uncle Augusto; to have a nickname and spend light evenings joking on the bridges and watch for that knitted sweater to come from the kitchen and go out into the orchard, then spend an hour or two next day unloading sacks for the spaghetti factory; yes, we realized why he always regretted this place when he was back home.

I would have been able to appreciate all this too, if I'd been a youth and had no worries, or been well settled with the family. But as we were, with the baby only just recovered from his illness, and work still to find, we could do no more than notice the things that had made Uncle Augusto call himself happy; and just noticing them was perhaps rather sad, for it made us feel the difference between our own wretched state and the contented world around. Little things, often of no importance, worried us lest they should suddenly make matters worse (before we knew anything about the ants); the endless instructions given us by the owner, Signora Mauro, while showing us over the rooms, increased this feeling we had of entering troubled waters. I remember a long talk she gave us about the gas meter, and how carefully we listened to what she said.

'Yes, Signora Mauro . . . We'll be very careful, Signora Mauro . . . Let's hope not, Signora Mauro . . .'

So that we did not take any notice when (though we remember it clearly now) she gave a quick glance all over the wall as if reading something there, then passed the tip of her finger over it, and brushed it afterwards as if she had touched something wet, sandy, or dusty. She did not mention the word 'ants' though, I'm certain of that; perhaps she considered it natural for ants to be there in the walls and roof; but my wife and I think now that she was trying to hide them from us as long as possible and that all her chatter and instructions were just a smoke screen to make other things seem important, and so direct our attention away from the ants.

When Signora Mauro had gone, I carried the mattresses inside. My wife wasn't able to move the cupboard by herself and called me to help. Then she wanted to begin cleaning out the little kitchen at once and got down on her knees to start, but I said: 'What's the point, at this hour? We'll see to that tomorrow; let's just arrange things as best we can for tonight.' The baby was whimpering and very sleepy, and the first thing to do was get his basket ready and put him to bed. At home we use a long basket for babies, and had brought one with us here; we emptied out the linen with which we'd filled it, and found a good place on the window ledge, where it wasn't damp or too far off the ground should it fall.

Our son soon went to sleep, and my wife and I began looking over our new home (one room divided in two by a partition – four walls and a roof), which was already showing signs of our occupation. 'Yes, yes, whitewash it, of course we must whitewash it,' I replied to my wife, glancing at the ceiling and at the same time taking her outside by an elbow. She wanted to have another good look at the toilet, which was in a little shack to the left, but I wanted to take a turn over the surrounding plot; for our house stood on a piece of land consisting of two large flower, or rather rough seed beds, with a path down the middle covered with an iron trellis, now bare and made perhaps for some dried-up climbing plants of gourds or vines. Signora Mauro had said she would let me have this plot to cultivate as a kitchen garden, without asking any rent, as it had been abandoned for so long; she had not mentioned this to us today, however, and we had not said anything as there were already too many other irons in the fire.

My intention now, by this first evening's walk of ours around the plot, was to acquire a sense of familiarity with the place, even of ownership in a way; for the first time in our lives the idea of continuity seemed possible, of walking evening after evening among beds of seeds as our circumstances gradually improved. Of course I didn't speak of those things to my wife; but I was anxious to see whether she felt them too; and that stroll of ours did, in fact, seem to have the effect on her which I had hoped. We began talking quietly, between long pauses, and we linked arms – a gesture symbolic of happier times.

Strolling along like this we came to the end of the plot, and over the hedge saw our neighbour, Signor Reginaudo, busy spraying around the outside of his house with a pair of bellows. I had met Signor Reginaudo a few months earlier when I had come to discuss my tenancy with Signora Mauro. I went up to greet him and introduce him to my wife. 'Good evening, Signor Reginaudo,' I said. 'D'you remember me?'

'Of course I do,' he said. 'Good evening! So you are our new neighbour now?' He was a short man with spectacles, in pyjamas and a straw hat.

'Yes, neighbours, and among neighbours . . .' My wife began producing a few vague pleasant phrases, to be polite: it was a long time since I'd heard her talk like that; I didn't particularly like it, but it was better than hearing her complain.

'Claudia,' called our neighbour, 'come here. Here are the new tenants of the Casa Laureri!' I had never heard our new home called that (Laureri, I learned later, was a previous owner), and the name made it sound strange. Signora Reginaudo, a big woman, now came out, drying her hands on her apron; they were an easygoing couple and very friendly.

"And what are you doing there with those bellows, Signor Reginaudo?' I asked him.

'Oh . . . the ants . . . these ants . . .' he said, and laughed as if not wanting to make it sound important.

'Ants?' repeated my wife in the polite detached tone she used with strangers to give the impression she was paying attention to what they were saying; a tone she never used with me, not even, as far as I can remember, when we first met.

We then took a ceremonious leave of our neighbours. But we did not seem to be enjoying really fully the fact of having neighbours, and such affable and friendly ones with whom we could chat so pleasantly.

On getting home we decided to go to bed at once. 'D'you hear?' said my wife. I listened and could still hear the squeak of Signor Reginaudo's bellows. My wife went to the washbasin for a glass of water. 'Bring me one too,' I called, and took off my shirt.

'Oh!' she screamed. 'Come here!' She had seen ants on the faucet and a stream of them coming up the wall.

We put on the light, a single bulb for the two rooms. The stream of ants on the wall was very thick; they were coming from the top of the door, and might originate anywhere. Our hands were now covered with them, and we held them out open in front of our eyes, trying to see exactly what they were like, these ants, moving our wrists all the time to prevent them from crawling up our arms. They were tiny wisps of ants, in ceaseless movement, as if urged along by the same little itch they gave us. It was only then that a name came to my mind: 'Argentine ants', or rather, 'the Argentine ant', that's what they called them; and now I came to think of it I must have heard someone saying that this was the country of 'the Argentine ant'. It was only now that I connected the name with a sensation, this irritating tickle spreading in every direction, which one couldn't get rid of by clenching one's fists or rubbing one's hands together as there always seemed to be some stray ant running up one's arm, or on one's clothes. When the ants were crushed, they became little black dots that fell like sand, leaving a strong acid smell on one's fingers.

'It's the Argentine ant, you know . . .' I said to my wife. 'It comes from South America . . .' Unconsciously my voice had taken on the inflection I used when wanting to teach her something; as soon as I'd realized this I was sorry, for I knew that she could not bear that tone in my voice and always reacted sharply, perhaps sensing that I was never very sure of myself when using it.

But instead she scarcely seemed to have heard me; she was frenziedly trying to destroy or disperse that stream of ants on the wall, but all she managed to do was get numbers of them on herself and scatter others around. Then she put her hand under the faucet and tried to squirt water at them, but the ants went on walking over the wet surface; she couldn't even get them off by washing her hands.

'There, we've got ants in the house!' she repeated. 'They were here before, too, and we didn't see them!' – as if things would have been very different if we had seen them before.

I said to her: 'Oh, come, just a few ants! Let's go to bed now and think about it tomorrow!' And it occurred to me also to add: 'There, just a few Argentine ants!' because by calling them by the exact name I wanted to suggest that their presence was already expected, and in a certain sense normal.

But the expansive feeling by which my wife had let herself be carried away during that stroll around the garden had now completely vanished; she had become distrustful of everything again and made her usual face. Nor was going to bed in our new home what I had hoped; we hadn't the pleasure now of feeling we were starting a new life, only a sense of dragging on into a future full of new troubles.

'All for a couple of ants,' was what I was thinking – what I thought I was thinking, rather, for everything seemed different now for me too.

Exhaustion finally overcame our agitation, and we dozed off. But in the middle of the night the baby cried; at first we lay there in bed, always hoping it might stop and go to sleep again; this, however, never happened and we began asking ourselves: 'What can be the matter? What's wrong with him?' Since he was better he had stopped crying at night.

'He's covered with ants!' cried my wife, who had gone and taken him in her arms. I got out of bed too. We turned the whole basket upside down and undressed the baby completely. To get enough light for picking the ants off, half blind as we were from sleep, we had to stand under the bulb in the draught coming from the door. My wife was saying: 'Now he'll catch cold.' It was pitiable looking for ants on that skin which reddened as soon as it was rubbed. There was a stream of ants going along the windowsill. We searched all the sheets until we could not find another ant and then said: 'Where shall we put him to sleep now?' In our bed we were so squeezed up against each other we would have crushed him. I inspected the chest of drawers and, as the ants had not got into that, pulled it away from the wall, opened a drawer, and prepared a bed for the baby there. When we put him in he had already gone to sleep. If we had only thrown ourselves on the bed we would have soon dozed off again, but my wife wanted to look at our provisions.

'Come here, come here! God! Full of 'em! Everything's black! Help!' What was to be done? I took her by the shoulders. 'Come along, we'll think about that tomorrow, we can't even see now, tomorrow we'll arrange everything, we'll put it all in a safe place, now come back to bed!'

'But the food. It'll be ruined!'

'It can go to the devil! What can we do now? Tomorrow we'll destroy the ants' nest. Don't worry.'

But we could no longer find peace in bed, with the thought of those insects everywhere, in the food, in all our things; perhaps by now they had crawled up the legs of the chest of drawers and reached the baby . . . We got off to sleep as the cocks were crowing, but before long we had again started moving about and scratching ourselves and feeling we had ants in the bed; perhaps they had climbed up there, or stayed on us after all our handling of them. And so even the early morning hours were no refreshment, and we were very soon up, nagged by the thought of the things we had to do, and of the nuisance, too, of having to start an immediate battle against the persistent imperceptible enemy which had taken over our home.

The first thing my wife did was see to the baby: examine him for any bites (luckily, there did not seem to be any), dress and feed him – all this while moving around in the ant-infested house. I knew the effort of self-control she was making not to let out a scream every time she saw, for example, ants going around the rims of the cups left in the sink, and the baby's bib, and the fruit. She did scream, though, when she uncovered the milk: 'It's black!' On top there was a veil of drowned or swimming ants. 'It's all on the surface,' I said. 'One can skim them off with a spoon.' But even so we did not enjoy the milk; it seemed to taste of ants.

I followed the stream of ants on the walls to see where they came from. My wife was combing and dressing herself, with occasional little cries of hastily suppressed anger. 'We can't arrange the furniture till we've got rid of the ants,' she said.

'Keep calm. I'll see that everything is all right. I'm just going to Signor Reginaudo, who has that powder, and ask him for a little of it. We'll put the powder at the mouth of the ants' nest. I've already seen where it is, and we'll soon be rid of them. But let's wait till a little later as we may be disturbing the Reginaudos at this hour.'

My wife calmed down a little, but I didn't. I had said I'd seen the entrance to the ants' nest to console her, but the more I looked, the more new ways I discovered by which the ants came and went. Our new home, although it looked so smooth and solid on the surface, was in fact porous and honeycombed with cracks and holes.

I consoled myself by standing on the threshold and gazing at the plants with the sun pouring down on them; even the brushwood covering the ground cheered me, as it made me long to get to work on it: to clean everything up thoroughly, then hoe and sow and transplant. 'Come,' I said to my son. 'You're getting mouldy here.' I took him in my arms and went out into the 'garden'. Just for the pleasure of starting the habit of calling it that, I said to my wife:

'I'm taking the baby into the garden for a moment,' then corrected myself: 'Into our garden,' as that seemed even more possessive and familiar.

The baby was happy in the sunshine and I told him: 'This is a carob tree, this is a persimmon,' and lifted him up onto the branches. 'Now Papa will teach you to climb.' He burst out crying. 'What's the matter? Are you frightened?' But I saw the ants; the sticky tree was covered with them. I pulled the baby down at once. 'Oh, lots of dear little ants . . .' I said to him, but meanwhile, deep in thought, I was following the line of ants down the trunk, and saw that the silent and almost invisible swarm continued along the ground in every direction between the weeds. How, I was beginning to wonder, shall we ever be able to get the ants out of the house when over this piece of ground, which had seemed so small yesterday but now appeared enormous in relation to the ants, the insects formed an uninterrupted veil, issuing from what must be thousands of underground nests and feeding on the thick sticky soil and the low vegetation? Wherever I looked I'd see nothing at first glance and would be giving a sigh of relief when I'd look closer and discover an ant approaching and find it formed part of a long procession, and was meeting others, often carrying crumbs and tiny bits of material much larger than themselves. In certain places, where they had perhaps collected some plant juice or animal remains, there was a guarding crust of ants stuck together like the black scab of a wound.

I returned to my wife with the baby at my neck, almost at a run, feeling the ants climbing up from my feet. And she said: 'Look, you've made the baby cry. What's the matter?'

'Nothing, nothing,' I said hurriedly. 'He saw a couple of ants on a tree and is still affected by last night, and thinks he's itching.'

'Oh, to have this to put up with too!' my wife cried. She was following a line of ants on the wall and trying to kill them by pressing the ends of her fingers on each one. I could still see the millions of ants surrounding us on that plot of ground, which now seemed immeasurable to me, and found myself shouting at her angrily: 'What're you doing? Are you mad? You won't get anywhere that way.'

She burst out in a flash of rage too. 'But Uncle Augusto! Uncle Augusto never said a word to us! What a couple of fools we were! To pay any attention to that old liar!' In fact, what could Uncle

Augusto have told us? The word 'ants' for us then could never have even suggested the horror of our present situation. If he had mentioned ants, as perhaps he had – I won't exclude the possibility – we would have imagined ourselves up against a concrete enemy that could be numbered, weighed, crushed. Actually, now I think about the ants in our own parts, I remember them as reasonable little creatures, which could be touched and moved like cats or rabbits. Here we were face to face with an enemy like fog or sand, against which force was useless.

Our neighbour, Signor Reginaudo, was in his kitchen pouring liquid through a funnel. I called him from outside, and reached the kitchen window panting hard.

'Ah, our neighbour!' exclaimed Reginaudo. 'Come in, come in. Forgive this mess! Claudia, a chair for our neighbour.'

I said to him quickly: 'I've come . . . please forgive the intrusion, but you know, I saw that you had some of that powder . . . all last night, the ants . . .'

'Oh, oh . . . the ants!' Signora Reginaudo burst out laughing as she came in, and her husband echoed her with a slight delay, it seemed to me, though his guffaws were noisier when they came. 'Ha, ha, ha! . . . You have ants, too! Ha, ha, ha!'

Without wanting to, I found myself giving a modest smile, as if realizing how ridiculous my situation was, but now I could do nothing about it; this was in point of fact true, as I'd had to come and ask for help.

'Ants! You don't say so, my dear neighbour!' exclaimed Signor Reginaudo, raising his hands.

'You don't say so, dear neighbour, you don't say so!' exclaimed his wife, pressing her hands to her breast but still laughing with her husband.

'But you have a remedy, haven't you?' I asked, and the quiver in my voice could, perhaps, have been taken for a longing to laugh, and not for the despair I could feel coming over me.

'A remedy, ha, ha, ha!' The Reginaudos laughed louder than ever. 'Have we a remedy? We've twenty remedies! A hundred . . . each, ha, ha, ha, each better than the other!'

They led me into another room lined with dozens of cartons and tins with brilliant-coloured labels.

'D'you want some Profosfan? Or Mirminec? Or perhaps Tiobroflit? Or Arsopan in powder or liquid form?' And still roaring with laughter he passed his hand over sprinklers with pistons, brushes, sprays, raising clouds of yellow dust, tiny beads of moisture, and a smell that was a mixture of a pharmacy and an agricultural depot.

'Have you really something that does the job?' I asked.

They stopped laughing. 'No, nothing,' he replied.

Signor Reginaudo patted me on the shoulder, the Signora opened the blinds to let the sun in. Then they took me around the house.

He was wearing pink-striped pyjama trousers tied over his fat little stomach, and a straw hat on his bald head. She wore a faded dressing gown, which opened every now and then to reveal the shoulder straps of her undershirt; the hair around her big red face was fair, dry, curly, and dishevelled. They both talked loudly and expansively; every corner of their house had a story which they recounted, repeating and interrupting each other with gestures and exclamations as if each episode had been a huge joke. In one place they had put down Arfanax diluted two to a thousand and the ants had vanished for two days but returned on the third day; then he had used a concentrate of ten to a thousand, but the ants had simply avoided that part and circled around by the doorframe; they had isolated another corner with Crisotan powder, but the wind blew it away and they used three kilos a day; on the stairs they had tried Petrocid, which seemed at first to kill them at one blow, but instead it had only sent them to sleep; in another corner they put down Formikill and the ants went on passing over it, then one morning they found a mouse poisoned there; in one spot they had put down liquid Zimofosf, which had acted as a definite blockade, but his wife had put Italmac powder on top which had acted as an antidote and completely nullified the effect.

Our neighbours used their house and garden as a battlefield, and their passion was to trace lines beyond which the ants could not pass, to discover the new detours they made, and to try out new mixtures and powders, each of which was linked to the memory of some strange episode or comic occurrence, so that one of them only had to pronounce a name 'Arsepit! Mirxidol!' for them both to burst out laughing with winks and comments. As for the actual killing of the ants, that, if they had ever attempted it, they seemed to have given up, seeing that their efforts were useless; all they tried to do was bar them from certain passages and turn them aside, frighten them or keep them at bay. They always had a new labyrinth traced out with different substances which they prepared from day to day, and for this game ants were a necessary element.

'There's nothing else to be done with the creatures, nothing,' they said, 'unless one deals with them like the captain . . .'

'Ah, yes, we certainly spend a lot of money on these insecticides,' they said. 'The captain's system is much more economical, you know.'

'Of course, we can't say we've defeated the Argentine ant yet,' they added, 'but d'you really think that captain is on the right road? I doubt it.'

'Excuse me,' I asked. 'But who is the captain?'

'Captain Brauni; don't you know him? Oh, of course, you only arrived yesterday! He's our neighbour there on the right, in that little white villa . . . an inventor . . .' They laughed. 'He's invented a system to exterminate the Argentine ant . . . lots of systems, in fact. And he's still perfecting them. Go and see him.'

The Reginaudos stood there, plump and sly among their few square yards of garden which was daubed all over with streaks and splashes of dark liquids, sprinkled with greenish powder, encumbered with watering cans, fumigators, masonry basins filled with some indigo-coloured preparation; in the disordered flower beds were a few little rosebushes covered with insecticide from the tips of the leaves to the roots. The Reginaudos raised contented and amused eyes to the limpid sky. Talking to them, I found myself slightly heartened; although the ants were not just something to laugh at, as they seemed to think, neither were they so terribly serious, anything to lose heart about. 'Oh, the ants!' I now thought. 'Just ants after all! What harm can a few ants do?' Now I'd go back to my wife and tease her a bit: 'What on earth d'you think you've seen, with those ants . . . ?'

I was mentally preparing a talk in this tone while returning across our piece of ground with my arms full of cartons and tins lent by our neighbours for us to choose the ones that wouldn't harm the baby, who put everything in his mouth. But when I saw my wife outside the house holding the baby, her eyes glassy and her cheeks hollow, and realized the battle she must have fought, I lost all desire to smile and joke.

'At last you've come back,' she said, and her quiet tone impressed me more painfully than the angry accent I had expected. 'I didn't know what to do here any more . . . if you saw . . . I really didn't know . . .'

'Look, now we can try this,' I said to her, 'and this and this and this . . .' and I put down my cans on the step in front of the house, and at once began hurriedly explaining how they were to be used, almost afraid of seeing too much hope rising in her eyes, not wanting either to deceive or undeceive her. Now I had another idea: I wanted to go at once and see that Captain Brauni.

'Do it the way I've explained; I'll be back in a minute.'

'You're going away again? Where are you off to?'

'To another neighbour's. He has a system. You'll see soon.'

And I ran off towards a metal fence covered with ramblers bounding our land to the right. The sun was behind a cloud. I looked through the fence and saw a little white villa surrounded by a tiny neat garden, with gravel paths encircling flower beds, bordered by wrought iron painted green as in public gardens, and in the middle of every flower bed a little black orange or lemon tree.

Everything was quiet, shady, and still. I was standing there, uncertain whether to go away, when bending over a well-clipped hedge, I saw a head covered with a shapeless white linen beach hat, pulled forward to a wavy brim above a pair of steel-framed glasses on a spongy nose, and then a sharp flashing smile of false teeth, also made of steel. He was a thin, shrivelled man in a pullover, with trousers clamped at the ankles by bicycle clips, and sandals on his feet. He went up to examine the trunk of one of the orange trees, looking silent and circumspect, still with his tight-lipped smile. I looked out from behind the rambler and called: 'Good day, Captain.' The man raised his head with a start, no longer smiling, and gave me a cold stare.

'Excuse me, are you Captain Brauni?' I asked him. The man nodded. 'I'm the new neighbour, you know, who's rented the Casa Laureri . . . May I trouble you for a moment, since I've heard that your system . . .'

The captain raised a finger and beckoned me to come nearer; I jumped through a gap in the iron fence. The captain was still holding up his finger, while pointing with the other hand to the spot he was observing. I saw that hanging from the tree, perpendicular to the trunk, was a short iron wire. At the end of the wire hung a piece – it seemed to me – of fish remains, and in the middle was a bulge at an acute angle pointing downward. A stream of ants was going to and fro on the trunk and the wire. Underneath the end of the wire was hanging a sort of meat can.

'The ants,' explained the captain, 'attracted by the smell of fish, run across the piece of wire; as you see, they can go to and fro on it without bumping into each other. But it's that *V* turn that is dangerous; when an ant going up meets one coming down on the turn of the *V*, they both stop, and the smell of the gasoline in this can stuns them; they try to go on their way but bump into each other, fall, and are drowned in the gasoline. Tic, tic.' (This 'tic, tic' accompanied the fall of two ants.) 'Tic, tic, tic . . .' continued the captain with his steely, stiff smile; and every 'tic' accompanied the fall of an ant into the can where, on the surface of an inch of gasoline, lay a black crust of shapeless insect bodies.

'An average of forty ants are killed per minute,' said Captain Brauni, 'twenty-four hundred per hour. Naturally, the gasoline must be kept clean, otherwise the dead ants cover it and the ones that fall in afterward can save themselves.'

I could not take my eyes off that thin but regular trickle of ants dropping off; many of them got over the dangerous point and returned dragging bits of fish back with them by the teeth, but there was always one which stopped at that point, waved its antennae, and then plunged into the depths. Captain Brauni, with a fixed stare behind his lenses, did not miss the slightest movement of the insects; at every fall he gave a tiny uncontrollable start and the tightly stretched corners of his almost lipless mouth twitched. Often he could not resist putting out his hands, either to correct the angle of the wire or to stir the gasoline around the crust of dead ants on the sides, or even to give his instruments a little shake to accelerate the victims' fall. But this last gesture must have seemed to him almost like breaking the rules, for he quickly drew back his hand and looked at me as if to justify his action.

'This is an improved model,' he said, leading me to another tree from which hung a wire with a horsehair tied to the top of the *V*: the ants thought they could save themselves on the horsehair, but the smell of the gasoline and the unexpectedly tenuous support confused them to the point of making the fatal drop. This expedient of the horsehair or bristle was applied to many other traps that the captain showed me: a third piece of wire would suddenly end in a piece of thin horsehair, and the ants would be confused by the change and lose their balance; he had even constructed a trap by which the corner was reached over a bridge made of a half-broken bristle, which opened under the weight of the ant and let it fall in the gasoline.

Applied with mathematical precision to every tree, every piece of tubing, every balustrade and column in this silent and neat garden, were wire contraptions with cans of gasoline underneath, and the standard-trained rosebushes and latticework of ramblers seemed only a careful camouflage for this parade of executions.

'Aglaura!' cried the captain, going up to the kitchen door, and to me: 'Now I'll show you our catch for the last few days.'

Out of the door came a tall, thin, pale woman with frightened, malevolent eyes, and a handkerchief knotted down over her forehead.

'Show our neighbour the sack,' said Brauni, and I realized she was not a servant but the captain's wife, and greeted her with a nod and a murmur, but she did not reply. She went into the house and came out again dragging a heavy sack along the ground, her muscular arms showing a greater strength than I had attributed to her at first glance. Through the half-closed door I could see a pile of sacks like this one stacked about; the woman had disappeared, still without saying a word.

The captain opened the mouth of the sack; it looked as if it contained garden loam or chemical manure, but he put his arm in and brought out a handful of what seemed to be coffee grounds and let this trickle into his other hand; they were dead ants, a soft red-black sand of dead ants all rolled up in tight little balls, reduced to spots in which one could no longer distinguish the head from the legs. They gave out a pungent acid smell. In the house there were hundredweights, pyramids of sacks like this one, all full.

'It's incredible,' I said. 'You've exterminated all of these, so . . .'

'No,' said the captain calmly. 'It's no use killing the worker ants. There are ants' nests everywhere with queen ants that breed millions of others.'

'What then?'

I squatted down beside the sack; he was seated on a step below me and to speak to me had to raise his head; the shapeless brim of his white hat covered the whole of his forehead and part of his round spectacles.

'The queens must be starved. If you reduce to a minimum the number of workers taking food to the ants' nests, the queens will be left without enough to eat. And I tell you that one day we'll see the queens come out of their ants' nests in high summer and crawl around searching for food with their own claws . . . That'll be the end of them all, and then . . .'

He shut the mouth of the sack with an excited gesture and got up. I got up too. 'But some people think they can solve it by letting the ants escape.' He threw a glance towards the Reginaudos' little house, and showed his steel teeth in a contemptuous laugh. 'And there are even those who prefer fattening them up . . . That's one way of dealing with them, isn't it?'

I did not understand his second allusion.

'Who?' I asked. 'Why should anyone want to fatten them up?'

'Hasn't the ant man been to you?'

What man did he mean? 'I don't know,' I said. 'I don't think so . . .'

'Don't worry, he'll come to you too. He usually comes on Thursdays, so if he wasn't here this morning he will be in the afternoon. To give the ants a tonic, ha, ha!'

I smiled to please him, but did not follow. Then as I had come to him with a purpose I said: 'I'm sure yours is the best possible system. D'you think I could try it at my place too?'

'Just tell me which model you prefer,' said Brauni, and led me back into the garden. There were numbers of his inventions that I had not yet seen. Swinging wire which when loaded with ants made contact with a battery that electrocuted the lot; anvils and hammers covered with honey which clashed together at the release of a spring and squashed all the ants left in between; wheels with teeth which the ants themselves put in motion, tearing their brethren to pieces until they in their turn were churned up by the pressure of those coming after. I couldn't get used to the idea of so much art and perseverance being needed to carry out such a simple operation as catching ants; but I realized that the important thing was to carry on continually and methodically. Then I felt discouraged as no one, it seemed to me, could ever equal this neighbour of ours in terrible determination.

'Perhaps one of the simpler models would be best for us,' I said, and Brauni snorted, I didn't know whether from approval or sympathy with the modesty of my ambition.

'I must think a bit about it,' he said. 'I'll make some sketches.'

There was nothing else left for me to do but thank him and take my leave. I jumped back over the hedge; my house, infested as it was, I felt for the first time to be really my home, a place where one returned saying: 'Here I am at last.'

But at home the baby had eaten the insecticide and my wife was in despair.

'Don't worry, it's not poisonous!' I quickly said.

No, it wasn't poisonous, but it wasn't good to eat either; our son was screaming with pain. He had to be made to vomit; he vomited in the kitchen, which at once filled with ants again, and my wife had just cleaned it up. We washed the floor, calmed the baby, and put him to sleep in the basket, isolated him all around with insect powder, and covered him with a mosquito net tied tight, so that if he awoke he couldn't get up and eat any more of the stuff.

My wife had done the shopping but had not been able to save the basket from the ants, so everything had to be washed first, even the sardines in oil and the cheese, and each ant sticking to them picked off one by one. I helped her, chopped the wood, tidied the kitchen, and fixed the stove while she cleaned the vegetables. But it was impossible to stand still in one place; every minute either she or I jumped and said: 'Ouch! They're biting,' and we had to scratch ourselves and rub off the ants or put our arms and legs under the faucet. We did not know where to set the table; inside it would attract more ants, outside we'd be covered with ants in no time. We ate standing up, moving about, and everything tasted of ants, partly from the ones still left in the food and partly because our hands were impregnated with their smell.

After eating I made a tour of the piece of land, smoking a cigarette. From the Reginaudos' came a tinkling of knives and forks; I went over and saw them sitting at table under an umbrella, looking shiny and calm, with checked napkins tied around their necks, eating a custard and drinking glasses of clear wine. I wished them a good appetite and they invited me to join them. But around the table I saw sacks and cans of insecticide, and everything covered with nets sprinkled with yellowish or whitish powder, and that smell of chemicals rose to my nostrils. I thanked them and said I no longer had any appetite, which was true. The Reginaudos' radio was playing softly and they were chattering in high voices, pretending to celebrate.

From the steps which I'd gone up to greet them I could also see a piece of the Braunis' garden; the captain must already have finished eating; he was coming out of his house with his cup of coffee, sipping and glancing around, obviously to see if all his instruments of torture were in action and if the ants' death agonies were continuing with their usual regularity. Suspended between two trees I saw a white hammock and realized that the bony, disagreeable-looking Signora Aglaura must be lying in it, though I could see only a wrist and a hand waving a ribbed fan. The hammock ropes were suspended in a system of strange rings, which must certainly have been some sort of defence against the ants; or perhaps the hammock itself was a trap for the ants, with the captain's wife put there as bait.

I did not want to discuss my visit to the Braunis with the Reginaudos, as I knew they would only have made the ironic comments that seemed usual in the relations between our neighbours. I looked up at Signora Mauro's garden above us on the crest of the hills, and at her villa surmounted by a revolving weathercock. 'I wonder if Signora Mauro has ants up there too,' I said.

The Reginaudos' gaiety seemed rather more subdued during their meal; they only gave a little quiet laugh or two and said no more than: 'Ha, ha, she must have them too. Ha, ha, yes, she must have them, lots of them . . .'

My wife called me back to the house, as she wanted to put a mattress on the table and try to get a little sleep. With the mattress on the floor it was impossible to prevent the ants from crawling up, but with the table we just had to isolate the four legs to keep them off, for a bit at least. She lay down to rest and I went out, with the thought of looking for some people who might know of some job for me, but in fact because I longed to move about and get out of the rut of my thoughts.

But as I went along the road, things all around seemed different from yesterday; in every kitchen garden, in every house I sensed streams of ants climbing the walls, covering the fruit trees, wriggling their antennae towards everything sweet or greasy; and my newly trained eyes now noticed at once mattresses put outside houses to beat because the ants had got into them, a spray of insecticide in an old woman's hand, a saucerful of poison, and then, straining my eyes, the rows of ants marching imperturbably around the door frames.

Yet this had been Uncle Augusto's ideal countryside. Unloading sacks, an hour for one employer and an hour for another, eating on the benches at the inn, going around in the evening in search of gaiety and a mouth organ, sleeping wherever he happened to be, wherever it was cool and soft, what bother could the ants have been to him?

As I walked along I tried to imagine myself as Uncle Augusto and to move along the road as he would have done on an afternoon like this. Of course, being like Uncle Augusto meant first being like him physically: squat and sturdy, that is, with rather monkeylike arms that opened and remained suspended in mid-air in an extravagant gesture, and short legs that stumbled when he turned to look at a girl, and a voice which when he got excited repeated the local slang all out of tune with his own accent. In him body and soul were all one; how nice it would have been, gloomy and worried as I was, to have been able to move and joke like Uncle Augusto. I could always pretend to be him mentally, though, and say to myself: 'What a sleep I'll have in that hayloft! What a bellyful of sausage and wine I'll have at the inn!' I imagined myself pretending to stroke the cats I saw, then shouting 'Booo!' to frighten them unexpectedly; and calling out to the servant girls: 'Hey, would you like me to come and give you a hand, Signorina?' But the game wasn't much fun; the more I tried to imagine how simple life was for Uncle Augusto here, the more I realized he was a different type, a man who never had my worries: a home to set up, a permanent job to find, an ailing baby, a long-faced wife, and a bed and kitchen full of ants.

I entered the inn where we had already been, and asked the girl in the white sweater if the men I'd talked to the day before had come yet. It was shady and cool in there; perhaps it wasn't a place for ants. I sat down to wait for those men, as she suggested, and asked, looking as casual as I could: 'So you haven't any ants here, then?'

She was passing a duster over the counter. 'Oh, people come and go here, no one's ever paid any attention.'

'But what about you who live here all the time?'

The girl shrugged her shoulders. 'I'm grown up, why should I be frightened of ants?'

Her air of dismissing the ants, as if they were something to be ashamed of, irritated me more and more, and I insisted: 'But don't you put any poison down?'

'The best poison against ants,' said a man sitting at another table, who, I noted now, was one of those friends of Uncle Augusto's to whom I'd spoken the evening before, 'is this,' and he raised his glass and drank it in one gulp.

Others came in and wanted to stand me a drink as they hadn't been able to put me on to any jobs. We talked about Uncle Augusto and one of them asked: 'And what's that old *lingera* up to?' '*Lingera*' is a local word meaning vagabond and scamp, and they all seemed to approve of this definition of him and to hold my uncle in great esteem as a *lingera*. I was a little confused at this reputation being attributed to a man whom I knew to be in fact considerate and modest, in spite of his disorganized way of life. But perhaps this was part of the boasting, exaggerated attitude common to all these people, and it occurred to me in a confused sort of way that this was somehow linked with the ants, that pretending they lived in a world of great movement and adventure was a way of insulating themselves from petty annoyances.

What prevented me from entering their state of mind, I was thinking on my way home, was my wife, who had always been opposed to any fantasy. And I thought what an influence she had had on my life, and how nowadays I could never get drunk on words and ideas any more.

She met me on the doorstep looking rather alarmed, and said; 'Listen, there's a surveyor here.' I, who still had in my ears the sound of superiority of those blusterers at the inn, said almost without listening: 'What now, a surveyor . . . Well, I'll just . . .'

She went on: 'A surveyor's come to take measurements.' I did not understand and went in. 'Ah, now I see. It's the captain!'

It was Captain Brauni who was taking measurements with a yellow tape measure, to set up one of his traps in our house. I introduced him to my wife and thanked him for his kindness.

'I wanted to have a look at the possibilities here,' he said. 'Everything must be done in a strictly mathematical way.' He even measured the basket where the baby was sleeping, and woke it up. The child was frightened at seeing the yellow yardstick levelled over his head and began to cry. My wife tried to put him to sleep again. The baby's crying made the captain nervous, though I tried to distract him. Luckily, he heard his wife calling him and went out. Signora Aglaura was leaning over the hedge and shouting: 'Come here! Come here! There's a visitor! Yes, the ant man!'

Brauni gave me a glance and a meaningful smile from his thin lips, and excused himself for having to return to his house so soon. 'Now, he'll come to you too,' he said, pointing towards the place where this mysterious ant man was to be found. 'You'll soon see,' and he went away.

I did not want to find myself face to face with this ant man without knowing exactly who he was and what he had come to do. I went to the steps that led to Reginaudo's land; our neighbour was just at that moment returning home; he was wearing a white coat and a straw hat, and was loaded with sacks and cartons. I said to him: 'Tell me, has the ant man been to you yet?'

'I don't know,' said Reginaudo, 'I've just got back, but I think he must have, because I see molasses everywhere. Claudia!'

His wife leaned out and said: 'Yes, yes, he'll come to the Casa Laureri too, but don't expect him to do very much!'

As if I was expecting anything at all! I asked: 'But who sent this man?'

'Who sent him?' repeated Reginaudo. 'He's the man from the Argentine Ant Control Corporation, their representative who comes and puts molasses all over the gardens and houses. Those little plates over there, do you see them?'

My wife said: 'Poisoned molasses . . .' and gave a little laugh as if she expected trouble.

'Does it kill them?' These questions of mine were just a deprecating joke. I knew it all already. Every now and then everything would seem on the point of clearing up, then complications would begin all over again.

Signor Reginaudo shook his head as if I'd said something improper. 'Oh no . . . just minute doses of poison, you understand . . . ants love sugary molasses. The worker ants take it back to the nest and feed the queens with these little doses of poison, so that sooner or later they're supposed to die from poisoning.'

I did not want to ask if, sooner or later, they really did die. I realized that Signor Reginaudo was informing me of this proceeding in the tone of one who personally holds a different view but feels that he should give an objective and respectful account of official opinion. His wife, however, with the habitual intolerance of women, was quite open about showing her aversion to the molasses system and interrupted her husband's remarks with little malicious laughs and ironic comments; this attitude of hers must have seemed to him out of place or too open, for he tried by his voice and manner to attenuate her defeatism, though not actually contradicting her entirely – perhaps because in private he said the same things, or worse – by making little compensating remarks such as: 'Come now, you exaggerate, Claudia . . . It's certainly not very effective, but it may help . . . Then, they do it for nothing. One must wait a year or two before judging . . .'

'A year or two? They've been putting that stuff down for twenty years, and every year the ants multiply.'

Signor Reginaudo, rather than contradict her, preferred to turn the conversation to other services performed by the Corporation; and he told me about the boxes of manure which the ant man put in the gardens for the queens to go and lay their eggs in, and how they then came and took them away to burn.

I realized that Signor Reginaudo's tone was the best to use in explaining matters to my wife, who is suspicious and pessimistic by nature, and when I got back home I reported what our neighbour had said, taking care not to praise the system as in any way miraculous or speedy, but also avoiding Signora Claudia's ironic comments. My wife is one of those women who, when she goes by train, for example, thinks that the timetable, the make-up of the train, the requests of the ticket collectors, are all stupid and ill planned, without any possible justification, but to be accepted with submissive rancour; so though she considered this business of molasses to be absurd and ridiculous, she made ready for the visit of the ant man (who, I gathered, was called Signor Baudino), intending to make no protest or useless request for help.

The man entered our plot of land without asking permission, and we found ourselves face to face while we were still talking about him, which caused rather an unpleasant embarrassment. He was a little man of about fifty, in a worn, faded black suit, with rather a drunkard's face, and hair that was still dark, parted like a child's. Half-closed lids, a rather greasy little smile, reddish skin around his eyes and at the sides of his nose, prepared us for the intonations of a clucking, rather priestlike voice with a strong lilt of dialect. A nervous tic made the wrinkles pulsate at the corner of his mouth and nose.

If I describe Signor Baudino in such detail, it's to try to define the strange impression that he made on us; but was it strange, really? For it seemed to us that we'd have picked him out among thousands as the ant man. He had large, hairy hands; in one he held a sort of coffeepot and in the other a pile of little earthenware plates. He told us about the molasses he had to put down, and his voice betrayed a lazy indifference to the job; even the soft and dragging way he had of pronouncing the word 'molasses' showed both disdain for the straits we were in and the complete lack of faith with which he carried out his task. I noticed that my wife was displaying exemplary calm as she showed him the main places where the ants passed. For myself, seeing him move so hesitantly, repeating again and again those few gestures of filling the dishes one after the other, nearly made me lose my patience. Watching him like that, I realized why he had made such a strange impression on me at first sight: he looked like an ant. It's difficult to tell exactly why, but he certainly did; perhaps it was because of the dull black of his clothes and hair, perhaps because of the proportions of that squat body of his, or the trembling at the corners of his mouth corresponding to the continuous quiver of antennae and claws. There was, however, one characteristic of the ant which he did not have, and that was their continuous busy movement. Signor Baudino moved slowly and awkwardly, as he now began daubing the house in an aimless way with a brush dipped in molasses.

As I followed the man's movements with increasing irritation I noticed that my wife was no longer with me; I looked around and saw her in a corner of the garden where the hedge of the Reginaudos' little house joined that of the Braunis'. Leaning over their respective hedges were Signora Claudia and Signora Aglaura, deep in talk, with my wife standing in the middle listening. Signor Baudino was now working on the yard at the back of the house, where he could mess around as much as he liked without having to be watched, so I went up to the women and heard Signora Brauni holding forth to the accompaniment of sharp angular gestures.

'He's come to give the ants a tonic, that man has; a tonic, not poison at all!'

Signora Reginaudo now chimed in, rather mellifluously: 'What will the employees of the Corporation do when there are no more ants? So what can you expect of them, my dear Signora?'

'They just fatten the ants, that's what they do!' concluded Signora Aglaura angrily.

My wife stood listening quietly, as both the neighbours' remarks were addressed to her, but the way in which she was dilating her nostrils and curling her lips told me how furious she was at the deceit she was being forced to put up with. And I, too, I must say, found myself very near believing that this was more than women's gossip.

'And what about the boxes of manure for the eggs?' went on Signora Reginaudo. 'They take them away, but do you think they'll burn them? Of course not!'

'Claudia, Claudia!' I heard her husband calling. Obviously these indiscreet remarks of his wife made him feel uneasy. Signora Reginaudo left us with an 'Excuse me,' in which vibrated a note of disdain for her husband's conventionality, while I thought I heard a kind of sardonic laugh echoing back from over the other hedge, where I caught sight of Captain Brauni walking up the gravelled paths and correcting the slant of his traps. One of the earthenware dishes just filled by Signor Baudino lay overturned and smashed at his feet by a kick which might have been accidental or intended.

I don't know what my wife had brewing inside her against the ant man as we were returning towards the house; probably at that moment I should have done nothing to stop her, and might even have supported her. But on glancing around the outside and inside of the house, we realized that Signor Baudino had disappeared; and I remembered hearing our gate creaking and shutting as we came along. He must have gone that moment without saying goodbye, leaving behind him those bowls of sticky, reddish molasses, which spread an unpleasant sweet smell, completely different from that of the ants, but somehow linked to it, I could not say how.

Since our son was sleeping, we thought that now was the moment to go up and see Signora Mauro. We had to go and visit her, not only as a duty call but to ask her for the key of a certain storeroom. The real reasons, though, why we were making this call so soon were to remonstrate with her for having rented us a place invaded with ants without warning us in any way, and chiefly to find out how our landlady defended herself against this scourge.

Signora Mauro's villa had a big garden running up the slope under tall palms with yellowed fanlike leaves. A winding path led to the house, which was all glass verandas and dormer windows, with a rusty weathercock turning creakily on its hinge on top of the roof, far less responsive to the wind than the palm leaves which waved and rustled at every gust.

My wife and I climbed the path and gazed down from the balustrade at the little house where we lived and which was still unfamiliar to us, at our patch of uncultivated land and the Reginaudos' garden looking like a warehouse yard, at the Braunis' garden looking as regular as a cemetery. And standing up there we could forget that all those places were black with ants; now we could see how they might have been without that menace which none of us could get away from even for an instant. At this distance it looked almost like a paradise, but the more we gazed down the more we pitied our life there, as if living in that wretched narrow valley we could never get away from our wretched narrow problems.

Signora Mauro was very old, thin, and tall. She received us in half darkness, sitting on a high-backed chair by a little table which opened to hold sewing things and writing materials. She was dressed in black, except for a white mannish collar; her thin face was lightly powdered, and her hair drawn severely back. She immediately handed us the key she had promised us the day before, but did not ask if we were all right, and this – it seemed to us – was a sign that she was already exepcting our complaints.

'But the ants that there are down there, Signora . . .' said my wife in a tone which this time I wished had been less humble and resigned. Although she can be quite hard and often even aggressive, my wife is seized by shyness every now and then, and seeing her at these moments always makes me feel uncomfortable too.

I came to her support, and assuming a tone full of resentment, said: 'You've rented us a house, Signora, which if I'd known about all those ants, I must tell you frankly . . .' and stopped there, thinking that I'd been clear enough.

The Signora did not even raise her eyes. 'The house has been unoccupied for a long time,' she said. 'It's understandable that there are a few Argentine ants in it . . . they get wherever . . . wherever things aren't properly cleaned. You,' she turned to me, 'kept me waiting for four months before giving me a reply. If you'd taken the place immediately, there wouldn't be any ants by now.'

We looked at the room, almost in darkness because of the half-closed blinds and curtains, at the high walls covered with antique tapestry, at the dark, inlaid furniture with the silver vases and teapots gleaming on top, and it seemed to us that this darkness and these heavy hangings served to hide the presence of streams of ants which must certainly be running through the old house from foundations to roof.

'And here . . .' said my wife, in an insinuating, almost ironic tone, 'you haven't any ants?'

Signora Mauro drew in her lips. 'No,' she said curtly; and then as if she felt she was not being believed, explained: 'Here we keep everything clean and shining as a mirror. As soon as any ants enter the garden, we realize it and deal with them at once.'

'How?' my wife and I quickly asked in one voice, feeling only hope and curiosity now.

'Oh,' said the Signora, shrugging her shoulders, 'we chase them away, chase them away with brooms.' At that moment her expression of studied impassiveness was shaken as if by a spasm of physical pain, and we saw that, as she sat, she suddenly moved her weight to another side of the chair and arched in her waist. Had it not contradicted her affirmations I'd have said that an Argentine ant was passing under her clothes and had just given her a bite; one or perhaps several ants were surely crawling up her body and making her itch, for in spite of her efforts not to move from the chair it was obvious that she was unable to remain calm and composed as before – she sat there tensely, while her face showed signs of sharper and sharper suffering.

'But that bit of land in front of us is black with 'em,' I said hurriedly, 'and however clean we keep the house, they come from the garden in their thousands . . .'

'Of course,' said the Signora, her thin hand closing over the arm of the chair, 'of course it's rough uncultivated ground that makes the ants increase so; I intended to put the land in order four months ago. You made me wait, and now the damage is done; it's not only damaged you, but everyone else around, because the ants breed . . .'

'Don't they breed up here too?' asked my wife, almost smiling.

'No, not here!' said Signora Mauro, going pale, then, still holding her right arm against the side of the chair, she began making a little rotating movement of the shoulder and rubbing her elbow against her ribs.

It occurred to me that the darkness, the ornaments, the size of the room, and her proud spirit were this woman's defences against the ants, the reason why she was stronger then we were in face of them; but that everything we saw around us, beginning with her sitting there, was covered with ants even more pitiless than ours; some kind of African termite, perhaps, which destroyed everything and left only the husks, so that all that remained of this house were tapestries and curtains almost in powder, all on the point of crumbling into bits before her eyes.

'We really came to ask you if you could give us some advice on how to get rid of the pests,' said my wife, who was now completely self-possessed.

'Keep the house clean and dig away at the ground. There's no other remedy. Work, just work,' and she got to her feet, the sudden decision to say goodbye to us coinciding with an instinctive start, as if she could keep still no longer. Then she composed herself and a shadow of relief passed over her pale face.

We went down through the garden, and my wife said: 'Anyway, let's hope the baby hasn't waked up.' I, too, was thinking of the baby. Even before we reached the house we heard him crying. We ran, took him in our arms, and tried to quiet him, but he went on crying shrilly. An ant had got into his ear; we could not understand at first why he cried so desperately without any apparent reason. My wife had said at once: 'It must be an ant!' but I could not understand why he went on crying so, as we could find no ants on him or any signs of bites or irritation, and we'd undressed and carefully inspected him. We found some in the basket, however; I'd done my very best to isolate it properly, but we had overlooked the ant man's molasses – one of the clumsy streaks made by Signor Baudino seemed to have been put down on purpose to attract the insects up from the floor to the child's cot.

What with the baby's tears and my wife's cries, we had attracted all the neighbouring women to the house: Signora Reginaudo, who was really very kind and sweet, Signora Brauni, who, I must say, did everything she could to help us, and other women I'd never seen before. They all gave ceaseless advice; to pour warm oil in his ear, make him hold his mouth open, blow his nose, and I don't know what else. They screamed and shouted and ended by giving us more trouble than help, although they'd been a certain comfort at first; and the more they fussed around our baby the more bitter we all felt against the ant man. My wife had blamed and cursed him to the four winds of heaven; and the neighbours all agreed with her that the man deserved all that was coming to him, and that he was doing all he could to help the ants increase so as not to lose his job, and that he was perfectly capable of having done this on purpose, because now he was always on the side of the ants and not on that of human beings. Exaggeration, of course, but in all this excitement, with the baby crying, I agreed too, and if I'd laid hands on Signor Baudino then I couldn't say what I'd have done to him either.

The warm oil got the ant out; the baby, half stunned with crying, took up a celluloid toy, waved it about, sucked it, and decided to forget us. I, too, felt the same need to be on my own and relax my nerves, but the women were still continuing their diatribe against Baudino, and they told my wife that he could probably be found in an enclosure nearby, where he had his warehouse. My wife exclaimed: 'Ah, I'll go and see him, yes, go and see him and give him what he deserves!'

Then they formed a small procession, with my wife at the head and I, naturally, beside her, without giving any opinion on the usefulness of the undertaking, and other women who had incited my wife following and sometimes overtaking her to show her the way. Signora Claudia offered to hold the baby and waved to us from the gate; I realized later that Signora Aglaura was not with us either, although she had declared herself to be one of Baudino's most violent enemies, and that we were accompanied by a little group of women we had not seen before. We went along a sort of alley, flanked by wooden hovels, chicken coops, and vegetable gardens half full of rubbish. One or two of the women, in spite of all they'd said, stopped when they got to their own homes, stood on the threshold excitedly pointing out our direction, then retired inside calling to the dirty children playing on the ground, or disappeared to feed the chickens. Only a couple of women followed us as far as Baudino's enclosure; but when the door opened after heavy knocks by my wife we found that she and I were the only ones to go in, though we felt ourselves followed by the other women's eyes from windows or chicken coops; they seemed to be continuing to incite us, but in very low voices and without showing themselves at all.

The ant man was in the middle of his warehouse, a shack three-quarters destroyed, to whose one surviving wooden wall was tacked a yellow notice with letters a foot and a half long: 'Argentine Ant Control Corporation'. Lying all around were piles of those dishes for molasses and tins and bottles of every description, all in a sort of rubbish heap full of bits of paper with fish remains and other refuse, so that it immediately occurred to one that this was the source of all the ants in the area. Signor Baudino stood in front of us half smiling in an irritating questioning way, showing the gaps in his teeth.

'You,' my wife attacked him, recovering herself after a moment of hesitation. 'You should be ashamed of yourself! Why d'you come to our house and dirty everything and let the baby get an ant in his ear with your molasses?'

She had her fists under his face, and Signor Baudino, without ceasing to give that decayed-looking smile of his, made the movements of a wild animal trying to keep its escape open, at the same time shrugging his shoulders and glancing and winking around to me, since there was no one else in sight, as if to say: 'She's bats.' But his voice only uttered generalities and soft denials like: 'No . . . No . . . Of course not.'

'Why does everyone say that you give the ants a tonic instead of poisoning them?' shouted my wife, so he slipped out of the door into the road with my wife following him and screaming abuse. Now the shrugging and winking of Signor Baudino were addressed to the women of the surrounding hovels, and it seemed to me that they were playing some kind of double game, agreeing to be witnesses for him that my wife was insulting him; and yet when my wife looked at them they incited her, with sharp little jerks of the head and movements of the brooms, to attack the ant man. I did not intervene; what could I have done? I certainly did not want to lay hands on the little man, as my wife's fury with him was already roused enough; nor could I try to moderate it, as I did not want to defend Baudino. At last my wife in another burst of anger cried: 'You've done my baby harm!' grasped him by his collar, and shook him hard.

I was just about to throw myself on them and separate them; but without touching her, he twisted around with movements that were becoming more and more antlike, until he managed to break away. Then he went off with a clumsy, running step, stopped, pulled himself together, and went on again, still shrugging his shoulders and muttering phrases like: 'But what behaviour . . . But who . . .' and making a gesture as if to say 'She's crazy,' to the people in the nearby hovels. From those people, the moment my wife threw herself on him, there rose an indistinct but confused mutter which stopped as soon as the man freed himself, then started up again in phrases not so much of protest and threat as of complaint and almost of supplication or sympathy, shouted out as if they were proud proclamations. 'The ants are eating us alive . . . Ants in the bed, ants in the dishes, ants every day, ants every night. We've little enough to eat anyway and have to feed them too . . .'

I had taken my wife by the arm. She was still shaking her fist every now and again and shouting: 'That's not the last of it! We know who is swindling whom! We know whom to thank!' and other threatening phrases which did not echo back, as the windows and doors of the hovels on our path closed again, and the inhabitants returned to their wretched lives with the ants.

So it was a sad return, as could have been foreseen. But what had particularly disappointed me was the way those women had behaved. I swore I'd never go around complaining about ants again in my life. I longed to shut myself up in silent tortured pride like Signora Mauro – but she was rich and we were poor. I had not yet found any solution to how we could go on living in these parts; and it seemed to me that none of the people here, who seemed so superior a short time ago, had found it, or were even on the way to finding it either.

We reached home; the baby was sucking his toy. My wife sat down on a chair. I looked at the ant-infested field and hedges, and beyond them at the cloud of insect powder rising from Signor Reginaudo's garden; and to the right there was the shady silence of the captain's garden, with that continuous dripping of his victims. This was my new home. I took my wife and child and said: 'Let's go for a walk, let's go down to the sea.'

It was evening. We went along alleys and streets of steps. The sun beat down on a sharp corner of the old town, on grey, porous stone, with lime-washed cornices to the windows and roofs green with moss. The town opened like a fan, undulating over slopes and hills, and the space between was full of limpid air, copper-coloured at this hour. Our child was turning around in amazement at everything, and we had to pretend to take part in his marvelling; it was a way of bringing us together, of reminding us of the mild flavour that life has at moments, and of reconciling us to the passing days.

We met old women balancing great baskets resting on head pads, walking rigidly with straight backs and lowered eyes; and in a nuns' garden a group of sewing girls ran along a railing to see a toad in a basin and said: 'How awful!'; and behind an iron gate, under the wistaria, some young girls dressed in white were throwing a beach ball to and fro with a blind man; and a half-naked youth with a beard and hair down to his shoulders was gathering prickly pears from an old cactus with a forked stick; and sad and spectacled children were making soap bubbles at the window of a rich house; it was the hour when the bell sounded in the old folks' home and they began climbing up the steps, one behind the other with their sticks, their straw hats on their heads, each talking to himself; and then there were two telephone workers, and one was holding a ladder and saying to the other on the pole: 'Come on down, time's up, we'll finish the job tomorrow.'

And so we reached the port and the sea. There was also a line of palm trees and some stone benches. My wife and I sat down and the baby was quiet. My wife said: 'There are no ants here.' I replied: 'And there's a fresh wind; it's pleasant.'

The sea rose and fell against the rocks of the mole, making the fishing boats sway, and dark-skinned men were filling them with red nets and lobster pots for the evening's fishing. The water was calm, with just a slight continual change of colour, blue and black, darker farthest away. I thought of the expanses of water like this, of the infinite grains of soft sand down there at the bottom of the sea where the currents leave white shells washed clean by the waves.

*Translated from the Italian by Archibald Colquhoun.*

# The Lady on the Grey

## John Collier

*Dr Moreau's hobby of turning animals into people, and its reverse, Circe's hobby of turning people into animals, are frequent themes in John Collier's writings. His novel* His Monkey Wife or Married to a Chimp *(1930) is also a love story and its closing lines are a good example of the seriousness of Collier's fantasy: 'Under her long and scanty hair, he caught glimpses of a plum-blue skin. Into the depths of those all-dark lustrous eyes, his spirit slid with no sound of splash. She uttered a few low words, rapidly, in her native tongue. The candle, guttering beside the bed, was strangled in the grasp of a prehensile foot, and darkness received, like a ripple in velvet, the final happy sigh.'*

*Anthony Burgess called Collier 'a creator of very wayward miniatures, and all that can be done with these is to enjoy them.'*

Ringwood was the last of an Anglo-Irish family which had played the devil in County Clare for a matter of three centuries. At last all their big houses were sold up, or burned down by the long-suffering Irish, and of all their thousands of acres not a single foot remained. Ringwood, however, had a few hundred a year of his own, and if the family estates had vanished he at least inherited a family instinct which prompted him to regard all Ireland as his domain and to rejoice in its abundance of horses, foxes, salmon, game, and girls.

In pursuit of these delights, Ringwood ranged and roved from Donegal to Wexford through all the seasons of the year. There were not many hunts he had not led at some time or other on a borrowed mount, nor many bridges he had not leaned over through half a May morning, nor many inn parlours where he had not snored away a wet winter afternoon in front of the fire.

He had an intimate by the name of Bates, who was another of the same breed and the same kidney. Bates was equally long and lean, and equally hard-up, and he had the same wind-flushed bony face, the same shabby arrogance, and the same seignorial approach to the little girls in the cottages and cowsheds.

Neither of these blades ever wrote a letter, but each generally knew where the other was to be found. The ticket collector, respectfully blind as he snipped Ringwood's third-class ticket in a first-class compartment, would mention that Mr Bates had travelled that way only last Tuesday, stopping off at Killorglin for a week or two after the snipe. The chambermaid, coy in the clammy bedroom of a fishing inn, would find time to tell Bates that Ringwood had gone on up to Lough Corrib for a go at the pike. Policemen, priests, bagmen, gamekeepers, even the tinkers on the roads, would pass on this verbal *pateran*. Then, if it seemed his friend was on to a good thing, the other would pack up his battered kitbag, put rods and guns into their cases, and drift off to join in the sport.

So it happened that one winter afternoon, when Ringwood was strolling back from a singularly blank day on the bog of Ballyneary, he was hailed by a one-eyed horse dealer of his acquaintance, who came trotting by in a gig, as people still do in Ireland. This worthy told our friend that he had just come down from Galway, where he had seen Mr Bates, who was on his way to a village called Knockderry, and who had told him very particularly to mention it to Mr Ringwood if he came across him.

Ringwood turned this message over in his mind, and noted that it was a very particular one, and that no mention was made as to whether it was fishing or shooting his friend was engaged in, or whether he had met with some Croesus who had a string of hunters that he was prepared to lend. 'He certainly would have put a name to it if it was anything of that sort! I'll bet my life it's a pair of sisters he's got on the track of. It must be!'

At this thought, he grinned from the tip of his long nose like a fox, and he lost no time in packing his bag and setting off for this place Knockderry, which he had never visited before in all his roving up and down the country in pursuit of fur, feather, and girls.

He found it was a long way off the beaten track, and a very quiet place when he got to it. There were the usual low, bleak hills all around, and a river running along the valley, and the usual ruined tower up on a slight rise, girdled with a straggly wood and approached by the remains of an avenue.

The village itself was like many another: a few groups of shabby cottages, a decaying mill, half-a-dozen beer shops, and one inn at which a gentleman, hardened to rural cookery, might conceivably put up.

Ringwood's hired car deposited him there, and he strode in and found the landlady in the kitchen, and asked for his friend Mr Bates.

'Why, sure, your honour,' said the landlady, 'the gentleman's staying here. At least, he is, so to speak, and then, now, he isn't.'

'How's that?' said Ringwood.

'His bag's here,' said the landlady, 'and his things are here, and my grandest room taken up with them (though I've another every bit as good), and himself staying in the house best part of a week. But the day before yesterday he went out for a bit of a constitutional, and – would you believe it, sir? – we've seen neither hide nor hair of him since.'

'He'll be back,' said Ringwood. 'Show me a room, and I'll stay here and wait for him.'

Accordingly, he settled in, and waited all the evening, but Bates failed to appear. However, that sort of thing bothers no one in Ireland, and Ringwood's only impatience was in connection with the pair of sisters, whose acquaintance he was extremely anxious to make.

During the next day or two he employed his time in strolling up and down all the lanes and bypaths in the neighbourhood, in the hope of discovering these beauties, or else some other. He was not particular as to which it should be, but on the whole he would have preferred a cottage girl, because he had no wish to waste time on elaborate approaches.

It was on the second afternoon, just as the early dusk was falling he was about a mile outside the village and he met a straggle of muddy cows coming along the road, and a girl driving them. Our friend took a look at this girl, and stopped dead in his tracks, grinning more like a fox than ever.

This girl was still a child in her teens, and her bare legs were spattered with mud and scratched by brambles, but she was so pretty that the seignorial blood of all the Ringwoods boiled in the veins of their last descendant, and he felt an overmastering desire for a cup of milk. He therefore waited a minute or two, and then followed leisurely along the lane, meaning to turn in as soon as he saw the byre, and beg the favour of this innocent refreshment, and perhaps a little conversation into the bargain.

They say, though, that blessings never come singly, any more than misfortunes. As Ringwood followed his charmer, swearing to himself that there couldn't be such another in the whole county, he heard the fall of a horse's hoofs, and looked up, and there, approaching him at a walking pace, was a grey horse, which must have turned in from some bypath or other, because there certainly had been no horse in sight a moment before.

A grey horse is no great matter, especially when one is so urgently in need of a cup of milk, but this grey horse differed from all others of its species and colour in two respects. First, it was no sort of a horse at all, neither hack nor hunter, and it picked up its feet in a queer way, and yet it had an arch to its neck and a small head and a wide nostril that were not entirely without distinction. And, second – and this distracted Ringwood from all curiosity as to breed and bloodline – this grey horse carried on its back a girl who was obviously and certainly the most beautiful girl he had ever seen in his life.

Ringwood looked at her, and as she came slowly through the dusk she raised her eyes and looked at Ringwood. He at once forgot the little girl with the cows. In fact, he forgot everything else in the world.

The horse came nearer, and still the girl looked, and Ringwood looked, and it was not a mere exchange of glances, it was wooing and a marriage, all complete and perfect in a mingling of the eyes.

Next moment the horse had carried her past him, and, quickening its pace a little, it left him standing on the road. He could hardly run after it, or shout; in any case, he was too overcome to do anything but stand and stare.

He watched the horse and rider go on through the wintry twilight, and he saw her turn in at a broken gateway just a little way along the road. Just as she passed through, she turned her head and whistled, and Ringwood noticed that her dog had stopped by him, and was sniffing about his legs. For a moment he thought it was a smallish wolfhound, but then he saw it was just a tall, lean, hairy lurcher. He watched it run limping after her, with its tail down, and it struck him that the poor creature had had an appalling thrashing not so long ago; he had noticed the marks where the hair was thin on its ribs.

However, he had little thought to spare for the dog. As soon as he got over his first excitement, he moved on in the direction of the gateway. The girl was already out of sight when he got there, but he recognized the neglected avenue which led up to the battered tower on the shoulder of the hill.

Ringwood thought that was enough for the day, so he made his way back to the inn. Bates was still absent, but that was just as well. Ringwood wanted the evening to himself in order to work out a plan of campaign.

'That horse never cost two ten-pound notes of anybody's money,' said he to himself. 'So, she's not so rich. So much the better! Besides, she wasn't dressed up much; I don't know what she had on – a sort of cloak or something. Nothing out of Bond Street, anyway. And lives in that old tower! I should have thought it was all tumbled down. Still, I suppose there's a room or two left at the bottom. Poverty Hall! One of the old school, blue blood and no money, pining away in this godforsaken hole, miles away from everybody. Probably she doesn't see a man from one year's end to another. No wonder she gave me a look. God! If I was sure she was there by herself, I wouldn't need much of an introduction. Still, there might be a father or a brother or somebody. Never mind, I'll manage it.'

When the landlady brought in the lamp: 'Tell me,' said he, 'Who's the young lady who rides the cobby-looking, old-fashioned-looking grey?'

'A young lady, sir?' said the landlady doubtfully. 'On a grey?'

'Yes,' said he. 'She passed me on the lane up there. She turned in on the old avenue, going up to the tower.'

'Oh, Mary bless and keep you!' said the good woman. 'That's the beautiful Murrough lady you must have seen.'

'Murrough?' said he. 'Is that the name? Well! Well! Well! That's a fine old name in the West here.'

'It is so, indeed,' said the landlady. 'For they were kings and queens in Connaught before the Saxon came. And herself, sir, has the face of a queen, they tell me.'

'They're right,' said Ringwood. 'Perhaps you'll bring me in the whiskey and water, Mrs Doyle, and I shall be comfortable.'

He had an impulse to ask if the beautiful Miss Murrough had anything in the shape of a father or a brother at the tower, but his principle was, 'Least said, soonest mended,' especially in little affairs of this sort. So he sat by the fire, recapturing and savouring the look the girl had given him, and he decided he needed only the barest excuse to present himself at the tower.

Ringwood had never any shortage of excuses, so the next afternoon he spruced himself up and set out in the direction of the old avenue. He turned in the gate, and went along under the forlorn and dripping trees, which were so ivied and overgrown that the darkness was already thickening under them. He looked ahead for a sight of the tower, but the avenue took a turn at the end, and it was still hidden among the clustering trees.

Just as he got to the end, he saw someone standing there, and he looked again, and it was the girl herself, standing as if she was waiting for him. 'Good afternoon, Miss Murrough,' said he, as soon as he got into earshot. 'Hope I'm not intruding. The fact is, I think I had the pleasure of meeting a relation of yours, down in Cork, only last month . . .' By this time he had got close enough to see the look in her eyes again, and all this nonsense died away in his mouth, for this was something beyond any nonsense of that sort.

'I thought you would come,' said she.

'My god!' said he. 'I had to. Tell me – are you all by yourself here?'

'All by myself,' said she, and she put out her hand as if to lead him along with her.

Ringwood, blessing his lucky stars, was about to take it, when her lean dog bounded between them and nearly knocked him over.

'Down!' cried she, lifting her hand. 'Get back!' The dog cowered and whimpered, and slunk behind her, creeping almost on its belly. 'He's not a dog to be trusted,' she said.

'He's all right,' said Ringwood. 'He looks a knowing old fellow. I like a lurcher. Clever dogs. What? Are you trying to talk to me, old boy?'

Ringwood always paid a compliment to a lady's dog, and in fact the creature really was whining and whimpering in the most extraordinary fashion.

'Be quiet!' said the girl, raising her hand again, and the dog was silent.

'A cur,' said she to Ringwood. 'Did you come here to sing the praises of a half-bred cur?' With that, she gave him her eyes again, and he forgot the wretched dog, and she gave him her hand, and this time he took it and they walked toward the tower.

Ringwood was in seventh heaven. 'What luck!' thought he. 'I might at this moment be fondling that little farm wench in some damp and smelly cowshed. And ten to one she'd be snivelling and crying and running home to tell her mammy. This is something different.'

At that moment, the girl pushed open a heavy door, and, bidding the dog lie down, she led our friend through a wide, bare, stone-flagged hall and into a small vaulted room which certainly had no resemblance to a cowshed except perhaps it smelt a little damp and mouldy, as these old stone places so often do. All the same, there were logs burning on the open hearth, and a broad, low couch before the fireplace. For the rest, the room was furnished with the greatest simplicity, and very much in the antique style. 'A touch of the Cathleen Ni Houlihan,' thought Ringwood. 'Well, well! Sitting in the Celtic twilight, dreaming of love. She certainly doesn't make much bones about it.'

The girl sat down on the couch and motioned him down beside her. Neither of them said anything; there was no sound but the wind outside, and the dog scratching and whimpering timidly at the door of the chamber.

At last, the girl spoke. 'You are of the Saxon,' said she gravely.

'Don't hold it against me,' said Ringwood. 'My people came here in 1656. Of course, that's yesterday to the Gaelic League, but still I think we can say we have a stake in the country.'

'Yes, through its heart,' said she.

'Is it politics we're going to talk?' said he, putting an Irish turn to his tongue. 'You and I, sitting here in the firelight?'

'It's love you'd rather be talking of,' said she with a smile. 'But you're the man to make a byword and a mockery of the poor girls of Eire.'

'You misjudge me entirely,' said Ringwood. 'I'm the man to live alone and sorrowful, waiting for the one love, though it seemed something beyond hoping for.'

'Yes,' said she. 'But yesterday you were looking at one of the Connell girls as she drove her kine along the lane.'

'Looking at her? I'll go so far as to say I did,' said he. 'But when I saw you I forgot her entirely.'

'That was my wish,' said she, giving him both her hands. 'Will you stay with me here?'

'Ah, that I will!' cried he in rapture.

'Always?' said she.

'Always,' cried Ringwood. 'Always and for ever!' For he felt it better to be guilty of a slight exaggeration than to be lacking in courtesy to a lady. But as he spoke she fixed her eyes on him, looking so much as if she believed him that he positively believed himself.

'Ah,' he cried. 'You bewitch me!' And he took her in his arms.

He pressed his lips to hers, and at once he was over the brink. Usually he prided himself on being a pretty cool hand, but this was an intoxication too strong for him; his mind seemed to dissolve in sweetness and fire, and at last the fire was gone, and his senses went with it. As they failed, he heard her saying, 'For ever! For ever!' and then everything was gone and he fell asleep.

He must have slept some time. It seemed he was awakened by the heavy opening and closing of a door. For a moment, he was all confused and hardly knew where he was.

The room was now quite dark, and the fire had sunk to a dim glow. He blinked, and shook his ears, trying to shake some sense into his head. Suddenly he heard Bates talking to him, muttering as if he, too, was half asleep, or half drunk more likely. 'You *would* come here,' said Bates. 'I tried hard enough to stop you.'

'Hullo!' said Ringwood, thinking he must have dozed off by the fire in the inn parlour. 'Bates? God, I must have slept heavy! I feel queer. Damn it – so it was all a dream! Strike a light, old boy. It must be late. I'll yell for supper.'

'Don't, for heaven's sake,' said Bates, in his altered voice. 'Don't yell. She'll thrash us if you do.'

'What's that?' said Ringwood. 'Thrash us? What the hell are you talking about?'

At that moment a log rolled on the hearth, and a little flame flickered up, and he saw his long and hairy forelegs, and he knew.

# The Queen of Spades

## Alexander Pushkin

*Pushkin was a kind of Lord Byron who wrote better prose than Byron and was certainly as good a poet. He was master of the short story and the epic poem; his tragedy* Boris Godunov *broke the traditions of eighteenth-century Russian theatre. He was born in Moscow in 1799 and was shot dead in a duel on January 29, 1837.*

*'The Queen of Spades' deals with the confrontation between a gambler and a ghost. Ghosts can be a punishment for others, an instrument of the Fates to haunt the living – something of a mixture of the bogey under the bed and the ever-present Eye of Big Brother. I remember a terrifying Spanish nursery rhyme we used to sing:*

> *Watch it! God is watching you!*
> *Watch it now and then!*
> *Watch it! You will die one day,*
> *But you don't know when!*

*Pushkin's story is about an avenging ghost, but also about a passion, gambling, the game of the Fates. I knew a gambler once; we were in high school together. He believed that every game was a duel between himself and something else which he could not define. Each card was to him a living creature; each had specific qualities and a hidden soul, like the Greek gods. He feared some cards and loved others, and he believed in their reality as much as in that of an Argentina torn by a monstrous civil war. He died some ten years ago, shot down by soldiers while trying to hold up a petrol station near the frontier of Bolivia.*

# I

*When bleak was the weather*
*They would meet together*
*For cards – God forgive them!*
*Some would win, others lost,*
*And they chalked up the cost*
*In bleak autumn weather*
*When they met together.*

There was a card party in the rooms of Narumov, an officer of the Horse Guards. The long winter night had passed unnoticed and it was after four in the morning when the company sat down to supper. Those who had won enjoyed their food; the others sat absent-mindedly in front of empty plates. But when the champagne appeared conversation became more lively and general.

'How did you fare, Surin?' Narumov asked.

'Oh I lost, as usual. I must confess, I have no luck: I stick to *mirandole*, never get excited, never lose my head, and yet I never win.'

'Do you mean to tell me you were not once tempted to back the red the whole evening? Your self-control amazes me.'

'But look at Hermann,' exclaimed one of the party, pointing to a young officer of the Engineers. 'Never held a card in his hands, never made a bet in his life, and yet he sits up till five in the morning watching us play.'

'Cards interest me very much,' said Hermann, 'but I am not in a position to risk the necessary in the hope of acquiring the superfluous.'

'Hermann is a German: he's careful, that's what that is!' remarked Tomsky. 'But if there is one person I can't understand it is my grandmother, Countess Anna Fedotovna.'

'Why is that?' the guests cried.

'I cannot conceive how it is that my grandmother does not play.'

'But surely there is nothing surprising in an old lady in the eighties not wanting to gamble?' said Narumov.

'Then you don't know about her?'

'No, nothing, absolutely nothing!'

'Well, listen then. I must tell you that some sixty years ago my grandmother went to Paris and was quite the rage there. People would run after her to catch a glimpse of *la Vénus moscovite*; Richelieu was at her beck and call, and grandmamma maintains that he very nearly blew his brains out because of her cruelty to him. In those days ladies used to play faro. One evening at the Court she lost a very considerable sum to the Duke of Orleans. When she got home she told my grandfather of her loss while removing the beauty spots from her face and untying her farthingale, and commanded him to pay her debt. My grandfather, so far as I remember, acted as a sort of major-domo to my grandmother. He feared her like fire; however, when he heard of such a frightful gambling loss he almost went out of his mind, fetched the bills they owed and pointed out to her that in six months they had spent half a million roubles and that in Paris they had neither their Moscow nor their Saratov estates upon which to draw, and flatly refused to pay. Grandmamma gave him a box on the ear and retired to bed without him as a sign of her displeasure. The following morning she sent for her husband, hoping that the simple punishment had had its effect, but she found him as obdurate as ever. For the first time in her life she went so far as to reason with him and explain, thinking to rouse his conscience and arguing with condescension, that there were debts and debts, and that a prince was different from a coach-builder. But it was not a bit of good – grandfather just would not hear of it. "Once and for all, no!" Grandmamma did not know what to do. Among her close acquaintances was a very remarkable man. You have heard of Count Saint-Germain, about whom so many marvellous stories are told. You know that he posed as the Wandering Jew and claimed to have discovered the elixir of life and the philosopher's stone, and so on. People laughed at him as a charlatan, and Casanova in his *Memoirs* says that he was a spy. Be that as it may, Saint-Germain, in spite of the mystery that surrounded him, had a most dignified appearance and was a very amiable person in society. Grandmamma is still to this day quite devoted to his memory and gets angry if anyone speaks of him with disrespect. Grandmamma knew that Saint-Germain had plenty of money at his disposal. She decided to appeal to him, and wrote a note asking him to come and see her immediately. The eccentric old man came at once and found her in terrible distress. She described in the blackest colours her husband's inhumanity, and ended by declaring that she laid all her hopes on his friendship and kindness. Saint-Germain pondered. "I could oblige you with the sum you want," he said, "but I know that you would not be easy until you had repaid me, and I should not like to involve you in fresh trouble. There is another way out – you could win it back."

' "But, my dear count," answered grandmamma, "I tell you I have no money at all."

' "That does not matter," Saint-Germain replied. "Listen now to what I am going to tell you."

'And he revealed to her a secret which all of us would give a great deal to know . . .'

The young gamblers redoubled their attention. Tomsky lit his pipe, puffed away for a moment and continued:

'That very evening grandmamma appeared at Versailles, at the *jeu de la reine*. The Duke of Orleans kept the bank. Grandmamma lightly excused herself for not having brought the money to pay off her debt, inventing some little story by way of explanation, and began to play against him. She selected three cards and played them one after the other: all three won, and grandmamma retrieved her loss completely.'

'Luck!' said one of the party.

'A fairy tale!' remarked Hermann.

'Marked cards, perhaps,' put in a third.

'I don't think so,' replied Tomsky impressively.

'What!' said Narumov. 'You have a grandmother who knows how to hit upon three lucky cards in succession, and you haven't learnt her secret yet?'

'That's the deuce of it!' Tomsky replied. 'She had four sons, one of whom was my father; all four were desperate gamblers, and yet she did not reveal her secret to a single one of them, though it would not have been a bad thing for them, or for me either. But listen to what my uncle, Count Ivan Ilyich, used to say, assuring me on his word of honour that it was true. Tchaplitsky – you know him, he died a pauper after squandering millions – as a young man once lost three hundred thousand roubles, to Zorich, if I remember rightly. He was in despair. Grandmamma was always very severe on the follies of young men, but somehow she took pity on Tchaplitsky. She gave him three cards, which he was to play one after the other, at the same time exacting from him a promise that he would never afterwards touch a card so long as he lived. Tchaplitsky went to Zorich's; they sat down to play. Tchaplitsky staked fifty thousand on his first card and won; doubled his stake and won; did the same again, won back his loss and ended up in pocket . . .

'But, I say, it's time to go to bed: it is a quarter to six already.'

And indeed dawn was breaking. The young men emptied their glasses and went home.

# II

*'Il paraît que monsieur est décidément pour les suivantes.'*
*'Que voulez-vous, madame? Elles sont plus fraîches.'*

FROM A SOCIETY CONVERSATION

The old Countess X was seated before the looking-glass in her dressing-room. Three maids were standing round her. One held a pot of rouge, another a box of hairpins, and the third a tall cap with flame-coloured ribbons. The countess had not the slightest pretensions to beauty – it had faded long ago – but she still preserved all the habits of her youth, followed strictly the fashion of the seventies, and gave as much time and care to her toilette as she had sixty years before. A young girl whom she had brought up sat at an embroidery frame by the window.

'Good morning, *grand'maman!*' said a young officer, coming into the room. '*Bonjour, Mademoiselle Lise. Grand'maman*, I have a favour to ask of you.'

'What is it, Paul?'

'I want you to let me introduce to you a friend of mine and bring him to your ball on Friday.'

'Bring him straight to the ball and introduce him to me then. Were you at the princess's last night?'

'Of course I was! It was most enjoyable: we danced until five in the morning. Mademoiselle Yeletsky looked enchanting!'

'Come, my dear! What is there enchanting about her? She isn't a patch on her grandmother, Princess Daria Petrovna. By the way, I expect Princess Daria Petrovna must have aged considerably?'

'How do you mean, aged?' Tomsky replied absentmindedly. 'She's been dead for the last seven years.'

The girl at the window raised her head and made a sign to the young man. He remembered that they concealed the deaths of her contemporaries from the old countess, and bit his lip. But the countess heard the news with the utmost indifference.

'Dead! I didn't know,' she said. 'We were maids of honour together, and as we were being presented the Empress . . .'

And for the hundredth time the countess repeated the story to her grandson.

'Well, Paul,' she said at the end; 'now help me to my feet. *Lise*, where is my snuff-box?'

And the countess went with her maids behind the screen to finish dressing. Tomsky was left *à deux* with the young girl.

'Who is it you want to introduce?' Lizaveta Ivanovna asked softly.

'Narumov. Do you know him?'

'No. Is he in the army?'

'Yes.'

'In the Engineers?'

'No, Horse Guards. What made you think he was in the Engineers?'

The girl laughed and made no answer.

'Paul!' the countess called from behind the screen. 'Send me a new novel to read, only pray not one of those modern ones.'

'How do you mean, *grand'maman*?'

'I want a book in which the hero does not strangle either his father or his mother, and where there are no drowned corpses. I have a horror of drowned persons.'

'There aren't any novels of that sort nowadays. Wouldn't you like something in Russian?'

'Are there any Russian novels? . . . Send me something, my dear fellow, please send me something!'

'Excuse me, *grand'maman*: I must hurry . . . Good-bye, Lizaveta Ivanovna! I wonder, what made you think Narumov was in the Engineers?'

And Tomsky departed from the dressing-room.

Lizaveta Ivanovna was left alone. She abandoned her work and began to look out of the window. Soon, round the corner of a house on the other side of the street, a young officer appeared. Colour flooded her cheeks; she took up her work again, bending her head over her embroidery-frame. At that moment the countess came in, having finished dressing.

'Order the carriage, *Lise*,' she said, 'and let us go for a drive.'

Lizaveta Ivanovna rose from her embroidery-frame and began putting away her work.

'What is the matter with you, my child, are you deaf?' the countess cried. 'Be quick and order the carriage.'

'I will go at once,' the young girl answered quietly and ran into the ante-room.

A servant came in and handed the countess a parcel of books from Prince Paul Alexandrovich.

'Good! Tell him I am much obliged,' said the countess. '*Lise*, *Lise*, where are you off to?'

'To dress.'

'There is plenty of time, my dear. Sit down here. Open the first volume and read to me.'

The girl took the book and read a few lines.

'Louder!' said the countess. 'What is the matter with you, my dear? Have you lost your voice, or what? Wait a minute . . . Give me that footstool. A little closer. That will do!'

Lizaveta Ivanovna read two more pages. The countess yawned.

'Throw that book away,' she said. 'What nonsense it is! Send it back to Prince Paul with my thanks . . . What about the carriage?'

'The carriage is ready,' said Lizaveta Ivanovna, glancing out into the street.

'How is it you are not dressed?' the countess said. 'You always keep people waiting. It really is intolerable!'

Liza ran to her room. Hardly two minutes passed before the countess started ringing with all her might. Three maids rushed in at one door and a footman at the other.

'Why is it you don't come when you are called?' the countess said to them. 'Tell Lizaveta Ivanovna I am waiting.'

Lizaveta Ivanovna returned, wearing a hat and a pelisse.

'At last, my dear!' said the countess. 'Why the finery? What is it for? . . . For whose benefit? . . . And what is the weather like? Windy, isn't it?'

'No, your ladyship,' the footman answered, 'there is no wind at all.'

'You say anything that comes into your head! Open the window. Just as I thought: there is a wind, and a very cold one too! Dismiss the carriage. *Lise*, my child, we won't go out – you need not have dressed up after all.'

'And this is my life!' Lizaveta Ivanovna thought to herself.

Indeed, Lizaveta Ivanovna was a most unfortunate creature. 'Another's bread is bitter to the taste,' says Dante, 'and his staircase hard to climb'; and who should know the bitterness of dependence better than a poor orphan brought up by an old lady of quality? The countess was certainly not bad-hearted but she had all the caprices of a woman spoiled by society, she was stingy and coldly selfish, like all old people who have done with love and are out of touch with life around them. She took part in all the vanities of the fashionable world, dragged herself to balls, where she sat in a corner, rouged and attired after some bygone mode, like a misshapen but indispensable ornament of the ballroom. On their arrival the guests all went up to her and bowed low, as though in accordance with an old-established rite, and after that no one took any more notice of her. She received the whole town at her house, observing the strictest etiquette and not recognizing the faces of any of her guests. Her numerous servants, grown fat and grey in her entrance hall and the maids' quarters, did what they liked and vied with each other in robbing the decrepit old woman. Lizaveta Ivanovna was the household martyr. She poured out tea and was reprimanded for using too much sugar; she read novels aloud to the countess and was blamed for all the author's mistakes; she accompanied the countess on her drives and was answerable for the weather and the state of the roads. She was supposed to receive a salary, which was never paid in full and yet she was expected to be as well dressed as everyone else – that is, as very few indeed. In society she played the most pitiable role. Everybody knew her and nobody gave her any thought. At balls she danced only when someone was short of a partner, and the ladies would take her by the arm each time they wanted to go to the cloakroom to rearrange some detail of their toilette. She was sensitive and felt her position keenly, and looked about impatiently for a deliverer to come; but the young men, calculating in their empty-headed frivolity, honoured her with scant attention though Lizaveta Ivanovna was a hundred times more charming than the cold, brazen-faced heiresses they ran after. Many a time she crept away from the tedious, glittering drawing-room to go and weep in her humble little attic with its wallpaper screen, chest of drawers, small looking-glass and painted wooden bedstead, and where a tallow-candle burned dimly in a brass candlestick.

One morning, two days after the card party described at the beginning of this story and a week before the scene we have just witnessed – one morning Lizaveta Ivanovna, sitting at her embroidery-frame by the window, happened to glance out into the street and see a young Engineers officer standing stock-still gazing at her window. She lowered her head and went on with her work. Five minutes afterwards she looked out again – the young officer was still on the same spot. Not being in the habit of coquetting with passing officers, she looked out no more and went on sewing for a couple of hours without raising her head. Luncheon was announced. She got up to put away her embroidery-frame and, glancing casually into the street, saw the officer again. This seemed to her somewhat strange. After luncheon she went to the window with a certain feeling of uneasiness, but the officer was no longer there, and she forgot about him . . .

A day or so later, just as she was stepping into the carriage with the countess, she saw him again. He was standing right by the front door, his face hidden by his beaver collar; his dark eyes sparkled beneath his fur cap. Lizaveta Ivanovna felt alarmed, though she did not know why, and seated herself in the carriage, inexplicably agitated.

On returning home she ran to the window – the officer was standing in his accustomed place, his eyes fixed on her. She drew back, consumed with curiosity and excited by a feeling quite new to her.

Since then not a day had passed without the young man appearing at a certain hour beneath the windows of their house, and between him and her a sort of mute acquaintance was established. Sitting at her work she would sense his approach, and lifting her head she looked at him longer and longer every day. The young man seemed to be grateful to her for looking out: with the keen eyes of youth she saw the quick flush of his pale cheeks every time their glances met. By the end of the week she had smiled at him . . .

When Tomsky asked the countess's permission to introduce a friend of his the poor girl's heart beat violently. But hearing that Narumov was in the Horse Guards, not the Engineers, she regretted the indiscreet question by which she had betrayed her secret to the irresponsible Tomsky.

Hermann was the son of a German who had settled in Russia and who left him some small capital sum. Being firmly convinced that it was essential for him to make certain of his independence, Hermann did not touch even the interest on his income but lived on his pay, denying himself the slightest extravagance. But since he was reserved and ambitious his companions rarely had any opportunity for making fun of his extreme parsimony. He had strong passions and an ardent imagination, but strength of character preserved him from the customary mistakes of youth. Thus, for instance, though a gambler at heart he never touched cards, having decided that his means did not allow him (as he put it) 'to risk the necessary in the hope of acquiring the superfluous'. And yet he spent night after night at the card tables, watching with feverish anxiety the vicissitudes of the game.

The story of the three cards had made a powerful impression upon his imagination and it haunted his mind all night. 'Supposing,' he thought to himself the following evening as he wandered about Petersburg, 'supposing the old countess were to reveal her secret to me? Or tell me the three winning cards! Why shouldn't I try my luck . . . Get introduced to her, win her favour – become her lover, perhaps. But all that would take time, and she is eighty-seven. She might be dead next week, or the day after tomorrow even! . . . And the story itself? Is it likely? No, economy, moderation and hard work are my three winning cards. With them I can treble my capital – increase it sevenfold and obtain for myself leisure and independence!' Musing thus, he found himself in one of the main streets of Petersburg, in front of a house of old-fashioned architecture. The street was lined with carriages which followed one another up to the lighted porch. Out of the carriages stepped now the shapely little foot of a young beauty, now a military boot with clinking spur, or a diplomat's striped stockings and buckled shoes. Fur coats and cloaks passed in rapid procession before the majestic-looking concierge. Hermann stopped.

'Whose house is that?' he asked a watchman in his box at the corner.

'The Countess X's,' the man told him. It was Tomsky's grandmother.

Hermann started. The strange story of the three cards came into his mind again. He began walking up and down past the house, thinking of its owner and her wonderful secret. It was late when he returned to his humble lodgings; he could not get to sleep for a long time, and when sleep did come he dreamed of cards, a green baize table, stacks of bank-notes and piles of gold. He played card after card, resolutely turning down the corners, winning all the time. He raked in the gold and stuffed his pockets with bank-notes.

Waking late in the morning, he sighed over the loss of his fantastic wealth, and then, sallying forth to wander about the town again, once more found himself outside the countess's house. It was as though some supernatural force drew him there. He stopped and looked up at the windows. In one of them he saw a dark head bent over a book or some needlework. The head was raised. Hermann caught sight of a rosy face and a pair of black eyes. That moment decided his fate.

# III

*Vous m'écrivez, mon ange, des lettres de quatre pages plus vite que je ne puis les lire.*

FROM A CORRESPONDENCE

Lizaveta Ivanovna had scarcely taken off her hat and mantle before the countess sent for her and again ordered the carriage. They went out to take their seats. Just as the two footmen were lifting the old lady and helping her through the carriage door Lizaveta Ivanovna saw her Engineers officer standing by the wheel. He seized her hand; before she had recovered from her alarm the young man had disappeared, leaving a letter between her fingers. She hid it in her glove, and for the rest of the drive neither saw nor heard anything. It was the countess's habit when they were out in the carriage to ask a constant stream of questions: 'Who was that we met?' – 'What bridge is this?' – 'What does that signboard say?' This time Lizaveta Ivanovna returned such random and irrelevant answers that the countess grew angry with her.

'What is the matter with you, my dear? Have you taken leave of your senses? Don't you hear me or understand what I say? . . . I speak distinctly enough, thank heaven, and am not in my dotage yet!'

Lizaveta Ivanovna paid no attention to her. When they returned home she ran up to her room and drew the letter out of her glove: it was unsealed. She read it. The letter contained a declaration of love: it was tender, respectful and had been copied word for word from a German novel. But Lizaveta Ivanovna did not know any German and she was delighted with it.

For all that, the letter troubled her greatly. For the first time in her life she was embarking upon secret and intimate relations with a young man. His boldness appalled her. She reproached herself for her imprudent behaviour, and did not know what to do: ought she to give up sitting at the window and by a show of indifference damp the young man's inclination to pursue her further? Should she return his letter to him? Or answer it coldly and firmly? There was nobody to whom she could turn for advice: she had neither female friend nor preceptor. Lizaveta Ivanovna decided to reply to the letter.

She sat down at her little writing-table, took pen and paper – and began to ponder. Several times she made a start and then tore the paper across: what she had written seemed to her either too indulgent or too harsh. At last she succeeded in composing a few lines with which she felt satisfied. 'I am sure,' she wrote, 'that your intentions are honourable and that you had no wish to hurt me by any thoughtless conduct; but our acquaintance ought not to have begun in this manner. I return you your letter, and hope that in future I shall have no cause to complain of being shown a lack of respect which is undeserved.'

Next day, as soon as she saw Hermann approaching, Lizaveta Ivanovna got up from her embroidery-frame, went into the drawing-room, opened the little ventilating window and threw the letter into the street, trusting to the young officer's alertness. Hermann ran forward, picked the letter up and went into a confectioner's shop. Breaking the seal, he found his own letter and Lizaveta Ivanovna's reply. It was just what he had expected and he returned home engrossed in his plot.

Three days after this a sharp-eyed young person brought Lizaveta Ivanovna a note from a milliner's establishment. Lizaveta Ivanovna opened it uneasily, fearing it was a demand for money, and suddenly recognized Hermann's handwriting.

'You have made a mistake, my dear,' she said. 'This note is not for me.'

'Oh yes it is for you!' retorted the girl boldly, not troubling to conceal a knowing smile. 'Please read it.'

Lizaveta Ivanovna glanced at the letter. In it Hermann wanted her to meet him.

'Impossible!' she cried, alarmed at the request, at its coming so soon, and at the means employed to transmit it. 'I am sure this was not addressed to me.' And she tore the letter into fragments.

'If the letter was not for you, why did you tear it up?' said the girl. 'I would have returned it to the sender.'

'Be good enough, my dear,' said Lizaveta Ivanovna, flushing
crimson at her remark, 'not to bring me any more letters. And tell
the person who sent you that he ought to be ashamed . . .'

But Hermann did not give in. Every day Lizaveta Ivanovna
received a letter from him by one means or another. They were no
longer translated from the German. Hermann wrote them inspired
by passion and in a style which was his own: they reflected both
his inexorable desire and the disorder of an unbridled imagination.
Lizaveta Ivanovna no longer thought of returning them: she drank
them in eagerly and took to answering – and the notes she sent
grew longer and more affectionate every hour. At last she threw out
of the window to him the following letter:

*There is a ball tonight at the Embassy. The countess will be there.
We shall stay until about two o'clock. Here is an opportunity for
you to see me alone. As soon as the countess is away the servants
are sure to go to their quarters, leaving the concierge in the hall
but he usually retires to his lodge. Come at half past eleven. Walk
straight up the stairs. If you meet anyone in the ante-room, ask if
the countess is at home. They will say 'No', but there will be no
help for it – you will have to go away. But probably you will not
meet anyone. The maids all sit together in the one room. Turn to
the left out of the ante-room and keep straight on until you reach
the countess's bedroom. In the bedroom, behind a screen, you will
find two small doors: the one on the right leads into the study where
the countess never goes; and the other on the left opens into a
passage with a narrow winding staircase up to my room.*

Hermann waited for the appointed hour like a tiger trembling for
its prey. By ten o'clock in the evening he was already standing
outside the countess's house. It was a frightful night: the wind
howled, wet snow fell in big flakes; the street lamps burned dimly;
the streets were deserted. From time to time a sledge drawn by a
sorry-looking hack passed by, the driver on the watch for a belated
fare. Hermann stood there without his great-coat, feeling neither
the wind nor the snow. At last the countess's carriage was brought
round. Hermann saw the old woman wrapped in sables being lifted
into the vehicle by two footmen; then Liza in a light cloak, with
natural flowers in her hair, flitted by. The carriage doors banged.
The vehicle rolled heavily over the wet snow. The concierge closed
the street-door. The lights in the windows went out. Hermann

started to walk to and fro outside the deserted house; he went up to a street-lamp and glanced at his watch: it was twenty minutes past eleven. He stood still by the lamp-post, his eyes fixed on the hand of the watch. Precisely at half past eleven Hermann walked up the steps of the house and entered the brightly lit vestibule. The concierge was not there. Hermann ran up the stairs, opened the door of the ante-room and saw a footman asleep in a soiled, old-fashioned armchair by the side of a lamp. With a light, firm tread Hermann passed quickly by him. The ballroom and drawing-room were in darkness but the lamp in the ante-room shed a dim light into them. Hermann entered the bedroom. Ancient icons filled the icon-stand before which burned a golden lamp. Armchairs upholstered in faded damask and sofas with down cushions, the tassels of which had lost their gilt, were ranged with depressing symmetry round the walls hung with Chinese wallpaper. On one of the walls were two portraits painted in Paris by Madame Lebrun: the first of a stout, red-faced man of some forty years of age, in a light-green uniform with a star on his breast; the other – a beautiful young woman with an aquiline nose and a rose in the powdered hair drawn back over her temples. Every corner was crowded with porcelain shepherdesses, clocks made by the celebrated Leroy, little boxes, roulettes, fans and all the thousand and one playthings invented for ladies of fashion at the end of the last century together with Montgolfier's balloon and Mesmer's magnetism. Hermann stepped behind the screen. A small iron bedstead stood there; to the right was the door into the study – to the left, the other door into the passage. Hermann opened it and saw the narrow winding staircase leading to poor little Liza's room. But he turned about and went into the dark study.

The time passed slowly. Everything was quiet. The drawing-room clock struck twelve; the clocks in the other rooms chimed twelve, one after the other, and all was still again. Hermann stood leaning against the cold stove. He was quite calm: his heart beat evenly, like that of a man resolved upon a dangerous but inevitable undertaking. The clocks struck one, and then two, and he heard the distant rumble of a carriage. In spite of himself he was overcome with agitation. The carriage drove up to the house and stopped. He heard the clatter of the carriage-steps being lowered. In the house all was commotion. Servants ran to and fro, there was a confusion of voices, and lights appeared everywhere. Three ancient lady's

maids bustled into the bedroom, followed by the countess who, half
dead with fatigue, sank into a Voltaire armchair. Hermann watched
through a crack in the door. Lizaveta Ivanovna passed close by him
and he heard her footsteps hurrying up the stairs to her room. For
a moment something akin to remorse assailed him but he quickly
hardened his heart again.

The countess began undressing before the looking-glass. Her
maids took off the cap trimmed with roses and lifted the powdered
wig from her grey, closely-cropped head. Pins showered about her.
The silver-trimmed yellow dress fell at her puffy feet. Hermann
witnessed the hideous mysteries of her toilet; at last the countess
put on bed jacket and night-cap, and in this attire, more suited to
her age, she seemed less horrible and ugly.

Like most old people the countess suffered from sleeplessness.
Having undressed, she sat down in a big armchair by the window
and dismissed her maids. They took away the candles, leaving only
the lamp before the icons to light the room. The countess sat there,
her skin sallow with age, her flabby lips twitching, her body swaying
to and fro. Her dim eyes were completely vacant and looking at her
one might have imagined that the dreadful old woman was rocking
her body not from choice but owing to some secret galvanic
mechanism.

Suddenly an inexplicable change came over the death-like face.
The lips ceased to move, the eyes brightened: before the countess
stood a strange young man.

'Do not be alarmed, for heaven's sake, do not be alarmed!' he
said in a low, clear voice. 'I have no intention of doing you any
harm, I have come to beg a favour of you.'

The old woman stared at him in silence, as if she had not heard.
Hermann thought she must be deaf and bending down to her ear
he repeated what he had just said. The old woman remained silent
as before.

'You can ensure the happiness of my whole life,' Hermann went
on, 'and at no cost to yourself. I know that you can name three
cards in succession . . .'

Hermann stopped. The countess appeared to have grasped what
he wanted and to be seeking words to frame her answer.

'It was a joke,' she said at last. 'I swear to you it was a joke.'

'No, madam,' Hermann retorted angrily. 'Remember
Tchaplitsky, and how you enabled him to win back his loss.'

The countess was plainly perturbed. Her face expressed profound agitation; but soon she relapsed into her former impassivity.

'Can you not tell me those three winning cards?' Hermann went on.

The countess said nothing. Hermann continued:

'For whom would you keep your secret? For your grandsons? They are rich enough already: they don't appreciate the value of money. Your three cards would not help a spendthrift. A man who does not take care of his inheritance will die a beggar though all the demons of the world were at his command. I am not a spendthrift: I know the value of money. Your three cards would not be wasted on me. Well? . . .

He paused, feverishly waiting for her reply. She was silent. Hermann fell on his knees.

'If your heart has ever known what it is to love, if you can remember the ecstasies of love, if you have ever smiled tenderly at the cry of your new-born son, if any human feeling has ever stirred in your breast, I appeal to you as wife, beloved one, mother – I implore you by all that is holy in life not to reject my prayer: tell me your secret. Of what use is it to you? Perhaps it is bound up with some terrible sin, with the loss of eternal salvation, with some bargain with the devil . . . Reflect – you are old: you have not much longer to live, and I am ready to take your sin upon my soul. Only tell me your secret. Remember that a man's happiness is in your hands; that not only I, but my children and my children's children will bless your memory and hold it sacred . . .'

The old woman answered not a word.

Hermann rose to his feet.

'You old hag!' he said, grinding his teeth. 'Then I will make you speak . . .'

With these words he drew a pistol from his pocket. At the sight of the pistol the countess for the second time showed signs of agitation. Her head shook and she raised a hand as though to protect herself from the shot . . . Then she fell back . . . and was still.

'Come, an end to this childish nonsense!' said Hermann, seizing her by the arm. 'I ask you for the last time – will you tell me those three cards? Yes or no?'

The countess made no answer. Hermann saw that she was dead.

# IV

*7 mai 18—*
*Homme sans mœurs et sans religion!*

FROM A CORRESPONDENCE

Lizaveta Ivanovna was sitting in her room, still in her ball dress, lost in thought. On returning home she had made haste to dismiss the sleepy maid who reluctantly offered to help her, saying that she would undress herself, and with trembling heart had gone to her own room, expecting to find Hermann and hoping that she would not find him. A glance convinced her he was not there, and she thanked fate for having prevented their meeting. She sat down without undressing and began to recall the circumstances that had led her so far in so short a time. It was not three weeks since she had first caught sight of the young man from the window – and yet she was carrying on a correspondence with him, and he had already succeeded in inducing her to agree to a nocturnal tryst! She knew his name only because he had signed some of his letters; she had never spoken to him, did not know the sound of his voice, had never heard him mentioned . . . until that evening. Strange to say, that very evening at the ball, Tomsky, piqued with the young Princess Pauline for flirting with somebody else instead of with him as she usually did, decided to revenge himself by a show of indifference. He asked Lizaveta Ivanovna to be his partner and danced the interminable mazurka with her. And all the time he kept teasing her about her partiality for officers of the Engineers, assuring her that he knew far more than she could suppose, and some of his sallies so found their mark that several times Lizaveta Ivanovna thought he must know her secret.

'Who told you all this?' she asked, laughing.

'A friend of someone you know,' Tomsky answered, 'a very remarkable person.'

'And who is this remarkable man?'

'His name is Hermann.'

Lizaveta Ivanovna said nothing; but her hands and feet turned to ice.

'This Hermann,' continued Tomsky, 'is a truly romantic figure: he has the profile of a Napoleon and the soul of a Mephistopheles.

I think there must be at least three crimes on his conscience. How pale you look!'

'I have a bad headache . . . Well, and what did this Hermann – or whatever his name is – tell you?'

'Hermann is very annoyed with his friend: he says that in his place he would act quite differently . . . I suspect in fact that Hermann has designs upon you himself; at any rate he listens to his friend's ecstatic exclamations with anything but indifference.'

'But where has he seen me?'

'In church, perhaps, or when you were out walking . . . heaven only knows! – in your own room, maybe, while you were asleep, for there is nothing he—'

Three ladies coming up to invite Tomsky to choose between *'oubli ou regret?'* interrupted the conversation which had become so painfully interesting to Lizaveta Ivanovna.

The lady chosen by Tomsky was the Princess Pauline herself. She succeeded in effecting a reconciliation with him while they danced an extra turn and spun round once more before she was conducted to her chair. When he returned to his place neither Hermann nor Lizaveta Ivanovna was in Tomsky's thoughts. Lizaveta Ivanovna longed to resume the interrupted conversation but the mazurka came to an end and shortly afterwards the old countess took her departure.

Tomsky's words were nothing more than the usual small-talk of the ballroom; but they sank deep into the girl's romantic heart. The portrait sketched by Tomsky resembled the picture she had herself drawn, and thanks to the novels of the day the commonplace figure both terrified and fascinated her. She sat there with her bare arms crossed and with her head, still adorned with flowers, sunk upon her naked bosom . . . Suddenly the door opened and Hermann came in . . . She shuddered.

'Where were you?' she asked in a frightened whisper.

'In the old countess's bedroom,' Hermann answered. 'I have just left her. The countess is dead.'

'Merciful heavens! . . . what are you saying?'

'And I think,' added Hermann, 'that I am the cause of her death.'

Lizaveta darted a glance at him, and heard Tomsky's words echo in her soul: '. . . there must be at least three crimes on his conscience'. Hermann sat down in the window beside her and related all that had happened.

Lizaveta Ivanovna listened to him aghast. So all those passionate letters, those ardent pleas, the bold, determined pursuit had not been inspired by love! Money! – that was what his soul craved! It was not she who could satisfy his desires and make him happy! Poor child, she had been nothing but the blind tool of a thief, of the murderer of her aged benefactress! . . . She wept bitterly in a vain agony of repentance. Hermann watched in silence: he too was suffering torment; but neither the poor girl's tears nor her indescribable charm in her grief touched his hardened soul. He felt no pricking of conscience at the thought of the dead old woman. One thing only horrified him: the irreparable loss of the secret which was to have brought him wealth.

'You are a monster!' said Lizaveta Ivanovna at last.

'I did not mean her to die,' Hermann answered. 'My pistol was not loaded.'

Both were silent.

Morning came. Lizaveta Ivanovna blew out the candle which had burned down. A pale light illumined the room. She wiped her tear-stained eyes and looked up at Hermann: he was sitting on the window-sill with his arms folded, a menacing frown on his face. In this attitude he bore a remarkable likeness to the portrait of Napoleon. The likeness struck even Lizaveta Ivanovna.

'How shall I get you out of the house?' she said at last. 'I had thought of taking you down the secret staircase but that means going through the bedroom, and I am afraid.'

'Tell me how to find this secret staircase – I will go alone.'

Lizaveta rose, took a key from the chest of drawers and gave it to Hermann with precise instructions. Hermann pressed her cold, unresponsive hand, kissed her bowed head and left her.

He walked down the winding stairway and entered the countess's bedroom again. The dead woman sat as though turned to stone. Her face wore a look of profound tranquillity. Hermann stood in front of her and gazed long and earnestly at her, as though trying to convince himself of the terrible truth. Then he went into the study, felt behind the tapestry for the door and began to descend the dark stairway, excited by strange emotions. 'Maybe some sixty years ago, at this very hour,' he thought, 'some happy youth – long since turned to dust – was stealing up this staircase into that very bedroom, in an embroidered tunic, his hair dressed *à l'oiseau royal*, pressing his three-cornered hat to his breast; and today the heart of his aged mistress has ceased to beat . . .'

At the bottom of the stairs Hermann saw a door which he opened with the same key, and found himself in a passage leading to the street.

# V

*That night the dead Baroness von W. appeared before me. She was all in white and said: 'How do you do, Mr Councillor?'*

SWEDENBORG

Three days after that fatal night, at nine o'clock in the morning, Hermann repaired to the Convent of — , where the last respects were to be paid to the mortal remains of the dead countess. Though he felt no remorse he could not altogether stifle the voice of conscience which kept repeating to him: 'You are the old woman's murderer!' Having very little religious faith, he was exceedingly superstitious. Believing that the dead countess might exercise a malignant influence on his life, he decided to go to her funeral to beg and obtain her forgiveness.

The church was full. Hermann had difficulty in making his way through the crowd. The coffin rested on a rich catafalque beneath a canopy of velvet. The dead woman lay with her hands crossed on her breast, in a lace cap and a white satin robe. Around the bier stood the members of her household: servants in black clothes, with armorial ribbons on their shoulders and lighted candles in their hands; relatives in deep mourning – children, grandchildren and great-grandchildren. No one wept: tears would have been *une affectation*. The countess was so old that her death could not have taken anybody by surprise, and her family had long ceased to think of her as one of the living. A famous preacher delivered the funeral oration. In simple and touching phrases he described the peaceful passing of the saintly woman whose long life had been a quiet, touching preparation for a Christian end. 'The angel of death,' he declared, 'found her vigilant in devout meditation, awaiting the midnight coming of the bridegroom.' The service was concluded in melancholy decorum. First the relations went forward to bid farewell of the corpse. They were followed by a long procession of all those who had come to render their last homage to one who had for so many years been a participator in their frivolous amusements. After them came the members of the countess's household. The last of these was an old woman-retainer the same age as the deceased. Two young girls supported her by the arms. She had not strength to prostrate herself – and she was the only one to shed tears as she kissed her mistress's cold hand. Hermann decided to approach the coffin after her. He knelt down on the cold stone strewed with branches of spruce-fir, and remained in that position for some minutes; at last he rose to his feet and, pale as the deceased herself, walked up the steps of the catafalque and bent over the corpse . . . At that moment it seemed to him that the dead woman darted a mocking look at him and winked her eye. Hermann drew back, missed his footing and crashed headlong to the floor. They picked him up. At the same time Lizaveta Ivanovna was carried out of the church in a swoon. This incident momentarily upset the solemnity of the mournful rite. There was a dull murmur among the congregation, and a tall thin man in the uniform of a court-chamberlain, a close relative of the deceased, whispered in the ear of an Englishman who was standing near him that the young officer was the natural son of the countess, to which the Englishman coldly replied, 'Oh?'

The whole of that day Hermann was strangely troubled. Repairing to a quiet little tavern to dine, he drank a great deal of wine, contrary to his habit, in the hope of stifling his inner agitation. But the wine only served to excite his imagination. Returning home, he threw himself on his bed without undressing, and fell heavily asleep.

It was night when he woke and the moon was shining into his room. He glanced at the time: it was a quarter to three. Sleep had left him; he sat on the bed and began thinking of the old countess's funeral.

Just then someone in the street looked in at him through the window and immediately walked on. Hermann paid no attention. A moment later he heard the door of his ante-room open. Hermann thought it was his orderly, drunk as usual, returning from some nocturnal excursion, but presently he heard an unfamiliar footstep: someone was softly shuffling along the floor in slippers. The door opened and a woman in white came in. Hermann mistook her for his old nurse and wondered what could have brought her at such an hour. But the woman in white glided across the room and stood before him – and Hermann recognized the countess!

'I have come to you against my will,' she said in a firm voice: 'but I am commanded to grant your request. The three, the seven and the ace will win for you if you play them in succession, provided that you do not stake more than one card in twenty-four hours and never play again as long as you live. I forgive you my death, on condition that you marry my ward, Lizaveta Ivanovna.'

With these words she turned softly, rustled to the door in her slippers, and disappeared. Hermann heard the street-door click and again saw someone peeping in at him through the window.

It was a long time before he could pull himself together and go into the next room. His orderly was asleep on the floor: Hermann had difficulty in waking him. The man was drunk as usual: there was no getting any sense out of him. The street-door was locked. Hermann returned to his room and, lighting a candle, wrote down all the details of his vision.

# VI

'Attendez!'
*'How dare you say* "Attendez!" *to me?'*
'Your Excellency, I said "Attendez", *sir.'*

Two *idées fixes* cannot co-exist in the moral world any more than two physical bodies can occupy one and the same space. 'The three, the seven, the ace' soon drove all thought of the dead woman from Hermann's mind. 'Three, seven, ace' were perpetually in his head and on his lips. If he saw a young girl he would say, 'How graceful she is! A regular three of hearts!' Asked the time, he would reply, 'Five minutes to seven.' Every stout man reminded him of the ace. 'Three, seven, ace' haunted his dreams, assuming all sorts of shapes. The three blossomed before him like a luxuriant flower, the seven took the form of a Gothic portal, and aces became gigantic spiders. His whole attention was focused on one thought: how to make use of the secret which had cost him so dear. He began to consider resigning his commission in order to go and travel abroad. In the public gambling-houses in Paris he would compel fortune to give him his magical treasure. Chance spared him the trouble.

A circle of wealthy gamblers existed in Moscow, presided over by the celebrated Tchekalinsky, who had spent his life at the card-table and amassed millions, accepting promissory notes when he won and paying his losses in ready money. His long experience inspired the confidence of his fellow-players, while his open house, his famous chef and his gay and friendly manner secured for him the general respect of the public. He came to Petersburg. The young men of the capital flocked to his rooms, forsaking balls for cards and preferring the excitement of gambling to the seductions of flirting. Narumov brought Hermann to him.

They passed through a succession of magnificent rooms full of attentive servants. The place was crowded. Several generals and privy councillors were playing whist; young men smoking long pipes lounged about on sofas upholstered in damask. In the drawing-room some twenty gamblers jostled round a long table at which the master of the house was keeping bank. Tchekalinsky was a man of about sixty years of age and most dignified appearance; he had silvery-grey hair, a full, florid face with a kindly expression, and sparkling eyes which were always smiling. Narumov introduced Hermann. Shaking hands cordially, Tchekalinsky requested him not to stand on ceremony, and went on dealing.

The game continued for some while. On the table lay more than thirty cards. Tchekalinsky paused after each round to give the players time to arrange their cards and note their losses, listened courteously to their observations and more courteously still straightened the corner of a card that some careless hand had turned down. At last the game finished. Tchekalinsky shuffled the cards and prepared to deal again.

'Will you allow me to take a card?' said Hermann, stretching out his hand from behind a stout gentleman who was punting.

Tchekalinsky smiled and bowed graciously, in silent token of consent. Narumov laughingly congratulated Hermann on breaking his long abstention from cards and wished him a lucky start.

'There!' said Hermann, chalking some figures on the back of his card.

'How much?' asked the banker, screwing up his eyes. 'Excuse me, I cannot see.'

'Forty-seven thousand,' Hermann answered.

At these words every head was turned in a flash, and all eyes were fixed on Hermann.

'He has taken leave of his senses!' thought Narumov.

'Allow me to point out to you,' said Tchekalinsky with his unfailing smile, 'that you are playing rather high: nobody here has ever staked more than two hundred and seventy five at a time.'

'Well?' returned Hermann. 'Do you accept my card or not?'

Tchekalinsky bowed with the same air of humble acquiescence.

'I only wanted to observe,' he said, 'that, being honoured with the confidence of my friends, I can only play against ready money. For my own part, of course, I am perfectly sure that your word is sufficient but for the sake of the rules of the game and our accounts I must request you to place the money on your card.'

Hermann took a bank-note from his pocket and handed it to Tchekalinsky, who after a cursory glance placed it on Hermann's card. He began to deal. On the right a nine turned up, and on the left a three.

'I win!' said Hermann, pointing to his card.

There was a murmur of astonishment among the company. Tchekalinsky frowned, but the smile quickly reappeared on his face.

'Would you like me to settle now?' he asked Hermann.

'If you please.'

Tchekalinsky took a number of bank-notes out of his pocket and paid there and then. Hermann picked up his money and left the table. Narumov could not believe his eyes. Hermann drank a glass of lemonade and departed home.

The following evening he appeared at Tchekalinsky's again. The host was dealing. Hermann walked up to the table; the players immediately made room for him. Tchekalinsky bowed graciously. Hermann waited for the next deal, took a card and placed on it his original forty-seven thousand together with his winnings of the day before. Tchekalinsky began to deal. A knave turned up on the right, a seven on the left.

Hermann showed his seven.

There was a general exclamation. Tchekalinsky was obviously disconcerted. He counted out ninety-four thousand and handed them to Hermann, who pocketed them in the coolest manner and instantly withdrew.

The next evening Hermann again made his appearance at the table. Every one was expecting him; the generals and privy council-lors left their whist to watch such extraordinary play. The young officers leaped up from their sofas and all the waiters collected in the drawing-room. Every one pressed round Hermann. The other players left off punting, impatient to see what would happen. Hermann stood at the table, prepared to play alone against Tchekalinsky, who was pale but still smiling. Each broke the seal of a pack of cards. Tchekalinsky shuffled. Hermann took a card and covered it with a pile of bank-notes. It was like a duel. Deep silence reigned in the room.

Tchekalinsky began dealing; his hands trembled. A queen fell on the right, an ace on the left.

'Ace wins!' said Hermann, and showed his card.

'Your queen has lost,' said Tchekalinsky gently.

Hermann started: indeed, instead of an ace there lay before him the queen of spades. He could not believe his eyes or think how he could have made such a mistake.

At that moment it seemed to him that the queen of spades opened and closed her eye, and mocked him with a smile. He was struck by the extraordinary resemblance . . .

'The old woman!' he cried in terror.

Tchekalinsky gathered up his winnings. Hermann stood rooted to the spot. When he left the table every one began talking at once.

'A fine game, that!' said the players.

Tchekalinsky shuffled the cards afresh and the game resumed as usual.

# Conclusion

Hermann went out of his mind. He is now in room number 17 of the Obuhov Hospital. He returns no answer to questions put to him but mutters over and over again, with incredible rapidity: 'Three, seven, ace! Three, seven, queen!'

Lizaveta Ivanovna has married a very pleasant young man; he is in the civil service somewhere and has a good income. He is the son of the old countess's former steward. Lizaveta Ivanovna in her turn is bringing up a poor relative.

And Tomsky, who has been promoted to the rank of captain, has married the Princess Pauline.

*Translated from the Russian by Rosemary Edmonds.*

# Of a Promise Kept

## Lafcadio Hearn

*'I am pledging myself to the worship of the Odd, the Queer, the Strange, the Exotic, the Monstrous,' said Lafcadio Hearn in one of his many letters.*

*Born on the Ionian coast of Leucadia (hence his given name), Lafcadio Hearn learned his first prayers in Italian and demotic Greek, studied in England and France, and became a Japanese subject at the age of forty-six – he is now buried in a Buddhist cemetery in Tokyo. Lafcadio Hearn could have chosen any of a number of different nationalities, but he always considered himself an American writer – his parents' homeland was the United States. His subject matter, though, was the Orient: not the Orient of chinoiseries and local colour, but the other, more secret and quiet universe rarely discovered by foreigners. He acquired a profound knowledge of Japanese history and culture and became so immersed in these traditions that today the younger Japanese consider him too traditional for their taste.*

*'Of a Promise Kept' appeared in 1901 in his collection* A Japanese Miscellany.

I shall return in the early autumn, said Akana Soyëmon several hundred years ago – when bidding goodbye to his brother by adoption, young Hasébé Samon. The time was spring; and the place was the village of Kato in the province of Harima. Akana was an Izumo samurai; and he wanted to visit his birthplace.

Hasébé said:

'Your Izumo – the Country of the Eight-Cloud Rising – is very distant. Perhaps it will therefore be difficult for you to promise to return here upon any particular day. But, if we were to know the exact day, we should feel happier. We could then prepare a feast of welcome and we could watch at the gateway for your coming.'

'Why, as for that,' responded Akana, 'I have been so much

accustomed to travel that I can usually tell beforehand how long it will take me to reach a place; and I can safely promise you to be here upon a particular day. Suppose we say the day of the festival Chōyō?'

'That is the ninth day of the ninth month,' said Hasébé; – 'then the chrysanthemums will be in bloom, and we can go together to look at them. How pleasant! . . . So you promise to come back on the ninth day of the ninth month?'

'On the ninth day of the ninth month,' repeated Akana, smiling farewell. Then he strode away from the village of Kato in the province of Harima; – and Hasébé Samon and the mother of Hasébé looked after him with tears in their eyes.

'Neither the Sun nor the Moon,' says an old Japanese proverb, 'ever halt upon their journey.' Swiftly the months went by; and the autumn came – the season of chrysanthemums. And early upon the morning of the ninth day of the ninth month Hasébé prepared to welcome his adopted brother. He made ready a feast of good things, bought wine, decorated the guest-room, and filled the vases of the alcove with chrysanthemums of two colours. Then his mother, watching him, said: 'The province of Izumo, my son, is more than one hundred ri from this place; and the journey thence over the mountains is difficult and weary; and you cannot be sure that Akana will be able to come today. Would it not be better, before you take all this trouble, to wait for his coming?' 'Nay, mother!' Hasébé made answer – 'Akana promised to be here today: he could not break a promise! And if he were to see us beginning to make preparation after his arrival, he would know that we had doubted his word; and we should be put to shame.'

The day was beautiful, the sky without a cloud, and the air so pure that the world seemed to be a thousand miles wider than usual. In the morning many travellers passed through the village – some of them samurai; and Hasébé, watching each as he came, more than once imagined that he saw Akana approaching. But the temple-bells sounded the hour of midday; and Akana did not appear. Through the afternoon also Hasébé watched and waited in vain. The sun set; and still there was no sign of Akana. Nevertheless Hasébé remained at the gate, gazing down the road. Later his mother went to him, and said, 'The mind of a man, my son – as our proverb declares –

may change as quickly as the sky of autumn. But your chrysan-
themum-flowers will still be fresh tomorrow. Better now to sleep;
and in the morning you can watch again for Akana, if you wish.'
'Rest well, mother,' returned Hasébé – 'but I still believe that he
will come.' Then the mother went to her own room; and Hasébé
lingered at the gate.

The night was pure as the day had been: all the sky throbbed
with stars; and the white River of Heaven shimmered with unusual
splendour. The village slept; – the silence was broken only by the
noise of a little brook, and by the far-away barking of peasants'
dogs. Hasébé still waited – waited until he saw the thin moon sink
behind the neighbouring hills. Then at last he began to doubt and
to fear. Just as he was about to re-enter the house, he perceived in
the distance a tall man approaching – very lightly and quickly; and
in the next moment he recognized Akana.

'Oh!' cried Hasébé, springing to meet him – 'I have been waiting
for you from the morning until now! . . . So you really did keep
your promise after all . . . But you must be tired, poor brother! –
come in; – everything is ready for you.' He guided Akana to the
place of honour in the guest-room, and hastened to trim the lights,
which were burning low. 'Mother,' continued Hasébé, 'felt a little
tired this evening, and she has already gone to bed; but I shall
awaken her presently.' Akana shook his head, and made a little
gesture of disapproval. 'As you will, brother,' said Hasébé; and he
set warm food and wine before the traveller. Akana did not touch
the food or the wine, but remained motionless and silent for a short
time. Then, speaking in a whisper – as if fearful of awakening the
mother, he said:

'Now I must tell you how it happened that I came thus late.
When I returned to Izumo I found that the people had almost
forgotten the kindess of our former ruler, the good Lord Enya, and
were seeking the favour of the usurper Tsunéhisa, who had
possessed himself of the Tonda Castle. But I had to visit my cousin,
Akana Tanji, though he had accepted service under Tsunéhisa, and
was living, as a retainer, within the castle grounds. He persuaded
me to present myself before Tsunéhisa: I yielded chiefly in order to
observe the character of the new ruler, whose face I had never seen.
He is a skilled soldier, and of great courage; but he is cunning and
cruel. I found it necessary to let him know that I could never enter
into his service. After I left his presence he ordered my cousin to

detain me – to keep me confined within the house. I protested that I had promised to return to Harima upon the ninth day of the ninth month; but I was refused permission to go. I then hoped to escape from the castle at night; but I was constantly watched; and until today I could find no way to fulfill my promise . . .'

'Until today!' exclaimed Hasébé in bewilderment; – the castle is more than a hundred ri from here!'

'Yes,' returned Akana; 'and no living man can travel on foot a hundred ri in one day. But I felt that, if I did not keep my promise, you could not think well of me; and I remembered the ancient proverb. '*Tama yoku ichi nichi ni sen ri wo yuku*' (The soul of a man can journey a thousand ri in a day). Fortunately I had been allowed to keep my sword; – thus only was I able to come to you . . . Be good to our mother.'

With these words he stood up, and in the same instant disappeared.

Then Hasébé knew that Akana had killed himself in order to fulfill the promise.

At earliest dawn Hasébé Samon set out for the Castle Tonda, in the province of Izumo. Reaching Matsué, he there learned that, on the night of the ninth day of the ninth month, Akana Soyëmon had performed harakiri in the house of Akana Tanji, in the grounds of the castle. Then Hasébé went to the house of Akana Tanji, and reproached Akana Tanji for the treachery done, and slew him in the midst of his family, and escaped without hurt. And when the Lord Tsunéhisa had heard the story, he gave commands that Hasébé should not be pursued. For, although an unscrupulous and cruel man himself, the Lord Tsunéhisa could respect the love of truth in others, and could admire the friendship and the courage of Hasébé Samon.

# The Wizard Postponed

Juan Manuel

*The fourteenth-century Spanish writer Don Juan Manuel was the grandson of King Fernando III and the nephew of Alfonso X. He was unscrupulous in politics (he sought the alliance of the Muslim king of Granada to serve his own ends) and notoriously brutal to each of his three successive wives. He built a monastery for the Dominican order near his fortress in Peñafiel and ordered the monks to keep his original manuscripts there so that corrupt versions of his work could, if necessary, be amended by reference to the master copy. He is the first Spanish author whose portrait survives: he is shown, together with his daughter Juana, queen of Castille, as a donor on a painting of St Lucia in the cathedral of Murcia.*

*'The Wizard Postponed' appears in a collection of moral tales by Juan Manuel traditionally known as* The Book of Examples of Count Lucanor. *Jorge Luis Borges discovered it and made it his own in his first collection of short stories,* A Universal History of Infamy, *meant, according to Borges, 'for popular consumption'. Borges' stories appeared first in a Buenos Aires newspaper,* Crítica, *in the early 1930s.*

*Borges has no qualms about adopting other people's writings; for him, reading is simply another form of making literature. The introduction to his first book of poems,* Fervor de Buenos Aires, *says, 'If the pages of this book allow a few happy verses, may the reader forgive me the discourtesy of having first usurped them myself. Our nothings are barely different; it is a trivial and fortuitous circumstance that you be the reader, I the writer, of these exercises.'*

In the city of Santiago, there was a dean who had a burning desire to learn the art of magic. Hearing that don Illán of Toledo knew more about magic than anyone else, the dean went to Toledo in search of him.

The very morning he arrived, he went straight to don Illán's and found him reading in a room at the back of his house. Don Illán received the dean cordially and asked him to postpone telling him the object of his visit until after they had eaten. Showing his guest into pleasant quarters, don Illán said he felt very happy about the dean's visit. After their meal, the dean told don Illán why he had come, and he begged to be taught the craft of magic. Don Illán said that he already knew that his guest was a dean, a man of good standing and of good prospects, but that were he to teach him all his knowledge, the day might come when the dean would fail to repay his services – as men in high places are often wont to do. The dean swore that he would never forget Don Illán's bounty and that he would always be at his call. Once they came to an agreement, don Illán explained that the magic arts could not be learned save in a place of deep seclusion, and, taking the dean by the hand, he led him to the next room, in whose floor there was a large iron ring. Before this, however, he told the serving maid to prepare partridges for supper but not to put them on to roast until he so ordered.

Don Illán and his guest lifted the ring and went down a well-worn, winding stairway until it seemed to the dean they had gone down so far that the bed of the Tagus must now be above them. At the foot of the staircase was a cell, and in it were a library of books and a kind of cabinet with magic instruments. They were leafing through the books, when suddenly two men appeared bearing a letter for the dean, written by the bishop, his uncle, in which the bishop informed him that he was gravely ill, and that if the dean wanted to find him alive he should not tarry. The news was very upsetting to the dean – for one thing, because of his uncle's illness; for another, because he would be forced to interrupt his studies. In the end, choosing to stay, he wrote an apology and sent it to the bishop.

Three days passed, and there arrived several men in mourning bearing further letters for the dean, in which he read that the bishop had died, that a successor was being chosen, and that they hoped by the grace of God that the dean would be elected. The letters advised him to remain where he was, it seeming better that he be absent during his election.

Ten days elapsed, and two finely dressed squires came, throwing themselves down at the dean's feet and kissing his hands and greeting him as bishop. When don Illán saw these things, he turned to the new prelate with great joy and said that he thanked the Lord that such good news should have come to his house. He then asked for the now vacant deanery for his son. The bishop answered that he had already set aside the deanery for his own brother but that he would find the son some post in the Church, and he begged that they all three leave together for Santiago.

They made their way to the city of Santiago, where they were received with honours. Six months passed, and messengers from the pope came to the bishop, offering him the archbishopric of Toulouse and leaving in his hands the naming of a successor. When don Illán heard this, he reminded the archbishop of his old promise and asked for the vacated title for his son. The archbishop told him that he had already set aside the bishopric for his own uncle, his father's brother, but that as he had given his word to shed favour on don Illán, they should, together with the son, all leave for Toulouse. Don Illán had no recourse but to agree.

The three set out for Toulouse, where they were received with honours and Masses. Two years passed, and messengers from the pope came to the archbishop, elevating him to the cardinalate and leaving in his hands the naming of a successor. When don Illán learned this, he reminded the cardinal of his old promise and asked for the vacant title for his son. The cardinal told him that he had already set aside the archbishopric for his own uncle, his mother's brother – a good old man – but that if don Illán and his son were to accompany him to Rome, surely some favourable opportunity would present itself. Don Illán protested, but in the end he was forced to agree.

The three then set out for Rome, where they were received with honours, Masses, and processions. Four years elapsed, and the pope died, and our cardinal was elected to the papacy by all the other cardinals. Learning of this, don Illán kissed His Holiness's feet, reminded him of his old promise, and asked for the vacant cardinal's office for his son. The pope told don Illán that by now he was weary of his continued requests and that if he persisted in importuning him he would clap him in gaol, since he knew full well that don Illán was no more than a wizard and that in Toledo he had been a teacher of the arts of magic.

Poor don Illán could only answer that he was going back to Spain, and he asked the pope for something to eat during the long sea journey. Once more the pope refused him, whereupon don Illán (whose face had changed in a strange fashion) said in an unwavering voice, 'In that case, I shall have to eat the partridges that I ordered for tonight.'

The serving maid came forward, and don Illán ordered the partridges roasted. Immediately the pope found himself in the underground cell in Toledo, no more than dean of Santiago, and so taken aback with shame that he did not know what to say. Don Illán said that this test was sufficient, refused the dean his share of the partridges, and saw him to the door, where, taking leave of him with great courtesy, he wished him a safe journey home.

*Translated from the Spanish by Norman Thomas di Giovanni.*

# The Monkey's Paw

## W. W. Jacobs

*It is a curious fact that although the number of arguments that can be developed in fiction are countless, certain stories are taken up again and again in different countries and in different centuries. The story of a hero's quest appears in the cycle of the Holy Grail and can be found in* Moby Dick; *the story of Cain and Abel is told in* King Lear *and in Steinbeck's* East of Eden; *Dido, abandoned by Aeneas, is also Hans Christian Andersen's Little Mermaid and Flaubert's Madame Bovary. There seems to be, in the adult reader, the child's delight in being told the same story over and over again, with changes of costume or scenery and clever new twists to an old and relished yarn.*

*The tale of the three wishes appears very early in literature; Egyptian mothers probably told it to their children while the pyramids were being built, and under the shadow of other, smaller pyramids, the Aztecs made it into a song. Boccaccio knew it, and so did the Brothers Grimm. It is, like so many of the world's best-loved stories, very simple: three wishes are granted to someone by a power not of this Earth; the first wish is futile, the second terrible, the third necessary to abolish the second.*

*William Wymark Jacobs was not a very good writer and 'The Monkey's Paw', tucked away among half a dozen remarkably poor stories in his collection* The Lady of the Barge (1902), *comes as a shock because it is certainly one of the best fantastic horror stories ever written. Nothing else Jacobs ever wrote had nearly the same power and charm, and – as if he realized that his Muse had abandoned him – in his later years he wrote very little and published almost nothing.*

# I

Without, the night was cold and wet, but in the small parlour of Laburnum Villa the blinds were drawn and the fire burned brightly. Father and son were at chess; the former, who possessed ideas about the game involving radical changes, putting his king into such sharp and unnecessary perils that it even provoked comment from the white-haired old lady knitting placidly by the fire.

'Hark at the wind,' said Mr White, who, having seen a fatal mistake after it was too late, was amiably desirous of preventing his son from seeing it.

'I'm listening,' said the latter, grimly surveying the board as he stretched out his hand. 'Check.'

'I should hardly think that he'd come tonight,' said his father, with his hand poised over the board.

'Mate,' replied the son.

'That's the worst of living so far out,' bawled Mr White, with sudden and unlooked-for violence; 'of all the beastly, slushy, out-of-the-way places to live in, this is the worst. Path's a bog, and the road's a torrent. I don't know what people are thinking about. I suppose because only two houses in the road are let, they think it doesn't matter.'

'Never mind, dear,' said his wife soothingly; 'perhaps you'll win the next one.'

Mr White looked up sharply, just in time to intercept a knowing glance between mother and son. The words died away on his lips, and he hid a guilty grin in his thin grey beard.

'There he is,' said Herbert White, as the gate banged to loudly and heavy footsteps came towards the door.

The old man rose with hospitable haste, and opening the door, was heard condoling with the new arrival. The new arrival also condoled with himself, so that Mrs White said, 'Tut, tut!' and coughed gently as her husband entered the room, followed by a tall, burly man, beady of eye and rubicund of visage.

'Sergeant-Major Morris,' he said, introducing him.

The sergeant-major shook hands, and taking the proffered seat by the fire, watched contentedly while his host got out whisky and tumblers and stood a small copper kettle on the fire.

At the third glass his eyes got brighter, and he began to talk, the little family circle regarding with eager interest this visitor from distant parts, as he squared his broad shoulders in the chair and spoke of wild scenes and doughty deeds; of wars and plagues and strange peoples.

'Twenty-one years of it,' said Mr White, nodding at his wife and son. 'When he went away he was a slip of a youth in the warehouse. Now look at him.'

'He don't look to have taken much harm,' said Mrs White politely.

'I'd like to go to India myself,' said the old man, 'just to look round a bit, you know.'

'Better where you are,' said the sergeant-major, shaking his head. He put down the empty glass, and sighing softly, shook it again.

'I should like to see those old temples and fakirs and jugglers,' said the old man. 'What was that you started telling me the other day about a monkey's paw or something, Morris?'

'Nothing,' said the soldier hastily. 'Leastways nothing worth hearing.'

'Monkey's paw?' said Mrs White curiously.

'Well, it's just a bit of what you might call magic, perhaps,' said the sergeant-major offhandedly.

His three listeners leaned forward eagerly. The visitor absent-mindedly put his empty glass to his lips and then set it down again. His host filled it for him.

'To look at,' said the sergeant-major, fumbling in his pocket, 'it's just an ordinary little paw, dried to a mummy.'

He took something out of his pocket and proffered it. Mrs White drew back with a grimace, but her son, taking it, examined it curiously.

'And what is there special about it?' inquired Mr White as he took it from his son, and having examined it, placed it upon the table.

'It had a spell put on it by an old fakir,' said the sergeant-major, 'a very holy man. He wanted to show that fate ruled people's lives, and that those who interfered with it did so to their sorrow. He put a spell on it so that three separate men could each have three wishes from it.'

His manner was so impressive that his hearers were conscious that their light laughter jarred somewhat.

'Well, why don't you have three, sir?' said Herbert White cleverly.

The soldier regarded him in the way that middle age is wont to regard presumptuous youth. 'I have,' he said quietly, and his blotchy face whitened.

'And did you really have the three wishes granted?' asked Mrs White.

'I did,' said the sergeant-major, and his glass tapped against his strong teeth.

'And has anybody else wished?' persisted the old lady.

'The first man had his three wishes. Yes,' was the reply; 'I don't know what the first two were, but the third was for death. That's how I got the paw.'

His tones were so grave that a hush fell upon the group.

'If you've had your three wishes, it's no good to you now, then, Morris,' said the old man at last. 'What do you keep it for?'

The soldier shook his head. 'Fancy, I suppose,' he said slowly. 'I did have some idea of selling it, but I don't think I will. It has caused enough mischief already. Besides, people won't buy. They think it's a fairy tale, some of them; and those who do think anything of it want to try it first and pay me afterward.'

'If you could have another three wishes,' said the old man, eyeing him keenly, 'would you have them?'

'I don't know,' said the other. 'I don't know.'

He took the paw, and dangling it between his forefinger and thumb, suddenly threw it upon the fire. White, with a slight cry, stooped down and snatched it off.

'Better let it burn,' said the soldier solemnly.

'If you don't want it, Morris,' said the other, 'give it to me.'

'I won't,' said his friend doggedly. 'I threw it on the fire. If you keep it, don't blame me for what happens. Pitch it on the fire again like a sensible man.'

The other shook his head and examined his new possession closely. 'How do you do it?' he inquired.

'Hold it up in your right hand and wish aloud,' said the sergeant-major, 'but I warn you of the consequences.'

'Sounds like the *Arabian Nights*,' said Mrs White, as she rose and began to set the supper. 'Don't you think you might wish for four pairs of hands for me.'

Her husband drew the talisman from his pocket, and then all three burst into laughter as the sergeant-major, with a look of alarm on his face, caught him by the arm.

'If you must wish,' he said gruffly, 'wish for something sensible.'

Mr White dropped it back in his pocket, and placing chairs, motioned his friend to the table. In the business of supper the talisman was partly forgotten, and afterward the three sat listening in an enthralled fashion to a second instalment of the soldier's adventures in India.

'If the tale about the monkey's paw is not more truthful than those he has been telling us,' said Herbert, as the door closed behind their guest, just in time to catch the last train, 'we shan't make much out of it.'

'Did you give him anything for it, father?' inquired Mrs White, regarding her husband closely.

'A trifle,' said he, colouring slightly. 'He didn't want it, but I made him take it. And he pressed me again to throw it away.'

'Likely,' said Herbert, with pretended horror. 'Why, we're going to be rich, and famous, and happy. Wish to be an emperor, father, to begin with; then you can't be henpecked.'

He darted round the table, pursued by the maligned Mrs White armed with an antimacassar.

Mr White took the paw from his pocket and eyed it dubiously. 'I don't know what to wish for, and that's a fact,' he said slowly. 'It seems to me I've got all I want.'

'If you only cleared the house, you'd be quite happy, wouldn't you!' said Herbert, with his hand on his shoulder. 'Well, wish for two hundred pounds, then; that'll just do it.'

His father, smiling shamefacedly at his own credulity, held up the talisman, as his son, with a solemn face, somewhat marred by a wink at his mother, sat down at the piano and struck a few impressive chords.

'I wish for two hundred pounds,' said the old man distinctly.

A fine crash from the piano greeted the words, interrupted by a shuddering cry from the old man. His wife and son ran toward him.

'It moved,' he cried, with a glance of disgust at the object as it lay on the floor. 'As I wished, it twisted in my hand like a snake.'

'Well, I don't see the money,' said his son, as he picked it up and placed it on the table, 'and I bet I never shall.'

'It must have been your fancy, father,' said his wife, regarding him anxiously.

He shook his head. 'Never mind, though; there's no harm done, but it gave me a shock all the same.'

They sat down by the fire again while the two men finished their pipes. Outside, the wind was higher than ever, and the old man started nervously at the sound of a door banging upstairs. A silence unusual and depressing settled upon all three, which lasted until the old couple rose to retire for the night.

'I expect you'll find the cash tied up in a big bag in the middle of your bed,' said Herbert, as he bade them good night, 'and something horrible squatting up on top of the wardrobe watching you as you pocket your ill-gotten gains.'

He sat alone in the darkness, gazing at the dying fire, and seeing faces in it. The last face was so horrible and so simian that he gazed at it in amazement. It got so vivid that, with a little uneasy laugh, he felt on the table for a glass containing a little water to throw over it. His hand grasped the monkey's paw, and with a little shiver he wiped his hand on his coat and went up to bed.

# II

In the brightness of the wintry sun next morning as it streamed over the breakfast table he laughed at his fears. There was an air of prosaic wholesomeness about the room which it had lacked on the previous night, and the dirty, shrivelled little paw was pitched on the side-board with a carelessness which betokened no great belief in its virtues.

'I suppose all old soldiers are the same,' said Mrs White. 'The idea of our listening to such nonsense! How could wishes be granted in these days? And if they could, how could two hundred pounds hurt you, father?'

'Might drop on his head from the sky,' said the frivolous Herbert.

'Morris said the things happened so naturally,' said his father, 'that you might if you so wished attribute it to coincidence.'

'Well, don't break into the money before I come back,' said Herbert as he rose from the table. 'I'm afraid it'll turn you into a mean, avaricious man, and we shall have to disown you.'

His mother laughed, and following him to the door, watched him down the road; and returning to the breakfast table, was very happy at the expense of her husband's credulity. All of which did not prevent her from scurrying to the door at the postman's knock, nor prevent her from referring somewhat shortly to retired sergeant-majors of bibulous habits when she found that the post brought a tailor's bill.

'Herbert will have some more of his funny remarks, I expect, when he comes home,' she said, as they sat at dinner.

'I dare say,' said Mr White, pouring himself out some beer; 'but for all that, the thing moved in my hand; that I'll swear to.'

'You thought it did,' said the old lady soothingly.

'I say it did,' replied the other. 'There was no thought about it; I had just— What's the matter?'

His wife made no reply. She was watching the mysterious movements of a man outside, who, peering in an undecided fashion at the house, appeared to be trying to make up his mind to enter. In mental connexion with the two hundred pounds, she noticed that the stranger was well dressed, and wore a silk hat of glossy newness. Three times he paused at the gate, and then walked on again. The fourth time he stood with his hand upon it, and then with sudden resolution flung it open and walked up the path. Mrs White at the same moment placed her hands behind her, and hurriedly unfastening the strings of her apron, put that useful article of apparel beneath the cushion of her chair.

She brought the stranger, who seemed ill at ease, into the room. He gazed at her furtively, and listened in a preoccupied fashion as the old lady apologized for the appearance of the room, and her husband's coat, a garment which he usually reserved for the garden. She then waited as patiently as her sex would permit for him to broach his business, but he was at first strangely silent.

'I – was asked to call,' he said at last, and stooped and picked a piece of cotton from his trousers. 'I come from "Maw and Meggins".'

The old lady started. 'Is anything the matter?' she asked breathlessly. 'Has anything happened to Herbert? What is it? What is it?'

Her husband interposed. 'There, there, mother,' he said hastily. 'Sit down, and don't jump to conclusions. You've not brought bad news, I'm sure, sir,' and he eyed the other wistfully.

'I'm sorry— ' began the visitor.

'Is he hurt?' demanded the mother wildly.

The visitor bowed in assent. 'Badly hurt,' he said quietly, 'but he is not in any pain.'

'Oh, thank God!' said the old woman, clasping her hands. 'Thank God for that! Thank— '

She broke off suddenly as the sinister meaning of the assurance dawned upon her and she saw the awful confirmation of her fears in the other's averted face. She caught her breath, and turning to her slower-witted husband, laid her trembling old hand upon his. There was a long silence.

'He was caught in the machinery,' said the visitor at length in a low voice.

'Caught in the machinery,' repeated Mr White, in a dazed fashion, 'yes.'

He sat staring blankly out of the window, and taking his wife's hand between his own, pressed it as he had been wont to do in their old courting days nearly forty years before.

'He was the only one left to us,' he said, turning gently to the visitor. 'It is hard.'

The other coughed, and rising, walked slowly to the window. 'The firm wished me to convey their sincere sympathy with you in your great loss,' he said, without looking round. 'I beg that you will understand I am only their servant and merely obeying orders.'

There was no reply; the old woman's face was white, her eyes staring, and her breath inaudible; on the husband's face was a look such as his friend the sergeant might have carried into his first action.

'I was to say that Maw and Meggins disclaim all responsibility,' continued the other. 'They admit no liability at all, but in consideration of you son's services, they wish to present you with a certain sum as compensation.'

Mr White dropped his wife's hand, and rising to his feet, gazed with a look of horror at his visitor. His dry lips shaped the words, 'How much?'

'Two hundred pounds,' was the answer.

Unconscious of his wife's shriek, the old man smiled faintly, put out his hands like a sightless man, and dropped, a senseless heap, to the floor.

# III

In the huge new cemetery, some two miles distant, the old people buried their dead, and came back to the house steeped in shadow and silence. It was all over so quickly that at first they could hardly realize it, and remained in a state of expectation as though of something else to happen – something else which was to lighten this load, too heavy for old hearts to bear.

But the days passed, and expectation gave place to resignation – the hopeless resignation of the old, sometimes miscalled apathy. Sometimes they hardly exchanged a word, for now they had nothing to talk about, and their days were long to weariness.

It was about a week after that the old man, waking suddenly in the night, stretched out his hand and found himself alone. The room was in darkness, and the sound of subdued weeping came from the window. He raised himself in bed and listened.

'Come back,' he said tenderly. 'You will be cold.'

'It is colder for my son,' said the old woman, and wept afresh.

The sound of her sobs died away on his ears. The bed was warm, and his eyes heavy with sleep. He dozed fitfully, and then slept until a sudden wild cry from his wife awoke him with a start.

'*The paw!*' she cried wildly. 'The monkey's paw!'

He started up in alarm. 'Where? Where is it? What's the matter?'

She came stumbling across the room toward him. 'I want it,' she said quietly. 'You've not destroyed it?'

'It's in the parlour, on the bracket,' he replied, marvelling. 'Why?'

She cried and laughed together, and bending over, kissed his cheek.

'I only just thought of it,' she said hysterically. 'Why didn't I think of it before? Why didn't *you* think of it?'

'Think of what?' he questioned.

'The other two wishes,' she replied rapidly. 'We've only had one.'

'Was not that enough?' he demanded fiercely.

'No,' she cried triumphantly; 'we'll have one more. Go down and get it quickly, and wish our boy alive again.'

The man sat up in bed and flung the bedclothes from his quaking limbs. 'Good God, you are mad!' he cried, aghast.

'Get it,' she panted; 'get it quickly, and wish— Oh, my boy, my boy!'

Her husband struck a match and lit the candle. 'Get back to bed,' he said unsteadily. 'You don't know what you are saying.'

'We had the first wish granted,' said the old woman feverishly; 'why not the second?'

'A coincidence,' stammered the old man.

'Go and get it and wish,' cried his wife, quivering with excitement.

The old man turned and regarded her, and his voice shook. 'He has been dead ten days, and besides he – I would not tell you else, but – I could only recognize him by his clothing. If he was too terrible for you to see then, how now?'

'Bring him back,' cried the old woman, and dragged him towards the door. 'Do you think I fear the child I have nursed?'

He went down in the darkness, and felt his way to the parlour, and then to the mantelpiece. The talisman was in its place, and a horrible fear that the unspoken wish might bring his mutilated son before him ere he could escape from the room seized upon him, and he caught his breath as he found that he had lost the direction of the door. His brow cold with sweat, he felt his way round the table, and groped along the wall until he found himself in the small passage with the unwholesome thing in his hand.

Even his wife's face seemed changed as he entered the room. It was white and expectant, and to his fears seemed to have an unnatural look upon it. He was afraid of her.

'*Wish!*' she cried, in a strong voice.

'It is foolish and wicked,' he faltered.

'*Wish!*' repeated his wife.

He raised his hand. 'I wish my son alive again.'

The talisman fell to the floor, and he regarded it fearfully. Then he sank trembling into a chair as the old woman, with burning eyes, walked to the window and raised the blind.

He sat until he was chilled with the cold, glancing occasionally at the figure of the old woman peering through the window. The candle-end, which had burned below the rim of the china candle-stick, was throwing pulsating shadows on the ceiling and walls, until, with a flicker larger than the rest, it expired. The old man, with an unspeakable sense of relief at the failure of the talisman, crept back to his bed, and a minute or two afterward the old woman came silently and apathetically beside him.

Neither spoke, but lay silently listening to the ticking of the clock. A stair creaked, and a squeaky mouse scurried noisily through the wall. The darkness was oppressive, and after lying for some time screwing up his courage, he took the box of matches, and striking one, went downstairs for a candle.

At the foot of the stairs the match went out, and he paused to strike another; and at the same moment a knock, so quiet and stealthy as to be scarcely audible, sounded on the front door.

The matches fell from his hand and spilled in the passage. He stood motionless, his breath suspended until the knock was repeated. Then he turned and fled swiftly back to his room, and closed the door behind him. A third knock sounded through the house.

'*What's that?*' cried the old woman, starting up.

'A rat,' said the old man in shaking tones – 'a rat. It passed me on the stairs.'

His wife sat up in bed listening. A loud knock resounded through the house.

'It's Herbert!' she screamed. 'It's Herbert!'

She ran to the door, but her husband was before her, and catching her by the arm, held her tightly.

'What are you going to do?' he whispered hoarsely.

'It's my boy; it's Herbert!' she cried, struggling mechanically. 'I forgot it was two miles away. What are you holding me for? Let go. I must open the door.'

'For God's sake don't let it in,' cried the old man, trembling.

'You're afraid of your own son,' she cried, struggling. 'Let me go. I'm coming Herbert; I'm coming.'

There was another knock, and another. The old woman with a sudden wrench broke free and ran from the room. Her husband followed to the landing, and called after her appealingly as she hurried downstairs. He heard the chain rattle back and the bottom bolt drawn slowly and stiffly from the socket. Then the old woman's voice, strained and panting.

'The bolt,' she cried loudly. 'Come down. I can't reach it.'

But her husband was on his hands and knees groping wildly on the floor in search of the paw. If he could only find it before the thing outside got in. A perfect fusillade of knocks reverberated through the house, and he heard the scraping of a chair as his wife put it down in the passage against the door. He heard the creaking of the bolt as it came slowly back, and at the same moment he found the monkey's paw, and frantically breathed his third and last wish.

The knocking ceased suddenly, although the echoes of it were still in the house. He heard the chair drawn back, and the door opened. A cold wind rushed up the staircase, and a long loud wail of disappointment and misery from his wife gave him courage to run down to her side, and then to the gate beyond. The street lamp flickering opposite shone on a quiet and deserted road.

# The Bottle Imp

## Robert Louis Stevenson

*Under the mistaken impression that the hot (and humid) South Seas' air
was an ideal treatment for tuberculosis, Robert Louis Stevenson, who
had suffered from that illness almost since his birth, accepted the* New
York Sun's *generous offer of $10,000 to sail away to the South Pacific
and write a series of letters about the cruise. Stevenson, his ageing
mother, his strong-willed wife Fanny, and Lloyd Osborne, her son from a
previous marriage, embarked on the* Casco *on June 28, 1888, in San
Francisco and set sail for the Marquesas, scene of Melville's* Typee, *one
of Stevenson's favourite books. Hawaii, Tahiti, the Tuamotus seemed
to Stevenson the garden of Eden. The family changed ships and on the
Equator reached Samoa in 1889. This was to be Stevenson's home until
his death at the age of forty-four: on December 3, 1894, 'the teller of
tales' (Tusitala as the natives called him) collapsed in an apoplectic fit.
The Samoans mounted guard around his body all night, and next day
carried the coffin up to the hilltop Stevenson himself had chosen for his
final resting-place.*

*The* Island Night Entertainments (*the title recalls Stevenson's much-
loved* Arabian Nights) *were written in Samoa. They include 'The Beach
of Falesà' (which Stevenson thought his best short story), 'The Bottle
Imp' and 'The Isle of Voices.' In a letter to Conan Doyle dated August
23, 1893, Stevenson wrote that he had told his Samoan overseer the
Sherlock Holmes' story 'The Engineer's Thumb' and that the overseer
had taken it to be true, because the Samoans could not grasp the notion
of fiction. Not even when 'The Bottle Imp' was translated into Samoan
did the natives think a story could be an invention; whenever they
visited Stevenson's house they would politely admire the furniture and the
paintings, and then ask, with touching faith, 'Yes, but where is the
Bottle?'*

There was a man of the Island of Hawaii, whom I shall call Keawe; for the truth is, he still lives, and his name must be kept secret; but the place of his birth was not far from Honaunau, where the bones of Keawe the Great lie hidden in a cave. This man was poor, brave, and active; he could read and write like a schoolmaster; he was a first-rate mariner besides, sailed for some time in the island steamers, and steered a whaleboat on the Hamakua coast. At length it came in Keawe's mind to have a sight of the great world and foreign cities, and he shipped on a vessel bound to San Francisco.

This is a fine town, with a fine harbour, and rich people uncountable; and, in particular, there is one hill which is covered with palaces. Upon this hill Keawe was one day taking a walk with his pocket full of money, viewing the great houses upon either hand with pleasure. 'What fine houses these are!' he was thinking, 'and how happy must those people be who dwell in them, and take no care for the morrow!' The thought was in his mind when he came abreast of a house that was smaller than some others, but all finished and beautified like a toy; the steps of that house shone like silver, and the borders of the garden bloomed like garlands, and the windows were bright like diamonds; and Keawe stopped and wondered at the excellence of all he saw. So stopping, he was aware of a man that looked forth upon him through a window so clear that Keawe could see him as you see a fish in a pool upon the reef. The man was elderly, with a bald head and a black beard; and his face was heavy with sorrow, and he bitterly sighed. And the truth of it is, that as Keawe looked in upon the man, and the man looked out upon Keawe, each envied the other.

All of a sudden, the man smiled and nodded, and beckoned Keawe to enter, and met him at the door of the house.

'This is a fine house of mine,' said the man, and bitterly sighed. 'Would you not care to view the chambers?'

So he led Keawe all over it, from the cellar to the roof, and there was nothing there that was not perfect of its kind, and Keawe was astonished.

'Truly,' said Keawe, 'this is a beautiful house; if I lived in the like of it, I should be laughing all day long. How comes it, then, that you should be sighing?'

'There is no reason,' said the man, 'why you should not have a house in all points similar to this, and finer, if you wish. You have some money, I suppose?'

'I have fifty dollars,' said Keawe; 'but a house like this will cost more than fifty dollars.'

The man made a computation. 'I am sorry you have no more,' said he, 'for it may raise you trouble in the future; but it shall be yours at fifty dollars.'

'The house?' asked Keawe.

'No, not the house,' replied the man; 'but the bottle. For, I must tell you, although I appear to you so rich and fortunate, all my fortune, and this house itself and its garden, came out of a bottle not much bigger than a pint. This is it.'

And he opened a lockfast place, and took out a round-bellied bottle with a long neck; the glass of it was white like milk, with changing rainbow colours in the grain. Withinsides something obscurely moved, like a shadow and a fire.

'This is the bottle,' said the man; and, when Keawe laughed, 'You do not believe me?' he added. 'Try, then, for yourself. See if you can break it.'

So Keawe took the bottle up and dashed it on the floor till he was weary; but it jumped on the floor like a child's ball, and was not injured.

'This is a strange thing,' said Keawe. 'For by the touch of it, as well as by the look, the bottle should be of glass.'

'Of glass it is,' replied the man, sighing more heavily than ever; 'but the glass of it was tempered in the flames of hell. An imp lives in it, and that is the shadow we behold there moving; or so I suppose. If any man buy this bottle the imp is at his command; all that he desires – love, fame, money, houses like this house, ay, or a city like this city – all are his at the word uttered. Napoleon had this bottle, and by it he grew to be the king of the world; but he sold it at the last, and fell. Captain Cook had this bottle, and by it he found his way to so many islands; but he, too, sold it, and was slain upon Hawaii. For, once it is sold, the power goes and the protection; and unless a man remain content with what he has, ill will befall him.'

'And yet you talk of selling it yourself?' Keawe said.

'I have all I wish, and I am growing elderly,' replied the man. 'There is one thing the imp cannot do – he cannot prolong life; and, it would not be fair to conceal from you, there is a drawback to the bottle; for if a man die before he sells it, he must burn in hell for ever.'

'To be sure, that is a drawback and no mistake,' cried Keawe. 'I would not meddle with the thing. I can do without a house, thank God; but there is one thing I could not be doing with one particle, and that is to be damned.'

'Dear me, you must not run away with things,' returned the man. 'All you have to do is to use the power of the imp in moderation, and then sell it to someone else, as I do to you, and finish your life in comfort.'

'Well, I observe two things,' said Keawe. 'All the time you keep sighing like a maid in love, that is one; and, for the other, you sell this bottle very cheap.'

'I have told you already why I sigh,' said the man. 'It is because I fear my health is breaking up; and, as you said yourself, to die and go to the devil is a pity for anyone. As for why I sell so cheap, I must explain to you there is a peculiarity about the bottle. Long ago, when the devil brought it first upon earth, it was extremely expensive, and was sold first of all to Prester John for many millions of dollars; but it cannot be sold at all, unless sold at a loss. If you sell it for as much as you paid for it, back it comes to you again like a homing pigeon. It follows that the price has kept falling in these centuries, and the bottle is now remarkably cheap. I bought it myself from one of my great neighbours on this hill, and the price I paid was only ninety dollars. I could sell it for as high as eighty-nine dollars and ninety-nine cents, but not a penny dearer, or back the thing must come to me. Now, about this there are two bothers. First, when you offer a bottle so singular for eighty odd dollars, people suppose you to be jesting. And second – but there is no hurry about that – and I need not go into it. Only remember it must be coined money that you sell it for.'

'How am I to know that this is all true?' asked Keawe.

'Some of it you can try at once,' replied the man. 'Give me your fifty dollars, take the bottle, and wish your fifty dollars back into your pocket. If that does not happen, I pledge you my honour I will cry off the bargain and restore your money.'

'You are not deceiving me?' said Keawe.

The man bound himself with a great oath.

'Well, I will risk that much,' said Keawe, 'for that can do no harm.' And he paid over his money to the man, and the man handed him the bottle.

'Imp of the bottle,' said Keawe, 'I want my fifty dollars back.'

And sure enough he had scarce said the word before his pocket was as heavy as ever.

'To be sure this is a wonderful bottle,' said Keawe.

'And now, good morning to you, my fine fellow, and the devil go with you for me!' said the man.

'Hold on,' said Keawe, 'I don't want any more of this fun. Here, take your bottle back.'

'You have bought it for less than I paid for it,' replied the man, rubbing his hands. 'It is yours now; and, for my part, I am only concerned to see the back of you.' And with that he rang for his Chinese servant, and had Keawe shown out of the house.

Now, when Keawe was in the street, with the bottle under his arm, he began to think. 'If all is true about this bottle, I may have made a losing bargain,' thinks he. 'But perhaps the man was only fooling me.' The first thing he did was to count his money; the sum was exact – forty-nine dollars American money, and one Chili piece. 'That looks like the truth,' said Keawe. 'Now I will try another part.'

The streets in that part of the city were as clean as a ship's decks, and though it was noon, there were no passengers. Keawe set the bottle in the gutter and walked away. Twice he looked back, and there was the milky, round-bellied bottle where he left it. A third time he looked back, and turned a corner; but he had scarce done so, when something knocked upon his elbow, and behold! it was the long neck sticking up; and as for the round belly, it was jammed into the pocket of his pilot-coat.

'And that looks like the truth,' said Keawe.

The next thing he did was to buy a cork-screw in a shop, and go apart into a secret place in the fields. And there he tried to draw the cork, but as often as he put the screw in, out it came again, and the cork as whole as ever.

'This is some new sort of cork,' said Keawe, and all at once he began to shake and sweat, for he was afraid of that bottle.

On his way back to the port-side, he saw a shop where a man sold shells and clubs from the wild islands, old heathen deities, old coined money, pictures from China and Japan, and all manner of things that sailors bring in their sea-chests. And here he had an idea. So he went in and offered the bottle for a hundred dollars. The man of the shop laughed at him at the first, and offered him five; but, indeed, it was a curious bottle – such glass was never blown in any human glass-works, so prettily the colours shone under the milky white, and so strangely the shadow hovered in the midst; so, after he had disputed awhile after the manner of his kind, the shopman gave Keawe sixty silver dollars for the thing, and set it on a shelf in the midst of his window.

'Now,' said Keawe, 'I have sold that for sixty which I bought for fifty – or, to say truth, a little less, because one of my dollars was from Chili. Now I shall know the truth upon another point.'

So he went back on board his ship, and, when he opened his chest, there was the bottle, and had come more quickly than himself. Now Keawe had a mate on board whose name was Lopaka.

'What ails you?' said Lopaka, 'that you stare in your chest?'

They were alone in the ship's forecastle, and Keawe bound him to secrecy, and told all.

'This is a very strange affair,' said Lopaka; 'and I fear you will be in trouble about this bottle. But there is one point very clear – that you are sure of the trouble, and you had better have the profit in the bargain. Make up your mind what you want with it; give the order, and if it is done as you desire, I will buy the bottle myself; for I have an idea of my own to get a schooner, and go trading through the islands.'

'That is not my idea,' said Keawe; 'but to have a beautiful house and garden on the Kona Coast, where I was born, the sun shining in at the door, flowers in the garden, glass in the windows, pictures on the walls, and toys and fine carpets on the tables, for all the world like the house I was in this day – only a storey higher, and with balconies all about like the King's palace; and to live there without care and make merry with my friends and relatives.'

'Well,' said Lopaka, 'let us carry it back with us to Hawaii, and if all comes true, as you suppose, I will buy the bottle, as I said, and ask a schooner.'

Upon that they were agreed, and it was not long before the ship returned to Honolulu, carrying Keawe and Lopaka, and the bottle. They were scarce come ashore when they met a friend upon the beach, who began at once to condole with Keawe.

'I do not know what I am to be condoled about,' said Keawe.

'Is it possible you have not heard,' said the friend, 'your uncle – that good old man – is dead, and your cousin – that beautiful boy – was drowned at sea?'

Keawe was filled with sorrow, and, beginning to weep and to

lament he forgot about the bottle. But Lopaka was thinking to himself, and presently, when Keawe's grief was a little abated, 'I have been thinking,' said Lopaka. 'Had not your uncle lands in Hawaii, in the district of Kaü?'

'No,' said Keawe, 'not in Kaü; they are on the mountain-side – a little way south of Hookena.'

'These lands will now be yours?' asked Lopaka.

'And so they will,' says Keawe, and began again to lament for his relatives.

'No,' said Lopaka, 'do not lament at present. I have a thought in my mind. How if this should be the doing of the bottle? For here is the place ready for your house.'

'If this be so,' cried Keawe, 'it is a very ill way to serve me by killing my relatives. But it may be, indeed; for it was in just such a station that I saw the house with my mind's eye.'

'The house, however, is not yet built,' said Lopaka.

'No, nor like to be!' said Keawe; 'for though my uncle has some coffee and ava and bananas, it will not be more than will keep me in comfort; and the rest of that land is the black lava.'

'Let us go to the lawyer,' said Lopaka; 'I have still this idea in my mind.'

Now, when they came to the lawyer's, it appeared Keawe's uncle had grown monstrous rich in the last days, and there was a fund of money.

'And here is the money for the house!' cried Lopaka.

'If you are thinking of a new house,' said the lawyer, 'here is the card of a new architect, of whom they tell me great things.'

'Better and better!' cried Lopaka. 'Here is all made plain for us. Let us continue to obey orders.'

So they went to the architect, and he had drawings of houses on his table.

'You want something out of the way,' said the architect. 'How do you like this?' and he handed a drawing to Keawe.

Now, when Keawe set eyes on the drawing, he cried out aloud, for it was the picture of his thought exactly drawn.

'I am in for this house,' thought he. 'Little as I like the way it comes to me, I am in for it now, and I may as well take the good along with the evil.'

So he told the architect all that he wished, and how he would have that house furnished, and about the pictures on the wall and the knick-knacks on the tables; and he asked the man plainly for how much he would undertake the whole affair.

The architect put many questions, and took his pen and made a computation; and when he had done he named the very sum that Keawe had inherited.

Lopaka and Keawe looked at one another and nodded.

'It is quite clear,' thought Keawe, 'that I am to have this house, whether or no. It comes from the devil, and I fear I will get little good by that; and of one thing I am sure, I will make no more wishes as long as I have this bottle. But with the house I am saddled, and I may as well take the good along with the evil.'

So he made his terms with the architect, and they signed a paper; and Keawe and Lopaka took ship again and sailed to Australia; for it was concluded between them they should not interfere at all, but leave the architect and the bottle imp to build and to adorn that house at their own pleasure.

The voyage was a good voyage, only all the time Keawe was holding in his breath, for he had sworn he would utter no more wishes, and take no more favours from the devil. The time was up when they got back. The architect told them that the house was ready, and Keawe and Lopaka took a passage in the *Hall*, and went down Kona way to view the house, and see if all had been done fitly according to the thought that was in Keawe's mind.

Now, the house stood on the mountain-side, visible to ships. Above, the forest ran up into the clouds of rain; below, the black lava fell in cliffs, where the kings of old lay buried. A garden bloomed about that house with every hue of flowers; and there was an orchard of papaia on the one hand and an orchard of breadfruit on the other, and right in front, toward the sea, a ship's mast had been rigged up and bore a flag. As for the house, it was three storeys high, with great chambers and broad balconies on each. The windows were of glass, so excellent that it was as clear as water and as bright as day. All manner of furniture adorned the chambers. Pictures hung upon the wall in golden frames: pictures of ships, and men fighting, and of the most beautiful women, and of singular places; nowhere in the world are there pictures of so bright a colour as those Keawe found hanging in his house. As for the knick-knacks, they were extraordinary fine; chiming clocks and musical boxes, little men with nodding heads, books filled with pictures, weapons of price from all quarters of the world, and the most elegant puzzles to entertain the leisure of a solitary man. And as no one would care to live in such chambers, only to walk through and view them, the balconies were made so broad that a whole town might have lived upon them in delight; and Keawe knew not which to prefer, whether the back porch, where you got the land breeze, and looked upon the orchards and the flowers, or the front balcony, where you could drink the wind of the sea, and look down the steep wall of the mountain and see the *Hall* going by once a week or so between Hookena and the hills of Pele, or the schooners plying up the coast for wood and ava and bananas.

When they had viewed all, Keawe and Lopaka sat on the porch.

'Well,' asked Lopaka, 'is it all as you designed?'

'Words cannot utter it,' said Keawe. 'It is better than I dreamed, and I am sick with satisfaction.'

'There is but one thing to consider,' said Lopaka; 'all this may be quite natural, and the bottle imp have nothing whatever to say to it. If I were to buy the bottle, and got no schooner after all, I should have put my hand in the fire for nothing. I gave you my word, I know; but yet I think you would not grudge me one more proof.'

'I have sworn I would take no more favours,' said Keawe. 'I have gone already deep enough.'

'This is no favour I am thinking of,' replied Lopaka. 'It is only to see the imp himself. There is nothing to be gained by that, and so nothing to be ashamed of; and yet, if I once saw him, I should be sure of the whole matter. So indulge me so far, and let me see the imp; and, after that, here is the money in my hand, and I will buy it.'

'There is only one thing I am afraid of,' said Keawe. 'The imp may be very ugly to view; and if you once set eyes upon him you might be very undesirous of the bottle.'

'I am a man of my word,' said Lopaka. 'And here is the money betwixt us.'

'Very well,' replied Keawe. 'I have a curiosity myself. So come, let us have one look at you, Mr Imp.'

Now as soon as that was said, the imp looked out of the bottle, and in again, swift as a lizard; and there sat Keawe and Lopaka turned to stone. The night had quite come, before either found a thought to say or voice to say it with; and then Lopaka pushed the money over and took the bottle.

'I am a man of my word,' said he, 'and had need to be so, or I would not touch this bottle with my foot. Well, I shall get my schooner and a dollar or two for my pocket; and then I will be rid of this devil as fast as I can. For to tell you the plain truth, the look of him has cast me down.'

'Lopaka,' said Keawe, 'do not you think any worse of me than you can help; I know it is night, and the roads bad, and the pass by the tombs an ill place to go by so late, but I declare since I have seen that little face, I cannot eat or sleep or pray till it is gone from me. I will give you a lantern, and a basket to put the bottle in, and any picture or fine thing in all my house that takes your fancy; – and be gone at once, and go sleep at Hookena with Nahinu.'

'Keawe,' said Lopaka, 'many a man would take this ill; above all, when I am doing you a turn so friendly, as to keep my word and buy the bottle; and for that matter, the night and the dark, and the way by the tombs, must be all tenfold more dangerous to a man with such a sin upon his conscience, and such a bottle under his arm. But for my part, I am so extremely terrified myself, I have not the heart to blame you. Here I go then; and I pray God you may be happy in your house, and I fortunate with my schooner, and both get to heaven in the end in spite of the devil and his bottle.'

So Lopaka went down the mountain; and Keawe stood in his front balcony, and listened to the clink of the horse's shoes, and watched the lantern go shining down the path, and along the cliff of caves where the old dead are buried; and all the time he trembled and clasped his hands, and prayed for his friend, and gave glory to God that he himself was escaped out of that trouble.

But the next day came very brightly, and that new house of his was so delightful to behold that he forgot his terrors. One day followed another, and Keawe dwelt there in perpetual joy. He had his place on the back porch; it was there he ate and lived, and read the stories in the Honolulu newspapers; but when anyone came by they would go in and view the chambers and the pictures. And the fame of the house went far and wide; it was called *Ka-Hale Nui* – the Great House – in all Kona; and sometimes the Bright House, for Keawe kept a Chinaman, who was all day dusting and furbishing; and the glass, and the gilt, and the fine stuffs, and the pictures, shone as bright as the morning. As for Keawe himself, he could not walk in the chambers without singing, his heart was so enlarged; and when ships sailed by upon the sea, he would fly his colours on the mast.

So time went by, until one day Keawe went upon a visit as far as Kailua to certain of his friends. There he was well feasted; and left as soon as he could the next morning, and rode hard, for he was impatient to behold his beautiful house; and, besides, the night then coming on was the night in which the dead of old days go abroad in the sides of Kona; and having already meddled with the devil, he was the more chary of meeting with the dead. A little beyond Honaunau, looking far ahead, he was aware of a woman bathing in the edge of the sea; and she seemed a well-grown girl, but he thought no more of it. Then he saw her white shift flutter as she put it on, and then her red holoku; and by the time he came abreast of her she was done with her toilet, and had come up from the sea, and stood by the track-side in her red holoku, and she was all freshened with the bath, and her eyes shone and were kind. Now Keawe no sooner beheld her than he drew rein.

'I thought I knew everyone in this country,' said he. 'How comes it that I do not know you?'

'I am Kokua, daughter of Kiano,' said the girl, 'and I have just returned from Oahu. Who are you?'

'I will tell you who I am in a little,' said Keawe, dismounting from his horse, 'but not now. For I have a thought in my mind, and if you knew who I was, you might have heard of me, and would not give me a true answer. But tell me, first of all, one thing: Are you married?'

At this Kokua laughed out aloud. 'It is you who ask questions,' she said. 'Are you married yourself?'

'Indeed, Kokua, I am not,' replied Keawe, 'and never thought to be until this hour. But here is the plain truth. I have met you here at the roadside, and I saw your eyes, which are like the stars, and my heart went to you as swift as a bird. And so now, if you want none of me, say so, and I will go on to my own place; but if you think me no worse than any other young man, say so, too, and I will turn aside to your father's for the night, and tomorrow I will talk with the good man.'

Kokua said never a word, but she looked at the sea and laughed.

'Kokua,' said Keawe, 'if you say nothing, I will take that for the good answer; so let us be stepping to your father's door.'

She went on ahead of him, still without speech; only sometimes she glanced back and glanced away again, and she kept the strings of her hat in her mouth.

Now, when they had come to the door, Kiano came out on his verandah, and cried out and welcomed Keawe by name. At that the girl looked over, for the fame of the great house had come to her ears; and, to be sure, it was a great temptation. All that evening they were very merry together; and the girl was as bold as brass under the eyes of her parents, and made a mock of Keawe, for she had a quick wit. The next day he had a word with Kiano, and found the girl alone.

'Kokua,' said he, 'you made a mock of me all the evening; and it is still time to bid me go. I would not tell you who I was, because I have so fine a house, and I feared you would think too much of that house and too little of the man that loves you. Now you know all, and if you wish to have seen the last of me, say so at once.'

'No,' said Kokua; but this time she did not laugh, nor did Keawe ask for more.

This was the wooing of Keawe; things had gone quickly; but so an arrow goes, and the ball of a rifle swifter still, and yet both may strike the target. Things had gone fast, but they had gone far also, and the thought of Keawe rang in the maiden's head; she heard his voice in the breach of the surf upon the lava, and for this young man that she had seen but twice she would have left father and mother and her native islands. As for Keawe himself, his horse flew up the path of the mountain under the cliff of tombs, and the sound of the hoofs, and the sound of Keawe singing to himself for pleasure, echoed in the caverns of the dead. He came to the Bright House, and still he was singing. He sat and ate in the broad balcony, and the Chinaman wondered at his master, to hear how he sang between the mouthfuls. The sun went down into the sea, and the night came; and Keawe walked the balconies by lamplight, high on the mountains, and the voice of his singing startled men on ships.

'Here am I now upon my high place,' he said to himself. 'Life may be no better; this is the mountain top; and all shelves about me toward the worse. For the first time I will light up the chambers, and bathe in my fine bath with the hot water and the cold, and sleep alone in the bed of my bridal chamber.'

So the Chinaman had word, and he must rise from sleep and light the furnaces; and as he wrought below, besides the boilers, he heard his master singing and rejoicing above him in the lighted chambers.

When the water began to be hot the Chinaman cried to his master; and Keawe went into the bathroom; and the Chinaman heard him sing as he filled the marble basin; and heard him sing, and the singing broken, as he undressed; until of a sudden, the song ceased. The Chinaman listened, and listened; he called up the house to Keawe to ask if all were well, and Keawe answered him 'Yes,' and bade him go to bed; but there was no more singing in the Bright House; and all night long, the Chinaman heard his master's feet go round and round the balconies without repose.

Now the truth of it was this: as Keawe undressed for his bath, he spied upon his flesh a patch like a patch of lichen on a rock, and it was then that he stopped singing. For he knew the likeness of that patch, and knew that he was fallen in the Chinese Evil.*

Now, it is a sad thing for any man to fall into this sickness. And it would be a sad thing for anyone to leave a house so beautiful and so commodious, and depart from all his friends to the north coast of Molokai between the mighty cliff and the sea-breakers. But what was that to the case of the man Keawe, he who had met his love but yesterday, and won her but that morning, and now saw all his hopes break, in a moment, like a piece of glass?

Awhile he sat upon the edge of the bath; then sprang, with a cry, and ran outside; and to and fro, to and fro, along the balcony, like one despairing.

'Very willingly could I leave Hawaii, the home of my fathers,' Keawe was thinking. 'Very lightly could I leave my house, the high-placed, the many-windowed, here upon the mountains. Very bravely could I go to Molokai, to Kalaupapa by the cliffs, to live with the smitten and to sleep there, far from my fathers. But what wrong have I done, what sin lies upon my soul, that I should have encountered Kokua coming cool from the sea-water in the evening? Kokua, the soul ensnarer! Kokua, the light of my life! Her may I never wed, her may I look upon no longer, her may I no more handle with my loving hand; and it is for this, it is for you, O Kokua! that I pour my lamentations!'

Now you are to observe what sort of a man Keawe was, for he might have dwelt there in the Bright House for years, and no one been the wiser of his sickness; but he reckoned nothing of that, if

* Leprosy.

he must lose Kokua. And again, he might have wed Kokua even as he was; and so many would have done, because they have the souls of pigs; but Keawe loved the maid manfully, and he would do her no hurt and bring her in no danger.

A little beyond the midst of the night, there came in his mind the recollection of that bottle. He went round to the back porch, and called to memory the day when the devil had looked forth; and at the thought ice ran in his veins.

'A dreadful thing is the bottle,' thought Keawe, 'and dreadful is the imp, and it is a dreadful thing to risk the flames of hell. But what other hope have I to cure my sickness or to wed Kokua? What!' he thought, 'would I beard the devil once, only to get me a house, and not face him again to win Kokua?'

Thereupon he called to mind it was the next day the *Hall* went by on her return to Honolulu. 'There must I go first,' he thought, 'and see Lopaka. For the best hope that I have now is to find that same bottle I was so pleased to be rid of.'

Never a wink could he sleep; the food stuck in his throat; but he sent a letter to Kiano, and about the time when the steamer would be coming, rode down beside the cliff of the tombs. It rained; his horse went heavily; he looked up at the black mouths of the caves, and he envied the dead that slept there and were done with trouble; and called to mind how he had galloped by the day before, and was astonished. So he came down to Hookena, and there was all the country gathered for the steamer as usual. In the shed before the store they sat and jested and passed the news; but there was no matter of speech in Keawe's bosom, and he sat in their midst and looked without on the rain falling on the houses, and the surf beating among the rocks, and the sighs arose in his throat.

'Keawe of the Bright House is out of spirits,' said one to another. Indeed, and so he was, and little wonder.

Then the *Hall* came, and the whaleboat carried him on board. The after-part of the ship was full of Haoles* who had been to visit the volcano, as their custom is; and the midst was crowded with Kanakas, and the forepart with wild bulls from Hilo and horses from Kaü; but Keawe sat apart from all in his sorrow, and watched for the house of Kiano. There it sat, low upon the shore in the

---

* Whites.

black rocks, and shaded by the cocoa palms, and there by the door was a red holoku, no greater than a fly, and going to and fro with a fly's busyness.

'Ah, queen of my heart,' he cried, 'I'll venture my dear soul to win you!'

Soon after, darkness fell, and the cabins were lit up, and the Haoles sat and played at the cards and drank whisky as their custom is; but Keawe walked the deck all night; and all the next day, as they steamed under the lee of Maui or of Molokai, he was still pacing to and fro like a wild animal in a menagerie.

Towards evening they passed Diamond Head, and came to the pier of Honolulu. Keawe stepped out among the crowd and began to ask for Lopaka. It seemed he had become the owner of a schooner – none better in the islands – and was gone upon an adventure as far as Pola-Pola or Kahiki; so there was no help to be looked for from Lopaka. Keawe called to mind a friend of his, a lawyer in the town (I must not tell his name), and inquired of him. They said he was grown suddenly rich, and had a fine new house upon Waikiki shore; and this put a thought in Keawe's head, and he called a hack and drove to the lawyer's house.

The house was all brand new, and the trees in the garden no greater than walking-sticks, and the lawyer, when he came, had the air of a man well pleased.

'What can I do to serve you?' said the lawyer.

'You are a friend of Lopaka's,' replied Keawe, 'and Lopaka purchased from me a certain piece of goods that I thought you might enable me to trace.'

The lawyer's face became very dark. 'I do not profess to misunderstand you, Mr Keawe,' said he, 'though this is an ugly business to be stirring in. You may be sure I know nothing, but yet I have a guess, and if you would apply in a certain quarter I think you might have news.'

And he named the name of a man, which, again, I had better not repeat. So it was for days, and Keawe went from one to another, finding everywhere new clothes and carriages, and fine new houses and men everywhere in great contentment, although, to be sure, when he hinted at his business their faces would cloud over.

'No doubt I am upon the track,' thought Keawe. 'These new clothes and carriages are all the gifts of the little imp, and these glad faces are the faces of men who have taken their profit and got rid of the accursed thing in safety. When I see pale cheeks and hear sighing, I shall know that I am near the bottle.'

So it befell at last that he was recommended to a Haole in Beritania Street. When he came to the door, about the hour of the evening meal, there were the usual marks of the new house, and the young garden, and the electric light shining in the windows; but when the owner came, a shock of hope and fear ran through Keawe; for here was a young man, white as a corpse, and black about the eyes, the hair shedding from his head, and such a look in his countenance as a man may have when he is waiting for the gallows.

'Here it is, to be sure,' thought Keawe, and so with this man he noways veiled his errand. 'I am come to buy the bottle,' said he.

At the word, the young Haole of Beritania Street reeled against the wall.

'The bottle!' he gasped. 'To buy the bottle!' Then he seemed to choke, and seizing Keawe by the arm carried him into a room and poured out wine in two glasses.

'Here is my respects,' said Keawe, who had been much about with Haoles in his time. 'Yes,' he added, 'I am come to buy the bottle. What is the price by now?'

At that word the young man let his glass slip through his fingers, and looked upon Keawe like a ghost.

'The price,' says he; 'the price! You do not know the price?'

'It is for that I am asking you,' returned Keawe. 'But why are you so much concerned? Is there anything wrong about the price?'

'It has dropped a great deal in value since your time, Mr Keawe,' said the young man, stammering.

'Well, well, I shall have the less to pay for it,' says Keawe. 'How much did it cost you?'

The young man was as white as a sheet. 'Two cents,' said he.

'What?' cried Keawe, 'two cents? Why, then, you can only sell it for one. And he who buys it— ' The words died upon Keawe's tongue; he who bought it could never sell it again, the bottle and the bottle imp must abide with him until he died, and when he died must carry him to the red end of hell.

The young man of Beritania Street fell upon his knees. 'For God's sake buy it!' he cried. 'You can have all my fortune in the bargain. I was mad when I bought it at that price. I had embezzled money at my store; I was lost else; I must have gone to jail.'

'Poor creature,' said Keawe, 'you would risk your soul upon so desperate an adventure, and to avoid the proper punishment of your own disgrace; and you think I could hesitate with love in front of me. Give me the bottle, and the change which I make sure you have all ready. Here is a five-cent piece.'

It was as Keawe supposed; the young man had the change ready in a drawer; the bottle changed hands, and Keawe's fingers were no sooner clasped upon the stalk than he had breathed his wish to be a clean man. And, sure enough, when he got home to his room, and stripped himself before a glass, his flesh was whole like an infant's. And here was the strange thing: he had no sooner seen this miracle, than his mind was changed within him, and he cared naught for the Chinese Evil, and little enough for Kokua; and had but the one thought, that here he was bound to the bottle imp for time and for eternity, and had no better hope but to be a cinder for ever in the flames of hell. Away ahead of him he saw them blaze with his mind's eye, and his soul shrank, and darkness fell upon the light.

When Keawe came to himself a little, he was aware it was the night when the band played at the hotel. Thither he went, because he feared to be alone; and there, among happy faces, walked to and fro, and heard the tunes go up and down, and saw Berger beat the measure, and all the while he heard the flames crackle, and saw the red fire burning in the bottomless pit. Of a sudden the band played *Hiki-ao-ao;* that was a song that he had sung with Kokua, and at the strain courage returned to him.

'It is done now,' he thought, 'and once more let me take the good along with the evil.'

So it befell that he returned to Hawaii by the first steamer, and as soon as it could be managed he was wedded to Kokua, and carried her up the mountain side to the Bright House.

Now it was so with these two, that when they were together, Keawe's heart was stilled; but so soon as he was alone he fell into a brooding horror, and heard the flames crackle, and saw the red fire burn in the bottomless pit. The girl, indeed, had come to him wholly; her heart leapt in her side at sight of him, her hand clung to his; and she was so fashioned from the hair upon her head to the nails upon her toes that none could see her without joy. She was pleasant in her nature. She had the good word always. Full of song she was, and went to and fro in the Bright House, the brightest thing in its three storeys, carolling like the birds. And Keawe beheld and heard her with delight, and then must shrink upon one side, and weep and groan to think upon the price that he had paid for her; and then he must dry his eyes, and wash his face, and go and sit with her on the broad balconies joining in her songs, and, with a sick spirit, answering her smiles.

There came a day when her feet began to be heavy and her songs more rare; and now it was not Keawe only that would weep apart, but each would sunder from the other and sit in opposite balconies with the whole width of the Bright House betwixt. Keawe was so sunk in his despair, he scarce observed the change, and was only glad he had more hours to sit alone and brood upon his destiny, and was not so frequently condemned to pull a smiling face on a sick heart. But one day, coming softly through the house, he heard the sound of a child sobbing, and there was Kokua rolling her face upon the balcony floor, and weeping like the lost.

'You do well to weep in this house, Kokua,' he said. 'And yet I would give the head off my body that you (at least) might have been happy.'

'Happy!' she cried. 'Keawe, when you lived alone in your Bright House, you were the word of the island for a happy man; laughter and song were in your mouth, and your face was as bright as the sunrise. Then you wedded poor Kokua; and the good God knows what is amiss in her – but from that day you have not smiled. Oh!' she cried, 'what ails me? I thought I was pretty, and I knew I loved him. What ails me that I throw this cloud upon my husband?'

'Poor Kokua,' said Keawe. He sat down by her side, and sought to take her hand; but that she plucked away. 'Poor Kokua,' he said, again. 'My poor child – my pretty. And I thought all this while to spare you! Well, you shall know all. Then, at least, you will pity poor Keawe; then you will understand how much he loved you in the past – that he dared hell for your possession – and how much he loves you still (the poor condemned one), that he can yet call up a smile when he beholds you.'

With that, he told her all, even from the beginning.

'You have done this for me?' she cried. 'Ah, well then what do I care!' – and she clasped and wept upon him.

'Ah, child!' said Keawe, 'and yet, when I consider of the fire of hell, I care a good deal!'

'Never tell me,' said she; 'no man can be lost because he loved Kokua, and no other fault. I tell you, Keawe, I shall save you with these hands, or perish in your company. What! you loved me, and gave your soul, and you think I will not die to save you in return?'

'Ah, my dear! you might die a hundred times, and what difference would that make?' he cried, 'except to leave me lonely till the time comes of my damnation?'

'You know nothing,' said she. 'I was educated in a school in Honolulu; I am no common girl. And I tell you, I shall save my lover. What is this you say about a cent? But all the world is not American. In England they have a piece they call a farthing, which is about half a cent. Ah! sorrow!' she cried, 'that makes it scarcely better, for the buyer must be lost, and we shall find none so brave as my Keawe! But, then, there is France; they have a small coin there which they call a centime, and these go five to the cent or thereabout. We could not do better. Come, Keawe, let us go to the French islands; let us go to Tahiti, as fast as ships can bear us. There we have four centimes, three centimes, two centimes, one centime; four possible sales to come and go on; and two of us to push the bargain. Come, my Keawe! kiss me, and banish care. Kokua will defend you.'

'Gift of God!' he cried. 'I cannot think that God will punish me for desiring aught so good! Be it as you will, then; take me where you please: I put my life and my salvation in your hands.'

Early the next day Kokua was about her preparations. She took Keawe's chest that he went with sailoring; and first she put the bottle in a corner; and then packed it with the richest of their clothes and the bravest of the knick-knacks in the house. 'For,' said she, 'we must seem to be rich folks, or who will believe in the bottle?' All the time of her preparation she was as gay as a bird; only when she looked upon Keawe, the tears would spring in her eye, and she must run and kiss him. As for Keawe, a weight was off his soul; now that he had his secret shared, and some hope in front of him, he seemed like a new man, his feet went lightly on the earth, and his breath was good to him again. Yet was terror still at his elbow; and ever and again, as the wind blows out a taper, hope died in him, and he saw the flames toss and the red fire burn in hell.

It was given out in the country they were gone pleasuring to the States, which was thought a strange thing, and yet not so strange as the truth, if any could have guessed it. So they went to Honolulu in the *Hall*, and thence in the *Umatilla* to San Francisco with a crowd of Haoles, and at San Francisco took their passage by the mail brigantine, the *Tropic Bird*, for Papeete,.the chief place of the French in the south islands. Thither they came, after a pleasant voyage, on a fair day of the Trade Wind, and saw the reef with the surf breaking, and Motuiti with its palms, and the schooner riding within-side, and the white houses of the town low down along the shore among green trees, and overhead the mountains and the clouds of Tahiti, the wise island.

It was judged the most wise to hire a house, which they did accordingly, opposite the British Consul's, to make a great parade of money, and themselves conspicuous with carriages and horses. This it was very easy to do, so long as they had the bottle in their possession; for Kokua was more bold than Keawe, and, whenever she had a mind, called on the imp for twenty or a hundred dollars. At this rate they soon grew to be remarked in the town; and the strangers from Hawaii, their riding and their driving, the fine holokus and the rich lace of Kokua, became the matter of much talk.

They got on well after the first with the Tahitian language, which is indeed like to the Hawaiian, with a change of certain letters; and as soon as they had any freedom of speech, began to push the bottle. You are to consider it was not an easy subject to introduce; it was not easy to persuade people you were in earnest, when you offered to sell them for four centimes the spring of health and riches inexhaustible. It was necessary besides to explain the dangers of the bottle; and either people disbelieved the whole thing and laughed, or they thought the more of the darker part, became overcast with gravity, and drew away from Keawe and Kokua, as from persons who had dealings with the devil. So far from gaining ground, these two began to find they were avoided in the town; the children ran away from them screaming, a thing intolerable to Kokua; Catholics crossed themselves as they went by; and all persons began with one accord to disengage themselves from their advances.

Depression fell upon their spirits. They would sit at night in their new house, after a day's weariness, and not exchange one word, or the silence would be broken by Kokua bursting suddenly into sobs. Sometimes they would pray together; sometimes they would have the bottle out upon the floor, and sit all evening watching how the shadow hovered in the midst. At such times they would be afraid to go to rest. It was long ere slumber came to them, and, if either dozed off, it would be to wake and find the other silently weeping in the dark, or, perhaps, to wake alone, the other having fled from the house and the neighbourhood of that bottle, to pace under the bananas in the little garden, or to wander on the beach by moonlight.

One night it was so when Kokua awoke. Keawe was gone. She felt in the bed and his place was cold. Then fear fell upon her, and she sat up in bed. A little moonshine filtered through the shutters. The room was bright, and she could spy the bottle on the floor. Outside it blew high, the great trees of the avenue cried aloud, and the fallen leaves rattled in the verandah. In the midst of this Kokua was aware of another sound; whether of a beast or of a man she could scarce tell, but it was as sad as death, and cut her to the soul. Softly she arose, set the door ajar, and looked forth into the moonlit yard. There, under the bananas, lay Keawe, his mouth in the dust, and as he lay he moaned.

It was Kokua's first thought to run forward and console him; her second potently withheld her. Keawe had borne himself before his wife like a brave man; it became her little in the hour of weakness to intrude upon his shame. With the thought she drew back into the house.

'Heaven!' she thought, 'how careless have I been – how weak! It is he, not I, that stands in this eternal peril; it was he, not I, that took the curse upon his soul. It is for my sake, and for the love of a creature of so little worth and such poor help, that he now beholds so close to him the flames of hell – ay, and smells the smoke of it, lying without there in the wind and moonlight. Am I so dull of spirit that never till now I have surmised my duty, or have I seen it before and turned aside? But now, at least, I take up my soul in both the hands of my affection; now I say farewell to the white steps of heaven and the waiting faces of my friends. A love for a love, and let mine be equalled with Keawe's! A soul for a soul, and be it mine to perish!'

She was a deft woman with her hands, and was soon apparelled. She took in her hands the change – the precious centimes they kept ever at their side; for this coin is little used, and they had made provision at a Government office. When she was forth in the avenue clouds came on the wind, and the moon was blackened. The town slept, and she knew not whither to turn till she heard one coughing in the shadow of the trees.

'Old man,' said Kokua, 'what do you here abroad in the cold night?'

The old man could scarce express himself for coughing, but she made out that he was old and poor, and a stranger in the island.

'Will you do me a service?' said Kokua. 'As one stranger to another, and as an old man to a young woman, will you help a daughter of Hawaii?'

'Ah,' said the old man. 'So you are the witch from the eight islands, and even my old soul you seek to entangle. But I have heard of you, and defy your wickedness.'

'Sit down here,' said Kokua, 'and let me tell you a tale.' And she told him the story of Keawe from the beginning to the end.

'And now,' said she, 'I am his wife, whom he bought with his soul's welfare. And what should I do? If I went to him myself and offered to buy it, he would refuse. But if you go, he will sell it eagerly; I will await you here; you will buy it for four centimes, and I will buy it again for three. And the Lord strengthen a poor girl!'

'If you meant falsely,' said the old man, 'I think God would strike you dead.'

'He would!' cried Kokua. 'Be sure he would. I could not be so treacherous – God would not suffer it.'

'Give me the four centimes and await me here,' said the old man.

Now, when Kokua stood alone in the street, her spirit died. The wind roared in the trees, and it seemed to her the rushing of the flames of hell; the shadows tossed in the light of the street lamp, and they seemed to her the snatching hands of evil ones. If she had had the strength, she must have run away, and if she had had the breath she must have screamed aloud; but, in truth, she could do neither, and stood and trembled in the avenue, like an affrighted child.

Then she saw the old man returning, and he had the bottle in his hand.

'I have done your bidding,' said he. 'I left your husband weeping like a child; tonight he will sleep easy.' And he held the bottle forth.

'Before you give it me,' Kokua panted, 'take the good with the evil – ask to be delivered from your cough.'

'I am an old man,' replied the other, 'and too near the gate of the grave to take a favour from the devil. But what is this? Why do you not take the bottle? Do you hesitate?'

'Not hesitate!' cried Kokua. 'I am only weak. Give me a moment. It is my hand resists, my flesh shrinks back from the accursed thing. One moment only!'

The old man looked upon Kokua kindly. 'Poor child!' said he, 'you fear; your soul misgives you. Well, let me keep it. I am old, and can never more be happy in this world, and as for the next—'

'Give it me!' gasped Kokua. 'There is your money. Do you think I am so base as that? Give me the bottle.'

'God bless you, child,' said the old man.

Kokua concealed the bottle under her holoku, said farewell to the old man, and walked off along the avenue, she cared not whither. For all roads were now the same to her, and led equally to hell. Sometimes she walked, and sometimes ran; sometimes she screamed out loud in the night, and sometimes lay by the wayside in the dust and wept. All that she had heard of hell came back to her; she saw the flames blaze, and she smelt the smoke, and her flesh withered on the coals.

Near day she came to her mind again, and returned to the house. It was even as the old man said – Keawe slumbered like a child. Kokua stood and gazed upon his face.

'Now, my husband,' said she, 'it is your turn to sleep. When you wake it will be your turn to sing and laugh. But for poor Kokua, alas! that meant no evil – for poor Kokua no more sleep, no more singing, no more delight, whether in earth or heaven.'

With that she lay down in the bed by his side, and her misery was so extreme that she fell in a deep slumber instantly.

Late in the morning her husband woke her and gave her the good news. It seemed he was silly with delight, for he paid no heed to her distress, ill though she dissembled it. The words stuck in her mouth, it mattered not; Keawe did the speaking. She ate not a bite, but who was to observe it? for Keawe cleared the dish. Kokua saw and heard him, like some strange thing in a dream; there were times when she forgot or doubted, and put her hands to her brow; to know herself doomed and hear her husband babble, seemed so monstrous.

All the while Keawe was eating and talking, and planning the time of their return, and thanking her for saving him, and fondling her, and calling her the true helper after all. He laughed at the old man that was fool enough to buy that bottle.

'A worthy old man he seemed,' Keawe said. 'But no one can judge by appearances. For why did the old reprobate require the bottle?'

'My husband,' said Kokua, humbly, 'his purpose may have been good.'

Keawe laughed like an angry man.

'Fiddle-de-dee!' cried Keawe. 'An old rogue, I tell you; and an old ass to boot. For the bottle was hard enough to sell at four centimes; and at three it will be quite impossible. The margin is not broad enough, the thing begins to smell of scorching – brrr!' said he, and shuddered. 'It is true I bought it myself at a cent, when I knew not there were smaller coins. I was a fool for my pains; there will never be found another: and whoever has that bottle now will carry it to the pit.'

'O my husband!' said Kokua. 'Is it not a terrible thing to save oneself by the eternal ruin of another? It seems to me I could not laugh. I would be humbled. I would be filled with melancholy. I would pray for the poor holder.'

Then Keawe, because he felt the truth of what she said, grew the more angry. 'Heighty-teighty!' cried he. 'You may be filled with melancholy if you please. It is not the mind of a good wife. If you thought at all of me, you would sit shamed.'

Thereupon he went out, and Kokua was alone.

What chance had she to sell that bottle at two centimes? None, she perceived. And if she had any, here was her husband hurrying her away to a country where there was nothing lower than a cent. And here – on the morrow of her sacrifice – was her husband leaving her and blaming her.

She would not even try to profit by what time she had, but sat in the house, and now had the bottle out and viewed it with unutterable fear, and now, with loathing, hid it out of sight.

By-and-by, Keawe came back, and would have her take a drive.

'My husband, I am ill,' she said. 'I am out of heart. Excuse me, I can take no pleasure.'

Then was Keawe more wroth than ever. With her, because he thought she was brooding over the case of the old man; and with himself, because he thought she was right, and was ashamed to be so happy.

'This is your truth,' cried he, 'and this your affection! Your husband is just saved from eternal ruin, which he encountered for the love of you – and you take no pleasure! Kokua, you have a disloyal heart.'

He went forth again furious, and wandered in the town all day. He met friends, and drank with them; they hired a carriage and drove into the country, and there drank again. All the time Keawe was ill at ease, because he was taking this pastime while his wife was sad, and because he knew in his heart that she was more right than he; and the knowledge made him drink the deeper.

Now there was an old brutal Haole drinking with him, one that had been a boatswain of a whaler, a runaway, a digger in gold mines, a convict in prisons. He had a low mind and a foul mouth; he loved to drink and to see others drunken; and he pressed the glass upon Keawe. Soon there was no more money in the company.

'Here, you!' says the boatswain, 'you are rich, you have been always saying. You have a bottle or some foolishness.'

'Yes,' says Keawe, 'I am rich; I will go back and get some money from my wife, who keeps it.'

'That's a bad idea, mate,' said the boatswain. 'Never you trust a petticoat with dollars. They're all as false as water; you keep an eye on her.'

Now, this word struck in Keawe's mind; for he was muddled with what he had been drinking.

'I should not wonder but she was false, indeed,' thought he. 'Why else should she be so cast down at my release? But I will show her I am not the man to be fooled. I will catch her in the act.'

Accordingly, when they were back in town, Keawe bade the boatswain wait for him at the corner, by the old calaboose, and went forward up the avenue alone to the door of his house. The night had come again; there was a light within, but never a sound; and Keawe crept about the corner, opened the back door softly, and looked in.

There was Kokua on the floor, the lamp at her side, before her was a milk-white bottle, with a round belly and a long neck; and as she viewed it, Kokua wrung her hands.

A long time Keawe stood and looked in the doorway. At first he was struck stupid; and then fear fell upon him that the bargain had been made amiss, and the bottle had come back to him as it came at San Francisco; and at that his knees were loosened, and the fumes of the wine departed from his head like mists off a river in the morning. And then he had another thought; and it was a strange one, that made his cheeks to burn.

'I must make sure of this,' thought he.

So he closed the door, and went softly round the corner again, and then came noisily in, as though he were but now returned. And, lo! by the time he opened the front door no bottle was to be seen; and Kokua sat in a chair and started up like one awakened out of sleep.

'I have been drinking all day and making merry,' said Keawe. 'I have been with good companions, and now I only come back for money, and return to drink and carouse with them again.'

Both his face and voice were as stern as judgement, but Kokua was too troubled to observe.

'You do well to use your own, my husband,' said she, and her words trembled.

'O, I do well in all things,' said Keawe, and he went straight to the chest and took out money. But he looked besides in the corner where they kept the bottle, and there was no bottle there.

At that the chest heaved upon the floor like a sea-billow, and the house span about him like a wreath of smoke, for he saw he was lost now, and there was no escape. 'It is what I feared,' he thought. 'It is she who has bought it.'

And then he came to himself a little and rose up; but the sweat streamed on his face as thick as the rain and as cold as the well-water.

'Kokua,' said he, 'I said to you today what ill became me. Now I return to carouse with my jolly companions,' and at that he laughed a little quietly. 'I will take more pleasure in the cup if you forgive me.'

She clasped his knees in a moment; she kissed his knees with flowing tears.

'O,' she cried, 'I asked but a kind word!'

'Let us never one think hardly of the other,' said Keawe, and was gone out of the house.

Now, the money that Keawe had taken was only some of that store of centime pieces they had laid in at their arrival. It was very sure he had no mind to be drinking. His wife had given her soul for him, now he must give his for hers; no other thought was in the world with him.

At the corner, by the old calaboose, there was the boatswain waiting.

'My wife has the bottle,' said Keawe, 'and, unless you help me to recover it, there can be no more money and no more liquor tonight.'

'You do not mean to say you are serious about that bottle?' cried the boatswain.

'There is the lamp,' said Keawe. 'Do I look as if I was jesting?'

'That is so,' said the boatswain. 'You look as serious as a ghost.'

'Well, then,' said Keawe, 'here are two centimes; you must go to my wife in the house, and offer her these for the bottle, which (if I am not much mistaken) she will give you instantly. Bring it to me here, and I will buy it back from you for one; for that is the law with this bottle, that it still must be sold for a less sum. But whatever you do, never breathe a word to her that you have come from me.'

'Mate, I wonder are you making a fool of me?' asked the boatswain.

'It will do you no harm if I am,' returned Keawe.

'That is so, mate,' said the boatswain.

'And if you doubt me,' added Keawe, 'you can try. As soon as you are clear of the house, wish to have your pocket full of money, or a bottle of the best rum, or what you please, and you will see the virtue of the thing.'

'Very well, Kanaka,' says the boatswain. 'I will try; but if you are having your fun out of me, I will take my fun out of you with a belaying pin.'

So the whaler-man went off up the avenue; and Keawe stood and waited. It was near the same spot where Kokua had waited the night before; but Keawe was more resolved, and never faltered in his purpose; only his soul was bitter with despair.

It seemed a long time he had to wait before he heard a voice singing in the darkness of the avenue. He knew the voice to be the boatswain's; but it was strange how drunken it appeared upon a sudden.

Next, the man himself came stumbling into the light of the lamp. He had the devil's bottle buttoned in his coat; another bottle was in his hand; and even as he came in view he raised it to his mouth and drank.

'You have it,' said Keawe. 'I see that.'

'Hands off!' cried the boatswain, jumping back. 'Take a step near me, and I'll smash your mouth. You thought you could make a cat's-paw of me, did you?'

'What do you mean?' cried Keawe.

'Mean?' cried the boatswain. 'This is a pretty good bottle, this is; that's what I mean. How I got it for two centimes I can't make out; but I'm sure you shan't have it for one.'

'You mean you won't sell?' gasped Keawe.

'No, *sir!*' cried the boatswain. 'But I'll give you a drink of the rum, if you like.'

'I tell you,' said Keawe, 'the man who has that bottle goes to hell.'

'I reckon I'm going anyway,' returned the sailor; 'and this bottle's the best thing to go with I've struck yet. 'No, sir!' he cried again, 'this is my bottle now, and you can go and fish for another.'

'Can this be true?' Keawe cried. 'For your own sake, I beseech you, sell it me!'

'I don't value any of your talk,' replied the boatswain. 'You thought I was a flat; now you see I'm not; and there's an end. If you won't have a swallow of the rum, I'll have one myself. Here's your health, and goodnight to you!'

So off he went down the avenue towards town, and there goes the bottle out of the story.

But Keawe ran to Kokua light as the wind; and great was their joy that night; and great, since then, has been the peace of all their days in the Bright House.

# The Rocking-horse Winner

## D. H. Lawrence

*Frieda, Lawrence's voluminous muse, was angered by the fact that Lawrence always seemed to make martyrs out of his male heroes, killing them off in the last chapters, the world blind to their glory. 'Let your hero become ordinary,' she wrote to him. 'Always this superiority and death.'*

*In the hero of 'The Rocking-horse Winner' Lawrence has managed to combine in one character the traits of an ordinary child in need of love, with the mysterious gift of prophecy. As in his novels, his poems, his essays, even his paintings, Lawrence applies his relentless eye for detail, bringing out the finer shades of his characters' personalities: 'the subtle changes of the spirit' which he minutely chronicled.*

There was a woman who was beautiful, who started with all the advantages, yet she had no luck. She married for love, and the love turned to dust. She had bonny children, yet she felt they had been thrust upon her, and she could not love them. They looked at her coldly, as if they were finding fault with her. And hurriedly she felt she must cover up some fault in herself. Yet what it was that she must cover up she never knew. Nevertheless, when her children were present, she always felt the centre of her heart go hard. This troubled her, and in her manner, she was all the more gentle and anxious for her children, as if she loved them very much. Only she herself knew that at the centre of her heart was a hard little place that could not feel love, no, not for anybody. Everybody else said of her. 'She is such a good mother. She adores her children.' Only she herself, and her children themselves, knew it was not so. They read it in each other's eyes.

There was a boy and two little girls. They lived in a pleasant house, with a garden, and they had discreet servants, and felt themselves superior to anyone in the neighbourhood.

Although they lived in style, they felt always an anxiety in the house. There was never enough money. The mother had a small income, and the father had a small income, but not nearly enough for the social position which they had to keep up. The father went into town to some office. But though he had good prospects, these prospects never materialized. There was always the grinding sense of the shortage of money, though the style was always kept up.

At last the mother said, 'I will see if *I* can't make something.' But she did not know where to begin. She racked her brains, and tried this thing and the other, but could not find anything successful. The failure made deep lines come into her face. Her children were growing up, they would have to go to school. There must be more money, there must be more money. The father, who was always very handsome and expensive in his tastes, seemed as if he never *would* be able to do anything worth doing. And the mother, who had a great belief in herself, did not succeed any better, and her tastes were just as expensive.

And so the house came to be haunted by the unspoken phrase: *There must be more money! There must be more money!* The children could hear it all the time, though nobody said it aloud. They heard it at Christmas, when the expensive and splendid toys filled the nursery. Behind the shining modern rocking-horse, behind the smart doll's-house, a voice would start whispering, 'There *must* be more money! There *must* be more money!' And the children would stop playing, to listen for a moment. They would look into each other's eyes, to see if they had all heard. And each one saw in the eyes of the other two that they too had heard. 'There *must* be more money! There *must* be more money!'

It came whispering from the springs of the still-swaying rocking-horse, and even the horse, bending his wooden, champing head, heard it. The big doll, sitting so pink and smirking in her new pram, could hear it quite plainly, and seemed to be smirking all the more self-consciously because of it. The foolish puppy too, that took the place of the teddy-bear, he was looking so extraordinarily foolish for no other reason but that he heard the secret whisper all over the house. 'There *must* be more money.'

Yet nobody ever said it aloud. The whisper was everywhere, and therefore no one spoke it. Just as no one ever says: 'We are breathing!' in spite of the fact that breath is coming and going all the time.

'Mother!' said the boy Paul one day. 'Why don't we keep a car of our own? Why do we always use uncle's or else a taxi?'

'Because we're the poor members of the family,' said the mother.

'But *why* are we, Mother?'

'Well – I suppose,' she said slowly and bitterly, 'it's because your father has no luck.'

The boy was silent for some time.

'Is luck money, Mother?' he asked, rather timidly.

'No, Paul! Not quite. It's what causes you to have money.'

'Oh!' said Paul vaguely. 'I thought when Uncle Oscar said *filthy lucker*, it meant money.'

'*Filthy lucre* does mean money,' said the mother. 'But it's lucre, not luck.'

'Oh!' said the boy. 'Then what *is* luck, Mother?'

'It's what causes you to have money. If you're lucky you have money. That's why it's better to be born lucky than rich. If you're rich, you may lose your money. But if you're lucky, you will always get more money.'

'Oh! Will you! And is Father not lucky?'

'Very unlucky, I should say,' she said, bitterly.

The boy watched her with unsure eyes.

'Why?' he asked.

'I don't know. Nobody ever knows why one person is lucky and another unlucky.'

'Don't they? Nobody at all? Does *nobody* know?'

'Perhaps God! But He never tells.'

'He ought to, then. And aren't you lucky either, Mother?'

'I can't be, if I married an unlucky husband.'

'But by yourself, aren't you?'

'I used to think I was, before I married. Now I think I am very unlucky indeed.'

'Why?'

'Well – never mind! Perhaps I'm not really,' she said.

The child looked at her, to see if she meant it. But he saw, by the lines of her mouth, that she was only trying to hide something from him.

'Well, anyhow,' he said stoutly. 'I'm a lucky person.'

'Why?' said his mother, with a sudden laugh.

He stared at her. He didn't even know why he had said it.

'God told me,' he asserted, brazening it out.

'I hope He did, dear!' she said, again with a laugh, but rather bitter.

'He did, Mother!'

'Excellent!' said the mother, using one of her husband's exclamations.

The boy saw she did not believe him; or rather, that she paid no attention to his assertion. This angered him somewhere, and made him want to compel her attention.

He went off by himself, vaguely, in a childish way, seeking for the clue to 'luck'. Absorbed, taking no heed of other people, he went about with a sort of stealth, seeking inwardly for luck. He wanted luck, he wanted it, he wanted it. When the two girls were playing dolls, in the nursery, he would sit on his big rocking-horse, charging madly into space, with a frenzy that made the little girls peer at him uneasily. Wildly the horse careered, the waving dark hair of the boy tossed, his eyes had a strange glare in them. The little girls dared not speak to him.

When he had ridden to the end of his mad little journey, he climbed down and stood in front of his rocking-horse, staring fixedly into its lowered face. Its red mouth was slightly open, its big eye was wide and glassy bright.

'Now!' he would silently command the snorting steed. 'Now take me where there is luck! Now take me!'

And he would slash the horse on the neck with the little whip he had asked Uncle Oscar for. He *knew* the horse could take him to where there was luck, if only he forced it. So he would mount again, and start on his furious ride, hoping at last to get there. He knew he could get there.

'You'll break your horse, Paul!' said the nurse.

'He's always riding like that! I wish he'd leave off!' said his elder sister Joan.

But he only glared down on them in silence. Nurse gave him up. She could make nothing of him. Anyhow he was growing beyond her.

One day his mother and his Uncle Oscar came in when he was on one of his furious rides. He did not speak to them.

'Hallo! you young jockey! Riding a winner?' said his uncle.

'Aren't you growing too big for a rocking-horse? You're not a very little boy any longer, you know,' said his mother.

But Paul only gave a blue glare from his big, rather close-set eyes.

He would speak to nobody when he was in full tilt. His mother watched him with an anxious expression on her face.

At last he suddenly stopped forcing his horse into the mechanical gallop, and slid down.

'Well, I got there!' he announced fiercely, his blue eyes still flaring, and his sturdy long legs straddling apart.

'Where did you get to?' asked his mother.

'Where I wanted to go to,' he flared back at her.

'That's right, son!' said Uncle Oscar. 'Don't you stop till you get there. What's the horse's name?'

'He doesn't have a name,' said the boy.

'Gets on without all right?' asked the uncle.

'Well, he has different names. He was called Sansovino last week.'

'Sansovino, eh? Won the Ascot. How did you know his name?'

'He always talks about horse-races with Bassett,' said Joan.

The uncle was delighted to find that his small nephew was posted with all the racing news. Bassett, the young gardener who had been wounded in the left foot in the war, and had got his present job through Oscar Cresswell, whose batman he had been, was a perfect blade of the 'turf'. He lived in the racing events, and the small boy lived with him.

Oscar Cresswell got it all from Bassett.

'Master Paul comes and askes me, so I can't do more than tell him, sir,' said Bassett, his face terribly serious, as if he were speaking of religious matters.

'And does he ever put anything on a horse he fancies?'

'Well – I don't want to give him away – he's a young sport, a fine sport, sir. Would you mind asking him himself? He sort of takes a pleasure in it, and perhaps he'd feel I was giving him away, sir, if you don't mind.'

Bassett was serious as a church.

The uncle went back to his nephew, and took him off for a ride in the car.

'Say, Paul, old man, do you ever put anything on a horse?' the uncle asked.

The boy watched the handsome man closely.

'Why, do you think I oughtn't to?' he parried.

'Not a bit of it! I thought perhaps you might give me a tip for the Lincoln.'

The car sped on into the country, going down to Uncle Oscar's place in Hampshire.

'Honour bright?' said the nephew.

'Honour bright, son!' said the uncle.

'Well, then, Daffodil.'

'Daffodil! I doubt it, sonny. What about Mirza?'

'I only know the winner,' said the boy. 'That's Daffodil!'

'Daffodil, eh?'

There was a pause. Daffodil was an obscure horse, comparatively.

'Uncle!'

'Yes, son?'

'You won't let it go any further, will you? I promised Bassett.'

'Bassett be damned, old man! What's he got to do with it?'

'We're partners! We've been partners from the first! Uncle, he lent me my first five shillings, which I lost. I promised him, honour bright, it was only between me and him: only you gave me that ten-shilling note I started winning with, so I thought you were lucky. You won't let it go any further, will you?'

The boy gazed at his uncle from those big, hot, blue eyes, set rather close together. The uncle stirred and laughed uneasily.

'Right you are, son! I'll keep your tip private. Daffodil, eh! How much are you putting on him?'

'All except twenty pounds,' said the boy. 'I keep that in reserve.'

The uncle thought it a good joke.

'You keep twenty pounds in reserve, do you, you young romancer? What are you betting, then?'

'I'm betting three hundred,' said the boy gravely. 'But it's between you and me, Uncle Oscar! Honour bright?'

The uncle burst into a roar of laughter.

'It's between you and me all right, you young Nat Gould,' he said, laughing. 'But where's your three hundred?'

'Bassett keeps it for me. We're partners.'

'You are, are you! And what is Bassett putting on Daffodil?'

'He won't go quite as high as I do, I expect. Perhaps he'll go a hundred and fifty.'

'What, pennies?' laughed the uncle.

'Pounds,' said the child, with a surprised look at his uncle. 'Bassett keeps a bigger reserve than I do.'

Between wonder and amusement, Uncle Oscar was silent. He

pursued the matter no further, but he determined to take his nephew with him to the Lincoln races.

'Now, son,' he said. 'I'm putting twenty on Mirza, and I'll put five for you on any horse you fancy. What's your pick?'

'Daffodil, uncle!'

'No, not the fiver on Daffodil!'

'I should if it was my own fiver,' said the child.

'Good! Good! Right you are! A fiver for me and a fiver for you on Daffodil.'

The child had never been to a race-meeting before, and his eyes were blue fire. He pursed his mouth tight, and watched. A Frenchman just in front had put his money on Lancelot. Wild with excitement, he flared his arms up and down, yelling '*Lancelot! Lancelot!*' in his French accent.

Daffodil came in first, Lancelot second, Mirza third. The child, flushed and with eyes blazing, was curiously serene. His uncle brought him five five-pound notes: four to one.

'What am I to do with these?' he cried, waving them before the boy's eyes.

'I suppose we'll talk to Bassett,' said the boy. 'I expect I have fifteen hundred now: and twenty in reserve: and this twenty.'

His uncle studied him for some moments.

'Look here, son!' he said. 'You're not serious about Bassett and that fifteen hundred, are you?'

'Yes, I am. But it's between you and me, uncle! Honour bright!'

'Honour bright, all right, son! But I must talk to Bassett.'

'If you'd like to be a partner, uncle, with Bassett and me, we could all be partners. Only you'd have to promise, honour bright, uncle, not to let it go beyond us three. Bassett and I are lucky, and you must be lucky, because it was your ten shillings I started winning with . . .'

Uncle Oscar took both Bassett and Paul into Richmond Park for an afternoon, and there they talked.

'It's like this, you see, sir,' Bassett said. 'Master Paul would get me talking about racing events, spinning yarns, you know, sir. And he was always keen on knowing if I'd made or if I'd lost. It's about a year since, now, that I put five shillings on Blush of Dawn for him: and we lost. Then the luck turned, with that ten shillings he had from you: that we put on Singhalese. And since that time, it's been pretty steady, all things considering. What do you say, Master Paul?'

'We're all right when we're *sure*,' said Paul. 'It's when we're not quite sure that we go down.'

'Oh, but we're careful then,' said Bassett.

'But when are your *sure*?' smiled Uncle Oscar.

'It's Master Paul, sir,' said Bassett, in a secret, religious voice. 'It's as if he had it from heaven. Like Daffodil, now, for the Lincoln. That was as sure as eggs.'

'Did you put anything on Daffodil?' asked Oscar Cresswell.

'Yes, sir. I made my bit.'

'And my nephew?'

Bassett was obstinately silent, looking at Paul.

'I made twelve hundred, didn't I, Bassett? I told uncle I was putting three hundred on Daffodil.'

'That's right,' said Bassett, nodding.

'But where's the money?' asked the uncle.

'I keep it safe locked up, sir. Master Paul, he can have it any minute he likes to ask for it.'

'What, fifteen hundred pounds?'

'And twenty! And *forty*, that is, with the twenty he made on the course.'

'It's amazing,' said the uncle.

'If Master Paul offers you to be partners, sir, I would, if I were you: if you'll excuse me,' said Bassett.

Oscar Cresswell thought about it.

'I'll see the money,' he said.

They drove home again, and sure enough, Bassett came round to the garden-house with fifteen hundred pounds in notes. The twenty pounds reserve was left with Joe Glee, in the Turf Commission deposit.

'You see, it's all right, uncle, when I'm *sure*! Then we go strong, for all we're worth. Don't we, Bassett?'

'We do that, Master Paul.'

'And when are you sure?' said the uncle, laughing.

'Oh well, sometimes I'm absolutely 'sure, like about Daffodil,' said the boy; 'and sometimes I have an idea; and sometimes I haven't an idea, have I, Bassett? Then we're careful, because we mostly go down.'

'You do, do you! And when you're sure, like about Daffodil, what makes you sure, sonny?'

'Oh, well, I don't know,' said the boy uneasily. 'I'm sure, you know, uncle; that's all.'

'It's as if he had it from heaven, sir,' Bassett reiterated.

'I should say so!' said the uncle.

But he became a partner. And when the Leger was coming on, Paul was 'sure' about Lively Spark, which was a quite inconsiderable horse. The boy insisted on putting a thousand on the horse, Bassett went for five hundred, and Oscar Cresswell two hundred. Lively Spark came in first and the betting had been ten to one against him. Paul had made ten thousand.

'You see', he said, 'I was absolutely sure of him.'

Even Oscar Cresswell had cleared two thousand.

'Look here, son,' he said, 'this sort of thing makes me nervous.'

'It needn't, uncle! Perhaps I shan't be sure again for a long time.'

'But what are you going to do with your money?' asked the uncle.

'Of course,' said the boy, 'I started it for Mother. She said she had no luck, because Father is unlucky, so I thought if I was lucky, it might stop whispering.'

'What might stop whispering?'

'Our house! I *hate* our house for whispering.'

'What does it whisper?'

'Why – why' – the boy fidgeted – 'why I don't know! But it's always short of money, you know, uncle.'

'I know it, son, I know it.'

'You know people send Mother writs, don't you uncle?'

'I'm afraid I do,' said the uncle.

'And then the house whispers like people laughing at you behind your back. It's awful, that is! I thought if I was lucky—'

'You might stop it,' added the uncle.

The boy watched him with big blue eyes, that had an uncanny cold fire in them, and he said never a word.

'Well, then!' said the uncle. 'What are we doing?'

'I shouldn't like Mother to know I was lucky,' said the boy.

'Why not, son?'

'She'd stop me.'

'I don't think she would.'

'Oh!' – and the boy writhed in an odd way – 'I *don't* want her to know, uncle.'

'All right, son! We'll manage it without her knowing.'

They managed it very easily. Paul, at the other's suggestion, handed over five thousand pounds to his uncle, who deposited it with the family lawyer, who was then to inform Paul's mother that a relative had put five thousand pounds into his hands, which sum was to be paid out a thousand pounds at a time, on the mother's birthday, for the next five years.

'So she'll have a birthday present of a thousand pounds for five successive years,' said Uncle Oscar.

'I hope it won't make it all the harder for her later.'

Paul's mother had her birthday in November. The house had been 'whispering' worse than ever lately, and even in spite of his luck, Paul could not bear up against it. He was very anxious to see the effect of the birthday letter, telling his mother about the thousand pounds.

When there were no visitors, Paul now took his meals with his parents, as he was beyond the nursery control. His mother went into town nearly every day. She had discovered that she had an odd knack of sketching furs and dress materials, so she worked secretly in the studio of a friend who was the chief 'artist' for the leading drapers. She drew the figures of ladies in furs and ladies in silk and sequins for the newspaper advertisements. This young woman artist earned several thousand pounds a year, but Paul's mother only made several hundreds, and she was again dissatisfied. She so wanted to be first in something, and she did not succeed, even in making sketches for drapery advertisements.

She was down to breakfast on the morning of her birthday. Paul watched her face as she read her letters. He knew the lawyer's letter. As his mother read it, her face hardened and became more expressionless. Then a cold, determined look came on her mouth. She hid the letter under the pile of others, and said not a word about it.

'Didn't you have anything nice in the post for your birthday, Mother?' said Paul.

'Quite moderately nice,' she said, her voice cold and absent.

She went away to town without saying more.

But in the afternoon Uncle Oscar appeared. He said Paul's mother had had a long interview with the lawyer, asking if the whole five thousand could not be advanced at once, as she was in debt.

'What do you think, uncle?' said the boy.

'I leave it to you, son.'

'Oh, let her have it, then! We can get some more with the other,' said the boy.

'A bird in the hand is worth two in the bush, laddie!' said Uncle Oscar.

'But I'm sure to *know* for the Grand National; or the Lincolnshire; or else the Derby. I'm sure to know for *one* of them,' said Paul.

So Uncle Oscar signed the agreement, and Paul's mother touched the whole five thousand. Then something very curious happened. The voices in the house suddenly went mad, like a chorus of frogs on a spring evening. There were certain new furnishings, and Paul had a tutor. He was *really* going to Eton, his father's school, in the following autumn. There were flowers in the winter, and a blossoming of the luxury Paul's mother had been used to. And yet the voices in the house, behind the sprays of mimosa and almond-blossom, and from under the piles of iridescent cushions, simply trilled and screamed in a sort of ecstasy: 'There *must* be more money! Oh-h-h! There *must* be more money! Oh, now, now-w! now-w-w – there *must* be more money! – more than ever! More than ever!'

It frightened Paul terribly. He studied away at his Latin and Greek with his tutors. But his intense hours were spent with Bassett. The Grand National had gone by; he had not 'known', and had lost a hundred pounds. Summer was at hand. He was in agony for the Lincoln. But even for the Lincoln he didn't 'know', and he lost fifty pounds. He became wild-eyed and strange, as if something were going to explode in him.

'Let it alone, son! Don't you bother about it!' urged Uncle Oscar. But it was as if the boy couldn't really hear what his uncle was saying.

'I've got to know for the Derby! I've *got* to know for the Derby!' the child reiterated, his big blue eyes blazing with a sort of madness.

His mother noticed how overwrought he was.

'You'd better go to the seaside. Wouldn't you like to go now to the seaside, instead of waiting? I think you'd better,' she said, looking down at him anxiously, her heart curiously heavy because of him.

But the child lifted his uncanny blue eyes.

'I couldn't possibly go before the Derby, Mother!' he said. 'I couldn't possibly!'

'Why not?' she said, her voice becoming heavy when she was opposed. 'Why not? You can still go from the seaside to see the Derby with your Uncle Oscar if that's what you wish. No need for you to wait here. Besides, I think you care too much about these races. It's a bad sign. My family has been a gambling family, and you won't know till you grow up how much damage it has done. But it has done damage. I shall have to send Bassett away and ask Uncle Oscar not to talk racing to you, unless you promise to be reasonable about it; go away to the seaside and forget it. You're all nerves!'

'I'll do what you like, Mother, so long as you don't send me away till after the Derby,' the boy said.

'Send you away from where? Just from this house?'

'Yes,' he said, gazing at her.

'Why, you curious child, what makes you care about this house so much, suddenly? I never knew you loved it!'

He gazed at her without speaking. He had a secret within a secret, something he had not divulged, even to Bassett or to his Uncle Oscar.

But his mother, after standing undecided and a little bit sullen for some moments, said:

'Very well, then! Don't go to the seaside till after the Derby, if you don't wish it. But promise me you won't let your nerves go to pieces! Promise you won't think so much about horse-racing and *events*, as you call them!'

'Oh no!' said the boy, casually. 'I won't think much about them, Mother. You needn't worry. I wouldn't worry, Mother, if I were you.'

'If you were me and I were you,' said his mother, 'I wonder what we *should* do!'

'But you know you needn't worry, Mother, don't you?' the boy repeated.

'I should be awfully glad to know it,' she said wearily.

'Oh, well, you can, you know. I mean you ought to know you needn't worry!' he insisted.

'Ought I? Then I'll see about it,' she said.

Paul's secret of secrets was his wooden horse, that which had no name. Since he was emancipated from a nurse and a nursery governess, he had had his rocking-horse removed to his own bedroom at the top of the house.

'Surely you're too big for a rocking-horse,' his mother had remonstrated.

'Well, you see, Mother, till I can have a *real* horse, I like to have *some* sort of animal about,' had been his quaint answer.

'Do you feel he keeps you company?' she laughed.

'Oh yes! He's very good, he always keeps me company, when I'm there,' said Paul.

So the horse, rather shabby, stood in an arrested prance in the boy's bedroom.

The Derby was drawing near, and the boy grew more and more tense. He hardly heard what was spoken to him, he was very frail, and his eyes were really uncanny. His mother had sudden strange seizures of uneasiness about him. Sometimes, for half an hour, she would feel a sudden anxiety about him that was almost anguish. She wanted to rush to him at once, and know he was safe.

Two nights before the Derby, she was at a big party in town, when one of her rushes of anxiety about her boy, her first-born, gripped her heart till she could hardly speak. She fought with the feeling, might and main, for she believed in common-sense. But it was too strong. She had to leave the dance and go downstairs to telephone to the country. The children's nursery governess was terribly surprised and startled at being rung up in the night.

'Are the children all right, Miss Wilmot?'

'Oh yes, they are quite all right.'

'Master Paul? Is he all right?'

'He went to bed as right as a trivet. Shall I run up and look at him?'

'No!' said Paul's mother reluctantly. 'No! Don't trouble. It's all right. Don't sit up. We shall be home fairly soon.' She did not want her son's privacy intruded upon.

'Very good,' said the governess.

It was about one o'clock when Paul's mother and father drove up to their house. All was still. Paul's mother went to her room and slipped off her white fur cloak. She had told the maid not to wait up for her. She heard her husband downstairs, mixing a whisky-and-soda.

And then, because of the strange anxiety at her heart, she stole upstairs to her son's room. Noiselessly, she went along the upper corridor. Was there a faint noise? What was it?

She stood, with arrested muscles, outside his door, listening.

There was a strange, heavy, and yet not loud noise. Her heart stood still. It was a soundless noise, yet rushing and powerful. Something huge, in violent, hushed motion. What was it? What in God's Name was it? She ought to know. She felt she *knew* the noise. She knew what it was.

Yet she could not place it. She couldn't say what it was. And on and on it went, like a madness.

Softly, frozen with anxiety and fear, she turned the door-handle.

The room was dark. Yet in the space near the window, she heard and saw something plunging to and fro. She gazed in fear and amazement.

Then suddenly she switched on the light, and saw her son, in his green pyjamas, madly surging on his rocking-horse. The blaze of light suddenly lit him up, as he urged the wooden horse, and lit her up, as she stood, blonde, in her dress of pale green and crystal, in the doorway.

'Paul!' she cried. 'Whatever are you doing?'

'It's Malabar!' he screamed, in a powerful, strange voice. 'It's Malabar!'

His eyes blazed at her for one strange and senseless second, as he ceased urging his wooden horse. Then he fell with a crash to the ground, and she, all her tormented motherhood flooding upon her, rushed to gather him up.

But he was unconscious, and unconscious he remained, with some brain-fever. He talked and tossed, and his mother sat stonily by his side.

'Malabar! It's Malabar! Bassett, Bassett, I *know*: it's Malabar!'

So the child cried, trying to get up and urge the rocking-horse that gave him his inspiration.

'What does he mean by Malabar?' asked the heart-frozen mother.

'I don't know,' said the father stonily.

'What does he mean by Malabar?' she asked her brother Oscar.

'It's one of the horses running for the Derby,' was the answer.

And, in spite of himself Oscar Cresswell spoke to Bassett, and himself put a thousand on Malabar: at fourteen to one.

The third day of the illness was critical: they were watching for a change. The boy, with his rather long, curly hair, was tossing ceaselessly on the pillow. He neither slept nor regained consciousness, and his eyes were like blue stones. His mother sat, feeling her heart had gone, turned actually into a stone.

In the evening, Oscar Cresswell did not come, but Bassett sent a message, saying could he come up for one moment, just one moment? Paul's mother was very angry at the intrusion, but on second thoughts she agreed. The boy was the same. Perhaps Bassett might bring him to consciousness.

The gardener, a shortish fellow with a little brown moustache and sharp little brown eyes, tiptoed into the room, touched his imaginary cap to Paul's mother, and stole to the bedside, staring with glittering, smallish eyes at the tossing, dying child.

'Master Paul!' he whispered. 'Master Paul! Malabar came in first all right, a clean win. I did as you told me. You've made over seventy thousand pounds, you have; you've got over eighty thousand. Malabar came in all right, Master Paul.'

'Malabar! Malabar! Did I say Malabar, Mother? Did I say Malabar! Do you think I'm lucky, Mother? I knew Malabar, didn't I? Over eighty thousand pounds! I call that lucky, don't you, Mother? Over eighty thousand pounds! I knew, didn't I know I knew? Malabar came in all right. If I ride my horse till I'm sure, then I tell you, Bassett, you can go as high as you like. Did you go for all you were worth, Bassett?'

'I went a thousand on it, Master Paul.'

'I never told you, Mother, that if I can ride my horse, and *get there*, then I'm absolutely sure – oh, absolutely! Mother, did I ever tell you? I *am* lucky!'

'No, you never did,' said the mother.

But the boy died in the night.

And even as he lay dead, his mother heard her brother's voice saying to her: 'My God, Hester, you're eighty-odd thousand to the good, and a poor devil of a son to the bad. But, poor devil, poor devil, he's best gone out of a life where he rides his rocking-horse to find a winner.

# Certain Distant Suns

## Joanne Greenburg

*In Lawrence's story the miracle ends in death; gifts must be paid for and faith does not call for reward. For the child faith is something tangible, almost physical – as tangible and physical as the lack of it in Joanne Greenberg's story. Faith and lack of faith are powerful levers. H. Kepler's* History of Judaism *tells the following story about faith. In the year 1160, during the reign of the Caliphs of Baghdad, a certain David Al-Roi of Amadia, Persia, declared himself Prince of the Jews and called upon the children of Abraham to come to him, for he had been sent by God to free them from the Muslim yoke and lead them to Jerusalem. His calling was short-lived: at the request of the Sultan of Persia, his father-in-law murdered him in his sleep. After his death his followers set up a circle in Baghdad, convinced that David Al-Roi would come back from the dead and set them free. Taking advantage of their faith, a pair of swindlers produced a forged letter signed by the departed leader, which stated that the hour of freedom was at hand and would arrive a few minutes before midnight on the following Sabbath. All Jews were supposed to dress themselves in green, climb on to the roofs of their houses, lift their arms towards Heaven and wait there for a strong wind that would carry them to Jerusalem. Full of hope, the Jews gave the swindlers all their possessions and at the stipulated hour climbed on to their roofs. Only after dawn had broken and no miraculous wind had appeared did the Jews realize their mistake and climb down. The inhabitants of Baghdad called 1160 'the Year of the Flight'.*

*'Certain Distant Suns' comes from Joanne Greenburg's collection* High Crimes and Misdemeanours, *published after her best-selling novel* I Never Promised You a Rose Garden.

The planning of the Passover Seder was a tradition in our family. My mother and three aunts, dressed in their best, would go downtown. They would conduct their deliberations at a fancy restaurant over drinks, and this included a complete springtime going-over of every other member of the family. Mother usually returned from these sessions snapping with vigour and virtue, but on March 12, 1970, she came home later than usual, slammed the door, slammed into the kitchen, and began to fix supper with a lethal whacking of pots. 'Bessie has refused!' she cried to us over a half-cooked, half-burnt meal. 'There are four sisters. Each one gives the Seder every fourth year. This is Bessie's year, and she has refused.'

'Is something the matter with Abe?' my father asked.

'No! She has the house, the health, the time, and the money. Those are requirements. The rest is her own headache, not a family matter. Not, when it comes down to it, a religious matter; not a requirement!'

In the end we found out that Aunt Bessie, in the fifty-sixth year of her life and three weeks before the Seder, had stopped believing in God.

Had we been Hasidim, Bessie's loss of faith might have been the prelude to one of their thrilling lawsuits against the Almighty. Had we been Orthodox, her denial would have been the occasion for breast-beating and bowed heads, but we were then as we are now: modern American Jews, tangled in compromise, passing the past and the heritage hand to hand like a hot potato and wincing with pain between the toss and the catch. Our belief or nonbelief was different from Bessie's only in degree. She hadn't weakened us spiritually; she had only annoyed us, and she had broken the solidarity of the family. Minnie gave the Seder. Eyebrows were raised but no voices. Bessie stayed away; her husband and children came and sat stiff and uncomfortable at the table. She was a stronger presence there than Elijah. My mother sighed and shook her head. I was nineteen; I thought it was wonderful.

As time passed, we learned to live around Bessie's peculiarity. To all secular family events she came as generously and happily as before. Presents on birthdays, soup in sickness. She would ring the bell with a kind of snap – 'Bessie's ring' – and would hurry in as though propelled from behind, her wiry hair unkempt and flying, her plucked eyebrows drawn on again in black pencil with a perpetually upshot line, her voice rich as a singer's (although she couldn't carry a tune – too impatient, I think). When the High Holy Days were glimpsed over the heat-watering horizon of summer and plans were made for the sharing of dinners and the attendance at services, Bessie dwindled to the point of disappearance. As the Lord rose in the web of the year, Aunt Bessie diminished only to reappear when the holy days were past.

The name of God disappeared from her lips. I was the first to notice this – such secular usages that we don't even remember Whose Name it is: Goodbye, Goddammit, for God's sake, Lord knows. No hint of Him. Not any of His Names. She did not tell us what had led to this loss of belief or the more bizarre divorcing of herself from the most common associations with the Name. To my knowledge, no one asked her. Which is, for us, unusual. Ours is a family that allows few secrets and no evasions. We are skilled and merciless trackers. We corner the secret-keepers at funerals and feasts and drive the diffident to the wall. We will not wait for the truth to out; we hector it forth with whatever force is necessary. Except, because we are Jews, for that most subtle of links, broken and rewoven a hundred times a day: belief. We did not examine the broken link.

And Bessie was getting along splendidly without the Lord. She travelled lighter, unburdened of the baggage of belief. We milled away at our compromises, grinding them now coarser, now finer; we were caught surprised as holidays loomed up suddenly from ambush to overwhelm us. We blurred the Sabbath and felt guilty; we violated the laws of kashrut and felt defensive. Bessie sailed past it all and never looked better. Her house was as spotless as ever. The houseplants thrived under her hands; her soufflés fell not, neither did her custards fail. The re-zoning of Martin Park stopped four blocks from her house, raising its value by a third.

Occasionally, my mother would mention some religious matter in Bessie's presence and would give one of her significant looks in Bessie's direction. Since belief was not truly an issue – Bessie was incontrovertibly and immutably a Jew by Jewish Law – all that remained for discussion was her uncooperativeness. Unfortunately, Bessie, in secular matters, was remarkably cooperative and the soul of considerate sisterliness. When anyone needed help Bessie was there, and when she heard that my parents were going to the banquet for the national-headquarters people in my father's firm, she came running over with Great Grandma's garnets.

I turned the mammoth ring over in my hand.

'Try on the earrings, darling,' Bessie said to me. 'They're just right with your colouring.'

'No thanks,' I said quickly and handed the things back. 'The ring alone would slow anybody down.'

'I'll wear them for the evening,' my mother said to Bessie, 'and I'll return them this weekend.'

'Keep them as long as you like,' Bessie said. 'Since I gave up the safety-deposit box they're only in my way.'

'You're not changing banks again, are you?' (Bessie was a sucker for the free premiums.)

'Which bank is it this time, Aunt Bessie, the one on Tyler Avenue?'

'No,' Bessie said cheerfully. 'I've decided that I really don't believe in all that anymore, the savings and the safety and the capital and the principal and the interest and the stocks and the bonds and the balances. I've closed my account in the banks and turned in my charge cards. Money is real. Money in the hand is real – coins and bills. The rest I don't believe in, and I don't think I ever did, really. What's a cheque after all, but a promise – mine, the bank's. Me, I know, but the bank? You know how quick those tellers change down there; you don't even get to know their names before they leave. Them I should trust?'

'But if you can't think of the convenience,' my mother cried, 'think of the danger. Money in the house, money in your purse. Think of fire and theft. What if—'

'What if,' Bessie said and waved her hand, dismissing it all, 'what if no one could be sure of anything!'

Had we been Hasidim we would have awaited the lightning stroke or a case of boils. Had we been Orthodox, we would have searched for the first faint whiff of corruption in her, some hint of moral or ethical disintegration, perhaps for symptoms, physical or psychiatric, that would show us that she was despairing or alienated – not that she had ceased believing in banks, but that she seemed actively to be calling down destruction upon herself, a condition from which

Jews have always turned in abhorrence. We make poor martyrs and worse ascetics. As it was, we could only wait and watch without knowing what we should wait and watch for.

The months passed. Bessie's housekeeping money went in a coffee can. The stock dividends from the family business were cashed and put in other coffee cans. The IRS got a mailing envelope crammed with bills representing their dividend of her dividends. Bills were paid in person. Neither did fire strike, nor criminals spring from the shadows upon her as my father predicted. In my thoughts, Bessie began to fill a larger space than the other aunts. I saw her as younger, happier, freer than they. The petty details that were weighing my mother down year after year – rules and laws, record keeping, busywork – did not touch Bessie. She had fought free of them, and her courage was keeping her young and heroic and outlined against the family background in sharper relief. When the consciousness-raising seminars came to our school and I sat and heard my 'sister' talk about the heroic women of the past, none of those women were Jews. Sojourner Truth and Harriet Tubman and the Quaker ladies of concern and the early defenders of women's rights held sway, but I was sure that had the underground railway gone through our time and place, Bessie would have been one of the conductors.

Spring came and the women of our family became narrow-eyed and diligent. Roach paste was painted around the bathroom pipes and in the corners. Stiff-jointed ladies bent themselves double to clean the sinister places behind the sinks and toilets and plotted elaborate stratagems against beetles, ants, and silverfish. Bessie knelt at no open cabinets, genuflected beneath no plumbing. As the ground warmed and the hundred million flies of the new generation remembered us, screens went up in all the windows of the neighbourhood. Except one. Fly killer in sprays, bricks, strips, candles, flares, and lightbulbs appeared in every shopping cart and was stocked in the newly cleaned cabinets of every dwelling. Except one. Fear of disease, plague, filth, and corruption (ritual and actual) haunted the half sleep of every householder. Except one. Bessie had given up germs.

'My God!, Bessie,' my mother cried, 'you won't last the summer! Flies in the food – every disease known to man!'

'Germs is a theory,' Bessie answered with her usual vigour. 'It says so in the books – the germ theory. I stopped believing in the theory, and I won't let it bother me anymore. Think about the people in the olden days. Did they use fly spray? Did they worry about pollution and disease all the time? No. They lived until they were ninety-five, some of them, in the middle of cities that teemed with rats and flies. Show me a rat as big as I am and I'll be afraid of it. Show me a germ and I'll believe in it all.'

'In a microscope—'

'I'll live in a microscope and I'll believe in the germs there.'

'My aunt is at one, in harmony, with the natural order,' I said to my sisters at a meeting. 'My sister is crazy,' my mother said. 'What bad things have happened to me?' Bessie asked. 'Am I sick? Have plagues fallen on me? You see that I am fine – better than ever. I sleep better and eat better because I don't have to worry about supernatural punishments or money or sickness.'

And it was true. The cataclysms predicted by my parents were not forthcoming. The flies in Bessie's house came in no greater numbers than those in ours in spite of all our care and her uncaring. I know, because after making a bet with my father, I counted them for him and all the family prophets of disaster who seemed obscurely disappointed that Bessie and Abe lived on unafflicted. In early August Bessie put up six quarts of pickles without steam scouring the crocks or boiling the jars. Mould formed and floated serenely on the tops of the crocks, but when Bessie skimmed it away, I found the pickles delicious and unspoiled. And Bessie wasn't sick. No colds or flu or aching joints or fevers or chills or swollen ears or congestions, inflammations, or eruptions. She was healthier than she had ever been, her skin clearer, her face less lined. She seemed lighter, too, freer, head up in the street even in bad weather while most of the other women in the neighbourhood passed by, eyes down, bodies hunched against the rain, frightened by the cough of the passenger next to them on the bus, the dirty nails of the shop-keeper, the sneeze of the postman. Bessie's fearlessness was wonderful to me, and it showed even brighter against the nervousness and hypochondria of the rest of the family. After seeing Bessie, how much poorer and sicker the rest of them looked to me! Aunt Dorothy was afraid of being mugged in the street, Aunt Minnie of what she called 'getting a condition' in fear of which she marshalled a pharmacopeia sufficient to supply a city. My mother was terrified of being caught somewhere without any money and died night after night in a hundred old-age homes without the dime for a phone call out. I seldom argued Bessie's case to the family – it only made my father laugh at her more and my mother shake her head. I showed my loyalty by visiting her often and my courage by staying for supper. In my parents' house dark and evil forces went to work on any food left out of a refrigerator for thirty seconds. Bessie's casual attitude was exciting to me. Would there be souring? Sickness? Plague? In a life insufficiently precarious, I felt I was a hostage to comfort. Bessie's danger was a tonic to my soul.

We had one brief cooling, a hiatus in our relationship. It happened when Ray and I, bowing to pressure from both our families, consented to stop living together and get married. Once the decision was made we found ourselves happy with it, eager for the status we had always ridiculed, the granting of full man-and-womanhood to us by our families. We even enjoyed helping to plan the wedding. When I told Bessie, she beamed and invited us over for a meal. Bessie's husband Abe worked long hours at his store. We seldom saw him, but Bessie promised he would be there for the dinner and for my wedding. 'Surely you'll be there too . . .'

But the wedding was to be a Jewish wedding – a religious ceremony – and Bessie must have known it. I was the foolish one. I had supposed that because it was to be *my* wedding, because I was her favourite niece, she would come. I had always admired her stand, her refusal to compromise with what she had no belief in, yet when it came to me, I wanted her love to suspend her disbelief. She stayed away. Abe came. He had an easygoing attitude towards Bessie, which was lucky under the circumstances. But I was hurt and Bessie knew it. She had sent us a huge chafing dish. It was the gift I had known it would be – exuberant, impractical, no compromise. I set it up on top of the kitchen cabinet in our small apartment against the day when we would entertain on such a scale. When I next saw her she was so free of guilt or explanation or reproach that I couldn't really stay angry – my anger seemed unreal. Her absence at my wedding seemed unreal. I soon stopped believing in it.

I did not see my relatives for a while. I assumed that they were standing in the positions in which I had left them, unchanging. It is enough of a shock that the people we see daily change before our eyes; it is unthinkable that the rest of reality is so far beyond our control. One day in April my mother brought over my old summer clothes and some of her own to alter on my machine. We work well together on projects like that, chatting companionably over our decisions, planning the alterations for the things we keep, fitting and refitting. Our tastes are similar, and we laugh and remember the days and events at which we wore this outfit or that. I had been looking forward to a peaceful afternoon. I had taken off from work for it. There was a nice lunch made.

But when I saw her at the door the pleasure went out of the day. She looked worried and frightened. I helped her unload the boxes she had brought from the car. 'What's the matter?'

'Later, later,' she said.

When we were upstairs, I asked again.

'It's Bessie. It's gone too far this time – Bessie has given up electricity.'

I think I laughed. 'No one "gives up" electricity. A person who "gives up" electricity has no neural function. That person is dead.'

'Stop being childish,' my mother said angrily. 'Bessie is alive enough, but she has stopped believing in electricity, and strange things are happening in that house!'

'What strange things? What does Uncle Abe say?' She was too upset to tell me any more. I could see that she was frightened and a little angry and also that she was angry at me. I had encouraged Bessie with my admiration, goaded her on from one selfishness to another with my shining-eyed approval. She had played to my youth and eagerness; perhaps it is easy for a middle-aged woman to fall into such a trap, to forget that she is middle-aged, too old for nonsense, for beliefs or disbeliefs that put a strain on the family. 'Should I go and see her?' I asked before my mother left.

'You might as well,' my mother said, as though she meant, 'See what you have started.'

But I hadn't started it and I wasn't to blame. Could I help it if I admired idealism, honesty, and independence? Could I help it if these were Bessie's virtues and if they are also virtues of the young? I admired her still, I would help and encourage her if I could. The next day I called in sick and went over to Bessie's house.

Bessie's street was a quietly decaying side street of two-family houses with small back gardens and great old trees. Going up the slightly tilted steps I thought I heard the TV with its warm, male drone. Most of the sets in this neighbourhood were on during the day. The neighbourhood was old, the street full of widows who filled their houses with the sounds of genial, sympathetic men – the suffering doctors of soap operas and the spruce hosts of game shows. If Bessie wasn't using electricity anymore, perhaps the sound was coming from the Galindas in the other half of the house. I rang Bessie's harsh, old-fashioned bell. There was no sound. Oh, yes, electricity. I knocked. After a minute or so I heard Bessie's footsteps going from the worn rug to the foyer floor. Then the door opened.

I studied her for changes. There was something, although I couldn't put my finger on it, and I cursed the curiosity that made me want to peer in through her defenses. Her hair was standing up around her head as usual, her movements were brisk, and she greeted me in that rich, loud voice of hers. 'Come on in; you look wonderful! I've been fixing up Danny's old bedroom and I could use a break.'

'I thought I heard voices in here when I was at the door,' I said. There was silence now. Bessie's face clouded. 'I like a little company when I work, that's all. Your mother has been blabbing about it all over town, and my big-mouth sister Minnie, too.' She had hurried into the kitchen and was filling a kettle at the sink. I saw her hand tremble a little. It could have been anger at my mother and Aunt Minnie, but there was something else on her face, an expression I couldn't read. 'What if a person wants to hear some programmes – have some company while she works! What's so wrong about that?' She was really upset now and almost in tears – not tears of sorrow but of anger and frustration.

'Aunt Bessie, what's the matter?' I cried.

'Well, if you really want to know, I'll show you, but please don't make more of it than there really is!' She took me into the living room.

It was a modest room; Uncle Abe worked hard but he was not very successful. The furniture came mostly from my grandparents' house. Serviceable, Bessie called it. In the corner was an old TV, black-and-white. As I looked at it, I remembered the furore that Bessie had made when my parents had finally gone to colour. Uncle Abe liked this set, which he had gotten with the twenty-one-inch screen when the rest of us still had nineteen-inch. Now Bessie

sometimes called herself 'the only sister without colour'. I noticed
that the set was unplugged. Bessie turned the knob. 'What do you
want to see?' she asked.

'What's on?' I smiled, thinking that she was perhaps going to tell
a joke.

'What do you want to see?' she asked impatiently. 'Pick something you want to see.'

'I don't know – you pick something.'

Medical shows. Doctors. In colour – brilliant, clear colour.
Transfixed, I saw 'Medic', 'Ben Casey', 'Dr Kildare', 'The Nurses'.
I saw brain operations, heart seizures, epidural hematomas. The
crises poured out upon us without snow, flopover, or distortion. All
the doctors spoke in Yiddish. All the nurses looked familiar; I
realized that they all resembled our family. Midway through a
lateral-transor-bital-shunt procedure, I asked Bessie why, except for
medical terms, Dr Ben Casey wasn't speaking English. 'Shush!' she
said, 'Wait for the commercial!'

During the commercial she told me some of the limitations of her
set. 'Radio shows I can get on TV also, but then I don't get a
picture. Fibber McGee I get in the daytime, never in Yiddish.
Benny and Berle I get in Yiddish. The doctors I can get in either
language, but they are more sympathetic in Yiddish. I always like
to have Dr Ben Casey and Marcus Welby in Yiddish.'

'I don't understand how you do it – how it happens,' I cried.
'Especially when nothing is plugged in.'

'Well,' she said, 'I don't believe in electricity – in wires carrying
power from a waterfall somewhere, but I believe in colour and I
believe in Ben Casey and the good work he does. I believe in Fibber
McGee and his closet and I believe in Jack Benny, how stingy he
is and how he tries to stay thirty-nine years old. Oh, I know no
doctor could be like Marcus Welby, but I believe in it anyway. A
person shouldn't have to accept anything he doesn't believe in.'

'Can you get the iron and the toaster to work without plugging
them in?'

'Nothing will work but this. Still, people were cleaning their
houses and washing their clothes years before electricity. I clean in
the old way, and Abe takes the clothes out to—'

As we spoke a black-and-white figure came on the screen. I saw
it for only a second before Bessie leaped up from the couch where
we sat and turned off the set with a curse. The picture did not go

away immediately but went black-red like an afterimage from the sun, and slowly the figure, arm raised as though to defend or to exhort, faded soundlessly from the set. Bessie watched it with a look of bitterness I had never seen on her face in all the years I had known her. 'What was that?' I asked uncomfortably.

'A commercial!' she hissed. I did not dare ask anymore.

Ours is a family of large egos. We gossip because we feel our smallest news must be as fascinating to everyone else as it is to us. Deliverymen and storekeepers know every grandchild's new tooth, every symptom. Each day the family's vital signs are broadcast to everyone who will listen. This habit fooled me into thinking that we could not keep a secret. I was wrong. If you want to keep a secret, bury it in talk. Neither the family, the children, nor even my husband, Ray, knew about Bessie's arcane gift. We who shared the secret had a never-mentioned horror of reporters, psychic investigators, universities, parapsychologists, and all the other interested (self– or otherwise) persons besieging the family to test and probe and question, document, report, explore, explode, destroy. Luckily, the lights worked in the house – Bessie believed in light. They had a gas stove, and she cooked in the usual way. Thank God for small favours.

Sometimes women in my consciousness-raising group would ask me about Bessie. In the past I had used her as an example of a woman heroically above the demeaning adjustments that threaten us all. The group, still fragile and unsure, wanted Founders, Roots, History. These women saw in Bessie, or in my stories of Bessie, a 'resource', as they called it, something as natural as a mineral, as usable as water. And suddenly I was frightened and silent. I said she was sick. It was a good excuse. Illness is not part of the image of the liberated woman. It reminds young people of dependence, real and sham, of limitations. Of compromise.

And then I got sick. Suddenly the sure things – health, strength, that organs would do their work silently and automatically – all these things were suddenly not sure at all. There was dizziness and weakness, sudden sweats and sudden chills. 'A renal crisis' the doctor said. In essence I had begun to poison myself. I went to the hospital.

After several false starts, the treatment took effect. The weakness drew away slowly, but I was now on notice that anywhere, at any time, any one of a thousand ills could fall on me like an eagle falling upon a feeding rabbit; could take me and transform me in moments into an invalid, a person not myself, a person at the mercy of blood-washing machines, pumps, tubes, and wires. It was more than a renal crisis. It was crisis of belief exactly the opposite of Bessie's . . . where was Bessie?

'Where's Aunt Bessie? Why hasn't she come?'

'You always said you hated that in our family, everyone checking off who sent things and who came and who called and what excuses people gave—'

'I'm not doing that; I only want to see her – I need to see her.'

'Cousin Grace has been here almost every day—'

'Cousin Grace is not Bessie. I can't stand one more description of Cousin Grace's canals – she doesn't visit the sick, she haunts them. Where is Aunt Bessie?'

Had I not been weak and ill I would not have seen my mother's discomfort. Skilled cornerers make skilled prevaricators, but my mother couldn't play that game now. You can lie to people; not to machines. I was half machine. My mother was stumped. She came close to the bed. 'Don't tell Ray—' she whispered. I think I must have gone very pale.

'What is it, Ma?'

'Bessie can't come to see you. She would if she could. She can't leave the house at all anymore. Bessie has stopped believing in gravity.'

As soon as I was out of the hospital I went to see her. I was still weak, still separated by a great unmeasured gulf from the world, from anyone who has no serious doubts about rising whole the next morning and who tranquilly says 'I will come', 'I will go', as though he could make such promises.

I was shocked at the change in Bessie's house. It was autumn, and the corpses of dried leaves were banked against the sides of the steps in little heaps. Bessie would never have allowed that had something not been terribly wrong. The outside of her house had always been immaculate. In a neighbourhood of two-family houses the façades, walks, steps, and doorways are a matter of intense rivalry among the housewives. I had grown up hearing Bessie mutter about 'the slut' three houses down 'who didn't sweep until noon, practically'. Now, all down the row, the clean steps of the other houses mocked her, and I shivered.

Looking up into Bessie's parlour window, I saw that the off-white curtains were limp and dingy. I began to formulate reasons for my visit. This in itself made me nervous. Excuses had never been needed. Aunt Bessie's house had always been as free to me as my own, sometimes more so, while I was growing up and often at odds with my mother. I wanted to run up the stairs freely and eagerly as I had countless times before to give and take confidences and laughter over cake and milk. But I stopped at the leaf-strewn steps, uncertain and listening. Maybe the TV would be on – 'Our Gal Sunday' as a Polish immigrant girl speaking a sweet Litvak Yiddish, or Dr Marcus Welby, comforting in the mother tongue. There was silence. Only the accusing leaves whispered and rustled in the warm afternoon. I rang the bell and, remembering again, knocked, feeling like a stranger.

I didn't hear the familiar steps. Instead the door swung open and I saw nothing. I stood at the opening. 'Aunt Bessie?'

'Come in!' a voice hissed from where I could not tell. I stepped into the dark foyer, light-blinded. It was a while before I saw her.

She lay prone in the air above me, hand on the knob. When the door closed, the wind of its closing blew her up and into a lazy somersault, back and forth. She banked and turned and slowly brought herself upright to face me. Her skin was grey. 'Come into the kitchen,' she said. 'It's better in the kitchen.' With a kind of swimming stroke she breasted her way before me. She had not greeted me or looked to see if I was well. She hadn't smiled. Her eyes hadn't lit up at my presence. I sat down at the table. Bessie bobbed in the air beside me, up and down, now oblique to the right, now overbalancing to the left – never still. It embarrassed me to look and, even more, to turn my head away. I gave a quick glance around the once-familiar kitchen.

For some people it might have been a passable kitchen before the morning cleanup. For Bessie in her present condition it must have been an agony. Crumbs lay in the corners and were picked out by the afternoon sun that shone in through the dusty window. Dishes stood in the sink, and there was a film of grease on the range top. She looked around at it all with a glare of disgust. 'It's a nightmare!' she said bitterly, 'a nightmare!'

'Oh, Aunt Bessie!' I cried.

Two tears formed in her eyes. She put her hand up to her face and then shook her head. The tears leaped away to hang in the air in two large drops and then fell with a splat to the floor. The motion of shaking her head had brought her up out of the chair, which she had been holding on to, and over into a roll from which she righted herself after several minutes. She sighed deeply but didn't say anything. Her situation was so unreal and her misery so real I cast around for anything I could offer to bring things under our control. 'Men in space—' I said, 'the astronauts – those men learn to adjust. They develop all kinds of ways of making peace with their condition—' (Why had I said that? It sounded like something a rabbi would say.)

'How?' she cried back at me in a kind of bitter triumph. 'Lead shoes? Weights? I've tried them all. As soon as I put anything on me, it becomes weightless, too.'

'Maybe someone could come in to help – until you get the feel of things—'

'Who? Who would come in to help a bouncing woman, a floating woman, a double- and triple-flip woman, and not go blabbing it all over town! Am I crazy? Do I want crowds at the windows watching me loop-the-loop? Abe helps – he shops a little now – your mother, Minnie, Dotty, and Cousin Clara, but I can't go out at all. I'm trapped in this house, and I can't stand to stay in here and look at this – this *pigsty*!' Once again tears formed in her eyes and wouldn't roll out until she tossed her head and went head over heels in recoil.

I had nothing to give her. I was unequipped for keeping company in grief, for weeping over what couldn't be changed. My training was all for answers, kindly and helpful suggestions, practical dispositions, for tactics, marches, petitions, and demands for redress. Surely somewhere was the solution, that certain, helpful thing, that method, formula, or hint that no one had thought of before and that would seem so right when I said it.

'Maybe,' I started . . .

'Do you know that when I make the bed I go up with the sheets? When I turn over in bed I turn for half an hour until I get sick, and if I'm sick enough to throw up I have to hang on or I fly away?'

'At least you don't *have* to go out. Uncle Abe does the shopping. Everyone is helping. I'll help too. You've got the radio and the TV in that wonderful colour – all the shows that ever were and every movie you ever saw. Maybe you could start to make your own movies, to be creative by—'

Bessie leaned close and whispered, and the force of her whispering caused her to bob up and down. 'I can't watch TV anymore, or radio. I can't because of the commercials!'

'The commercials – when I saw them on your set that day they were no different from—'

'That was before!' Bessie hissed. 'It's all different now! You think the sponsor would let such a chance go by, a helpless woman trapped in the house like I am?' She looked down at me, pinched, old, aggrieved. The energy of her hissing had pushed her up and away until she lay prone in the air again, near the ceiling. I found myself remembering the authority of her tread, the vigour of her ring. It was less than a year ago that her presence everywhere was heralded with so much certainty. Now there wouldn't even be a footfall.

'Everybody hates commercials.' Reasonable and lost and thinking that if only I were more reasonable I would not be so lost, I said, 'They drive me mad, especially when they interrupt something. We all—'

'No! No!' And she flailed her arms in impatience. In space all Italians, Jews, and Spaniards will be punished and the hand-mute Saxons will be vindicated by the God of Newton, who hates all wasted motion. Bessie began to spin and turn. Not humbled but enraged, she cried, 'Go turn on the set, Mrs Smarty, and see for yourself!' Hopelessly I went into the parlour and turned on the unplugged set.

The picture came on immediately. Bessie's black-and-white console erupted in luscious colour again. It was a movie called *Red Garters* with Rosemary Clooney. There was dancing and gaiety. There were lots of songs. No one spoke Yiddish in this one, but it was just the thing to raise the spirits – everyone was pretty or witty or graceful. The colour was richer than any I had ever seen on TV. I called Aunt Bessie in to watch. Surely this couldn't hurt her. She came swimming into the parlour disconsolately, and for a while we watched the dancing and the music. Once or twice I saw her smiling a little. After about fifteen minutes there was a station break. The movie stopped abruptly, and the call letters RUACH-TV came on the screen in black-and-white. I turned to Bessie. 'What station is that? I never heard of it before, and there's a picture of a shofar in the background.'

'Turn it off,' she said dully. A commercial or announcement of some kind began.

It had obviously been staged in the studio by rank amateurs. A slight, bent Hasidic Jew stood uncomfortably on one foot and then on the other. He took off his glasses and wiped them and then held them dangling from his hand. He could not have been an actor in costume. The clothes were too obviously his, although nothing matched – pants too short, sleeves too long, the beard bushy as though he had a chin full of grey foam. He spoke in Yiddish very slowly and haltingly, but it was a Yiddish unfamiliar to me, and the word I knew here and there gave me no clue. Bessie was floating up over me, hovering in the air.

'What's he saying?' I asked, looking up at her. She sighed. 'This is the sad one. At least he's better than the angry one, the one who squints.'

'Yes, but what's he saying?'

She began to interpret. ' "I'm pleading with all the people," he says, "in the vast television audience, not to renounce the universe along with the Master of the Universe, if for some reason they find it necessary to renounce Him. I realize," he says, "that in every relationship a certain amount of resentment builds up over the years and that this is especially true in regard to mankind and the Master of the Universe, since the relationship is so . . . so one-sided." He says, "I beg you, all of you, not to stop discussing the Master of the Universe, even if you can no longer praise Him. If it be in anger or despair or even, God forbid, in ridicule, keep His Name aloud in your mouths. It is possible that certain distant suns are powered by the mention of His Name." '

The movie began again; Bessie was crying and so was I, but I didn't want to turn off the set. When the angry one came on, the one with the squint, Bessie shook her fist at him and was pushed softly against the wall, bouncing slightly back and forth. There she stayed, answering his angry incomprehensible questions.

'You left Him!' the Rabbi shouted at last, in English. 'You sent Him away, abandoned Him, abandoned your part of Him, a part that can never be replaced!'

'I stopped believing in Him, what could I do?' Bessie shouted back.

'Foolish woman, a soul goes in and out of belief a hundred times a day. Belief is too fragile to weigh a minute on. You stopped running after Him, looking for Him, struggling with Him. Even His Laws you turned from!'

'If I did, why did He take it, why did He walk away like a whipped child? Is He no stronger than a fifty-year-old woman?'

'How can His relationship with you be any stronger than you are yourself? You think He made you for the fun of it – without needing you?'

'He let it happen, that's all I know! He didn't fight back. A *mensh* fights back!'

# The Third Bank of the River

## João Guimarães Rosa

*When* Grande Sertão: Veredas *was published in 1956 it was recognized at once as one of Brazil's finest novels and certainly as Guimarães Rosa's best book. Through the uninterrupted monologue of Riobaldo, leader of a group of bandits in Brazil's north-east, Guimarães Rosa unfolds a story of vengeance achieved by making a pact with the devil; the hero's triumph lies in his overwhelming faith in this mission of revenge.*

*Faith also moves the hero of 'The Third Bank of the River'. He chooses neither bank – neither left nor right: with blind faith he accomplishes a self-imposed, seemingly absurd mission until he is replaced by his now believing son.*

*A friend who knew Guimarães Rosa told me that they were once discussing the drudgery of reality, in a café in Manaos in 1967. My friend observed that in a place like Manaos – the baroque city of the Amazon – nothing fantastic ever took place. 'There are exceptions,' said Guimarães Rosa, and excused himself for a few minutes. My friend waited a while, then looked for him around the café, in the toilets, outside on the street. An hour passed, two hours. Guimarães Rosa never came back and never offered a word of explanation; he died a month later.*

My father was a dutiful, orderly, straightforward man. And according to several reliable people of whom I inquired, he had had these qualities since adolescence or even childhood. By my own recollection, he was neither jollier nor more melancholy than the other men we knew. Maybe a little quieter. It was Mother, not Father, who ruled the house. She scolded us daily – my sister, my brother, and me. But it happened one day that Father ordered a boat.

He was very serious about it. It was to be made specially for him, of mimosa wood. It was to be sturdy enough to last twenty or thirty years and just large enough for one person. Mother carried on plenty about it. Was her husband going to become a fisherman all of a sudden? Or a hunter? Father said nothing. Our house was less than a mile from the river, which around there was deep, quiet, and so wide you couldn't see across it.

I can never forget the day the rowboat was delivered. Father showed no joy or other emotion. He just put on his hat as he always did and said goodbye to us. He took along no food or bundle of any sort. We expected Mother to rant and rave, but she didn't. She looked very pale and bit her lip, but all she said was: 'If you go away, stay away. Don't ever come back!'

Father made no reply. He looked gently at me and motioned me to walk along with him. I feared Mother's wrath, yet I eagerly obeyed. We headed towards the river together. I felt bold and exhilarated, so much so that I said: 'Father, will you take me with you in your boat?'

He just looked at me, gave me his blessing, and by a gesture, told me to go back. I made as if to do so but, when his back was turned, I ducked behind some bushes to watch him. Father got into the boat and rowed away. Its shadow slid across the water like a crocodile, long and quiet.

Father did not come back. Nor did he go anywhere, really. He just rowed and floated across and around, out there in the river. Everyone was appalled. What had never happened, what could not possibly happen, was happening. Our relatives, neighbours, and friends came over to discuss the phenomenon.

Mother was ashamed. She said little and conducted herself with great composure. As a consequence, almost everyone thought (though no one said it) that Father had gone insane. A few, however, suggested that Father might be fulfilling a promise he had made to God or to a saint, or that he might have some horrible disease, maybe leprosy, and that he left for the sake of the family, at the same time wishing to remain fairly near them.

Travellers along the river and people living near the bank on one side or the other reported that Father never put foot on land, by day or night. He just moved about on the river, solitary, aimless, like a derelict. Mother and our relatives agreed that the food which he had doubtless hidden in the boat would soon give out and that then he would either leave the river and travel off somewhere (which would be at least a little more respectable) or he would repent and come home.

How far from the truth they were! Father had a secret source of provisions: me. Every day I stole food and brought it to him. The first night after he left, we all lit fires on the shore and prayed and called to him. I was deeply distressed and felt a need to do something more. The following day I went down to the river with a loaf of corn bread, a bunch of bananas, and some bricks of raw brown sugar. I waited impatiently a long, long hour. Then I saw the boat, far off, alone, gliding almost imperceptibly on the smoothness of the river. Father was sitting in the bottom of the boat. He saw me but he did not row toward me or make any gesture. I showed him the food and then I placed it in a hollow rock on the river bank; it was safe there from animals, rain, and dew. I did this day after day, on and on and on. Later I learned, to my surprise, that Mother knew what I was doing and left food around where I could easily steal it. She had a lot of feelings she didn't show.

Mother sent for her brother to come and help on the farm and in business matters. She had the school-teacher come and tutor us children at home because of the time we had lost. One day, at her request, the priest put on his vestments, went down to the shore, and tried to exorcise the devils that had got into my father. He shouted that Father had a duty to cease his unholy obstinacy. Another day she arranged to have two soldiers come and try to frighten him. All to no avail. My father went by in the distance, sometimes so far away he could barely be seen. He never replied to anyone and no one ever got close to him. When some newspapermen came in a launch to take his picture, Father headed his boat to the other side of the river and into the marshes, which he knew like the palm of his hand but in which other people quickly got lost. There in his private maze, which extended for miles with heavy foliage overhead and rushes on all sides, he was safe.

We had to get accustomed to the idea of Father's being out on the river. We had to but we couldn't, we never could. I think I was the only one who understood to some degree what our father wanted and what he did not want. The thing I could not understand at all was how he stood the hardship. Day and night, in sun and rain, in heat and in the terrible midyear cold spells, with his old hat on his head and very little other clothing, week after week, month after month, year after year, unheedful of the waste and emptiness in which his life was slipping by. He never set foot on earth or grass, on isle or mainland shore. No doubt he sometimes tied up the boat at a secret place, perhaps at the tip of some island, to get a little sleep. He never lit a fire or even struck a match and he had no flashlight. He took only a small part of the food that I left in the hollow rock – not enough, it seemed to me, for survival. What could his state of health have been? How about the continual drain on his energy, pulling and pushing the oars to control the boat? And how did he survive the annual floods, when the river rose and swept along with it all sorts of dangerous objects – branches of trees, dead bodies of animals – that might suddenly crash against his little boat?

He never talked to a living soul. And we never talked about him. We just thought. No, we could never put our father out of mind. If for a short time we seemed to, it was just a lull from which we would be sharply awakened by the realization of his frightening situation.

My sister got married, but Mother didn't want a wedding party. It would have been a sad affair, for we thought of him every time we ate some especially tasty food. Just as we thought of him in our cozy beds on a cold, stormy night – out there, alone and unprotected, trying to bail out the boat with only his hands and a gourd. Now and then someone would say that I was getting to look more and more like my father. But I knew that by then his hair and beard must have been shaggy and his nails long. I pictured him thin and sickly, black with hair and sunburn, and almost naked despite the articles of clothing I occasionally left for him.

He didn't seem to care about us at all. But I felt affection and respect for him, and, whenever they praised me because I had done something good, I said: 'My father taught me to act that way.'

It wasn't exactly accurate but it was a truthful sort of lie. As I said, Father didn't seem to care about us. But then why did he stay around there? Why didn't he go up the river or down the river, beyond the possibility of seeing us or being seen by us? He alone knew the answer.

My sister had a baby boy. She insisted on showing Father his grandson. One beautiful day we all went down to the riverbank, my sister in her white wedding dress, and she lifted the baby high. Her husband held a parasol above them. We shouted to Father and waited. He did not appear. My sister cried; we all cried in each other's arms.

My sister and her husband moved far away. My brother went to live in a city. Times changed, with their usual imperceptible rapidity. Mother finally moved too: she was old and went to live with her daughter. I remained behind, a leftover. I could never think of marrying. I just stayed there with the impedimenta of my life. Father, wandering alone and forlorn on the river, needed me. I knew he needed me, although he never even told me why he was doing it. When I put the question to people bluntly and insistently, all they told me was that they heard that Father had explained it to the man who made the boat. But now this man was dead and nobody knew or remembered anything. There was just some foolish talk, when the rains were especially severe and persistent, that my father was wise like Noah and had the boat built in anticipation of a new flood; I dimly remember people saying this. In any case, I would not condemn my father for what he was doing. My hair was beginning to turn grey.

I have only sad things to say. What bad had I done, what was my great guilt? My father always away and his absence always with me. And the river, always the river, perpetually renewing itself. The river, always. I was beginning to suffer from old age, in which life is just a sort of lingering. I had attacks of illness and of anxiety. I had a nagging rheumatism. And he? Why, why was he doing it? He must have been suffering terribly. He was so old. One day, in his failing strength, he might let the boat capsize; or he might let the current carry it downstream, on and on, until it plunged over the waterfall to the boiling turmoil below. It pressed upon my heart. He was out there and I was forever robbed of my peace. I am guilty of I know not what, and my pain is an open wound inside me. Perhaps I would know – if things were different. I began to guess what was wrong.

Out with it! Had I gone crazy? No, in our house that word was never spoken, never through all the years. No one called anybody crazy, for nobody is crazy. Or maybe everybody. All I did was go there and wave a handkerchief so he would be more likely to see me. I was in complete command of myself. I waited. Finally he appeared in the distance, there, then over there, a vague shape sitting in the back of the boat. I called to him several times. And I said what I was so eager to say, to state formally and under oath. I said it as loud as I could:

'Father, you have been out there long enough. You are old . . . Come back, you don't have to do it anymore . . . Come back and I'll go instead. Right now, if you want. Any time. I'll get into the boat. I'll take your place.'

And when I had said this my heart beat more firmly.

He heard me. He stood up. He manoeuvred with his oars and headed the boat towards me. He had accepted my offer. And suddenly I trembled, down deep. For he had raised his arm and waved – the first time in so many, so many years. And I couldn't . . . In terror, my hair on end, I ran, I fled madly. For he seemed to come from another world. And I'm begging forgiveness, begging, begging.

I experienced the dreadful sense of cold that comes from deadly fear, and I became ill. Nobody ever saw or heard about him again. Am I a man, after such a failure? I am what never should have been. I am what must be silent. I know it is too late. I must stay in the deserts and unmarked plains of my life, and I fear I shall shorten it. But when death comes I want them to take me and put me in a little boat in this perpetual water between the long shores; and I, down the river, lost in the river, inside the river . . . the river . . .

*Translated from the Portuguese by William L. Grossman.*

# Home

## Hilaire Belloc

*I found the following short story hidden in a book of Belloc's essays called* On Something. *It is not as ferociously funny as his verse –* Cautionary Tales, *for instance – but it has the same undertone of mock seriousness. The story of the search for a place in which we have known happiness is also the search for Paradise Lost; it appears again in H. G. Wells's 'The Door in the Wall' which follows 'Home' in this anthology.*

*Belloc collaborated frequently with his friend G. K. Chesterton who, like Belloc, advertised his Catholic faith in his writings; together they wrote satirical novels which Chesterton illustrated. Bernard Shaw called them the Chesterbelloc, a monstrous animal that opposed the socialism of Wells and of Shaw himself.*

There is a river called the Eure which runs between low hills often wooded, with a flat meadow floor in between. It so runs for many miles. The towns that are set upon it are for the most part small and rare, and though the river is well known by name, and though one of the chief cathedrals of Europe stands near its source, for the most part it is not visited by strangers.

In this valley one day as I was drawing a picture of the woods I found a wandering Englishman who was in the oddest way. He seemed by the slight bend at his knees and the leaning forward of his head to have no very great care how much further he might go. He was in the clothes of an English tourist, which looked odd in such a place, as, for that matter, they do anywhere. He had upon his head a pork-pie hat which was of the same colour and texture as his clothes, a speckly brown. He carried a thick stick. He was a man over fifty years of age, his face was rather hollow and worn; his eyes were very simple and pale; he was bearded with a weak beard and in his expression there appeared a constrained but kindly weariness. This was the man who came up to me as I was drawing my picture. I had heard him scrambling in the undergrowth of the woods just behind me.

He came out and walked to me across the few yards of meadow. The haying was over, so he did the grass no harm. He came and stood near me, irresolutely, looking vaguely up and across the valley towards the further woods, and then gently towards what I was drawing. When he had so stood still and so looked for a moment he asked me in French the name of the great house whose roof showed above the more ordered trees beyond the river, where a park emerged from and mixed with the forest. I told him the name of the house, whereupon he shook his head and said that he had once more come to the wrong place.'

I asked him what he meant, and he told me, sitting down slowly and carefully upon the grass, this adventure:

'First,' said he, 'are you always quite sure whether a thing is really there or not?'

'I am always quite sure,' said I; 'I am always positive.'

He sighed and added: 'Could you understand how a man might feel that things were really there when they were not?'

'Only,' said I, 'in some very vivid dream, and even then I think a man knows pretty well inside his own mind that he is dreaming.' I said that it seemed to me rather like the question of the cunning of lunatics; most of them know at the bottom of their silly minds that they are cracked, as you may see by the way they plot and pretend.

'You are not sympathetic with me,' he said slowly, 'but I will nevertheless tell you what I want to tell you, for it will relieve me, and it will explain to you why I have again come into this valley.'

'Why do you say "again"?' said I.

'Because,' he answered gently, 'whenever my work gives me the opportunity I do the same thing. I go up the valley of the Seine by train from Dieppe; I get out at the station at which I got out on that day, and I walk across these low hills, hoping that I may strike just the path and just the mood – but I never do.'

'What path and what mood?' said I.

'I was telling you,' he answered patiently, 'only you were so brutal about reality.' And then he sighed. He put his stick across his knees as he sat there on the grass, held it with a hand on either side of his knees, and so sitting bunched up began his tale once more.

'It was ten years ago, and I was extremely tired, for you must know that I am a Government servant, and I find my work most wearisome. It was just this time of year that I took a week's holiday. I intended to take it in Paris, but I thought on my way, as the weather was so fine, that I would do something new and that I would walk a little way off the track. I had often wondered what country lay behind the low and steep hills on the right of the railway line.

'I had crossed the Channel by night,' he continued, a little sorry for himself, 'to save the expense. It was dawn when I reached Rouen, and there I very well remember drinking some coffee which I did not like, and eating some good bread which I did. I changed carriages at Rouen because the express did not stop at any of the little stations beyond. I took a slower train, which came immediately behind it, and stopped at most of the stations. I took my ticket rather at random for a little station between Pont de l'Arche and Mantes. I got out at that little station, and it was still early – only midway through the morning.

'I was in an odd mixture of fatigue and exhilaration: I had not slept and I would willingly have done so, but the freshness of the new day was upon me, and I have always had a very keen curiosity to see new sights and to know what lies behind the hills.

'The day was fine and already rather hot for June. I did not stop in the village near the station for more than half an hour, just the time to take some soup and a little wine; then I set out into the woods to cross over into this parallel valley. I knew that I should come to it and to the railway line that goes down it in a very few miles. I proposed when I came to that other railway line on the far side of the hills to walk quietly down it as nearly parallel to it as I could get, and at the first station to take the next train for Chartres, and then the next day to go from Chartres to Paris. That was my plan.

'The road up into the woods was one of those great French roads which sometimes frighten me and always weary me by their length and insistence: men seem to have taken so much trouble to make them, and they make me feel as though I had to take trouble myself; I avoid them when I walk. Therefore, so soon as this great road had struck the crest of the hills and was well into the woods (cutting through them like the trench of a fortification, with the tall trees on either side) I struck out into a ride which had been cut through them many years ago and was already half overgrown, and I went along this ride for several miles.

'It did not matter to me how I went, since my design was so simple and since any direction more or less westward would enable me to fulfil it, that is, to come down upon the valley of the Eure and to find the single railway line which leads to Chartres. The woods were very pleasant on that June noon, and once or twice I was inclined to linger in their shade and sleep an hour. But – note this clearly – I did not sleep. I remember every moment of the way, though I confess my fatigue oppressed me somewhat as the miles continued.

'At last by the steepness of a new descent I recognized that I had crossed the watershed and was coming down into the valley of this river. The ride had dwindled to a path, and I was wondering where the path would lead me when I noticed that it was getting more orderly: there were patches of sand, and here and there a man had cut and trimmed the edges of the way. Then it became more orderly still. It was all sanded, and there were artificial bushes here and there – I mean bushes not native to the forest, until at last I was aware that my ramble had taken me into someone's own land, and that I was in a private ground.

'I saw no great harm in this, for a traveller, if he explains himself, will usually be excused; moreover, I had to continue, for I knew no other way, and this path led me westward also. Only, whether because my trespassing worried me or because I felt my own dishevelment more acutely, the lack of sleep and the strain upon me increased as I pursued those last hundred yards, until I came out suddenly from behind a screen of rosebushes upon a large lawn, and at the end of it there was a French country house with a moat round it, such as they often have, and a stone bridge over the moat.

'The château was simple and very grand. The mouldings upon it pleased me, and it was full of peace. Upon the further side of the lawn, so that I could hear it but not see it, a fountain was playing into a basin. By the sound it was one of those high French fountains which the people who built such houses as these two hundred years ago delighted in. The plash of it was very soothing, but I was so tired and drooping that at one moment it sounded much further than at the next.

'There was an iron bench at the edge of the screen of roses, and hardly knowing what I did – for it was not the right thing to do in

another person's place – I sat down on this bench, taking pleasure
in the sight of the moat and the house with its noble roof, and the
noise of the fountain. I think I should have gone to sleep there and
at that moment – for I felt upon me worse than ever the strain of
that long hot morning and that long night journey – had not a very
curious thing happened.'

Here the man looked up at me oddly, as though to see whether
I disbelieved him or not; but I did not disbelieve him.

I was not even very much interested, for I was trying to make
the trees to look different one from the other, which is an extremely
difficult thing: I had not succeeded and I was niggling away. He
continued with more assurance:

'The thing that happened was this: a young girl came out of the
house dressed in white, with a blue scarf over her head and crossed
round her neck. I knew her face as well as possible: it was a face I
had known all my youth and early manhood – but for the life of
me I could not remember her name!'

'When one is very tired,' I said, 'that does happen to one: a name
one knows as well as one's own escapes one. It is especially the
effect of lack of sleep.'

'It is,' said he, sighing profoundly; 'but the oddness of my feeling
it is impossible to describe, for there I was meeting the oldest and
perhaps the dearest and certainly the most familiar of my friends,
whom,' he added, hesitating a moment, 'I had not seen for many
years. It was a very great pleasure . . . it was a sort of comfort and
an ending. I forgot, the moment I saw her, why I had come over
the hills, and all about how I meant to get to Chartres . . . And
now I must tell you,' added the man a little awkwardly, 'that my
name is Peter.'

'No doubt,' said I gravely, for I could not see why he should not
bear that name.

'My Christian name,' he continued hurriedly.

'Of course,' said I, as sympathetically as I could. He seemed
relieved that I had not even smiled at it.

'Yes,' he went on rather quickly, 'Peter – my name is Peter. Well,
this lady came up to me and said, "Why, Peter, we never thought
you would come!" She did not seem very much astonished, but
rather as though I had come earlier than she had expected. "I will
get Philip," she said. "You remember Philip?" Here I had another
little trouble with my memory: I did remember that there was a

Philip, but I could not place him. That was odd, you know. As for her, oh, I knew *her* as well as the colour of the sky: it was her name that my brain missed, as it might have missed my own name or my mother's.

'Philip came out as she called him, and there was a familiarity between them that seemed natural to me at the time, but whether he was a brother or a lover or a husband, or what, I could not for the life of me remember.

' "You look tired," he said to me in a kind voice that I liked very much and remembered clearly. "I am," said I, "dog tired." "Come in with us," he said, "and we will give you some wine and water. When would you like to eat?" I said I would rather sleep than eat. He said that could easily be arranged.

'I strolled with them towards the house across that great lawn, hearing the noise of the fountain, now dimmer, now nearer; sometimes it seemed miles away and sometimes right in my ears. Whether it was their conversation or my familiarity with them or my fatigue, at any rate, as I crossed the moat I could no longer recall anything save their presence. I was not even troubled by the desire to recall anything; I was full of a complete contentment, and this surging up of familiar things, this surging up of it in a foreign place, without excuse or possible connection or any explanation whatsoever, seemed to me as natural as breathing.

'As I crossed the bridge I wholly forgot whence I came or whither I was going, but I knew myself better than ever I had known myself, and every detail of the place was familiar to me.

'Here I had passed (I thought) many hours of my childhood and my boyhood and my early manhood also. I ceased considering the names and the relation of Philip and the girl.

'They gave me cold meat and bread and excellent wine, and water to mix with it, and as they continued to speak even the last adumbrations of care fell off me altogether, and my spirit seemed entirely released and free. My approaching sleep beckoned to me like an easy entrance into Paradise. I should wake from it quite simply into the perpetual enjoyment of this place and its companionship. Oh, it was an absolute repose!

'Philip took me to a little room on the ground floor fitted with the exquisite care and the simplicity of the French: there was a curtained bed, a thing I love. He lent me night clothes, though it was broad day, because he said that if I undressed and got into the bed I should be much more rested; they would keep everything quiet at that end of the house, and the gentle fall of the water into the moat outside would not disturb me. I said on the contrary it would soothe me, and I felt the benignity of the place possess me like a spell. Remember that I was very tired and had not slept for now thirty hours.

'I remember handling the white counterpane and noting the delicate French pattern upon it, and seeing at one corner the little red silk coronet embroidered, which made me smile. I remember putting my hand upon the cool linen of the pillow-case and smoothing it; then I got into that bed and fell asleep. It was broad noon, with the stillness that comes of a summer noon upon the woods; the air was cool and delicious above the water of the moat, and my windows were open to it.

'The last thing I heard as I dropped asleep was her voice calling to Philip in the corridor. I could have told the very place. I knew that corridor so well. We used to play there when we were children. We used to play at travelling, and we used to invent the names of railway stations for the various doors. Remembering this and smiling at the memory, I fell at once into a blessed sleep.

' . . . I do not want to annoy you,' said the man apologetically, 'but I really had to tell you this story, and I hardly know how to tell you the end of it.'

'Go on,' said I hurriedly, for I had gone and made two trees one exactly like the other (which in nature was never seen) and I was annoyed with myself.

'Well,' said he, still hesitating and sighing with real sadness, 'when I woke up I was in a third-class carriage; the light was that of late afternoon, and a man had woken me by tapping my shoulder and telling me that the next station was Chartres . . . That's all.'

He sighed again. He expected me to say something. So I did. I said without much originality: 'You must have dreamed it.'

'No,' said he, very considerably put out, 'that is the point! I didn't! I tell you I can remember exactly every stage from when I left the railway train in the Seine Valley until I got into that bed.'

'It's all very odd,' said I.

'Yes,' said he, 'and so was my mood; but it was real enough. It was the second or third most real thing that has ever happened to me. I am quite certain that it happened to me.'

I remained silent, and rubbed out the top of one of my trees so

as to invent a new top for it, since I could not draw it as it was.
Then, as he wanted me to say something more, I said: 'Well, you
must have got into the train somehow.'

'Of course,' said he.

'Well, where did you get into the train?'

'I don't know.'

'Your ticket would have told you that.'

'I think I must have given it up to the man,' he answered doubtfully, 'the guard who told me that the next station was Chartres.'

'Well, it's all very mysterious,' I said.

'Yes,' he said, getting up rather weakly to go on again, 'it is.'
And he sighed again. 'I come here every year. I hope,' he added a
little wistfully, 'I hope, you see, that it may happen to me again
. . . but it never does.'

'It will at last,' said I to comfort him.

And, will you believe it, that simple sentence made him in a
moment radiantly happy; his face beamed, and he positively thanked
me, thanked me warmly.

'You speak like one inspired,' he said. (I confess I did not feel
like it at all.) 'I shall go much lighter on my way after that sentence
of yours.'

He bade me goodbye with some ceremony and slouched off, with
his eyes set towards the west and the more distant hills.

# The Door in the Wall

## H. G. Wells

*H. G. Wells was on the opposite side of the political field from Belloc.
He was an optimist whose logical mind led him to write like a pessimist.
He prophesied the Second World War, he gave a grim picture of man
in* The Fate of Homo Sapiens, *and even in his fantastic novels the
outcome is always depressing: in* The Sleeper Wakes *the world of the
future is a soulless, fascist society; in* The Time Machine *it is divided
between a race of cruel masters and docile slaves; in* The War of the
Worlds *the Earth is conquered and destroyed. However, his optimism
appears in the portrayal of his characters: they always have a saving
grace and show in the gloom a glimmer of hope.*

*'The Door in the Wall' is my favourite Wells story. I was a bit
discomfited by the pastoral scene behind the first door, smacking a little
of good fairies with magic wands and hideous hairstyles, but the door
itself, the idea of this opening towards happiness, is truly wonderful.
Algernon Blackwood uses a similar theme in 'The Old Man of Visions'
but the result is not as effective because Blackwood is not as good a
craftsman as Wells. 'Please God I may dream of the garden' is not the
least frequent of my prayers.*

# I

One confidential evening, not three months ago, Lionel Wallace
told me this story of the Door in the Wall. And at the time I thought
that so far as he was concerned it was a true story.

He told it me with such direct simplicity of conviction that I
could not do otherwise than believe in him. But in the morning, in
my own flat, I woke to a different atmosphere; and as I lay in bed
and recalled the things he had told me, stripped of the glamour of
his earnest slow voice, denuded of the focused, shaded table light,
the shadowy atmosphere that wrapped about him and me, and the

pleasant bright things, the dessert and glasses and napery of the dinner we had shared, making them for the time a bright little world quite cut off from everyday realities, I saw it all as frankly incredible. 'He was mystifying!' I said, and then: 'How well he did it! . . . It isn't quite the thing I should have expected of him, of all people, to do well.'

Afterwards as I sat up in bed and sipped my morning tea, I found myself trying to account for the flavour of reality that perplexed me in his impossible reminiscences, by supposing they did in some way suggest, present, convey – I hardly know which word to use – experiences it was otherwise impossible to tell.

Well, I don't resort to that explanation now. I have got over my intervening doubts. I believe now, as I believed at the moment of telling, that Wallace did to the very best of his ability strip the truth of his secret for me. But whether he himself saw, or only thought he saw, whether he himself was the possessor of an inestimable privilege or the victim of a fantastic dream, I cannot pretend to guess. Even the facts of his death, which ended my doubts for ever, throw no light on that.

That much the reader must judge for himself.

I forget now what chance comment or criticism of mine moved so reticent a man to confide in me. He was, I think, defending himself against an imputation of slackness and unreliability I had made in relation to a great public movement, in which he had disappointed me. But he plunged suddenly. 'I have,' he said, 'a preoccupation – '

'I know,' he went on, after a pause, 'I have been negligent. The fact is – it isn't a case of ghosts or apparitions – but – it's an odd thing to tell of, Redmond – I am haunted. I am haunted by something – that rather takes the light out of things, that fills me with longings . . .'

He paused, checked by that English shyness that so often overcomes us when we speak of moving or grave or beautiful things. 'You were at Saint Athelstan's all through,' he said, and for a moment that seemed to me quite irrelevant. 'Well' – and he paused. Then very haltingly at first, but afterwards more easily, he began to tell of the thing that was hidden in his life, the haunting memory of a beauty and happiness that filled his heart with insatiable longings, that made all the interests and spectacle of worldly life seem dull and tedious and vain to him.

Now that I have the clue to it, the thing seems written visibly in his face. I have a photograph in which that look of detachment has been caught and intensified. It reminds me of what a woman once said of him – a woman who had loved him greatly. 'Suddenly,' she said, 'the interest goes out of him. He forgets you. He doesn't care a rap for you – under his very nose . . .'

Yet the interest was not always out of him, and when he was holding his attention to a thing Wallace could contrive to be an extremely successful man. His career, indeed, is set with successes. He left me behind him long ago; he soared up over my head, and cut a figure in the world that I couldn't cut – anyhow. He was still a year short of forty, and they say now that he would have been in office and very probably in the new Cabinet if he had lived. At school he always beat me without effort – as it were by nature. We were at school together at Saint Athelstan's College in West Kensington for almost all our school-time. He came into the school as my co-equal, but he left far above me, in a blaze of scholarships and brilliant performance. Yet I think I made a fair average running. And it was at school I heard first of the 'Door in the Wall' – that I was to hear of a second time only a month before his death.

To him at least the Door in the Wall was a real door, leading through a real wall to immortal realities. Of that I am now quite assured.

And it came into his life quite early, when he was a little fellow between five and six. I remember how, as he sat making his confession to me with a slow gravity, he reasoned and reckoned the date of it. 'There was,' he said, 'a crimson Virginia creeper in it – all one bright uniform crimson, in a clear amber sunshine against a white wall. That came into the impression somehow, though I don't clearly remember how, and there were horse-chestnut leaves upon the clean pavement outside the green door. They were blotched yellow and green, you know, not brown nor dirty, so that they must have been new fallen. I take it that means October. I look out for horse-chestnut leaves every year and I ought to know.

'If I'm right in that, I was about five years and four months old.'

He was, he said, rather a precocious little boy – he learned to talk at an abnormally early age, and he was so sane and 'old-fashioned', as people say, that he was permitted an amount of initiative that most children scarcely attain by seven or eight. His mother died when he was two, and he was under the less vigilant and authoritative care of a nursery governess. His father was a stern, preoccupied lawyer, who gave him little attention and expected great things of him. For all his brightness he found life grey and dull, I think. And one day he wandered.

He could not recall the particular neglect that enabled him to get away, nor the course he took among the West Kensington roads. All that had faded among the incurable blurs of memory. But the white wall and the green door stood out quite distinctly.

As his memory of that childish experience ran, he did at the very first sight of that door experience a peculiar emotion, an attraction, a desire to get to the door and open it and walk in. And at the same time he had the clearest conviction that either it was unwise or it was wrong of him – he could not tell which – to yield to this attraction. He insisted upon it as a curious thing that he knew from the very beginning – unless memory has played him the queerest trick – that the door was unfastened, and that he could go in as he chose.

I seem to see the figure of that little boy, drawn and repelled. And it was very clear in his mind, too, though why it should be so was never explained, that his father would be very angry if he went in through that door.

Wallace described all these moments of hesitation to me with the utmost particularity. He went right past the door, and then, with his hands in his pockets and making an infantile attempt to whistle, strolled right along beyond the end of the wall. There he recalls a number of mean dirty shops, and particularly that of a plumber and decorator with a dusty disorder of earthenware pipes, sheet lead, ball taps, pattern books of wallpaper, and tins of enamel. He stood pretending to examine these things, and *coveting*, passionately desiring, the green door.

Then, he said, he had a gust of emotion. He made a run for it, lest hesitation should grip him again; he went plumb with outstretched hand through the green door and let it slam behind him. And so, in a trice, he came into the garden that has haunted all his life.

It was very difficult for Wallace to give me his full sense of that garden into which he came.

There was something in the very air of it that exhilarated, that gave one a sense of lightness and good happening and well-being; there was something in the sight of it that made all its colour clean and perfect and subtly luminous. In the instant of coming into it one was exquisitely glad – as only in rare moments, and when one is young and joyful one can be glad in this world. And everything was beautiful there . . .

Wallace mused before he went on telling me. 'You see,' he said, with the doubtful inflection of a man who pauses at incredible things, 'there were two great panthers there . . . Yes, spotted panthers. And I was not afraid. There was a long wide path with marble-edged flower borders on either side, and these two huge velvety beasts were playing there with a ball. One looked up and came towards me, a little curious as it seemed. It came right up to me, rubbed its soft round ear very gently against the small hand I held out, and purred. It was, I tell you, an enchanted garden. I know. And the size? Oh! it stretched far and wide, this way and that. I believe there were hills far away. Heaven knows where West Kensington had suddenly got to. And somehow it was just like coming home.

'You know, in the very moment the door swung to behind me, I forgot the road with its fallen chestnut leaves, its cabs and tradesmen's carts, I forgot the sort of gravitational pull back to the discipline and obedience of home, I forgot all hesitations and fear, forgot discretion, forgot all the intimate realities of this life. I became in a moment a very glad and wonder-happy little boy – in another world. It was a world with a different quality, a warmer, more penetrating, and mellower light, with a faint clear gladness in its air, and wisps of sun-touched cloud in the blueness of its sky. And before me ran this long wide path, invitingly, with weedless beds on either side, rich with untended flowers, and these two great panthers. I put my little hands fearlessly on their soft fur, and caressed their round ears and the sensitive corners under their ears, and played with them, and it was as though they welcomed me home. There was a keen sense of homecoming in my mind, and when presently a tall, fair girl appeared in the pathway and came to meet me, smiling, and said, "Well?" to me, and lifted me and kissed me and put me down and led me by the hand, there was no amazement, but only an impression of delightful rightness, of being reminded of happy things that had in some strange way been overlooked. There were broad red steps, I remember, that came into view between spikes of delphinium, and up these we went to a great avenue between very old and shady dark trees. All down this avenue, you know, between the red chapped stems, were marble seats of honour and statuary, and very tame and friendly white doves.

'Along this cool avenue my girl-friend led me, looking down – I recall the pleasant lines, the finely-modelled chin of her sweet kind face – asking me questions in a soft, agreeable voice, and telling me things, pleasant things, I know, though what they were I was never able to recall . . . Presently a Capuchin monkey, very clean, with a fur of ruddy brown and kindly hazel eyes, came down a tree to us and ran beside me, looking up at me and grinning, and presently leaped to my shoulder. So we two went on our way in great happiness.'

He paused.

'Go on,' I said.

'I remember little things. We passed an old man musing among laurels, I remember, and a place gay with parakeets, and came through a broad shaded colonnade to a spacious cool palace, full of pleasant fountains, full of beautiful things, full of the quality and promise of heart's desire. And there were many things and many people, some that still seem to stand out clearly and some that are vaguer; but all these people were beautiful and kind. In some way – I don't know how – it was conveyed to me that they all were kind to me, glad to have me there, and filling me with gladness by their gestures, by the touch of their hands, by the welcome and love in their eyes. Yes – '

He mused for a while. 'Playmates I found there. That was much to me, because I was a lonely little boy. They played delightful games in a grass-covered court where there was a sundial set about with flowers. And as one played one loved . . .

'But – it's odd – there's a gap in my memory. I don't remember the games we played. I never remembered. Afterwards, as a child, I spent long hours trying, even with tears, to recall the form of that happiness. I wanted to play it all over again – in my nursery – by myself. No! All I remember is the happiness and two dear play-fellows who were most with me . . . Then presently came a sombre dark woman, with a grave, pale face and dreamy eyes, a sombre woman, wearing a soft long robe of pale purple, who carried a book, and beckoned and took me aside with her into a gallery above a hall – though my playmates were loth to have me go, and ceased their game and stood watching as I was carried away. "Come back to us!" they cried. "Come back to us soon!" I looked up at her face, but she heeded them not at all. Her face was very gentle and grave. She took me to a seat in the gallery, and I stood beside her, ready to look at her book as she opened it upon her knee. The pages fell open. She pointed, and I looked, marvelling, for in the living pages of that book I saw myself; it was a story about myself, and in it were all the things that had happened to me since ever I was born . . .

'It was wonderful to me, because the pages of that book were not pictures, you understand, but realities.'

Wallace paused gravely – looked at me doubtfully.

'Go on,' I said. 'I understand.'

'They were realities – yes, they must have been; people moved and things came and went in them; my dear mother, whom I had near forgotten; then my father, stern and upright, the servants, the nursery, all the familiar things of home. Then the front door and the busy streets, with traffic to and fro. I looked and marvelled, and looked half doubtfully again into the woman's face and turned the pages over, skipping this and that, to see more of this book and more, and so at last I came to myself hovering and hesitating outside the green door in the long white wall, and felt again the conflict and the fear.

' "And next?" ' I cried, and would have turned on, but the cool hand of the grave woman delayed me.

' "Next?" ' I insisted, and struggled gently with her hand, pulling up her fingers with all my childish strength, and as she yielded and the page came over she bent down upon me like a shadow and kissed my brow.

'But the page did not show the enchanted garden, nor the panthers, nor the girl who had led me by the hand, nor the play-fellows who had been so loth to let me go. It showed a long grey street in West Kensington, in that chill hour of afternoon before the lamps are lit; and I was there, a wretched little figure, weeping aloud, for all that I could do to restrain myself, and I was weeping because I could not return to my dear playfellows who had called after me, "Come back to us! Come back to us soon!" I was there. This was no page in a book, but harsh reality; that enchanted place and the restraining hand of the grave mother at whose knee I stood had gone – whither had they gone?'

He halted again, and remained for a time staring into the fire.

'Oh! the woefulness of that return!' he murmured.

'Well?' I said, after a minute or so.

'Poor little wretch I was! – brought back to this grey world again! As I realized the fullness of what had happened to me, I gave way to quite ungovernable grief. And the shame and humiliation of that public weeping and my disgraceful home-coming remain with me still. I see again the benevolent-looking old gentleman in gold spectacles who stopped and spoke to me – prodding me first with his umbrella. "Poor little chap," said he; "and are you lost then?" – and me a London boy of five and more! And he must needs bring in a kindly young policeman and make a crowd of me, and so march me home. Sobbing, conspicuous, and frightened, I came back from the enchanted garden to the steps of my father's house.

'That is as well as I can remember my vision of that garden – the garden that haunts me still. Of course, I can convey nothing of that indescribable quality of translucent unreality, that difference from the common things of experience that hung about it all; but that – that is what happened. If it was a dream, I am sure it was a day-time and altogether extraordinary dream . . . H'm! – naturally there followed a terrible questioning, by my aunt, my father, the nurse, the governess – everyone . . .

'I tried to tell them, and my father gave me my first thrashing for telling lies. When afterwards I tried to tell my aunt, she punished me again for my wicked persistence. Then, as I said, everyone was forbidden to listen to me, to hear a word about it. Even my fairy-tale books were taken away from me for a time – because I was too "imaginative". Eh! Yes, they did that! My father belonged to the old school . . . And my story was driven back upon myself. I whispered it to my pillow – my pillow that was often damp and salt to my whispering lips with childish tears. And I added always to my official and less fervent prayers this one heartfelt request: "Please God I may dream of the garden. O! take me back to my garden." Take me back to my garden! I dreamt often of the garden. I may have added to it, I may have changed it; I do not know . . . All this, you understand, is an attempt to reconstruct from fragmentary memories a very early experience. Between that and the other consecutive memories of my boyhood there is a gulf. A time came when it seemed impossible I should ever speak of that wonder glimpse again.'

I asked an obvious question.

'No,' he said. 'I don't remember that I ever attempted to find my way back to the garden in those early years. This seems odd to me now, but I think that very probably a closer watch was kept on my movements after this misadventure to prevent my going astray. No, it wasn't till you knew me that I tried for the garden again. And I believe there was a period – incredible as it seems now – when I forgot the garden altogether – when I was about eight or nine it may have been. Do you remember me as a kid at Saint Athelstan's?'

'Rather!'

'I didn't show any signs, did I, in those days of having a secret dream?'

# II

He looked up with a sudden smile.

'Did you ever play North-West Passage with me? . . . No, of course you didn't come my way!

'It was the sort of game,' he went on, 'that every imaginative child plays all day. The idea was the discovery of a North-West Passage to school. The way to school was plain enough; the game consisted of finding some way that wasn't plain, starting off ten minutes early in some almost hopeless direction, and working my way round through unaccustomed streets to my goal. And one day I got entangled among some rather low-class streets on the other side of Campden Hill, and I began to think that for once the game would be against me and that I should get to school late. I tried rather desperately a street that seemed a cul-de-sac, and found a passage at the end. I hurried through that with renewed hope. "I shall do it yet," I said, and passed a row of frowsy little shops that were inexplicably familiar to me, and behold! there was my long white wall and the green door that led to the enchanted garden!

'The thing whacked upon me suddenly. Then, after all, that garden, that wonderful garden, wasn't a dream!'

He paused.

'I suppose my second experience with the green door marks the world of difference there is between the busy life of a schoolboy and the infinite leisure of a child. Anyhow, this second time I didn't for a moment think of going in straight away. You see— For one thing, my mind was full of the idea of getting to school in time – set on not breaking my record for punctuality. I must surely have felt *some* little desire at least to try the door – yes. I must have felt that . . . But I seem to remember the attraction of the door mainly as another obstacle to my overmastering determination to get to school. I was immensely interested by this discovery I had made, of course – I went on with my mind full of it – but I went on. It didn't check me. I ran past, tugging out my watch, found I had ten minutes still to spare, and then I was going downhill into familiar surroundings. I got to school, breathless, it is true, and wet with perspiration, but in time. I can remember hanging up my coat and hat . . . Went right by it and left it behind me. Odd, eh?'

He looked at me thoughtfully. 'Of course I didn't know then that it wouldn't always be there. Schoolboys have limited imaginations. I suppose I thought it was an awfully jolly thing to have it there, to know my way back to it; but there was the school tugging at me. I expect I was a good deal distraught and inattentive that morning, recalling what I could of the beautiful strange people I should presently see again. Oddly enough I had no doubt in my mind that they would be glad to see me . . . Yes, I must have thought of the garden that morning just as a jolly sort of place to which one might resort in the interludes of a strenuous scholastic career.

'I didn't go that day at all. The next day was a half-holiday, and that may have weighed with me. Perhaps, too, my state of inattention brought down impositions upon me, and docked the margin of time necessary for the *détour*. I don't know. What I do know is that in the meantime the enchanted garden was so much upon my mind that I could not keep it to myself.

'I told – what was his name? – a ferrety-looking youngster we used to call Squiff.'

'Young Hopkins,' said I.

'Hopkins it was. I did not like telling him. I had a feeling that in some way it was against the rules to tell him, but I did. He was walking part of the way home with me; he was talkative, and if we had not talked about the enchanted garden we should have talked of something else, and it was intolerable to me to think about any other subject. So I blabbed.

'Well, he told my secret. The next day in the play interval I found myself surrounded by half a dozen bigger boys, half teasing, and wholly curious to hear more of the enchanted garden. There was that big Fawcett – you remember him? – and Carnaby and Morley Reynolds. You weren't there by any chance? No, I think I should have remembered if you were . . .

'A boy is a creature of odd feelings. I was, I really believe, in spite of my secret self-disgust, a little flattered to have the attention of these big fellows. I remember particularly a moment of pleasure caused by the praise of Crawshaw – you remember Crawshaw major, the son of Crawshaw the composer? – who said it was the best lie he had ever heard. But at the same time there was a really painful undertow of shame at telling what I felt was indeed a sacred secret. That beast Fawcett made a joke about the girl in green—'

Wallace's voice sank with the keen memory of that shame. 'I pretended not to hear,' he said. 'Well, then Carnaby suddenly called me a young liar, and disputed with me when I said the thing was true. I said I knew where to find the green door, could lead them all there in ten minutes. Carnaby became outrageously virtuous, and said I'd have to – and bear out my words or suffer. Did you ever have Carnaby twist your arm? Then perhaps you'll understand how it went with me. I swore my story was true. There was nobody in the school then to save a chap from Carnaby, though Crawshaw put in a word or so. Carnaby had got his game. I grew excited and red-eared, and a little frightened. I behaved altogether like a silly little chap, and the outcome of it all was that instead of starting alone for my enchanted garden, I led the way presently – cheeks flushed, ears hot, eyes smarting, and my soul one burning misery and shame – for a party of six mocking, curious, and threatening schoolfellows.

'We never found the white wall and the green door . . .'

'You mean – '

'I mean I couldn't find it. I would have found it if I could.

'And afterwards when I could go alone I couldn't find it. I never found it. I seem now to have been always looking for it through my schoolboy days, but I never came upon it – never.'

'Did the fellows – make it disagreeable?'

'Beastly . . . Carnaby held a council over me for wanton lying. I remember how I sneaked home and upstairs to hide the marks of my blubbering. But when I cried myself to sleep at last it wasn't for Carnaby, but for the garden, for the beautiful afternoon I had hoped for, for the sweet friendly women and the waiting playfellows, and the game I had hoped to learn again, that beautiful forgotten game . . .

'I believed firmly that if I had not told— I had bad times after that – crying at night and wool-gathering by day. For two terms I slacked and had bad reports. Do you remember? Of course you would! It was *you* – your beating me in mathematics that brought me back to the grind again.'

# III

For a time my friend stared silently into the red heart of the fire. Then he said: 'I never saw it again until I was seventeen.

'It leaped upon me for the third time – as I was driving to Paddington on my way to Oxford and a scholarship. I had just one momentary glimpse. I was leaning over the apron of my hansom smoking a cigarette, and no doubt thinking myself no end of a man of the world, and suddenly there was the door, the wall, the dear sense of unforgettable and still attainable things.

'We clattered by – I too taken by surprise to stop my cab until we were well past and round a corner. Then I had a queer moment, a double and divergent movement of my will: I tapped the little door in the roof of the cab, and brought my arm down to pull out my watch. "Yes, sir!" said the cabman smartly. "Er – well – it's nothing," I cried. "*My* mistake! We haven't much time! Go on!" And he went on . . .

'I got my scholarship. And the night after I was told of that I sat over my fire in my little upper room, my study, in my father's house, with his praise – his rare praise – and his sound counsels ringing in my ears, and I smoked my favourite pipe – the formidable bulldog of adolescence – and thought of that door in the long white wall. "If I had stopped," I thought, "I should have missed my scholarship, I should have missed Oxford – muddled all the fine career before me! I begin to see things better!" I fell to musing deeply, but I did not doubt then this career of mine was a thing that merited sacrifice.

'Those dear friends and that clear atmosphere seemed very sweet to me, very fine but remote. My grip was fixing now upon the world. I saw another door opening – the door of my career.'

He stared again into the fire. Its red light picked out a stubborn strength in his face for just one flickering moment, and then it vanished again.

'Well,' he said and sighed, 'I have served that career. I have done – much work, much hard work. But I have dreamt of the enchanted garden a thousand dreams, and seen its door, or at least glimpsed its door, four times since then. Yes – four times. For a while this world was so bright and interesting, seemed so full of meaning and opportunity, that the half-effaced charm of the garden was by comparison gentle and remote. Who wants to pat panthers on the way to dinner with pretty women and distinguished men? I came down to London from Oxford, a man of bold promise that I have done something to redeem. Something – and yet there have been disappointments . . .

'Twice I have been in love – I will not dwell on that – but once, as I went to some one who, I knew, doubted whether I dared to come, I took a short cut at a venture through an unfrequented road near Earl's Court, and so happened on a white wall and a familiar green door. "Odd!" said I to myself, "but I thought this place was on Campden Hill. It's the place I never could find somehow – like counting Stonehenge – the place of that queer daydream of mine." And I went by it intent upon my purpose. It had no appeal to me that afternoon.

'I had just a moment's impulse to try the door, three steps aside were needed at the most – though I was sure enough in my heart that it would open to me – and then I thought that doing so might delay me on the way to that appointment in which my honour was involved. Afterwards I was sorry for my punctuality – I might at least have peeped in and waved a hand to those panthers, but I knew enough by this time not to seek again belatedly that which is not found by seeking. Yes, that time made me very sorry . . .

'Years of hard work after that, and never a sight of the door. It's only recently it has come back to me. With it there has come a sense as though some thin tarnish had spread itself over my world. I began to think of it as a sorrowful and bitter thing that I should never see that door again. Perhaps I was suffering a little from overwork – perhaps it was what I've heard spoken of as the feeling of forty. I don't know. But certainly the keen brightness that makes effort easy has gone out of things recently, and that just at a time – with all these new political developments – when I ought to be working. Odd, isn't it? But I do begin to find life toilsome, its rewards, as I come near them, cheap. I began a little while ago to want the garden quite badly. Yes – and I've seen it three times.'

'The garden?'

'No – the door! And I haven't gone in!'

He leaned over the table to me, with an enormous sorrow in his voice as he spoke. 'Thrice I have had my chance – *thrice!* If ever that door offers itself to me again, I swore, I will go in, out of this dust and heat, out of this dry glitter of vanity, out of these toilsome futilities. I will go and never return. This time I will stay . . . I swore it, and when the time came – I *didn't* go.

'Three times in one year I have passed that door and failed to enter. Three times in the last year.

'The first time was on the night of the snatch division on the Tenants' Redemption Bill, on which the Government was saved by a majority of three. You remember? No one on our side – perhaps very few on the opposite side – expected the end that night. Then the debate collapsed like egg-shells. I and Hotchkiss were dining with his cousin at Brentford; we were both unpaired, and we were called up by telephone, and set off at once in his cousin's motor. We got in barely in time, and on the way we passed my wall and door – livid in the moonlight, blotched with hot yellow as the glare of our lamps lit it, but unmistakable. "My God!" cried I. "What?" said Hotchkiss. "Nothing!" I answered, and the moment passed.

' "I've made a great sacrifice," I told the whip as I got in. "They all have," he said, and hurried by.

'I do not see how I could have done otherwise then. And the next occasion was as I rushed to my father's bedside to bid that stern old man farewell. Then, too, the claims of life were imperative. But the third time was different; it happened a week ago. It fills me with hot remorse to recall it. I was with Gurker and Ralphs – it's no secret now, you know, that I've had my talk with Gurker. We had been dining at Frobisher's, and the talk had become intimate between us. The question of my place in the reconstructed Ministry lay always just over the boundary of the discussion. Yes – yes. That's all settled. It needn't be talked about yet, but there's no reason to keep a secret from you . . . Yes – thanks! thanks! But let me tell you my story.

'Then, on that night things were very much in the air. My position was a very delicate one. I was keenly anxious to get some definite word from Gurker, but was hampered by Ralphs' presence. I was using the best power of my brain to keep that light and careless talk not too obviously directed to the point that concerned me. I had to. Ralphs' behaviour since has more than justified my caution . . . Ralphs, I knew, would leave us beyond the Kensington High Street, and then I could surprise Gurker by a sudden frankness.

One has sometimes to resort to these little devices . . . And then it was that in the margin of my field of vision I became aware once more of the white wall, the green door before us down the road.

'We passed it talking. I passed it. I can still see the shadow of Gurker's marked profile, his opera hat tilted forward over his prominent nose, the many folds of his neck wrap going before my shadow and Ralphs' as we sauntered past.

'I passed within twenty inches of the door. "If I say goodnight to them, and go in," I asked myself, "what will happen?" And I was all a-tingle for that word with Gurker.

'I could not answer that question in the tangle of my other problems. "They will think me mad," I thought. "And suppose I vanish now? – Amazing disappearance of a prominent politician!" That weighed with me. A thousand inconceivable petty worldlinesses weighed with me in that crisis.'

Then he turned on me with a sorrowful smile, and, speaking slowly, 'Here I am!' he said.

'Here I am!' he repeated, 'and my chance has gone from me. Three times in one year the door has been offered me – that door that goes into peace, into delight, into a beauty beyond dreaming, a kindness no man on earth can know. And I have rejected it, Redmond, and it has gone—'

'How do you know?'

'I know. I know. I am left now to work it out, to stick to the tasks that held me so strongly when my moments came. You say I have success – this vulgar, tawdry, irksome, envied thing. I have it.' He had a walnut in his big hand. 'If that was my success,' he said, and crushed it, and held it out for me to see.

'Let me tell you something, Redmond. This loss is destroying me. For two months, for ten weeks nearly now, I have done no work at all, except the most necessary and urgent duties. My soul is full of inappeasable regrets. At nights – when it is less likely I shall be recognized – I go out. I wander. Yes. I wonder what people would think of that if they knew. A Cabinet Minister, the responsible head of that most vital of all departments, wandering alone – grieving – sometimes near audibly lamenting – for a door, for a garden!'

# IV

I can see now his rather pallid face, and the unfamiliar sombre fire that had come into his eyes. I see him very vividly tonight. I sit recalling his words, his tones, and last evening's *Westminster Gazette* still lies on my sofa, containing the notice of his death. At lunch today the club was busy with his death. We talked of nothing else.

They found his body very early yesterday morning in a deep excavation near East Kensington Station. It is one of two shafts that have been made in connection with an extension of the railway southward. It is protected from the intrusion of the public by a hoarding upon the high road, in which a small doorway has been cut for the convenience of some of the workmen who live in that direction. The doorway was left unfastened through a misunderstanding between two gangers, and through it he made his way.

My mind is darkened with questions and riddles.

It would seem he walked all the way from the House that night – he has frequently walked home during the past Session – and so it is I figure his dark form coming along the late and empty streets, wrapped up, intent. And then did the pale electric lights near the station cheat the rough planking into a semblance of white? Did that fatal unfastened door awaken some memory?

Was there, after all, ever any green door in the wall at all?

I do not know. I have told his story as he told it to me. There are times when I believe that Wallace was no more than the victim of the coincidence between a rare but not unprecedented type of hallucination and a careless trap, but that indeed is not my profoundest belief. You may think me superstitious, if you will, and foolish; but, indeed, I am more than half convinced that he had, in truth, an abnormal gift, and a sense, something – I know not what – that in the guise of a wall and door offered him an outlet, a secret and peculiar passage of escape into another and altogether more beautiful world. At any rate, you will say, it betrayed him in the end. But did it betray him? There you touch the inmost mystery of these dreamers, these men of vision and the imagination. We see our world fair and common, the hoarding and the pit. By our daylight standard he walked out of security into darkness, danger, and death.

But did he see like that?

# The Friends

## Silvina Ocampo

*Silvina Ocampo is one of the most original writers in the Spanish language. Her short stories, seemingly simple, are in fact carefully contrived traps in which she snares the reader. We enter them carelessly because they seem artificial, and we are caught by their impeccable, terrifying logic. Her themes, which she herself has listed, are 'love, time, the bewilderment of feelings, the entanglements of human relationships. And sometimes themes that I don't want to take on, but which come to me on their own: themes of revenge, jealousy, the hold one human being has over another, deceit. Also nature: animals, animal life, childhood.'*

*Silvina Ocampo has translated Horace, Ronsard, Alexander Pope, Andrew Marvell, Baudelaire, Nerval and Emily Dickinson, and together with Bioy Casares and Borges she compiled the essential* Anthology of Fantastic Literature *which in 1940 established the rules of the genre in Latin America.*

Many unfortunate things happened in our town. A flood cut us off from the town centre. I remember that for two months we were not able to go to school, not even to the chemist. Then the following year a typhoid epidemic killed my aunt – a strict but pious woman –, our schoolmistress, and the parish priest whom my parents held in high esteem. In less than three weeks there were over thirty fatal cases. Almost the entire town was in mourning; the cemetery looked like a horticultural bazaar and the streets were the stage for a bell-ringing concert.

My friend Cornelio lived on the upper floor of our house. We were both seven years old and, because our families were so close to each other, we were more like brothers than friends. We shared our games, our parents, our aunts, our meals. We went to school together. Cornelio learnt his lessons easily, but I knew he disliked school. I loved school, but had great difficulty in learning. I had been very fond of the schoolmistress, but I knew Cornelio had hated her.

'He's bound to become a saint,' Aunt Fermina would mutter dolefully.

'He'll get over it,' Aunt Claudia, who looked very like an ostrich, would answer. 'Not to worry.' And like an ostrich shakes its wings, she would shake her shoulders as she spoke.

'What's wrong with being a saint?' my mother would snap back.

'If he were *your* son, I'm sure *you* wouldn't like it,' Cornelio's mother would argue.

'Why not? Isn't it a good thing to be in God's grace?'

'Hair-cloth, fasting, seclusion.' Cornelio's mother would utter the words slowly, with both fear and delight.

'Would you rather it were drink, women and politics? Are you afraid that they will take your son away from you? Well, either God or the world will do just that.'

Our mothers would smile sadly, as if they had reached an agreement, and I would listen in silence. I had seen Cornelio with his white school pinafore, a prayer-book in his hand, kneeling by the window, night and day, praying. When I entered the room he would blush and pretend to be studying a grammar or history-book, and would quickly hide the prayer-book under a seat or in a drawer so that I wouldn't see it. I used to ask myself: why is he ashamed of his pious feelings? Did he feel that praying was like playing with dolls? He never confided in me and we never discussed religion, though, in spite of our age, we spoke quite openly of girlfriends, marriage and sex. I felt a contradiction in his mystical manners and his outspokenness.

'When I pray for a miracle, it's always granted,' he said to me one day, in a proud, sing-song voice.

I repeated his words to my aunts and for some time they spoke of nothing else. They attributed Cornelio's remark to the deep shock they imagined he had suffered when the flood and the epidemic struck our town: when a child our age witnesses, in so short a period, so many deaths, the experience is likely to leave traces in his soul. And if these events had not influenced my own character, it was because of my insensitive and slightly wicked nature. But I knew that Cornelio's mysticism had begun well before the flood and the epidemic; it was absurd to attribute it to those catastrophes. I darkly realized the mistake these grown-ups were making, but I was

accustomed to hold my tongue and accept things as they came. I
bowed therefore to my role as the wicked child, in contrast with
Cornelio who appeared to be the very incarnation of sensitivity and
kindness. I felt both jealousy and admiration. I would lock myself
up in my room and cry for my sins, begging God to make me a
little more like my friend.

Cornelio's hold over me was immense. I tried not to upset him,
or displease him or hurt him, but he seemed to demand that I upset
him, displease him and even hurt him. One day he got angry with
me because I had taken his penknife away from him. (I had to
resort to tricks like this so that he would not despise me.) Another
time, when I got hold of his pencilcase, he hit me and scratched
my face.

'If you touch one of my things ever again, I'll pray for you to
die,' he said. I laughed. 'Don't you believe me? Wasn't there a
flood, and then a plague? You think that was by chance?'

'The flood?' I asked.

'I brought it on. It was my doing.'

Perhaps he didn't use these very words, but he spoke like a
grown-up man and his words were precise.

'Why?'

'Not to go to school, of course. Why else? Why else does one
pray?'

'And the plague?' I whispered, holding my breath.

'That too. That gave me even less trouble.'

'But why?'

'To kill our teacher and our aunt. And I could make *you* die, if
I felt like it.'

I laughed, because I knew he'd think me worthless if I didn't.
In the mirror on the cupboard door, opposite us, I saw that I was
pulling a face. As soon as I could, I went to tell my aunts what he
had said. The aunts laughed at my worries.

'It's just a joke,' they said. 'That child's a saint.'

But Rita, my cousin, who looked like a little old lady and was
always listening in on conversations, butted in:

'He's no saint. And he doesn't pray to God. He's made a pact
with the Devil. Haven't you seen his prayer-book? The cover is the
same as that of any other prayer-book, but the writing inside is
different. You can't understand a word of what is scribbled on those

horrible pages. You want to see it? Bring the book,' she ordered me. 'It's in the chest-of-drawers, wrapped up in a handkerchief.'

I hesitated. How could I betray Cornelio? Secrets are sacred. But my weakness got the better of me. I went to Cornelio's room and trembling brought out the prayer-book wrapped up in the handkerchief. My aunt Claudia untied the corners of the handkerchief and took out the book. A page was stuck over the original fly-leaf. I managed to catch a glimpse of the inscrutable characters and the demoniacal scribbles that Rita had described.

'What shall we do?' said my aunts.

Cornelio's mother handed the book to me. 'Put it back where you found it,' she ordered. And turning to Rita, said sharply, 'You deserve to be imprisoned for slander. Ah, if only we were in England!'

My aunts hissed like offended owls.

'The child is a saint. He probably has his own language in which he speaks to God,' said my mother, looking sternly at Rita who was choking on a mint.

'And if he manages to make me die?' I stammered.

The women all laughed, even Rita who seconds ago was saying that there was a pact between Cornelio and the Devil.

What seriousness was there in the words of grown-ups? Who would believe me or take me seriously? Rita had made fun of me. To prove that I was telling the truth, I went up to Cornelio's room and instead of putting the book back in the drawer, I put it in my pocket and took from the drawer the object he loved the most: a plastic watch with movable hands.

I remember it was late when we sat down to dinner with the family. As it was in the summer, after dinner I went out into the garden with my aunt. Probably Cornelio hadn't yet gone to his room and noticed that something was missing.

What power did Cornelio have that his prayers should be answered? What death would he ask for me? Fire, water, blood? The words flashed through my mind as I heard steps on the stairs and in his room. The blunt tapping of shoes overlapped the beating of my heart. I was about to run away, to bury the book and the watch in the garden, but I knew I couldn't deceive Cornelio – Cornelio who had sought alliance with someone greater than us. I heard him call my name: his voice was a roar. I climbed the stairs to his room. I stopped for a moment on the landing, trying to see his movements through the door that stood ajar; then I braved the wobbly staircase that led to the attic. Cornelio, from the landing, called me; instead of answering I threw the book and the watch in his face. He didn't say a word. He picked them up. He knelt down and eagerly read from the pages. For the first time Cornelio didn't seem to be ashamed of being seen in prayer. The step on which I stood creaked and suddenly gave way: as I fell, I hit my head against the iron bars of the railing.

When I came to my senses the entire family was there, surrounding me. Cornelio sat motionless in a corner, with his arms crossed.

I felt that I was going to die because I could see, as from the bottom of a well, the faces leaning over me.

'Why don't you ask God to save your little friend?' my Aunt Fermina dared whisper. 'Don't you say God grants you anything you ask him?'

Cornelio knelt down and bent over, like a muslim. He hit his head against the floor and, like a spoiled child, pouted. 'I can only obtain sickness or death.'

My mother stared at him in horror and, kneeling down beside him, pulled back his hair as if he were a dog and said:

'Please try, my dear. It can't hurt to pray. God *must* hear you.'

For several days I drifted in a pink and blue limbo, between life and death. The voices had grown faint. I could no longer recognize the faces: they continued to quiver above the surface of what seemed like water.

Two months later I recovered. They all thanked Cornelio for my good fortune: according to our aunts and mothers he had saved me. Again I heard Cornelio's praises sung. They no longer remembered the tears they had shed for me, nor the pity they had felt. Again I became the insensitive, wicked child, so inferior to his friend.

Through my aunts, through the seamstress and through several friends of the family, contradictory details about what had happened reached the town. Someone pointed out Cornelio's mystical inclinations. Several others said my friend was a saint; yet others that he was a warlock and that it wasn't wise to visit our house because of his evil spells. When my Aunt Claudia married nobody came to the wedding.

Was Cornelio a warlock or was he a saint? At night, tossing and turning in my bed, trying to find a cool place on my pillow, I would wonder about his saintliness or his demoniacal powers. Had even Rita forgotten her suspicions?

One day we went to Willow Brook, to fish. We took a picnic basket with us, planning to spend the day there. Andres, our neighbour, who was fond of the sport, was sitting on the bank with his fishing-rod ready. A dog came up to us and began sniffing around, as dogs do when they're lost. Andres said he would take him home as a pet; Cornelio said that *he* would. They began to fight. Cornelio fell to the ground and Andres, proud as a peacock, packed his gear, picked up the dog in his arms, and left. From the ground Cornelio began muttering his curses: his lips made a noise like that of a liquid about to boil over. Andres had barely taken twenty steps when he collapsed; foam spurted from his mouth. The dog, feeling free, ran to us. Afterwards we learnt that Andres had suffered an epileptic fit.

Now, when Cornelio and I walked down the street, people would whisper. One Good Friday the other children didn't let us go into the church and threw stones at us.

I wanted to find a way of punishing Cornelio. Would I succeed only with my own death, as witness to my truth and his perversions? In a flash I imagined his life ruined for ever, haunted by the memory of me, like Cain by Abel. I tried to make him angry: I had to force him to curse me again. I was sorry, however, that my death would prevent me from witnessing his repentance once his will was done. Would it prevent him from ever again uttering his wicked prayers?

We were once again on the bank of Willow Brook. We were looking at a kingfisher as he dived into the water, again and again, at a dazzling speed. We each had a slingshot. We aimed: Cornelio, at the kingfisher; I, in the air, so as to miss. Cornelio, who was a good marksman, hit the bird on the head. We plunged into the water to get it. Back on the bank we argued about who had killed it. I firmly mantained that the catch was mine.

There was a deep spot in the brook where we couldn't touch bottom. I knew where it was because a sort of whirlpool marked the place, and my father had pointed it out to me. I picked up the bird, ran along the bank until I got to where the mysterious movement in the water could be seen. Andres was sitting nearby, fishing as usual. I stopped and threw the bird into the whirlpool. Cornelio, who was running after me, fell to his knees. I heard the terrifying whisper on his lips: he was repeating my name. A cold sweat bathed my neck, my arms, my hair. The fields, the trees, the banks, the brook, Andres – all began to shake, to spin. Then I heard Cornelio uttering his own name. I didn't notice – my surprise was too great – that Cornelio had thrown himself into the brook; he wasn't trying to reach the bird, he was struggling in the water, he was sinking, he couldn't swim. Andres shouted at him, without flinching, in a bitter voice like that of a parrot:

'You idiot, so much for your witchcraft!'

Only after many years did I understand that at the last moment Cornelio had changed the contents of his prayer: to save me, instead of asking for my death which perhaps had already been granted, he had asked for his own.

*Translated from the Spanish by Alberto Manguel.*

# Et in Sempiternum Pereant

## Charles Williams

*I owe the discovery of this story to* Visions of Wonder, *an anthology edited by R. H. Boyer and K. J. Zahorski. The editors say that this is Williams's only short story, inspired by Canto 34 of Dante's Inferno.*

*Charles Williams was an editor at Oxford University Press; he lectured at Oxford University and was awarded an honorary M.A. He formed part of the Oxford literary circle known as 'the Inklings', with, among others, J. R. R. Tolkien and C. S. Lewis. He wrote several novels, all fantastic, and critical works on Dante. Dorothy L. Sayers (who apart from writing her Lord Peter Wimsey detective novels also translated the* Divine Comedy) *quotes Williams on Canto 34 of the* Inferno: *according to Williams the very pit of Hell is 'willed' by those who suffer there – it is, in effect, a creation of their minds. The title of this story translates roughly as 'And may they be for ever damned.'*

Lord Arglay came easily down the road. About him the spring was as gaudy as the restraint imposed by English geography ever lets it be. The last village lay a couple of miles behind him; as far in front, he had been told, was a main road on which he could meet a motor bus to carry him near his destination. A casual conversation in a club had revealed to him, some months before, that in a country house of England there were supposed to lie a few yet unpublished legal opinions of the Lord Chancellor Bacon. Lord Arglay, being no longer Chief Justice, and having finished and published his *History of Organic Law*, had conceived that the editing of these papers might provide a pleasant variation upon his present business of studying the more complex parts of the Christian Schoolmen. He had taken advantage of a weekend spent in the neighbourhood to arrange, by the good will of the owner, a visit of inspection; since, as the owner had remarked, with a bitterness due to his financial problems, 'everything that is smoked isn't Bacon'. Lord Arglay had

smiled – it hurt him a little to think that he had smiled – and said,
which was true enough, that Bacon himself would not have made
a better joke.

It was a very deserted part of the country through which he was
walking. He had been careful to follow the directions given him,
and in fact there were only two places where he could possibly have
gone wrong, and at both of them Lord Arglay was certain he had
not gone wrong. But he seemed to be taking a long time – a longer
time than he had expected. He looked at his watch again, and noted
with sharp disapproval of his own judgement that it was only six
minutes since he had looked at it last. It had seemed more like
sixteen. Lord Arglay frowned. He was usually a good walker, and
on that morning he was not conscious of any unusual weariness.
His host had offered to send him in a car, but he had declined. For
a moment, as he put his watch back, he was almost sorry he had
declined. A car would have made short time of this road, and at
present his legs seemed to be making rather long time of it. 'Or,'
Lord Arglay said aloud, 'making time rather long.' He played a
little, as he went on, with the fancy that every road in space had a
corresponding measure in time; that it tended, merely of itself, to
hasten or delay all those that drove or walked upon it. The nature
of some roads, quite apart from their material effectiveness, might
urge men to speed, and of others to delay. So that the intentions of
all travellers were counterpointed continually by the media they
used. The courts, he thought, might reasonably take that into consideration in case of offences against right speed, and a man who
accelerated upon one road would be held to have acted under the
improper influence of the way, whereas one who did the same on
another would be known to have defied and conquered the way.

Lord Arglay just stopped himself looking at his watch again. It
was impossible that it should be more than five minutes since he
had last done so. He looked back to observe, if possible, how far
he had since come. It was not possible; the road narrowed and
curved too much. There was a cloud of trees high up behind him;
it must have been half an hour ago that he passed through it, yet
it was not merely still in sight, but the trees themselves were in
sight. He could remark them as trees; he could almost, if he were
a little careful, count them. He thought, with some irritation, that
he must be getting old more quickly, and more unnoticeably, than
he had supposed. He did not much mind about the quickness, but

he did mind about the unnoticeableness. It had given him pleasure to watch the various changes which age tended to bring; to be as stealthy and as quick to observe those changes as they were to come upon him – the slower pace, the more meditative voice, the greater reluctance to decide, the inclination to fall back on habit, the desire for the familiar which is the first skirmishing approach of unfamiliar death. He neither welcomed nor grudged such changes; he only observed them with a perpetual interest in the curious nature of the creation. The fantasy of growing old, like the fantasy of growing up, was part of the ineffable sweetness, touched with horror, of existence, itself the lordliest fantasy of all. But now, as he stood looking back over and across the hidden curves of the road, he felt suddenly that time had outmarched and out-twisted him, that it was spreading along the countryside and doubling back on him, so that it troubled and deceived his judgement. In an unexpected and unusual spasm of irritation he put his hand to his watch again. He felt as if it were a quarter of an hour since he had looked at it; very well, making just allowance for his state of impatience, he would expect the actual time to be five minutes. He looked; it was only two.

Lord Arglay made a small mental effort, and almost immediately recognized the effort. He said to himself: 'This is another mark of age. I am losing my sense of duration.' He said also: 'It is becoming an effort to recognize these changes.' Age was certainly quickening its work in him. It approached him now doubly; not only his method of experience, but his awareness of experience was attacked. His knowledge of it comforted him – perhaps, he thought, for the last time. The knowledge would go. He would savour it then while he could. Still looking back at the trees, 'It seems I'm decaying,' Lord Arglay said aloud. 'And that anyhow is one up against decay. Am I procrastinating? I am, and in the circumstances procrastination is a proper and pretty game. It is the thief of time, and quite right too! Why should time have it all its own way?'

He turned to the road again, and went on. It passed now between open fields; in all those fields he could see no one. It was pasture, but there were no beasts. There was about him a kind of void, in which he moved, hampered by this growing oppression of duration. Things *lasted*. He had exclaimed, in his time, against the too swift passage of the world. This was a new experience; it was lastingness – almost, he could have believed, everlastingness. The measure of it was but his breathing, and his breathing, as it grew slower and heavier, would become the measure of everlasting labour – the labour of Sisyphus, who pushed his own slow heart through each infinite moment, and relaxed but to let it beat back and so again begin. It was the first touch of something Arglay had never yet known, of simple and perfect despair.

At that moment he saw the house. The road before him curved sharply, and as he looked he wondered at the sweep of the curve; it seemed to make a full half-circle and so turn back in the direction that he had come. At the farthest point there lay before him, tangentially, another path. The sparse hedge was broken by an opening which was more than footpath and less than road. It was narrow, even when compared with the narrowing way by which he had come, yet hard and beaten as if by the passage of many feet. There had been innumerable travellers, and all solitary, all on foot. No cars or carts could have taken that path; if there had been burdens, they had been carried on the shoulders of their owners. It ran for no long distance, no more than in happier surroundings might have been a garden path from gate to door. There, at the end, was the door.

Arglay, at the time, took all this in but half-consciously. His attention was not on the door but on the chimney. The chimney, in the ordinary phrase, was smoking. It was smoking effectively and continuously. A narrow and dense pillar of dusk poured up from it, through which there glowed, every now and then, a deeper undershade of crimson, as if some trapped genius almost thrust itself out of the moving prison that held it. The house itself was not much more than a cottage. There was a door, shut; on the left of it a window, also shut; above, two little attic windows, shut, and covered within by some sort of dark hanging, or perhaps made opaque by smoke that filled the room. There was no sign of life anywhere, and the smoke continued to mount to the lifeless sky. It seemed to Arglay curious that he had not noticed this grey pillar in his approach, that only now when he stood almost in the straight and narrow path leading to the house did it become visible, an exposition of tall darkness reserved to the solitary walkers upon that wearying road.

Lord Arglay was the last person in the world to look for responsibilities. He shunned them by a courteous habit; a responsibility had to present itself with a delicate emphasis before he acceded to it.

But when any so impressed itself he was courteous in accepting as in declining; he sought friendship with necessity, and as young lovers call their love fatal, so he turned fatality of life into his love. It seemed to him, as he stood and gazed at the path, the shut door, the smoking chimney, that here perhaps was a responsibility being delicately emphatic. If everyone was out – if the cottage had been left for an hour – ought he to do something? Of course, they might be busy about it within; in which case a thrusting stranger would be inopportune. Another glow of crimson in the pillar of cloud decided him. He went up the path.

As he went he glanced at the little window, but it was blurred by dirt; he could not very well see whether the panes did or did not hide smoke within. When he was so near the threshold that the window had almost passed out of his vision, he thought he saw a face looking out of it – at the extreme edge, nearest the door – and he checked himself, and went back a step to look again. It had been only along the side of his glance that the face, if face it were, had appeared, a kind of sudden white scrawl against the blur, as if it were a mask hung by the window rather than any living person, or as if the glass of the window itself had looked sideways at him, and he had caught the look without understanding its cause. When he stepped back, he could see no face. Had there been a sun in the sky he would have attributed the apparition to a trick of the light, but in the sky over this smoking house there was no sun. It had shone brightly that morning when he started; it had paled and faded and finally been lost to him as he had passed along his road. There was neither sun nor peering face. He stepped back to the threshold, and knocked with his knuckles on the door.

There was no answer. He knocked again and again waited, and as he stood there he began to feel annoyed. The balance of Lord Arglay's mind had not been achieved without the creation of a considerable counter energy to the violence of Lord Arglay's natural temper. There had been people whom he had once come very near hating, hating with a fury of selfish rage and detestation; for instance, his brother-in-law. His brother-in-law had not been a nice man; Lord Arglay, as he stood by the door and for no earthly reason, remembered him, admitted it. He admitted, at the same moment, that no lack of niceness on that other's part could excuse any indulgence of vindictive hate on his own, nor could he think why, then and there, he wanted him, wanted to have him merely to hate. His brother-in-law was dead. Lord Arglay almost regretted it. Almost he desired to follow, to be with him, to provoke and torment him, to . . .

Lord Arglay struck the door again. 'There is,' he said to himself, 'entire clarity in the Omnipotence.' It was his habit of devotion, his means of recalling himself into peace out of the angers, greeds, sloths and perversities that still too often possessed him. It operated: the temptation passed into the benediction of the Omnipotence and disappeared. But there was still no answer from within. Lord Arglay laid his hand on the latch. He swung the door, and, lifting his hat with his other hand, looked into the room – a room empty of smoke as of fire, and of all as of both.

Its size and appearance were those of a rather poor cottage, rather indeed a large brick hut than a cottage. It seemed much smaller within than without. There was a fireplace – at least, there was a place for a fire – on his left. Opposite the door, against the right-hand wall, there was a ramshackle flight of wooden steps, going up to the attics, and at its foot, swinging on a broken hinge, a door which gave a way presumably to a cellar. Vaguely, Arglay found himself surprised; he had not supposed that a dwelling of this sort would have a cellar. Indeed, from where he stood, he could not be certain. It might only be a cupboard. But, unwarrantably, it seemed more, a hinted unseen depth, as if the slow slight movement of the broken wooden door measured that labour of Sisyphus, as if the road ran past him and went coiling spirally into the darkness of the cellar. In the room there was no furniture, neither fragment of paper nor broken bit of wood; there was no sign of life, no flame in the grate nor drift of smoke in the air. It was completely and utterly void.

Lord Arglay looked at it. He went back a few steps and looked up again at the chimney. Undoubtedly the chimney was smoking. It was received into a pillar of smoke; there was no clear point where the dark chimney ended and the dark smoke began. House leaned to roof, roof to chimney, chimney to smoke, and smoke went up for ever and ever over those roads where men crawled infinitely through the smallest measurements of time. Arglay returned to the door, crossed the threshold, and stood in the room. Empty of flame, empty of flame's material, holding within its dank air the very opposite of flame, the chill of ancient years, the room lay round him. Lord Arglay contemplated it. 'There's no smoke without fire,' he said aloud. 'Only apparently there is. Thus one lives and learns. Unless indeed this is the place where one lives without learning.'

The phrase, leaving his lips, sounded oddly about the walls and in the corners of the room. He was suddenly revolted by his own chance words – 'a place where one lives without learning', where no courtesy or integrity could any more be fined or clarified. The echo daunted him; he made a sharp movement, he took a step aside towards the stairs, and before the movement was complete, was aware of a change. The dank chill became a concentration of dank and deadly heat, pricking at him, entering his nostrils and his mouth. The fantasy of life without knowledge materialized, inimical, in the air, life without knowledge, corrupting life without knowledge, jungle and less than jungle, and though still the walls of the bleak chamber met his eyes, a shell of existence, it seemed that life, withdrawn from all those normal habits of which the useless memory was still drearily sustained by the thin phenomenal fabric, was collecting and corrupting in the atmosphere behind the door he had so rashly passed – outside the other door which swung crookedly at the head of the darker hole within.

He had recoiled from the heat, but not so as to escape it. He had even taken a step or two up the stairs, when he heard from without a soft approach. Light feet were coming up the beaten path to the house. Some other Good Samaritan, Arglay thought, who would be able to keep his twopence in his pocket. For certainly, whatever was the explanation of all this and wherever it lay, in the attics above or in the pit of the cellar below, responsibility was gone. Lord Arglay did not conceive that either he or anyone else need rush about the country in an anxious effort to preserve a house which no one wanted and no one used. Prematurely enjoying the discussion, he waited. Through the doorway someone came in.

It was, or seemed to be, a man of ordinary height, wearing some kind of loose dark overcoat that flapped about him. His head was bare; so, astonishingly, were his legs and feet. At first, as he stood just inside the door, leaning greedily forward, his face was invisible, and for a moment Arglay hesitated to speak. Then the stranger lifted his face and Arglay uttered a sound. It was emaciated beyond imagination; it was astonishing, at the appalling degree of hunger revealed, that the man could walk or move at all, or even stand as he was now doing, and turn that dreadful skull from side to side.

Arglay came down the steps of the stair in one jump; he cried out
again, he ran forward, and as he did so the deep burning eyes in
the turning face of bone met his full and halted him. They did not
see him, or if they saw did not notice; they gazed at him and moved
on. Once only in his life had Arglay seen eyes remotely like those;
once, when he had pronounced the death sentence upon a wretched
man who had broken under the long strain of his trial and filled the
court with shrieks. Madness had glared at Lord Arglay from that
dock, but at least it had looked at him and seen him; these eyes did
not. They sought something – food, life, or perhaps only a form
and something to hate, and in that energy the stranger moved. He
began to run round the room. The bones that were his legs and feet
jerked up and down. The head turned from side to side. He ran
circularly, round and again round, crossing and recrossing, looking
up, down, around, and at last, right in the centre of the room,
coming to a halt, where, as if some terrible pain of starvation gripped
him, he bent and twisted downward until he squatted grotesquely
on the floor. There, squatting and bending, he lowered his head
and raised his arm, and as the fantastic black coat slipped back,
Arglay saw a wrist, saw it marked with scars. He did not at first
think what they were; only when the face and wrist of the figure
swaying in its pain came together did he suddenly know. They were
teeth marks; they were bites; the mouth closed on the wrist and
gnawed. Arglay cried out and sprang forward, catching the arm,
trying to press it down, catching the other shoulder, trying to press
it back. He achieved nothing. He held, he felt, he grasped; he could
not control. The long limb remained raised, the fierce teeth gnawed.
But as Arglay bent, he was aware once more of that effluvia of heat
risen round him, and breaking out with the more violence, when
suddenly the man, if it were a man, cast his arm away, and with a
jerk of movement rose once more to his feet. His eyes, as the head
went back, burned close into Arglay's, who, what with the heat,
the eyes, and his sickness at the horror, shut his own against them,
and was at the same moment thrown from his balance by the rising
form, and sent staggering a step or two away, with upon his face
the sensation of a light hot breath, so light that only in the utter
stillness of time could it be felt, so hot that it might have been the
inner fire from which the pillar of smoke poured outward to the
world.

He recovered his balance; he opened his eyes; both motions

brought him into a new corner of that world. The odd black coat
the thing had worn had disappeared, as if it had been a covering
imagined by a habit of mind. The thing itself, a wasted flicker of
pallid movement, danced and gyrated in white flame before him.
Arglay saw it still, but only now as a dreamer may hear, half-asleep
and half-awake, the sound of dogs barking or the crackling of fire
in his very room. For he opened his eyes not to such things, but to
the thing that on the threshold of this place, some seconds earlier
or some years, he had felt and been pleased to feel, to the reality
of his hate. It came in a rush within him, a fountain of fire, and
without and about him images of the man he hated swept in a thick
cloud of burning smoke. The smoke burned his eyes and choked
his mouth; he clutched at it, at images within it – at his greedy
loves and greedy hates – at the cloud of the sin of his life, yearning
to catch but one image and renew again the concentration for which
he yearned. He could not. The smoke blinded and stifled him, yet
more than stifling or blinding was the hunger for one true thing to
lust after or hate. He was starving in the smoke, and all the hut
was full of smoke, for the hut and the world were smoke, pouring
up round him, from him and all like him – a thing once wholly,
and still a little, made visible to his corporeal eyes in forms which
they recognized, but in itself of another nature. He swung and
twisted and crouched. His limbs ached from long wrestling with
the smoke, for as the journey to this place had prolonged itself
infinitely, so now, though he had no thought of measurements, the
clutch of his hands and the growing sickness that invaded him
struck through him the sensation of the passage of years and the
knowledge of the passage of moments. The fire sank within him,
and the sickness grew, but the change could not bring him nearer
to any end. The end here was not at the end, but in the beginning.
There was no end to this smoke, to this fever and this chill, to
crouching and rising and searching, unless the end was now. *Now*
– *now* was the only possible other fact, chance, act. He cried out,
defying infinity, '*Now!*'

Before his voice the smoke of his prison yielded, and yielded two
ways at once. From where he stood he could see in one place an
alteration in that perpetual grey, an alternate darkening and light-
ening as if two ways, of descent and ascent, met. There was, he
remembered, a way in, therefore a path out; he had only to walk
along it. But also there was a way still farther in, and he could walk

along that. Two doors had swung, to his outer senses, in that small room. From every gate of hell there was a way to heaven, yes, and in every way to heaven there was a gate to deeper hell.

Yet for a moment he hesitated. There was no sign of the phenomenon by which he had discerned the passage of that other spirit. He desired – very strongly he desired – to be of use to it. He desired to offer himself to it, to make a ladder of himself, if that should be desired, by which it might perhaps mount from the nature of the lost, from the dereliction of all minds that refuse living and learning, postponement and irony, whose dwelling is necessarily in their undying and perishing selves. Slowly, unconsciously, he moved his head as if to seek his neighbour.

He saw, at first he felt, nothing. His eyes returned to that vibrating oblong of an imagined door, the heart of the smoke beating in the smoke. He looked at it; he remembered the way; he was on the point of movement, when the stinging heat struck him again, but this time from behind. It leapt through him; he was seized in it and loosed from it; its rush abandoned him. The torrent of its fiery passage struck the darkening hollow in the walls. At the instant that it struck, there came a small sound; there floated up a thin shrill pipe, too short to hear, too certain to miss, faint and quick as from some single insect in the hedgerow or the field, and yet more than single – a weak wail of multitudes of the lost. The shrill lament struck his ears, and he ran. He cried as he sprang: 'Now is God: now is glory in God,' and as the dark door swung before him it was the threshold of the house that received his flying feet. As he passed, another form slipped by him, slinking hastily into the house, another of the hordes going so swiftly up that straight way, hard with everlasting time; each driven by his own hunger, and each alone. The vision, a face looking in as a face had looked out, was gone. Running still; but more lightly now, and with some communion of peace at heart, Arglay came into the curving road. The trees were all about him; the house was at their heart. He ran on through them beyond, he saw, he reached, the spring day and the sun. At a little distance a motor bus, gaudy within and without, was coming down the road. The driver saw him. Lord Arglay instinctively made a sign, ran, mounted. As he sat down, breathless and shaken, '*E quindi uscimmo*,' his mind said, '*a riveder le stelle.*'

# The Captives of Longjumeau

## Léon Bloy

*Léon Bloy was an antisemite who believed that the Jews were going to save the world (he wrote* Salvation through the Jews *in 1904); he was a bourgeois who fiercely attacked bourgeois society (in* The Ungrateful Beggar, *1892–95, and* The Poor Woman, *1897); he wrote wonderful French prose which is hardly read in France today. Speaking about him to a friend, Kafka remarked: 'Léon Bloy possesses a fire that brings to mind the ardour of the prophets – an even greater ardour, I should say. Of course that is easily explained: his fire is nurtured by the dung-heap of modern times.'*

*'The Captives of Longjumeau', like Kafka's* The Castle, *is the story of a seemingly simple but unsuccessful endeavour: in the former the task consists of leaving a city, in the latter of reaching a castle. Both prove impossible, but in both cases unrewarded efforts are in themselves presented as a triumph and achieve the grandeur of a minor epic.*

Yesterday the *Longjumeau Echo* announced the deplorable demise of the Fourmis. This commendable periodical – commendable both because of the abundance as well as the quality of its information – seemed at a loss to explain the mysterious causes that had driven this apparently happy couple to suicide.

They had married young, and every day had been to them like the dawn of a new honeymoon. They had never left the city, not even for a day.

Spared by a generous parental allowance from the financial troubles that so often poison the life of a young couple – amply provided for, indeed, with everything that makes possible a certain kind of legitimate wedded bliss which allows no room for those amorous adventures fickle human beings commonly relish – the Fourmis were, in the eyes of the world, a miracle of eternal infatuation.

One beautiful afternoon in May they arrived in Longjumeau by the local train, accompanied by their parents who had come to help them settle into the delightful property that was to be their love-nest.

All pure-hearted Longjumeaunians looked fondly on the pretty couple, whom the veterinarian did not hesitate to compare to Romeo and Juliet. They did indeed look splendid, like the pale children of a feudal lord.

Mr Piceu, the district's most important attorney, had acquired for them, at the gates of the city, a minuscule green bower that the dead themselves would have envied. In truth it must be said that the garden did look a little like an abandoned cemetery, but this could not have displeased them since they never made any efforts to change it, allowing the plants to overgrow it at will.

If I may use one of Mr Piceu's profoundly original phrases, the Fourmis lived with their heads in the clouds, seeing no one – not through malice or scorn but simply because the thought of other people never crossed their minds. Also, in order to lead any sort of social life they would have had to let go of each other for a few hours or minutes, and interrupt their amorous ecstasies, and . . . well, reflecting on the brevity of life, they lacked the courage to do so.

One of the greatest men of the Middle Ages, John Tauler, tells the story of a hermit who was asked by a visitor to get something from his cell. The hermit entered his cell to look for whatever it was, but once inside he forgot what he was looking for, because the image of exterior objects could not root itself in his brain. He came out and asked the visitor to repeat his request. The visitor did so. Once more the hermit entered his cell and once more he forgot what he was looking for. After several unsuccessful tries he was forced to say to the importunate visitor, 'Come in and look for whatever it is you want yourself, because I, dear sir, cannot manage to hold on to its image long enough to do as you ask.'

Frequently Mr and Mrs Fourmi reminded me of the hermit. They would have happily granted anyone's request if only they had been able to remember it. Their absent-mindedness was famous, and spoken of as far as Corbeil. And yet it did not seem to affect them. Because of this, the 'grim' resolution that put an end to their much-envied lives seems inexplicable to most.

A letter, now old, from the unfortunate Fourmi himself – whom I had known as a bachelor – has allowed me to reconstruct by inference their whole woeful tale. Here follows the letter. Perhaps it will at last be admitted that my friend was neither a madman nor a fool:

'. . . For the tenth or twentieth time, my dear fellow, we have broken our word. For all your patience, you must by now be more than weary of inviting us again and again. The truth is that, like last time, like so many times before, my wife and I have no excuse to offer. We had written to you to expect us and we had no other engagements. Nevertheless, as on every other occasion, we missed our train.

'For the past *fifteen years* we have missed every train and every other public transport we have tried to catch, no matter what we do. It is horribly stupid, it is unbearably ridiculous, but I am starting to think that this affliction has no cure. We are victims of a grotesque fatality. All is useless. Let me give you an example. To catch the eight o'clock train we have tried getting up at three in the morning; we have even tried to spend the night awake. And – well, my friend, at the very last moment the chimney would catch fire, or half-way to the station I would twist an ankle, or Juliet's dress would get caught on a bramble, or we would fall asleep in the waiting-room and neither the arrival of the train nor the cries of the porter would manage to wake us up in time; and so on and so on and so on.

'Last time I forgot my wallet. Why carry on? As I say, this has lasted fifteen years, and I feel that here lies the beginning of our end. Because of this scourge, as you know, I have bungled everything. I am on bad terms with everyone, I am taken to be a monster of egotism, and my poor Juliet is of course dragged along by the same tide of disapproval. Since our arrival at this cursed place we have missed seventy-four funerals, twelve weddings, thirty christenings, a thousand social calls or meetings which were of the highest importance. I let my mother-in-law pass away without once going to see her even though she lay in her sick-bed for over a year, thereby losing three quarters of her inheritance which she furiously denied us, the very day before her death, in a codicil to her will.

'There is no end to my list of *faux pas* and failures due to the incredible fact that we have never been able to leave Longjumeau. To put it plainly, we are *prisoners*, hopeless prisoners, and we see the time coming in which this galley-slave life will become unbearable . . .'

I suppress the rest of the letter in which my sad friend confided things too intimate to be published. But I give my word that he was not a vulgar man, that he fully merited his wife's adoration, and that both deserved a better fate than ending their lives in such a stupid and untidy way.

Certain peculiarities which I cannot permit myself to reveal lead me to think that the unfortunate Fourmis were in fact victims of the Enemy of man, who led them, by means of an evidently infernal attorney, to that evil corner of Longjumeau from which no power in this world could wrench them. I truly believe that they *could not* escape, that surrounding their house was a barrier of invisible *troops* carefully selected to besiege them, and against which all efforts were useless.

The sign, for me, of a diabolical influence was the fact that the Fourmis were consumed by a passion for travelling. These captives were, by nature, essentially migrant creatures.

Before uniting they had felt a lust for other lands. Only days after becoming engaged they visited Enghien, Choisy-le-Roi, Meudon, Clamart, Montretout. Once they even reached Saint-Germain.

In Longjumeau, which seemed to them a South Sea island, this craving for daring exploration, for adventures on land and sea, became even greater. Their house was crammed full of globes and maps of the world, and English and German atlases. They even had a map of the moon published in Gotha and edited by a blockhead called Justus Perthes.

When they were not busy with their love they would read together the chronicles of famous navigators – practically the only books in their library. There was no travel journal, no *Tour du Monde*, no geographical society bulletin to which they had not subscribed. Their house was showered with railway timetables and travel agencies' brochures.

Incredible as it may seem, their trunks were always packed. They were always on the point of departure, always about to begin their endless journeys to the most distant and unexplored lands of this earth.

I have received some forty telegrams announcing their imminent departure for Borneo, Tierra del Fuego, New Zealand or British Columbia. Many a time, it is true, they really were on the point of leaving. But the fact is that they did not leave, that they never left, because they could not and were not meant to leave. Atoms and molecules formed alliances to hold them back.

One day, however, some ten years ago, they finally thought they had managed to escape. They had succeeded, against all hope, in climbing into a first-class carriage bound for Versailles. Freedom at last! There, no doubt, the magic circle would break.

The train started to move but they did not. Naturally they had found a seat in a carriage that was to remain in the station. They had to start all over again. The only voyage they were destined not to miss was the one they have just started and, dear me, their character, which I knew so well, leads me to believe that they prepared for it trembling.

*Translated from the French by Alberto Manguel.*

# The Visit to the Museum

## Vladimir Nabokov

*In the thirteenth century Alfonso X, king of Castile, wrote some four hundred* cantigas, *or poems to be set to music.* Cantiga *103 tells of a monk who begs Our Lady to allow him to taste, during his life, the delights of Paradise. One afternoon, while walking through the monastery garden, he sees a fountain of clear water and hears the song of a small bird which delights him. When he returns to the monastery, believing it is time for supper, he finds everything changed; he is told that three hundred years have elapsed between his departure and his return.*

*In Nabokov's story the hero enters not the future but simply a world which exists far away, a world which Nabokov himself abandoned when he left Russia in 1919, after his family's fortunes collapsed with the October Revolution. After studying in England he emigrated to the United States and began writing in English.* Laughter in the Dark, Lolita, Ada *and* Pale Fire *are some of his great novels. To help us understand one important detail in 'The Visit to the Museum' (written originally in Russian and translated by Nabokov himself) the author provides the following note: 'At one point the unfortunate narrator notices a shop sign and realizes he is not in the Russia of his past, but in the Russia of the Soviets. What gives that shop sign away is the absence of the letter that used to decorate the end of a word after a consonant in old Russia but is omitted in the reformed orthography adopted by the Soviets today.'*

Several years ago a friend of mine in Paris – a person with oddities, to put it mildly – learning that I was going to spend two or three days at Montisert, asked me to drop in at the local museum where there hung, he was told, a portrait of his grandfather by Leroy. Smiling and spreading out his hands, he related a rather vague story to which I confess I paid little attention, partly because I do not like other people's obtrusive affairs, but chiefly because I had always had doubts about my friend's capacity to remain this side of fantasy. It went more or less as follows: after the grandfather died in their St Petersburg house back at the time of the Russo-Japanese War, the contents of his apartment in Paris were sold at auction. The portrait, after some obscure peregrinations, was acquired by the museum of Leroy's native town. My friend wished to know if the portrait was really there; if there, if it could be ransomed; and if it could, for what price. When I asked why he did not get in touch with the museum, he replied that he had written several times, but had never received an answer.

I made an inward resolution not to carry out the request – I could always tell him I had fallen ill or changed my itinerary. The very notion of seeing sights, whether they be museums or ancient buildings, is loathsome to me; besides, the good freak's commission seemed absolute nonsense. It so happened, however, that, while wandering about Montisert's empty streets in search of a stationery store, and cursing the spire of a long-necked cathedral, always the same one, that kept popping up at the end of every street, I was caught in a violent downpour which immediately went about accelerating the fall of the maple leaves, for the fair weather of a southern October was holding on by a mere thread. I dashed for cover and found myself on the steps of the museum.

It was a building of modest proportions, constructed of many-coloured stones, with columns, a gilt inscription over the frescoes of the pediment, and a lion-legged stone bench on either side of the bronze door. One of its leaves stood open, and the interior seemed dark against the shimmer of the shower. I stood for a while on the steps, but, despite the overhanging roof, they were gradually growing speckled. I saw that the rain had set in for good, and so, having nothing better to do, I decided to go inside. No sooner had I trod on the smooth, resonant flagstones of the vestibule than the clatter of a moved stool came from a distant corner, and the custodian – a banal pensioner with an empty sleeve – rose to meet me, laying aside his newspaper and peering at me over his spectacles. I paid my franc and, trying not to look at some statues at the entrance (which were as traditional and as insignificant as the first number in a circus programme), I entered the main hall.

Everything was as it should be: grey tints, the sleep of substance, matter dematerialized. There was the usual case of old, worn coins resting in the inclined velvet of their compartments. There was, on top of the case, a pair of owls, Eagle Owl and Long-eared, with their French names reading 'Grand Duke' and 'Middle Duke' if translated. Venerable minerals lay in their open graves of dusty papier-mâché; a photograph of an astonished gentleman with a pointed beard dominated an assortment of strange black lumps of various sizes. They bore a great resemblance to frozen frass, and I paused involuntarily over them, for I was quite at a loss to guess their nature, composition and function. The custodian had been following me with felted steps, always keeping a respectful distance; now, however, he came up, with one hand behind his back and the ghost of the other in his pocket, and gulping, if one judged by his Adam's apple.

'What are they?' I asked.

'Science has not yet determined,' he replied, undoubtedly having learned the phrase by rote. 'They were found,' he continued in the same phony tone, 'in 1895, by Louis Pradier, Municipal Councillor and Knight of the Legion of Honour,' and his trembling finger indicated the photograph.

'Well and good,' I said, 'but who decided, and why, that they merited a place in the museum?'

'And now I call your attention to this skull!' the old man cried energetically, obviously changing the subject.

'Still, I would be interested to know what they are made of,' I interrupted.

'Science . . .' he began anew, but stopped short and looked crossly at his fingers, which were soiled with dust from the glass.

I proceeded to examine a Chinese vase, probably brought back by a naval officer; a group of porous fossils; a pale worm in clouded alcohol; a red-and-green map of Montisert in the seventeenth century; and a trio of rusted tools bound by a funereal ribbon – a spade, a mattock and a pick. 'To dig in the past,' I thought absentmindedly, but this time did not seek clarification from the custodian, who was following me noiselessly and meekly, weaving in and out among the display cases. Beyond the first hall there was another, apparently the last, and in its centre a large sarcophagus stood like a dirty bathtub, while the walls were hung with paintings.

At once my eye was caught by the portrait of a man between two abominable landscapes (with cattle and 'atmosphere'). I moved closer and, to my considerable amazement, found the very object whose existence had hitherto seemed to me but the figment of an unstable mind. The man, depicted in wretched oils, wore a frock coat, whiskers and a large pince-nez on a cord; he bore a likeness to Offenbach, but, in spite of the work's vile conventionality, I had the feeling one could make out in his features the horizon of a resemblance, as it were, to my friend. In one corner, meticulously traced in carmine against a black background, was the signature *Leroy* in a hand as commonplace as the work itself.

I felt a vinegarish breath near my shoulder, and turned to meet the custodian's kindly gaze. 'Tell me,' I asked, 'supposing someone wished to buy one of these paintings, whom should he see?'

'The treasures of the museum are the pride of the city,' replied the old man, 'and pride is not for sale.'

Fearing his eloquence, I hastily concurred, but nevertheless asked for the name of the museum's director. He tried to distract me with the story of the sarcophagus, but I insisted. Finally he gave me the name of one M. Godard and explained where I could find him.

Frankly, I enjoyed the thought that the portrait existed. It is fun to be present at the coming true of a dream, even if it is not one's own. I decided to settle the matter without delay. When I get in the spirit, no one can hold me back. I left the museum with a brisk, resonant step, and found that the rain had stopped, blueness had spread across the sky, a woman in besplattered stockings was spinning along on a silver-shining bicycle, and only over the surrounding hills did clouds still hang. Once again the cathedral began playing hide-and-seek with me, but I outwitted it. Barely escaping the onrushing tyres of a furious red bus packed with singing youths, I crossed the asphalt thoroughfare and a minute later was ringing at the garden gate of M. Godard. He turned out to be a thin, middle-aged gentleman in high collar and dickey, with a pearl in the knot of his tie, and a face very much resembling a Russian wolfhound; as if that were not enough, he was licking his chops in a most doglike manner, while sticking a stamp on an envelope, when I entered his small but lavishly furnished room with its malachite inkstand on the desk and a strangely familiar Chinese vase on the mantel. A pair of fencing foils hung crossed over the mirror, which reflected the narrow grey back of his head. Here and there photographs of a warship pleasantly broke up the blue flora of the wallpaper.

'What can I do for you?' he asked, throwing the letter he had just sealed into the wastebasket. This act seemed unusual to me;

however, I did not see fit to interfere. I explained in brief my reason for coming, even naming the substantial sum with which my friend was willing to part, though he had asked me not to mention it, but wait instead for the museum's terms.

'All this is delightful,' said M. Godard. 'The only thing is, you are mistaken – there is no such picture in our museum.'

'What do you mean there is no such picture? I have just seen it! Portrait of a Russian nobleman, by Gustave Leroy.'

'We do have one Leroy,' said M. Godard when he had leafed through an oilcloth notebook and his black fingernail had stopped at the entry in question. 'However, it is not a portrait but a rural landscape: *The Return of the Herd.*'

I repeated that I had seen the picture with my own eyes five minutes before and that no power on earth could make me doubt its existence.

'Agreed,' said M. Godard, 'but I am not crazy either. I have been curator of our museum for almost twenty years now and know this catalogue as well as I know the Lord's Prayer. It says here *Return of the Herd* and that means the herd is returning, and, unless perhaps your friend's grandfather is depicted as a shepherd, I cannot conceive of his portrait's existence in our museum.'

'He is wearing a frock coat,' I cried. 'I swear he is wearing a frock coat!'

'And how did you like our museum in general?' M. Godard asked suspiciously. 'Did you appreciate the sarcophagus?'

'Listen,' I said (and I think there was already a tremor in my voice), 'do me a favour – let's go there this minute, and let's make an agreement that if the portrait is there, you will sell it.'

'And if not?' inquired M. Godard.

'I shall pay you the sum anyway.'

'All right,' he said. 'Here, take this red-and-blue pencil and using the red – the red, please – put it in writing for me.'

In my excitement I carried out his demand. Upon glancing at my signature, he deplored the difficult pronunciation of Russian names. Then he appended his own signature and, quickly folding the sheet, thrust it into his waistcoat pocket.

'Let's go,' he said, freeing a cuff.

On the way he stepped into a shop and bought a bag of sticky-looking caramels which he began offering me insistently; when I flatly refused, he tried to shake out a couple of them into my hand.

I pulled my hand away. Several caramels fell on the pavement; he stopped to pick them up and then overtook me at a trot. When we drew near the museum we saw the red tourist bus (now empty) parked outside.

'Aha,' said M. Godard, pleased. 'I see we have many visitors today.'

He doffed his hat and, holding it in front of him, walked decorously up the steps.

All was not well at the museum. From within issued rowdy cries, lewd laughter, and even what seemed like the sound of a scuffle. We entered the first hall; there the elderly custodian was restraining two sacrilegists who wore some kind of festive emblems in their lapels and were altogether very purple-faced and full of pep as they tried to extract the municipal councillor's merds from beneath the glass. The rest of the youths, members of some rural athletics organization, were making noisy fun, some of the worm in alcohol, others of the skull. One joker was in rapture over the pipes of the steam radiator, which he pretended was an exhibit; another was taking aim at an owl with his fist and forefinger. There were about thirty of them in all, and their motion and voices created a condition of crush and thick noise.

M. Goddard clapped his hands and pointed at a sign reading 'Visitors to the Museum must be decently attired.' Then he pushed his way, with me following, into the second hall. The whole company immediately swarmed after us. I steered Godard to the portrait; he froze before it, chest inflated, and then stepped back a bit, as if admiring it, and his feminine heel trod on somebody's foot.

'Splendid picture,' he exclaimed with genuine sincerity. 'Well, let's not be petty about this. You were right, and there must be an error in the catalogue.'

As he spoke, his fingers, moving as it were on their own, tore up our agreement into little bits which fell like snowflakes into a massive spittoon.

'Who's the old ape?' asked an individual in a striped jersey, and, as my friend's grandfather was depicted holding a glowing cigar, another funster took out a cigarette and prepared to borrow a light from the portrait.

'All right, let us settle on the price,' I said, 'and, in any case, let's get out of here.'

'Make way, please!' shouted M. Godard, pushing aside the curious.

There was an exit, which I had not noticed previously, at the end of the hall and we thrust our way through to it.

'I can make no decision,' M. Godard was shouting above the din. 'Decisiveness is a good thing only when supported by law. I must first discuss the matter with the mayor, who has just died and has not yet been elected. I doubt that you will be able to purchase the portrait but nonetheless I would like to show you still other treasures of ours.'

We found ourselves in a hall of considerable dimensions. Brown books, with a half-baked look and coarse, foxed pages, lay open under glass on a long table. Along the walls stood dummy soldiers in jack boots with flared tops.

'Come, let's talk it over,' I cried out in desperation, trying to direct M. Godard's evolutions to a plush-covered sofa in a corner. But in this I was prevented by the custodian. Flailing his one arm, he came running after us, pursued by a merry crowd of youths, one of whom had put on his head a copper helmet with a Rembrandtesque gleam.

'Take it off, take it off!' shouted M. Godard, and someone's shove made the helmet fly off the hooligan's head with a clatter.

'Let us move on,' said M. Godard, tugging at my sleeve, and we passed into the section of Ancient Sculpture.

I lost my way for a moment among some enormous marble legs, and twice ran around a giant knee before I again caught sight of M. Godard, who was looking for me behind the white ankle of a neighbouring giantess. Here a person in a bowler, who must have clambered up her, suddenly fell from a great height to the stone floor. One of his companions began helping him up, but they were both drunk, and, dismissing them with a wave of the hand, M. Godard rushed on to the next room, radiant with Oriental fabrics; there hounds raced across azure carpets, and a bow and quiver lay on a tiger skin.

Strangely, though, the expanse and motley only gave me a feeling of oppressiveness and imprecision, and, perhaps because new visitors kept dashing by or perhaps because I was impatient to leave the unnecessarily spreading museum and amid calm and freedom conclude my business negotiations with M. Godard, I began to experience a vague sense of alarm. Meanwhile we had transported ourselves into yet another hall, which must have been really enormous, judging by the fact that it housed the entire skeleton of a whale, resembling a frigate's frame; beyond were visible still other halls, with the oblique sheen of large paintings, full of storm clouds, among which floated the delicate idols of religious art in blue and pink vestments; and all this resolved itself in an abrupt turbulence of misty draperies, and chandeliers came aglitter and fish with translucent frills meandered through illuminated aquariums. Racing up a staircase, we saw, from the gallery above, a crowd of grey-haired people with umbrellas examining a gigantic mock-up of the universe.

At last, in a sombre but magnificent room dedicated to the history of steam machines, I managed to halt my carefree guide for an instant.

'Enough!' I shouted. 'I'm leaving. We'll talk tomorrow.'

He had already vanished. I turned and saw, scarcely an inch from me, the lofty wheels of a sweaty locomotive. For a long time I tried to find the way back among models of railroad stations. How strangely glowed the violet signals in the gloom beyond the fan of wet tracks, and what spasms shook my poor heart! Suddenly everything changed again: in front of me stretched an infinitely long passage, containing numerous office cabinets and elusive, scurrying people. Taking a sharp turn, I found myself amid a thousand musical instruments; the walls, all mirror, reflected an enfilade of grand pianos, while in the centre there was a pool with a bronze Orpheus atop a green rock. The aquatic theme did not end here as, racing back, I ended up in the Section of Fountains and Brooks, and it was difficult to walk along the winding, slimy edges of those waters.

Now and then, on one side or the other, stone stairs, with puddles on the steps, which gave me a strange sensation of fear, would descend into misty abysses, whence issued whistles, the rattle of dishes, the clatter of typewriters, the ring of hammers and many other sounds, as if, down there, were exposition halls of some kind or other, already closing or not yet completed. Then I found myself in darkness and kept bumping into unknown furniture until I finally saw a red light and walked out on to a platform that clanged under me – and suddenly, beyond it, there was a bright parlour, tastefully furnished in Empire style, but not a living soul, not a living soul . . . By now I was indescribably terrified, but every time I turned

and tried to retrace my steps along the passages, I found myself in
hitherto unseen places – a greenhouse with hydrangeas and broken
windowpanes with the darkness of artificial light showing through
beyond; or a deserted laboratory with dusty alembics on its tables.
Finally I ran into a room of some sort with coat-racks monstrously
loaded down with black coats and astrakhan furs; from beyond a
door came a burst of applause, but when I flung the door open,
there was no theatre, but only a soft opacity and splendidly counter-
feited fog with the perfectly convincing blotches of indistinct street-
lights. More than convincing! I advanced, and immediately a joyous
and unmistakable sensation of reality at last replaced all the unreal
trash amid which I had just been dashing to and fro. The stone
beneath my feet was real sidewalk, powdered with wonderfully
fragrant, newly fallen snow, in which the infrequent pedestrians
had already left fresh black tracks. At first the quiet and the snowy
coolness of the night, somehow strikingly familiar, gave me a pleasant feeling after my feverish wanderings. Trustfully, I started to
conjecture just where I had come out, and why the snow, and what
were those lights exaggeratedly but indistinctly beaming here and
there in the brown darkness. I examined and, stooping, even
touched a round spur stone on the curb, then glanced at the palm
of my hand, full of wet granular cold, as if hoping to read an
explanation there. I felt how lightly, how naïvely I was clothed, but
the distinct realization that I had escaped from the museum's maze
was still so strong that, for the first two or three minutes, I experienced neither surprise nor fear. Continuing my leisurely examination, I looked up at the house beside which I was standing and was
immediately struck by the sight of iron steps and railings that
descended into the snow on their way to the cellar. There was a
twinge in my heart, and it was with a new, alarmed curiosity that
I glanced at the pavement, at its white cover along which stretched
black lines, at the brown sky across which there kept sweeping a
mysterious light, and at the massive parapet some distance away. I
sensed that there was a drop beyond it; something was creaking and
gurgling down there. Further on, beyond the murky cavity,
stretched a chain of fuzzy lights. Scuffling along the snow in my
soaked shoes, I walked a few paces, all the time glancing at the dark
house on my right; only in a single window did a lamp glow softly
under its green-glass shade. Here, a locked wooden gate . . . There,
what must be the shutters of a sleeping shop . . . And by the light

of a streetlamp whose shape had long been shouting to me its impossible message, I made out the ending of a sign – ' . . . *inka Sapog*' (' . . . *oe Repair*') but no, it was not the snow that had obliterated the 'hard sign' at the end. 'No, no, in a minute I shall wake up,' I said aloud, and, trembling, my heart pounding, I turned, walked on, stopped again. From somewhere came the receding sound of hooves, the snow sat like a skullcap on a slightly leaning spur stone and indistinctly showed white on the woodpile on the other side of the fence, and already I knew, irrevocably, where I was. Alas, it was not the Russia I remembered, but the factual Russia of today, forbidden to me, hopelessly slavish, and hopelessly my own native land. A semiphantom in a light foreign suit, I stood on the impassive snow of an October night, somewhere on the Moyka or the Fontanka Canal, or perhaps on the Obvodny, and I had to do something, go somewhere, run; desperately protect my fragile, illegal life. Oh, how many times in my sleep I had experienced a similar sensation! Now, though, it was reality. Everything was real – the air that seemed to mingle with scattered snowflakes, the still unfrozen canal, the floating fish house, and that peculiar squareness of the darkened and the yellow windows. A man in a fur cap, with a briefcase under his arm, came towards me out of the fog, gave me a startled glance, and turned to look again when he had passed me. I waited for him to disappear and then, with a tremendous haste, began pulling out everything I had in my pockets, ripping up papers, throwing them into the snow and stamping them down. There were some documents, a letter from my sister in Paris, five hundred francs, a handkerchief, cigarettes; however, in order to shed all the integument of exile, I would have to tear off and destroy my clothes, my linen, my shoes, everything, and remain ideally naked; and, even though I was already shivering from my anguish and from the cold, I did what I could.

But enough. I shall not recount how I was arrested, nor tell of my subsequent ordeals. Suffice it to say that it cost me incredible patience and effort to get back abroad, and that, ever since, I have foresworn carrying out commissions entrusted one by the insanity of others.

# 'Autumn Mountain'

## Ryunosuke Akutagawa

*Akutagawa is best known for* Rashomon, *a film based on two of his stories, 'Rashomon' and 'In a Grove'. He was the leading Japanese intellectual of the early twentieth century, reviving the public's interest in old traditional tales, and adapting Western works; inspired by* Gulliver's Travels, *he wrote his successful novel* Kappa. *He committed suicide at the age of thirty-five, leaving in his farewell note the names of famous historical suicides, including Christ among them.*

' *"Autumn Mountain"* ' *deals with the theme of beauty that cannot be perceived; like Lovecraft's horrors, which become effective through the alleged impossibility of describing them, Akutagawa creates the expectation of something which is wonderful because it will never be attained.*

'And speaking of Ta Ch'ih, have you ever seen his *Autumn Mountain* painting?'

One evening, Wang Shih-ku, who was visiting his friend Yün Nan-t'ien, asked this question.

'No, I have never seen it. And you?'

Ta Ch'ih, together with Mei-tao-jen and Huang-hao-shan-ch'iao, had been one of the great painters of the Mongol dynasty. As Yün Nan-t'ien replied, there passed before his eyes images of the artist's famous works, the *Sandy Shore* painting and the *Joyful Spring* picture scroll.

'Well, strange to say,' said Wang Shih-ku, 'I'm really not sure whether or not I have seen it. In fact . . .'

'You don't know whether you have seen it or you haven't?' said Yün Nan-t'ien, looking curiously at his guest. 'Do you mean that you've seen an imitation?'

'No, not an imitation. I saw the original. And it is not I alone who have seen it. The great critics Yen-k'o and Lien-chou both became involved with the *Autumn Mountain*.' Wang Shih-ku sipped his tea and smiled thoughtfully. 'Would it bore you to hear about it?'

'Quite the contrary,' said Yün Nan-t'ien, bowing his head politely. He stirred the flame in the copper lamp.

At that time (began Wang Shih-ku) the old master Yüan Tsai was still alive. One evening while he was discussing paintings with Yen-k'o, he asked him whether he had ever seen Ta Ch'ih's *Autumn Mountain*. As you know, Yen-k'o made a veritable religion of Ta Ch'ih's painting and was certainly not likely to have missed any of his works. But he had never set eyes on this *Autumn Mountain*.

'No, I haven't seen it,' he answered shamefacedly, 'and I've never even heard of its existence.'

'In that case,' said Yüan Tsai, 'please don't miss the first opportunity you have of seeing it. As a work of art it's on an even higher level than his *Summer Mountain* or *Wandering Storm*. In fact, I'm not sure that it isn't the finest of all Ta Ch'ih's paintings.'

'Is it really such a masterpiece? Then I must do my best to see it. May I ask who owns this painting?'

'It's in the house of a Mr Chang in the County of Jun. If you ever have occasion to visit the Chin-shan Temple, you should call on him and see the picture. Allow me to give you a letter of introduction.'

As soon as Yen-k'o received Yüan Tsai's letter, he made plans to set out for the County of Jun. A house which harboured so precious a painting as this would, he thought, be bound to have other great works of different periods. Yen-k'o was quite giddy with anticipation as he started out.

When he reached the County of Jun, however, he was surprised to find that Mr Chang's house, though imposing in structure, was dilapidated. Ivy was coiled about the walls, and in the garden grass and weeds grew rank. As the old man approached, chicken, ducks, and other barnyard fowl looked up, as if surprised to see any stranger enter here. For a moment he could not help doubting Yüan Tsai's words and wondering how a masterpiece of Ta Ch'ih's could possibly have found its way into such a house. Upon a servant's answering his knock, he handed over the letter, explaining that he had come from far in the hope of seeing the *Autumn Mountain*.

He was led almost immediately into the great hall. Here again, though the divans and tables of red sandalwood stood in perfect order, a mouldy smell hung over everything and an atmosphere of desolation had settled even on the tiles. The owner of the house, who now appeared, was an unhealthy-looking man; but he had a pleasant air about him and his pale face and delicate hands bore signs of nobility. Yen-k'o, after briefly introducing himself, lost no time in telling his host how grateful he would be if he might be shown the famous Ta Ch'ih painting. There was an urgency in the master's words, as if he feared that were he not to see the great painting at once, it might somehow vanish like a mist.

Mr Chang assented without hesitation and had the painting hung on the bare wall of the great hall.

'This,' he said, 'is the *Autumn Mountain* to which you refer.'

At the first glance Yen-k'o let out a gasp of admiration. The dominant colour was a dark green. From one end to the other a river ran its twisting course; bridges crossed the river at various places and along its banks were little hamlets. Dominating it all rose the main peak of the mountain range, before which floated peaceful wisps of autumn cloud. The mountain and its neighbouring hills were fresh green, as if newly washed by rain, and there was an uncanny beauty in the red leaves of the bushes and thickets scattered along their slopes. This was no ordinary painting, but one in which both design and colour had reached an apex of perfection. It was a work of art instinct with the classical sense of beauty.

'Well, what do you think of it? Does it please you?' said Mr Chang, peering at Yen-k'o with a smile.

'Oh, it is truly of godlike quality!' cried Yen-k'o, while he stared at the picture in awe. 'Yüan Tsai's lavish praise was more than merited. Compared to this painting, everything I have seen until now seems second-rate.'

'Really? You find it such a masterpiece?'

Yen-k'o could not help turning a surprised look at his host. 'Can you doubt it?'

'Oh no, it isn't that I have any doubts,' said Mr Chang, and he blushed with confusion like a schoolboy. Looking almost timidly at the painting, he continued: 'The fact is that each time I look at this picture I have the feeling that I am dreaming, though my eyes are wide open. I cannot help feeling that it is I alone who see its beauty, which is somehow too intense for this world of ours. What you just said brought back these strange feelings.'

But Yen-k'o was not much impressed by his host's evident attempt at self-vindication. His attention was absorbed by the painting, and Mr Chang's speech seemed to him merely designed to hide a deficiency in critical judgement.

Soon after, Yen-k'o left the desolate house.

As the weeks passed, the vivid image of the *Autumn Mountain* remained fresh in Yen-k'o's mind (continued Wang Shih-ku after accepting another cup of tea). Now that he had seen Ta Ch'ih's masterpiece, he felt ready to give up anything whatsoever to possess it. Inveterate collector that he was, he knew that not one of the great works that hung in his own house – not even Li Ying-ch'iu's *Floating Snowflakes*, for which he had paid five hundred taels of silver – could stand comparison with that transcendent *Autumn Mountain*.

While still sojourning in the County of Jun, he sent an agent to the Chang house to negotiate for the sale of the painting. Despite repeated overtures, he was unable to persuade Mr Chang to enter into any arrangement. On each occasion that pallid gentleman would reply that while he deeply appreciated the master's admiration of the *Autumn Mountain* and while he would be quite willing to lend the painting, he must ask to be excused from actually parting with it.

These refusals only served to strengthen the impetuous Yen-k'o's resolve. 'One day,' he promised himself, 'that great picture will hang in my own hall.' Confident of the eventual outcome, he finally resigned himself to returning home and temporarily abandoning the *Autumn Mountain*.

'About a year later, in the course of a further visit to the County of Jun, he tried calling once more at the house of Mr Chang. Nothing had changed: the ivy was still coiled in disorder about the walls and fences, and the garden was covered with weeds. But when the servant answered his knock, Yen-k'o was told that Chang was not in residence. The old man asked if he might have another look at the *Autumn Mountain* despite the owner's absence, but his importunacy was of no avail: the servant repeated that he had no authority to admit anyone until his master returned. As Yen-k'o persisted, the man finally shut the door in his face. Overcome with chagrin, Yen-k'o had to leave the house and the great painting that lay somewhere in one of the dilapidated rooms.

Wang Shih-ku paused for a moment.

'All that I have related so far,' he said, 'I heard from the master Yen-k'o himself.'

'But tell me,' said Yün Nan-t'ien, stroking his white beard, 'did Yen-k'o ever really see the *Autumn Mountain*?'

'He said that he saw it. Whether or not he did, I cannot know for certain. Let me tell you the sequel, and then you can judge for yourself.'

Wang Shih-ku continued his story with a concentrated air, and now he was no longer sipping his tea.

When Yen-k'o told me all this (said Wang Shih-ku) almost fifty years had passed since his visits to the County of Jun. The master Yüan Tsai was long since dead and Mr Chang's large house had already passed into the hands of two successive generations of his family. There was no telling where the *Autumn Mountain* might be – nor if the best parts of the scroll might not have suffered hopeless deterioration. In the course of our talk old Yen-k'o described that mysterious painting so vividly that I was almost convinced I could see it before my eyes. It was not the details that had impressed the master but the indefinable beauty of the picture as a whole. Through the words of Yen-k'o, that beauty had entered into my heart as well as his.

It happened that, about a month after my meeting with Yen-k'o, I had myself to make a journey to the southern provinces, including the County of Jun. When I mentioned this to the old man, he suggested that I go and see if I could not find the *Autumn Mountain*. 'If that painting ever comes to light again,' he said, 'it will indeed be a great day for the world of art.'

Needless to say, by this time I also was anxious to see the painting, but my journey was crowded and it soon became clear that I would not find time to visit Mr Chang's house. Meanwhile, however, I happened to hear a report that the *Autumn Mountain* had come into the hands of a certain nobleman by the name of Wang. Having learned of the painting, Mr Wang had despatched a messenger with greetings to Chang's grandson. The latter was said to have sent back with the messenger not only the ancient family documents and the great ceremonial cauldron which had been in the family for countless generations, but also a painting which fitted the description of Ta Ch'ih's *Autumn Mountain*. Delighted with these gifts, Mr Wang had arranged a great banquet for Chang's grandson, at which he had placed the young man in the seat of honour and regaled him with the choicest delicacies, gay music, and lovely girls; in addition he had given him one thousand pieces of gold.

On hearing this report I almost leaped with joy. Despite the vicissitudes of half a century, it seemed that the *Autumn Mountain* was still safe! Not only that, but it actually had come within my range. Taking along only the barest necessities, I set out at once to see the painting.

I still vividly remember the day. It was a clear, calm afternoon in early summer and the peonies were proudly in bloom in Mr Wang's garden. On meeting Mr Wang, my face broke into a smile of delight even before I had completed my ceremonial bow. 'To think that the *Autumn Mountain* is in this very house!' I cried. 'Yen-k'o spent all those years in vain attempts to see it again – and now I am to satisfy my own ambition without the slightest effort . . .'

'You come at an auspicious time,' replied Mr Wang. 'It happens that today I am expecting Yen-k'o himself, as well as the great critic Lien-chou. Please come inside, and since you are the first to arrive you shall be the first to see the painting.'

Mr Wang at once gave instructions for the *Autumn Mountain* to be hung on the wall. And then it all leaped forth before my eyes: the little villages on the river, the flocks of white cloud floating over the valley, the green of the towering mountain range which extended into the distance like a succession of folding-screens – the whole world, in fact, that Ta Ch'ih had created, a world far more wonderful than our own. My heart seemed to beat faster as I gazed intently at the scroll on the wall.

These clouds and mists and hills and valleys were unmistakably the work of Ta Ch'ih. Who but Ta Ch'ih could carry the art of drawing to such perfection that every brush-stroke became a thing alive? Who but he could produce colours of such depth and richness, and at the same time hide all mechanical trace of brush and paint? And yet . . . and yet I felt at once that this was not the same painting that Yen-k'o had seen once long ago. No, no, a magnificent painting it surely was, yet just as surely not the unique painting which he had described with such religious awe!

Mr Wang and his entourage had gathered around me and were watching my expression, so I hastened to express my enthusiasm. Naturally I did not want him to doubt the authenticity of his picture, yet it was clear that my words of praise failed to satisfy him. Just then Yen-k'o himself was announced – he who had first spoken to me of this *Autumn Mountain*. As the old man bowed to Mr Wang, I could sense the excitement inside him, but no sooner had his eyes settled on the scroll than a cloud seemed to pass before his face.

'What do you think of it, Master?' asked Mr Wang, who had been carefully observing him. 'We have just heard the teacher Wang Shih-ku's enthusiastic praise, but . . .'

'Oh, you are, sir, a very fortunate man to have acquired this painting,' answered Yen-k'o promptly. 'Its presence in your house will add lustre to all your other treasures.'

Yen-k'o's courteous words only seemed to deepen Mr Wang's anxiety; he, like me, must have heard in them a note of insincerity. I think we were all a bit relieved when Lien-chou, the famous critic, made his appearance at this juncture. After bowing to us, he turned to the scroll and stood looking at it silently, chewing his long moustaches.

'This, apparently, is the same painting that the master Yen-k'o last saw half a century ago,' Mr Wang explained to him. 'Now I would much like to hear your opinion of the work. Your candid opinion,' Mr Wang added, forcing a smile.

Lien-chou sighed and continued to look at the picture. Then he took a deep breath and, turning to Mr Wang, said: 'This, sir, is probably Ta Ch'ih's greatest work. Just see how the artist has shaded those clouds. What power there was in his brush! Note also the colour of his trees. And then that distant peak which brings the whole composition to life.' As he spoke, Lien-chou pointed to various outstanding features of the painting, and needless to say, a look of relief, then of delight, spread over Mr Wang's face.

Meanwhile I secretly exchanged glances with Yen-k'o. 'Master,' I whispered, 'is that the real *Autumn Mountain*?' Almost imperceptibly the old man shook his head, and there was a twinkle in his eyes.

'It's all like a dream,' he murmured. 'I really can't help wondering if that Mr Chang wasn't some sort of hobgoblin.'

'So that is the story of the *Autumn Mountain*,' said Wang Shih-ku after a pause, and took a sip of his tea. 'Later on it appears that Mr Wang made all sorts of exhaustive enquiries. He visited Mr Chang, but when he mentioned to him the *Autumn Mountain*, the young man denied all knowledge of any other version. So one cannot tell if that *Autumn Mountain* which Yen-k'o saw all those years ago is not even now hidden away somewhere. Or perhaps the whole thing was just a case of faulty memory on an old man's part. It would seem unlikely, though, that Yen-k'o's story about visiting Mr Chang's house to see the *Autumn Mountain* was not based on solid fact.'

'Well, in any case the image of that strange painting is no doubt engraved for ever on Yen-k'o's mind. And on yours too.'

'Yes,' said Wang Shih-ku, 'I still see the dark green of the mountain rock, as Yen-k'o described it all those years ago. I can see the red leaves of the bushes as if the painting were before my eyes this very moment.'

'So even if it never existed, there is not really much cause for regret!'

The two men laughed and clapped their hands with delight.

*Translated from the Japanese by Ivan Morris.*

# The Sight

## Brian Moore

*Cassandra's gift is of course a curse. The Trojan priestess who could foretell the future (but whom no one would believe) is haunted by the evils that will come and the knowledge that nothing can prevent them. She shares her curse with the condemned in Hell – they also know what they can expect from the days ahead, and they also lack all hope. In Brian Moore's story, Cassandra appears in an unexpected light.*

*Brian Moore has written a number of highly successful novels – including* The Lonely Passion of Judith Hearne, Catholics, The Great Victorian Collection *– and is claimed as a national writer by Ireland (where he was born), Canada (where he worked) and the United States (where he now lives).*

Benedict Chipman never took a drink before five and never drank after midnight. He ate only a light lunch, avoided bread and potatoes, and drank decaffeinated coffee. These self-regulations were, he sometimes thought, the only set rules he observed. Otherwise, he did as he liked.

Yet on the morning he returned to his eight-room apartment on Fifth Avenue after four days in hospital, his first act was to tell his housekeeper to bring some Scotch and ice into the library. When she brought it, he was standing by the window, looking out at Central Park. He did not turn around.

'Will that be all, sir?'

'Yes, thanks, Mrs Leahy.'

Chipman was fifty-two and a partner in a New York law firm. A few weeks ago, during his annual medical check-up, his doctor had noticed a large mole on his back and had recommended its removal. The operation was minor but, for Chipman who had never been in hospital before, the invasion of his bodily privacy by doctors, nurses, and attendants had been humiliating and vaguely upsetting. Then, to complicate matters, while the biopsy showed the mole to be probably benign, the pathologist advised that 'to be completely sure', the surgeon should repeat the procedure but, this time, make a wider incision. The second biopsy had been scheduled for the end of the month. 'There's nothing to worry about,' the surgeon said. 'Just relax and come back ten days from now.'

But Chipman did not feel like relaxing. He felt nervous and irritable. As he poured the Scotch, he looked at the tray containing his mail. The first letter on the pile was postmarked Bishopsgate, N.H. He had been born in Bishopsgate and for some reason he could not explain the sight of the postmark disturbed him. The letter was from his brother, Blake, who wrote that he and his wife were coming to New York to visit their son Buddy, a journalism major at Columbia. Buddy, it seemed, had learned that his uncle had been in hospital and Blake wrote that all three of them would like to call tomorrow afternoon. The letter irritated Chipman. He had no wish to see Blake and his family. He thought of his brother as a man who had never in his life owned a hundred dollars he didn't know about and whose relations with himself were sycophantic rather than fraternal, largely because of loans which Blake had not repaid.

At the library door, Mrs Leahy announced herself with a small prefatory cough. 'Mrs Kirwen is here, sir.'

'Show her in. And ask if she'd like something to drink.'

As he put his brother's letter down and rose to greet Geraldine, he heard her chatting with Mrs Leahy in the front hall.

'Is *he* having one? Oh, well then, a sherry, I think. By the way, how's your nephew, Mrs Leahy?'

'He still has the pleurisy, ma'am. But he'll be all right.'

'Good, that's good news.'

'Thank you, Mrs Kirwen.'

I never knew Mrs Leahy had a nephew, Chipman said to himself. But, come to think of it, he didn't know much about Mrs Leahy, although she had been with him for almost ten years. Lately, he had decided that his interest in other people was limited to the extent of their contributions to his purse, his pleasure, or his self-esteem. He had a weakness for such aphoristic judgements. But in this instance he also remembered another aphorist's warning: lack of interest in others is a first sign of age.

'Ben, darling, how are you? Shouldn't you have your feet up or something? You mustn't overdo it on your first day home.'

'Stop fussing.'

'I'm not fussing. Dr Wilking told me you should take it easy.'

'When was Wilking talking to *you*?'

'I met him in the corridor yesterday. Remember, he thinks I'm your wife.'

The surgeon, who did not know Chipman, had come in on them unexpectedly the night after the biopsy and found Geraldine, the buttons of her dress undone, lying on the hospital bed with Chipman. The surgeon had tactfully assumed she was Chipman's wife and had addressed her as such in the subsequent conversation. No one had contradicted him. 'That was a mistake,' Chipman said now, remembering. 'I should have said something.'

'Oh, what's it matter?'

'Well, my own doctor, Dr Loeb, knows I'm not married.'

'Oh, Ben. Who cares nowadays?'

At that point Mrs Leahy brought Geraldine's sherry. Geraldine, sipping it, put her long legs up on a yellow silk footstool. In this posture her skirt fell back, revealing her elegant thighs. Although impromptu erotic views normally pleased Chipman, this morning he was not pleased: he was irritated. 'Why can't you sit properly?'

'That's not a very nice thing to say when I've given up an important job to be with you today.'

'What job?'

'Remember I tried out for the Phil Lewis show last week? Well, my agent called and said they want me for a second audition this afternoon. He says that usually means you've got the job. But, I'm not going.'

'Why not?'

'Because if I got the job it would mean I'd be on the coast for the next seven weeks. I'm not going to be three thousand miles away while you're in and out of hospital.'

'I'm not in and out of hospital. I'm just going back for a couple of days, that's all. Now, be a good girl. Phone and say you'll be glad to audition this afternoon.'

'No,' she said, suddenly looking as though she might begin to cry.

'But why not?'

'Because I've realized something, Ben. I'm in love with you. I don't want to be separated from you.'

In love with him? He remembered La Rochefoucauld's maxim that nothing is more natural or more mistaken than to suppose that we are loved. He knew Geraldine did not love him. She was an unsuccessful young actress, divorced from a television producer and in receipt of a reasonable alimony. His own role in her life was that of a suitable escort, an older man capable of providing presents and a good time, a friend who was good for a small loan and might not expect to see his money again. This sudden protestation of love was, he decided, no more than the familiar feminine need to justify having gone to bed with him. Geraldine would not give up her alimony: he did not want her to. The present arrangement suited him perfectly.

Nevertheless when she said that she loved him, for one moment he felt strangely elated. Then put his glass back on the silver tray and in its surface saw his face, which seemed distorted, white, old. This foolishness must stop. 'Now, don't talk nonsense. Go and phone those people.'

'Are you trying to get rid of me?'

'Of course not. But if you go out to Hollywood this week it might work out very well. I was thinking of going to Puerto Rico. I thought I'd take a vacation. Lie in the sun until I have to go back into hospital.'

'Do you know people in Puerto Rico, is that it?'

'No. No. Look, Geraldine, you're *not* in love with me. My God, I'm twenty years older than you.'

'Age has nothing to do with being in love with someone.'

'Maybe not at your age. But at my age it has everything to do with it. Now go and make that phone call. Then I'll take you out and buy you lunch.'

She stood and picked up the otter coat he had helped pay for, trailing it behind her on the carpet as she moved across the room. At the door, she turned. 'So that's what you want? To go to Puerto Rico alone?'

'Yes.'

'Okay.'

She went into the hall. He listened to hear the tinkle as she picked up the phone, but instead heard the front door slam. He started across the room, thinking to go after her and bring her back, but stopped. He realized that he was close to the almost forgotten sensation of tears. Dammit, he'd just invented Puerto Rico to help her make up her mind about the audition. But now, as he felt himself tremble with anger – or was it weakness? – he decided a short vacation in the sun might be the ideal way to wait out the next ten days. Maybe with Geraldine. He decided to suggest it at the office when he went in tomorrow.

There might be a little ill-feeling, though. He had already had a long vacation this summer. But what could they do? In the seventeen years he had been a member of the firm he had frequently demonstrated that his interests were not the law or the success of the partnership, but women, music, and his collection of paintings. However, on the day he joined the partnership he brought with him, as a wedding present from his father-in-law, an insurance company which dwarfed all other clients the firm did business with. And although his marriage had subsequently broken up (his wife died eight years later in an alcoholic clinic, driven there, some said, by Chipman's behaviour with other women) his father-in-law had not held it against him. He still represented the insurance company and this power, coupled with his disregard for the firm's other clients, had driven his partners to revenge themselves on him in the only way they knew. They no longer invited him to their homes or, indeed, to any social function. Their boycott amused him: they bored him. They knew that he was amused and bored. Their dislike of him, he guessed, had long ago turned to hatred.

Yet on the following morning when he went to the office he was surprised to see George Geddes, the senior partner, come in at his doorway, eager, out of breath, and smiling like a job applicant. 'Ben, how are you, how're you feeling?'

'Hello, George.'

'So, how did it go?'

Directly behind Geddes, Chipman's secretary was at her desk in the outer office. He did not want her to hear what he had to say and so beckoned Geddes in and shut the door. 'Matter of fact, George, I wanted to have a word with you about that. Everything went very well, but they want me to go back, just as a precaution, and have a wider excision made. They've scheduled it for the thirty-first. I don't know. I'm feeling a little knocked out. I thought, if you don't mind, I might go and lie in the sun for a week. Not really come back to the office until next month.'

As he spoke he noticed that Geddes was already nodding agreement as though helping someone with a speech impediment. 'Of course, Ben, of course. No sense sitting around here. Good idea.'

'Well, thanks. Of course there are a few things I can clear up before I go.'

'No, no,' Geddes said. 'Let the juniors do some work for a change. Get on your feet again, that's the main thing.'

After Geddes had left, Chipman phoned a travel agency. He booked a double room with patio and pool in a first-class Puerto Rico resort hotel, starting the following Monday. He called in his juniors and reviewed their current handling of his clients' affairs. At noon he told his secretary that he was leaving and would not be back until the first week in December. Then he took a taxi to his apartment and for the second morning in a row broke his rule and made himself a drink.

But now his reason was celebratory. What a relief it had been to find Geddes agreeable for once. And there was a note saying Geraldine had telephoned. Obviously, her temper tantrum had not lasted. After pouring a Scotch he picked up the phone and dialled her number.

'Geraldine? Ben. First of all, I'm sorry about yesterday.'

'No, darling, it was my fault. Why shouldn't you go on a trip if you want to? When are you going, by the way?'

'No, tell me first, how was your audition?'

'I didn't go. It's a long story, I won't bore you with it.'

'Does that mean you might be free to join me in Puerto Rico?'

'Ben, do you mean it?'

'Of course. I booked a double room with patio and pool in the Caribe Imperial. Or would you rather I got you a room of your own?'

'No, no.'

'Good. And what about the week-end? Are you free?'

'Do you mean now? Yes. Completely.'

'Well, so am I. Or, almost. I have to be here tomorrow afternoon when my brother and his family are coming. But that shouldn't take more than an hour.'

'Are we thinking of the same thing?'

'I hope so.'

'All right, darling. Come on down. I'll be waiting.'

'I'll be right there.'

His brother's hand, tentative at first, went out to finger the Steinway's polished surface, then boldly stroked the wood. His brother's head turned, afternoon sunlight merciless on the thin grey hair, the pink skull-cap of skin beneath. His brother smiled, ingratiate and falsely intimate. 'Beautiful piano, eh, Ben?' his brother said. 'You must play something for us before we go. I mean, if you feel up to it.'

'Oh yes, Ben, you must,' said his brother's wife who, he knew, did not care at all for music.

If he felt up to it. What would they say if they knew he had come up from the village two hours ago after a night of screwing that would exhaust anyone? Perhaps it would not exhaust Blake's wife, though. One summer, when their son Buddy was still a brat in rompers, Chipman had gone to visit them at their summer cottage on Cape Cod. He was sunbathing in the dunes when Blake's wife came up from the beach, drying her hair on a towel, her shoulder-straps undone, her swimsuit wet from the sea. She did not see him until she stumbled on him and when he reached up and pulled her down she did not say a word. Later they walked hand in hand over the dunes towards the cottage. Blake was sitting on a deck-chair on the lawn, reading a book, and the child was on the porch playing with an old inner tube. Man and child looked up and his brother's wife at once let go of his hand and ran to kiss her child. She avoided Chipman for the rest of that evening and the following morning he thought it wise to pretend a business engagement in Boston. He had not been to stay with them since.

'Let Buddy play something,' he said, knowing that Buddy's atrocious playing would please them much more than his own. And so Buddy obediently flopped down on the piano bench, looked disdainfully at the music scores in front of him, then poised his large hands over the keys. 'What'll it be, Uncle Ben?'

'You choose,' Chipman said. Years ago, prodded by Blake's wistful hints about the child's musical inclinations, he had paid for a series of piano lessons for Buddy. The money had been wasted for Buddy's musical talents were a myth, the first of a long series of efforts on his parents' part to make Chipman feel a special affection for the boy. All had failed. Buddy's only effect on his uncle was to relieve him of any regrets about not having had a son of his own.

But now he pretended to listen as Buddy stumbled through some

Cole Porter tunes, noticing as he mimed attention that Buddy's parents seemed nervous as though they had quarrelled before coming and were now trying to cover it up by a surfeit of polite remarks to each other. Chipman was uninterested. He simply wanted them to go and so, when Blake glanced at last in his direction, he pretended drowsiness. It worked. As his son thumped to a pause in the music, Blake stood up. 'Thanks, Bud, but we'd better not overtire your uncle. Besides, your mother and I want to catch that Wyeth show at the Met before our train leaves.'

Then he turned to Chipman. 'Ben, could I have a word with you?'

As on signal both Buddy and his mother left the room. It was, Chipman knew, the usual prelude to Blake's asking for money, but today a loan seemed well worth it to get rid of them. He went to his desk, aware that Blake, if left to his own devices, would take at least five minutes to come to the point. He opened a drawer and took out his cheque-book.

'What's that for?' Blake asked sharply.

'Nothing.'

'Put that away, will you,' Blake said. 'I'm ashamed that I owe you so much. As a matter of fact, Ben, it wasn't that at all. It was just that we wondered if you'd like to come up to Bishopsgate to convalesce until you go back into the hospital.'

'Thanks, but I'm going to Puerto Rico.'

'Oh. Puerto Rico?'

'Yes, I thought I'd like to lie in the sun for a few days.'

'Oh, that's a pity, we were looking forward to the thought of having you. You and I haven't spent much time together these last years.'

'I know. Well, maybe some other time.'

'Any time,' Blake said. 'I'd like us to go for walks around the old place and have talks and all that. I'd like that a lot.'

And then, abruptly, Blake took hold of his hand and squeezed it. 'I'd really like it, Ben.'

'Well, we'll do it,' Chipman said, uneasily, beginning to move towards the hallway where the others waited. As they came out he saw Blake's wife glance at her husband and saw Blake give a small, almost imperceptible shake of his head. Buddy came forward, hand out, smiling. 'Goodbye, sir.'

'Goodbye,' Chipman said. 'Goodbye, Blake.'

His sister-in-law came towards him. He held out his hand. She ignored it and reached up to kiss him on the cheek. He was astonished. 'Goodbye,' his sister-in-law said. 'Take care of yourself.'

The elevator came. They went down.

Confused, Chipman closed the door of his apartment. It was as though he had found an interesting passage in a dull book and had seen it snatched away before he had time to finish it. Why had Blake's wife kissed him, she who had so carefully avoided kissing him ever since that summer on the beach? And why had Blake come up with this unprecedented invitation to visit them at Bishopsgate? Why were they being so kind all of a sudden? Come to think of it, everyone had been abnormally kind these past two days – Geraldine, Geddes, Blake. It was irritating, dammit, to be treated as though, all of a sudden, he were made of glass. How did La Rochefoucauld put it? *Pride does not wish to owe, nor vanity to pay.* He didn't want favours from anyone. So, why did they try?

He had reached the library door before the thought and the answer came to him. He was going to die. That was why they were all being so gentle. They knew something he didn't know. A wider excision, that was what the surgeon said. 'To be completely sure,' the pathologist said. They hadn't told him the truth, that was it. 'Just relax,' the surgeon said.

He must not panic. He must call Dr Loeb, his internist, and put the question to him quite casually, implying that he already knew all about it. He must go to the phone now and clear things up.

He went into his bedroom and closed the door so that Mrs Leahy would not overhear him. He phoned Dr Loeb but the answering service said Dr Loeb was out of town for the weekend and a Dr Slattery was taking his calls. So that was no use. The surgeon's name was Wilking. He looked up the number. The answering service said Dr Wilking wasn't in, but would he leave a message. He left his name and number and lay down on the bed, worrying. After five minutes he telephoned again and said it was an emergency. He must reach Dr Wilking at once. This time, the answering service gave him a number to call. Dr Wilking answered.

'Dr Wilking, this is Benedict Chipman speaking. Now, I know this may sound silly to you, but was there anything about that operation of mine that I should know about?'

'Why do you ask, Mr Chipman?'

'I just want to know the truth. It's important, doctor.'

'Well, look, Mr Chipman, it's pretty much as I told you. I don't think you have anything to worry about.'

'Is that the truth? I want the truth.'

'Yes, what can I say? Look, Mr Chipman. The best thing you can do now is relax. Your wife mentioned you might go off for a short vacation. I think that's a good idea.'

'How the hell can I take it easy? For God's sake, doctor, that's like telling a man to take it easy in the condemned cell while you decide whether or not he's to be reprieved.'

'Oh, come on now, Mr Chipman, I wouldn't say that.'

'Of course, you wouldn't,' Chipman shouted. 'And that girl isn't my wife, do you hear? So anything you have to say, just say it to me!'

He put the receiver down without waiting to hear the surgeon's reply. He looked at his bed. This was the bed he might die in. He turned from it and went into his library. Small picture-lights lit his collection of Krieghoff landscapes. When he died these pictures would be sent to the Bishopsgate Art Gallery to be exhibited in a special room with a brass plaque over the door, identifying him as their donor. They would arrive after his body, which would be buried under a plain headstone in the episcopal cemetery, next to his parents' grave. How many people ever read donors' plaques or the names on headstones? A year from now he would be forgotten.

But wasn't that jumping the gun, giving in to a bad case of jitters unsupported by any evidence? How could they know he was going to die when they hadn't even done the second biopsy yet? What were they keeping from him? Whatever it was had frightened Geraldine into suddenly declaring her love. But she doesn't love me, Chipman decided, she pities me. Pity is what everyone feels for me now: Geraldine, Geddes, Blake, Blake's wife. Yet how could they all know this thing about me? Geraldine has never met Geddes. Or Buddy. Who told Buddy, for instance?

Chipman went to his desk, searched it, and then went to the telephone table in the hall. He knew he had a number for Buddy someplace, and when he found it and dialled it, it was a fraternity house. No one answered for a long time and then some boy told him Buddy wasn't in, and that he didn't know when he would be back. As Chipman replaced the receiver, Mrs Leahy passed him in the hall, going down the corridor to her own room. Only one person might have spoken to Buddy, to Geddes, to Geraldine. One person who would answer the phone when people called here to ask how he was. He went down the corridor to the far end of the apartment and stopped outside Mrs Leahy's door. He almost never came into this part of the apartment, near the pantry and wine cellar, and past the kitchen. He stood for a moment and then, without knocking, he opened the door.

He had not seen the inside of Mrs Leahy's room for years. Sometimes he heard the television sound, turned low, and sometimes she would leave the door open, at night, when she went to answer the phone. Now, his eyes went from the television set to the horrid rose and green curtains, the cheap coloured lithograph of some saint, to the crucifix, entwined with fading palm, which hung over what seemed to be a sewing-table. It was the sort of room he used to glimpse through upper-storey windows, years ago, when he still rode the subways, a room which screamed a sudden mockery of all other rooms in his elegant apartment. And its occupant, her back to him, unaware of his presence, was the perfect figure in this interior. In her pudgy fingers, the surprise of a cigarette: on her lap, inevitably, the garish headlines of the *Daily News*.

'Mrs Leahy?'

She turned. Her grey head was that of a stranger's, utterly changed by the absence of her uniform cap. 'Oh, did you ring, sir? Is the bell not working?'

'No, I didn't ring.'

'Can I get you something, sir? Are you all right?'

By this time she had stubbed her cigarette and had pinned on the familiar housemaid's cap. 'A little whisky?' she said. 'Or, are you hungry, sir? Would you like a sandwich?'

'Whisky,' he said. 'And I want to talk to you.'

'Yes, Mr Chipman.' Swiftly she moved past him going down the corridor to the monastic neatness of her kitchen. She did not, of course, expect him to follow her into the kitchen and looked up, surprised, when he did.

'A little water with it, sir? I'll bring it into the library, will I?'

'No. Sit down, Mrs Leahy. Please.'

As she placed the bottle of Scotch, ice, and a glass and pitcher of water on a tray, he drew out one of the chrome and leather kitchen chairs, indicating that she should sit in at the table. As she did, he saw a red rash of embarrassment rise from her neck to her cheeks. They had never been informal together. He sat opposite her and poured himself a Scotch. 'Now,' he said. 'Let me ask you something. Are you the person who's been telling people I have cancer?'

'Me, sir?'

'Yes, you.'

She did not answer him at once. She put her veiny old hands on the table, joined them as in an attitude of prayer, then looked at him with the calculating, ready-to-bolt caution of a rodent. He had never before noticed this animal quality of hers. Why, she's a hedgehog, he decided. She's Mrs Tiggy-winkle.

'Yes, sir. It was me.'

He must keep calm. He must not let her know that he was ignorant of all the facts of his illness. 'I see. And who told *you* that I might have cancer?'

'Mrs Kirwen, sir.'

'And what did she say, exactly?'

'Ah, she didn't say you had cancer, she said they were going to operate on you again just to be sure. There was always the chance, she said. And I said to her I thought I should let Mr Buddy know. On account of your brother, sir. And then Mr Geddes rang up about you. And I told him. To let him know, like.'

'Oh, you did, did you? Well, I like the way you let them know. They think I'm going to die. I could see it on my brother's face this afternoon. He thinks I'm going to die.'

'I'm very sorry, now, Mr Chipman.'

'Mrs Kirwen *didn't* say to you I had cancer, did she? She didn't say the doctors had told her something they hadn't told me. Or, did she?'

'Ah, no, sir. Mrs Kirwen never said you were going to die. 'Tis not Mrs Kirwen's fault at all. 'Tis my fault, and I'm very sorry now.'

'Tell me Mrs Leahy. Do you dislike me?'

'Oh, no, sir.'

'Then why did you tell these people that I'm going to die?'

'Ah, well, sir, that's a long story. And I'm very sorry to be bringing you news like that. But them doctors don't know everything, now do they?'

'What do you mean?' He was shouting, but he could not stop himself. 'Just exactly what the hell do you mean, Mrs Leahy?'

Mrs Leahy, avoiding his eye, stared down at her joined hands.

'Well, sir, you see, I have something now, something not many people have. And there's times I wish I didn't, let me tell you.'

'Didn't what? Didn't have what?'

'I have the sight, sir. The second sight.'

'Second sight?' Chipman repeated the words with the joy of a man repeating the punch line of a joke. 'Well. And there I was . . .' Beginning to shake with amusement, he lifted his glass and drank a great swallow of whisky. 'You mean you dreamed it, or something like that?'

'Yes, sir. Last Monday, the night before your operation.'

'Now let me get this straight,' Chipman said. 'Mrs Kirwen told you nothing except what you've told me. The truth is nobody *knows* I have cancer. There's absolutely no proof of it at all.'

'That's right, sir.'

'My God, do you realize the mischief you've caused?'

'I'm very sorry, now. I see I shouldn't have said anything. I beg your pardon, sir.'

'It was a disgraceful thing to do!'

'Yes, sir. I'm sorry, sir. Maybe I should give you my notice?'

'No, no.' Chipman poured himself a second drink. Suddenly, he felt like laughing again. 'Well, now,' he said. Unconsciously, and for the first time in their acquaintance, he found himself slipping into an imitation of her Irish brogue. 'And how long have you had this "sight"?'

'Ah, a long time, now. I noticed it first when I was only fourteen.'

'You dream about things and then they happen, is that it?'

'In a way, sir.'

'What do you mean? Tell me.'

'I'd rather not, now, sir. I'm sorry about speaking to those people. I only meant it for your sake, sir.'

'Now, wait. I'm just interested in this premonition of yours. Now, what happened in my case? You had a dream?'

'Yes, just the dream, sir. Nothing else.'

'What do you mean, nothing else?'

'Well you see, first there's the dream. And then, later on, you see, there's a second sign.'

'And what's this second sign?'

'It's a look I do see on the person's face.'

'A look?'

'Yes. When the trouble is very close.'

Chipman, in the act of downing his second Scotch, looked at her over the rim of his glass. Ignorant, stupid old creature with her hedgehog eyes and butterfat brogue. Some primitive folk nonsense, typically Irish, he supposed; it was their religion that encouraged these fairy-tales. 'When it's close,' he said. 'What does that mean?'

'When it's close to the time, sir.'

'So, I take it you haven't seen this look on my face. Not yet.'

'That's right, sir.'

'When do you think you'll see it?'

'I don't know that, sir. Better not be asking me things like that. It's no pleasure to me to be seeing the things I do see. That's the God's own truth, sir.'

'But how do you know you'll see it? Do you always see it after you have this dream?'

'I'd say so, sir.'

'Give me an example.'

'Well, I saw it on my own sister, sir, the night before she died. I had a dream and saw her in the dream, and when I woke up she was sleeping in the bed with me and I lit the lamp and looked at her face. I saw it in her face. And the very next night she was killed by a bus on her way home. I was fourteen at the time.'

'Tell me about another time.'

'Ah, now, what's the use, sir?'

'No, you started this, Mrs Leahy. I want to hear more.'

'And I don't want to tell you, sir.'

'But you told Mrs Kirwen and Mr Geddes and my nephew. You weren't afraid to tell them this fairy-tale.'

'Ah, I didn't tell them that at all, sir. Sure they wouldn't believe it. I just said I had information, I couldn't say more. But that the doctors were very worried about you.'

'*Did* you?' Again, he felt furious at her. 'How dare you, Mrs Leahy!'

'I'm sorry, sir. I wanted to be a help to you, sir. I mean I wanted Mrs Kirwen, and your family and all, to be good to you now in your time of trouble.'

I must *not* lose my temper with a servant, Chipman told himself. 'All right,' he said. 'You told me about your sister. Give me another example.'

'My husband, sir, God rest his soul. I dreamed about him June second, 1946, and he was took on the second of November, the same year. And on the first of November I saw the look on his face. I begged him not to go to work the next day, but he didn't heed me. He fell off a scaffolding. He never lived to see a priest.'

'Wait,' Chipman said. 'Both these deaths were from accidents, not illnesses.'

'Yes, sir.'

'Well, have you had any premonitions about deaths from illness?'

'Well, Jimmy, one of the doormen in this building. I saw him in a dream four months before he died of heart disease. And on the day he was taken I went to see him in the hospital. And I saw the look on him.'

'Indeed.' Slowly, Chipman finished his Scotch.

'Of course, 'tis not always departures. Deaths. Sometimes I do see arrivals. Do you remember, sir, the night you came home from Washington, last New Year's it was? I had your dinner waiting for you. I dreamed the night before that you would come at nine, wanting your dinner. And you did.'

As a matter of fact, Chipman thought, I remember it well. I remember thinking she'd prepared that roast lamb for herself and some crony. Extra-sensory perception, premonition: of course all that was only one jump away from teacup reading, table turning, spiritualistic quacks. But she dreamed of my death.

'So, Mrs Leahy. You dreamed of me, again, the other night. But this time it wasn't about my arrival?'

She nodded.

'Tell me the dream.'

'Ah, don't be asking, sir.'

'But I am asking. If you go around telling false stories to people about my death, you have the obligation to tell me the truth about what prompted you to do it. Now, what did you see in this dream?'

'I saw the shroud, sir. You came in the room and you were wearing the shroud.'

'A shroud. That means death.'

'Yes, sir.'

'When?'

'Ah, now, I don't know that, sir.'

'But you will know, as soon as you see this look on my face, is that it?'

'Yes, sir. I'd know the time, then.'

'I see,' Chipman said. 'And now I suppose you'd like me to cross your palm with silver, so that you'll tell me when I must make my funeral arrangements. Well, Mrs Leahy, I'm going to disappoint you. A few minutes ago, when I thought of the mischief you've done and the worry you've caused my family and friends, I was quite prepared to let you go. But, believe me, I wouldn't let you go now for all the gold in Fort Knox. A year from now, Mrs Leahy, you and I will sit here together. We'll have a drink together, this time, this date, one year from now.'

'God willing and we will, sir.'

He stood up, suddenly feeling his drink, his chair making a screeching noise on the linoleum floor. 'And now,' he said, 'I'd better phone Mrs Kirwen and those other people and explain what's really happened.'

'Yes, sir. I'm very sorry.'

He went back into the library. There was no point in being angry with her, it was a joke really. He should be celebrating. The doctors weren't alarmed, and even if they found some malignancy, there are all sorts of treatments, cobalt bombs, chemotherapy and so on. To think that stupid old hedgehog had set all this in motion – Geddes, Buddy, even Geraldine. Poor Geraldine.

He went to his shelves, took down a volume of the *Encyclopaedia Britannica* and read the entry under *cancer*. He then read the entry under *clairvoyance*. When he had finished, he replaced the books and rang the bell.

'Yes, sir.'

She stood at the door, her uniform cap on straight, the perfect housekeeper, a treasure, his women friends said. 'I'd like some ice and water,' he said.

She nodded and smiled. Mrs Tiggy-winkle. When she came back with the tray, he tried to affect a bantering tone. 'Now, just in theory, mind you, just for curiosity's sake. When do you think you'll see that look on my face?'

'I don't know, sir. I hope it will be a long, long time off. Was there anything else, sir?'

'No.'

'Goodnight, sir.'

She bobbed her head in her usual half-curtsey of withdrawal. When she had gone he made himself a fresh drink, then went to the window and stood looking down at Fifth Avenue. People in evening dress were getting out of rental Cadillac limousines in front of his building, laughing and joking, going to some function.

An hour later, he was still standing there. The room behind him was quite dark. He heard no sound in the apartment. He walked into the lighted hallway and went towards the kitchen. She was not there. He went past the kitchen, going towards her room. He stood in front of her door, trembling with excitement. He knocked.

'Yes, sir.'

She was sitting in her armchair, stitching the hem of an apron. The television set had been turned off.

'You were waiting for me, weren't you?'

'No, sir. Would you be wanting dinner, sir?'

'You should know I don't want dinner. I thought knowing things like that was one of your specialities.'

She bent to her sewing.

'Mrs Leahy, I want to ask you something. What if I fired you tonight? You'd never see the look, would you?'

'I suppose not, sir.'

'Then you'd never know if you'd been right. I mean supposing you never saw my death in the paper. You wouldn't know, would you?'

She bit the edge of her thread.

'Well, answer me.'

'Yes, sir, I'd know.'

'Look at me!' Even to himself, his voice sounded strange. 'You haven't looked at me since I came into the room.'

She folded the apron, placed it on the sewing-table and turned around. He went towards her, his face drained. As her eyes met his, he thought again of an animal. An animal does not think: it knows or it does not know. He sat on the edge of a worn sofa, facing her.

'Well?' His voice was hoarse.

'Well what, sir?'

'You know what. Am I still all right?'

'Yes, sir.'

'Mrs Leahy,' he said. 'You wouldn't lie to me, would you? I mean, you'd tell me if you saw it?'

'I suppose so, sir. I might be afraid to worry you, though.'

His hands gripped hers. 'No, no, I want to know. You must tell me. Promise me you'll tell me when the time comes?'

Tears, the unfamiliar tears of dependence, blurred his vision: made the room tremble. Gently, she nodded her head.

# Clorinda

## André Pieyre de Mandiargues

*In the second half of the sixteenth century, Torquato Tasso, an Italian contemporary of Shakespeare, wrote the epic* Jerusalem Delivered. *It tells the story of the First Crusade, in which Tancred, a brave Christian knight, falls in love with Clorinda, a Saracen lady warrior. Clorinda, who doesn't love him, tries to burn down the Christian camp. Tancred, not recognizing his beloved, attacks her with his sword. Before she dies, Clorinda reveals herself to Tancred and asks him to baptize her. The poem brought Tasso fame and insanity. He died mad in Rome in 1595.*

*André Pieyre de Mandiargues conjures up Tasso's Clorinda in the following story – a modern version of Pygmalion, perhaps the fable of a writer and his creations – taken from his collection* Soleil des Loups *('Sun of the Wolves', a metaphor for the moon). Mandiargues has written several volumes of short stories, literary and art criticism, and novels. His* Girl on a Motorcycle *was translated into English and made into a film.*

*In memory of Tasso*

*Plumeless, Clorinda has dressed herself (an evil omen)
in armour of black and rust.*

You lie asleep, like an ox. Last night you got drunk again and now the vapours of rum knock down the flies swarming around the light bulb. Dawn is breaking; outside the window the glare of the street-lamp fades. You forgot to draw the blinds. On the marble top of the chest of drawers, next to the narrow bed in which you lie, a glass bell covers a number of objects. I can make out three or four dried butterflies, a hawk-moth, a piece of wood – once resinous but now eaten away by the larvae of God-knows-what insects – and finally, on a strip of moss, a tiny iron helmet inlaid with red gold, no larger than a thimble, which an armourer would perhaps recognize as of very old German craftsmanship.

Life for you is obviously a thing of the past; the days you now drag out are numbered. You drink, then you fall asleep rolled up in a horse-blanket thrown over a sheetless mattress. As soon as the caretaker who cleans your room knocks on the door, you feverishly grab a book that lies next to your hand, or pretend to write (though the paper is still blank), because you fear the secret judgement of this old woman whom you have never heard utter a single word and who looks like a bundle of black thorny twigs. And since you will soon be dead I shall try to write on these loose sheets of paper (because *you* never will) the story you told me last night after having begged me to help you home, before you got hold of the now empty bottle which the sloping floor rolls back to me every time I try to kick it under the lowest drawer of the dressing-table.

One very warm day early last autumn, when you were walking through a splendid forest with the vague intention of picking mushrooms (though they were not yet in season), you suddenly noticed on top of a small mound an object which reminded you of a fort, complete with ramparts, towers and battlements, like those one can see in Victor Hugo's drawings. It was nothing but a piece of wood, however, standing on a bed of fine moss, blanched by the rains of several winters and ridden with galleries drilled by the jaws of termite ants. A sudden curiosity made you lift it off the moss, turn it round and shake it. It let out a cloud of dust as fine as flour. Inside the wood you heard, much to your surprise, a sort of metal clang, and from one of the holes sprang forth a shining, living creature which at first you took to be an insect. 'A large cricket,' you thought, unable to believe your own eyes and to admit the existence of this miniature knight locked from head to foot inside armour with dark golden inlays, who, standing on what seemed to you a rampart, unsheathed a formidable sword, held it with both hands and began to wave it about dangerously close to your fingers.

You watched with amazement and fear. The knight seemed so sure of himself, so capable of slicing your thumb to the bone (or splitting your thumbnail in half – an idea as painful as the wound itself). A nervous jerk of your hand as you tried to avoid the blade upset the creature's balance – from the height of your chest the little warrior fell to the ground and hit his head on a stone. You saw him lying motionless, and quickly crouching down, almost flat on your stomach, you picked him up and held him in the palm of your hand. Afraid that he might have hurt himself, you tried to open his armour. Your fingers, at first clumsy, finally managed to find the catch of the helmet and lift the vizor. And what an unexpected wonder! Behind the opening appeared the beautiful face of a young girl.

Taking great care not to injure the fainted beauty, you undid the breastplate, which was closed at the back with hinges, like a corset, and then holding the tiny woman by the waist as carefully as your fingers could manage you took off the rest of her armour (a familiar gesture, you noticed, like taking shrimp-meat out of its shell). The creature wore nothing but a shirt of what seemed to you an extraordinarily delicate material, but which was really, in proportion to the body, a heavy, roughly knit cloth. The shirt hung down to the middle of her thighs, and its collar barely hid the shape of her golden neck.

She soon came back to life, and as you were sitting on the ground in order to examine her it was a simple trick for the little warrior to jump from your hand on to your knee, and from there down to the mossy patch, in an effort to escape. But a tangle of moss stood in her way and you had no trouble catching her again. She struggled angrily, shaking her thick black hair which came down to her shoulders, pounding with her fists on your fingernails, trying to bite you. To keep her quiet you tore two bits of wool off your coat: one of them (still rust-coloured in your memory) you used to tie her hands behind her back, the other (of a beautiful deep blue) you tied to her ankle and to a rather heavy stone, thereby leaving her no hope of escape. Kneeling on the moss next to her stone, you knew, even though she could not stretch her arms towards you, that she was begging you to free her. This made you wish to see her naked. You took a penknife out of your pocket, held the little warrior in mid-air, and split the shirt from back to front and sideways (not forgetting the shoulders). The wind carried away the pieces and you returned your prisoner to her bed of moss.

She lay on her back, closed her eyes and adopted the resigned attitude of women 'of the great class' (that is how, in your own language, you used to call your women) when they know it is too late to feel ashamed (or even make believe they feel ashamed), when they abandon all modesty. Your eyes ran over her, meeting no resistance, fixing themselves on the previously glimpsed oriental neck, measuring the slender waist which a wedding-ring would have girdled, stroking the polished beauty of her knees and thighs, venturing into the dark and curly triangle so lustrous and thick that it almost seemed to belong to a wild animal. As if your eyes were not enough, you put your nose next to her belly: her body exuded a perfume similar to that of the *reseda odorata*. You would have given anything to become as small as the tiny creature, to fall, with her, on the moss, next to her, to hold her in your arms, because tied up as she was she had become easy prey for the first passing stranger – provided he were the same size.

At last you could no longer restrain your desire, so intense that it made you shake with impotent rage. Certain of finding your prisoner again whenever you wanted her, you ran into the forest like a madman, embracing the pine trees in your path, falling into ditches, tearing up carpets of moss, pressing your lips against the earth amid the grass and wild flowers. But when your frenzy died out and, dirty with mud and leaves, you returned to where you had left her whom you considered yours (like a hedgehog or a lizard caught during an idle walk), you found that she had disappeared. There was no doubt about the place. The piece of blue wool and the stone had not been moved from the bed of moss. But the wool had been torn, and its loose end lay now in a glistening drop of fresh blood.

Never for a moment did you suspect the pine-tree ants, one of which you could see running among the pine needles not far away, because there were no bones left on the moss and it is a well-known fact that these ants do not carry away their larger prey but devour it on the spot. But with unspeakable horror you thought of the beak of a bird. Painfully and precisely, pecking at your conscience as you imagined it pecking at the body of your tiny woman, you thought immediately of the beak of a warbler.

'Why,' later you asked me, 'do the idiots who write stories or songs, why do asinine naturalists give the warbler the reputation of being a pretty bird with graceful manners, a reputation it uses to deceive all those who cannot see the truth? Even its song is not as beautiful as we are told. Its name alone should tell us how evil this creature is, outside the imaginary world built by poets. All you need do,' you told me, 'is say aloud these three words, *wolf, weasel, warbler*, to realize immediately the slyness, the cruelty and blood-thirstiness of that vile bird of prey.' While looking for a trace of her whom you had lost, you found at your feet the tiny helmet. You wrapped it up in your handkerchief – there where you would have wished to wrap up, warm and living, the warrior who had worn it – and brought it home.

As for the rest of the armour, where had it fallen? In spite of your efforts you never found it again.

And now what a pitiful thing your life has become. What every man vaguely dreams of and desires was granted to you on a fine autumn day, among the pine trees of a forest on the moor, but you lost it, maddened by your senses. Now you have nothing to look forward to except death. And while you wait for death to come and fetch you, you get drunk on rum, like a wild beast, and fall asleep.

*Translated from the French by Alberto Manguel.*

# The Pagan Rabbi

## Cynthia Ozick

*I interviewed Cynthia Ozick briefly, in New York, in the summer of 1983. One of the questions I asked her was how, as a Jewish writer, she had become so attracted to the pagan world of magic and the fantastic. 'In my daily life,' she said, 'as a thinking, breathing person, I am Jewish; as a writer, like the Pagan Rabbi, I am a pagan. I could only be a pagan, being a writer.'*

*'The Pagan Rabbi', written in the sixties, was published, together with other stories, in 1970. 'Curiously enough,' Cynthia Ozick recalled, 'it came out of an emotion, but this emotion took the form of an idea. I wanted to explore what happens to somebody who is committed to a mode of restraint, a system of ethics, when he releases himself from it and enters the truly mystical world. What would happen to such a person?'*

Rabbi Jacob said: 'He who is walking alone and studying, but then breaks off to remark, "How lovely is that tree!" or "How beautiful is that fallowfield!"? – Scripture regards such a one as having hurt his own being.' From *The Ethics of the Fathers*

When I heard that Isaac Kornfeld, a man of piety and brains, had hanged himself in the public park, I put a token in the subway stile and journeyed out to see the tree.

We had been classmates in the rabbinical seminary. Our fathers were both rabbis. They were also friends, but only in a loose way of speaking: in actuality our fathers were enemies. They vied with one another in demonstrations of charitableness, in the captious glitter of their scholiae, in the number of their adherents. Of the two, Isaac's father was the milder. I was afraid of my father; he had a certain disease of the larynx, and if he even uttered something so trivial as 'Bring the tea' to my mother, it came out splintered, clamorous, and vindictive.

Neither man was philosophical in the slightest. It was the one thing they agreed on. 'Philosophy is an abomination,' Isaac's father used to say. 'The Greeks were philosophers, but they remained children playing with their dolls. Even Socrates, a monotheist, nevertheless sent money down to the temple to pay for incense to their doll.'

'Idolatry is the abomination,' Isaac argued, 'not philosophy.'

'The latter is the corridor to the former,' his father said.

My own father claimed that if not for philosophy I would never have been brought to the atheism which finally led me to withdraw, in my second year, from the seminary. The trouble was not philosophy – I had none of Isaac's talent: his teachers later said of him that his imagination was so remarkable he could concoct holiness out of the fine line of a serif. On the day of his funeral the president of his college was criticized for having commented that although a suicide Isaac Kornfeld was *ipso facto* consecrated. It should be noted that Isaac hanged himself several weeks short of his thirty-sixth birthday: he was then at the peak of his renown; and the president, of course, did not know the whole story. He judged by Isaac's reputation, which was at no time more impressive than just before his death.

I judged by the same, and marvelled that all that holy genius and intellectual surprise should in the end be raised no higher than the next-to-lowest limb of a delicate young oak, with burly roots like the toes of a gryphon exposed in the wet ground.

The tree was almost alone in a long rough meadow, which sloped down to a bay filled with sickly clams and a bad smell. The place was called Trilham's Inlet, and I knew what the smell meant: that cold brown water covered half the city's turds.

On the day I came to see the tree the air was bleary with fog. The weather was well into autumn and, though it was Sunday, the walks were empty. There was something historical about the park just then, with its rusting grasses and deserted monuments. In front of a soldier's cenotaph a plastic wreath left behind months before by some civic parade stood propped against a stone frieze of identical marchers in the costume of an old war. A banner across the wreath's belly explained that the purpose of war is peace. At the margins of the park they were building a gigantic highway. I felt I was making my way across a battlefield silenced by the victory of the peace machines. The bulldozers had bitten far into the park, and the rolled carcasses of the sacrificed trees were already cut up into logs. There were dozens of felled maples, elms, and oaks. Their moist inner wheels breathed out a fragrance of barns, countryside, decay.

In the bottommost meadow fringing the water I recognized the tree which had caused Isaac to sin against his own life. It looked curiously like a photograph – not only like that newspaper photograph I carried warmly in my pocket, which showed the field and its markers – the drinking-fountain a few yards off, the ruined brick wall of an old estate behind. The caption-writer had particularly remarked on the 'rope'. But the rope was no longer there; the widow had claimed it. It was his own prayer-shawl that Isaac, a short man, had thrown over the comely neck of the next-to-lowest limb. A Jew is buried in his prayer-shawl; the police had handed it over to Sheindel. I observed that the bark was rubbed at that spot. The tree lay back against the sky like a licked postage-stamp. Rain began to beat it flatter yet. A stench of sewage came up like a veil in the nostril. It seemed to me I was a man in a photograph standing next to a grey blur of tree. I would stand through eternity beside Isaac's guilt if I did not run, so I ran that night to Sheindel herself.

I loved her at once. I am speaking now of the first time I saw her, though I don't exclude the last. The last – the last together with Isaac – was soon after my divorce; at one stroke I left my wife and my cousin's fur business to the small upstate city in which both had repined. Suddenly Isaac and Sheindel and two babies appeared in the lobby of my hotel – they were passing through: Isaac had a lecture engagement in Canada. We sat under scarlet neon and Isaac told how my father could now not speak at all.

'He keeps his vow,' I said.

'No, no, he's a sick man,' Isaac said. 'An obstruction in the throat.'

'I'm the obstruction. You know what he said when I left the seminary. He meant it, never mind how many years it is. He's never addressed a word to me since.'

'We were reading together. He blamed the reading, who can blame *him*? Fathers like ours don't know how to love. They live too much indoors.'

It was an odd remark, though I was too much preoccupied with my own resentments to notice. 'It wasn't what we read,' I objected.

'Torah tells that an illustrious man doesn't have an illustrious son. Otherwise he wouldn't be humble like other people. This much scholarly stuffing I retain. Well, so my father always believed he was more illustrious than anybody, especially more than your father. *There*fore,' I delivered in Talmudic cadence, 'what chance did I have? A nincompoop and no *sitz fleish*. Now you, you could answer questions that weren't even invented yet. Then you invented them.'

'Torah isn't a spade,' Isaac said. 'A man should have a livelihood. You had yours.'

'The pelt of a dead animal isn't a living either, it's an indecency.'

All the while Sheindel was sitting perfectly still; the babies, female infants in long stockings, were asleep in her arms. She wore a dark thick woollen hat – it was July – that covered every part of her hair. But I had once seen it in all its streaming black shine.

'And Jane?' Isaac asked finally.

'Speaking of dead animals. Tell my father – he won't answer a letter, he won't come to the telephone – that in the matter of the marriage he was right, but for the wrong reason. If you share a bed with a Puritan you'll come into it cold and you'll go out of it cold. Listen, Isaac, my father calls me an atheist, but between the conjugal sheets every Jew is a believer in miracles, even the lapsed.'

He said nothing then. He knew I envied him his Sheindel and his luck. Unlike our fathers, Isaac had never condemned me for my marriage, which his father regarded as his private triumph over my father, and which my father, in his public defeat, took as an occasion for declaring me as one dead. He rent his clothing and sat on a stool for eight days, while Isaac's father came to watch him mourn, secretly satisfied, though aloud he grieved for all apostates. Isaac did not like my wife. He called her a tall yellow straw. After we were married he never said a word against her, but he kept away.

I went with my wife to his wedding. We took the early train down especially, but when we arrived the feast was well under way, and the guests far into the dancing.

'Look, look, they don't dance together,' Jane said.

'Who?'

'The men and the women. The bride and the groom.'

'Count the babies,' I advised. 'The Jews are also Puritans, but only in public.'

The bride was enclosed all by herself on a straight chair in the centre of a spinning ring of young men. The floor heaved under their whirl. They stamped, the chandeliers shuddered, the guests cried out, the young men with linked arms spiralled and their skullcaps came flying off like centrifugal balloons. Isaac, a mist of black suit, a stamping foot, was lost in the planet's wake of black suits and emphatic feet. The dancing young men shouted bridal songs, the floor leaned like a plate, the whole room teetered.

Isaac had told me something of Sheindel. Before now I had never seen her. Her birth was in a concentration camp, and they were about to throw her against the electrified fence when an army mobbed the gate; the current vanished from the terrible wires, and she had nothing to show for it afterwards but a mark on her cheek like an asterisk, cut by a barb. The asterisk pointed to certain dry footnotes: she had no mother to show, she had no father to show, but she had, extraordinarily, God to show – she was known to be, for her age and sex, astonishingly learned. She was only seventeen.

'What pretty hair she has,' Jane said.

Now Sheindel was dancing with Isaac's mother. All the ladies made a fence, and the bride, twirling with her mother-in-law, lost a shoe and fell against the long laughing row. The ladies lifted their glistering breasts in their lacy dresses and laughed; the young men, stamping two by two, went on shouting their wedding songs. Sheindel danced without her shoe, and the black river of her hair followed her.

'After today she'll have to hide it all,' I explained.

Jane asked why.

'So as not to be a temptation to men,' I told her, and covertly looked for my father. There he was, in a shadow, apart. My eyes discovered his eyes. He turned his back and gripped his throat.

'It's a very anthropological experience,' Jane said.

'A wedding is a wedding,' I answered her, 'among us even more so.'

'Is that your father over there, that little scowly man?'

To Jane all Jews were little. 'My father the man of the cloth. Yes.'

'A wedding is not a wedding,' said Jane: we had had only a licence and a judge with bad breath.

'Everybody marries for the same reason.'

'No,' said my wife. 'Some for love and some for spite.'

'And everybody for bed.'

'Some for spite,' she insisted.

'I was never cut out for a man of the cloth,' I said. 'My poor father doesn't see that.'

'He doesn't speak to you.'

'A technicality. He's losing his voice.'

'Well, he's not like you. He doesn't do it for spite,' Jane said.

'You don't know him,' I said.

He lost it altogether the very week Isaac published his first remarkable collection of responsa. Isaac's father crowed like a passionate rooster, and packed his wife and himself off to the Holy Land to boast on the holy soil. Isaac was a little relieved; he had just been made Professor of Mishnaic History, and his father's whims and pretences and foolish rivalries were an embarrassment. It is easy to honour a father from afar, but bitter to honour one who is dead. A surgeon cut out my father's voice, and he died without a word.

Isaac and I no longer met. Our ways were too disparate. Isaac was famous, if not in the world, certainly in the kingdom of jurists and scholars. By this time I had acquired a partnership in a small book store in a basement. My partner sold me his share, and I put up a new sign: 'The Book Cellar'; for reasons more obscure than filial (all the same I wished my father could have seen it) I established a department devoted especially to not-quite-rare theological works, chiefly in Hebrew and Aramaic, though I carried some Latin and Greek. When Isaac's second volume reached my shelves (I had now expanded to street level), I wrote him to congratulate him, and after that we corresponded, not with any regularity. He took to ordering all his books from me, and we exchanged awkward little jokes. 'I'm still in the jacket business,' I told him, 'but now I feel I'm where I belong. Last time I went too fur.' 'Sheindel is well, and Naomi and Esther have a sister,' he wrote. And later: 'Naomi, Esther, and Miriam have a sister,' And still later: 'Naomi, Esther, Miriam, and Ophra have a sister.' It went on until there were seven girls. There's nothing in Torah that prevents an illustrious man from having illustrious daughters,' I wrote him when he said he had given up hope of another rabbi in the family. 'But where do you find seven illustrious husbands?' he asked. Every order brought another quip, and we bantered back and forth in this way for some years.

I noticed that he read everything. Long ago he had inflamed my taste, but I could never keep up. No sooner did I catch his joy in Saadia Gaon, than he had already sprung ahead to Yehudah Halevi. One day he was weeping with Dostoyevski and the next leaping in the air over Thomas Mann. He introduced me to Hegel and Nietzsche while our fathers wailed. His mature reading was no more peaceable than those frenzies in his youth, when I would come upon him in an abandoned classroom at dusk, his stocking feet on the window sill, the light already washed from the lowest city clouds, wearing the look of a man half-sotted with print.

But when the widow asked me – covering a certain excess of alertness or irritation – whether to my knowledge Isaac had lately been ordering any books on horticulture, I was astonished.

'He bought so much,' I demurred.

'Yes, yes, yes,' she said. 'How could you remember?'

She poured the tea and then, with a discreetness of gesture, lifted my dripping raincoat from the chair where I had thrown it and took it out of the room. It was a crowded apartment, not very neat, far from slovenly, cluttered with dolls and tiny dishes and an array of tricycles. The dining table was as large as a desert. An old-fashioned crocheted lace runner divided it into two nations, and on the end of this, in the neutral zone, so to speak, Sheindel had placed my cup. There was no physical relic of Isaac: not even a book.

She returned. 'My girls are all asleep, we can talk. What an ordeal for you, weather like this and going out so far to that place.'

It was impossible to tell whether she was angry or not. I had rushed in on her like the rainfall itself, scattering drops, my shoes stuck all over with leaves.

'I comprehend exactly why you went out there. The impulse of a detective,' she said. Her voice contained an irony that surprised me. It was brilliantly and unmistakably accented, and because of this jaggedly precise. It was as if every word emitted a quick white thread of great purity, like hard silk, which she was then obliged to bite cleanly off. 'You went to find something? An atmosphere? The sadness itself?'

'There was nothing to see,' I said, and thought I was lunatic to have put myself in her way.

'Did you dig in the ground? He might have buried a note for goodbye.'

'Was there a note?' I asked, startled.

'He left nothing behind for ordinary humanity like yourself.'

I saw she was playing with me. 'Rebbetzin Kornfeld,' I said, standing up, 'forgive me. My coat, please, and I'll go.'

'Sit,' she commanded. 'Isaac read less lately, did you notice that?'

I gave her a civil smile. 'All the same he was buying more and more.'

'Think,' she said. 'I depend on you. You're just the one who might know. I had forgotten this. God sent you perhaps.'

'Rebbetzin Kornfeld, I'm only a bookseller.'

'God in his judgement sent me a bookseller. For such a long time Isaac never read at home. Think! Agronomy?'

'I don't remember anything like that. What would a Professor of Mishnaic History want with agronomy?'

'If he had a new book under his arm he would take it straight to the seminary and hide it in his office.'

'I mailed to his office. If you like I can look up some of the titles—'

'You were in the park and you saw nothing?'

'Nothing.' Then I was ashamed. 'I saw the tree.'

'And what is that? A tree is nothing.'

'Rebbetzin Kornfeld,' I pleaded, 'It's a stupidity that I came here. I don't know myself why I came, I beg your pardon, I had no idea—'

'You came to learn why Isaac took his life. Botany? Or even, please listen, even mycology? He never asked you to send something on mushrooms? Or having to do with herbs? Manure? Flowers? A certain kind of agricultural poetry? A book about gardening? Forestry? Vegetables? Cereal growing?'

'Nothing, nothing like that,' I said excitedly. 'Rebbetzin Kornfeld, your husband was a rabbi!'

'I know what my husband was. Something to do with vines? Arbors? Rice? Think, think, think! Anything to do with land – meadows – goats – a farm, hay – anything at all, anything rustic or lunar—'

'Lunar! My God! Was he a teacher or a nurseryman? Goats! Was he a furrier? Sheindel, are you crazy? *I* was the furrier! What do you want from the dead?'

Without a word she replenished my cup, though it was more than half full, and sat down opposite me, on the other side of the lace boundary-line. She leaned her face into her palms, but I saw her eyes. She kept them wide.

'Rebbetzin Kornfeld,' I said, collecting myself, 'with a tragedy like this—'

'You imagine I blame the books. I don't blame the books, what-

ever they were. If he had been faithful to his books he would have
lived.'

'He lived,' I cried, 'in books, what else?'

'No,' said the widow.

'A scholar. A rabbi. A remarkable Jew!'

At this she spilled a furious laugh. 'Tell me, I have always been
very interested and shy to inquire. Tell me about your wife.'

I intervened: 'I haven't had a wife in years.'

'What are they like, those people?'

'They're exactly like us, if you can think what we would be if we
were like them.'

'We are not like them. Their bodies are more to them than ours
are to us. Our books are holy, to them their bodies are holy.'

'Jane's was so holy she hardly ever let me get near it,' I muttered
to myself.

'Isaac used to run in the park, but he lost his breath too quickly.
Instead he read in a book about runners with hats made of leaves.'

'Sheindel, Sheindel, what did you expect of him? He was a
student, he sat and he thought, he was a Jew.'

She thrust her hands flat. 'He was not.'

I could not reply. I looked at her merely. She was thinner now
than in her early young-womanhood, and her face had an in-between
cast, poignant still at the mouth and jaw, beginning to grow coarse
on either side of the nose.

'I think he was never a Jew,' she said.

I wondered whether Isaac's suicide had unbalanced her.

'I'll tell you a story,' she resumed. 'A story about stories. These
were the bedtime stories Isaac told Naomi and Esther: about mice
that danced and children who laughed. When Miriam came he
invented a speaking cloud. With Ophra it was a turtle that married
a blade of withered grass. By Leah's time the stones had tears for
their leglessness. Rebecca cried because of a tree that turned into a
girl and never grew colours again in the autumn. Shiphrah, the
littlest, believes that a pig has a soul.'

'My own father used to drill me every night in sacred recitation.
It was a terrible childhood.'

'He insisted on picnics. Each time we went farther and farther
into the country. It was a madness. Isaac never troubled to learn to
drive a car, and there was always a clumsiness of baskets to carry
and a clutter of buses and trains and seven exhausted wild girls.

And he would look for special places – we couldn't settle just here or there, there had to be a brook or such-and-such a slope or else a little grove. And then, though he said it was all for the children's pleasure, he would leave them and go off alone and never come back until sunset when everything was spilled and the air freezing and the babies crying.'

'I was a grown man before I had the chance to go on a picnic,' I admitted.

'I'm speaking of the beginning,' said the widow. 'Like you, wasn't I fooled? I was fooled, I was charmed. Going home with our baskets of berries and flowers we were a romantic huddle. Isaac's stories on those nights were full of dark invention. May God preserve me, I even begged him to write them down. Then suddenly he joined a club, and Sunday mornings he was up and away before dawn.'

'A club? So early? What library opens at that hour?' I said, stunned that a man like Isaac should ally himself with anything so doubtful.

'Ah, you don't follow, you don't follow. It was a hiking club, they met under the moon. I thought it was a pity, the whole week Isaac was so inward, he needed air for the mind. He used to come home too fatigued to stand. He said he went for the landscape. I was like you, I took what I heard, I heard it all and never followed. He resigned from the hikers finally, and I believed all that strangeness was finished. He told me it was absurd to walk at such a pace, he was a teacher and not an athlete. Then he began to write.'

'But he always wrote,' I objected.

'Not this way. What he wrote was only fairy tales. He kept at it and for a while he neglected everything else. It was the strangeness in another form. The stories surprised me, they were so poor and dull. They were a little like the ideas he used to scare the girls with, but choked all over with notes, appendices, prefaces. It struck me then he didn't seem to understand he was only doing fairy tales. Yet they were really very ordinary – full of sprites, nymphs, gods, everything ordinary and old.'

'Will you let me see them?'

'Burned, all burned.'

'Isaac burned them?'

'You don't think I did! I see what you think.'

It was true that I was marvelling at her hatred. I supposed she was one of those born to dread imagination. I was overtaken by a coldness for her, though the sight of her small hands with their tremulous staves of fingers turning and turning in front of her face like a gate on a hinge reminded me of where she was born and who she was. She was an orphan and had been saved by magic and had a terror of it. The coldness fled. 'Why should you be bothered by little stories?' I inquired. 'It wasn't the stories that killed him.'

'No, no, not the stories,' she said. 'Stupid corrupt things. I was glad when he gave them up. He piled them in the bathtub and lit them with a match. Then he put a notebook in his coat pocket and said he would walk in the park. Week after week he tried all the parks in the city. I didn't dream what he could be after. One day he took the subway and rode to the end of the line, and this was the right park at last. He went every day after class. An hour going, an hour back. Two, three in the morning he came home. "Is it exercise?" I said. I thought he might be running again. He used to shiver with the chill of night and the dew. "No, I sit quite still," he said. "Is it more stories you do out there?" "No, I only jot down what I think." "A man should meditate in his own house, not by night near bad water," I said. Six, seven in the morning he came home. I asked him if he meant to find his grave in that place.'

She broke off with a cough, half artifice and half resignation, so loud that it made her crane toward the bedrooms to see if she had awakened a child. 'I don't sleep any more,' she told me. 'Look around you. Look, look everywhere, look on the windowsills. Do you see any plants, any common houseplants? I went down one evening and gave them to the garbage collector. I couldn't sleep in the same space with plants. They are like little trees. Am I deranged? Take Isaac's notebook and bring it back when you can.'

I obeyed. In my own room, a sparse place, with no ornaments but a few pretty stalks in pots, I did not delay and seized the notebook. It was a tiny affair, three inches by five, with ruled pages that opened on a coiled wire. I read searchingly, hoping for something not easily evident. Sheindel by her melancholy innuendo had made me believe that in these few sheets Isaac had revealed the reason for his suicide. But it was all a disappointment. There was not a word of any importance. After a while I concluded that, whatever her motives, Sheindel was playing with me again. She meant to punish me for asking the unaskable. My inquisitiveness offended her; she had given me Isaac's notebook not to enlighten but to rebuke. The handwriting was recognizable yet oddly formed, shaky and even senile, like that of a man outdoors and deskless who scribbles in his palm or on his lifted knee or leaning on a bit of bark; and there was no doubt that the wrinkled leaves, with their ragged corners, had been in and out of someone's pocket. So I did not mistrust Sheindel's mad anecdote; this much was true: a park, Isaac, a notebook, all at once, but signifying no more than that a professor with a literary turn of mind had gone for a walk. There was even a green stain straight across one of the quotations, as if the pad had slipped grassward and been trod on.

I have forgotten to mention that the notebook, though scantily filled, was in three languages. The Greek I could not read at all, but it had the shape of verse. The Hebrew was simply a miscellany, drawn mostly from Leviticus and Deuteronomy. Among these I found the following extracts, transcribed not quite verbatim:

> Ye shall utterly destroy all the places of the gods, upon the high mountains, and upon the hills, and under every green tree.

> And the soul that turneth after familiar spirits to go a-whoring after them, I will cut him off from among his people.

These, of course, were ordinary unadorned notes, such as any classroom lecturer might commonly make to remind himself of the text, with a phrase cut out here and there for the sake of speeding his hand. Or I thought it possible that Isaac might at that time have been preparing a paper on the Talmudic commentaries for these passages. Whatever the case, the remaining quotations, chiefly from English poetry, interested me only slightly more. They were the elegiac favourites of a closeted Romantic. I was repelled by Isaac's Nature: it wore a capital letter, and smelled like my own Book Cellar. It was plain to me that he had lately grown painfully academic: he could not see a weed's tassel without finding a classical reference for it. He had put down a snatch of Byron, a smudge of Keats (like his Scriptural copyings, these too were quick and fragmented), a pair of truncated lines from Tennyson, and this unmarked and clumsy quatrain:

> And yet all is not taken. Still one Dryad
> >   Flits through the wood, one Oread skims the hill;
> > White in the whispering stream still gleams a Naiad;
> >   The beauty of the earth is haunted still.

All of this was so cloying and mooning and ridiculous, and so pedantic besides, that I felt ashamed for him. And yet there was almost nothing else, nothing to redeem him and nothing personal, only a sentence or two in his rigid self-controlled scholar's style, not unlike the starched little jokes of our correspondence. 'I am writing at dusk sitting on a stone in Trilham's Inlet Park, within sight of Trilham's Inlet, a bay to the north of the city, and within two yards of a slender tree, *Quercus velutina*, the age of which, should one desire to measure it, can be ascertained by (God forbid) cutting the bole and counting the rings. The man writing is thirty-five years old and ageing too rapidly, which may be ascertained by counting the rings under his poor myopic eyes.' Below this, deliberate and readily more legible than the rest, appeared three curious words:

Great Pan lives.

That was all. In a day or so I returned the notebook to Sheindel. I told myself that she had seven orphans to worry over, and repressed my anger at having been cheated.

She was waiting for me. 'I am so sorry, there was a letter in the notebook, it had fallen out. I found it on the carpet after you left.'

'Thank you, no,' I said. 'I've read enough out of Isaac's pockets.'

'Then why did you come to see me to begin with?'

'I came,' I said, 'just to see you.'

'You came for Isaac.' But she was more mocking than distraught. 'I gave you everything you needed to see what happened and still you don't follow. Here.' She held out a large law-sized paper. 'Read the letter.'

'I've read his notebook. If everything I need to fathom Isaac is in the notebook I don't need the letter.'

'It's a letter he wrote to explain himself,' she persisted.

'You told me Isaac left you no notes.'

'It was not written to me.'

I sat down on one of the dining room chairs and Sheindel put the page before me on the table. It lay face up on the lace divider. I did not look at it.

'It's a love letter,' Sheindel whispered. 'When they cut him down they found the notebook in one pocket and the letter in the other.'

I did not know what to say.

'The police gave me everything,' Sheindel said. 'Everything to keep.'

'A love letter?' I repeated.

'That is what such letters are commonly called.'

'And the police – they gave it to you, and that was the first you realized what' – I floundered after the inconceivable – 'what could be occupying him?'

'What could be occupying him,' she mimicked. 'Yes. Not until they took the letter and the notebook out of his pocket.'

'My God. His habit of life, his mind . . . I can't imagine it. You never guessed?'

'No.'

'These trips to the park—'

'He had become aberrant in many ways. I have described them to you.'

'But the park! Going off like that, alone – you didn't think he might be meeting a woman?'

'It was not a woman.'

Disgust like a powder clotted my nose. 'Sheindel, you're crazy.'

'I'm crazy, is that it? Read his confession! Read it! How long can I be the only one to know this thing? Do you want my brain to melt? Be my confidant,' she entreated so unexpectedly that I held my breath.

'You've said nothing to anyone?'

'Would they have recited such eulogies if I had? Read the letter!'

'I have no interest in the abnormal,' I said coldly.

She raised her eyes and watched me for the smallest space. Without any change in the posture of her suppliant head her laughter began; I have never since heard sounds like those – almost mouselike in density for fear of waking her sleeping daughters, but so rational in intent that it was like listening to astonished sanity rendered into a cackling fugue. She kept it up for a minute and then calmed herself. 'Please sit where you are. Please pay attention. I will read the letter to you myself.'

She plucked the page from the table with an orderly gesture. I saw that this letter had been scrupulously prepared; it was closely written. Her tone was cleansed by scorn.

' "My ancestors were led out of Egypt by the hand of God," ' she read.

'Is this how a love letter starts out?'

She moved on resolutely. ' "We were guilty of so-called abominations well-described elsewhere. Other peoples have been nourished on their mythologies. For aeons we have been weaned from all traces of the same." '

I felt myself becoming impatient. The fact was I had returned with a single idea: I meant to marry Isaac's widow when enough time had passed to make it seemly. It was my intention to court her with great subtlety at first, so that I would not appear to be presuming on her sorrow. But she was possessed. 'Sheindel, why do you want to inflict this treatise on me? Give it to the seminary, contribute it to a symposium of professors.'

'I would sooner die.'

At this I began to attend in earnest.

' "I will leave aside the wholly plausible position of so-called animism within the concept of the One God. I will omit a historical illumination of its continuous but covert expression even within the Fence of the Law. Creature, I leave these aside—" '

'What?' I yelped.

' "Creature," ' she repeated, spreading her nostrils. ' "What is human history? What is our philosophy? What is our religion? None of these teaches us poor human ones that we are alone in the universe, and even without them we would know that we are not. At a very young age I understood that a foolish man would not believe in a fish had he not had one enter his experience. Innumerable forms exist and have come to our eyes, and to the still deeper eye of the lens of our instruments; from this minute perception of what already is, it is easy to conclude that further forms are possible, that all forms are probable. God created the world not for Himself alone, or I would not now possess this consciousness with which I am enabled to address thee, Loveliness." '

'Thee,' I echoed, and swallowed a sad bewilderment.

'You must let me go on,' Sheindel said, and grimly went on. ' "It is false history, false philosophy, and false religion which declare to us human ones that we live among Things. The arts of physics and chemistry begin to teach us differently, but their way of compassion is new, and finds few to carry fidelity to its logical and beautiful end. The molecules dance inside all forms, and within the molecules dance the atoms, and within the atoms dance still profounder sources of divine vitality. There is nothing that is Dead. There is no Non-life. Holy life subsists even in the stone, even in the bones of dead dogs and dead men. Hence in God's fecundating Creation there is no possibility of Idolatry, and therefore no possibility of committing this so-called abomination." '

'My God, my God,' I wailed. 'Enough, Sheindel, it's more than enough, no more—'

'There is more,' she said.

'I don't want to hear it.'

'He stains his character for you? A spot, do you think? You will hear.' She took up in a voice which all at once reminded me of my father's: it was unforgiving. ' "Creature, I rehearse these matters though all our language is a breath to thee; as baubles for the juggler. Where we struggle to understand from day to day, and contemplate the grave for its riddle, the other breeds are born fulfilled in wisdom. Animal races conduct themselves without self-investigations; instinct is a higher and not a lower thing. Alas that we human ones — but for certain pitifully primitive approximations in those few reflexes and involuntary actions left to our bodies — are born bare of instinct! All that we unfortunates must resort to through science, art, philosophy, religion, all our imaginings and tormented strivings, all our meditations and vain questionings, all! — are expressed naturally and rightly in the beasts, the plants, the rivers, the stones. The reason is simple, it is our tragedy: our soul is included in us, it inhabits us, we contain it, when we seek our soul we must seek in ourselves. To *see* the soul, to confront it — that is divine wisdom. Yet how can we see into our dark selves? With the other races of being it is differently ordered. The soul of the plant does not reside in the chlorophyll, it may roam if it wishes, it may choose whatever form or shape it pleases. Hence the other breeds, being largely free of their soul and able to witness it, can live in peace. To see one's soul is to know all, to know all is to own the peace our philosophies futilely envisage. Earth displays two categories of soul: the free and the indwelling. We human ones are cursed with the indwelling—" '

'Stop!' I cried.

'I will not,' said the widow.

'Please, you told me he burned his fairy tales.'

'Did I lie to you? Will you say I lied?'

'Then for Isaac's sake why didn't you? If this isn't a fairy tale what do you want me to think it could be?'

'Think what you like.'

'Sheindel,' I said, 'I beg you, don't destroy a dead man's honour. Don't look at this thing again, tear it to pieces, don't continue with it.'

'I don't destroy his honour. He had none.'

'Please! Listen to yourself! My God, who was the man? Rabbi Isaac Kornfeld! Talk of honour! Wasn't he a teacher? Wasn't he a scholar?'

'He was a pagan.'

Her eyes returned without hesitation to their task. She commenced: ' "All these truths I learned only gradually, against my will and desire. Our teacher Moses did not speak of them; much may be said under this head. It was not out of ignorance that Moses failed to teach about those souls that are free. If I have learned what Moses knew, is this not because we are both men? He was a man, but God addressed him; it was God's will that our ancestors should no longer be slaves. Yet our ancestors, being stiffnecked, would not have abandoned their slavery in Egypt had they been taught of the free souls. They would have said: 'Let us stay, our bodies will remain enslaved in Egypt, but our souls will wander at their pleasure in Zion. If the cactus-plant stays rooted while its soul roams, why not also a man?' And if Moses had replied that only the world of Nature has the gift of the free soul, while man is chained to his, and that a man, to free his soul, must also free the body that is its vessel, they would have scoffed. 'How is it that men, and men alone, are different from the world of Nature? If this is so, then the condition of men is evil and unjust, and if this condition of ours is evil and unjust in general, what does it matter whether we are slaves in Egypt or citizens in Zion?' And they would not have done God's will and abandoned their slavery. Therefore Moses never spoke to them of the free souls, lest the people not do God's will and go out from Egypt." '

In an instant a sensation broke in me – it was entirely obscure, there was nothing I could compare it with, and yet I was certain I recognized it. And then I did. It hurtled me into childhood – it was the crisis of insight one experiences when one has just read out, for the first time, that conglomeration of figurines which makes a word. In that moment I penetrated beyond Isaac's alphabet into his language. I saw that he was on the side of possibility: he was both sane and inspired. His intention was not to accumulate mystery but to dispel it.

'All that part is brilliant,' I burst out.

Sheindel meanwhile had gone to the sideboard to take a sip of cold tea that was standing there. 'In a minute,' she said, and pursued her thirst. 'I have heard of drawings surpassing Rembrandt daubed by madmen who when released from the fit couldn't hold the chalk. What follows is beautiful, I warn you.'

'The man was a genius.'

'Yes.'

'Go on,' I urged.

She produced for me her clownish jeering smile. She read: ' "Sometimes in the desert journey on the way they would come to a watering-place, and some quick spry boy would happen to glimpse the soul of the spring (which the wild Greeks afterwards called naiad), but not knowing of the existence of the free souls he would suppose only that the moon had cast a momentary beam across the water. Loveliness, with the same innocence of accident I discovered thee. Loveliness, Loveliness." '

She stopped.

'Is that all?'

'There is more.'

'Read it.'

'The rest is the love letter.'

'Is it hard for you?' But I asked with more eagerness than pity.

'I was that man's wife, he scaled the Fence of the Law. For this God preserved me from the electric fence. Read it for yourself.'

Incontinently I snatched the crowded page.

' "Loveliness, in thee the joy, substantiation, and supernal succour of my theorem. How many hours through how many years I walked over the cilia-forests of our enormous aspiring vegetable-star, this light rootless seed that crawls in its single furrow, this shaggy mazy unimplanted cabbage-head of our earth! – never, all that time, all those days of unfulfilment, a white space like a desert thirst, never, never to grasp. I thought myself abandoned to the intrigue of my folly. At dawn, on a hillock, what seemed the very shape and seizing of the mound's nature – what was it? Only the haze of the sunball growing great through hoarfrost. The oread slipped from me, leaving her illusion; or was never there at all; or was there but for an instant, and ran away. What sly ones the free souls are! They have a comedy we human ones cannot dream: the laughing drunkard feels in himself the shadow of the shadow of the shadow of their wit, and only because he has made himself a vessel, as the two banks and the bed of a rivulet are the naiad's vessel. A naiad I may indeed have viewed whole: all seven of my daughters were once wading in a stream in a compact but beautiful park, of which I had much hope. The youngest being not yet two, and fretful, the older ones were told to keep her always by the hand, but they did not obey. I, having passed some way into the woods behind, all at once heard a scream and noise of splashes, and caught sight of a tiny body flying down into the water. Running back through the trees I could see the others bunched together, afraid, as the baby dived helplessly, all these little girls frozen in a garland – when suddenly one of them (it was too quick a movement for me to recognize which) darted to the struggler, who was now underwater, and pulled her up, and put an arm around her to soothe her. The arm was blue – blue. As blue as a lake. And fiercely, from my spot on the bank, panting, I began to count the little girls. I counted eight, thought myself not mad but delivered, again counted, counted seven, knew I had counted well before, knew I counted well even now. A blue-armed girl had come to wade among them. Which is to say the shape of a girl. I questioned my daughters: each in her fright believed one of the others had gone to pluck up the tiresome baby. None wore a dress with blue sleeves." '

'Proofs,' said the widow. 'Isaac was meticulous, he used to account for all his proofs always.'

'How?' My hand in tremor rustled Isaac's letter; the paper bleated as though whipped.

'By eventually finding a principle to cover them,' she finished maliciously. 'Well, don't rest even for me, you don't oblige me. You have a long story to go, long enough to make a fever.'

'Tea,' I said hoarsely.

She brought me her own cup from the sideboard, and I believed as I drank that I swallowed some of her mockery and gall.

'Sheindel, for a woman so pious you're a great sceptic.' And now the tremor had command of my throat.

'An atheist's statement,' she rejoined. 'The more piety, the more scepticism. A religious man comprehends this. Superfluity, excess of custom, and superstition would climb like a choking vine on the Fence of the Law if scepticism did not continually hack them away to make freedom for purity.'

I then thought her fully worthy of Isaac. Whether I was worthy of her I evaded putting to myself; instead I gargled some tea and returned to the letter.

' "It pains me to confess," ' I read, ' "how after that I moved from clarity to doubt and back again. I had no trust in my conclusions because all my experiences were evanescent. Everything certain I attributed to some other cause less certain. Every voice out of the moss I blamed on rabbits and squirrels. Every motion among leaves I called a bird, though there positively was no bird. My first sight of the Little People struck me as no more than a shudder of literary delusion, and I determined they could only be an instantaneous crop of mushrooms. But one night, a little after ten o'clock at the crux of summer – the sky still showed strings of light – I was wandering in this place, this place where they will find my corpse—" '

'Not for my sake,' said Sheindel when I hesitated.

'It's terrible,' I croaked, 'terrible.'

'Withered like a shell,' she said, as though speaking of the cosmos; and I understood from her manner that she had a fanatic's acquaintance with this letter, and knew it nearly by heart. She appeared to be thinking the words faster than I could bring them out, and for some reason I was constrained to hurry the pace of my reading.

' " – where they will find my corpse withered like the shell of an insect," ' I rushed on. ' "The smell of putrefaction lifted clearly from the bay. I began to speculate about my own body after I was dead – whether the soul would be set free immediately after the departure of life, or whether only gradually, as decomposition proceeded and more and more of the indwelling soul was released to freedom. But when I considered how a man's body is no better than a clay pot, a fact which none of our sages has ever contradicted, it seemed to me then that an indwelling soul by its own nature would be obliged to cling to its bit of pottery until the last crumb and grain had vanished into earth. I walked through the ditches of that black meadow grieving and swollen with self-pity. It came to me that while my poor bones went on decaying at their ease, my soul would have to linger inside them, waiting, despairing, longing to join the free ones. I cursed it for its gravity-despoiled, slow, interminably languishing purse of flesh; better to be encased in vapour, in wind, in a hair of a coconut! Who knows how long it takes the body of a man to shrink into gravel, and the gravel into sand, and the sand into vitamin? A hundred years? Two hundred, three hundred? A thousand perhaps! Is it not true that bones nearly intact are constantly being dug up by the palaeontologists two million years after burial?" – Sheindel,' I interrupted, 'this is death, not love. Where's the love letter to be afraid of here? I don't find it.'

'Continue,' she ordered. And then: 'You see I'm not afraid.'

'Not of love?'

'No. But you recite much too slowly. Your mouth is shaking. Are you afraid of death?'

I did not reply.

'Continue,' she said again. 'Go rapidly. The next sentence begins with an extraordinary thought.'

' "An extraordinary thought emerged in me. It was luminous, profound, and practical. More than that, it had innumerable precedents; the mythologies had documented it a dozen dozen times over. I recalled all those mortals reputed to have coupled with gods (a collective word, showing much common sense, signifying what our philosophies more abstrusely call Shekhina), and all that poignant miscegenation represented by centaurs, satyrs, mermaids, fauns, and so forth, not to speak of that even more famous mingling in Genesis, whereby the sons of God took the daughters of men for brides, producing giants and possibly also those abortions leviathan and behemoth of which we read in Job, along with unicorns and other chimeras and monsters abundant in Scripture, hence far from fanciful. There existed also the example of the succubus Lilith, who was often known to couple in the medieval ghetto even with pre-pubescent boys. By all these evidences I was emboldened in my confidence that I was surely not the first man to conceive such a desire in the history of our earth. Creature, the thought that took hold of me was this: if only I could couple with one of the free souls, the strength of the connection would likely wrest my own soul from my body – seize it, as if by a tongs, draw it out, so to say, to its own freedom. The intensity and force of my desire to capture one of these beings now became prodigious. I avoided my wife—" '

Here the widow heard me falter.

'Please,' she commanded, and I saw creeping in her face the completed turn of a sneer.

' " – lest I be depleted of potency at that moment (which might occur in any interval, even, I assumed, in my own bedroom) when

I should encounter one of the free souls. I was borne back again and again to the fetid viscosities of the Inlet, borne there as if on the rising stink of my own enduring and tedious putrefaction, the idea of which I could no longer shake off – I envisaged my soul as trapped in my last granule, and that last granule itself perhaps petrified, never to dissolve, and my soul condemned to minister to it throughout eternity! It seemed to me my soul must be released at once or be lost to sweet air forever. In a gleamless dark, struggling with this singular panic, I stumbled from ditch to ditch, strained like a blind dog for the support of solid verticality; and smacked my palm against bark. I looked up and in the black could not fathom the size of the tree – my head lolled forward, my brow met the trunk with all its gravings. I busied my fingers in the interstices of the bark's cuneiform. Then with forehead flat on the tree, I embraced it with both arms to measure it. My hands united on the other side. It was a young narrow weed, I did not know of what family. I reached to the lowest branch and plucked a leaf and made my tongue travel meditatively along its periphery to assess its shape: oak. The taste was sticky and exaltingly bitter. A jubilation lightly carpeted my groin. I then placed one hand (the other I kept around the tree's waist, as it were) in the bifurcation (disgustingly termed crotch) of that lowest limb and the elegant and devoutly firm torso, and caressed that miraculous juncture with a certain languor, which gradually changed to vigour. I was all at once savagely alert and deeply daring: I chose that single tree together with the ground near it for an enemy which in two senses would not yield: it would neither give nor give in. 'Come, come,' I called aloud to Nature. A wind blew out a braid of excremental malodour into the heated air. 'Come,' I called, 'couple with me, as thou didst with Cadmus, Rhoecus, Tithonus, Endymion, and that king Numa Pompilius to whom thou didst give secrets. As Lilith comes without a sign, so come thou. As the sons of God came to copulate with women, so now let a daughter of Shekhina the Emanation reveal herself to me. Nymph, come now, come now.'

' "Without warning I was flung to the ground. My face smashed into earth, and a flaky clump of dirt lodged in my open mouth. For the rest, I was on my knees, pressing down on my hands, with the fingernails clutching dirt. A superb ache lined my haunch. I began to weep because I was certain I had been ravished by some sinewy animal. I vomited the earth I had swallowed and believed I was defiled, as it is written: 'Neither shalt thou lie with any beast.' I lay sunk in the grass, afraid to lift my head to see if the animal still lurked. Through some curious means I had been fully positioned and aroused and exquisitely sated, all in half a second, in a fashion impossible to explain, in which, though I performed as with my own wife, I felt as if a preternatural rapine had been committed upon me. I continued prone, listening for the animal's breathing. Meanwhile, though every tissue of my flesh was gratified in its inmost awareness, a marvellous voluptuousness did not leave my body; sensual exultations of a wholly supreme and paradisal order, unlike anything our poets have ever defined, both flared and were intensely satisfied in the same moment. This salubrious and delightful perceptiveness excited my being for some time: a conjoining not dissimilar (in metaphor only; in actuality it cannot be described) from the magical contradiction of the tree and its issuance-of-branch at the point of bifurcation. In me were linked, *in the same instant*, appetite and fulfilment, delicacy and power, mastery and submissiveness, and other paradoxes of entirely remarkable emotional import.

' "Then I heard what I took to be the animal treading through the grass quite near my head, all cunningly: it withheld its breathing, then snored it out in a cautious and wisplike whirr that resembled a light wind through rushes. With a huge energy (my muscular force seemed to have increased) I leaped up in fear of my life; I had nothing to use for a weapon but – oh, laughable! – the pen I had been writing with in a little notebook I always carried about with me in those days (and still keep on my person as a self-shaming souvenir of my insipidness, my bookishness, my pitiable conjecture and wishfulness in a time when, not yet knowing thee, I knew nothing). What I saw was not an animal but a girl no older than my oldest daughter, who was then fourteen. Her skin was as perfect as an eggplant's and nearly of that colour. In height she was half as tall as I was. The second and third fingers of her hands – this I noticed at once – were peculiarly fused, one slotted into the other, like the ligula of a leaf. She was entirely bald and had no ears but rather a type of gill or envelope, one only, on the left side. Her toes displayed the same oddity I had observed in her fingers. She was neither naked nor clothed – that is to say, even though a part of her body, from hip to just below the breasts (each of which appeared to be a kind of velvety colourless pear, suspended from a very short, almost invisible stem), was luxuriantly covered with a flossy or spore-like material, this was a natural efflorescence in the manner of, with us, hair. All her sexual portion was wholly visible, as in any field flower. Aside from these express deviations, she was commandingly human in aspect, if unmistakably flowerlike. She was, in fact, the reverse of our hackneyed euphuism, as when we say a young girl blooms like a flower – she, on the contrary, seemed a flower transfigured into the shape of the most stupendously lovely child I had ever seen. Under the smallest push of wind she bent at her superlative waist; this, I recognized, and not the exhalations of some lecherous beast, was the breathlike sound that had alarmed me at her approach: these motions of hers made the blades of grass collide. (She herself, having no lungs, did not 'breathe'.) She stood bobbing joyfully before me, with a face as tender as a morning-glory, strangely phosphorescent: she shed her own light, in effect, and I had no difficulty in confronting her beauty.

' "Moreover, by experiment I soon learned that she was not only capable of language, but that she delighted in playing with it. This she literally could do – if I had distinguished her hands before anything else, it was because she had held them out to catch my first cry of awe. She either caught my words like balls or let them roll, or caught them and then darted off to throw them into the Inlet. I discovered that whenever I spoke I more or less pelted her; but she liked this, and told me ordinary human speech only tickled and amused, whereas laughter, being highly plosive, was something of an assault. I then took care to pretend much solemnity, though I was lightheaded with rapture. Her own 'voice' I apprehended rather than heard – which she, unable to imagine how we human ones are prisoned in sensory perception, found hard to conceive. Her sentences came to me not as a series of differentiated frequencies but (impossible to develop this idea in language) as a diffused cloud of field fragrances; yet to say that I assimilated her thought through the olfactory nerve would be a pedestrian distortion. All the same it was clear that whatever she said reached me in a shimmer of pellucid perfumes, and I understood her meaning with an immed-iacy of glee and with none of the ambiguities and suspiciousness of motive that surround our human communication.

' "Through this medium she explained that she was a dryad and that her name was Iripomonoéià (as nearly as I can render it in our narrowly limited orthography, and in this dunce's alphabet of ours which is notoriously impervious to odoriferous categories). She told me what I had already seized: that she had given me her love in response to my call.

' " 'Wilt thou come to any man who calls?' I asked.

' " 'All men call, whether realizing it or not. I and my sisters sometimes come to those who do not realize. Almost never, unless for sport, do we come to that man who calls knowingly – he wishes only to inhabit us out of perversity or boastfulness or to indulge a dreamed-of-disgust.'

' " 'Scripture does not forbid sodomy with the plants,' I exclaimed, but she did not comprehend any of this and lowered her hands so that my words would fly past her uncaught. 'I too called thee knowingly, not for perversity but for love of Nature.'

' " 'I have caught men's words before as they talked of Nature, you are not the first. It is not Nature they love so much as Death they fear. So Corylylyb my cousin received it in a season not long ago coupling in a harbour with one of your kind, one called Spinoza, one that had catarrh of the lung. I am of Nature and immortal and so I cannot pity your deaths. But return tomorrow and say Iripomonoéià.' Then she chased my last word to where she had kicked it, behind the tree. She did not come back. I ran to the tree and circled it diligently but she was lost for that night.

" 'Loveliness, all the foregoing, telling of my life and meditations until now, I have never before recounted to thee or any other. The rest is beyond mean telling: those rejoicings from midnight to dawn, when the greater phosphorescence of the whole shouting sky frightened thee home! How in a trance of happiness we coupled in the ditches, in the long grasses, behind a fountain, under a broken wall, once recklessly on the very pavement, with a bench for roof and trellis! How I was taught by natural arts to influence certain chemistries engendering explicit marvels, blisses, and transports no man has slaked himself with since Father Adam pressed out the forbidden chlorophyll of Eden! Loveliness, Loveliness, none like thee. No brow so sleek, no elbow-crook so fine, no eye so green, no waist so pliant, no limbs so pleasant and acute. None like immortal Iripomonoéià.

' "Creature, the moon filled and starved twice, and there was still no end to the glorious archaic newness of Iripomonoéià.

' "Then last night. Last night! I will record all with simplicity.

' "We entered a shallow ditch. In a sweet-smelling voice of

extraordinary redolence – so intense in its sweetness that even the barbaric stinks and wind-lifted farts of the Inlet were overpowered by it – Iripomonoéià inquired of me how I felt without my soul. I replied that I did not know this was my condition. 'Oh yes, your body is now an empty packet, that is why it is so light. Spring.' I sprang in air and rose effortlessly. 'You have spoiled yourself, spoiled yourself with confusions,' she complained, 'now by morning your body will be crumpled and withered and ugly, like a leaf in its sere hour, and never again after tonight will this place see you.' 'Nymph!' I roared, amazed by levitation. 'Oh, oh, that damaged,' she cried, 'you hit my eye with that noise,' and she wafted a deeper aroma, a leeklike mist, one that stung the mucous membranes. A white bruise disfigured her petally lid. I was repentant and sighed terribly for her injury. 'Beauty marred is for our kind what physical hurt is for yours,' she reproved me. 'Where you have pain, we have ugliness. Where you profane yourselves by immorality, we are profaned by ugliness. Your soul has taken leave of you and spoils our pretty game.' 'Nymph!' I whispered, 'heart, treasure, if my soul is separated how is it I am unaware?'

' " 'Poor man,' she answered, 'you have only to look and you will see the thing.' Her speech had now turned as acrid as an herb, and all that place reeked bitterly. 'You know I am a spirit. You know I must flash and dart. All my sisters flash and dart. Of all races we are the quickest. Our very religion is all-of-a-sudden. No one can hinder us, no one may delay us. But yesterday you undertook to detain me in your embrace, you stretched your kisses into years, you called me your treasure and your heart endlessly, your soul in its slow greed kept me close and captive, all the while knowing well how a spirit cannot stay and will not be fixed. I made to leap from you, but your obstinate soul held on until it was snatched straight from your frame and escaped with me. I saw it hurled out on to the pavement, the blue beginning of day was already seeping down, so I ran away and could say nothing until this moment.'

' " 'My soul is free? Free entirely? And can be seen?'

' " 'Free. If I could pity any living thing under the sky I would pity you for the sight of your soul. I do not like it, it conjures against me.'

' " 'My soul loves thee,' I urged in all my triumph, 'it is freed from the thousand-year grave!' I jumped out of the ditch like a frog, my legs had no weight; but the dryad sulked in the ground, stroking her ugly violated eye. 'Iripomonoéià, my soul will follow thee with thankfulness into eternity.'

' " 'I would sooner be followed by the dirty fog. I do not like that soul of yours. It conjures against me. It denies me, it denies every spirit and all my sisters and every nereid of the harbour, it denies all our multiplicity, and all gods diversiform, it spites even Lord Pan, it is an enemy, and you, poor man, do not know your own soul. Go, look at it, there it is on the road.'

' "I scudded back and forth under the moon.

' " 'Nothing, only a dusty old man trudging up there.'

' " 'A quite ugly old man?'

' " 'Yes, that is all. My soul is not there.'

' " 'With a matted beard and great fierce eyebrows?'

' " 'Yes, yes, one like that is walking on the road. He is half bent over under the burden of a dusty old bag. The bag is stuffed with books – I can see their ravelled bindings sticking out.'

' " 'And he reads as he goes?'

' " 'Yes, he reads as he goes.'

' " 'What is it he reads?'

' " 'Some huge and terrifying volume, heavy as a stone.' I peered forward in the moonlight. 'A Tractate. A Tractate of the Mishnah. Its leaves are so worn they break as he turns them, but he does not turn them often because there is much matter on a single page. He is so sad! Such antique weariness broods in his face! His throat is striped from the whip. His cheeks are folded like ancient flags, he reads the Law and breathes the dust.'

' " 'And are there flowers on either side of the road?'

' " 'Incredible flowers! Of every colour! And noble shrubs like mounds of green moss! And the cricket crackling in the field. He passes indifferent through the beauty of the field. His nostrils sniff his book as if flowers lay on the clotted page, but the flowers lick his feet. His feet are bandaged, his notched toenails gore the path. His prayer-shawl droops on his studious back. He reads the Law and breathes the dust and doesn't see the flowers and won't heed the cricket spitting in the field.'

' " 'That,' said the dryad, 'is your soul.' And was gone with all her odours.

' "My body sailed up to the road in a single hop. I alighted near the shape of the old man and demanded whether he were indeed the soul of Rabbi Isaac Kornfeld. He trembled but confessed. I asked if he intended to go with his books through the whole future without change, always with his Tractate in his hand, and he answered that he could do nothing else.

' " 'Nothing else! You, who I thought yearned for the earth! You, an immortal, free, and caring only to be bound to the Law!'

' "He held a dry arm fearfully before his face, and with the other arm hitched up his merciless bag on his shoulder. 'Sir,' he said, still quavering, 'didn't you wish to see me with your own eyes?'

' " 'I know your figure!' I shrieked. 'Haven't I seen that figure a hundred times before? On a hundred roads? It is not mine! I will not have it be mine!'

' " 'If you had not contrived to be rid of me, I would have stayed with you till the end. The dryad, who does not exist, lies. It was not I who clung to her but you, my body. Sir, all that has no real existence lies. In your grave beside you I would have sung you David's songs, I would have moaned Solomon's voice to your last grain of bone. But you expelled me, your ribs exile me from their fate, and I will walk here alone always, in my garden' – he scratched on his page – 'with my precious birds' – he scratched at the letters – 'and my darling trees' – he scratched at the tall side-column of commentary.

' "He was so impudent in his bravery – for I was all fleshliness and he all floppy wraith – that I seized him by the collar and shook him up and down, while the books on his back made a vast rubbing one on the other, and bits of shredding leather flew out like a rain.

' " 'The sound of the Law,' he said, 'is more beautiful than the crickets. The smell of the Law is more radiant than the moss. The taste of the Law exceeds clear water.'

' "At this nervy provocation – he more than any other knew my despair – I grabbed his prayer-shawl by its tassels and whirled around him once or twice until I had unwrapped it from him altogether, and wound it on my own neck and in one bound came to the tree.

' " 'Nymph!' I called to it. 'Spirit and saint! Iripomonoéià, come! None like thee, no brow so sleek, no elbow-crook so fine, no eye so green, no waist so pliant, no limbs so pleasant and acute. For pity of me, come, come.'

' "But she does not come.

' " 'Loveliness, come.'

' "She does not come.

' "Creature, see how I am coiled in the snail of this shawl as if in a leaf. I crouch to write my words. Let soul call thee lie, but body . . .

' " . . . body . . .

' " . . . fingers twist, knuckles dark as wood, tongue dries like grass, deeper now into silk . . .

' " . . . silk of pod of shawl, knees wilt, knuckles wither, neck . . ." '

Here the letter suddenly ended.

'You see? A pagan!' said Sheindel, and kept her spiteful smile. It was thick with audacity.

'You don't pity him,' I said, watching the contempt that glittered in her teeth.

'Even now you don't see? You can't follow?'

'Pity him,' I said.

'He who takes his own life does an abomination.'

For a long moment I considered her, 'You don't pity him? You don't pity him at all?'

'Let the world pity me.'

'Goodbye,' I said to the widow.

'You won't come back?'

I gave what amounted to a little bow of regret.

'I told you you came just for Isaac! But Isaac' – I was in terror of her cough, which was unmistakably laughter – 'Isaac disappoints. "A scholar. A rabbi. A remarkable Jew!" Ha! he disappoints you?'

'He was always an astonishing man.'

'But not what you thought,' she insisted. 'An illusion.'

'Only the pitiless are illusory. Go back to that park, Rebbetzin,' I advised her.

'And what would you like me to do there? Dance around a tree and call Greek names to the weeds?'

'Your husband's soul is in that park. Consult it.' But her low derisive cough accompanied me home: whereupon I remembered her earlier words and dropped three green houseplants down the toilet; after a journey of some miles through conduits they straightway entered Trilham's Inlet, where they decayed amid the civic excrement.

# The Fisherman and his Soul

## Oscar Wilde

*Wilde's stories are so full of joy and contentment that one is struck by
the odd contrast they make with the outcome of his life. He is one of
those writers, like Stevenson, with whom one wishes one could have been
friends. In* A Sort of Life, *Graham Greene tells the following anecdote
about his parents' visit to Naples in the 1890s: 'Once they had a curious
encounter. A stranger hearing them speak English asked whether he
might join them over their coffee. There was something familiar and to
them vaguely disagreeable about his face, but he kept them charmed by
his wit for more than an hour before he said goodbye. They didn't
exchange names even at parting and he left them to pay for his drink
which was certainly not coffee. It was some time before they realized in
whose company they had been. The stranger was Oscar Wilde, who not
very long before had been released from prison.'*

Every evening the young Fisherman went out upon the sea, and
threw his nets into the water.

When the wind blew from the land he caught nothing, or but
little at best, for it was a bitter and black-winged wind, and rough
waves rose up to meet it. But when the wind blew to the shore, the
fish came in from the deep, and swam into the meshes of his nets,
and he took them to the market-place and sold them.

Every evening he went out upon the sea, and one evening the net
was so heavy that hardly could he draw it into the boat. And he
laughed, and said to himself, 'Surely I have caught all the fish that
swim, or snared some dull monster that will be a marvel to men,
or some thing of horror that the great Queen will desire,' and
putting forth all his strength, he tugged at the coarse ropes till, like
lines of blue enamel round a vase of bronze, the long veins rose up
on his arms. He tugged at the thin ropes, and nearer and nearer

came the circle of flat corks, and the net rose at last to the top of the water.

But no fish at all was in it, nor any monster or thing of horror, but only a little Mermaid lying fast asleep.

Her hair was as a wet fleece of gold, and each separate hair as a thread of fine gold in a cup of glass. Her body was as white ivory, and her tail was of silver and pearl. Silver and pearl was her tail, and the green weeds of the sea coiled round it; and like sea-shells were her ears, and her lips were like sea-coral. The cold waves dashed over her cold breasts, and the salt glistened upon her eyelids.

So beautiful was she that when the young Fisherman saw her he was filled with wonder, and he put out his hand and drew the net close to him, and leaning over the side he clasped her in his arms. And when he touched her, she gave a cry like a startled seagull, and woke, and looked at him in terror with her mauve-amethyst eyes, and struggled that she might escape. But he held her tightly to him, and would not suffer her to depart.

And when she saw that she could in no way escape from him, she began to weep, and said, 'I pray thee let me go, for I am the only daughter of a King, and my father is aged and alone.'

But the young Fisherman answered, 'I will not let thee go save thou makest me a promise that whenever I call thee, thou wilt come and sing to me, for the fish delight to listen to the song of the Sea-folk and so shall my nets be full.'

'Wilt thou in very truth let me go, if I promise thee this?' cried the Mermaid.

'In very truth I will let thee go,' said the young Fisherman.

So she made him the promise he desired, and sware it by the oath of the Sea-folk. And he loosened his arms from about her, and she sank down into the water, trembling with a strange fear.

Every evening the young Fisherman went out upon the sea, and called to the Mermaid, and she rose out of the water and sang to him. Round and round her swam the dolphins, and the wild gulls wheeled above her head.

And she sang a marvellous song. For she sang of the Sea-folk who drive their flocks from cave to cave, and carry the little calves on their shoulders; of the Tritons who have long green beards, and hairy breasts, and blow through twisted conchs when the King passes by; of a palace of the King which is all of amber, with a roof of clear emerald, and a pavement of bright pearl; and of the gardens of the sea where the great filigrane fans of coral wave all day long, and the fish dart about like silver birds, and the anemones cling to the rocks, and the pinks bourgeon in the ribbed yellow sand. She sang of the big whales that come down from the north seas and have sharp icicles hanging to their fins; of the Sirens who tell of such wonderful things that the merchants have to stop their ears with wax lest they should hear them, and leap into the water and be drowned; of the sunken galleys with their tall masts, and the frozen sailors clinging to the rigging, and the mackerel swimming in and out of the open portholes; of the little barnacles who are great travellers, and cling to the keels of the ships and go round and round the world; and of the cuttlefish who live in the sides of the cliffs and stretch out their long black arms, and can make night come when they will it. She sang of the nautilus who has a boat of her own that is carved out of an opal and steered with a silken sail; of the happy Mermen who play upon harps and can charm the great Kraken to sleep; of the little children who catch hold of the slippery porpoises and ride laughing upon their backs; of the Mermaids who lie in the white foam and hold out their arms to the mariners; and of the sea-lions with their curved tusks, and the sea-horses with their floating manes.

And as she sang, all the tunny-fish came in from the deep to listen to her, and the young Fisherman threw his nets round them and caught them, and others he took with a spear. And when his boat was well-laden, the Mermaid would sink down into the sea, smiling at him.

Yet would she never come near him that he might touch her. Oftentimes he called to her and prayed of her, but she would not; and when he sought to seize her she dived into the water as a seal might dive, nor did he see her again that day. And each day the sound of her voice became sweeter to his ears. So sweet was her voice that he forgot his nets and his cunning, and had no care of his craft. Vermilion-finned and with eyes of bossy gold, the tunnies went by in shoals, but he heeded them not. His spear lay by his side unused, and his baskets of plaited osier were empty. With lips parted, and eyes dim with wonder, he sat idle in his boat and listened, listening till the sea-mists crept round him and the wandering moon stained his brown limbs with silver.

And one evening he called to her, and said: 'Little Mermaid, little Mermaid, I love thee. Take me for thy bridegroom for I love thee.'

But the Mermaid shook her head. 'Thou hast a human Soul,' she answered. 'If only thou wouldst send away thy Soul, then could I love thee.'

And the young Fisherman said to himself, 'Of what use is my Soul to me? I cannot see it. I may not touch it. I do not know it. Surely I will send it away from me, and much gladness shall be mine.' And a cry of joy broke from his lips, and standing up in the painted boat, he held out his arms to the Mermaid. 'I will send my Soul away,' he cried, 'and you shall be my bride, and I will be thy bridegroom, and in the depth of the sea we will dwell together, and all that thou hast sung of thou shalt show me, and all that thou desirest I will do, nor shall our lives be divided.'

And the little Mermaid laughed for pleasure and hid her face in her hands.

'But how shall I send my Soul from me?' cried the young Fisherman. 'Tell me how I may do it, and lo! it shall be done.'

'Alas! I know not,' said the little Mermaid: 'the Sea-folk have no souls.' And she sank down into the deep, looking wistfully at him.

Now early on the next morning, before the sun was the span of a man's hand above the hill, the young Fisherman went to the house of the Priest and knocked three times at the door.

The novice looked out through the wicket, and when he saw who it was, he drew back the latch and said to him, 'Enter.'

And the young Fisherman passed in, and knelt down on the sweet-smelling rushes on the floor, and cried to the Priest who was reading out of the Holy Book and said to him, 'Father, I am in love with one of the Sea-folk, and my Soul hindereth me from having my desire. Tell me how I can send my Soul away from me, for in truth I have no need of it. Of what value is my Soul to me? I cannot see it. I may not touch it. I do not know it.'

And the Priest beat his breast, and answered, 'Alack, alack, thou art mad, or hast eaten of some poisonous herb, for the Soul is the noblest part of man, and was given to us by God that we should nobly use it. There is no thing more precious than a human Soul, nor any earthly thing that can be weighed with it. It is worth all the gold that is in the world, and is more precious than the rubies of the kings. Therefore, my son, think not any more of this matter, for it is a sin that may not be forgiven. And as for the Sea-folk, they are lost, and they who would traffic with them are lost also. They are the beasts of the field that know not good from evil, and for them the Lord has not died.'

The young Fisherman's eyes filled with tears when he heard the bitter words of the Priest, and he rose up from his knees and said to him, 'Father, the Fauns live in the forest and are glad, and on the rocks sit the Mermen with their harps of red gold. Let me be as they are, I beseech thee, for their days are as the days of flowers. And as for my Soul, what doth my Soul profit me, if it stand between me and the thing that I love?'

'The love of the body is vile,' cried the Priest, knitting his brows, 'and vile and evil are the pagan things God suffers to wander through His world. Accursed be the Fauns of the woodland, and accursed be the singers of the sea! I have heard them at night-time, and they have sought to lure me from my beads. They tap at the window and laugh. They whisper into my ears the tale of their perilous joys. They tempt me with temptations, and when I would pray they make mouths at me. They are lost, I tell thee, they are lost. For them there is no heaven or hell, and in neither shall they praise God's name.'

'Father,' cried the young Fisherman, 'thou knowest not what thou sayest. Once in my net I snared the daughter of a King. She is fairer than the morning star, and whiter than the moon. For her body I would give my Soul, and for her love I would surrender heaven. Tell me what I ask of thee, and let me go in peace.'

'Away! Away!' cried the Priest: 'thy leman is lost, and thou shalt be lost with her.' And he gave him no blessing, but drove him from his door.

And the young Fisherman went down into the market-place, and he walked slowly, and with bowed head, as one who is in sorrow.

And when the merchants saw him coming, they began to whisper to each other, and one of them came forth to meet him, and called him by name, and said to him, 'What hast thou to sell?'

'I will sell thee my Soul,' he answered: 'I pray thee buy it off me, for I am weary of it. Of what use is my Soul to me? I cannot see it. I may not touch it. I do not know it.'

But the merchants mocked at him, and said, 'Of what use is a man's Soul to us? It is not worth a clipped piece of silver. Sell us thy body for a slave, and we will clothe thee in sea purple, and put a ring upon thy finger, and make thee the minion of the great Queen. But talk not of the Soul, for to us it is nought, nor has it any value for our service.'

And the young Fisherman said to himself: 'How strange a thing this is! The Priest telleth me that the Soul is worth all the gold in the world, and the merchants say that it is not worth a clipped piece of silver.' And he passed out of the market-place, and went down to the shore of the sea, and began to ponder on what he should do.

And at noon he remembered how one of his companions, who was a gatherer of samphire, had told him of a certain young Witch who dwelt in a cave at the head of the bay and was very cunning in her witcheries. And he set to and ran, so eager was he to get rid of his Soul, and a cloud of dust followed him as he sped round the sand of the shore. By the itching of her palm the young Witch knew his coming, and she laughed and let down her red hair. With her red hair falling around her, she stood at the opening of the cave, and in her hand she had a spray of wild hemlock that was blossoming.

'What d'ye lack? What d'ye lack?' she cried, as he came panting up the steep, and bent down before her. 'Fish for thy net, when the wind is foul? I have a little reed-pipe, and when I blow on it the mullet come sailing into the bay. But it has a price, pretty boy, it has a price. What d'ye lack? What d'ye lack? A storm to wreck the ships, and wash the chests of rich treasure ashore? I have more storms than the wind has, for I serve one who is stronger than the wind, and with a sieve and a pail of water I can send the great galleys to the bottom of the sea. But I have a price, pretty boy, I have a price. What d'ye lack? What d'ye lack? I know a flower that grows in the valley, none knows it but I. It has purple leaves, and a star in its heart, and its juice is as white as milk. Shouldst thou touch with this flower the hard lips of the Queen, she would follow thee all over the world. Out of the bed of the King she would rise, and over the whole world she would follow thee. And it has a price, pretty boy, it has a price. What d'ye lack? What d'ye lack? I can pound a toad in a mortar, and make broth of it, and stir the broth with a dead man's hand. Sprinkle it on thine enemy while he sleeps, and he will turn into a black viper, and his own mother will slay him. With a wheel I can draw the Moon from heaven, and in a crystal I can show thee Death. What d'ye lack? What d'ye lack?

Tell me thy desire, and I will give it thee, and thou shalt pay me a price, pretty boy, thou shalt pay me a price.'

'My desire is but for a little thing,' said the young Fisherman, 'yet hath the Priest been wroth with me, and driven me forth. It is but for a little thing, and the merchants have mocked at me, and denied me. Therefore am I come to thee, though men call thee evil, and whatever be thy price I shall pay it.'

'What wouldst thou?' asked the Witch, coming near to him.

'I would send my Soul away from me,' answered the young Fisherman.

The Witch grew pale, and shuddered, and hid her face in her blue mantle. 'Pretty boy, pretty boy,' she muttered, 'that is a terrible thing to do.'

He tossed his brown curls and laughed. 'My Soul is nought to me,' he answered. 'I cannot see it. I may not touch it. I do not know it.'

'What wilt thou give me if I tell thee?' asked the Witch, looking down at him with her beautiful eyes.

'Five pieces of gold,' he said, 'and my nets, and the wattled house where I live, and the painted boat in which I sail. Only tell me how to get rid of my Soul, and I will give thee all that I possess.'

She laughed mockingly at him, and struck him with the spray of hemlock. 'I can turn the autumn leaves into gold,' she answered, 'and I can weave the pale moonbeams into silver if I will it. He whom I serve is richer than all the kings of this world, and has their dominions.'

'What then shall I give thee,' he cried, 'if thy price be neither gold nor silver?'

The Witch stroked his hair with her thin white hand. 'Thou must dance with me, pretty boy,' she murmured, and she smiled at him as she spoke.

'Nought but that?' cried the young Fisherman in wonder, and he rose to his feet.

'Nought but that,' she answered, and she smiled at him again.

'Then at sunset in some secret place we shall dance together,' he said, 'and after that we have danced thou shalt tell me the thing which I desire to know.'

She shook her head. 'When the moon is full, when the moon is full,' she muttered. Then she peered all round, and listened. A blue bird rose screaming from its nest and circled over the dunes, and three spotted birds rustled through the coarse grey grass and whistled to each other. There was no other sound save the sound of a wave fretting the smooth pebbles below. So she reached out her hand, and drew him near to her and put her dry lips close to his ear.

'Tonight thou must come to the top of the mountain,' she whispered. 'It is a Sabbath, and He will be there.'

The young Fisherman started and looked at her, and she showed her white teeth and laughed. 'Who is He of whom thou speakest?' he asked.

'It matters not,' she answered. 'Go thou tonight, and stand under the branches of the hornbeam, and wait for my coming. If a black dog runs towards thee, strike it with a rod of willow, and it will go away. If an owl speak to thee, make it no answer. When the moon is full I shall be with thee, and we will dance together on the grass.'

'But wilt thou swear to me to tell me how I may send my Soul from me?' he made question.

She moved out into the sunlight, and through her red hair rippled the wind. 'By the hoofs of the goat I swear it,' she made answer.

'Thou art the best of the witches,' cried the young Fisherman, 'and I will surely dance with thee tonight on the top of the mountain. I would indeed that thou hadst asked of me either gold or silver. But such as thy price is thou shalt have it, for it is but a little thing.' And he doffed his cap to her, and bent his head low, and ran back to the town filled with a great joy.

And the Witch watched him as he went, and when he had passed from her sight she entered her cave, and having taken a mirror from a box of carved cedarwood, she set it up on a frame, and burned vervain on lighted charcoal before it, and peered through the coils of the smoke. And after a time she clenched her hands in anger. 'He should have been mine,' she muttered, 'I am as fair as she is.'

And that evening, when the moon had risen, the young Fisherman climbed up to the top of the mountain, and stood under the branches of the hornbeam. Like a targe of polished metal the round sea lay at his feet, and the shadows of the fishing-boats moved in the little bay. A great owl, with yellow sulphurous eyes, called to him by his name, but he made it no answer. A black dog ran towards him and snarled. He struck it with a rod of willow, and it went away whining.

At midnight the witches came flying through the air like bats. 'Phew!' they cried, as they lit upon the ground, 'there is some one here we know not!' and they sniffed about, and chattered to each other, and made signs. Last of all came the young Witch, with her red hair streaming in the wind. She wore a dress of gold tissue embroidered with peacocks' eyes, and a little cap of green velvet was on her head.

'Where is he, where is he?' shrieked the witches when they saw her, but she only laughed, and ran to the hornbeam, and taking the Fisherman by the hand she led him out into the moonlight and began to dance.

Round and round they whirled, and the young Witch jumped so high that he could see the scarlet heels of her shoes. Then right across the dancers came the sound of the galloping of a horse, but no horse was to be seen, and he felt afraid.

'Faster,' cried the Witch, and she threw her arms about his neck, and her breath was hot upon his face. 'Faster, faster!' she cried, and the earth seemed to spin beneath his feet, and his brain grew troubled, and a great terror fell on him, as of some evil thing that was watching him, and at last he became aware that under the shadow of a rock there was a figure that had not been there before.

It was a man dressed in a suit of black velvet, cut in the Spanish fashion. His face was strangely pale, but his lips were like a proud red flower. He seemed weary, and was leaning back toying in a listless manner with the pommel of his dagger. On the grass beside him lay a plumed hat, and a pair of riding-gloves gauntleted with gilt lace, and sewn with seed-pearls wrought into a curious device. A short cloak lined with sables hung from his shoulder, and his delicate white hands were gemmed with rings. Heavy eyelids drooped over his eyes.

The young Fisherman watched him, as one snared in a spell. At last their eyes met, and wherever he danced it seemed to him that the eyes of the man were upon him. He heard the Witch laugh, and caught her by the waist, and whirled her madly round and round.

Suddenly a dog bayed in the wood, and the dancers stopped, and going up two by two, knelt down, and kissed the man's hands. As they did so, a little smile touched his proud lips, as a bird's wing touches the water and makes it laugh. But there was disdain in it. He kept looking at the young Fisherman.

'Come! Let us worship,' whispered the Witch, and she led him up, and a great desire to do as she besought him seized on him, and he followed her. But when he came close, and without knowing why he did it, he made on his breast the sign of the Cross, and called upon the holy name.

No sooner had he done so than the witches screamed like hawks and flew away, and the pallid face that had been watching him twitched with a spasm of pain. The man went over to a little wood, and whistled. A jennet with silver trappings came running to meet him. As he leapt upon the saddle he turned round, and looked at the young Fisherman sadly.

And the Witch with the red hair tried to fly away also, but the Fisherman caught her by her wrists, and held her fast.

'Loose me,' she cried, 'and let me go. For thou hast named what should not be named, and shown the sign that may not be looked at.'

'Nay,' he answered, 'but I will not let thee go till thou hast told me the secret.'

'What secret?' said the Witch, wrestling with him like a wild cat, and biting her foam-flecked lips.

'Thou knowest,' he made answer.

Her grass-green eyes grew dim with tears, and she said to the Fisherman, 'Ask me anything but that!'

He laughed, and held her all the more tightly.

And when she saw that she could not free herself, she whispered to him, 'Surely I am as fair as the daughter of the sea, and as comely as those that dwell in the blue waters,' and she fawned on him and put her face close to his.

But he thrust her back frowning, and said to her, 'If thou keepest not the promise that thou madest to me I will slay thee for a false witch.'

She grew grey as a blossom of the Judas tree, and shuddered. 'Be it so,' she muttered. 'It is thy Soul and not mine. Do with it as thou wilt.' And she took from her girdle a little knife that had a handle of green viper's skin, and gave it to him.

'What shall this serve me?' he asked of her, wondering.

She was silent for a few moments, and a look of terror came over her face. Then she brushed her hair back from her forehead, and smiling strangely she said to him, 'What men call the shadow of the body is not the shadow of the body, but is the body of the Soul. Stand on the seashore with thy back to the moon, and cut away from around thy feet thy shadow, which is thy Soul's body, and bid thy soul leave thee, and it will do so.'

The young Fisherman trembled. 'Is this true?' he murmured.

'It is true, and I would that I had not told thee of it,' she cried, and she clung to his knees weeping.

He put her from him and left her in the rank grass, and going to the edge of the mountain he placed the knife in his belt and began to climb down.

And his Soul that was within him called out to him and said, 'Lo! I have dwelt with thee for all these years, and have been thy servant. Send me not away from thee now, for what evil have I done thee?'

And the young Fisherman laughed. 'Thou hast done me no evil, but I have no need of thee,' he answered. 'The world is wide, and there is Heaven also, and Hell, and that dim twilight house that lies between. Go wherever thou wilt, but trouble me not, for my love is calling to me.'

And his Soul besought him piteously, but he heeded it not, but leapt from crag to crag, being surefooted as a wild goat, and at last he reached the level ground and the yellow shore of the sea.

Bronze-limbed and well-knit, like a statue wrought by a Grecian, he stood on the sand with his back to the moon, and out of the foam came white arms that beckoned to him, and out of the waves rose dim forms that did him homage. Before him lay his shadow, which was the body of his Soul, and behind him hung the moon in the honey-coloured air.

And his Soul said to him, 'If indeed thou must drive me from thee, send me not forth without a heart. The world is cruel, give me thy heart to take with me.'

He tossed his head and smiled. 'With what should I love my love if I gave thee my heart?' he cried.

'Nay, but be merciful,' said his Soul: 'give me thy heart, for the world is very cruel, and I am afraid.'

'My heart is my love's,' he answered, 'therefore tarry not, but get thee gone.'

'Should I not love also?' asked his Soul.

'Get thee gone, for I have no need of thee,' cried the young Fisherman, and he took the little knife with its handle of green viper's skin, and cut away his shadow from around his feet, and it rose up and stood before him, and looked at him, and it was even as himself.

He crept back, and thrust the knife into his belt, and a feeling of awe came over him. 'Get thee gone,' he murmured, 'and let me see thy face no more.'

'Nay, but we must meet again,' said the Soul. Its voice was low and flute-like, and its lips hardly moved while it spake.

'How shall we meet?' cried the young Fisherman. 'Thou wilt not follow me into the depths of the sea?'

'Once every year I will come to this place, and call to thee,' said the Soul. 'It may be that thou wilt have need of me.'

'What need should I have of thee?' cried the young Fisherman, 'but be it as thou wilt,' and he plunged into the water, and the Tritons blew their horns, and the little Mermaid rose up to meet him, and put her arms around his neck and kissed him on the mouth.

And the Soul stood on the lonely beach and watched them. And when they had sunk down into the sea, it went weeping away over the marshes.

And after a year was over the Soul came down to the shore of the sea and called to the young Fisherman, and he rose out of the deep, and said, 'Why dost thou call to me?'

And the Soul answered, 'Come nearer, that I may speak with thee, for I have seen marvellous things.'

So he came nearer, and couched in the shallow water, and leaned his head upon his hand and listened.

And the Soul said to him, 'When I left thee I turned my face to the East and journeyed. From the East cometh everything that is wise. Six days I journeyed, and on the morning of the seventh day I came to a hill that is in the country of the Tartars. I sat down under the shade of a tamarisk tree to shelter myself from the sun. The land was dry and burnt up with the heat. The people went to and fro over the plains like flies crawling upon a disk of polished copper.

'When it was noon a cloud of red dust rose up from the flat rim of the land. When the Tartars saw it, they strung their painted bows, and having leapt upon their little horses they galloped to meet it. The women fled screaming to the waggons, and hid themselves behind the felt curtains.

'At twilight the Tartars returned, but five of them were missing, and of those that came back not a few had been wounded. They harnessed their horses to the waggons and drove hastily away. Three jackals came out of a cave and peered after them. Then they sniffed up the air with their nostrils, and trotted off in the opposite direction.

'When the moon rose I saw a camp-fire burning on the plain, and went towards it. A company of merchants were seated round it on carpets. Their camels were picketed behind them, and the Negroes who were their servants were pitching tents of tanned skin upon the sand, and making a high wall of the prickly pear.

'As I came near them, the chief of the merchants rose up and drew his sword and asked me my business.

'I answered that I was a Prince in my own land, and that I had escaped from the Tartars, who had sought to make me their slave. The chief smiled, and showed me five heads fixed upon long reeds of bamboo.

'Then he asked me who was the prophet of God, and I answered him Mohammed.

'When he heard the name of the false prophet, he bowed and took me by the hand, and placed me by his side. A Negro brought me some mare's milk in a wooden dish, and a piece of lamb's flesh roasted.

'At daybreak we started on our journey. I rode on a red-haired camel by the side of the chief, and a runner ran before us carrying a spear. The men of war were on either hand, and the mules followed with the merchandise. There were forty camels in the caravan, and the mules were twice forty in number.

'We went from the country of the Tartars into the country of those who curse the Moon. We saw the Gryphons guarding their gold on the white rocks, and the scaled Dragons sleeping in their caves. As we passed over the mountains we held our breath lest the snows might fall on us, and each man tied a veil of gauze before his eyes. As we passed through the valleys the Pygmies shot arrows at us from the hollows of the trees, and at night-time we heard the wild men beating on their drums. When we came to the Tower of Apes we set fruits before them, and they did not harm us. When we came to the Tower of Serpents we gave them warm milk in bowls of brass, and they let us go by. Three times in our journey we came to the banks of the Oxus. We crossed it on rafts of wood with great bladders of blown hide. The river-horses raged against us and sought to slay us. When the camels saw them they trembled.

'The kings of each city levied tolls on us, but would not suffer us to enter their gates. They threw us bread over the walls, little maizecakes baked in honey and cakes of fine flour filled with dates. For every hundred baskets we gave them a bead of amber.

'When the dwellers in the villages saw us coming, they poisoned the wells and fled to the hill-summits. We fought with the Magadae who are born old, and grow younger and younger every year, and die when they are little children; and with the Laktroi who say that they are the sons of tigers, and paint themselves yellow and black; and with the Aurantes who bury their dead on the tops of trees, and themselves live in dark caverns lest the Sun, who is their god, should slay them; and with the Krimnians who worship a crocodile, and give it ear-rings of green grass, and feed it with butter and fresh fowls; and with the Agazonbae, who are dog-faced; and with the Sibans, who have horses' feet, and run more swiftly than horses. A third of our company died in battle, and a third died of want. The rest murmured against me, and said that I had brought them an evil fortune. I took a horned adder from beneath a stone and let it sting me. When they saw that I did not sicken they grew afraid.

'In the fourth month we reached the city of Illel. It was night-time when we came to the grove that is outside the walls, and the air was sultry, for the Moon was travelling in Scorpion. We took the ripe pomegranates from the trees, and brake them, and drank their sweet juices. Then we lay down on our carpets and waited for the dawn.

'And at dawn we rose and knocked at the gate of the city. It was wrought out of red bronze, and carved with sea-dragons and dragons that have wings. The guards looked down from the battlements and asked us our business. The interpreter of the caravan answered that we had come from the island of Syria with much merchandise. They took hostages, and told us that they would open the gate to us at noon, and bade us tarry till then.

'When it was noon they opened the gate, and as we entered in the people came crowding out of the houses to look at us, and a crier went round the city crying through a shell. We stood in the market-place, and the Negroes uncorded the bales of figured cloths and opened the carved chests of sycamore. And when they had ended their task, the merchants set forth their strange wares, the waxed linen from Egypt, and the painted linen from the country of the Ethiops, the purple sponges from Tyre and the blue hangings from Sidon, the cups of cold amber and the fine vessels of glass and the curious vessels of burnt clay. From the roof of a house a company of women watched us. One of them wore a mask of gilded leather.

'And on the first day the priests came and bartered with us, and on the second day came the nobles, and on the third day came the craftsmen and the slaves. And this is their custom with all merchants as long as they tarry in the city.

'And we tarried for a moon, and when the moon was waning, I wearied and wandered away through the streets of the city and came to the garden of its god. The priests in their yellow robes moved silently through the green trees, and on a pavement of black marble stood the rose-red house in which the god had his dwelling. Its doors were of powdered lacquer, and bulls and peacocks were wrought on them in raised and polished gold. The tilted roof was of sea-green porcelain and the jutting eaves were festooned with little bells. When the white doves flew past, they struck the bells with their wings and made them tinkle.

'In front of the temple was a pool of clear water paved with veined onyx. I lay down beside it, and with my pale fingers I touched the broad leaves. One of the priests came towards me and stood behind me. He had sandals on his feet, one of soft serpent-skin and the other of birds' plumage. On his head was a mitre of black felt decorated with silver crescents. Seven yellows were woven into his robe, and his frizzed hair was stained with antimony.

'And after a little while he spake to me, and asked me my desire.

'I told him that my desire was to see the god.

' "The god is hunting," said the priest, looking strangely at me with his small slanting eyes.

' "Tell me in what forest, and I will ride with him," I answered.

'He combed out the soft fringes of his tunic with his long pointed nails. "The god is asleep," he murmured.

' "Tell me on what couch, and I will watch by him," I answered.

' "The god is at the feast," he cried.

' "If the wine be sweet, I will drink it with him, and if it be bitter I will drink it with him also," was my answer.

'He bowed his head in wonder, and, taking me by the hand, he raised me up, and led me into the temple.

'And in the first chamber I saw an idol seated on a throne of jasper bordered with great orient pearls. It was carved out of ebony, and in stature was of the stature of a man. On its forehead was a ruby, and thick oil dripped from its hair on to its thighs. Its feet were red with the blood of a newly-slain kid, and its loins girt with a copper belt that was studded with seven beryls.

'And I said to the priest, "Is this the god?" And he answered me, "This is the god."

' "Show me the god," I cried, "or I will surely slay thee." And I touched his hand, and it became withered.

'And the priest besought me, saying, "Let my lord heal his servant, and I will show him the god."

'So I breathed with my breath upon his hand, and it became whole again, and he trembled and led me into the second chamber, and I saw an idol standing on a lotus of jade hung with great emeralds. It was carved out of ivory, and in stature was twice the stature of a man. On its forehead was a chrysolite, and its breasts were smeared with myrrh and cinnamon. In one hand it held a crooked sceptre of jade, and in the other a round crystal. It wore buskins of brass, and its thick neck was circled with a circle of selenites.

'And I said to the priest, "Is this the god?" And he answered me, "This is the god."

' "Show me the god," I cried, "or I will surely slay thee." And I touched his eyes, and they became blind.

'And the priest besought me, saying, "Let my lord heal his servant, and I will show him the god."

'So I breathed with my breath upon his eyes, and the sight came back to them, and he trembled again, and led me into the third chamber, and lo! there was no idol in it, nor image of any kind, but only a mirror of round metal set on an altar of stone.

'And I said to the priest, "Where is the god?"

'And he answered me: "There is no god but this mirror that thou seest, for this is the Mirror of Wisdom. And it reflecteth all things that are in heaven and on earth, save only the face of him who looketh into it. This it reflecteth not, so that he who looketh into it may be wise. Many other mirrors are there, but they are mirrors of Opinion. This only is the Mirror of Wisdom. And they who possess this mirror know everything, nor is there anything hidden from them. And they who possess it not have not Wisdom. Therefore is it the god, and we worship it." And I looked into the mirror, and it was even as he had said to me.

'And I did a strange thing, but what I did matters not, for in a valley that is but a day's journey from this place have I hidden the

Mirror of Wisdom. Do but suffer me to enter into thee again and be thy servant, and thou shalt be wiser than all the wise men, and Wisdom shall be thine. Suffer me to enter into thee, and none will be as wise as thou.'

But the young Fisherman laughed. 'Love is better than Wisdom,' he cried, 'and the little Mermaid loves me.'

'Nay, but there is nothing better than Wisdom,' said the Soul.

'Love is better,' answered the young Fisherman, and he plunged into the deep, and the Soul went weeping away over the marshes.

And after the second year was over, the Soul came down to the shore of the sea, and called to the young Fisherman and he rose out of the deep and said, 'Why dost thou call to me?'

And the Soul answered, 'Come nearer, that I may speak with thee, for I have seen marvellous things.'

So he came nearer, and couched in the shallow water, and leaned his head upon his hand and listened.

And the Soul said to him, 'When I left thee, I turned my face to the South and journeyed. From the South cometh everything that is precious. Six days I journeyed along the highways that lead to the city of Ashter, along the dusty red-dyed highways by which the pilgrims are wont to go did I journey, and on the morning of the seventh day I lifted up my eyes, and lo! the city lay at my feet, for it is in a valley.

'There are nine gates to this city, and in front of each gate stands a bronze horse that neighs when the Bedouins come down from the mountains. The walls are cased with copper, and the watch-towers on the wall are roofed with brass. In every tower stands an archer with a bow in his hand. At sunrise he strikes with an arrow on a gong, and at sunset he blows through a horn of horn.

'When I sought to enter, the guards stopped me and asked of me who I was. I made answer that I was a Dervish and on my way to the city of Mecca, where there was a green veil on which the Koran was embroidered in silver letters by the hands of the angels. They were filled with wonder, and entreated me to pass in.

'Inside it is even as a bazaar. Surely thou shouldst have been with me. Across the narrow streets the gay lanterns of paper flutter like large butterflies. When the wind blows over the roofs they rise and fall as painted bubbles do. In front of their booths sit the merchants on silken carpets. They have straight black beards, and their turbans are covered with golden sequins, and long strings of amber and carved peach-stones glide through their cool fingers. Some of them sell galbanum and nard, and curious perfumes from the islands of the Indian Sea, and the thick oil of red roses, and myrrh and little nail-shaped cloves. When one stops to speak to them, they throw pinches of frankincense upon a charcoal brazier and make the air sweet. I saw a Syrian who held in his hands a thin rod like a reed. Grey threads of smoke came from it, and its odour as it burned was as the odour of the pink almond in spring. Others sell silver bracelets embossed all over with creamy blue turquoise stones, and anklets of brass wire fringed with little pearls, and tigers' claws set in gold, and the claws of that gilt cat, the leopard, set in gold also, and ear-rings of pierced emerald, and finger-rings of hollowed jade. From the tea-houses comes the sound of the guitar, and the opium-smokers with their white smiling faces look out at the passers-by.

'Of a truth thou shouldst have been with me. The wine-sellers elbow their way through the crowd with great black skins on their shoulders. Most of them sell the wine of Schiraz, which is as sweet as honey. They serve it in little metal cups and strew rose leaves upon it. In the market-place stand the fruitsellers, who sell all kinds of fruit: ripe figs, with their bruised purple flesh, melons, smelling of musk and yellow as topazes, citrons and rose-apples and clusters of white grapes, round red-gold oranges, and oval lemons of green gold. Once I saw an elephant go by. Its trunk was painted with vermilion and turmeric, and over its ears it had a net of crimson silk cord. It stopped opposite one of the booths and began eating the oranges, and the man only laughed. Thou canst not think how strange a people they are. When they are glad they go to the bird-sellers and buy of them a caged bird, and set it free that their joy may be greater, and when they are sad they scourge themselves with thorns that their sorrow may not grow less.

'One evening I met some Negroes carrying a heavy palanquin through the bazaar. It was made of gilded bamboo, and the poles were of vermilion lacquer studded with brass peacocks. Across the windows hung thin curtains of muslin embroidered with beetles' wings and with tiny seed-pearls, and as it passed by a pale-faced Circassian looked out and smiled at me. I followed behind, and the Negroes hurried their steps and scowled. But I did not care. I felt a great curiosity come over me.

'At last they stopped at a square white house. There were no windows to it, only a little door like the door of a tomb. They set down the palanquin and knocked three times with a copper hammer. An Armenian in a caftan of green leather peered through the wicket, and when he saw them he opened, and spread a carpet on the ground, and the woman stepped out. As she went in, she turned round and smiled at me again. I had never seen any one so pale.

'When the moon rose I returned to the same place and sought for the house, but it was no longer there. When I saw that, I knew who the woman was, and wherefore she had smiled at me.

'Certainly thou shouldst have been with me. On the feast of the New Moon the young Emperor came forth from his palace and went into the mosque to pray. His hair and beard were dyed with rose-leaves, and his cheeks were powdered with a fine gold dust. The palms of his feet and hands were yellow with saffron.

'At sunrise he went forth from his palace in a robe of silver, and at sunset he returned to it again in a robe of gold. The people flung themselves on the ground and hid their faces, but I would not do so. I stood by the stall of a seller of dates and waited. When the Emperor saw me, he raised his painted eyebrows and stopped. I stood quite still, and made him no obeisance. The people marvelled at my boldness, and counselled me to flee from the city. I paid no heed to them, but went and sat with the sellers of strange gods, who by reason of their craft are abominated. When I told them what I had done, each of them gave me a god and prayed me to leave them.

'That night, as I lay on a cushion in the tea-house that is in the Street of Pomegranates, the guards of the Emperor entered and led me to the palace. As I went in they closed each door behind me, and put a chain across it. Inside was a great court with an arcade running all round. The walls were of white alabaster, set here and there with blue and green tiles. The pillars were of green marble, and the pavement of a kind of peach-blossom marble. I had never seen anything like it before.

'As I passed across the court two veiled women looked down from a balcony and cursed me. The guards hastened on, and the butts of the lances rang upon the polished floor. They opened a gate of wrought ivory, and I found myself in a watered garden of seven terraces. It was planted with tulip-cups and moon-flowers, and silver-studded aloes. Like a slim reed of crystal a fountain hung in the dusky air. The cypress-trees were like burnt-out torches. From one of them a nightingale was singing.

'At the end of the garden stood a little pavilion. As we approached it two eunuchs came out to meet us. Their fat bodies swayed as they walked, and they glanced curiously at me with their yellow-lidded eyes. One of them drew aside the captain of the guard, and in a low voice whispered to him. The other kept munching scented pastilles, which he took with an affected gesture out of an oval box of lilac enamel.

'After a few moments the captain of the guard dismissed the soldiers. They went back to the palace, the eunuchs following slowly behind and plucking the sweet mulberries from the trees as they passed. Once the elder of the two turned round, and smiled at me with an evil smile.

'Then the captain of the guard motioned me towards the entrance of the pavilion. I walked on without trembling, and drawing the heavy curtain aside I entered in.

'The young Emperor was stretched on a couch of dyed lion skins, and a ger-falcon perched upon his wrist. Behind him stood a brass-turbaned Nubian, naked down to the waist, and with heavy ear-rings in his split ears. On a table by the side of the couch lay a mighty scimitar of steel.

'When the Emperor saw me he frowned, and said to me, "What is thy name? Knowest thou not that I am Emperor of this city?" But I made him no answer.

'He pointed with his finger at the scimitar, and the Nubian seized it, and rushing forward struck at me with great violence. The blade whizzed through me, and did me no hurt. The man fell sprawling on the floor, and when he rose up his teeth chattered with terror and he hid himself behind the couch.

'The Emperor leapt to his feet, and taking a lance from a stand of arms, he threw it at me. I caught it in its flight, and brake the shaft into two pieces. He shot at me with an arrow, but I held up my hands and it stopped in mid-air. Then he drew a dagger from a belt of white leather, and stabbed the Nubian in the throat lest the slave should tell of his dishonour. The man writhed like a trampled snake, and a red foam bubbled from his lips.

'As soon as he was dead the Emperor turned to me, and when he had wiped away the bright sweat from his brow with a little napkin of purfled and purple silk, he said to me, "Art thou a prophet, that I may not harm thee, or the son of a prophet, that I can do thee no hurt? I pray thee leave my city tonight, for while thou art in it I am no longer its lord."

'And I answered him, "I will go for half of thy treasure. Give me half of thy treasure, and I will go away."

'He took me by the hand, and led me out into the garden. When the captain of the guard saw me, he wondered. When the eunuchs saw me, their knees shook and they fell upon the ground in fear.

'There is a chamber in the palace that has eight walls of red porphyry, and a brass-scaled ceiling hung with lamps. The Emperor touched one of the walls and it opened, and we passed down a corridor that was lit with many torches. In niches upon each side stood great wine-jars filled to the brim with silver pieces. When we reached the centre of the corridor the Emperor spake the word that may not be spoken, and a granite door swung back on a secret spring, and he put his hands before his face lest his eyes should be dazzled.

'Thou couldst not believe how marvellous a place it was. There were huge tortoise-shells full of pearls, and hollowed moonstones of great size piled up with red rubies. The gold was stored in coffers of elephant-hide, and the gold-dust in leather bottles. There were opals and sapphires, the former in cups of crystal, and the latter in cups of jade. Round green emeralds were ranged in order upon thin plates of ivory, and in one corner were silk bags filled, some with turquoise-stones, and others with beryls. The ivory horns were heaped with purple amethysts, and the horns of brass with chalcedonies and sards. The pillars, which were of cedar, were hung with strings of yellow lynx-stones. In the flat oval shields there were carbuncles, both wine-coloured and coloured like grass. And yet I have told thee but a tithe of what was there.

'And when the Emperor had taken away his hands from before his face he said to me: "This is my house of treasure, and half that is in it is thine, even as I promised to thee. And I will give thee camels and camel drivers, and they shall do thy bidding and take thy share of the treasure to whatever part of the world thou desirest to go. And the thing shall be done tonight, for I would not that the Sun, who is my father, should see that there is in my city a man whom I cannot slay."

'But I answered him, "The gold that is here is thine, and the silver also is thine, and thine are the precious jewels and the things of price. As for me, I have no need of these. Nor shall I take aught from thee but that little ring that thou wearest on the finger of thy hand."

'And the Emperor frowned. "It is but a ring of lead," he cried, "nor has it any value. Therefore take thy half of the treasure and go from my city."

' "Nay," I answered, "but I will take nought but that leaden ring, for I know what is written within it, and for what purpose."

'And the Emperor trembled, and besought me and said, "Take all the treasure and go from my city. The half that is mine shall be thine also."

'And I did a strange thing, but what I did matters not, for in a cave that is but a day's journey from this place have I hidden the Ring of Riches. It is but a day's journey from this place, and it waits for thy coming. He who has this Ring is richer than all the kings of the world. Come therefore and take it, and the world's riches shall be thine.'

But the young Fisherman laughed. 'Love is better than Riches,' he cried, 'and the little Mermaid loves me.'

'Nay, but there is nothing better than Riches,' said the Soul.

'Love is better,' answered the young Fisherman, and he plunged into the deep, and the Soul went weeping away over the marshes.

And after the third year was over, the Soul came down to the shore of the sea, and called to the young Fisherman, and he rose out of the deep and said, 'Why dost thou call to me?'

And the Soul answered, 'Come nearer, that I may speak with thee, for I have seen marvellous things.'

So he came nearer, and couched in the shallow water, and leaned his head upon his hand and listened.

And the Soul said to him, 'In a city that I know of there is an inn that standeth by a river. I sat there with sailors who drank of two different-coloured wines, and ate bread made of barley, and little salt fish served in bay leaves with vinegar. And as we sat and made merry, there entered to us an old man bearing a leathern carpet and a lute that had two horns of amber. And when he had laid out the carpet on the floor, he struck with a quill on the wire strings of his lute, and a girl whose face was veiled ran in and began to dance before us. Her face was veiled with a veil of gauze, but her feet were naked. Naked were her feet, and they moved over the carpet like white pigeons. Never have I seen anything so marvellous, and the city in which she dances is but a day's journey from this place.'

Now when the young Fisherman heard the words of his Soul, he remembered that the little Mermaid had no feet and could not dance. And a great desire came over him, and he said to himself, 'It is but a day's journey, and I can return to my love,' and he laughed and stood up in the shallow water, and strode towards the shore.

And when he had reached the dry shore he laughed again, and held out his arms to his Soul. And his Soul gave a great cry of joy and ran to meet him, and entered into him, and the young Fisherman saw stretched before him upon the sand that shadow of the body that is the body of the Soul.

And his Soul said to him, 'Let us not tarry, but get hence at once, for the Sea-gods are jealous, and have monsters that do their bidding.'

So they made haste, and all that night they journeyed beneath the moon, and all the next day they journeyed beneath the sun, and on the evening of the day they came to a city.

And the young Fisherman said to his Soul, 'Is this the city in which she dances of whom thou didst speak to me?'

And his Soul answered him, 'It is not this city, but another. Nevertheless let us enter in,'

So they entered in and passed through the streets, and as they passed through the Street of the Jewellers the young Fisherman saw a fair silver cup set forth in a booth. And his Soul said to him, 'Take that silver cup and hide it.'

So he took the cup and hid it in the fold of his tunic, and they went hurriedly out of the city.

And after that they had gone a league from the city, the young Fisherman frowned, and flung the cup away, and said to his Soul, 'Why didst thou tell me to take this cup and hide it, for it was an evil thing to do?'

But his Soul answered him, 'Be at peace, be at peace.'

And on the evening of the second day they came to a city, and the young Fisherman said to his Soul, 'Is this the city in which she dances of whom thou didst speak to me?'

And his Soul answered him, 'It is not this city, but another. Nevertheless let us enter in.'

So they entered in, and passed through the streets, and as they passed through the Street of the Sellers of Sandals, the young Fisherman saw a child standing by a jar of water. And his Soul said to him, 'Smite that child.' So he smote the child till it wept, and when he had done this they went hurriedly out of the city.

And after that they had gone a league from the city the young Fisherman grew wroth, and said to his Soul, 'Why didst thou tell me to smite the child, for it was an evil thing to do?'

But his Soul answered him, 'Be at peace, be at peace.'

And on the evening of the third day they came to a city, and the young Fisherman said to his Soul, 'Is this the city in which she dances of whom thou didst speak to me?'

And his Soul answered him, 'It may be that it is in this city, therefore let us enter in.'

So they entered in and passed through the streets, but nowhere could the young Fisherman find the river or the inn that stood by its side. And the people of the city looked curiously at him, and he grew afraid and said to his Soul, 'Let us go hence, for she who dances with white feet is not here.'

But his Soul answered, 'Nay, but let us tarry, for the night is dark and there will be robbers on the way.'

So he sat him down in the market-place and rested, and after a time there went by a hooded merchant who had a cloak of cloth of Tartary, and bare a lantern of pierced horn at the end of a jointed reed. And the merchant said to him, 'Why does thou sit in the market-place, seeing that the booths are closed and the bales corded?'

And the young Fisherman answered him, 'I can find no inn in this city, nor have I any kinsman who might give me shelter.'

'Are we not all kinsmen?' said the merchant. 'And did not one God make us? Therefore come with me, for I have a guest-chamber.'

So the young Fisherman rose up and followed the merchant to his house. And when he had passed through a garden of pomegranates and entered into the house, the merchant brought him rosewater in a copper dish that he might wash his hands, and ripe melons that he might quench his thirst, and set a bowl of rice and a piece of roasted kid before him.

And after that he had finished, the merchant led him to the

guest-chamber, and bade him sleep and be at rest. And the young Fisherman gave him thanks, and kissed the ring that was on his hand, and flung himself down on the carpets of dyed goat's-hair. And when he had covered himself with a covering of black lamb's-wool he fell asleep.

And three hours before dawn, and while it was still night, his Soul waked him and said to him, 'Rise up and go to the room of the merchant, even to the room in which he sleepeth, and slay him, and take from him his gold, for we have need of it.'

And the young Fisherman rose up and crept towards the room of the merchant, and over the feet of the merchant there was lying a curved sword, and the tray by the side of the merchant held nine purses of gold. And he reached out his hand and touched the sword, and when he touched it the merchant started and awoke, and leaping up seized himself the sword and cried to the young Fisherman, 'Dost thou return evil for good, and pay with the shedding of blood for the kindness that I have shown thee?'

And his Soul said to the young Fisherman, 'Strike him,' and he struck him so that he swooned, and he seized then the nine purses of gold, and fled hastily through the garden of pomegranates, and set his face to the star that is the star of morning.

And when they had gone a league from the city, the young Fisherman beat his breast, and said to his Soul, 'Why didst thou bid me slay the merchant and take his gold? Surely thou art evil.'

But his Soul answered him, 'Be at peace, be at peace.'

'Nay,' cried the young Fisherman, 'I may not be at peace, for all that thou hast made me to do I hate. Thee also I hate, and I bid thee tell me wherefore thou hast wrought with me in this wise.'

And his Soul answered him, 'When thou didst send me forth into the world thou gavest me no heart, so I learned to do all these things and love them.'

'What sayest thou?' murmured the young Fisherman.

'Thou knowest,' answered his Soul, 'thou knowest it well. Hast thou forgotten that thou gavest me no heart? I trow not. And so trouble not thyself nor me, but be at peace, for there is no pain that thou shalt not give away, nor any pleasure that thou shalt not receive.'

And when the young Fisherman heard these words he trembled and said to his Soul, 'Nay, but thou art evil, and hast made me forget my love, and hast tempted me with temptations, and hast set my feet in the ways of sins.'

And his Soul answered him, 'Thou hast not forgotten that when thou didst send me forth into the world thou gavest me no heart. Come, let us go to another city, and make merry, for we have nine purses of gold.'

But the young Fisherman took the nine purses of gold, and flung them down, and trampled on them.

'Nay,' he cried, 'but I will have nought to do with thee, nor will I journey with thee anywhere, but even as I sent thee away before, so will I send thee away now, for thou hast wrought me no good.' And he turned his back to the moon, and with the little knife that had the handle of green viper's skin he strove to cut from his feet that shadow of the body which is the body of the Soul.

Yet his Soul stirred not from him, nor paid heed to his command, but said to him, 'The spell that the Witch told thee avails thee no more, for I may not leave thee, nor mayest thou drive me forth. Once in his life may a man send his Soul away, but he who receiveth back his Soul must keep it with him for ever, and this is his punishment and his reward.'

And the young Fisherman grew pale and clenched his hands and cried, 'She was a false Witch in that she told me not that.'

'Nay,' answered his Soul, 'but she was true to Him she worships, and whose servant she will be ever.'

And when the young Fisherman knew that he could no longer get rid of his Soul, and that it was an evil Soul, and would abide with him always, he fell upon the ground weeping bitterly.

And when it was day, the young Fisherman rose up and said to his Soul, 'I will bind my hands that I may not do thy bidding, and close my lips that I may not speak thy words, and I will return to the place where she whom I love has her dwelling. Even to the sea will I return, and to the little bay where she is wont to sing, and I will call to her and tell her the evil I have done and the evil thou hast wrought on me.'

And his Soul tempted him and said, 'Who is thy love, that thou shouldst return to her? The world has many fairer than she is. There are the dancing-girls of Samaris who dance in the manner of all kinds of birds and beasts. Their feet are painted with henna, and in their hands they have little copper bells. They laugh while they dance, and their laughter is as clear as the laughter of water. Come with me and I will show them to thee. For what is this trouble of thine about the things of sin? Is that which is pleasant to eat not made for the eater? Is there poison in that which is sweet to drink? Trouble not thyself, but come with me to another city. There is a little city hard by in which there is a garden of tulip-trees. And there dwell in this comely garden white peacocks and peacocks that have blue breasts. Their tails when they spread them to the sun are like disks of ivory and like gilt disks. And she who feeds them dances for pleasure, and sometimes she dances on her hands and at other times she dances with her feet. Her eyes are coloured with stibium, and her nostrils are shaped like the wings of a swallow. From a hook in one of her nostrils hangs a flower that is carved out of a pearl. She laughs while she dances, and the silver rings that are about her ankles tinkle like bells of silver. And so trouble not thyself any more, but come with me to this city.'

But the young Fisherman answered not his Soul, but closed his lips with the seal of silence and with a tight cord bound his hands, and journeyed back to the place from which he had come, even to the little bay where his love had been wont to sing. And ever did his Soul tempt him by the way, but he made it no answer, nor would he do any of the wickedness that it sought to make him do, so great was the power of the love that was within him.

And when he had reached the shore of the sea, he loosed the cord from his hands, and took the seal of silence from his lips, and called to the little Mermaid. But she came not to his call, though he called to her all day long and besought her.

And his Soul mocked him and said, 'Surely thou hast but little joy out of thy love. Thou art as one who in time of death pours water into a broken vessel. Thou gavest away what thou hast, and nought is given to thee in return. It were better for thee to come with me, for I know where the Valley of Pleasure lies, and what things are wrought there.'

But the young Fisherman answered not his Soul, but in a cleft of rock he built himself a house of wattles, and abode there for the space of a year. And every morning he called to the Mermaid, and every noon he called to her again, and at night-time he spake her name. Yet never did she rise out of the sea to meet him, nor in any place of the sea could he find her though he sought for her in the caves and in the green water, in the pools of the tide and in the wells that are at the bottom of the deep.

And ever did his Soul tempt him with evil, and whisper of terrible things. Yet did it not prevail against him, so great was the power of his love.

And after the year was over, the Soul thought within himself, 'I have tempted my master with evil, and his love is stronger than I am. I will tempt him now with good, and it may be that he will come with me.'

So he spake to the young Fisherman and said, 'I have told thee of the joy of the world, and thou hast turned a deaf ear to me. Suffer me now to tell thee of the world's pain, and it may be that thou wilt hearken. For of a truth pain is the Lord of this world, nor is there any one who escapes from its net. There be some who lack raiment, and others who lack bread. There be widows who sit in purple, and widows who sit in rags. To and fro over the fens go the lepers, and they are cruel to each other. The beggars go up and down on the highways, and their wallets are empty. Through the streets of the cities walks Famine, and the Plague sits at their gates. Come, let us go forth and mend these things, and make them not to be. Wherefore shouldst thou tarry here calling to thy love, seeing she comes not to thy call? And what is love, that thou shouldst set this high store upon it?'

But the young Fisherman answered it nought, so great was the power of his love. And every morning he called to the Mermaid, and every noon he called to her again, and at night-time he spake her name. Yet never did she rise out of the sea to meet him, nor in any place of the sea could he find her, though he sought for her in the rivers of the sea, and in the valleys that are under the waves, in the sea that the night makes purple, and in the sea that the dawn leaves grey.

And after the second year was over, the Soul said to the young Fisherman at night-time, and as he sat in the wattled house alone, 'Lo! now I have tempted thee with evil, and I have tempted thee with good, and thy love is stronger than I am. Wherefore will I tempt thee no longer, but I pray thee to suffer me to enter thy heart, that I may be one with thee even as before.'

'Surely thou mayest enter,' said the young Fisherman, 'for in the days when with no heart thou didst go through the world thou must have much suffered.'

'Alas!' cried his Soul, 'I can find no place of entrance, so compassed about with love is this heart of thine.'

'Yet I would that I could help thee,' said the young Fisherman. And as he spake there came a great cry of mourning from the sea, even the cry that men hear when one of the Sea-folk is dead. And the young Fisherman leapt up, and left his wattled house, and ran down to the shore. And the black waves came hurrying to the shore, bearing with them a burden that was whiter than silver. White as the surf it was, and like a flower it tossed on the waves. And the surf took it from the waves, and the foam took it from the the surf, and the shore received it, and lying at his feet the young Fisherman saw the body of the little Mermaid. Dead at his feet it was lying.

Weeping as one smitten with pain he flung himself down beside it, and he kissed the cold red of the mouth, and toyed with the wet amber of the hair. He flung himself down beside it on the sand, weeping as one trembling with joy, and in his brown arms he held it to his breast. Cold were the lips, yet he kissed them. Salt was the honey of the hair, yet he tasted it with a bitter joy. He kissed the closed eyelids, and the wild spray that lay upon their cups was less salt than his tears.

And to the dead thing he made confession. Into the shells of its ears he poured the harsh wine of his tale. He put the little hands round his neck, and with his fingers he touched the thin reed of the throat. Bitter, bitter was his joy, and full of strange gladness was his pain.

The black sea came nearer, and the white foam moaned like a leper. With white claws of foam the sea grabbled at the shore. From the palace of the Sea-King came the cry of mourning again, and far out upon the sea the great Tritons blew hoarsely upon their horns.

'Flee away,' said his Soul, 'for ever doth the sea come nigher, and if thou tarriest it will slay thee. Flee away, for I am afraid, seeing that thy heart is closed against me by reason of the greatness of thy love. Flee away to a place of safety. Surely thou wilt not send me without a heart into another world?'

But the young Fisherman listened not to his Soul, but called on the little Mermaid and said, 'Love is better than wisdom, and more precious than riches, and fairer than the feet of the daughters of men. The fires cannot destroy it, nor can the waters quench it. I called on thee at dawn, and thou didst come to my call. The moon heard thy name, yet hadst thou no heed of me. For evilly had I left thee, and to my own hurt had I wandered away. Yet ever did thy love abide with me, and ever was it strong, nor did aught prevail against it, though I have looked upon evil and looked upon good. And now that thou art dead, surely I will die with thee also.'

And his Soul besought him to depart, but he would not, so great was his love. And the sea came nearer, and sought to cover him with its waves, and when he knew that the end was at hand he kissed with mad lips the cold lips of the Mermaid, and the heart that was within him brake. And as through the fullness of his love his heart did break, the Soul found an entrance and entered in, and was one with him even as before. And the sea covered the young Fisherman with its waves.

And in the morning the Priest went forth to bless the sea, for it had been troubled. And with him went the monks and the musicians, and the candle-bearers, and the swingers of censers, and a great company.

And when the Priest reached the shore he saw the young Fisherman lying drowned in the surf, and clasped in his arms was the body of the little Mermaid. And he drew back frowning, and having made the sign of the Cross, he cried aloud and said, 'I will not bless the sea nor anything that is in it. Accursed be the Sea-folk, and accursed be all they who traffic with them. And as for him who for love's sake forsook God, and so lieth here with his leman slain by God's judgement, take up his body and the body of his leman, and bury them in the corner of the Field of the Fullers, and set no mark above them, nor sign of any kind, that none may know the place of their resting. For accursed were they in their lives, and accursed shall they be in their deaths also.'

And the people did as he commanded them, and in the corner of the Field of the Fullers, where no sweet herbs grew, they dug a deep pit, and laid the dead things within it.

And when the third year was over, and on a day that was a holy day, the Priest went up to the chapel, that he might show to the people the wounds of the Lord, and speak to them about the wrath of God.

And when he had robed himself with his robes, and entered in and bowed himself before the altar, he saw that the altar was covered with strange flowers that never had been seen before. Strange were they to look at, and of curious beauty, and their beauty troubled him, and their odour was sweet in his nostrils, and he felt glad, and understood not why he was glad.

And after that he had opened the tabernacle, and incensed the monstrance that was in it, and shown the fair wafer to the people, and hid it again behind the veil of veils, he began to speak to the people, desiring to speak to them of the wrath of God. But the beauty of the white flowers troubled him, and their odour was sweet in his nostrils, and there came another word into his lips, and he spake not of the wrath of God, but of the God whose name is love. And why he so spake, he knew not.

And when he had finished his word the people wept, and the Priest went back to his sacristy, and his eyes were full of tears. And the deacons came in and began to unrobe him, and took from him the alb and the girdle, the maniple and the stole. And he stood as one in a dream.

And after that they had unrobed him, he looked at them and said, 'What are the flowers that stand on the altar, and whence do they come?'

And they answered him, 'What flowers they are we cannot tell, but they come from the corner of the Fullers' Field.' And the Priest trembled, and returned to his own house and prayed.

And in the morning, while it was still dawn, he went forth with the monks and the musicians, and the candle-bearers and the swingers of censers, and a great company, and came to the shore of the sea, and blessed the sea, and all the wild things that are in it. The Fauns also he blessed, and the little things that dance in the woodland, and the bright-eyed things that peer through the leaves. All the things in God's world he blessed, and the people were filled with joy and wonder. Yet never again in the corner of the Fullers' Field grew flowers of any kind, but the field remained barren even as before. Nor came the Sea-folk into the bay as they had been wont to do, for they went to another part of the sea.

# The Bureau d'Echange de Maux

## Lord Dunsany

*'I never write of the things I have seen,' said Edward John Moreton Drax Plunkett, 18th Baron Dunsany, 'only of things I have imagined.' Like William Blake and J. R. R. Tolkien, he created a world of gods, myths and wonders, but he also wrote fantastic tales with realistic settings and bizarre plays like* The Glittering Gate *(1909) which anticipated the theatre of Ionesco.*

*'The Bureau d'Echange de Maux' ('The Office Where Ills Are Exchanged') possesses the quality of folk or fairy tales, and yet is firmly rooted in a world of things we know, evoking an indefinable atmosphere of menacing power.*

I often think of the Bureau d'Echange de Maux and the wondrously evil old man that sate therein. It stood in a little street that there is in Paris, its doorway made of three brown beams of wood, the top one overlapping the others like the Greek letter pi, all the rest painted green, a house far lower and narrower than its neighbours and infinitely stranger, a thing to take one's fancy. And over the doorway on the old brown beam in faded yellow letters this legend ran, 'Bureau Universel d'Echange de Maux'.

I entered at once and accosted the listless man that lolled on a stool by his counter. I demanded the wherefore of his wonderful house, what evil wares he exchanged, with many other things that I wished to know, for curiosity led me: and indeed had it not I had gone at once from the shop, for there was so evil a look in that fattened man, in the hang of his fallen cheeks and his sinful eye, that you would have said he had had dealings with Hell and won the advantage by sheer wickedness.

Such a man was mine host, but above all the evil of him lay in his eyes, which lay so still, so apathetic, that you would have sworn that he was drugged or dead; like lizards motionless on a wall they lay, then suddenly they darted, and all his cunning flamed up and revealed itself in what one moment before seemed no more than a sleepy and ordinary wicked old man. And this was the object and trade of that peculiar shop, the Bureau Universel d'Echange de Maux: you paid twenty francs, which the old man proceeded to take from me, for admission to the bureau, and then had the right to exchange any evil or misfortune with anyone on the premises for some evil or misfortune that he 'could afford', as the old man put it.

There were four or five men in the dingy ends of that low-ceilinged room who gesticulated and muttered softly in twos as men who make a bargain, and now and then more came in, and the eyes of the flabby owner of the house leaped up at them as they entered, seemed to know their errands at once and each one's peculiar need, and fell back again into somnolence, receiving his twenty francs in an almost lifeless hand and biting the coin as though in pure absence of mind.

'Some of my clients,' he told me. So amazing to me was the trade of this extraordinary shop that I engaged the old man in conversation, repulsive though he was, and from his garrulity I gathered these facts. He spoke in perfect English though his utterance was somewhat thick and heavy, no language seemed to come amiss to him. He had been in business a great many years, how many he would not say, and was far older than he looked. All kinds of people did business in his shop. What they exchanged with each other he did not care, except that it had to be evils; he was not empowered to carry on any other kind of business.

There was no evil, he told me, that was not negotiable there; no evil the old man knew had ever been taken away in despair from his shop. A man might have to wait and come back again next day and next day and the day after, paying twenty francs each time, but the old man had the addresses of his clients and shrewdly knew their needs, and soon the right two met and eagerly changed their commodities. 'Commodities' was the old man's terrible word, said with a gruesome smack of his heavy lips, for he took a pride in his business and evils to him were goods.

I learned from him in ten minutes very much of human nature, more than I had ever learned from any other man; I learned from him that a man's own evil is to him the worst thing that there is or could be, and that an evil so unbalances all men's minds that they always seek for extremes in that small grim shop. A woman that had no children had exchanged with an impoverished half-maddened creature with twelve. On one occasion a man had exchanged wisdom for folly.

'Why on earth did he do that?' I said.

'None of my business,' the old man answered in his heavy indolent way. He merely took his twenty francs from each and ratified the agreement in the little room at the back opening out of the shop where his clients do business. Apparently the man that had parted with wisdom had left the shop upon the tips of his toes with a happy though foolish expression all over his face, but the other went thoughtfully away wearing a troubled and very puzzled look. Almost always it seemed they did business in opposite evils.

But the thing that puzzled me most in all my talks with that unwieldy man, the thing that puzzles me still, is that none that had once done business in that shop ever returned again; a man might come day after day for many weeks, but once do business and he never returned; so much the old man told me, but, when I asked him why, he only muttered that he did not know.

It was to discover the wherefore of this strange thing, and for no other reason at all, that I determined myself to do business sooner or later in the little room at the back of that mysterious shop. I determined to exchange some very trivial evil for some evil equally slight, to seek for myself an advantage so very small as scarcely to give Fate as it were a grip; for I deeply distrusted these bargains, knowing well that man has never yet benefited by the marvellous and that the more miraculous his advantage appears to be the more securely and tightly do the gods or the witches catch him. In a few days more I was going back to England and I was beginning to fear that I should be sea-sick: this fear of sea-sickness, not the actual malady but only the mere fear of it, I decided to exchange for a suitably little evil. I did not know with whom I should be dealing, who in reality was the head of the firm (one never does when shopping), but I decided that no one could make very much on so small a bargain as that.

I told the old man my project, and he scoffed at the smallness of my commodity, trying to urge me on to some darker bargain, but could not move me from my purpose. And then he told me tales with a somewhat boastful air of the big business, the great bargains, that had passed through his hands. A man had once run in there to try to exchange death; he had swallowed poison by accident and had only twelve hours to live. That sinister old man had been able to oblige him. A client was willing to exchange the commodity.

'But what did he give in exchange for death?' I said.

'Life,' said that grim old man with a furtive chuckle.

'It must have been a horrible life,' I said.

'That was not my affair,' the proprietor said, lazily rattling together as he spoke a little pocketful of twenty-franc pieces.

Strange business I watched in that shop for the next few days, the exchange of odd commodities, and heard strange mutterings in corners amongst couples who presently rose and went to the back room, the old man following to ratify.

Twice a day for a week I paid my twenty francs, watching life with its great needs and its little needs morning and afternoon spread out before me in all its wonderful variety.

And one day I met a comfortable man with only a little need, he seemed to have the very evil I wanted. He always feared the lift was going to break. I knew too much of hydraulics to fear things as silly as that, but it was not my business to cure his ridiculous fear. Very few words were needed to convince him that mine was the evil for him, he never crossed the sea, and I, on the other hand, could always walk upstairs, and I also felt at the time, as many must feel in that shop, that so absurd a fear could never trouble me. And yet at times it is almost the curse of my life. When we both had signed the parchment in the spidery back room and the old man had signed and ratified (for which we had to pay him fifty francs each) I went back to my hotel, and there I saw the deadly thing in the basement. They asked me if I would go upstairs in the lift; from force of habit I risked it, and I held my breath all the way up and clenched my hands. Nothing will induce me to try such a journey again. I would sooner go up to my room in a balloon. And why? Because if a balloon goes wrong you have a chance, it may spread out into a parachute after it has burst, it may catch in a tree, a hundred and one things may happen, but if the lift falls down its shaft you are done. As for sea-sickness I shall never be sick again, I cannot tell you why except that I know that it is so.

And the shop in which I made this remarkable bargain, the shop to which none return when their business is done: I set out for it next day. Blindfold I could have found my way to the unfashionable quarter out of which a mean street runs, where you take the alley at the end, whence runs the cul-de-sac where the queer shop stood. A shop with pillars, fluted and painted red, stands on its near side, its other neighbour is a low-class jeweller's with little silver brooches in the window. In such incongruous company stood the shop with beams, with its walls painted green.

In half an hour I stood in the cul-de-sac to which I had gone twice a day for the last week. I found the shop with the ugly painted pillars and the jeweller that sold brooches, but the green house with the three beams was gone.

Pulled down, you will say, although in a single night. That can never be the answer to the mystery, for the house of the fluted pillars painted on plaster, and the low-class jeweller's shop with its silver brooches (all of which I could identify one by one) were standing side by side.

# The Ones Who Walk Away From Omelas

## Ursula K. LeGuin

*Ursula K. LeGuin, author of the* Earthsea *books and many science-fiction novels, has also written a number of fantastic short stories. The following is from* The Wind's Twelve Quarters, *and is subtitled 'Variations on a theme by William James'. Ursula K. LeGuin herself provides the introduction: 'The central idea of this psychomyth, the scapegoat, turns up in Dostoyevsky's* Brothers Karamazov *and several people have asked me, rather suspiciously, why I gave the credit to William James. The fact is, I haven't been able to re-read Dostoyevsky, much as I loved him, since I was twenty-five, and I'd simply forgotten he used the idea. But when I met it in James's 'The Moral Philosopher and the Moral Life', it was with a shock of recognition. Here is how James puts it:*

> *Or if the hypothesis were offered us of a world in which Messrs Fourier's and Bellamy's and Morris's utopias should all be outdone, and millions kept permanently happy on the one simple condition that a certain lost soul on the far-off edge of things should lead a life of lonely torment, what except a specific and independent sort of emotion can it be which would make us immediately feel, even though an impulse arose within us to clutch at the happiness so offered, how hideous a thing would be its enjoyment when deliberately accepted as the fruit of such a bargain?*

*'The dilemma of the American conscience can hardly be better stated. Dostoyevsky was a great artist, and a radical one, but his early social radicalism reversed itself, leaving him a violent reactionary. Whereas the American James, who seems so mild, so naïvely gentlemanly – look how he says 'us', assuming all his readers are as decent as himself! – was, and remained, and remains, a genuinely radical thinker. Directly after the 'lost soul' passage he goes on,*

*All the higher, more penetrating ideals are revolutionary. They
present themselves far less in the guise of effects of past experience
than in that of probable causes of future experiences, factors to
which the environment and the lessons it has so far taught us must
learn to bend.*

*The application of those two sentences to this story, and to science fiction,
and to all thinking about the future, is quite direct. Ideals as 'the probable
causes of future experience' – that is a subtle and an exhilarating remark!*
*'Of course I didn't read James and sit down and say, Now I'll write
a story about the "lost soul". It seldom works that simply. I sat down
and started the story, just because I felt like it, with nothing but the
word "Omelas" in mind. It came from a road sign: Salem (Oregon)
backwards. Don't you read road signs backwards? POTS. WOLS
nerdlihc. Ocsicnarf Nas . . . Salem equals schelomo equals salaam equals
Peace. Melas. O melas. Omelas, Homme hélas. "Where do you get your
ideas from, Ms LeGuin?" From forgetting Dostoyevsky and reading road
signs backwards, naturally. Where else?'*

With a clamour of bells that set the swallows soaring, the Festival
of Summer came to the city Omelas, bright-towered by the sea. The
rigging of the boats in harbour sparkled with flags. In the streets
between houses with red roofs and painted walls, between old moss-
grown gardens and under avenues of trees, passed great parks and
public buildings, processions moved. Some were decorous: old
people in long stiff robes of mauve and grey, grave master workmen,
quiet, merry women carrying their babies and chatting as they
walked. In other streets the music beat faster, a shimmering of gong
and tambourine, and the people went dancing, the procession was
a dance. Children dodged in and out, their high calls rising like the
swallows' crossing flights over the music and the singing. All the
processions wound towards the north side of the city, where on the
great water-meadow called the Green Fields boys and girls, naked
in the bright air, with mud-stained feet and ankles and long, lithe
arms, exercised their restive horses before the race. The horses wore
no gear at all but a halter without bit. Their manes were braided
with streamers of silver, gold, and green. They flared their nostrils
and pranced and boasted to one another; they were vastly excited,

the horse being the only animal who has adopted our ceremonies as his own. Far off to the north and west the mountains stood up half encircling Omelas on her bay. The air of morning was so clear that the snow still crowning the Eighteen Peaks burned with white-gold fire across the miles of sunlit air, under the dark blue of the sky. There was just enough wind to make the banners that marked the racecourse snap and flutter now and then. In the silence of the broad green meadows one could hear the music winding through the city streets, farther and nearer and ever approaching, a cheerful faint sweetness of the air that from time to time trembled and gathered together and broke out into the great joyous clanging of the bells.

Joyous! How is one to tell about joy? How describe the citizens of Omelas?

They were not simple folk, you see, though they were happy. But we do not say the words of cheer much any more. All smiles have become archaic. Given a description such as this one tends to make certain assumptions. Given a description such as this one tends to look next for the King, mounted on a splendid stallion and surrounded by his noble knights, or perhaps in a golden litter borne by great-muscled slaves. But there was no king. They did not use swords, or keep slaves. They were not barbarians. I do not know the rules and laws of their society, but I suspect that they were singularly few. As they did without monarchy and slavery, so they also got on without the stock exchange, the advertisement, the secret police, and the bomb. Yet I repeat that these were not simple folk, not dulcet shepherds, noble savages, bland utopians. They were not less complex than us. The trouble is that we have a bad habit, encouraged by pedants and sophisticates, of considering happiness as something rather stupid. Only pain is intellectual, only evil interesting. This is the treason of the artist: a refusal to admit the banality of evil and the terrible boredom of pain. If you can't lick 'em, join 'em. If it hurts, repeat it. But to praise despair is to condemn delight, to embrace violence is to lose hold of everything else. We have almost lost hold; we can no longer describe a happy man, nor make any celebration of joy. How can I tell you about the people of Omelas? They were not naïve and happy children – though their children were, in fact, happy. They were mature, intelligent, passionate adults whose lives were not wretched. O miracle! but I wish I could describe it better. I wish I could convince you. Omelas sounds in my words like a city in a fairy tale, long ago and far away, once upon a time. Perhaps it would be best if you imagined it as your own fancy bids, assuming it will rise to the occasion, for certainly I cannot suit you all. For instance, how about technology? I think that there would be no cars or helicopters in and above the streets; this follows from the fact that the people of Omelas are happy people. Happiness is based on a just discrimination of what is necessary, what is neither necessary nor destructive, and what is destructive. In the middle category, however – that of the unnecessary but undestructive, that of comfort, luxury, exuberance, etc. – they could perfectly well have central heating, subway trains, washing machines, and all kinds of marvellous devices not yet invented here, floating light-sources, fuelless power, a cure for the common cold. Or they could have none of that: it doesn't matter. As you like it. I incline to think that people from towns up and down the coast have been coming in to Omelas during the last days before the Festival on very fast little trains and double-decked trams and that the train station of Omelas is actually the handsomest building in town, though plainer than the magnificent Farmers' Market. But even granted trains, I fear that Omelas so far strikes some of you as goody-goody. Smiles, bells, parades, horse, bleh. If so, please add an orgy. If an orgy would help, don't hesitate. Let us not, however, have temples from which issue beautiful nude priests and priestesses already half in ecstasy and ready to copulate with any man or woman, lover or stranger, who desires union with the deep godhead of the blood, although that was my first idea. But really it would be better not to have any temples in Omelas – at least, not manned temples. Religion yes, clergy no. Surely the beautiful nudes can just wander about, offering themselves like divine soufflés to the hunger of the needy and the rapture of the flesh. Let them join the processions. Let tambourines be struck above the copulations, and the glory of desire be proclaimed upon the gongs, and (a not unimportant point) let the offspring of these delightful rituals be beloved and looked after by all. One thing I know there is none of in Omelas is guilt. But what else should there be? I thought at first there were no drugs, but that is puritanical. For those who like it, the faint insistent sweetness of *drooz* may perfume the ways of the city, *drooz* which first brings a great lightness and brilliance to the mind and limbs, and then after some hours a dreamy languor, and wonderful visions at last of the very arcana and inmost secrets of the Universe, as well as exciting the pleasure of sex beyond all belief; and it is not habit-forming. For more modest tastes I think there ought to be beer. What else, what else belongs in the joyous city? The sense of victory, surely, the celebration of courage. But as we did without clergy, let us do without soldiers. The joy built upon successful slaughter is not the right kind of joy; it will not do, it is fearful and it is trivial. A boundless and generous contentment, a magnanimous triumph felt not against some outer enemy but in communion with the finest and fairest in the souls of all men everywhere and the splendour of the world's summer: this is what swells the hearts of the people of Omelas, and the victory they celebrate is that of life. I really don't think many of them need to take *drooz*.

Most of the processions have reached the Green Fields by now. A marvellous smell of cooking goes forth from the red and blue tents of the provisioners. The faces of small children are amiably sticky; in the benign grey beard of a man a couple of crumbs of rich pastry are entangled. The youths and girls have mounted their horses and are beginning to group around the starting line of the course. An old woman, small, fat, and laughing is passing out flowers from a basket, and tall young men wear her flowers in their shining hair. A child of nine or ten sits at the edge of the crowd, alone, playing on a wooden flute. People pause to listen, and they smile, but they do not speak to him, for he never ceases playing and never sees them, his dark eyes wholly rapt in the sweet, thin magic of the tune.

He finishes and slowly lowers his hands holding the wooden flute.

As if that little private silence were the signal, all at once a trumpet sounds from the pavilion near the starting line: imperious, melancholy, piercing. The horses rear on their slender legs, and some of them neigh in answer. Sober-faced, the young riders stroke the horses' necks and soothe them, whispering, 'Quiet, quiet, there my beauty, my hope . . . ' They begin to form in rank along the starting line. The crowds along the racecourse are like a field of grass and flowers in the wind. The Festival of Summer has begun.

Do you believe? Do you accept the festival, the city, the joy? No? Then let me describe one more thing.

In a basement under one of the beautiful public buildings of Omelas, or perhaps in the cellar of one of its spacious private homes, there is a room. It has one locked door, and no window. A little light seeps in dustily between cracks in the boards, second-hand from a cobwebbed window somewhere across the cellar. In one corner of the little room a couple of mops, with stiff, clotted, foul-smelling heads, stand near a rusty bucket. The floor is dirt, a little damp to the touch, as cellar dirt usually is. The room is about three paces long and two wide: a mere broom closet or disused tool room. In the room a child is sitting. It could be a boy or a girl. It looks about six, but actually is nearly ten. It is feeble-minded. Perhaps it was born defective, or perhaps it has become imbecile through fear, malnutrition, and neglect. It picks its nose and occasionally fumbles vaguely with its toes or genitals, as it sits hunched in the corner farthest from the bucket and the two mops. It is afraid of the mops. It finds them horrible. It shuts its eyes, but it knows the mops are still standing there; and the door is locked; and nobody will come. The door is always locked; and nobody ever comes, except that sometimes – the child has no understanding of time or interval – sometimes the door rattles terribly and opens, and a person, or several people, are there. One of them may come in and kick the child to make it stand up. The others never come close, but peer in at it with frightened, disgusted eyes. The food bowl and the water jug are hastily filled, the door is locked, the eyes disappear. The people at the door never say anything, but the child, who has not always lived in the tool room, and can remember sunlight and its mother's voice, sometimes speaks. 'I will be good,' it says. 'Please let me out. I will be good!' They never answer. The child used to scream for help at night, and cry a good deal, but now it only makes a kind of whining, 'eh-haa, eh-haa,' and it speaks less and less often. It is so thin there are no calves to its legs; its belly protrudes; it lives on a half-bowl of corn meal and grease a day. It is naked. Its buttocks and thighs are a mass of festered sores, as it sits in its own excrement continually.

They all know it is there, all the people of Omelas. Some of them have come to see it, others are content merely to know it is there. They all know that it has to be there. Some of them understand why, and some do not, but they all understand that their happiness, the beauty of their city, the tenderness of their friendships, the health of their children, the wisdom of their scholars, the skill of their makers, even the abundance of their harvest and the kindly weathers of their skies, depend wholly on this child's abominable misery.

This is usually explained to children when they are between eight and twelve, whenever they seem capable of understanding; and most of those who come to see the child are young people, though often enough an adult comes, or comes back, to see the child. No matter how well the matter has been explained to them, these young spectators are always shocked and sickened at the sight. They feel disgust, which they had thought themselves superior to. They feel anger, outrage, impotence, despite all the explanations. They would like to do something for the child. But there is nothing they can do. If the child were brought up into the sunlight out of that vile place, if it were cleaned and fed and comforted, that would be a good thing, indeed; but if it were done, in that day and hour all the prosperity and beauty and delight of Omelas would wither and be destroyed. Those are the terms. To exchange all the goodness and grace of every life in Omelas for that single, small improvement: to throw away the happiness of thousands for the chance of the happiness of one: that would be to let guilt within the walls indeed.

The terms are strict and absolute; there may not even be a kind word spoken to the child.

Often the young people go home in tears, or in a tearless rage, when they have seen the child and faced this terrible paradox. They may brood over it for weeks or years. But as time goes on they begin to realize that even if the child could be released, it would not get much good of its freedom: a little vague pleasure of warmth and food, no doubt, but little more. It is too degraded and imbecile to know any real joy. It has been afraid too long ever to be free of fear. Its habits are too uncouth for it to respond to humane treatment. Indeed, after so long it would probably be wretched without walls about it to protect it, and darkness for its eyes, and its own excrement to sit in. Their tears at the bitter injustice dry when they begin to perceive the terrible justice of reality, and to accept it. Yet it is their tears and anger, the trying of their generosity and the acceptance of their helplessness, which are perhaps the true source of the splendour of their lives. Theirs is no vapid, irresponsible happiness. They know that they, like the child, are not free. They know compassion. It is the existence of the child, and their knowledge of its existence, that makes possible the nobility of their architecture, the poignancy of their music, the profundity of their science. It is because of the child that they are so gentle with children. They know that if the wretched one were not there snivelling in the dark, the other one, the flute-player, could make no joyful music as the young riders line up in their beauty for the race in the sunlight of the first morning of summer.

Now do you believe in them? Are they not more credible? But there is one more thing to tell, and this is quite incredible.

At times one of the adolescent girls or boys who go to see the child does not go home to weep or rage, does not, in fact, go home at all. Sometimes also a man or woman much older falls silent for a day or two, and then leaves home. These people go out into the street, and walk down the street alone. They keep walking, and walk straight out of the city of Omelas, through the beautiful gates. They keep walking across the farmlands of Omelas. Each one goes alone, youth or girl, man or woman. Night falls; the traveller must pass down village streets, between the houses with yellow-lit windows, and on out into the darkness of the fields. Each alone, they go west or north, towards the mountains. They go on. They leave Omelas, they walk ahead into the darkness, and they do not come back. The place they go towards is a place even less imaginable to most of us than the city of happiness. I cannot describe it at all. It is possible that it does not exist. But they seem to know where they are going, the ones who walk away from Omelas.

# In the Penal Colony

## Franz Kafka

*Kafka is one of the great masters of fantastic literature: he makes the fantastic seem horribly real and thereby become more effective. Some of his stories, for example 'In the Penal Colony', are 'almost' possible. 'I fix images in order to drain them from my spirit,' said Kafka. 'Writing stories is my own way of closing my eyes.'*

*In September 1914 Kafka read the first chapters of The Trial to his friend Max Brod; in November he read him 'In the Penal Colony'. Kafka worked on the novel and the story at the same time; both deal with the concept of Justice. 'Since the Book of Job in the Bible,' wrote Brod, 'God has never been so savagely striven with as in Kafka's The Trial . . . or in his story 'In the Penal Colony'. In the latter, Justice is presented in the image of a machine thought out with refined cruelty, an inhuman, almost devilish machine . . . Just as in the Book of Job, God does what seems absurd and unjust to man. But it is only to man that this seems so.' And Brod ends his note on Kafka saying, 'Of all believers he was the freest from illusions, and among all those who see the world as it is, without illusions, he was the most unshakeable believer.'*

'It's a curious device,' said the officer to the traveller, surveying with a look almost of admiration the device with which he was of course so familiar. The traveller appeared to have acted purely out of politeness in complying with the commandant's request that he attend the execution of a soldier condemned for insubordination and insulting a superior. Interest in the execution was clearly not very great even within the penal colony itself. At least, the only persons present in that deep sandy valley with its barren slopes all around were, apart from the officer and the traveller, the condemned man, a stolid, broad-mouthed individual with a look of neglect about his hair and face, and a soldier who held the heavy chain gathering up the little chains that were fixed to the condemned man's ankles, wrists and neck as well as being fastened to each other by interconnecting chains. In fact the condemned man had an air of such doglike subservience as to suggest that one could have given him the run of the surrounding slopes and a mere whistle would have fetched him back when the execution was due to begin.

The traveller was not greatly interested in the device, and his uninvolvement was little short of obvious as he paced up and down behind the condemned man while the officer attended to the final preparations, now crawling underneath the device, which was sunk some way into the earth, now climbing a ladder to inspect its upper parts. These were tasks that could really have been left to a mechanic, yet the officer performed them with enormous enthusiasm, either because he was a particular devotee of this device or because there were other reasons why the work could be entrusted to no one else. 'All ready now!' he called out at last, stepping down from the ladder. He was dreadfully tired, his mouth hung wide open as he breathed, and he had wedged two delicate lady's handkerchiefs inside the collar of his uniform. 'They're too heavy for the tropics, those uniforms,' said the traveller instead of, as the officer had expected him to, asking questions about the device. 'That's right,' said the officer as he washed the oil and grease from his hands in the bucket of water that stood there for the purpose, 'but they mean home; we don't want to lose touch with home. Now, take a look at this device,' he went on briskly, drying his hands on a towel and at the same time pointing at the device. 'Up to now I've still had to do some things by hand, but from here onwards the device is entirely automatic.' The traveller nodded and followed the officer. To cover himself against all eventualities, the latter added, 'We get the odd breakdown of course. I hope nothing will happen today, but one has to be prepared for it; after all, the device is required to run for twelve hours without interruption. But even if breakdowns do occur they're only very minor and we repair them straight away. Won't you take a seat?' he asked in conclusion, pulling a cane chair out of a pile of such chairs and offering it to the traveller, who could not refuse.

He found himself sitting at the edge of a pit, into which he cast a quick glance. It was not very deep. On one side of the pit the excavated earth had been piled up to form an embankment; on the other side stood the device. 'I don't know,' the officer said, 'whether the commandant has already explained the device to you.' The traveller gestured vaguely, which was all the officer wanted because now he could go ahead and explain the device himself. 'This device,' he said, grasping a connecting-rod and leaning his weight on it, 'is an invention of the late commandant's. I worked on the very first experiments, and I was involved at every stage of the job up to its completion, but the credit for the invention is his and his alone. Have you heard of our late commandant? No? Well, I'm not exaggerating when I say that the entire set-up here is his work. We, his friends, knew when he died that the whole way the penal colony had been constituted was so complete, so self-contained, that his successor, no matter how many new projects he had in mind, would be able to alter nothing of the original concept for many years at least. And we were right; the new commandant has had to admit as much. What a shame you never knew our late commandant! But,' the officer interrupted himself, 'here am I, blathering on, and we have his device before us. It consists, as you see, of three parts. Over the years each of those parts has acquired a popular name, as it were. The bottom part is called the bed, the top part the scriber, and this middle part, suspended between them, is known as the harrow.' 'The harrow?' inquired the traveller. He had not been paying full attention; the valley was without shade and trapped too much sun, which made it difficult to collect one's thoughts. All the greater was his admiration for the officer, who in his tight parade-ground tunic with its heavy epaulettes and loops of braid was explaining his job with such enthusiasm while at the same time, screwdriver in hand, also busying himself with the odd screw here and there. The soldier appeared to be in much the same state as the traveller. He had wound the condemned man's chain round both his wrists and was leaning with one hand on his rifle, head flung back, paying no attention to anything. The traveller was not surprised at this, because the language the officer was speaking was French, which surely neither the soldier nor the condemned man understood. It did, however, make all the more remarkable the fact that the condemned man was nevertheless doing his utmost to follow the officer's explanations. With a kind of drowsy obstinacy he would direct his gaze wherever the officer happened to be pointing, and when the latter was interrupted by a question from the traveller he too, like the officer, turned to look in the traveller's direction.

'The harrow, yes,' said the officer. 'It's a good name. The needles are set in the same pattern as on a harrow, and the whole thing is driven in much the same way except that it stays in one place and works much more neatly and efficiently. You'll get the picture in a moment. The condemned man is laid on the bed here. You see, I want to describe the device first and then afterwards have it go through the actual process. You'll be able to follow it better then. Also one of the cogwheels in the scriber is rather worn; it grates badly as it turns, and one can hardly hear oneself speak; spares are difficult to get hold of here, unfortunately. Right, here's the bed, as I was saying. It is completely covered with a layer of cotton wool, you'll discover why later. The condemned man is laid on the cotton wool on his stomach – naked, naturally; these straps here are for his hands, his feet, and his neck, to fasten him down. Here at the head end of the bed, where as I've said the man starts off lying on his face, there's this little stub of felt that can be easily adjusted to push right into the man's mouth. The object of that is to prevent screaming and biting of the tongue. The man has to take the felt, of course, because otherwise the neck straps would break his neck.' 'That's cotton wool?' asked the traveller, leaning forward. 'Oh, yes,' said the officer with a smile. 'Feel'. And he took the traveller's hand and passed it over the surface of the bed. 'It's a specially treated type of cotton wool, which is why it looks so different; I'll come back to what it's for in a moment.' The device was beginning to capture the traveller's imagination; using his hand to keep the sun out of his eyes, he stared up at it. It was a sizable structure. The bed and the scriber were about equally large and resembled two dark-coloured chests. The scriber was mounted some two metres above the bed, and the two were joined at the corners by four brass rods that almost shone in the sun. Suspended between the two chests on a steel strap was the harrow.

The officer, who had hardly noticed the traveller's earlier indifference, evidently sensed these first stirrings of interest and paused in his elucidations to give the traveller time to view the device at his ease. The condemned man aped what the traveller was doing except that, being unable to put his hand over his eyes, he blinked upwards with his eyes unprotected.

'All right, the man's lying there,' said the traveller; he leant back in his chair and crossed his legs.

'Yes,' said the officer, tipping his cap back and passing a hand over his hot face, 'now, listen to this! Both the bed and the scriber have their own batteries, the bed for itself, the scriber for the harrow. As soon as the man is fastened down, the bed is set in motion. It quivers with tiny, very rapid jerks from side to side and at the same time up and down. You'll have seen similar devices in sanatoria; the only difference is, with our bed all the movements are painstakingly calculated; they have to be, to mesh in with the movements of the harrow. But it's this part, the harrow, that actually carries out the sentence.'

'What is the sentence, in fact?' asked the traveller. 'You don't even know that?' said the astonished officer, beginning to bite his lips. 'Forgive me – my explanations are perhaps a trifle muddled. I'm very sorry, I really am. The commentary always used to be given by the commandant, but the new commandant has been evading his duty in this respect. Still, that so eminent a visitor as yourself' – the traveller tried with both hands to parry this distinction, but the officer insisted – 'that so eminent a visitor as yourself should not even have been told about the form our sentence takes is yet another innovation on his part that—' There was an oath on his lips, but he recovered himself and said merely, 'I wasn't informed; it's not my fault. In point of fact I am the person best qualified to explain our sentences because I have here' – he tapped his breast pocket – 'the relevant drawings in the late commandant's own hand.'

'Drawings in his own hand?' the traveller asked. 'Did he do everything, then? Was he soldier, judge, mechanical engineer, chemist, draftsman?'

'He certainly was,' said the officer, nodding with a fixed, thoughtful look. Then he examined his hands; they did not seem to him clean enough to touch the drawings; so he went to the bucket and washed them a second time. Then he pulled out a small leather wallet and said, 'Our sentence doesn't sound particularly severe. The condemned man has the law that he has broken inscribed on his body with the harrow. This man, for instance – the officer pointed to him – 'will have "Honour your superiors!" inscribed on his body.'

The traveller cast a quick glance at the condemned man; his head was bowed as the officer pointed at him, and he appeared to be straining his ears in an attempt to learn something, though it was evident from the movements of his thick, pouting lips that he understood nothing. The traveller had various questions in mind but at the sight of the man asked only, 'Does he know his sentence?'

'No,' said the officer. He was about to go on with his explanations, but the traveller cut him short: 'He doesn't know his own sentence?' 'No,' the officer said again; he was still for a moment as if expecting the traveller to volunteer some reason for his question, then he said, 'There would be no sense in telling him. He experiences it on his own body.' The traveller, who would have said no more, became aware that the condemned man was looking at him, apparently to ask whether he was able to sanction the process being described. The traveller therefore bent forward again, having leant back in his seat, and asked another question: 'But he knows he has been sentenced?' 'He doesn't know that either,' said the officer, smiling at the traveller as if in anticipation of further strange disclosures on his part. 'You mean,' said the traveller, passing a hand over his forehead, 'that even now the man doesn't know how his defence was received?' 'He's had no opportunity to defend himself,' said the officer, looking away as if he were talking to himself and did not wish to humiliate the traveller with an account of things that, to him, were self-evident. 'But he must have had an opportunity to defend himself,' the traveller said, rising to his feet.

The officer, recognizing the risk of a serious hold-up as far as his explaining the device was concerned, went over to the traveller, placed an arm in his, pointed to the condemned man, who was standing stiffly erect, now that he was so obviously the centre of attention – also the soldier was pulling on the chain – and said, 'It's like this. I hold the office of judge here in the penal colony. In spite of my youth. The reason being that I used to help the late commandant with all the criminal cases, and I also know the device better than anyone else. The principle on which I base my decisions is: guilt is invariably beyond doubt. Other courts are unable to abide by this principle because they consist of several persons and also have higher courts above them. This is not the case here, or at least it wasn't under the late commandant; the new one has shown signs of wanting to meddle in my jurisdiction, but so far I have managed to ward him off, and I shall continue to do so. You wanted to know about this case; it's as straightforward as they all are. A captain laid a charge this morning to the effect that this man, who is assigned to him as a servant and sleeps outside his door, had been asleep on duty. Part of his duty, you see, is to get up every time the hour strikes and salute the captain's door. A simple enough duty, surely, but a very necessary one because for both watching over and waiting on his superior the man has to remain alert. Last night the captain wanted to check whether the servant was performing his duty. Opening the door on the stroke of two, he found him curled up asleep. He fetched the horsewhip and hit him in the face. Instead of then standing up and apologizing the man seized his master round the legs, shook him, and yelled, 'Drop that whip or I'll make mincemeat of you!' Those are the facts. The captain came to me an hour ago; I wrote down his statement and immediately after it the sentence. Then I had the man put in chains. It was all very simple. Had I first called the man in and questioned him it would only have led to confusion. He would have lied; when I succeeded in refuting the lies he would have told fresh ones in their stead; and so on. Now, though, I've got him and I won't let him go. Does that explain everything? But time's getting on, we ought to be starting with the execution, and I haven't finished explaining the device.' Urging the traveller to resume his seat, he went back to the device and began, 'As you can see, the harrow is in the shape of a man; here is the harrow for the abdomen, here are the harrows for the legs. For the head there's just this one little cutter. Is that clear?' He leant amiably towards the traveller, ready to supply the fullest possible explanations.

The traveller was looking at the harrow with a frown. The information about the trial procedure had failed to satisfy him. He had to admit, of course, that this was a penal colony, that therefore special measures were called for, and that the procedure must be military throughout. On the other hand he had placed a certain amount of hope in the new commandant, who clearly intended, however slowly, to introduce a new form of procedure, which was beyond this officer's limited understanding. Pursuing this train of thought, the traveller asked, 'Will the commandant be attending the execution?' 'It's not certain,' said the officer, embarrassed by the abrupt question, his friendly features twisting into a grimace. 'That's why we have to get a move on. I shall even, much against my will, have to cut short my remarks. But I could fill in the details tomorrow, when the device has been cleaned – that's the only trouble with it, that it gets in such a mess. All right, just the essentials now. When the man is lying on the bed and the bed has started vibrating, the harrow is lowered onto the body. It sets itself automatically with the tips of the needles just touching the body. Once it is set, this hawser tautens to form a rod. Now we're in business. Outwardly the layman sees no difference between the punishments. The harrow appears to operate quite uniformly, vibrating away and stabbing its needles into the body as the body, itself quivering, is offered up by the bed. Now, to enable everyone to study the execution of the sentence the harrow is made of glass. Mounting the needles presented one or two technical snags, but after a lot of experimenting we eventually managed it. No effort was spared, you understand. And now everyone can watch through the glass as the inscription is made on the body. Come over here, won't you, and have a closer look at the needles.'

The traveller got slowly to his feet, walked forward, and bent over the harrow. 'You have here,' the officer said, 'two sorts of needle in a multiple arrangement. Each long one has a short one beside it. The long one writes, you see, and the short one squirts out water to wash away the blood and keep the writing clear at all times. The blood water is then channelled through a system of little gutters into this main gutter here and down the drainpipe into the pit.' The officer's finger indicated the precise path the mixture of blood and water must take. When in the interests of maximum clarity he actually made as if to catch it in his cupped hands at the mouth of the pipe, the traveller raised his head and, feeling behind him with one hand, began to back towards his chair. He saw then to his horror that the condemned man had likewise accepted the officer's invitation to inspect the harrow at close quarters. He had pulled the sleepy soldier forward a little way on the chain and was leaning over the glass. One could see him searching with a puzzled look in his eyes for what the two gentlemen had just spotted and, without the accompanying explanation, failing to find it. He was leaning this way and that, running his gaze repeatedly over the glass. The traveller wanted to push him back because he was surely committing a punishable offence. The officer, however, restraining the traveller with one hand, used the other to pick up a clod from the embankment and hurl it at the soldier. The latter looked up with a start, saw what the condemned man had dared to do, dropped his rifle, dug his heels in, hauled the condemned man back so that he fell over, and stood looking down at him as he writhed about in his clinking chains. 'Stand him up!' the officer shouted, aware that the traveller was being very seriously distracted by the condemned man. Indeed he was even leaning out over the harrow again, taking no notice of it but merely trying to see what was happening to the condemned man. 'Careful with him!' the officer shouted again. He ran round the device, grasped the condemned man under the armpits, and with the soldier's help, and after much slipping and sliding on the condemned man's part, stood him on his feet.

'Now I know all about it,' said the traveller as the officer came back. 'All but the most important thing,' the latter replied, grasping the traveller's arm and pointing upwards. 'The scriber there houses the machinery that governs the movements of the harrow, and that machinery is geared up to match the drawing on which the sentence is set out. I still use the late commandant's drawings. Here they are – he pulled several sheets from the leather wallet – only I'm afraid I can't let you handle them yourself; they're my most treasured possession. Sit down and I'll show you them from here; you'll see everything perfectly.' He held up the first sheet. The traveller would have liked to say something appreciative, but all he could see was a maze of criss-cross lines covering the paper so closely that it was difficult to make out the white spaces between. 'Read it,' said the officer. 'I can't,' said the traveller. 'But it's quite clear,' said the officer. 'It's most artistic,' the traveller said evasively, 'but I can't decipher it.' 'Right,' said the officer, putting the wallet away with a chuckle. 'This is no copybook calligraphy. It takes a lot of reading. Even you could make it out in the end, I'm sure. It can't be plain lettering, you see; it's not supposed to kill straight away but only after a twelve-hour period, on average, with the turning-point calculated to occur at the sixth hour. So the actual lettering has to be accompanied by a great deal of embellishment. The text itself forms only a narrow band running round the waist, the rest of the body being set aside for flourishes. Are you in a position now, do you think, to appreciate the work of the harrow and of the device as a whole? Well, watch!' He shinned up the ladder, spun a wheel, called down, 'Out of the way, please!' and the whole thing started working. Had the wheel not grated, it would have been magnificent. As if the offending wheel had come as a surprise to him, the officer threatened it with his fist, then spread his arms apologetically for the traveller's benefit and came hurrying down the ladder to observe the operation of the device from below. Something was still not right, though only he was aware of it; he climbed up again, reached inside the scriber with both hands, and then, to get down faster, instead of using the ladder, slid down one of the poles and started yelling in the traveller's ear as loudly as he could in order to make himself heard: 'Do you understand the process? The harrow starts to write; as soon as it has completed the first draft of the inscription on the man's back the cotton-wool layer rolls round and turns the body slowly on to its side, offering a fresh area for the harrow to work on. Meanwhile the parts already inscribed are presented to the cotton wool, which being specially treated immediately staunches the bleeding and prepares the way for a deepening of the inscription. These teeth here along the edge of the harrow then catch the cotton wool as the body rolls on round, hook it out of the wounds, toss it into the pit, and the harrow can get to work again. So it goes on, for the full twelve hours, writing deeper and deeper all the time. For the first six hours the condemned man lives almost as before; he merely suffers pain. After two hours the felt is removed because the man no longer has the strength to scream. Here in this electrically-heated bowl at the head end we put warm rice pudding, from which, if he wishes, the man can help himself to as much as he can reach with his tongue. Not one of them passes up the chance. I know of none, and my experience is considerable. Not until around the sixth hour does the man lose his pleasure in eating. I usually kneel down here at that point and observe the phenomenon. The man seldom swallows the last bite, he simply turns it round in his mouth and spits it into the pit. I have to duck then, otherwise I get it in the face. How quiet the man becomes, though, around that sixth hour! The dimmest begin to catch on. It starts around the eyes. From there it gradually spreads. A sight to make you feel like lying down beside him under the harrow. Nothing else happens; the man is simply beginning to decipher the text, pursing his lips as if listening. It's not easy, as you saw, to decipher the text when looking at it; our man, remember, is doing it with his wounds. There's a good deal of work involved, of course; he needs six hours to complete the job. But then the harrow runs him right through, hoists him up, and throws him into the pit, where he lands with a splash in the blood water and the cotton wool. Judgement is then complete, and we, the soldier and I, shovel a bit of earth on top of him.'

The traveller, one ear inclined towards the officer, stood with his hands in his pockets, watching the machine in operation. The condemned man was watching too, but uncomprehendingly. Bent forward slightly, he was trying to follow the swaying needles when the soldier, at a signal from the officer, took out a knife and slit the condemned man's shirt and trousers open from behind so that they fell from his body; he tried to grab them as they fell in order to cover his nakedness, but the soldier lifted him up and shook the remaining rags off him. The officer stopped the machine, and in the ensuing silence the condemned man was laid beneath the harrow. The chains were removed and the straps done up instead, which for the condemned man seemed at first almost to be a relief. The harrow now came down a little lower, because this was a thin man. As the points made contact a shudder ran over his skin; he stretched out his left hand – the soldier was busy with his right – not knowing in which direction; but it was towards where the traveller was standing. The officer was looking steadily at the traveller from the side as if trying to tell from his face what impression the execution, which he had now at least superficially explained, was having on him.

The strap that was meant to go round the wrist tore; probably the soldier had pulled it too tight. The soldier held up the broken piece of strap, appealing to the officer for help. The officer went over to him and said, looking at the traveller, 'The machine is extremely complex; something's bound to give here and there; one shouldn't let that cloud one's overall judgement. In any case, for the straps we can find a substitute straight away; I'll use a chain, though of course it will spoil the subtlety of the oscillations as far as the right arm is concerned.' And as he fixed the chain he added, 'The money available for upkeep is very limited now. Under the late commandant I had access to a special fund set aside for the purpose. There used to be a storage depot here that stocked all kinds of spares. I admit I made almost extravagant use of it – before, I mean; not now, as the new commandant claims, but then for him everything's an excuse to attack ancient institutions. Now he administers the machine fund himself, and if I send for a new strap I have to submit the old one as evidence, the new one takes ten days to arrive, and when it does it's of inferior quality and not much use to me. How I'm supposed to operate the machine without straps in the meantime doesn't appear to bother anyone.'

The traveller thought: it is always a serious matter, intervening decisively in other people's affairs. He was neither a citizen of the penal colony nor a citizen of the country to which it belonged. Were he to attempt to pass judgement on or, worse, prevent this execution, they could have told him: be quiet, you're a foreigner. He would have had no rejoinder; he could only have added that in this instance he found his own behaviour puzzling, travelling as he did purely for the purpose of seeing things and not at all, for example, in order to alter the way in which other countries constituted their legal systems. Here, though, the circumstances were extremely tempting. The injustice of the procedure and the inhumanity of the execution were beyond doubt. No one could presume self-interest of any kind on the traveller's part since the condemned man was a stranger to him, not even a fellow countryman, and by no means a person to inspire sympathy. The traveller himself carried letters of recommendation from people in high places, he had been most courteously received here, and the fact that he had been invited to attend the execution even seemed to indicate that his opinion of this trial was sought after. This was all the more likely in view of the commandant's being, as he had just heard in the clearest possible terms, no supporter of this procedure and maintaining an attitude almost of hostility towards the officer.

At this point the traveller heard the officer let out a yell of rage. He had just succeeded, not without difficulty, in shoving the stub of felt into the condemned man's mouth when the condemned man, nauseated beyond bearing, closed his eyes and vomited. Hastily the officer yanked him up off the stub and tried to turn his head towards the pit, but it was too late; vomit was already running down the machine. 'This is all the commandant's fault!' the officer yelled, shaking the front two brass rods in a blind fury. 'My machine's being fouled like a pigsty!' His hands trembled as he pointed out to the traveller what had happened. 'Have I not spent hours of my time trying to make the commandant see that for one day before the execution no further food is to be served? Oh, no: the new leniency begs to differ. The commandant's ladies stuff the man full of sweets before he is led away. His whole life he's lived on stinking fish and now he has to eat sweets. All right, I don't mind that, but why don't they get hold of a new felt as I've been asking them to do for the past three months? How can anyone take this piece in his mouth without feeling sick when upwards of a hundred men have sucked and chewed on it as they died?'

The condemned man had laid his head down again and was looking peaceful; the soldier was busy wiping the machine with the condemned man's shirt. The officer went over to the traveller, who in response to some premonition took a step backwards; the officer, however, grasped his hand and drew him aside. 'I want to tell you something in confidence,' he said. 'I may, I take it?' 'Certainly,' said the traveller, and he listened with lowered gaze.

'This procedure and this form of execution, which you now have the opportunity of admiring, currently have no open supporters left in our colony. I am their sole champion, just as I am the sole champion of the old commandant's legacy. Further improvement of the procedure is more than I can contemplate undertaking; it requires all my strength to maintain what we have. When the old commandant was alive the colony was full of his supporters. I have something of the old commandant's persuasiveness but none of his power; consequently the supporters have gone into hiding; there are still plenty of them but none will own up to the fact. If you go into the tea-house today – in other words, on an execution day – and listen to what the people are saying you may well hear nothing but ambiguous remarks. They'll all be supporters, but under the present commandant and given his present views they're completely useless as far as I'm concerned. And now I ask you: Is the achievement of a lifetime' – he indicated the machine – 'to be utterly ruined because of this commandant and the women who influence him? Is that something one can allow to happen? Even as a foreigner who is only visiting our island for a few days? But there's no time to be lost; they're planning something to curb my jurisdiction. Already discussions are being held in the commandant's office to which I am not invited to contribute; even your visit today strikes me as typical of the whole situation; the man's a coward and sends you, a foreigner, out to reconnoitre. How different it all used to be! A full day before the execution the entire valley would be crammed with people, all there just to watch; early in the morning the commandant appeared with his ladies; fanfares roused the entire camp; I reported that everything was ready; the top people – and every high-ranking official had to be there – took their places around the machine; the pile of cane chairs over there is a pathetic reminder of those days. The machine sparkled; it was always freshly cleaned, and I used to take new parts for nearly every execution. Hundreds of pairs of eyes – there were spectators standing on tiptoe all the way to the rising ground over there – watched as the condemned man was laid beneath the harrow by the commandant himself. What a common soldier is allowed to do today was then my job as presiding judge, and I counted it an honour. And then the execution began! No jarring note interfered with the work of the machine. Many people stopped watching altogether and lay down in the sand with their eyes closed; they all knew: Justice was being done. In the silence you could hear only the moaning of the condemned man, muffled by the felt. Nowadays the machine can no longer force a louder moan out of the condemned man than the felt is able to stifle, but then the scribing needles used to drip a caustic fluid that we're not allowed to use today. Ah, and then came the sixth hour! We couldn't possibly let everyone watch from close up that wanted to. The commandant in his wisdom gave orders that the children should be considered first; I was of course always allowed to be present by virtue of my job, and many were the times I squatted there with a little child in either arm. The way we all took in the look of enlightenment on the tortured face, the way we held our cheeks up to the glow of a justice accomplished at last and already beginning to fade! Those were the days, my friend!' The officer had evidently forgotten who was standing there; he had taken the traveller in his arms and pressed his face to the man's shoulder. The traveller, deeply embarrassed, was looking impatiently over the officer's head. The soldier had finished cleaning up and had just shaken some rice pudding into the bowl from a tin. As soon as he saw this the condemned man, now apparently quite recovered, began reaching for the pudding with his tongue. The soldier kept pushing him away, the pudding being probably intended for later, but surely it was also highly irregular that the soldier should stick his dirty hands in it and eat some before the eyes of his ravenous charge.

The officer quickly regained his composure. 'I didn't mean to upset you,' he said. 'I know how impossible it is to make anyone understand what times were like then. Anyway, the machine still works and is its own justification, even standing by itself in this valley. And the end is still that incredibly smooth flight of the corpse into the pit even when, unlike then, people are not swarming round the pit in their hundreds like flies. Then we had to have a stout railing running round the pit; it was pulled up long ago.'

The traveller wanted to conceal his face from the officer and looked aimlessly about him. The officer, thinking he was contemplating the desolation of the valley, seized his hands, moved round him to look into his eyes, and demanded, 'You see the shame of it?'

But the traveller said nothing. The officer left him alone for a moment; legs apart, hands on hips, he stood still and looked at the ground. Then he gave the traveller a cheery smile and said, 'I was not far away from you yesterday when the commandant invited you. I heard the invitation. I know the commandant. I saw immediately what he was trying to achieve by inviting you. Although he has the power to take steps against me he still dare not do so, yet he is quite prepared to expose me to the judgement of a distinguished foreigner such as yourself. He's worked it all out very carefully: this is your second day on the island, you didn't know the old commandant and the way his mind worked, you have your European preconceptions, possibly you're opposed on principle to the death penalty in general and this type of mechanical method of execution in particular, you're also seeing how the execution takes place with no public participation, joylessly, and on a somewhat damaged machine – might you not, in the light of all these things (thinks the commandant), very possibly be inclined to regard my procedure as wrong? And if you do regard it as wrong you will not fail (I'm still speaking from the commandant's point of view) to say so, because you surely have confidence in your tried and tested convictions. On the other hand you have seen and learnt to respect many peculiarities of many peoples, so you will probably not put your whole energy, as you might have done back in your own country, into speaking out against the procedures here. But the commandant doesn't even need that. A single unguarded remark will be enough. It need not even represent your conviction, as long as it appears to be in line with what he wants. He will question you with enormous cunning, I'm sure of that. And his ladies will sit around in a circle and prick up their ears; you'll say, for example, "Our trial procedure is different," or, "We examine the accused before passing sentence," or, "In our system the condemned man is told the sentence," or, "We have other punishments besides the death penalty," or, "In our country people were tortured only in the Middle Ages." All remarks that are as correct as they seem to you self-evident; innocent remarks that in no way impugn my procedure. But how will they be received by the commandant? I can see him, our excellent commandant, pushing his chair aside immediately and hurrying out to the balcony; I see his ladies go streaming out after him; I hear his voice – like thunder, as the ladies describe it – and what he says is: "One of the West's great explorers, appointed to investigate trial procedure in every country in the world, has just said that our procedure, based on ancient custom, is inhumane. Given this verdict by a person of such standing, I naturally cannot tolerate this procedure any longer. With effect from today I therefore give orders that – and so on." You want to intervene, you didn't say what he reported you as saying, you didn't call my procedure inhumane, on the contrary it is your deeply held conviction that it is the most humane and dignified procedure possible, you also admire this piece of machinery – but it's too late; you can't even get on to the balcony, which by now is full of ladies; you want to draw attention to yourself; you want to shout; but a lady's hand holds your mouth closed – and I and the old commandant's work are done for.'

The traveller had to suppress a smile; so it was that easy, the task he had thought would present such difficulty. He said evasively, 'You overestimate my influence; the commandant has read my letters of recommendation and knows I am no authority on legal procedures. Were I to express an opinion it would be the opinion of a private person, carrying no more weight than that of anyone else and certainly a great deal less than the opinion of the commandant, who has, I understand, very extensive rights in this penal colony. If his opinion regarding this procedure is as definite as you believe, then I am afraid the procedure is indeed doomed without my modest assistance being necessary.'

Did the officer understand now? No, he did not. He shook his head vigorously, glanced back at the condemned man and the soldier, both of whom flinched away from the rice, he went right up to the traveller, looking not in his face but at some point on his jacket, and said more quietly than before, 'You don't know the commandant; as far as he and all of us are concerned you're as it were – if you'll pardon the expression – untouchable: believe me, your influence cannot be rated too highly. I was delighted to learn that you were to attend the execution on your own. The commandant's directive was in fact aimed at me, but I'm going to turn it to my advantage. Undeterred by false insinuations and scornful looks – which given a bigger attendance at the execution would have been inevitable – you have listened to my explanations, seen the machine, and are now viewing the execution. Your mind, surely, is already made up: any lingering doubts will be removed as you watch the execution. So I now appeal to you: please take my side against the commandant!'

The traveller let him go no further. 'How could I?' he exclaimed. 'It's out of the question. I can no more be of use to you than I can damage your interests.'

'You can,' said the officer. The traveller saw with some alarm that the officer's fists were clenched. 'You can,' the officer repeated with even greater urgency. 'I have a plan that's sure to succeed. You don't think you wield sufficient influence. I know you do. But even accepting that you are right, if we are to save this procedure we surely need to mobilize all our resources, don't we, even the possibly inadequate? Let me tell you my plan. If we're to bring it off it's very important that, today in the colony, you should keep as quiet as possible about your opinion of the procedure. Unless you're asked straight out, you should say nothing at all; what you do say must be brief and noncommittal; let them see that you find it difficult to talk about it, that you feel bitter, that, were you to speak frankly, you would have almost to break out into cursing and swearing. I'm not asking you to tell lies; not at all; just to keep your answers brief, as, "Yes, I saw the execution," or, "Yes, I heard all the explanations." That's all, nothing more. There's reason enough, after all, for the bitterness we want them to hear in your voice, even if it's not quite what the commandant intended. He of course will get it completely wrong and interpret everything in his own way. That's the gist of my plan. Tomorrow there's to be a big meeting in the commandant's office, under the commandant's chairmanship, of all the top administrative officials. The commandant, of course, has managed to turn such meetings into a public spectacle. A gallery has been built and it's invariably packed. I am forced to take part in the discussions, though I shudder with loathing. Now, you are sure to be invited to the meeting, whatever happens, and if today you act in accordance with my plan the invitation will become an urgent request to attend. If, however, for some mysterious reason you should not be invited, you must certainly demand an invitation; that you will then receive one is beyond any doubt. So tomorrow there you are, sitting with the ladies in the commandant's box. He looks up repeatedly to satisfy himself that you are there. After various trifling, ridiculous items aimed solely at the audience – usually to do with harbour works, they're always talking about harbour works – the question of trial procedure comes up. If this fails to happen or takes too long to happen on the commandant's initiative, I shall make sure that it happens. I shall stand up and report today's execution. Very briefly, just saying it took place. It's not the usual thing to make such reports there, but I do so all the same. The commandant thanks me, as he always does, with a pleasant smile and then, unable to restrain himself, seizes his opportunity. "We have just" – this is what he'll say, or something like it – "had the report of the execution. I should merely like to add a note to the effect that this particular execution was attended by the great explorer of whose visit to our colony as well as the quite exceptional honour it does us you are all aware. Our meeting today is likewise lent greater significance by his presence. Why don't we now turn to this great explorer and ask him what he thinks of our traditional method of execution and the procedure leading up to it?" Lots of applause, of course; unanimous approval, with me making more noise than anyone. The commandant bows to you and says, "Then, sir, on behalf of us all I put that question to you." And now you step up to the rail. Put your hands where everyone can see them, otherwise the ladies will get hold of them and play with your fingers. And at last you speak. I don't know how I'm going to stand the tension of the intervening hours. In your speech you mustn't set yourself any limits; let the truth ring out, lean over the rail and shout at the commandant, really shout out your opinion, your unshakable opinion. But perhaps you'd rather not, it's not in your character, where you come from people may behave differently in such situations, that doesn't matter, that will do fine, don't even get up, merely say a few words, whisper them so that they just reach the ears of the officials sitting below you, that will be enough, you needn't even talk about the lack of attendance at the execution, the wheel that grates, the broken strap, the revolting felt, you needn't even mention those things yourself, I'll see to all the rest, and believe me, if my speech doesn't drive him from the room it'll force him to his knees: "Old commandant," it'll make him say, "I humble myself before you." That's my plan; will you help me carry it out? But of course you will – what am I saying – you must.' And the officer seized the traveller by both arms and stared into his face, panting for breath. The last few phrases had been yelled at such a pitch that even the soldier and the condemned man had begun to take notice; though they understood nothing they had paused in their eating and were staring across at the traveller, chewing.

The answer he must give had, as far as the traveller was concerned, been beyond doubt from the very beginning; he had

been through too much in his life for there to have been any question
of his wavering here; he was fundamentally honest, and he was not
afraid. Even so he did, at the sight of the soldier and the condemned
man, hesitate for a moment. But eventually he said, as he had to,
'No.' The officer blinked several times but without taking his eyes
off him. 'Do you want an explanation?' the traveller asked. The
officer nodded wordlessly. 'I am opposed to this procedure,' the
traveller went on. 'Even before you took me into your confidence
– a confidence that I shall of course under no circumstances abuse
– I was already wondering whether I had any right to intervene
against this procedure and whether my intervention had even the
remotest prospect of success. It was clear to me whom I must
approach first: the commandant, of course. You have made that
even clearer, though without doing anything in the way of strengthening my resolve; on the contrary, the sincerity of your conviction
affects me deeply, even if it cannot distract me from my purpose.'

The officer, still without a word, turned to the machine, grasped
one of the brass rods, and, leaning back slightly, looked up at the
scriber as if checking whether everything was in order. The soldier
and the condemned man appeared to have struck up a friendship:
the condemned man was making signs to the soldier, difficult though
this was with the straps pulled so tight; the soldier bent over him;
the condemned man whispered something to him, and the soldier
nodded.

The traveller went over to the officer and said, 'You don't know
yet what I intend to do. I shall certainly be telling the commandant
what I think of the procedure but not at a meeting; I shall do so in
private; nor shall I be staying here long enough to be called into
any meeting; I sail tomorrow morning or shall at least be rejoining
my ship then.'

It did not look as if the officer had been listening. 'So the procedure didn't convince you,' he murmured, smiling as an old man
smiles at the nonsense of a child and uses the smile to hide what
he is really thinking. 'The time has come, then,' he concluded, and
suddenly he looked at the traveller with eyes that were bright with
a kind of challenge, almost a call to complicity.

'The time for what?' the traveller asked uneasily, but he received
no answer.

'You're free,' the officer told the condemned man in his own
language. The man did not believe it at first. 'I said you're free,'

the officer repeated. For the first time genuine life came into the condemned man's face. Was this true? Was it just a whim of the officer's that might pass? Had the foreign visitor got him off? What was it? his face seemed to be asking. But not for long. Whatever it might be, he wanted, if he could, to be actually at liberty, and he began to shake himself about as much as the harrow allowed.

'You're tearing my straps!' the officer shouted. 'Keep still! We'll undo them for you!' He beckoned to the soldier, and the two of them set to work. The condemned man said nothing but chuckled quietly to himself, turning his face now to the left towards the officer, now to the right towards the soldier, and in between even towards the traveller.

'Pull him out,' the officer ordered the soldier. This had to be done with a certain amount of care because of the harrow. The condemned man already had a number of minor lacerations on his back as a result of his earlier impatience.

From this point on, however, the officer took very little notice of him. He went over to the traveller, pulled out the small leather wallet once more, leafed through it, eventually found the sheet he was looking for, and held it up for the traveller to look at. 'Read it,' he said. 'I can't,' said the traveller. 'I told you, I can't read those sheets.' 'Look carefully,' the officer said, moving round beside the traveller to read the sheet with him. When even this failed he stuck out his little finger and, holding it well away as if the sheet must not on any account be touched, ran it over the paper to make it easier for the traveller to read. The traveller really tried, hoping to be able to accommodate the officer at least in this respect, but he found it impossible. The officer then started spelling out what was written there and in the end read out the whole thing: ' "Be just," it says. Now you can read it, surely?' The traveller bent so low over the paper that the officer, afraid he might touch it, moved it farther away; the traveller said nothing more, but it was obvious that he had still not been able to read it. ' "Be just," it says,' the officer repeated. 'Possibly,' said the traveller. 'I believe you.' 'Right,' the officer said, partially satisfied at least, and he took the sheet with him and climbed the ladder; very carefully he bedded the sheet in the scriber and then appeared to rearrange the entire gear mechanism; this was an extremely laborious operation, some of the gear wheels evidently being very small, and from time to time the officer's head would disappear completely inside the scriber, so closely did he have to inspect the mechanism.

The traveller kept uninterrupted watch on the operation from below until his neck was stiff and his eyes ached from the sunlight flooding the sky. The soldier and the condemned man were concerned only with each other. The condemned man's shirt and trousers, which lay in the pit, were hauled out on the end of the soldier's bayonet. The shirt was horribly filthy, and the condemned man washed it in the bucket of water. When he then donned it and the trousers, neither the soldier nor he could refrain from laughing, because of course the garments had been slit up the back. Possibly in the belief that it was his duty to entertain the soldier, the condemned man pirouetted in front of him in his ruined clothing; the soldier, squatting on the ground, slapped his knees as he laughed. With the gentlemen present, however, they kept themselves under control.

When the officer had finally finished up on top, he smilingly surveyed the whole thing once more, part by part, slammed the scriber lid shut this time, it having been open until now, climbed down, looked into the pit and then at the condemned man, saw to his satisfaction that the latter had taken his clothes out, walked over to the bucket of water to wash his hands, noticed the revolting filth too late, was distressed that he could not now wash his hands, finally plunged them – it was an inadequate substitute but he had to bow to circumstances – into the sand, then stood up and began unbuttoning his tunic. As he did so the two lady's handkerchiefs that he had wedged inside the collar fell out into his hands. 'Here – your handkerchiefs,' he said, tossing them to the condemned man. And for the traveller's benefit he explained. 'Presents from the ladies.'

Despite the evident haste in which he removed his tunic and then all the rest of his clothes, he handled each garment with great care, even running his fingers deliberately over the silver braid of the tunic and shaking the odd tassel straight. It was then rather out of keeping with his carefulness that, as soon as he had finished with a garment, he tossed it into the pit with an impatient jerk. The last thing he was left with was his short sword on its sling. He unsheathed it, broke it into pieces, then, gathering everything together, the bits of sword, the scabbard, and the sling, hurled it all from him with such force that it hit the bottom of the pit with a clang.

He stood there, naked. The traveller bit his lips and said nothing. He knew what was going to happen, but he had no right to hinder the officer in any way. If the trial procedure to which the officer was so attached was really on the point of being abolished – possibly in consequence of actions to which the traveller, for his part, felt committed in advance – then he was acting quite properly; the traveller would have acted no differently in his place.

The soldier and the condemned man, understanding nothing, at first did not even watch. The condemned man was delighted to have his handkerchiefs back. His delight was short-lived, though, the soldier snatching them back with a swift, unforseeable movement. The condemned man then tried to pull the handkerchiefs out from behind the soldier's belt, where the latter had put them for safe keeping, but the soldier was on his guard. They went on struggling like this, half jokingly, and it was not until the officer was completely naked that they began to take notice. The condemned man in particular appeared to have sensed some kind of major reversal. What had been happening to him was now happening to the officer. Perhaps this time it would be taken to the last extreme. Probably the foreign traveller had given the order. Vengeance, then. Without himself having suffered all the way he was going to be revenged all the way. A broad, soundless laugh materialized on his face and stayed there.

The officer, meanwhile, had turned to the machine. It had been clear enough all along how well he understood the machine, but now one might almost have been staggered by his handling of it and by its response. All he did was to hold a hand out towards the harrow and it raised and lowered itself several times until it was in the right position to receive him; he simply gripped the edge of the bed and it began to vibrate; the stub of felt moved towards him, you could see that the officer did not really want to take it, but after only a moment's hesitation he submitted and accepted it in his mouth. Everything was ready, except that the straps still hung down at the sides, but they were clearly superfluous; the officer did not need to be strapped down. The condemned man, however, noticing that the straps were undone and feeling that the execution was incomplete if the straps were not fastened, beckoned officiously to the soldier, and they ran to strap the officer down. The officer had already stretched out a foot to kick at the crank handle that would start the scriber, but when he saw them coming he withdrew the foot and allowed himself to be strapped down. Now, of course, he could no longer reach the crank handle; neither the soldier nor the condemned man would find it, and the traveller was determined not to move. There was no need; hardly was the last strap attached when the machine went into operation; the bed vibrated, the needles danced over the skin, the harrow swung to and fro. The traveller had been staring at the sight for some time before he remembered that a wheel in the scriber ought to have been grating; all was quiet, however, with not even the faintest whirring to be heard.

Operating so quietly, the machine literally escaped the traveller's attention. He looked across at the soldier and the condemned man. The condemned man was the livelier of the two, interested in everything about the machine, bending down, stretching up, always with his index finger extended to point something out to the soldier. The traveller found this embarrassing. He was determined to stay to the end, but he could not have put up with the sight of those two for long. 'Go home,' he said. The soldier might have been prepared to do so, but the condemned man felt the order to be almost a punishment. Clasping his hands together, he begged to be allowed to stay, and when the traveller shook his head in adamant refusal he even sank to his knees. Realizing that orders were useless here, the traveller was about to go over and chase the pair of them away when he became aware of a noise in the scriber. He looked up. Was that gear-wheel giving trouble after all? No, this was something else. Slowly the lid of the scriber rose higher and higher until it fell open completely. The cogs of a gear-wheel became visible, rising up, soon the whole wheel could be seen, it was as if some mighty force were squeezing the scriber, there was no room for this wheel, the wheel turned till it reached the edge of the scriber, tumbled down, rolled a little way in the sand, then fell over and lay still. But up in the scriber another was already emerging, many more followed, big ones, little ones, others virtually indistinguishable in size, the same thing happening to them all; surely the scriber must be empty now, you kept thinking, but then another, even more numerous cluster of them rose up, came tumbling down, rolled in the sand, and lay flat. Meanwhile the condemned man had forgotten all about the traveller's order; fascinated by the gear-wheels, he kept trying to catch one, urging the soldier to help him, but he drew his hand back in alarm each time because right behind came another wheel that, at least as it first started to roll, gave him a fright.

As for the traveller, he was deeply uneasy; the machine was obviously disintegrating; its easy action was an illusion; he felt he ought to be looking after the officer, now that the latter was no longer in a position to fend for himself. But while the fall of the gear-wheels had been occupying his whole attention he had neglected to keep an eye on the rest of the machine; now, the last gear-wheel having left the scriber, as he bent over the harrow he received another, even nastier surprise. The harrow was not inscribing, merely stabbing, and the bed, instead of turning the body over, merely thrust it, quivering, up at the needles. The traveller wanted to intervene, possibly to stop the whole process; this was not the torture the officer had wanted to achieve, this was plain murder. He reached out. But the harrow, with the body skewered on it, was already canting up and over to one side, as it normally did only in the twelfth hour. Blood flowed in a hundred streams (unmixed with water, the water ducts too having failed this time). And now the last thing went wrong as well: the body failed to come off the long needles and, still gushing blood, hung above the pit without falling. The harrow tried to return to its original position, appeared to become aware that it was not yet free of its burden, and remained suspended over the pit. 'Come and help!' the traveller shouted to the soldier and the condemned man as he himself took hold of the officer's feet. He meant to push against the feet at his end, he wanted the others to go to the other side and take hold of the officer's head, and between them they would slowly lift him off the needles. The others, however, could not make up their minds to come; the condemned man actually turned away; the traveller had to go over to them and forcibly move them to the officer's head. In doing so he caught an almost involuntary glimpse of the face of the corpse. It was just as it had been in life, with no sign of the promised deliverance; what all the others had found in the machine, the officer had not found; his lips were pressed firmly together, his eyes were open and had the look of being alive, the expression in them was one of calm conviction, the tip of the great iron spike stuck out of his forehead.

As the traveller, with the soldier and the condemned man behind him, reached the first houses of the colony the soldier pointed to one and said, 'That's the tea-house.'

The ground floor of one of the buildings was occupied by a deep, low, cave-like room with smoke-blackened walls and ceiling. On the street side it was open along its whole width. There was little to distinguish the tea-house from the rest of the colony's buildings, which including the palatial quarters of the commandant were all in an advanced state of disrepair, yet on the traveller it had the effect of a reminder of the past, and he felt the power of an earlier age. He drew nearer, passed with his two attendants between the empty tables that stood in the street in front of the tea-house, and inhaled the cool, moist air coming from inside. 'The old man's buried here,' said the soldier. 'Chaplain wouldn't give him a plot in the cemetery. For a while they couldn't decide where to bury him, then in the end they buried him here. The officer won't have told you anything about that, because of course it's what he was most ashamed of. Once or twice he even tried to dig the old man up at night, but he always got chased away.' 'Where is the grave?' the traveller asked, unable to believe the soldier. Immediately the two of them, the soldier and the condemned man, ran ahead and pointed with outstretched hands to where the grave was. They led the traveller over to the rear wall, where customers were sitting at several of the tables. These were probably dockers, powerfully-built men with short, gleaming black beards. All sat jacketless, and their shirts were torn; they were poor, oppressed folk. As the traveller approached, some of them stood up, backed against the wall, and watched him expectantly. 'A foreigner,' went the whisper all around him, 'come to look at the grave.' They pushed one of the tables aside, and underneath there really was a gravestone. It was a simple stone and low enough to be concealed beneath a table. It bore an inscription in very small letters; the traveller had to kneel down to read it. It read: 'Here lies the old commandant. His followers, who now may bear no name, dug this grave for him and set up this stone. It is prophesied that the commandant will rise again after a certain number of years have elapsed and lead his followers out from this house to reconquer the colony. Wait in faith!' When the traveller, having read this, rose to his feet he saw the men standing around him and smiling as if they had read the inscription with him, found it ridiculous, and were inviting him to share their view. The traveller pretended not to have noticed, distributed a few coins among them, waited till the table had been pushed back over the grave, left the tea-house, and made his way to the harbour.

The soldier and the condemned man had come across acquaintances in the tea-house who detained them. They must have quickly torn themselves away, however, because the traveller had only got as far as the middle of the long flight of stairs leading to the boats before they appeared in pursuit. Probably they wanted to make the traveller take them with him at the last moment. While he was negotiating with a boatman at the foot of the steps to take him out to the steamer, the other two came racing down the steps in silence, not daring to shout. But by the time they reached the bottom the traveller was already in the boat and the boatman was casting off. They could have leapt into the boat, but the traveller, picking up a heavy length of knotted rope from the floor of the boat and threatening them with it, prevented them from making the attempt.

*Translated from the German by J. A. Underwood.*

# A Dog in Dürer's Etching
## 'The Knight, Death and The Devil'

## Marco Denevi

*In 1966 I was working for Galerna, a small publishing company in Buenos Aires. I had almost total freedom and, full of enthusiasm, I set up a short, and ultimately unsuccessful, series called 'Variations on a Theme'. The idea was to choose one subject per volume (the subject might be anything – a newspaper clipping, a painting) and offer it to a dozen writers who would then make their own 'variation' on that given theme. For one of the volumes I chose Dürer's engraving* The Knight, Death and The Devil; *among the authors I asked to write on the theme was Marco Denevi.*

*Denevi had become famous in Argentina through two books: a superb detective novel badly translated into English as* Rose at Ten O'Clock, *and a novella,* Secret Ceremony, *which won* Life *magazine's prize for the best Latin-American short story in 1960 – and which was then completely changed by a Joseph Losey gone haywire in his terrible film of the same name.*

*Denevi called me back barely a day later and said that my 'order' was ready. I went to his office to collect it (he was then working as an insurance broker, dressed in impeccable black) and I read the typewritten pages on the bus on my way back home. I remember the thrill of the first lines, the enjoyment of the virtuoso performance that revealed itself almost immediately, the happiness of the last fifty words that round up the story like a symphonic finale. In all these years my enthusiasm for this subtle, fantastic tale has not waned.*

The knight (as we all know) is back from the war, the Seven Years' War, the Thirty Years' War, the War of the Roses, the War of the Three Henrys, a dynastic or religious war, or a gallant war, in the Palatinate, in the Netherlands, in Bohemia, no matter where, no matter when, all wars are fragments of a single war, all wars make up the nameless war, simply the war, the War, so that although the knight returns from travelling through a fragment of the war, it is as if he had journeyed through all wars and all the war, because all wars, even if they seem different when seen from close to, seen from a distance only repeat the same infamies and the same clamour, so let us not be scrupulous about names or dates, let us not worry if out of the Plantagenets and the Hohenstaufen we make one wayward family, if we mix lansquenets with grenadiers, crossbow-men with archers, or if we muddle our geography and mix cities with cities, castles with castles, towers with towers, and so returning to the knight we were saying that at last he is back from the war, back from a link in the chain of war, believing the war to be the very last link, not knowing that the chain is endless, or that it has an end but, being circular, that Time makes it turn as if it were endless, for he left young and brave and war returns him old, wizened and bald, although this is nothing new, war lacks imagina-tion and repeats its tricks, so the knight, like all knights who have been through a war without falling into Death's trap, is unshaven, grimy, smelling of sweat, blood and filth, his armpits infested with fleas, a rash burning the insides of his thighs, coughing greenish phlegm marbled with scarlet threads, speaking in a voice made harsh by frost, fire, hard drinking, oaths, cries of terror and courage, he can no longer utter two words without swearing, he has forgotten the florid language of his childhood when he served as a page at the court of some margrave or archbishop, he has forgotten the beautiful manners and graceful bows with which he charmed the ladies because now he no longer asks women for love, he asks them for wine, food, a bed, and while his soldiers rape the girls he drinks alone, in silence, until the soldiers come back yawning, and then he slams his hand on the table and curses, he curses the little kings fleeing pale and tattered on panting horses, those kings who will return in triumph as soon as the battle is over, dressed in cloth of gold, under a golden canopy, in the midst of an army of pennants and banners, he curses the Popes dressed in ermine who from the height of their gestatorial chairs sprinkle holy water on the scarlet seals of alliances and coalitions, he curses the Emperor whom he once saw walking between spears erect as phalluses at the sight of that damsel of war, and the knight jumps to his feet, knocks over his chair, knocks over the table, the glasses and the jug of wine, a violent quarrel flares up, the tavern or whatever is burnt to the ground, the innkeeper beaten, and the troop led by the knight rides on once more, and now it passes through a forest in the moonlight but the knight no longer curses, no longer makes a sound, he rides on, silent, his eyes staring deep into the night, and one by one the soldiers stop talking, they fall asleep in their saddles, each dreaming alone with his head fallen on his breastplate, one hearing perhaps a distant music, the music of his childhood in a village in the Duchy of Milan or in Catalonia, while another hears voices which call to him, the voice of his mother, the voice of his wife or his sweetheart, and another cries out and wakens with a start, but the knight doesn't stop, he doesn't turn to see who cried, as if the cry were the cry of a bird in the wood, he rides on with his eyes fixed upon the darkness, the moon polishing his armour, and the soldier behind him, the one nearest to him, the one carrying a tattered flag burnt by gunpowder, a flag now hanging over the rump of his horse like a filthy rag, that soldier, a blond youth very much like a minstrel, suddenly has a strange thought, he thinks that perhaps the knight's armour is riding empty, that the knight has vanished and all that is left is the armour like a hollow iron doll, or that perhaps the armour has overpowered the knight, sucked him up like a sponge, sucked his blood, crushed his bones, and now is an empty fleshless shell riding on, and he imagines this because he has never seen the knight without his armour and his spear, without his greaves and his gauntlets that point to the north of war, without his howling helmet beneath which lies a tangle of hair, but hair that belongs perhaps to a faceless beard, hair that is perhaps the helmet's stuffing, perhaps the whole armour is stuffed with hair, and the thought makes the blond soldier laugh because it occurs to him that the knight may have dried up in his armour a long time ago, that the armour became empty a long time ago and they, the soldiers, never learnt the truth, and they, the soldiers, have tramped behind this empty armour from battle to battle, defying Death in the firm belief that the knight would protect them from Death, and, as the blond standard-bearer laughs, like a sleep-walker or a drunkard the knight hoists himself on the edge of his stirrups and utters a curse, as if guessing the reason for the standard-bearer's laughter, trying to show him that deep down inside the armour he is still alive, or maybe to rebuke him for dreaming, and the blond soldier shrinks in fright until he realizes that the knight has not even woken, that he isn't cursing because of his laughter but because the trees in the forest, which up to that moment seemed frozen under the moon and under the winter snow, have suddenly burst into flower and are covered with fruit, which is to say – even though the image is old and you have all understood – that the trees have flowered with the blossoms that the heat of war brings forth in all four seasons, in good and in bad weather, in fertile lands as in waste lands, that the trees have been covered with that fruit which is always in season, always ripe for plucking or picking, I mean the enemy, I mean the unquenchable enemy who waits patiently, stubbornly, hidden in the shadow, blurred by the fog and the smoke, and then the slumbering horses turn in a flash – but all this has already happened, all this is over now and the knight has returned to his castle, without the clashing of metal, of horses and of men that followed him in his journey through one of the provinces of war, he has left behind the shouting, he has freed himself for ever from the soggy camps, the plundering, the ambushes, from hunger, terror, lack of sleep, he has kept nothing of the war except his horse, his panoply, his spear with the fox-skin at one end to stop the blood from dripping down and soaking his hand, he has kept the smell of sweat and filth, the lice, the rash, the exhaustion, the feebleness, old age and memories, memories out of the loud tableau of war, like that youth fallen on the grass, face skywards, sinking both his legs up to the knees in an uncaring river, the Rhine, the Tajo, the Arno, and the water passing by the body, lifting the legs, softening and tearing at them until it carries them downstream transformed into ravelled threads, first crimson, then pink, finally grey and ochre, or like those ten gallows in a dark and empty square, a body hanging from each one, ten dangling objects with their tongues out, and the wind made music with the bodies while in the steeple a bell sounded one same hour out of Time, or like the old man crouched to empty his bowels on the hard ground covered in frost and suddenly collapsing over a blossom of blood and feces, the ancient rose of dysentery, or like that lofty tower, square and built of bricks, rising against a row of cypresses, the jet of burning pitch spewing from one of the battlements, falling on the knights dressed in white tunics with a red cross on their chests, on the knights who were all so refined and beautiful and who had attended mass only a short while before, a mass conducted by an archbishop studded with precious stones, and the black crater dug by the boiling pitch, the hole smoking and crackling like a pan on the fire, until he, our knight, became aware of a sweetish smell, a smell of frying and burnt cloth, and felt a sting, and saw that a little piece of meat had landed on his hand, a little piece of flesh from one of those knights who a short while before had heard mass and commended themselves to God, because that is what the war had been for him, though perhaps for the little kings it had been something else and something else again for the Popes and the Emperors, perhaps a game of chess played at a distance, each of them locked up in a city, in a fortress, in a palace until the game is over and they come out and meet and shake hands like good sportsmen and split their share of harvested land, but now the knight has jumped off the chessboard of Popes and Emperors, now he returns to his castle, to his wife whom he left young and whom he expects to find as young as when he left her, to the sumptuously laden table and the warm well-made bed, to the falcon that used to perch on his gloved fist on the morning of the hunt, to the lute he once plucked, singing at a court in Provence or Sicily the roundelays of Cino de Pistoia, to the castle where he will at last cast off his armour like a dried scab, where he will take off his helmet like an alien head that could do nothing but swear and seek the track of the enemy's army, he returns to his castle where the little kings whom he saved from the ignominy of defeat will cover him with honours, where the Pope and the Emperor who move the pieces on the chessboard of war will make him duke or count palatine, and then, turning a bend in the road, he sees upon an untouched hill his untouched castle, he sees around it the fields and the peasants bent over the soil, he sees a dog, a domestic dog, a stray dog belonging to no one, a dog running among the stones, stopping here and there to sniff the traces of other dogs, and confronted with the idyllic picture of the castle, the peasants and the dog, the knight thinks that just as he cannot grasp the true key to war, held fast in the hands of Popes and Emperors and furiously coveted by little kings, these peasants bent over their furrows are denied the knowledge of the terrible task of war which has been his for so long, because for these peasants war will have been a blurred rumour, the glow of a fire in the distance, the marching of troops down the road, and as for the dog, the knight thinks, it did not even know there was a war, it did not even know there was plunder and murder, treaties blessed by the Pope, an Emperor who made spears rise like phalluses, it would have carried on eating, sleeping, coupling with other dogs and ignoring the fact that far away, where the knight was fighting, the frontiers were being undone in order to be done up again in another pattern, indeed the dog would never know that a Vicar of Christ was being dragged bleeding through the streets or that an Emperor was kneeling, day and night, naked, outside a door that never opened, it would never know that the flower of Christendom had been fried alive in pitch and oil and that a chime of hanged men tolled the hours on a dark and empty square, because for the dog the thunder of war made the same terrible noise as the thunder of a storm, and had the dog seen the damsel of war it would have barked at her as it would bark at a stranger, or wagged its tail if it had found her friendly or been given some food, and now the knight feels proud of being a knight, of having been one of the pieces on the chessboard of war, of belonging to History even though his name will not appear in History, even though only the names of the Popes and Emperors will appear in the Annals of History, and in smaller letters the names of the little kings, and the knight feels sorry for the peasants who do not even belong to History, and amazed at the dog, contemporary of Popes and Emperors, who will never know there have been Popes and Emperors, who will never even know there have been knights, he feels a kind of awe seeing this dog who comes to greet him as it would come to greet a peasant or an Emperor without distinguishing one from the other, who comes to greet him without suspecting the disasters and heroic deeds that girdle his armour, and following his thought, following this train of thought that begins with the dog, the knight thinks that perhaps the last links in the chain are not the Popes or the Emperors, because in the same way that the dog ignores what the peasants know, in the same way that the peasants ignore what the knight knows, and in the same way that the knight ignores what the little kings know, and the little kings what the Popes and the Emperors know, in the same way the Popes and the Emperors ignore what only God knows as a whole and in the perfection of Truth, and thinking this of war, believing that for God too war is something different from that which Popes and Emperors see, fills the knight with hope, hope that, in God's mind, History will include the knight's name, hope that if the Pope and the Emperor, masters of the game of war, will make him, the knight, a duke or a count in recognition of his bravery, then God, master of the game of Popes and Emperors, will absolve him of the murders, the rapes and the plunders, in recognition of his suffering, his hunger and his lack of sleep, and will receive him in Paradise, and this hope makes him smile, it comforts him and makes the past ills of the war seem worthwhile, when all of a sudden, just as hope is comforting the knight and making him smile, the dog, running to meet him, stops in its tracks as in front of a wall, digs its paws into the ground, its hackles rise, its jaws part in a snarl and it bares its fangs and starts to howl mournfully, but the knight attributes its behaviour to some insignificant circumstance, he attributes it to the fact that the dog does not know him and is frightened of the horse, or the armour, or the spear with the fox's tail hanging from one end, it's hardly surprising that this peasant's dog should be frightened of a knight dressed in iron, and of a horse adorned with head-stall and snaffle, so the knight pays no attention to the dog's behaviour and follows the road that leads to the hill on top of which stands his castle, and the hoofs of his horse are about to trample the dog but it jumps to one side at the last minute and continues to howl, continues to whimper and bare its teeth, while the knight remembers again his young wife, his falcon and his love-lute, and has forgotten about the dog, the dog now left behind him like the war, and what the knight will never know is that the dog has smelt on the knight's armour the stench of Death and Hell, because the dog already knows what the knight does not know, it knows that in the knight's groin a pustule has begun to distil the juices of the Plague, and that Death and the Devil are waiting for the knight at the foot of the hill to take him with them, because if the knight could read what I now write he would perhaps think, following an analogous train of thought but in reverse, he would think that just as the dog stopped there where he rides on so knights perhaps stop there where Popes and Emperors ride on, and perhaps therefore the Popes and Emperors will ignore his heroic deeds and not make him a duke or a count, he would think that the war of knights is, for Popes and Emperors, like the stench of Death and the Devil that only dogs can smell, and still within the circle of this reasoning the knight would think that perhaps Popes and Emperors stop there where God rides on, that perhaps they play a game of chess which God does not take into account, I mean which God does not watch, perhaps God does not even see their chessboard, and the sacrifice of the pieces serves no purpose in God's eyes and the knight will not be absolved of his sins nor admitted into Paradise, I mean that if the knight reasoned in this manner he would think that perhaps for God the realities that trap men form a web which cannot trap God, in the same way that the knight had passed through, without seeing it, the web in which the dog became entangled, even though the web was woven for the knight and not for the dog, even though the prayers, the hopes and sufferings of men are woven for God, but the knight will never read what I now write and he reaches the bottom of the hill, happy with the hope that his valour has woven a web that will trap the fly Pope, the fly Emperor, happy with the hope that Popes and Emperors have woven another web that will trap the fly God, while down there, on the road, the dog who confuses the thunder of war with the thunder of a storm continues to wage another, vaster war, in which the knight confuses the barking of Death with the barking of a dog.

*Translated from the Spanish by Alberto Manguel.*

# The Large Ant

## Howard Fast

*It comes as a surprise to realize that Howard Fast, the author of such vast bestsellers as* Spartacus, Citizen Tom Paine, My Glorious Brothers *and* Moses, Prince of Egypt – *readable but not remarkable historical novels – is also the author of wonderful fantastic stories such as 'The Martian Shop', 'The Cold, Cold Box', 'Cato the Martian', 'The Trap', and 'The Large Ant'. They have been collected under the title* Time and the Riddle *(echoing perhaps Thomas Wolfe's famous novel) and subtitled 'Twenty-One Zen Stories' – but this should not deter the reader. 'After a lifetime of writing fiction,' says Fast, 'I find it most engaging to clothe whatever philosophy and conclusions my life has brought me in stories that primarily entertain.'*

There had been all kinds of notions and guesses as to how it would end. One held that sooner or later there would be too many people; another that we would do each other in, and the atom bomb made that a very good likelihood. All sorts of notions, except the simple fact that we were what we were. We could find a way to feed any number of people and perhaps even a way to avoid wiping each other out with the bomb; those things we are very good at, but we have never been any good at changing ourselves or the way we behave.

I know. I am not a bad man or a cruel man; quite to the contrary, I am an ordinary, humane person, and I love my wife and my children and I get along with my neighbours. I am like a great many other men, and I do the things they would do and just as thoughtlessly. There it is in a nutshell.

I am also a writer, and I told Lieberman, the curator, and Fitzgerald, the government man, that I would like to write down the story. They shrugged their shoulders. 'Go ahead,' they said, 'because it won't make one bit of difference.'

'You don't think it would alarm people?'

'How can it alarm anyone when nobody will believe it?'

'If I could have a photograph or two.'

'Oh, no,' they said then. 'No photographs.'

'What kind of sense does that make?' I asked them. 'You are willing to let me write the story – why not the photographs so that people could believe me?'

'They still won't believe you. They will just say you faked the photographs, but no one will believe you. It will make for more confusion, and if we have a chance of getting out of this, confusion won't help.'

'What will help?'

They weren't ready to say that, because they didn't know. So here is what happened to me, in a very straightforward and ordinary manner.

Every summer, sometime in August, four good friends of mine and I go for a week's fishing on the St Regis chain of lakes in the Adirondacks. We rent the same shack each summer; we drift around in canoes, and sometimes we catch a few bass. The fishing isn't very good, but we play cards well together, and we cook out and generally relax. This summer past, I had some things to do that couldn't be put off. I arrived three days late, and the weather was so warm and even and beguiling that I decided to stay on by myself for a day or two after the others left. There was a small flat lawn in front of the shack, and I made up my mind to spend at least three or four hours at short putts. That was how I happened to have the putting iron next to my bed.

The first day I was alone, I opened a can of beans and a can of beer for my supper. Then I lay down on my bed with *Life on the Mississippi*, a pack of cigarettes, and an eight-ounce chocolate bar. There was nothing I had to do, no telephone, no demands and no newspapers. At the moment, I was about as contented as any man can be in these nervous times.

It was still light outside, and enough light came in through the window above my head for me to read by. I was just reaching for a fresh cigarette, when I looked up and saw it on the foot of my bed. The edge of my hand was touching the golf club, and with a single motion I swept the club over and down, struck it a savage and accurate blow, and killed it. This is what I referred to before. Whatever kind of a man I am, I react as a man does. I think that any man, black, white or yellow, in China, Africa or Russia, would have done the same thing.

First I found that I was sweating all over, and then I knew I was going to be sick. I went outside to vomit, recalling that this hadn't happened to me since 1943, on my way to Europe on a tub of a Liberty Ship. Then I felt better and was able to go back into the shack and look at it. It was quite dead, but I had already made up my mind that I was not going to sleep alone in this shack.

I couldn't bear to touch it with my bare hands. With a piece of brown paper, I picked it up and dropped it into my fishing creel. That, I put into the trunk case of my car, along with what luggage I carried. Then I closed the door of the shack, got into my car and drove back to New York. I stopped once along the road, just before I reached the Thruway, to nap in the car for a little over an hour. It was almost dawn when I reached the city, and I had shaved, had a hot bath and changed my clothes before my wife awoke.

During breakfast, I explained that I was never much of a hand at the solitary business, and since she knew that, and since driving alone all night was by no means an extraordinary procedure for me, she didn't press me with any questions. I had two eggs, coffee and a cigarette. Then I went into my study, lit another cigarette, and contemplated my fishing creel, which sat upon my desk.

My wife looked in, saw the creel, remarked that it had too ripe a smell, and asked me to remove it to the basement.

'I'm going to dress,' she said. The kids were still at camp. 'I have a date with Ann for lunch – I had no idea you were coming back. Shall I break it?'

'No, please don't. I can find things to do that have to be done!'

Then I sat and smoked some more, and finally I called the Museum, and asked who the curator of insects was. They told me his name was Bertram Lieberman, and I asked to talk to him. He had a pleasant voice. I told him that my name was Morgan, and that I was a writer, and he politely indicated that he had seen my name and read something that I had written. That is formal procedure when a writer introduces himself to a thoughtful person.

I asked Lieberman if I could see him, and he said that he had a busy morning ahead of him. Could it be tomorrow?

'I am afraid it has to be now,' I said firmly.

'Oh? Some information you require.'

'No, I have a specimen for you.'

'Oh?' The 'oh' was a cultivated, neutral interval. It asked and answered and said nothing. You have to develop that particular 'oh'.

'Yes. I think you will be interested.'

'An insect?' he asked mildly.

'I think so.'

'Oh? Large?'

'Quite large,' I told him.

'Eleven o'clock? Can you be here then? On the main floor, to the right, as you enter.'

'I'll be there,' I said.

'One thing – dead?'

'Yes, it's dead.'

'Oh?' again. 'I'll be happy to see you at eleven o'clock, Mr Morgan.'

My wife was dressed now. She opened the door of my study and said firmly, 'Do get rid of the fishing creel. It smells.'

'Yes, darling. I'll get rid of it.'

'I should think you'd want to take a nap after driving all night.'

'Funny, but I'm not sleepy,' I said. 'I think I'll drop around to the museum.'

My wife said that was what she liked about me, that I never tired of places like museums, police courts and third-rate night clubs.

Anyway, aside from a racetrack, a museum is the most interesting and unexpected place in the world. It was unexpected to have two other men waiting for me, along with Mr Lieberman, in his office. Lieberman was a skinny, sharp-faced man of about sixty. The government man, Fitzgerald, was small, dark-eyed, and wore gold-rimmed glasses. He was very alert, but he never told me what part of the government he represented. He just said 'we', and it meant the government. Hopper, the third man, was comfortable-looking, pudgy, and genial. He was a United States senator with an interest in entomology, although before this morning I would have taken better than even money that such a thing not only wasn't, but could not be.

The room was large and square and plainly furnished, with shelves and cupboards on all walls.

We shook hands, and then Lieberman asked me, nodding at the creel. 'Is that it?'

'That's it.'

'May I?'

'Go ahead,' I told him. 'It's nothing that I want to stuff for the parlour. I'm making you a gift of it.'

'Thank you, Mr Morgan,' he said, and then he opened the creel and looked inside. Then he straightened up, and the other two men looked at him inquiringly.

He nodded. 'Yes.'

The senator closed his eyes for a long moment. Fitzgerald took off his glasses and wiped them industriously. Lieberman spread a piece of plastic on his desk, and then lifted the thing out of my creel and laid it on the plastic. The two men didn't move. They just sat where they were and looked at it.

'What do you think it is, Mr Morgan?' Lieberman asked me.

'I thought that was your department.'

'Yes, of course. I only wanted your impression.'

'An ant. That's my impression. It's the first time I saw an ant fourteen, fifteen inches long. I hope it's the last.'

'An understandable wish,' Lieberman nodded.

Fitzgerald said to me, 'May I ask you how you killed it, Mr Morgan?'

'With an iron. A golf club, I mean. I was doing a little fishing with some friends up at St Regis in the Adirondacks, and I brought the iron for my short shots. They're the worst part of my game, and when my friends left I intended to stay on at our shack and do four or five hours of short putts. You see—'

'There's no need to explain,' Hopper smiled, a trace of sadness on his face. 'Some of our very best golfers have the same trouble.'

'I was lying in bed, reading, and I saw it at the foot of my bed. I had the club—'

'I understand,' Fitzgerald nodded.

'You avoid looking at it,' Hopper said.

'It turns my stomach.'

'Yes – yes, I suppose so.'

Lieberman said, 'Would you mind telling us why you killed it, Mr Morgan.'

'Why?'

'Yes – why?'

'I don't understand you,' I said. 'I don't know what you're driving at?'

'Sit down, please, Mr Morgan,' Hopper nodded. 'Try to relax. I'm sure this has been very trying.'

'I still haven't slept. I want a chance to dream before I say how trying.'

'We are not trying to upset you, Mr Morgan,' Lieberman said. 'We do feel, however, that certain aspects of this are very important. That is why I am asking you why you killed it. You must have had a reason. Did it seem about to attack you?'

'No.'

'Or make any sudden motion towards you?'

'No. It was just there.'

'Then why?'

'This is to no purpose,' Fitzgerald put in. 'We know why he killed it.'

'Do you?'

'The answer is very simple, Mr Morgan. You killed it because you are a human being.'

'Oh?'

'Yes. Do you understand?'

'No. I don't.'

'Then why did you kill it?' Hopper put in.

'I was scared to death. I still am, to tell the truth.'

Lieberman said, 'You are an intelligent man, Mr Morgan. Let me show you something.' He then opened the doors of one of the wall cupboards, and there were eight jars of formaldehyde and in each jar a specimen like mine – and in each case mutilated by the violence of its death. I said nothing. I just stared.

Lieberman closed the cupboard doors. 'All in five days,' he shrugged.

'A new race of ants,' I whispered stupidly.

'No. They're not ants. Come here!' He motioned me to the desk and the other two joined me. Lieberman took a set of dissecting instruments out of his drawer, used one to turn the thing over and then pointed to the underpart of what would be the thorax in an insect.

'That looks like part of him, doesn't it, Mr Morgan?'

'Yes, it does.'

Using two of the tools, he found a fissure and pried the bottom apart. It came open like the belly of a bomber; it was a pocket, a pouch, a receptacle that the thing wore, and in it were four beautiful little tools or instruments or weapons, each about an inch and a half long. They were beautiful the way any object of functional purpose and loving creation is beautiful – the way the creature itself would have been beautiful, had it not been an insect and myself a man. Using tweezers, Lieberman took each instrument off the brackets that held it, offering each to me. And I took each one, felt it, examined it, and then put it down.

I had to look at the ant now, and I realized that I had not truly looked at it before. We don't look carefully at a thing that is horrible or repugnant to us. You can't look at anything through a screen of hatred. But now the hatred and the fear was dilute, and as I looked, I realized it was not an ant although like an ant. It was nothing that I had ever seen or dreamed of.

All three men were watching me, and suddenly I was on the defensive. 'I didn't know! What do you expect when you see an insect that size?'

Lieberman nodded.

'What in the name of God is it?'

From his desk, Lieberman produced a bottle and four small glasses. He poured and we drank it neat. I would not have expected him to keep good Scotch in his desk.

'We don't know,' Hopper said. 'We don't know what it is.'

Lieberman pointed to the broken skull from which a white substance oozed. 'Brain material – a great deal of it.'

'It could be a very intelligent creature,' Hopper nodded.

Lieberman said, 'It is an insect in developmental structure. We know very little about intelligence in our insects. It's not the same as what we call intelligence. It's a collective phenomenon – as if you were to think of the component parts of our bodies. Each part is alive, but the intelligence is a result of the whole. If that same pattern were to extend to creatures like this one—'

I broke the silence. They were content to stand there and stare at it.

'Suppose it were?'

'What?'

'The kind of collective intelligence you were talking about.'

'Oh? Well, I couldn't say. It would be something beyond our wildest dreams. To us – well, what we are to an ordinary ant.'

'I don't believe that,' I said shortly, and Fitzgerald, the government man, told me quietly, 'Neither do we. We guess.'

'If it's that intelligent, why didn't it use one of those weapons on me?'

'Would that be a mark of intelligence?' Hopper asked mildly.

'Perhaps none of these are weapons,' Lieberman said.

'Don't you know? Didn't the others carry instruments?'

'They did,' Fitzgerald said shortly.

'Why? What were they?'

'We don't know,' Lieberman said.

'But you can find out. We have scientists, engineers – good God, this is an age of fantastic instruments. Have them taken apart!'

'We have.'

'Then what have you found out?'

'Nothing'.

'Do you mean to tell me,' I said, 'that you can find out nothing about these instruments – what they are, how they work, what their purpose is?'

'Exactly,' Hopper nodded. 'Nothing, Mr Morgan. They are meaningless to the finest engineers and technicians in the United States. You know the old story – suppose you gave a radio to Aristotle? What would he do with it? Where would he find power? And what would he receive with no one to send? It is not that these instruments are complex. They are actually very simple. We simply have no idea of what they can or should do.'

'But they must be a weapon of some kind.'

'Why?' Lieberman demanded. 'Look at yourself, Mr Morgan – a cultured and intelligent man, yet you cannot conceive of a mentality that does not include weapons as a prime necessity. Yet a weapon is an unusual thing, Mr Morgan. An instrument of murder. We don't think that way, because the weapon has become the symbol of the world we inhabit. Is that civilized, Mr Morgan? Or is the weapon and civilization in the ultimate sense incompatible? Can you imagine a mentality to which the concept of murder is impossible – or let me say absent. We see everything through our own subjectivity. Why shouldn't some other – this creature, for example – see the process of mentation out of his subjectivity? So he approaches a creature of our world – and he is slain. Why? What explanation? Tell me, Mr Morgan, what conceivable explanation could we offer a wholly rational creature for this—' pointing to the thing on his desk. 'I am asking you the question most seriously. What explanation?'

'An accident?' I muttered.

'And the eight jars in my cupboard? Eight accidents?'

'I think, Dr Lieberman,' Fitzgerald said, 'that you can go a little too far in that direction.'

'Yes, you would think so. It's a part of your own background. Mine is as a scientist. As a scientist, I try to be rational when I can. The creation of a structure of good and evil, or what we call morality and ethics, is a function of intelligence – and unquestionably the ultimate evil may be the destruction of conscious intelligence. That is why, so long ago, we at least recognized the injunction, "thou shalt not kill!" even if we never gave more than lip service to it. But to a collective intelligence, such as this might be a part of, the concept of murder would be monstrous beyond the power of thought.'

I sat down and lit a cigarette. My hands were trembling. Hopper apologized. 'We have been rather rough with you, Mr Morgan. But over the past days, eight other people have done just what you did. We are caught in the trap of being what we are.'

'But tell me – where do these things come from?'

'It almost doesn't matter where they come from,' Hopper said hopelessly. 'Perhaps from another planet – perhaps from inside this one – or the moon or Mars. That doesn't matter. Fitzgerald thinks they come from a smaller planet, because their movements are apparently slow on earth. But Dr Lieberman thinks that they move slowly because they have not discovered the need to move quickly. Meanwhile, they have the problem of murder and what to do with it. Heaven knows how many of them have died in other places – Africa, Asia, Europe.'

'Then why don't you publicize this? Put a stop to it before it's too late!'

'We've thought of that,' Fitzgerald nodded. 'What then – panic, hysteria, charges that this is the result of the atom bomb? We can't change. We are what we are.'

'They may go away,' I said.

'Yes, they may,' Lieberman nodded. 'But if they are without the curse of murder, they may also be without the curse of fear. They may be social in the highest sense. What does society do with a murderer?'

'There are societies that put him to death – and there are other societies that recognize his sickness and lock him away, where he can kill no more,' Hopper said. 'Of course, when a whole world is on trial, that's another matter. We have atom bombs now and other things, and we are reaching out to the stars—'

'I'm inclined to think that they'll run,' Fitzgerald put it. 'They may just have that curse of fear, Doctor.'

'They may,' Lieberman admitted. 'I hope so.'

But the more I think of it the more it seems to me that fear and hatred are the two sides of the same coin. I keep trying to think back, to recreate the moment when I saw it standing at the foot of my bed in the fishing shack. I keep trying to drag out of my memory a clear picture of what it looked like, whether behind that chitinous face and the two gently swaying antennae there was any evidence of fear and anger. But the clearer the memory becomes, the more I seem to recall a certain wonderful dignity and repose. Not fear and not anger.

And more and more, as I go about my work, I get the feeling of what Hopper called 'a world on trial'. I have no sense of anger myself. Like a criminal who can no longer live with himself, I am content to be judged.

# The Lemmings

## Alex Comfort

*The uncomfortable feeling that arises in us when we read Howard Fast's 'The Large Ant' comes from realizing that faced with a similar situation, we would react in exactly the same way. The fantastic story can bring to light an underlying strain in man's character and transform it into a guilt-ridden nightmare, as in Alex Comfort's 'The Lemmings'.*

*Alex Comfort, doctor of social psychology, gerontologist and writer, appears in his poems and novels as a staunch pacifist of anarchist beliefs. He refused military service during World War Two and became deeply involved with the 'New Romanticism' movement in England; he was influenced by Herbert Read, whose one remarkable novel* The Green Child *is among other things a fantastic vision of that better world for which Comfort seems to strive. In 1973 Alex Comfort published the huge best-seller,* The Joy of Sex.

It is an extremely long time since I was on that particular island, but I understand that what I am about to describe continues to occur periodically, though no longer regularly every five years as was formerly the case.

I had travelled a considerable distance from the nearest steamer port in a small boat rowed by a native fisherman. Upon coming in sight of the island I noticed nothing unusual, but one of the rowers maintained that he could see greater activity than usual in the colony which extended along a line of yellow rocks running to westward. I could see the chimneys of the Keeper's house, however, and as we approached the jetty, which was constructed of bamboo poles and very flimsy, I noticed the Keeper himself hastening down a path through the woods to meet us. I also noticed that the path and the garden of the house was everywhere surrounded with high wire mesh fences, which, so far as I could judge by the recently turned earth at their bases, were continued to some depth underground.

My anxiety to meet the Keeper was extremely great. I had heard the most remarkable stories on the boat both of the spectacle I had come so far to witness and of the extraordinary personality of this man – of his almost supernatural influence over his charges, who on account of the shortage of food on the island would probably have gnawed to death any other human visitor not under his protection – and of his alleged power of conversing with the creatures in their own language, an assertion which I am unable any longer to doubt.

'You are just in time,' he remarked, shaking me by both hands as I stepped ashore. 'Had you been a day late you might well have missed the whole performance. As it is we are in ample time. You will be able to lunch with me, I think: I doubt if they will begin before tea-time. Please bring your bag to my house, and instruct the crew to fetch you in two days' time. Their arrival sooner might disturb the proceedings.'

Examining the Keeper I found him to be a middle-aged man, bald, extremely – and at times, indeed, effusively – genial, wearing a blue uniform with red-piped edges, similar to that which postmen at home are accustomed to wear. The most singular feature of his attire, however, was a clerical collar, much soiled – owing, I suppose, to the infrequency of trade with that island: he also wore a stout leather belt, from which was suspended a whistle and an object which I took to be a sugar stick, but I saw upon closer inspection that it was a life-preserver, painted white with coloured spiral stripes like those upon a barber's pole. Seeing that my gaze rested upon these objects he smiled apologetically and explained their use.

'I assumed the collar,' he said, 'not out of religious conviction, but because, for some reason or other, I find it makes them less restive. You could imagine no shier animals. They take the most violent objection to some minor articles of dress – by the way, I must ask you if you have a watch or clock with you?'

I told him that I had.

'Then you will be so kind as to leave it at the house if we are to go down among them. It's a prejudice I have never been able to understand. As for this truncheon, I have to carry it, for even I am not entirely safe – their numbers are so great – but I feel that to carry it openly might diminish their confidence in me. That confidence,' he said, 'is my major joy in life. I could never do anything which might diminish it. I have been on this island for

nearly fifty years, alone, and I find these creatures my truest friends.'
A large tear ran down the piping on his collar.

'But what can have made you select so lonely and unremunerative
an office?' I asked him.

'I do not know,' he replied. 'But the creatures chose me
themselves.'

'Chose you?'

'Yes, indeed. Please be careful of that hole. There are others near
here, and my sight is not good enough to point them all out to you.
The wire is defective. Very defective. Yes, you must know that
formerly the office of keeper here was hereditary. When it was
thrown open for applications, I was the first to submit my name,
together with a Scotsman. The retiring keeper stood us on the
beach. There were thousands of them – the rocks and the sand were
brown with them. Suddenly at a word from the Keeper they came
forward, flowing over the rocks like hairy treacle. It was too much
for the Scotsman. He turned to get behind the wire, but the old
Keeper tripped him up, and they were all over him in a few seconds.
He only managed to kill one. When they went away, his brain was
the only part of him they had been unable to reach. My first duty,
when the old Keeper had given me his whistle and truncheon and
been rowed away, was to bury this separately. I have some of the
bones in my study. They show the most interesting tooth-prints.'

We were by now approaching the house, which was large and
well built. It was surmounted by a watch-tower which, being the
highest point of the island, dominated the shore in all directions.
There was an elaborate system of trenches, nets, and wires crossing
in every direction throughout the garden of the house, and upon
coming accidentally in contact with one of these I was surprised to
receive a sharp electric shock.

'I regret these defensive measures,' said my host. 'They are so
unsightly. But I fear they are extremely necessary.'

Having let us in with a key, my host guided me to my room and
invited me to join him on top of the tower in a few minutes' time.
From this eminence, as I have said, the entire island was revealed.
I found my host leaning over the balcony examining a distant part
of the coast through a pair of fieldglasses. Being unassisted by any
such appliance, I could see nothing, except an appearance resembling a reddish-brown smoke which was passing along a small rocky
valley among the trees to our right. There were a number of small

bare hills of a sandy soil, and I noticed that these were studded in all directions with circular black mouths of holes, and with the mounds of yellow soil thrown up in the course of their excavation.

'I think,' the Keeper was remarking, 'they are going to start from that bay over there, Skull Bay. Yes, I am sure they are. You are going to be privileged. You will have a perfect view of the entire performance. Look over there, look over there . . . They are assembling in their thousands.'

As, however, he retained the glasses pressed closely to his eyes, I could be certain of nothing, only it appeared to me that along every defile a column of the same brownish smoke was making its way to the spot which he indicated. The spit of rocks at the far side of this bay, the same which I had remarked on approaching the island, was encrusted with a thick moving deposit of the same colour, like live fur. I mentioned this appearance to the Keeper, in the hope of getting the loan of his glasses.

'It is live fur,' he remarked, retaining them. 'You would never imagine the intelligence of the creatures, the love and patience which they have expended in preparing for this day. The females have swum for miles removing the weeds from the bay and the rocks. The males have been digging and refilling holes with almost human industry to prepare themselves. I ought to explain to you exactly what will happen. Very soon they will begin to gather in groups, as if to be addressed by their leaders. But they are waiting for me to give the signal. They have taken me into their confidence throughout. I have witnessed this event no less than nine times. I know by now what sort of things please them. I carve them little medals out of the tops of condensed milk tins and hang them from ribbons. For weeks beforehand they wait at my back door to drag the medals away to their holes. In their enthusiasm to make preparations they do irreparable damage to the island – that, I suppose, is partly responsible for the food shortage – but one has not the heart to stop them.'

'But what exactly will they do?' I asked him.

'When they have been addressed by their leaders they will go down to the shore, all together, and stand along the edge of the sea. By that time it will be sundown, and they will call to me. I will then hoist a flag upon the pole which you see upon that hill. Then the leaders will enter the water, a few at a time. Gradually they will pass through the line of breakers and begin to swim out towards the setting sun and the open sea. Others will follow, squeaking with confidence. I tell you I have watched this spectacle no less than nine times, and on every occasion I have been struck and inspired by the expression of confidence upon the faces of every individual animal, even the females and the extremely young. You must forgive my sentimental and unscientific approach, but I have come to regard the creatures with affection, and I can interpret their expressions as you can those of a man.'

'And what then?' I asked.

'They continue to swim out to sea.'

'For how long?'

'Until the last one has sunk. It is a most touching business. For weeks later the island is abnormally quiet, and I go round collecting and skinning the corpses with which the windward side is littered. The white sand on those beaches is almost entirely composed of pulverized bone.'

I pondered for a moment this astounding biological phenomenon. 'But how is it,' I asked him, 'that the species does not become extinct?'

'A certain number remain behind, of course,' he told me. 'The malformed and the sick, some of the extremely aged – though I have noticed the enthusiasm with which these lead the march to the shore, though hardly able to stagger along and quite unable to participate by swimming. And there are a certain number of abnormal adults who seem to have no urge to join in the migration. These are quite often killed by the others, though. I may be able to show you a few tonight.' He put away the glasses, as by now the sun was not far from the water of the bay, and he found it dazzling. 'If we go now,' he said, 'we shall have time for a meal before the migration begins.'

Accordingly we went downstairs. The Keeper's imported food was excellent, and he diverted me throughout the meal with the exhibition and explanation of the curiosities with which the room was filled, including the Scotsman's bones, and a number of curious objects washed ashore by the sea. So much, however, was I wearied by my journey, that in the course of his talking I fell fast asleep.

I was awakened by my host bending over me and shaking me. I noticed, although the light was rapidly failing, that he had large tears running down his face. 'Come,' he said, 'they are waiting for me.' He removed a red flag from a small locker and opened the front door. We passed at a run through a gate in the high wire fence, which my host unlocked, and on among the trunks of the small trees with which the island is covered. On a number of occasions I fell as a result of catching my feet in holes or mounds of earth. The woods were entirely deserted, but I could detect a multiplicity of footprints all running the same way as we were running. My companion seemed to know every inch of the ground, for he never stumbled until we found ourselves on the summit of the small hole-riddled hill overlooking the bay, where the pole stood. 'We are in time,' he gasped.

I looked down on to the beach below me, utterly astounded by what I saw, a sight that in every way surpassed my expectations. The arena of white sand was illuminated by the oblique red light of the sun under a cloud bank, and both it and the spit of seaward rocks were flowing and undulating with an immense crowd of small red furry animals. They surged over the stones at the foot of the low cliffs, and fresh contingents continued to arrive in streams which poured out of several defiles and paths leading to the beach rather like a viscous fluid. There was a tide-mark of them creeping and climbing on the rocks. The beach itself was so congested that a number of the animals were jammed into cracks in the stones, while a long brown fringe undulated with each successive wave. My host was enraptured. 'I never, never saw so many,' was all he was capable of saying at first. Then he began to talk rapidly in my ear, pointing out to me facts which I would not otherwise have observed. I noted that the animals were engaged in crowding into groups, in the centres of which larger and older individuals could be seen. I could smell an overpowering smell of small rodent. The air was full of a minute shuffling and the dry noise of claws and tails crossing on stones. Turning my attention to individual animals closer to myself, I noticed that many were cleaning their fur, while the females brushed and licked their young and marshalled them in the direction of the shore. I noticed – or rather the Keeper pointed out to me with pride – that one of the larger lemmings was dragging a tin medal from a bedraggled ribbon between his prominent front teeth. I observed also the complacent, if not confident, expression upon the faces of the rodents, though being unfamiliar with their normal appearance I am unable to state its significance.

'Look there,' said the Keeper, 'that's the oldest animal I've seen. He's at the centre of a group. And do you see—' Here he broke off short, watching closely a small group of animals on the top of a low dune, separated from the rest. Their fur was noticeably less kempt than that of the others, and they were huddled into a group. As I watched, a larger lemming, passing, dragged one of them down into the crowd, and after a while his corpse was thrown out and rolled down the dune. 'Those are some of the abnormals I told you of,' said the Keeper. 'They're apparently refusing to go.'

Suddenly he stiffened, and caught my arm, pointing out to sea. The lower limb of the sun, elliptical in form, had touched the horizon. There was an instant cessation of movement below us, except where at the periphery of the crowd a few latecomers hastened to take their places. Then suddenly a shrill dry squeaking commenced at the end of the spit in the far distance and approached, until its volume was terrible. I put my hands to my ears, but could not exclude it. The Keeper spoke but I could not hear his words. With feverish hands he attached the flag to its halliard and hoisted it.

Instantly the sound ceased. There was a long quiet pause. And then the first lemming entered the water, and swam resolutely out, its head and paws jerking, and a red arrowhead of ripple coming from its chin. It swam about three yards alone, and then a second followed it, and another. Within a few moments the surface of the bay was covered with the minute black wedges of heads and intersecting V-shaped ripples, and the entire gathering began to crowd down the beach to the water, calling quietly to one another, the females administering a final preen to their young, the adults ruffling and smoothing their coats. They began to pass below us, headed out to sea. The Keeper took off his cap and held it before him, weeping and clapping his hands. After a while one or two of the animals ceased to swim and sank, many of them at a point immediately below our hill. I noticed that whenever one appeared on the point of sinking, two of the larger lemmings would rush towards him and attempt to reach him in time to hang round his neck one of the tin medals, the weight and encumbrance of which usually caused him to sink at once, though here and there the ribbon remained floating, suggesting that in these instances the medal was of wood. Before many moments had passed, there remained on the beach only the small group on their dune, and a solitary infant which rushed to and fro and finally entered the water, sinking just off the rocks below our viewpoint. The Keeper was shouting at the top of his voice, 'Wonderful, wonderful!' By this time the squeaking was dying away, and the light fading. Only the net of ripples marked the progress of the lemmings out to sea.

The Keeper hauled down the flag, trembling with emotion. Already a few bodies were being returned by the water along the line of the tide. I gave him my promise to assist him the following day in the collection and preservation of the valuable skins, and thanked him for his hospitality and the unique opportunity I had enjoyed. By now it was dark, and the island extremely quiet.

# The Grey Ones

## J. B. Priestley

*Under the influence of Dunne's* An Experiment with Time *(where it is suggested that memory can flow forwards as well as backwards), J. B. Priestley wrote four splendid fantastic plays:* Dangerous Corner *(1932),* Time and the Conways *(1937),* I Have Been Here Before *(also 1937) and* An Inspector Calls *(1945). His novels, however, are not fantastic and 'The Grey Ones' is, to the best of my knowledge, Priestley's only fantastic short story.*

*Guy de Maupassant died insane in 1893 having published over three hundred short stories during his lifetime. One of these, 'The Horla' (he wrote two versions of the same story), deals with a man who believes that the world is being taken over by a mysterious creature. Priestley's story on a similar theme is more convincing. The end, admittedly, is forseeable, but the nagging question remains: what if what we see is not what it seems to be? What if our world is a deception?*

'And your occupation, Mr Patson?' Dr Smith asked, holding his beautiful fountain pen a few inches from the paper.

'I'm an exporter,' said Mr Patson, smiling almost happily. Really this wasn't too bad at all. First, he had drawn Dr Smith instead of his partner Dr Meyenstein. Not that he had anything against Dr Meyenstein, for he had never set eyes on him, but he had felt that it was at least a small piece of luck that Dr Smith had been free to see him and Dr Meyenstein hadn't. If he had to explain himself to a psychiatrist, then he would much rather have one simply and comfortably called Smith. And Dr Smith, a broad-faced man about fifty with giant rimless spectacles, had nothing forbidding about him, and looked as if he might have been an accountant, a lawyer, or a dentist. His room, too, was reassuring, with nothing frightening in it; rather like a sitting room in a superior hotel. And that fountain pen really was a beauty. Mr Patson had already made a mental note to ask Dr Smith where he had bought that pen. And surely a man who could make such a mental note, right off, couldn't have much wrong with him?

'It's a family business,' Mr Patson continued, smiling away. 'My grandfather started it. Originally for the Far East. Firms abroad, especially in rather remote places, send us orders for all manner of goods, which we buy here on commission for them. It's not the business it was fifty years ago, of course, but on the other hand we've been helped to some extent by all these trade restrictions and systems of export licences, which people a long way off simply can't cope with. So we cope for them. Irritating work often, but not uninteresting. On the whole I enjoy it.'

'That is the impression you've given me,' said Dr Smith, making a note. 'And you are reasonably prosperous, I gather? We all have our financial worries these days, of course. I know I have.' He produced a mechanical sort of laugh, like an actor in a comedy that had been running too long, and Mr Patson echoed him like another bored actor. Then Dr Smith looked grave and pointed his pen at Mr Patson as if he might shoot him with it. 'So I think we can eliminate all that side, Mr Patson – humph?'

'Oh yes – certainly – certainly,' said Mr Patson hurriedly, not smiling now.

'Well now,' said Dr Smith, poising his pen above the paper again, 'tell me what's troubling you.'

Mr Patson hesitated. 'Before I tell you the whole story, can I ask you a question?'

Dr Smith frowned, as if his patient had made an improper suggestion. 'If you think it might help—'

'Yes, I think it would,' said Mr Patson, 'because I'd like to know roughly where you stand before I begin to explain.' He waited a moment. 'Dr Smith, do you believe there's a kind of Evil Principle in the universe, a sort of super devil, that is working hard to ruin humanity, and has its agents, who must really be minor devils or demons, living among us as people? Do you believe that?'

'Certainly not,' replied Dr Smith without any hesitation at all. 'That's merely a superstitious fancy, for which there is no scientific evidence whatever. It's easy to understand – though we needn't go into all that now – why anybody, even today, suffering from emotional stress, might be possessed by such an absurd belief, but of course it's mere fantasy, entirely subjective in origin. And the notion that this Evil Principle could have its agents among us might be very dangerous indeed. It could produce very serious antisocial effects. You realize that, Mr Patson?'

'Oh – yes – I do. I mean, at certain times when – well, when I've been able to look at it as you're looking at it, doctor. But most times I can't. And that, I suppose,' Mr Patson added, with a wan smile, 'is why I'm here.'

'Quite so,' Dr Smith murmured, making some notes. 'And I think you have been well advised to ask for some psychiatric treatment. These things are apt to be sharply progressive, although their actual progress might be described as regressive. But I won't worry you with technicalities, Mr Patson. I'll merely say that you – or was it Mrs Patson? – or shall I say both of you? – are to be congratulated on taking this very sensible step in good time. And now you know, as you said, where I stand, perhaps you had better tell me all about it. Please don't omit anything for fear of appearing ridiculous. I can only help you if you are perfectly frank with me, Mr Patson. I may ask a few questions, but their purpose will be to make your account clearer to me. By the way, here we don't adopt the psychoanalytic methods – we don't sit behind our patients while they relax on a couch – but if you would find it easier not to address me as you have been doing – face to face—'

'No, that's all right,' said Mr Patson, who was relieved to discover he would not have to lie on the couch and murmur at the opposite wall. 'I think I can talk to you just like this. Anyhow, I'll try.'

'Good! And remember, Mr Patson, try to tell me everything relevant. Smoke if it will help you to concentrate.'

'Thanks, I might later on.' Mr Patson waited a moment, surveying his memories as if they were some huge glittering sea, and then waded in. 'It began about a year ago. I have a cousin who's a publisher, and one night he took me to dine at his club – the Burlington. He thought I might like to dine there because it's a club used a great deal by writers and painters and musicians and theatre people. Well, after dinner we played bridge for an hour or two, then we went down into the lounge for a final drink before leaving. My cousin was claimed by another publisher, so I was left alone for about a quarter of an hour. It was then that I overheard Firbright – you know, the famous painter – who was obviously full of drink, although you couldn't exactly call him drunk, and was holding forth to a little group at the other side of the fireplace.

Apparently he'd just come back from Syria or somewhere around there, and he'd picked this idea up from somebody there though he said it only confirmed what he'd been thinking himself for some time.'

Dr Smith gave Mr Patson a thin smile. 'You mean the idea of an Evil Principle working to ruin humanity?'

'Yes,' said Mr Patson. 'Firbright said that the old notion of a scarlet and black sulphuric Satan, busy tempting people, was of course all wrong, though it might have been right at one time, perhaps in the Middle Ages. Then the devils were all fire and energy. Firbright quoted the poet Blake – I've read him since – to show that these weren't real devils and their hell wasn't the real hell. Blake, in fact, according to Firbright, was the first man here to suggest we didn't understand the Evil Principle, but in his time it had hardly made a start. It's during the last few years, Firbright said, that the horrible thing has really got to work on us.'

'Got to work on us?' Dr Smith raised his eyebrows. 'Doing what?'

'The main object, I gathered from what Firbright said,' Mr Patson replied earnestly, 'is to make mankind go the way the social insects went, to turn us into automatic creatures, mass beings without individuality, soulless machines of flesh and blood.'

The doctor seemed amused. 'And why should the Evil Principle want to do that?'

'To destroy the soul of humanity,' said Mr Patson, without an answering smile. 'To eliminate certain states of mind that belong essentially to the Good. To wipe from the face of this earth all wonder, joy, deep feeling, the desire to create, to praise life. Mind you, that is what Firbright said.'

'But you believed him?'

'I couldn't help feeling, even then, that there was something in it. I'd never thought on those lines before – I'm just a plain business man and not given to fancy speculation – but I had been feeling for some time that things were going wrong and that somehow they seemed to be out of our control. In theory I suppose we're responsible for the sort of lives we lead, but in actual practice we find ourselves living more and more the kind of life we don't like. It's as if,' Mr Patson continued rather wildly, avoiding the doctor's eye, 'we were all compelled to send our washing to one huge sinister laundry, which returned everything with more and more colour bleached out of it until it was all a dismal grey.'

'I take it,' said Dr Smith, 'that you are now telling me what you thought and felt yourself, and not what you overheard this man Firbright say?'

'About the laundry – yes. And about things never going the right way. Yes, that's what I'd been feeling. As if the shape and colour and smell of things were going. Do you understand what I mean, doctor?'

'Oh – yes – it's part of a familiar pattern. Your age may have something to do with it—'

'I don't think so,' said Mr Patson sturdily. 'This is something quite different. I've made all allowance for that.'

'So far as you can, no doubt,' said Dr Smith smoothly, without any sign of resentment. 'You must also remember that the English middle class, to which you obviously belong, has suffered recently from the effects of what has been virtually an economic and social revolution. Therefore any member of that class – and I am one myself – can't help feeling that life does not offer the same satisfactions as it used to do, before the war.'

'Dr Smith,' cried Mr Patson, looking straight at him now, 'I know all about that – my wife and her friends have enough to say about it, never stop grumbling. But this is something else. I may tell you, I've always been a Liberal and believed in social reform. And if this was a case of one class getting a bit less, and another class getting a bit more, my profits going down and my clerk's and warehousemen's wages going up, I wouldn't lose an hour's sleep over it. But what I'm talking about is something quite different. Economics and politics and social changes may come into it, but *they're just being used.*'

'I don't follow you there, Mr Patson.'

'You will in a minute, doctor. I want to get back to what I overheard Firbright saying, that night. I got away from it just to make the point that I couldn't help feeling at once there was something in what he said. Just because for the first time somebody had given me a reason why these things were happening.' He regarded the other man earnestly.

Smiling thinly, Dr Smith shook his head. 'The hypothesis of a mysterious but energetic Evil Principle, Mr Patson, doesn't offer us much of a reason.'

'It's a start,' replied Mr Patson, rather belligerently. 'And of course that wasn't all, by any means. Now we come to these agents.'

'Ah – yes – the agents.' Dr Smith looked very grave now. 'It was Firbright who gave you that idea, was it?'

'Yes, it would never have occurred to me, I'll admit. But if this Evil Principle was trying to make something like insects out of us, it could do it in two ways. One – by a sort of remote control, perhaps by a sort of continuous radio programme, never leaving our minds alone, telling us not to attempt anything new, to play safe, not to have any illusions, to keep to routine, not to waste time and energy wondering and brooding and being fanciful, and all that.'

'Did Firbright suggest something of that sort was happening?'

'Yes, but it wasn't his own idea. The man he'd been talking about before I listened to him, somebody he'd met in the Near East, had told him definitely all that non-stop propaganda was going on. But the other way – direct control, you might call it – was by the use of these agents – a sort of evil fifth column – with more and more of 'em everywhere, hard at work.'

'Devils?' enquired the doctor, smiling. 'Demons? What?'

'That's what they amount to,' said Mr Patson, not returning the smile but frowning a little. 'Except that it gives one a wrong idea of them – horns and tails and that sort of thing. These are quite different, Firbright said. All you can definitely say is that they're not human. They don't belong to us. They don't like us. They're working against us. They have their orders. They know what they're doing. They work together in teams. They arrange to get jobs for one another, more and more influence and power. So what chance have we against them?' And Mr Patson asked this question almost at the top of his voice.

'If such beings existed,' Dr Smith replied calmly, 'we should soon be at their mercy, I agree. But then they don't exist – except of course as figures of fantasy, although in that capacity they can do a great deal of harm. I take it, Mr Patson, that you have thought about – or shall we say *brooded over* – these demonic creatures rather a lot lately? Quite so. By the way, what do you call them? It might save time and possible confusion if we can give them a name.'

'They're the Grey Ones,' said Mr Patson without any hesitation.

'Ah – the Grey Ones.' Dr Smith frowned again and pressed his thin lips together, perhaps to show his disapproval of such a prompt reply. 'You seem very sure about this, Mr Patson.'

'Well, why shouldn't I be? You ask me what I call them, so I tell you. Of course, I don't know what they call themselves. And I didn't invent that name for them.'

'Oh – this is Firbright again, is it?'

'Yes, that's what I heard him calling them, and it seemed to me a very good name for them. They're trying to give everything a grey look, aren't they? And there's something essentially grey about these creatures themselves – none of your gaudy, red and black, Mephistopheles stuff about *them*. Just quiet grey fellows busy greying everything – that's them.'

'Is it indeed? Now I want to be quite clear about this, Mr Patson. As I suggested earlier, this idea of the so-called Grey Ones is something I can't dismiss lightly, just because it might have very serious antisocial effects. It is one thing to entertain a highly fanciful belief in some mysterious Evil Principle working on us for its own evil ends. It is quite another thing to believe that actual fellow citizens, probably highly conscientious and useful members of the community, are not human beings at all but so many masquerading demons. You can see that, can't you?'

'Of course I can,' said Mr Patson, with a flick of impatience. 'I'm not stupid, even though I may have given you the impression that I am. This idea of the Grey Ones – well, it brings the whole thing home to you, doesn't it? Here they are, busy as bees, round every corner, you might say.'

The doctor smiled. 'Yet you've never met one. Isn't that highly suggestive? Doesn't that make you ask yourself what truth there can be in this absurd notion? All these Grey Ones, seeking power over us, influencing our lives, and yet you've never actually come into contact with one. Now – now – Mr Patson—' And he wagged a finger.

'Who says I've never met one?' Mr Patson demanded indignantly. 'Where did you get that idea from, doctor?'

'Do you mean to tell me—?'

'Certainly I mean to tell you. I know at least a dozen of 'em. My own brother-in-law is one.'

Dr Smith looked neither shocked nor surprised. He merely stared searchingly for a moment or two, then rapidly made some notes. And now he stopped sounding like a rather playful schoolmaster and became a doctor in charge of a difficult case. 'So that's how it is, Mr Patson. You know at least a dozen Grey Ones, and one of them is your brother-in-law. That's correct, isn't it? Good! Very well, let us begin with your brother-in-law. When and how did you make the discovery that he is a Grey One?'

'Well, I'd wondered about Harold for years,' said Mr Patson slowly. 'I'd always disliked him but I never quite knew why. He'd always puzzled me too. He's one of those chaps who don't seem to have any centre you can understand. They don't act from any ordinary human feeling. They haven't motives you can appreciate. It's as if there was nothing inside 'em. They seem to tick over like automatic machines. Do you know what I mean, doctor?'

'It would be better now if you left me out of it. Just tell me what you thought and felt – about Harold, for instance.'

'Yes, Harold. Well, he was one of them. No centre, no feeling, no motives. I'd try to get closer to him, just for my wife's sake, although they'd never been close. I'd talk to him at home, after dinner, and sometimes I'd take him out. You couldn't call him unfriendly – that at least would have been *something*. He'd listen, up to a point, while I talked. If I asked him a question, he'd make some sort of reply. He'd talk himself in a kind of fashion, rather like a leading article in one of the more cautious newspapers. Chilly stuff, grey stuff. Nothing exactly wrong with it, but nothing right about it either. And after a time, about half an hour or so, I'd find it hard to talk to him, even about my own affairs. I'd begin wondering what to say next. There'd be a sort of vacuum between us. He had a trick, which I've often met elsewhere, of deliberately not encouraging you to go on, of just staring, waiting for you to say something silly. Now I put this down to his being a public official. When I first knew him, he was one of the assistants to the clerk of our local borough council. Now he's the clerk, quite a good job, for ours is a big borough. Well, a man in that position has to be more careful than somebody like me has. He can't let himself go, has too many people to please – or rather, not to offend. And one thing was certain about Harold – and that ought to have made him more human, but somehow it didn't – and that was that he meant to get on. He had ambition, but there again it wasn't an ordinary human ambition, with a bit of fire and nonsense in it somewhere, but a sort of cold determination to keep on moving up. You see what I mean? Oh – I forgot – no questions. Well, that's how he was – and is. But then I noticed another thing about Harold. And even my wife had to agree about this. He was what we called a damper. If you took him out to enjoy something, he not only didn't enjoy it himself, but he contrived somehow to stop you from enjoying it. I'm very fond of a good show – and don't mind seeing a really good one several times – but if I took Harold along then it didn't matter what it was, I couldn't enjoy it. He wouldn't openly attack it or sneer at it, but somehow by just being there, sitting beside you, he'd cut it down and take all the colour and fun out of it. You'd wonder why you'd wasted your evening and your money on such stuff. It was the same if you tried him with a football or cricket match, you'd have a boring afternoon. And if you asked him to a little party, it was fatal. He'd be polite, quite helpful, do whatever you asked him to do, but the party would never get going. It would be just as if he was invisibly spraying us with some devilish composition that made us all feel tired and bored and depressed. Once we were silly enough to take him on a holiday with us motoring through France and Italy. It was the worst holiday we ever had. He killed it stone dead. Everything he looked at seemed smaller and duller and greyer than it ought to have been. Chartres, the Loire country, Provence, the Italian Riviera, Florence, Siena – they were all cut down and greyed over, so that we wondered why we'd ever bothered to arrange such a trip and hadn't stuck to Torquay and Bournemouth. Then, before I'd learnt more sense, I'd talk to him about various plans I had for improving the business, but as soon as I'd described any scheme to Harold I could feel my enthusiasm ebbing away. I felt – or he made me feel – any possible development wasn't worth the risk. Better stick to the old routine. I think I'd have been done for now if I hadn't had sense enough to stop talking to Harold about the business. If he asked me about any new plans, I'd tell him I hadn't any. Now all this was long before I knew about the Grey Ones. But I had Harold on my mind, particularly as he lived and worked so close to us. When he became clerk to the council, I began to take more interest in our municipal affairs, just to see what influence Harold was having on them. I made almost a detective job of it. For instance, we'd had a go-ahead, youngish chief education officer, but he left and in his place a dull timid fellow was appointed. And I found out that Harold had worked that. Then we had a lively chap as entertainments officer, who'd brightened things up a bit, but Harold got rid of him too. Between them, he and his friend, the treasurer, who was another of them, managed to put an end to everything that added a little colour and sparkle to life round our way. Of course they always had a good excuse – economy and all that. But I noticed that Harold and the treasurer only made economies in one direction, on what you might call the anti-grey side, and never stirred themselves to save money in other directions, in what was heavily official, pompous, interfering, irritating, depressing, calculated to make you lose heart. And you must have noticed yourself that we never do save money in those directions, either in municipal or national affairs, and that what I complained of in our borough was going on all over the country – yes, and as far as I can make out, in a lot of other countries too.'

Dr Smith waited a moment or two, and then said rather sharply: 'Please continue, Mr Patson. If I wish to make a comment or ask a question, I will do so.'

'That's what I meant earlier,' said Mr Patson, 'when I talked about economies and politics and social changes just being used. I've felt all the time there was something behind 'em. If we're doing it for ourselves, it doesn't make sense. But the answer is of course that we're not doing it for ourselves, we're just being manipulated. Take communism. The Grey Ones must have almost finished the job in some of those countries – they hardly need to bother any more. All right, we don't like communism. We must make every possible effort to be ready to fight it. So what happens? More and more of the Grey Ones take over. This is their chance. So either way they win and we lose. We're farther along the road we never wanted to travel. Nearer the bees, ants, termites. Because we're being pushed. My God – doctor – can't you feel it yourself?'

'No, I can't, but never mind about me. And don't become too general, please. What about your brother-in-law, Harold? When did you decide he was a Grey One?'

'As soon as I began thinking over what Firbright said,' replied Mr Patson. 'I'd never been able to explain Harold before – and God knows I'd tried often enough. Then I saw at once he was a Grey One. He wasn't born one, of course, for that couldn't possibly be how it works. My guess is that sometime while he was still young, the soul or essence of the real Harold Sothers was drawn out and a Grey One slipped in. That must be going on all the time now, there are so many of them about. Of course they recognize each other and help each other, which makes it easy for them to handle us humans. They know exactly what they're up to. They receive and give orders. It's like having a whole well-disciplined secret army

working against us. And our only possible chance now is to bring
'em out into the open and declare war on 'em.'

'How can we do that,' asked Dr Smith, smiling a little, 'if they're
secret?'

'I've thought a lot about that,' said Mr Patson earnestly, 'and it's
not so completely hopeless as you might think. After a time you
begin to recognize a few. Harold, for instance. And our borough
treasurer. I'm certain he's one. Then, as I told you at first, there
are about a dozen more that I'd willingly stake a bet on. Yes, I
know what you're wondering, doctor. If they're all officials, eh?
Well no, they aren't, though seven or eight of 'em are – and you
can see why – because that's where the power is now. Another two
are up-and-coming politicians – and not in the same party neither.
One's a banker I know in the city – and he's a Grey One all right.
I wouldn't have been able to spot them if I hadn't spent so much
time either with Harold or wondering about him. They all have the
same cutting down and bleaching stare, the same dead touch. Wait
till you see a whole lot of 'em together, holding a conference.' Then
Mr Patson broke off abruptly, as if he felt he had said too much.

Dr Smith raised his eyebrows so that they appeared above his
spectacles, not unlike hairy caterpillars on the move. 'Perhaps you
would like a cigarette now, Mr Patson. No, take one of these. I'm
no smoker myself but I'm told they're excellent. Ah – you have a
light. Good! Now take it easy for a minute or two because I think
you're tiring a little. And it's very important you should be able to
finish your account of these – er – Grey Ones, if possible without
any hysterical overemphasis. No, no – Mr Patson – I didn't mean
to suggest there'd been any such overemphasis so far. You've done
very well indeed up to now, bearing in mind the circumstances.
And it's a heavy sort of day, isn't it? We seem to have too many
days like this, don't we? Or is it simply that we're not getting any
younger?' He produced his long-run actor's laugh. Then he brought
his large white hands together, contrived to make his lips smile
without taking the hard stare out of his eyes, and said finally: 'Now
then, Mr Patson. At the point you broke off your story, shall we
call it, you had suggested that you had seen a whole lot of Grey
Ones together, holding a conference. I think you might very usefully
enlarge that rather astonishing suggestion, don't you?'

Mr Patson looked and sounded troubled. 'I'd just as soon leave
that, if you don't mind, doctor. You see, if it's all nonsense, then

there's no point in my telling you about that business. If it isn't all nonsense—'

'Yes,' said Dr Smith, after a moment, prompting him, 'if it isn't all nonsense—?'

'Then I might be saying too much.' And Mr Patson looked about for an ashtray as if to hide his embarrassment.

'There – at your elbow, Mr Patson. Now please look at me. And remember what I said earlier. I am not interested in fanciful theories of the universe or wildly imaginative interpretations of present world conditions. All I'm concerned with here, in my professional capacity, is your state of mind, Mr Patson. That being the case, it's clearly absurd to suggest that you might be saying too much. Unless you are perfectly frank with me, it will be very difficult for me to help you. Come now, we agreed about that. So far you've followed my instructions admirably. All I ask now is for a little more cooperation. Did you actually attend what you believed to be a conference of these Grey Ones?'

'Yes, I did,' said Mr Patson, not without some reluctance. 'But I'll admit I can't prove anything. The important part may be something I imagined. But if you insist, I'll tell you what happened. I overheard Harold and our borough treasurer arranging to travel together to Maundby Hall, which is about fifteen miles north of where I live. I'd never been there myself but I'd heard of it in connection with various summer schools and conferences and that sort of thing. Perhaps you know it, Dr Smith?'

'As a matter of fact, I do. I had to give a paper there one Saturday night. It's a rambling early Victorian mansion, with a large ballroom that's used for the more important meetings.'

'That's the place. Well, it seems they were going there to attend a conference of the New Era Community Planning Association. And when I overheard them saying that, first I told myself how lucky I was not to be going too. Then afterward, thinking it over, I saw that if you wanted to hold a meeting that no outsider in his senses would want to attend, you couldn't do better than hold it in a country house that's not too easy to get at, and call it a meeting or conference of the New Era Community Planning Association. I know if anybody said to me "Come along with me and spend the day listening to the New Era Community Planning Association," I'd make any excuse to keep away. Of course it's true that anybody like Harold couldn't be bored. The Grey Ones are never bored, which is one reason why they are able to collar and hold down so many jobs nowadays, the sort of jobs that reek of boredom. Well, this New Era Community Planning Association might be no more than one of the usual societies of busybodies, cranks, and windbags. But then again it might be something very different, and I kept thinking about it in connection with the Grey Ones. Saturday was the day of the conference. I went down to my office in the morning, just to go through the post and see if there was anything urgent, and then went home to lunch. In the middle of the afternoon I felt I had to know what was happening out at Maundby Hall, so off I went in my car. I parked it just outside the grounds, scouted round a bit, then found an entrance through a little wood at the back. There was nobody about, and I sneaked into the house by way of a servants' door near the pantries and larders. There were some catering people around there, but nobody bothered me. I went up some back stairs and after more scouting, which I enjoyed as much as anything I've done this year, I was guided by the sound of voices to a small door in a corridor upstairs. This door was locked on the inside, but a fellow had once shown me how to deal with a locked door when the key's still in the lock on the other side. You slide some paper under the door, poke the key out so that it falls on to the paper and then slide the paper back with the key on it. Well, this trick worked and I was able to open the door, which I did very cautiously. It led to a little balcony overlooking the floor of the ballroom. There was no window near this balcony so that it was rather dark up there and I was able to creep down to the front rail without being seen. There must have been between three and four hundred of them in that ballroom, sitting on little chairs. This balcony was high above the platform, so I had a pretty good view of them as they sat facing it. They looked like Grey Ones, but of course I couldn't be sure. And for the first hour or so, I couldn't be sure whether this really was a meeting of the New Era Community Planning Association or a secret conference of Grey Ones. The stuff they talked would have done for either. That's where the Grey Ones are so damnably clever. They've only to carry on doing what everybody expects them to do, in their capacity as sound conscientious citizens and men in authority, to keep going with their own hellish task. So there I was, getting cramp, no wiser. Another lot of earnest busybodies might be suggesting new ways of robbing us of our individuality. Or an organized covey of masquerading devils and demons might be making plans to bring us nearer to the insects, to rob us of our souls. Well, I was just about to creep back up to the corridor, giving it up as a bad job, when something happened.' He stopped, and looked dubiously at his listener.

'Yes, Mr Patson,' said Dr Smith encouragingly, 'then something happened?'

'This is the part you can say I imagined, and I can't prove I didn't. But I certainly didn't dream it, because I was far too cramped and aching to fall asleep. Well, the first thing I noticed was a sudden change in the atmosphere of the meeting. It was as if somebody very important had arrived, although I didn't see anybody arriving. And I got the impression that the *real* meeting was about to begin. Another thing – I knew for certain now that this was no random collection of busybodies and windbags, that they were all Grey Ones. If you asked me to tell you in detail how I knew, I couldn't begin. But I noticed something else, after a minute or two. These Grey Ones massed together down there had now a positive quality of their own, which I'd never discovered before. It wasn't that they were just negative, not human, as they were at ordinary times; they had this positive quality, which I can't describe except as a sort of chilly hellishness. As if they'd stopped pretending to be human and were letting themselves go, recovering their demon natures. And here I'm warning you, doctor, that my account of what happened from then is bound to be sketchy and peculiar. For one thing, I wasn't really well placed up in that balcony; not daring to show myself and only getting hurried glimpses; and for another thing, I was frightened. Yes, doctor, absolutely terrified. I was crouching there just above three or four hundred creatures from some cold hell. That quality I mentioned, that chilly hellishness, seemed to come rolling over me in waves. I might have been kneeling on the edge of a pit of iniquity a million miles deep. I felt the force of this hellishness not on the outside but inside, as if the very essence of me was being challenged and attacked. One slip, a blackout, and then I might waken up to find myself running a concentration camp, choosing skins for lamp shades. Then somebody, something, arrived. Whoever or whatever they'd been waiting for was down there on the platform. I knew that definitely. But I couldn't see him or it. All I could make out was a sort of thickening and whirling of the air down there. Then out of that a voice spoke, the voice of the leader they had been expecting. But this voice didn't come from outside, through my ears. It spoke inside me, right in the centre, so that it came out to my attention, if you see what I mean. Rather like a small, very clear voice on a good telephone line, but coming from inside. I'll tell you frankly I didn't want to stay there and listen, no matter what big secrets were coming out; all I wanted to do was to get away from there as soon as I could; but for a few minutes I was too frightened to make the necessary moves.'

'Then you heard what this – er – voice was saying, Mr Patson?' the doctor asked.

'Some of it – yes.'

'Excellent! Now this is important.' And Dr Smith pointed his beautiful fountain pen at Mr Patson's left eye. 'Did you learn from it anything you hadn't known before? Please answer me carefully.'

'I'll tell you one thing you won't believe,' cried Mr Patson. 'Not about the voice – we'll come to that – but about those Grey Ones. I risked a peep while the voice was talking, and what I saw nearly made me pass out. There they were – three or four hundred of 'em – not looking human at all, not making any attempt; they'd all gone back to their original shapes. They looked – this is the nearest I can get to it – like big semitransparent toads – and their eyes were like six hundred electric lamps burning under water, all greeny, unblinking, and shining out of hell.'

'But what did you hear the voice say?' Dr Smith was urgent now. 'How much can you remember? That's what I want to know. Come along, man.'

Mr Patson passed a hand across his forehead and then looked at the edge of this hand with some astonishment, as if he had not known it would be so wet. 'I heard it thank them in the name of Adaragraffa – Lord of the Creeping Hosts. Yes, I could have imagined it – only I never knew I'd that sort of imagination. And what is imagination anyhow?'

'What else – what else – did you hear, man?'

'Ten thousand more were to be drafted into the Western Region. There would be promotions for some there who'd been on continuous duty longest. There was to be a swing over from the assault by way of social conditions, which could almost look after itself now, to the draining away of character, especially in the young of the doomed species. Yes, those were the very words,' Mr Patson shouted, jumping up and waving his arms. 'Especially in the young of the doomed species. Us – d'you understand – us. And I tell you

– we haven't a chance unless we start fighting back now – *now* –
yes, and with everything we've got left. Grey Ones. And more and
more of them coming, taking charge of us, giving us a push here,
a shove there – down – down – down—'

Mr Patson found his arms strongly seized and held by the doctor,
who was clearly a man of some strength. The next moment he was
being lowered into his chair. 'Mr Patson,' said the doctor sternly,
'you must not excite yourself in this fashion. I cannot allow it. Now
I must ask you to keep still and quiet for a minute while I speak to
my partner, Dr Meyenstein. It's for your own good. Now give me
your promise.'

'All right, but don't be long,' said Mr Patson, who suddenly felt
quite exhausted. As he watched the doctor go out, he wondered if
he had not said either too much or not enough. Too much, he felt,
if he was to be accepted as a sensible business man who happened
to be troubled by some neurotic fancies. Not enough, perhaps, to
justify, in view of the doctor's obvious scepticism, the terrible
shaking excitement that had possessed him at the end of their
interview. No doubt, round the corner, Drs Smith and Meyenstein
were having a good laugh over this rubbish about Grey Ones. Well,
they could try and make him laugh too. He would be only too
delighted to join them, if they could persuade him he had been
deceiving himself. Probably that is what they would do now.

'Well, Mr Patson,' said Dr Smith, at once brisk and grave, as he
returned with two other men, one of them Dr Meyenstein and the
other a bulky fellow in white who might be a male nurse. All three
moved forward slowly as Dr Smith spoke to him. 'You must realize
that you are a very sick man – sick in mind if not yet sick in body.
So you must put yourself in our hands.'

Even as he nodded in vague agreement, Mr Patson saw what he
ought to have guessed before, that Dr Smith was a Grey One and
that now he had brought two more Grey Ones with him. There was
a fraction of a moment, as the three of them bore down upon him
to silence his warning for ever, when he thought he caught another
glimpse of the creature in the ballroom, three of them now like big
semitransparent toads, six eyes like electric lamps burning under
water, all greeny, unblinking, shining triumphantly out of hell . . .

# The Feather Pillow

## Horacio Quiroga

*Like Edgar Allan Poe, to whom he has often been compared, Horacio Quiroga had a life dogged by tragedy. His father was killed in a shooting accident, his first wife committed suicide, and Quiroga himself accidentally shot his best friend. In 1937, after discovering that he was suffering from cancer, Quiroga committed suicide in Buenos Aires.*

*Born in Uruguay, he spent most of his life in the everglade jungles of north-eastern Argentina, the setting of many of his best stories: 'Anaconda' (the adventures of one of South America's largest and deadliest serpents, told in the style of Kipling's* Jungle Book, *'The Dead Man' and 'Sunstroke', laconic tales of violence and death. 'The Feather Pillow', with its icily perfect last line, shows Quiroga at his most haunting and powerful.*

Her entire honeymoon gave her hot and cold shivers. A blonde, angelic, and timid young girl, the childish fancies she had dreamed about being a bride had been chilled by her husband's rough character. She loved him very much, nonetheless, although sometimes she gave a light shudder when, as they returned home through the streets together at night, she cast a furtive glance at the impressive stature of her Jordan, who had been silent for an hour. He, for his part, loved her profoundly but never let it be seen.

For three months – they had been married in April – they lived in a special kind of bliss. Doubtless she would have wished less severity in the rigorous sky of love, more expansive and less cautious tenderness, but her husband's impassive manner always restrained her.

The house in which they lived influenced her chills and shuddering to no small degree. The whiteness of the silent patio – friezes, columns, and marble statues – produced the wintry impression of an enchanted palace. Inside, the glacial brilliance of stucco, the completely bare walls, affirmed the sensation of unpleasant coldness. As one crossed from one room to another, the echo of his steps reverberated throughout the house, as if long abandonment had sensitized its resonance.

Alicia passed the autumn in this strange love nest. She had determined, however, to cast a veil over her former dreams and live like a sleeping beauty in the hostile house, trying not to think about anything until her husband arrived each evening.

It is not strange that she grew thin. She had a light attack of influenza that dragged on insidiously for days and days: after that Alicia's health never returned. Finally one afternoon she was able to go into the garden, supported on her husband's arm. She looked around listlessly. Suddenly Jordan, with deep tenderness, ran his hand very slowly over her head, and Alicia instantly burst into sobs, throwing her arms around his neck. For a long time she cried out all the fears she had kept silent, redoubling her weeping at Jordan's slightest caress. Then her sobs subsided, and she stood a long while, her face hidden in the hollow of his neck, not moving or speaking a word.

This was the last day Alicia was well enough to be up. On the following day she awakened feeling faint. Jordan's doctor examined her with minute attention, prescribing calm and absolute rest.

'I don't know,' he said to Jordan at the street door. 'She has a great weakness that I am unable to explain. And with no vomiting, nothing . . . if she wakes tomorrow as she did today, call me at once.'

When she awakened the following day, Alicia was worse. There was a consultation. It was agreed there was an anemia of incredible progression, completely inexplicable. Alicia had no more fainting spells, but she was visibly moving towards death. The lights were lighted all day long in her bedroom, and there was complete silence. Hours went by without the slightest sound. Alicia dozed. Jordan virtually lived in the drawing-room, which was also always lighted. With tireless persistence he paced ceaselessly from one end of the room to the other. The carpet swallowed his steps. At times he entered the bedroom and continued his silent pacing back and forth alongside the bed, stopping for an instant at each end to regard his wife.

Suddenly Alicia began to have hallucinations, vague images, at first seeming to float in the air, then descending to floor level. Her eyes excessively wide, she stared continuously at the carpet on either side of the head of her bed. One night she suddenly focused on one spot. Then she opened her mouth to scream, and pearls of sweat suddenly beaded her nose and lips.

'Jordan! Jordan!' she clamoured, rigid with fright, still staring at the carpet.

Jordan ran to the bedroom, and, when she saw him appear, Alicia screamed with terror.

'It's I, Alicia, it's I!'

Alicia looked at him confusedly; she looked at the carpet; she looked at him once again; and after a long moment of stupefied confrontation, she regained her senses. She smiled and took her husband's hand in hers, caressing it, trembling, for half an hour.

Among her most persistent hallucinations was that of an anthropoid poised on his fingertips on the carpet, staring at her.

The doctors returned, but to no avail. They saw before them a diminishing life, a life bleeding away day by day, hour by hour, absolutely without their knowing why. During their last consultation Alicia lay in a stupor while they took her pulse, passing her inert wrist from one to another. They observed her a long time in silence and then moved into the dining room.

'Phew . . . ' The discouraged chief physician shrugged his shoulders. 'It is an inexplicable case. There is little we can do . . . '

'That's my last hope!' Jordan groaned. And he staggered blindly against the table.

Alicia's life was fading away in the subdelirium of anemia, a delirium which grew worse throughout the evening hours but which let up somewhat after dawn. The illness never worsened during the daytime, but each morning she awakened pale as death, almost in a swoon. It seemed only at night that her life drained out of her in new waves of blood. Always when she awakened she had the sensation of lying collapsed in the bed with a million-pound weight on top of her. Following the third day of this relapse she never left her bed again. She could scarcely move her head. She did not want her bed to be touched, not even to have her bedcovers arranged. Her crepuscular terrors advanced now in the form of monsters that dragged themselves towards the bed and laboriously climbed upon the bedspread.

Then she lost consciousness. The final two days she raved ceaselessly in a weak voice. The lights funereally illuminated the bedroom and drawing room. In the deathly silence of the house the only sound was the monotonous delirium from the bedroom and the dull echoes of Jordan's eternal pacing.

Finally, Alicia died. The servant, when she came in afterward to strip the now empty bed, stared wonderingly for a moment at the pillow.

'Sir!' she called Jordan in a low voice. 'There are stains on the pillow that look like blood.'

Jordan approached rapidly and bent over the pillow. Truly, on the case, on both sides of the hollow left by Alicia's head, were two small dark spots.

'They look like punctures,' the servant murmured after a moment of motionless observation.

'Hold it up to the light,' Jordan told her.

The servant raised the pillow but immediately dropped it and stood staring at it, livid and trembling. Without knowing why, Jordan felt the hair rise on the back of his neck.

'What is it?' he murmured in a hoarse voice.

'It's very heavy,' the servant whispered, still trembling.

Jordan picked it up; it was extraordinarily heavy. He carried it out of the room, and on the dining room table he ripped open the case and the ticking with a slash. The top feathers floated away, and the servant, her mouth opened wide, gave a scream of horror and covered her face with her clenched fists: in the bottom of the pillowcase, among the feathers, slowly moving its hairy legs, was a monstrous animal, a living, viscous ball. It was so swollen one could scarcely make out its mouth.

Night after night, since Alicia had taken to her bed, this abomination had stealthily applied its mouth – its proboscis one might better say – to the girl's temples, sucking her blood. The puncture was scarcely perceptible. The daily plumping of the pillow had doubtlessly at first impeded its progress, but as soon as the girl could no longer move, the suction became vertiginous. In five days, in five nights, the monster had drained Alicia's life away.

These parasites of feathered creatures, diminutive in their habitual environment, reach enormous proportions under certain conditions. Human blood seems particularly favourable to them, and it is not rare to encounter them in feather pillows.

*Translated from the Spanish by Margaret Sayers Peden.*

# Seaton's Aunt

## Walter de la Mare

*'I remember,' says Chesterton in one of his hundreds of essays, 'the real literary thrill which I felt long ago when reading* The Turn of the Screw, *and how it woke within me again long after under the suffocating vividness of "Seaton's Aunt".' It is the vividness of something undefined: we never know exactly who or what Seaton's aunt is, we simply feel her presence as terrible and menacing, like an unopened door in a bad dream. Dreams were one of de la Mare's lifelong preoccupations; they appear again and again in his stories and poems, so much so that the poet Stephen Spender expressed doubts as to whether de la Mare was a real person – or a dream. 'He already has so much the air of being an inhabitant of the shades,' said Spender, who met him in the fifties. Walter de la Mare died in England in 1956.*

I had heard rumours of Seaton's aunt long before I actually encountered her. Seaton, in the hush of confidence, or at any little show of toleration on our part, would remark, 'My aunt', or 'My old aunt, you know', as if his relative might be a kind of cement to an *entente cordiale*.

He had an unusual quantity of pocket-money; or, at any rate, it was bestowed on him in unusually large amounts; and he spent it freely, though none of us would have described him as an 'awfully generous chap'. 'Hullo, Seaton,' we would say, 'the old Begum?' At the beginning of term, too, he used to bring back surprising and exotic dainties in a box with a trick padlock that accompanied him from his first appearance at Gummidge's in a billycock hat to the rather abrupt conclusion of his schooldays.

From a boy's point of view he looked distastefully foreign with his yellowish skin, slow chocolate-coloured eyes, and lean weak figure. Merely for his looks he was treated by most of us true-blue Englishmen with condescension, hostility, or contempt. We used to

call him 'Pongo', but without any much better excuse for the nickname than his skin. He was, that is, in one sense of the term what
he assuredly was not in the other sense, a sport.

Seaton and I, as I may say, were never in any sense intimate at
school; our orbits only intersected in class. I kept deliberately aloof
from him. I felt vaguely he was a sneak, and remained quite unmol-
lified by advances on his side, which, in a boy's barbarous fashion,
unless it suited me to be magnanimous, I haughtily ignored.

We were both of us quick-footed, and at Prisoner's Base used
occasionally to hide together. And so I best remember Seaton – his
narrow watchful face in the dusk of a summer evening; his peculiar
crouch, and his inarticulate whisperings and mumblings. Otherwise
he played all games slackly and limply; used to stand and feed at
his locker with a crony or two until his 'tuck' gave out; or waste
his money on some outlandish fancy or other. He bought, for
instance, a silver bangle, which he wore above his left elbow, until
some of the fellows showed their masterly contempt of the practice
by dropping it nearly red-hot down his neck.

It needed, therefore, a rather peculiar taste, and a rather rare
kind of schoolboy courage and indifference to criticism, to be much
associated with him. And I had neither the taste nor, probably, the
courage. None the less, he did make advances, and on one memorable occasion went to the length of bestowing on me a whole pot of
some outlandish mulberry-coloured jelly that had been duplicated
in his term's supplies. In the exuberance of my gratitude I promised
to spend the next half-term holiday with him at his aunt's house.

I had clean forgotten my promise when, two or three days before
the holiday, he came up and triumphantly reminded me of it.

'Well, to tell you the honest truth, Seaton, old chap—' I began
graciously: but he cut me short.

'My aunt expects you,' he said; 'she is very glad you are coming.
She's sure to be quite decent to *you*, Withers.'

I looked at him in sheer astonishment; the emphasis was so
uncalled for. It seemed to suggest an aunt not hitherto hinted at,
and a friendly feeling on Seaton's side that was far more disconcerting than welcome.

We reached his aunt's house partly by train, partly by a lift in an
empty farm-cart, and partly by walking. It was a whole-day holiday,
and we were to sleep the night; he lent me extraordinary night-gear,

I remember. The village street was unusually wide, and was fed
from a green by two converging roads, with an inn, and a high
green sign at the corner. About a hundred yards down the street
was a chemist's shop – a Mr Tanner's. We descended the two steps
into his dusky and odorous interior to buy, I remember, some rat
poison. A little beyond the chemist's was the forge. You then walked
along a very narrow path, under a fairly high wall, nodding here
and there with weeds and tufts of grass, and so came to the iron
garden-gates, and saw the high flat house behind its huge sycamore.
A coach-house stood on the left of the house, and on the right a
gate led into a kind of rambling orchard. The lawn lay away over
to the left again, and at the bottom (for the whole garden sloped
gently to a sluggish and rushy pond-like stream) was a meadow.

We arrived at noon, and entered the gates out of the hot dust
beneath the glitter of the dark-curtained windows. Seaton led me
at once through the little garden-gate to show me his tadpole pond,
swarming with what (being myself not in the least interested in low
life) seemed to me the most horrible creatures – of all shapes,
consistencies, and sizes, but with which Seaton was obviously on
the most intimate of terms. I can see his absorbed face now as,
squatting on his heels he fished the slimy things out in his sallow
palms. Wearying at last of these pets, we loitered about awhile in
an aimless fashion. Seaton seemed to be listening, or at any rate
waiting, for something to happen or for someone to come. But
nothing did happen and no one came.

That was just like Seaton. Anyhow, the first view I got of his
aunt was when, at the summons of a distant gong, we turned from
the garden, very hungry and thirsty, to go into luncheon. We were
approaching the house when Seaton suddenly came to a standstill.
Indeed, I have always had the impression that he plucked at my
sleeve. Something, at least, seemed to catch me back, as it were, as
he cried, 'Look out, there she is!'

She was standing at an upper window which opened wide on a
hinge, and at first sight she looked an excessively tall and overwhelming figure. This, however, was mainly because the window
reached all but to the floor of her bedroom. She was in reality rather
an undersized woman, in spite of her long face and big head. She
must have stood, I think, unusually still, with eyes fixed on us,
though this impression may be due to Seaton's sudden warning and
to my consciousness of the cautious and subdued air that had fallen

on him at sight of her. I know that without the least reason in the world I felt a kind of guiltiness, as if I had been 'caught'. There was a silvery star pattern sprinkled on her black silk dress, and even from the ground I could see the immense coils of her hair and the rings on her left hand which was held fingering the small jet buttons of her bodice. She watched our united advance without stirring, until, imperceptibly, her eyes raised and lost themselves in the distance, so that it was out of an assumed reverie that she appeared suddenly to awaken to our presence beneath her when we drew close to the house.

'So this is your friend, Mr Smithers, I suppose?' she said, bobbing to me.

'Withers, Aunt,' said Seaton.

'It's much the same,' she said, with eyes fixed on me. 'Come in, Mr Withers, and bring him along with you.'

She continued to gaze at me – at least, I think she did so. I know that the fixity of her scrutiny and her ironical 'Mr' made me feel peculiarly uncomfortable. None the less she was extremely kind and attentive to me, though, no doubt, her kindness and attention showed up more vividly against her complete neglect of Seaton. Only one remark that I have any recollection of she made to him: 'When I look on my nephew, Mr Smithers, I realize that dust we are, and dust shall become. You are hot, dirty, and incorrigible, Arthur.'

She sat at the head of the table, Seaton at the foot, and I, before a wide waste of damask tablecloth, between them. It was an old and rather close dining-room, with windows thrown wide to the green garden and a wonderful cascade of fading roses. Miss Seaton's great chair faced this window, so that its rose-reflected light shone full on her yellowish face, and on just such chocolate eyes as my schoolfellow's, except that hers were more than half-covered by unusually long and heavy lids.

There she sat, steadily eating, with those sluggish eyes fixed for the most part on my face; above them stood the deep-lined fork between her eyebrows; and above that the wide expanse of a remarkable brow beneath its strange steep bank of hair. The lunch was copious, and consisted, I remember, of all such dishes as are generally considered too rich and too good for the schoolboy digestion – lobster mayonnaise, cold game sausages, an immense veal and ham pie farced with eggs, truffles, and numberless delicious flavours;

besides kickshaws, creams and sweetmeats. We even had a wine, a half-glass of old darkish sherry each.

Miss Seaton enjoyed and indulged an enormous appetite. Her example and a natural schoolboy voracity soon overcame my nervousness of her, even to the extent of allowing me to enjoy to the best of my bent so rare a spread. Seaton was singularly modest; the greater part of his meal consisted of almonds and raisins, which he nibbled surreptitiously and as if he found difficulty in swallowing them.

I don't mean that Miss Seaton 'conversed' with me. She merely scattered trenchant remarks and now and then twinkled a baited question over my head. But her face was like a dense and involved accompaniment to her talk. She presently dropped the 'Mr', to my intense relief, and called me now Withers, or Wither, now Smithers, and even once towards the close of the meal distinctly Johnson, though how on earth my name suggested it, or whose face mine had reanimated in memory, I cannot conceive.

'And is Arthur a good boy at school, Mr Wither?' was one of her many questions. 'Does he please his masters? Is he first in his class? What does the reverend Dr Gummidge think of him, eh?'

I knew she was jeering at him, but her face was adamant against the least flicker of sarcasm or facetiousness. I gazed fixedly at a blushing crescent of lobster.

'I think you're eighth, aren't you, Seaton?'

Seaton moved his small pupils towards his aunt. But she continued to gaze with a kind of concentrated detachment at me.

'Arthur will never make a brilliant scholar, I fear,' she said, lifting a dexterously burdened fork to her wide mouth . . .

After luncheon she preceded me up to my bedroom. It was a jolly little bedroom, with a brass fender and rugs and a polished floor, on which it was possible, I afterwards found, to play 'snow-shoes'. Over the washstand was a little black-framed water-colour drawing, depicting a large eye with an extremely fishlike intensity in the spark of light on the dark pupil; and in 'illuminated' lettering beneath was printed very minutely, 'Thou God Seest ME', followed by a long looped monogram, 'S.S.', in the corner. The other pictures were all of the sea: brigs on blue water; a schooner overtopping chalk cliffs; a rocky island of prodigious steepness, with two tiny sailors dragging a monstrous boat up a shelf of beach.

'This is the room, Withers, my poor dear brother William died in when a boy. Admire the view!'

I looked out of the window across the tree-tops. It was a day hot with sunshine over the green fields, and the cattle were standing swishing their tails in the shallow water. But the view at the moment was no doubt made more vividly impressive by the apprehension that she would presently enquire after my luggage, and I had brought not even a toothbrush. I need have had no fear. Hers was not that highly civilized type of mind that is stuffed with sharp, material details. Nor could her ample presence be described as in the least motherly.

'I would never consent to question a schoolfellow behind my nephew's back,' she said, standing in the middle of the room, 'but tell me, Smithers, why is Arthur so unpopular? You, I understand, are his only close friend.' She stood in a dazzle of sun, and out of it her eyes regarded me with such leaden penetration beneath their thick lids that I doubt if my face concealed the least thought from her. 'But there, there,' she added very suavely, stooping her head a little, 'don't trouble to answer me. I never extort an answer. Boys are queer fish. Brains might perhaps have suggested his washing his hands before luncheon; but – not my choice, Smithers. God forbid! And now, perhaps, you would like to go into the garden again. I cannot actually see from here, but I should not be surprised if Arthur is now skulking behind that hedge.'

He was. I saw his head come out and take a rapid glance at the windows.

'Join him, Mr Smithers; we shall meet again, I hope, at the tea-table. The afternoon I spend in retirement.'

Whether or not, Seaton and I had not been long engaged with the aid of two green switches in riding round and round a lumbering old grey horse we found in the meadow, before a rather bunched-up figure appeared, walking along the fieldpath on the other side of the water, with a magenta parasol studiously lowered in our direction throughout her slow progress, as if that were the magnetic needle and we the fixed Pole. Seaton at once lost all nerve and interest. At the next lurch of the old mare's heels he toppled over into the grass, and I slid off the sleek broad back to join him where he stood, rubbing his shoulder and sourly watching the rather pompous figure till it was out of sight.

'Was that your aunt, Seaton?' I enquired; but not till then.

He nodded.

'Why didn't she take any notice of us, then?'

'She never does.'

'Why not?'

'Oh, she knows all right, without; that's the damn awful part of it.' Seaton was one of the very few fellows at Gummidge's who had the ostentation to use bad language. He had suffered for it too. But it wasn't, I think, bravado. I believe he really felt certain things more intensely than most of the other fellows, and they were generally things that fortunate and average people do not feel at all – the peculiar quality, for instance, of the British schoolboy's imagination.

'I tell you, Withers,' he went on moodily, slinking across the meadow with his hands covered up in his pockets, 'she sees everything. And what she doesn't see she knows without.'

'But how?' I said, not because I was much interested, but because the afternoon was so hot and tiresome and purposeless, and it seemed more of a bore to remain silent. Seaton turned gloomily and spoke in a very low voice.

'Don't appear to be talking of her, if you wouldn't mind. It's – because she's in league with the Devil.' He nodded his head and stooped to pick up a round flat pebble. 'I tell you,' he said, still stooping, 'you fellows don't realize what it is. I know I'm a bit close and all that. But so would you be if you had that old hag listening to every thought you think.'

I looked at him, then turned and surveyed one by one the windows of the house.

'Where's your *pater*?' I said awkwardly.

'Dead, ages and ages ago, and my mother too. She's not my aunt even by rights.'

'What is she, then?'

'I mean she's not my mother's sister, because my grandmother married twice; and she's one of the first lot. I don't know what you call her, but anyhow she's not my real aunt.'

'She gives you plenty of pocket-money.'

Seaton looked steadfastly at me out of his flat eyes. 'She can't give me what's mine. When I come of age half of the whole lot will be mine; and what's more' – he turned his back on the house – 'I'll make her hand over every blessed shilling of it.'

I put my hands in my pockets and stared at Seaton. 'Is it much?'

He nodded.

'Who told you?' He got suddenly very angry; a darkish red came into his cheeks, his eyes glistened, but he made no answer, and we loitered listlessly about the garden until it was time for tea . . .

Seaton's aunt was wearing an extraordinary kind of lace jacket when we sidled sheepishly into the drawing-room together. She greeted me with a heavy and protracted smile, and bade me bring a chair close to the little table.

'I hope Arthur has made you feel at home,' she said as she handed me my cup in her crooked hand. 'He don't talk much to me; but then I'm an old woman. You must come again, Wither, and draw him out of his shell. You old snail!' She wagged her head at Seaton, who sat munching cake and watching her intently.

'And we must correspond, perhaps.' She nearly shut her eyes at me. 'You must write and tell me everything behind the creature's back.' I confess I found her rather disquieting company. The evening drew on. Lamps were brought in by a man with a nondescript face and very quiet footsteps. Seaton was told to bring out the chessmen. And we played a game, she and I, with her big chin thrust over the board at every move as she gloated over the pieces and occasionally croaked 'Check!' – after which she would sit back inscrutably staring at me. But the game was never finished. She simply hemmed me in with a gathering cloud of pieces that held me impotent, and yet one and all refused to administer to my poor flustered old king a merciful *coup de grâce*.

'There,' she said, as the clock struck ten – 'a drawn game, Withers. We are very evenly matched. A very creditable defence, Withers. You know your room. There's supper on a tray in the dining-room. Don't let the creature over-eat himself. The gong will sound three-quarters of an hour *before* a punctual breakfast.' She held out her cheek to Seaton, and he kissed it with obvious perfunctoriness. With me she shook hands.

'An excellent game,' she said cordially, 'but my memory is poor, and' – she swept the pieces helter-skelter into the box – 'the result will never be known.' She raised her great head far back. 'Eh?'

It was a kind of challenge, and I could only murmur: 'Oh, I was absolutely in a hole, you know!' when she burst our laughing and waved us both out of the room.

Seaton and I stood and ate our supper, with one candlestick to light us, in a corner of the dining-room. 'Well, and how would you like it?' he said very softly, after cautiously poking his head round the doorway.

'Like what?'

'Being spied on – every blessed thing you do and think?'

'I shouldn't like it at all,' I said, 'if she does.'

'And yet you let her smash you up at chess!'

'I didn't let her!' I said indignantly.

'Well, you funked it, then.'

'And I didn't funk it either,' I said, 'she's so jolly clever with her knights.'

Seaton stared at the candle. 'Knights,' he said slowly. 'You wait, that's all.' And we went upstairs to bed.

I had not been long in bed, I think, when I was cautiously awakened by a touch on my shoulder. And there was Seaton's face in the candlelight – and his eyes looking into mine.

'What's up?' I said, lurching on to my elbow.

'*Ssh!* Don't scurry,' he whispered. 'She'll hear. I'm sorry for waking you, but I didn't think you'd be asleep so soon.'

'Why, what's the time, then?' Seaton wore, what was then rather unusual, a night-suit, and he hauled his big silver watch out of the pocket in his jacket.

'It's a quarter to twelve. I never get to sleep before twelve – not here.'

'What do you do, then?'

'Oh, I read: and listen.'

'Listen?'

Seaton stared into his candle-flame as if he were listening even then. 'You can't guess what it is. All you read in ghost stories, that's all rot. You can't see much, Withers, but you know all the same.'

'Know what?'

'Why, that they're there.'

'Who's there?' I asked fretfully, glancing at the door.

'Why, in the house. It swarms with 'em. Just you stand still and listen outside my bedroom door in the middle of the night. I have, dozens of times; they're all over the place.'

'Look here, Seaton,' I said, 'you asked me to come here, and I didn't mind chucking up a leave just to oblige you and because I'd promised; but don't get talking a lot of rot, that's all, or you'll know the difference when we get back.'

'Don't fret,' he said coldly, turning away. 'I shan't be at school long. And what's more, you're here now, and there isn't anybody else to talk to. I'll chance the other.'

'Look here, Seaton,' I said, 'you may think you're going to scare me with a lot of stuff about voices and all that. But I'll just thank you to clear out; and you may please yourself about pottering about all night.'

He made no answer; he was standing by the dressing-table looking across his candle into the looking-glass; he turned and stared slowly round the walls.

'Even this room's nothing more than a coffin. I suppose she told you – "It's all exactly the same as when my brother William died" – trust her for that! And good luck to him, say I. Look at that.' He raised his candle close to the little water-colour I have mentioned. 'There's hundreds of eyes like that in this house; and even if God does see you, He takes precious good care you don't see Him. And it's just the same with them. I tell you what, Withers, I'm getting sick of all this. I shan't stand it much longer.'

The house was silent within and without, and even in the yellowish radiance of the candle a faint silver showed through the open window on my blind. I slipped off the bedclothes, wide awake, and sat irresolute on the bedside.

'I know you're only guying me,' I said angrily, 'but why is the house full of – what you say? Why do you hear – what you *do* hear? Tell me that, you silly fool!'

Seaton sat down on a chair and rested his candlestick on his knee. He blinked at me calmly. 'She brings them,' he said, with lifted eyebrows.

'Who? Your aunt?'

He nodded.

'How?'

'I told you,' he answered pettishly. 'She's in league. You don't know. She as good as killed my mother; I know that. But it's not only her by a long chalk. She just sucks you dry. I know. And that's what she'll do for me; because I'm like her – like my mother, I mean. She simply hates to see me alive. I wouldn't be like that old she-wolf for a million pounds. And so' – he broke off, with a comprehensive wave of his candlestick – 'they're always here. Ah, my boy, wait till she's dead! She'll hear something then, I can tell you. It's all very well now, but wait till then! I wouldn't be in her shoes when she has to clear out – for something. Don't you go and believe I care for ghosts, or whatever you like to call them. We're all in the same box. We're all under her thumb.'

He was looking almost nonchalantly at the ceiling at the moment, when I saw his face change, saw his eyes suddenly drop like shot birds and fix themselves on the cranny of the door he had left just ajar. Even from where I sat I could see his cheek change colour; it went greenish. He crouched without stirring, like an animal. And I, scarcely daring to breathe, sat with creeping skin, sourly watching him. His hands relaxed, and he gave a kind of sigh.

'Was *that* one?' I whispered, with a timid show of jauntiness. He looked round, opened his mouth, and nodded. 'What?' I said. He jerked his thumb with meaningful eyes, and I knew that he meant that his aunt had been there listening at our door cranny.

'Look here, Seaton,' I said once more, wriggling to my feet. 'You may think I'm a jolly noodle; just as you please. But your aunt has been civil to me and all that, and I don't believe a word you say about her, that's all, and never did. Every fellow's a bit off his pluck at night, and you may think it a fine sport to try your rubbish on me. I heard your aunt come upstairs before I fell asleep. And I'll bet you a level tanner she's in bed now. What's more, you can keep your blessed ghosts to yourself. It's a guilty conscience, I should think.'

Seaton looked at me intently, without answering for a moment. 'I'm not a liar, Withers; but I'm not going to quarrel either. You're the only chap I care a button for; or, at any rate, you're the only chap that's ever come here; and it's something to tell a fellow what you feel. I don't care a fig for fifty thousand ghosts, although I swear on my solemn oath that I know they're here. But she' – he turned deliberately – 'you laid a tanner she's in bed, Withers; well, I know different. She's never in bed much of the night, and I'll prove it, too, just to show you I'm not such a nolly as you think I am. Come on!'

'Come on where?'

'Why, to see.'

I hesitated. He opened a large cupboard and took out a small dark dressing-gown and a kind of shawl-jacket. He threw the jacket on the bed and put on the gown. His dusky face was colourless, and I could see by the way he fumbled at the sleeves he was shivering. But it was no good showing the white feather now. So I threw the tasselled shawl over my shoulders and, leaving our candle brightly burning on the chair, we went out together and stood in the corridor.

'Now then, listen!' Seaton whispered.

We stood leaning over the staircase. It was like leaning over a well, so still and chill the air was all around us. But presently, as I suppose happens in most old houses, began to echo and answer in my ears a medley of infinite small stirrings and whisperings. Now out of the distance an old timber would relax its fibres, or a scurry die away behind the perishing wainscot. But amid and behind such sounds as these I seemed to begin to be conscious, as it were, of the lightest of footfalls, sounds as faint as the vanishing remembrance of voices in a dream. Seaton was all in obscurity except his face; out of that his eyes gleamed darkly, watching me.

'You'd hear, too, in time, my fine soldier,' he muttered. 'Come on!'

He descended the stairs, slipping his lean fingers lightly along the balusters. He turned to the right at the loop, and I followed him barefooted along a thickly carpeted corridor. At the end stood a door ajar. And from here we very stealthily and in complete blackness ascended five narrow stairs. Seaton, with immense caution, slowly pushed open a door, and we stood together, looking into a great pool of duskiness, out of which, lit by the feeble clearness of a night-light, rose a vast bed. A heap of clothes lay on the floor; beside them two slippers dozed, with noses each to each, a foot or two apart. Somewhere a little clock ticked huskily. There was a close smell; lavender and eau de Cologne, mingled with the fragrance of ancient sachets, soap, and drugs. Yet it was a scent even more peculiarly compounded than that.

And the bed! I stared warily in; it was mounded gigantically, and it was empty.

Seaton turned a vague pale face, all shadows: 'What did I say?' he muttered. 'Who's – who's the fool now, I say? How are we going to get back without meeting her, I say? Answer me that! Oh, I wish to God you hadn't come here, Withers.'

He stood audibly shivering in his skimpy gown, and could hardly speak for his teeth chattering. And very distinctly, in the hush that followed his whisper, I heard approaching a faint unhurried voluminous rustle. Seaton clutched my arm, dragged me to the right across the room to a large cupboard, and drew the door close to on us. And, presently, as with bursting lungs I peeped out into the long, low, curtained bedroom, waddled in that wonderful great head and body. I can see her now, all patched and lined with shadow, her tied-up hair (she must have had enormous quantities of it for so old a woman), her heavy lids above those flat, slow, vigilant eyes. She just passed across my ken in the vague dusk; but the bed was out of sight.

We waited on and on, listening to the clock's muffled ticking. Not the ghost of a sound rose up from the great bed. Either she lay archly listening or slept a sleep serener than an infant's. And when, it seemed, we had been hours in hiding and were cramped, chilled, and half suffocated, we crept out on all fours, with terror knocking at our ribs, and so down the five narrow stairs and back to the little candle-lit blue-and-gold bedroom.

Once there, Seaton gave in. He sat livid on a chair with closed eyes.

'Here,' I said, shaking his arm, 'I'm going to bed; I've had enough of this foolery; I'm going to bed.' His lips quivered, but he made no answer. I poured out some water into my basin and, with that cold pictured azure eye fixed on us, bespattered Seaton's sallow face and forehead and dabbled his hair. He presently sighed and opened fish-like eyes.

'Come on!' I said. 'Don't get shamming, there's a good chap. Get on my back, if you like, and I'll carry you into your bedroom.'

He waved me away and stood up. So, with my candle in one hand, I took him under the arm and walked him along according to his direction down the corridor. His was a much dingier room than mine, and littered with boxes, paper, cages, and clothes. I huddled him into bed and turned to go. And suddenly, I can hardly explain it now, a kind of cold and deadly terror swept over me. I almost ran out of the room, with eyes fixed rigidly in front of me, blew out my candle, and buried my head under the bedclothes.

When I awoke, roused not by a gong, but by a long-continued tapping at my door, sunlight was raying in on cornice and bedpost, and birds were singing in the garden. I got up, ashamed of the night's folly, dressed quickly, and went downstairs. The breakfast room was sweet with flowers and fruit and honey. Seaton's aunt was standing in the garden beside the open French window, feeding a great flutter of birds. I watched her for a moment, unseen. Her face was set in a deep reverie beneath the shadow of a big loose sun-hat. It was deeply lined, crooked, and, in a way I can't describe, fixedly vacant and strange. I coughed politely, and she turned with a prodigious smiling grimace to ask how I had slept. And in that mysterious fashion by which we learn each other's secret thoughts without a syllable said, I knew that she had followed every word and movement of the night before, and was triumphing over my affected innocence and ridiculing my friendly and too easy advances.

We returned to school, Seaton and I, lavishly laden, and by rail all the way. I made no reference to the obscure talk we had had, and resolutely refused to meet his eyes or to take up the hints he let fall. I was relieved – and yet I was sorry – to be going back, and strode on as fast as I could from the station, with Seaton almost trotting at my heels. But he insisted on buying more fruit and sweets – my share of which I accepted with a very bad grace. It was uncomfortably like a bribe, and, after all, I had no quarrel with his rum old aunt, and hadn't really believed half the stuff he had told me.

I saw as little of him as I could after that. He never referred to our visit or resumed his confidences, though in class I would sometimes catch his eye fixed on mine, full of a mute understanding, which I easily affected not to understand. He left Gummidge's, as I have said, rather abruptly, though I never heard of anything to his discredit. And I did not see him or have any news of him again till by chance we met one summer afternoon in the Strand.

He was dressed rather oddly in a coat too large for him and a bright silky tie. But we instantly recognized one another under the awning of a cheap jeweller's shop. He immediately attached himself to me and dragged me off, not too cheerfully, to lunch with him at an Italian restaurant near by. He chattered about our old school, which he remembered only with dislike and disgust; told me cold-bloodedly of the disastrous fate of one or two of the older fellows who had been among his chief tormentors; insisted on an expensive wine and the whole gamut of the foreign menu; and finally informed me, with a good deal of niggling, that he had come up to town to buy an engagement-ring.

And of course: 'How is your aunt?' I enquired at last.

He seemed to have been awaiting the question. It fell like a stone into a deep pool, so many expressions flitted across his long, sad, sallow, un-English face.

'She's aged a good deal,' he said softly, and broke off.

'She's been very decent,' he continued presently after, and paused again. 'In a way.' He eyed me fleetingly. 'I dare say you heard that – she – that is, that we – had lost a good deal of money.'

'No,' I said.

'Oh, yes!' said Seaton, and paused again.

And somehow, poor fellow, I knew in the clink and clatter of glass and voices that he had lied to me; that he did not possess, and never had possessed, a penny beyond what his aunt had squandered on his too ample allowance of pocket-money.

'And the ghosts?' I enquired quizzically.

He grew instantly solemn, and, though it may have been my fancy, slightly yellowed. But 'You are making game of me, Withers,' was all he said.

He asked for my address, and I rather reluctantly gave him my card.

'Look here, Withers,' he said, as we stood together in the sunlight on the kerb, saying goodbye, 'here I am, and – and it's all very well. I'm not perhaps as fanciful as I was. But you are practically the only friend I have on earth – except Alice. . . And there – to make a clean breast of it, I'm not sure that my aunt cares much about my getting married. She doesn't say so, of course. You know her well enough for that.' He looked sidelong at the rattling gaudy traffic.

"What I was going to say is this: Would you mind coming down? You needn't stay the night unless you please, though, of course, you know you would be awfully welcome. But I should like you to meet my – to meet Alice; and then, perhaps, you might tell me your honest opinion of – of the other too.'

I vaguely demurred. He pressed me. And we parted with a half promise that I would come. He waved his ball-topped cane at me and ran off in his long jacket after a bus.

A letter arrived soon after, in his small weak handwriting, giving me full particulars regarding route and trains. And without the least curiosity, even perhaps with some little annoyance that chance should have thrown us together again, I accepted his invitation and arrived one hazy midday at his out-of-the-way station to find him sitting on a low seat under a clump of 'double' hollyhocks, awaiting me.

He looked preoccupied and singularly listless; but seemed, none the less, to be pleased to see me.

We walked up the village street, past the little dingy apothecary's and the empty forge, and, as on my first visit, skirted the house together, and, instead of entering by the front door, made our way down the green path into the garden at the back. A pale haze of cloud muffled the sun; the garden lay in a grey shimmer – its old trees, its snap-dragoned faintly glittering walls. But now there was an air of slovenliness where before all had been neat and methodical. In a patch of shallowly dug soil stood a worn-down spade leaning against a tree. There was an old decayed wheelbarrow. The roses had run to leaf and briar; the fruit-trees were unpruned. The goddess of neglect had made it her secret resort.

'You ain't much of a gardener, Seaton,' I said at last, with a sigh of relief.

'I think, do you know, I like it best like this,' said Seaton. 'We haven't any man now, of course. Can't afford it.' He stood staring at his little dark oblong of freshly turned earth. 'And it always seems to me,' he went on ruminatingly, 'that, after all, we are all nothing better than interlopers on the earth, disfiguring and staining wherever we go. It may sound shocking blasphemy to say so; but then it's different here, you see. We are further away.'

'To tell you the truth, Seaton, I *don't* quite see,' I said; 'but it isn't a new philosophy, is it? Anyhow, it's a precious beastly one.'

'It's only what I think,' he replied, with all his odd old stubborn meekness. 'And one thinks as one *is*.'

We wandered on together, talking little, and still with that expression of uneasy vigilance on Seaton's face. He pulled out his watch as we stood gazing idly over the green meadows and the dark motionless bulrushes.

'I think, perhaps, it's nearly time for lunch,' he said. 'Would you like to come in?'

We turned and walked slowly towards the house, across whose windows I confess my own eyes, too, went restlessly meandering in search of its rather disconcerting inmate. There was a pathetic look of bedraggledness, of want of means and care, rust and overgrowth and faded paint. Seaton's aunt, a little to my relief, did not share our meal. So he carved the cold meat, and dispatched a heaped-up plate by an elderly servant for his aunt's private consumption. We talked little and in half-suppressed tones, and sipped some Madeira which Seaton after listening for a moment or two fetched out of the great mahogany sideboard.

I played him a dull and effortless game of chess, yawning between the moves he himself made almost at haphazard, and with attention elsewhere engaged. Towards five o'clock came the sound of a distant ring, and Seaton jumped up, overturning the board, and so ended a game that else might have fatuously continued to this day. He effusively excused himself, and after some little while returned with a slim, dark, pale-faced girl of about nineteen, in a white gown and hat, to whom I was presented with some little nervousness as his 'dear old friend and schoolfellow'.

We talked on in the golden afternoon light, still, as it seemed to me, and even in spite of our efforts to be lively and gay, in a half-suppressed, lack-lustre fashion. We all seemed, if it were not my fancy, to be expectant, to be almost anxiously awaiting an arrival, the appearance of someone whose image filled our collective consciousness. Seaton talked least of all, and in a restless interjectory way, as he continually fidgeted from chair to chair. At last he proposed a stroll in the garden before the sun should have quite gone down.

Alice walked between us. Her hair and eyes were conspicuously dark against the whiteness of her gown. She carried herself not ungracefully, and yet with peculiarly little movement of her arms and body, and answered us both without turning her head. There was a curious provocative reserve in that impassive melancholy face. It seemed to be haunted by some tragic influence of which she herself was unaware.

And yet somehow I knew – I believe we all knew – that this walk, this discussion of their future plans was a futility. I had nothing to base such scepticism on, except only a vague sense of oppression, a foreboding consciousness of some inert invincible power in the background, to whom optimistic plans and love-making and youth are as chaff and thistledown. We came back, silent, in the last light. Seaton's aunt was there – under an old brass lamp. Her hair was as barbarously massed and curled as ever. Her eyelids, I think, hung even a little heavier in age over their slow-moving inscrutable pupils. We filed in softly out of the evening, and I made my bow.

'In this short interval, Mr Withers,' she remarked amiably, 'you have put off youth, put on the man. Dear me, how sad it is to see the young days vanishing! Sit down. My nephew tells me you met by chance – or act of Providence, shall we call it? – and in my beloved Strand! You, I understand, are to be best man – yes, best man! Or am I divulging secrets?' She surveyed Arthur and Alice with overwhelming graciousness. They sat apart on two low chairs and smiled in return.

'And Arthur – how do you think Arthur is looking?'

'I think he looks very much in need of a change,' I said.

'A change! Indeed?' She all but shut her eyes at me and with an exaggerated sentimentality shook her head. 'My dear Mr Withers! Are we not *all* in need of a change in this fleeting, fleeting world?' She mused over the remark like a connoisseur. 'And you,' she continued, turning abruptly to Alice, 'I hope you pointed out to Mr Withers all my pretty bits?'

'We only walked round the garden,' the girl replied; then, glancing at Seaton, added almost inaudibly, 'it's a very beautiful evening.'

'*Is* it?' said the old lady, starting up violently. 'Then on this very beautiful evening we will go in to supper. Mr Withers, your arm; Arthur, bring your bride.'

We were a queer quartet, I thought to myself, as I solemnly led the way into the faded, chilly dining-room, with this indefinable old creature leaning wooingly on my arm – the large flat bracelet on the yellow-laced wrist. She fumed a little, breathing heavily, but as if with an effort of the mind rather than of the body; for she had grown much stouter and yet little more proportionate. And to talk into that great white face, so close to mine, was a queer experience in the dim light of the corridor, and even in the twinkling crystal of the candles. She was naïve – appallingly naïve; she was crafty and challenging; she was even arch; and all these in the brief, rather puffy passage from one room to the other, with these two tongue-tied children bringing up the rear. The meal was tremendous. I have never seen such a monstrous salad. But the dishes were greasy and over-spiced, and were indifferently cooked. One thing only was quite unchanged – my hostess's appetite was as gargantuan as ever. The heavy silver candelabra that lighted us stood before her high-backed chair. Seaton sat a little removed, his plate almost in darkness.

And throughout this prodigious meal his aunt talked, mainly to me, mainly *at* him, but with an occasional satirical sally at Alice and muttered explosions of reprimand to the servant. She had aged, and yet, if it be not nonsense to say so, seemed no older. I suppose to the Pyramids a decade is but as the rustling down of a handful of dust. And she reminded me of some such unshakeable prehistoricism. She certainly was an amazing talker – rapid, egregious, with a delivery that was perfectly overwhelming. As for Seaton – her flashes of silence were for him. On her enormous volubility would suddenly fall a hush; acid sarcasm would be left implied; and she would sit softly moving her great head, with eyes fixed full in a dreamy smile; but with her whole attention, one could see, slowly, joyously absorbing his mute discomfiture.

She confided in us her views on a theme vaguely occupying at the moment, I suppose, all our minds. 'We have barbarous institutions, and so must put up, I suppose, with a never-ending procession of fools – of fools *ad infinitum*. Marriage, Mr Withers, was instituted in the privacy of a garden; *sub rosa*, as it were. Civilization flaunts it in the glare of day. The dull marry the poor; the rich the effete; and so our New Jerusalem is peopled with naturals, plain and coloured, at either end. I detest folly; I detest still more (if I must be frank, dear Arthur) mere cleverness. Mankind has simply become a tailless host of uninstinctive animals. We should never have taken to Evolution, Mr Withers. "Natural Selection!" – little gods and fishes! – the deaf for the dumb. We should have used our brains – intellectual pride, the ecclesiastics call it. And by brains I mean – what do I mean, Alice? – I mean, my dear child,' and she laid two gross fingers on Alice's narrow sleeve, 'I mean courage. Consider it, Arthur. I read that the scientific world is once more beginning to be afraid of spiritual agencies. Spiritual agencies that tap, and actually float, bless their hearts! I think just one more of those mulberries – thank you.

'They talk about "blind Love",' she ran on derisively as she helped herself, her eyes roving over the dish, 'but why blind? I think, Mr Withers, from weeping over its rickets. After all, it is we plain women that triumph, is it not so – beyond the mockery of time. Alice, now! Fleeting, fleeting is youth, my child. What's that you were confiding to your plate, Arthur? Satirical boy. He laughs at his old aunt: nay, but thou didst laugh. He detests all sentiment. He whispers the most acid asides. Come, my love, we will leave these cynics; we will go and commiserate with each other on our sex. The choice of two evils, Mr Smithers!' I opened the door, and she swept out as if borne on a torrent of unintelligible indignation; and Arthur and I were left in the clear four-flamed light alone.

For a while we sat in silence. He shook his head at my cigarette-case, and I lit a cigarette. Presently he fidgeted in his chair and poked his head forward into the light. He paused to rise, and shut again the shut door.

'How long will you be?' he asked me.

I laughed.

'Oh, it's not that!' he said, in some confusion. 'Of course, I like to be with her. But it's not that. The truth is, Withers, I don't care about leaving her too long with my aunt.'

I hesitated. He looked at me questioningly.

'Look here, Seaton,' I said, 'you know well enough that I don't want to interfere in your affairs, or to offer advice where it is not wanted. But don't you think perhaps you may not treat your aunt quite in the right way? As one gets old, you know, a little give and take. I have an old godmother, or something of the kind. She's a bit queer, too . . . A little allowance; it does no harm. But hang it all, I'm no preacher.'

He sat down with his hands in his pockets and still with his eyes fixed almost incredulously on mine. 'How?' he said.

'Well, my dear fellow, if I'm any judge – mind, I don't say that I am – but I can't help thinking she thinks you don't care for her; and perhaps takes your silence for – for bad temper. She has been very decent to you, hasn't she?'

' "Decent"? My God!' said Seaton.

I smoked on in silence; but he continued to look at me with that peculiar concentration I remembered of old.

'I don't think, perhaps, Withers,' he began presently, 'I don't think you quite understand. Perhaps you are not quite our kind. You always did, just like the other fellows, guy me at school. You laughed at me that night you came to stay here – about the voices and all that. But I don't mind being laughed at – because I know.'

'Know what?' It was the same old system of dull question and evasive answer.

'I mean I know that what we see and hear is only the smallest fraction of what is. I know she lives quite out of this. She *talks* to you; but it's all make-believe. It's all a "parlour game". She's not really with you; only pitting her outside wits against yours and enjoying the fooling. She's living on inside on what you're rotten without. That's what it is – a cannibal feast. She's a spider. It doesn't much matter what you call it. It means the same kind of thing. I tell you, Withers, she hates me; and you can scarcely dream what that hatred means. I used to think I had an inkling of the reason. It's oceans deeper than that. It just lies behind: herself against myself. Why, after all, how much do we really understand of anything? We don't even know our own histories, and not a tenth, not a tenth of the reasons. What has life been to me? – nothing but a trap. And when one sets oneself free for a while, it only begins again. I thought you might understand; but you are on a different level: that's all.'

'What on earth are you talking about?' I said contemptuously, in spite of myself.

'I mean what I say,' he said gutturally. 'All this outside's only make-believe – but there! what's the good of talking? So far as this is concerned I'm as good as done. You wait.'

Seaton blew out three of the candles and, leaving the vacant room in semi-darkness, we groped our way along the corridor to the drawing-room. There a full moon stood shining in at the long garden windows. Alice sat stooping at the door, with her hands clasped in her lap, looking out, alone.

'Where is she?' Seaton asked in a low tone.

She looked up; and their eyes met in a glance of instantaneous understanding, and the door immediately afterwards opened behind us.

'*Such* a moon!' said a voice, that once heard, remained unforgettably on the ear. 'A night for lovers, Mr Withers, if ever there was one. Get a shawl, my dear Arthur, and take Alice for a little promenade. I dare say we old cronies will manage to keep awake. Hasten, hasten, Romeo! My poor, poor Alice, how laggard a lover!'

Seaton returned with a shawl. They drifted out into the moonlight. My companion gazed after them till they were out of hearing, turned to me gravely, and suddenly twisted her white face into such a convulsion of contemptuous amusement that I could only stare blankly in reply.

'Dear innocent children!' she said, with inimitable unctuousness. 'Well, well, Mr Withers, we poor seasoned old creatures must move with the times. Do you sing?'

I scouted the idea.

'Then you must listen to my playing. Chess' – she clasped her forehead with both cramped hands – 'chess is now completely beyond my poor wits.'

She sat down at the piano and ran her fingers in a flourish over the keys. 'What shall it be? How shall we capture them, those passionate hearts? That first fine careless rapture? Poetry itself.' She gazed softly into the garden a moment, and presently, with a shake of her body, began to play the opening bars of Beethoven's 'Moonlight' Sonata. The piano was old and woolly. She played without music. The lamplight was rather dim. The moonbeams from the window lay across the keys. Her head was in shadow. And whether it was simply due to her personality or to some really occult skill in her playing I cannot say; I only know that she gravely and deliberately set herself to satirize the beautiful music. It brooded on the air, disillusioned, charged with mockery and bitterness. I stood at the window; far down the path I could see the white figure glimmering in that pool of colourless light. A few faint stars shone, and still that amazing woman behind me dragged out of the unwilling keys her wonderful grotesquerie of youth and love and beauty. It came to an end. I knew the player was watching me. 'Please, please, go on!' I murmured, without turning. '*Please* go on playing, Miss Seaton.'

No answer was returned to this honeyed sarcasm, but I realized in some vague fashion that I was being acutely scrutinized, when suddenly there followed a procession of quiet, plaintive chords which broke at last softly into the hymn, 'A Few More Years Shall Roll.'

I confess it held me spellbound. There is a wistful, strained plangent pathos in the tune; but beneath those masterly old hands it cried softly and bitterly the solitude and desperate estrangement of the world. Arthur and his lady-love vanished from my thoughts. No one could put into so hackneyed an old hymn tune such an appeal who had never known the meaning of the words. Their meaning, anyhow, isn't commonplace.

I turned a fraction of an inch to glance at the musician. She was leaning forward a little over the keys, so that at the approach of my silent scrutiny she had but to turn her face into the thin flood of moonlight for every feature to become distinctly visible. And so, with the tune abruptly terminated, we steadfastly regarded one another; and she broke into a prolonged chuckle of laughter.

'Not quite so seasoned as I supposed, Mr Withers. I see you are a real lover of music. To me it is too painful. It evokes too much thought . . .'

I could scarcely see her little glittering eyes under their penthouse lids.

'And now,' she broke off crisply, 'tell me, as a man of the world, what do you think of my new niece?'

I was not a man of the world, nor was I much flattered in my stiff and dullish way of looking at things by being called one; and I could answer her without the least hesitation.

'I don't think, Miss Seaton, I'm much of a judge of character. She's very charming.'

'A brunette?'

'I think I prefer dark women.'

'And why? Consider, Mr Withers; dark hair, dark eyes, dark cloud, dark night, dark vision, dark death, dark grave, dark DARK!'

Perhaps the climax would have rather thrilled Seaton, but I was too thick-skinned. 'I don't know much about all that,' I answered rather pompously. 'Broad daylight's difficult enough for most of us.'

'Ah,' she said, with a sly inward burst of satirical laughter.

'And I suppose,' I went on, perhaps a little nettled, 'it isn't the actual darkness one admires, it's the contrast of the skin, and the colour of the eyes, and – and their shining. Just as,' I went blundering on, too late to turn back, 'just as you only see the stars in the dark. It would be a long day without any evening. As for death and the grave, I don't suppose we shall much notice that.' Arthur and his sweetheart were slowly returning along the dewy path. 'I believe in making the best of things.'

'How very interesting!' came the smooth answer. 'I see you are a philosopher, Mr Withers. H'm! "As for death and the grave, I don't suppose we shall much notice that." Very interesting . . . And I'm sure,' she added in a particularly suave voice, 'I profoundly hope so.' She rose slowly from her stool. 'You will take pity on me again, I hope. You and I would get on famously – kindred spirits – elective affinities. And, of course, now that my nephew's going to leave me, now that his affections are centred on another, I shall be a very lonely old woman . . . Shall I not, Arthur?'

Seaton blinked stupidly. 'I didn't hear what you said, Aunt.'

'I was telling our old friend, Arthur, that when you are gone I shall be a very lonely old woman.'

'Oh, I don't think so,' he said in a strange voice.

'He means, Mr Withers, he means, my dear child,' she said, sweeping her eyes over Alice, 'he means that I shall have memory for company – heavenly memory – the ghosts of other days. Sentimental boy! And did you enjoy our music, Alice? Did I really stir that youthful heart? . . . O, O, O,' continued the horrible old creature, 'you billers and cooers, I have been listening to such flatteries, such confessions! Beware, beware, Arthur, there's many a slip.' She rolled her little eyes at me, she shrugged her shoulders at Alice, and gazed an instant stonily into her nephew's face.

I held out my hand. 'Good night, good night!' she cried. 'He that fights and runs away. Ah, good night, Mr Withers; come again soon!' She thrust out her cheek at Alice, and we all three filed slowly out of the room.

Black shadow darkened the porch and half the spreading sycamore. We walked without speaking up the dusty village street. Here and there a crimson window glowed. At the fork of the high-road I said goodbye. But I had taken hardly more than a dozen paces when a sudden impulse seized me.

'Seaton!' I called.

He turned in the cool stealth of the moonlight.

'You have my address; if by any chance, you know, you should care to spend a week or two in town between this and the – the Day, we should be delighted to see you.'

'Thank you, Withers, thank you,' he said in a low voice.

'I dare say' – I waved my stick gallantly at Alice – 'I dare say you will be doing some shopping; we could all meet,' I added, laughing.

'Thank you, thank you, Withers – immensely,' he repeated.

And so we parted.

But they were out of the jog-trot of my prosaic life. And being of a stolid and incurious nature, I left Seaton and his marriage, and even his aunt, to themselves in my memory, and scarcely gave a thought to them until one day I was walking up the Strand again, and passed the flashing gloaming of the second-rate jeweller's shop where I had accidentally encountered my old schoolfellow in the summer. It was one of those stagnant autumnal days after a night of rain. I cannot say why, but a vivid recollection returned to my mind of our meeting and of how suppressed Seaton had seemed, and of how vainly he had endeavoured to appear assured and eager. He must be married by now, and had doubtless returned from his honeymoon. And I had clean forgotten my manners, had sent not a word of congratulation, nor – as I might very well have done, and as I knew he would have been pleased at my doing – even the ghost of a wedding present. It was just as of old.

On the other hand, I pleaded with myself, I had had no invitation. I paused at the corner of Trafalgar Square, and at the bidding of one of those caprices that seize occasionally on even an unimaginative mind, I found myself pelting after a green bus, and actually bound on a visit I had not in the least intended or foreseen.

The colours of autumn were over the village when I arrived. A beautiful late afternoon sunlight bathed thatch and meadow. But it was close and hot. A child, two dogs, a very old woman with a heavy basket I encountered. One or two incurious tradesmen looked idly up as I passed by. It was all so rural and remote, my whimsical impulse had so much flagged, that for a while I hesitated to venture under the shadow of the sycamore-tree to enquire after the happy pair. Indeed I first passed by the faint-blue gates and continued my walk under the high, green and tufted wall. Hollyhocks had attained their topmost bud and seeded in the little cottage gardens beyond; the Michaelmas daisies were in flower; a sweet warm aromatic smell of fading leaves was in the air. Beyond the cottages lay a field where cattle were grazing, and beyond that I came to a little churchyard. Then the road wound on, pathless and houseless, among gorse and bracken. I turned impatiently and walked quickly back to the house and rang the bell.

The rather colourless elderly woman who answered my enquiry informed me that Miss Seaton was at home, as if only taciturnity forbade her adding, 'But she doesn't want to see *you*.'

'Might I, do you think, have Mr Arthur's address?' I said.

She looked at me with quiet astonishment, as if waiting for an explanation. Not the faintest of smiles came into her thin face.

'I will tell Miss Seaton,' she said after a pause. 'Please walk in.'

She showed me into the dingy undusted drawing-room, filled with evening sunshine and with the green-dyed light that penetrated the leaves overhanging the long French windows. I sat down and waited on and on, occasionally aware of a creaking footfall overhead. At last the door opened a little, and the great face I had once known peered round at me. For it was enormously changed; mainly, I think, because the aged eyes had rather suddenly failed, and so a kind of stillness and darkness lay over its calm and wrinkled pallor.

'Who is it?' she asked.

I explained myself and told her the occasion of my visit.

She came in, shut the door carefully after her, and, though the fumbling was scarcely perceptible, groped her way to a chair. She had on an old dressing-gown, like a cassock, of a patterned cinnamon colour.

'What is it you want?' she said, seating herself and lifting her blank face to mine.

'Might I just have Arthur's address?' I said deferentially. 'I am so sorry to have disturbed you.'

'H'm. You have come to see my nephew?'

'Not necessarily to see him, only to hear how he is, and, of course, Mrs Seaton, too. I am afraid my silence must have appeared . . .'

'He hasn't noticed your silence,' croaked the old voice out of the great mask; 'besides, there isn't any Mrs Seaton.'

'Ah, then,' I answered, after a momentary pause, 'I have not seemed so black as I painted myself! And how is Miss Outram?'

'She's gone into Yorkshire,' answered Seaton's aunt.

'And Arthur too?'

She did not reply, but simply sat blinking at me with lifted chin, as if listening, but certainly not for what I might have to say. I began to feel rather at a loss.

'You were no close friend of my nephew's, Mr Smithers?' she said presently.

'No,' I answered, welcoming the cue, 'and yet, do you know, Miss Seaton, he is one of the very few of my old school-fellows I have come across in the last few years, and I suppose as one gets older one begins to value old associations . . .' My voice seemed to trail off into a vacuum. 'I thought Miss Outram,' I hastily began again, 'a particularly charming girl. I hope they are both quite well.'

Still the old face solemnly blinked at me in silence.

'You must find it very lonely, Miss Seaton, with Arthur away?'

'I was never lonely in my life,' she said sourly. 'I don't look to flesh and blood for my company. When you've got to be my age, Mr Smithers (which God forbid), you'll find life a very different affair from what you seem to think it is now. You won't seek company then, I'll be bound. It's thrust on you.' Her face edged round into the clear green light, and her eyes groped, as it were, over my vacant, disconcerted face. 'I dare say, now,' she said, composing her mouth, 'I dare say my nephew told you a good many tarradiddles in his time. Oh, yes, a good many, eh? He was always a liar. What, now, did he say of me? Tell me, now.' She leant forward as far as she could, trembling, with an ingratiating smile.

'I think he is rather superstitious,' I said coldly, 'but, honestly, I have a very poor memory, Miss Seaton.'

'Why?' she said. '*I* haven't.'

'The engagement hasn't been broken off, I hope.'

'Well, between you and me,' she said, shrinking up and with an immensely confidential grimace, 'it has.'

'I'm sure I'm very sorry to hear it. And where is Arthur?'

'Eh?'

'Where is Arthur?'

We faced each other mutely among the dead old bygone furniture. Past all my analysis was that large, flat, grey, cryptic countenance. And then, suddenly, our eyes for the first time really met. In some indescribable way out of that thick-lidded obscurity a far small something stooped and looked out at me for a mere instant of time that seemed of almost intolerable protraction. Involuntarily I blinked and shook my head. She muttered something with great rapidity, but quite inarticulately; rose and hobbled to the door. I thought I heard, mingled in broken mutterings, something about tea.

'Please, please, don't trouble,' I began, but could say no more, for the door was already shut between us. I stood and looked out on the long-neglected garden. I could just see the bright weedy greenness of Seaton's tadpole pond. I wandered about the room. Dusk began to gather, the last birds in that dense shadowiness of trees had ceased to sing. And not a sound was to be heard in the house. I waited on and on, vainly speculating. I even attempted to ring the bell; but the wire was broken, and only jangled loosely at my efforts.

I hesitated, unwilling to call or to venture out, and yet more unwilling to linger on, waiting for a tea that promised to be an exceedingly comfortless supper. And as darkness drew down, a feeling of the utmost unease and disquietude came over me. All my talks with Seaton returned on me with a suddenly enriched meaning. I recalled again his face as we had stood hanging over the staircase, listening in the small hours to the inexplicable stirrings of the night. There were no candles in the room; every minute the autumnal darkness deepened. I cautiously opened the door and listened, and with some little dismay withdrew, for I was uncertain of my way out. I even tried the garden, but was confronted under a veritable thicket of foliage by a padlocked gate. It would be a little too ignominious to be caught scaling a friend's garden fence!

Cautiously returning into the still and musty drawing-room, I took out my watch, and gave the incredible old woman ten minutes in which to reappear. And when that tedious ten minutes had ticked by I could scarcely distinguish its hands. I determined to wait no longer, drew open the door and, trusting to my sense of direction, groped my way through the corridor that I vaguely remembered led to the front of the house.

I mounted three or four stairs and, lifting a heavy curtain, found myself facing the starry fanlight of the porch. From here I glanced into the gloom of the dining-room. My fingers were on the latch of the outer door when I heard a faint stirring in the darkness above the hall. I looked up and became conscious of, rather than saw, the huddled old figure looking down on me.

There was an immense hushed pause. Then, 'Arthur, Arthur,' whispered an inexpressibly peevish rasping voice, 'is that you? Is that you, Arthur?'

I can scarcely say why, but the question horribly startled me. No conceivable answer occurred to me. With head craned back, hand clenched on my umbrella, I continued to stare up into the gloom, in this fatuous confrontation.

'Oh, oh,' the voice croaked. 'It is *you*, is it? *That* disgusting man! . . . Go away out. Go away out.'

At this dismissal, I wrenched open the door and, rudely slamming it behind me, ran out into the garden, under the gigantic old sycamore, and so out at the open gate.

I found myself half up the village street before I stopped running. The local butcher was sitting in his shop reading a piece of newspaper by the light of a small oil-lamp. I crossed the road and enquired the way to the station. And after he had with minute and needless care directed me, I asked casually if Mr Arthur Seaton still lived with his aunt at the big house just beyond the village. He poked his head in at the little parlour door.

'Here's a gentleman enquiring after young Mr Seaton, Millie,' he said. 'He's dead, ain't he?'

'Why, yes, bless you,' replied a cheerful voice from within. 'Dead and buried these three months or more – young Mr Seaton. And just before he was to be married, don't you remember, Bob?'

I saw a fair young woman's face peer over the muslin of the little door at me.

'Thank you,' I replied, 'then I go straight on?'

'That's it, sir; past the pond, bear up the hill a bit to the left, and then there's the station lights before your eyes.'

We looked intelligently into each other's faces in the beam of the smoky lamp. But not one of the many questions in my mind could I put into words.

And again I paused irresolutely a few paces further on. It was not, I fancy, merely a foolish apprehension of what the raw-boned butcher might 'think' that prevented my going back to see if I could find Seaton's grave in the benighted churchyard. There was precious little use in pottering about in the muddy dark merely to discover where he was buried. And yet I felt a little uneasy. My rather horrible thought was that, so far as I was concerned – one of his extremely few friends – he had never been much better than 'buried' in my mind.

# The Friends of the Friends

## Henry James

*On the eve of the American Civil War Henry James' family returned to their homeland after spending five years in Europe, and settled briefly in Providence, Rhode Island. The eighteen-year-old Henry James injured his back while helping to fight a fire, and this prevented him from volunteering for service in the army. It also gave him what he called his 'obscure hurt'; he became 'a detached but concerned observer' of the war, an attitude also apparent in his writings. His profound, convoluted novels and short stories seem always written by someone not fully concerned or even fully aware of what is going on. This is especially true of his fantastic stories: among others, his masterpiece* The Turn of the Screw, *his oft-anthologized 'The Jolly Corner', and 'The Friends of the Friends'.*

I find, as you prophesied, much that's interesting, but little that helps the delicate question – the possibility of publication. Her diaries are less systematic than I hoped; she only had a blessed habit of noting and narrating. She summarized, she saved; she appears seldom indeed to have let a good story pass without catching it on the wing. I allude of course not so much to things she heard as to things she saw and felt. She writes sometimes of herself, sometimes of others, sometimes of the combination. It's under this last rubric that she's usually most vivid. But it's not, you'll understand, when she's most vivid that she's always most publishable. To tell the truth she's fearfully indiscreet, or has at least all the material for making *me* so. Take as an instance the fragment I send you after dividing it for your convenience into several small chapters. It's the contents of a thin blank-book which I've had copied out and which has the merit of being nearly enough a rounded thing, an intelligible whole. These pages evidently date from years ago. I've read with the liveliest wonder the statement they so circumstantially make and done my best to swallow the prodigy they leave to be inferred. These things would be striking, wouldn't they? to any reader; but can you imagine for a moment my placing such a document before the world, even though, as if she herself had desired the world should have the benefit of it, she has given her friends neither name nor initials? Have you any sort of clue to their identity? I leave her the floor.

# I

I know perfectly of course that I brought it upon myself; but that doesn't make it any better. I was the first to speak of her to him – he had never even heard her mentioned. Even if I had happened not to speak some one else would have made up for it: I tried afterwards to find comfort in that reflection. But the comfort of reflections is thin: the only comfort that counts in life is not to have been a fool. That's a beatitude I shall doubtless never enjoy. 'Why you ought to meet her and talk it over' is what I immediately said. 'Birds of a feather flock together.' I told him who she was and that they were birds of a feather because if he had had in youth a strange adventure she had had about the same time just such another. It was well known to her friends – an incident she was constantly called on to describe. She was charming clever pretty unhappy; but it was none the less the thing to which she had originally owed her reputation.

Being at the age of eighteen somewhere abroad with an aunt she had had a vision of one of her parents at the moment of death. The parent was in England hundreds of miles away and so far as she knew neither dying nor dead. It was by day, in the museum of some great foreign town. She had passed alone, in advance of her companions, into a small room containing some famous work of art and occupied at that moment by two other persons. One of these was an old custodian; the second, before observing him, she took for a stranger, a tourist. She was merely conscious that he was bareheaded and seated on a bench. The instant her eyes rested on him, however, she beheld to her amazement her father, who, as if he had long waited for her, looked at her in singular distress and an impatience that was akin to reproach. She rushed to him with a bewildered cry, 'Papa, what *is* it?' but this was followed by an exhibition of still livelier feeling when on her movement he simply vanished, leaving the custodian and her relations, who were by that time at her heels, to gather round her in dismay. These persons, the official, the aunt, the cousins, were therefore in a manner witnesses of the fact – the fact at least of the impression made on her; and there was the further testimony of a doctor who was attending one of the party and to whom it was immediately afterwards communicated. He gave her a remedy for hysterics, but said to the aunt privately: 'Wait and see if something doesn't happen at home.' Something *had* happened – the poor father, suddenly and violently seized, had died that morning. The aunt, the mother's sister, received before the day was out a telegram announcing the event and requesting her to prepare her niece for it. Her niece was already prepared, and the girl's sense of this visitation remained of course indelible. We had all, as her friends, had it conveyed to us and had conveyed it creepily to each other. Twelve years had elapsed, and as a woman who had made an unhappy marriage and lived apart from her husband she had become interesting from other sources; but since the name she now bore was a name frequently borne, and since moreover her judicial separation, as things were going, could hardly count as a distinction, it was usual to qualify her as 'the one, you know, who saw her father's ghost'.

As for him, dear man, he had seen his mother's – so there you are! I had never heard of that till this occasion on which our closer, our pleasanter acquaintance led him, through some turn of the subject of our talk, to mention it and to inspire me in so doing with the impulse to let him know that he had a rival in the field – a person with whom he could compare notes. Later on his story became for him, perhaps because of my unduly repeating it, likewise a convenient worldly label; but it hadn't a year before been the ground on which he was introduced to me. He had other merits, just as she, poor thing, had others. I can honestly say that I was quite aware of them from the first – I discovered them sooner than he discovered mine. I remember how it struck me even at the time that his sense of mine was quickened by my having been able to match, though not indeed straight from my own experience, his curious anecdote. It dated, this anecdote, as hers did, from some dozen years before – a year in which, at Oxford, he had for some reason of his own been staying on into the 'Long'. He had been in the August afternoon on the river. Coming back into his room while it was still distinct daylight he found his mother standing there as if her eyes had been fixed on the door. He had had a letter from her that morning out of Wales, where she was staying with her father. At the sight of him she smiled with extraordinary radiance and extended her arms to him, and then as he sprang forward and joyfully opened his own she vanished from the place. He wrote to her that night, telling her what had happened; the letter had been carefully preserved. The next morning he heard of her death. He was through this chance of our talk extremely struck with the little prodigy I was able to produce for him. He had never encountered another case. Certainly they ought to meet, my friend and he; certainly they would have something in common. I would arrange this, wouldn't I? – if *she* didn't mind; for himself he didn't mind in the least. I had promised to speak to her of the matter as soon as possible, and within the week I was able to do so. She 'minded' as little as he; she was perfectly willing to see him. And yet no meeting was to occur – as meetings are commonly understood.

## II

That's just half my tale – the extraordinary way it was hindered. This was the fault of a series of accidents; but the accidents, persisting for years, became, to me and to others, a subject of mirth with either party. They were droll enough at first, then they grew rather a bore. The odd thing was that both parties were amenable; it wasn't a case of their being indifferent, much less of their being indisposed. It was one of the caprices of chance, aided I suppose by some rather settled opposition of their interests and habits. His were centred in his office, his eternal inspectorship, which left him small leisure, constantly calling him away and making him break engagements. He liked society, but he found it everywhere and took it at a run. I never knew at a given moment where he was, and there were times when for months together I never saw him. She was on her side practically suburban: she lived at Richmond and never went 'out'. She was a woman of distinction, but not of fashion, and felt, as people said, her situation. Decidedly proud and rather whimsical, she lived her life as she had planned it. There were things one could do with her, but one couldn't make her come to one's parties. One went indeed a little more than seemed quite convenient to hers, which consisted of her cousin, a cup of tea and the view. The tea was good; but the view was familiar, though perhaps not, like the cousin – a disagreeable old maid who had been of the group at the museum and with whom she now lived – offensively so. This connexion with an inferior relative, which had partly an economic motive – she proclaimed her companion a marvellous manager – was one of the little perversities we had to forgive her. Another was her estimate of the proprieties created by her rupture with her husband. That was extreme – many persons called it even morbid. She made no advances; she cultivated scruples; she suspected, or I should perhaps rather say she remembered, slights: she was one of the few women I've known whom that particular predicament had rendered modest rather than bold. Dear thing, she had some delicacy! Especially marked were the limits she had set to possible attentions from men: it was always her thought that her husband only waited to pounce on her. She discouraged if she didn't forbid the visits of male persons not senile: she said she could never be too careful.

When I first mentioned to her that I had a friend whom fate had distinguished in the same weird way as herself I put her quite at liberty to say 'Oh bring him out to see me!' I should probably have been able to bring him, and a situation perfectly innocent or at any rate comparatively simple would have been created. But she uttered no such word; she only said: 'I must meet him certainly; yes, I shall look out for him!' That caused the first delay, and meanwhile various things happened. One of them was that as time went on she made, charming as she was, more and more friends, and that it regularly befell that these friends were sufficiently also friends of his to bring him up in conversation. It was odd that without belonging, as it were, to the same world, or, according to the horrid term, the same set, my baffled pair should have happened in so many cases to fall in with the same people and make them join in the droll chorus. She had friends who didn't know each other but who inevitably and punctually recommended *him*. She had also the sort of originality, the intrinsic interest, that led her to be kept by each of us as a private resource, cultivated jealously, more or less in secret, as a person whom one didn't meet in society, whom it was not for every one – whom it was not for the vulgar – to approach, and with whom therefore acquaintance was particularly difficult and particularly precious. We saw her separately, with appointments and conditions, and found it made on the whole for harmony not to tell each other. Somebody had always had a note from her still later than somebody else. There was some silly woman who for a long time, among the unprivileged, owed to three simple visits to Richmond a reputation for being intimate with 'lots of awfully clever out-of-the-way people'.

Every one has had friends it has seemed a happy thought to bring together, and every one remembers that his happiest thoughts have not been his greatest successes; but I doubt if there was ever a case in which the failure was in such direct proportion to the quantity of influence set in motion. It's really perhaps here the quantity of influence that was most remarkable. My lady and my gentleman each pronounced it to me and others quite a subject for a roaring farce. The reason first given had with time dropped out of sight and fifty better ones flourished on top of it. They were so awfully alike: they had the same ideas and tricks and tastes, the same prejudices and superstitions and heresies; they said the same things and sometimes did them; they liked and disliked the same persons and places, the same books, authors and styles; there were touches of resemblance even in their looks and features. It established much of a propriety that they were in common parlance equally 'nice' and almost equally handsome. But the great sameness, for wonder and chatter, was their rare perversity in regard to being photographed. They were the only persons ever heard of who had never been 'taken' and who had a passionate objection to it. They just *wouldn't* be – no, not for anything any one could say. I had loudly complained of this; him in particular I had so vainly desired to be able to show on my drawing-room chimney-piece in a Bond Street frame. It was at any rate the very liveliest of all the reasons why they ought to know each other – all the lively reasons reduced to naught by the strange law that had made them bang so many doors in each other's face, made them the buckets in the well, the two ends of the see-saw, the two parties in the State, so that when one was up the other was down, when one was out the other was in; neither by any possibility entering a house till the other had left it or leaving it all unawares till the other was at hand. They only arrived when they had been given up, which was precisely also when they departed. They were in a word alternate and incompatible; they missed each other with an inveteracy that could be explained only by its being preconcerted. It was however so far from preconcerted that it had ended – literally after several years – by disappointing and annoying them. I don't think their curiosity was lively till it had been proved utterly vain. A great deal was of course done to help them, but it merely laid wires for them to trip. To give examples I should have to have taken notes; but I happen to remember that neither had even been able to dine on the right occasion. The right occasion for each was the occasion that would be wrong for the other. On the wrong one they were most punctual and there were never any but wrong ones. The very elements conspired and the constitution of man re-enforced them. A cold, a headache, a bereavement, a storm, a fog, an earthquake, a cataclysm, infallibly intervened. The whole business was beyond a joke.

Yet as a joke it had still to be taken, though one couldn't help feeling that the joke had made the situation serious, had produced on the part of each a consciousness, an awkwardness, a positive dread of the last accident of all, the only one with any freshness left, the accident that *would* bring them together. The final effect of its predecessors had been to kindle this instinct. They were quite ashamed – perhaps even a little of each other. So much preparation, so much frustration: what indeed could be good enough for it all to lead up to? A mere meeting would be mere flatness. Did I see them at the end of years, they often asked, just stupidly confronted? If they were bored by the joke they might be worse bored by something else. They made exactly the same reflections and each in some manner was sure to hear of the other's. I really think it was this peculiar diffidence that finally controlled the situation. I mean that if they had failed for the first year or two because they couldn't help it, they kept up the habit because they had – what shall I call it? – grown nervous. It really took some lurking volition to account for anything both so regular and so ridiculous.

# III

When to crown our long acquaintance I accepted his renewed offer of marriage it was humorously said, I know, that I had made the gift of his photograph a condition. This was so far true that I had refused to give him mine without it. At any rate I had him at last, in his high distinction, on the chimney-piece, where the day she called to congratulate me she came nearer than she had ever done to seeing him. He had in being taken set her an example that I invited her to follow; he had sacrificed his perversity – wouldn't she sacrifice hers? She too must give me something on my engagement – wouldn't she give me the companion-piece? She laughed and

shook her head; she had headshakes whose impulse seemed to come
from as far away as the breeze that stirs a flower. The companion-
piece to the portrait of my future husband was the portrait of his
future wife. She had taken her stand – she could depart from it as
little as she could explain it. It was a prejudice, an *entêtement*, a vow
– she would live and die unphotographed. Now too she was alone
in that state: this was what she liked; it made her so much more
original. She rejoiced in the fall of her late associate and looked a
long time at his picture, about which she made no memorable
remark, though she even turned it over to see the back. About our
engagement she was charming – full of cordiality and sympathy.
'You've known him even longer than I've *not*,' she said, 'and that
seems a very long time.' She understood how we had jogged together
over hill and dale and how inevitable it was that we should now rest
together. I'm definite about all this because what followed is so
strange that it's a kind of relief to me to mark the point up to which
our relations were as natural as ever. It was I myself who in a
sudden madness altered and destroyed them. I see now that she
gave me no pretext and that I only found one in the way she looked
at the fine face in the Bond Street frame. How then would I have
had her look at it? What I had wanted from the first was to make
her care for him. Well, that was what I still wanted – up to the
moment of her having promised me she would on this occasion
really aid me to break the silly spell that had kept them asunder. I
had arranged with him to do his part if she would as triumphantly
do hers. I was on a different footing now – I was on a footing to
answer for him. I would positively engage that at five on the
following Saturday he should be on that spot. He was out of town
on pressing business, but, pledged to keep his promise to the letter,
would return on purpose and in abundant time. 'Are you perfectly
sure?' I remember she asked, looking grave and considering: I
thought she had turned a little pale. She was tired, she was indisposed: it was a pity he was to see her after all at so poor a moment.
If he only *could* have seen her five years before! However, I replied
that this time I was sure and that success therefore depended simply
on herself. At five o'clock on the Saturday she would find him in a
particular chair I pointed out, the one in which he usually sat and
in which – though this I didn't mention – he had been sitting when,
the week before, he put the question of our future to me in the way
that had brought me round. She looked at it in silence, just as she

had looked at the photograph, while I repeated for the twentieth time that it was too preposterous one shouldn't somehow succeed in introducing to one's dearest friend one's second self. '*Am* I your dearest friend?' she asked with a smile that for a moment brought back her beauty. I replied by pressing her to my bosom; after which she said: 'Well, I'll come. I'm extraordinarily afraid, but you may count on me.'

When she had left me I began to wonder what she was afraid of, for she had spoken as if she fully meant it. The next day, late in the afternoon, I had three lines from her: she had found on getting home the announcement of her husband's death. She hadn't seen him for seven years, but she wished me to know it in this way before I should hear of it in another. It made however in her life, strange and sad to say, so little difference that she would scrupulously keep her appointment. I rejoiced for her – I supposed it would make at least the difference of her having more money; but even in this diversion, far from forgetting she had said she was afraid, I seemed to catch sight of a reason for her being so. Her fear, as the evening went on, became contagious, and the contagion took in my breast the form of a sudden panic. It wasn't jealousy – it just was the dread of jealousy. I called myself a fool for not having been quiet till we were man and wife. After that I should somehow feel secure. It was only a question of waiting another month – a trifle surely for people who had waited so long. It had been plain enough she was nervous, and now she was free her nervousness wouldn't be less. What was it therefore but a sharp foreboding? She had been hitherto the victim of interference, but it was quite possible she would henceforth be the source of it. The victim in that case would be my simple self. What had the interference been but the finger of Providence pointing out a danger? The danger was of course for poor *me*. It had been kept at bay by a series of accidents unexampled in their frequency; but the reign of accident was now visibly at an end. I had an intimate conviction that both parties would keep the tryst. It was more and more impressed on me that they were approaching, converging. They were like the seekers for the hidden object in the game of blindfold; they had one and the other begun to 'burn'. We had talked about breaking the spell; well, it would be effectually broken – unless indeed it should merely take another form and overdo their encounters as it had overdone their escapes. This was something I couldn't sit still for thinking of; it kept me awake – at midnight I was full of unrest. At last I felt there was only one way of laying the ghost. If the reign of accident was over I must just take up the succession. I sat down and wrote a hurried note which would meet him on his return and which, as the servants had gone to bed, I sallied forth bareheaded into the empty gusty street to drop into the nearest pillar-box. It was to tell him that I shouldn't be able to be at home in the afternoon as I had hoped and that he must postpone his visit till dinner-time. This was an implication that he would find me alone.

# IV

When accordingly at five she presented herself I naturally felt false and base. My act had been a momentary madness, but I had at least, as they say, to live up to it. She remained an hour: he of course never came; and I could only persist in my perfidy. I had thought it best to let her come; singular as this now seems to me I held it diminished my guilt. Yet as she sat there so visibly white and weary, stricken with a sense of everything her husband's death had opened up, I felt a really piercing pang of pity and remorse. If I didn't tell her on the spot what I had done it was because I was too ashamed. I feigned astonishment – I feigned it to the end; I protested that if ever I had had confidence I had had it that day. I blush as I tell my story – I take it as my penance. There was nothing indignant I didn't say about him; I invented suppositions, attenuations; I admitted in stupefaction, as the hands of the clock travelled, that their luck hadn't turned. She smiled at this vision of their 'luck', but she looked anxious – she looked unusual: the only thing that kept me up was the fact that, oddly enough, she wore mourning – no great depths of crape, but simple and scrupulous black. She had in her bonnet three small black feathers. She carried a little muff of astrakhan. This put me, by the aid of some acute reflection, a little in the right. She had written to me that the sudden event made no difference for her, but apparently it made as much difference as that. If she was inclined to the usual forms why didn't she observe that of not going the first day or two out to tea? There was some one she wanted so much to see that she couldn't wait till her husband was buried. Such a betrayal of eagerness made me hard and cruel enough to practise my odious deceit, though at the same time, as the hour waxed and waned, I suspected in her something deeper still than disappointment and somewhat less successfully concealed. I mean a strange underlying relief, the soft low emission of the breath that comes when a danger is past. What happened as she spent her barren hour with me was that at last she gave him up. She let him go for ever. She made the most graceful joke of it that I've ever seen made of anything; but it was for all that a great date in her life. She spoke with her mild gaiety of all the other vain times, the long game of hide-and-seek, the unprecedented queerness of such a relation. For it *was*, or had been, a relation, wasn't it, hadn't it? That was just the absurd part of it. When she got up to go I said to her that it was more a relation than ever, but that I hadn't the face after what had occurred to propose to her for the present another opportunity. It was plain that the only valid opportunity would be my accomplished marriage. Of course she would be at my wedding? It was even to be hoped that *he* would.

'If *I* am, he won't be!' – I remember the high quaver and the little break of her laugh. I admitted there might be something in that. The thing was therefore to get us safely married first. 'That won't help us. Nothing will help us!' she said as she kissed me farewell: 'I shall never, never see him!' It was with those words she left me.

I could bear her disappointment as I've called it; but when a couple of hours later I received him at dinner I discovered I couldn't bear his. The way my manoeuvre might have affected him hadn't been particularly present to me; but the result of it was the first word of reproach that had ever yet dropped from him. I say 'reproach' because that expression is scarcely too strong for the terms in which he conveyed to me his surprise that under the extraordinary circumstances I shouldn't have found some means not to deprive him of such an occasion. I might really have managed either not to be obliged to go out or to let their meeting take place all the same. They would probably have got on, in my drawing-room, well enough without me. At this I quite broke down – I confessed my iniquity and the miserable reason of it. I hadn't put her off and I hadn't gone out; she had been there and, after waiting for him an hour, had departed in the belief that he had been absent by his own fault.

'She must think me a precious brute!' he exclaimed. 'Did she say of me' – and I remember the just perceptible catch of breath in his pause – 'what she had a right to say?'

'I assure you she said nothing that showed the least feeling. She looked at your photograph, she even turned round the back of it, on which your address happens to be inscribed. Yet it provoked her to no demonstration. She doesn't care so much as all that.'

'Then why are you afraid of her?'

'It wasn't of her I was afraid. It was of you.'

'Did you think I'd be so sure to fall in love with her? You never alluded to such a possibility before,' he went on as I remained silent. 'Admirable person as you pronounced her, that wasn't the light in which you showed her to me.'

'Do you mean that if it *had* been you'd have managed by this time to catch a glimpse of her? I didn't fear things then,' I added. 'I hadn't the same reason.'

He kissed me at this, and when I remembered that she had done so an hour or two before I felt for an instant as if he were taking from my lips the very pressure of hers. In spite of kisses the incident had shed a certain chill, and I suffered horribly from the sense that he had seen me guilty of a fraud. He had seen it only through my frank avowal, but I was as unhappy as if I had a stain to efface. I couldn't get over the manner of his looking at me when I spoke of her apparent indifference to his not having come. For the first time since I had known him he seemed to have expressed a doubt of my word. Before we parted I told him that I'd undeceive her – start the first thing in the morning for Richmond and there let her know he had been blameless. At this he kissed me again. I'd expiate my sin, I said; I'd humble myself in the dust: I'd confess and ask to be forgiven. At this he kissed me once more.

# V

In the train the next day this struck me as a good deal for him to have consented to; but my purpose was firm enough to carry me on. I mounted the long hill to where the view begins, and then I knocked at her door. I was a trifle mystified by the fact that her blinds were still drawn, reflecting that if in the stress of my compunction I had come early I had certainly yet allowed people time to get up.

'At home, mum? She has left home for ever.'

I was extraordinarily startled by this announcement of the elderly parlour-maid. 'She has gone away?'

'She's dead, mum, please.' Then as I gasped at the horrible word: 'She died last night.'

The loud cry that escaped me sounded even in my own ears like some harsh violation of the hour. I felt for the moment as if I had killed her; I turned faint and saw through a vagueness the woman hold out her arms to me. Of what next happened I've no recollection, nor of anything but my friend's poor stupid cousin, in a darkened room, after an interval that I suppose very brief, sobbing at me in a smothered accusatory way. I can't say how long it took me to understand, to believe and then to press back with an immense effort that pang of reponsibility which, superstitiously, insanely, had been at first almost all I was conscious of. The doctor, after the fact, had been superlatively wise and clear: he was satisfied of a long-latent weakness of the heart, determined probably years before by the agitation and terrors to which her marriage had introduced her. She had had in those days cruel scenes with her husband, she had been in fear of her life. All emotion, everything in the nature of anxiety and suspense had been after that to be strongly depre-cated, as in her marked cultivation of a quiet life she was evidently well aware; but who could say that any one, especially a 'real lady', might be successfully protected from *every* little rub? She had had one a day or two before in the news of her husband's death – since there were shocks of all kinds, not only those of grief and surprise. For that matter she had never dreamed of so near a release: it had looked uncommonly as if he would live as long as herself. Then in the evening, in town, she had manifestly had some misadventure: something must have happened there that it would be imperative to clear up. She had come back very late – it was past eleven o'clock, and on being met in the hall by her cousin, who was extremely anxious, had allowed she was tired and must rest a moment before mounting the stairs. They had passed together into the dining-room, her companion proposing a glass of wine and bustling to the sideboard to pour it out. This took but a moment, and when my informant turned round our poor friend had not had time to seat herself. Suddenly, with a small moan that was barely audible, she dropped upon the sofa. She was dead. What unknown 'little rub' had dealt her the blow? What concussion, in the name of wonder, *had* awaited her in town? I mentioned immediately the one thinkable ground of disturbance – her having failed to meet at my house, to which by invitation for the purpose she had come at five o'clock, the gentleman I was to be married to, who had been accidentally kept away and with whom she had no acquaintance whatever. This obviously counted for little; but something else might easily have occurred: nothing in the London streets was more possible than an accident, especially an accident in those desperate cabs. What had she done, where had she gone on leaving my house? I had taken for granted she had gone straight home. We both presently remembered that in her excursions to town she sometimes, for convenience, for refreshment, spent an hour or two at the 'Gentlewomen', the quiet little ladies' club, and I promised that it should be my first care to make at that establishment an earnest appeal. Then we entered the dim and dreadful chamber where she lay locked up in death and where, asking after a little to be left alone with her, I remained for half an hour. Death had made her, had kept her beautiful; but I felt above all, as I knelt at her bed, that it had made her, had kept her silent. It had turned the key on something I was concerned to know.

On my return from Richmond and after another duty had been performed I drove to his chambers. It was the first time, but I had often wanted to see them. On the staircase, which, as the house contained twenty sets of rooms, was unrestrictedly public, I met his servant, who went back with me and ushered me in. At the sound of my entrance he appeared in the doorway of a further room, and the instant we were alone I produced my news: 'She's dead!'

'Dead?' He was tremendously struck, and I noticed he had no need to ask whom, in this abruptness, I meant.

'She died last evening – just after leaving me.'

He stared with the strangest expression, his eyes searching mine as for a trap. 'Last evening – after leaving you?' He repeated my words in stupefaction. Then he brought out, so that it was in stupefaction I heard, 'Impossible! I saw her.'

'You "saw" her?'

'On that spot – where you stand.'

This called back to me after an instant, as if to help me to take it in, the great wonder of the warning of his youth. 'In the hour of death – I understand: as you so beautifully saw your mother.'

'Ah *not* as I saw my mother – not that way, not that way!' He was deeply moved by my news – far more moved, it was plain, than he would have been the day before: it gave me a vivid sense that, as I had then said to myself, there was indeed a relation between them and that he had actually been face to face with her. Such an idea, by its reassertion of his extraordinary privilege, would have suddenly presented him as painfully abnormal hadn't he vehemently insisted on the difference. 'I saw her living. I saw her to speak to her. I saw her as I see you now.'

It's remarkable that for a moment, though only for a moment, I found relief in the more personal, as it were, but also the more natural, of the two odd facts. The next, as I embraced this image of her having come to him on leaving me and of just what it accounted for in the disposal of her time, I demanded with a shade of harshness of which I was aware: 'What on earth did she come for?'

He had now a minute to think – to recover himself and judge of effects, so that if it was still with excited eyes he spoke he showed a conscious redness and made an inconsequent attempt to smile away the gravity of his words. 'She came just to see me. She came – after what had passed at your house – so that we *should*, nevertheless, at last meet. The impulse seemed to me exquisite, and that was the way I took it?

I looked round the room where she had been – where *she* had been and I never had till now. 'And was the way you took it the way she expressed it?'

'She only expressed it by being here and by letting me look at her. That was enough!' he cried with an extraordinary laugh.

I wondered more and more. 'You mean she didn't speak to you?'

'She said nothing. She only looked at me as I looked at her.'

'And you didn't speak either?'

He gave me again his painful smile. 'I thought of *you*. The situation was every way delicate. I used the finest tact. But she saw she had pleased me.' He even repeated his dissonant laugh.

'She evidently "pleased" you!' Then I thought a moment. 'How long did she stay?'

'How can I say? It seemed twenty minutes, but it was probably a good deal less.'

'Twenty minutes of silence!' I began to have my definite view, and now in fact quite to clutch at it. 'Do you know you're telling me a thing positively monstrous?'

He had been standing with his back to the fire; at this, with a pleading look, he came to me. 'I beseech you, dearest, to take it kindly.'

I could take it kindly, and I signified as much, but I couldn't somehow, as he rather awkwardly opened his arms, let him draw me to him. So there fell between us for an appreciable time the discomfort of a great silence.

# VI

He broke it by presently saying: 'There's absolutely no doubt of her death?'

'Unfortunately none. I've just risen from my knees by the bed where they've laid her out.'

He fixed his eyes hard on the floor; then he raised them to mine. 'How does she look?'

'She looks – at peace.'

He turned away again while I watched him; but after a moment he began: 'At what hour then—?'

'It must have been near midnight. She dropped as she reached her house – from an affection of the heart which she knew herself and her physician knew her to have, but of which, patiently, bravely, she had never spoken to me.'

He listened intently and for a minute was unable to speak. At last he broke out with an accent of which the almost boyish confidence, the really sublime simplicity, rings in my ears as I write: 'Wasn't she *wonderful*!' Even at the time I was able to do it justice enough to answer that I had always told him so; but the next minute, as if after speaking he had caught a glimpse of what he might have made me feel, he went on quickly: 'You can easily understand that if she didn't get home till midnight—'

I instantly took him up. 'There was plenty of time for you to have seen her? How so,' I asked, 'when you didn't leave my house till late? I don't remember the very moment – I was preoccupied. But you know that though you said you had lots to do you sat for some time after dinner. She, on her side, was all the evening at the "Gentlewomen". I've just come from there – I've ascertained. She had tea there; she remained a long long time.'

'What was she doing all the long long time?'

I saw him eager to challenge at every step my account of the matter: and the more he showed this the more I was moved to emphasize that version, to prefer with apparent perversity an explanation which only deepened the marvel and the mystery, but which, of the two prodigies it had to choose from, my reviving jealousy found easiest to accept. He stood there pleading with a candour that now seems to me beautiful for the privilege of having in spite of supreme defeat known the living woman; while I, with a passion I wonder at today, though it still smoulders in a manner in its ashes, could only reply that, through a strange gift shared by her with his mother and on her own side likewise hereditary, the miracle of his youth had been renewed for him, the miracle of hers for her. She had been to him – yes, and by an impulse as charming as he liked; but oh she hadn't been in the body! It was a simple question of evidence. I had had, I maintained, a definite statement of what she had done – most of the time – at the little club. The place was almost empty, but the servants had noticed her. She had sat motionless in a deep chair by the drawing-room fire; she had leaned back her head, she had closed her eyes, she had seemed softly to sleep.

'I see. But till what o'clock?'

'There,' I was obliged to answer, 'the servants fail me a little. The portress in particular is unfortunately a fool, even though she too is supposed to be a Gentlewoman. She was evidently at that period of the evening, without a substitute and against regulations, absent for some little time from the cage in which it's her business to watch the comings and goings. She's muddled, she palpably prevaricates, so I can't positively, from her observation, give you an hour. But it was remarked towards half-past ten that our poor friend was no longer in the club.'

It suited him down to the ground. She came straight here, and from here she went straight to the train.

'She couldn't have run it so close,' I declared. 'That was a thing she particularly never did.'

'There was no need of running it close, my dear – she had plenty of time. Your memory's at fault about my having left you late: I left you, as it happens, unusually early. I'm sorry my stay with you seemed long, for I was back here by ten.'

'To put yourself into your slippers,' I retorted, 'and fall asleep in your chair. You slept till morning – you saw her in a dream!' He looked at me in silence and with sombre eyes – eyes that showed me he had some irritation to repress. Presently I went on: 'You had a visit, at an extraordinary hour, from a lady – *soit*: nothing in the world's more probable. But there are ladies and ladies. How in the name of goodness, if she was unannounced and dumb and you had into the bargain never seen the least portrait of her – how could you identify the person we're talking of?'

'Haven't I to absolute satiety heard her described? I'll describe her for you in every particular.'

'Don't!' I cried with a promptness that made him laugh once more. I coloured at this, but I continued: 'Did your servant introduce her?'

'He wasn't here – he's always away when he's wanted. One of the features of this big house is that from the street-door the different floors are accessible practically without challenge. My servant makes love to a young person employed in the rooms above these, and he had a long bout of it last evening. When he's out on that job he leaves my outer door, on the staircase, so much ajar as to enable him to slip back without a sound. The door then only requires a push. She pushed it – that simply took a little courage.'

'A little? It took tons! And it took all sorts of impossible calculations.'

'Well, she had them – she made them. Mind you, I don't deny for a moment,' he added, 'that it was very very wonderful!'

Something in his tone kept me a time from trusting myself to speak. At last I said: 'How did she come to know where you live?'

'By remembering the address on the little label the shop-people happily left sticking to the frame I had had made for my photograph.'

'And how was she dressed?'

'In mourning, my own dear. No great depths of crape, but simple and scrupulous black. She had in her bonnet three small black feathers. She carried a little muff of astrakhan. She has near the left eye,' he continued, 'a tiny vertical scar—'

I stopped him short. 'The mark of a caress from her husband.' Then I added: 'How close you must have been to her!' He made no answer to this, and I thought he blushed, observing which I broke straight off. 'Well, goodbye.'

'You won't stay a little?' He came to me again tenderly, and this time I suffered him. 'Her visit had its beauty,' he murmured as he held me, 'but yours has a greater one.'

I let him kiss me, but I remembered, as I had remembered the day before, that the last kiss she had given, as I supposed, in this world had been for the lips he touched. 'I'm life, you see,' I answered. 'What you saw last night was death.'

'It was life – it was life!'

He spoke with a soft stubbornness – I disengaged myself. We stood looking at each other hard. 'You describe the scene – so far as you describe it at all – in terms that are incomprehensible. She was in the room before you knew it?'

'I looked up from my letter-writing – at that table under the lamp I had been wholly absorbed in it – and she stood before me.'

'Then what did you do?'

'I sprang up with an ejaculation, and she, with a smile, laid her finger, ever so warningly, yet with a sort of delicate dignity, to her lips. I knew it meant silence, but the strange thing was that it seemed immediately to explain and to justify her. We at any rate stood for a time that, as I've told you, I can't calculate, face to face. It was just as you and I stand now.'

'Simply staring?'

He shook an impatient head. 'Ah! *we're* not staring!'

'Yes, but we're talking.'

'Well, *we* were – after a fashion.' He lost himself in the memory of it. 'It was as friendly as this.' I had on my tongue's end to ask if that was saying much for it, but I made the point instead that what they had evidently done was to gaze in mutual admiration. Then I asked if his recognition of her had been immediate. 'Not quite,' he replied, 'for of course I didn't expect her; but it came to me long before she went who she was – who only she could be.'

I thought a little. 'And how did she at last go?'

'Just as she arrived. The door was open behind her and she passed out.'

'Was she rapid – slow?'

'Rather quick. But looking behind her,' he smiled to add. 'I let her go, for I perfectly knew I was to take it as she wished.'

I was conscious of exhaling a long vague sigh. 'Well, you must take it now as *I* wish – you must let *me* go.'

At this he drew near me again, detaining and persuading me, declaring with all due gallantry that I was a very different matter. I'd have given anything to have been able to ask him if he had touched her, but the words refused to form themselves: I knew to the last tenth of a tone how horrid and vulgar they'd sound. I said something else – I forget exactly what; it was feebly tortuous and intended, meanly enough, to make him tell me without my putting the question. But he didn't tell me; he only repeated, as from a glimpse of the propriety of soothing and consoling me the sense of his declaration of some minutes before – the assurance that she was indeed exquisite, as I had always insisted, but that I was his 'real' friend and his very own for ever. This led me to reassert, in the spirit of my previous rejoinder, that I had at least the merit of being alive; which in turn drew from him again the flash of contradiction I dreaded. 'Oh *she* was alive! She was, she was!'

'She was dead, she was dead!' I asseverated with an energy, a determination it should *be* so, which comes back to me now almost as grotesque. But the sound of the word as it rang out filled me suddenly with horror, and all the natural emotion the meaning of it might have evoked in other conditions gathered and broke in a flood. It rolled over me that here was a great affection quenched, and how much I had loved and trusted her. I had a vision at the same time of the lonely beauty of her end. 'She's gone – she's lost to us for ever!' I burst into sobs.

'That's exactly what I feel,' he exclaimed, speaking with extreme kindness and pressing me to him for comfort. 'She's gone; she's lost to us for ever: so what does it matter now?' He bent over me, and when his face had touched mine I scarcely knew if it were wet with my tears or with his own.

# VII

It was my theory, my conviction, it became, as I may say, my attitude, that they had still never 'met'; and it was just on this ground I felt it generous to ask him to stand with me at her grave. He did so very modestly and tenderly, and I assumed, though he himself clearly cared nothing for the danger, that the solemnity of the occasion, largely made up of persons who had known them both and had a sense of the long joke, would sufficiently deprive his presence of all light association. On the question of what had happened the evening of her death little more passed between us; I had been taken by a horror of the element of evidence. On either hypothesis it was gross and prying. He on his side lacked producible corroboration – everything, that is, but a statement of his house-porter, on his own admission a most casual and intermittent personage – that between the hours of ten o'clock and midnight no less than three ladies in deep black had flitted in and out of the place. This proved far too much; we had neither of us any use for three. He knew I considered I had accounted for every fragment of her time, and we dropped the matter as settled; we abstained from further discussion. What *I* knew however was that he abstained to please me rather than because he yielded to my reasons. He didn't yield – he was only indulgent; he clung to his interpretation because he liked it better. He liked it better, I held, because it had more to say to his vanity. That, in a similar position, wouldn't have been its effect on me, though I had doubtless quite as much; but these are things of individual humour and as to which no person can judge for another. I should have supposed it more gratifying to be the subject of one of those inexplicable occurrences that are chronicled in thrilling books and disputed about at learned meetings; I could conceive, on the part of a being just engulfed in the infinite and still vibrating with human emotion, of nothing more fine and pure, more high and august, than such an impulse of reparation, of admonition, or even of curiosity. *That* was beautiful, if one would, and I should in his place have thought more of myself for being so distinguished and so selected. It was public that he had already, that he had long figured in that light, and what was such a fact in itself but almost a proof? Each of the strange visitations contributed to establish the other. He had a different feeling; but he had also, I hasten to add, an unmistakable desire not to make a stand or, as they say, a fuss about it. I might believe what I liked – the more so that the whole thing was in a manner a mystery of my producing. It was an event of my history, a puzzle of my consciousness, not of his; therefore he would take about it any tone that struck me as convenient. We had both at all events other business on hand: we were pressed with preparations for our marriage.

Mine were assuredly urgent, but I found as the days went on that to believe what I 'liked' was to believe what I was more and more intimately convinced of. I found also that I didn't like it so much as that came to, or that the pleasure at all events was far from being the cause of my conviction. My obsession, as I may really call it and as I began to perceive, refused to be elbowed away, as I had hoped, by my sense of paramount duties. If I had a great deal to do, I had still more to think of, and the moment came when my occupations were gravely menaced by my thoughts. I see it all now, I feel it, I live it over. It's terribly void of joy, it's full indeed to overflowing of bitterness; and yet I must do myself justice – I couldn't have been other than I was. The same strange impressions, had I to meet them again, would produce the same deep anguish, the same sharp doubts, the same still sharper certainties. Oh it's all easier to remember than to write, but even could I retrace the business hour by hour could I find terms for the inexpressible, the ugliness and the pain would quickly stay my hand. Let me then note very simply and briefly that a week before our wedding-day, three weeks after her death, I knew in all my fibres that I had something very serious to look in the face and that if I was to make this effort I must make it on the spot and before another hour should elapse. My unextinguished jealousy – that was the Medusa-mask. It hadn't died with her death, it had lividly survived, and it was fed by suspicions unspeakable. They *would* be unspeakable today, that is, if I hadn't felt the sharp need of uttering them at the time. This need took possession of me – to save me, as it seemed, from my fate. When once it had done so I saw – in the urgency of the case, the diminishing hours and shrinking interval – only one issue, that of absolute promptness and frankness. I could at least not do him the wrong of delaying another day; I could at least treat my difficulty as too fine for a subterfuge. Therefore very quietly, but none the less abruptly and hideously, I put it before him on a certain evening that we must reconsider our situation and recognize that it had completely altered.

He stared bravely, 'How in the world altered?'

·'Another person has come between us.'

He took but an instant to think. 'I won't pretend not to know whom you mean.' He smiled in pity for my aberration, but he meant to be kind. 'A woman dead and buried!'

'She's buried, but she's not dead. She's dead for the world – she's dead for me. But she's not dead for you.'

'You hark back to the different construction we put on her appearance that evening?'

'No,' I answered, 'I hark back to nothing. I've no need of it. I've more than enough with what's before me.'

'And pray, darling, what may that be?'

'You're completely changed.'

'By that absurdity?' he laughed.

'Not so much by that one as by other absurdities that have followed it.'

'And what may *they* have been?'

We had faced each other fairly, with eyes that didn't flinch; but his had a dim strange light, and my certitude triumphed in his perceptible paleness. 'Do you really pretend,' I asked, 'not to know what they are?'

'My dear child,' he replied, 'you describe them too sketchily!'

I considered a moment. 'One may well be embarrassed to finish the picture! But from that point of view – and from the beginning – what was ever more embarrassing than your idiosyncrasy?'

He invoked his vagueness – a thing he always did beautifully. 'My idiosyncrasy?'

'Your notorious, your peculiar power.'

He gave a great shrug of impatience, a groan of overdone disdain. 'Oh my peculiar power!'

'Your accessibility to forms of life,' I coldly went on, 'your command of impressions, appearances, contacts, closed – for our gain or our loss – to the rest of us. That was originally a part of the deep interest with which you inspired me – one of the reasons I was amused – I was indeed positively proud, to know you. It was a magnificent distinction: it's a magnificent distinction still. But of course I had no prevision then of the way it would operate now; and even had that been the case I should have had none of the extraordinary way in which its action would affect me.'

'To what in the name of goodness,' he pleadingly inquired, 'are you fantastically alluding?' Then as I remained silent, gathering a tone for my charge, 'How in the world *does* it operate?' he went on; 'and how in the world are you affected?'

'She missed you for five years,' I said, 'but she never misses you now. You're making it up!'

'Making it up?' He had begun to turn from white to red.

'You see her – you see her: you see her every night!' He gave a loud sound of derision, but I felt it ring false. 'She comes to you as she came that evening,' I declared; 'having tried it she found she liked it!' I was able, with God's help, to speak without blind passion or vulgar violence; but those were the exact words – and far from 'sketchy' they then appeared to me – that I uttered. He had turned away in his laughter, clapping his hands at my folly, but in an instant he faced me again with a change of expression that struck me. 'Do you dare to deny,' I then asked, 'that you habitually see her?'

He had taken the line of indulgence, of meeting me half-way and kindly humouring me. At all events he to my astonishment suddenly said: 'Well, my dear, what if I do?'

'It's your natural right: it belongs to your constitution and to your wonderful if not perhaps quite enviable fortune. But you'll easily understand that it separates us. I unconditionally release you.'

'Release me?'

'You must choose between me and her.'

He looked at me hard. 'I see.' Then he walked away a little, as if grasping what I had said and thinking how he had best treat it. At last he turned on me afresh. 'How on earth do you know such an awfully private thing?'

'You mean because you've tried so hard to hide it? It *is* awfully private, and you may believe I shall never betray you. You've done your best, you've acted your part, you've behaved, poor dear! loyally and admirably. Therefore I've watched you in silence, playing my part too; I've noted every drop in your voice, every absence in your eyes, every effort in your indifferent hand: I've waited till I was utterly sure and miserably unhappy. How *can* you hide it when you're abjectly in love with her, when you're sick almost to death with the joy of what she gives you?' I checked his quick protest with a quicker gesture. 'You love her as you've *never* loved, and, passion for passion, she gives it straight back! She rules you, she holds you, she has you all! A woman, in such a case as mine, divines and feels and sees; she's not a dull dunce who has to be "credibly informed". You come to me mechanically, compunctiously, with the dregs of your tenderness and the remnant of your life. I can renounce you, but I can't share you: the best of you is hers, I know what it is and freely give you up to her for ever!'

He made a gallant fight, but it couldn't be patched up; he repeated his denial, he retracted his admission, he ridiculed my charge, of which I freely granted him moreover the indefensible extravagance. I didn't pretend for a moment that we were talking of common things, I didn't pretend for a moment that he and she were common people. Pray, if they *had* been, how should I ever have cared for them? They had enjoyed a rare extension of being and they had caught me up in their flight; only I couldn't breathe in such air and I promptly asked to be set down. Everything in the facts was monstrous, and most of all my lucid perception of them; the only thing allied to nature and truth was my having to act on that perception. I felt after I had spoken in this sense that my assurance was complete; nothing had been wanting to it but the sight of my effect on him. He disguised indeed the effect in a cloud of chaff, a diversion that gained him time and covered his retreat. He challenged my sincerity, my sanity, almost my humanity, and that of course widened our breach and confirmed our rupture. He did everything in short but convince me either that I was wrong or that he was unhappy: we separated, and I left him to his inconceivable communion.

He never married, any more than I've done. When six years later, in solitude and silence, I heard of his death I hailed it as a direct contribution to my theory. It was sudden, it was never properly accounted for, it was surrounded by circumstances in which – for oh I took them to pieces – I distinctly read an intention, the mark of his own hidden hand. It was the result of a long necessity, of an unquenchable desire. To say exactly what I mean, it was a response to an irresistible call.

# The Travelling Companion

## Hans Christian Andersen

*Mainly read as children's stories, Hans Christian Andersen's fairy tales are in fact more than simple fables. They use traditional characters — fairies, princesses, goblins, mermaids — but they deal with fears and passions that usually come later in life. 'The Little Mermaid', 'The Snow Queen', 'The Garden of Eden', 'The Travelling Companion' can also be read as adult fantastic tales that hint at deeper meanings. 'The Travelling Companion' is a profoundly optimistic story: it suggests that we are not alone, that someone watches over us, that there is always hope of finding help, even far away along a solitary road. Charles Dickens, in whose house Andersen spent five weeks in 1857, called the story 'a modern version of the Guardian Angel, the kindest of the celestial hosts'.*

Poor John was very sad; for his father was so ill, he had no hope of his recovery. John sat alone with the sick man in the little room, and the lamp had nearly burnt out; for it was late in the night.

'You have been a good son, John,' said the sick father, 'and God will help you on in the world.' He looked at him, as he spoke, with mild, earnest eyes, drew a deep sigh, and died; yet it appeared as if he still slept.

John wept bitterly. He had no one in the wide world now; neither father, mother, brother, nor sister. Poor John! he knelt down by the bed, kissed his dead father's hand, and wept many, many bitter tears. But at last his eyes closed, and he fell asleep with his head resting against the hard bedpost. Then he dreamed a strange dream; he thought he saw the sun shining upon him, and his father alive and well, and even heard him laughing as he used to do when he was very happy. A beautiful girl, with a golden crown on her head, and long, shining hair, gave him her hand; and his father said, 'See what a bride you have won. She is the loveliest maiden on the whole earth.' Then he awoke, and all the beautiful things vanished before his eyes, his father lay dead on the bed, and he was all alone. Poor John!

During the following week the dead man was buried. The son walked behind the coffin which contained his father, whom he so dearly loved, and would never again behold. He heard the earth fall on the coffin-lid, and watched it till only a corner remained in sight, and at last that also disappeared. He felt as if his heart would break with its weight of sorrow, till those who stood round the grave sang a psalm, and the sweet, holy tones brought tears into his eyes, which relieved him. The sun shone brightly down on the green trees, as if it would say, 'You must not be so sorrowful, John. Do you see the beautiful blue sky above you? Your father is up there, and he prays to the loving Father of all, that you may do well in the future.'

'I will always be good,' said John, 'and then I shall go to be with my father in heaven. What joy it will be when we see each other again! How much I shall have to relate to him, and how many things he will be able to explain to me of the delights of heaven, and teach me as he once did on earth. Oh, what joy it will be!'

He pictured it all so plainly to himself, that he smiled even while the tears ran down his cheeks.

The little birds in the chestnut-trees twittered, 'Tweet, tweet'; they were so happy, although they had seen the funeral; but they seemed as if they knew that the dead man was now in heaven, and that he had wings much larger and more beautiful than their own; and he was happy now, because he had been good here on earth, and they were glad of it. John saw them fly away out of the green trees into the wide world, and he longed to fly with them; but first he cut out a large wooden cross, to place on his father's grave; and when he brought it there in the evening, he found the grave decked out with gravel and flowers. Strangers had done this; they who had known the good old father who was now dead, and who had loved him very much.

Early the next morning, John packed up his little bundle of clothes, and placed all his money, which consisted of fifty dollars and a few shillings, in his girdle; with this he determined to try his fortune in the world. But first he went into the churchyard; and, by his father's grave, he offered up a prayer, and said, 'Farewell'.

As he passed through the fields, all the flowers looked fresh and beautiful in the warm sunshine, and nodded in the wind, as if they wished to say, 'Welcome to the green wood, where all is fresh and bright.'

Then John turned to have one more look at the old church, in which he had been christened in his infancy, and where his father had taken him every Sunday to hear the service and join in singing the psalms. As he looked at the old tower, he espied the ringer standing at one of the narrow openings, with his little pointed red cap on his head, and shading his eyes from the sun with his bent arm. John nodded farewell to him, and the little ringer waved his red cap, laid his hand on his heart, and kissed his hand to him a great many times, to show that he felt kindly towards him, and wished him a prosperous journey.

John continued his journey, and thought of all the wonderful things he should see in the large, beautiful world, till he found himself farther away from home than ever he had been before. He did not even know the names of the places he passed through, and could scarcely understand the language of the people he met, for he was far away, in a strange land. The first night he slept on a haystack, out in the fields, for there was no other bed for him; but it seemed to him so nice and comfortable that even a king need not wish for a better. The field, the brook, the haystack, with the blue sky above, formed a beautiful sleeping-room. The green grass, with the little red and white flowers, was the carpet; the elder-bushes and the hedges of wild roses looked like garlands on the walls; and for a bath he could have the clear, fresh water of the brook; while the rushes bowed their heads to him, to wish him good morning and good evening. The moon, like a large lamp, hung high up in the blue ceiling, and he had no fear of its setting fire to his curtains. John slept here quite safely all night; and when he awoke, the sun was up, and all the little birds were singing round him, 'Good morning, good morning. Are you not up yet?'

It was Sunday, and the bells were ringing for church. As the people went in, John followed them; he heard God's word, joined in singing the psalms, and listened to the preacher. It seemed to him just as if he were in his own church, where he had been christened, and had sung the psalms with his father. Out in the churchyard were several graves, and on some of them the grass had grown very high. John thought of his father's grave, which he knew at last would look like these, as he was not there to weed and attend to it. Then he set to work, pulled up the high grass, raised the wooden crosses which had fallen down, and replaced the wreaths which had been blown away from their places by the wind, thinking all the time, 'Perhaps some one is doing the same for my father's grave, as I am not there to do it.'

Outside the church door stood an old beggar, leaning on his crutch. John gave him his silver shillings, and then he continued his journey, feeling lighter and happier than ever. Towards evening, the weather became very stormy, and he hastened on as quickly as he could, to get shelter; but it was quite dark by the time he reached a little lonely church which stood on a hill. 'I will go in here,' he said, 'and sit down in a corner; for I am quite tired, and want rest.'

So he went in, and seated himself; then he folded his hands, and offered up his evening prayer, and was soon fast asleep and dreaming, while the thunder rolled and the lightning flashed without. When he awoke, it was still night; but the storm had ceased, and the moon shone in upon him through the windows. Then he saw an open coffin standing in the centre of the church, which contained a dead man, waiting for burial. John was not at all timid; he had a good conscience, and he knew also that the dead can never injure any one. It is living wicked men who do harm to others. Two such wicked persons stood now by the dead man, who had been brought to the church to be buried. Their evil intentions were to throw the poor dead body outside the church door, and not leave him to rest in his coffin.

'Why do you do this?' asked John, when he saw what they were going to do; 'it is very wicked. Leave him to rest in peace, in Christ's name.'

'Nonsense,' replied the two dreadful men. 'He has cheated us; he owed us money which he could not pay, and now he is dead we shall not get a penny; so we mean to have our revenge, and let him lie like a dog outside the church door.'

'I have only fifty dollars,' said John, 'it is all I possess in the world, but I will give it to you if you will promise me faithfully to leave the dead man in peace. I shall be able to get on without the money; I have strong and healthy limbs, and God will always help me.'

'Why, of course,' said the horrid men, 'if you will pay his debt we will both promise not to touch him. You may depend upon that;' and then they took the money he offered them, laughed at him for his good nature, and went their way.

Then he laid the dead body back in the coffin, folded the hands, and took leave of it; and went away contentedly through the great forest. All around him he could see the prettiest little elves dancing in the moonlight, which shone through the trees. They were not disturbed by his appearance, for they knew he was good and harmless among men. They are wicked people only who can never obtain a glimpse of fairies. Some of them were not taller than the breadth of a finger, and they wore golden combs in their long, yellow hair. They were rocking themselves two together on the large dew-drops with which the leaves and the high grass were sprinkled. Sometimes the dew-drops would roll away, and then they fell down between the stems of the long grass, and caused a great deal of laughing and noise among the other little people. It was quite charming to watch them at play. Then they sang songs, and John remembered that he had learnt those pretty songs when he was a little boy. Large speckled spiders, with silver crowns on their heads, were employed to spin suspension bridges and palaces from one hedge to another, and when the tiny drops fell upon them, they glittered in the moonlight like shining glass. This continued till sunrise. Then the little elves crept into the flower-buds, and the wind seized the bridges and palaces, and fluttered them in the air like cobwebs.

As John left the wood, a strong man's voice called after him, 'Hallo, comrade, where are you travelling?'

'Into the wide world,' he replied; 'I am only a poor lad, I have neither father nor mother, but God will help me.'

'I am going into the wide world also,' replied the stranger; 'shall we keep each other company?'

'With all my heart,' he said, and so they went on together. Soon they began to like each other very much, for they were both good; but John found out that the stranger was much more clever than himself. He had travelled all over the world, and could describe almost everything. The sun was high in the heavens when they seated themselves under a large tree to eat their breakfast, and at the same moment an old woman came towards them. She was very old and almost bent double. She leaned upon a stick and carried on her back a bundle of firewood, which she had collected in the forest; her apron was tied round it, and John saw three great stems of fern and some willow twigs peeping out. Just as she came close up to them, her foot slipped and she fell to the ground screaming loudly; poor old woman, she had broken her leg! John proposed directly that they should carry the old woman home to her cottage; but the stranger opened his knapsack and took out a box, in which he said he had a salve that would quickly make her leg well and strong again, so that she would be able to walk home herself, as if her leg had never been broken. And all that he would ask in return was the three fern stems which she carried in her apron.

'That is rather too high a price,' said the old woman, nodding her head quite strangely. She did not seem at all inclined to part with the fern stems. However, it was not very agreeable to lie there with a broken leg, so she gave them to him; and such was the power of the ointment, that no sooner had he rubbed her leg with it than the old mother rose up and walked even better than she had done before. But then this wonderful ointment could not be bought at a chemist's.

'What can you want with those three fern rods?' asked John of his fellow-traveller.

'Oh, they will make capital brooms,' said he; 'and I like them because I have strange whims sometimes.' Then they walked on together for a long distance.

'How dark the sky is becoming,' said John; 'and look at those thick, heavy clouds.'

'Those are not clouds,' replied his fellow-traveller; 'they are mountains – large lofty mountains – on the tops of which we should be above the clouds, in the pure, free air. Believe me, it is delightful to ascend so high, tomorrow we shall be there.' But the mountains were not so near as they appeared; they had to travel a whole day before they reached them, and pass through black forests and piles of rock as large as a town. The journey had been so fatiguing that John and his fellow-traveller stopped to rest at a roadside inn, so that they might gain strength for their journey on the morrow. In the large public room of the inn a great many persons were assembled to see a comedy performed by dolls. The showman had just erected his little theatre, and the people were sitting round the room to witness the performance. Right in front, in the very best place, sat a stout butcher, with a great bull-dog by his side who seemed very much inclined to bite. He sat staring with all his eyes, and so indeed did every one else in the room. And then the play began. It was a pretty piece, with a king and a queen in it, who sat on a beautiful throne, and had gold crowns on their heads. The trains to their dresses were very long, according to the fashion; while the prettiest of wooden dolls, with glass eyes and large moustaches, stood at the doors, and opened and shut them, that the fresh air might come into the room. It was a very pleasant play, not at all mournful; but just as the queen stood up and walked across the stage, the great bull-dog, who should have been held back by his master, made a spring forward, and caught the queen in the teeth by the slender wrist, so that it snapped in two. This was a very dreadful disaster. The poor man, who was exhibiting the dolls, was much annoyed, and quite sad about his queen; she was the prettiest doll he had, and the bull-dog had broken her head and shoulders off. But after all the people were gone away, the stranger, who came with John, said that he could soon set her to rights. And then he brought out his box and rubbed the doll with some of the salve with which he had cured the old woman when she broke her leg. As soon as this was done the doll's back became quite right again; her head and shoulders were fixed on, and she could even move her limbs herself: there was now no occasion to pull the wires, for the doll acted just like a living creature excepting that she could not speak. The man to whom the show belonged was quite delighted at having a doll who could dance of herself without being pulled by the wires: none of the other dolls could do this.

During the night, when all the people at the inn were gone to bed, some one was heard to sigh so deeply and painfully, and the sighing continued for so long a time, that every one got up to see what could be the matter. The showman went at once to his little theatre and found that it proceeded from the dolls, who all lay on the floor sighing piteously, and staring with their glass eyes: they all wanted to be rubbed with the ointment, so that, like the queen, they might be able to move of themselves. The queen threw herself on her knees, took off her beautiful crown, and, holding it in her hand, cried, 'Take this from me, but do rub my husband and his courtiers.'

The poor man who owned the theatre could scarcely refrain from weeping: he was so sorry that he could not help them. Then he immediately spoke to John's comrade, and promised him all the money he might receive at the next evening's performance, if he would only rub the ointment on four or five of his dolls. But the fellow-traveller said he did not require anything in return, excepting the sword which the showman wore by his side. As soon as he received the sword he anointed six of the dolls with the ointment, and they were able immediately to dance so gracefully that all the living girls in the room could not help joining in the dance. The coachman danced with the cook, and the waiters with the chambermaids, and all the strangers joined: even the tongs and the fire-shovel made an attempt, but they fell down after the first jump. So after all it was a very merry night. The next morning John and his companion left the inn to continue their journey through the great pine-forests and over the high mountains. They arrived at last at such a great height that towns and villages lay beneath them, and the church steeples looked like little specks between the green trees. They could see for miles round, far away to places they had never visited and John saw more of the beautiful world than he had ever known before. The sun shone brightly in the blue firmament above, and through the clear mountain air came the sound of the huntsman's horn, and the soft, sweet notes brought tears into his eyes and he could not help exclaiming. 'How good and loving God is to give us all this beauty and loveliness in the world to make us happy.'

His fellow-traveller stood by with folded hands gazing on the dark wood and the towns bathed in the warm sunshine. At this moment there sounded over their heads sweet music. They looked up and discovered a large white swan hovering in the air, and singing as never bird sang before. But the song soon became weaker and weaker, the bird's head drooped, and he sunk slowly down, and lay dead at their feet.

'It is a beautiful bird,' said the traveller, 'and these large white wings are worth a great deal of money. I will take them with me. You see now that a sword will be very useful.'

So he cut off the wings of the dead swan with one blow, and carried them away with him.

They now continued their journey over the mountains for many miles, till they at length reached a large city, containing hundreds of towers, that shone in the sunshine like silver. In the midst of the city stood a splendid marble palace, roofed with pure red gold, in which dwelt the king. John and his companion would not go into the town immediately; so they stopped at an inn outside the town, to change their clothes; for they wished to appear respectable as they walked through the streets. The landlord told them that the king was a very good man, who never injured any one; but as to his daughter, 'Heaven defend us!'

She was indeed a wicked princess. She possessed beauty enough

– nobody could be more elegant or prettier than she was; but what of that? for she was a wicked witch; and in consequence of her conduct many noble young princes had lost their lives. Any one was at liberty to make her an offer; were he a prince or a beggar, it mattered not to her. She would ask him to guess three things which she had just thought of, and if he succeed, he was to marry her, and be king over all the land when her father died; but if he could not guess these three things, then she ordered him to be hanged or to have his head cut off. The old king, her father, was very much grieved at her conduct, but he could not prevent her from being so wicked, because he once said he would have nothing more to do with her lovers; she might do as she pleased. Each prince who came and tried the three guesses, so that he might marry the princess, had been unable to find them out, and had been hanged or beheaded. They had all been warned in time, and might have left her alone, if they would. The old king became at last so distressed at all these dreadful circumstances, that for a whole day every year he and his soldiers knelt and prayed that the princess might become good; but she continued as wicked as ever. The old women who drank brandy would colour it quite black before they drank it, to show how they mourned; and what more could they do?

'What a horrible princess!' said John; 'she ought to be well flogged. If I were the old king, I would have her punished in some way.'

Just then they heard the people outside shouting, 'Hurrah!' and, looking out, they saw the princess passing by; and she was really so beautiful that everybody forgot her wickedness, and shouted 'Hurrah!' Twelve lovely maidens in white silk dresses, holding golden tulips in their hands, rode by her side on coal-black horses. The princess herself had a snow-white steed, decked with diamonds and rubies. Her dress was of cloth of gold, and the whip she held in her hand looked like a sunbeam. The golden crown on her head glittered like the stars of heaven, and her mantle was formed of thousands of butterflies' wings sewn together. Yet she herself was more beautiful than all.

When John saw her, his face became as red as a drop of blood, and he could scarcely utter a word. The princess looked exactly like the beautiful lady with the golden crown of whom he had dreamed on the night his father died. She appeared to him so lovely that he could not help loving her.

'It could not be true,' he thought, 'that she was really a wicked witch, who ordered people to be hanged or beheaded, if they could not guess her thoughts. Every one has permission to go and ask her hand, even the poorest beggar. I shall pay a visit to the palace,' he said; 'I must go, for I cannot help myself.'

Then they all advised him not to attempt it; for he would be sure to share the same fate as the rest. His fellow-traveller also tried to persuade him against it; but John seemed quite sure of success. He brushed his shoes and his coat, washed his face and his hands, combed his soft flaxen hair, and then went out alone into the town, and walked to the palace.

'Come in,' said the king, as John knocked at the door. John opened it, and the old king, in a dressing gown and embroidered slippers, came towards him. He had the crown on his head, carried his sceptre in one hand, and the orb in the other. 'Wait a bit,' said he, and he placed the orb under his arm, so that he could offer the other hand to John; but when he found that John was another suitor, he began to weep so violently, that both the sceptre and the orb fell to the floor, and he was obliged to wipe his eyes with his dressing gown. Poor old king! 'Let her alone,' he said; 'you will fare as badly as all the others. Come, I will show you.' Then he led him out into the princess's pleasure gardens, and there he saw a frightful sight. On every tree hung three or four king's sons who had wooed the princess, but had not been able to guess the riddles she gave them. Their skeletons rattled in every breeze, so that the terrified birds never dared to venture into the garden. All the flowers were supported by human bones instead of sticks, and human skulls in the flowerpots grinned horribly. It was really a doleful garden for a princess. 'Do you see all this?' said the old king; 'your fate will be the same as those who are here, therefore do not attempt it. You really make me very unhappy – I take these things to heart so very much.'

John kissed the good old king's hand, and said he was sure it would be all right, for he was quite enchanted with the beautiful princess. Then the princess herself came riding into the palace yard with all her ladies, and he wished her 'Good morning'. She looked wonderfully fair and lovely when she offered her hand to John, and he loved her more than ever. How could she be a wicked witch, as all the people asserted? He accompanied her into the hall, and the little pages offered them gingerbread nuts and sweetmeats, but the old king was so unhappy he could eat nothing, and besides, gingerbread nuts were too hard for him. It was decided that John should come to the palace the next day, when the judges and the whole of the counsellors would be present, to try if he could guess the first riddle. If he succeeded, he would have to come a second time; but if not, he would lose his life – and no one had ever been able to guess even one. However, John was not at all anxious about the result of his trial; on the contrary, he was very merry. He thought only of the beautiful princess, and believed that in some way he should have help, but how he knew not, and did not like to think about it; so he danced along the high-road as he went back to the inn, where he had left his fellow-traveller waiting for him. John could not refrain from telling him how gracious the princess had been, and how beautiful she looked. He longed for the next day so much, that he might go to the palace and try his luck at guessing the riddles. But his comrade shook his head, and looked very mournful. 'I do so wish you to do well,' said he; 'we might have continued together much longer, and now I am likely to lose you: you poor dear John! I could shed tears, but I will not make you unhappy on the last night we may be together. We will be merry, really merry, this evening; tomorrow, after you are gone, I shall be able to weep undisturbed.'

It was very quickly known among the inhabitants of the town that another suitor had arrived for the princess, and there was great sorrow in consequence. The theatre remained closed, the women who sold sweetmeats tied crape round the sugar-sticks, and the king and the priests were on their knees in the church. There was a great lamentation, for no one expected John to succeed better than those who had been suitors before.

In the evening John's comrade prepared a large bowl of punch, and said, 'Now let us be merry, and drink to the health of the princess.' But after drinking two glasses, John became so sleepy, that he could not possibly keep his eyes open, and fell fast asleep. Then his fellow-traveller lifted him gently out of his chair, and laid him on the bed; and as soon as it was quite dark, he took the two large wings which he had cut from the dead swan, and tied them firmly to his own shoulders. Then he put into his pocket the largest of the three rods which he had obtained from the old woman who had fallen and broken her leg. After this he opened the window, and flew away over the town, straight towards the palace, and seated himself in a corner, under the window which looked into the bedroom of the princess.

The town was perfectly still when the clocks struck a quarter to twelve. Presently the window opened, and the princess, who had large black wings to her shoulders, and a long white mantle, flew away over the city towards a high mountain. The fellow-traveller, who had made himself invisible, so that she could not possibly see him, flew after her through the air, and whipped the princess with his rod, so that the blood came whenever he struck her. Ah, it was a strange flight through the air! The wind caught her mantle, so that it spread out on all sides, like the large sail of a ship, and the moon shone through it. 'How it hails, to be sure!' said the princess, at each blow she received from the rod; and it served her right to be whipped.

At last she reached the side of the mountain, and knocked. The mountain opened with a noise like the roll of thunder, and the princess went in. The traveller followed her; no one could see him, as he had made himself invisible. They went through a long, wide passage. A thousand gleaming spiders ran here and there on the walls, causing them to glitter as if they were illuminated with fire. They next entered a large hall built of silver and gold. Large red and blue flowers shone on the walls, looking like sunflowers in size, but no one could dare to pluck them, for the stems were hideous poisonous snakes, and the flowers were flames of fire, darting out of their jaws. Shining glow-worms covered the ceiling, and sky-blue bats flapped their transparent wings. Altogether the place had a frightful appearance. In the middle of the floor stood a throne supported by four skeleton horses, whose harness had been made by fiery-red spiders. The throne itself was made of milk-white glass, and the cushions were little black mice, each biting the other's tail. Over it hung a canopy of rose-coloured spider's webs, spotted with the prettiest little green flies, which sparkled like precious stones. On the throne sat an old magician with a crown on his ugly head, and a sceptre in his hand. He kissed the princess on the forehead, seated her by his side on the splendid throne, and then the music commenced. Great black grasshoppers played the mouth organ, and the owl struck herself on the body instead of a drum. It was altogether a ridiculous concert. Little black goblins with false lights in their caps danced about the hall; but no one could see the traveller, and he had placed himself just behind the throne where he could see and hear everything. The courtiers who came in afterwards looked noble and grand; but any one with common sense could see what they really were, only broomsticks, with cabbages for heads. The magician had given them life, and dressed them in embroidered robes. It answered very well, as they were only wanted for show. After there had been a little dancing, the princess told the magician that she had a new suitor, and asked him what she could think of for the suitor to guess when he came to the castle the next morning.

'Listen to what I say,' said the magician, 'you must choose something very easy, he is less likely to guess it then. Think of one of your shoes, he will never imagine it is that. Then cut his head off; and mind you do not forget to bring his eyes with you tomorrow night, that I may eat them.'

The princess curtsied low, and said she would not forget the eyes.

The magician then opened the mountain and she flew home again, but the traveller followed and flogged her so much with the rod, that she sighed quite deeply about the heavy hailstorm, and made as much haste as she could to get back to her bedroom through the window. The traveller then returned to the inn where John still slept, took off his wings and laid down on the bed, for he was very tired. Early in the morning John awoke, and when his fellow-traveller got up, he said that he had a very wonderful dream about the princess and her shoe, he therefore advised John to ask her if she had not thought of her shoe. Of course the traveller knew this from what the magician in the mountain had said.

'I may as well say that as anything,' said John. 'Perhaps your dream may come true; still I will say farewell, for if I guess wrong I shall never see you again.'

Then they embraced each other, and John went into the town and walked to the palace. The great hall was full of people, and the judges sat in armchairs, with eider-down cushions to rest their heads upon, because they had so much to think of. The old king stood near, wiping his eyes with his white pocket-handkerchief. When the princess entered, she looked even more beautiful than she had appeared the day before, and greeted every one present most gracefully; but to John she gave her hand, and said, 'Good morning to you.'

Now came the time for John to guess what she was thinking of; and oh, how kindly she looked at him as she spoke. But when he uttered the single word shoe, she turned as pale as a ghost; all her wisdom could not help her, for he had guessed rightly. Oh, how pleased the old king was! It was quite amusing to see how he capered about. All the people clapped their hands, both on his account and John's, who had guessed rightly the first time. His fellow-traveller was glad also, when he heard how successful John had been. But John folded his hands, and thanked God, who, he felt quite sure, would help him again; and he knew he had to guess twice more. The evening passed pleasantly like the one preceding. While John slept, his companion flew behind the princess to the mountain, and flogged her even harder than before; this time he had taken two rods with him. No one saw him go in with her, and he heard all that was said. The princess this time was to think of a glove, and he told John as if he had again heard it in a dream. The next day, therefore, he was able to guess correctly the second time, and it caused great rejoicing at the palace. The whole court jumped about as they had seen the king do the day before, but the princess lay on the sofa, and would not say a single word. All now depended upon John. If he only guessed rightly the third time, he would marry the princess, and reign over the kingdom after the death of the old king; but if he failed, he would lose his life, and the magician would have his beautiful blue eyes. That evening John said his prayers and went to bed very early, and soon fell asleep calmly. But his companion tied on his wings to his shoulders, took three rods, and, with his sword at his side, flew to the palace. It was a very dark night, and so stormy that the tiles flew from the roofs of the houses, and the trees in the garden upon which the skeletons hung bent themselves like reeds before the wind. The lightning flashed, and the thunder rolled in one long-continued peal all night. The window of the castle opened, and the princess flew out. She was pale as death, but she laughed at the storm as if it were not bad enough. Her white mantle fluttered in the wind like a large sail, and the traveller flogged her with the three rods till the blood trickled down, and at last she could scarcely fly; she contrived, however, to reach the mountain. 'What a hailstorm!' she said, as she entered; 'I have never been out in such weather as this.'

'Yes, there may be too much of a good thing sometimes,' said the magician.

Then the princess told him that John had guessed rightly the second time, and if he succeeded the next morning, he would win, and she could never come to the mountain again, or practice magic as she had done, and therefore she was quite unhappy. 'I will find out something for you to think of which he will never guess, unless he is a greater conjuror than myself. But now let us be merry.'

Then he took the princess by both hands, and they danced with all the little goblins and Jack-o'-lanterns in the room. The red spiders sprang here and there on the walls quite as merrily, and the flowers of fire appeared as if they were throwing out sparks. The owl beat the drum, the crickets whistled and the grasshoppers played the mouth-organ. It was a very ridiculous ball. After they had danced enough, the princess was obliged to go home, for fear she should be missed at the palace. The magician offered to go with her, that they might be company to each other on the way. Then they flew away through the bad weather, and the traveller followed them, and broke his three rods across their shoulders. The magician had never been out in such a hailstorm as this. Just by the palace the magician stopped to wish the princess farewell, and to whisper in her ear, 'Tomorrow think of my head.'

But the traveller heard it, and just as the princess slipped through the window into her bedroom, and the magician turned round to fly back to the mountain, he seized him by the long black beard, and with his sabre cut off the wicked conjuror's head just behind the shoulders, so that he could not even see who it was. He threw the body into the sea to the fishes, and after dipping the head into the water, he tied it up in a silk handkerchief, took it with him to the inn, and then went to bed. The next morning he gave John the handkerchief, and told him not to untie it till the princess asked him what she was thinking of. There were so many people in the great hall of the palace that they stood as thick as radishes tied together in a bundle. The council sat in their armchairs with the white cushions. The old king wore new robes, and the golden crown and sceptre had been polished up so that he looked quite smart. But the princess was very pale, and wore a black dress as if she were going to a funeral.

'What have I thought of?' asked the princess, of John. He immediately untied the handkerchief, and was himself quite frightened when he saw the head of the ugly magician. Every one shuddered, for it was terrible to look at; but the princess sat like a statue, and could not utter a single word. At length she rose and gave John her hand, for he had guessed rightly.

She looked at no one, but sighed deeply, and said, 'You are my master now; this evening our marriage must take place.'

'I am very pleased to hear it,' said the old king. 'It is just what I wish.'

Then all the people shouted 'Hurrah.' The band played music in the streets, the bells rang, and the cake-women took the black crape off the sugar-sticks. There was universal joy. Three oxen, stuffed with ducks and chickens, were roasted whole in the market-place, where every one might help himself to a slice. The fountains spouted forth the most delicious wine, and whoever bought a penny loaf at the baker's received six large buns, full of raisins, as a present. In the evening the whole town was illuminated. The soldiers fired off cannons, and the boys let off crackers. There was eating and drinking, dancing and jumping everywhere. In the palace, the high-born gentlemen and beautiful ladies danced with each other, and they could be heard at a great distance singing the following song:

Here are maidens, young and fair,
Dancing in the summer air;
Like two spinning-wheels at play,
Pretty maidens dance away—
Dance the spring and summer through
Till the sole falls from your shoe.

But the princess was still a witch, and she could not love John. His fellow-traveller had thought of that, so he gave John three feathers out of the swan's wings, and a little bottle with a few drops in it. He told him to place a large bath full of water by the princess's bed, and put the feathers and the drops into it. Then, at the moment she was about to get into bed, he must give her a little push, so that she might fall into the water, and then dip her three times. This would destroy the power of the magician, and she would love him very much. John did all that his companion told him to do. The princess shrieked aloud when he dipped her under the water the first time, and struggled under his hands in the form of a great black swan with fiery eyes. As she rose the second time from the water, the swan had become white, with a black ring round its neck. John allowed the water to close once more over the bird, and at the same time it changed into a most beautiful princess. She was more lovely even than before, and thanked him, while her eyes sparkled with tears, for having broken the spell of the magician. The next day, the king came with the whole court to offer their congratulations, and stayed till quite late. Last of all came the travelling-companion; he had his staff in his hand and his knapsack on his back. John kissed him many times and told him he must not go, he must remain with him, for he was the cause of all his good fortune. But the traveller shook his head, and said gently and kindly, 'No: my time is up now. I have only paid my debt to you. Do you remember the dead man whom the bad people wished to throw out of his coffin? You gave all you possessed that he might rest in his grave. I am that man.' As he said this, he vanished.

The wedding festivities lasted a whole month. John and his princess loved each other dearly, and the old king lived to see many a happy day, when he took their little children on his knees and let them play with his sceptre. And John became king over the whole country.

*Translated from the Danish by H. Oskar Sommer.*

# The Curfew Tolls

## Stephen Vincent Benét

*Although Stephen Vincent Benét's long, boring epic poem 'John Brown's Body' was awarded the Pulitzer Prize in 1928, he was not a very good poet.*

> *My father, he was a mountaineer,*
> *His fist was a knotty hammer;*
> *He was quick on his feet as a running deer,*
> *And he spoke with a Yankee stammer.*

*But he was an excellent short-story writer. 'The Devil and Daniel Webster' is a hilarious folk-tale told in excellent slang: it was made into a musical comedy, an opera and a film. 'Jacob and the Indians' is a tribute to the Jewish pioneers. 'The Curfew Tolls' makes use of the possibilities fantastic literature has of twisting the course of time, and shows Benét at his best.*

*It is not enough to be the possessor of genius – the time and the man must conjoin. An Alexander the Great, born into an age of profound peace, might scarce have troubled the world – a Newton, grown up in a thieves' den, might have devised little but a new and ingenious picklock . . .*

*Diversions of Historical Thought*
John Cleveland Cotton

(The following extracts have been made from the letters of General Sir Charles William Geoffrey Estcourt, CB, to his sister Harriet, Countess of Stokely, by permission of the Stokely family. Omissions are indicated by triple dots, thus . . .)

★

*St Philippe-des-Bains, September 3rd, 1788*

My Dear Sister: . . . I could wish that my excellent Paris physician had selected some other spot for my convalescence. But he swears by the waters of St Philip and I swear by him, so I must resign myself to a couple of yawning months ere my constitution mends. Nevertheless, you will get long letters from me, though I fear they may be dull ones. I cannot bring you the gossip of Baden or Aix – except for its baths, St Philip is but one of a dozen small white towns on this agreeable coast. It has its good inn and its bad inn, its dusty, little square with its dusty, fleabitten beggar, its posting-station and its promenade of scrubby lindens and palms. From the heights one may see Corsica on a clear day, and the Mediterranean is of an unexampled blue. To tell the truth, it is all agreeable enough and an old Indian campaigner, like myself, should not complain. I am well treated at the Cheval Blanc – am I not an English milord? – and my excellent Gaston looks after me devotedly. But there is a bluebottle drowsiness about small watering places out of season, and our gallant enemies, the French, know how to bore themselves more exquisitely in their provinces than any nation on earth. Would you think that the daily arrival of the diligence from Toulon would be an excitement? Yet it is to me, I assure you, and to all St Philip. I walk, I take the waters, I read Ossian, I play piquet with Gaston, and yet I seem to myself but half-alive . . .

. . . You will smile and say to me, 'Dear brother, you have always plumed yourself on being a student of human nature. Is there no society, no character for you to study, even in St Philippe-des-Bains?' My dear sister, I bend myself earnestly to that end, yet so far with little result. I have talked to my doctor – a good man but unpolished; I have talked to the curé – a good man but dull. I have even attempted the society of the baths, beginning with Monsieur le Marquis de la Percedragon, who has ninety-six quarterings, soiled wristbands, and a gloomy interest in my liver, and ending with Mrs Macgregor Jenkins, a worthy and red-faced lady whose conversation positively cannonades with dukes and duchesses. But, frankly, I prefer my chair in the garden and my Ossian to any of them, even at the risk of being considered a bear. A witty scoundrel would be the veriest godsend to me, but do such exist in St Philip? I trow not. As it is, in my weakened condition, I am positively agog when Gaston comes in every morning with his budget of village scandal. A pretty pass to come to, you will say, for a man who has served with Eyre Coote and but for the mutabilities of fortune, not to speak of a most damnable cabal . . . (A long passage dealing with General Estcourt's East Indian services and his personal and unfavourable opinion of Warren Hastings is here omitted from the manuscript.) . . . But, at fifty, a man is either a fool or a philosopher. Nevertheless, unless Gaston provides me with a character to try my wits on, shortly, I shall begin to believe that they too have deteriorated with Indian suns . . .

*September 21st, 1788.* My Dear Sister: . . . Believe me, there is little soundness in the views of your friend, Lord Martindale. The French monarchy is not to be compared with our own, but King Louis is an excellent and well-beloved prince, and the proposed summoning of the States-General cannot but have the most salutary effect . . . (Three pages upon French politics and the possibility of cultivating sugar-cane in Southern France are here omitted.) . . . As for news of myself, I continue my yawning course, and feel a decided improvement from the waters . . . So I shall continue them though the process is slow . . .

You ask me, I fear a trifle mockingly, how my studies in human nature proceed?

Not so ill, my dear sister – I have, at least, scraped acquaintance with one odd fish, and that, in St Philip, is a triumph. For some time, from my chair in the promenade, I have observed a pursy little fellow, of my age or thereabouts, stalking up and down between the lindens. His company seems avoided by such notables of the place as Mrs Macgregor Jenkins and at first I put him down as a retired actor, for there is something a little theatrical in his dress and walk. He wears a wide-brimmed hat of straw, loose nankeen trousers and a quasi-military coat, and takes his waters with as much ceremony as Monsieur le Marquis, though not quite with the same *ton*. I should put him down as a Meridional, for he has the quick, dark eye, the sallow skin, the corpulence and the rodomontish airs that mark your true son of the Midi, once he has passed his lean and hungry youth.

And yet, there is some sort of unsuccessful oddity about him, which sets him off from your successful bourgeois. I cannot put my finger on it yet, but it interests me.

At any rate, I was sitting in my accustomed chair, reading Ossian, this morning, as he made his solitary rounds of the promenade.

Doubtless I was more than usually absorbed in my author, for I must have pronounced some lines aloud as he passed. He gave me a quick glance at the time, but nothing more. But on his next round, as he was about to pass me, he hesitated for a moment, stopped, and then, removing his straw hat, saluted me very civilly.

'Monsieur will pardon me,' he said, with a dumpy hauteur, 'but surely monsieur is English? And surely the lines that monsieur just repeated are from the great poet, Ossian?'

I admitted both charges, with a smile, and he bowed again.

'Monsieur will excuse the interruption,' he said, 'but I myself have long admired the poetry of Ossian' – and with that he continued my quotation to the end of the passage, in very fair English, too, though with a strong accent. I complimented him, of course, effusively – after all, it is not every day that one runs across a fellow-admirer of Ossian on the promenade of a small French watering place – and after that, he sat down in the chair beside me and we fell into talk. He seems, astonishingly for a Frenchman, to have an excellent acquaintance with our English poets – perhaps he has been a tutor in some English family. I did not press him with questions on this first encounter, though I noted that he spoke French with a slight accent also, which seems odd.

There is something a little rascally about him, to tell you the truth, though his conversation with me was both forceful and elevated. An ill man, too, and a disappointed one, or I miss my mark, yet his eyes, when he talks, are strangely animating. I fancy I would not care to meet him in a *guetapens*, and yet, he may be the most harmless of broken pedagogues. We took a glass of waters together, to the great disgust of Mrs Macgregor Jenkins, who ostentatiously drew her skirts aside. She let me know, afterwards, in so many words, that my acquaintance was a noted bandit, though, when pressed, she could give no better reason than that he lives a little removed from the town, that 'nobody knows where he comes from' and that his wife is 'no better than she should be', whatever that portentous phrase entails. Well, one would hardly call him a gentleman, even by Mrs Macgregor's somewhat easy standards, but he has given me better conversation than I have had in a month – and if he is a bandit, we might discuss thuggee together. But I hope for nothing so stimulating, though I must question Gaston about him . . .

*October 11th* . . . But Gaston could tell me little, except that my acquaintance comes from Sardinia or some such island originally, has served in the French army, and is popularly supposed to possess the evil eye. About Madame he hinted that he could tell me a great deal, but I did not labour the point. After all, if my friend has been c-ck-ld-d – do not blush, my dear sister! – that, too, is the portion of a philosopher, and I find his wide range of conversation much more palatable than Mrs Macgregor Jenkins' rewarmed London gossip. Nor has he tried to borrow money from me yet, something which, I am frank to say, I expected and was prepared to refuse . . .

*November 20th* . . . Triumph! My character is found – and a character of the first water, I assure you! I have dined with him in his house, and a very bad dinner it was. Madame is not a good housekeeper, whatever else she may be. And what she has been, one can see at a glance – she has all the little faded coquetries of the garrison coquette. Good-tempered, of course, as such women often are, and must have been pretty in her best days, though with shocking bad teeth. I suspect her of a touch of the tarbrush, though there I may be wrong. No doubt she caught my friend young – I have seen the same thing happen in India often enough – the experienced woman and the youngster fresh from England. Well, 'tis an old story – an old one with him, too – and no doubt Madame has her charms, though she is obviously one reason why he has not risen.

After dinner, Madame departed, not very willingly, and he took me into his study for a chat. He had even procured a bottle of port, saying he knew the Englishman's taste for it, and while it was hardly the right Cockburn, I felt touched by the attention. The man is desperately lonely – one reads that in his big eyes. He is also desperately proud, with the quick, touchy sensitiveness of the failure, and I quite exerted myself to draw him out.

And indeed, the effort repaid me. His own story is simple enough. He is neither bandit nor pedagogue, but, like myself, a broken soldier – a major of the French Royal Artillery, retired on half pay for some years. I think it creditable of him to have reached so respectable a rank, for he is of foreign birth – Sardinian, I think I told you – and the French service is by no means as partial to foreigners as they were in the days of the first Irish Brigade. Moreover, one simply does not rise in that service, unless one is a gentleman of quarterings, and that he could hardly claim. But the passion of his life has been India, and that is what interests me. And, 'pon my honour, he was rather astonishing about it.

As soon as, by a lucky chance, I hit upon the subject, his eyes lit up and his sickness dropped away. Pretty soon he began to take maps from a cabinet in the wall and ply me with questions about my own small experiences. And very soon indeed, I am abashed to state, I found myself stumbling in my answers. It was all book knowledge on his part, of course, but where the devil he could have got some of it, I do not know. Indeed, he would even correct me, now and then, as cool as you please. 'Eight twelve pounders, I think, on the north wall of the old fortifications of Madras—' and the deuce of it is, he would be right. Finally, I could contain myself no longer.

'But, major, this is incredible,' I said. 'I have served twenty years with John Company and thought that I had some knowledge. But one would say you had fought over every inch of Bengal!'

He gave me a quick look, almost of anger, and began to roll up his maps.

'So I have, in my mind,' he said, shortly, 'but, as my superiors have often informed me, my hobby is a tedious one.'

'It is not tedious to me,' I said boldly. 'Indeed, I have often marvelled at your government's neglect of their opportunities in India. True, the issue is settled now—'

'It is by no means settled,' he said, interrupting me rudely. I stared at him.

'It was settled, I believe, by Baron Clive, at a spot named Plassey,' I said frigidly. 'And afterwards, by my own old general, Eyre Coote, at another spot named Wandewash.'

'Oh, yes – yes – yes,' he said impatiently, 'I grant you Clive – Clive was a genius and met the fate of geniuses. He steals an empire for you, and your virtuous English Parliament holds up its hands in horror because he steals a few lakhs of rupees for himself as well. So he blows out his brains in disgrace – you inexplicable English! – and you lose your genius. A great pity. I would not have treated Clive so. But then, if I had been Milord Clive, I would not have blown out my brains.'

'And what would you have done, had you been Clive?' I said, for the man's calm, staring conceit amused me.

His eyes were dangerous for a moment and I saw why the worthy Mrs Macgregor Jenkins had called him a bandit.

'Oh,' he said coolly, 'I would have sent a file of grenadiers to your English Parliament and told it to hold its tongue. As Cromwell did. Now there was a man. But your Clive – faugh! – he had the ball at his feet and he refused to kick it. I withdraw the word genius. He was a nincompoop. At the least, he might have made himself a rajah.'

This was a little too much, as you may imagine. 'General Clive had his faults,' I said icily, 'but he was a true Briton and a patriot.'

'He was a fool,' said my puffy little major, flatly, his lower lip stuck out. 'As big a fool as Dupleix, and that is saying much. Oh, some military skill, some talent for organization, yes. But a genius would have brushed him into the sea! It was possible to hold Arcot, it was possible to win Plassey – look!' and, with that, he ripped another map from his cabinet and began to expound to me eagerly exactly what he would have done in command of the French forces in India, in 1757, when he must have been but a lad in his twenties. He thumped the paper, he strewed corks along the table for his troops – corks taken from a supply in a tin box, so it must be an old game with him. And, as I listened, my irritation faded, for the man's monomania was obvious. Nor was it, to tell the truth, an ill-designed plan of campaign, for corks on a map. Of course these things are different, in the field.

I could say, with honesty, that his plan had features of novelty, and he gulped the words down hungrily – he has a great appetite for flattery.

'Yes, yes,' he said. 'That is how it should be done – the thickest skull can see it. And, ill as I am, with a fleet and ten thousand picked men—' He dreamed, obviously, the sweat of his exertions on his waxy face – it was absurd and yet touching to see him dream.

'You would find a certain amount of opposition,' I said, in an amused voice.

'Oh, yes, yes,' he said quickly, 'I do not underrate the English. Excellent horse, solid foot. But no true knowledge of cannon, and I am a gunner—'

I hated to bring him down to earth and yet I felt that I must.

'Of course, major,' I said, 'you have had great experience in the field.'

He looked at me for a moment, his arrogance quite unshaken.

'I have had very little,' he said, quietly, 'but one knows how the thing should be done or one does not know. And that is enough.'

He stared at me for an instant with his big eyes. A little mad, of course. And yet I found myself saying, 'But surely, major – what happened?'

'Why,' he said, still quietly, 'what happens to folk who have naught but their brains to sell? I staked my all on India when I was young – I thought that my star shone over it. I ate dirty puddings – *corpo di Bacco!* – to get there – I was no De Rohan or Soubise to win the king's favour! And I reached there indeed, in my youth, just in time to be included in the surrender of Pondicherry.' He laughed, rather terribly, and sipped at his glass.

'You English were very courteous captors,' he said. 'But I was not released till the Seven Years' War had ended – that was in '63. Who asks for the special exchange of an unknown artillery lieutenant? And then ten years odd of garrison duty at Mauritius. It was there that I met Madame – she is a Creole. A pleasant spot, Mauritius. We used to fire the cannon at the sea birds when we had enough ammunition for target practice,' and he chuckled drearily. 'By then I was thirty-seven. They had to make me a captain – they even brought me back to France. To garrison duty. I have been on garrison duty, at Toulon, at Brest, at—' He ticked off the names on his fingers but I did not like his voice.

'But surely,' I said, 'the American war, though a small affair – there were opportunities—'

'And who did they send?' he said quickly. 'Lafayette – Rochambeau – De Grasse – the sprigs of the nobility. Oh, at Lafayette's age, I would have volunteered like Lafayette. But one should be successful in youth – after that, the spring is broken. And when one is over forty, one has responsibilities. I have a large family, you see, though not of my own begetting,' and he chuckled as if at a secret joke. 'Oh, I wrote the Continental Congress,' he said reflectively, 'but they preferred a dolt like Von Steuben. A good dolt, an honest dolt, but there you have it. I also wrote your British War Office,' he said in an even voice. 'I must show you that plan of campaign – sometime – they could have crushed General Washington with it in three weeks.'

I stared at him, a little appalled.

'For an officer who has taken his king's shilling to send to an enemy nation a plan for crushing his own country's ally,' I said, stiffly – 'well, in England, we would call that treason.'

'And what is treason?' he said lightly. 'If we call it unsuccessful ambition we shall be nearer the truth.' He looked at me, keenly. 'You are shocked, General Estcourt,' he said, 'I am sorry for that. But have you never known the curse' – and his voice vibrated – 'the curse of not being employed when you should be employed? The curse of being a hammer with no nail to drive? The curse – the curse of sitting in a dusty garrison town with dreams that would split the brain of a Caesar, and no room on earth for those dreams?'

'Yes,' I said, unwillingly, for there was something in him that demanded the truth, 'I have known that.'

'Then you know hells undreamed of by the Christian,' he said, with a sigh, 'and if I committed treason – well, I have been punished for it. I might have been a brigadier, otherwise – I had Choiseul's ear for a few weeks, after great labour. As it is, I am here on half pay, and there will not be another war in my time. Moreover, M. de Ségur has proclaimed that all officers now must show sixteen quarterings. Well, I wish them joy of those officers, in the next conflict. Meanwhile, I have my corks, my maps and my family ailment.' He smiled and tapped his side. 'It killed my father at thirty-nine – it has not treated me quite so ill, but it will come for me soon enough.'

And indeed, when I looked at him, I could well believe it, for the light had gone from his eyes and his cheeks were flabby. We chatted a little on indifferent subjects after that, then I left him, wondering whether to pursue the acquaintance. He is indubitably a character, but some of his speeches leave a taste in my mouth. Yet he can be greatly attractive – even now, with his mountainous failure like a cloak upon him. And yet why should I call it mountainous? His conceit is mountainous enough, but what else could he have expected of his career? Yet I wish I could forget his eyes . . . To tell the truth, he puzzles me and I mean to get to the bottom of him . . .

*February 12th, 1789* . . . I have another sidelight on the character of my friend, the major. As I told you, I was half of a mind to break off the acquaintance entirely, but he came up to me so civilly, the following day, that I could find no excuse. And since then, he has made me no embarrassingly treasonable confidences, though whenever we discuss the art of war, his arrogance in unbelievable. He even informed me, the other day, that while Frederick of Prussia was a fair general, his tactics might have been improved upon. I merely laughed and turned the question. Now and then I play a war game with him, with his corks and maps, and when I let him win, he is as pleased as a child . . . His illness increases visibly, despite the waters, and he shows an eagerness for my company which I cannot but find touching . . . After all, he is a man of intelligence, and the company he has had to keep must have galled him at times . . .

Now and then I amuse myself by speculating what might have happened to him, had he chosen some other profession than that of arms. He has, as I have told you, certain gifts of the actor, yet his stature and figure must have debarred him from tragic parts, while he certainly does not possess the humours of the comedian. Perhaps his best choice would have been the Romish church, for there, the veriest fisherman may hope, at least, to succeed to the keys of St Peter . . . And yet, Heaven knows, he would have made a very bad priest! . . .

But, to my tale. I had missed him from our accustomed walks for some days and went to his house – St Helen's it is called; we lived in a pother of saints' names hereabouts – one evening to inquire. I did not hear the quarrelling voices till the tousle-haired servant had admitted me and then it was too late to retreat. Then my friend bounced down the corridor, his sallow face bored and angry.

'Ah, General Estcourt!' he said, with a complete change of expression as soon as he saw me. 'What fortune! I was hoping you would pay us a call – I wish to introduce you to my family!'

He had told me previously of his pair of stepchildren by Madame's first marriage, and I must confess I felt curious to see them. But it was not of them he spoke, as I soon gathered.

'Yes,' he said. 'My brothers and sisters, or most of them, are here for a family council. You come in the nick of time!' He pinched my arm and his face glowed with the malicious naïveté of a child. 'They do not believe that I really know an English general – it will be a great blow to them!' he whispered as we passed down the corridor. 'Ah, if you had only worn your uniform and your Garters! But one cannot have everything in life!'

Well, my dear sister, what a group, when we entered the salon!

It is a small room, tawdrily furnished in the worst French taste, with a jumble of Madame's femininities and souvenirs from the Island of Mauritius, and they were all sitting about in the French after-dinner fashion, drinking tisane and quarrelling. And, indeed, had the room been as long as the nave of St Peter's it would yet have seemed too small for such a crew! An old mother, straight as a ramrod and as forbidding, with the burning eyes and the bitter dignity one sees on the faces of certain Italian peasants – you could see that they were all a little afraid of her except my friend, and he, I must say, treated her with a filial courtesy that was greatly to his credit. Two sisters, one fattish, swarthy and spiteful, the other with the wreck of great beauty and the evident marks of a certain profession on her shabby-fine *toilette* and her pinkened cheeks. An innkeeper brother-in-law called Buras or Durat, with a jowlish, heavily handsome face and the manners of a cavalry sergeant – he is married to the spiteful sister. And two brothers, one sheep-like, one fox-like, yet both bearing a certain resemblance to my friend.

The sheep-like brother is at least respectable, I gathered – a provincial lawyer in a small way of business whose great pride is that he has actually appeared before the Court of Appeals at Marseilles. The other, the fox-like one, makes his living more dubiously – he seems the sort of fellow who orates windily in tap-rooms about the Rights of Man, and other nonsense of M. Rousseau's. I would certainly not trust him with my watch, though he is trying to get himself elected to the States-General. And, as regards family concord, it was obvious at first glance that not one of them trusted the others. And yet, that is not all of the tribe. There are, if you will believe me, two other brothers living, and this family council was called to deal with the affairs of the next-to-youngest, who seems, even in this mélange, to be a black sheep.

I can assure you, my head swam, and when my friend introduced me, proudly, as a Knight of the Garters, I did not even bother to contradict him. For they admitted me to their intimate circle at once – there was no doubt about that. Only the old lady remained aloof, saying little and sipping her camomile tea as if it were the blood of her enemies. But, one by one, the others related to me, with an unasked-for frankness, the most intimate and scandalous details of their brothers' and sisters' lives. They seemed united only on two points, jealousy of my friend, the major, because he is his mother's favourite, and dislike of Madame Josephine because she gives herself airs. Except for the haggard beauty – I must say, that, while her remarks anent her sister-in-law were not such as I would care to repeat, she seemed genuinely fond of her brother, the major, and expounded his virtues to me through an overpowering cloud of scent.

It was like being in a nest of Italian smugglers, or a den of quarrelsome foxes, for they all talked, or rather barked at once, even the brother-in-law, and only Madame Mère could bring silence among them. And yet, my friend enjoyed it. It was obvious he showed them off before me as he might have displayed the tricks of a set of performing animals. And yet with a certain fondness, too – that is the inexplicable part of it. I do not know which sentiment was upmost in my mind – respect for this family feeling or pity for his being burdened with such a clan.

For though not the eldest, he is the strongest among them, and they know it. They rebel, but he rules their family conclaves like a petty despot. I could have laughed at the farce of it, and yet, it was nearer tears. For here, at least, my friend was a personage.

I got away as soon as I could, despite some pressing looks from the haggard beauty. My friend accompanied me to the door.

'Well, well,' he said, chuckling and rubbing his hands, 'I am infinitely obliged to you, general. They will not forget this in a hurry. Before you entered, Joseph' – Joseph is the sheep-like one – 'was boasting about his acquaintance with a *sous-intendant*, but an English general, bah! Joseph will have green eyes for a fortnight!' And he rubbed his hands again in a perfect paroxysm of delight.

It was too childlike to make me angry. 'I am glad, of course, to have been of any service,' I said.

'Oh, you have been a great service,' he said. 'They will not plague my poor Josie for at least half an hour. Ah, this is a bad business of Louis' – a bad business!' – Louis is the black sheep – 'but we will patch it up somehow. Hortense is worth three of him – he must go back to Hortense!'

'You have a numerous family, major,' I said, for want of something better to say.

'Oh, yes,' he said, cheerfully. 'Pretty numerous – I am sorry you could not meet the others. Though Louis is a fool – I pampered him in his youth. Well! He was a baby – and Jerome a mule. Still, we haven't done so badly for ourselves; not badly. Joseph makes a go of his law practice – there are fools enough in the world to be impressed by Joseph – and if Lucien gets to the States-General, you may trust Lucien to feather his nest! And there are the grandchildren, and a little money – not much,' he said, quickly. 'They mustn't expect that from me. But it's a step up from where we started – if papa had lived, he wouldn't have been so ill-pleased. Poor Elisa's gone, but the rest of us have stuck together, and, while we may seem a little rough, to strangers, our hearts are in the right place. When I was a boy,' and he chuckled again, 'I had other ambitions for them. I thought, with luck on my side, I could make them all kings and queens. Funny, isn't it, to think of a numbskull like Joseph as a king! Well, that was the boy of it. But, even so, they'd all be eating chestnuts back on the island without me, and that's something.'

He said it rather defiantly, and I did not know which to marvel at most – his preposterous pride in the group or his cool contempt of them. So I said nothing but shook his hand instead. I could not help doing the latter. For surely, if anyone started in life with a millstone about his neck . . . and yet they are none of them ordinary people . . .

*March 13th, 1789* . . . My friend's complaint has taken a turn for the worse and it is I who pay him visits now. It is the act of a Christian to do so and, to tell the truth, I have become oddly attached to him, though I can give no just reason for the attachment. He makes a bad patient, by the way, and is often abominably rude to both myself and Madame, who nurses him devotedly though unskilfully. I told him yesterday that I could have no more of it and he looked at me with his strangely luminous eyes. 'So,' he said, 'even the English desert the dying.' . . . Well, I stayed; after that, what else might a gentleman do? . . . Yet I cannot feel that he bears me any real affection – he exerts himself to charm, on occasion, but one feels he is playing a game . . . yes, even upon his deathbed, he plays a game . . . a complex character . . .

*April 28th, 1789* . . . My friend the major's malady approaches its term – the last few days find him fearfully enfeebled. He knows that the end draws nigh; indeed he speaks of it often, with remarkable calmness. I had thought it might turn his mind towards religion, but while he has accepted the ministrations of his Church, I fear it is without the sincere repentance of a Christian. When the priest had left him, yesterday, he summoned me, remarking, 'Well, all that is over with,' rather more in the tone of a man who has just reserved a place in a coach than one who will shortly stand before his Maker.

'It does no harm,' he said, reflectively. 'And, after all, it might be true. Why not?' and he chuckled in a way that repelled me. Then he asked me to read to him – not the Bible, as I had expected, but some verses of the poet Gray. He listened attentively, and when I came to the passage, 'Hands, that the rod of empire might have swayed,' and its successor, 'Some mute inglorious Milton here may rest,' he asked me to repeat them. When I had done so, he said, 'Yes, yes. That is true, very true. I did not think so in boyhood – I thought genius must force its own way. But your poet is right about it.'

I found this painful, for I had hoped that his illness had brought him to a juster, if less arrogant, estimate of his own abilities.

'Come, major,' I said, soothingly, 'we cannot all be great men, you know. And you have no need to repine. After all, as you say, you have risen in the world—'

'Risen?' he said, and his eyes flashed. 'Risen? Oh, God, that I should die alone with my one companion an Englishman with a soul of suet! Fool, if I had had Alexander's chance, I would have bettered Alexander! And it will come, too, that is the worst of it. Already Europe is shaking with a new birth. If I had been born under the Sun-King, I would be a Marshal of France; if I had been born twenty years ago, I would mould a new Europe with my fists in the next half-dozen years. Why did they put my soul in my body at this infernal time? Do you not understand, imbecile? Is there no one who understands?'

I called Madame at this, as he was obviously delirious, and, after some trouble, we got him quieted.

*May 8th, 1789* . . . My poor friend is gone, and peacefully enough at the last. His death, oddly enough, coincided with the date of the opening of the States-General at Versailles. The last moments of life are always painful for the observer, but his end was as relatively serene as might be hoped for, considering his character. I was watching at one side of the bed and a thunderstorm was raging at the time. No doubt, to his expiring consciousness, the cracks of the thunder sounded like artillery, for, while we were waiting the death-struggle, he suddenly raised himself in the bed and listened intently. His eyes glowed, a beatific expression passed over his features. 'The army! Head of the army!' he whispered ecstatically, and, when we caught him, he was lifeless . . . I must say that, while it may not be very Christian, I am glad that death brought him what life could not, and that, in the very article of it, he saw himself at the head of victorious troops. Ah, Fame – delusive spectre . . . (A page of disquisition by General Estcourt on the vanities of human ambition is here omitted.) . . . The face, after death, was composed, with a certain majesty, even . . . one could see that he might have been handsome as a youth . . .

*May 26th, 1789* . . . I shall return to Paris by easy stages and reach Stokely sometime in June. My health is quite restored and all that has kept me here this long has been the difficulty I have met with in attempting to settle my poor friend, the major's, affairs. For one thing, he appears to have been originally a native of Corsica, not of Sardinia as I had thought, and while that explains much in his character, it has also given occupation to the lawyers. I have met his rapacious family, individually and in conclave, and, if there are further grey hairs on my head, you may put it down to them . . . However, I have finally assured the major's relict of her legitimate rights in his estate, and that is something – my one ray of comfort in the matter being the behaviour of her son by the former marriage, who seems an excellent and virtuous young man . . .

 . . . You will think me a very soft fellow, no doubt, for wasting so much time upon a chance acquaintance who was neither, in our English sense, a gentleman nor a man whose Christian virtues counterbalanced his lack of true breeding. Yet there was a tragedy about him beyond his station, and that verse of Gray's rings in my head. I wish I could forget the expression on his face when he spoke of it. Suppose a genius born in circumstances that made the development of that genius impossible – well, all this is the merest moonshine . . .

 . . . To revert to more practical matters, I discover that the major has left me his military memoirs, papers and commentaries, including his maps. Heaven knows what I shall do with them! I cannot, in courtesy, burn them *sur-le-champ*, and yet they fill two huge packing cases and the cost of transporting them to Stokely will be considerable. Perhaps I will take them to Paris and quietly

dispose of them there to some waste-paper merchant . . . In return
for this unsought legacy, Madame has consulted me in regard to a
stone and epitaph for her late husband, and, knowing that otherwise
the family would squabble over the affair for weeks, I have drawn
up a design which I hope meets with their approval. It appears that
he particularly desired that the epitaph should be writ in English,
saying that France had had enough of him, living – a freak of dying
vanity for which one must pardon him. However, I have produced
the following, which I hope will answer.

> Here lies
> NAPOLEONE BUONAPARTE
> Major of the Royal Artillery
> of France.
> Born August 15th, 1737
> at Ajaccio, Corsica.
> Died May 5th, 1789
> at St Philippe-des-Bains

'Rest, perturbed spirit . . .'

. . . I had thought, for some hours, of excerpting the lines of Gray's
– the ones that still ring in my head. But, on reflection, though they
suit well enough, they yet seem too cruel to the dust.

# The State of Grace

## Marcel Aymé

*What would Napoleon have been had he not had access to power?*
*Stephen Vincent Benét plays the game of 'what would have happened*
*if . . .', a device used many times in short stories and novels, particularly*
*thrillers. Kipling, in A St Helena Lullaby, pictures Napoleon as a child*
*still capable of choosing his future:*

> *'How far is St Helena from a little child at play?'*
> *What makes you want to wander there with all the world between?*
> *Oh! Mother, call your child again or else he'll run away,*
> *(No one thinks of winter when the grass is green.)*

*But becoming Napoleon is perhaps not a choice, but a gift. 'The State*
*of Grace' is about such a gift, about a man selected by God to bear the*
*mark of His appreciation.*

*Marcel Aymé is probably the best-loved of French humorists. His*
*sardonic style and his brilliant imagination combine in his work to*
*produce some of the finest fantastic literature of our time. After the success*
*of his novel* The Green Mare *in 1933 he dedicated himself entirely to*
*writing. When he died in 1967 he had published over thirty novels, many*
*plays and several collections of short stories.*

In the year 1939 the best Christian in the Rue Gabrielle, and indeed
in all Montmartre, was a certain Monsieur Duperrier, a man of such
piety, uprightness and charity that God, without awaiting his death,
and while he was still in the prime of life, crowned his head with a
halo which never left it by day or by night. Like those in paradise
this halo, although made of some immaterial substance, manifested
itself in the form of a whitish ring which looked as though it might
have been cut out of fairly stiff cardboard, and shed a tender light.
M. Duperrier wore it gratefully, with devout thanks to Heaven for
a distinction which, however, his modesty did not permit him to

regard as a formal undertaking in respect of the hereafter. He would have been unquestionably the happiest of men had his wife, instead of rejoicing in this signal mark of the Divine approval, not received it with outspoken resentment and exasperation.

'Well really, upon my word,' the lady said, 'what do you think you look like going round in a thing like that, and what do you suppose the neighbours and the tradespeople will say, not to mention my cousin Léopold? I never in my life saw anything so ridiculous. You'll have the whole neighbourhood talking.'

Mme Duperrier was an admirable woman, of outstanding piety and impeccable conduct, but she had not yet understood the vanity of the things of this world. Like so many people whose aspirations to virtue are marred by a certain lack of logic, she thought it more important to be esteemed by her concierge than by her Creator. Her terror lest she should be questioned on the subject of the halo by one of the neighbours or by the milkman had from the very outset an embittering effect upon her. She made repeated attempts to snatch away the shimmering plate of light that adorned her husband's cranium, but with no more effect than if she had tried to grasp a sunbeam, and without altering its position by a hair's-breadth. Girdling the top of his forehead where the hair began, the halo hung low over the back of his neck, with a slight tilt which gave it a coquettish look.

The foretaste of beatitude did not cause Duperrier to overlook the consideration he owed to his wife's peace of mind. He himself possessed too great a sense of discretion and modesty not to perceive that there were grounds for her disquiet. The gifts of God, especially when they wear a somewhat gratuitous aspect, are seldom accorded the respect they deserve, and the world is all too ready to find in them a subject of malicious gossip. Duperrier did his utmost, so far as the thing was possible to make himself at all times inconspicuous. Regretfully putting aside the bowler hat which he had hitherto regarded as an indispensable attribute of his accountant's calling, he took to wearing a large felt hat, light in colour, of which the wide brim exactly covered the halo provided he wore it rakishly on the back of his head. Thus clad, there was nothing startlingly out-of-the-way in his appearance to attract the attention of the passer-by. The brim of his hat merely had a slight phosphorescence which by daylight might pass for the sheen on the surface of smooth felt. During office hours he was equally successful in avoiding the notice of his employer and fellow-workers. His desk, in the small shoe factory in Ménilmontant where he kept the books, was situated in a glass-paned cubby hole between two workshops, and his state of isolation saved him from awkward questions. He wore the hat all day, and no one was sufficiently interested to ask him why he did so.

But these precautions did not suffice to allay his wife's misgivings. It seemed to her that the halo must already be a subject of comment among the ladies of the district, and she went almost furtively about the streets adjoining the Rue Gabrielle, her buttocks contracted and her heart wrung with agonizing suspicions, convinced that she heard the echo of mocking laughter as she passed. To this worthy woman who had never had any ambition other than to keep her place in a social sphere ruled by the cult of the absolute norm, the glaring eccentricity with which her husband had been afflicted rapidly assumed catastrophic proportions. Its very improbability made it monstrous. Nothing would have induced her to accompany him out of doors. The evenings and Sunday afternoons which they had previously devoted to small outings and visits to friends were now passed in a solitary intimacy which became daily more oppressive. In the living-room of light oak where between meals the long leisure hours dragged by, Mme Duperrier, unable to knit a single stitch, would sit bitterly contemplating the halo, while Duperrier, generally reading some work of devotion and feeling the brush of angels' wings, wore an expression of beatific rapture which added to her fury. From time to time, however, he would glance solicitously at her, and noting the expression of angry disapproval on her face would feel a regret which was incompatible with the gratitude he owed to Heaven, so that this in its turn inspired him with a feeling of remorse at one remove.

So painful a state of affairs could not long continue without imperilling the unhappy woman's mental equilibrium. She began presently to complain that the light of the halo, bathing the pillows, made it impossible for her to sleep at nights. Duperrier, who sometimes made use of the divine illumination to read a chapter of the Scriptures, was obliged to concede the justice of this grievance, and he began to be afflicted with a sense of guilt. Finally, certain events, highly deplorable in their consequences, transformed this state of unease into one of acute crisis.

Upon setting out for the office one morning, Duperrier passed a funeral in the Rue Gabrielle, within a few yards of their house. He had become accustomed, outrageous though it was to his natural sense of courtesy, to greet acquaintances by merely raising a hand to his hat; but being thus confronted by the near presence of the dead he decided, after thinking the matter over, that nothing could relieve him of the obligation to uncover himself entirely. Several shopkeepers, yawning in their doorways, blinked at the sight of the halo, and gathered together to discuss the phenomenon. When she came out to do her shopping Mme Duperrier was assailed with questions, and in a state of extreme agitation uttered denials whose very vehemence appeared suspect. Upon his return home at midday her husband found her in a state of nervous crisis which caused him to fear for her reason.

'Take off that halo!' she cried. 'Take it off instantly! I never want to see it again!'

Duperrier gently reminded her that it was not in his power to remove it, whereupon she cried still more loudly:

'If you had any consideration for me you'd find some way of getting rid of it. You're simply selfish, that's what you are!' These words, to which he prudently made no reply, gave Duperrier much food for thought. And on the following day a second incident occurred to point to the inevitable conclusion. Duperrier never missed early morning Mass, and since he had become endowed with the odour of sanctity he had taken to hearing it at the Basilica of the Sacré-Coeur. Here he was obliged to remove his hat, but the church is a large one and at that hour of the morning the congregation was sufficiently sparse to make it a simple matter for him to hide behind a pillar. On this particular occasion, however, he must have been less circumspect than usual. As he was leaving the church after the service an elderly spinster flung herself at his feet crying: 'St Joseph! St Joseph!', and kissed the hem of his overcoat. Duperrier beat a hasty retreat, flattered but considerably put out at recognizing his adorer, who lived only a few doors away. A few hours later the devoted creature burst into the apartment, where Mme Duperrier was alone, uttering cries of – 'St Joseph! I want to see St Joseph!'

Although somewhat lacking in brilliant and picturesque qualities, St Joseph is nevertheless an excellent saint: but his unsensational merits, with their flavour of solid craftsmanship and passive good-will, seem to have brought upon him some degree of injustice.

There are indeed persons, some of the utmost piety, who, without even being conscious of it, associate the notion of naïve complaisance with the part he played in the Nativity. This impression of simple-mindedness is further enchanced by the habit of superimposing upon the figure of the saint the recollection of that other Joseph who resisted the advances of Potiphar's wife. Mme Duperrier had no great respect for the presumed sanctity of her husband, but this fervour of adoration which with loud cries invoked him by the name of St Joseph seemed to her to add the finishing touch to his shame and absurdity. Goaded into a state of almost demented fury, she chased the visitor out of the apartment with an umbrella and then smashed several piles of plates. Her first act upon her husband's return was to have hysterics, and when finally she had regained her self-control she said in a decided voice:

'For the last time I ask you to get rid of that halo. You can do it if you choose. You know you can.'

Duperrier hung his head, not daring to ask how she thought he should go about it, and she went on:

'It's perfectly simple. You only have to sin.'

Uttering no word of protest, Duperrier withdrew to the bedroom to pray.

'Almighty God,' he said in substance, 'you have granted me the highest reward that man may hope for upon earth, excepting martyrdom. I thank you, Lord, but I am married and I share with my wife the bread of tribulation which you deign to send us, no less than the honey of your favour. Only thus can a devout couple hope to walk in your footsteps. And it so happens that my wife cannot endure the sight or even the thought of my halo, not at all because it is a gift bestowed by Heaven but simply because it's a halo. You know what women are. When some unaccustomed happening does not chance to kindle their enthusiasm it is likely to upset all the store of rules and harmonies which they keep lodged in their little heads. No one can prevent this, and though my wife should live to be a hundred there will never be any place for my halo in her scheme of things. Oh God, you who see into my heart, you know how little store I set by my personal tranquillity and the evening slippers by the fireside. For the rapture of wearing upon my head the token of your goodwill I would gladly suffer even the most violent domestic upheavals. But, alas, it is not my own peace of mind that is imperilled. My wife is losing all taste for life. Worse

still, I can see the day approaching when her hatred of my halo will
cause her to revile Him who bestowed it upon me. Am I to allow
the life-companion you chose for me to die and damn her soul for
all eternity without making an effort to save her? I find myself today
at the parting of the ways, and the safe road does not appear to me
to be the more merciful. That your spirit of infinite justice may talk
to me with the voice of my conscience is the prayer which in this
hour of my perplexity I lay at your radiant feet, oh Lord.'

Scarcely had Duperrier concluded this prayer than his conscience
declared itself in favour of the way of sin, making of this an act of
duty demanded by Christian charity. He returned to the living-
room, where his wife awaited him, grinding her teeth.

'God is just,' he said, with his thumbs in the armholes of his
waistcoat. 'He knew what he was doing when he gave me my halo.
The truth is that I deserve it more than any man alive. They don't
make men like me in these days. When I reflect upon the vileness
of the human herd and then consider the manifold perfections
embodied in myself I am tempted to spit in the faces of the people
in the street. God has rewarded me, it is true, but if the Church
had any regard for justice I should be an archbishop at the very
least.'

Duperrier had chosen the sin of pride, which enabled him, while
exalting his own merits, in the same breath to praise God, who had
singled him out. His wife was not slow to realize that he was sinning
deliberately and at once entered into the spirit of the thing.

'My angel,' she said, 'you will never know how proud I am of
you. My cousin Léopold, with his car and his villa at Le Vésinet,
is not worthy to unloose the latchet of your shoe.'

'That is precisely my own opinion. If I had chosen to concern
myself with sordid matters I could have amassed a fortune as easily
as any man, and a much bigger one than Léopold's, but I chose to
follow a different road and my triumph is of another kind. I despise
his money as I despise the man himself and all the countless other
half-wits who are incapable of perceiving the grandeur of my modest
existence. They have eyes and see not.'

The utterance of sentiments such as these, spoken at first from
half-closed lips, his heart rent with shame, became within a short
time a simple matter for Duperrier, a habit costing him no effort at
all. And such is the power of words over the human mind that it

was not long before he accepted them as valid currency. His wife, however, anxiously watching the halo, and seeing that its lustre showed no sign of diminishing, began to suspect that her husband's sin was lacking in weight and substance. Duperrier readily agreed with this.

'Nothing could be more true,' he said. 'I thought I was giving way to pride when in fact I was merely expressing the most simple and obvious of truths. When a man has attained to the uttermost degree of perfection, as I have done, the word "pride" ceases to have any meaning.'

This did not prevent him from continuing to extol his merits, but at the same time he recognized the necessity for embarking upon some other form of sin. It appeared to him that gluttony was, of the Deadly Sins, the one most suited to his purpose, which was to rid himself of the halo without too far forfeiting the goodwill of Heaven. He was supported in this conclusion by the recollection, from his childhood days, of gentle scoldings for excessive indulgence in jam or chocolate. Filled with hope his wife set about the preparation of rich dishes whose variety enhanced their savour. The Duperriers' dinner-table was loaded with game, pâté, river-trout, lobster, sweets, pastries and vintage wines. Their meals lasted twice as long as hitherto, if not three times. Nothing could have been more hideous and revolting than the spectacle of Duperrier, his napkin tied round his neck, his face crimson and his eyes glazed with satiation, loading his plate with a third helping, washing down roast and stuffing with great gulps of claret, belching, dribbling sauce and gravy, and perspiring freely under his halo. Before long he had developed such a taste for good cooking and rich repasts that he frequently rebuked his wife for an over-cooked joint or an unsuccessful mayonnaise. One evening, annoyed by his incessant grumbling, she said sharply:

'Your halo seems to be flourishing. Anyone would think it was growing fat on my cooking, just as you are. It looks to me as though gluttony isn't a sin after all. The only thing against it is that it costs money, and I can see no reason why I shouldn't put you back on vegetable soup and spaghetti.'

'That's enough of that!' roared Duperrier. 'Put me back on vegetable soup and spaghetti, will you? By God, I'd like to see you try! Do you think I don't know what I'm doing? Put me back on spaghetti, indeed! The insolence! Here am I, wallowing in sin just to oblige you, and that's the way you talk. Don't let me hear another word. It would serve you right if I slapped your face.'

One sin leads to another, in short, and thwarted greed, no less than pride, promotes anger. Duperrier allowed himself to fall into this new sin without knowing whether he was doing it for his wife's sake or because he enjoyed it. This man who had hitherto been distinguished by the gentleness and equability of his nature now became given to thunderous rages; he smashed the crockery and on occasions went so far as to strike his wife. He even swore, invoking the name of his Creator. But his outbursts, growing steadily more frequent, did not save him from being both arrogant and gluttonous. He was, in fact, now sinning in three different ways, and Mme Duperrier mused darkly on God's infinite indulgence.

The fact is that the noblest of virtues can continue to flourish in a soul sullied by sin. Proud, gluttonous and choleric, Duperrier nevertheless remained steeped in Christian charity, nor had he lost anything of his lofty sense of duty as a man and a husband. Finding that Heaven remained unmoved by his anger, he resolved to be envious as well. To tell the truth, without his knowing it, envy had already crept into his soul. Rich feeding, which puts a burden on the liver, and pride, which stirs the sense of injustice, may dispose even the best of men to envy his neighbour. And anger lent a note of hatred to Duperrier's envy. He became jealous of his relations, his friends, his employer, the shopkeepers of the neighbourhood and even the stars of sport and screen whose photographs appeared in the papers. Everything infuriated him, and he was known to tremble with ignoble rage at the thought that the people next door possessed a cutlery service with silver handles, whereas his own were only of bone. But the halo continued to glow with undiminished brightness. Instead of being dismayed by this, he concluded that his sins were lacking in reality, and he had no difficulty in reasoning that his supposed gluttony did not in fact exceed the natural demands of a healthy appetite, while his anger and his envy merely bore witness to a lofty craving for justice. It was the halo itself, however, which furnished him with the most solid arguments.

'I'm bound to say I would have expected Heaven to be a little more fussy,' his wife said. 'If all your gluttony and boasting and brutality and malice have done nothing to dim your halo, it doesn't look as though I need worry about *my* place in Paradise.'

'Hold your tongue!' roared the furious man. 'How much longer have I got to listen to you nagging? I'm fed up with it. You think it funny, do you, that a saintly character like myself should have to plunge into sin for the sake of your blasted peace of mind? Stow it, d'you hear me?'

The tone of these replies was clearly lacking in that suavity which may rightly be looked for in a man enhaloed by the glory of God. Since he had entered upon the paths of sin Duperrier had become increasingly given to strong language. His formerly ascetic countenance was becoming bloated with rich food. Not only was his vocabulary growing coarse, but a similar vulgarity was invading his thoughts. His vision of Paradise, for example, had undergone a notable transformation. Instead of appearing to him as a symphony of souls in robes of cellophane, the dwelling-place of the elect came to look more and more like a vast dining-room. Mme Duperrier did not fail to observe the changes that were overtaking her husband and even to feel some anxiety for the future. Nevertheless, the thought of his possible descent into the abyss still did not outweigh in her mind the horror of singularity. Rather than an enhaloed Duperrier she would have preferred a husband who was an atheist, a debauchée and as crude of speech as her cousin Léopold. At least she would not then have to blush for him before the milkman.

No especial decision was called for on the part of Duperrier for him to lapse into the sin of sloth. The arrogant belief that he was required at the office to perform tasks unworthy of his merits, together with the drowsiness caused by heavy eating and drinking, made him naturally disposed to be idle; and since he had sufficient conceit to believe that he must excel in all things, even the worst, he very soon became a model of indolence. The day his indignant employer sacked him, he received the sentence with his hat in his hand.

'What's that on your head?' his employer asked.

'A halo,' said Duperrier.

'Is it indeed? And I suppose that's what you've been fooling around with when you were supposed to be working?'

When he told his wife of his dismissal, she asked him what he intended to do next.

'It seems to me that this would be a good moment to try the sin of avarice,' he answered gaily.

Of all the Deadly Sins, avarice was the one that called for the greatest effort of willpower on his part. To those not born avaricious it is the vice offering the fewest easy allurements, and when it is adopted on principle there is nothing to distinguish it, at least in the early stages, from that most sterling of all virtues, thrift. Duperrier subjected himself to severe disciplines, such as confining himself to gluttony, and thus succeeded in gaining a solid reputation for avarice among his friends and acquaintances. He really liked money for its own sake, and was better able than most people to experience the malicious thrill which misers feel at the thought that they control a source of creative energy and prevent it from functioning. Counting up his savings, the fruit of a hitherto laborious existence, he came by degrees to know the hideous pleasure of harming others by damming a current of exchange and of life. This outcome, simply because it was painfully achieved, filled Mme Duperrier with hope. Her husband had yielded so easily to the seductions of the other sins that God, she thought, could not condemn him very severely for an innocent, animal surrender which made him appear rather a victim deserving of compassion. His deliberate and patient progress along the road of avarice, on the other hand, could only be the fruit of a perverse desire which was like a direct challenge to Heaven. Nevertheless, although Duperrier became miserly to the point of putting trouser-buttons in the collection-bag, the brilliance and size of the halo remained unimpaired. This new setback, duly noted, plunged husband and wife into despair.

Proud, gluttonous, angry, envious, slothful and avaricious, Duperrier felt that his soul was still perfumed with innocence. Deadly though they were, the six sins he had thus far practised were nevertheless such as a first communicant may confess to without despairing. The deadliest of all, lust, filled him with horror. The others, it seemed to him, might be said to exist almost outside the sphere of God's notice. In the case of each, sin or peccadillo, it all depended on the size of the dose. But lust, the sin of the flesh, meant unqualified acceptance of the Devil's work. The enchantments of the night were a foretaste of the burning shades of Hell, the darting tongues were like the flames of eternity, the moans of ecstasy, the writhing bodies, these did but herald the wailing of the damned and the convulsions of flesh racked by endless torment. Duperrier had not deliberately reserved the sin of the flesh to the last: he had simply refused to contemplate it. Mme Duperrier herself could not think of it without disquiet. For many years the pair had lived in a state of delicious chastity, their nightly rest attended, until the coming of the halo, by dreams as pure as the driven snow. As she thought of it, the recollection of those years of continence was a source of considerable annoyance to Mme Duperrier, for she did not doubt that the halo was the result. Plainly that lily-white nimbus could be undone by lust alone.

Duperrier, after obstinately resisting his wife's persuasions, at length allowed himself to be overborne. Once again his sense of duty cast out fear. Having reached the decision, he was embarrassed by his ignorance; but his wife, who thought of everything, bought him a revolting book in which all the essentials were set forth in the form of plain and simple instruction. The night-time spectacle of that saintly man, the halo encircling his head, reading a chapter of the abominable work to his wife, was a poignant one indeed. Often his voice trembled at some infamous word or some image more hideously evocative than the rest. Having thus achieved a theoretical mastery of the subject, he still delayed while he considered whether this last sin should be consummated in domestic intimacy or elsewhere. Mme Duperrier took the view that it should be done at home, adducing reasons of economy which did not fail to weigh with him; but having considered all the pros and cons, he concluded that he had no need to involve her in vile practices which might be prejudicial to her own salvation. As a loyal husband he valiantly resolved that he alone should run the risks.

Thereafter Duperrier spent most of his nights in disreputable hotels where he pursued his initiation in company with the professionals of the quarter. The halo, which he could not conceal from these wretched associates, led to his finding himself in various odd situations, sometimes embarrassing and sometimes advantageous. In the beginning, owing to his anxiety to conform to the instructions in his manual, he sinned with little exaltation but rather with the methodical application of a dancer learning a new step or figure of choreography. However, the desire for perfection to which his pride impelled him soon achieved its lamentable reward in the notoriety which he gained among the women with whom he consorted. Although he came to take the liveliest pleasure in these pursuits, Duperrier nevertheless found them expensive and was cruelly afflicted in his avarice. One evening on the Place Pigalle he made the acquaintance of a creature twenty years of age, already a lost soul, whose name was Marie-Jannick. It was for her, so it is

believed, that the poet Maurice Fombeure wrote the charming
lines:

> It's Marie-Jannick
> Of Landivisoo
> Who kills mosquitoes
> With her shoe.

Marie-Jannick had come from Brittany six months previously to
go into service as maid-of-all-work in the home of a municipal
councillor who was both a socialist and an atheist. Finding herself
unable to endure the life of this godless household, she had given
notice and was now courageously earning her living on the Boulevard de Clichy. As was to be expected, the halo made a deep
impression on that little religious soul. To Marie-Jannick, Duperrier
seemed the equal of St Yves and St Ronan, and he, on his side,
was not slow to perceive the influence he had over her and to turn
it to profit.

Thus it is that on this very day, the 22nd February of the year
1944, amid the darkness of winter and of war, Marie-Jannick, who
will shortly be twenty-five, may be seen walking her beat on the
Boulevard de Clichy. During the black-out hours the stroller
between the Place Pigalle and the Rue des Martyrs may be startled
to observe, floating and swaying in the darkness a mysterious circle
of light that looks rather like a ring of Saturn. It is Duperrier, his
head adorned with the glorious halo which he no longer seeks to
conceal from the curiosity of all and sundry; Duperrier, burdened
with the weight of the seven Deadly Sins, who, lost to all shame,
supervises the labours of Marie-Jannick, administering a smart kick
in the pants when her zeal flags, and waiting at the hotel door to
count her takings by the light of the halo. But from the depths of
his degradation, through the dark night of his conscience, a murmur
yet arises from time to time to his lips, a prayer of thanksgiving for
the absolute gratuity of the gifts of God.

*Translated from the French by Norman Denny.*

# The Story of a Panic

## E.M. Forster

*With six novels (notably* A Passage to India), *three volumes of short stories and a few volumes of essays and biographies, Edward Morgan Forster established himself as one of the greatest modern English writers. He was a member of the Bloomsbury Group, but his writing is highly personal. (Although the Group's Bible was G. E. Moore's* Principia Ethica, *shortly before his death Forster confessed to never having read it.) A powerful characteristic of his novels and short stories ('The Story of a Panic', for example) is the contrast between the freedom of paganism and the restrained codes of civilized England, the world of 'telegrams and anger'.*

*I would have liked to include a certain story Forster never published (an uncorrected version appeared posthumously), because it could have been fantastic. Forster heard it in Cornwall and then waited too long to write it, and when he did it was a total disaster. 'No editor would look at it,' he said. 'It was about a man who was saved from drowning by some fishermen, and knew not how to reward them. What is your life worth? Five pounds? Five thousand pounds? He ended by giving nothing, and lived among them, hated and despised.'*

# I

Eustace's career – if career it can be called – certainly dates from that afternoon in the chestnut woods above Ravello. I confess at once that I am a plain, simple man, with no pretensions to literary style. Still, I do flatter myself that I can tell a story without exaggerating, and I have therefore decided to give an unbiased account of the extraordinary events of eight years ago.

Ravello is a delightful place with a delightful little hotel in which we met some charming people. There were the two Miss Robinsons, who had been there for six weeks with Eustace, their nephew, then a boy of about fourteen. Mr Sandbach had also been there some time. He had held a curacy in the north of England, which he had been compelled to resign on account of ill-health, and while he was recruiting at Ravello he had taken in hand Eustace's education – which was then sadly deficient – and was endeavouring to fit him for one of our great public schools. Then there was Mr Leyland, a would-be artist, and, finally, there was the nice landlady, Signora Scafetti, and the nice English-speaking waiter, Emmanuele – though at the time of which I am speaking Emmanuele was away, visiting a sick father.

To this little circle, I, my wife, and my two daughters made, I venture to think, a not unwelcome addition. But though I liked most of the company well enough, there were two of them to whom I did not take at all. They were the artist, Leyland, and the Miss Robinsons' nephew, Eustace.

Leyland was simply conceited and odious, and, as those qualities will be amply illustrated in my narrative, I need not enlarge upon them here. But Eustace was something besides: he was indescribably repellent.

I am fond of boys as a rule, and was quite disposed to be friendly. I and my daughters offered to take him out – 'No, walking was such a fag.' Then I asked him to come and bathe – 'No, he could not swim.'

'Every English boy should be able to swim,' I said, 'I will teach you myself.'

'There, Eustace dear,' said Miss Robinson; 'here is a chance for you.'

But he said he was afraid of the water! – a boy afraid! – and of course I said no more.

I would not have minded so much if he had been a really studious boy, but he neither played hard nor worked hard. His favourite occupations were lounging on the terrace in an easy chair and loafing along the high road, with his feet shuffling up the dust and his shoulders stooping forward. Naturally enough, his features were pale, his chest contracted, and his muscles undeveloped. His aunts thought him delicate; what he really needed was discipline.

That memorable day we all arranged to go for a picnic up in the chestnut woods – all, that is, except Janet, who stopped behind to finish her water-colour of the Cathedral – not a very successful attempt, I am afraid.

I wander off into these irrelevant details because in my mind I cannot separate them from an account of the day; and it is the same with the conversation during the picnic: all is imprinted on my brain together. After a couple of hours' ascent, we left the donkeys that had carried the Miss Robinsons and my wife, and all proceeded on foot to the head of the valley – Vallone Fontana Caroso is its proper name, I find.

I have visited a good deal of fine scenery before and since, but have found little that has pleased me more. The valley ended in a vast hollow, shaped like a cup, into which radiated ravines from the precipitous hills around. Both the valley and the ravines and the ribs of hill that divided the ravines were covered with leafy chestnut, so that the general appearance was that of a many-fingered green hand, palm upwards, which was clutching convulsively to keep us in its grasp. Far down the valley we could see Ravello and the sea, but that was the only sign of another world.

'Oh, what a perfectly lovely place,' said my daughter Rose. 'What a picture it would make!'

'Yes,' said Mr Sandbach. 'Many a famous European gallery would be proud to have a landscape a tithe as beautiful as this upon its walls.'

'On the contrary,' said Leyland, 'it would make a very poor picture. Indeed, it is not paintable at all.'

'And why is that?' said Rose, with far more deference than he deserved.

'Look, in the first place,' he replied, 'how intolerably straight against the sky is the line of the hill. It would need breaking up and diversifying. And where we are standing the whole thing is out of perspective. Besides, all the colouring is monotonous and crude.'

'I do not know anything about pictures,' I put in, 'and I do not pretend to know: but I know what is beautiful when I see it, and I am thoroughly content with this.'

'Indeed, who could help being contented!' said the elder Miss Robinson; and Mr Sandbach said the same.

'Ah!' said Leyland, 'you all confuse the artistic view of Nature with the photographic.'

Poor Rose had brought her camera with her, so I thought this positively rude. I did not wish any unpleasantness; so I merely turned away and assisted my wife and Miss Mary Robinson to put out the lunch – not a very nice lunch.

'Eustace dear,' said his aunt, 'come and help us here.'

He was in a particularly bad temper that morning. He had, as usual, not wanted to come, and his aunts had nearly allowed him to stop at the hotel to vex Janet. But I, with their permission, spoke to him rather sharply on the subject of exercise; and the result was that he had come, but was even more taciturn and moody than usual.

Obedience was not his strong point. He invariably questioned every command, and only executed it grumbling. I should always insist on prompt and cheerful obedience, if I had a son.

'I'm – coming – Aunt – Mary,' he at last replied, and dawdled to cut a piece of wood to make a whistle, taking care not to arrive till we had finished.

'Well, well, sir!' said I. 'You stroll in at the end and profit by our labours.' He sighed, for he could not endure being chaffed. Miss Mary, very unwisely, insisted on giving him the wing of the chicken, in spite of all my attempts to prevent her. I remember that I had a moment's vexation when I thought that, instead of enjoying the sun, and the air, and the woods, we were all engaged in wrangling over the diet of a spoilt boy.

But, after lunch, he was a little less in evidence. He withdrew to a tree trunk, and began to loosen the bark from his whistle. I was thankful to see him employed, for once in a way. We reclined, and took a *dolce far niente*.

Those sweet chestnuts of the South are puny striplings compared with our robust Northerners. But they clothed the contours of the hills and valleys in a most pleasing way, their veil being only broken by two clearings, in one of which we were sitting.

And because these few trees were cut down, Leyland burst into a petty indictment of the proprietor.

'All the poetry is going from Nature,' he cried, 'her lakes and marshes are drained, her seas banked up, her forests cut down. Everywhere we see the vulgarity of desolation spreading.'

I have had some experience of estates, and answered that cutting was very necessary for the health of the larger trees. Besides, it was unreasonable to expect the proprietor to derive no income from his lands.

'If you take the commercial side of landscape, you may feel pleasure in the owner's activity. But to me the mere thought that a tree is convertible into cash is disgusting.'

'I see no reason,' I observed politely, 'to despise the gifts of Nature because they are of value.'

It did not stop him. 'It is no matter,' he went on, 'we are all hopelessly steeped in vulgarity. I do not except myself. It is through us, and to our shame, that the Nereids have left the waters and the Oreads the mountains, that the woods no longer give shelter to Pan.'

'Pan!' cried Mr Sandbach, his mellow voice filling the valley as if it had been a great green church, 'Pan is dead. That is why the woods do not shelter him.' And he began to tell the striking story of the mariners who were sailing near the coast at the time of the birth of Christ, and three times heard a loud voice saying: 'The great God Pan is dead.'

'Yes. The great God Pan is dead,' said Leyland. And he abandoned himself to that mock misery in which artistic people are so fond of indulging. His cigar went out, and he had to ask me for a match. 'How very interesting,' said Rose. 'I do wish I knew some ancient history.'

'It is not worth your notice,' said Mr Sandbach. 'Eh, Eustace?'

Eustace was finishing his whistle. He looked up, with the irritable frown in which his aunts allowed him to indulge, and made no reply.

The conversation turned to various topics and then died out. It was a cloudless afternoon in May, and the pale green of the young chestnut leaves made a pretty contrast with the dark blue of the sky. We were all sitting at the edge of the small clearing for the sake of the view, and the shade of the chestnut saplings behind us was manifestly insufficient. All sounds died away – at least that is my account: Miss Robinson says that the clamour of the birds was the first sign of uneasiness that she discerned. All sounds died away, except that, far in the distance, I could hear two boughs of a great chestnut grinding together as the tree swayed. The grinds grew shorter and shorter, and finally that sound stopped also. As I looked over the green fingers of the valley, everything was absolutely motionless and still; and that feeling of suspense which one so often experiences when Nature is in repose began to steal over me.

Suddenly we were all electrified by the excruciating noise of Eustace's whistle. I never heard any instrument give forth so ear-splitting and discordant a sound.

'Eustace dear,' said Miss Mary Robinson, 'you might have thought of your poor Aunt Julia's head.'

Leyland, who had apparently been asleep, sat up.

'It is astonishing how blind a boy is to anything that is elevating or beautiful,' he observed. 'I should not have thought he could have found the wherewithal out here to spoil our pleasure like this.'

Then the terrible silence fell upon us again. I was now standing up and watching a cat's-paw of wind that was running down one of the ridges opposite, turning the light green to dark as it travelled. A fanciful feeling of foreboding came over me; so I turned away, to find to my amazement, that all the others were also on their feet, watching it too.

It is not possible to describe coherently what happened next: but I, for one, am not ashamed to confess that, though the fair blue sky was above me, and the green spring woods beneath me, and the kindest of friends around me, yet I became terribly frightened, more frightened than I ever wish to become again, frightened in a way I never have known either before or after. And in the eyes of the others, too, I saw blank, expressionless fear, while their mouths strove in vain to speak and their hands to gesticulate. Yet, all around us were prosperity, beauty, and peace, and all was motionless, save the cat's-paw of wind, now travelling up the ridge on which we stood.

Who moved first has never been settled. It is enough to say that in one second we were tearing away along the hillside. Leyland was in front, then Mr Sandbach, then my wife. But I only saw for a brief moment; for I ran across the little clearing and through the woods and over the undergrowth and the rocks and down the dry torrent beds into the valley below. The sky might have been black as I ran, and the trees, short grass, and the hillside a level road; for I saw nothing and heard nothing and felt nothing, since all the channels of sense and reason were blocked. It was not the spiritual fear that one has known at other times, but brutal, overmastering, physical fear, stopping up the ears, and dropping clouds before the eyes, and filling the mouth with foul tastes. And it was no ordinary humiliation that survived; for I had been afraid, not as a man, but as a beast.

# II

I cannot describe our finish any better than our start; for our fear passed away as it had come, without cause. Suddenly I was able to see, and hear, and cough, and clear my mouth. Looking back, I saw that the others were stopping too; and, in a short time, we were all together, though it was long before we could speak, and longer before we dared to

No one was seriously injured. My poor wife had sprained her ankle, Leyland had torn one of his nails on a tree trunk, and I myself had scraped and damaged my ear. I never noticed it till I had stopped.

We were all silent, searching one another's faces. Suddenly Miss Mary Robinson gave a terrible shriek. 'Oh, merciful heavens! Where is Eustace?' And then she would have fallen if Mr Sandbach had not caught her.

'We must go back, we must go back at once,' said my Rose, who was quite the most collected of the party. 'But I hope – I feel he is safe.'

Such was the cowardice of Leyland, that he objected. But, finding himself in a minority, and being afraid of being left alone, he gave in. Rose and I supported my poor wife, Mr Sandbach and Miss Robinson helped Miss Mary, and we returned slowly and silently, taking forty minutes to ascend the path that we had descended in ten.

Our conversation was naturally disjointed, as no one wished to offer an opinion on what had happened. Rose was the most talkative: she startled us all by saying that she had very nearly stopped where she was.

'Do you mean to say that you weren't – that you didn't feel compelled to go?' said Mr Sandbach.

'Oh, of course, I did feel frightened' – she was the first to use the word – 'but I somehow felt that if I could stop on it would be quite different, that I shouldn't be frightened at all, so to speak.' Rose never did express herself clearly: still, it is greatly to her credit that she, the youngest of us, should have held on so long at that terrible time.

'I should have stopped, I do believe,' she continued, 'if I had not seen mamma go.'

Rose's experience comforted us a little about Eustace. But a feeling of terrible foreboding was on us all as we painfully climbed the chestnut-covered slopes and neared the little clearing. When we reached it our tongues broke loose. There, at the farther side, were the remains of our lunch, and close to them, lying motionless on his back, was Eustace.

With some presence of mind I at once cried out: 'Hey, you young monkey! Jump up!' But he made no reply, nor did he answer when his poor aunts spoke to him. And, to my unspeakable horror, I saw one of those green lizards dart out from under his shirt-cuff as we approached.

We stood watching him as he lay there so silently, and my ears began to tingle in expectation of the outbursts of lamentations and tears.

Miss Mary fell on her knees beside him and touched his hand, which was convulsively entwined in the long grass.

As she did so, he opened his eyes and smiled.

I have often seen that peculiar smile since, both on the possessor's face and on the photographs of him that are beginning to get into the illustrated papers. But, till then, Eustace had always worn a peevish, discontented frown; and we were all unused to this disquieting smile, which always seemed to be without adequate reason.

His aunts showered kisses on him, which he did not reciprocate and then there was an awkward pause. Eustace seemed so natural and undisturbed; yet, if he had not had astonishing experiences himself, he ought to have been all the more astonished at our extraordinary behaviour. My wife, with ready tact, endeavoured to behave as if nothing had happened.

'Well, Mr Eustace,' she said, sitting down as she spoke, to ease her foot, 'how have you been amusing yourself since we have been away?'

'Thank you, Mrs Tytler, I have been very happy.'

'And where have you been?'

'Here.'

'And lying down all the time, you idle boy?'

'No, not all the time.'

'What were you doing before?'

'Oh; standing or sitting.'

'Stood and sat doing nothing! Don't you know the poem "Satan finds some mischief still for—" '

'Oh, my dear madam, hush! hush!' Mr Sandbach's voice broke in; and my wife, naturally mortified by the interruption, said no more and moved away. I was surprised to see Rose immediately take her place, and, with more freedom than she generally displayed, ran her fingers through the boy's tousled hair.

'Eustace! Eustace!' she said hurriedly, 'tell me everything – every single thing.'

Slowly he sat up – till then he had lain on his back.

'Oh, Rose—' he whispered, and, my curiosity being aroused, I moved nearer to hear what he was going to say. As I did so, I caught sight of some goat's footmarks in the moist earth beneath the trees.

'Apparently you have had a visit from some goats,' I observed. 'I had no idea they fed up here.'

Eustace laboriously got on to his feet and came to see; and when he saw the footmarks he lay down and rolled on them, as a dog rolls in dirt.

After that there was a grave silence, broken at length by the solemn speech of Mr Sandbach.

'My dear friends,' he said, 'it is best to confess the truth bravely. I know that what I am going to say now is what you are all now feeling. The Evil One has been very near us in bodily form. Time may yet discover some injury that he has wrought among us. But, at present, for myself at all events, I wish to offer up thanks for a merciful deliverance.'

With that he knelt down, and, as the others knelt, I knelt too, though I do not believe in the Devil being allowed to assail us in visible form, as I told Mr Sandbach afterwards. Eustace came too, and knelt quietly enough between his aunts after they had beckoned to him. But when it was over he at once got up, and began hunting for something.

'Why! Someone has cut my whistle in two,' he said. (I had seen Leyland with an open knife in his hand – a superstitious act which I could hardly approve.)

'Well, it doesn't matter,' he continued.

'And why doesn't it matter?' said Mr Sandbach, who has ever since tried to entrap Eustace into an account of that mysterious hour.

'Because I don't want it any more.'

'Why?'

At that he smiled; and, as no one seemed to have anything more to say, I set off as fast as I could through the wood, and hauled up a donkey to carry my poor wife home. Nothing occurred in my absence, except that Rose had again asked Eustace to tell her what had happened; and he, this time, had turned away his head, and had not answered her a single word.

As soon as I returned, we all set off. Eustace walked with difficulty, almost with pain, so that, when we reached the other donkeys, his aunts wished him to mount one of them and ride all the way home. I make it a rule never to interfere between relatives, but I put my foot down at this. As it turned out, I was perfectly right, for the healthy exercise, I suppose, began to thaw Eustace's sluggish mood and loosen his stiffened muscles. He stepped out manfully, for the first time in his life, holding his head up and taking deep draughts of air into his chest. I observed with satisfaction to Miss Mary Robinson that Eustace was at last taking some pride in his personal appearance.

Mr Sandbach sighed, and said that Eustace must be carefully watched, for we none of us understood him yet. Miss Mary Robinson being very much – over much, I think – guided by him, sighed too.

'Come, come, Miss Robinson,' I said, 'there's nothing wrong with Eustace. Our experiences are mysterious, not his. He was astonished at our sudden departure, that's why he was so strange when we returned. He's right enough – improved, if anything.'

'And is the worship of athletics, the cult of insensate activity to be counted as an improvement?' put in Leyland, fixing a large, sorrowful eye on Eustace, who had stopped to scramble on to a rock to pick some cyclamen. 'The passionate desire to rend from Nature the few beauties that have been still left her – that is to be counted as an improvement too?'

It is mere waste of time to reply to such remarks, especially when they come from an unsuccessful artist suffering from a damaged finger. I changed the conversation by asking what we should say at the hotel. After some discussion, it was agreed that we should say nothing, either there or in our letters home. Importunate truth-telling, which brings only bewilderment and discomfort to the hearers, is, in my opinion, a mistake; and, after a long discussion, I managed to make Mr Sandbach acquiesce in my view.

Eustace did not share in our conversation. He was racing about, like a real boy, in the wood to the right. A strange feeling of shame prevented us from openly mentioning our fright to him. Indeed, it seemed almost reasonable to conclude that it had made but little impression on him. So it disconcerted us when he bounded back with an armful of flowering acanthus, calling out:

'Do you suppose Gennaro'll be there when we get back?'

Gennaro was the stop-gap waiter, a clumsy, impertinent fisher-lad, who had been had up from Minori in the absence of the nice English-speaking Emmanuele. It was to him that we owed our scrappy lunch; and I could not conceive why Eustace desired to see him, unless it was to make mock with him of our behaviour.

'Yes, of course he will be there,' said Miss Robinson. 'Why do you ask, dear?'

'Oh, I thought I'd like to see him.'

'And why?' snapped Mr Sandbach.

'Because, because I do, I do; because, because I do.' He danced away into the darkening wood to the rhythm of his words.

'This is very extraordinary,' said Mr Sandbach. 'Did he like Gennaro before?'

'Gennaro has been here only two days,' said Rose, 'and I know that they haven't spoken to each other a dozen times.'

Each time Eustace returned from the wood his spirits were higher. Once he came whooping down on us as a wild Indian, and another time he made believe to be a dog. The last time he came back with a poor dazed hare, too frightened to move, sitting on his arm. He was getting too uproarious, I thought; and we were all glad to leave the wood, and start upon the steep staircase path that leads down into Ravello. It was late and turning dark and we made all the speed we could, Eustace scurrying in front of us like a goat.

Just where the staircase path debouches on the white high road, the next extraordinary incident of this extraordinary day occurred. Three old women were standing by the wayside. They, like ourselves, had come down from the woods, and they were resting their heavy bundles of fuel on the low parapet of the road. Eustace stopped in front of them, and, after a moment's deliberation, stepped forward and – kissed the left-hand one on the cheek!

'My good fellow!' exclaimed Mr Sandbach, 'are you quite crazy?'

Eustace said nothing, but offered the old woman some of his flowers, and then hurried on. I looked back; and the old woman's companions seemed as much astonished at the proceeding as we were. But she herself had put the flowers in her bosom, and was murmuring blessings.

This salutation of the old lady was the first example of Eustace's strange behaviour, and we were both surprised and alarmed. It was useless talking to him, for he either made silly replies, or else bounded away without replying at all.

He made no reference on the way home to Gennaro, and I hoped that that was forgotten. But when we came to the piazza, in front of the cathedral, he screamed out: 'Gennaro! Gennaro!' at the top of his voice, and began running up the little alley that led to the hotel. Sure enough, there was Gennaro at the end of it, with his arms and legs sticking out of the nice little English-speaking waiter's dress suit, and a dirty fisherman's cap on his head – for, as the poor landlady truly said, however much she superintended his toilette, he always managed to introduce something incongruous into it before he had done.

Eustace sprang to meet him, and leapt right up into his arms, and put his own arms round his neck. And this in the presence, not only of us, but also of the landlady, the chambermaid, the facchino, and of two American ladies who were coming for a few days' visit to the little hotel.

I always make a point of behaving pleasantly to Italians, however little they may deserve it; but this habit of promiscuous intimacy was perfectly intolerable, and could only lead to familiarity and mortification for all. Taking Miss Robinson aside, I asked her permission to speak seriously to Eustace on the subject of intercourse with social inferiors. She granted it; but I determined to wait till the absurd boy had calmed down a little from the excitement of the day. Meanwhile, Gennaro, instead of attending to the wants of the two new ladies, carried Eustace into the house, as if it was the most natural thing in the world.

'Ho capito,' I heard him say as he passed me. 'Ho capito' is the Italian for 'I have understood'; but, as Eustace had not spoken to him, I could not see the force of the remark. It served to increase our bewilderment, and, by the time we sat down at the dinner-table, our imaginations and our tongues were alike exhausted.

I omit from this account the various comments that were made, as few of them seem worthy of being recorded. But, for three or four hours, seven of us were pouring forth our bewilderment in a stream of appropriate and inappropriate exclamations. Some traced a connexion between our behaviour in the afternoon and the behaviour of Eustace now. Others saw no connexion at all. Mr

Sandbach still held to the possibility of infernal influences, and also said that he ought to have a doctor. Leyland only saw the development of 'that unspeakable Philistine, the boy'. Rose maintained, to my surprise, that everything was excusable; while I began to see that the young gentleman wanted a sound thrashing. The poor Miss Robinsons swayed helplessly about between these diverse opinions; inclining now to careful supervision, now to acquiescence, now to corporal chastisement now to Eno's Fruit Salt.

Dinner passed off fairly well, though Eustace was terribly fidgety, Gennaro as usual dropping the knives and spoons, and hawking and clearing his throat. He only knew a few words of English, and we were all reduced to Italian for making known our wants. Eustace, who had picked up a little somehow, asked for some oranges. To my annoyance, Gennaro, in his answer, made use of the second person singular – a form only used when addressing those who are both intimates and equals. Eustace had brought it on himself; but an impertinence of this kind was an affront to us all, and I was determined to speak, and to speak at once.

When I heard him clearing the table I went in, and, summoning up my Italian, or rather Neapolitan – the Southern dialects are execrable – I said, 'Gennaro! I heard you address Signor Eustace with "Tu".'

'It is true.'

'You are not right. You must use "Lei" or "Voi" – more polite forms. And remember that, though Signor Eustace is sometimes silly and foolish – this afternoon for example – yet you must always behave respectfully to him; for he is a young English gentleman, and you are a poor Italian fisherboy.'

I know that speech sounds terribly snobbish, but in Italian one can say things that one would never dream of saying in English. Besides, it is no good speaking delicately to persons of that class. Unless you put things plainly, they take a vicious pleasure in mis-understanding you.

An honest English fisherman would have landed me one in the eye in a minute for such a remark, but the wretched downtrodden Italians have no pride. Gennaro only sighed, and said: 'It is true.'

'Quite so,' I said, and turned to go. To my indignation I heard him add: 'But sometimes it is not important.'

'What do you mean?' I shouted.

He came close up to me with horrid gesticulating fingers.

'Signor Tytler, I wish to say this. If Eustazio asks me to call him "Voi", I will call him "Voi". Otherwise, no.'

With that he seized up a tray of dinner things, and fled from the room with them; and I heard two more wine-glasses go on the courtyard floor.

I was now fairly angry, and strode out to interview Eustace. But he had gone to bed, and the landlady, to whom I also wished to speak, was engaged. After more vague wonderings obscurely expressed owing to the presence of Janet and the two American ladies, we all went to bed, too, after a harassing and most extraordinary day.

# III

But the day was nothing to the night.

I suppose I had slept for about four hours, when I woke suddenly thinking I heard a noise in the garden. And, immediately, before my eyes were open, cold terrible fear seized me – not fear of something that was happening, like the fear in the wood, but fear of something that might happen.

Our room was on the first floor, looking out on to the garden – or terrace, it was rather a wedge-shaped block of ground covered with roses and vines, and intersected with little asphalt paths. It was bounded on the small side by the house; round the two long sides ran a wall, only three feet above the terrace level, but with a good twenty feet drop over it into the olive yards, for the ground fell very precipitously away.

Trembling all over, I stole to the window. There, pattering up and down the asphalt paths, was something white. I was too much alarmed to see clearly; and in the uncertain light of the stars the thing took all manner of curious shapes. Now it was a great dog, now an enormous white bat, now a mass of quickly travelling cloud. It would bounce like a ball, or take short flights like a bird, or glide slowly like a wraith. It gave no sound – save the pattering sound of what, after all, must be human feet. And at last the obvious explanation forced itself upon my disordered mind; and I realized that Eustace had got out of bed, and that we were in for something more.

I hastily dressed myself, and went down into the dining-room which opened upon the terrace. The door was already unfastened.

My terror had almost entirely passed away, but for quite five minutes I struggled with a curious cowardly feeling, which bade me not interfere with the poor strange boy, but leave him to his ghostly patterings, and merely watch him from the window to see he took no harm.

But better impulses prevailed and, opening the door, I called out: 'Eustace! what on earth are you doing? Come in at once.'

He stopped his antics and said: 'I hate my bedroom. I could not stop in it, it is too small.'

'Come! come! I'm tired of affectation. You've never complained of it before.'

'Besides, I can't see anything – no flowers, no leaves, no sky: only a stone wall.' The outlook of Eustace's room certainly was limited; but, as I told him, he had never complained of it before.

'Eustace, you talk like a child. Come in! Prompt obedience, if you please.'

He did not move.

'Very well: I shall carry you in by force,' I added, and made a few steps towards him. But I was soon convinced of the futility of pursuing a boy through a tangle of asphalt paths, and went in instead to call Mr Sandbach and Leyland to my aid.

When I returned with them he was worse than ever. He would not even answer us when we spoke, but began singing and chattering to himself in a most alarming way.

'It's a case for the doctor now,' said Mr Sandbach, gravely tapping his forehead.

He had stopped his running, and was singing, first low, then loud – singing five-finger exercises, scales, hymn tunes, scraps of Wagner – anything that came into his head. His voice – a very untuneful voice – grew stronger and stronger, and he ended with a tremendous shout which boomed like a gun among the mountains, and awoke everyone who was still sleeping in the hotel. My poor wife and the two girls appeared at their respective windows, and the American ladies were heard violently ringing their bell.

'Eustace,' we all cried, 'stop! Stop, dear boy, and come into the house.'

He shook his head, and started off again – talking this time. Never have I listened to such an extraordinary speech. At any other time it would have been ludicrous, for here was a boy, with no sense of beauty and a puerile command of words, attempting to tackle themes which the greatest poets have found almost beyond their power. Eustace Robinson, aged fourteen, was standing in his nightshirt saluting, praising, and blessing the great forces and manifestations of Nature.

He spoke first of night and the stars and planets above his head, of the swarms of fireflies below him, of the invisible sea below the fireflies, of the great rocks covered with anemones and shells that were slumbering in the invisible sea. He spoke of the rivers and waterfalls, of the ripening bunches of grapes, of the smoking cone of Vesuvius and the hidden fire-channels that made the smoke, of the myriads of lizards who were lying curled up in the crannies of the sultry earth, of the showers of white rose-leaves that were tangled in his hair. And then he spoke of the rain and the wind by which all things are changed, of the air through which all things live, and of the woods in which all things can be hidden.

Of course, it was all absurdly high faluting: yet I could have kicked Leyland for audibly observing that it was 'a diabolical carica-ture of all that was most holy and beautiful in life'.

'And then' – Eustace was going on in the pitiable conversational doggerel which was his only mode of expression – 'and then there are men, but I can't make them out so well.' He knelt down by the parapet, and rested his head on his arms.

'Now's the time,' whispered Leyland. I hate stealth, but we darted forward and endeavoured to catch hold of him from behind, He was away in a twinkling, but turned round at once to look at us. As far as I could see in the starlight, he was crying. Leyland rushed at him again, and we tried to corner him among the asphalt paths, but without the slightest approach to success.

We returned, breathless and discomfited, leaving him to his madness in the farther corner of the terrace. But my Rose had an inspiration.

'Papa,' she called from the window, 'if you get Gennaro, he might be able to catch him for you.'

I had no wish to ask a favour of Gennaro, but, as the landlady had by now appeared on the scene, I begged her to summon him from the charcoal-bin in which he slept, and make him try what he could do.

She soon returned, and was shortly followed by Gennaro, attired in a dress coat, without either waistcoat, shirt, or vest, and a ragged pair of what had been trousers, cut short above the knees for purposes of wading. The landlady, who had quite picked up English ways, rebuked him for the incongruous and even indecent appearance which he presented.

'I have a coat and I have trousers. What more do you desire?'

'Never mind, Signora Scafetti,' I put in. 'As there are no ladies here, it is not of the slightest consequence.' Then, turning to Gennaro, I said: 'The aunts of Signor Eustace wish you to fetch him into the house.'

He did not answer.

'Do you hear me? He is not well. I order you to fetch him into the house.'

'Fetch! Fetch!' said Signora Scafetti, and shook him roughly by the arm.

'Eustazio is well where he is.'

'Fetch! Fetch!' Signora Scafetti screamed, and let loose a flood of Italian, most of which, I am glad to say, I could not follow. I glanced up nervously at the girls' window, but they hardly know as much as I do, and I am thankful to say that none of us caught one word of Gennaro's answer.

The two yelled and shouted at each other for quite ten minutes, at the end of which Gennaro rushed back to his charcoal-bin and Signora Scafetti burst into tears, as well she might, for she greatly valued her English guests.

'He says,' she sobbed, 'that Signor Eustace is well where he is, and that he will not fetch him. I can do no more.'

But I could, for, in my stupid British way, I have got some insight into the Italian character. I followed Mr Gennaro to his place of repose, and found him wriggling down on to a dirty sack.

'I wish you to fetch Signor Eustace to me,' I began.

He hurled at me an unintelligible reply.

'If you fetch him, I will give you this.' And out of my pocket I took a new ten-lira note.

This time he did not answer.

'This note is equal to ten lire in silver,' I continued, for I knew that the poor-class Italian is unable to conceive of a single large sum.

'I know it.'

'That is, two hundred soldi.'

'I do not desire them. Eustazio is my friend.'

I put the note into my pocket.

'Besides, you would not give it me.'

'I am an Englishman. The English always do what they promise.'

'That is true.' It is astonishing how the most dishonest of nations trust us. Indeed, they often trust us more than we trust one another. Gennaro knelt up on his sack. It was too dark to see his face, but I could feel his warm garlicky breath coming out in gasps, and I knew that the eternal avarice of the South had laid hold upon him. 'I could not fetch Eustazio to the house. He might die there.'

'You need not do that,' I replied patiently. 'You need only bring him to me; and I will stand outside in the garden.' And to this, as if it were something quite different, the pitiable youth consented.

'But give me first the ten lire.'

'No' – for I knew the kind of person with whom I had to deal. Once faithless, always faithless.

We returned to the terrace, and Gennaro, without a single word, pattered off towards the pattering that could be heard at the remoter end. Mr Sandbach, Leyland, and myself moved away a little from the house, and stood in the shadow of the white climbing roses, practically invisible.

We heard 'Eustazio' called, followed by absurd cries of pleasure from the poor boy. The pattering ceased, and we heard them talking. Their voices got nearer, and presently I could discern them through the creepers, the grotesque figure of the young man, and the slim little white-robed boy. Gennaro had his arm round Eustace's neck, and Eustace was talking away in his fluent, slip-shod Italian.

'I understand almost everything,' I heard him say. 'The trees, hills, stars, water, I can see all. But isn't it odd! I can't make out men a bit. Do you know what I mean?'

'Ho capito,' said Gennaro gravely, and took his arm off Eustace's shoulder. But I made the new note crackle in my pocket; and he heard it. He stuck his hand out with a jerk; and the unsuspecting Eustace gripped it in his own.

'It is odd!' Eustace went on – they were quite close now – 'It almost seems as if – as if—'

I darted out and caught hold of his arm, and Leyland got hold of the other arm, and Mr Sandbach hung on to his feet. He gave shrill heart-piercing screams; and the white roses, which were falling early that year, descended in showers on him as we dragged him into the house.

As soon as we entered the house he stopped shrieking; but floods of tears silently burst forth and spread over his upturned face.

'Not to my room,' he pleaded. 'It is so small.'

His infinitely dolorous look filled me with strange pity, but what could I do? Besides, his window was the only one that had bars to it.

'Never mind, dear boy,' said kind Mr Sandbach. 'I will bear you company till the morning.'

At this his convulsive struggles began again. 'Oh, please, not that. Anything but that. I will promise to lie still and not to cry more than I can help, if I am left alone.'

So we laid him on the bed, and drew the sheets over him, and left him sobbing bitterly, and saying: 'I nearly saw everything, and now I can see nothing at all.'

We informed the Miss Robinsons of all that had happened, and returned to the dining-room, where we found Signora Scafetti and Gennaro whispering together. Mr Sandbach got pen and paper, and began writing to the English doctor at Naples. I at once drew out the note, and flung it down on the table to Gennaro.

'Here is your pay,' I said sternly, for I was thinking of the Thirty Pieces of Silver.

'Thank you very much, sir,' said Gennaro, and grabbed it.

He was going off, when Leyland, whose interest and indifference were always equally misplaced, asked him what Eustace had meant by saying 'he could not make out men a bit'.

'I cannot say. Signor Eustazio' (I was glad to observe a little deference at last) 'has a subtle brain. He understands many things.'

'But I heard you say you understood,' Leyland persisted.

'I understand, but I cannot explain. I am a poor Italian fisherlad. Yet, listen: I will try.' I saw to my alarm that his manner was changing, and tried to stop him. But he sat down on the edge of the table and started off, with some absolutely incoherent remarks.

'It is sad,' he observed at last. 'What has happened is very sad. But what can I do? I am poor. It is not I.'

I turned away in contempt. Leyland went on asking questions. He wanted to know who it was that Eustace had in his mind when he spoke.

'That is easy to say,' Gennaro gravely answered. 'It is you, it is I. It is all in this house, and many outside it. If he wishes for mirth, we discomfort him. If he asks to be alone, we disturb him. He

longed for a friend, and found none for fifteen years. Then he found
me, and the first night I – I who have been in the woods and
understood things too – betray him to you and send him in to die.
But what could I do?'

'Gently, gently,' said I.

'Oh, assuredly he will die. He will lie in the small room all night,
and in the morning he will be dead. That I know for certain.'

'There, that will do,' said Mr Sandbach. 'I shall be sitting with
him.'

'Filomena Giusti sat all night with Caterina, but Caterina was
dead in the morning. They would not let her out, though I begged,
and prayed, and cursed, and beat the door, and climbed the wall.
They were ignorant fools, and thought I wished to carry her away.
And in the morning she was dead.'

'What is all this?' I asked Signora Scafetti.

'All kinds of stories will get about,' she replied, 'and he, least of
anyone, has reason to repeat them.'

'And I am alive now,' he went on, 'because I had neither parents
nor relatives nor friends, so that, when the first night came, I could
run through the woods, and climb the rocks, and plunge into the
water, until I had accomplished my desire!'

We heard a cry from Eustace's room – a faint but steady sound,
like the sound of wind in a distant wood heard by one standing in
tranquillity.

'That,' said Gennaro, 'was the last noise of Caterina. I was
hanging on to her window then, and it blew out past me.'

And, lifting up his hand, in which my ten-lira note was safely
packed, he solemnly cursed Mr Sandbach, and Leyland, and myself,
and Fate, because Eustace was dying in the upstairs room. Such is
the working of the Southern mind; and I verily believe that he
would not have moved even then, had not Leyland, that unspeakable idiot, upset the lamp with his elbow. It was a patent self-
extinguishing lamp, bought by Signora Scafetti, at my special
request, to replace the dangerous thing that she was using. The
result was, that it went out; and the mere physical change from
light to darkness had more power over the ignorant animal nature
of Gennaro than the most obvious dictates of logic and reason.

I felt, rather than saw, that he had left the room, and shouted
out to Mr Sandbach: 'Have you got the key to Eustace's room in
your pocket?' But Mr Sandbach and Leyland were both on the

floor, having mistaken each other for Gennaro, and some more precious time was wasted in finding a match. Mr Sandbach had only just time to say that he had left the key in the door, in case the Miss Robinsons wished to pay Eustace a visit, when we heard a noise on the stairs, and there was Gennaro, carrying Eustace down.

We rushed out and blocked up the passage, and they lost heart and retreated to the upper landing.

'Now they are caught,' cried Signora Scafetti. 'There is no other way out.'

We were cautiously ascending the staircase, when there was a terrific scream from my wife's room, followed by a heavy thud on the asphalt path. They had leapt out of her window.

I reached the terrace just in time to see Eustace jumping over the parapet of the garden wall. This time I knew for certain he would be killed. But he alighted in an olive tree, looking like a great white moth, and from the tree he slid on to the earth. And as soon as his bare feet touched the clods of earth he uttered a strange loud cry, such as I should not have thought the human voice could have produced, and disappeared among the trees below.

'He has understood and he is saved,' cried Gennaro, who was still sitting on the asphalt path. 'Now, instead of dying he will live!'

'And you, instead of keeping the ten lire, will give them up,' I retorted, for at this theatrical remark I could contain myself no longer.

'The ten lire are mine,' he hissed back in a scarcely audible voice. He clasped his hand over his breast to protect his ill-gotten gains, and, as he did so, he swayed forward and fell upon his face on the path. He had not broken any limbs, and a leap like that would never have killed an Englishman, for the drop was not great. But those miserable Italians have no stamina. Something had gone wrong inside him, and he was dead.

The morning was still far off, but the morning breeze had begun, and more rose leaves fell on us as we carried him in. Signora Scafetti burst into screams at the sight of the dead body, and, far down the valley towards the sea, there still resounded the shouts and the laughter of the escaping boy.

# An Invitation to the Hunt

## George Hitchcock

'*The laws of Heaven and Hell are versatile,*' *says Silvina Ocampo.*
'*Going to one place or the other depends on the tiniest detail. I know
people who because of a broken key or a wicker cage have gone to Hell,
and others who because of a bit of newspaper or a cup of milk have
gone to Heaven.*'

*Punishment that we cannot understand, reprisal for unknown sin, is
one of the themes of Kafka's 'In the Penal Colony', and also of George
Hitchcock's 'An Invitation to the Hunt'. The ending is perhaps expected
but not for that reason less frightening and horrible.*

His first impulse upon receiving it had been to throw it in the fire.
They did not travel in the same social set and he felt it presumptuous
of them, on the basis of a few words exchanged in the shopping
centre and an occasional chance meeting on the links, to include
him in their plans. Of course, he had often seen them – moving
behind the high iron grillwork fence that surrounded their estates,
the women in pastel tea-gowns serving martinis beneath the striped
lawn umbrellas and the men suave and bronzed in dinner jackets
or sailing togs – but it had always been as an outsider, almost as a
Peeping Tom.

'The most charitable interpretation,' he told Emily, 'would be to
assume that it is a case of mistaken identity.'

'But how could it be?' his wife answered holding the envelope in
her slender reddened fingers. 'There is only one Fred Perkins in
Marine Gardens and the house number is perfectly accurate.'

'But there's no earthly reason for it. Why *me* of all people?'

'I should think,' said Emily helping him on with his coat and
fitting the two sandwiches neatly wrapped in aluminium foil into
his pocket, 'that you would be delighted. It's a real step upward for

you. You've often enough complained of our lack of social contacts since we moved out of the city.'

'It's fantastic,' Perkins said, 'and of course I'm not going,' and he ran out of his one-storey shingled California ranch cottage to join the car pool which waited for him at the kerb.

All the way to the city, like a dog with a troublesome bone, he worried and teased at the same seemingly insoluble problem: how had he attracted their notice? What was there in his appearance or manner which had set him apart from all the rest? There had been, of course, that day the younger ones had come in off the bay on their racing cutter, when by pure chance (as it now seemed) he had been the one man on the pier within reach of the forward mooring line. He recalled the moment with satisfaction – the tanned, blonde girl leaning out from the bow-sprit with a coil of manila in her capable hand. 'Catch!' she had cried and at the same instant spun the looping rope towards him through the air. He had caught it deftly and snubbed it about the bitt, easing the cutter's forward motion. 'Thanks!' she had called across the narrowing strip of blue water, but there had been no sign of recognition in her eyes, nor had she when a moment later the yacht was securely tied to the wharf invited him aboard or even acknowledged his continuing presence on the pier. No, that could hardly have been the moment he sought.

Once at the Agency and there bedded down in a day of invoices, he tried to put the problem behind him, but it would not rest. At last, victim of a fretful pervasive anxiety which ultimately made concentration impossible, he left his desk and made his way to the hall telephone (years ago a written reproof from Henderson had left him forever scrupulous about using the Agency phone for private business) where he deposited a dime and rang his golf partner, Bianchi.

They met for lunch at a quiet restaurant on Maiden Lane. Bianchi was a young man recently out of law school and still impressed by the improbable glitter of society. This will give him a thrill, Perkins thought, he's a second generation Italian and it isn't likely that he's ever laid eyes on one of these.

'The problem is,' he said aloud, 'that I'm not sure why they invited me. I hardly know them. At the same time I don't want to do anything that might be construed as – well – as – '

'Defiance?' Bianchi supplied.

'Perhaps. Or call it unnecessary rudeness. We can't ignore their influence.'

'Well, first let's have a look at it,' Bianchi said finishing his vermouth. 'Do you have it with you?'

'Of course'.

'Well, let's see it.'

Poor Bianchi! It was obvious that he was dying for an invitation himself and just as obvious from his slurred, uncultivated English and his skin acne that he would never receive one. Perkins took the envelope from his notecase and extracted the stiff silver-edged card which he lay face up on the table.

'It's engraved,' he pointed out.

'They always are,' Bianchi said putting on his shell-rimmed reading glasses, 'but that doesn't prove a thing. They aren't the real article without the watermark.' He held the envelope up against the table lamp hoping, Perkins imagined, that the whole thing would prove fraudulent.

'It's there,' he admitted, 'by God, it's there.' And Perkins detected a note of grudging respect in his voice as he pointed out the two lions rampant and the neatly quartered shield. 'It's the real McCoy and no mistake.'

'But what do I do now?' Perkins asked with a hint of irritation.

'First let's see the details,' Bianchi studied the engraved Old English script:

*The pleasure of your company at the hunt*
*is requested*
*on August sixteenth of this year*

R.S.V.P.                    *Appropriate attire ob.*

'The "ob" ' he explained, 'is for "obligatory".'

'I know that.'

'Well?'

'The problem is,' Perkins said in an unnecessarily loud voice, 'that I have no intention of going.'

He was aware that Bianchi was staring at him incredulously but this merely strengthened his own stubbornness.

'It's an imposition. I don't know them and it happens I have other plans for the sixteenth.'

'All right, all right,' Bianchi said soothingly, 'no need to shout. I can hear you perfectly well.'

With a flush of embarrassment Perkins looked about the restaurant and caught the reproving gaze of the waiters. Obviously he had become emotionally involved in his predicament to the extent of losing control; he hastily reinserted the invitation in its envelope and returned it to his notecase. Bianchi had arisen and was folding his napkin.

'Do as you like,' he said, 'but I know a dozen men around town who would give their right arm for that invitation.'

'But I don't hunt!'

'You can always learn,' Bianchi said coldly and signalling for the waiter, paid his cheque and left.

Meanwhile, word of the invitation had apparently gotten around the Agency, for Perkins noticed that he was treated with new interest and concern. Miss Nethersole, the senior librarian, accosted him by the water-cooler in deep thrush-like tones.

'I'm so thrilled for you, Mr Perkins! There is no one else in the whole office who deserves it more.'

'That's very sweet of you,' he answered attempting to hide his embarrassment by bending over the faucet, 'but the truth is I'm not going.'

'Not going?' The rich pear-shaped tones (the product of innumerable diction lessons) broke into a cascade of rippling laughter. 'How can you say that with a straight face? Have you seen the rotogravure section?'

'No,' Perkins said shortly.

'It's all there. The guests, the caterers, even a map of the course, I should give anything to be invited!'

No doubt you would, Perkins thought, looking at her square masculine breastless figure, it's just the sort of sport which would entertain you, but aloud he merely said, 'I have other commitments,' and went back to his desk.

After lunch he found the rotogravure section stuck under the blotter on his desk. Aware that every eye in the office was secretly on him he did not dare unfold it but stuck it in his coat pocket and only later after he had arisen casually and strolled down the long row of desks to the men's room, did he in the privacy of a locked cubicle and with trembling hands spread it out on his knees. Miss Nethersole had been right: the guest list was truly staggering. It filled three columns in six point type; titles gleamed like diamonds in the newsprint; there were generals, statesmen, manufacturers and university presidents; editors of great magazines, movie queens and polar explorers; radiocasters, regents, prize-winning novelists – but Perkins could not begin to digest the list. His eyes ferreted among the jumbled syllables and at last with a little catch of delight he came upon the one he had unconsciously sought: 'Mr Fred Perkins.' That was all, no identification, no LID nor Pres. Untd Etc. Corp. He read his one name over four times and then neatly folded the paper and put it back in his pocket.

'Well,' he said with a thin-lipped smile, 'I'm not going and that's that.'

But apparently Emily, too, had seen the paper.

'The phone has been ringing all day,' she informed him as soon as he entered the house and deposited his briefcase on the cane-bottomed chair by the TV set. 'Of course everyone is furiously envious but they don't dare admit it so I've been receiving nothing but congratulations.'

She helped him off with his coat.

'Come into the dining-room,' she said mysteriously, 'I've a little surprise for you.' The telephone rang. 'No, wait, you mustn't go in without me. It will only be a minute.'

He stood uneasily shifting from one foot to the other until she returned.

'It was the Corrigans,' she announced. 'Beth wants us to come to a little dinner party on the seventeenth. Naturally,' she added, 'the date isn't accidental. They expect to pump you for all the details before anyone else in the subdivision hears about it. Now come on—' and like a happy child on Christmas morning she took his hand and led him into the dining-room.

Perkins followed her with mumbled protestations.

'Isn't it gorgeous?'

There, spread out on the mahogany table (not yet fully paid for) were a pair of tan whipcord breeches, a tattersall vest and a bright pink coat with brass buttons. In the centre of the table where the floral piece usually stood was a gleaming pair of boots.

'And here's the stock,' she said waving a bright bit of yellow silk under his eyes. 'You can wear one of my stickpins, the one with the onyx in the jade setting I think would be best. And I've ordered a riding crop with a silver handle, it's to be delivered tomorrow.'

'You're taking a great deal for granted,' Perkins said. He picked up the boots and felt the soft pliable waxed leather. 'They must be very expensive. Where did you get the money for them?'

Emily laughed. 'They're on time, silly, we have twelve months to pay.'

'I'll look ridiculous in that coat.'

'No, you won't. You're a very handsome man and I've always said you would cut a fine figure anywhere.'

'Well,' said Perkins hesitantly, 'I suppose we can send them back if I decide not to go.'

After dinner Bianchi drove by in his old Studebaker and obviously a bit fuzzy from too many cocktails. Emily opened the door for him.

'Fred is in the bedroom trying on his new hunting outfit,' she said, 'he'll be out in a moment.'

'Who is it?' Perkins shouted and when she answered he hastily took off the pink coat (which was a bit tight under the arms anyway) and slipped on his smoking-jacket. He remembered the scene in the restaurant and felt ashamed to let Bianchi see that his resolution was wavering.

'Look, Fred,' Bianchi said when they were seated in the living-room over their Old Fashioneds, 'I hope you've finally changed your mind – about—' He glanced at Emily to see how much she knew of the invitation.

'Go ahead. I've told her everything,' Perkins said.

'Well, you can certainly decline if you feel strongly about it,' said Bianchi in his best legal manner, 'but I don't advise it. If they once get the idea you're snubbing them they can make things pretty unpleasant for you – and in more ways than one.'

'But this is ridiculous!' Emily interrupted. 'He is not going to decline. Are you darling?'

'Well,' Perkins said.

She caught the indecision in his voice and went on vehemently, 'This is the first social recognition you've ever had, Fred, you can't think of declining. Think what it will mean for the children! In a few years they'll be ready for college. And you know what that means. And do you seriously plan to remain in this house for the rest of your life?'

'There's nothing wrong with this house,' Perkins said defensively, reflecting that the house was not yet paid for but already Emily was finding fault with it.

'Suppose the invitation was a mistake,' Emily continued. 'I'm not saying that it was, but suppose it just for a minute. Is that any the less reason why you shouldn't accept?'

'But I don't like hunting,' Perkins interjected weakly. 'And I'll look ridiculous on a horse.'

'No more ridiculous than ninety per cent of the other guests. Do you suppose Senator Gorman will exactly look like a centaur? And what about your boss, Mr Henderson? He's certainly no polo player.'

'Is he going?' Perkins asked in surprise.

'He certainly is. If you had paid the slightest attention to the guest list you would have noticed it.'

'All right, all right,' Perkins said, 'then I'll go.'

'I think that's the wisest course,' said Bianchi with a slightly blurry attempt at the judicial manner.

He wrote his acceptance that evening, in pen and ink on a plain stiff card with untinted edges.

'It's all right for them to use silvered edges,' Emily pointed out, 'but they're apt to think it shows too much swank if you do.' She phoned a messenger service – explaining, 'it's not the sort of thing you deliver by mail' - and the next morning a uniformed messenger dropped his acceptance off at the gatekeeper's lodge.

The ensuing week passed swiftly. Emily fitted the pink coat and the tan breeches, marked them with chalk and sent them out for alterations. The yellow stock, she decided, would not do after all – 'a bit too flashy,' she observed – so it was replaced by one in conservative cream. The alteration necessitated a change in stickpin and cufflinks to simple ones of hammered silver which she selected in the village. The expense was ruinous but she over-rode his objections. 'So much depends upon your making a good impression and after all if it goes well you will be invited again and can always use the same clothes. And the cufflinks will be nice with a dinner jacket,' she added as an afterthought.

At the Agency he found that he basked in a new glow of respect. On Monday Mr Presby, the office manager, suggested that he might be more comfortable at a desk nearer the window.

'Of course, with air-conditioning it doesn't make as much difference as it did in the old days, but still there's a bit of a view and it helps break the monotony.'

Perkins thanked him for his thoughtfulness.

'Not at all,' Presby answered, 'it's a small way of showing it, but we appreciate your services here, Mr Perkins.'

And on Friday afternoon Henderson himself, the Agency chief and reputedly high in the councils of Intercontinental Guaranty & Trust, stopped by his desk on his way home. Since in a dozen years he had received scarcely a nod from Henderson, Perkins was understandably elated.

'I understand we'll be seeing each other tomorrow,' Henderson said resting one buttock momentarily on the corner of Perkins' desk.

'Looks like it,' Perkins said noncommittally.

'I damn well hope they serve whisky,' Henderson said. 'I suppose hot punch is strictly in the old hunting tradition but it gives me gas.'

'I think I'll take a flask of my own,' said Perkins as if it were his longstanding habit at hunts.

'Good idea,' Henderson said getting up. And as he left the office he called back over his shoulder, 'Save a nip for me, Fred!'

After dinner that evening Emily put the children to bed and the two of them then strolled to the edge of Marine Gardens and gazed across the open fields towards the big houses behind their iron grills. Even from that distance they could see signs of bustle and activity. The driveway under the elms seemed full of long black limousines and on the spreading lawns they could make out the caterer's assistants setting up green tables for the morrow's breakfast. As they watched, an exercise boy on a chestnut mare trotted by outside the fence leading a string of some forty sleek brown and black horses toward the distant stables.

'The weather will be gorgeous,' Emily said as they turned back. 'There's just a hint of autumn in the air already.'

Perkins did not answer her. He was lost in his own reflections. He had not wanted to go, part of him still did not want to go. He realized that he was trembling with nervous apprehension; but of course that might have been expected – the venture into new surrounding, the fear of failure, of committing some social gaffe, of not living up to what they must certainly expect of him – these were causes enough for his trembling hands and the uneven palpitations of his heart.

'Let's go to bed early,' Emily said, 'you'll need a good night's sleep.'

Perkins nodded and they went into their house. But despite the obvious necessity, Perkins slept very little that night. He tossed about envisaging every conceivable social humiliation until his wife at last complained, 'you kick and turn so that I can't get a bit of sleep,' and took her pillow and a blanket and went into the children's room.

He had set the alarm for six – an early start was called for – but it was long before that when he was awakened.

'Perkins? Fred Perkins?'

He sat bolt upright in bed.

'Yes?'

It was light but the sun had not yet risen. There were two men standing in his bedroom. The taller of them, he who had just shaken his shoulder, was dressed in a black leather coat and wore a cap divided into pie-shaped slices of yellow and red.

'Come on, get up!' the man said.

'Hurry along with it,' added the second man, shorter and older but dressed also in leather.

'What is it?' Perkins asked. He was fully awake now and the adrenalin charged his heart so that it pumped with a terrible urgency.

'Get out of bed,' said the larger man and seizing the covers with one hand jerked them back. As he did so Perkins saw the two lions rampant and the quartered shield stamped in gilt on the breast of his leather coat. Trembling, and naked except for his shorts, he rose from his bed into the cool, crisp morning.

'What is it?' he repeated senselessly.

'The hunt, the hunt, it's for the hunt,' said the older man.

'Then let me get my clothes,' Perkins stammered and moved towards the dresser where in the dim light he could see the splendid pink coat and whipcord breeches spread out awaiting his limbs. But as he turned he was struck a sharp blow by the short taped club which he had not observed in the large man's hand.

'You won't be needing them,' his attacker laughed, and out of the corner of his eye Perkins saw the older man pick up the pink coat and holding it by the tails rip it up the centre.

'Look here!' he began but before he could finish the heavy man in black leather twisted his arm sharply behind his back and pushed him out of the French doors into the cold clear sunless air. Behind him he caught a glimpse of Emily in night-clothes appearing suddenly in the door, heard her terrified scream and the tinkle of glass from one of the panes which broke as the short man slammed the door shut. He broke loose and ran in a frenzy across the lawn but the two gamekeepers were soon up with him. They seized him under the armpits and propelled him across the street to the point where Marine Gardens ended and the open country began. There they threw him on to the stubbled ground and the short one drew out a whip.

'Now, run! You son of a bitch, run!' screamed the large man.

Perkins felt the sharp agony of the whip across his bare back. He stumbled to his feet and began to lope across the open fields. The grass cut his bare feet, sweat poured down his naked chest and his mouth was filled with incoherent syllables of protest and outrage, but he ran, he ran, he ran. For already across the rich summery fields he heard the hounds baying and the clear alto note of the huntsman's horn.

# From the 'American Notebooks'

## Nathaniel Hawthorne

*For many years Hawthorne wrote down his impressions and comments, details of things that had struck him and ideas for stories, in a number of small notebooks; his wife published a selection in 1868, four years after his death, and the complete collection was published in 1932. 'These Notebooks are a very singular series of volumes,' wrote Henry James in his book on Hawthorne. 'I doubt whether there is anything exactly corresponding to them in the whole body of literature . . . I am at a loss to perceive how they came to be written.'*

*The reader is struck by the powerful imagination of his ideas; his outlines make up a wonderful collection of never-written tales (though Poe used one as a basis for his story 'Hop-Frog'). Reading someone else's stories we become accomplices in the act of creation; Hawthorne's outlines allow us, more generously than a finished work, an even greater sense of freedom.*

To write a dream, which shall resemble the real course of a dream, with all its inconsistency, its eccentricities and aimlessness – with nevertheless a leading idea running through the whole. Up to this old age of the world, no such thing has ever been written.

Some man of powerful character to command a person, morally subjected to him, to perform some act. The commanding person to suddenly die; and, for all the rest of his life, the subjected one continues to perform that act.

The situation of a man in the midst of a crowd, yet as completely in the power of another, life and all, as if they two were in the deepest solitude.

In an old house, a mysterious knocking might be heard on the wall, where had formerly been a doorway, now bricked up.

A person to be writing a tale, and to find that it shapes itself against his intentions: that the characters act otherwise than he thought: that unforeseen events occur; and a catastrophe comes which he strives in vain to avert. It might shadow forth his own fate – he having made himself one of the personages.

An old looking-glass. Somebody finds out the secret of making all the images that have been reflected in it pass back again across its surface.

A steam engine in a factory to be supposed to possess a malignant spirit; it catches one man's arm, and pulls it off; seizes another by the coat-tails, and almost grapples him bodily; catches a girl by the hair, and scalps her; and finally draws a man, and crushes him to death.

# The Dream

## O. Henry

*William Sydney Porter, who signed his work O. Henry, was one of America's most prolific writers. He was an orphan, and he worked at his uncle's drugstore, then as a ranch-hand, as a singer and finally as a writer. He served a disputed sentence in the federal penitentiary of Columbus, Ohio, for embezzlement, and in 1899 published his first short story, 'Whistling Dick's Christmas Stocking', which included what came to be known as the 'O. Henry twist', or surprise ending.*

*'The Dream' was O. Henry's last story. He left it unfinished; it was completed by the editor of* Cosmopolitan *magazine where it was published in 1910.*

Murray dreamed a dream.

Both psychology and science grope when they would explain to us the strange adventures of our immaterial selves when wandering in the realm of 'Death's twin brother, sleep.' This story will not attempt to be illuminative; it is no more than a record of Murray's dream. One of the most puzzling phases of that strange waking sleep is that dreams which seem to cover months or even years may take place within a few seconds or minutes.

Murray was waiting in his cell in the ward of the condemned. An electric arc light in the ceiling of the corridor shone brightly upon his table. On a sheet of white paper an ant crawled wildly here and there as Murray blocked its way with an envelope. The electrocution was set for eight o'clock in the evening. Murray smiled at the antics of the wisest of insects.

There were seven other condemned men in the chamber. Since he had been there Murray had seen three taken out to their fate; one gone mad and fighting like a wolf caught in a trap; one, no less mad, offering up a sanctimonious lip-service to Heaven; the third, a weakling, collapsed and strapped to a board. He wondered with what credit to himself his own heart, foot, and face would meet his punishment; for this was his evening. He thought it must be nearly eight o'clock.

Opposite his own in the two rows of cells was the cage of Bonifacio, the Sicilian slayer of his betrothed and of two officers who came to arrest him. With him Murray had played checkers many a long hour, each calling his move to his unseen opponent across the corridor.

Bonifacio's great booming voice with its indestructible singing quality called out:

'Eh, Meestro Murray; how you feel – all-a right – yes?'

'All right, Bonifacio,' said Murray steadily, as he allowed the ant to crawl upon the envelope and then dumped it gently on the stone floor.

'Dat's good-a, Meestro Murray. Men like us, we must-a die like-a men. My time come nex'-a week. All-a right. Remember, Meestro Murray, I beat-a you dat las' game of de check. Maybe we play again some-a time. I don'-a know. Maybe we have to call-a de move damn-a loud to play de check where dey goin' send us.'

Bonifacio's hardened philosophy, followed closely by his deafening musical peal of laughter, warmed rather than chilled Murray's numbed heart. Yet, Bonifacio had until next week to live.

The cell-dwellers heard the familiar, loud click of the steel bolts as the door at the end of the corridor was opened. Three men came to Murray's cell and unlocked it. Two were prison guards; the other was 'Len' – no; that was in the old days; now the Reverend Leonard Winston, a friend and neighbour from their barefoot days.

'I got them to let me take the prison chaplain's place,' he said, as he gave Murray's hand one short, strong grip. In his left hand he held a small Bible, with his forefinger marking a page.

Murray smiled slightly and arranged two or three books and some pen-holders orderly on his small table. He would have spoken, but no appropriate words seemed to present themselves to his mind.

The prisoners had christened this cellhouse, eighty feet long, twenty-eight feet wide, Limbo Lane. The regular guard of Limbo Lane, an immense, rough, kindly man, drew a pint bottle of whisky from his pocket and offered it to Murray, saying:

'It's the regular thing, you know. All has it who feel like they need a bracer. No danger of it becoming a habit with 'em, you see.'

Murray drank deep into the bottle.

'That's the boy!' said the guard. 'Just a little nerve tonic, and everything goes smooth as silk.'

They stepped into the corridor, and each one of the doomed seven knew. Limbo Lane is a world on the outside of the world; but it had learned, when deprived of one or more of the five senses, to make another sense supply the deficiency. Each one knew that it was nearly eight, and that Murray was to go to the chair at eight. There is also in the many Limbo Lanes an aristocracy of crime. The man who kills in the open, who beats his enemy or pursuer down, flushed by the primitive emotions and the ardour of combat, holds in contempt the human rat, the spider, and the snake.

So, of the seven condemned only three called their farewells to Murray as he marched down the corridor between the two guards – Bonifacio, Marvin, who had killed a guard while trying to escape from the prison, and Bassett, the train-robber, who was driven to it because the express-messenger wouldn't raise his hands when ordered to do so. The remaining four smouldered, silent, in their cells, no doubt feeling their social ostracism in Limbo Lane society more keenly than they did the memory of their less picturesque offences against the law.

Murray wondered at his own calmness and nearly indifference. In the execution room were about twenty men, a congregation made up of prison officers, newspaper reporters, and lookers-on who had succeeded

Here, in the very middle of a sentence, the hand of Death interrupted the telling of O. Henry's last story. He had planned to make this story different from his others, the beginning of a new series in a style he had not previously attempted. 'I want to show the public,' he said, 'that I can write something new – new for me, I mean – a story without slang, a straightforward dramatic plot treated in a way that will come nearer my idea of real story-writing.' Before starting to write the present story, he outlined briefly how he intended to develop it: Murray, the criminal accused and convicted of the brutal murder of his sweetheart – a murder prompted by jealous rage – at first faces the death penalty, calm, and, to all outward appearances, indifferent to his fate. As he nears the electric chair he is overcome by a revulsion of feeling. He is left dazed, stupefied, stunned. The entire scene in the death-chamber – the witnesses, the spectators, the preparations for execution – become unreal to him. The thought flashes through his brain that a terrible mistake is being made. Why is he being strapped to the chair? What has he done? What crime has he committed? In the few moments while the straps are being adjusted a vision comes to him. He dreams a dream. He sees a little country cottage, bright, sunlit, nestling in a bower of flowers. A woman is there, and a little child. He speaks with them and finds that they are his wife, his child – and the cottage their home. So, after all, it is a mistake. Some one has frightfully, irretrievably blundered. The accusation, the trial, the conviction, the sentence to death in the electric chair – all a dream. He takes his wife in his arms and kisses the child. Yes, here is happiness. It was a dream. Then – at a sign from the prison warden – the fatal current is turned on.

Murray had dreamed the wrong dream.

# The Authors

*Most of the following biographical information has been taken from the Oxford Companions to English, American, Spanish, French, German and Canadian Literature, and from the Penguin Companion to Literature. A.M.*

**Akutagawa, Ryunosuke**. Japanese novelist (1892–1927), translator of many Western writers. His best-known novel is *Kappa* (1927). His collected tales include 'Rashomon' (1915), 'The Nose' (1916), 'Hell Screen' (1918), 'In a Grove' (1922) and 'Tobacco and the Devil' (1917).

**Alarcón, Pedro Antonio De**. Spanish novelist (1833–91). He achieved popular success with *Journal of an eye-witness of the war in Africa* (1859) and fame with two short novels: *The Three-cornered Hat* (1874) and *Captain Poison* (1881). He is the author of several short stories.

**Andersen, Hans Christian**. Danish writer of fairy tales (1805–75). Among his most famous stories are 'The Ugly Duckling', 'The Tinderbox', 'The Princess and the Pea', 'The Emperor's New Clothes'. He also wrote six novels, several travel books and autobiographies, poems and plays.

**Aymé, Marcel**. French writer (1902–67). His novels include *The Green Mare* (1933), *Other People's Faces* (1952) and *The Stowaway Ox* (1939). He was a master of the humorous short story, of which he published several collections, and entertaining plays. His books for children are very popular in France.

**Beerbohm, Max**. English writer and caricaturist (1872–1956). His books include *A Christmas Garland*, a book of parodies (1912), *The Works of Max Beerbohm* (1896), *The Happy Hypocrite* (1897), *Seven Men* (1919). His only novel is the fantastic comedy *Zuleika Dobson* (1911).

**Belloc, Hilaire**. English essayist, historian, novelist and poet (1870–1953). He was born in France of an English mother and a

French father, but educated in England. His most famous works are the *Bad Child's Book of Beasts* (1896), *The Four Men* (1912) and his biographies of Napoleon (1932) and Cromwell (1934).

**Benét, Stephen Vincent**. American writer (1898–1943). His epic poem 'John Brown's Body' won him the Pulitzer Prize in 1928. Of his short stories, 'The Devil and Daniel Webster' is the best known.

**Bioy Casares, Adolfo**. Argentine novelist and short-story writer (1914– ). His novels include *The Invention of Morel* (1940), *Heroes Dream* (1954) and *Journal of the War of the Pig* (1969). His short stories were published in Spanish in two collections: *Fantastic Tales* and *Love Stories*.

**Bloy, Léon**. French novelist (1846–1917). His many books include *The Poor Woman* (1897), *The Last Pillars of the Church* (1903), *Poorman's Blood* (1909), and the intimate, beautifully written *Journal* (from 1892 to 1917).

**Borges, Jorge Luis**. Argentine essayist, poet and short-story writer (1899– ). Two collections of short stories, *Fictions* (1944) and *The Aleph* (1949), are among the most important books of this century. He also wrote *A Universal History of Infamy* (1935), *Dreamtigers* (1960) and *Doctor Brodie's Report* (1970)

**Bradbury, Ray**. American writer of fantastic literature (1920– ). Among his already classic books are *The Martian Chronicles* (1950), *The Illustrated Man* (1951), *Farenheit 451* (1953), and *Dandelion Wine* (1957).

**Calvino, Italo**. Italian writer born in Cuba (1923– ). His first books are neo-realistic: *The Path of Spiders' Nests* (1947) and *Adam One Afternoon* (1949), but from then onwards his style is fantastic. *The Cloven Viscount* (1952), *The Baron in the Trees* (1957), *The Non-Existent Knight* (1959), *The Castle of Crossed Destinies* (1969), *Invisible Cities* (1972), and *If on a Winter's Night a Traveller* (1979). He also collected a volume of *Italian Folktales* (1975).

**Cocteau, Jean**. French filmmaker, writer and painter (1889–1963). His films are brilliant, personal works of art: *The Blood of a Poet* (1932), *Beauty and the Beast* (1945), *Orpheus* (1949) and *The Testament of Orpheus* (1959). His plays include *The Human Voice* (1930),

*The Infernal Machine* (1934), *The Holy Terrors* (1940). He wrote novels, books of essays and many collections of poetry.

**Collier, John.** American short-story writer and novelist, born in England (1901– ). Two novels, *His Monkey Wife* (1930) and *Defy the Foul Fiend* (1934), established his reputation. His short stories have been edited by Anthony Burgess.

**Comfort, Alexander.** English writer and doctor of medicine (1920– ). He has published *France and Other Poems* (1942), *A Wreath for the Living* (1943) and *The Power House* (1944), as well as the best-selling *The Joy of Sex* (1973) and its sequel *More Joy* (1974).

**Cortázar, Julio.** Argentine writer born in Brussels (1914–84). His novel *Hopscotch* (1965) is his most famous but not his best book. His collections of short stories are excellent: *End of Game* (1964), *The Secret Arms* (1964), *Bestiary* (1951), *All Fires the Fire* (1966), *Cronopios and Famas* (1962). Cortázar translated Poe and Marguerite Yourcenar into Spanish.

**De la Mare, Walter.** English writer and anthologist, born in Kent of an old Huguenot family (1873–1956). He published some fifty volumes of poetry, tales and fantasies, children's stories, novels and essays.

**Denevi, Marco.** Argentine novelist, short-story writer and playwright (1922– ). His detective novel *Rose at Ten* won the Kraft prize in 1955, and in 1960 he was awarded the *Life* magazine prize for his short story 'Secret Ceremony'.

**Dickens, Charles.** English novelist (1812–70). Among his most famous books are *Oliver Twist* (1838), *Nicholas Nickelby* (1839), *David Copperfield* (1850), *A Tale of Two Cities* (1859) *Great Expectations* (1861), and the unfinished *The Mystery of Edwin Drood* (1870).

**Dinesen, Isak.** (Pseud. of the Danish writer Baroness Karen Blixen-Finecke) (1885–1962). She achieved success with the publication of *Seven Gothic Tales* (1934), written in English. Other titles include *Winter's Tales* (1942), *Anecdotes of Destiny* (1958), and the autobiographical *Out of Africa* (1937).

**Du Maurier, Daphne.** English writer (1907– ). She is the author of many successful novels: *Jamaica Inn* (1936), *Rebecca* (1938), *My*

*Cousin Rachel* (1951), several collections of short stories and volumes of memoirs.

**Dunsany, Lord.** Irish dramatist and short-story writer (1878–1957). He was the eighteenth Baron Dunsany, ferociously aristocratic, a big-game hunter, cricketer and a master at chess. He is best known for his many volumes of plays and stories: *Time and the Gods* (1906), *Fifty-One Tales* (1915), *The Curse of the Wise Woman* (1933), among others.

**Fast, Howard.** American novelist (1914– ). After the Depression he became a leading left-wing activist and his writings often deal with revolutionary situations. He wrote *The Unvanquished* (1942), *Citizen Tom Paine* (1943), *My Glorious Brothers* (1948), *Spartacus* (1952) and *Power* (1963).

**Forster, Edward Morgan.** English novelist and essayist (1879–1970). Most of his short stories have been collected in *The Celestial Omnibus* (1911) and *The Eternal Moment* (1928). His novels include *Where Angels Fear to Tread* (1905), *A Room with a View* (1908), *The Longest Journey* (1907), *Howards End* (1910) and *A Passage to India* (1924).

**Garnett, David.** English novelist and publisher (1892– ). *Lady Into Fox* was his first book, published in 1922. Apart from his autobiography in several volumes, he has written *A Man in the Zoo* (1924), *Go She Must!* (1927), *The Grasshoppers Come* (1931), *A Rabbit in the Air* (1932), and *Ulterior Motives* (1966).

**Greenburg, Joanne.** American novelist and short-story writer (1932– ). Under the name Hannah Green she published *I Never Promised You a Rose Garden* (1964). She has written four other novels and several collections of short stories. Two of the best collections are *Rites of Passage* (1972) and *High Crimes and Misdemeanours* (1980).

**Greene, Graham.** English novelist (1904– ). He has also written short stories, plays, essays, film and literary criticism and children's stories. Among his best novels are *The Power and the Glory* (1940), *The End of the Affair* (1951), *The Quiet American* (1955), *Travels with my Aunt* (1969), *The Honorary Consul* (1973), *The Human Factor* (1978), and *Monsignor Quixote* (1982).

**Guimarães Rosá, João.** Brazilian novelist (1908–67). He studied medicine and served as a diplomat. His books include several collections of short stories: *Dance Group* (1956), *Sagarana* (1961) and *First Tales* (1962) and the ambitious novel *Grande Sertāo: Veredas* (1956), translated into English as *The Devil to Pay in the Backlands* (New York, 1963).

**Hartley, Lesley Poles.** English novelist (1895–1973). His *Collected Stories* appeared in 1968. His novels include *Simonetta Perkins* (1925), *The Shrimp and the Anemone* (1944), *The Sixth Heaven* (1946), *Eustace and Hilda* (1947), *The Boat* (1949), *The Go-Between* (1953), and *The Brickfield* (1964).

**Hawthorne, Nathaniel.** American novelist and short-story writer (1804–64). *Twice-Told Tales* (1837) made him famous and his novel *The Scarlet Letter* (1850) established his reputation. He also published *The Marble Faun* (1860), *The House of the Seven Gables* (1851) and *The Blithedale Romance* (1852).

**Hearn, Lafcadio.** American writer (1850–1904). His first book was a translation of Theophile Gautier, *One of Cleopatra's Nights* (1882). His work includes *Stray Leaves from Strange Literature* (1884), *Some Chinese Ghosts* (1887), *Glimpses of Unfamiliar Japan* (1893), *In Ghostly Japan* (1899) and *Letters from the Raven* (posth. 1907).

**Henry, Oliver** (pseud. of William Sidney Porter). American short-story writer, one of the most prolific authors in the US (1862–1910). His first book was *Cabbages and Kings* (1904). He also wrote *The Four Million* (1906), *The Voice of the City* (1908), *Roads of Destiny* (1909) and several other collections published posthumously.

**Hesse, Hermann.** German novelist and poet (1877–1962). After a visit to India in 1911 he lived in Switzerland for the rest of his life, and was awarded the Nobel Prize in 1946. He wrote *Under the Wheel* (1905), *Rosshalde* (1914), *Demian* (1919), *Siddhartha* (1922), *Steppenwolf* (1927), *Narziss und Goldmund* (1930), and *Magister Ludi* (1950).

**Hichens, Robert Smythe.** English writer (1864–1950). His novels include *The Green Carnation* (1894), *The Garden of Allah* (1904) and *Bella Donna* (1909).

**Hitchcock, George.** American poet, playwright and novelist born in 1914. Among his books are *Tactics of Survival and other poems* (1964), *The Dolphin with the Revolver in its Teeth* (1967), *Lessons in Alchemy* (1976) and *The Piano Beneath the Skin* (1978). His plays include *The Busy Martyr* (1962) and *The Counterfeit Rose* (1975).

**Ireland, I. A.** English scholar (1871– ? ). Among his books are *A Brief History of Nightmares* (1899), *Spanish Literature* (1911), *The Tenth Book of the Annals of Tacitus, newly done into English* (1911) and *Visitations* (1919).

**Jacobs, William Wymark.** English short-story writer (1863–1943). His first collection, *Many Cargoes* (1896) was a popular success, followed by twenty more volumes. Among these are *Light Freights* (1901), *The Lady of the Barge* (1902), *Short Cruises* (1907) and *Night Watches* (1914).

**James, Henry.** English writer born in America (1843–1916). His many novels include *The Europeans* (1878), *Daisy Miller* (1879), *Washington Square* (1880), *The Portrait of a Lady* (1881), *The Princess Casamassima* (1886), *The Golden Bowl* (1904). At the time of his death he left two unfinished novels: *The Ivory Tower* and *The Sense of the Past*.

**James, Montague Rhodes.** English scholar and short-story writer (1862–1936). He wrote on the Apocrypha and on medieval subjects, but is best known for his ghost stories: *Ghost Stories of an Antiquary* (1904 and 1911), *A Thin Ghost and Others* (1919), *Twelve Medieval Ghost Stories* (1922) and *The Five Jars* (1922).

**Kafka, Franz.** Czech novelist who wrote in German (1883–1924). His work, a keystone of modern literature, includes the novels *The Trial* (posth. 1925), *The Castle* (posth. 1926) and *America* (posth. 1927) and many brilliant short stories such as 'Metamorphosis' (1912).

**King, Francis.** English writer born in Switzerland in 1923. He spent his childhood in India and later studied in Oxford. He is a fellow of the Royal Society of Literature and has won both the Somerset Maugham Award and the Katherine Mansfield Short Story Award.

**Kipling, Rudyard.** One of the greatest English writers of the turn of the century, born in Bombay in 1865. He published his first stories in India and was hailed as a genius when he arrived in London at the age of twenty-four. His collected works comprise thirty-five volumes of which the best are his poems and short stories – *Plain Tales From the Hills* (1890), *Life's Handicap* (1891), *Many Inventions* (1893), *The Jungle Books* (1894–5), *Traffics and Discoveries* (1904), *Actions and Reactions* (1909), and the novel *Kim* (1901). Kipling died in London in 1936.

**Lawrence, David Herbert.** English novelist and poet (1885–1930), an explorer of the finer shades of human relationships and feelings. His first poems were published by Ford Madox Ford. His novels include *The White Peacock* (1911), *Sons and Lovers* (1913), *The Rainbow* (1915), *Women in Love* (1920), *The Plumed Serpent* (1926) and several versions of *Lady Chatterley's Lover*, of which the final version was privately printed in Florence in 1928. There are several collections of his short stories.

**LeGuin, Ursula Kroeber.** American novelist and short-story writer, born in Berkley, California, in 1929. Her best-known books are *The Earthsea Trilogy* (1968, 1971, and 1972), *Orsinian Tales* (1976) and *The Word for World is Forest* (1972). She won the Nebula and Hugo awards twice: in 1969 for *The Left Hand of Darkness* and in 1975 for *The Dispossessed*.

**Mandiargues, André Pieyre de.** French writer born in Paris in 1909. He has published *Le Musée Noir* (1946), *Soleil des Loups* (1951), *La Marge* (Prix Goncourt, 1967) and many others. He entered André Breton's surrealist group in 1947. Mandiargues has translated into French the works of Mishima and W. B. Yeats.

**Manuel, Juan.** Spanish prince, grandson of King Fernando III and nephew of King Alfonso X (1282–1348). He was joint regent during the minority of King Alfonso XI and being unscrupulous in politics, he made an alliance with the Muslim King of Granada. His most important books (which have survived) are *The Book of Examples of Count Lucanor*, *Treatise on the Asumption* and *The Manners of Love*. He also wrote books on hunting and heraldry.

**Maugham, William Somerset.** English novelist, short-story writer and playwright, born in Paris (1874–1965). He studied medicine, but never practised. His first novel, *Liza of Lambeth* (1897), makes use of his medical knowledge, but is less successful than his later work: *Of Human Bondage* (1915), *The Moon and Sixpence* (1919), *Cakes and Ale* (1930). His best short stories are extraordinary, and so are the selections of his diaries published as *A Writer's Notebook* (1949).

**Moore, Brian**. Born in Belfast (Northern Ireland) in 1921, he emigrated to Canada in 1948 and lived in Montreal till his departure for the US in 1959. His novels include *The Feast of Lupercal* (1957), *The Luck of Ginger Coffey* (1960), *The Emperor of Ice-Cream* (1965), *Catholics* (1972) and *Cold Heaven* (1983).

**Mujica Lainez, Manuel**. Argentine novelist and short-story writer (1910–1984). He studied in France and England; back in Argentina he set out to chronicle the history of his homeland in two collections of related stories – *Here They Lived* (1949) and *Mysterious Buenos Aires* (1950) – and in several novels including *The House* (1954) and *Guests in Paradise* (1957). Some of his best novels, however, deal with the history of other countries: *The Wandering Unicorn* (1965), *Bomarzo* (1962) and *The Scarab* (1982).

**Nabokov, Vladimir**. American novelist born in St Petersburg to an eminent Russian family who went into exile in 1919 (1899–1977). His first novels were written in Russian: *Maskenka* (1926), *King, Queen, Knave* (1928) and others. After *The Gift* (1937) Nabokov began to write in English: *The Real Life of Sebastian Knight* (1941), *Bend Sinister* (1948), *Pnin* (1957), *Pale Fire* (1962), *Ada* (1969). His most popular, though perhaps not his best novel, is *Lolita* (1955).

**O'Brien, Flann** (pseud. of Brian O'Nolan). Irish novelist and humorist (1911–66). He attended University College in Dublin and gained notoriety after publishing an obscene epic in Old Irish, escaping punishment because the prosecuting authorities, including the president of the college, could not read the ancient tongue. Two novels secure his fame: *At Swim-Two-Birds* (1939) and *The Third Policeman* (published posthumously in 1967 because he could not find a publisher during his lifetime).

**Ocampo, Silvina**. Argentine poet, short-story writer and painter, born in Buenos Aires in 1906. Her books of poems include *Forgotten Journey* (1937), *The Garden Sonnets* (1946), *Poems of Desperate Love* (1949), *Yellow blue* (1972); her collections of short stories include *Autobiography of Irene* (1948), *The Fury* (1959), *The Guests* (1961),

*The Days of Night* (1970). With her husband, Adolfo Bioy Casares, she wrote a detective novel, *Those who love, hate* (1946), and with J. R. Wilcock a play in verse, *The Traitors* (1956).

**Ozick, Cynthia**. American essayist, novelist and short-story writer, born 1928. She established her reputation as one of America's finest stylists with her novel, *Trust* (1966), but her best work lies in her volumes of shorter pieces: *The Pagan Rabbi and Other Stories* (1971), *Bloodshed and Three Novellas* (1976) and *Levitation* (1982).

**Papini, Giovanni**. Italian essayist and short-story writer (1881–1956). He wrote over sixty books on philosophical and religious matters. His best-known titles are *Life of Christ* (1921), *The Devil* (1954), *A Man – Finished* (1912), *The Blind Pilot* (1907), *Dante Alive* (1933).

**Piñera, Virgilio**. Cuban playwright, novelist and short-story writer (1914– ). He spent a long exile in Argentina, where he published his first novel *René's Flesh* (1952) and the collection of short stories *Cold Tales* (1956). After returning to Cuba he published another novel, *Minor Manoeuvres* (1963).

**Poe, Edgar Allan**. American poet, short-story writer and critic, born in Boston (1809–49). He invented the detective story and set the rules for the tale of horror. His poetry had a powerful influence both in France and in Latin America. His complete works contain seventeen volumes. His only novel, *The Narrative of Arthur Gordon Pym of Nantucket*, was published in 1838.

**Priestley, John Boynton**. English novelist and dramatist, born in 1894. His many novels include *Benighted* (1927), *The Good Companions* (1929), *Angel Pavement* (1930), *The Magician* (1954). Of his many plays perhaps the most popular is *An Inspector Calls* (1945).

**Pushkin, Aleksandr Sergeyevich**. Russian writer born in Moscow in 1799, died in St Petersburg in 1837. His main works are a novel in verse, *Eugene Onegin* (1833), and an historical drama, *Boris Godunov* (1831).

**Quiroga, Horacio**. Uruguayan writer (1878–1937). He lived in the jungles of north-eastern Argentina and wrote under the influence of Poe. His books include *Tales of Love, Madness and Death* (1917),

*Anaconda* (1921), *The Exiles* (1926), *The Coral Reef* (1901), *The Savage* (1920) and *Jungle Tales* (1918).

**Saki** (pseud. of Hector Hugh Munro). English writer and journalist born in Burma (1870–1916). He wrote *The Rise of the Russian Empire* (1900) but is best known for his collections of short stories: *Reginald* (1904), *The Chronicles of Clovis* (1912), *Beasts and Super-Beasts* (1914), and *The Square Egg and Other Sketches* (1924). *The Unbearable Bassington*, a novel, was published 1912.

**Schulz, Bruno.** Polish writer (1892–1942). He translated Kafka's *The Trial* into Polish. Two of his works have survived: *The Street of Crocodiles* (1934) and *Sanatorium under the Sign of the Hourglass* (1937). At his death he was working on a novel, *The Messiah*, of which nothing remains.

**Stevenson, Robert Louis.** Scottish writer born in Edinburgh (1850–94). His novels combine the thrill of wonderful adventures with the delight of an impeccable literary style. He wrote travel books: *An Inland Voyage* (1878), *Travels with a Donkey in the Cevennes* (1879); novels: *Treasure Island* (1883), *Kidnapped* (1886), *The Strange Case of Dr Jekyll and Mr Hyde* (1886), *The Master of Ballantrae* (1889), *Catriona* (1893); essays: *Viriginibus Puerisque* (1881), *Familiar Studies of Men and Books* (1882); verse: *A Child's Garden of Verses* (1885), *Ballads* (1890).

**Tanizaki, Junichiro.** Japanese novelist (1886–1965). Under the influence of Edgar Allan Poe and Oscar Wilde he opposed the Naturalist movement in Japan and developed a personal style of fantastic sensuality. Among his books are *Some Prefer Nettles* (1928), *Ashikari* (1932), *Shunkinsho* (1933), *The Makioka Sisters* (1943–8). Tanizaki also wrote an adaptation of *Genji-monogatari*, the famous eleventh-century Japanese novel.

**Verne, Jules.** French novelist (1828–1905). His many fine adventure stories include: *Five Weeks in a Balloon* (1863), *Journey to the Centre of the Earth* (1864), *From the Earth to the Moon* (1865), *The Adventures of Captain Hatteras* (1866), *The Children of Captain Grant* (1867), *Twenty Thousand Leagues Under the Seas* (1870), *A Floating City* (1871), *Around the World in Eighty Days* (1873), *Michel Strogoff* (1876), *Two Years Holiday* (1888), *Master of the World* (1904).

**Wells, Herbert George.** English novelist and biologist (1866–1946).

He wrote more than a hundred books, many of them novels. Among the most famous are: *The Time Machine* (1895), *The Invisible Man* (1897), *In the Days of the Comet* (1906), *The Shape of Things to Come* (1933), *The History of Mr Polly* (1910), *Ann Veronica* (1909). In 1919 (rev. 1930) he published *The Outline of History*.

**Wharton, Edith**. American writer born in New York (1862–1937). Her themes are taken from the leisured life of the rich, both in the US and in Europe. Her books include *The House of Mirth* (1905), *Ethan Frome* (1911), *The Reef* (1912), *The Custom of the Country* (1913), *The Age of Innocence* (1920), *The World Over* (1936). Her autobiography was published in 1934 under the title *A Backward Glance*.

**Wilde, Oscar**. Irish dramatist, short-story writer and humorist (1854–1900). Among his plays are *Lady Windermere's Fan* (1892), *A Woman of No Importance* (1893), *The Importance of Being Earnest* (1895). His short stories are included in three collections: *The Happy Prince* (1888), *Lord Arthur Savile's Crime* (1891) and *The House of Pomegranates* (1891). His novel *The Picture of Dorian Gray* was also published in 1891.

**Williams, Charles**. English writer (1886–1945). He worked as an editor for the Oxford University Press and wrote several novels which include *War in Heaven* (1930), *Many Dimensions* (1931), *The Place of the Lion* (1932), *Descent into Hell* (1937). He also wrote two narrative poems, a number of historical plays and critical works on Dante.

**Williams, Tennessee**. (pseud. of Thomas Lanier Williams). American playwright and short-story writer (1914–83). His first success came with *The Glass Menagerie* (1945). Other plays include *A Streetcar Named Desire* (1947), *Summer and Smoke* (1948), *The Rose Tattoo* (1951), *Cat on a Hot Tin Roof* (1955), *Orpheus Descending* (1957), *Sweet Bird of Youth* (1959). Among his novels and collections of short stories are: *The Roman Spring of Mrs Stone* (1950), *Hard Candy* (1954), *Three Players of a Summer Game* (1960). *In The Winter of Cities* (1956) is a collection of poems.

**Yourcenar, Marguerite** (pseud. of Marguerite de Criayencourt). French novelist born in Brussels, Belgium, in 1903. In 1980 she became the first woman ever to be elected a member of the French

Academy of Letters. Her novels include *Alexis* (1929), *The New Eurydice* (1931), *Coin of Dreams* (1934), *Memoirs of Hadrian* (1951). She has translated a selection of Negro spirituals, and poems by the Greek poet Constantin Cavafy.